FICTIONS

THIRD EDITION

FICTIONS

THIRD EDITION

Joseph F. Trimmer

Ball State University

C. Wade Jennings

Ball State University

Harcourt Brace College Publishers
Fort Worth Philadelphia San Diego New York
Orlando Austin San Antonio
Toronto Montreal London Sydney Tokyo

Publisher:	Ted Buchholz
Acquisitions Editor:	Stephen T. Jordan
Developmental Editor:	Helen Triller
Production Manager:	Debra A. Jenkin
Cover Designer:	Jim Taylor
Editorial & Production Services:	Michael Bass & Associates
Cover Image:	Lawrence, Jacob: *The Library,* 1960. National Museum of American Art, Washington, D.C./Art Resource, NY. Copyright VAGA

Printed in the United States of America

Library of Congress Catalog Card Number: 93-29769

ISBN: 0-15-500121-3

3 4 5 6 7 8 9 0 1 2 016 9 8 7 6 5 4 3 2 1

Preface

Fictions is an anthology of short fiction designed for college courses in which the short story and the novella are the principal subjects for discussion and writing. This collection of 99 stories includes some of the most memorable work of the world's classic and contemporary writers. Many of the selections are masterpieces that have fascinated students of literature for generations. Others, while less well known, possess similar virtues and may thus achieve a comparable position within our literary tradition. This edition is three stories shorter than the previous editions to accommodate the inclusion of some longer stories, such as those by Harrison and Ozick.

The stories are arranged alphabetically by author, with an alternative table of contents provided for those who wish to analyze stories according to thematic grouping. The Thematic Table of Contents has been moved to the front of the book in this edition. Seven writers—Nathaniel Hawthorne, Franz Kafka, D. H. Lawrence, Flannery O'Connor, Katherine Anne Porter, Alice Walker, and Eudora Welty—are represented by three stories each to allow students to compare the way an individual writer varies theme and technique; ten other writers are represented by two. The collection also includes a generous selection of novellas to enable students to experience works of greater length and complexity.

The Introduction, "Reading and Writing about Short Stories," begins by defining the five basic elements of fiction—plot, characterization, setting, point of view, and theme. Each element is discussed clearly and simply and is illustrated concretely with examples from the stories in the text. The introduction continues with a set of guidelines or practical strategies for reading, analyzing, and interpreting a story. Kate Chopin's minor classic, "The Story of an Hour," is then reprinted in its entirety, along with a headnote and study questions, so that students can apply their knowledge of literary terminology and test their ability to use the recommended reading strategies on one very short and relatively straightforward example.

The second part of this chapter introduces students to the process of writing an essay about a short story. Using actual student responses to the Chopin story, the section illustrates how the various steps in the process—keeping a journal, brainstorming, restricting a topic, planning the outline, writing the first draft, and revising the first draft—lead to a successful essay.

The rest of the editorial apparatus is, by design, minimal. A brief headnote provides students with essential information about the author and includes a reference to the story's source and date. Five study questions follow the story, one each for the five elements of fiction discussed in the introduction. These questions are not meant to be exhaustive; they are simply attempts to open up the story for discussion and possible writing assignments. A glossary of critical terms concludes the text.

The Instructor's Manual, by Vanessa Haley of Mary Washington College, is available upon request to any instructor using *Fictions.*

It is a pleasure to acknowledge the many people who have helped prepare *Fictions.* For their assistance in helping us read and formulate useful questions about the stories in this collection, we thank our students—in particular, the students who allowed us to reprint their work in the introductory essay. For her assistance in researching and typing the headnotes, we thank Karen Taylor. At Harcourt Brace, we thank Stephen Jordan, Helen Triller, and Eleanor Garner for their editorial endeavors. For his inspiration and guidance, we owe a special debt of gratitude to Bill McLane. For their forthright responses to our *Fictions* questionnaire, we thank the following:

Joseph A. Alvarez
Central Piedmont Community College

Nancy G. Anderson
Auburn University at Montgomery

William M. Applebaum
State University of New York, Cobleskill

Melissa E. Barth
Appalachian State University

Brian Beck
University of Wisconsin, Whitewater

Steve Blades
Evergreen Valley College

Barbara R. Brown
Marshall University

Catherine Calloway
Arkansas State University

Karen M. Carney
University of Illinois at Champaign-Urbana

Donna R. Cheney
Weber State University

Jerry Clements
Christian Brothers College

Claire M. Crabtree
University of Detroit

Mary Lou Cutrera
Louisiana State University

Robert Dees
Orange Coast College

ty

New York, Albany

Marshall Bruce Gentry
University of Indianapolis

Joan Gilson
University of Missouri at Kansas City

Jean Gravelle
State University of New York, Brockport

Huey S. Guagliardo
Louisiana State University at Eunice

John Hildebrand
University of Wisconsin at Eau Claire

Gerald A. Iannotti
Fulton Montgomery Community College

Edith Johnsen
Monterey Peninsula College

Kenneth G. Johnston
Kansas State University

Brigit Keefe
Monmouth College

Joyce Kessel
Villa Maria College

C. H. Knoblauch
State University of New York, Albany

Martha McGowan
University of Lowell

Jeremy McNamara
Monmouth College

Dianne S. Metzar
Broome Community College

James H. Miesen
Alpena Community College

Don Moore
Louisiana State University

Ann D. Moorefield
Presbyterian College

Creston Munger
Green Mountain College

John Pastoor
Montcalm Community College

Barry Phillips
University of Massachusetts, Boston

Susan Pepper Robbins
Hampden-Sydney College

Patricia R. Robertson
University of Southwestern Louisiana

James E. Rocks
Loyola University

James S. Rodgers
Lawrence Technological University

Joyce Schenk
El Camino College

Beverly J. Slaughter
Brevard Community College

Constance Fletcher Smith
Mary Washington College

Doug Spainhower
Weber State University

Robert Spiegel
Central Connecticut State University

Cruce Stark
University of Delaware

Michael L. Storey
College of Notre Dame of Maryland

Marlys M. Styne
Wright College

John S. Terhes
Chemeketa Community College

Felicity Trueblood
University of Florida

Wayne Ude
Old Dominion University

Mike Vause
Weber State University

Diane Wahto
Butler County Community College

Gary Willhardt
Monmouth College

Carolyn Zerboni
Mission College

Philip L. Zweifel
University of Wisconsin Center, Waukesha

Joseph F. Trimmer
C. Wade Jennings

Contents

Preface v

Thematic Table of Contents xiii

Introduction: Reading and Writing about Short Stories 1

Discussing Short Stories: The Basic Elements 1
- Plot 2
- Characterization 3
- Setting 4
- Point of View 5
- Theme 7

Guidelines for Reading Short Stories 9
- Preview the Story 9
- Read the Story Actively 10
- Respond Promptly to the Story 10

Sample Story: "The Story of an Hour," Kate Chopin 11

Two Sample Student Responses 14

Writing an Essay on a Topic of Your Own Choice 16
- Brainstorm about the Story 17
- Restrict Your Topic 18
- Plan Your Essay 19
- Develop Your Paragraphs 20
- Sample Rough Draft 21
- Sample Revision Strategy 23
- Sample Revised Essay 24

Writing an Essay on an Assigned Topic 26

A Final Word 27

The Stories

1 CHINUA ACHEBE *Vengeful Creditor* 28

2 ISABEL ALLENDE *Two Words* 39

3 ISABEL ALLENDE *Walimai* 45

4 SHERWOOD ANDERSON *The Egg* 50

5 MARGARET ATWOOD *The Age of Lead* 57
6 JAMES BALDWIN *Sonny's Blues* 67
7 TONI CADE BAMBARA *The Lesson* 90
8 AMBROSE BIERCE *An Occurrence at Owl Creek Bridge* 96
9 HEINRICH BÖLL *Christmas Not Just Once a Year* 103
10 ARNA BONTEMPS *A Summer Tragedy* 118
11 JORGE LUIS BORGES *The Garden of Forking Paths* 125
12 ELIZABETH BOWEN *The Demon Lover* 133
13 KAY BOYLE *Astronomer's Wife* 138
14 LARRY BROWN *Kubuku Rides (This Is It)* 142
15 ALBERT CAMUS *The Guest* 153
16 ETHAN CANIN *The Year of Getting to Know Us* 162
17 ETHAN CANIN *We Are Nighttime Travelers* 176
18 RAYMOND CARVER *A Small, Good Thing* 186
19 WILLA CATHER *Paul's Case* 203
20 JOHN CHEEVER *The Swimmer* 217
21 ANTON CHEKHOV *The Lady with the Dog* 225
22 SANDRA CISNEROS *Never Marry a Mexican* 237
23 JOSEPH CONRAD *Heart of Darkness* 246
24 STEPHEN CRANE *The Open Boat* 303
25 STEPHEN CRANE *The Blue Hotel* 321
26 ARTHUR CONAN DOYLE *The Adventure of the Speckled Band* 341
27 RALPH ELLISON *Battle Royal* 358
28 RALPH ELLISON *King of the Bingo Game* 369
29 WILLIAM FAULKNER *A Rose for Emily* 376
30 WILLIAM FAULKNER *Barn Burning* 384
31 F. SCOTT FITZGERALD *Babylon Revisited* 396
32 MARY WILKINS FREEMAN *The Revolt of "Mother"* 411
33 ERNEST J. GAINES *The Sky Is Gray* 423
34 GABRIEL GARCIA MARQUEZ *A Very Old Man with Enormous Wings* 444
35 ELLEN GILCHRIST *Revenge* 449
36 CHARLOTTE PERKINS GILMAN *The Yellow Wallpaper* 459
37 GAIL GODWIN *Dream Children* 471
38 NADINE GORDIMER *The Train from Rhodesia* 481

39 JIM HARRISON *The Woman Lit by Fireflies* 485
40 NATHANIEL HAWTHORNE *Young Goodman Brown* 522
41 NATHANIEL HAWTHORNE *The Birthmark* 532
42 NATHANIEL HAWTHORNE *Rappaccini's Daughter* 543
43 ERNEST HEMINGWAY *The Short Happy Life of Francis Macomber* 563
44 SHIRLEY JACKSON *The Lottery* 584
45 SARAH ORNE JEWETT *A White Heron* 591
46 CHARLES JOHNSON *Moving Pictures* 599
47 JAMES JOYCE *Araby* 603
48 JAMES JOYCE *The Dead* 608
49 FRANZ KAFKA *A Hunger Artist* 636
50 FRANZ KAFKA *The Metamorphosis* 643
51 FRANZ KAFKA *In the Penal Colony* 674
52 D. H. LAWRENCE *The Rocking-Horse Winner* 691
53 D. H. LAWRENCE *The Horse Dealer's Daughter* 703
54 D. H. LAWRENCE *Odour of Chrysanthemums* 714
55 URSULA K. LE GUIN *The Ones Who Walk Away from Omelas* 728
56 DORIS LESSING *A Woman on a Roof* 733
57 JACK LONDON *To Build a Fire* 741
58 CARSON McCULLERS *A Tree, a Rock, a Cloud* 752
59 DENNIS McFARLAND *Nothing to Ask For* 758
60 JAMES ALAN McPHERSON *The Silver Bullet* 769
61 BERNARD MALAMUD *The Magic Barrel* 780
62 KATHERINE MANSFIELD *Her First Ball* 792
63 BOBBIE ANN MASON *Shiloh* 797
64 GUY DE MAUPASSANT *The Necklace* 808
65 HERMAN MELVILLE *Bartleby the Scrivener* 814
66 YUKIO MISHIMA *Patriotism* 839
67 ALICE MUNRO *How I Met My Husband* 856
68 JOYCE CAROL OATES *Where Are You Going, Where Have You Been?* 869
69 JOYCE CAROL OATES *The Lady with the Pet Dog* 882
70 FLANNERY O'CONNOR *A Good Man Is Hard to Find* 894
71 FLANNERY O'CONNOR *Revelation* 906
72 FLANNERY O'CONNOR *Everything That Rises Must Converge* 921

73	FRANK O'CONNOR	*Guests of the Nation*	932
74	TILLIE OLSEN	*I Stand Here Ironing*	941
75	CYNTHIA OZICK	*Puttermesser Paired*	947
76	DOROTHY PARKER	*The Waltz*	982
77	EDGAR ALLAN POE	*The Fall of the House of Usher*	985
78	EDGAR ALLAN POE	*The Cask of Amontillado*	999
79	KATHERINE ANNE PORTER	*The Jilting of Granny Weatherall*	1004
80	KATHERINE ANNE PORTER	*The Grave*	1011
81	KATHERINE ANNE PORTER	*Holiday*	1016
82	PHILIP ROTH	*Defender of the Faith*	1035
83	ISAAC BASHEVIS SINGER	*Gimpel the Fool*	1056
84	JOHN STEINBECK	*The Chrysanthemums*	1066
85	JAMES THURBER	*The Catbird Seat*	1075
86	LEO TOLSTOY	*The Death of Ivan Ilych*	1082
87	WILLIAM TREVOR	*The Ballroom of Romance*	1120
88	JOHN UPDIKE	*A & P*	1133
89	JOHN UPDIKE	*A Sandstone Farmhouse*	1139
90	ABRAHAM VERGHESE	*Lilacs*	1156
91	KURT VONNEGUT, JR.	*Harrison Bergeron*	1165
92	ALICE WALKER	*Everyday Use*	1171
93	ALICE WALKER	*To Hell with Dying*	1178
94	ALICE WALKER	*Really,* Doesn't *Crime Pay?*	1183
95	EUDORA WELTY	*A Worn Path*	1191
96	EUDORA WELTY	*Petrified Man*	1198
97	EUDORA WELTY	*Why I Live at the P.O.*	1208
98	EDITH WHARTON	*Roman Fever*	1217
99	RICHARD WRIGHT	*The Man Who Was Almost a Man*	1227
Glossary of Critical Terms			1237

Thematic Table of Contents

Initiation and Maturation
MARGARET ATWOOD *The Age of Lead*
TONI CADE BAMBARA *The Lesson*
WILLA CATHER *Paul's Case*
WILLIAM FAULKNER *Barn Burning*
ERNEST J. GAINES *The Sky Is Gray*
ELLEN GILCHRIST *Revenge*
JAMES JOYCE *Araby*
CARSON McCULLERS *A Tree, a Rock, a Cloud*
JAMES ALAN McPHERSON *The Silver Bullet*
KATHERINE MANSFIELD *Her First Ball*
KATHERINE ANNE PORTER *The Grave*
ISAAC BASHEVIS SINGER *Gimpel the Fool*
JOHN UPDIKE *A & P*
RICHARD WRIGHT *The Man Who Was Almost a Man*

Parents and Children
SHERWOOD ANDERSON *The Egg*
ETHAN CANIN *The Year of Getting to Know Us*
RAYMOND CARVER *A Small, Good Thing*
WILLIAM FAULKNER *Barn Burning*
F. SCOTT FITZGERALD *Babylon Revisited*
ERNEST J. GAINES *The Sky Is Gray*
GAIL GODWIN *Dream Children*
FLANNERY O'CONNOR *Everything That Rises Must Converge*
TILLIE OLSEN *I Stand Here Ironing*
KATHERINE ANNE PORTER *Holiday*
JOHN UPDIKE *A Sandstone Farmhouse*
ALICE WALKER *Everyday Use*
EUDORA WELTY *Why I Live at the P.O.*
EDITH WHARTON *Roman Fever*

Men and Women
KAY BOYLE *Astronomer's Wife*
ANTON CHEKHOV *The Lady with the Dog*
MARY WILKINS FREEMAN *The Revolt of "Mother"*
JIM HARRISON *The Woman Lit by Fireflies*
JAMES JOYCE *The Dead*

D. H. LAWRENCE *The Horse Dealer's Daughter*
DORIS LESSING *A Woman on a Roof*
BERNARD MALAMUD *The Magic Barrel*
BOBBIE ANN MASON *Shiloh*
GUY DE MAUPASSANT *The Necklace*
ALICE MUNRO *How I Met My Husband*
JOYCE CAROL OATES *The Lady with the Pet Dog*
CYNTHIA OZICK *Puttermesser Paired*
DOROTHY PARKER *The Waltz*
JOHN STEINBECK *The Chrysanthemums*
JAMES THURBER *The Catbird Seat*
EUDORA WELTY *Petrified Man*

The Individual and Society
CHINUA ACHEBE *Vengeful Creditor*
ISABEL ALLENDE *Walimai*
HEINRICH BÖLL *Christmas Not Just Once a Year*
ALBERT CAMUS *The Guest*
JOHN CHEEVER *The Swimmer*
JOSEPH CONRAD *Heart of Darkness*
STEPHEN CRANE *The Blue Hotel*
WILLIAM FAULKNER *A Rose for Emily*
NATHANIEL HAWTHORNE *Young Goodman Brown*
SHIRLEY JACKSON *The Lottery*
FRANZ KAFKA *In the Penal Colony*
URSULA K. LE GUIN *The Ones Who Walk Away from Omelas*
HERMAN MELVILLE *Bartleby the Scrivener*
YUKIO MISHIMA *Patriotism*
FLANNERY O'CONNOR *Revelation*
FLANNERY O'CONNOR *Everything That Rises Must Converge*
FRANK O'CONNOR *Guests of the Nation*
ABRAHAM VERGHESE *Lilacs*
KURT VONNEGUT, JR. *Harrison Bergeron*

The Minority Experience
ISABEL ALLENDE *Two Words*
JAMES BALDWIN *Sonny's Blues*
TONI CADE BAMBARA *The Lesson*
ARNA BONTEMPS *A Summer Tragedy*
LARRY BROWN *Kubuku Rides (This Is It)*
SANDRA CISNEROS *Never Marry a Mexican*
RALPH ELLISON *Battle Royal*
RALPH ELLISON *King of the Bingo Game*
NADINE GORDIMER *The Train from Rhodesia*
DENNIS McFARLAND *Nothing to Ask For*

JAMES ALAN McPHERSON *The Silver Bullet*
FRANK O'CONNOR *Guests of the Nation*
PHILIP ROTH *Defender of the Faith*
WILLIAM TREVOR *The Ballroom of Romance*

The Artist and Art
ISABEL ALLENDE *Two Words*
JAMES BALDWIN *Sonny's Blues*
HEINRICH BÖLL *Christmas Not Just Once a Year*
JORGE LUIS BORGES *The Garden of Forking Paths*
ETHAN CANIN *We Are Nighttime Travelers*
NADINE GORDIMER *The Train from Rhodesia*
NATHANIEL HAWTHORNE *Rappaccini's Daughter*
CHARLES JOHNSON *Moving Pictures*
FRANZ KAFKA *A Hunger Artist*
CYNTHIA OZICK *Puttermesser Paired*
EDGAR ALLAN POE *The Fall of the House of Usher*
JOHN STEINBECK *The Chrysanthemums*
ALICE WALKER *Everyday Use*
ALICE WALKER *"Really,* Doesn't *Crime Pay?"*

The Ordeal of Nature
ARNA BONTEMPS *A Summer Tragedy*
ETHAN CANIN *We Are Nighttime Travelers*
JOHN CHEEVER *The Swimmer*
JOSEPH CONRAD *Heart of Darkness*
STEPHEN CRANE *The Open Boat*
MARY WILKINS FREEMAN *The Revolt of "Mother"*
NATHANIEL HAWTHORNE *Young Goodman Brown*
NATHANIEL HAWTHORNE *The Birthmark*
ERNEST HEMINGWAY *The Short Happy Life of Francis Macomber*
SARAH ORNE JEWETT *A White Heron*
D. H. LAWRENCE *Odour of Chrysanthemums*
JOHN UPDIKE *A Sandstone Farmhouse*
EUDORA WELTY *A Worn Path*

The Extraordinary and the Fantastic
ISABEL ALLENDE *Walimai*
MARGARET ATWOOD *The Age of Lead*
HEINRICH BÖLL *Christmas Not Just Once a Year*
ARTHUR CONAN DOYLE *The Adventure of the Speckled Band*
RALPH ELLISON *King of the Bingo Game*
GABRIEL GARCIA MARQUEZ *A Very Old Man with Enormous Wings*
CHARLOTTE PERKINS GILMAN *The Yellow Wallpaper*
GAIL GODWIN *Dream Children*
JIM HARRISON *The Woman Lit by Fireflies*

NATHANIEL HAWTHORNE *The Birthmark*
NATHANIEL HAWTHORNE *Rappaccini's Daughter*
SHIRLEY JACKSON *The Lottery*
FRANZ KAFKA *A Hunger Artist*
FRANZ KAFKA *The Metamorphosis*
FRANZ KAFKA *In the Penal Colony*
D. H. LAWRENCE *The Rocking-Horse Winner*
URSULA K. LE GUIN *The Ones Who Walk Away from Omelas*
HERMAN MELVILLE *Bartleby the Scrivener*
EDGAR ALLAN POE *The Cask of Amontillado*
KURT VONNEGUT, JR. *Harrison Bergeron*

Terror and Violence
CHINUA ACHEBE *Vengeful Creditor*
ISABEL ALLENDE *Walimai*
ELIZABETH BOWEN *The Demon Lover*
LARRY BROWN *Kubuku Rides (This Is It)*
ARTHUR CONAN DOYLE *The Adventure of the Speckled Band*
RALPH ELLISON *Battle Royal*
FRANZ KAFKA *In the Penal Colony*
JAMES ALAN McPHERSON *The Silver Bullet*
YUKIO MISHIMA *Patriotism*
JOYCE CAROL OATES *Where Are You Going, Where Have You Been?*
FLANNERY O'CONNOR *A Good Man Is Hard to Find*
EDGAR ALLAN POE *The Fall of the House of Usher*
JAMES THURBER *The Catbird Seat*

Aging and Dying
AMBROSE BIERCE *An Occurrence at Owl Creek Bridge*
ARNA BONTEMPS *A Summer Tragedy*
ETHAN CANIN *We Are Nighttime Travelers*
WILLIAM FAULKNER *A Rose for Emily*
JAMES JOYCE *The Dead*
FRANZ KAFKA *The Metamorphosis*
JACK LONDON *To Build a Fire*
DENNIS McFARLAND *Nothing to Ask For*
KATHERINE ANNE PORTER *The Jilting of Granny Weatherall*
KATHERINE ANNE PORTER *The Grave*
LEO TOLSTOY *The Death of Ivan Ilych*
JOHN UPDIKE *A Sandstone Farmhouse*
ABRAHAM VERGHESE *Lilacs*
ALICE WALKER *To Hell with Dying*
EUDORA WELTY *A Worn Path*

Introduction

Reading and Writing about Short Stories

One of the most enduring pleasures in life is a well-told story. From childhood on, we crave accounts of people, experiences, ways of living that lie beyond our own immediate lives, probably because we are insatiably curious about the possibilities of human existence. Whatever the reason, we spend a significant amount of our time and money in order to live imaginatively in created worlds.

Our bargain with story-tellers is a simple one: we give them our time, our attention, and our cooperation in the imagining process; they give us the pleasure of a story that interests and involves us—that intensifies our experience with life as we already know it or gives us a taste of life as we have not experienced it. Our first response is basic: either we like the story—a reaction usually implying that it has stirred our imaginations, thoughts, and feelings—or it bores us, unpleasantly confuses us, or introduces us to worlds and people we don't want to know.

Although it may be strong, this first response is often entirely private. We may not feel any need to explain or justify our reaction to anyone else. If we are asked for an opinion, our reply may be terse: "It was all right." "Not worth the time." "A lot of fun." "Interesting." Often such a reply is all anybody really wants to know. On other occasions, we may want to say more about a story, either because we want to understand our own reaction more clearly or because something in the story has affected us so strongly that we want the pleasure of discussing it with others. And finally, of course, students in literature classes are often required to talk or write about their experiences with a story.

Whatever the reason, when we move from our strong but unexpressed *private* reaction to some sort of developed response addressed to other people—our *public* reaction—we need to have the language that allows us to say directly and precisely what we mean. We need not only clarify what our response was, but also explain *why* we responded as we did. This introduction will explain the basic terminology used to discuss short fiction and will then illustrate various strategies that can be used to write about it.

DISCUSSING SHORT STORIES: The Basic Elements

One of the most difficult terms to explain is the basic one: what is a *short story*? Arbitrary definitions are convenient but not very accurate. We can say that a short story is a work of prose fiction that is less than 40,000 words in length. Obviously, however, a story of 41,000 words is not magically transformed into some wholly different kind of creation.

Nor would we care to term such things as biblical parables or Aesop's fables short stories, even though they are short works of prose fiction.

We need to add to our definition. Traditionally, the short story has been defined as a work of fiction that is unified by a structured *plot* in which a chain of circumstances and events is separated from the rest of human experience and treated as a coherent whole. We expect the *characters* in such a story to be developed enough for us to understand both what they do and why. We usually expect that the people and their actions in the story will lead to some understanding on our part of why these things matter—a sense of meaning or *theme.* We also expect the writer to give us a clear sense of the *setting* of the story—the place, time, and social circumstances within which the narrative unfolds. Finally, we have to know from whose perspective we are seeing the events and the characters—the *point of view* in the story. These five elements—plot, characters, theme, setting, and point of view—almost always work together to achieve the short story's purpose, direction, and movement, so we call them the *basic elements* of the traditional short story.

Any full consideration of short stories will probably touch on all five elements, though individually they vary in importance from story to story. In a well-crafted short story there is no separation of these elements: we expect what happens in the plot to be at least in part a result of what characters choose; we understand that setting may influence profoundly the development of a character; and we see that our understanding of theme in a story is often dependent on the point of view from which we have seen the situation. For the sake of clarity, however, we may often choose to consider each of these elements in turn, both as an end in itself and as a means of deepening our overall understanding of the story. When we divide a story into its elements for the sake of such examination, we have begun the process of *critical analysis.* Since the basic elements are important to our reading, discussing, and writing about the short stories in this collection, we will begin with a brief discussion of each.

Plot

In the events of a traditional short story, unlike the events of life, we expect to find a clear-cut pattern, an order. The *plot* often provides the essential structure in the story by arranging its action in a unified order from the beginning through the middle to the end. The writer must begin by showing us where and when the story takes place, who the characters are, and what the initial situation in the story is. This introductory material is termed *exposition.* In some instances it may be brief, since the writer expects us to understand immediately most things about the setting and circumstances. In "A & P," for example, John Updike does not need to spend much time showing his readers what a supermarket is like, what a cashier does, or how adolescent boys respond to attractive girls. On the other hand, in "Heart of Darkness," Joseph Conrad has to provide a lengthy exposition to prepare his readers for the significance of a mysterious trip up the Congo River.

After the writer has established the original situation in the story, we expect complications to arise. These complications are almost always the result of *conflicts*—among characters, between a character and his or her environment, or among the thoughts, needs, and emotions of a single character. In some cases, all three kinds of conflicts may occur together. In "A & P" the central character has a disagreement with his manager, he runs afoul of the rules of the supermarket, and he cannot decide in his own mind whether he is acting the fool or the hero.

In a traditional story, the conflicts develop to a moment of crisis—often a moment in which a choice must be made, an action performed, or a recognition achieved that will in some way focus and then resolve the conflict. This moment of crisis, the *climax* of the story, usually marks an end of the development of the major action of the story. In whatever remains of the plot, we expect the writer to show us the consequences of the action that occurred in the climax. This final section of the plot is the *denouement,* a French word meaning the untangling of a knot. The denouement may add a surprising twist or turn to the plot, but often it does not add any significant new action or conflict.

In addition to these essential elements of plot, writers may add suspense or richness to their plots by using such techniques as *foreshadowing* and *flashback*. In the first technique, writers provide hints or clues early in the story of events that will occur later. In the second, they interrupt the forward flow of the story to introduce a scene or episode from the past that explains or comments on the present situation. Writers may also add to our pleasure in the story by building *situational irony* into the plot, letting us believe that events will move in one direction when in fact they will take a surprising and contradictory turn. Overall, however, a traditional plot should satisfy us by being coherent, unified, and meaningful—by making a pattern. But some modern fiction writers are seriously challenging this premise by experimenting with new forms of structure, as in the stories in this collection by writers such as Jorge Luis Borges.

Characterization

Many readers often believe that plot is the most crucial element to their enjoyment of a story, but most of us soon recognize that no matter how exciting, eventful, or surprising the plot of a short story may be, we care most about finding convincing portrayals of human nature in action. We have to care about the *characters,* the people in the stories, before we can care about what happens to them. The methods by which writers create, reveal, and develop characters is called *characterization.*

In short fiction, writers usually focus on a single character and show us the complexities, contradictions, and difficulties in that person's life and personality. Sometimes this central character, the *protagonist,* undergoes little change in the story: he or she is simply revealed more fully. More often, however, this character is changed in some ways by experience. Characters who remain relatively unchanged are called *static.* Those who go through some development are called *dynamic.*

The central characters in most short stories are *round:* they have fully developed, complex personalities that may defy simple analysis or description. Less significant characters in the story are likely to be *flat:* we see only the surface, so for us they have no real depth or complexity. At times a writer may employ a type of flat character known as a *stereotype.* This stock type—the shrewish wife, the town drunk, the Don Juan—we already know from earlier experiences as readers or viewers.

Writers develop their characters in a number of ways. When concerned primarily with the *external reality* of their characters, writers describe their physical appearance, dramatize their actions or conversations, and summarize their previous histories for us. In portraying the external reality, writers give us what other characters in the story see, hear, and know about the character. However, in most short fiction, writers also penetrate the minds and hearts of some characters, particularly the protagonist, to show their *inner reality*—the thoughts and feelings of which others in the story may be unaware. This portrayal of inner reality is often more complex and more central to the major concern in the story than external reality. In fact, there may be a large difference between the two, a discrepancy between what the character appears to be and what we finally know him or her to be. Our perception of this difference results from *dramatic irony,* in which writers allow us to know more about their characters than the characters themselves know. In John Cheever's "The Swimmer," for example, we suspect early in the story that Neddy Merrill's cross-country swim is a symptom of some unacknowledged personal crisis.

Not all short stories focus exclusively on one protagonist, of course. In some stories the emphasis may instead be on relationships in a group or on particular roles that people play in society. When the fiction writer is primarily interested in *why* characters choose and respond as they do—their *motivation*—we as readers must respond by seeking an explanation for their behavior. On the other hand, if the writer's main intent is to explore relationships among characters as they interact in groups or in socially defined roles, our emphasis as readers must be to understand that outer reality. Of course, many stories approach characters from both these directions.

Finally, some characters in fiction lend themselves to neither kind of analysis. Instead they may represent abstractions or ideas rather than complex human beings in action. Particularly in *allegories,* stories in which all the elements have symbolic meanings, characters may also be *symbols,* and our chief concern will be with those ideas or qualities they represent. In Ursula K. Le Guin's "The Ones Who Walk Away from Omelas," for instance, the suffering child is a scapegoat, a traditional symbol of the innocent who suffers for the collective sins of others.

Setting

In simple terms, *setting* is the time, place, and social reality within which a story takes place. Setting seems to be an insignificant element in some stories; they could take place just as well in any time or place. In other stories—most, in fact—setting is much more important. We have to understand where the characters are, in which period of time, in which society and at which level in that society if we are to interpret correctly the other elements in the story.

In stories in which *place* is the important element of setting, the writer usually provides specific, sometimes extended descriptions of the place. In Arthur Conan Doyle's "The Adventure of the Speckled Band," the solution of the mystery depends on our having a minutely detailed understanding of the layout of one wing of the house and of certain features of each room in that wing. Doyle devotes so much attention to this setting that we can't mistake its importance. On the other hand, Hawthorne provides almost no description of the interior of Young Goodman Brown's house, since that part of the setting is irrelevant to his main purpose. We understand, therefore, that in well-crafted short stories, descriptions of place matter and should be noted as carefully as any other part of the story.

In other stories, the *time period* is more significant than place. Again, in the Hawthorne story we have to know that we are in New England in the time of the Puritans if we are to understand the events in the story, the outlook and motivation of the central character, and the story's theme. In such a story as Poe's "The Fall of the House of Usher," however, we recognize no clearly discernible time. We don't need to know whether the action takes place in the fifteenth or the nineteenth century. The time period is irrelevant.

Just as important as place and time, sometimes even more important, is the *social context* in the story, often a product of time and place. We must understand enough about the society—its customs, values, and possibilities—to know what constraints the characters face, what they are free to choose, and what they may not do. American readers unfamiliar with Japanese society will be disturbed and confused by the action in Yukio Mishima's "Patriotism" until they understand the tradition of ritualized suicide at times when dishonor is the only alternative.

Setting is also an important element in establishing the *tone* in a work of fiction, the writer's attitude toward the situations and characters in a story. In describing the law offices in "Bartleby the Scrivener," for instance, Herman Melville sets a tone of tame, even boring, ordinariness. The extraordinary events that unfold in this world have greater intensity for us because they contrast so markedly with the matter-of-fact tone that the opening description has established.

Like other elements in a story, setting may, of course, be used occasionally for symbolic purposes. The dark wood in "Young Goodman Brown" has demonic connotations for Puritans. We understand, therefore, that by walking in the woods at night, Brown is courting evil consequences. Likewise, the jungle in Joseph Conrad's "Heart of Darkness" comes to represent the impenetrable mystery of Africa and the human heart.

Point of View

When we read a successful work of fiction, its *point of view*—the perspective from which readers will view events—often seems inevitable, as though no other is possible. For example, it is almost inconceivable that Ernest Gaines's "The Sky Is Gray" could be told from anyone else's point of view than that of eight-year-old James. We often forget that selecting this perspective is one of the most important decisions writers make. Each potential point of view offers significant advantages and corresponding limitations. In fact, when writers choose their point of view, they often choose their theme and even their protagonist as well.

A writer must first decide whether the story will be told by a narrator who is outside the story or by one of the characters within the world created in the story. An outside point of view provides greater flexibility and suggests a greater sense of objectivity. An inside point of view provides a more intimate, often more engrossing narration. Since the character narrating is within the story, he or she may be incorrectly informed or may have some motive for misrepresenting events; therefore, we cannot always trust his or her account as we generally can that of an outside narrator.

Perhaps because it gives them greater scope, writers often choose the third-person *omniscient* point of view. In such cases the all-knowing narrator is usually assumed to be the writer, so that he or she can move at will from time to time and place to place within the story's world, telling us not only of the external events in the story but also of the inner reality of any or all of the characters—their very thoughts and feelings. The advantages of such a point of view are clear: we can know anything that the writer wants us to know; we are not limited by the experience or understanding of any of the characters. The disadvantages may be less obvious: we usually don't have the opportunity to grow gradually in understanding along with the characters through sharing their experience. The omniscience we share with the writer therefore provides the pleasure of absolute knowledge but takes away the pleasure of learning and of interpreting experience as we do in life. Willa Cather's "Paul's Case" illustrates the advantages of the omniscient point of view. In the first scene of the story, not only can we "see" the events that transpire, we can "hear" the thoughts and feelings of some of the characters.

If writers wish to maintain some objectivity while permitting readers a gradual understanding, they may give up omniscience and choose the third-person *limited omniscient* point of view, which is restricted to the external experiences and internal thoughts of one character. We remain with that character throughout the entire story, seeing what he or she sees, knowing what he or she knows, though the narrator remains separate from that character. This point of view may at times be frustrating because we cannot know fully what is happening outside a character's experience. For that very reason, however, we—like the character—must interpret others' motives and assimilate information to reach conclusions about what others have done. A detective story is especially well suited to this point of view, of course, since there would be no suspense—no "mystery"—if we were to know more than the detective about the facts of the case.

In some instances, writers choose the *objective* point of view—that is, they limit themselves exclusively to exterior reality, to those things a sound camera might record if it was placed in the scene. Like a camera, the story records without comment and interpretation. All that we understand we must gather from observation and inference. The detachment provided by this point of view removes us from direct confrontation with the characters' emotions except as we interpret them. Nadine Gordimer's "The Train from Rhodesia" illustrates the effect of this technique: we see the events in the village and inside the train, hear what the characters say to one another, and then see how they react to these circumstances. We are provided with no explanation of those events, no interpretation that might guide our thinking except for the protagonist's brief meditation near the story's conclusion. We must therefore actively enter the creative process and make some of the choices that the writer usually makes. We lack the security of *knowing,* but we have the pleasure of *seeing.*

If writers choose to have one of their characters tell us the story, thus employing the *first-person* point of view, they then have other decisions to make. They may have the protagonists tell their own stories or have a secondary character do so. First-person narrators may even be bystanders, or they may recount stories they have heard from others. In all of these cases, however, we as readers have some questions to answer: how reliable is our narrator? Does he or she mean to tell the truth? Is he or she clever enough to know what matters in the story? Does he or she have personal prejudices or emotional biases that make for unreliability? These are all vital questions if we are to understand stories using the first-person point of view. To answer them, we must learn to know our narrators, perhaps better than they know themselves. In a first-person narrative, we must pay attention to small things as well as to those the narrator emphasizes. We must differentiate between the narrator's interpretation and our own. The process is a complex one, but it is one we are familiar with already since we do the same thing in our daily lives when responding to what others tell us.

The first-person point of view often works especially well in stories where the writer intends to emphasize the difference between a character's view of a situation and the reader's view of the same matters. In Updike's "A & P," for example, the nineteen-year-old cashier who tells us his story has only fleeting glimpses of himself as he really is. He obviously thinks of himself as hard-nosed, realistic, knowledgeable in the ways of the world. But beneath his pose we see a tender-hearted, callow, and highly romantic boy—we see the difference between what he means to be and what he is, a distinction that is emphasized by the point of view.

In some instances, we have an almost impersonal first-person narrator. In William Faulkner's "A Rose for Emily," we know almost nothing about the narrator except that he is a long-time resident of the Southern town where the story is set. He obviously stands for the point of view of the town itself, or at least that part which understands and values the old ways. We come to know the town, therefore, rather than the individual narrator as he tells us Miss Emily's story and the town's reaction to it.

No matter what the point of view in the story, we usually find that we come to recognize the narrator's *voice* and style—the way he or she uses words, the things he or she chooses to include or omit from the account. Whether we believe that voice to be the writer's own, as in Ursula K. Le Guin's story, or that of a created character, as in Updike's story, our response to that personality, that voice, may do as much as anything else in the story to color our intellectual and emotional response to it. A good reader, therefore, tries to recognize and interpret voice as an important part of the reading experience.

Theme

By *theme* we mean the central and unifying idea about human experience that grows out of all the other elements in the story. Since a good short story is likely to raise a number of related issues and pose a number of complex questions for perceptive readers, we may find it difficult to decide which is the most important theme, which potential statement of theme best integrates all our perceptions and insights about the story. Because the question of theme is often the most difficult as well as one of the most important ones to consider, we may differ more as readers and writers in our consideration of this element than of any of the others. These differences may be instructive, however, if they send us back to the story itself to reexamine our thinking about its central idea.

Some particular techniques may help us discover and state theme. For example, we should look closely at the generalizations about human experience that the author makes in the story, either directly or through one of the characters. Occasionally, we will find that the writer has already provided a statement of theme that we find entirely satisfactory. In "The Open Boat," for instance, Stephen Crane writes of an experience in which men battle nature—the sea—for their lives. The correspondent, the character we come to know the best, is irresolute during much of the story. He is unsure whether nature is either basically friendly, in which case the men must be saved; or basically cruel, in which case they will be destroyed. He finally comes to the following recognition, one that might serve as a statement of theme in the story: "She [nature] did not seem cruel to him then, nor beneficient, nor treacherous, nor wise. But she was indifferent, flatly indifferent."

If we find no such authorial statement of theme, we may have to ask ourselves what the central characters have learned from their experiences, since the story's beginning, or what *we* have learned that the characters did not perceive as a result of this experience. In "Young Goodman Brown," the protagonist concludes that all human beings are hopelessly corrupt, totally damned, and must therefore be rejected. As readers, however, we may arrive at a different conclusion, one that might serve as a statement of theme: since no human being is without sin, we must learn to accept and love one another because of our shared weakness and mutual need.

We may also gain an insight into theme by the ways in which writers use literary devices that compress a good deal of meaning into a small space. A *symbol,* for example, is a thing, a person, or an action that has both a literal significance and an additional abstract meaning. Symbols often reveal or emphasize major themes. For instance, in Ralph Ellison's story "King of the Bingo Game," the prize wheel that the protagonist spins is a symbol of all that he most wants in life—escape from his desperation, his poverty, his isolation. We know therefore that his doomed attempt to win at the wheel symbolizes a central traumatic loss in his life, not merely a momentary setback. The prize wheel, which we recognize as a symbol of the universal wheel of fortune, suggests a dark theme—that we cannot expect salvation from our fate.

An *allusion,* or reference, is another device that often suggests a thematic connection between something in the story and something similar in literature, history, or myth. In "Babylon Revisited," F. Scott Fitzgerald compares the Paris that Charlie knew in the twenties to the biblical Babylon, a place of ungodliness, temptation, and threatened spiritual destruction. By means of the allusion in his title, Fitzgerald suggests that the story deals with a spiritual crisis. Recognizing this will sharpen our consideration of theme in that story.

In other stories, particularly in modern experimental ones, the main themes may not arise directly from our responses to the plot and characters, but from the relationship between the writer, the reader, and the story told. Often in such cases, the writer deliberately reminds readers that they are not dealing with reality but with fiction, an artifice, a creation. Fiction that insists upon our recognizing it as creation rather than reality is often termed *reflexive.* The writers of reflexive fiction may share with their readers some personal thoughts about the choices they are making, or they may even address readers directly, asking them to cooperate in the fiction-making process. In Le Guin's "The Ones Who Walk Away from Omelas," for example, the narrator at one point says to the reader, "Perhaps it would be best if you imagine it as your own fancy bids."

Writers traditionally have tried to make their fictions seem like credible reports of reality, and some readers at first may be annoyed or confused by the violation of that convention in reflexive fiction. But such fiction offers its own stimulation and pleasure, encouraging readers to consider the nature of imagination and creation, the relationship between writer and reader in the process of story making, and the complex connection between fiction and reality. These issues necessarily become major themes in reflexive fiction.

Borges's "The Garden of Forking Paths" provides a good example of reflexive fiction. The narrator in the story discovers that the novel written by an illustrious ancestor and the maze created by that same man are in fact the same creation—the work of fiction *is* the intricate maze. The rest of the short story illustrates this point in various ways. The narrator takes us into a world of apparent contradictions, unexplained conflicts and motivations, and uncertain resolutions. We have no clear sense of traditional character, plot, or theme. As the image in the title suggests, we eventually understand that Borges is choosing among a vast number of paths that his story might follow, and he allows us to contemplate that creative process while the story is forming. The process of choosing, therefore, becomes more important than any of the particular paths chosen. The thematic connection between the process of fiction making and the process of living is, of course, obvious and important in such stories.

Our view of theme finally must be broad enough to include the whole story and all its implications. We may in fact discover that a discussion of theme will necessarily involve a consideration of all of the other basic elements of the short story.

As convenient and useful as it may be for us to separate these basic elements so that we can consider them individually, it is important to recognize that they interact with one another in rich and diverse ways to produce works that are greater than the sum of their parts. After the process of separation and discovery, the critical analysis best ends with an attempt to reintegrate the story in our own minds, to find all the reinforcing connections that exist among the elements of the story, and—very important—to understand and respond to the whole experience with appropriate emotions.

GUIDELINES FOR READING SHORT STORIES

While you have already discovered ways of reading that no doubt work for you, the following section will provide some practical advice that may help you as you read the stories in this book.

Preview the Story

It is possible to learn several important things about a story before you even read the first sentence.

1. Begin with a close consideration of the title. Since it provides our first impression of the world we are about to enter, the title gives important clues about what to expect. For instance, García Márquez's title "A Very Old Man with Enormous Wings" should prepare us for a story that will challenge our usual sense of reality, while Updike's "A & P" suggests a familiar world about which we may learn more. Cather's title "Paul's Case" tells us which character most matters in her story, while John Cheever's impersonal title "The Swimmer" may suggest more focus on the role the character plays in his world than on his individual nature. You should of course reconsider the significance of the title after you read the story to see how accurate your first impression may have been.

2. Ask what you know about the author of the story. If you recognize the name because you have read other things by that same writer, you may already have some expectations about the story. Or if you know the writer by reputation, your initial insight may again prove valuable. Readers who know that William Faulkner wrote almost exclusively about the South, for example, may enter into his world more quickly than those who have to discover that fact by reading the story.
3. Read the headnote carefully. The biography of the writer in the headnote may amplify what you already know or tell you significant facts about that person. In addition to helping you understand the writer, each headnote concludes with a statement that will help you focus on the central situation or theme in the story that follows.

Read the Story Actively

There is a difference between passively absorbing words on a page and seriously engaging the situation and ideas that those words convey. If you find that you are not always an active reader, the following techniques will help you.

1. Always read with a pen or pencil in your hand. Underline the things in a story that seem to you important: clues to a character's motivation, for instance, or a generalization that may serve as a statement of theme; a description of setting that helps to establish a particular tone, or a choice of words that gives us a sense of the narrator's voice. You will find that even after brief practice you will become adept at spotting many such significant details in a story and that your reading will improve because you have paid attention. When you underline, it is a good practice also to make a marginal notation that will help you understand later why you thought the marked material significant. Many experienced readers work out a private code that allows them to make brief but meaningful marginal notations, but at first you may have to jot down phrases that connect the underlined passages to such things as the basic elements in the story: *character* as a marginal note in "The Sky Is Gray," for instance, helps you remember why the passage mattered, but *James's character* may be a more useful notation. You may also note questions, ambiguities, your own reactions. Anything that you mark or write that reflects your active reading of the story is likely to be useful later. At the very least, the process of annotating keeps you alert.
2. Keep asking questions as you read. Sometimes you may want to write them in the margins. Other times you may simply pause in the reading to ask them of yourself. You should wonder as you read, for example, how a sequence of events is likely to turn out, whether a character has made a wise decision, whether the narrator is to be trusted in this instance. All such questions indicate that you are reading actively, that you are cooperating imaginatively in the creative process with the writer. Your reading will inevitably be more pleasurable and more illuminating as a consequence.

Respond Promptly to the Story

1. Write out, preferably in complete sentences, a few initial responses as soon as you finish the story. The responses may take the form of questions or statements or both, but they should reflect your strongest immediate impressions, including your basic

attitude toward the story. Did you like it or not? Even more important, why did you like it or not? You will be writing about yourself as well as the story, but also try to consider all five of the basic elements as part of these initial written responses.

You may find it useful to keep an informal journal in which you record such first impressions as well as later, more considered responses. Such a journal provides much useful raw material when you move from your private response to the public response of discussing or writing about the story.

2. Consult the questions at the end of the story to see how other active readers have responded. Your editors are, like you, readers who have tried to understand what has happened in a story and why it matters. Their questions, like yours, represent an attempt to open their response to your consideration and to stimulate further private response on your part. You may find that you have already answered some of the questions in your own reading and preliminary response. Other questions, however, may send you back to the story to look more closely at parts you may not have examined fully in your first reading. You may find it helpful on occasion to write out responses to certain questions in order to clarify your own understanding.

Now test the advice we have given you by reading the following story, including the headnote. Then answer the questions that follow the story.

KATE CHOPIN

The Story of an Hour

KATE CHOPIN (1851–1904) was born in St. Louis, the daughter of an Irish immigrant father who was killed in a train wreck when she was four. She was raised by her mother's French-speaking Creole family and educated at the local Academy of the Sacred Heart. At the age of eighteen, she traveled to New Orleans where she met and two years later married Oscar Chopin, a cotton trader. After her husband's death by swamp fever in 1882, Chopin and her six children returned to St. Louis where she began to write about her experiences in the South. These local-color stories appeared in magazines such as *Century* and *Harper's,* and some of them were collected in *Bayou Folk* (1894) and *A Night in Acadie* (1897). Chopin's work was well received until the publication of *The Awakening* (1899). This novel, a classic study of a woman's struggle for personal freedom, was condemned by contemporary reviewers for its realistic treatment of adultery. Shocked by this critical reaction, Chopin published little in the remaining years of her life. "The Story of an Hour," first published in *Vogue* magazine in 1894, is a brief portrait of a woman's reaction to the inevitability of death and the possibility of freedom.

Knowing that Mrs. Mallard was afflicted with a heart trouble, great care was taken to break to her as gently as possible the news of her husband's death.

It was her sister Josephine who told her, in broken sentences; veiled hints that revealed in half concealing. Her husband's friend Richards was there, too, near her. It was he who had been in the newspaper office when intelligence of the railroad disaster was received, with Brently Mallard's name leading the list of "killed." He had only taken the time to assure himself of its truth by a second telegram, and had hastened to forestall any less careful, less tender friend in bearing the sad message.

She did not hear the story as many women have heard the same, with a paralyzed inability to accept its significance. She wept at once, with sudden, wild abandonment, in her sister's arms. When the storm of grief had spent itself she went away to her room alone. She would have no one follow her.

There stood, facing the open window, a comfortable, roomy armchair. Into this she sank, pressed down by a physical exhaustion that haunted her body and seemed to reach into her soul.

She could see in the open square before her house the tops of trees that were all aquiver with the new spring life. The delicious breath of rain was in the air. In the street below a peddler was crying his wares. The notes of a distant song which some one was singing reached her faintly, and countless sparrows were twittering in the eaves.

There were patches of blue sky showing here and there through the clouds that had met and piled one above the other in the west facing her window.

She sat with her head thrown back upon the cushion of the chair, quite motionless, except when a sob came up into her throat and shook her, as a child who has cried itself to sleep continues to sob in its dreams.

She was young, with a fair, calm face, whose lines bespoke repression and even a certain strength. But now there was a dull stare in her eyes, whose gaze was fixed away off yonder on one of those patches of blue sky. It was not a glance of reflection, but rather indicated a suspension of intelligent thought.

There was something coming to her and she was waiting for it, fearfully. What was it? She did not know; it was too subtle and elusive to name. But she felt it, creeping out of the sky, reaching toward her through the sounds, the scents, the color that filled the air.

Now her bosom rose and fell tumultuously. She was beginning to recognize this thing that was approaching to possess her, and she was striving to beat it back with her will—as powerless as her two white slender hands would have been.

When she abandoned herself a little whispered word escaped her slightly parted lips. She said it over and over under her breath: "free, free, free!" The vacant stare and the look of terror that had followed it went from her eyes. They stayed keen and bright. Her pulses beat fast, and the coursing blood warmed and relaxed every inch of her body.

She did not stop to ask if it were or were not a monstrous joy that held her. A clear and exalted perception enabled her to dismiss the suggestion as trivial.

She knew that she would weep again when she saw the kind, tender hands folded in death; the face that had never looked save with love upon her, fixed and gray and dead. But she saw beyond that bitter moment a long procession of years to come that would belong to her absolutely. And she opened and spread her arms out to them in welcome.

There would be no one to live for her during those coming years; she would live for herself. There would be no powerful will bending hers in that blind persistence with which men and women believe they have a right to impose a private will upon a fellow-creature. A kind intention or a cruel intention made the act seem no less a crime as she looked upon it in that brief moment of illumination.

And yet she had loved him—sometimes. Often she had not. What did it matter! What could love, the unsolved mystery, count for in face of this possession of self-assertion which she suddenly recognized as the strongest impulse of her being!

"Free! Body and soul free!" she kept whispering.

Josephine was kneeling before the closed door with her lips to the keyhole, imploring for admission. "Louise, open the door! I beg; open the door—you will make yourself ill. What are you doing, Louise? For heaven's sake open the door."

"Go away. I am not making myself ill." No; she was drinking in a very elixir of life through that open window.

Her fancy was running riot along those days ahead of her. Spring days, and summer days, and all sorts of days that would be her own. She breathed a quick prayer that life might be long. It was only yesterday she had thought with a shudder that life might be long.

She arose at length and opened the door to her sister's importunities. There was a feverish triumph in her eyes, and she carried herself unwittingly like a goddess of Victory. She clasped her sister's waist, and together they descended the stairs. Richards stood waiting for them at the bottom.

Some one was opening the front door with a latchkey. It was Brently Mallard who entered, a little travel-stained, composedly carrying his gripsack and umbrella. He had been far from the scene of accident, and did not even know there had been one. He stood amazed at Josephine's piercing cry; at Richards' quick motion to screen him from the view of his wife.

But Richards was too late.

When the doctors came they said she had died of heart disease—of joy that kills.

QUESTIONS FOR DISCUSSION AND WRITING

1. The major divisions of the story are marked by movements from downstairs to upstairs to downstairs again. What is the difference between the kind of action that takes place in the two locations?
2. What important things do we learn about Mrs. Mallard from the very brief description of her face? How does this description help us understand what she has been and what she might be?
3. Why does Chopin contrast Mrs. Mallard's profound grief with the details of the scene she sees through the bedroom window?
4. What attitudes distinguish the points of view of Mrs. Mallard and those who are concerned with her welfare?
5. What do we discover about the connection between freedom and death during the "hour" of the story?

TWO SAMPLE STUDENT RESPONSES

What was your initial response to "The Story of an Hour"? How did you respond to it intellectually and emotionally? What ambiguous feelings did it arouse in you? Was there anything you are not sure you understood? Can you analyze this story by submitting it to the critical process we outlined earlier and looking at its basic elements individually? Compare your own basic response to the story with the two journal entries that follow, in which two student readers responded privately to the story in entirely different ways. Since they knew these entries were to be read by a teacher, their responses are perhaps a little more formal than yours may be. Both entries accomplish their major purpose, however: they show active readers responding intellectually and emotionally to the story.

Student A

My first reaction to the story is one of amazement. I cannot imagine anyone being so elated about his or her spouse dying. Even if she really had not loved him there was a bond that had kept her there. This woman must have been a very selfish person. If she had wanted her husband out of her life so she could be free, she should have left him or divorced the poor man, instead of being joyous at the news of his death.

When she is in her room alone, it seems as if for the first time in her life she can hear things she had never heard before and see things she had never paid much attention to before. I can relate to this in some sense. My father died from cancer when I was eleven. The night he died I couldn't bear to stay in the house so I went outside and sat by myself. Now, when I look back I never remember a night that was so dark or so quiet, yet I could hear the birds chirping in the trees so distinctly. I never liked birds before, but my father adored them. That night I felt as if a part of my father were coming out in me.

As you can tell, I have experienced the loss of someone very close and I cannot understand why anyone would be delighted over someone's death. If the person has been suffering with a terminal illness, I can understand that the family and friends would be relieved because he is not suffering any more, but to be overjoyed by the death, I think not.

I didn't particularly like the woman in the story so I think it was ironic that she died from the shock that her husband was not dead. If her life with him had been miserable, his life with her probably was too, so maybe he was grateful that she died.

If I were to write a formal essay on the story I would write on her feelings when she was alone.

Student B

Kate Chopin's "The Story of an Hour" is realistic in both situation and character. The situation, a woman's husband thought to be dead from a tragic accident, can and continues to happen even today. Her emotions are experienced by everyone. Though not willing to admit it, women who break up relationships often rationalize their feelings like the woman in the story. The thoughts "I can live without him" and "I'm free" are the two common feelings shared by both the audience and the writer. These two elements combined add to the meaning of the story.

I think the writer's purpose here was to put down on paper what no one would admit to feeling. I think she is also asking us, "How many times do you really feel the way others want you to feel?"

My overall response to this story is enjoyment. I liked the truthfulness, the non-typical response from the widow, and especially the ending. I thrive on surprise endings.

The first of these responses is somewhat ambiguous. The writer is "amazed" by what he perceives to be the central character's callous indifference to the death of her husband. On the other hand, he knows from his own experience that the death of a loved one may indeed sharpen one's awareness of the world. His observation that Mrs. Mallard should have left or divorced her husband if she was not happy in the marriage reveals a misunderstanding of the social values of the nineteenth-century setting, a misunderstanding that somewhat distorts his understanding of the character and the theme of the story.

The second response is more emphatic: this reader believes that Chopin has touched a truth in this story which is commonly felt but rarely expressed—that many people feel trapped in relationships that look happy to others. This writer also reveals an interesting fact about her own taste in plots when she tells us she "thrives" on surprise endings.

Obviously these two readers would have a great deal to discuss with each other about this story. No doubt they would be stimulated to reconsider their own views and perhaps return to the story to find the evidence that led them to these responses.

Equally important, both of these writers have done a good deal to move from private to public responses. Both have offered not only initial responses but also some explanation of those responses. If they were asked to write an essay-length public response to the story as the next step in the process of discovery, both would find that they had already made a number of observations worth further exploration. For example, both are obviously interested in the contradictions in the characterization of the protagonist. Both see that she is responding in a surprising way to the death of a spouse, and both understand something of the difference between the reality of that response and others' views of it. While the first reader concludes that Mrs. Mallard is "very selfish," he also acknowledges the credibility of her heightened awareness at a time of crisis. The second reader sees Mrs. Mallard as a much more sympathetic and understandable character, one whose reaction is in fact usual rather than amazing, though no one speaks of such feelings.

Which of these two views of character is more valid? We would have to return to the story to test them—the first step in any theorizing we do about short fiction. Perhaps this time, Student A would notice the time period indicated in the headnote and realize that Mrs. Mallard was trapped by social realities in a marriage that she couldn't simply leave at will. Given such facts, this reader would have to reconsider his amazement at the character's thoughts and feelings, though he might still conclude that Chopin has given us a limited, selfish woman in Mrs. Mallard.

Student B would have to find further evidence to support her contention that the protagonist's reaction was as normal as she suggests. She would have to show what details Chopin provides that allow a careful reader to form such a conclusion.

In short, both these readers have begun an exploration of characterization in the story, one that they might choose to pursue in further writing assignments. Both also touch on theme, raising other issues worth consideration. Student A, for example, writes of the intensification of life in the face of death, certainly one of the story's surprising points. Student B sees clearly the point that all of us lead buried lives, experiencing feelings that we are not permitted to express. This recognition of emotional alienation is another theme that she might choose to pursue at length in a subsequent essay.

If you are asked to write an essay about the Chopin story or one of the other stories in this book, your private response can be an extremely useful beginning point whether you choose the topic of the essay or whether it is assigned by your teacher. The following section presents some practical suggestions for approaching and developing both types of topics. Again, we'll use the Chopin story as an example.

WRITING AN ESSAY ON A TOPIC OF YOUR OWN CHOICE

If you have followed the guidelines in the previous section, you have already performed the crucial first step in selecting and developing a topic. You know well the story you are going to write about, you have thought about its implications from several perspectives, and you have considered the ways in which it achieves its purpose. Now you can begin exploring several potential topics.

Brainstorm about the Story

It is often a mistake to choose a topic too quickly since your first choice may not be the best. One way to see how many options you have is to *brainstorm* about the story—that is, in a limited amount of time—fifteen to twenty minutes—list as many points as occur to you about the story you have just read. You may discover that you have many more perceptions and possibilities than you supposed, and in addition to finding a variety of potential topics in this way, you will also generate a number of sub-points that may well be useful to you in developing the topic you finally select.

Once you have exhausted your first reactions, go back and look at the list your brainstorming has produced. Ask yourself how you might group your responses into logical units. For example, you may wish to use the five basic elements to cluster and arrange your perceptions. You may discover that some points overlap: some you can group under characterization and setting; others involve both plot and theme. Experiment with arranging the points in several ways. Consider the following brainstorming list that one reader generated after her initial reading of the Chopin headnote, story, and questions.

```
Louise Mallard
    Cries like a child
    Gazes out at nature
    Young, fair, calm face
Setting
    1800's—no divorce laws, I think. Check this.
    The house—two stories. Seems like a comfortable
      place. Why?
    Nature—spring outside, storm breaking up
Theme
    The big question: why does she feel "monstrous
      joy"?
    What about love for husband?
    She knows grief and will again, but feels freedom.
    Others don't know the truth about why she dies.
Plot
    Question points out movement from downstairs to
      upstairs, back again: why is that significant?
    Stages in the plot?
    Foreshadowing about "heart trouble" in opening.
```

```
        Stages of her response: shock, grief, joy, grief
          again, death? (Is this characterization, or
          plot?)
        Climax? When she accepts what she feels or when
          she finds out husband is not dead?
    Point of View
        Third-person, limited omniscient. Why?
        Difference in her point of view about events and
          those of others in the story (character point?)
        Why not first-person? Objectivity, advantages of
          seeing her in part from outside.
```

As you see, this reader has grouped even these first responses into categories suggested by the basic elements. She recognizes, however, that these categories are not hard and fast, that some of her observations seem to connect in one way or another to several elements. She wisely notes those overlappings in her first list, and may discover other points as she reconsiders and rearranges her list. Since the brainstorming session is only a preliminary step, however, it is a good idea to cut it short after a limited amount of time and go on to the selection stage.

Restrict Your Topic

The first and most important step in moving from loosely grouped ideas to an organized essay is to express a significant point about the story drawn from those observations—a *thesis sentence* that will give direction, shape, and purpose to the entire essay.

The thesis is a one-sentence statement of the central idea in your essay. A clear, unified, and specific thesis sentence focuses the topic so that both you and your readers know just exactly how you intend to interpret the story. It guides you in your selection of material to include and in your choices of what to exclude from consideration. It may even suggest the rhetorical method by which your topic will be developed.

A good thesis sentence has a clearly stated subject and a strong verb. It is expressed in concrete, specific words, and it commits the writer to a particular task in the paper. A weak thesis sentence is vague in diction and meaning and leaves so many options open that the writer must *still* make hard decisions about what to include or omit. Consider the two pairs of thesis statements below. Which ones would be really useful to a writer planning an essay? Which ones would provide little focus?

1a. Mrs. Mallard is a woman facing a unique situation.

1b. We see Mrs. Mallard from contrasting perspectives—the exterior view that others have of her and the interior view that we gain through Chopin's revelation of her thoughts.

2a. The description of the spring day outside is pleasant and happy.

2b. The description of the spring day outside Mrs. Mallard's window suggests the theme of the story, that even in the face of death life renews itself in a strong, joyous manner.

Sentence **1a** obviously provides no significant focus. Words like *unique, interesting,* and *nice* are empty, conveying little meaning. They should therefore be avoided in thesis statements.

Sentence **1b** offers a much more specific and focused point: we can see the writer's intention to contrast the view that other characters have of Mrs. Mallard and our final understanding of her. In this case, we understand not only the point of the essay to follow, but also the method by which it will be developed.

Sentence **2a** states a bland, pointless fact. It leads nowhere.

Sentence **2b,** however, suggests a connection between that observation and the theme of the story. The writer means to show us not only *what* Chopin has described, an obvious point, but also *why* she has described it, a matter that requires interpretation.

Since the thesis statement is so crucial to the success of the paper, you will need to spend time and thought working it out, but don't stop with the first one you compose. Consider other possibilities that you discovered during brainstorming. Try to transform each promising item on the list into a solid thesis statement. If, after you have made the effort, you find that you really cannot express a thesis idea that seems worth developing, discard the topic, but don't give up too quickly or easily. Sometimes the thesis statements that have cost you the most effort to compose turn out to be the best.

Plan Your Essay

As soon as you have several promising thesis statements, you should test them by projecting plans for the essays that arrange and develop these ideas. At this stage you should again go back to the story, your notes, your initial private response, your answers to the editors' questions, and your brainstorming. The essential question you must answer for your readers is how you arrived at the conclusion you have stated in the thesis sentence. What evidence in the story made that conclusion logical, even inevitable? After all, you mean to convince your readers of the validity of your analysis by sharing with them the evidence that led to your interpretation.

Begin by breaking the thesis idea into its logical parts. Like other essays you write, this essay will have an introductory paragraph that will state or imply the thesis point, followed by a number of paragraphs in which you will present evidence to clarify, develop, and illustrate that point. Each of those paragraphs will have a topic idea that will be a logical subdivision of the thesis idea. Like the thesis sentence itself, the topic sentence of a paragraph should be clear, specific, and unified: you should know exactly what you mean to accomplish in the paragraph. As part of your plan, then, work out topic sentences for each of your paragraphs. Since you must be certain that you will have a focused, clear point for each paragraph in the final paper, it's a good idea to write out these topic ideas as complete sentences. You will find that you are less likely to fool yourself about what you mean to do in the paragraph if you have stated its purpose explicitly and fully at the beginning. Also check carefully to see that the topic sentence is indeed a logical subdivision of the thesis idea.

Consider the thesis statement below. Is it clear and focused? Do the sample topic sentences seem to be logical subdivisions of the thesis point? Do they express specific ideas that are suitable for development in single paragraphs? Or will they require several paragraphs to develop in sufficient detail?

Thesis: While Mrs. Mallard's friends and relatives see her as the victim of life and of her own emotions, the reader knows that she has experienced an internal victory.

Topic Sentence 1. Those around Mrs. Mallard see her as a victim of circumstances.

Topic Sentence 2. The reader sees her as strong enough to face the truth about herself and to triumph over circumstances.

Develop Your Paragraphs

Once you have a thesis and topic sentences that meet the criteria we have discussed, you are ready to move to the next stage in the writing process—gathering the specific details and illustrations that best develop the topic ideas. This step also involves selection and arrangement. You will want the most relevant details and the strongest illustrations, of course; and you will want to arrange them in a coherent, logical manner. If you were searching for evidence to develop the first topic sentence above, you would find the following details to develop your point about the exterior view of Mrs. Mallard: she has a heart condition; the family friend is so worried about her that he means to deliver the news himself so that it can be broken gently to her; her sister is very concerned about her while she is alone in her room; her sister supports her physically when she comes back downstairs; the doctor assumes that her own emotion of joy has killed her when she sees her husband. Since these details are drawn from the story in the order in which they occurred, chronological order might well be the method in which you choose to develop the paragraph. On the other hand, you might also consider alternative methods. For instance, you might choose climactic order, in which you first discuss the most objective view—that of the doctor and the medical profession; then the closer, warmer point of view of the family friend; and finally the most intimate and sympathetic of the exterior points of view, that of her sister. Whichever method of organization you choose, you will have ample evidence to develop your topic idea in the paragraph. Your plan for that paragraph might now look like this:

1. Those around Mrs. Mallard see her as a victim of circumstances and her own weakness.
   a. The doctor sees her as a frail patient with a weak heart.
   b. Her friend sees her as an emotionally and physically fragile woman who must be protected from shock.
   c. Her sister sees her as a pitiful creature who must be watched over and supported at all times.

The plan here guarantees that you have both a point worth developing and a means of developing it in an organized, coherent paragraph. Having made those decisions, you will be able to concentrate on such other things as precise diction and clear syntax when you actually write the paragraph.

You will discover with only a little practice that you can go through all the stages from brainstorming to complete plan in a reasonably brief time. You can even make two or three plans for the development of thesis ideas you like so that finally you can select the one that seems most interesting, insightful, and useful.

When you write the first draft of your paper, however, you may find other points more worthy of making than the ones included in your plan. View the early draft as an experiment, a way of discovering more about the story, rather than as a finished product slavishly based on a plan. Be prepared to rethink, replan, and rewrite.

Notice how the following student writer critically responds to her own first draft and then rewrites it, avoiding weaknesses and developing strengths.

Sample Rough Draft

Two Views of Mrs. Mallard

"The Story of an Hour" was written by Kate Chopin. Mrs. Mallard, its central character, was really two different people. She was the woman other people saw. This is her external character. She was also what the reader saw. This is her internal character. The two were very different. The others think of her as kind of weak, not able to take care of herself. Upstairs by herself, she is much stronger. She develops that after she finds out about the death of her husband in a train accident. She finds that inside she is happy and strong. The other characters do not know this, however, because she dies before she can tell them. That is the irony in the story. The irony is not humorous—it's more tragic. No one ever really gets to know her. But the important thing is that Chopin gives us the two different pictures of Mrs. Mallard.

The others think of her as weak. The doctor thinks she is so frail that she might die of shock. The author tells us at the very beginning of the story that she has a heart condition. This is foreshadowing. That's why the friend comes to the house to tell her about the accident. Her husband has been killed and he wants to keep the news from her—or to have somebody tell her gently, I guess. I believe that this shows how weak he thinks she is. Her sister does too. She even listens at her keyhole. This is after she goes upstairs. The sister isn't snooping. She's genuinely concerned about her sister. She thinks she is too weak to bear it. At the end the doctor says she died of joy. This shows the exterior view one more time.

Up in her room, Mrs. Mallard goes through a big change. She first feels grief. That's understandable. Any wife who has lost a husband is likely to feel really bad about it at first. Mrs. Mallard does. She also feels something creeping up on her and that makes her uncomfortable. I think what she is seeing at first is that she will also be free because her husband is dead. She thinks she will be "free, free, free." This thought surprises her, but I think it's believable. After all, she is living in a time when wives weren't very free, so it's natural for her to like it. When she goes back downstairs like a "goddess of Victory," she has obviously changed a lot. This is what I see about her interior character.

I think Chopin did a good job of contrasting the two Mrs. Mallards. I like the ending because I think it shows how different a person may be from what that person seems to be. Not even close friends or relatives may see what's really there. In a way, other people keep them from being themselves. It's joy that kills Mrs. Mallard all right. But it's not the kind the doctor thinks. It's joy that comes from finding strength and freedom.

Although the writer may recognize that her essay does not express her thoughts clearly and well, she may not know how to improve it. At this point the response of other readers may help her. Following her teacher's directions, she exchanged essays with another student in her class so that they could clarify problems and suggest solutions by giving one another objective comments.

The student critic made three major observations about the essay: it sounded rough, didn't read smoothly and naturally; it rambled and didn't seem to come to a clear point; and the writer was probably wrong about Mrs. Mallard's having felt relief at her husband's death.

The writer agreed with the first two observations and knew that these were problems that had to be resolved in the next draft. She disagreed, however, with her critic's point about the character; she understood the other point of view but felt that the story justified her interpretation. The writer has therefore benefitted from criticism, but she has not blindly accepted every suggestion for revision. She understands that finally it is *her* view of the story that must be expressed.

The writer next talked with her teacher about the ways in which she might effectively revise. Her teacher pointed out that the most significant problem is focus: the essay does not clearly establish the unifying purpose of the details that the writer has used. The reader may wind up thinking "So what?" The teacher simply asked at this point, "What is the most important thing you have discovered about why Chopin thought this story worth telling?" Such simple but basic questions at this stage in the writing process often take the writer back to a consideration of the central thesis.

The teacher also made some suggestions about improving style and coherence, especially by using more dependent clauses for the less significant points and more transitions as she moves from point to point. After a little practice with material drawn from the rough draft, the writer felt confident that she could make such revisions easily.

However valuable the writer finds the criticism of others, however, she must not lose sight of the fact that the essay is ultimately hers—her ideas, style, and purpose. The next step therefore is for her to go through the essay, incorporating suggestions but asking her own questions and devising her own strategy for revision. In the following notes, the student comments on problems in the first draft that she can resolve in the next version.

Sample Revision Strategy

Title: Meaning is not clear here. It should say more about the thesis point.

Introduction: There are too many short sentences, and I get off the subject. The big problem is that I don't really have a clear thesis point here.

Second paragraph: This is a mess. Too many short sentences again, and it doesn't really go anywhere. I need to give more specific information to illustrate what others think about her. I need a clear topic sentence that relates back to the thesis idea.

Third paragraph: This one is a little better than the second one because there's a little more detail in it, but I need more. I should prove that she is strong and that she has found joy in her freedom. Combine some of the short sentences so it will read better and be easier to understand.

Conclusion: I say more here than in the introduction about what I really see happening in the story. The

```
point is that the writer shows two views of the
character to illustrate that grief can lead to joy
and that we don't really know each other well. No,
those are two ideas. Which one is worth developing?
Can I combine them? Anyway, that's where I'll get my
thesis point from.
```

The writer is correct in noting that her most important discovery is the connection between the characterization of the protagonist and the theme of the story, a point that she doesn't fully recognize until she expresses it in the conclusion. In trying to express that thesis idea, she came up with the following statements. Which is the richest and clearest thesis sentence?

1. Mrs. Mallard has been living a false life because others have not recognized her joy and strength.

   Obviously this statement is still not entirely clear. What is a "false life"? Is the problem that *others* haven't recognized her strength? This statement still suggests that the exterior view is correct, that she is a victim of others.

2. Mrs. Mallard finds in her response to grief that she has the strength to embrace the freedom that her life has earlier lacked.

   This statement provides a clear statement of the change that takes place in the character, but it doesn't connect clearly to the exterior and interior views of character that the writer began with and wants to keep as part of the thesis statement.

3. Although Mrs. Mallard and those around her believe that she is a weak and helpless victim of circumstances, she discovers in herself the strength to embrace life and freedom joyfully.

   This thesis statement is comprehensive enough to include almost all the points that the writer has made in her draft of the essay. It requires that the writer first show the limited view that everyone had of the character, then show the change that takes place within the character's mind and heart, and finally the implicit thematic point of this change.

Having revised her thesis sentence to her satisfaction, the writer can now reconstruct her plan. She does not have to change the basic structure, but she will devise new topic sentences that will reflect the change in the thesis idea. As she rewrites the essay, she will also make changes based on her earlier criticism of the first draft. The following essay is the product of this restructuring and revising process.

Sample Revised Essay

```
        The Significance of the Two Mrs. Mallards
  In her short story "The Story of an Hour," Kate
Chopin gives contrasting views of Mrs. Mallard, her
central character, in order to develop the theme that
```

a person can find a renewed sense of life and joy if he or she has the strength to face the truth. The others in the story feel that Mrs. Mallard is a frail victim of circumstances, but the reader sees that she has found the strength in herself to admit that in her loss and grief she has found freedom and joy.

The view that others have of Mrs. Mallard is clearly presented in the first few paragraphs. The doctor sees her only as a woman with a heart condition. A friend of the family who hears of her husband's death in the train accident brings the news to the house himself, probably to avoid the risk of giving her a shock that might kill her. Finally, her sister assists her up the stairs and later checks on her by speaking to her through the keyhole. All of these people, from the impersonal doctor to the sister who seems to love her very much, seem to agree that Mrs. Mallard is a physically and emotionally frail woman who will have great difficulty accepting the reality of her life. When she dies of a heart attack at the end of the story, they feel their view of her is confirmed.

The reader has no reason to doubt this interpretation of Mrs. Mallard until the scene when she is alone in her room. The description Chopin provides at this point suggests that the earlier view is not entirely correct: "She was young, with a fair, calm face, whose lines bespoke repression and even a certain strength." We see that strength emerge after she has given in to her grief for a while. Then she has to face a new thought that seems to be coming against her will, something "too subtle and elusive to name." Mrs. Mallard doesn't want to face this perception, whatever it is, and if she was really as weak as the others think she is, she would probably hide from it or call in others to distract her from it. Instead, she has the strength to face it and is surprised to discover that what she feels is "free, free, free!" Recognizing that she is free "body and

```
soul" gives her joy finally, even though such a
reaction is contrary to everything conventional women
are supposed to feel, particularly in Chopin's time.
She therefore has the strength not only to face the
truth but to accept what others would find shocking.
  Chopin's portrayal of Mrs. Mallard from the exterior
and interior points of view helps to develop her major
theme, that human beings should not be bound by the
view of others since freedom and joy come only to
those strong enough to face and accept the truth.
The fact that Mrs. Mallard is physically frail and
ironically dies "of joy" at the end of the story does
not change the fact that in a single hour she has
found herself and her own kind of victory.
```

While the writer will want to reread, edit, and again revise this draft, she has already greatly improved the focus, coherence, and development in this essay.

WRITING AN ESSAY ON AN ASSIGNED TOPIC

If your teacher assigns a topic about a short story, your task as a writer may be easier in some respects, and it will almost certainly be a bit shorter. If the topic is a congenial one—one that immediately prompts a clear and directed response from you—you may find that you can quickly review your notes, your private responses, and your answers to the relevant questions at the end of the story and rapidly come up with a workable plan.

If you find the topic uncongenial at first, you may have to go through a process of analyzing, planning, and writing. Assume, for example, that your teacher asks you to answer the following question in a five- or six-hundred-word essay: "Why does Chopin show us the difference between the exterior view of Mrs. Mallard and her inner reality?" You might logically approach this assigned task by breaking it down into the following steps:

1. Analyze the topic carefully to see what it asks you to do—and what it restricts you from doing. Obviously this topic is about characterization in the story, and that element must be given first consideration. If you later find that you must also deal with elements such as theme to answer the question fully, be sure you connect those points to your initial concern with characterization.
2. Determine if the wording of the topic suggests one of the standard rhetorical methods of organization. The topic above quite clearly asks you to *contrast* exterior and interior character, and that approach will provide all or at least the major part of the basic structure of your essay.

3. Consider any special terminology in the assigned topic and be certain you understand its meaning before going on. The question in this case asks you to write about a character's *exterior* and *interior reality*; you would therefore review those terms in the Introduction or the Glossary if you had any doubt about their meaning.
4. Reread the story in light of the assigned topic, paying particular attention to your earlier notations that seem relevant to that topic. You may discover, however, that you will need to underline some passages you have previously neglected and make further notes, given the new focus the topic provides.
5. Review your private responses and your answers to the questions at the end of the story to see if you have already discovered relevant detail.
6. Proceed with the same process of prewriting, writing, and revising described earlier, this time limiting yourself to the given topic. Brainstorm by developing several potential thesis sentences and projecting plans for those that are most promising. Choose the one that seems most directly to respond to the assigned topic. Select evidence from the sources earlier reviewed and organize this information in the ways we earlier suggested. Then write your rough draft. In criticizing your rough draft, make particularly sure that every part clearly focuses on the assigned topic. Writing and proofreading your final draft will of course involve much the same process already described.

A FINAL WORD

Writing about short stories is as much a process of discovery as it is reporting what has been discovered. We hope our suggestions will be helpful to you, particularly if you have not had much experience in writing about literature. You will find, however, that with practice you will develop your own methods of discovering, organizing, and developing your ideas. Remember that all critics have a single purpose: to lend their minds to their readers, to give others a way of seeing more clearly or with more pleasure matters of mutual interest. Your manner of writing must finally be shaped by the unique point of view which you alone can offer your readers.

1

CHINUA ACHEBE

Vengeful Creditor

CHINUA ACHEBE was born in 1930 in Ogidi, Nigeria, and educated at Government College, Umuahia; University College, Ibadan; and London University. After studying broadcasting at the BBC, he worked as a writer for the Nigerian Broadcasting Corporation and as the founder and director of Voice of Nigeria. His first novel, *Things Fall Apart* (1958), quickly established him as the most widely discussed contemporary African novelist. This modern classic was followed by *No Longer at Ease* (1960), *Arrow of God* (1964), and *A Man of the People* (1966). He has also written three books for children—*Chike and the River* (1966), *The Flute* (1978), and *The Drum* (1978); two volumes of poetry—*Beware, Soul Brother, and Other Poems* (1971) and *Christmas in Biafra, and Other Poems* (1973); and two collections of essays—*Morning Yet on Creation Day* (1975) and *Hopes and Impediments* (1988). His short stories have been collected in *The Sacrificial Egg, and Other Stories* (1962) and *Girls at War* (1973). Achebe has been a prominent spokesman for his own Igbo people, who tried to secede from Nigeria to form the independent nation of Biafra. His most recent novel, *Anthills of the Savannah* (1987), was nominated for the Booker Prize. In "Vengeful Creditor," reprinted from *Girls at War,* Achebe dramatizes the personal and public controversies created by the native African desire for education.

Madame, this way," sang the alert, high-wigged salesgirl minding one of a row of cash machines in the supermarket. Mrs. Emenike veered her full-stacked trolley ever so lightly to the girl.

"Madame, you were coming to me," complained the cheated girl at the next machine.

"Ah, sorry my dear. Next time."

"Good afternoon, Madame," sang the sweet-voiced girl already unloading Madame's purchases on to her counter.

"Cash or account, Madame?"

"Cash."

She punched the prices as fast as lightning and announced the verdict. Nine pounds fifteen and six. Mrs. Emenike opened her handbag, brought out from it a wallet, unzipped it and held out two clean and crisp five-pound notes. The girl punched again and the machine released a tray of cash. She put Madame's money away and gave her her change and a foot-long receipt. Mrs. Emenike glanced at the bottom of the long strip of paper where the polite machine had registered her total spending with the words THANK YOU COME AGAIN, and nodded.

It was at this point that the first hitch occurred. There seemed to be nobody around to load Madame's purchases into a carton and take them to her car outside.

"Where are these boys?" said the girl almost in distress. "Sorry, Madame. Many of our carriers have gone away because of this free primary . . . John!" she called out, as she caught sight of one of the remaining few, "Come and pack Madame's things!"

John was a limping forty-year-old boy sweating profusely even in the air-conditioned comfort of the supermarket. As he put the things into an empty carton he grumbled aloud.

"I don talk say make una tell Manager make e go fin' more people for dis monkey work."

"You never hear say everybody don go to free primary?" asked the wigged girl, jovially.

"All right-o. But I no go kill myself for sake of free primary."

Out in the car-park he stowed the carton away in the boot of Mrs. Emenike's grey Mercedes and then straightened up to wait while she opened her handbag and then her wallet and stirred a lot of coins there with one finger until she found a three-penny piece, pulled it out between two fingers and dropped it into the carrier's palm. He hesitated for a while and then limped away without saying a word.

Mrs. Emenike never cared for these old men running little boys' errands. No matter what you gave them they never seemed satisfied. Look at this grumbling cripple. How much did he expect to be given for carrying a tiny carton a few yards? That was what free primary education had brought. It had brought even worse to the homes. Mrs. Emenike had lost three servants including her baby-nurse since the beginning of the school year. The baby-nurse problem was of course the worst. What was a working woman with a seven-month-old baby supposed to do?

However the problem did not last. After only a term of free education the government withdrew the scheme for fear of going bankrupt. It would seem that on the advice of its experts the Education Ministry had planned initially for eight hundred thousand children. In the event one million and a half turned up on the first day of school. Where did all the rest come from? Had the experts misled the government? The chief statistician, interviewed on the radio, said it was nonsense to talk about a miscalculation. The trouble was simply that children from neighbouring states had been brought in in thousands and registered dishonestly by unscrupulous people, a clear case of sabotage.

Whatever the reason the government cancelled the scheme. The *New Age* wrote an editorial praising the Prime Minister for his statesmanship and courage but pointing out that the whole dismal affair could have been avoided if the government had listened in the first place to the warning of many knowledgeable and responsible citizens. Which was true enough, for these citizens had written on the pages of the *New Age* to express their doubt and reservation about free education. The newspaper, on throwing open its pages to a thorough airing of views on the matter, had pointed out that it did so in the national cause and, mounting an old hobby-horse, challenged those of its critics who could see no merit whatever in a newspaper owned by foreign capital to come forward and demonstrate an equal or a higher order of national commitment and patriotism, a challenge that none of those critics took up. The offer of space by the *New Age* was taken up eagerly and in the course of ten days at the rate of two or even three articles a day a large number of responsible citizens—lawyers, doctors, merchants, engineers, salesmen, insurance brokers, university lecturers, etc.—had written in criticism of the scheme. No one was against education for the kids, they said, but free education was premature. Someone said that not even the United States of America in all its wealth and power had introduced it yet, how much less . . .

Mr. Emenike read the various contributions with boyish excitement. "I wish civil servants were free to write to the papers," he told his wife at least on three occasions during those ten days.

"This is not bad, but he should have mentioned that this country has made tremendous strides in education since independence because parents know the value of education and will make any sacrifice to find school fees for their children. We are not a nation of Oliver Twists."

His wife was not really interested in all the argument at that stage, because somehow it all seemed to hang in the air. She had some vague, personal doubts about free education, that was all.

"Have you looked at the paper? Mike has written on this thing," said her husband on another occasion.

"Who is Mike?"

"Mike Ogudu."

"Oh, what does he say?"

"I haven't read it yet . . . Oh yes, you can trust Mike to call a spade a spade. See how he begins: 'Free primary education is tantamount to naked Communism'? That's not quite true but that's Mike all over. He thinks someone might come up to nationalize his shipping line. He is so scared of Communism."

"But who wants Communism here?"

"Nobody. That's what I told him the other evening at the Club. But he is so scared. You know one thing? Too much money is bad-o."

The discussion in the Emenike family remained at this intellectual level until one day their "Small Boy," a very bright lad of twelve helping out the cook and understudying the steward, announced he must go home to see his sick father.

"How did you know your Father was sick?" asked Madame.

"My brodder come tell me."

"When did your brother come?"

"Yesterday for evening-time."

"Why didn't you bring him to see me?"

"I no no say Madame go wan see am."

"Why you no talk since yesterday?" asked Mr. Emenike looking up from his newspaper.

"At first I tink say I no go go home. But today one mind tell me say make you go see-am-o; perhaps e de sick too much. So derefore . . ."

"All right. You can go but make sure you are back by tomorrow afternoon otherwise . . ."

"I must return back by morning-time sef."

He didn't come back. Mrs. Emenike was particularly angry because of the lies. She didn't like being outwitted by servants. Look at that little rat imagining himself clever. She should have suspected something from the way he had been carrying on of late. Now he had gone with a full month's pay which he should lose in lieu of notice. It went to show that kindness to these people did not pay in the least.

A week later the gardener gave notice. He didn't try to hide anything. His elder brother had sent him a message to return to their village and register for free education. Mr. Emenike tried to laugh him out of this ridiculous piece of village ignorance.

"Free primary education is for children. Nobody is going to admit an old man like you. How old are you?"

"I am fifteen years of old, sir."

"You are three," sneered Mrs. Emenike. "Come and suck breast."

"You are not fifteen," said Mr. Emenike. "You are at least twenty and no headmaster will admit you into a primary school. If you want to go and try, by all means do. But don't come back here when you've gone and failed."

"I no go fail, oga," said the gardener. "One man for our village wey old pass my fader sef done register everyting finish. He just go for Magistrate Court and pay dem five shilling and dey swear-am for Court juju wey no de kill porson; e no fit kill rat sef."

"Well it's entirely up to you. Your work here has been good but . . ."

"Mark, what is all that long talk for? He wants to go, let him go."

"Madame, no be say I wan go like dat. But my senior brodder . . ."

"We have heard. You can go now."

"But I no de go today. I wan give one week notice. And I fit find anoder gardener for Madame."

"Don't worry about notice or gardener. Just go away."

"I fit get my pay now or I go come back for afternoon-time?"

"What pay?"

"Madame, for dis ten days I don work for dis mont."

"Don't annoy me any further. Just go away."

But real annoyance was yet to come for Mrs. Emenike. Abigail, the baby-nurse, came up to her two mornings later as she was getting ready for work and dumped the baby in her lap and took off. Abigail of all people! After all she had done for her. Abigail who came to her full of craw-craw, who used rags for sanitary towels, who was so ignorant she gave the baby a full bowl of water to stop it crying and dropped some through its nose. Now Abigail was a lady; she could sew and bake, wear a bra and clean pants, put on powder and perfumes and stretch her hair; and she was ready to go.

From that day Mrs. Emenike hated the words "free primary" which had suddenly become part of everyday language, especially in the villages where they called it "free primadu." She was particularly angry when people made jokes about it and had a strong urge to hit them on the head for a lack of feeling and good taste. And she hated the Americans and the embassies (but particularly the Americans) who threw their money around and enticed the few remaining servants away from Africans. This began when she learnt later that her gardener had not gone to school at all but to a Ford Foundation man who had offered him seven pounds, and bought him a bicycle and a Singer sewing-machine for his wife.

"Why do they do it?" she asked. She didn't really want or need an answer but her husband gave one all the same.

"Because," said he, "back home in America they couldn't possibly afford a servant. So when they come out here and find them so cheap they go crazy. That's why."

Three months later free primary ended and school fees were brought back. The government was persuaded by then that its "piece of hare-brained socialism" as the *New Age* called it was unworkable in African conditions. This was a jibe at the Minister of Education who was notorious for his leftist sympathies and was perpetually at war with the formidable Minister of Finance.

"We cannot go through with this scheme unless we are prepared to impose new taxes," said the Finance Minister at a Cabinet meeting.

"Well then, let's impose the taxes," said the Minister of Education, which provoked derisive laughter from all his colleagues and even from Permanent Secretaries like Mr. Emenike who were in attendance and who in strict protocol should not participate in debate or laughter.

"We can't," said the Finance Minister indulgently with laughter still in his mouth. "I know my right honourable friend here doesn't worry whether or not this government lasts its full term, but some of us others do. At least I want to be here long enough to retire my election debts . . ."

This was greeted with hilarious laughter and cries of "Hear! Hear!" In debating skill Education was no match for Finance. In fact Finance had no equal in the entire Cabinet, the Prime Minister included.

"Let us make no mistake about it," he continued with a face and tone now serious, "if any one is so foolish as to impose new taxes now on our long-suffering masses . . ."

"I thought we didn't have masses in Africa," interrupted the Minister of Education starting a meagre laughter that was taken up in good sport by one or two others.

"I am sorry to trespass in my right honourable friend's territory; communist slogans are so infectious. But as I was saying we should not talk lightly about new taxes unless we are prepared to bring the Army out to quell tax riots. One simple fact of life which we have come to learn rather painfully and reluctantly—and I'm not so sure even now that we have all learnt it—is that people do riot against taxes but not against school fees. The reason is simple. Everybody, even a motor-park tout, knows what school fees are for. He can see his child going to school in the morning and coming back in the afternoon. But you go and tell him about general taxation and he immediately thinks that government is stealing his money from him. One other point, if a man doesn't want to pay school fees he doesn't have to. After all this is a democratic society. The worst that can happen is that his child stays at home which he probably doesn't mind at all. But taxes are different; everybody must pay whether they want to or not. The difference is pretty sharp. That's why mobs riot." A few people said "Hear! Hear!" Others just let out exhalations of relief or agreement. Mr. Emenike who had an unrestrainable admiration for the Finance Minister and had been nodding like a lizard through his speech shouted his "Hear! Hear!" too loud and got a scorching look from the Prime Minister.

A few desultory speeches followed and the government took its decision not to abolish free primary education but to suspend it until all the relevant factors had been thoroughly examined.

One little girl of ten, named Veronica, was brokenhearted. She had come to love school as an escape from the drabness and arduous demands of home. Her mother, a near-destitute widow who spent all hours of the day in the farm and, on market days, in the market, left Vero to carry the burden of caring for the younger children. Actually only the youngest, aged one, needed much looking after. The other two, aged seven and four, being old enough to fend for themselves, picking palm-kernels and catching grasshoppers to eat, were no problem at all to Vero. But Mary was different. She cried a lot even after she had been fed her midmorning foo-foo and soup saved for her (with a little addition of water to the soup) from breakfast, which was itself a diluted left-over from last night's supper. Mary could not manage palm-kernels on her own account yet so Vero half-chewed them first before passing them on to her. But even after the food and the kernels and grasshoppers and the bowls of water, Mary was rarely satisfied, even though her belly would be big and tight like a drum and shine like a mirror.

Their widowed mother, Martha, was a hard-luck woman. She had had an auspicious beginning long, long ago as a pioneer pupil at St. Monica's, then newly founded by white women missionaries to train the future wives of native evangelists. Most of her school mates of those days had married young teachers and were now wives of pastors and one or two even of bishops. But Martha, encouraged by her teacher, Miss Robinson, had married a young carpenter trained by white artisan-missionaries at the Onitsha Industrial Mission, a trade school founded in the fervent belief that if the black man was to be redeemed he needed to learn the Bible alongside manual skills. (Miss Robinson was very keen on the Industrial Mission whose Principal she herself later married.) But in spite of the bright hopes of those early evangelical days carpentry never developed very much in the way teaching and clerical jobs were to develop. So when Martha's husband died (or as those missionary artisans who taught him long ago might have put it—when he was called to higher service in the heavenly mansions by Him who was Himself once a Carpenter on earth) he left her in complete ruins. It had been a bad-luck marriage from the start. To begin with she had had to wait twenty whole years after their marriage for her first child to be born, so that now she was virtually an old woman with little children to care for and little strength left for her task. Not that she was bitter about that. She was simply too overjoyed that God in His mercy had lifted her curse of barrenness to feel a need to grumble. What she nearly did grumble about was the disease that struck her husband and paralysed his right arm for five years before his death. It was a trial too heavy and unfair.

Soon after Vero withdrew from school Mr. Mark Emenike, the big government man of their village who lived in the capital, called on Martha. His Mercedes 220S pulled up on the side of the main road and he walked the 500 yards or so of a narrow unmotorable path to the widow's hut. Martha was perplexed at the visit of such a great man and as she bustled about for kolanut she kept wondering. Soon the great man himself in the hurried style of modern people cleared up the mystery.

"We have been looking for a girl to take care of our new baby and today someone told me to inquire about your girl . . ."

At first Martha was reluctant, but when the great man offered her £5 for the girl's services in the first year—plus feeding and clothing and other things—she began to soften.

"Of course it is not money I am concerned about," she said, "but whether my daughter will be well cared for."

"You don't have to worry about that, Ma. She will be treated just like one of our own children. My wife is a Social Welfare Officer and she knows what it means to care for children. Your daughter will be happy in our home, I can tell you that. All she will be required to do is carry the little baby and give it its milk while my wife is away at the office and the older children at school."

"Vero and her sister Joy were also at school last term," said Martha without knowing why she said it.

"Yes, I know. That thing the government did is bad, very bad. But my belief is that a child who will be somebody will be somebody whether he goes to school or not. It is all written here, in the palm of the hand."

Martha gazed steadily at the floor and then spoke without raising her eyes. "When I married I said to myself: My daughters will do better than I did. I read Standard Three in those days and I said they will all go to College. Now they will not have even the little I had thirty years ago. When I think of it my heart wants to burst."

"Ma, don't let it trouble you too much. As I said before, what anyone of us is going to be is all written here, no matter what the difficulties."

"Yes, I pray God that what is written for these children will be better than what He wrote for me and my husband."

"Amen! . . . And as for this girl if she is obedient and good in my house what stops my wife and me sending her to school when the baby is big enough to go about on his own? Nothing. And she is still a small girl. How old is she?"

"She is ten."

"You see? She is only a baby. There is plenty of time for her to go to school."

He knew that the part about sending her to school was only a manner of speaking. And Martha knew too. But Vero who had been listening to everything from a dark corner of the adjoining room did not. She actually worked out in her mind the time it would take the baby to go about on his own and it came out quite short. So she went happily to live in the capital in a great man's family and looked after a baby who would soon be big enough to go about on his own and then she would have a chance to go to school.

Vero was a good girl and very sharp. Mr. Emenike and his wife were very pleased with her. She had the sense of a girl twice her age and was amazingly quick to learn.

Mrs. Emenike, who had almost turned sour over her recent difficulty in getting good servants, was now her old self again. She could now laugh about the fiasco of free primadu. She told her friends that now she could go anywhere and stay as long as she liked without worrying about her little man. She was so happy with Vero's work and manners that she affectionately nicknamed her "Little Madame." The nightmare of the months following Abigail's departure was mercifully at an end. She had sought high and low then for another baby-nurse and just couldn't find one. One rather over-ripe young lady had presented herself and asked for seven pounds a month. But it wasn't just the money. It was her general air—a kind of labour-exchange attitude which knew all the rights in the labour code, including presumably the right to have abortions in your servants' quarters and even have a go at your husband. Not that Mark was that way but the girl just wasn't right. After her no other person had turned up until now.

Every morning as the older Emenike children—three girls and a boy—were leaving for school in their father's Mercedes or their mother's little noisy Fiat, Vero would bring the baby out to the steps to say bye-bye. She liked their fine dresses and shoes—she'd never worn any shoes in her life—but what she envied them most was simply the going away every morning, going away from home, from familiar things and tasks. In the first months this envy was very, very mild. It lay beneath the joy of the big going away from the village, from her mother's drab hut, from eating palm-kernels that twisted the intestines at midday, from bitter-leaf soup without fish. That going away was something enormous. But as the months passed the hunger grew for these other little daily departures in fine dresses and shoes and sandwiches and biscuits wrapped in beautiful paper-napkins in dainty little school bags. One morning, as the Fiat took the children away and little Goddy began to cry on Vero's back, a song sprang into her mind to quieten him:

Little noisy motor-car
If you're going to the school
Please carry me
Pee—pee—pee!—poh—poh—poh!

All morning she sang her little song and was pleased with it. When Mr. Emenike dropped the other children home at one o'clock and took off again Vero taught them her new song. They all liked it and for days it supplanted "Baa Baa Black Sheep" and "Simple Simon" and the other songs they brought home from school.

"The girl is a genius," said Mr. Emenike when the new song finally got to him. His wife who heard it first had nearly died from laughter. She had called Vero and said to her, "So you make fun of my car, naughty girl." Vero was happy because she saw not anger but laughter in the woman's eyes.

"She is a genius," said her husband. "And she hasn't been to school."

"And besides she knows you ought to buy me a new car."

"Never mind, dear. Another year and you can have that sports car."

"Na so."

"So you don't believe me? Just you wait and see."

More weeks and months passed and little Goddy was beginning to say a few words but still no one spoke about Vero's going to school. She decided it was Goddy's fault, that he wasn't growing fast enough. And he was becoming rather too fond of riding on her back even though he could walk perfectly well. In fact his favourite words were "Cayi me." Vero made a song about that too and it showed her mounting impatience:

Carry you! Carry you!
Every time I carry you!
If you no wan grow again
I mus leave you and go school

Because Vero e don tire!
Tire, tire e don tire!

She sang it all morning until the other children returned from school and then she stopped. She only sang this one when she was alone with Goddy.

One afternoon Mrs. Emenike returned from work and noticed a redness on Vero's lips.

"Come here," she said, thinking of her expensive lipstick. "What is that?"

It turned out, however, not to be lipstick at all, only her husband's red ink. She couldn't help a smile then.

"And look at her finger-nails! And toes too! So, Little Madame, that's what you do when we go out and leave you at home to mind the baby? You dump him somewhere and begin to paint yourself. Don't ever let me catch you with that kind of nonsense again; do you hear?" It occurred to her to strengthen her warning somehow, if only to neutralize the smile she had smiled at the beginning.

"Do you know that red ink is poisonous? You want to kill yourself. Well, little lady you have to wait till you leave my house and return to your mother."

That did it, she thought in glowing self-satisfaction. She could see that Vero was suitably frightened. Throughout the rest of that afternoon she walked about like a shadow.

When Mr. Emenike came home she told him the story as he ate a late lunch. And she called Vero for him to see.

"Show him your finger-nails," she said. "And your toes, Little Madame!"

"I see," he said waving Vero away. "She is learning fast. Do you know the proverb which says that when mother-cow chews giant grass her little calves watch her mouth?"

"Who is a cow? You rhinoceros!"

"It is only a proverb, my dear."

A week or so later Mrs. Emenike just home from work noticed that the dress she had put on the baby in the morning had been changed into something much too warm.

"What happened to the dress I put on him?"

"He fell down and soiled it. So I changed him," said Vero. But there was something very strange in her manner. Mrs. Emenike's first thought was that the child must have had a bad fall.

"Where did he fall?" she asked in alarm. "Where did he hit on the ground? Bring him to me! What is all this? Blood? No? What is it? My God has killed me! Go and bring me the dress. At once!"

"I washed it," said Vero beginning to cry, a thing she had never done before. Mrs. Emenike rushed out to the line and brought down the blue dress and the white vest both heavily stained red!

She seized Vero and beat her in a mad frenzy with both hands. Then she got a whip and broke it all on her until her face and arms ran with blood. Only then did Vero admit making the child drink a bottle of red ink. Mrs. Emenike collapsed into a chair and began to cry.

Mr. Emenike did not wait to have lunch. They bundled Vero into the Mercedes and drove her the forty miles to her mother in the village. He had wanted to go alone but his wife insisted on coming, and taking the baby too. He stopped on the main road as usual. But he didn't go in with the girl. He just opened the door of the car, pulled her out and his wife threw her little bundle of clothes after her. And they drove away again.

Martha returned from the farm tired and grimy. Her children rushed out to meet her and to tell her that Vero was back and was crying in their bedroom. She practically dropped her basket and went to see; but she couldn't make any sense of her story.

"You gave the baby red ink? Why? So that you can go to school? How? Come on. Let's go to their place. Perhaps they will stay in the village overnight. Or else they will have told somebody there what happened. I don't understand your story. Perhaps you stole something. Not so?"

"Please Mama don't take me back there. They will kill me."

"Come on, since you won't tell me what you did."

She seized her wrist and dragged her outside. Then in the open she saw all the congealed blood on whip-marks all over her head, face, neck and arms. She swallowed hard.

"Who did this?"

"My Madame."

"And what did you say you did? You must tell me."

"I gave the baby red ink."

"All right, then let's go."

Vero began to wail louder. Martha seized her by the wrist again and they set off. She neither changed her work clothes nor even washed her face and hands. Every woman—and sometimes the men too—they passed on the way screamed on seeing Vero's whip-marks and wanted to know who did it. Martha's reply to all was "I don't know yet. I am going to find out."

She was lucky. Mr. Emenike's big car was there, so they had not returned to the capital. She knocked at their front door and walked in. Mrs. Emenike was sitting there in the parlour giving bottled food to the baby but she ignored the visitors completely neither saying a word to them nor even looking in their direction. It was her husband who descended the stairs a little later who told the story. As soon as the meaning dawned on Martha—that the red ink was given to the baby *to drink* and that the motive was to encompass its death—she screamed, with two fingers plugging her ears, that she wanted to hear no more. At the same time she rushed outside, tore a twig off a flowering shrub and by clamping her thumb and forefinger at one end and running them firmly along its full length stripped it of its leaves in one quick movement. Armed with the whip she rushed back to the house crying "I have heard an abomination!" Vero was now screaming and running round the room.

"Don't touch her here in my house," said Mrs. Emenike, cold and stern as an oracle, noticing her visitors for the first time. "Take her away from here at once. You want to show me your shock. Well I don't want to see. Go and show your anger in your own house. Your daughter did not learn murder here in my house."

This stung Martha deep in her spirit and froze her in mid-stride. She stood rooted to the spot, her whip-hand lifeless by her side. "My Daughter," she said finally addressing the younger woman, "as you see me here I am poor and wretched but I am not a murderer. If my daughter Vero is to become a murderer God knows she cannot say she learnt from me."

"Perhaps it's from me she learnt," said Mrs. Emenike showing her faultless teeth in a terrible false smile, "or maybe she snatched it from the air. That's right, she snatched it from the air. Look, woman, take your daughter and leave my house."

"Vero, let's go; come, let's go!"

"Yes, please go!"

Mr. Emenike who had been trying vainly to find an opening for the clearly needed male intervention now spoke.

"It is the work of the devil," he said. "I have always known that the craze for education in this country will one day ruin all of us. Now even children will commit murder in order to go to school."

This clumsy effort to mollify all sides at once stung Martha even more. As she jerked Vero homewards by the hand she clutched her unused whip in her other hand. At first she rained abuses on the girl, called her an evil child that entered her mother's womb by the back of the house.

"Oh God, what have I done?" Her tears began to flow now. "If I had had a child with other women of my age, that girl that calls me murderer might have been no older than my daughter. And now she spits in my face. That's what you brought me to," she said to the crown of Vero's head, and jerked her along more violently.

"I will kill you today. Let's get home first."

Then a strange revolt, vague, undirected began to well up at first slowly inside her. "And that thing that calls himself a man talks to me about the craze for education. All his children go to school, even the one that is only two years; but that is no craze. Rich people have no craze. It is only when the children of poor widows like me want to go with the rest that it becomes a craze. What is this life? To God, what is it? And now my child thinks she must kill the baby she is hired to tend before she can get a chance. Who put such an abomination into her belly? God, you know I did not."

She threw away the whip and with her freed hand wiped her tears.

QUESTIONS FOR DISCUSSION AND WRITING

1. How does the possibility of free education create social crisis in the story? How does Martha's "strange revolt" bring that crisis to a climax?
2. How do Mrs. Emenike's behavior at the grocery store and Mr. Emenike's reaction to the newspaper stories reveal their attitudes toward race and class?
3. How does Achebe use the parliamentary debates to extend the social setting for the story?
4. How does the narrator's introduction of Veronica make it clear that his sympathy lies with her and her family?
5. How does Achebe want us to interpret Veronica's attempt to murder the baby? How does this episode fit into the larger political conflict?

2

ISABEL ALLENDE

Two Words

ISABEL ALLENDE was born in 1942 in Lima, Peru, the daughter of a Chilean diplomat and the niece of Chile's former President Salvador Allende. After completing her education at a private school in Santiago, Chile, she first worked as a secretary for the United Nations Food and Agricultural Organization and later as a journalist and television commentator. In 1973, as part of a military coup, her uncle was assassinated and her family fled to Venezuela. She began to contribute a newspaper column to *El Nacional* (Caracas, Venezuela) and then completed her first novel, *The House of Spirits* (1982). Her subsequent novels include *Of Love and Shadows* (1984) and *Eva Luna* (1987). In 1985, Allende began teaching creative writing at universities such as the University of Virginia, Barnard College, and the University of California, Berkeley. Her most recent novel, *The Infinite Plan* (1993), is set in the United States. "Two Words," reprinted from *The Stories of Eva Luna* (1989), dramatizes the ambiguous relationship between language and politics in South America. "Walimai," reprinted from the same collection, evokes the tension between the culture of the "white ones" and the traditions of the native people.

She went by the name of Belisa Crepusculario, not because she had been baptized with that name or given it by her mother, but because she herself had searched until she found the poetry of "beauty" and "twilight" and cloaked herself in it. She made her living selling words. She journeyed through the country from the high cold mountains to the burning coasts, stopping at fairs and in markets where she set up four poles covered by a canvas awning under which she took refuge from the sun and rain to minister to her customers. She did not have to peddle her merchandise because from having wandered far and near, everyone knew who she was. Some people waited for her from one year to the next, and when she appeared in the village with her bundle beneath her arm, they would form a line in front of her stall. Her prices were fair. For five centavos she delivered verses from memory; for seven she improved the quality of dreams; for nine she wrote love letters; for twelve she invented insults for irreconcilable enemies. She also sold stories, not fantasies but long, true stories she recited at one telling, never skipping a word. This is how she carried news from one town to another. People paid her to add a line or two: our son was born; so-and-so died; our children got married; the crops burned in the field. Wherever she went a small crowd gathered around to listen as she began to speak, and that was how they learned about each others' doings, about distant relatives, about what was going on in the civil war. To anyone who paid her fifty centavos in trade, she gave the gift of a secret word to drive away melancholy. It was not the same word for everyone, naturally, because that would have been collective deceit. Each person received his or her own word, with the assurance that no one else would use it that way in this universe or the Beyond.

Belisa Crepusculario had been born into a family so poor they did not even have names to give their children. She came into the world and grew up in an inhospitable land where some years the rains became avalanches of water that bore everything away before them and others when not a drop fell from the sky and the sun swelled to fill the horizon and the world became a desert. Until she was twelve, Belisa had no occupation or virtue other than having withstood hunger and the exhaustion of centuries. During one interminable drought, it fell to her to bury four younger brothers and sisters; when she realized that her turn was next, she decided to set out across the plains in the direction of the sea, in hopes that she might trick death along the way. The land was eroded, split with deep cracks, strewn with rocks, fossils of trees and thorny bushes, and skeletons of animals bleached by the sun. From time to time she ran into families who, like her, were heading south, following the mirage of water. Some had begun the march carrying their belongings on their back or in small carts, but they could barely move their own bones, and after a while they had to abandon their possessions. They dragged themselves along painfully, their skin turned to lizard hide and their eyes burned by the reverberating glare. Belisa greeted them with a wave as she passed, but she did not stop, because she had no strength to waste in acts of compassion. Many people fell by the wayside, but she was so stubborn that she survived to cross through that hell and at long last reach the first trickles of water, fine, almost invisible threads that fed spindly vegetation and farther down widened into small streams and marshes.

Belisa Crepusculario saved her life and in the process accidentally discovered writing. In a village near the coast, the wind blew a page of newspaper at her feet. She picked up the brittle yellow paper and stood a long while looking at it, unable to determine its purpose, until curiosity overcame her shyness. She walked over to a man who was washing his horse in the muddy pool where she had quenched her thirst.

"What is this?" she asked.

"The sports page of the newspaper," the man replied, concealing his surprise at her ignorance.

The answer astounded the girl, but she did not want to seem rude, so she merely inquired about the significance of the fly tracks scattered across the page.

"Those are words, child. Here it says that Fulgencio Barba knocked out El Negro Tiznao in the third round."

That was the day Belisa Crepusculario found out that words make their way in the world without a master, and that anyone with a little cleverness can appropriate them and do business with them. She made a quick assessment of her situation and concluded that aside from becoming a prostitute or working as a servant in the kitchens of the rich there were few occupations she was qualified for. It seemed to her that selling words would be an honorable alternative. From that moment on, she worked at that profession, and was never tempted by any other. At the beginning, she offered her merchandise unaware that words could be written outside of newspapers. When she learned otherwise, she calculated the infinite possibilities of her trade and with her savings paid a priest twenty pesos to teach her to read and write; with her three remaining coins she bought a dictionary. She poured over it from A to Z and then threw it into the sea, because it was not her intention to defraud her customers with packaged words.

One August morning several years later, Belisa Crepusculario was sitting in her tent in the middle of a plaza, surrounded by the uproar of market day, selling legal arguments to an old man who had been trying for sixteen years to get his pension. Suddenly she heard yelling and thudding hoofbeats. She looked up from her writing and saw, first, a cloud of dust, and then a band of horsemen come galloping into the plaza. They were the Colonel's men, sent under orders of El Mulato, a giant known throughout the land for the speed of his knife and his loyalty to his chief. Both the Colonel and El Mulato had spent their lives fighting in the civil war, and their names were ineradicably linked to devastation and calamity. The rebels swept into town like a stampeding herd, wrapped in noise, bathed in sweat, and leaving a hurricane of fear in their trail. Chickens took wing, dogs ran for their lives, women and children scurried out of sight, until the only living soul left in the market was Belisa Crepusculario. She had never seen El Mulato and was surprised to see him walking toward her.

"I'm looking for you," he shouted, pointing his coiled whip at her; even before the words were out, two men rushed her—knocking over her canopy and shattering her inkwell—bound her hand and foot, and threw her like a sea bag across the rump of El Mulato's mount. Then they thundered off toward the hills.

Hours later, just as Belisa Crepusculario was near death, her heart ground to sand by the pounding of the horse, they stopped, and four strong hands set her down. She tried to stand on her feet and hold her head high, but her strength failed her and she slumped to the ground, sinking into a confused dream. She awakened several hours later to the murmur of night in the camp, but before she had time to sort out the sounds, she opened her eyes and found herself staring into the impatient glare of El Mulato, kneeling beside her.

"Well, woman, at last you've come to," he said. To speed her to her senses, he tipped his canteen and offered her a sip of liquor laced with gunpowder.

She demanded to know the reason for such rough treatment, and El Mulato explained that the Colonel needed her services. He allowed her to splash water on her face, and then led her to the far end of the camp where the most feared man in all the land was lazing in a hammock strung between two trees. She could not see his face, because he lay in a deceptive shadow of the leaves and the indelible shadow of all his years as a bandit, but she imagined from the way his gigantic aide addressed him with such humility that he must have a very menacing expression. She was surprised by the Colonel's voice, as soft and well-modulated as a professor's.

"Are you the woman who sells words?" he asked.

"At your service," she stammered, peering into the dark and trying to see him better.

The Colonel stood up, and turned straight toward her. She saw dark skin and the eyes of a ferocious puma, and she knew immediately that she was standing before the loneliest man in the world.

"I want to be President," he announced.

The Colonel was weary of riding across that godforsaken land, waging useless wars and suffering defeats that no subterfuge could transform into victories. For years he had been sleeping in the open air, bitten by mosquitoes, eating iguanas and snake soup, but those minor inconveniences were not why he wanted to change his destiny. What truly troubled him was the terror he saw in people's eyes. He longed to ride into a town beneath a triumphal arch with bright flags and flowers everywhere; he wanted to be cheered, and be given newly laid eggs and freshly baked bread. Men fled at the sight of him, children trembled, and women miscarried from fright; he had had enough, and so he had decided to become President. El Mulato had suggested that they ride to the capital, gallop up to the Palace, and take over the government, the way they had taken so many other things without anyone's permission. The Colonel, however, did not want to be just another tyrant; there had been enough of those before him and, besides, if he did that, he would never win people's hearts. It was his aspiration to win the popular vote in the December elections.

"To do that, I have to talk like a candidate. Can you sell me the words for a speech?" the Colonel asked Belisa Crepusculario.

She had accepted many assignments, but none like this. She did not dare refuse, fearing that El Mulato would shoot her between the eyes, or worse still, that the Colonel would burst into tears. There was more to it than that, however; she felt the urge to help him because she felt a throbbing warmth beneath her skin, a powerful desire to touch that man, to fondle him, to clasp him in her arms.

All night and a good part of the following day, Belisa Crepusculario searched her repertory for words adequate for a presidential speech, closely watched by El Mulato, who could not take his eyes from her firm wanderer's legs and virginal breasts. She discarded harsh, cold words, words that were too flowery, words worn from abuse, words that offered improbable promises, untruthful and confusing words, until all she had left were words sure to touch the minds of men and women's intuition. Calling upon the knowledge she had purchased from the priest for twenty pesos, she wrote the speech on a sheet of paper and then signaled El Mulato to untie the rope that bound her ankles to a tree. He led her once more to the Colonel, and again she felt the throbbing anxiety that had seized her when she first saw him. She handed him the paper and waited while he looked at it, holding it gingerly between thumbs and fingertips.

"What the shit does this say?" he asked finally.

"Don't you know how to read?"

"War's what I know," he replied.

She read the speech aloud. She read it three times, so her client could engrave it on his memory. When she finished, she saw the emotion in the faces of the soldiers who had gathered round to listen, and saw that the Colonel's eyes glittered with enthusiasm, convinced that with those words the presidential chair would be his.

"If after they've heard it three times, the boys are still standing there with their mouths hanging open, it must mean the thing's damn good, Colonel," was El Mulato's approval.

"All right, woman. How much do I owe you?" the leader asked.

"One peso, Colonel."

"That's not much," he said, opening the pouch he wore at his belt, heavy with proceeds from the last foray.

"The peso entitles you to a bonus. I'm going to give you two secret words," said Belisa Crepusculario.

"What for?"

She explained that for every fifty centavos a client paid, she gave him the gift of a word for his exclusive use. The Colonel shrugged. He had no interest at all in her offer, but he did not want to be impolite to someone who had served him so well. She walked slowly to the leather stool where he was sitting, and bent down to give him her gift. The man smelled the scent of a mountain cat issuing from the woman, a fiery heat radiating from her hips, he heard the terrible whisper of her hair, and a breath of sweetmint murmured into his ear the two secret words that were his alone.

"They are yours, Colonel," she said as she stepped back. "You may use them as much as you please."

El Mulato accompanied Belisa to the roadside, his eyes as entreating as a stray dog's, but when he reached out to touch her, he was stopped by an avalanche of words he had never heard before; believing them to be an irrevocable curse, the flame of his desire was extinguished.

During the months of September, October, and November the Colonel delivered his speech so many times that had it not been crafted from glowing and durable words it would have turned to ash as he spoke. He traveled up and down and across the country, riding into cities with a triumphal air, stopping in even the most forgotten villages where only the dump heap betrayed a human presence, to convince his fellow citizens to vote for him. While he spoke from a platform erected in the middle of the plaza, El Mulato and his men handed out sweets and painted his name on all the walls in gold frost. No one paid the least attention to those advertising ploys; they were dazzled by the clarity of the Colonel's proposals and the poetic lucidity of his arguments, infected by his powerful wish to right the wrongs of history, happy for the first time in their lives. When the Candidate had finished his speech, his soldiers would fire their pistols into the air and set off firecrackers, and when finally they rode off, they left behind a wake of hope that lingered for days on the air, like the splendid memory of a comet's tail. Soon the Colonel was the favorite. No one had ever witnessed such a phenomenon: a man who surfaced from the civil war, covered with scars and speaking like a professor, a man whose fame spread to every corner of the land and captured the nation's heart. The press focused their attention on him. Newspapermen came from far away to interview him and repeat his phrases, and the number of his followers and enemies continued to grow.

"We're doing great, Colonel," said El Mulato, after twelve successful weeks of campaigning.

But the Candidate did not hear. He was repeating his secret words, as he did more and more obsessively. He said them when he was mellow with nostalgia; he murmured them in his sleep; he carried them with him on horseback; he thought them before delivering his famous speech; and he caught himself savoring them in his leisure time. And every time he thought of those two words, he thought of Belisa Crepusculario, and his senses were inflamed with the memory of her feral scent, her fiery heat, the whisper of her hair, and her sweetmint breath in his ear, until he began to go around like a sleepwalker, and his men realized that he might die before he ever sat in the presidential chair.

"What's got hold of you, Colonel," El Mulato asked so often that finally one day his chief broke down and told him the source of his befuddlement: those two words that were buried like two daggers in his gut.

"Tell me what they are and maybe they'll lose their magic," his faithful aide suggested.

"I can't tell them, they're for me alone," the Colonel replied.

Saddened by watching his chief decline like a man with a death sentence on his head, El Mulato slung his rifle over his shoulder and set out to find Belisa Crepusculario. He followed her trail through all that vast country, until he found her in a village in the far south, sitting under her tent reciting her rosary of news. He planted himself, spraddle-legged, before her, weapon in hand.

"You! You're coming with me," he ordered.

She had been waiting. She picked up her inkwell, folded the canvas of her small stall, arranged her shawl around her shoulders, and without a word took her place behind El Mulato's saddle. They did not exchange so much as a word in all the trip; El Mulato's desire for her had turned into rage, and only his fear of her tongue prevented his cutting her to shreds with his whip. Nor was he inclined to tell her that the Colonel was in a fog, and that a spell whispered into his ear had done what years of battle had not been able to do. Three days later they arrived at the encampment, and immediately, in view of all the troops, El Mulato led his prisoner before the Candidate.

"I brought this witch here so you can give her back her words, Colonel," El Mulato said, pointing the barrel of his rifle at the woman's head. "And then she can give you back your manhood."

The Colonel and Belisa Crepusculario stared at each other, measuring one another from a distance. The men knew then that their leader would never undo the witchcraft of those accursed words, because the whole world could see the voracious-puma eyes soften as the woman walked to him and took his hand in hers.

QUESTIONS FOR DISCUSSION AND WRITING

1. Why does Allende end the story where she does? Has it reached its logical conclusion? If so, how does that conclusion comment on the major conflict in the story?
2. How are animals and other natural images used to characterize the relationships between Belisa, the Colonel, and El Mulato?
3. How does the civil war create the social setting for the story? How does the social setting compare with the natural environment?
4. How does the combining of supernatural and realistic details complicate the point of view in the story?
5. How does the story demonstrate the transforming power of language? How has Belisa used this power to save the Colonel and the land?

3

ISABEL ALLENDE

Walimai

The name given me by my father is Walimai, which in the tongue of our brothers in the north means "wind." I can tell it to you, since now you are like my own daughter and you have my permission to call my name, although only when we are among family. The names of persons and living creatures demand respect, because when we speak them we touch their heart and become a part of their life force. This is how we blood kinsmen greet each other. I cannot understand the ease with which the white ones call each others' names, with no fear; not only does it show a lack of respect, it can also lead to grave danger. I have noted that these persons speak unthinkingly, not realizing that to speak is also to be. Word and gesture are man's thought. We should not speak without reason; this I have taught my sons and daughters, but they do not always listen to my counsel. Long ago, taboos and traditions were respected. My grandfathers, and the grandfathers of my grandfathers, received all necessary knowledge from their grandfathers. Nothing changed. A man with a good memory could recall every teaching he had received and thus knew what to do in any situation. But then came the white ones speaking against the wisdom of the grandfathers, and pushing us off our land. We move always deeper into the jungle, but always they overtake us; sometimes years pass, but finally they come again, and we must destroy our planted fields, put our children on our back, bind our animals, and depart. So it has been as long as I have memory: leave everything, and run away like mice—not like the mighty warriors and gods who inhabited these lands in days of old. Some of our young are curious about the whites, and while we travel deeper into the forest to continue to live as our ancestors did, others undertake a different path. We think of those who leave as if they were dead, because very few return, and those who do have changed so that we cannot recognize them as kinsmen.

They tell that in the years before I came into the world not enough women were born to our people, and thus my father had to travel long roads to seek a wife from a different tribe. He journeyed through the forests, following the marks of others who had traveled that route before him and for the same purpose and returned with women not of our blood. After much traveling, when my father had begun to lose hope of finding a life companion, he saw a girl standing by a tall waterfall, a river that fell from the sky. Staying some distance away, in order not to frighten her, he spoke to her in the tone that hunters use to calm their prey, and explained his need to marry her. She made signs that he might come near, studied him openly, and must have been pleased by the face of the traveler, because she decided that the idea of marriage was not a rash one. My father had to work for his father-in-law until he paid for the woman's value. After they had fulfilled the rituals of marriage, they made the return journey to our village.

I grew up with my brothers and sisters beneath the canopies of tall trees, never seeing the sun. Sometimes a wounded tree would fall, leaving an opening in the thick dome of the forest; at those times we saw the blue eye of the sky. My father and mother told me stories; they sang songs to me, and taught me what a man must know to survive alone, with nothing but his bow and his arrows. I was free. We, the Children of the Moon, cannot live unless we are free. When we are closed inside walls or bars we collapse inward; we become blind and deaf, and in a few days our spirit detaches itself from the bones of our chest and abandons us. At those times we become like miserable beasts and, almost always, we prefer to die. That is why our houses have no walls, only a sloped roof to stop the wind and shed the rain; beneath it we hang our hammocks close together, because we like to listen to the dreams of the women and the children and feel the breath of the monkeys and dogs and pigs that sleep beneath the same shelter. In the earliest times we lived in the jungles without knowing that there was a world beyond the cliffs and rivers. Friends came to visit from other tribes, and told us rumors of Boa Vista and El Plantanal, of the white ones and their customs, but we believed these were only stories to make us laugh. I reached manhood, and my turn came to find a wife, but I decided to wait, because I liked being with the bachelors; we were happy, and lived well. Even so, I could not devote myself solely to games and resting as the others did, because my family is very large: brothers and sisters, cousins, nieces and nephews, many mouths to feed, and much work for a hunter.

One day a group of the pale men came to our village. They hunted with powder, from far away, without skill or courage; they could not climb a tree or spear a fish in the water; they moved clumsily through the jungle, they were always getting tangled in their packs, their weapons, even their own feet. They did not clothe themselves in air, as we do, but wore wet and stinking clothing; they were dirty and they did not know the laws of decency, but they insisted on telling us of their knowledge and their gods. We compared them with what we had been told about the white men, and we verified the truth of that gossip. Soon we realized that these men were not missionaries, or soldiers or rubber collectors: they were mad. They wanted the land; they wanted to carry away the wood; they were also searching for stones. We explained that the jungle is not something to be tossed over your shoulder and transported like a dead bird, but they did not want to hear our arguments. They made camp near our village. Each one of them was like a wind of catastrophe; he destroyed everything he touched; he left a trail of waste behind him; he disturbed animals and people. At first we obeyed the laws of courtesy, and pleased them, because they were our guests; but they were never satisfied, they wanted always more, until, weary of their games, we declared war with all traditional ceremonies. They are not good warriors; they are easily frightened and their fragile skullbones could not withstand the clubbing we gave them. Afterward we abandoned our village and we journeyed to the east where the forest is impenetrable, traveling for long stretches through the tops of the trees so their companions could not find us. We had been told that they are vengeful, and that for each one of them who dies, even in fair battle, they are capable of eliminating an entire tribe, including the children. We discovered a place to establish a new village. It was not as good—the women had to walk hours to find clean water—but we stayed there because we believed that no one would come so far to search for us. A year later I was far from our village following the track of a puma, when I approached too near a camp of soldiers. I was tired, and had not eaten in several days; for this reason, I used poor judgment. Instead of turning back when I glimpsed the strangers, I lay down to rest. The soldiers caught me. They did not mention the men we had clubbed to death. In fact, they asked me nothing; perhaps they did not know those men or did not know that I am Walimai. They pressed me into work with the rubber collectors, with many men from other tribes, men they had dressed in trousers and driven to work with no thought for their wishes. The rubber demands much care, and there were not enough people to do the work; that was why they forced us. That was a time without freedom, and I do not want to speak of it. I stayed only to see whether I could learn anything, but from the beginning I knew I would return to my people. Nothing can long hold a warrior against his will.

We worked from sun to sun, some bleeding the trees to drain their life drop by drop, others cooking the liquid to thicken it and form it into great balls. The air outdoors was sick with the stench of the burned sap, and the air indoors in the sleeping quarters foul with the sweat of the men. No one could draw a deep breath in that place. They gave us maize to eat, and bananas, and the strange contents of some cans, which I never tasted, because nothing good for humans can grow in tins. At one end of the camp they had built a large hut where they kept the women. After two weeks of working with the raw rubber, the boss handed me a slip of paper and sent me where the women were. He also gave me a cup of liquor, which I turned out on the ground, because I have seen how that water destroys a man's good sense. I stood in line with the others. I was the last, and when it came my turn to enter the hut, the sun had gone down and night begun, with its clamor of frogs and parrots.

She was of the tribe of the Ila, the people of gentle heart, from which the most delicate girls come. Some men travel months on end to find the Ila; they take them gifts and hunt for them in the hope of obtaining one of their women. She looked like a lizard lying there, but I recognized her because my mother, too, was an Ila woman. She lay naked on her straw mat, tied by one ankle to a chain staked in the ground, sluggish, as if she had breathed in the *yopo* of the acacia; she had the smell of sick dogs, and she was wet with the dew of all the men who had covered her before me. She was the size of a young boy, and her bones clicked like small stones in the river. The Ila women remove all their bodily hair, even their eyelashes; they adorn their ears with feathers and flowers; they thrust polished sticks through their cheeks and nose; they paint designs over all their body in the reds of the annatto, the deep purple of the palm, and the black of carbon. But she had none of that. I placed my machete on the ground, and greeted her as a sister, imitating some songbirds and the sound of rivers. She did not respond. I pounded her chest, to see whether her spirit still resonated in her rib cage, but there was no echo; her soul was very weak and could not answer me. Kneeling beside her, I gave her water to drink and spoke to her in my mother's tongue. She opened her eyes, and stared at me a long time. I understood.

First of all, I washed myself without wasting the clean water. I took a good draft into my mouth and sprinkled it in small streams onto my hands, which I rubbed carefully and then wet to clean my face. I did the same with her, to cleanse the men's dew from her body. I removed the trousers the boss had given me. From a cord at my waist hung my sticks for making fire, the tips of arrows, my roll of tobacco, my wooden knife with a rat's tooth in the point, and a bag of strong leather in which I carried a small amount of curare. I spread a bit of that paste on the point of my knife, bent over the woman and, with the poisoned instrument, opened a small cut in her neck. Life is a gift from the gods. The hunter kills to feed his family; he tries not to eat the flesh of his prey but prefers to eat what another hunter offers him. At times, tragically, a man kills another in war, but he never harms a woman or a child. She looked at me with large eyes yellow as honey, and I thought she tried to smile, gratefully. For her I had violated the first taboo of the Children of the Moon, and I would have to pay for my shame with many labors of expiation. I held my ear to her mouth, and she murmured her name. I repeated it twice in my mind to be very sure, but did not speak it aloud; it is not good to mention the dead or disturb their peace, and she was already dead even though her heart still beat. Soon I saw the muscles of her belly, her chest, her arms stiffen with paralysis; she stopped breathing, and changed color. A sigh escaped her, and her body died without a struggle, as small creatures die.

Immediately, I felt her spirit leave through her nostrils and enter mine, anchoring itself to my breastbone. All her weight fell upon me, and I had to struggle to get to my feet. I moved very slowly, as if I were under water. I arranged her body in the position of the last rest, with her knees touching her chin. I bound her with fibers from the mat, then made a mound with the rest of the straw and used my sticks to make fire. When I saw that the fire was blazing intensely, I left the hut slowly, laboriously climbed the camp fence—because she kept dragging me down—and walked into the forest. I had reached the first trees when I heard the alarm bells.

I walked all the first day without stopping. On the second day I fashioned a bow and arrows so I could hunt for her, and for myself as well. The warrior who bears the weight of another human life must fast for ten days; in this way the spirit of the dead one grows weak; finally it lets go and journeys to the land of souls. If the warrior does not do this, the spirit grows fat on the food it is fed and grows inside the man until it suffocates him. I have seen men of great courage die this way. But before I fulfilled those conditions, I had to lead the spirit of the Ila woman into the thickest jungle where she would never be found. I ate very little, barely enough not to kill her a second time. Each mouthful tasted like spoiled meat, and every sip of water was bitter, but I forced myself to swallow, to nourish the two of us. For one complete cycle of the moon I traveled deep into the jungle, carrying inside me the soul of the woman who weighed more each day. We spoke often. The tongue of the Ila is uninhibited and resounds beneath the trees with a long echo. We communicated singing, with our body, with our eyes, our waist, our feet. I repeated to her the legends I had learned from my mother and my father; I told her my past, and she told me of the first part of her life, when she was a happy girl playing with her brothers and sisters, rolling in the mud and swinging from the high branches. Out of courtesy, she did not mention her recent past of misfortune and humiliation. I caught a white bird; I plucked the finest feathers and made adornments for her ears. At night I kept a small fire burning so she would not be cold, and so jaguars or serpents would not disturb her sleep. I bathed her in the river with care, rubbing her with ash and crushed flowers, to take away her bad memories.

Finally one day we reached the perfect spot, and had no further excuse to continue walking. There the jungle was so dense that in places I had to open a path by slashing the undergrowth with my machete, even my teeth, and we had to speak in a low voice not to alter the silence of time. I chose a place near a thread of water; I put up a roof of leaves and made a hammock for her from three long strips of bark. With my knife I shaved my head and began my fast.

During the time we had walked together the woman and I had come to love one another so much that we did not want to part; but man does not control life, not even his own, and so I had to fulfill my obligation. For many days, I took nothing in my mouth except a few sips of water. As I grew weak, she slipped from my embrace, and her spirit, ever more ethereal, did not weigh upon me as before. After five days, while I dozed, she took her first steps, but she was not ready to continue her journey alone, and she returned to me. She repeated those brief travels on several occasions, each time venturing a little farther. The sorrow of her parting was as terrible as a deep burn, and I had to call on all the courage I had learned from my father not to call her name aloud and bring her back to me forever. After twelve days I dreamed that she was flying like a toucan above the treetops, and I awakened feeling very light, and wanting to weep. She was gone. I picked up my weapons and walked for many hours until I reached a branch of the river. I walked into the water up to my waist; I speared a small fish with a sharp stick and swallowed it whole, scales, tail, and all. I immediately vomited it up with a little blood; it was as it should be. I was not sad now. I had learned that sometimes death is more powerful than love. Then I went to hunt, so I would not return to my village with empty hands.

QUESTIONS FOR DISCUSSION AND WRITING

1. If Walimai is the protagonist in the story, how is the conflict resolved in the story? If, however, Walimai's *people* are the protagonists, how will the conflict most likely be resolved beyond the frame of the story?
2. How does Walimai compare the behavior, motives, and values of "the white ones" with his own people?
3. What does the jungle mean to "the white ones"? What does it mean to the people who live there?
4. How does Walimai establish his reliability as a narrator within his world? What does the reader find out that reveals the limits of his understanding?
5. How does Walimai's killing of the girl reflect the values of his culture?

4

SHERWOOD ANDERSON

The Egg

SHERWOOD ANDERSON (1876–1941) was born in Camden, Ohio, and spent most of his childhood in small Midwestern towns where his father worked intermittently as a harness maker and sign painter. Anderson's formal education ended at the age of fourteen when he began working as an errand boy and stable groom. At nineteen, he left home to work at a series of odd jobs in Chicago before enlisting in the Spanish American War. After the war he worked as an advertising writer and then purchased an interest in a paint factory, trying for the next several years to combine his business interests with his growing aspirations to become a serious writer. In 1912, following a nervous breakdown, Anderson gave up his business to devote his full attention to writing. After three mildly successful books—*Windy McPherson's Sons* (1916), *Marching Men* (1917), and *Mid-American Chants* (1918)—he published *Winesburg, Ohio* (1919), a set of related short stories exploring the deforming effects of disillusionment. Its novel lyric style and psychological realism established Anderson's reputation as one of America's major writers. His later work includes two novels, *Poor White* (1920) and *Dark Laughter* (1925), and three volumes of short stories, *The Triumph of the Egg* (1921), *Horses and Men* (1923), and *Death in the Woods* (1933). In "The Egg," reprinted from *The Triumph of the Egg*, a young narrator recounts his parents' unsuccessful attempts to triumph over disillusionment and fulfill their dreams.

My father was, I am sure, intended by nature to be a cheerful, kindly man. Until he was thirty-four years old he worked as a farm-hand for a man named Thomas Butterworth whose place lay near the town of Bidwell, Ohio. He had then a horse of his own and on Saturday evenings drove into town to spend a few hours in social intercourse with other farm-hands. In town he drank several glasses of beer and stood about in Ben Head's saloon—crowded on Saturday evenings with visiting farm-hands. Songs were sung and glasses thumped on the bar. At ten o'clock father drove home along a lonely country road, made his horse comfortable for the night and himself went to bed, quite happy in his position in life. He had at that time no notion of trying to rise in the world.

It was in the spring of his thirty-fifth year that father married my mother, then a country school-teacher, and in the following spring I came wriggling and crying into the world. Something happened to the two people. They became ambitious. The American passion for getting up in the world took possession of them.

It may have been that mother was responsible. Being a school-teacher she had no doubt read books and magazines. She had, I presume, read of how Garfield, Lincoln, and other Americans rose from poverty to fame and greatness and as I lay beside her—in the days of her lying-in—she may have dreamed that I would some day rule men and cities. At any rate she induced father to give up his place as a farm-hand, sell his horse and embark on an independent enterprise of his own. She was a tall silent woman with a long nose and troubled grey eyes. For herself she wanted nothing. For father and myself she was incurably ambitious.

The first venture into which the two people went turned out badly. They rented ten acres of poor stony land on Grigg's Road, eight miles from Bidwell, and launched into chicken raising. I grew into boyhood on the place and got my first impressions of life there. From the beginning they were impressions of disaster and if, in my turn, I am a gloomy man inclined to see the darker side of life, I attribute it to the fact that what should have been for me the happy joyous days of childhood were spent on a chicken farm.

One unversed in such matters can have no notion of the many and tragic things that can happen to a chicken. It is born out of an egg, lives for a few weeks as a tiny fluffy thing such as you will see pictured on Easter cards, then becomes hideously naked, eats quantities of corn and meal bought by the sweat of your father's brow, gets diseases called pip, cholera, and other names, stands looking with stupid eyes at the sun, becomes sick and dies. A few hens and now and then a rooster, intended to serve God's mysterious ends, struggle through to maturity. The hens lay eggs out of which come other chickens and the dreadful cycle is thus made complete. It is all unbelievably complex. Most philosophers must have been raised on chicken farms. One hopes for so much from a chicken and is so dreadfully disillusioned. Small chickens, just setting out on the journey of life, look so bright and alert and they are in fact so dreadfully stupid. They are so much like people they mix one up in one's judgments of life. If disease does not kill them they wait until your expectations are thoroughly aroused and then walk under the wheels of a wagon—to go squashed and dead back to their maker. Vermin infest their youth, and fortunes must be spent for curative powders. In later life I have seen how a literature has been built up on the subject of fortunes to be made out of the raising of chickens. It is intended to be read by the gods who have just eaten of the tree of the knowledge of good and evil. It is a hopeful literature and declares that much may be done by simple ambitious people who own a few hens. Do not be led astray by it. It was not written for you. Go hunt for gold on the frozen hills of Alaska, put your faith in the honesty of a politician, believe if you will that the world is daily growing better and that good will triumph over evil, but do not read and believe the literature that is written concerning the hen. It was not written for you.

I, however, digress. My tale does not primarily concern itself with the hen. If correctly told it will center on the egg. For ten years my father and mother struggled to make our chicken farm pay and then they gave up that struggle and began another. They moved into the town of Bidwell, Ohio, and embarked in the restaurant business. After ten years of worry with incubators that did not hatch, and with tiny—and in their own way lovely—balls of fluff that passed on into semi-naked pullethood and from that into dead henhood, we threw all aside and packing our belongings on a wagon drove down

Grigg's Road toward Bidwell, a tiny caravan of hope looking for a new place from which to start on our upward journey through life.

We must have been a sad looking lot, not, I fancy, unlike refugees fleeing from a battlefield. Mother and I walked in the road. The wagon that contained our goods had been borrowed for the day from Mr. Albert Griggs, a neighbor. Out of its sides stuck the legs of cheap chairs and at the back of the pile of beds, tables, and boxes filled with kitchen utensils was a crate of live chickens, and on top of that the baby carriage in which I had been wheeled about in my infancy. Why we stuck to the baby carriage I don't know. It was unlikely other children would be born and the wheels were broken. People who have few possessions cling tightly to those they have. That is one of the facts that make life so discouraging.

Father road on top of the wagon. He was then a bald-headed man of forty-five, a little fat and from long association with mother and the chickens he had become habitually silent and discouraged. All during our ten years on the chicken farm he had worked as a laborer on neighboring farms and most of the money he had earned had been spent for remedies to cure chicken diseases, on Wilmer's White Wonder Cholera Cure or Professor Bidlow's Egg Producer or some other preparations that mother found advertised in the poultry papers. There were two little patches of hair on father's head just above his ears. I remember that as a child I used to sit looking at him when he had gone to sleep in a chair before the stove on Sunday afternoons in the winter. I had at that time already begun to read books and have notions of my own and the bald path that led over the top of his head was, I fancied, something like a broad road, such a road as Caesar might have made on which to lead his legions out of Rome and into the wonders of an unknown world. The tufts of hair that grew above father's ears were, I thought, like forests. I fell into a half-sleeping, half-waking state and dreamed I was a tiny thing going along the road into a far beautiful place where there were no chicken farms and where life was a happy eggless affair.

One might write a book concerning our flight from the chicken farm into town. Mother and I walked the entire eight miles—she to be sure that nothing fell from the wagon and I to see the wonders of the world. On the seat of the wagon beside father was his greatest treasure. I will tell you of that.

On a chicken farm where hundreds and even thousands of chickens come out of eggs surprising things sometimes happen. Grotesques are born out of eggs as out of people. The accident does not often occur—perhaps once in a thousand births. A chicken is, you see, born that has four legs, two pairs of wings, two heads or what not. The things do not live. They go quickly back to the hand of their maker that has for a moment trembled. The fact that the poor little things could not live was one of the tragedies of life to father. He had some sort of notion that if he could but bring into henhood or roosterhood a five-legged hen or a two-headed rooster his fortune would be made. He dreamed of taking the wonder about to county fairs and of growing rich by exhibiting it to other farm-hands.

At any rate he saved all the little monstrous things that had been born on our chicken farm. They were preserved in alcohol and put each in its own glass bottle. These he had carefully put into a box and on our journey into town it was carried on the wagon seat beside him. He drove the horses with one hand and with the other clung to the box. When we got to our destination the box was taken down at once and the bottles removed. All during our days as keepers of a restaurant in the town of Bidwell, Ohio, the grotesques in their little glass bottles sat on a shelf back of the counter. Mother sometimes protested but father was a rock on the subject of his treasure. The grotesques were, he declared, valuable. People, he said, liked to look at strange and wonderful things.

Did I say that we embarked in the restaurant business in the town of Bidwell, Ohio? I exaggerated a little. The town itself lay at the foot of a low hill and on the shore of a small river. The railroad did not run through the town and the station was a mile away to the north at a place called Pickleville. There had been a cider mill and pickle factory at the station, but before the time of our coming they had both gone out of business. In the morning and in the evening busses came down to the station along a road called Turner's Pike from the hotel on the main street of Bidwell. Our going to the out of the way place to embark in the restaurant business was mother's idea. She talked of it for a year and then one day went off and rented an empty store building opposite the railroad station. It was her idea that the restaurant would be profitable. Travelling men, she said, would be always waiting around to take trains out of town and town people would come to the station to await incoming trains. They would come to the restaurant to buy pieces of pie and drink coffee. Now that I am older I know that she had another motive in going. She was ambitious for me. She wanted me to rise in the world, to get into a town school and become a man of the towns.

At Pickleville father and mother worked hard as they always had done. At first there was the necessity of putting our place into shape to be a restaurant. That took a month. Father built a shelf on which he put tins of vegetables. He painted a sign on which he put his name in large red letters. Below his name was the sharp command—"EAT HERE"—that was so seldom obeyed. A show case was bought and filled with cigars and tobacco. Mother scrubbed the floor and the walls of the room. I went to school in the town and was glad to be away from the farm and from the presence of the discouraged, sad-looking chickens. Still I was not very joyous. In the evening I walked home from school along Turner's Pike and remembered the children I had seen playing in the town school yard. A troop of little girls had gone hopping about and singing. I tried that. Down along the frozen road I went hopping solemnly on one leg. "Hippity Hop To The Barber Shop," I sang shrilly. Then I stopped and looked doubtfully about. I was afraid of being seen in my gay mood. It must have seemed to me that I was doing a thing that should not be done by one who, like myself, had been rasied on a chicken farm where death was a daily visitor.

Mother decided that our restaurant should remain open at night. At ten in the evening a passenger train went north past our door followed by a local freight. The freight crew had switching to do in Pickleville and when the work was done they came to our restaurant for hot coffee and food. Sometimes one of them ordered a fried egg. In the morning at four they returned north-bound and again visited us. A little trade began to grow up. Mother slept at night and during the day tended the restaurant and fed our boarders while father slept. He slept in the same bed mother had occupied during the night and I went off to the town of Bidwell and to school. During the long nights, while mother and I slept, father cooked meats that were to go into sandwiches for the lunch baskets of our boarders. Then an idea in regard to getting up in the world came into his head. The American spirit took hold of him. He also became ambitious.

In the long nights when there was little to do father had time to think. That was his undoing. He decided that he had in the past been an unsuccessful man because he had not been cheerful enough and that in the future he would adopt a cheerful outlook on life. In the early morning he came upstairs and got into bed with mother. She woke and the two talked. From my bed in the corner I listened.

It was father's idea that both he and mother should try to entertain the people who came to eat at our restaurant. I cannot now remember his words, but he gave the impression of one about to become in some obscure way a kind of public entertainer. When people, particularly young people from the town of Bidwell, came into our place, as on very rare occasions they did, bright entertaining conversation was to be made. From father's words I gathered that something of the jolly inn-keeper effect was to be sought. Mother must have been doubtful from the first, but she said nothing discouraging. It was father's notion that a passion for the company of himself and mother would spring up in the breasts of the younger people of the town of Bidwell. In the evening bright happy groups would come singing down Turner's Pike. They would troop shouting with joy and laughter into our place. There would be song and festivity. I do not mean to give the impression that father spoke so elaborately of the matter. He was as I have said an uncommunicative man. "They want some place to go. I tell you they want some place to go," he said over and over. That was as far as he got. My own imagination has filled in the blanks.

For two or three weeks this notion of father's invaded our house. We did not talk much, but in our daily lives tried earnestly to make smiles take the place of glum looks. Mother smiled at the boarders and I, catching the infection, smiled at our cat. Father became a little feverish in his anxiety to please. There was no doubt, lurking somewhere in him, a touch of the spirit of the showman. He did not waste much of his ammunition on the railroad men he served at night but seemed to be waiting for a young man or woman from Bidwell to come in to show what he could do. On the counter in the restaurant there was a wire basket kept always filled with eggs, and it must have been before his eyes when the idea of being entertaining was born in his brain. There was something pre-natal about the way eggs kept themselves connected with the development of his idea. At any rate an egg ruined his new impulse in life. Late one night I was awakened by a roar of anger coming from father's throat. Both mother and I sat upright in our beds. With trembling hands she lighted a lamp that stood on a table by her head. Downstairs the front door of our restaurant went shut with a bang and in a few minutes father tramped up the stairs. He held an egg in his hand and his hand trembled as though he were having a chill. There was a half insane light in his eyes. As he stood glaring at us I was sure he intended throwing the egg at either mother or me. Then he laid it gently on the table beside the lamp and dropped on his knees beside mother's bed. He began to cry like a boy and I, carried away by his grief, cried with him. The two of us filled the little upstairs room with our wailing voices. It is ridiculous, but of the picture we made I can remember only the fact that mother's hand continually stroked the bald path that ran across the top of his head. I have forgotten what mother said to him and how she induced him to tell her of what had happened downstairs. His explanation also has gone out of my mind. I remember only my own grief and fright and the shiny path over father's head glowing in the lamp light as he knelt by the bed.

As to what happened downstairs. For some unexplainable reason I know the story as well as though I had been a witness to my father's discomfiture. One in time gets to know many unexplainable things. On that evening young Joe Kane, son of a merchant of Bidwell, came to Pickleville to meet his father, who was expected on the ten o'clock evening train from the South. The train was three hours late and Joe came into our place to loaf about and to wait for its arrival. The local freight train came in and the freight crew were fed. Joe was left alone in the restaurant with father.

From the moment he came into our place the Bidwell young man must have been puzzled by my father's actions. It was his notion that father was angry at him for hanging around. He noticed that the restaurant keeper was apparently disturbed by his presence and he thought of going out. However, it began to rain and he did not fancy the long walk to town and back. He bought a five-cent cigar and ordered a cup of coffee. He had a newspaper in his pocket and took it out and began to read. "I'm waiting for the evening train. It's late," he said apologetically.

For a long time father, whom Joe Kane had never seen before, remained silently gazing at his visitor. He was no doubt suffering from an attack of stage fright. As so often happens in life he had thought so much and so often of the situation that now confronted him that he was somewhat nervous in its presence.

For one thing, he did not know what to do with his hands. He thrust one of them nervously over the counter and shook hands with Joe Kane. "How-de-do," he said. Joe Kane put his newspaper down and stared at him. Father's eye lighted on the basket of eggs that sat on the counter and he began to talk. "Well," he began hesitatingly, "well, you have heard of Christopher Columbus, eh?" He seemed to be angry. "That Christopher Columbus was a cheat," he declared emphatically. "He talked of making an egg stand on its end. He talked, he did, and then he went and broke the end of the egg."

My father seemed to his visitor to be beside himself at the duplicity of Christopher Columbus. He muttered and swore. He declared it was wrong to teach children that Christopher Columbus was a great man when, after all, he cheated at the critical moment. He had declared he would make an egg stand on end and then when his bluff had been called he had done a trick. Still grumbling at Columbus, father took an egg from the basket on the counter and began to walk up and down. He rolled the egg between the palms of his hands. He smiled genially. He began to mumble words regarding the effect to be produced on an egg by the electricity that comes out of the human body. He declared that without breaking its shell and by virtue of rolling it back and forth in his hands he could stand the egg on its end. He explained that the warmth of his hands and the gentle rolling movement he gave the egg created a new center of gravity, and Joe Kane was mildly interested. "I have handled thousands of eggs," father said. "No one knows more about eggs than I do."

He stood the egg on the counter and it fell on its side. He tried the trick again and again, each time rolling the egg between the palms of his hands and saying the words regarding the wonders of electricity and the laws of gravity. When after a half hour's effort he did succeed in making the egg stand for a moment he looked up to find that his visitor was no longer watching. By the time he had succeeded in calling Joe Kane's attention to the success of his effort the egg had again rolled over and lay on its side.

Afire with the showman's passion and at the same time a good deal disconcerted by the failure of his first effort, father now took the bottles containing the poultry monstrosities down from their place on the shelf and began to show them to his visitor. "How would you like to have seven legs and two heads like this fellow?" he asked, exhibiting the most remarkable of his treasures. A cheerful smile played over his face. He reached over the counter and tried to slap Joe Kane on the shoulder as he had seen men do in Ben Head's saloon when he was a young farm-hand and drove to town on Saturday evenings. His visitor was made a little ill by the sight of the body of the terribly deformed bird floating in the alcohol in the bottle and got up to go. Coming from behind the counter father took hold of the young man's arm and led him back to his seat. He grew a little angry and for a moment had to turn his face away and force himself to smile. Then he put the bottles back on the shelf. In an outburst of generosity he fairly compelled Joe Kane to have a fresh cup of coffee and another cigar at his expense. Then he took a pan and filling it with vinegar, taken from a jug that sat beneath the counter, he declared himself about to do a new trick. "I will heat this egg in this pan of vinegar," he said. "Then I will put it through the neck of a bottle without breaking the shell. When the egg is inside the bottle it will resume its normal shape and the shell will become hard again. Then I will give the bottle with the egg in it to you. You can take it about with you wherever you go. People will want to know how you got the egg in the bottle. Don't tell them. Keep them guessing. That is the way to have fun with this trick."

Father grinned and winked at his visitor. Joe Kane decided that the man who confronted him was mildly insane but harmless. He drank the cup of coffee that had been given him and began to read his paper again. When the egg had been heated in vinegar father carried it on a spoon to the counter and going into a back room got an empty bottle. He was angry because his visitor did not watch him as he began to do his trick, but nevertheless went cheerfully to work. For a long time he struggled, trying to get the egg to go through the neck of the bottle. He put the pan of vinegar back on the stove, intending to reheat the egg, then picked it up and burned his fingers. After a second bath in the hot vinegar the shell of the egg had been softened a little but not enough for his purpose. He worked and worked and a spirit of desperate determination took possession of him. When he thought that at last the trick was about to be consummated the delayed train came in at the station and Joe Kane started to go nonchalantly out the door. Father made a last desperate effort to conquer the egg and make it do the thing that would establish his reputation as one who knew how to entertain guests who came into his restaurant. He worried the egg. He attempted to be somewhat rough with it. He swore and the sweat stood out on his forehead. The egg broke under his hand. When the contents spurted over his clothes, Joe Kane, who had stopped at the door, turned and laughed.

A roar of anger rose from my father's throat. He danced and shouted a string of inarticulate words. Grabbing another egg from the basket on the counter, he threw it, just missing the head of the young man as he dodged through the door and escaped.

Father came upstairs to mother and me with an egg in his hand. I do not know what he intended to do. I imagine he had some idea of destroying it, of destroying all eggs, and that he intended to let mother and me see him begin. When, however, he got into the presence of mother something happened to him. He laid the egg gently on the table and dropped on his knees by the bed as I have already explained. He later decided to close the restaurant for the night and to come upstairs and get into bed. When he did so he blew out the light and after much muttered conversation both he and mother went to sleep. I suppose I went to sleep also, but my sleep was troubled. I awoke at dawn and for a long time looked at the egg that lay on the table. I wondered why eggs had to be and why from the egg came the hen who again laid the egg. The question got into my blood. It has stayed there, I imagine, because I am the son of my father. At any rate, the problem remains unsolved in my mind. And that, I conclude, is but another evidence of the complete and final triumph of the egg—at least as far as my family is concerned.

QUESTIONS FOR DISCUSSION AND WRITING

1. Who and what are responsible for the family's decision to make each change in its lifestyle? How does the father's failure to perform the trick tie together the various elements of the story's plot?
2. How does the narrator characterize his father at the beginning of the story? What changes the father's character? How does the narrator characterize his mother?
3. How does the narrator's detailed description of the chicken ranch prepare us for the disasters at the restaurant?
4. Why does Anderson choose the son's point of view to tell the story? How does the son account for his "gloomy" perspective on life?
5. What larger mystery does the egg come to represent to the narrator? What relationship does the narrator see between the egg and the bottled chicks?

5

MARGARET ATWOOD

The Age of Lead

MARGARET ATWOOD was born in Ottawa, Ontario, in 1939, and educated at the University of Toronto, Radcliffe College, and Harvard University. She has taught at the University of British Columbia and York University and served as writer-in-residence at the University of Alabama and Macquarie University, Australia. Although she has written over a dozen volumes of poetry, several

books for children and works of nonfiction, she is best known for her novels, including *Surfacing* (1972), the best selling and controversial *The Handmaid's Tale* (1985), and *Cat's Eye* (1989). Her short stories have been collected in *Dancing Girls and Other Stories* (1977), *Bluebird's Egg* (1983), *Murder in the Dark* (1983), and *Wilderness Tips* (1991). In "The Age of Lead," reprinted from *Wilderness Tips,* Atwood's main character sees significant parallels between a failed expedition and her own attempt to live a life without consequences.

The man has been buried for a hundred and fifty years. They dug a hole in the frozen gravel, deep into the permafrost, and put him down there so the wolves couldn't get to him. Or that is the speculation.

When they dug the hole the permafrost was exposed to the air, which was warmer. This made the permafrost melt. But it froze again after the man was covered up, so that when he was brought to the surface he was completely enclosed in ice. They took the lid off the coffin and it was like those maraschino cherries you used to freeze in ice-cube trays for fancy tropical drinks: a vague shape, looming through a solid cloud.

Then they melted the ice and he came to light. He is almost the same as when he was buried. The freezing water has pushed his lips away from his teeth into an astonished snarl, and he's a beige colour, like a gravy stain on linen, instead of pink, but everything is still there. He even has eyeballs, except that they aren't white but the light brown of milky tea. With these tea-stained eyes he regards Jane: an indecipherable gaze, innocent, ferocious, amazed, but contemplative, like a werewolf meditating, caught in a flash of lightning at the exact split second of his tumultuous change.

Jane doesn't watch very much television. She used to watch it more. She used to watch comedy series, in the evenings, and when she was a student at university she would watch afternoon soaps about hospitals and rich people, as a way of procrastinating. For a while, not so long ago, she would watch the evening news, taking in the disasters with her feet tucked up on the chesterfield, a throw rug over her legs, drinking a hot milk and rum to relax before bed. It was all a form of escape.

But what you can see on the television, at whatever time of day, is edging too close to her own life; though in her life, nothing stays put in those tidy compartments, comedy here, seedy romance and sentimental tears there, accidents and violent deaths in thirty-second clips they call *bites,* as if they were chocolate bars. In her life, everything is mixed together. *Laugh, I thought I'd die,* Vincent used to say, a very long time ago, in a voice imitating the banality of mothers; and that's how it's getting to be. So when she flicks on the television these days, she flicks it off again soon enough. Even the commercials, with their surreal dailiness, are beginning to look sinister, to suggest meanings behind themselves, behind their façade of cleanliness, lusciousness, health, power, and speed.

Tonight she leaves the television on, because what she is seeing is so unlike what she usually sees. There is nothing sinister behind this image of the frozen man. It is entirely itself. *What you sees is what you gets,* as Vincent also used to say, crossing his eyes, baring his teeth at one side, pushing his nose into a horror-movie snout. Although it never was, with him.

The man they've dug up and melted was a young man. Or still is: it's difficult to know what tense should be applied to him, he is so insistently present. Despite the distortions caused by the ice and the emaciation of his illness, you can see his youthfulness, the absence of toughening, of wear. According to the dates painted carefully onto his nameplate, he was only twenty years old. His name was John Torrington. He was, or is, a sailor, a seaman. He wasn't an able-bodied seaman though; he was a petty officer, one of those marginally in command. Being in command has little to do with the ableness of the body.

He was one of the first to die. This is why he got a coffin and a metal nameplate, and a deep hole in the permafrost—because they still had the energy, and the piety, for such things, that early. There would have been a burial service read over him, and prayers. As time went on and became nebulous and things did not get better, they must have kept the energy for themselves; and also the prayers. The prayers would have ceased to be routine and become desperate, and then hopeless. The later dead ones got cairns of piled stones, and the much later ones not even that. They ended up as bones, and as the soles of boots and the occasional button, sprinkled over the frozen stony treeless relentless ground in a trail heading south. It was like the trails in fairy tales, of bread crumbs or seeds or white stones. But in this case nothing had sprouted or lit up in the moonlight, forming a miraculous pathway to life; no rescuers had followed. It took ten years before anyone knew even the barest beginnings of what had been happening to them.

All of them together were the Franklin Expedition. Jane has seldom paid much attention to history except when it has overlapped with her knowledge of antique furniture and real estate—"19th C. pine harvest table," or "Prime location Georgian centre hall, impeccable reno"—but she knows what the Franklin Expedition was. The two ships with their bad-luck names have been on stamps—the *Terror,* the *Erebus.* Also she took it in school, along with a lot of other doomed expeditions. Not many of those explorers seemed to have come out of it very well. They were always getting scurvy, or lost.

What the Franklin Expedition was looking for was the Northwest Passage, an open seaway across the top of the Arctic, so people, merchants, could get to India from England without going all the way around South America. They wanted to go that way because it would cost less and increase their profits. This was much less exotic than Marco Polo or the headwaters of the Nile; nevertheless, the idea of exploration appealed to her then: to get onto a boat and just go somewhere, somewhere mapless, off into the unknown. To launch yourself into fright; to find things out. There was something daring and noble about it, despite all of the losses and failures, or perhaps because of them. It was like having sex, in high school, in those days before the Pill, even if you took precautions. If you were a girl, that is. If you were a boy, for whom such a risk was fairly minimal, you had to do other things: things with weapons or large amounts of alcohol, or high-speed vehicles, which at her suburban Toronto high school, back then at the beginning of the sixties, meant switchblades, beer, and drag races down the main streets on Saturday nights.

Now, gazing at the television as the lozenge of ice gradually melts and the outline of the young sailor's body clears and sharpens, Jane remembers Vincent, sixteen and with more hair then, quirking one eyebrow and lifting his lip in a mock sneer and saying, "Franklin, my dear, I don't give a damn." He said it loud enough to be heard, but the history teacher ignored him, not knowing what else to do. It was hard for the teachers to keep Vincent in line, because he never seemed to be afraid of anything that might happen to him.

He was hollow-eyed even then; he frequently looked as if he'd been up all night. Even then he resembled a very young old man, or else a dissipated child. The dark circles under his eyes were the ancient part, but when he smiled he had lovely small white teeth, like the magazine ads for baby foods. He made fun of everything, and was adored. He wasn't adored the way other boys were adored, those boys with surly lower lips and greased hair and a studied air of smouldering menace. He was adored like a pet. Not a dog, but a cat. He went where he liked, and nobody owned him. Nobody called him Vince.

Strangely enough, Jane's mother approved of him. She didn't usually approve of the boys Jane went out with. Maybe she approved of him because it was obvious to her that no bad results would follow from Jane's going out with him: no heartaches, no heaviness, nothing burdensome. None of what she called *consequences.* Consequences: the weightiness of the body, the growing flesh hauled around like a bundle, the tiny frill-framed goblin head in the carriage. Babies and marriage, in that order. This was how she understood men and their furtive, fumbling, threatening desires, because Jane herself had been a consequence. She had been a mistake, she had been a war baby. She had been a crime that had needed to be paid for, over and over.

By the time she was sixteen, Jane had heard enough about this to last her several lifetimes. In her mother's account of the way things were, you were young briefly and then you fell. You plummeted downwards like an overripe apple and hit the ground with a squash; you fell, and everything about you fell too. You got fallen arches and a fallen womb, and your hair and teeth fell out. That's what having a baby did to you. It subjected you to the force of gravity.

This is how she remembers her mother, still: in terms of a pendulous, drooping, wilting motion. Her sagging breasts, the downturned lines around her mouth. Jane conjures her up: there she is, as usual, sitting at the kitchen table with a cup of cooling tea, exhausted after her job clerking at Eaton's department store, standing all day behind the jewellery counter with her bum stuffed into a girdle and her swelling feet crammed into the mandatory medium-heeled shoes, smiling her envious, disapproving smile at the spoiled customers who turned up their noses at pieces of glittering junk she herself could never afford to buy. Jane's mother sighs, picks at the canned spaghetti Jane has heated up for her. Silent words waft out of her like stale talcum powder: *What can you expect,* always a statement, never a question. Jane tries at this distance for pity, but comes up with none.

As for Jane's father, he'd run away from home when Jane was five, leaving her mother in the lurch. That's what her mother called it—"running away from home"—as if he'd been an irresponsible child. Money arrived from time to time, but that was the sum total of his contribution to family life. Jane resented him for it, but she didn't blame him. Her mother inspired in almost everyone who encountered her a vicious desire for escape.

Jane and Vincent would sit out in the cramped backyard of Jane's house, which was one of the squinty-windowed little stuccoed wartime bungalows at the bottom of the hill. At the top of the hill were the richer houses, and the richer people: the girls who owned cashmere sweaters, at least one of them, instead of the Orlon and lambswool so familiar to Jane. Vincent lived about halfway up the hill. He still had a father, in theory.

They would sit against the back fence, near the spindly cosmos flowers that passed for a garden, as far away from the house itself as they could get. They would drink gin, decanted by Vincent from his father's liquor hoard and smuggled in an old military pocket flask he'd picked up somewhere. They would imitate their mothers.

"I pinch and I scrape and I work my fingers to the bone, and what thanks do I get?" Vincent would say peevishly. "No help from you, Sonny Boy. You're just like your father. Free as the birds, out all night, do as you like and you don't care one pin about anyone else's feelings. Now take out that garbage."

"It's love that does it to you," Jane would reply, in the resigned, ponderous voice of her mother. "You wait and see, my girl. One of these days you'll come down off your devil-may-care high horse." As Jane said this, and even though she was making fun, she could picture love, with a capital L, descending out of the sky towards her like a huge foot. Her mother's life had been a disaster, but in her own view an inevitable disaster, as in songs and movies. It was Love that was responsible, and in the face of Love, what could be done? Love was like a steamroller. There was no avoiding it, it went over you and you came out flat.

Jane's mother waited, fearfully and uttering warnings, but with a sort of gloating relish, for the same thing to happen to Jane. Every time Jane went out with a new boy her mother inspected him as a potential agent of downfall. She distrusted most of these boys; she distrusted their sulky, pulpy mouths, their eyes half-closed in the up-drifting smoke of their cigarettes, their slow, sauntering manner of walking, their clothing that was too tight, too full: too full of their bodies. They looked this way even when they weren't putting on the sulks and swaggers, when they were trying to appear bright-eyed and industrious and polite for Jane's mother's benefit, saying goodbye at the front door, dressed in their shirts and ties and their pressed heavy-date suits. They couldn't help the way they looked, the way they were. They were helpless; one kiss in a dark corner would reduce them to speechlessness; they were sleepwalkers in their own liquid bodies. Jane, on the other hand, was wide awake.

Jane and Vincent did not exactly go out together. Instead they made fun of going out. When the coast was clear and Jane's mother wasn't home, Vincent would appear at the door with his face painted bright yellow, and Jane would put her bathrobe on back to front and they would order Chinese food and alarm the delivery boy and eat sitting cross-legged on the floor, clumsily, with chopsticks. Or Vincent would turn up in a threadbare thirty-year-old suit and a bowler hat and a cane, and Jane would rummage around in the cupboard for a discarded church-going hat of her mother's, with smashed cloth violets and a veil, and they would go downtown and walk around, making loud remarks about the passersby, pretending to be old, or poor, or crazy. It was thoughtless and in bad taste, which was what they both liked about it.

Vincent took Jane to the graduation formal, and they picked out her dress together at one of the second-hand clothing shops Vincent frequented, giggling at the shock and admiration they hoped to cause. They hesitated between a flame-red with falling-off sequins and a backless hip-hugging black with a plunge front, and chose the black, to go with Jane's hair. Vincent sent a poisonous-looking lime-green orchid, the colour of her eyes, he said, and Jane painted her eyelids and fingernails to match. Vincent wore white tie and tails, and a top hat, all frayed Sally-Ann issue and ludicrously too large for him. They tangoed around the gymnasium, even though the music was not a tango, under the tissue-paper flowers, cutting a black swath through the sea of pastel tulle, unsmiling, projecting a corny sexual menace, Vincent with Jane's long pearl necklace clenched between his teeth.

The applause was mostly for him, because of the way he was adored. Though mostly by the girls, thinks Jane. But he seemed to be popular enough among the boys as well. Probably he told them dirty jokes, in the proverbial locker room. He knew enough of them.

As he dipped Jane backwards, he dropped the pearls and whispered in her ear, "No belts, no pins, no pads, no chafing." It was from an ad for tampons, but it was also their leitmotif. It was what they both wanted: freedom from the world of mothers, the world of precautions, the world of burdens and fate and heavy female constraints upon the flesh. They wanted a life without consequences. Until recently, they'd managed it.

The scientists have melted the entire length of the young sailor now, at least the upper layer of him. They've been pouring warm water over him, gently and patiently; they don't want to thaw him too abruptly. It's as if John Torrington is asleep and they don't want to startle him.

Now his feet have been revealed. They're bare, and white rather than beige; they look like the feet of someone who's been walking on a cold floor, on a winter day. That is the quality of the light that they reflect: winter sunlight, in early morning. There is something intensely painful to Jane about the absence of socks. They could have left him his socks. But maybe the others needed them. His big toes are tied together with a strip of cloth; the man talking says this was to keep the body tidily packaged for burial, but Jane is not convinced. His arms are tied to his body, his ankles are tied together. You do that when you don't want a person walking around.

This part is almost too much for Jane; it is too reminiscent. She reaches for the channel switcher, but luckily the show (it is only a show, it's only another show) changes to two of the historical experts, analyzing the clothing. There's a close-up of John Torrington's shirt, a simple, high-collared, pin-striped white-and-blue cotton, with mother-of-pearl buttons. The stripes are a printed pattern, rather than a woven one; woven would have been more expensive. The trousers are grey linen. Ah, thinks Jane. Wardrobe. She feels better: this is something she knows about. She loves the solemnity, the reverence, with which the stripes and buttons are discussed. An interest in the clothing of the present is frivolity, an interest in the clothing of the past is archaeology; a point Vincent would have appreciated. After high school, Jane and Vincent both got scholarships to university, although Vincent had appeared to study less, and did better. That summer they did everything together. They got summer jobs at the same hamburger heaven, they went to movies together after work, although Vincent never paid for Jane. They still occasionally dressed up in old clothes and pretended to be a weird couple, but it no longer felt careless and filled with absurd invention. It was beginning to occur to them that they might conceivably end up looking like that.

In her first year at university Jane stopped going out with other boys: she needed a part-time job to help pay her way, and that and the schoolwork and Vincent took up all her time. She thought she might be in love with Vincent. She thought that maybe they should make love, to find out. She had never done such a thing, entirely; she had been too afraid of the untrustworthiness of men, of the gravity of love, too afraid of consequences. She thought, however, that she might trust Vincent.

But things didn't go that way. They held hands, but they didn't hug; they hugged, but they didn't pet; they kissed, but they didn't neck. Vincent liked looking at her, but he liked it so much he would never close his eyes. She would close hers and then open them, and there would be Vincent, his own eyes shining in the light from the streetlamp or the moon, peering at her inquisitively as if waiting to see what odd female thing she would do next, for his delighted amusement. Making love with Vincent did not seem altogether possible.

(Later, after she had flung herself into the current of opinion that had swollen to a river by the late sixties, she no longer said "making love"; she said "having sex." But it amounted to the same thing. You had sex, and love got made out of it whether you liked it or not. You woke up in a bed or more likely on a mattress, with an arm around you, and found yourself wondering what it might be like to keep on doing it. At that point Jane would start looking at her watch. She had no intention of being left in any lurches. She would do the leaving herself. And she did.)

Jane and Vincent wandered off to different cities. They wrote each other postcards. Jane did this and that. She ran a co-op food store in Vancouver, did the financial stuff for a diminutive theatre in Montreal, acted as managing editor for a small publisher, ran the publicity for a dance company. She had a head for details and for adding up small sums—having to scrape her way through university had been instructive—and such jobs were often available if you didn't demand much money for doing them. Jane could see no reason to tie herself down, to make any sort of soul-stunting commitment, to anything or anyone. It was the early seventies; the old heavy women's world of girdles and precautions and consequences had been swept away. There were a lot of windows opening, a lot of doors: you could look in, then you could go in, then you could come out again.

She lived with several men, but in each of the apartments there were always cardboard boxes, belonging to her, that she never got around to unpacking; just as well, because it was that much easier to move out. When she got past thirty she decided it might be nice to have a child, some time, later. She tried to figure out a way of doing this without becoming a mother. Her own mother had moved to Florida, and sent rambling, grumbling letters, to which Jane did not often reply.

Jane moved back to Toronto, and found it ten times more interesting than when she'd left it. Vincent was already there. He'd come back from Europe, where he'd been studying film; he'd opened a design studio. He and Jane met for lunch, and it was the same: the same air of conspiracy between them, the same sense of their own potential for outrageousness. They might still have been sitting in Jane's garden, beside the cosmos flowers, drinking forbidden gin and making fun.

Jane found herself moving in Vincent's circles, or were they orbits? Vincent knew a great many people, people of all kinds; some were artists and some wanted to be, and some wanted to know the ones who were. Some had money to begin with, some made money; they all spent it. There was a lot more talk about money, these days, or among these people. Few of them knew how to manage it, and Jane found herself helping them out. She developed a small business among them, handling their money. She would gather it in, put it away safely for them, tell them what they could spend, dole out an allowance. She would note with interest the things they bought, filing their receipted bills: what furniture, what clothing, which *objets.* They were delighted with their money, enchanted with it. It was like milk and cookies for them, after school. Watching them play with their money, Jane felt responsible and indulgent, and a little matronly. She stored her own money carefully away, and eventually bought a townhouse with it.

All this time she was with Vincent, more or less. They'd tried being lovers but had not made a success of it. Vincent had gone along with this scheme because Jane had wanted it, but he was elusive, he would not make declarations. What worked with other men did not work with him: appeals to his protective instincts, pretences at jealousy, requests to remove stuck lids from jars. Sex with him was more like a musical workout. He couldn't take it seriously, and accused her of being too solemn about it. She thought he might be gay, but was afraid to ask him; she dreaded feeling irrelevant to him, excluded. It took them months to get back to normal.

He was older now, they both were. He had thinning temples and a widow's peak, and his bright inquisitive eyes had receded even farther into his head. What went on between them continued to look like a courtship, but was not one. He was always bringing her things: a new, peculiar food to eat, a new grotesquerie to see, a new piece of gossip, which he would present to her with a sense of occasion, like a flower. She in her turn appreciated him. It was like a yogic exercise, appreciating Vincent; it was like appreciating an anchovy, or a stone. He was not everyone's taste.

There's a black-and-white print on the television, then another: the nineteenth century's version of itself, in etchings. Sir John Franklin, older and fatter than Jane had supposed; the *Terror* and the *Erebus,* locked fast in the crush of the ice. In the high Arctic, a hundred and fifty years ago, it's the dead of winter. There is no sun at all, no moon; only the rustling northern lights, like electronic music, and the hard little stars.

What did they do for love, on such a ship, at such a time? Furtive solitary gropings, confused and mournful dreams, the sublimation of novels. The usual, among those who have become solitary.

Down in the hold, surrounded by the creaking of the wooden hull and the stale odours of men far too long enclosed, John Torrington lies dying. He must have known it; you can see it on his face. He turns toward Jane his tea-coloured look of puzzled reproach.

Who held his hand, who read to him, who brought him water? Who, if anyone, loved him? And what did they tell him about whatever it was that was killing him? Consumption, brain fever, Original Sin. All those Victorian reasons, which meant nothing and were the wrong ones. But they must have been comforting. If you are dying, you want to know why.

In the eighties, things started to slide. Toronto was not so much fun any more. There were too many people, too many poor people. You could see them begging on the streets, which were clogged with fumes and cars. The cheap artists' studios were torn down or converted to coy and upscale office space; the artists had migrated elsewhere. Whole streets were torn up or knocked down. The air was full of windblown grit.

People were dying. They were dying too early. One of Jane's clients, a man who owned an antique store, died almost overnight of bone cancer. Another, a woman who was an entertainment lawyer, was trying on a dress in a boutique and had a heart attack. She fell over and they called the ambulance, and she was dead on arrival. A theatrical producer died of AIDS, and a photographer; the lover of the photographer shot himself, either out of grief or because he knew he was next. A friend of a friend died of emphysema, another of viral pneumonia, another of hepatitis picked up on a tropical vacation, another of spinal meningitis. It was as if they had been weakened by some mysterious agent, a thing like a colourless gas, scentless and invisible, so that any germ that happened along could invade their bodies, take them over.

Jane began to notice news items of the kind she'd once skimmed over. Maple groves dying of acid rain, hormones in the beef, mercury in the fish, pesticides in the vegetables, poison sprayed on the fruit, God knows what in the drinking water. She subscribed to a bottled spring-water service and felt better for a few weeks, then read in the paper that it wouldn't do her much good, because whatever it was had been seeping into everything. Each time you took a breath, you breathed some of it in. She thought about moving out of the city, then read about toxic dumps, radioactive waste, concealed here and there in the countryside and masked by the lush, deceitful green of waving trees.

Vincent has been dead for less than a year. He was not put into the permafrost or frozen in ice. He went into the Necropolis, the only Toronto cemetery of whose general ambience he approved; he got flower bulbs planted on top of him, by Jane and others. Mostly by Jane. Right now John Torrington, recently thawed after a hundred and fifty years, probably looks better than Vincent.

A week before Vincent's forty-third birthday, Jane went to see him in the hospital. He was in for tests. Like fun he was. He was in for the unspeakable, the unknown. He was in for a mutated virus that didn't even have a name yet. It was creeping up his spine, and when it reached his brain it would kill him. It was not, as they said, responding to treatment. He was in for the duration.

It was white in his room, wintry. He lay packed in ice, for the pain. A white sheet wrapped him, his white thin feet poked out the bottom of it. They were so pale and cold. Jane took one look at him, laid out on ice like a salmon, and began to cry.

"Oh Vincent," she said. "What will I do without you?" This sounded awful. It sounded like Jane and Vincent making fun, of obsolete books, obsolete movies, their obsolete mothers. It also sounded selfish: here she was, worrying about herself and her future, when Vincent was the one who was sick. But it was true. There would be a lot less to do, altogether, without Vincent.

Vincent gazed up at her; the shadows under his eyes were cavernous. "Lighten up," he said, not very loudly, because he could not speak very loudly now. By this time she was sitting down, leaning forward; she was holding one of his hands. It was thin as the claw of a bird. "Who says I'm going to die?" He spent a moment considering this, revised it. "You're right," he said. "They got me. It was the Pod People from outer space. They said, 'All I want is your poddy.' "

Jane cried more. It was worse because he was trying to be funny. "But what *is* it?" she said. "Have they found out yet?"

Vincent smiled his ancient, jaunty smile, his smile of detachment, of amusement. There were his beautiful teeth, juvenile as ever. "Who knows?" he said. "It must have been something I ate."

Jane sat with the tears running down her face. She felt desolate: left behind, stranded. Their mothers had finally caught up to them and been proven right. There were consequences after all; but they were the consequences to things you didn't even know you'd done.

The scientists are back on the screen. They are excited, their earnest mouths are twitching, you could almost call them joyful. They know why John Torrington died; they know, at last, why the Franklin Expedition went so terribly wrong. They've snipped off pieces of John Torrington, a fingernail, a lock of hair, they've run them through machines and come out with the answers.

There is a shot of an old tin can, pulled open to show the seam. It looks like a bomb casing. A finger points: it was the tin cans that did it, a new invention back then, a new technology, the ultimate defence against starvation and scurvy. The Franklin Expedition was excellently provisioned with tin cans, stuffed full of meat and soup and soldered together with lead. The whole expedition got lead-poisoning. Nobody knew it. Nobody could taste it. It invaded their bones, their lungs, their brains, weakening them and confusing their thinking, so that at the end those that had not yet died in the ships set out in an idiotic trek across the stony, icy ground, pulling a lifeboat laden down with toothbrushes, soap, handkerchiefs, and slippers, useless pieces of junk. When they were found ten years later, they were skeletons in tattered coats, lying where they'd collapsed. They'd been heading back towards the ships. It was what they'd been eating that had killed them.

Jane switches off the television and goes into her kitchen—all white, done over the year before last, the outmoded butcher-block counters from the seventies torn out and carted away—to make herself some hot milk and rum. Then she decides against it; she won't sleep anyway. Everything in here looks ownerless. Her toaster oven, so perfect for solo dining, her microwave for the vegetables, her espresso maker—they're sitting around waiting for her departure, for this evening or forever, in order to assume their final, real appearances of purposeless objects adrift in the physical world. They might as well be pieces of an exploded spaceship orbiting the moon.

She thinks about Vincent's apartment, so carefully arranged, filled with the beautiful or deliberately ugly possessions he once loved. She thinks about his closet, with its quirky particular outfits, empty now of his arms and legs. It has all been broken up now, sold, given away.

Increasingly the sidewalk that runs past her house is cluttered with plastic drinking cups, crumpled soft-drink cans, used take-out plates. She picks them up, clears them away, but they appear again overnight, like a trail left by an army on the march or by the fleeing residents of a city under bombardment, discarding the objects that were once thought essential but are now too heavy to carry.

QUESTIONS FOR DISCUSSION AND WRITING

1. In what sense is Jane's life an expedition? How would you compare it to the various stages of the Franklin Expedition?
2. What qualities do Jane and Vincent share? How are Vincent and the frozen corpse alike?
3. How does the story establish the changing values of the sixties, seventies, and eighties? Does Jane see one decade as better than another? Explain your answer.
4. Why does the narrator shift verb tenses as she tells Jane's story? Why is it "difficult to know what tense" to apply to the frozen sailor?
5. In what sense do both Jane and the dead sailor suffer the consequences of living in an "age of lead"?

6

JAMES BALDWIN

Sonny's Blues

JAMES BALDWIN (1924–1987) was born in New York City's Harlem and attended DeWitt Clinton High School. After working at a number of odd jobs, he moved to Paris in 1948 where he felt the social and artistic environment gave him the freedom to pursue his career as a writer. He remained in self-exile for ten years, writing about his personal struggle to establish his identity as a black American man in novels such as *Go Tell It on the Mountain* (1953) and essays such as those collected in *Notes of a Native Son* (1955). In 1957, Baldwin returned to the United States and became actively involved in the civil rights movement. His essays during this period, *Nobody Knows My Name* (1961), *More Notes of a Native Son* (1961), and *The Fire Next Time* (1963), propelled Baldwin into the public spotlight as one of the most forceful and perceptive essayists in our time. His fiction includes the novels *Tell Me How Long the Train's Been Gone* (1968) and *If Beale Street Could Talk* (1974), and the short-story collections *Blues for Mister Charlie* (1964) and *The Amen Corner* (1965). His later publications include *The Devil Finds Work* (1976), *Just Above My Head* (1979), and a collection of poems, *Jimmy Blues* (1985). In "Sonny's Blues,"

excerpted from *Going to Meet the Man* (1957), an older brother begins to understand his own troubles as he watches his younger brother live and then play "the blues."

I read about it in the paper, in the subway, on my way to work. I read it, and I couldn't believe it, and I read it again. Then perhaps I just stared at it, at the newsprint spelling out his name, spelling out the story. I stared at it in the swinging lights of the subway car, and in the faces and bodies of the people, and in my own face, trapped in the darkness which roared outside.

It was not to be believed and I kept telling myself that, as I walked from the subway station to the high school. And at the same time I couldn't doubt it. I was scared, scared for Sonny. He became real to me again. A great block of ice got settled in my belly and kept melting there slowly all day long, while I taught my classes algebra. It was a special kind of ice. It kept melting, sending trickles of ice water all up and down my veins, but it never got less. Sometimes it hardened and seemed to expand until I felt my guts were going to come spilling out or that I was going to choke or scream. This would always be at a moment when I was remembering some specific thing Sonny had once said or done.

When he was about as old as the boys in my class his face had been bright and open, there was a lot of copper in it; and he'd had wonderfully direct brown eyes, and great gentleness and privacy. I wondered what he looked like now. He had been picked up, the evening before, in a raid on an apartment downtown, for peddling and using heroin.

I couldn't believe it: but what I mean by that is that I couldn't find any room for it anywhere inside me. I had kept it outside me for a long time. I hadn't wanted to know. I had had suspicions, but I didn't name them, I kept putting them away. I told myself that Sonny was wild, but he wasn't crazy. And he'd always been a good boy, he hadn't ever turned hard or evil or disrespectful, the way kids can, so quick, so quick, especially in Harlem. I didn't want to believe that I'd ever see my brother going down, coming to nothing, all that light in his face gone out, in the condition I'd already seen so many others. Yet it had happened and here I was, talking about algebra to a lot of boys who might, every one of them for all I knew, be popping off needles every time they went to the head. Maybe it did more for them than algebra could.

I was sure that the first time Sonny had ever had horse, he couldn't have been much older than these boys were now. These boys, now, were living as we'd been living then, they were growing up with a rush and their heads bumped abruptly against the low ceiling of their actual possibilities. They were filled with rage. All they really knew were two darknesses, the darkness of their lives, which was now closing in on them, and the darkness of the movies, which had blinded them to that other darkness, and in which they now, vindictively, dreamed, at once more together than they were at any other time, and more alone.

When the last bell rang, the last class ended, I let out my breath. It seemed I'd been holding it for all that time. My clothes were wet—I may have looked as though I'd been sitting in a steam bath, all dressed up, all afternoon. I sat alone in the classroom a long time. I listened to the boys outside, downstairs, shouting and cursing and laughing. Their laughter struck me for perhaps the first time. It was not the joyous laughter which—God knows why—one associates with children. It was mocking and insular, its intent was to denigrate. It was disenchanted, and in this, also, lay the authority of their curses. Perhaps I was listening to them because I was thinking about my brother and in them I heard my brother. And myself.

One boy was whistling a tune, at once very complicated and very simple, it seemed to be pouring out of him as though he were a bird, and it sounded very cool and moving through all that harsh, bright air, only just holding its own through all those other sounds.

I stood up and walked over to the window and looked down into the courtyard. It was the beginning of the spring and the sap was rising in the boys. A teacher passed through them every now and again, quickly, as though he or she couldn't wait to get out of that courtyard, to get those boys out of their sight and off their minds. I started collecting my stuff. I thought I'd better get home and talk to Isabel.

The courtyard was almost deserted by the time I got downstairs. I saw this boy standing in the shadow of a doorway, looking just like Sonny. I almost called his name. Then I saw that it wasn't Sonny, but somebody we used to know, a boy from around our block. He's been Sonny's friend. He's never been mine, having been too young for me, and, anyway, I'd never liked him. And now, even though he was a grown-up man, he still hung around that block, still spent hours on the street corners, was always high and raggy. I used to run into him from time to time and he'd often work around to asking me for a quarter or fifty cents. He always had some real good excuse, too, and I always gave it to him, I don't know why.

But now, abruptly, I hated him. I couldn't stand the way he looked at me, partly like a dog, partly like a cunning child. I wanted to ask him what the hell he was doing in the school courtyard.

He sort of shuffled over to me, and he said, "I see you got the papers. So you already know about it."

"You mean about Sonny? Yes, I already know about it. How come they didn't get you?"

He grinned. It made him repulsive and it also brought to mind what he'd looked like as a kid. "I wasn't there. I stay away from them people."

"Good for you." I offered him a cigarette and I watched him through the smoke. "You come all the way down here just to tell me about Sonny?"

"That's right." He was sort of shaking his head and his eyes looked strange, as though they were about to cross. The bright sun deadened his damp dark brown skin and it made his eyes look yellow and showed up the dirt in his kinked hair. He smelled funky. I moved a little away from him and I said, "Well, thanks. But I already know about it and I got to get home."

"I'll walk you a little ways," he said. We started walking. There were a couple of kids still loitering in the courtyard and one of them said goodnight to me and looked strangely at the boy beside me.

"What're you going to do?" he asked me. "I mean, about Sonny?"

"Look. I haven't seen Sonny for over a year, I'm not sure I'm going to do anything. Anyway, what the hell *can* I do?"

"That's right," he said quickly, "ain't nothing you can do. Can't much help old Sonny no more, I guess."

It was what I was thinking and so it seemed to me he had no right to say it.

"I'm surprised at Sonny, though," he went on—he had a funny way of talking, he looked straight ahead as though he were talking to himself—"I thought Sonny was a smart boy, I thought he was too smart to get hung."

"I guess he thought so too," I said sharply, "and that's how he got hung. And how about you? You're pretty goddamn smart, I bet."

Then he looked directly at me, just for a minute. "I ain't smart," he said. "If I was smart, I'd have reached for a pistol a long time ago."

"Look. Don't tell *me* your sad story, if it was up to me, I'd give you one." Then I felt guilty—guilty, probably, for never having supposed that the poor bastard *had* a story of his own, much less a sad one, and I asked, quickly, "What's going to happen to him now?"

He didn't answer this. He was off by himself some place. "Funny thing," he said, and from his tone we might have been discussing the quickest way to get to Brooklyn, "when I saw the papers this morning, the first thing I asked myself was if I had anything to do with it. I felt sort of responsible."

I began to listen more carefully. The subway station was on the corner, just before us, and I stopped. He stopped, too. We were in front of a bar and he ducked slightly, peering in, but whoever he was looking for didn't seem to be there. The juke box was blasting away with something black and bouncy and I half watched the barmaid as she danced her way from the juke box to her place behind the bar. And I watched her face as she laughingly responded to something someone said to her, still keeping time to the music. When she smiled one saw the little girl, one sensed the doomed, still-struggling woman beneath the battered face of the semi-whore.

"I never *give* Sonny nothing," the boy said finally, "but a long time ago I come to school high and Sonny asked me how it felt." He paused, I couldn't bear to watch him, I watched the barmaid, and I listened to the music which seemed to be causing the pavement to shake. "I told him it felt great." The music stopped, the barmaid paused and watched the juke box until the music began again. "It did."

All this way carrying me some place I didn't want to go. I certainly didn't want to know how it felt. It filled everything, the people, the houses, the music, the dark, quicksilver barmaid, with menace; and this menace was their reality.

"What's going to happen to him now?" I asked again.

"They'll send him away some place and they'll try to cure him." He shook his head. "Maybe he'll even think he's kicked the habit. Then they'll let him loose"—he gestured, throwing his cigarette into the gutter. "That's all."

"What do you mean, that's *all?*"

But I knew what he meant.

"I *mean*, that's *all.*" He turned his head and looked at me, pulling down the corners of his mouth. "Don't you know what I mean?" he asked, softly.

"How the hell *would* I know what you mean?" I almost whispered it, I don't know why.

"That's right," he said to the air, "how would *he* know what I mean?" He turned toward me again, patient and calm, and yet I somehow felt him shaking, shaking as though he were going to fall apart. I felt that ice in my guts again, the dread I'd felt all afternoon;

and again I watched the barmaid, moving about the bar, washing glasses, and singing. "Listen. They'll let him out and then it'll just start all over again. That's what I mean."

"You mean—they'll let him out. And then he'll just start working his way back in again. You mean he'll never kick the habit. Is that what you mean?"

"That's right," he said, cheerfully. "*You* see what I mean."

"Tell me," I said at last, "why does he want to die? He must want to die, he's killing himself, why does he want to die?"

He looked at me in surprise. He licked his lips. "He don't want to die. He wants to live. Don't nobody want to die, ever."

Then I wanted to ask him—too many things. He could not have answered, or if he had, I could not have borne the answers. I started walking. "Well, I guess it's none of my business."

"It's going to be rough on old Sonny," he said. We reached the subway station. "This is your station?" he asked. I nodded. I took one step down. "Damn!" he said, suddenly. I looked up at him. He grinned again. "Damn it if I didn't leave all my money home. You ain't got a dollar on you, have you? Just for a couple of days, is all."

All at once something inside gave and threatened to come pouring out of me. I didn't hate him any more. I felt that in another moment I'd start crying like a child.

"Sure," I said. "Don't swear." I looked in my wallet and didn't have a dollar, I only had a five. "Here," I said. "That hold you?"

He didn't look at it—he didn't want to look at it. A terrible, closed look came over his face, as though he were keeping the number on the bill a secret from him and me. "Thanks," he said, and now he was dying to see me go. "Don't worry about Sonny. Maybe I'll write him or something."

"Sure," I said. "You do that. So long."

"Be seeing you," he said. I went down the steps.

And I didn't write Sonny or send him anything for a long time. When I finally did, it was just after my little girl died, he wrote me back a letter which made me feel like a bastard.

Here's what he said:

> Dear Brother,
>
> You don't know how much I needed to hear from you. I wanted to write you many a time but I dug how much I must have hurt you and so I didn't write. But now I feel like a man who's been trying to climb up out of some deep, real deep and funky hole and just saw the sun up there, outside. I got to get outside.
>
> I can't tell you much about how I got here. I mean I don't know how to tell you. I guess I was afraid of something or I was trying to escape from something and you know I have never been very strong in the head (smile). I'm glad Mama and Daddy are dead and can't see what's happened to their son and I swear if I'd known what I was doing I would never have hurt you so, you and a lot of other fine people who were nice to me and who believed in me.
>
> I don't want you to think it had anything to do with me being a musician. It's more than that. Or maybe less than that. I can't get anything straight in my head down here

> and I try not to think about what's going to happen to me when I get outside again. Sometime I think I'm going to flip and *never* get outside and sometime I think I'll come straight back. I tell you one thing, though, I'd rather blow my brains out than go through this again. But that's what they all say, so they tell me. If I tell you when I'm coming to New York and if you could meet me, I sure would appreciate it. Give my love to Isabel and the kids and I was sure sorry to hear about little Gracie. I wish I could be like Mama and say the Lord's will be done, but I don't know it seems to me that trouble is the one thing that never does get stopped and I don't know what good it does to blame it on the Lord. But maybe it does some good if you believe it.
>
> Your brother,
> Sonny

Then I kept in constant touch with him and I sent him whatever I could and I went to meet him when he came back to New York. When I saw him many things I thought I had forgotten came flooding back to me. This was because I had begun, finally, to wonder about Sonny, about the life that Sonny lived inside. This life, whatever it was, had made him older and thinner and it had deepened the distant stillness in which he had always moved. He looked very unlike my baby brother. Yet, when he smiled, when we shook hands, the baby brother I'd never known looked out from the depths of his private life, like an animal waiting to be coaxed into the light.

"How you been keeping?" he asked me.

"All right. And you?"

"Just fine." He was smiling all over his face. "It's good to see you again."

"It's good to see you."

The seven years' difference in our ages lay between us like a chasm: I wondered if these years would ever operate between us as a bridge. I was remembering, and it made it hard to catch my breath, that I had been there when he was born; and I had heard the first words he had ever spoken. When he started to walk, he walked from our mother straight to me. I caught him just before he fell when he took the first steps he ever took in this world.

"How's Isabel?"

"Just fine. She's dying to see you."

"And the boys?"

"They're fine, too. They're anxious to see their uncle."

"Oh, come on. You know they don't remember me."

"Are you kidding? Of course they remember you."

He grinned again. We got into a taxi. We had a lot to say to each other, far too much to know how to begin.

As the taxi began to move, I asked, "You still want to go to India?"

He laughed. "You still remember that. Hell, no. This place is Indian enough for me."

"It used to belong to them," I said.

And he laughed again. "They damn sure knew what they were doing when they got rid of it."

Years ago, when he was around fourteen, he'd been all hipped on the idea of going to India. He read books about people sitting on rocks, naked, in all kinds of weather, but mostly bad, naturally, and walking barefoot through hot coals and arriving at wisdom. I used to say that it sounded to me as though they were getting away from wisdom as fast as they could. I think he sort of looked down on me for that.

"Do you mind," he asked, "if we have the driver drive alongside the park? On the west side—I haven't seen the city in so long."

"Of course not," I said. I was afraid that I might sound as though I were humoring him, but I hoped he wouldn't take it that way.

So we drove along, between the green of the park and the stony, lifeless elegance of hotels and apartment buildings, toward the vivid, killing streets of our childhood. These streets hadn't changed, though housing projects jutted up out of them now like rocks in the middle of a boiling sea. Most of the houses in which we had grown up had vanished, as had the stores from which we had stolen, the basements in which we had first tried sex, the rooftops from which we hurled tin cans and bricks. But houses exactly like the houses of our past yet dominated the landscape, boys exactly like the boys we once had been found themselves smothering in these houses, came down into the streets for light and air and found themselves encircled by disaster. Some escaped the trap, most didn't. Those who got out always left something of themselves behind, as some animals amputate a leg and leave it in the trap. It might be said, perhaps, that I had escaped, after all, I was a school teacher; or that Sonny had, he hadn't lived in Harlem for years. Yet, as the cab moved uptown through streets which seemed, with a rush, to darken with dark people, and as I covertly studied Sonny's face, it came to me that what we both were seeking through our separate cab windows was that part of ourselves which had been left behind. It's always at the hour of trouble and confrontation that the missing member aches.

We hit 110th Street and started rolling up Lenox Avenue. And I'd known this avenue all my life, but it seemed to me again, as it had seemed on the day I'd first heard about Sonny's trouble, filled with a hidden menace which was its very breath of life.

"We almost there," said Sonny.

"Almost." We were both too nervous to say anything more.

We lived in a housing project. It hasn't been up long. A few days after it was up it seemed uninhabitably new, now, of course, it's already rundown. It looks like a parody of the good, clean, faceless life—God knows the people who live in it do their best to make it a parody. The beat-looking grass lying around isn't enough to make their lives green, the hedges will never hold out the streets, and they know it. The big windows fool no one, they aren't big enough to make space out of no space. They don't bother with the windows, they watch the TV screen instead. The playground is most popular with the children who don't play at jacks, or skip rope, or roller skate, or swing, and they can be found in it after dark. We moved in partly because it's not too far from where I teach, and partly for the kids; but it's really just like the houses in which Sonny and I grew up. The same things happen, they'll have the same things to remember. The moment Sonny and I started into the house I had the feeling that I was simply bringing him back into the danger he had almost died trying to escape.

Sonny has never been talkative. So I don't know why I was sure he'd be dying to talk to me when supper was over the first night. Everything went fine, the oldest boy remembered him, and the youngest boy liked him, and Sonny had remembered to bring something for each of them; and Isabel, who is really much nicer than I am, more open and giving, had gone to a lot of trouble about dinner and was genuinely glad to see him. And she's always been able to tease Sonny in a way that I haven't. It was nice to see her face so vivid again and to hear her laugh and watch her make Sonny laugh. She wasn't, or, anyway, she didn't seem to be, at all uneasy or embarrassed. She chatted as though there were no subject which had to be avoided and she got Sonny past his first, faint stiffness. And thank God she was there, for I was filled with that icy dread again. Everything I did seemed awkward to me, and everything I said sounded freighted with hidden meaning. I was trying to remember everything I'd heard about dope addiction and I couldn't help watching Sonny for signs. I wasn't doing it out of malice. I was trying to find out something about my brother. I was dying to hear him tell me he was safe.

"Safe!" my father grunted, whenever Mama suggested trying to move to a neighborhood which might be safer for children. "Safe, hell! Ain't no place safe for kids, nor nobody."

He always went on like this, but he wasn't, ever, really as bad as he sounded, not even on weekends, when he got drunk. As a matter of fact, he was always on the lookout for "something a little better," but he died before he found it. He died suddenly, during a drunken weekend in the middle of the war, when Sonny was fifteen. He and Sonny hadn't ever got on too well. And this was partly because Sonny was the apple of his father's eye. It was because he loved Sonny so much and was frightened for him, that he was always fighting with him. It doesn't do any good to fight with Sonny. Sonny just moves back, inside himself, where he can't be reached. But the principal reason that they never hit it off is that they were so much alike. Daddy was big and rough and loud-talking, just the opposite of Sonny, but they both had—that same privacy.

Mama tried to tell me something about this, just after Daddy died. I was home on leave from the army.

This was the last time I ever saw my mother alive. Just the same, this picture gets all mixed up in my mind with pictures I had of her when she was younger. The way I always see her is the way she used to be on a Sunday afternoon, say, when the old folks were talking after the big Sunday dinner. I always see her wearing pale blue. She'd be sitting on the sofa. And my father would be sitting in the easy chair, not far from her. And the living room would be full of church folks and relatives. There they sit, in chairs all around the living room, and the night is creeping up outside, but nobody knows it yet. You can see the darkness growing against the windowpanes and you hear the street noises every now and again, or maybe the jangling beat of a tambourine from one of the churches close by, but it's real quiet in the room. For a moment nobody's talking, but every face looks darkening, like the sky outside. And my mother rocks a little from the waist, and my father's eyes are closed. Everyone is looking at something a child can't see. For a minute they've forgotten the children. Maybe a kid is lying on the rug, half asleep. Maybe somebody's got a kid in his lap and is absent-mindedly stroking the kid's head. Maybe there's a kid, quiet and big-eyed, curled up in a big chair in the corner. The silence, the darkness coming, and the darkness in the faces frightens the child obscurely. He hopes that the hand which strokes his forehead will never stop—will never die. He hopes that there will never come a time when the old folks won't be sitting around the living room, talking about where they've come from, and what they've seen, and what's happened to them and their kinfolk.

But something deep and watchful in the child knows that this is bound to end, is already ending. In a moment someone will get up and turn on the light. Then the old folks will remember the children and they won't talk any more that day. And when light fills the room, the child is filled with darkness. He knows that every time this happens he's moved just a little closer to that darkness outside. The darkness outside is what the old folks have been talking about. It's what they've come from. It's what they endure. The child knows that they won't talk any more because if he knows too much about what's happened to *them*, he'll know too much too soon, about what's going to happen to *him*.

The last time I talked to my mother, I remember I was restless. I wanted to get out and see Isabel. We weren't married then and we had a lot to straighten out between us.

There Mama sat, in black, by the window. She was humming an old church song, *Lord, you brought me from a long ways off.* Sonny was out somewhere. Mama kept watching the streets.

"I don't know," she said, "if I'll ever see you again, after you go off from here. But I hope you'll remember the things I tried to teach you."

"Don't talk like that," I said, and smiled. "You'll be here a long time yet."

She smiled, too, but she said nothing. She was quiet for a long time. And I said, "Mama, don't you worry about nothing. I'll be writing all the time, and you be getting the checks . . ."

"I want to talk to you about your brother," she said, suddenly. "If anything happens to me he ain't going to have nobody to look out for him."

"Mama," I said, "ain't nothing going to happen to you *or* Sonny. Sonny's all right. He's a good boy and he's got good sense."

"It ain't a question of his being a good boy," Mama said, "nor of his having good sense. It ain't only the bad ones, nor yet the dumb ones that gets sucked under." She stopped, looking at me. "Your Daddy once had a brother," she said, and she smiled in a way that made me feel she was in pain. "You didn't never know that, did you?"

"No," I said, "I never knew that," and I watched her face.

"Oh, yes," she said, "your Daddy had a brother." She looked out of the window again. "I know you never saw your Daddy cry. But *I* did—many a time, through all these years."

I asked her, "What happened to his brother? How come nobody's ever talked about him?"

This was the first time I ever saw my mother look old.

"His brother got killed," she said, "when he was just a little younger than you are now. I knew him. He was a fine boy. He was maybe a little full of the devil, but he didn't mean nobody no harm."

Then she stopped and the room was silent, exactly as it had sometimes been on those Sunday afternoons. Mama kept looking out into the streets.

"He used to have a job in the mill," she said, "and, like all young folks, he just liked to perform on Saturday nights. Saturday nights, him and your father would drift around to different places, go to dances and things like that, or just sit around with people they knew, and your father's brother would sing, he had a fine voice, and play along with himself on his guitar. Well, this particular Saturday night, him and your father was coming home from some place, and they were both a little drunk and there was a moon that night, it was bright like day. Your father's brother was feeling kind of good, and he was whistling to himself, and he had his guitar slung over his shoulder. They was coming down a hill and beneath them was a road that turned off from the highway. Well, your father's brother, being always kind of frisky, decided to run down this hill, and he did, with that guitar banging and clanging behind him, and he ran across the road, and he was making water behind a tree. And your father was sort of amused at him and he was still coming down the hill, kind of slow. Then he heard a car motor and that same minute his brother stepped from behind the tree, into the road, in the moonlight. And he started to cross the road. And your father started to run down the hill, he says he don't know why. This car was full of white men. They was all drunk, and when they seen your father's brother they let out a great whoop and holler and they aimed the car straight at him. They was having fun, they just wanted to scare him, the way they do sometimes, you know. But they was drunk. And I guess the boy, being drunk, too, and scared, kind of lost his head. By the time he jumped it was too late. Your father says he heard his brother scream when the car rolled over him, and he heard the wood of that guitar when it give, and he heard them strings go flying, and he heard them white men shouting, and the car kept on a-going and it ain't stopped till this day. And, time your father got down the hill, his brother weren't nothing but blood and pulp."

Tears were gleaming on my mother's face. There wasn't anything I could say.

"He never mentioned it," she said, "because I never let him mention it before you children. Your Daddy was like a crazy man that night and for many a night thereafter. He says he never in his life seen anything as dark as that road after the lights of that car had gone away. Weren't nothing; weren't nobody on that road, just your Daddy and his brother and that busted guitar. Oh, yes. Your Daddy never did really get right again. Till the day he died he weren't sure but that every white man he saw was the man that killed his brother."

She stopped and took out her handkerchief and dried her eyes and looked at me.

"I ain't telling you all this," she said, "to make you scared or bitter or to make you hate nobody. I'm telling you this because you got a brother. And the world ain't changed."

I guess I didn't want to believe this. I guess she saw this in my face. She turned away from me, toward the window again, searching those streets.

"But I praise my Redeemer," she said at last, "that He called your Daddy home before me. I ain't saying it to throw no flowers at myself, but, I declare, it keeps me from feeling too cast down to know I helped your father get safely through this world. Your father always acted like he was the roughest, strongest man on earth. And everybody took him to be like that. But if he hadn't had *me* there—to see his tears!"

She was crying again. Still, I couldn't move. I said, "Lord, Lord, Mama, I didn't know it was like that."

"Oh, honey," she said, "There's a lot that you don't know. But you are going to find out." She stood up from the window and came over to me. "You got to hold on to your brother," she said, "and don't let him fall, no matter what it looks like is happening to him and no matter how evil you gets with him. You going to be evil with him many a time. But don't you forget what I told you, you hear?"

"I won't forget," I said. "Don't you worry, I won't forget. I won't let nothing happen to Sonny."

My mother smiled as though she were amused at something she saw in my face. Then, "You may not be able to stop nothing from happening. But you got to let him know you's *there*."

Two days later I was married, and then I was gone. And I had a lot of things on my mind and I pretty well forgot my promise to Mama until I got shipped home on a special furlough for her funeral.

And, after the funeral, with just Sonny and me alone in the empty kitchen, I tried to find out something about him.

"What do you want to do?" I asked him.

"I'm going to be a musician," he said.

For he had graduated, in the time I had been away, from dancing to the juke box to finding out who was playing what, and what they were doing with it, and he had bought himself a set of drums.

"You mean, you want to be a drummer?" I somehow had the feeling that being a drummer might be all right for other people but not for my brother Sonny.

"I don't know," he said, looking at me very gravely, "that I'll ever be a good drummer. But I think I can play a piano."

I frowned. I'd never played the role of the older brother quite so seriously before, had scarcely ever, in fact, *asked* Sonny a damn thing. I sensed myself in the presence of something I didn't really know how to handle, didn't understand. So I made my frown a little deeper as I asked: "What kind of musician do you want to be?"

He grinned. "How many kinds do you think there are?"

"Be *serious,*" I said.

He laughed, throwing his head back, and then looked at me. "I *am* serious."

"Well, then, for Christ's sake, stop kidding around and answer a serious question. I mean, do you want to be a concert pianist, you want to play classical music and all that, or—or what?" Long before I finished he was laughing again. "For Christ's *sake,* Sonny!"

He sobered, but with difficulty. "I'm sorry. But you sound so—*scared!*" and he was off again.

"Well, you may think it's funny now, baby, but it's not going to be so funny when you have to make your living at it, let me tell you *that*." I was furious because I knew he was laughing at me and I didn't know why.

"No," he said, very sober now, and afraid, perhaps, that he'd hurt me, "I don't want to be a classical pianist. That isn't what interests me. I mean"—he paused, looking hard at me, as though his eyes would help me to understand, and then gestured helplessly, as though perhaps his hand would help—"I mean, I'll have a lot of studying to do, and I'll have to study *everything,* but, I mean, I want to play *with*—jazz musicians." He stopped. "I want to play jazz," he said.

Well, the word had never before sounded as heavy, as real, as it sounded that afternoon in Sonny's mouth. I just looked at him and I was probably frowning a real frown by this time. I simply couldn't see why on earth he'd want to spend his time hanging around nightclubs, clowning around on bandstands, while people pushed each other around a dance floor. It seemed—beneath him, somehow. I had never thought about it before, had never been forced to, but I suppose I had always put jazz musicians in a class with what Daddy called "goodtime people."

"Are you *serious?*"

"Hell, *yes*, I'm serious."

He looked more helpless than ever, and annoyed, and deeply hurt.

I suggested, helpfully: "You mean—like Louis Armstrong?"

His face closed as though I'd struck him. "No. I'm not talking about none of that old-time, down home crap."

"Well, look, Sonny, I'm sorry, don't get mad. I just don't altogether get it, that's all. Name somebody—you know, a jazz musician you admire."

"Bird."

"Who?"

"Bird! Charlie Parker! Don't they teach you nothing in the goddamn army?"

I lit a cigarette. I was surprised and then a little amused to discover that I was trembling. "I've been out of touch," I said. "You'll have to be patient with me. Now. Who's this Parker character?"

"He's just one of the greatest jazz musicians alive," said Sonny, sullenly, his hands in his pockets, his back to me. "Maybe *the* greatest," he added, bitterly, "that's probably why *you* never heard of him."

"All right," I said, "I'm ignorant. I'm sorry. I'll go out and buy all the cat's records right away, all right?"

"It don't," said Sonny, with dignity, "make any difference to me. I don't care what you listen to. Don't do me no favors."

I was beginning to realize that I'd never seen him so upset before. With another part of my mind I was thinking that this would probably turn out to be one of those things kids go through and that I shouldn't make it seem important by pushing it too hard. Still, I didn't think it would do any harm to ask: "Doesn't all this take a lot of time? Can you make a living at it?"

He turned back to me and half leaned, half sat, on the kitchen table. "Everything takes time," he said, "and—well, yes, sure, I can make a living at it. But what I don't seem to be able to make you understand is that it's the only thing I want to do."

"Well, Sonny," I said, gently, "you know people can't always do exactly what they *want* to do—"

"*No*, I don't know that," said Sonny, surprising me. "I think people *ought* to do what they want to do, what else are they alive for?"

"You getting to be a big boy," I said desperately, "it's time you started thinking about your future."

"I'm thinking about my future," said Sonny, grimly. "I think about it all the time."

I gave up. I decided, if he didn't change his mind, that we could always talk about it later. "In the meantime," I said, "you got to finish school." We had already decided that he'd have to move in with Isabel and her folks. I knew this wasn't the ideal arrangement because Isabel's folks are inclined to be dicty and they hadn't especially wanted Isabel to marry me. But I didn't know what else to do. "And we have to get you fixed up at Isabel's."

There was a long silence. He moved from the kitchen table to the windows. "That's a terrible idea. You know it yourself."

"Do you have a *better* idea?"

He just walked up and down the kitchen for a minute. He was as tall as I was. He had started to shave. I suddenly had the feeling that I didn't know him at all.

He stopped at the kitchen table and picked up my cigarettes. Looking at me with a kind of mocking, amusing defiance, he put one between his lips. "You mind?"

"You smoking already?"

He lit the cigarette and nodded, watching me through the smoke. "I just wanted to see if I'd have the courage to smoke in front of you." He grinned and blew a great cloud of smoke to the ceiling. "It was easy." He looked at my face. "Come on, now. I bet you was smoking at my age, tell the truth."

I didn't say anything but the truth was on my face, and he laughed. But now there was something very strained in his laugh. "Sure. And I bet that ain't all you was doing."

He was frightening me a little. "Cut the crap," I said. "We already decided that you was going to go and live at Isabel's. Now what's got into you all of a sudden?"

"*You* decided it," he pointed out. "*I* didn't decide nothing." He stopped in front of me, leaning against the stove, arms loosely folded. "Look, brother. I don't want to stay in Harlem no more, I really don't." He was very earnest. He looked at me, then over toward the kitchen window. There was something in his eyes I'd never seen before, some thoughtfulness, some worry all his own. He rubbed the muscle of one arm. "It's time I was getting out of here."

"Where do you want to *go*, Sonny?"

"I want to join the army. Or the navy, I don't care. If I say I'm old enough, they'll believe me."

Then I got mad. It was because I was so scared. "You must be crazy. You goddamn fool, what the hell do you want to go and join the *army* for?"

"I just told you. To get out of Harlem."

"Sonny, you haven't even finished *school*. And if you really want to be a musician, how do you expect to study if you're in the *army?*"

He looked at me, trapped, and in anguish. "There's ways. I might be able to work out some kind of deal. Anyway, I'll have the G.I. Bill when I come out."

"*If* you come out." We stared at each other. "Sonny, please. Be reasonable. I know the setup is far from perfect. But we got to do the best we can."

"I ain't learning nothing in school," he said. "Even when I go." He turned away from me and opened the window and threw his cigarette out into the narrow alley. I watched his back. "At least, I ain't learning nothing you'd want me to learn." He slammed the window so hard I thought the glass would fly out, and turned back to me. "And I'm sick of the stink of these garbage cans!"

"Sonny," I said, "I know how you feel. But if you don't finish school now, you're going to be sorry later that you didn't." I grabbed him by the shoulders. "And you only got another year. It ain't so bad. And I'll come back and I swear I'll help you do *whatever* you want to do. Just try to put up with it till I come back. Will you please do that? For me?"

He didn't answer and he wouldn't look at me.

"Sonny. You hear me?"

He pulled away. "I hear you. But you never hear anything *I* say."

I didn't know what to say to that. He looked out of the window and then back at me. "OK," he said, and sighed. "I'll try."

Then I said, trying to cheer him up a little, "They got a piano at Isabel's. You can practice on it."

And as a matter of fact, it did cheer him up for a minute. "That's right," he said to himself. "I forgot that." His face relaxed a little. But the worry, the thoughtfulness, played on it still, the way shadows play on a face which is staring into the fire.

But I thought I'd never hear the end of that piano. At first, Isabel would write me, saying how nice it was that Sonny was so serious about his music and how, as soon as he came in from school, or wherever he had been when he was supposed to be at school, he went straight to that piano and stayed there until suppertime. And, after supper, he went back to that piano and stayed there until everybody went to bed. He was at the piano all day Saturday and all day Sunday. Then he bought a record player and started playing records. He'd play one record over and over again, all day long sometimes, and he'd improvise along with it on the piano. Or he'd play one section of the record, one chord, one change, one progression, then he'd do it on the piano. Then back to the record. Then back to the piano.

Well, I really don't know how they stood it. Isabel finally confessed that it wasn't like living with a person at all, it was like living with sound. And the sound didn't make any sense to her, didn't make any sense to any of them—naturally. They began, in a way, to be afflicted by this presence that was living in their home. It was as though Sonny were some sort of god, or monster. He moved in an atmosphere which wasn't like theirs at all. They fed him and he ate, he washed himself, he walked in and out of their door; he certainly wasn't nasty or unpleasant or rude, Sonny isn't any of those things; but it was as though he were all wrapped up in some cloud, some fire, some vision all his own; and there wasn't any way to reach him.

At the same time, he wasn't really a man yet, he was still a child, and they had to watch out for him in all kinds of ways. They certainly couldn't throw him out. Neither did they dare to make a great scene about that piano because even they dimly sensed, as I sensed, from so many thousands of miles away, that Sonny was at that piano playing for his life.

But he hadn't been going to school. One day a letter came from the school board and Isabel's mother got it—there had, apparently, been other letters but Sonny had torn them up. This day, when Sonny came in, Isabel's mother showed him the letter and asked where he'd been spending his time. And she finally got it out of him that he'd been down in Greenwich Village, with musicians and other characters, in a white girl's apartment. And this scared her and she started to scream at him and what came up, once she began—though she denies it to this day—was what sacrifices they were making to give Sonny a decent home and how little he appreciated it.

Sonny didn't play the piano that day. By evening, Isabel's mother had calmed down but then there was the old man to deal with, and Isabel herself. Isabel says she did her best to be calm but she broke down and started crying. She says she just watched Sonny's face. She could tell, by watching him, what was happening with him. And what was happening was that they penetrated his cloud, they had reached him. Even if their fingers had been a thousand times more gentle than human fingers ever are, he could hardly help feeling that they had stripped him naked and were spitting on that nakedness. For he also had to see that his presence, that music, which was life or death to him, had been torture for them and that they had endured it, not at all for his sake, but only for mine. And Sonny couldn't take that. He can take it a little better today than he could then but he's still not very good at it and, frankly, I don't know anybody who is.

The silence of the next few days must have been louder than the sound of all the music ever played since time began. One morning, before she went to work, Isabel was in his room for something and she suddenly realized that all of his records were gone. And she knew for certain that he was gone. And he was. He went as far as the navy would carry him. He finally sent me a postcard from some place in Greece and that was the first I knew that Sonny was still alive. I didn't see him any more until we were both back in New York and the war had long been over.

He was a man by then, of course, but I wasn't willing to see it. He came by the house from time to time, but we fought almost every time we met. I didn't like the way he carried himself, loose and dreamlike all the time, and I didn't like his friends, and his music seemed to be merely an excuse for the life he led. It sounded just that weird and disordered.

Then we had a fight, a pretty awful fight, and I didn't see him for months. By and by I looked him up, where he was living, in a furnished room in the Village, and I tried to make it up. But there were lots of other people in the room and Sonny just lay on his bed, and he wouldn't come downstairs with me, and he treated these other people as though they were his family and I weren't. So I got mad and then he got mad, and then I told him that he might just as well be dead as live the way he was living. Then he stood up and he told me not to worry about him any more in life, that he *was* dead as far as I was concerned. Then he pushed me to the door and the other people looked on as though nothing were happening, and he slammed the door behind me. I stood in the hallway, staring at the door. I heard somebody laugh in the room and then the tears came to my eyes. I started down the steps, whistling to keep from crying, I kept whistling to myself, *You going to need me, baby, one of these cold, rainy days.*

I read about Sonny's trouble in the spring. Little Grace died in the fall. She was a beautiful little girl. But she only lived a little over two years. She died of polio and she suffered. She had a slight fever for a couple of days, but it didn't seem like anything and we just kept her in bed. And we would certainly have called the doctor, but the fever dropped, she seemed to be all right. So we thought it had just been a cold. Then, one day, she was up, playing, Isabel was in the kitchen fixing lunch for the two boys when they'd come in from school, and she heard Grace fall down in the living room. When you have a lot of children you don't always start running when one of them falls, unless they start screaming or something. And, this time, Grace was quiet. Yet, Isabel says that when she heard that *thump* and then that silence, something happened in her to make her afraid. And she ran to the living room and there was little Grace on the floor, all twisted up, and the reason she hadn't screamed was that she couldn't get her breath. And when she did scream, it was the worst sound, Isabel says, that she'd ever heard in all her life, and she still hears it sometimes in her dreams. Isabel will sometimes wake me up with a low, moaning, strangled sound and I have to be quick to awaken her and hold her to me and where Isabel is weeping against me seems a mortal wound.

I think I may have written Sonny the very day that little Grace was buried. I was sitting in the living room in the dark, by myself, and I suddenly thought of Sonny. My trouble made his real.

One Saturday afternoon, when Sonny had been living with us, or, anyway, been in our house, for nearly two weeks, I found myself wandering aimlessly about the living room, drinking from a can of beer, and trying to work up the courage to search Sonny's room. He was out, he was usually out whenever I was home, and Isabel had taken the children to see their grandparents. Suddenly I was standing still in front of the living room window, watching Seventh Avenue. The idea of searching Sonny's room made me still. I scarcely dared to admit to myself what I'd be searching for. I didn't know what I'd do if I found it. Or if I didn't.

On the sidewalk across from me, near the entrance to a barbecue joint, some people were holding an old-fashioned revival meeting. The barbecue cook, wearing a dirty white apron, his conked hair reddish and metallic in the pale sun, and a cigarette between his lips, stood in the doorway, watching them. Kids and older people paused in their errands and stood there, along with some older men and a couple of very tough-looking women who watched everything that happened on the avenue, as though they owned it, or were maybe owned by it. Well, they were watching this, too. The revival was being carried on by three sisters in black, and a brother. All they had were their voices and their Bibles and a tambourine. The brother was testifying and while he testified two of the sisters stood together, seeming to say, amen, and the third sister walked around with the tambourine outstretched and a couple of people dropped coins into it. Then the brother's testimony ended and the sister who had been taking up the collection dumped the coins into her palm and transferred them to the pocket of her long black robe. Then she raised both hands, striking the tambourine against the air, and then against one hand, and she started to sing. And the two other sisters and the brother joined in.

It was strange, suddenly, to watch, though I had been seeing these street meetings all my life. So, of course, had everybody else down there. Yet, they paused and watched and listened and I stood still at the window. "*Tis the old ship of Zion,*" they sang, and the sister with the tambourine kept a steady, jangling beat, "*it has rescued many a thousand!*" Not a soul under the sound of their voices was hearing this song for the first time, not one of them had been rescued. Nor had they seen much in the way of rescue work being done around them. Neither did they especially believe in the holiness of the three sisters and the brother, they knew too much about them, knew where they lived, and how. The woman with the tambourine, whose voice dominated the air, whose face was bright with joy, was divided by very little from the woman who stood watching her, a cigarette between her heavy, chapped lips, her hair a cuckoo's nest, her face scarred and swollen from many beatings, and her black eyes glittering like coal. Perhaps they both knew this, which was why, when, as rarely, they addressed each other, they addressed each other as Sister. As the singing filled the air the watching, listening faces underwent a change, the eyes focusing on something within; the music seemed to soothe a poison out of them; and time seemed, nearly, to fall away from the sullen, belligerent, battered faces, as though they were fleeing back to their first condition, while dreaming of their last. The barbecue cook half shook his head and smiled, and dropped his cigarette and disappeared into his joint. A man fumbled in his pockets for change and stood holding it in his hand impatiently, as though he had just remembered a pressing appointment further up the avenue. He looked furious. Then I saw Sonny, standing on the edge of the crowd. He was carrying a wide, flat notebook with a green cover, and it made him look, from where I was standing, almost like a schoolboy. The coppery sun brought out the copper in his skin, he was very faintly smiling, standing very still. Then the singing stopped, the tambourine turned into a collection plate again. The furious man dropped in his coins and vanished, so did a couple of the women, and Sonny dropped some change in the plate, looking directly at the woman with a little smile. He started across the avenue, toward the house. He has a slow, loping walk, something like the way Harlem hipsters walk, only he's imposed on this his own half-beat. I had never really noticed it before.

I stayed at the window, both relieved and apprehensive. As Sonny disappeared from my sight, they began singing again. And they were still singing when his key turned in the lock.

"Hey," he said.

"Hey, youself. You want some beer?"

"No. Well, maybe." But he came up to the window and stood beside me, looking out. "What a warm voice," he said.

They were singing *If I could only hear my mother pray again!*

"Yes," I said, "and she can sure beat that tambourine."

"But what a terrible song," he said, and laughed. He dropped his notebook on the sofa and disappeared into the kitchen. "Where's Isabel and the kids?"

"I think they went to see their grandparents. You hungry?"

"No." He came back into the living room with his can of beer. "You want to come some place with me tonight?"

I sensed, I don't know how, that I couldn't possibly say no. "Sure. Where?"

He sat down on the sofa and picked up his notebook and started leafing through it. "I'm going to sit in with some fellows in a joint in the Village."

"You mean, you're going to play, tonight?"

"That's right." He took a swallow of his beer and moved back to the window. He gave me a sidelong look. "If you can stand it."

"I'll try," I said.

He smiled to himself and we both watched as the meeting across the way broke up. The three sisters and the brother, heads bowed, were singing *God be with you till we meet again.* The faces around them were very quiet. Then the song ended. The small crowd dispersed. We watched the three women and the lone man walk slowly up the avenue.

"When she was singing before," said Sonny, abruptly, "her voice reminded me for a minute of what heroin feels like sometimes—when it's in your veins. It makes you feel sort of warm and cool at the same time. And distant. And—and sure." He sipped his beer, very deliberately not looking at me. I watched his face. "It makes you feel—in control. Sometimes you've got to have that feeling."

"Do you?" I sat down slowly in the easy chair.

"Sometimes." He went to the sofa and picked up his notebook again. "Some people do."

"In order," I asked, "to play?" And my voice was very ugly, full of contempt and anger.

"Well"—he looked at me with great, troubled eyes, as though, in fact, he hoped his eyes would tell me things he could never otherwise say—"they *think* so. And *if* they think so—!"

"And what do *you* think?" I asked.

He sat on the sofa and put his can of beer on the floor. "I don't know," he said, and I couldn't be sure if he were answering my question or pursuing his thoughts. His face didn't tell me. "It's not so much to *play*. It's to *stand* it, to be able to make it at all. On any level." He frowned and smiled: "In order to keep from shaking to pieces."

"But these friends of yours," I said, "they seem to shake themselves to pieces pretty goddamn fast."

"Maybe." He played with the notebook. And something told me that I should curb my tongue, that Sonny was doing his best to talk, that I should listen. "But of course you only know the ones that've gone to pieces. Some don't—or at least they haven't *yet* and that's just about all *any* of us can say." He paused. "And then there are some who just live, really, in hell, and they know it and they see what's happening and they go right on. I don't know." He sighed, dropped the notebook, folded his arms. "Some guys, you can tell from the way they play, they on something *all* the time. And you can see that, well, it makes something real for them. But of course," he picked up his beer from the floor and sipped it and put the can down again, "they *want* to, too, you've got to see that. Even some of them that say they don't—*some,* not all."

"And what about you?" I asked—I couldn't help it. "What about you? Do *you* want to?"

He stood up and walked to the window and remained silent for a long time. Then he sighed. "Me," he said. Then: "While I was downstairs before, on my way here, listening to that woman sing, it struck me all of a sudden how much suffering she must have had to go through—to sing like that. It's *repulsive* to think you have to suffer that much."

I said: "But there's no way not to suffer—is there, Sonny?"

"I believe not," he said and smiled, "but that's never stopped anyone from trying." He looked at me. "Has it?" I realized, with his mocking look, that there stood between us, forever, beyond the power of time or forgiveness, the fact that I had held silence—so long!—when he had needed human speech to help him. He turned back to the window. "No, there's no way not to suffer. But you try all kinds of ways to keep from drowning in it, to keep on top of it, and to make it seem—well, like *you.* Like you did something, all right, and now you're suffering for it. You know?" I said nothing. "Well you know," he said, impatiently, "Why *do* people suffer? Maybe it's better to do something to give it a reason, *any* reason."

"But we just agreed," I said, "that there's no way not to suffer. Isn't it better, then, just to—take it?"

"But nobody just takes it," Sonny cried, "that's what I'm telling you! *Everybody* tries not to. You're just hung up on the *way* some people try—it's not *your* way!"

The hair on my face began to itch, my face felt wet. "That's not true," I said, "that's not true. I don't give a damn what other people do, I don't even care how they suffer. I just care how *you* suffer." And he looked at me. "Please believe me," I said, "I don't want to see you—die—trying not to suffer."

"I won't," he said, flatly, "die trying not to suffer. At least, not any faster than anybody else."

"But there's no need," I said, trying to laugh, "is there? in killing yourself."

I wanted to say more, but I couldn't. I wanted to talk about will power and how life could be—well, beautiful. I wanted to say that it was all within; but was it? or, rather, wasn't that exactly the trouble? And I wanted to promise that I would never fail him again. But it would all have sounded—empty words and lies.

So I made the promise to myself and prayed that I would keep it.

"It's terrible sometimes, inside," he said, "that's what's the trouble. You walk these streets, black and funky and cold, and there's not really a living ass to talk to, and there's nothing shaking, and there's no way of getting it out—that storm inside. You can't talk it and you can't make love with it, and when you finally try to get with it and play it, you realize *nobody's* listening. So *you've* got to listen. You got to find a way to listen."

And then he walked away from the window and sat on the sofa again, as though all the wind had suddenly been knocked out of him. "Sometimes you'll do *anything* to play, even cut your mother's throat." He laughed and looked at me. "Or your brother's." Then he sobered. "Or your own." Then: "Don't worry. I'm all right now and I think I'll *be* all right. But I can't forget—where I've been. I don't mean just the physical place I've been, I mean where I've *been.* And *what* I've been."

"What have you been, Sonny?" I asked.

He smiled—but sat sideways on the sofa, his elbow resting on the back, his fingers playing with his mouth and chin, not looking at me. "I've been something I didn't recognize, didn't know I could be. Didn't know anybody could be." He stopped, looking inward, looking helplessly young, looking old. "I'm not talking about it now because I feel *guilty* or anything like that—maybe it would be better if I did, I don't know. Anyway, I can't really talk about it. Not to you, not to anybody," and now he turned and faced me. "Sometimes, you know, and it was actually when I was most *out* of the world, I felt that I was in it, that I was *with* it, really, and I could play or I didn't really have to *play,* it just came out of me, it was there. And I don't know how I played, thinking about it now, but I know I did awful things, those times, sometimes, to people. Or it wasn't that I *did* anything to them—it was that they weren't real." He picked up the beer can; it was empty; he rolled it between his palms: "And other times—well, I needed a fix, I needed to find a place to lean, I needed to clear a space to *listen*—and I couldn't find it, and I—went crazy, I did terrible things to *me*, I was terrible *for* me." He began pressing the beer can between his hands, I watched the metal begin to give. It glittered, as he played with it, like a knife, and I was afraid he would cut himself, but I said nothing. "Oh well. I can never tell you.

I was all by myself at the bottom of something, stinking and sweating and crying and shaking, and I smelled it, you know? *my* stink, and I thought I'd die if I couldn't get away from it and yet, all the same, I knew that everything I was doing was just locking me in with it. And I didn't know," he paused, still flattening the beer can, "I didn't know, I still *don't* know, something kept telling me that maybe it was good to smell your own stink, but I didn't think that *that* was what I'd been trying to do—and—who can stand it?" and he abruptly dropped the ruined beer can, looking at me with a small, still smile, and then rose, walking to the window as though it were the lodestone rock. I watched his face, he watched the avenue. "I couldn't tell you when Mama died—but the reason I wanted to leave Harlem so bad was to get away from drugs. And then, when I ran away, that's what I was running from—really. When I came back, nothing had changed. *I* hadn't changed, I was just—older." And he stopped, drumming with his fingers on the windowpane. The sun had vanished, soon darkness would fall. I watched his face. "It can come again," he said, almost as though speaking to himself. Then he turned to me. "It can come again," he repeated. "I just want you to know that."

"All right," I said, at last. "So it can come again, All right."

He smiled, but the smile was sorrowful. "I had to try to tell you," he said.

"Yes," I said. "I understand that."

"You're my brother," he said, looking straight at me, and not smiling at all.

"Yes," I repeated, "yes. I understand that."

He turned back to the window, looking out. "All that hatred down there," he said, "all that hatred and misery and love. It's a wonder it doesn't blow the avenue apart."

We went to the only nightclub on a short, dark street, downtown. We squeezed through the narrow, chattering, jam-packed bar to the entrance of the big room, where the bandstand was. And we stood there for a moment, for the lights were very dim in this room and we couldn't see. Then, "Hello, boy," said a voice and an enormous black man, much older than Sonny or myself, erupted out of all that atmospheric lighting and put an arm around Sonny's shoulder. "I been sitting right here," he said, "waiting for you."

He had a big voice, too, and heads in the darkness turned toward us.

Sonny grinned and pulled a little away, and said, "Creole, this is my brother. I told you about him."

Creole shook my hand. "I'm glad to meet you, son," he said, and it was clear that he was glad to meet me *there* for Sonny's sake. And he smiled, "You got a real musician in *your* family," and he took his arm from Sonny's shoulder and slapped him, lightly, affectionately, with the back of his hand.

"Well. Now I've heard it all," said a voice behind us. This was another musician, and a friend of Sonny's, a coal-black, cheerful-looking man, built close to the ground. He immediately began confiding to me, at the top of his lungs, the most terrible things about Sonny, his teeth gleaming like a lighthouse and his laugh coming up out of him like the beginning of an earthquake. And it turned out that everyone at the bar knew Sonny, or almost everyone; some were musicians, working there, or nearby, or not working, some were simply hangers-on, and some were there to hear Sonny play. I was introduced to all of them and they were all very polite to me. Yet, it was clear that, for them, I was only

Sonny's brother. Here, I was in Sonny's world. Or, rather: his kingdom. Here, it was not even a question that his veins bore royal blood.

They were going to play soon and Creole installed me, by myself, at a table in a dark corner. Then I watched them, Creole, and the little black man, and Sonny, and the others, while they horsed around, standing just below the bandstand. The light from the bandstand spilled just a little short of them and, watching them laughing and gesturing and moving about, I had the feeling that they, nevertheless, were being most careful not to step into that circle of light too suddenly: that if they moved into the light too suddenly, without thinking, they would perish in flame. Then, while I watched, one of them, the small, black man, moved into the light and crossed the bandstand and started fooling around with his drums. Then—being funny and being, also, extremely ceremonious—Creole took Sonny by the arm and led him to the piano. A woman's voice called Sonny's name and a few hands started clapping. And Sonny, also being funny and being ceremonious, and so touched, I think, that he could have cried, but neither hiding it nor showing it, riding it like a man, grinned, and put both hands to his heart and bowed from the waist.

Creole then went to the bass fiddle and a lean, very bright-skinned brown man jumped up on the bandstand and picked up his horn. So there they were, and the atmosphere on the bandstand and in the room began to change and tighten. Someone stepped up to the microphone and announced them. Then there were all kinds of murmurs. Some people at the bar shushed others. The waitress ran around, frantically getting in the last orders, guys and chicks got closer to each other, and the lights on the bandstand, on the quartet, turned to a kind of indigo. Then they all looked different there. Creole looked about him for the last time, as though he were making certain that all his chickens were in the coop, and then he—jumped and struck the fiddle. And there they were.

All I know about music is that not many people ever really hear it. And even then, on the rare occasions when something opens within, and the music enters, what we mainly hear, or hear corroborated, are personal, private, vanishing evocations. But the man who creates the music is hearing something else, is dealing with the roar rising from the void and imposing order on it as it hits the air. What is evoked in him, then, is of another order, more terrible because it has no words, and triumphant, too, for that same reason. And his triumph, when he triumphs, is ours. I just watched Sonny's face. His face was troubled, he was working hard, but he wasn't with it. And I had the feeling that, in a way, everyone on the bandstand was waiting for him, both waiting for him and pushing him along. But as I began to watch Creole, I realized that it was Creole who held them all back. He had them on a short rein. Up there, keeping the beat with his whole body, wailing on the fiddle, with his eyes half closed, he was listening to everything, but he was listening to Sonny. He was having a dialogue with Sonny. He wanted Sonny to leave the shoreline and strike out for the deep water. He was Sonny's witness that deep water and drowning were not the same thing—he had been there, and he knew. And he wanted Sonny to know. He was waiting for Sonny to do the things on the keys which would let Creole know that Sonny was in the water.

And, while Creole listened, Sonny moved, deep within, exactly like someone in torment. I had never before thought of how awful the relationship must be between the musician and his instrument. He has to fill it, this instrument, with the breath of life, his own. He has to make it do what he wants it to do. And a piano is just a piano. It's made out of so much wood and wires and little hammers and big ones, and ivory. While there's only so much you can do with it, the only way to find this out is to try; to try and make it do everything.

And Sonny hadn't been near a piano for over a year. And he wasn't on much better terms with his life, not the life that stretched before him now. He and the piano stammered, started one way, got scared, stopped; started another way, panicked, marked time, started again; then seemed to have found a direction, panicked again, got stuck. And the face I saw on Sonny I'd never seen before. Everything had been burned out of it, and, at the same time, things usually hidden were being burned in, by the fire and fury of the battle which was occurring in him up there.

Yet, watching Creole's face as they neared the end of the first set, I had the feeling that something had happened, something I hadn't heard. Then they finished, there was scattered applause, and then, without an instant's warning, Creole started into something else, it was almost sardonic, it was *Am I Blue*. And, as though he commanded, Sonny began to play. Something began to happen. And Creole let out the reins. The dry, low, black man said something awful on the drums, Creole answered, and the drums talked back. Then the horn insisted, sweet and high, slightly detached perhaps, and Creole listened, commenting now and then, dry, and driving, beautiful and calm and old. Then they all came together again, and Sonny was part of the family again. I could tell this from his face. He seemed to have found, right there beneath his fingers, a damn brand-new piano. It seemed that he couldn't get over it. Then, for awhile, just being happy with Sonny, they seemed to be agreeing with him that brand-new pianos certainly were a gas.

Then Creole stepped forward to remind them that what they were playing was the blues. He hit something in all of them, he hit something in me, myself, and the music tightened and deepened, apprehension began to beat the air. Creole began to tell us what the blues were all about. They were not about anything very new. He and his boys up there were keeping it new, at the risk of ruin, destruction, madness, and death, in order to find new ways to make us listen. For, while the tale of how we suffer, and how we are delighted, and how we may triumph is never new, it always must be heard. There isn't any other tale to tell, it's the only light we've got in all this darkness.

And this tale, according to that face, that body, those strong hands on those strings, has another aspect in every country, and a new depth in every generation. Listen, Creole seemed to be saying, listen. Now these are Sonny's blues. He made the little black man on the drums know it, and the bright, brown man on the horn. Creole wasn't trying any longer to get Sonny in the water. He was wishing him Godspeed. Then he stepped back, very slowly, filling the air with the immense suggestion that Sonny speak for himself.

Then they all gathered around Sonny and Sonny played. Every now and again one of them seemed to say, amen. Sonny's fingers filled the air with life, his life. But that life contained so many others. And Sonny went all the way back, he really began with the spare, flat statement of the opening phrase of the song. Then he began to make it his. It was very beautiful because it wasn't hurried and it was no longer a lament. I seemed to hear with what burning he had made it his, with what burning we had yet to make it ours, how we could cease lamenting. Freedom lurked around us and I understood, at last, that he could help us to be free if we would listen, that he would never be free until we did. Yet, there was no battle in his face now. I heard what he had gone through, and would continue to go through until he came to rest in earth. He had made it his: that long line, of which we knew only Mama and Daddy. And he was giving it back, as everything must be given back, so that, passing through death, it can live forever. I saw my mother's face again, and felt, for the first time, how the stones of the road she had walked on must have bruised her feet. I saw the moonlit road where my father's brother died. And it brought something else back to me, and carried me past it, I saw my little girl again and felt Isabel's tears again, and I felt my own tears begin to rise. And I was yet aware that this was only a moment, that the world waited outside, as hungry as a tiger, and that trouble stretched above us, longer than the sky.

Then it was over. Creole and Sonny let out their breath, both soaking wet, and grinning. There was a lot of applause and some of it was real. In the dark, the girl came by and I asked her to take drinks to the bandstand. There was a long pause, while they talked up there in the indigo light and after awhile I saw the girl put a Scotch and milk on top of the piano for Sonny. He didn't seem to notice it, but just before they started playing again, he sipped from it and looked toward me, and nodded. Then he put it back on top of the piano. For me, then, as they began to play again, it glowed and shook above my brother's head like the very cup of trembling.

QUESTIONS FOR DISCUSSION AND WRITING

1. How does Mama's story about Sonny's uncle help prepare us for the events of the story? In what way does the promise she extracts from the older brother complicate the plot?
2. How would you contrast the characters of Sonny and his brother? In what unexpected ways are they similar?
3. How does Baldwin characterize the risks and the rewards of living in Harlem? How does this setting shape the characters in the story?
4. How does the older brother's point of view change during the course of the story? How is his point of view toward his brother deepened by his own personal problems?
5. What relationship does Baldwin suggest exists between heroin, religion, and music? What do they promise? What do they provide? How do they help define "the blues"?

7
TONI CADE BAMBARA
The Lesson

TONI CADE BAMBARA was born in 1939 in New York City and educated at Queens College, the University of Florence, the Ecole de Mme. Etienne Decroux in Paris, and the City College of the City University of New York. She attended post-degree courses at the New School for Social Research, the Katherine Dunham Dance Studio, and the Studio Museum of Harlem Film Institute. Bambara's work experience has been extremely varied: a social investigator for the New York State Department of Welfare, a director of recreation in the psychiatry department of New York's Metropolitan Hospital, a visiting professor of Afro-American studies (Stephens College), and a consultant on women's studies (Emory University). Since 1971, she has been writer-in-residence at Spelman College in Atlanta. Bambara has contributed stories and essays to magazines as diverse as *Negro Digest, Prairie Schooner,* and *Redbook.* Her collections of short stories, *Gorilla, My Love* (1972), *The Sea Birds Are Still Alive: Collected Stories* (1977), and *The Salt Eaters* (1980) and novel, *If Blessing Comes* (1987), deal with the emerging sense of self of black women. "The Lesson," reprinted from *Gorilla, My Love,* focuses on the experiences of several black children who learn how much things "cost."

Back in the days when everyone was old and stupid or young and foolish and me and Sugar were the only ones just right, this lady moved on our block with nappy hair and proper speech and no makeup. And quite naturally we laughed at her, laughed the way we did at the junk man who went about his business like he was some big-time president and his sorry-ass horse his secretary. And we kinda hated her too, hated the way we did the winos who cluttered up our parks and pissed on our handball walls and stank up our hallways and stairs so you couldn't halfway play hide-and-seek without a goddamn gas mask. Miss Moore was her name. The only woman on the block with no first name. And she was black as hell, cept for her feet, which were fish-white and spooky. And she was always planning these boring-ass things for us to do, us being my cousin, mostly, who lived on the block cause we all moved North the same time and to the same apartment then spread out gradual to breathe. And our parents would yank our heads into some kinda shape and crisp up our clothes so we'd be presentable for travel with Miss Moore, who always looked like she was going to church, though she never did. Which is just one of the things the grownups talked about when they talked behind her back like a dog. But when she came calling with some sachet she'd sewed up or some gingerbread she'd made or some book, why then they'd all be too embarrassed to turn her down and we'd get handed over all spruced up. She'd been to college and said it was only right that she should take responsibility for the young ones' education, and she not even related by marriage or blood. So they'd go for it. Specially Aunt Gretchen. She was the main gofer in the family. You got some ole dumb shit foolishness you want somebody to go for, you send for Aunt Gretchen. She been screwed into the go-along for so long, it's a blood-deep natural thing with her. Which is how she got saddled with me and Sugar and Junior in the first place while our mothers were in a la-de-da apartment up the block having a good ole time.

So this one day, Miss Moore rounds us all up at the mailbox and it's puredee hot and she's knockin herself out about arithmetic. And school suppose to let up in summer I heard, but she don't never let up. And the starch in my pinafore scratching the shit outta me and I'm really hating this nappy-head bitch and her goddamn college degree. I'd much rather go to the pool or to the show where it's cool. So me and Sugar leaning on the mailbox being surly, which is a Miss Moore word. And Flyboy checking out what everybody brought for lunch. And Fat Butt already wasting his peanut-butter-and-jelly sandwich like the pig he is. And Junebug punchin on Q.T.'s arm for potato chips. And Rosie Giraffe shifting from one hip to the other waiting for somebody to step on her foot or ask her if she from Georgia so she can kick ass, preferably Mercedes'. And Miss Moore asking us do we know what money is, like we a bunch of retards. I mean real money, she say, like it's only poker chips or monopoly papers we lay on the grocer. So right away I'm tired of this and say so. And would much rather snatch Sugar and go to the Sunset and terrorize the West Indian kids and take their hair ribbons and their money too. And Miss Moore files that remark away for next week's lesson on brotherhood, I can tell. And finally I say we oughta get to the subway cause it's cooler and besides we might meet some cute boys. Sugar done swiped her mama's lipstick, so we ready.

So we heading down the street and she's boring us silly about what things cost and what our parents make and how much goes for rent and how money ain't divided up right in this country. And then she gets to the part about we all poor and live in the slums, which I don't feature. And I'm ready to speak on that, but she steps out in the street and hails two cabs just like that. Then she hustles half the crew in with her and hands me a five-dollar bill and tells me to calculate 10 percent tip for the driver. And we're off. Me and Sugar and Junebug and Flyboy hangin out the window and hollering to everybody, putting lipstick on each other cause Flyboy a faggot anyway, and making farts with our sweaty armpits. But I'm mostly trying to figure how to spend this money. But they all fascinated with the meter ticking and Junebug starts laying bets as to how much it'll read when Flyboy can't hold his breath no more. Then Sugar lays bets as to how much it'll be when we get there. So I'm stuck. Don't nobody want to go for my plan, which is to jump out at the next light and run off to the first bar-b-que we can find. Then the driver tells us to get the hell out cause we there already. And the meter reads eighty-five cents. And I'm stalling to figure out the tip and Sugar say give him a dime. And I decide he don't need it bad as I do, so later for him. But then he tries to take off with Junebug foot still in the door so we talk about his mamma something ferocious. Then we check out that we on Fifth Avenue and everybody dressed up in stockings. One lady in a fur coat, hot as it is. White folks crazy.

"This is the place," Miss Moore say, presenting it to us in the voice she uses at the museum. "Let's look in the windows before we go in."

"Can we steal?" Sugar asks very serious like she's getting the ground rules squared away before she plays. "I beg your pardon," say Miss Moore, and we fall out. So she leads us around the windows of the toy store and me and Sugar screamin, "This is mine, that's mine, I gotta have that, that was made for me, I was born for that," till Big Butt drowns us out.

"Hey, I'm goin to buy that there."

"That there? You don't even know what it is, stupid."

"I do so," he say punchin on Rosie Giraffe. "It's a microscope."

"Whatcha gonna do with a microscope, fool?"

"Look at things."

"Like what, Ronald?" ask Miss Moore. And Big Butt ain't got the first notion. So here go Miss Moore gabbing about the thousands of bacteria in a drop of water and the somethinorother in a speck of blood and the million and one living things in the air around us is invisible to the naked eye. And what she say that for? Junebug go to town on that "naked" and we rolling. Then Miss Moore ask what it cost. So we all jam into the window smudgin it up and the price tag say $300. So then she ask how long'd take for Big Butt and Junebug to save up their allowances. "Too long," I say. "Yeh," adds Sugar, "outgrown it by that time." And Miss Moore say no, you never outgrow learning instruments. "Why, even medical students and interns and," blah, blah, blah. And we ready to choke Big Butt for bringing it up in the first damn place.

"This here costs four hundred eighty dollars," say Rosie Giraffe. So we pile up all over her to see what she pointin out. My eyes tell me it's a chunk of glass cracked with something heavy, and different-color inks dripped into the splits, then the whole thing put into a oven or something. But for $480 it don't make sense.

"That's a paperweight made of semi-precious stones fused together under tremendous pressure," she explains slowly, with her hands doing the mining and all the factory work.

"So what's a paperweight?" ask Rosie Giraffe.

"To weigh paper with, dumbbell," say Flyboy, the wise man from the East.

"Not exactly," say Miss Moore, which is what she say when you warm or way off too. "It's to weigh paper down so it won't scatter and make your desk untidy." So right away me and Sugar curtsy to each other and then to Mercedes who is more the tidy type.

"We don't keep paper on top of the desk in my class," say Junebug, figuring Miss Moore crazy or lyin one.

"At home, then," she say. "Don't you have a calendar and a pencil case and a blotter and a letter-opener on your desk at home where you do your homework?" And she know damn well what our homes look like cause she nosys around in them every chance she gets.

"I don't even have a desk," say Junebug. "Do we?"

"No. And I don't get no homework neither," says Big Butt.

"And I don't even have a home," says Flyboy like he do at school to keep the white folks off his back and sorry for him. Send this poor kid to camp posters, is his specialty.

"I do," says Mercedes. "I have a box of stationery on my desk and a picture of my cat. My godmother bought the stationery and the desk. There's a big rose on each sheet and the envelopes smell like roses."

"Who wants to know about your smelly-ass stationery," say Rosie Giraffe fore I can get my two cents in.

"It's important to have a work area all your own so that . . ."

"Will you look at this sailboat, please," say Flyboy, cutting her off and pointin to the thing like it was his. So once again we tumble all over each other to gaze at this magnificent thing in the toy store which is just big enough to maybe sail two kittens across the pond if you strap them to the posts tight. We all start reciting the price tag like we in assembly. "Handcrafted sailboat of fiberglass at one thousand one hundred ninety-five dollars."

"Unbelievable," I hear myself say and am really stunned. I read it again for myself just in case the group recitation put me in a trance. Same thing. For some reason this pisses me off. We look at Miss Moore and she lookin at us, waiting for I dunno what.

"Who'd pay all that when you can buy a sailboat set for a quarter at Pop's, a tube of glue for a dime, and a ball of string for eight cents? It must have a motor and a whole lot else besides," I say. "My sailboat cost me about fifty cents."

"But will it take water?" say Mercedes with her smart ass.

"Took mine to Alley Pond Park once," say Flyboy. "String broke. Lost it. Pity."

"Sailed mine in Central Park and it keeled over and sank. Had to ask my father for another dollar."

"And you got the strap," laugh Big Butt. "The jerk didn't even have a string on it. My old man wailed on his behind."

Little Q.T. was staring hard at the sailboat and you could see he wanted it bad. But he too little and somebody'd just take it from him. So what the hell. "This boat for kids, Miss Moore?"

"Parents silly to buy something like that just to get all broke up," say Rosie Giraffe.

"That much money it should last forever," I figure.

"My father'd buy it for me if I wanted it."

"Your father, my ass," say Rosie Giraffe getting a chance to finally push Mercedes.

"Must be rich people shop here," say Q.T.

"You are a very bright boy," say Flyboy. "What was your first clue?" And he rap him on the head with the back of his knuckles, since Q.T. the only one he could get away with. Though Q.T. liable to come up behind you years later and get his licks in when you half expect it.

"What I want to know is," I says to Miss Moore though I never talk to her, I wouldn't give the bitch that satisfaction, "is how much a real boat costs? I figure a thousand'd get you a yacht any day."

"Why don't you check that out," she says, "and report back to the group?" Which really pains my ass. If you gonna mess up a perfectly good swim day least you could do is have some answers. "Let's go in," she say like she got something up her sleeve. Only she don't lead the way. So me and Sugar turn the corner to where the entrance is, but when we get there I kinda hang back. Not that I'm scared, what's there to be afraid of, just a toy store. But I feel funny, shame. But what I got to be shamed about? Got as much right to go in as anybody. But somehow I can't seem to get hold of the door, so I step away from Sugar to lead. But she hangs back too. And I look at her and she looks at me and this is ridiculous. I mean, damn, I have never ever been shy about doing nothing or going nowhere. But then Mercedes steps up and then Rosie Giraffe and Big Butt crowd in behind and shove, and next thing we all stuffed into the doorway with only Mercedes squeezing past us, smoothing out her jumper and walking right down the aisle. Then the rest of us tumble in like a glued-together jigsaw done all wrong. And people lookin at us. And it's like the time me and Sugar crashed into the Catholic church on a dare. But once we got in there and everything so hushed and holy and the candles and the bowin and the handkerchiefs on all the drooping heads, I just couldn't go through with the plan. Which was for me to run up to the altar and do a tap dance while Sugar played the nose flute and messed around in the holy water. And Sugar kept given me the elbow. Then later teased me so bad I tied her up in the shower and turned it on and locked her in. And she'd be there till this day if Aunt Gretchen hadn't finally figured I was lyin about the boarder takin a shower.

Same thing in the store. We all walkin on tiptoe and hardly touchin the games and puzzles and things. And I watched Miss Moore who is steady watchin us like she waitin for a sign. Like Mama Drewery watches the sky and sniffs the air and takes note of just how much slant is in the bird formation. Then me and Sugar bump smack into each other, so busy gazing at the toys, 'specially the sailboat. But we don't laugh and go into our fat-lady bump-stomach routine. We just stare at that price tag. Then Sugar run a finger over the whole boat. And I'm jealous and want to hit her. Maybe not her, but I sure want to punch somebody in the mouth.

"Watcha bring us here for, Miss Moore?"

"You sound angry, Sylvia. Are you mad about something?" Givin me one of them grins like she tellin a grown-up joke that never turns out to be funny. And she's lookin very closely at me like maybe she plannin to do my portrait from memory. I'm mad, but I won't give her that satisfaction. So I slouch around the store bein very bored and say, "Let's go."

Me and Sugar at the back of the train watchin the tracks whizzin by large then small then getting gobbled up in the dark. I'm thinkin about this tricky toy I saw in the store. A clown that somersaults on a bar then does chin-ups just cause you yank lightly at his leg. Cost $35. I could see me askin my mother for a $35 birthday clown. "You wanna who that costs what?" she'd say, cocking her head to the side to get a better view of the hole in my head. Thirty-five dollars could buy new bunk beds for Junior and Gretchen's boy. Thirty-five dollars and the whole household could go visit Granddaddy Nelson in the country. Thirty-five dollars would pay for the rent and the piano bill too. Who are these people that spend that much for performing clowns and $1000 for toy sailboats? What kinda work they do and how they live and how come we ain't in on it? Where we are is who we are, Miss Moore always pointin out. But it don't necessarily have to be that way, she always adds then waits for somebody to say that poor people have to wake up and demand their share of the pie and don't none of us know what kind of pie she talking about in the first damn place. But she ain't so smart cause I still got her four dollars from the taxi and she sure ain't gettin it. Messin up my day with this shit. Sugar nudges me in my pocket and winks.

Miss Moore lines us up in front of the mailbox where we started from, seem like years ago, and I got a headache for thinkin so hard. And we lean all over each other so we can hold up under the draggy-ass lecture she always finishes us off with at the end before we thank her for borin us to tears. But she just looks at us like she readin tea leaves. Finally she say, "Well, what did you think of F. A. O. Schwarz?"

Rosie Giraffe mumbles, "White folks crazy."

"I'd like to go there again when I get my birthday money," says Mercedes, and we shove her out the pack so she has to lean on the mailbox by herself.

"I'd like a shower. Tiring day," say Flyboy.

Then Sugar surprises me by sayin, "You know, Miss Moore, I don't think all of us here put together eat in a year what that sailboat costs." And Miss Moore lights up like somebody goosed her. "And?" she say, urging Sugar on. Only I'm standin on her foot so she don't continue.

"Imagine for a minute what kind of society it is in which some people can spend on a toy what it would cost to feed a family of six or seven. What do you think?"

"I think," say Sugar pushing me off her feet like she never done before, cause I whip her ass in a minute, "that this is not much of a democracy if you ask me. Equal chance to pursue happiness means an equal crack at the dough, don't it?" Miss Moore is besides herself and I am disgusted with Sugar's treachery. So I stand on her foot one more time to see if she'll shove me. She shuts up, and Miss Moore looks at me, sorrowfully I'm thinkin. And somethin weird is goin on, I can feel it in my chest.

"Anybody else learn anything today?" lookin dead at me. I walk away and Sugar has to run to catch up and don't even seem to notice when I shrug her arm off my shoulder.

"Well, we got four dollars anyway," she says.

"Uh, hunh."

"We could go to Hascombs and get a half a chocolate layer and then go to the Sunset and still have plenty money for potato chips and ice cream sodas."

"Uh hunh."

"Race you to Hascombs," she say.

We start down the block and she gets ahead which is O.K. by me cause I'm going to the West End and then over to the Drive to think this day through. She can run if she want to and even run faster. But ain't nobody gonna beat me at nuthin.

QUESTIONS FOR DISCUSSION AND WRITING

1. How does the cost of the sailboat help establish the conflict in the story?
2. How do the language and behavior of the kids in this story help characterize them? How do their reactions to Miss Moore help characterize her?
3. Why does Miss Moore take the kids out of their neighborhood to Fifth Avenue to teach them "the lesson"?
4. How does the narrator's point of view change once she enters the toy store? What emotions does she say she feels? How do these emotions affect her behavior?
5. What sign is Miss Moore waiting for as she watches the children in the toy store? What evidence can you find that she has seen the sign?

8

AMBROSE BIERCE

An Occurrence at Owl Creek Bridge

AMBROSE BIERCE (1842–1914?) was born on a farm in Ohio and raised in Indiana, where he worked briefly on an antislavery newspaper. He attended the Kentucky Military Institute for a year, but with the outbreak of the Civil War he enlisted as a private with the Ninth Indiana Volunteers and rose through the ranks to brevet major. Following the war, Bierce went west, where he wrote for and eventually edited the *San Francisco News-Letter.* In 1872 he married and moved to London where his slashing brand of journalism earned him the reputation of "Bitter Bierce." Bierce returned to the United States in 1876 to work for the San Francisco *Sunday Examiner* and began to write fiction. His stories, many of them based on his war experiences, were collected under the titles *Tales of Soldiers and Civilians* (1891) and *Can Such Things Be?* (1893). His *Devil's Dictionary* (1906), a collection of sardonic definitions, reflects the many tragedies that began to dominate his personal life. Bierce disappeared mysteriously while reporting on Pancho Villa's rebel army during the Mexican Revolution. "An Occurrence at Owl Creek Bridge," reprinted from *Tales of Soldiers and Civilians,* portrays the physical and psychological "occurrence" of a military execution.

1

A man stood upon a railroad bridge in northern Alabama, looking down into the swift water twenty feet below. The man's hands were behind his back, the wrists bound with a cord. A rope closely encircled his neck. It was attached to a stout cross-timber above his head and the slack fell to the level of his knees. Some loose boards laid upon the sleepers supporting the metals of the railway supplied a footing for him and his executioners—two private soldiers of the Federal army, directed by a sergeant who in civil life may have been a deputy sheriff. At a short remove upon the same temporary platform was an officer in the uniform of his rank, armed. He was a captain. A sentinel at each end of the bridge stood with his rifle in the position known as "support," that is to say, vertical in front of the left shoulder, the hammer resting on the forearm thrown straight across the chest—a formal and unnatural position, enforcing an erect carriage of the body. It did not appear to be the duty of these two men to know what was occurring at the center of the bridge; they merely blockaded the two ends of the foot planking that traversed it.

Beyond one of the sentinels nobody was in sight; the railroad ran straight away into a forest for a hundred yards, then, curving, was lost to view. Doubtless there was an outpost farther along. The other bank of the stream was open ground—a gentle acclivity topped with a stockade of vertical tree trunks, loopholed for rifles, with a single embrasure through which protruded the muzzle of a brass cannon commanding the bridge. Midway of the slope between bridge and fort were the spectators—a single company of infantry in line, at "parade rest," the butts of the rifles on the ground, the barrels inclining slightly backward against the right shoulder, the hands crossed upon the stock. A lieutenant stood at the right of the line, the point of his sword upon the ground, his left hand resting upon his right. Excepting the group of four at the centre of the bridge, not a man moved. The company faced the bridge, staring stonily, motionless. The sentinels, facing the banks of the stream, might have been statues to adorn the bridge. The captain stood with folded arms, silent, observing the work of his subordinates, but making no sign. Death is a dignitary who when he comes announced is to be received with formal manifestations of respect, even by those most familiar with him. In the code of military etiquette silence and fixity are forms of deference.

The man who was engaged in being hanged was apparently about thirty-five years of age. He was a civilian, if one might judge from his habit, which was that of a planter. His features were good—a straight nose, firm mouth, broad forehead, from which his long, dark hair was combed straight back, falling behind his ears to the collar of his well-fitting frock-coat. He wore a mustache and pointed beard, but no whiskers; his eyes were large and dark gray, and had a kindly expression which one would hardly have expected in one whose neck was in the hemp. Evidently this was no vulgar assassin. The liberal military code makes provision for hanging many kinds of persons, and gentlemen are not excluded.

The preparations being complete, the two private soldiers stepped aside and each drew away the plank upon which he had been standing. The sergeant turned to the captain, saluted and placed himself immediately behind that officer, who in turn moved apart one pace. These movements left the condemned man and the sergeant standing on the two ends of the same plank, which spanned three of the cross-ties of the bridge. The end upon which the civilian stood almost, but not quite, reached a fourth. This plank had been held in place by the weight of the captain; it was now held by that of the sergeant. At a signal from the former the latter would step aside, the plank would tilt and the condemned man go down between two ties. The arrangement commended itself to his judgment as simple and effective. His face had not been covered nor his eyes bandaged. He looked a moment at his "unsteadfast footing," then let his gaze wander to the swirling water of the stream racing madly beneath his feet. A piece of dancing driftwood caught his attention and his eyes followed it down the current. How slowly it appeared to move! What a sluggish stream!

He closed his eyes in order to fix his last thoughts upon his wife and children. The water, touched to gold by the early sun, the brooding mists under the banks at some distance down the stream, the fort, the soldiers, the piece of drift—all had distracted him. And now he became conscious of a new disturbance. Striking through the thought of his dear ones was a sound which he could neither ignore nor understand, a sharp, distinct, metallic percussion like the stroke of a blacksmith's hammer upon the anvil; it had the same ringing quality. He wondered what it was, and whether immeasurably distant or near by—it seemed both. Its recurrence was regular, but as slow as the tolling of a death knell. He awaited each stroke with impatience and—he knew not why—apprehension. The intervals of silence grew progressively longer; the delays became maddening. With their greater infrequency the sounds increased in strength and sharpness. They hurt his ear like the thrust of a knife; he feared he would shriek. What he heard was the ticking of his watch.

He unclosed his eyes and saw again the water below him. "If I could free my hands," he thought, "I might throw off the noose and spring into the stream. By diving I could evade the bullets and, swimming vigorously, reach the bank, take to the woods and get away home. My home, thank God, is as yet outside their lines; my wife and little ones are still beyond the invader's farthest advance."

As these thoughts, which have here to be set down in words, were flashed into the doomed man's brain rather than evolved from it the captain nodded to the sergeant. The sergeant stepped aside.

2

Peyton Farquhar was a well-to-do planter, of an old and highly respected Alabama family. Being a slave owner and like other slave owners a politician he was naturally an original secessionist and ardently devoted to the Southern cause. Circumstances of an imperious nature, which it is unnecessary to relate here, had prevented him from taking service with the gallant army that had fought the disastrous campaigns ending with the fall of Corinth, and he chafed under the inglorious restraint, longing for the release of his energies, the larger life of the soldier, the opportunity for distinction. That opportunity, he felt, would come, as it comes to all in war time. Meanwhile he did what he could. No service was too humble for him to perform in aid of the South, no adventure too perilous for him to undertake if consistent with the character of a civilian who was at heart a soldier, and who in good faith and without too much qualification assented to at least a part of the frankly villainous dictum that all is fair in love and war.

One evening while Farquhar and his wife were sitting on a rustic bench near the entrance to his grounds, a gray-clad soldier rode up to the gate and asked for a drink of water. Mrs. Farquhar was only too happy to serve him with her own white hands. While she was fetching the water her husband approached the dusty horseman and inquired eagerly for news from the front.

"The Yanks are repairing the railroads," said the man, "and are getting ready for another advance. They have reached the Owl Creek bridge, put it in order and built a stockade on the north bank. The commandant has issued an order, which is posted everywhere, declaring that any civilian caught interfering with the railroad, its bridges, tunnels or trains will be summarily hanged. I saw the order."

"How far is it to the Owl Creek bridge?" Farquhar asked.

"About thirty miles."

"Is there no force on this side of the creek?"

"Only a picket post half a mile out, on the railroad, and a single sentinel at this end of the bridge."

"Suppose a man—a civilian and student of hanging—should elude the picket post and perhaps get the better of the sentinel," said Farquhar, smiling, "what could he accomplish?"

The soldier reflected. "I was there a month ago," he replied. "I observed that the flood of last winter had lodged a great quantity of driftwood against the wooden pier at this end of the bridge. It is now dry and would burn like tow."

The lady had now brought the water, which the soldier drank. He thanked her ceremoniously, bowed to her husband and rode away. An hour later, after nightfall, he repassed the plantation, going northward in the direction from which he had come. He was a Federal scout.

3

As Peyton Farquhar fell straight downward through the bridge he lost consciousness and was as one already dead. From this state he was awakened—ages later, it seemed to him—by the pain of a sharp pressure upon his throat, followed by a sense of suffocation. Keen, poignant agonies seemed to shoot from his neck downward through every fibre of his body and limbs. These pains appeared to flash along well-defined lines of ramification and to beat with an inconceivably rapid periodicity. They seemed like streams of pulsating fire heating him to an intolerable temperature. As to his head, he was conscious of nothing but a feeling of fullness—of congestion. These sensations were unaccompanied by thought. The intellectual part of his nature was already effaced; he had power only to feel, and feeling was torment. He was conscious of motion. Encompassed in a luminous cloud, of which he was now merely the fiery heart, without material substance, he swung through unthinkable arcs of oscillation, like a vast pendulum. Then all at once, with terrible suddenness, the light about him shot upward with the noise of a loud plash; a frightful roaring was in his ears, and all was cold and dark. The power of thought was restored; he knew that the rope had broken and he had fallen into the stream. There was no additional strangulation; the noose about his neck was already suffocating him and kept the water from his lungs. To die of hanging at the bottom of a river!—the idea seemed to him ludicrous. He opened his eyes in the darkness and saw above him a gleam of light, but how distant, how inaccessible! He was still sinking, for the light became fainter and fainter until it was a mere glimmer. Then it began to grow and brighten, and he knew that he was rising toward the surface—knew it with reluctance, for he was now very comfortable. "To be hanged and drowned," he thought, "that is not so bad; but I do not wish to be shot. No; I will not be shot; that is not fair."

He was not conscious of an effort, but a sharp pain in his wrist apprised him that he was trying to free his hands. He gave the struggle his attention, as an idler might observe the feat of a juggler, without interest in the outcome. What splendid effort!—what magnificent, what superhuman strength! Ah, that was a fine endeavor! Bravo! The cord fell away; his arms parted and floated upward, the hands dimly seen on each side in the growing light. He watched them with a new interest as first one and then the other pounced upon the noose at his neck. They tore it away and thrust it fiercely aside, its undulations resembling those of a water-snake. "Put it back, put it back!" He thought he shouted these words to his hands, for the undoing of the noose had been succeeded by the direst pang that he had yet experienced. His neck arched horribly, his brain was on fire; his heart, which had been fluttering faintly, gave a great leap, trying to force itself out at his mouth. His whole body was racked and wrenched with an insupportable anguish! But his disobedient hands gave no heed to the command. They beat the water vigorously with quick, downward strokes, forcing him to the surface. He felt his head emerge; his eyes were blinded by the sunlight; his chest expanded convulsively, and with a supreme and crowning agony his lungs engulfed a great draught of air, which instantly he expelled in a shriek!

He was now in full possession of his physical senses. They were, indeed, preternaturally keen and alert. Something in the awful disturbance of his organic system had so exalted and refined them that they made record of things never before perceived. He felt the ripples upon his face and heard their separate sounds as they struck. He looked at the forest on the bank of the stream, saw the individual trees, the leaves and the veining of each leaf—saw the very insects upon them: the locusts, the brilliant-bodied flies, the gray spiders stretching their webs from twig to twig. He noted the prismatic colors in all the dewdrops upon a million blades of grass. The humming of the gnats that danced above the eddies of the stream, the beating of the dragon-flies' wings, the strokes of the water-spiders' legs, like oars which had lifted their boat—all these made audible music. A fish slid along beneath his eyes and he heard the rush of its body parting the water.

He had come to the surface facing down the stream; in a moment the visible world seemed to wheel slowly round, himself the pivotal point, and he saw the bridge, the fort, the soldiers upon the bridge, the captain, the sergeant, the two privates, his executioners. They were in silhouette against the blue sky. They shouted and gesticulated, pointing at him. The captain had drawn his pistol, but did not fire, the others were unarmed. Their movements were grotesque and horrible, their forms gigantic.

Suddenly he heard a sharp report and something struck the water smartly within a few inches of his head, spattering his face with spray. He heard a second report, and saw one of the sentinels with his rifle at his shoulder, a light cloud of blue smoke rising from the muzzle. The man in the water saw the eye of the man on the bridge gazing into his own through the sights of the rifle. He observed that it was a gray eye and remembered having read that gray eyes were keenest, and that all famous marksmen had them. Nevertheless, this one had missed.

A counter-swirl had caught Farquhar and turned him half round; he was again looking into the forest on the bank opposite the fort. The sound of a clear, high voice in a monotonous singsong now rang out behind him and came across the water with a distinctness that pierced and subdued all other sounds, even the beating of the ripples in his ears. Although no soldier, he had frequented camps enough to know the dread significance of that delicate, drawling, aspirated chant; the lieutenant on shore was taking a part in the morning's work. How coldly and pitilessly—with what an even, calm intonation, presaging, and enforcing tranquility in the men—with what accurately measured intervals fell those cruel words:

"Attention, company! . . . Shoulder arms! . . . Ready! . . . Aim! . . . Fire!"

Farquhar dived—dived as deeply as he could. The water roared in his ears like the voice of Niagara, yet he heard the dulled thunder of the volley and, rising again toward the surface, met shining bits of metal, singularly flattened, oscillating slowly downward. Some of them touched him on the face and hands, then fell away, continuing their descent. One lodged between his collar and neck; it was uncomfortably warm and he snatched it out.

As he rose to the surface, gasping for breath, he saw that he had been a long time under water; he was perceptibly farther down stream—nearer to safety. The soldiers had almost finished reloading; the metal ramrods flashed all at once in the sunshine as they were drawn from the barrels, turned in the air, and thrust into their sockets. The two sentinels fired again, independently and ineffectually.

The hunted man saw all this over his shoulder; he was now swimming vigorously with the current. His brain was as energetic as his arms and legs; he thought with the rapidity of lightning.

"The officer," he reasoned, "will not make that martinet's error a second time. It is as easy to dodge a volley as a single shot. He has probably already given the command to fire at will. God help me, I cannot dodge them all!"

An appalling plash within two yards of him was followed by a loud, rushing sound, *diminuendo,* which seemed to travel back through the air to the fort and died in an explosion which stirred the very river to its deeps! A rising sheet of water curved over him, fell down upon him, blinded him, strangled him! The cannon had taken a hand in the game. As he shook his head free from the commotion of the smitten water he heard the deflected shot humming through the air ahead, and in an instant it was cracking and smashing the branches in the forest beyond.

"They will not do that again," he thought; "the next time they will use a charge of grape. I must keep my eye upon the gun; the smoke will apprise me—the report arrives too late; it lags behind the missile. That is a good gun."

Suddenly he felt himself whirled round and round—spinning like a top. The water, the banks, the forests, the now distant bridge, fort and men—all were commingled and blurred. Objects were represented by their colors only; circular horizontal streaks of color—that was all he saw. He had been caught in a vortex and was being whirled on with a velocity of advance and gyration that made him giddy and sick. In a few moments he was flung upon the gravel at the foot of the left bank of the stream—the southern bank—and behind a projecting point which concealed him from his enemies. The sudden arrest of his motion, the abrasion of one of his hands on the gravel, restored him, and he wept with delight. He dug his fingers into the sand, threw it over himself in handfuls and audibly blessed it. It looked like diamonds, rubies, emeralds; he could think of nothing beautiful which it did not resemble. The trees upon the bank were giant garden plants; he noted a definite order in their arrangement, inhaled the fragrance of their blooms. A strange, roseate light shone through the spaces among their trunks and the wind made in their branches the music of aeolian harps. He had no wish to perfect his escape—was content to remain in that enchanting spot until retaken.

A whiz and rattle of grapeshot among the branches high above his head roused him from his dream. The baffled cannoneer had fired him a random farewell. He sprang to his feet, rushed up the sloping bank, and plunged into the forest.

All that day he traveled, laying his course by the rounding sun. The forest seemed interminable; nowhere did he discover a break in it, not even a woodman's road. He had not known that he lived in so wild a region. There was something uncanny in the revelation.

By night fall he was fatigued, footsore, famishing. The thought of his wife and children urged him on. At last he found a road which led him in what he knew to be the right direction. It was as wide and straight as a city street, yet it seemed untraveled. No fields bordered it, no dwelling anywhere. Not so much as the barking of a dog suggested human habitation. The black bodies of the trees formed a straight wall on both sides, terminating on the horizon in a point, like a diagram in a lesson in perspective. Overhead, as he looked up through this rift in the wood, shone great golden stars looking unfamiliar and grouped in strange constellations. He was sure they were arranged in some order which had a secret and malign significance. The wood on either side was full of singular noises, among which—once, twice, and again, he distinctly heard whispers in an unknown tongue.

His neck was in pain and lifting his hand to it he found it horribly swollen. He knew that it had a circle of black where the rope had bruised it. His eyes felt congested; he could no longer close them. His tongue was swollen with thirst; he relieved its fever by thrusting it forward from between his teeth into the cold air. How softly the turf had carpeted the untraveled avenue—he could no longer feel the roadway beneath his feet!

Doubtless, despite his suffering, he had fallen asleep while walking, for now he sees another scene—perhaps he has merely recovered from a delirium. He stands at the gate of his own home. All is as he left it, and all bright and beautiful in the morning sunshine. He must have traveled the entire night. As he pushes open the gate and passes up the wide white walk, he sees a flutter of female garments; his wife, looking fresh and cool and sweet, steps down from the veranda to meet him. At the bottom of the steps she stands waiting, with a smile of ineffable joy, an attitude of matchless grace and dignity. Ah, how beautiful she is! He springs forward with extended arms. As he is about to clasp her he feels a stunning blow upon the back of the neck; a blinding white light blazes all about him with a sound like the shock of a cannon—then all is darkness and silence!

Peyton Farquhar was dead; his body, with a broken neck, swung gently from side to side beneath the timbers of the Owl Creek bridge.

QUESTIONS FOR DISCUSSION AND WRITING

1. What is the relationship among the three major divisions of the story? What paragraph in part 2 prepares us for part 3?
2. What kind of person is Farquhar? How does Bierce characterize him in part 2? What do we learn about him in parts 2 and 3?
3. How does the execution change Peyton Farquhar's perception of the setting? How does the setting contrast with the events that transpire there?
4. What is the point of view in each of the three sections? How does the last sentence of the story explain the point of view of part 3?
5. What *occurs* at Owl Creek Bridge beyond the exterior action of the execution? How does facing death give a richer meaning to Farquhar's past life as well as present existence?

9

HEINRICH BÖLL

Christmas Not Just Once a Year

HEINRICH BÖLL (1917–1985) was born in Cologne, Germany, attended the University of Cologne, and worked briefly as an apprentice book dealer before he was unwillingly conscripted into the German army during World War II. Near the end of the war (1945), he became an American prisoner of war. His revulsion at the cruelties and injustices he witnessed under the Nazis appears throughout his writing, leading many critics to identify him as the conscience of his nation. His prolific writing includes novels *Adam, Where Art Thou?* (1951), *The Clown* (1965), *Group Portrait with Lady* (1971); essays *Missing Persons* (1977); an autobiography, *What's to Become of the Boy? Or Something to Do With Books* (1981); and several collections of short stories including *Traveller, If You Come to the Spa* (1950) and *Children are Civilians Too* (1970). "Christmas Not Just Once a Year," reprinted from *The Stories of Henrich Böll* (1986), documents a family's attempt to exchange an empty ritual of "Peace" for the destructive memories of war.

1

Among our relatives, symptoms of disintegration are beginning to show up that for a while we tried silently to ignore but the threat of which we are now determined to face squarely. I do not yet dare use the word "collapse," but the alarming facts are accumulating to the point where they represent a threat and compel me to speak of things that may sound strange to the ears of my contemporaries but whose reality no one can dispute. The mildew of decay has obtained a foothold under the thick, hard veneer of respectability, colonies of deadly parasites heralding the end of the integrity of an entire clan. Today we must regret having ignored the voice of our cousin Franz, who long ago began to draw attention to the terrible consequences of what was on the face of it a harmless event. This event was in itself so trivial that we are now shocked by the extent of its consequences. Franz warned us long ago. Unfortunately he lacked prestige in the family. He had chosen an occupation that had never before been pursued, would never have been permitted to be pursued, by any member of our entire clan: he became a boxer. Of a brooding melancholy even in his youth, and of a piety always described as "a pose of religious zeal," he set out early on paths that caused my Uncle Franz—that kindest of men—deep concern. It was Franz's wont to stay away from school with a frequency that could no longer be described as normal. He met regularly with shady characters in remote parks and dense undergrowth on the outskirts of town, where they practiced the tough rules of fistfighting, showing no concern for the fact that their humanistic heritage was being neglected. Already these young toughs were demonstrating the bad habits of their generation—one that has, needless to say, turned out to be good for nothing. The thrilling intellectual battles of previous centuries did not interest them, so totally were they preoccupied with the dubious thrills of their own century. At first, Franz's piety struck me as being incompatible with these regular exercises in passive and active brutality. But today, certain things are beginning to dawn on me. I shall have to return to this later.

So it was Franz who issued a timely warning, who dissociated himself from certain celebrations, describing it all as affectation and a pain in the neck, above all later refusing to participate in measures deemed necessary to preserve what he called a pain in the neck. However—as I have said—his prestige was not high enough for him to find a hearing among his relatives.

But now things have got so out of hand that we are at a total loss, not knowing how to put a curb on them.

Franz has long since become a famous boxer, yet today he rejects the praise heaped upon him by the family with the same indifference with which he at one time refused to accept any criticism.

His brother, however, my cousin Johannes—a man for whom I would at any time have vouched, a successful attorney, my uncle's favorite son—is said to have become involved with the Communist Party, a rumor I obstinately refuse to believe. My cousin Lucie, until now a normal woman, is said to spend her nights in disreputable places, accompanied by her helpless spouse, at dances for which I can find no other adjective than "existentialist." Even Uncle Franz, that kindest of men, is supposed to have said that he is tired of life—a man who was regarded by the entire clan as a model of vitality and as a paragon of what we have been taught to call a Christian businessman.

Medical bills pile up; psychiatrists, psychologists, are called in. Only my Aunt Milla, who must be cited as the originator of all these phenomena, enjoys the best of health, smiles, is as well and cheerful as she has almost always been. Her bright, cheery manner is now, after our years of heartfelt concern for her well-being, slowly beginning to get on our nerves. For there was a crisis in her life that threatened to become alarming. This is where I will have to go into more detail.

2

It is simple enough with hindsight to discern the origin of a disquieting trend—and, strangely enough, it is only now, when I observe the situation pragmatically, that the things which have been occurring in the family for almost two years seem unusual.

It might have struck us earlier that something was not right. In fact, something wasn't right, and if anything at all has ever been right—which I doubt—here things are occurring that fill me with horror. Throughout the family, Aunt Milla had always been known for her particular fondness for decorating the Christmas tree, a harmless if particular weakness that is fairly widespread in our Fatherland. Her weakness met with smiles all around, and the resistance displayed by Franz from his earliest youth to this "to-do" was always the object of vehement indignation, especially since Franz cut a disquieting figure anyway. He refused to help decorate the tree. Up to a certain point, all this took a normal course. My aunt had become accustomed to Franz's staying away from the pre-Christmas preparations, even from the actual celebration, appearing only for Christmas dinner. It was no longer even discussed.

At the risk of making myself unpopular, I must now mention a fact in defense of which I can only say that it really is one. During the years 1939 to 1945 there was a war on. In wartime there is a lot of singing, shooting, talking, fighting, starving, and dying—and bombs are dropped, all disagreeable things with which I have no intention of boring my contemporaries. I must merely mention them because the war had a bearing on the story I wish to tell. For the war was registered by my Aunt Milla merely as a force that began as early as Christmas 1939 to jeopardize her Christmas tree. Admittedly, her Christmas tree was unusually vulnerable.

The main attractions on my Aunt Milla's Christmas tree were glass dwarfs holding a cork hammer in their uplifted arms with a bell-shaped anvil at their feet. Under the dwarfs' feet, candles were affixed, and upon a certain temperature being reached, a hidden mechanism was set in motion, a hectic agitation was communicated to the dwarfs' arms, with their cork hammers they flailed away like crazy at the bell shaped anvils, thus, since they were about a dozen in number, producing a concerted elfin tinkling. Furthermore: from the tip of the Christmas tree hung a red-cheeked angel in a silvery dress, and at regular intervals the angel parted its lips to whisper "Peace," and again, "Peace." The mechanical secret of this angel, obstinately guarded, became known to me much later, although at the time I had the opportunity almost every week of admiring it. In addition, of course, my aunt's Christmas tree was also bedecked with sugar rings, cookies, angel hair, marzipan figures, and—last but not least—silver tinsel; and I can still remember that properly attaching the various ornaments took a great deal of effort, requiring the participation of the entire family, so that on Christmas Eve frayed nerves cost us all our appetite, and the mood was then—as one says—dismal, except in the case of my cousin Franz, who, of course, had taken no part in these preparations and was the only one to enjoy the roast and the asparagus, the whipped cream and ice cream.

When we duly arrived, then, for a visit the day after Christmas, and risked the bold assumption that the secret of the talking angel was based on the same mechanism that caused certain dolls to say "Mama" or "Papa," the only response was mocking laughter. Now it is easy to imagine that bombs falling close by posed an extreme hazard to such a vulnerable tree. There were terrible scenes when the dwarfs fell off the tree, and once even the angel toppled to the ground. My aunt was inconsolable. After every air raid she went to endless trouble to restore the tree completely and to maintain it at least over the Christmas holidays. But even in 1940 it was already a hopeless task. Again at the risk of making myself very unpopular, I must mention in passing that the number of air raids on our city was indeed considerable, to say nothing of their violence. At any rate, my aunt's Christmas tree fell victim—the thread of my narrative forbids my mentioning other victims—to modern warfare; foreign ballistic experts temporarily snuffed out its existence.

We were all genuinely sorry for our aunt, who was a charming, gracious woman. We felt sorry that, after bitter struggles, endless arguments, after many tears and scenes, she had to agree to renounce her tree for the duration of the war.

Fortunately—or should I say unfortunately?—that was almost the only impact the war had on her. The shelter built by my uncle was bombproof; moreover, there was always an automobile ready to whisk my Aunt Milla away to areas where nothing was to be seen of the immediate effects of the war. Everything was done to spare her the sight of the appalling destruction. My two cousins were lucky enough not to have to do their war service in its most rigorous form. Johannes quickly joined his uncle's business, which played a crucial role in supplying our city with vegetables. Moreover, he had a chronic gallbladder complaint. Franz, on the other hand, although he became a soldier, was entrusted only with guarding prisoners, an assignment he utilized to render himself unpopular with his military superiors—by treating Russians and Poles as human beings. In those days my cousin Lucie was still unmarried and helped in the business. One afternoon a week she did volunteer war work at a factory that embroidered swastikas. But this is not the place to enumerate the political sins of my relatives.

Anyway, all in all there was no lack of money or food or whatever was necessary for protection, and the only thing my aunt bitterly resented was having to give up her tree. My Uncle Franz, that kindest of men, spent almost fifty years acquiring considerable merit and profit by buying up oranges and lemons in tropical and subtropical countries and selling them with a suitable markup. During the war he expanded his business to include less valuable fruits and vegetables. But after the war the gratifying produce that was his main interest was once again available, and citrus fruit became the object of keenest interest at every level. At this point Uncle Franz succeeded in regaining his former influential position, and he was able to provide the population with the enjoyment of vitamins and himself with that of a respectable fortune.

But he was almost seventy and wanted to retire, to hand over the business to his son-in-law. That is when the event occurred which at the time we smiled at but which today seems to us to have been the cause of the whole wretched sequence of events.

My Aunt Milla started in about the Christmas tree again. That was harmless enough; even the perseverance with which she insisted that everything was to be "like in the old days" merely drew smiles from us. At first there was really no reason to take it all that seriously. Although the war had destroyed so much of which the restoration caused greater concern, why—we said to ourselves—deny a charming old lady this trifling pleasure?

Everyone knows how difficult it was at that time to obtain such things as butter and bacon. But even for my Uncle Franz, who enjoyed the best of connections, it was impossible in 1945 to obtain marzipan figures, chocolate rings, and candles. It was not until 1946 that all these things could be provided. Fortunately, a complete set of dwarfs and anvils as well as an angel had survived.

I well remember the day we were invited to my uncle's home. It was in January 1947, and bitterly cold outside. But indoors it was warm, and there was no shortage of things to eat. And when the lights were put out, the candles lit, when the dwarfs began to hammer, the angel whispered "Peace," and again, "Peace," I felt transported back into an era that I had assumed to be past.

Nevertheless, this experience, although surprising, was not extraordinary. What *was* extraordinary was the experience I had three months later. My mother—it was now the middle of March—had sent me over to find out whether there was anything my Uncle Franz "could do": she was looking for fruit. I strolled through the streets to the part of town where my uncle lived; the air was mild, it was dusk. All unsuspecting, I walked past overgrown piles of rubble and neglected parks and, opening the gate to my uncle's garden, stopped, dumbfounded. In the quiet of the evening, the sound of singing was clearly audible, coming from my uncle's living room. Singing is a good old German custom, and there are many songs about spring, but now I could clearly hear "Holy infant, so tender and mild . . ."

I must admit to being confused. Slowly I approached the house, waiting for the singing to end. The curtains were drawn shut; I bent down to the keyhole. At that moment the tinkling of the dwarfs' bells reached my ear, and I could clearly hear the whispering of the angel. I didn't have the courage to intrude, and walked slowly back home. In the family, my account produced general merriment. But it was not until Franz appeared and gave us the details that we found out what had happened.

Around Candlemas, the time when in our part of the country the Christmas trees are stripped and then thrown on the garbage pile, where they are picked up by good-for-nothing children to be dragged through ashes and other rubbish, and used for various games—it was around Candlemas that the terrible thing happened. When my cousin Johannes, on Candlemas Eve, after the tree had been lit for the last time, began to detach the dwarfs from their clips, my aunt, until then such a gentle soul, set up a pitiful wail, a wail so violent and sudden that my cousin was startled, and lost control over the gently swaying tree. Then it happened: there was a tinkling and a ringing, dwarfs and bells, anvils and all-surmounting angel—everything crashed to the floor, and my aunt screamed.

She screamed for almost a week. Neurologists were summoned by telegram, psychiatrists came racing up in taxis—but all, even the most famous of them, left the house shrugging their shoulders, although also somewhat alarmed. None of them had been able to put a stop to that shrill, discordant concert. Only the strongest medication yielded a few hours of quiet; however, the dose of Luminal that can be given daily to a sixty-year-old woman without endangering her life is unfortunately rather small. But it is torture to have in the house a woman screaming at the top of her voice; by the second day the family was already totally distraught. Even the comforting words of the priest, who always celebrated Christmas Eve with the family, had no effect: my aunt screamed.

Franz made himself especially unpopular by suggesting a regular exorcism. The priest scolded him, the family was dismayed by his medieval views, and for a few weeks his reputation for brutality outweighed his reputation as a boxer.

Meanwhile everything was being tried to relieve my aunt of her condition. She refused food, did not speak, did not sleep; they tried cold water, hot foot-baths, hot and cold compresses, and the doctors searched through their reference works looking for a name for this neurosis, but could not find it.

And my aunt screamed. She went on screaming until my Uncle Franz—really the kindest of men—hit on the idea of setting up a new Christmas tree.

3

The idea was excellent, but its execution proved to be extremely difficult. By this time it was almost the middle of February, and it is fairly difficult to find an acceptable Christmas tree for sale at that time. The entire business world has long since shifted—with gratifying speed, by the way—to other things. Carnival is approaching: masks and pistols, cowboy hats and crazy headdresses for Czardas princesses fill the store windows where earlier one had been able to admire angels and angel hair, candles and Nativity scenes. The confectionery stores have long since moved their Christmas items back into their storerooms, whereas carnival crackers now adorn their windows. In any event, Christmas trees are not available at this time of year on the regular market.

Eventually an expedition of rapacious grandchildren was equipped with pocket money and a sharp ax. These young people rode out into the state forest and returned late that afternoon, obviously in the best of moods, with a silver fir. But meanwhile it had been discovered that four dwarfs, six bell-shaped anvils, and the all-surmounting angel had been completely destroyed. The marzipan figures and the cookies had fallen victim to the greedy grandchildren. So this generation too, now growing up, is good for nothing; and if ever a generation has been good for something—which I doubt—I have come to the conclusion that it was the generation of our fathers.

Although there was no lack of cash, or of the necessary contacts, it took another four days to assemble all the accessories. Throughout this time, my aunt screamed incessantly. Telegrams to the German toy centers, which were just beginning to get back on their feet, were sent winging through the ether, urgent long-distance calls were made, express packages were delivered during the night by perspiring young postal assistants, bribery ensured an import license from Czechoslovakia at short notice.

Those days will be remembered in the annals of my uncle's family as days of an exceptionally high consumption of coffee, cigarettes, and nerves. Meanwhile my aunt was wasting away: her round face became hard and angular, her mild expression gave way to one of unyielding severity, she did not eat, did not drink, she screamed incessantly, was watched over by two nurses, and the dose of Luminal had to be increased every day.

Franz told us that the entire family was in the grip of a pathological tension when at last, on February 12, the Christmas tree decorations were once again complete. The candles were lit, the curtains drawn, my aunt was brought from her sickroom, and among those assembled only sobs and giggles were to be heard. My aunt's expression began to relax in the light of the candles, and, upon the right degree of warmth being reached, the little glass fellows started hammering away like crazy, and finally the angel whispered "Peace," and again, "Peace," the most beautiful smile lit up my aunt's face, and almost at once the whole family would strike up "O Christmas Tree!" In order to complete the picture, the priest had also been invited, since he normally spent Christmas Eve at Uncle Franz's. He too smiled; he too was relieved and joined in the singing.

No test, no psychologist's expertise, no specialist's disclosure of hidden traumata, had achieved it, but the sensitive heart of my uncle had hit upon the right thing. The Christmas tree therapy of that kindest of men had saved the situation.

My aunt had calmed down and was almost—it was hoped at the time—cured. After a few carols had been sung, a few dishes of cookies emptied, everyone was tired and withdrew for the night, and lo and behold: my aunt fell asleep without any tranquilizer. The two nurses were dismissed, the doctors shrugged their shoulders, everything seemed to be back to normal. My aunt was eating again, drinking again, was once again gracious and gentle. But the following evening, as the twilight hour approached, my uncle was sitting reading the paper beside his wife next to the tree, when she suddenly touched his arm gently and said, "So now let's light the candles and call in the children, I think it's time to begin." Later my uncle admitted to us that he was startled but that he got up to summon his children and grandchildren as quickly as possible and to send word to the priest. The priest arrived, somewhat out of breath and surprised, but the candles were lit, the dwarfs made to hammer, the angel was made to whisper, carols were sung, cookies were eaten—and everything seemed to be back to normal.

4

Now, all vegetation is subject to certain biological laws, and fir trees, when uprooted from their soil, are known to have the devastating tendency to drop their needles, especially when they are standing in warm rooms, and at my uncle's it was always warm. The life span of the silver fir is somewhat longer than that of the common fir, as has been proved in the well-known treatise *Abies vulgaris and abies nobilis,* by Dr. Hergenring. However, even the life span of the silver fir is not unlimited. With the approach of the carnival season, it became apparent that an attempt must be made to subject my aunt to new distress: the tree was rapidly losing its needles, and during the evening carol singing a slight frown was noticed on my aunt's forehead. At the advice of a really outstanding psychologist, the attempt was now made to speak, in a casual conversational tone, of a possible end to the Christmas season, especially now that trees were beginning to put forth their leaves, something generally acknowledged to be an indication of approaching spring, whereas in our latitudes the word "Christmas" is unquestionably associated with conceptions of winter. My very astute uncle suggested one evening that everyone join in singing the songs "Hark, the birds have all arrived!" and "Come, Lovely May," but even at the very first line of the first of those songs my aunt put on such a grim expression that everyone immediately broke off and intoned "O Christmas Tree!" Three days later, my cousin Johannes was instructed to undertake a mild act of spoliation; but no sooner had he reached out and taken the cork hammer from one of the dwarfs than my aunt started screaming so violently that the dwarf was immediately made whole again, the candles were lit, and, somewhat hastily but very loud, the carol "Silent Night" burst forth.

However, the nights were no longer silent. Loudly singing groups of youthful drunkards roamed through the city with trumpets and drums, everything was covered with streamers and confetti, and children in fancy dress filled the streets during the day, shooting, yelling, some of them singing too. According to private statistics there were at least sixty thousand cowboys and forty thousand Czardas princesses in our city. In short, it was carnival time, a feast we are accustomed to celebrate with a vigor equal to if not surpassing that of Christmas. But my aunt seemed to be blind and deaf: she deplored the carnival costumes that inevitably turn up in the clothes closets of our homes during this time; in a sad voice she complained of the decline of morality since people seemed unable, even during Christmastime, to refrain from these immoral goings-on; and when in my cousin's bedroom she discovered a balloon that, although deflated, still clearly showed a white jester's cap painted on it, she burst into tears and begged my uncle to put a stop to these unholy goings-on.

To its consternation, the family had to conclude that my aunt actually was under the delusion that it was "Christmas Eve." At any rate, my uncle called a family conclave, pleaded for forbearance toward his wife, consideration for her strange mental condition, and proceeded to organize another expedition in order at least to ensure the peace of the evening festivities.

While my aunt was asleep, the decorations were removed from the old tree and installed on the new one, and her condition remained gratifying.

5

But carnival time passed too, and spring really did arrive, and instead of the song "Come, Lovely May," one could have already sung "Lovely May, thou art now come." Then it was June. Four Christmas trees had already withered, and none of the more recently consulted doctors could promise any hope of improvement. My aunt was adamant. Even Dr. Bless, regarded as an international authority, had withdrawn with a shrug of his shoulders to his study after collecting his fee of 1,365 marks, thus supplying further evidence of his unworldliness. A few further, rather vague attempts to curtail or discontinue the celebration met with such screams on the part of my aunt that the family had once and for all to desist from such sacrilege.

The terrible part was that my aunt insisted on all those close to her being present. Among these were also the priest and the grandchildren. It was difficult enough to insist that members of the family turn up regularly, but the case of the priest presented still greater difficulties. For a few weeks, out of consideration for his old penitent, he had stuck it out without grumbling, but the time finally came when, with much hemming and hawing, he tried to explain to my uncle that the situation could not continue. Granted the actual ceremony was brief (it lasted some thirty-eight minutes), but in the long run even this brief ritual was becoming insupportable, the priest maintained. He had other obligations: evening gatherings with his confreres, parochial duties, to say nothing of taking confessions on Saturdays. For several weeks he had put up with having to rearrange his schedule, but toward the end of June he was making vigorous demands for his release. Franz went on the rampage in the family, looking for accomplices to his plan to have his mother placed in an institution, but he was met with rejection on all sides.

In short: problems began to mount. One evening the priest didn't show up, couldn't be reached by either telephone or messenger, and it became apparent that his absence was deliberate. My uncle cursed mightily, and he used the occasion to call the servants of the Church names that I must refuse to repeat. As a last resort, one of the curates, a person of humble origin, was asked to help out. He did so but behaved so appallingly that the result was almost a disaster. However, it must be borne in mind that it was June, in other words—hot; nevertheless, the curtains had been drawn shut in order at least to give the impression of winter darkness, and the candles had been lit. Then the ceremony began. Although the curate had already heard of these strange happenings, he could not really imagine them. With a good deal of trepidation, the family introduced the curate to my aunt, explaining that he was substituting for the priest. To their surprise she accepted this change in the program. So: the dwarfs hammered away, the angel whispered, "O Christmas Tree!" was sung, then cookies were eaten, the carol was sung again, and suddenly the curate was seized with uncontrollable laughter. Later he confessed that he hadn't been able to hear the line ". . . in winter too, when snowflakes fall," without laughing. He exploded with clerical foolishness, left the room, and was not seen again. Everyone looked breathlessly at my aunt, but in a resigned voice she merely said something about "yokels in priest's clothing," and popped a piece of marzipan into her mouth. At the time we too deplored the incident, but today I am inclined to call it an outburst of natural mirth.

At this point I must—if I am to do justice to the truth—insert that my uncle exploited his connections with the highest ecclesiastical authorities in order to complain about the priest as well as the curate. The matter was handled with the utmost punctiliousness; an action was brought over neglect of parochial duties and was won by both clerics. An appeal is still under consideration.

Fortunately a retired priest was found who lived in the neighborhood. This charming old gentleman graciously and unhesitatingly agreed to put himself at their disposal and complete the regular evening ritual. But I am anticipating. My Uncle Franz, who was sensible enough to realize that the situation was beyond any medical aid, and who also obstinately refused to attempt exorcism, was enough of a businessman to take the long view and to work out the most economical method. He began by putting a stop to the grandchildren's expeditions as early as mid-June, having established that they were costing too much. My ingenious cousin Johannes, who maintains excellent contacts with the business world at all levels, discovered the Fresh Christmas Tree Service provided by Söderbaum's, an efficient company that for the past two years has deserved high praise for relieving the nervous strain of my relatives. After only six months Söderbaum's converted the arrangement into an annual contract at a considerably reduced rate. Further, the company undertook to have the delivery dates precisely established by Dr. Alfast, their specialist in evergreen trees, so that now, three days before the old tree becomes unacceptable, the new one arrives and can be decorated at leisure. Furthermore, as a precautionary measure, two dozen dwarfs are kept in stock and three angels held in reserve. To this day, the confectionery has remained a sore point. It has a devastating tendency to melt and drip down from the tree, faster and more radically than melting wax. At least during the summer months. Every attempt to preserve their seasonal crispness by skillfully camouflaged cooling devices has so far failed, as has a series of experiments designed to test the possibility of embalming the tree. Nevertheless, the family is grateful for and open to any innovative suggestion that might reduce the cost of this permanent festivity.

6

In the meantime, the evening ceremonies at my uncle's home have acquired an almost professional inflexibility: the family assembles at or around the tree. My aunt comes in, the candles are lit, the dwarfs begin to hammer, and the angel whispers "Peace, peace"; then a few carols are sung, cookies are nibbled, there is some casual conversation, and everyone retires with a yawn and a "Merry Christmas, everyone!"—at which point the young people turn to seasonal diversions while my kindly uncle and Aunt Milla go to bed. Candle smoke remains behind in the room, together with the mild aroma of heated fir branches and the spicy odor of Christmas cookies. The dwarfs, slightly phosphorescent, stand stiffly in the darkness, their arms raised menacingly, and the angel glows in its silvery robe, which is apparently also phosphorescent.

It may be superfluous to remark that the whole family's pleasure in the real Christmas festivities has been greatly diminished. We can, if we so wish, admire a traditional Christmas tree at any time in our uncle's home—and it often happens, when we are sitting on the veranda on a summer evening, after the labors of the day, imbibing Uncle's mild orange punch, that the tinkling of glass bells comes from within, and in the dusk the dwarfs are to be seen hammering away like nimble little devils, while the angel whispers "Peace," and again, "Peace." And we are still taken aback when, in the middle of summer, my uncle suddenly calls out to his children: "Light the tree, please, Mother will be here any minute." At that point, usually right on time, the prelate arrives, a mild old gentleman whom we have all taken to our hearts because he plays his part so beautifully, assuming he even knows he is playing a part and which part. But never mind: he plays it, white-haired, smiling, and the patch of purple below his collar lends the last touch of refinement to his personality. And it is an unusual experience to hear, on warm summer nights, the anxious cry "The candle snuffer—quick, where's the candle snuffer?" It has happened more than once that, during a violent thunderstorm, the dwarfs suddenly felt impelled, without the effect of heat, to raise their arms and swing them wildly, thus providing a kind of unscheduled concert, a fact that the family tried to explain, without much imagination, by the dry word "electricity."

One not wholly inconsiderable aspect of this arrangement is the financial one. Even though, generally speaking, our family is not strapped for cash, such extraordinary expenditures upset all calculations. For, despite every precaution, the wear and tear on dwarfs, anvils, and hammers is, of course, enormous; and the sensitive mechanism enabling the angel to speak requires constant care and maintenance and must from time to time be replaced. Incidentally, I have meanwhile discovered the secret: the angel is connected by a cable to a microphone in the next room, and in front of the mike there is a constantly rotating phonograph record that whispers at intervals "Peace," and again, "Peace." All these items are especially costly in that they are designed for use on only a few days in the year but now have to stand up to hard wear all year round. I was amazed when my uncle told me one day that the dwarfs had actually to be renewed every three months and that a complete set cost no less than a hundred and twenty-eight marks. He had asked an engineer friend of his to reinforce them with a latex coating but without impairing the beauty of their sound. This attempt failed. The consumption of candles, spekulatius, and marzipan, the tree contract, medical bills, and the token of appreciation due every month to the prelate: all that, said my uncle, amounts to a daily average of eleven marks, not to mention the wear and tear on his nerves and other impairments to his health that were then beginning to make themselves felt. But that was in the fall, and these deleterious effects were ascribed to a certain autumnal sensitivity, a matter of quite common observation.

7

The actual Christmas celebrations went off normally. Something like a sigh of relief went through my uncle's family now that other families were to be seen gathered around

Christmas trees, other families had also to sing and eat spekulatius. But the relief lasted only for the duration of the Christmas season. As early as mid-January my cousin Lucie was afflicted by a strange malady: at the sight of the Christmas trees lying around on streets and garbage piles, she would burst into hysterical sobbing. This was followed by a regular attack of madness, which the family tried to pass off as a nervous breakdown. When a friend with whom she was having afternoon coffee smilingly offered her some spekulatius, she knocked the plate out of her hand. It is true, of course, that my cousin is what is known as a temperamental woman; so she knocked the plate out of her friend's hand, walked over to the Christmas tree, ripped it from its stand, and trampled on the glass baubles, artificial mushrooms, candles, and stars, a continuous howl issuing from her lips. The assembled ladies fled, including the hostess, and Lucie was left to rampage while they waited in the hall for the doctor, listening perforce to china being smashed inside the room. I find it difficult, but I must report here that Lucie was taken away in a straitjacket.

Although repeated hypnotic treatments arrested the malady, the actual cure progressed very slowly. Above all, the release from the evening ceremony, on which the doctor insisted, seemed to have a noticeably beneficial effect; after only a few days she began to thrive. After only ten days the doctor could risk at least mentioning spekulatius, but she obstinately refused to eat any. The doctor hit on the brilliant idea of feeding her pickles, offering her salads and hearty meat dishes. That was really poor Lucie's salvation. She laughed again, and she began to spice the endless therapeutic conversations with her doctor by adding ironic comments.

Although the gap caused by Lucie's absence from the evening ceremony was painful for my aunt, it was explained by a circumstance that can be accepted as a valid excuse for all women—pregnancy.

But Lucie had created what is called a precedent: she had proved that, although our aunt suffered when someone was absent, she did not start screaming right away, and my cousin Johannes and his brother-in-law Karl now tried to break out of the strict discipline by pleading illness or business commitments, or offering other more or less transparent reasons. But here my uncle was surprisingly adamant: with relentless severity he stipulated that only in exceptional cases could doctors' certificates be submitted and the briefest of dispensations applied for. My aunt immediately noticed any additional gap and would break into quiet but persistent weeping, giving rise to the most ominous concern.

After a month, Lucie returned and expressed her willingness to rejoin the daily ritual, but her doctor has insisted that a jar of pickles and a plate of hearty sandwiches be kept in readiness for her, her spekulatius trauma having proved to be incurable. Thus for a while all disciplinary problems were resolved by my uncle, who on this point turned out to be surprisingly adamant.

8

Soon after the first anniversary of the perpetual Christmas celebration, disturbing rumors began to circulate: my cousin Johannes was said to have obtained an expert opinion from a medical friend as to the foreseeable life span of my aunt—a truly sinister rumor that threw a disquieting light on a peaceful daily family gathering. The expert opinion was said to have been devastating for Johannes. All the vital organs of my aunt, whose life has been a model of sobriety, are completely intact; the life span of her father extended over seventy-eight years, that of her mother over eighty-six. My aunt herself is sixty-two, and there is therefore no reason to prophesy an early and blessed demise for her. Even less, in my opinion, to wish it for her. So when my aunt fell ill during the summer—vomiting and diarrhea plagued the poor woman—there were whisperings that she had been poisoned; but let me expressly declare that this rumor is nothing but a figment on the part of evil-minded relatives. It has been proved beyond a doubt that she suffered from an infection brought in by a grandson. Analyses of my aunt's feces showed not even the slightest trace of poison.

That same summer the first antisocial tendencies showed up in Johannes: he resigned from his choral society, declaring, in writing, that he no longer intended to devote himself to the cultivation of German songs. It is true, of course—if I may interject this here—that, despite his academic degree, he was an uncultured person. For the male choir Virhymnia, being deprived of his bass voice was a great loss.

Lucie's husband, Karl, began secretly to get in touch with emigration offices. The land of his dreams had to have certain qualities: no fir trees must grow there, and their import must be prohibited or made impossible by high tariffs; furthermore—this for his wife's sake—the secret of baking spekulatius must be unknown there and the singing of Christmas carols prohibited. Karl declared his willingness to accept hard manual labor.

Meanwhile his attempts have been released from the curse of secrecy because my uncle has undergone a complete and abrupt change. This took place on such a disagreeable level that we had every reason to be shocked. That respectable man, of whom I can only say that he is as stubborn as he is kind, was observed on paths that are unquestionably immoral and will remain so as long as the world continues to exist. Various things have become known about him, and attested to by witnesses, to which only the word "adultery" can be applied. And the most terrible part about it is that he no longer denies it but claims that he is living under circumstances and conditions that must justify exceptional moral standards. Awkwardly enough, this sudden change came to light at the very time when the appeal against the two clerics of his parish was due to be heard. As a witness, as a crypto-plaintiff, Uncle Franz must have made such an unprepossessing impression that he can be considered solely to blame for the fact that the appeal turned out in favor of the two clerics. But by this time all such things have ceased to interest Uncle Franz: the moral disintegration of Uncle Franz is complete, a *fait accompli*.

He was also the first to hit upon the idea of having an actor represent him at the evening ritual. He had dug up an unemployed bon vivant who imitated him for two weeks so perfectly that not even his wife was aware of the substitution. His children were not aware of it either. It was one of the grandsons who, during a short pause in the singing, suddenly called out, "Grandpa's wearing striped socks!", at the same time triumphantly raising the bon vivant's trouser leg. For the poor artist, this scene must have been terrible. The family too were aghast, and, in order to avert a disaster, they immediately—as already so often in embarrassing situations—struck up a carol. After my aunt had gone to bed, the identity of the artist was quickly established. It was the signal for an almost total collapse.

9

Still, one must bear in mind that eighteen months is a long time, and that midsummer had arrived again, the season in which my relatives find it hardest to participate in this charade. Listlessly they nibble in the heat at cinnamon stars and gingerbread, smiling fixedly while they crack dry nuts, listening to the tirelessly hammering dwarfs, and flinching when the red-cheeked angel whispers "Peace" above their heads, "Peace." But they carry on while, despite their summer clothing, the perspiration runs down their necks and cheeks and their shirts stick to their bodies. Or, rather, they used to carry on.

For the time being, money is no object—on the contrary, one might say. Now there are whispers that Uncle Franz has been resorting to business methods that virtually no longer permit the description "Christian businessman." He is determined not to allow any appreciable diminution of his fortune, a commitment that both reassures and alarms us.

The unmasking of the bon vivant led to a regular mutiny, the result of which was a compromise: Uncle Franz has undertaken to finance a small ensemble to replace himself, Johannes, my brother-in-law Karl, and Lucie; and an agreement has been reached whereby one of the four takes part in the evening ritual in person, in order to keep an eye on the children. So far the prelate has been quite unaware of this fraud, to which one can by no means apply the adjective "pious." Apart from my aunt and the children, he is the only original character in this charade.

A detailed plan has been worked out, known in the family as the "game plan"; and in view of the fact that one of them always does take part, the actors are also assured of certain free days. Meanwhile the family has noticed that the actors are not at all averse to lending themselves to the ritual and are happy to earn some extra money; consequently their fees have been successfully reduced, there being fortunately no lack of out-of-work actors. Karl has told me that there is a good chance of further reducing this item, and quite considerably, especially since the actors are offered a meal, and, as everybody knows, art doesn't put bread on the table.

10

I have already hinted at the disastrous trend taking place in Lucie: she now spends almost all her time gadding about in night spots, and, especially on days when she has been forced to take part in the ceremony at home, she throws all restraint to the winds. She wears cords, gaudy sweaters, runs around in sandals, and has cut off her glorious hair in favor of a plain square-cut style which, I now learn, has been in vogue more than once as "bangs." Although I have not yet been able to observe any overt immorality on her part, merely a certain exaltation that she herself calls "existentialism," I cannot see my way toward regarding this trend as desirable. I prefer women who are gentle, who move decorously to the rhythm of a waltz, who quote pleasant poetry, and whose diet does not consist exclusively of pickles and goulash overspiced with paprika. Karl's emigration plans seem to be crystallizing: he has discovered a country, not far from the equator, that promises to live up to his conditions, and Lucie is thrilled: in that country people wear clothes not unlike her own, love pungent spices, and dance to rhythms without which she maintains she is no longer able to live. Although it is somewhat shocking that this couple do not seem to cherish the idea of "Home, sweet home," I can understand their desire to get away from it all.

The situation with Johannes is even worse. Unfortunately the nasty rumor has turned out to be true: he has become a Communist. He has broken off all connection with his family, ignores all his obligations, and attends the evening ritual only by proxy: that of his double. His eyes have acquired a fanatical expression; he acts like a dervish at the public functions of his party, neglects his practice, and writes furious articles in appropriate journals. Strangely enough, he now quite often sees Franz, who tries vainly to convert him and whom he tries just as vainly to convert. Despite all spiritual alienation, they have grown somewhat closer on a personal level.

As for Franz, I have not seen him for a long time, only heard of him. He is said to have fallen into a deep depression, spending hours in dim churches, and I believe one is justified in describing his piety as exaggerated. He began to neglect his profession after his family became engulfed in its troubles; and just the other day I saw on the wall of a demolished building a faded poster announcing "Last fight of ex-champion Lenz vs. Lecoq. Lenz retiring from the ring." The poster was dated March, and we are now well into August. Franz is said to be in very poor shape. I believe he finds himself in a situation never before experienced in our family: he is poor. Fortunately he has remained single, so the social consequences of his irresponsible piety affect only himself. With amazing persistence he has been trying to arrange for Lucie's children to be placed under protective guardianship, believing as he does that they are threatened by the evening ritual. But his efforts have been in vain: we can be thankful that the children of well-to-do couples are not exposed to the interference of social institutions.

The one who has removed himself the least from the rest of the family is, in spite of some repulsive traits, Uncle Franz, although it is true that, in spite of his advanced age, he has a mistress, and his commercial practices are of a nature of which, while we may admire them, we can by no means approve. Recently he unearthed an out-of-work stage manager who supervises the evening ritual and sees to it that everything goes like clockwork. And it really does.

11

Meanwhile almost two years have passed: a long time. And I could not refrain, on one of my evening strolls, from walking past my uncle's house, where normal hospitality is no longer possible, now that unknown artist types are milling around in there every evening and the members of the family indulge in strange-seeming amusements. It was a warm summer's evening when I passed by there, and even as I turned the corner into the chestnut avenue I could hear the words "Christmas glitter decks the forests. . . ." A passing truck rendered the remainder inaudible. I crept slowly up to the house and looked through a gap in the curtains into the room: the resemblance of the playactors to the relatives they were representing was so startling that for a moment I could not make out who actually was in charge—as they call it—that evening. I could not see the dwarfs, but I could hear them. Their chirping tinkle is on wavelengths that penetrate every wall. The whispering of the angel was inaudible. My aunt seemed genuinely happy: she was chatting with the prelate, and it took a while for me to recognize my brother-in-law as the only, if I may so put it, real person. I recognized him by the way he puckered his lips when he blew out a match. There do seem to be unmistakable traits of individuality. It occurred to me that the actors are treated to cigars, cigarettes, and wine; moreover, asparagus is served every evening. If they take advantage of this—and which artist would not?—it means a considerable additional expense for my uncle. The children were playing with dolls and toy wagons in a corner of the room: they looked pale and wan. Perhaps something really should be done about them, after all. It occurred to me that they might be replaced by wax dummies, the kind used in drugstore windows to promote milk powder and skin cream. They always seem very lifelike to me.

So I decide to draw the attention of the family to the possible effects of this unusual daily stimulation on childish minds. Although, of course, a certain amount of discipline can do no harm, it would seem that inordinate demands are being placed upon them in this instance.

I left my observation post when they started to sing "Silent Night." I really couldn't stand that carol. The air was so mild—and for a moment I had the impression of being present at a gathering of ghosts. I was suddenly seized by a craving for pickles, which gave me an inkling of how greatly Lucie must have suffered.

12

Meanwhile I have been successful in having the children replaced by wax dummies. The acquisition proved to be expensive—Uncle Franz balked at it for a long time, but it would have been irresponsible to continue to allow the children to be fed marzipan every evening and make them sing carols that may eventually cause psychological damage. The acquisition of the dummies proved fortunate, since Karl and Lucie really did emigrate, and Johannes also withdrew his children from his father's household. Standing amid big steamer trunks, I said good-bye to Karl, Lucie, and the children; they seemed happy, although somewhat apprehensive. Johannes has also moved away from our city. He is busy somewhere reorganizing one of the regional branches of his party.

Uncle Franz is tired of life. In a plaintive voice he recently told me that they keep forgetting to dust the dummies. The servants are giving him enough trouble as it is, and the actors are beginning to get out of hand. They are drinking more than they are entitled to, and some of them have been caught pocketing cigars and cigarettes. I advised my uncle to serve them colored water and to obtain some cardboard cigars.

The only reliable ones are my aunt and the prelate. They chat about the good old days, titter, and seem to be having a good time, and they only break off their conversation when a carol is struck up.

In any event: the ritual is being continued.

My cousin Franz's career has taken a strange turn. He has been accepted as a lay brother in a nearby monastery. The first time I saw him in his monk's habit I got a shock: that tall figure with the broken nose and swollen lips, those brooding eyes—he reminded me more of a convict than of a monk. It almost seemed as if he had divined my thoughts. "Our life is our punishment," he said in a low voice. I followed him into the visitors' room. Our conversation was stiff and halting, and he was obviously relieved when the bell summoned him for prayers in the chapel. I stood there pensively as he left: he was hurrying, and his haste seemed to be genuine.

QUESTIONS FOR DISCUSSION AND WRITING

1. What stages in the plot mark the disintegration of "the entire clan"? Why is the narrator reluctant to conclude that the plot reveals the family's "collapse"?
2. How do the members of the family define themselves by their relationship to Aunt Milla? How does the family define itself by its willingness to be replaced by actors and wax figures?
3. What happened to most families in German society during the years 1939–1945? Why does the narrator feel that a discussion of these years might make him "unpopular"?
4. To what extent is the narrator a participant in the story he tells? How does his relationship to the family affect his interpretation of its behavior?
5. How does the family's unwillingness to face change lead to Franz's assertion that "our life is our punishment"?

10

ARNA BONTEMPS

A Summer Tragedy

ARNA BONTEMPS (1902–1973) was born in Alexandria, Louisiana, but grew up in California where he graduated from Pacific Union College. In the early 1920s, after completing graduate work at the University of Chicago, Bontemps moved to New York City and became associated with the talented black writers of the Harlem Renaissance. He explored his black American heritage in poems, stories, novels, plays, essays, and children's literature. He also preserved much of that heritage in anthologies of folklore, slave narratives, short stories, and poetry. In addition to writing and editing, Bontemps held several teaching jobs before becoming librarian at Fisk University, a position he held for over twenty years. His books include *God Sends Sunday* (1931), *Black Thunder* (1936), *Personals* (1963), and *The Old South* (1973). "A Summer Tragedy," reprinted from *The Old South,* describes an elderly couple's preparations to carry out a solemn decision.

Old Jeff Patton, the black share farmer, fumbled with his bow tie. His fingers trembled and the high, stiff collar pinched his throat. A fellow loses his hand for such vanities after thirty or forty years of simple life. Once a year, or maybe twice if there's a wedding among his kinfolks, he may spruce up, but generally fancy clothes do nothing but adorn the wall of the big room and feed the moths. That had been Jeff Patton's experience. He had not worn his stiff-bosomed shirt more than a dozen times in all his married life. His swallow-tailed coat lay on the bed beside him, freshly brushed and pressed, but it was as full of holes as the overalls in which he worked on weekdays. The moths had used it badly. Jeff twisted his mouth into a hideous toothless grimace as he contended with the obstinate bow. He stamped his good foot and decided to give up the struggle.

"Jennie," he called.

"What's that, Jeff?" His wife's shrunken voice came out of the adjoining room like an echo. It was hardly bigger than a whisper.

"I reckon you'll have to he'p me wid this heah bow tie, baby," he said meekly. "Dog if I can hitch it up."

Her answer was not strong enough to reach him, but presently the old woman came to the door, feeling her way with a stick. She had a wasted, dead-leaf appearance. Her body, as scrawny and gnarled as a string bean, seemed less than nothing in the ocean of frayed and faded petticoats that surrounded her. These hung an inch or two above the tops of her heavy unlaced shoes and showed little grotesque piles where the stockings had fallen down from her negligible legs.

"You oughta could do a heap mo' wid a thing like that'n me—beingst as you got yo' good sight."

"Looks like I oughta could," he admitted. "But my fingers is gone democrat on me. I get all mixed up in the looking glass an' can't tell wicha way to twist the devilish thing."

Jennie sat on the side of the bed, and old Jeff Patton got down on one knee while she tied the bow knot. It was a slow and painful ordeal for each of them in this position. Jeff's bones cracked, his knee ached, and it was only after a half dozen attempts that Jennie worked a semblance of a bow into the tie.

"I got to dress maself now," the old woman whispered. "These is ma old shoes an' stockings, and I ain't so much as unwrapped ma dress."

"Well, don't worry 'bout me no mo', baby," Jeff said. "That 'bout finishes me. All I gotta do now is slip on that old coat 'n ves' an' I'll be fixed to leave."

Jennie disappeared again through the dim passage into the shed room. Being blind was no handicap to her in that black hole. Jeff heard the cane placed against the wall beside the door and knew that his wife was on easy ground. He put on his coat, took a battered top hat from the bed post, and hobbled to the front door. He was ready to travel. As soon as Jennie could get on her Sunday shoes and her old black silk dress, they would start.

Outside the tiny log house, the day was warm and mellow with sunshine. A host of wasps were humming with busy excitement in the trunk of a dead sycamore. Gray squirrels were searching through the grass for hickory nuts, and blue jays were in the trees, hopping from branch to branch. Pine woods stretched away to the left like a black sea. Among them were scattered scores of log houses like Jeff's, houses of black share farmers.

Cows and pigs wandered freely among the trees. There was no danger of loss. Each farmer knew his own stock and knew his neighbor's as well as he knew his neighbor's children.

Down the slope to the right were the cultivated acres on which the colored folks worked. They extended to the river, more than two miles away, and they were today green with the unmade cotton crop. A tiny thread of a road, which passed directly in front of Jeff's place, ran through these green fields like a pencil mark.

Jeff, standing outside the door, with his absurd hat in his left hand, surveyed the wide scene tenderly. He had been forty-five years on these acres. He loved them with the unexplained affection that others have for the countries to which they belong.

The sun was hot on his head, his collar still pinched his throat, and the Sunday clothes were intolerably hot. Jeff transferred the hat to his right hand and began fanning with it. Suddenly the whisper that was Jennie's voice came out of the shed room.

"You can bring the car round front whilst you's waitin'," it said feebly. There was a tired pause; then it added, "I'll soon be fixed to go."

"A'right, baby," Jeff answered. "I'll get it in a minute."

But he didn't move. A thought struck him that made his mouth fall open. The mention of the car brought to his mind with new intensity, the trip he and Jennie were about to take. Fear came into his eyes; excitement took his breath. Lord, Jesus!

"Jeff. . . . O Jeff," the old woman's whisper called.

He awakened with a jolt. "Hunh, baby?"

"What you doin'?"

"Nuthin. Jes studyin'. I jes been turnin' things round 'n round in ma mind."

"You could be gettin' the car," she said.

"Oh yes, right away, baby."

He started round to the shed, limping heavily on his bad leg. There were three frizzly chickens in the yard. All his other chickens had been killed or stolen recently. But the frizzly chickens had been saved somehow. That was fortunate indeed, for these curious creatures had a way of devouring "poison" from the yard and in that way protecting against conjure and black luck and spells. But even the frizzly chickens seemed now to be in a stupor. Jeff thought they had some ailment; he expected all three of them to die shortly.

The shed in which the old T-model Ford stood was only a grass roof held up by four corner poles. It had been built by tremulous hands at a time when the little rattletrap car had been regarded as a peculiar treasure. And, miraculously, despite wind and downpour, it still stood.

Jeff adjusted the crank and put his weight upon it. The engine came to life with a sputter and bang that rattled the old car from radiator to tail light. Jeff hopped into the seat and put his foot on the accelerator. The sputtering and banging increased. The rattling became more violent. That was good. It was good banging, good sputtering and rattling, and it meant that the aged car was still in running condition. She could be depended on for this trip.

Again Jeff's thought halted as if paralyzed. The suggestion of the trip fell into the machinery of his mind like a wrench. He felt dazed and weak. He swung the car out into the yard, made a half turn, and drove around to the front door. When he took his hands off the wheel, he noticed that he was trembling violently. He cut off the motor and climbed to the ground to wait for Jennie.

A few minutes later she was at the window, her voice rattling against the pane like a broken shutter.

"I'm ready, Jeff."

He did not answer, but limped into the house and took her by the arm. He led her slowly through the big room, down the step, and across the yard.

"You reckon I'd oughta lock the do'?" he asked softly.

They stopped and Jennie weighed the question. Finally she shook her head.

"Ne' mind the do'," she said. "I don't see no cause to lock up things."

"You right," Jeff agreed. "No cause to lock up."

Jeff opened the door and helped his wife into the car. A quick shudder passed over him. Jesus! Again he trembled.

"How come you shaking so?" Jennie whispered.

"I don't know," he said.

"You mus' be scairt, Jeff."

"No, baby, I ain't scairt."

He slammed the door after her and went around to crank up again. The motor started easily. Jeff wished that it had not been so responsive. He would have liked a few more minutes in which to turn things around in his head. As it was, with Jennie chiding him about being afraid, he had to keep going. He swung the car into the little pencil-mark road and started off toward the river, driving very slowly, very cautiously.

Chugging across the green countryside, the small battered Ford seemed tiny indeed. Jeff felt a familiar excitement, a thrill, as they came down the first slope to the immense levels on which the cotton was growing. He could not help reflecting that the crops were good. He knew what that meant, too; he had made forty-five of them with his own hands. It was true that he had worn out nearly a dozen mules, but that was the fault of old man Stevenson, the owner of the land. Major Stevenson had the old notion that one mule was all a share farmer needed to work a thirty-acre plot. It was an expensive notion, the way it killed mules from overwork, but the old man held to it. Jeff thought it killed a good many share farmers as well as mules, but he had no sympathy for them. He had always been strong, and he had been taught to have no patience with weakness in men. Women or children might be tolerated if they were puny, but a weak man was a curse. Of course, his own children—

Jeff's thought halted there. He and Jennie never mentioned their dead children any more. And naturally, he did not wish to dwell upon them in his mind. Before he knew it, some remark would slip out of his mouth and that would make Jennie feel blue. Perhaps she would cry. A woman like Jennie could not easily throw off the grief that comes from losing five grown children within two years. Even Jeff was still staggered by the blow. His memory had not been much good recently. He frequently talked to himself. And, although he had kept it a secret, he knew that his courage had left him. He was terrified by the least unfamiliar sound at night. He was reluctant to venture far from home in the daytime. And that habit of trembling when he felt fearful was now far beyond his control. Sometimes he became afraid and trembled without knowing what had frightened him. The feeling would just come over him like a chill.

The car rattled slowly over the dusty road. Jennie sat erect and silent with a little absurd hat pinned to her hair. Her useless eyes seemed very large, very white in their deep sockets. Suddenly Jeff heard her voice, and he inclined his head to catch the words.

"Is we passed Delia Moore's house yet?" she asked.

"Not yet," he said.

"You must be drivin' mighty slow, Jeff."

"We just as well take our time, baby."

There was a pause. A little puff of steam was coming out of the radiator of the car. Heat wavered above the hood. Delia Moore's house was nearly half a mile away. After a moment Jennie spoke again.

"You ain't really scairt, is you, Jeff?"

"Nah, baby, I ain't scairt."

"You know how we agreed—we gotta keep on goin'."

Jewels of perspiration appeared on Jeff's forehead. His eyes rounded, blinked, became fixed on the road.

"I don't know," he said with a shiver, "I reckon it's the only thing to do."

"Hm."

A flock of guinea fowls, pecking in the road, were scattered by the passing car. Some of them took to their wings; others hid under bushes. A blue jay, swaying on a leafy twig, was annoying a roadside squirrel. Jeff held an even speed till he came near Delia's place. Then he slowed down noticeably.

Delia's house was really no house at all, but an abandoned stone building converted into a dwelling. It sat near a crossroads, beneath a single black cedar tree. There Delia, a cattish old creature of Jennie's age, lived alone. She had been there more years than anybody could remember, and long ago had won the disfavor of such women as Jennie. For in her young days Delia had been gayer, yellower, and saucier than seemed proper in those parts. Her ways with menfolks had been dark and suspicious. And the fact that she had had as many husbands as children did not help her reputation.

"Yonder's old Delia," Jeff said as they passed.

"What she doin'?"

"Jes sittin' in the do'," he said.

"She see us?"

"Hm," Jeff said. "Musta did."

That relieved Jennie. It strengthened her to know that her old enemy had seen her pass in her best clothes. That would give the old she-devil something to chew her gums and fret about, Jennie thought. Wouldn't she have a fit if she didn't find out? Old evil Delia! This would be just the thing for her. It would pay her back for being so evil. It would also pay her, Jennie thought, for the way she used to grin at Jeff—long ago, when her teeth were good.

The road became smooth and red, and Jeff could tell by the smell of the air that they were nearing the river. He could see the rise where the road turned and ran along parallel to the stream. The car chugged on monotonously. After a long silent spell, Jennie leaned against Jeff and spoke.

"How many bale o'cotton you think we got standin'?" she said.

Jeff wrinkled his forehead as he calculated.

"'Bout twenty-five, I reckon."

"How many you make las' year?"

"Twenty-eight," he said. "How come you ask that?"

"I's jes thinkin'," Jennie said quietly.

"It don't make a speck o'difference though," Jeff reflected. "If we get much or if we get little, we still gonna be in debt to old man Stevenson when he gets through counting up agin us. It's took us a long time to learn that."

Jennie was not listening to these words. She had fallen into a trancelike meditation. Her lips twitched. She chewed her gums and rubbed her gnarled hands nervously. Suddenly, she leaned forward, buried her face in the nervous hands, and burst into tears. She cried aloud in a dry, cracked voice that suggested the rattle of fodder on dead stalks. She cried aloud like a child, for she had never learned to suppress a genuine sob. Her slight old frame shook heavily and seemed hardly able to sustain such violent grief.

"What's the matter, baby?" Jeff asked awkwardly. "Why you cryin' like all that?"

"I's jes thinkin'," she said.

"So you the one what's scairt now, hunh?"

"I ain't scairt, Jeff. I's jes thinkin' 'bout leavin' eve'thing like this—eve'thing we been used to. It's right sad-like."

Jeff did not answer, and presently Jennie buried her face again and cried.

The sun was almost overhead. It beat down furiously on the dusty wagon-path road, on the parched roadside grass and the tiny battered car. Jeff's hands, gripping the wheel, became wet with perspiration; his forehead sparkled. Jeff's lips parted. His mouth shaped a hideous grimace. His face suggested the face of a man being burned. But the torture passed and his expression softened again.

"You mustn't cry, baby," he said to his wife. "We gotta be strong. We can't break down."

Jennie waited a few seconds, then said, "You reckon we oughta do it, Jeff? You reckon we oughta go 'head an' do it, really?"

Jeff's voice choked; his eyes blurred. He was terrified to hear Jennie say the thing that had been in his mind all morning. She had egged him on when he had wanted more than anything in the world to wait, to reconsider, to think things over a little longer. Now she was getting cold feet. Actually, there was no need of thinking the question through again. It would only end in making the same painful decision once more. Jeff knew that. There was no need of fooling around longer.

"We jes as well to do like we planned," he said. "They ain't nothin' else for us now—it's the bes' thing."

Jeff thought of the handicaps, the near impossibility of making another crop with his leg bothering him more and more each week. Then there was always the chance that he would have another stroke, like the one that had made him lame. Another one might kill him. The least it could do would be to leave him helpless. Jeff gasped—Lord Jesus! He could not bear to think of being helpless, like a baby, on Jennie's hands. Frail, blind Jennie.

The little pounding motor of the car worked harder and harder. The puff of steam from the cracked radiator became larger. Jeff realized that they were climbing a little rise. A moment later the road turned abruptly, and he looked down upon the face of the river.

"Jeff."

"Hunh?"

"Is that the water I hear?"

"Hm. Tha's it."

"Well, which way you goin' now?"

"Down this-a way," he said. "The road runs 'long 'side o' the water a lil piece."

She waited a while calmly. Then she said, "Drive faster."

"A'right, baby," Jeff said.

The water roared in the bed of the river. It was fifty or sixty feet below the level of the road. Between the road and the water there was a long smooth slope, sharply inclined. The slope was dry, the clay hardened by prolonged summer heat. The water below, roaring in a narrow channel, was noisy and wild.

"Jeff."

"Hunh?"

"How far you goin'?"

"Jes a lil piece down the road."

"You ain't scairt, is you, Jeff?"

"Nah, baby," he said trembling. "I ain't scairt."

"Remember how we planned it, Jeff. We gotta do it like we said. Brave-like."

"Hm."

Jeff's brain darkened. Things suddenly seemed unreal, like figures in a dream. Thoughts swam in his mind foolishly, hysterically, like little blind fish in a pool within a dense cave. They rushed again. Jeff soon became dizzy. He shuddered violently and turned to his wife.

"Jennie, I can't do it. I can't." His voice broke pitifully.

She did not appear to be listening. All the grief had gone from her face. She sat erect, her unseeing eyes wide open, strained and frightful. Her glossy black skin had become dull. She seemed as thin, as sharp and bony, as a starved bird. Now, having suffered and endured the sadness of tearing herself away from beloved things, she showed no anguish. She was absorbed with her own thoughts, and she didn't even hear Jeff's voice shouting in her ear.

Jeff said nothing more. For an instant there was light in his cavernous brain. The great chamber was, for less than a second, peopled by characters he knew and loved. They were simple, healthy creatures, and they behaved in a manner that he could understand. They had quality. But since he had already taken leave of them long ago, the remembrance did not break his heart again. Young Jeff Patton was among them, the Jeff Patton of fifty years ago who went down to New Orleans with a crowd of country boys to the Mardi Gras doings. The gay young crowd, boys with candy-striped shirts and rouged brown girls in noisy silks, was like a picture in his head. Yet it did not make him sad. On that very trip Slim Burns had killed Joe Beasley—the crowd had been broken up. Since then Jeff Patton's world had been the Greenbriar Plantation. If there had been other Mardi Gras carnivals, he had not heard of them. Since then there had been no time; the years had fallen on him like waves. Now he was old, worn out. Another paralytic stroke (like the one he had already suffered) would put him on his back for keeps. In that condition, with a frail blind woman to look after him, he would be worse off than if he were dead.

Suddenly Jeff's hands became steady. He actually felt brave. He slowed down the motor of the car and carefully pulled off the road. Below, the water of the stream boomed, a soft thunder in the deep channel. Jeff ran the car onto the clay slope, pointed it directly toward the stream, and put his foot heavily on the accelerator. The little car leaped furiously down the steep incline toward the water. The movement was nearly as swift and direct as a fall. The two old black folks, sitting quietly side by side, showed no excitement. In another instant the car hit the water and dropped immediately out of sight.

A little later it lodged in the mud of a shallow place. One wheel of the crushed and upturned little Ford became visible above the rushing water.

QUESTIONS FOR DISCUSSION AND WRITING

1. What is the first indication that Jeff and Jennie are planning something tragic on this summer day? How many times do they have second thoughts about their intentions?
2. How does the opening scene help characterize Jeff and Jennie? What specific details of action and dialogue reveal the nature of their relationship to one another?
3. Why is the couple no longer attached to the land where they have worked and lived for so many years?
4. Why is it appropriate that Jeff's point of view dominates the story? Where is there a shift in the point of view? Why is it included?
5. In how many senses does this story record a summer tragedy? What other summer tragedies have led the Pattons to enact this one? Do you think their decision is justifiable? Explain your answer.

11

JORGE LUIS BORGES

The Garden of Forking Paths

TRANSLATED BY DONALD A. YATES

For Victoria Ocampo

JORGE LUIS BORGES (1899–1986) was born in Buenos Aires, Argentina, and educated at the College de Geneve, Switzerland. After World War I, he traveled throughout Europe and associated with a Spanish literary movement called *Ultraisme.* Borges returned to Argentina in 1921 to lead various avant-garde literary movements and to publish his poems and essays. In the 1930s he began composing fiction that revealed the influence of Kafka and Joyce. In addition to writing, Borges worked as an editor, teacher,

and librarian. In 1946 dictator Juan Perón demoted him for political reasons to the rank of chicken inspector. With the fall of Perón's government in 1955, Borges was reappointed director of the National Library and professor of English and American Literature at the University of Buenos Aires. During the next thirty years Borges continued to teach and write in Europe, America, and Argentina. His writings include *Ficciones* (1944), *Labyrinths* (1962), *The Aleph and Other Stories* (1970), *Doctor Brodie's Report* (1972), *The Book of Sand* (1977), and *Six Problems for Don Isidro Parodi* (1981). In "The Garden of Forking Paths," reprinted from *Labyrinths,* Borges meditates on the infinitely complex relationship between writing history and fiction.

On page 22 of Liddell Hart's *History of World War I* you will read that an attack against the Serre-Montauban line by thirteen British divisions (supported by 1,400 artillery pieces), planned for the 24th of July, 1916, had to be postponed until the morning of the 29th. The torrential rains, Captain Liddell Hart comments, caused this delay, an insignificant one, to be sure.

The following statement, dictated, reread and signed by Dr. Yu Tsun, former professor of English at the *Hochschule* at Tsingtao, throws an unsuspected light over the whole affair. The first two pages of the document are missing.

". . . and I hung up the receiver. Immediately afterwards, I recognized the voice that had answered in German. It was that of Captain Richard Madden. Madden's presence in Viktor Runeberg's apartment meant the end of our anxieties and—but this seemed, *or should have seemed,* very secondary to me—also the end of our lives. It meant that Runeberg had been arrested or murdered.[1] Before the sun set on that day, I would encounter the same fate. Madden was implacable. Or rather, he was obliged to be so. An Irishman at the service of England, a man accused of laxity and perhaps of treason, how could he fail to seize and be thankful for such a miraculous opportunity: the discovery, capture, maybe even the death of two agents of the German Reich? I went up to my room; absurdly I locked the door and threw myself on my back on the narrow iron cot. Through the window I saw the familiar roofs and the cloud-shaded six o'clock sun. It seemed incredible to me that that day without premonitions or symbols should be the one of my inexorable death. In spite of my dead father, in spite of having been a child in a symmetrical garden of Hai Feng, was I—now—going to die? Then I reflected that everything happens to a man precisely, precisely *now.* Centuries of centuries and only in the present do things happen; countless men in the air, on the face of the earth and the sea, and all that really is happening is happening to me . . . The almost intolerable recollection of Madden's horse-like face banished these wanderings. In the midst of my hatred and terror (it means nothing to me now to speak of terror, now that I have mocked Richard Madden, now that my throat yearns for the noose) it occurred to me that that tumultuous and doubtless happy warrior did not suspect that I possess the Secret. The name of the exact location

[1]An hypothesis both hateful and odd. The Prussian spy Hans Rabener, alias Viktor Runeberg, attacked with drawn automatic the bearer of the warrant for his arrest, Captain Richard Madden. The latter, in self-defense, inflicted the wound which brought about Runeberg's death. (Borges's note.)

of the new British artillery park on the River Ancre. A bird streaked across the gray sky and blindly I translated it into an airplane and that airplane into many (against the French sky) annihilating the artillery station with vertical bombs. If only my mouth, before a bullet shattered it, could cry out that secret name so it could be heard in Germany . . . My human voice was very weak. How might I make it carry to the ear of the Chief? To the ear of that sick and hateful man who knew nothing of Runeberg and me save that we were in Staffordshire and who was waiting in vain for our report in his arid office in Berlin, endlessly examining newspapers . . . I said out loud: *I must flee.* I sat up noiselessly, in a useless perfection of silence, as if Madden were already lying in wait for me. Something—perhaps the mere vain ostentation of proving my resources were nil—made me look through my pockets. I found what I knew I would find. The American watch, the nickel chain and the square coin, the key ring with the incriminating useless keys to Runeberg's apartment, the notebook, a letter which I resolved to destroy immediately (and which I did not destroy), a crown, two shillings and a few pence, the red and blue pencil, the handkerchief, the revolver with one bullet. Absurdly, I took it in my hand and weighed it in order to inspire courage within myself. Vaguely I thought that a pistol report can be heard at a great distance. In ten minutes my plan was perfected. The telephone book listed the name of the only person capable of transmitting the message; he lived in a suburb of Fenton, less than a half hour's train ride away.

I am a cowardly man. I say it now, now that I have carried to its end a plan whose perilous nature no one can deny. I know its execution was terrible. I didn't do it for Germany, no. I care nothing for a barbarous country which imposed upon me the abjection of being a spy. Besides, I know of a man from England—a modest man—who for me is no less great than Goethe. I talked with him for scarcely an hour, but during that hour he was Goethe . . . I did it because I sensed that the Chief somehow feared people of my race—for the innumerable ancestors who merge within me. I wanted to prove to him that a yellow man could save his armies. Besides, I had to flee from Captain Madden. His hands and his voice could call at my door at any moment. I dressed silently, bade farewell to myself in the mirror, went downstairs, scrutinized the peaceful street and went out. The station was not far from my home, but I judged it wise to take a cab. I argued that in this way I ran less risk of being recognized; the fact is that in the deserted street I felt myself visible and vulnerable, infinitely so. I remember that I told the cab driver to stop a short distance before the main entrance. I got out with voluntary, almost painful slowness; I was going to the village of Ashgrove but I bought a ticket for a more distant station. The train left within a very few minutes, at eight-fifty. I hurried; the next one would leave at nine-thirty. There was hardly a soul on the platform. I went through the coaches; I remember a few farmers, a woman dressed in mourning, a young boy who was reading with fervor the *Annals* of Tacitus, a wounded and happy soldier. The coaches jerked forward at last. A man whom I recognized ran in vain to the end of the platform. It was Captain Richard Madden. Shattered, trembling, I shrank into the far corner of the seat, away from the dreaded window.

From this broken state I passed into an almost abject felicity. I told myself that the duel had already begun and that I had won the first encounter by frustrating, even if for forty minutes, even if by a stroke of fate, the attack of my adversary. I argued that this slightest of victories foreshadowed a total victory. I argued (no less fallaciously) that my cowardly felicity proved that I was a man capable of carrying out the adventure successfully. From this weakness I took strength that did not abandon me. I foresee that man will resign himself each day to more atrocious undertakings; soon there will be no one but warriors and brigands; I give them this counsel: *The author of an atrocious undertaking ought to imagine that he has already accomplished it, ought to impose upon himself a future as irrevocable as the past.* Thus I proceeded as my eyes of a man already dead registered the elapsing of that day, which was perhaps the last, and the diffusion of the night. The train ran gently along, amid ash trees. It stopped, almost in the middle of the fields. No one announced the name of the station. "Ashgrove?" I asked a few lads on the platform. "Ashgrove," they replied. I got off.

A lamp enlightened the platform but the faces of the boys were in shadow. One questioned me, "Are you going to Dr. Stephen Albert's house?" Without waiting for my answer, another said, "The house is a long way from here, but you won't get lost if you take this road to the left and at every crossroads turn again to your left." I tossed them a coin (my last), descended a few stone steps and started down the solitary road. It went downhill, slowly. It was of elemental earth; overhead the branches were tangled; the low, full moon seemed to accompany me.

For an instant, I thought that Richard Madden in some way had penetrated my desperate plan. Very quickly, I understood that that was impossible. The instructions to turn always to the left reminded me that such was the common procedure for discovering the central point of certain labyrinths. I have some understanding of labyrinths: not for nothing am I the great grandson of that Ts'ui Pên who was governor of Yunnan and who renounced wordly power in order to write a novel that might be even more populous than the *Hung Lu Meng* and to construct a labyrinth in which all men would become lost. Thirteen years he dedicated to these heterogeneous tasks, but the hand of a stranger murdered him—and his novel was incoherent and no one found the labyrinth. Beneath English trees I meditated on that lost maze: I imagined it inviolate and perfect at the secret crest of a mountain; I imagined it erased by rice fields or beneath the water; I imagined it infinite, no longer composed of octagonal kiosks and returning paths, but of rivers and provinces and kingdoms . . . I thought of a labyrinth of labyrinths, of one sinuous spreading labyrinth that would encompass the past and the future and in some way involve the stars. Absorbed in these illusory images, I forgot my destiny of one pursued. I felt myself to be, for an unknown period of time, an abstract perceiver of the world. The vague, living countryside, the moon, the remains of the day worked on me, as well as the slope of the road which eliminated any possibility of weariness. The afternoon was intimate, infinite. The road descended and forked among the now confused meadows. A high-pitched, almost syllabic music approached and receded in the shifting of the wind, dimmed by leaves and distance. I thought that a man can be an enemy of other men, of the moments of other men, but not of a country: not of fireflies, words, gardens, streams of water, sunsets. Thus I arrived before a tall, rusty gate. Between the iron bars I made out a poplar grove and a pavilion. I understood suddenly two things, the first trivial, the second almost unbelievable: the music came from the pavilion, and the music was Chinese. For precisely that reason I had openly accepted it without paying it any heed. I do not remember whether there was a bell or whether I knocked with my hand. The sparkling of the music continued.

From the rear of the house within a lantern approached: a lantern that the trees sometimes striped and sometimes eclipsed, a paper lantern that had the form of a drum and the color of the moon. A tall man bore it. I didn't see his face for the light blinded me. He opened the door and said slowly, in my own language: "I see that the pious Hsi P'êng persists in correcting my solitude. You no doubt wish to see the garden?"

I recognized the name of one of our consuls and I replied, disconcerted, "The garden?"

"The garden of forking paths."

Something stirred in my memory and I uttered with incomprehensible certainty, "The garden of my ancestor Ts'ui Pên."

"Your ancestor? Your illustrious ancestor? Come in."

The damp path zigzagged like those of my childhood. We came to a library of Eastern and Western books. I recognized bound in yellow silk several volumes of the Lost Encyclopedia, edited by the Third Emperor of the Luminous Dynasty but never printed. The record on the phonograph revolved next to a bronze phoenix. I also recall a *famille rose* vase and another, many centuries older, of that shade of blue which our craftsmen copied from the potters of Persia . . .

Stephen Albert observed me with a smile. He was, as I have said, very tall, sharp-featured, with gray eyes and a gray beard. He told me that he had been a missionary in Tientsin "before aspiring to become a Sinologist."

We sat down—I on a long, low divan, he with his back to the window and a tall circular clock. I calculated that my pursuer, Richard Madden, could not arrive for at least an hour. My irrevocable determination could wait.

"An astounding fate, that of Ts'ui Pên," Stephen Albert said. "Governor of his native province, learned in astronomy, in astrology and in the tireless interpretation of the canonical books, chess player, famous poet and calligrapher—he abandoned all this in order to compose a book and a maze. He renounced the pleasures of both tyranny and justice, of his populous couch, of his banquets and even of erudition—all to close himself up for thirteen years in the Pavilion of the Limpid Solitude. When he died, his heirs found nothing save chaotic manuscripts. His family, as you may be aware, wished to condemn them to the fire; but his executor—a Taoist or Buddhist monk—insisted on their publication."

"We descendants of Ts'ui Pên," I replied, "continue to curse that monk. Their publication was senseless. The book is an indeterminate heap of contradictory drafts. I examined it once: in the third chapter the hero dies, in the fourth he is alive. As for the other undertaking of Ts'ui Pên, his labyrinth . . ."

"Here is Ts'ui Pên's labyrinth," he said, indicating a tall lacquered desk.

"An ivory labyrinth!" I exclaimed. "A minimum labyrinth."

"A labyrinth of symbols," he corrected. "An invisible labyrinth of time. To me, a barbarous Englishman, has been entrusted the revelation of this diaphanous mystery. After more than a hundred years, the details are irretrievable; but it is not hard to conjecture what happened. Ts'ui Pên must have said once: *I am withdrawing to write a book.* And another time: *I am withdrawing to construct a labyrinth.* Every one imagined two works; to no one did it occur that the book and the maze were one and the same thing. The Pavilion of the Limpid Solitude stood in the center of a garden that was perhaps intricate;

that circumstance could have suggested to the heirs a physical labyrinth. Ts'ui Pên died; no one in the vast territories that were his came upon the labyrinth; the confusion of the novel suggested to me that *it* was the maze. Two circumstances gave me the correct solution of the problem. One: the curious legend that Ts'ui Pên had planned to create a labyrinth which would be strictly infinite. The other: a fragment of a letter I discovered."

Albert rose. He turned his back on me for a moment; he opened a drawer of the black and gold desk. He faced me and in his hands he held a sheet of paper that had once been crimson, but was now pink and tenuous and cross-sectioned. The fame of Ts'ui Pên as a calligrapher had been justly won. I read, uncomprehendingly and with fervor, these words written with a minute brush by a man of my blood: *I leave to the various futures (not to all) my garden of forking paths.* Wordlessly, I returned the sheet. Albert continued:

"Before unearthing this letter, I had questioned myself about the ways in which a book can be infinite. I could think of nothing other than a cyclic volume, a circular one. A book whose last page was identical with the first, a book which had the possibility of continuing indefinitely. I remembered too that night which is at the middle of the Thousand and One Nights when Scheherazade (through a magical oversight of the copyist) begins to relate word for word the story of the Thousand and One Nights, establishing the risk of coming once again to the night when she must repeat it, and thus on to infinity. I imagined as well a Platonic, hereditary work, transmitted from father to son, in which each new individual adds a chapter or corrects with pious care the pages of his elders. These conjectures diverted me; but none seemed to correspond, not even remotely, to the contradictory chapters of Ts'ui Pên. In the midst of this perplexity, I received from Oxford the manuscript you have examined. I lingered, naturally, on the sentence: *I leave to the various futures (not to all) my garden of forking paths.* Almost instantly, I understood: 'the garden of forking paths' was the chaotic novel; the phrase 'the various futures (not to all)' suggested to me the forking in time, not in space. A broad rereading of the work confirmed the theory. In all fictional works, each time a man is confronted with several alternatives, he chooses one and eliminates the others; in the fiction of Ts'ui Pên, he chooses—simultaneously—all of them. *He creates,* in this way, diverse futures, diverse times which themselves also proliferate and fork. Here, then, is the explanation of the novel's contradictions. Fang, let us say, has a secret; a stranger calls at his door; Fang resolves to kill him. Naturally, there are several possible outcomes: Fang can kill the intruder, the intruder can kill Fang, they both can escape, they both can die, and so forth. In the work of Ts'ui Pên, all possible outcomes occur; each one is the point of departure for other forkings. Sometimes, the paths of this labyrinth converge: for example, you arrive at this house, but in one of the possible pasts you are my enemy, in another, my friend. If you will resign yourself to my incurable pronunciation, we shall read a few pages."

His face, within the vivid circle of the lamplight, was unquestionably that of an old man, but with something unalterable about it, even immortal. He read with slow precision two versions of the same epic chapter. In the first, an army marches to a battle across a lonely mountain; the horror of the rocks and shadows makes the men undervalue their lives and they gain an easy victory. In the second, the same army traverses a palace where a great festival is taking place; the resplendent battle seems to them a continuation of the celebration and they win the victory. I listened with proper veneration to these ancient narratives, perhaps less admirable in themselves than the fact that they had been created by my blood and were being restored to me by a man of a remote empire, in the course of a desperate adventure, on a Western isle. I remember the last words, repeated in each version like a secret commandment: *Thus fought the heroes, tranquil their admirable hearts, violent their swords, resigned to kill and to die.*

From that moment on, I felt about me and within my dark body an invisible, intangible swarming. Not the swarming of the divergent, parallel and finally coalescent armies, but a more inaccessible, more intimate agitation that they in some manner prefigured. Stephen Albert continued:

"I don't believe that your illustrious ancestor played idly with these variations. I don't consider it credible that he would sacrifice thirteen years to the infinite execution of a rhetorical experiment. In your country, the novel is a subsidiary form of literature; in Ts'ui Pên's time it was a despicable form. Ts'ui Pên was a brilliant novelist, but he was also a man of letters who doubtless did not consider himself a mere novelist. The testimony of his contemporaries proclaims—and his life fully confirms—his metaphysical and mystical interests. Philosophic controversy usurps a good part of the novel. I know that of all problems, none disturbed him so greatly nor worked upon him so much as the abysmal problem of time. Now then, the latter is the only problem that does not figure in the pages of the *Garden*. He does not even use the word that signifies *time*. How do you explain this voluntary omission?"

I proposed several solutions—all unsatisfactory. We discussed them. Finally, Stephen Albert said to me:

"In a riddle whose answer is chess, what is the only prohibited word?"

I thought a moment and replied, "The word *chess*."

"Precisely," said Albert. "*The Garden of Forking Paths* is an enormous riddle, or parable, whose theme is time; this recondite cause prohibits its mention. To omit a word always, to resort to inept metaphors and obvious periphrases, is perhaps the most emphatic way of stressing it. That is the tortuous method preferred, in each of the meanderings of his indefatigable novel, by the oblique Ts'ui Pên. I have compared hundreds of manuscripts. I have corrected the errors that the negligence of the copyists has introduced. I have guessed the plan of this chaos, I have re-established—I believe I have re-established—the primordial organization, I have translated the entire work: it is clear to me that not once does he employ the word 'time.' The explanation is obvious: *The Garden of Forking Paths* is an incomplete, but not false, image of the universe as Ts'ui Pên conceived it. In contrast to Newton and Schopenhauer, your ancestor did not believe in a uniform, absolute time. He believed in an infinite series of times, in a growing, dizzying net of divergent, convergent and parallel times. This network of times which approached one another, forked, broke off, or were unaware of one another for centuries, embraces *all* possibilities of time. We do not exist in the majority of these times; in some you exist, and not I; in others I, and not you; in others, both of us. In the present one, which a favorable fate has granted me, you have arrived at my house; in another, while crossing the garden, you found me dead; in still another, I utter these same words, but I am a mistake, a ghost."

"In every one," I pronounced, not without a tremble to my voice, "I am grateful to you and revere you for your re-creation of the garden of Ts'ui Pên."

"Not in all," he murmured with a smile. "Time forks perpetually toward innumerable futures. In one of them I am your enemy."

Once again I felt the swarming sensation of which I have spoken. It seemed to me that the humid garden that surrounded the house was infinitely saturated with invisible persons. Those persons were Albert and I, secret, busy and multiform in other dimensions of time. I raised my eyes and the tenuous nightmare dissolved. In the yellow and black garden there was only one man; but this man was as strong as a statue . . . this man was approaching along the path and he was Captain Richard Madden.

"The future already exists," I replied, "but I am your friend. Could I see the letter again?"

Albert rose. Standing tall, he opened the drawer of the tall desk; for the moment his back was to me. I had readied the revolver. I fired with extreme caution. Albert fell uncomplainingly, immediately. I swear his death was instantaneous—a lightning stroke.

The rest is unreal, insignificant. Madden broke in, arrested me. I have been condemned to the gallows. I have won out abominably; I have communicated to Berlin the secret name of the city they must attack. They bombed it yesterday; I read it in the same papers that offered to England the mystery of the learned Sinologist Stephen Albert who was murdered by a stranger, one Yu Tsun. The Chief had deciphered this mystery. He knew my problem was to indicate (through the uproar of the war) the city called Albert, and that I had found no other means to do so than to kill a man of that name. He does not know (no one can know) my innumerable contrition and weariness.

QUESTIONS FOR DISCUSSION AND WRITING

1. Arrange the major events of the story in chronological order. Does this arrangement help explain the events narrated in the first two paragraphs? Explain your answer.

2. How do you explain the narrator's intense commitment to completing his mission in spite of the fact that he has no patriotic concern about the outcome of the war? How does the narrator characterize the man who means to prevent him from completing this mission?

3. In what ways do the house, garden, and study provide an appropriate setting for the discussion of the concept of forking paths?

4. How does Tsun's acknowledgment that "everything happens to a man precisely, precisely *now*" influence his point of view toward the events he narrates? What advice does he offer other people who attempt "atrocious undertakings"?

5. How is the concept of a labyrinth crucial to an understanding of the theme of the story? For example, how do the past accomplishments of Tsun's ancestor prefigure his present choices?

12

ELIZABETH BOWEN

The Demon Lover

ELIZABETH BOWEN (1899–1973) was born in Dublin, Ireland, and educated in England. During World War I she worked as a nurse in a military hospital in Dublin. Bowen returned to England and became a student at the London Council of Art. In 1923 she married Alan Cameron, a teacher in a school near Oxford. In the same year, Bowen published her first collection of short stories, *Encounters.* For the next twelve years she lived and wrote in Oxford, publishing *The Hotel* (1927), *The Last September* (1929), *Friends and Relations* (1931), and *The House in Paris* (1935). In 1935 the couple moved to London, where Bowen became acquainted with the Bloomsbury Group and in particular Virginia Woolf. During World War II Bowen worked for the Ministry of Information and contributed reviews and essays to *The New Statesman.* Her most acclaimed novel, *Death of the Heart* (1938), was followed by a series of short-story collections including *Look at All Those Roses* (1941), *The Demon Lover* (1945), and *Day in the Dark* (1965). "The Demon Lover," reprinted from *The Collected Stories of Elizabeth Bowen* (1974), recounts a woman's fateful encounter with a former lover.

Towards the end of her day in London Mrs. Drover went round to her shut-up house to look for several things she wanted to take away. Some belonged to herself, some to her family, who were by now used to their country life. It was late August; it had been a steamy, showery day: at the moment the trees down the pavement glittered in an escape of humid yellow afternoon sun. Against the next batch of clouds, already piling up ink dark, broken chimneys and parapets stood out. In her once familiar street, as in any unused channel, an unfamiliar queerness had silted up; a cat wove itself in and out of railings, but no human eye watched Mrs. Drover's return. Shifting some parcels under her arm, she slowly forced round her latchkey in an unwilling lock, then gave the door, which had warped, a push with her knee. Dead air came out to meet her as she went in.

The staircase window having been boarded up, no light came down into the hall. But one door, she could just see, stood ajar, so she went quickly through into the room and unshuttered the big window in there. Now the prosaic woman, looking about her, was more perplexed than she knew by everything that she saw, by traces of her long former habit of life—the yellow smoke-stain up the white marble mantelpiece, the ring left by a vase on the top of the escritoire; the bruise in the wallpaper where, on the door being thrown open widely, the china handle had always hit the wall. The piano, having gone away to be stored, had left what looked like claw-marks on its part of the parquet.

Though not much dust had seeped in, each object wore a film of another kind; and, the only ventilation being the chimney, the whole drawing-room smelled of the cold hearth. Mrs. Drover put down her parcels on the escritoire and left the room to proceed upstairs; the things she wanted were in a bedroom chest.

She had been anxious to see how the house was—the part-time caretaker she shared with some neighbours was away this week on his holiday, known to be not yet back. At the best of times he did not look in often, and she was never sure that she trusted him. There were some cracks in the structure, left by the last bombing, on which she was anxious to keep an eye. Not that one could do anything—

A shaft of refracted daylight now lay across the hall. She stopped dead and stared at the hall table—on this lay a letter addressed to her.

She thought first—then the caretaker *must* be back. All the same, who, seeing the house shuttered, would have dropped a letter in at the box? It was not a circular, it was not a bill. And the post office redirected, to the address in the country, everything for her that came through the post. The caretaker (even if he *were* back) did not know she was due in London today—her call here had been planned to be a surprise—so his negligence in the manner of this letter, leaving it to wait in the dusk and the dust, annoyed her. Annoyed, she picked up the letter, which bore no stamp. But it cannot be important, or they would know . . . She took the letter rapidly upstairs with her, without a stop to look at the writing till she reached what had been her bedroom, where she let in light. The room looked over the garden and other gardens: the sun had gone in; as the clouds sharpened and lowered, the trees and rank lawns seemed already to smoke with dark. Her reluctance to look again at the letter came from the fact that she felt intruded upon—and by someone contemptuous of her ways. However, in the tenseness preceding the fall of rain she read it: it was a few lines.

> Dear Kathleen: You will not have forgotten that today is our anniversary, and the day we said. The years have gone by at once slowly and fast. In view of the fact that nothing has changed, I shall rely upon you to keep your promise. I was sorry to see you leave London, but was satisfied that you would be back in time. You may expect me, therefore, at the hour arranged. Until then . . .
>
> K.

Mrs. Drover looked for the date: it was today's. She dropped the letter on to the bed-springs, then picked it up to see the writing again—her lips, beneath the remains of lipstick, beginning to go white. She felt so much the change in her own face that she went to the mirror, polished a clear patch in it and looked at once urgently and stealthily in. She was confronted by a woman of forty-four, with eyes starting out under a hat-brim that had been rather carelessly pulled down. She had not put on any more powder since she left the shop where she ate her solitary tea. The pearls her husband had given her on their marriage hung loose round her now rather thinner throat, slipping in the V of the pink wool jumper her sister knitted last autumn as they sat round the fire. Mrs. Drover's most normal expression was one of controlled worry, but of assent. Since the birth of the third of her little boys, attended by a quite serious illness, she had had an intermittent muscular flicker to the left of her mouth, but in spite of this she could always sustain a manner that was at once energetic and calm.

Turning from her own face as precipitately as she had gone to meet it, she went to the chest where the things were, unlocked it, threw up the lid and knelt to search. But as rain began to come crashing down she could not keep from looking over her shoulder at the stripped bed on which the letter lay. Behind the blanket of rain the clock of the church that still stood struck six—with rapidly heightening apprehension she counted each of the slow strokes. "The hour arranged . . . My God," she said, "*what* hour? How should I . . . ? After twenty-five years . . ."

The young girl talking to the soldier in the garden had not ever completely seen his face. It was dark; they were saying goodbye under a tree. Now and then—for it felt, from not seeing him at this intense moment, as though she had never seen him at all—she verified his presence for these few moments longer by putting out a hand, which he each time pressed, without very much kindness, and painfully, on to one of the breast buttons of his uniform. That cut of the button on the palm of her hand was, principally, what she was to carry away. This was so near the end of a leave from France that she could only wish him already gone. It was August 1916. Being not kissed, being drawn away from and looked at intimidated Kathleen till she imagined spectral glitters in the place of his eyes. Turning away and looking back up the lawn she saw, through branches of trees, the drawing-room window light: she caught a breath for the moment when she could go running back there into the safe arms of her mother and sister, and cry: "What shall I do, what shall I do? He has gone."

Hearing her catch her breath, her fiancé said, without feeling: "Cold?"

"You're going away such a long way."

"Not so far as you think."

"I don't understand?"

"You don't have to," he said. "You will. You know what we said."

"But that was—suppose you—I mean, suppose."

"I shall be with you," he said, "sooner or later. You won't forget that. You need do nothing but wait."

Only a little more than a minute later she was free to run up the silent lawn. Looking in through the window at her mother and sister, who did not for the moment perceive her, she already felt that unnatural promise drive down between her and the rest of all human kind. No other way of having given herself could have made her feel so apart, lost and foresworn. She could not have plighted a more sinister troth.

Kathleen behaved well when, some months later, her fiancé was reported missing, presumed killed. Her family not only supported her but were able to praise her courage without stint because they could not regret, as a husband for her, the man they knew almost nothing about. They hoped she would, in a year or two, console herself—and had it been only a question of consolation things might have gone much straighter ahead. But her trouble, behind just a little grief, was a complete dislocation from everything. She did not reject other lovers, for these failed to appear: for years she failed to attract men—and with the approach of her thirties she became natural enough to share her family's anxiousness on this score. She began to put herself out, to wonder; and at thirty-two she was very greatly relieved to find herself being courted by William Drover. She married him, and the two of them settled down in this quiet, arboreal part of Kensington: in this house the years piled up, her children were born and they all lived till they were driven out by the bombs of the next war. Her movements as Mrs. Drover were circumscribed, and she dismissed any idea that they were still watched.

As things were—dead or living the letter-writer sent her only a threat. Unable, for some minutes, to go on kneeling with her back exposed to the empty room, Mrs. Drover rose from the chest to sit on an upright chair whose back was firmly against the wall. The desuetude of her former bedroom, her married London home's whole air of being a cracked cup from which memory, with its reassuring power, had either evaporated or leaked away, made a crisis—and at just this crisis the letter-writer had, knowledgeably, struck. The hollowness of the house this evening cancelled years on years of voices, habits and steps. Through the shut windows she only heard rain fall on the roofs around. To rally herself, she said she was in a mood—and for two or three seconds shutting her eyes, told herself that she had imagined the letter. But she opened them—there it lay on the bed.

On the supernatural side of the letter's entrance she was not permitting her mind to dwell. Who, in London, knew she meant to call at the house today? Evidently, however, this had been known. The caretaker, *had* he come back, had had no cause to expect her: he would have taken the letter in his pocket, to forward it, at his own time, through the post. There was no other sign that the caretaker had been in—but, if not? Letters dropped in at doors of deserted houses do not fly or walk to tables in halls. They do not sit on the dust of empty tables with the air of certainty that they will be found. There is needed some human hand—but nobody but the caretaker had a key. Under circumstances she did not care to consider, a house can be entered without a key. It was possible that she was not alone now. She might be being waited for, downstairs. Waited for—until when? Until "the hour arranged". At least that was not six o'clock: six has struck.

She rose from the chair and went over and locked the door.

The thing was, to get out. To fly? No, not that: she had to catch her train. As a woman whose utter dependability was the keystone of her family life she was not willing to return to the country, to her husband, her little boys and her sister, without the objects she had come up to fetch. Resuming work at the chest she set about making up a number of parcels in a rapid, fumbling-decisive way. These, with her shopping parcels, would be too much to carry; these meant a taxi—at the thought of the taxi her heart went up and her normal breathing resumed. I will ring up the taxi now; the taxi cannot come too soon: I shall hear the taxi out there running its engine, till I walk calmly down to it through the hall. I'll ring up—But no: the telephone is cut off . . . She tugged at a knot she had tied wrong.

The idea of flight . . . He was never kind to me, not really. I don't remember him kind at all. Mother said he never considered me. He was set on me, that was what it was—not love. Not love, not meaning a person well. What did he do, to make me promise like that? I can't remember—But she found that she could.

She remembered with such dreadful acuteness that the twenty-five years since then dissolved like smoke and she instinctively looked for the weal left by the button on the palm of her hand. She remembered not only all that he said and did but the complete suspension of *her* existence during that August week. I was not myself—they all told me so at the time. She remembered—but with one white burning blank as where acid has dropped on a photograph: *under no conditions* could she remember his face.

So, wherever he may be waiting, I shall not know him. You have no time to run from a face you do not expect.

The thing was to get to the taxi before any clock struck what could be the hour. She would slip down the street and round the side of the square to where the square gave on the main road. She would return in the taxi, safe, to her own door, and bring the solid driver into the house with her to pick up the parcels from room to room. The idea of the taxi driver made her decisive, bold: she unlocked her door, went to the top of the staircase and listened down.

She heard nothing—but while she was hearing nothing the *passé* air of the staircase was disturbed by a draught that travelled up to her face. It emanated from the basement: down there a door or window was being opened by someone who chose this moment to leave the house.

The rain had stopped; the pavements steamily shone as Mrs. Drover let herself out by inches from her own front door into the empty street. The unoccupied houses opposite continued to meet her look with their damaged stare. Making towards the thoroughfare and the taxi, she tried not to keep looking behind. Indeed, the silence was so intense—one of those creeks of London silence exaggerated this summer by the damage of war—that no tread could have gained on hers unheard. Where her street debouched on the square where people went on living, she grew conscious of, and checked, her unnatural pace. Across the open end of the square two buses impassively passed each other: women, a perambulator, cyclists, a man wheeling a barrow signalized, once again, the ordinary flow of life. At the square's most populous corner should be—and was—the short taxi rank. This evening, only one taxi—but this, although it presented its blank rump, appeared already to be alertly waiting for her. Indeed, without looking round the driver started his engine as she panted up from behind and put her hand on the door. As she did so, the clock struck seven. The taxi faced the main road: to make the trip back to her house it would have to turn she had settled back on the seat and the taxi *had* turned before she, surprised by its knowing movement, recollected that she had not "said where". She leaned forward to scratch at the glass panel that divided the driver's head from her own.

The driver braked to what was almost a stop, turned round and slid the glass panel back: the jolt of this flung Mrs. Drover forward till her face was almost into the glass. Through the aperture driver and passenger, not six inches between them, remained for an eternity eye to eye. Mrs. Drover's mouth hung open for some seconds before she could issue her first scream. After that she continued to scream freely and to beat with her gloved hands on the glass all round as the taxi, accelerating without mercy, made off with her into the hinterland of deserted streets.

QUESTIONS FOR DISCUSSION AND WRITING

1. In what ways does the middle section of the story explain Mrs. Drover's "controlled worry" during the first part of the story? How does it prepare for the dramatic ending?
2. How does Mrs. Drover characterize her demon lover? In what way does Mrs. Drover's house characterize her life since the war?

3. How is the setting of the shut-up house and the deserted street important to our understanding of the story? For example, how does Mrs. Drover explain the appearance of the letter?
4. What is Mrs. Drover's point of view toward this experience? Is she really surprised by the appearance of her demon lover or has she been looking for him? Explain your answer.
5. What is the theme of this story? Can you explain it in realistic terms or do you have to consider the "supernatural side"?

13

KAY BOYLE

Astronomer's Wife

KAY BOYLE was born in 1902 in St. Paul, Minnesota, but spent her childhood in a number of cities in America and Europe. Boyle studied architecture at the Ohio Mechanics Institute and the violin at the Cincinnati Conservatory of Music before moving to New York to begin her writing career. In 1923 she married a French engineering student and spent the next twenty years living in various parts of Europe. After World War II, Boyle returned to the United States to write for magazines such as *Harper's, Broom,* and *The New Yorker,* and in 1963, she joined the English faculty at San Francisco State University. Although Boyle has written over a dozen novels, including *Plagued by the Nightingale* (1931), *Generation Without Farewell* (1960), and *The Underground Woman* (1970), she is known chiefly for her short stories, collected in memorable volumes such as *Wedding Day and Other Stories* (1930), *Thirty Stories* (1946), *Nothing Ever Breaks Except the Heart* (1966), and *Year Before Last* (1966). "Astronomer's Wife," reprinted from *The White Horses of Vienna and Other Stories* (1936), explores a woman's involvement in two masculine worlds.

There is an evil moment on awakening when all things seem to pause. But for women, they only falter and may be set in action by a single move: a lifted hand and the pendulum will swing, or the voice raised and through every room the pulse takes up its beating. The astronomer's wife felt the interval gaping and at once filled it to the brim. She fetched up her gentle voice and sent it warily down the stairs for coffee, swung her feet out upon the oval mat, and hailed the morning with her bare arms' quivering flesh drawn taut in rhythmic exercise: left, left, left my wife and fourteen children, right, right, right in the middle of the dusty road.

The day would proceed from this, beat by beat, without reflection, like every other day. The astronomer was still asleep, or feigning it, and she, once out of bed, had come into her own possession. Although scarcely ever out of sight of the impenetrable silence of his brow, she would be absent from him all the day in being clean, busy, kind. He was a man of other things, a dreamer. At times he lay still for hours, at others he sat upon the roof behind his telescope, or wandered down the pathway to the road and out across the mountains. This day, like any other, would go on from the removal of the spot left there from dinner on the astronomer's vest to the severe thrashing of the mayonnaise for lunch. That man might be each time the new arching wave, and woman the undertow that sucked him back, were things she had been told by his silence were so.

In spite of the earliness of the hour, the girl had heard her mistress's voice and was coming up the stairs. At the threshold of the bedroom she paused, and said: "Madame, the plumber is here."

The astronomer's wife put on her white and scarlet smock very quickly and buttoned it at the neck. Then she stepped carefully around the motionless spread of water in the hall.

"Tell him to come right up," she said. She laid her hands on the bannisters and stood looking down the wooden stairway. "Ah, I am Mrs. Ames," she said softly as she saw him mounting. "I am Mrs. Ames," she said softly, softly down the flight of stairs. "I am Mrs. Ames," spoken soft as a willow weeping. "The professor is still sleeping. Just step this way."

The plumber himself looked up and saw Mrs. Ames with her voice hushed, speaking to him. She was a youngish woman, but this she had forgotten. The mystery and silence of her husband's mind lay like a chiding finger on her lips. Her eyes were gray, for the light had been extinguished in them. The strange dim halo of her yellow hair was still uncombed and sideways on her head.

For all of his heavy boots, the plumber quieted the sound of his feet, and together they went down the hall, picking their way around the still lake of water that spread as far as the landing and lay docile there. The plumber was a tough, hardy man; but he took off his hat when he spoke to her and looked her fully, almost insolently in the eye.

"Does it come from the wash-basin," he said, "or from the other . . . ?"

"Oh, from the other," said Mrs. Ames without hesitation.

In this place the villas were scattered out few and primitive, and although beauty lay without there was no reflection of her face within. Here all was awkward and unfit; a sense of wrestling with uncouth forces gave everything an austere countenance. Even the plumber, dealing as does a woman with matters under hand, was grave and stately. The mountains round about seemed to have cast them into the shadow of great dignity.

Mrs. Ames began speaking of their arrival that summer in the little villa, mourning each event as it followed on the other.

"Then, just before going to bed last night," she said, "I noticed something was unusual."

The plumber cast down a folded square of sackcloth on the brimming floor and laid his leather apron on it. Then he stepped boldly onto the heart of the island it shaped and looked long into the overflowing bowl.

"The water should be stopped from the meter in the garden," he said at last.

"Oh, I did that," said Mrs. Ames, "the very first thing last night. I turned it off at once, in my nightgown, as soon as I saw what was happening. But all this had already run in."

The plumber looked for a moment at her red kid slippers. She was standing just at the edge of the clear, pure-seeming tide.

"It's no doubt the soil lines," he said severely. "It may be that something has stopped them, but my opinion is that the water seals aren't working. That's the trouble often enough in such cases. If you had a valve you wouldn't be caught like this."

Mrs. Ames did not know how to meet this rebuke. She stood, swaying a little, looking into the plumber's blue relentless eye.

"I'm sorry—I'm sorry that my husband," she said, "is still—resting and cannot go into this with you. I'm sure it must be very interesting. . . ."

"You'll probably have to have the traps sealed," said the plumber grimly, and at the sound of this Mrs. Ames' hand flew in dismay to the side of her face. The plumber made no move, but the set of his mouth as he looked at her seemed to soften. "Anyway, I'll have a look from the garden end," he said.

"Oh, do," said the astronomer's wife in relief. Here was a man who spoke of action and object as simply as women did! But however hushed her voice had been, it carried clearly to Professor Ames who lay, dreaming and solitary, upon his bed. He heard their footsteps come down the hall, pause, and skip across the pool of overflow.

"Katherine!" said the astronomer in a ringing tone. "There's a problem worthy of your mettle!"

Mrs. Ames did not turn her head, but led the plumber swiftly down the stairs. When the sun in the garden struck her face, he saw there was a wave of color in it, but this may have been anything but shame.

"You see how it is," said the plumber, as if leading her mind away. "The drains run from these houses right down the hill, big enough for a man to stand upright in them, and clean as a whistle too." There they stood in the garden with the vegetation flowering in disorder all about. The plumber looked at the astronomer's wife. "They come out at the torrent on the other side of the forest beyond there," he said.

But the words the astronomer had spoken still sounded in her in despair. The mind of man, she knew, made steep and sprightly flights, pursued illusion, took foothold in the nameless things that cannot pass between the thumb and finger. But whenever the astronomer gave voice to the thoughts that soared within him, she returned in gratitude to the long expanses of his silence. Desertlike they stretched behind and before the articulation of his scorn.

Life, life is an open sea, she sought to explain it in sorrow, and to survive women cling to the floating débris on the tide. But the plumber had suddenly fallen upon his knees in the grass and crooked his fingers through the rings of the drains' trap-door. When she looked down she saw that he was looking up into her face, and she saw too that his hair was as light as gold.

"Perhaps Mr. Ames," he said rather bitterly, "would like to come down with me and have a look around?"

"Down?" said Mrs. Ames in wonder.

"Into the drains," said the plumber brutally. "They're a study for a man who likes to know what's what."

"Oh, Mr. Ames," said Mrs. Ames in confusion. "He's still—still in bed, you see."

The plumber lifted his strong, weathered face and looked curiously at her. Surely it seemed to him strange for a man to linger in bed, with the sun pouring yellow as wine all over the place. The astronomer's wife saw his lean cheeks, his high, rugged bones, and the deep seams in his brow. His flesh was as firm and clean as wood, stained richly tan with the climate's rigor. His fingers were blunt, but comprehensible to her, gripped in the ring and holding the iron door wide. The backs of his hands were bound round and round with ripe blue veins of blood.

"At any rate," said the astronomer's wife, and the thought of it moved her lips to smile a little, "Mr. Ames would never go down there alive. He likes going up," she said. And she, in her turn, pointed, but impudently, towards the heavens. "On the roof. Or on the mountains. He's been up on the tops of them many times."

"It's a matter of habit," said the plumber, and suddenly he went down the trap. Mrs. Ames saw a bright little piece of his hair still shining, like a star, long after the rest of him had gone. Out of the depths, his voice, hollow and dark with foreboding, returned to her. "I think something has stopped the elbow," was what he said.

This was speech that touched her flesh and bone and made her wonder. When her husband spoke of height, having no sense of it, she could not picture it nor hear. Depth or magic passed her by unless a name were given. But madness in a daily shape, as elbow stopped, she saw clearly and well. She sat down on the grasses, bewildered that it should be a man who had spoken to her so.

She saw the weeds springing up, and she did not move to tear them up from life. She sat powerless, her senses veiled, with no action taking shape beneath her hands. In this way some men sat for hours on end, she knew, tracking a single thought back to its origin. The mind of man could balance and divide, weed out, destroy. She sat on the full, burdened grasses, seeking to think, and dimly waiting for the plumber to return.

Whereas her husband had always gone up, as the dead go, she knew now that there were others who went down, like the corporeal being of the dead. That men were then divided into two bodies now seemed clear to Mrs. Ames. This knowledge stunned her with its simplicity and took the uneasy motion from her limbs. She could not stir, but sat facing the mountains' rocky flanks, and harking in silence to lucidity. Her husband was the mind, this other man the meat, of all mankind.

After a little, the plumber emerged from the earth: first the light top of his head, then the burnt brow, and then the blue eyes fringed with whitest lash. He braced his thick hands flat on the pavings of the garden-path and swung himself completely from the pit.

"It's the soil lines," he said pleasantly. "The gases," he said as he looked down upon her lifted face, "are backing up the drains."

"What in the world are we going to do?" said the astronomer's wife softly. There was a young and strange delight in putting questions to which true answers would be given. Everything the astronomer had ever said to her was a continuous query to which there would be no response.

"Ah, come, now," said the plumber, looking down and smiling. "There's a remedy for every ill, you know. Sometimes it may be that," he said as if speaking to a child, "or sometimes the other thing. But there's always a help for everything a-miss."

Things come out of herbs and make you young again, he might have been saying to her; or the first good rain will quench any drought; or time of itself will put a broken bone together.

"I'm going to follow the ground pipe out right to the torrent," the plumber was saying. "The trouble's between here and there and I'll find it on the way. There's nothing at all that can't be done over for the caring," he was saying, and his eyes were fastened on her face in insolence, or gentleness, or love.

The astronomer's wife stood up, fixed a pin in her hair, and turned around towards the kitchen. Even while she was calling the servant's name, the plumber began speaking again.

"I once had a cow that lost her cud," the plumber was saying. The girl came out on the kitchen-step and Mrs. Ames stood smiling at her in the sun.

"The trouble is very serious, very serious," she said across the garden. "When Mr. Ames gets up, please tell him I've gone down."

She pointed briefly to the open door in the pathway, and the plumber hoisted his kit on his arm and put out his hand to help her down.

"But I made her another in no time," he was saying, "out of flowers and things and what-not."

"Oh," said the astronomer's wife in wonder as she stepped into the heart of the earth. She took his arm, knowing that what he said was true.

QUESTIONS FOR DISCUSSION AND WRITING

1. In what sense does the astronomer's single utterance explain the tension that produces the conflict in the story?
2. How does the astronomer's wife characterize her husband? What contrasts does she perceive in the plumber's character?
3. What is significant about the two settings referred to in the story—*up* and *down?* What does each setting represent? Why does the wife decide to go down?
4. What is the point of view of the astronomer's wife toward the day's events? Does she know what she is doing and why?
5. What has Mrs. Ames always assumed to be the difference between men and women? What surprising discovery does she make about men?

14

LARRY BROWN

Kubuku Rides (This Is It)

LARRY BROWN was born in 1951 in Oxford, Mississippi, where he attended the University of Mississippi. He has worked as a carpenter, lumberjack, house painter, and as a member of the Oxford Fire Department. He has contributed short stories to journals such as the *Mississippi Review, Fiction International,* and *Paris*

***Review.* He has published two novels, *Dirty Work* (1989) and *Joe* (1991), and two collections of short stories, *Facing the Music* (1988) and *Big Bad Love* (1990); and he is currently at work on a book of nonfiction, *Fire Notes.* "Kubuku Rides (This Is It)," reprinted from *Facing the Music,* portrays the destructive power of alcoholism.**

Angel hear the back door slam. It Alan, in from work. She start to hide the glass and then she don't hide the glass, he got a nose like a bloodhound and gonna smell it anyway, so she just keep sitting on the couch. She gonna act like nothing happening, like everything cool. Little boy in the yard playing, he don't know nothing. He think Mama in here watching Andy Griffith. Cooking supper. She better now anyway. Just wine, beer, no whiskey, no vodka. No gin. She getting well, she gonna make it. He have to be patient with her. She trying. He no rose garden himself anyway.

She start to get up and then she don't, it better if she stay down like nothing going on. She nervous, though. She know he looking, trying to catch her messing up. He watch her like a hawk, like somebody with eyes in the back of they head. He don't miss much. He come into the room and he see her. She smile, try to, but it wrong, she know it wrong, she guilty. He see it. He been out loading lumber or something all day long, he tired and ready for supper. But ain't no supper yet. She know all this and ain't said nothing. She scared to speak because she so guilty. But she mad over having to *feel* guilty, because some of this guilt *his* fault. Not all his fault. But some of it. Maybe half. Maybe less. This thing been going on a while. This thing nothing new.

"Hey honey," she say.

"I done unloaded two tons of two-by-fours today," he say.

"You poor baby," she say. "Come on and have a little drink with Mama." That the wrong thing to say.

"What?" he say. "You drinkin again? I done told you and told you and told you."

"It's just wine," she say.

"Well woman how many you done had?"

"This just my first one," she say, but she lying. She done had five and ain't even took nothing out the deep freeze. Wind up having a turkey pot pie or something. Something don't nobody want. She can't cook while she trying to figure out what to do. Don't know what to do. Ain't gonna drink nothing at all when she get up. Worries all day about drinking, then in the evening she done worried so much over *not* drinking she starts *in* drinking. She in one of them vicious circles. She done even thought about doing away with herself, but she hate to leave her husband and her little boy alone in the world. Probably mess her little boy up for the rest of his life. She don't want to die anyway. Angel ain't but about thirty years old. She still good-looking too. And love her husband like God love Jesus. Ain't no answer, that's it.

"Where that bottle?" he say.

Now she gonna act like she don't know what he talking about. "What bottle?" she say.

"Hell, woman. Bottle you drinkin from. What you mean what bottle?"

She scared now, frightened of his wrath. He don't usually go off. But he go off on her drinking in a minute. He put up with anything but her drinking.

"It's in the fridge," she say.

He run in there. She hear him open the door. He going to bust it in a million pieces. She get up and go after him, wobbly. She grabbing for doors and stuff, trying to get in there. He done took her money away, she can't have no more. He don't let her write no checks. He holding the bottle up where she can see it good. The contents of that bottle done trashed.

He say, "First glass my ass."

"Oh, Alan," she say. "That a old bottle."

"Old bottle? That what you say, old bottle?"

"I found it," she say.

"Lyin!" he say.

She shake her head no no no no no. She wanting that last drink because everything else hid.

"What you mean goin out buying some more?" he say. He got veins standing up in his neck. He mad, he madder than she ever seen him.

"Oh, Alan, please," she say. She hate herself begging like this. She ready to get down on her knees if she have to, though.

"I found it," she say.

"You been to the liquor store. Come on, now," he say. "You been to the liquor store, ain't you?"

Angel start to say something, start to scream something, but she see Randy come in from the front yard. He stop behind his daddy. Mama fixing to get down in the floor for that bottle. Daddy yelling stuff. Ain't no good time to come in. He eight year old but he know what going on. He tiptoe back out.

"Don't pour it out," she say. "Just let me finish it and I'll quit. Start supper," she say.

"Lie to me," he say. "Lie to me and take money and promise. How many times you promised?"

She go to him. He put the bottle behind his back, saying, "Don't, now, baby." He moaning, like.

"Alan *please,*" she say. She put one arm around his waist and try for that bottle. He stronger than her. It ain't fair! They stumble around in the kitchen. She trying for the bottle, he heading for the sink, she trying to get it. Done done this before. Ain't no fun no more.

He say, "I done told you what I'm goin to do."

She say, "Just let me finish it, Alan. Don't make me beg," she say. Ain't no way she hold him, he too strong. Lift weights three days a week. Runs. Got muscles like concrete. Know how to box but don't never hit her. She done hit him plenty with her little drunk fists, ain't hurt him, though. He turn away and start taking the cap off the bottle. She grab for it. She got both hands on it. He trying to pull it away. She panting. He pulling the bottle away, down in the sink so he can pour it out. They going to break it. Somebody going to get cut. May be him, may be her. Don't matter who. They tugging, back and forth, up and down. Ain't nobody in they right mind.

"Let go!" she say. She know Randy hearing it. He done run away once. Ain't enough for her. Ought to be but ain't.

He jerk it away and it hit the side of the sink and break. Blood gushing out of his hand. Mixing with the wine. Blood and wine all over the sink. Don't look good. Look bad. Look like maybe somebody have to kill theirself before it all get over with. Can't keep on like this. Done gone on too long.

"Godomightydamn," he say. Done sliced his hand wide open. It bad, she don't know how bad. Angel don't want to see. She run back to the living room for the rest of that glass. She don't drink it, he'll get it. She grab it. Pour it down. Two inches of wine. Then it all gone. She throw the glass into the mirror and everything break. Alan yell something in the kitchen and she run back in there and look. He got a bloody towel wrap around his hand. Done unloaded two tons of wood today and hospital bill gonna be more than he made. Won't take fifteen minutes. Emergency room robbery take longer than plain robbery but don't require no gun.

He shout, "This is it!" He crying and he don't cry. "Can't stand it! Sick of it!"

She sick too. He won't leave her alone. He love her. He done cut his hand wide open because of this love. He crying, little boy terrified. He run off again, somebody liable to snatch him up and they never see him again. Ought to be enough but ain't. Ain't never enough.

She flashing back now. She done had a wreck a few weeks ago. She done went out with some friends of hern, Betty and Glynnis and Sue. She done bought clothes for Randy and towels for her mama and cowboy boots for Alan. Pretty ones. Rhino's hide and hippo's toes. She working then, she still have a job then. It a Saturday. Randy and Alan at Randy's Little League game. She think she going over later, but she never make it. She get drunk instead.

They gone have just one little drink, her and Betty and Sue and them. One little drink ain't gone hurt nothing or nobody. Betty telling about her divorce and new men she checking out. She don't give no details, though. They drinking a light white wine but Angel having a double One Fifty-One and Coke. She ain't messing around. This a few weeks ago, she ain't got time for no wine. And she drink hers off real quick and order and get another one before they even get they wines down. She think maybe they won't even notice she done had two, they all so busy listening to Betty telling about these wimps she messing with. But it ain't even interesting and they notice right away. Angel going to the game, though. She definitely going to the game. She done promised everybody in the country. Time done come where she have to be straight. She got to quit breaking these promises. She got to quit all this lying and conniving.

Then before long they start talking about leaving. She ask them to stay, say Please, ya'll just stay and have one more. But naw, they got to go. Glynnis, she claim she got this hot date tonight. She talk like she got a hot date every night. Betty got this new man she going out with and she got to roll her hair and stuff. But Sue now is true. Angel done went to high school with her. They was in school together back when they was wearing hot pants and stuff. This like a old relationship. But Sue know what going on. She just hate to say anything. She just hate to bring it out in the wide open. She got to say something, though. She wait till the rest of them go and then she speak up.

She say, "I thought you goin to the ball game, girl." She look at her watch.

"Yeah," Angel say. "Honey, I'm goin. I wouldn't miss it for the world. But first I got to have me some more One Fifty-One and Coke."

Sue know she lying. She done lied to everybody about everything. This thing a problem can't keep quiet. She done had troubles at work. She done called in late, and sick, done called in and lied like a dog about her physical condition with these hungovers.

Now Angel hurting. She know Sue know the truth but too good to nag. She know Sue one good person she can depend on the rest of her life, but she know too Sue ain't putting up with her killing herself in her midst. She know Sue gone say something, but Sue don't say nothing until she finish her second wine. This after Angel ask her to have a third wine. Somebody got to stop her. She keep on, she be asking to stay for a eighth and a ninth wine. She be asking to stay till the place close down.

So Sue say, "You gone miss that ball game, girl."

She say she already late. She motion for another drink. Sue reach over and put her hand over Angel's glass and say, "Don't do that, girl."

"Late already," she say. "One more won't make no difference."

She know her speech and stuff messed up. It embarrassing, but the barmaid, she bring the drink. And Sue reach out, put her hand over the glass and say, "Don't you give her that shit, woman."

Girl back up and say, "*Ma'am?*" Real nice like.

"Don't you give her that," say Sue.

Girl say, "Yes'm, but ma'am, she order it, ma'am."

Girl look at Angel.

"Thank you, hon," she say. She reach and take the drink and give the girl some money. Then she tip her a dollar and the girl walk away. Angel grab this drink and slosh some of it out on her. She know it but she can't help it. She don't know what went wrong. She shopping and going to the ball game and now this done happened again. She ain't making no ball game. Ball game done shot to hell. She be in perhaps two three in the morning.

Sue now, she tired of this.

"When you goin to admit it?" she say.

"Admit what?"

"Girl, *you* know. Laying drunk. Runnin around here drinkin every night. Stayin out."

She say, "I don't know what you talkin about," like she huffy. She drinking every day. Even Sunday. Especially Sunday. Sunday the worst because ain't nothing open. She don't hit the liquor store Saturday night she climbing the walls Sunday afternoon. She done even got drunk and listened to the services on TV Sunday morning and got all depressed and passed out before dinnertime. Then Alan and Randy have to eat them turkey pot pies again.

"Alan and Randy don't understand me," she say.

"They love you," Sue say.

"And I love them," she say.

"Listen now," Sue tell her, "you gonna lose that baby and that man if you don't stop this messin around."

"Ain't gonna do that no such of a thing," she say, but she know Sue right. She still pouring that rum down, she ain't slacked off. She just have to deny the truth because old truth hurt too much to face.

Sue get up, she got tears in her eye and stuff, she dabbing with Kleenexes. Can't nobody talk sense to this fool.

"Yes you will," she say, and she leave. She ain't gone hang around and watch this self-destruction. Woman done turned into a time bomb ticking. She got to get away from here, so she run out the door. She booking home. Everybody looking.

Angel all alone now. She order two more singles and drink both of them. But she shitfaced time she drink that last one, she done been in the booth a hour and a half. Which has done caused some men to think about hitting on her, they done seen them thin legs and stuff she got. This one wimp done even come over to the table, he just assume she lonesome and want some male company, he think he gonna come over like he Robert Goulet or somebody and just invite himself to sit down. He done seen her wedding ring, but he thinking, Man, this woman horny or something, she wouldn't be sitting here all by her lonesome. And this fool almost sit down in the booth with her, he gonna buy her a drink, talk some trash to her, when he really thinking is he gonna get her in some motel room and take her panties off. But she done recognized his act, she ain't having nothing to do with this fool. She tell him off right quick. Of course he get huffy and leave. That's fine. Ain't asked that fool to sit down with her anyway.

Now she done decided she don't want to have another drink in this place. Old depression setting in. People coming in now to eat seafood with they families, little kids and stuff, grandmamas, she don't need to be hanging around in here no more. Waiters looking at her. She know they wanting her to leave before she give their place a bad name. Plus she taking up room in this booth where some family wanting to eat some filet catfish. She know all this stuff. She know she better leave before they ask her to. She done had embarrassment enough, don't need no more.

Ain't eat nothing yet. Don't want nothing to eat. Don't even eat at home much. Done lost weight, breasts done come down, was fine and full, legs even done got skinny. She know Alan notice it when she undress. She don't even weigh what she weigh on they wedding night when she give herself to Alan. She know he worried sick about her. He get her in the bed and squeeze her so tight he hurt her, but she don't say Let go.

She trying to walk straight when she go out to her car, but she look like somebody afflicted. Bumping into hoods and stuff. She done late already. Ball game over. It after six and Randy and Alan already home by now. Ain't no way she going home right now. She ain't gonna face them crying faces. And, too, she go home, Alan ain't letting her drink another drop. So she decide to get her a bottle and just ride around a while. She gonna ride around and sober up, then she gonna go home. And she need to do this anyway because this give her time to think something up like say the car tore up or something, why she late.

Only thing, she done gone in the liquor store so many times she ashamed to. She see these same people and she know they thinking: Damn, this woman done been in here four times this week. Drinking like a fish. She don't like to look in they eyes. So she hunt her up another store on the other side of town. She don't want to get too drunk, so she just get a sixer of beers and some schnapps. She going to ride around, cruise a little and sober up. That what she thinking.

She driving okay. Hitting them beers occasionally, hitting that peach schnapps every few minutes because it so good and ain't but forty-eight proof. It so weak it ain't gonna make her drunk. Not no half pint. She ain't gonna ride around but a hour. Then she gonna go home.

She afraid to take a drink when anybody behind her. She thinking the police gonna see her and throw them blue lights on her. Then she be in jail calling Alan to come bail her out. Which he already done twice before. She don't want to stay in town. She gonna drive out on the lake road. They not as much traffic out there. So she go off out there, on this blacktop road. She gonna ride out to the boat landing. Ain't nobody out there, it too cold to fish. She curve around through the woods three or four miles. She done finished one of them beers and throwed the bottle out the window. She get her another one and drink some more of that schnapps. That stuff go down so easy and so hard to stop on. Usually when she open a half pint, she throw the cap far as she can.

Angel weaving a little, but she ain't drunk. She just a little tired. She wishing she home in the bed right now. She know they gonna have a big argument when she get home. She dreading that. Alan, he have to fix supper for Randy and his mama ain't taught him nothing about cooking. Only thing he know how to do is warm up a TV dinner, and Randy just sull up when he have to eat one of them. She wishing now she'd just gone on home. Wouldn't have been so bad then. Going to be worse now, much worser than if she'd just gone on home after them double One Fifty-Ones. Way it is, though. Get started, can't stop. Take that first drink, she ain't gonna stop till she pass out or run out. She don't know what it is. She ain't even understand it herself. Didn't start out like this. Didn't use to be this way. Use to be a beer once in a while, little wine at New Year's. Things just get out of hand. Don't mean to be this way. Just can't help it. Alan used to would drink a little beer on weekends and it done turned him flat against it. He don't even want to be around nobody drinking now. Somebody offer him a drink now he tell em to get it out of his face. He done even lost some of his friends over this thing.

Angel get down to the boat ramp, ain't a soul there. Windy out there, water dark, scare her to death just to see it. What would it be to be out in them waves, them black waves closing over your head, ain't nobody around to hear you screaming. Coat be waterlogged and pulling you down. Hurt just a little and that's all. Just a brief pain. Be dead then, won't know nothing. Won't have no hurts. Easy way out. They get over it eventually. Could make it look like an accident. Drive her car right off in the water, everybody think it a mistake. Just a tragedy, that's all, a unfortunate thing. Don't want to hurt nobody. What so wrong with her life she do the things she do? Killing her baby and her man little at a time. And her ownself. But have to have it. Thinking things when she drinking she wouldn't think at all when she not drinking. But now she drinking all the time, and she thinking same way all the time.

She drink some more beer and schnapps, and then she pass out or go to sleep, she don't know which. Same thing. Sleeping she don't have to think no more. Ain't no hurting when she sleeping. Sleeping good, but can't sleep forever. Somebody done woke her up, knocking on the glass. Some boy out there. High school boy. Truck parked beside, some more kids in it. She scared at first, think something bad. But they look all right.

Don't look mean or nothing. Just look worried. She get up and roll her window down just a little, just crack it.

"Ma'am?" this boy say. "You all right, ma'am?"

"Yes," she say. "Fine, thank you."

"Seen you settin here," he say. "Thought your car tore up maybe."

"No," Angel say. "Just sleepy," she say. "Leaving now," she say, and she roll the window up. She turn the lights on, car still running, ain't even shut it off. Out in the middle of nowhere asleep, ain't locked the door. Somebody walk up and slit her throat, she not even know it. She crazy. She got to get home. She done been asleep no telling how long.

She afraid they gonna follow her out. They do. She can't stand for nobody to get behind her like that. Make her nervous. She decide she gonna speed up and leave them behind. She get up to about sixty-five. She start to pull away. She sobered up a little while she asleep. Be okay to get another one of them beers out the sack now. Beer sack down in the floor. Have to lean over and take her eyes off the road just a second to get that beer, no problem.

Her face hit the windshield, the seat slam her up. Too quick. Lights shining up against a tree. Don't even know what happened. Windshield broke all to pieces. Smoke coming out the hood. She wiping her face. Interior light on, she got blood all over her hands. Face bleeding. She look in the rearview mirror, she don't know her own self. Look like something in a monster movie. She screaming now. Face cut all to pieces. She black out again. She come to, she out on the ground. People helping her up. She screaming I'm ruint I'm ruint. Lights in her eyes, legs moving in front of her. Kids talking. One of them say she just drive right off the road into that tree. She don't believe it. Road move or something. Tree jump out in front of her. She a good driver. She drive too good for something like this.

Cost three thousand dollars to fix the car this time. Don't even drive right no more. Alan say the frame bent. Alan say it won't never drive right no more. And ain't even paid for. She don't know about no frame. She just know it jerk going down the road.

She in the hospital a while. She don't remember exactly, three or four days. They done had to sew her face up. People see them scars even through thick makeup the rest of her life. She bruised so bad she don't get out the bed for a week. Alan keep saying they lucky she ain't dead. He keep praising God his wife ain't dead. She know she just gonna have to go through it again now sometime, till a worse one happen. Police done come and talked to her. She lie her way out of it, though. Can't prove nothing. Alan keep saying we lucky.

Ain't lucky. Boss call, want to know when she coming back to work. She hem and haw. Done missed all them Mondays. She can't give no definite answer. He clear his throat. Maybe he should find somebody else for her position since she so vague. Well yessir, she say, yessir, if you think that the best thing.

Alan awful quiet after this happen. He just sit and stare. She touch him out on the porch, he just draw away. Like her hand a bad thing to feel on him. This go on about a week. Then he come home from work one evening and she sitting in the living room with a glass of wine in her hand.

He back now from having his hand sewed up. He sitting in the kitchen drinking coffee, he done bought some cigarettes and he smoking one after another. Done been quit two years, say it the hardest thing he ever done. He say he never stop wanting one, that he have to brace himself every day. Now he done started back. She know: This what she done to him.

Angel not drinking anything. Don't mean she don't have nothing. Just can't have it right now. He awake now. Later he be asleep. He think the house clean. House ain't clean. Lots of places to hide things, you want to hide them bad enough. Ain't like Easter eggs, like Christmas presents. Like life and death.

Wouldn't never think on her wedding night it ever be like this. She in the living room by herself, he in the kitchen by himself. TV on, she ain't watching it, some fool on Johnny Carson telling stuff ain't even funny. She ain't got the sound on. Ain't hear nothing, ain't see nothing. She hear him like choke in there once in a while. Randy in the bed asleep. Want so bad to get up and go in there and tell Alan, Baby I promise I will quit. Again. But ain't no use in saying it, she don't mean it. Just words. Don't mean nothing. Done lost trust anyway. Lose trust, a man and wife, done lost everything. Even if she quit now, stay quit, he always be looking over that shoulder, he always be smelling her breath. Lost his trust she won't never get it back.

He come in there where she at finally. He been crying, she tell it by looking at him. He not hurting for himself, he not hurting for his hand. He cut off his hand and throw it away she ask him to. He hurting for her. She know all this, don't nobody have to tell her. Why it don't do no good to talk to her. She know it all already.

"Baby," he say. "I goin to bed. Had a long day today."

His face look like he about sixty years old. He thirty-one. Weigh one sixty-five and bench press two-ninety. "You comin?" he say.

She want to. Morning be soon enough to drink something else. He be gone to work, Randy be gone to school. House be quiet by seven-thirty. She do what she want to then. Whole day be hers to do what she want to. Things be better tomorrow maybe. She cook them something good for supper, she make them a good old pie and have ice cream. She get better. They know she trying. She just weak, she just need some time. This thing not something you throw off like a cold. This thing deep, this thing beat more good people than her.

Angel say, "Not just yet, baby. I going to sit in here in the livin room a while. I so sorry you cut your hand," she say.

"You want to move?" he say. "Another state? Another country? You say the word I quit my job tomorrow. Don't matter. Just a job," he say.

"Don't want to move," she say. She trembling.

"Don't matter what people thinks," he say.

She think he gonna come over and get down on the floor and hug her knees and cry, but he don't. He look like he holding back to keep from doing that. And she glad he don't. He do that, she make them promises again. She promise anything if he just stop.

"Okay," he say. "I goin to bed now." He look beat.

He go. She by herself. It real quiet now. Hear anything. Hear walls pop, hear mice move. They eating something in the cabinet, she need to set some traps.

Time go by so slow. She know he in there listening. He listen for any step she make, which room she move into, which furniture she reach for. She have to wait. It risky now. He think she in here drinking, they gonna have it all over again. One time a night enough. Smart thing is go to bed. Get next to him. That what he want. Ought to be what she want. Use to be she did.

Thirty minutes a long time like this. She holding her breath when she go in there to look at him. He just a lump in the dark. Can't tell if he sleeping or not. Could be laying there looking at her. Too dark to tell. He probably asleep, though. He tired, he give out. He work so hard for them.

Tomorrow be better. Tomorrow she have to try harder. She know she can do it, she got will power. Just need a little time. They have to be patient with her. Ain't built Rome in a day. And she gonna be so good in the future, it ain't gonna hurt nothing to have a few cold beers tonight. Ain't drinking no whiskey now. Liquor store done closed anyway. Big Star still open. She just run down get some beer and then run right back. Don't need to drink what she got hid anyway. Probably won't need none later, she gonna quit anyway, but just in case.

She know where the checkbook laying. She ain't making no noise. If he awake he ain't saying nothing. If he awake he'd be done said something. He won't know she ever been gone. Won't miss no three dollar check no way. Put it in with groceries sometime.

Side door squeak every time. Don't never notice it in daytime. Squeak like hell at night. Porch light on. He always leave it on if she going to be out. Ain't no need to turn it off. She be back in ten minutes. He never know she gone. Car in the driveway. It raining. A little.

Ain't cold. Don't need no coat.

She get in, ease the door to. Trying to be quiet. He so tired, he need his rest. She look at the bedroom window when she turn the key. And the light come on in there.

Caught now. Wasn't even asleep. Trying to just catch her on purpose. Laying in there in the dark just making out like he asleep. Don't trust her. Won't never trust her. It like he making her slip around. Damn him anyway.

Ain't nothing to do but talk to him. He standing on the step in his underwear. She put it in reverse and back on up. She stop beside him and roll down the window. She hate to. Neighbors gonna see him out here in his underwear. What he think he doing anyway, can't leave her alone. Treat her like some baby he can't take his eye off of for five minutes.

"I just goin to the store," she say. "I be right back."

"Don't care for you goin to the store," he say. "Long as you come back. You comin back?"

He got his arms wrapped around him, he shivering in the night air. He look like he been asleep.

"I just goin after some cigarettes," she say. "I be back in ten minutes. Go on back to bed. I be right back. I promise."

He step off the porch and come next the car. He hugging himself and shaking, barefooted. Standing in the driveway getting wet.

"I won't say nothin about you drinkin if you just do it at home," he say. "Go git you somethin to drink. But come back home," he say. "Please," he say.

It hit her now, this enough. This enough to stop anything, anybody, everything. He done give up.

"Baby," he say, "know you ain't gone stop. Done said all I can say. Just don't get out on the road drinkin. Don't care about the car. Just don't hurt yourself."

"I done told you I be back in ten minutes," she say. "I be *back* in ten minutes."

Something cross his face. Can't tell rain from tears in this. But what he shivering from she don't think is cold.

"Okay, baby," he say, "okay," and he turn away. She relieved. Now maybe won't be no argument. Now maybe won't be no dread. She telling the truth anyway. Ain't going nowhere but Big Star. Be back in ten minutes. All this fussing for nothing. Neighbors probably looking out the windows.

He go up on the porch and put his hand on the door. He watching her back out the driveway, she watching him standing there half naked. All this foolishness over a little trip to Big Star. She shake her head while she backing out the driveway. It almost like he ain't even expecting her to come back. She almost laugh at this. Ain't nothing even open this late but bars, and she *ain't* going to none of them, no ma'am. She see him watch her again, and then she see him step inside. What he need to do. Go on back to bed, get him some rest. He got to go to work in the morning. All she got to do is sleep.

She turn the wipers on to see better. The porch light shining out there, yellow light showing rain, it slanting down hard. It shine on the driveway and on Randy's bicycle and on they barbecue grill setting there getting wet. It make her feel good to know this all hers, that she always got this to come back to. This light show her home, this warm place she own that mean everything to her. This light, it always on for her. That what she thinking when it go out.

QUESTIONS FOR DISCUSSION AND WRITING

1. How is the basic conflict in the story established in the first paragraph? How are flashback and foreshadowing used to suggest the likely outcome of Angel's story?

2. How does Brown maintain our sympathy for Angel even as she portrays her own self-destructiveness? What does our last glimpse of Alan reveal about his character?

3. How is the social and economic situation of the family established in the details of the story? For example, what will Alan's trip to the emergency room mean to the family?

4. Although this story appears to be told in the third person, what evidence can you supply that Angel is telling her own story?

5. What does Angel's self-assessment reveal about the power of addiction? How does her assessment suggest that mutual trust is essential to overcoming addiction? What thematic meaning do you find in the title of the story?

15

ALBERT CAMUS

The Guest

TRANSLATED BY JUSTIN O'BRIEN

ALBERT CAMUS (1913–1960) was born in Mondovi, Algeria, then still a colony of France, and was educated at the University of Algeria where he majored in philosophy and participated in the activities of a small theatrical company. During World War II he moved to France, joined the Resistance, and wrote for and edited the underground magazine *Combat.* His three novels, *The Stranger* (1942), *The Plague* (1947), and *The Fall* (1956), together with his first collection of philosophical essays, *The Myth of Sisyphus* (1942), established Camus as one of the primary spokesmen for existentialist philosophy. During the Algerian war in the 1950s, Camus's loyalties were divided between the Arab nationalists and the French colonists. His attempt to find a reasonable middle position between these extremes resulted in his major philosophical work, *The Rebel: An Essay on Man in Revolt* (1954), and in his selection for the Nobel Prize for literature in 1957. Camus was killed in an automobile accident near Paris in 1960. "The Guest," reprinted from Camus's collection of short stories, *Exile and the Kingdom* (1957), portrays the dilemma of a man trying to decide between conflicting responsibilities.

The schoolmaster was watching the two men climb toward him. One was on horseback, the other on foot. They had not yet tackled the abrupt rise leading to the schoolhouse built on the hillside. They were toiling onward, making slow progress in the snow, among the stones, on the vast expanse of the high, deserted plateau. From time to time the horse stumbled. Without hearing anything yet, he could see the breath issuing from the horse's nostrils. One of the men, at least, knew the region. They were following the trail although it had disappeared days ago under a layer of dirty white snow. The schoolmaster calculated that it would take them half an hour to get onto the hill. It was cold; he went back into the school to get a sweater.

He crossed the empty, frigid classroom. On the blackboard the four rivers of France, drawn with four different colored chalks, had been flowing toward their estuaries for the past three days. Snow had suddenly fallen in mid-October after eight months of drought without the transition of rain, and the twenty pupils, more or less, who lived in the villages scattered over the plateau had stopped coming. With fair weather they would return. Daru now heated only the single room that was his lodging, adjoining the classroom and giving also onto the plateau to the east. Like the class windows, his window looked to the south too. On that side the school was a few kilometers from the point where the plateau began to slope toward the south. In clear weather could be seen the purple mass of the mountain range where the gap opened onto the desert.

Somewhat warmed, Daru returned to the window from which he had first seen the two men. They were no longer visible. Hence they must have tackled the rise. The sky was not so dark, for the snow had stopped falling during the night. The morning had opened with a dirty light which had scarcely become brighter as the ceiling of clouds lifted. At two in the afternoon it seemed as if the day were merely beginning. But still this was better than those three days when the thick snow was falling amidst unbroken darkness with little gusts of wind that rattled the double door of the classroom. Then Daru had spent long hours in his room, leaving it only to go to the shed and feed the chickens or get some coal. Fortunately the delivery truck from Tadjid, the nearest village to the north, had brought his supplies two days before the blizzard. It would return in forty-eight hours.

Besides, he had enough to resist a siege, for the little room was cluttered with bags of wheat that the administration left as a stock to distribute to those of his pupils whose families had suffered from the drought. Actually they had all been victims because they were all poor. Every day Daru would distribute a ration to the children. They had missed it, he knew, during these bad days. Possibly one of the fathers or big brothers would come this afternoon and he could supply them with grain. It was just a matter of carrying them over to the next harvest. Now shiploads of wheat were arriving from France and the worst was over. But it would be hard to forget that poverty, that army of ragged ghosts wandering in the sunlight, the plateaus burned to a cinder month after month, the earth shriveled up little by little, literally scorched, every stone bursting into dust under one's foot. The sheep had died then by thousands and even a few men, here and there, sometimes without anyone's knowing.

In contrast with such poverty, he who lived almost like a monk in his remote schoolhouse, nonetheless satisfied with the little he had and with the rough life, had felt like a lord with his whitewashed walls, his narrow couch, his unpainted shelves, his well, and his weekly provision of water and food. And suddenly this snow, without warning, without the foretaste of rain. This is the way the region was, cruel to live in, even without men—who didn't help matters either. But Daru had been born here. Everywhere else, he felt exiled.

He stepped out onto the terrace in front of the schoolhouse. The two men were now halfway up the slope. He recognized the horseman as Balducci, the old gendarme he had known for a long time. Balducci was holding on the end of a rope an Arab who was walking behind him with hands bound and head lowered. The gendarme waved a greeting to which Daru did not reply, lost as he was in contemplation of the Arab dressed in a faded blue jellaba, his feet in sandals but covered with socks of heavy raw wool, his head surmounted by a narrow, short *chèche*. They were approaching. Balducci was holding back his horse in order not to hurt the Arab, and the group was advancing slowly.

Within earshot, Balducci shouted: "One hour to do the three kilometers from El Ameur!" Daru did not answer. Short and square in his thick sweater, he watched them climb. Not once had the Arab raised his head. "Hello," said Daru when they got up onto the terrace. "Come in and warm up." Balducci painfully got down from his horse without letting go the rope. From under his bristling mustache he smiled at the schoolmaster. His little dark eyes, deep-set under a tanned forehead, and his mouth surrounded with wrinkles made him look attentive and studious. Daru took the bridle, led the horse to the shed, and came back to the two men, who were now waiting for him in the school. He led them into his room. "I am going to heat up the classroom," he said. "We'll be more comfortable there." When he entered the room again, Balducci was on the couch. He had undone the rope tying him to the Arab, who had squatted near the stove. His hands still bound, the *chèche* pushed back on his head, he was looking toward the window. At first Daru noticed only his huge lips, fat, smooth, almost Negroid; yet his nose was straight, his eyes were dark and full of fever. The *chèche* revealed an obstinate forehead and, under the weathered skin now rather discolored by the cold, the whole face had a restless and rebellious look that struck Daru when the Arab, turning his face toward him, looked him straight in the eyes. "Go into the other room," said the schoolmaster, "and I'll make you some mint tea." "Thanks," Balducci said. "What a chore! How I long for retirement." And addressing his prisoner in Arabic: "Come on, you." The Arab got up and, slowly, holding his bound wrists in front of him, went into the classroom.

With the tea, Daru brought a chair. But Balducci was already enthroned on the nearest pupil's desk and the Arab had squatted against the teacher's platform facing the stove, which stood between the desk and the window. When he held out the glass of tea to the prisoner, Daru hesitated at the sight of his bound hands. "He might perhaps be untied." "Sure," said Balducci. "That was for the trip." He started to get to his feet. But Daru, setting the glass on the floor, had knelt beside the Arab. Without saying anything, the Arab watched him with his feverish eyes. Once his hands were free, he rubbed his swollen wrists against each other, took the glass of tea, and sucked up the burning liquid in swift little sips.

"Good," said Daru. "And where are you headed?"

Balducci withdrew his mustache from the tea. "Here, son."

"Odd pupils! And you're spending the night?"

"No. I'm going back to El Ameur. And you will deliver this fellow to Tinguit. He is expected at police headquarters."

Balducci was looking at Daru with a friendly little smile.

"What's this story?" asked the schoolmaster. "Are you pulling my leg?"

"No, son. Those are the orders."

"The orders? I'm not . . ." Daru hesitated, not wanting to hurt the old Corsican. "I mean, that's not my job."

"What! What's the meaning of that? In wartime people do all kinds of jobs."

"Then I'll wait for the declaration of war!"

Balducci nodded.

"O.K. But the orders exist and they concern you too. Things are brewing, it appears. There is talk of a forthcoming revolt. We are mobilized, in a way."

Daru still had his obstinate look.

"Listen, son," Balducci said. "I like you and you must understand. There's only a dozen of us at El Ameur to patrol throughout the whole territory of a small department and I must get back in a hurry. I was told to hand this guy over to you and return without delay. He couldn't be kept there. His village was beginning to stir; they wanted to take him back. You must take him to Tinguit tomorrow before the day is over. Twenty kilometers shouldn't faze a husky fellow like you. After that, all will be over. You'll come back to your pupils and your comfortable life."

Behind the wall the horse could be heard snorting and pawing the earth. Daru was looking out the window. Decidedly, the weather was clearing and the light was increasing over the snowy plateau. When all the snow was melted, the sun would take over again and once more would burn the fields of stone. For days, still, the unchanging sky would shed its dry light on the solitary expanse where nothing had any connection with man.

"After all," he said, turning around toward Balducci, "what did he do?" And, before the gendarme had opened his mouth, he asked: "Does he speak French?"

"No, not a word. We had been looking for him for a month, but they were hiding him. He killed his cousin."

"Is he against us?"

"I don't think so. But you can never be sure."

"Why did he kill?"

"A family squabble, I think. One owed the other grain, it seems. It's not at all clear. In short, he killed his cousin with a billhook. You know, like a sheep, *kreezk!*"

Balducci made the gesture of drawing a blade across his throat and the Arab, his attention attracted, watched him with a sort of anxiety. Daru felt a sudden wrath against the man, against all men with their rotten spite, their tireless hates, their blood lust.

But the kettle was singing on the stove. He served Balducci more tea, hesitated, then served the Arab again, who a second time, drank avidly. His raised arms made the jellaba fall open and the schoolmaster saw his thin, muscular chest.

"Thanks, kid," Balducci said. "And now, I'm off."

He got up and went toward the Arab, taking a small rope from his pocket.

"What are you doing?" Daru asked dryly.

Balducci, disconcerted, showed him the rope.

"Don't bother."

The old gendarme hesitated. "It's up to you. Of course, you are armed?"

"I have my shotgun."

"Where?"

"In the trunk."

"You ought to have it near your bed."

"Why? I have nothing to fear."

"You're crazy, son. If there's an uprising, no one is safe, we're all in the same boat."

"I'll defend myself. I'll have time to see them coming."

Balducci began to laugh, then suddenly the mustache covered the white teeth.

"You'll have time? O.K. That's just what I was saying. You have always been a little cracked. That's why I like you, my son was like that."

At the same time he took out his revolver and put it on the desk.

"Keep it; I don't need two weapons from here to El Ameur."

The revolver shone against the black paint of the table. When the gendarme turned toward him, the schoolmaster caught the smell of leather and horseflesh.

"Listen, Balducci," Daru said suddenly, "every bit of this disgusts me, and first of all your fellow here. But I won't hand him over. Fight, yes, if I have to. But not that."

The old gendarme stood in front of him and looked at him severely.

"You're being a fool," he said slowly. "I don't like it either. You don't get used to putting a rope on a man even after years of it, and you're even ashamed—yes, ashamed. But you can't let them have their way."

"I won't hand him over," Daru said again.

"It's an order, son, and I repeat it."

"That's right. Repeat to them what I've said to you: I won't hand him over."

Balducci made a visible effort to reflect. He looked at the Arab and at Daru. At last he decided.

"No, I won't tell them anything. If you want to drop us, go ahead; I'll not denounce you. I have an order to deliver the prisoner and I'm doing so. And now you'll just sign this paper for me."

"There's no need. I'll not deny that you left him with me."

"Don't be mean with me. I know you'll tell the truth. You're from hereabouts and you are a man. But you must sign, that's the rule."

Daru opened his drawer, took out a little square bottle of purple ink, the red wooden penholder with the "sergeant-major" pen he used for making models of penmanship, and signed. The gendarme carefully folded the paper and put it into his wallet. Then he moved toward the door.

"I'll see you off," Daru said.

"No," said Balducci. "There's no use being polite. You insulted me."

He looked at the Arab, motionless in the same spot, sniffed peevishly, and turned away toward the door. "Good-by, son," he said. The door shut behind him. Balducci appeared suddenly outside the window and then disappeared. His footsteps were muffled by the snow. The horse stirred on the other side of the wall and several chickens fluttered in fright. A moment later Balducci reappeared outside the window leading the horse by the bridle. He walked toward the little rise without turning around and disappeared from sight with the horse following him. A big stone could be heard bouncing down. Daru walked back toward the prisoner, who, without stirring, never took his eyes off him. "Wait," the schoolmaster said in Arabic and went toward the bedroom. As he was going through the door, he had a second thought, went to the desk, took the revolver, and stuck it in his pocket. Then, without looking back, he went into his room.

For some time he lay on his couch watching the sky gradually close over, listening to the silence. It was this silence that had seemed painful to him during the first days here, after the war. He had requested a post in the little town at the base of the foothills separating the upper plateaus from the desert. There, rocky walls, green and black to the north, pink and lavender to the south, marked the frontier of eternal summer. He had been named to a post farther north, on the plateau itself. In the beginning, the solitude and the silence had been hard for him on these wastelands peopled only by stones. Occasionally, furrows suggested cultivation, but they had been dug to uncover a certain kind of stone good for building. The only plowing here was to harvest rocks. Elsewhere a thin layer of soil accumulated in the hollows would be scraped out to enrich paltry village gardens. This is the way it was: bare rock covered three quarters of the region. Towns sprang up, flourished, then disappeared; men came by, loved one another or fought bitterly, then died. No one in this desert, neither he nor his guest, mattered. And yet, outside this desert neither of them, Daru knew, could have really lived.

When he got up, no noise came from the classroom. He was amazed at the unmixed joy he derived from the mere thought that the Arab might have fled and that he would be alone with no decision to make. But the prisoner was there. He had merely stretched out between the stove and the desk. With eyes open, he was staring at the ceiling. In that position, his thick lips were particularly noticeable, giving him a pouting look. "Come," said Daru. The Arab got up and followed him. In the bedroom, the schoolmaster pointed to a chair near the table under the window. The Arab sat down without taking his eyes off Daru.

"Are you hungry?"

"Yes," the prisoner said.

Daru set the table for two. He took flour and oil, shaped a cake in a frying-pan, and lighted the little stove that functioned on bottled gas. While the cake was cooking, he went out to the shed to get cheese, eggs, dates, and condensed milk. When the cake was done he sat it on the window sill to cool, heated some condensed milk diluted with water, and beat up the eggs into an omelette. In one of his motions he knocked against the revolver stuck in his right pocket. He set the bowl down, went into the classroom, and put the revolver in his desk drawer. When he came back to the room, night was falling. He put on the light and served the Arab. "Eat," he said. The Arab took a piece of the cake, lifted it eagerly to his mouth, and stopped short.

"And you?" he asked.

"After you. I'll eat too."

The thick lips opened slightly. The Arab hesitated, then bit into the cake determinedly.

The meal over, the Arab looked at the schoolmaster. "Are you the judge?"

"No, I'm simply keeping you until tomorrow."

"Why do you eat with me?"

"I'm hungry."

The Arab fell silent. Daru got up and went out. He brought back a folding bed from the shed, set it up between the table and the stove, perpendicular to his own bed. From a large suitcase which, upright in a corner, served as a shelf for papers, he took two blankets and arranged them on the camp bed. Then he stopped, felt useless, and sat down on his bed. There was nothing more to do or to get ready. He had to look at this man. He looked at him, therefore, trying to imagine his face bursting with rage. He couldn't do so. He could see nothing but the dark yet shining eyes and the animal mouth.

"Why did you kill him?" he asked in a voice whose hostile tone surprised him.

The Arab looked away.

"He ran away. I ran after him."

He raised his eyes to Daru again and they were full of a sort of woeful interrogation. "Now what will they do to me?"

"Are you afraid?"

He stiffened, turning his eyes away.

"Are you sorry?"

The Arab stared at him openmouthed. Obviously he did not understand. Daru's annoyance was growing. At the same time he felt awkward and self-conscious with his big body wedged between the two beds.

"Lie down there," he said impatiently. "That's your bed."

The Arab didn't move. He called to Daru:

"Tell me!"

The schoolmaster looked at him.

"Is the gendarme coming back tomorrow?"

"I don't know."

"Are you coming with us?"

"I don't know. Why?"

The prisoner got up and stretched out on top of the blankets, his feet toward the window. The light from the electric bulb shone straight into his eyes and he closed them at once.

"Why?" Daru repeated, standing beside the bed.

The Arab opened his eyes under the blinding light and looked at him, trying not to blink.

"Come with us," he said.

In the middle of the night, Daru was still not asleep. He had gone to bed after undressing completely; he generally slept naked. But when he suddenly realized that he had nothing on, he hesitated. He felt vulnerable and the temptation came to him to put his clothes back on. Then he shrugged his shoulders; after all, he wasn't a child and, if need be, he could break his adversary in two. From his bed he could observe him, lying on his back, still motionless with his eyes closed under the harsh light. When Daru turned out the light, the darkness seemed to coagulate all of a sudden. Little by little, the night came back to life in the window where the starless sky was stirring gently. The schoolmaster soon made out the body lying at his feet. The Arab still did not move, but his eyes seemed open. A faint wind was prowling around the schoolhouse. Perhaps it would drive away the clouds and the sun would reappear.

During the night the wind increased. The hens fluttered a little and then were silent. The Arab turned over on his side with his back to Daru, who thought he heard him moan. Then he listened for his guest's breathing, become heavier and more regular. He listened to that breath so close to him and mused without being able to go to sleep. In this room where he had been sleeping alone for a year, this presence bothered him. But it bothered him also by imposing on him a sort of brotherhood he knew well but refused to accept in the present circumstances. Men who share the same rooms, soldiers or prisoners, develop a strange alliance as if, having cast off their armor with their clothing, they fraternized every evening, over and above their differences, in the ancient community of dream and fatigue. But Daru shook himself; he didn't like such musings, and it was essential to sleep.

A little later, however, when the Arab stirred slightly, the schoolmaster was still not asleep. When the prisoner made a second move, he stiffened, on the alert. The Arab was lifting himself slowly on his arms with almost the motion of a sleepwalker. Seated upright in bed, he waited motionless without turning his head toward Daru, as if he were listening attentively. Daru did not stir; it had just occurred to him that the revolver was still in the drawer of his desk. It was better to act at once. Yet he continued to observe the prisoner, who, with the same slithery motion, put his feet on the ground, waited again, then began to stand up slowly. Daru was about to call out to him when the Arab began to walk, in a quite natural but extraordinarily silent way. He was heading toward the door at the end of the room that opened into the shed. He lifted the latch with precaution and went out, pushing the door behind him but without shutting it. Daru had not stirred. "He is running away," he merely thought. "Good riddance!" Yet he listened attentively. The hens were not fluttering; the guest must be on the plateau. A faint sound of water reached him, and he didn't know what it was until the Arab again stood framed in the doorway, closed the door carefully, and came back to bed without a sound. Then Daru turned his back on him and fell asleep. Still later he seemed, from the depths of his sleep, to hear furtive steps around the schoolhouse. "I'm dreaming! I'm dreaming!" he repeated to himself. And he went on sleeping.

When he awoke, the sky was clear; the loose window let in a cold, pure air. The Arab was asleep, hunched up under the blankets now, his mouth open, utterly relaxed. But when Daru shook him, he started dreadfully, staring at Daru with wild eyes as if he had never seen him and such a frightened expression that the schoolmaster stepped back. "Don't be afraid. It's me. You must eat." The Arab nodded his head and said yes. Calm had returned to his face, but his expression was vacant and listless.

The coffee was ready. They drank it seated together on the folding bed as they munched their pieces of the cake. Then Daru led the Arab under the shed and showed him the faucet where he washed. He went back into the room, folded the blankets and the bed, made his own bed and put the room in order. Then he went through the classroom and out onto the terrace. The sun was already rising in the blue sky; a soft, bright light was bathing the deserted plateau. On the ridge the snow was melting in spots. The stones were about to reappear. Crouched on the edge of the plateau, the schoolmaster looked at the deserted expanse. He thought of Balducci. He had hurt him, for he had sent him off in a way as if he didn't want to be associated with him. He could still hear the gendarme's farewell and, without knowing why, he felt strangely empty and vulnerable. At that moment, from the other side of the schoolhouse, the prisoner coughed. Daru listened to him almost despite himself and then, furious, threw a pebble that whistled through the air before sinking into the snow. That man's stupid crime revolted him, but to hand him over was contrary to honor. Merely thinking of it made him smart with humiliation. And he cursed at one and the same time his own people who had sent him this Arab and the Arab too who had dared to kill and not managed to get away. Daru got up, walked in a circle on the terrace, waited motionless, and then went back into the schoolhouse.

The Arab, leaning over the cement floor of the shed, was washing his teeth with two fingers. Daru looked at him and said: "Come." He went back into the room ahead of the prisoner. He slipped a hunting-jacket on over his sweater and put on walking-shoes. Standing, he waited until the Arab had put on his *chèche* and sandals. They went into the classroom and the schoolmaster pointed to the exit, saying: "Go ahead." The fellow didn't budge. "I'm coming," said Daru. The Arab went out. Daru went back into the room and made a package of pieces of rusk, dates, and sugar. In the classroom, before going out, he hesitated a second in front of his desk, then crossed the threshold and locked the door. "That's the way," he said. He started toward the east, followed by the prisoner. But, a short distance from the schoolhouse, he thought he heard a slight sound behind them. He retraced his steps and examined the surroundings of the house; there was no one there. The Arab watched him without seeming to understand. "Come on," said Daru.

They walked for an hour and rested beside a sharp peak of limestone. The snow was melting faster and faster and the sun was drinking up the puddles at once, rapidly cleaning the plateau, which gradually dried and vibrated like the air itself. When they resumed walking, the ground rang under their feet. From time to time a bird rent the space in front of them with a joyful cry. Daru breathed in deeply the fresh morning light. He felt a sort of rapture before the vast familiar expanse, now almost entirely yellow under its dome of blue sky. They walked an hour more, descending toward the south. They reached a level height made up of crumbly rocks. From there on, the plateau sloped down, eastward, toward a low plain where there were a few spindly trees and, to the south, toward outcroppings of rock that gave the landscape a chaotic look.

Daru surveyed the two directions. There was nothing but the sky on the horizon. Not a man could be seen. He turned toward the Arab, who was looking at him blankly. Daru held out the package to him. "Take it," he said. "There are dates, bread, and sugar. You can hold out for two days. Here are a thousand francs too." The Arab took the package and the money but kept his full hands at chest level as if he didn't know what to do with what was being given him. "Now look," the schoolmaster said as he pointed in the direction of the east, "there's the way to Tinguit. You have a two-hour walk. At Tinguit you'll find the administration and the police. They are expecting you." The Arab looked toward the east, still holding the package and the money against his chest. Daru took his elbow and turned him rather roughly toward the south. At the foot of the height on which they stood could be seen a faint path. "That's the trail across the plateau. In a day's walk from here you'll find pasturelands and the first nomads. They'll take you in and shelter you according to their law." The Arab had now turned toward Daru and a sort of panic was visible in his expression. "Listen," he said. Daru shook his head: "No, be quiet. Now I'm leaving you." He turned his back on him, took two long steps in the direction of the school, looked hesitantly at the motionless Arab, and started off again. For a few minutes he heard nothing but his own step resounding on the cold ground and did not turn his head. A moment later, however, he turned around. The Arab was still there on the edge of the hill, his arms hanging now, and he was looking at the schoolmaster. Daru felt something rise in his throat. But he swore with impatience, waved vaguely, and started off again. He had already gone some distance when he again stopped and looked. There was no longer anyone on the hill.

Daru hesitated. The sun was now rather high in the sky and was beginning to beat down on his head. The schoolmaster retraced his steps, at first somewhat uncertainly, then with decision. When he reached the little hill, he was bathed in sweat. He climbed it as fast as he could and stopped, out of breath, at the top. The rock-fields to the south stood out sharply against the blue sky, but on the plain to the east a steamy heat was already rising. And in that slight haze, Daru, with heavy heart, made out the Arab walking slowly on the road to prison.

A little later, standing before the window of the classroom, the schoolmaster was watching the clear light bathing the whole surface of the plateau, but he hardly saw it. Behind him on the blackboard, among the winding French rivers, sprawled the clumsily chalked-up words he had just read: "You handed over our brother. You will pay for this." Daru looked at the sky, the plateau, and, beyond, the invisible lands stretching all the way to the sea. In this vast landscape he had loved so much, he was alone.

QUESTIONS FOR DISCUSSION AND WRITING

1. The conflicts in this story arise from the choices Daru is forced to make. Which choice forms the climax of the story? Explain your answer.
2. How does Daru's request for an isolated post establish his character? What does Daru's attitude toward firearms reveal about him? How would Balducci characterize Daru and his motives?
3. In what ways do the three major characters differ in their understanding of their common environment?
4. Why does Camus choose a third-person omniscient rather than a first-person point of view for this story? How does this technique further emphasize Daru's isolation?
5. Why does Daru free the Arab to make his own choice? Has he, in fact, betrayed his "brother"? Explain your answer.

16

ETHAN CANIN

The Year of Getting to Know Us

ETHAN CANIN was born in 1960 in Ann Arbor, Michigan, and educated at Stanford University, the University of Iowa, and Harvard Medical School. Among the first to recognize Canin's talent was Danielle Steel, who taught at Canin's private school before her own novels began to sell widely. Her praise inspired Canin to write fiction throughout college and at the University of Iowa Writer's Workshop, where he drafted stories that were included in Houghton Mifflin's annual collection, *Best American Short Stories.* Despite this early success, Canin decided to pursue a more practical career in medicine. He was in the middle of exams when an editor from Houghton Mifflin called, suggesting that he publish a collection of his stories. *Emperor of the Air* (1988) became a best seller and Canin reclaimed his life as a writer. He continues to write stories for periodicals such as *The Atlantic Monthly* and *Esquire,*

and has published a novel, *Blue River* (1991). In "The Year of Getting to Know Us," reprinted from *Emperor of the Air,* a young man struggles to understand his relationship with his father. In "We Are Nighttime Travelers," from the same collection, an old man moves toward a reassessment of his relationship with his wife.

I told my father not to worry, that love is what matters, and that in the end, when he is loosed from his body, he can look back and say without blinking that he did all right by me, his son, and that I loved him.

And he said, "Don't talk about things you know nothing about."

We were in San Francisco, in a hospital room. IV tubes were plugged into my father's arms; little round Band-Aids were on his chest. Next to his bed was a table with a vase of yellow roses and a card that my wife, Anne, had brought him. On the front of the card was a photograph of a golf green. On the wall above my father's head an electric monitor traced his heartbeat. He was watching the news on a TV that stood in the corner next to his girlfriend, Lorraine. Lorraine was reading a magazine.

I was watching his heartbeat. It seemed all right to me: the blips made steady peaks and drops, moved across the screen, went out at one end, and then came back at the other. It seemed that this was all a heart could do. I'm an English teacher, though, and I don't know much about it.

"It looks strong," I'd said to my mother that afternoon over the phone. She was in Pasadena. "It's going right across, pretty steady. Big bumps. Solid."

"Is he eating all right?"

"I think so."

"Is *she* there?"

"Is Lorraine here, you mean?"

She paused. "Yes, Lorraine."

"No," I said. "She's not."

"Your poor father," she whispered.

I'm an only child, and I grew up in a big wood-frame house on Huron Avenue in Pasadena, California. The house had three empty bedrooms and in the back yard a section of grass that had been stripped and leveled, then seeded and mowed like a putting green. Twice a week a Mexican gardener came to trim it, wearing special moccasins my father had bought him. They had soft hide soles that left no imprints.

My father was in love with golf. He played seven times every week and talked about the game as if it were a science that he was about to figure out. "Cut through the outer rim for a high iron," he used to say at dinner, looking out the window into the yard while my mother passed him the carved-wood salad bowl, or "In hot weather hit a high-compression ball." When conversations paused, he made little putting motions with his hands. He was a top amateur and in another situation might have been a pro. When I was sixteen, the year I was arrested, he let me caddie for the first time. Before that all I knew about golf was his clubs—the Spalding made-to-measure woods and irons, Dynamiter sand wedge, St. Andrews putter—which he kept in an Abercrombie & Fitch bag in the trunk of his Lincoln, and the white leather shoes with long tongues and screw-in spikes, which he stored upside down in the hall closet. When he wasn't playing, he covered the club heads with socks that had little yellow dingo balls on the ends.

He never taught me to play. I was a decent athlete—could run, catch, throw a perfect spiral—but he never took me to the golf course. In the summer he played every day. Sometimes my mother asked if he would take me along with him. "Why should I?" he answered. "Neither of us would like it."

Every afternoon after work he played nine holes; he played eighteen on Saturday, and nine again on Sunday morning. On Sunday afternoon, at four o'clock, he went for a drive by himself in his white Lincoln Continental. Nobody was allowed to come with him on the drives. He was usually gone for a couple of hours. "Today I drove in the country," he would say at dinner, as he put out his cigarette, or "This afternoon I looked at the ocean," and we were to take from this that he had driven north on the coastal highway. He almost never said more, and across our blue-and-white tablecloth, when I looked at him, my silent father, I imagined in his eyes a pure gaze with which he read the waves and currents of the sea. He had made a fortune in business and owed it to being able to see the truth in any situation. For this reason, he said, he liked to drive with all the windows down. When he returned from his trips his face was red from the wind and his thinning hair lay fitfully on his head. My mother baked on Sunday afternoons while he was gone, walnut pies or macaroons that she prepared on the kitchen counter, which looked out over his putting green.

I teach English in a high school now, and my wife, Anne, is a journalist. I've played golf a half-dozen times in ten years and don't like it any more than most beginners, though the two or three times I've hit a drive that sails, that takes flight with its own power, I've felt something that I think must be unique to the game. These were the drives my father used to hit. Explosions off the tee, bird flights. But golf isn't my game, and it never has been, and I wouldn't think about it at all if not for my father.

Anne and I were visiting in California, first my mother, in Los Angeles, and then my father and Lorraine, north in Sausalito, and Anne suggested that I ask him to play nine holes one morning. She'd been wanting me to talk to him. It's part of the project we've started, part of her theory of what's wrong—although I don't think that much is. She had told me that twenty-five years changes things, and since we had the time, why not go out to California.

She said, "It's not too late to talk to him."

My best friend in high school was named Nickie Apple. Nickie had a thick chest and a voice that had been damaged somehow, made a little hoarse, and sometimes people thought he was twenty years old. He lived in a four-story house that had a separate floor for the kids. It was the top story, and his father, who was divorced and a lawyer, had agreed never to come up there. That was where we sat around after school. Because of the agreement, no parents were there, only kids. Nine or ten of us, usually. Some of them had slept the night on the big pillows that were scattered against the walls: friends of his older brothers', in Stetson hats and flannel shirts; girls I had never seen before.

Nickie and I went to Shrier Academy, where all the students carried around blue-and-gray notebooks embossed with the school's heraldic seal. SUMUS PRIMI the seal said. Our gray wool sweaters said it; our green exam books said it; the rear window decal my mother brought home said it. My father wouldn't put the sticker on the Lincoln, so she pressed in onto the window above her kitchen sink instead. PRIMI SUMUS I read whenever I washed my hands. At Shrier we learned Latin in the eighth grade and art history in the ninth, and in the tenth I started getting into some trouble. Little things: cigarettes, graffiti. Mr. Goldman, the student counselor, called my mother in for a premonition visit. "I have a premonition about Leonard," he told her in the counseling office one afternoon in the warm October when I was sixteen. The office was full of plants and had five floor-to-ceiling windows that let in sun like a greenhouse. They looked over grassy, bushless knolls. "I just have a feeling about him."

That October he started talking to me about it. He called me in and asked me why I was friends with Nickie Apple, a boy going nowhere. I was looking out the big windows, opening and closing my fists beneath the desk top. He said, "Lenny, you're a bright kid—what are you trying to tell us?" And I said, "Nothing. I'm not trying to tell you anything."

Then we started stealing, Nickie and I. He did it first, and took things I didn't expect: steaks, expensive cuts that we cooked on a grill by the window in the top story of his house; garden machinery; luggage. We didn't sell it and we didn't use it, but every afternoon we went someplace new. In November he distracted a store clerk and I took a necklace that we thought was diamonds. In December we went for a ride in someone else's car, and over Christmas vacation, when only gardeners were on the school grounds, we threw ten rocks, one by one, as if we'd paid for them at a carnival stand, through the five windows in Mr. Goldman's office.

"You look like a train station," I said to my father as he lay in the hospital bed. "All those lines coming and going everywhere."

He looked at me. I put some things down, tried to make a little bustle. I could see Anne standing in the hall just beyond the door.

"Are you comfortable, Dad?"

"What do you mean, 'comfortable'? My heart's full of holes, leaking all over the place. Am I comfortable? No, I'm dying."

"You're not dying," I said, and I sat down next to him. "You'll be swinging the five iron in two weeks."

I touched one of the tubes in his arm. Where it entered the vein, the needle disappeared under a piece of tape. I hated the sight of this. I moved the bedsheets a little bit, tucked them in. Anne had wanted me to be alone with him. She was in the hall, waiting to head off Lorraine.

"What's the matter with her?" he asked, pointing at Anne.

"She thought we might want to talk."

"What's so urgent?"

Anne and I had discussed it the night before. "Tell him what you feel," she said. "Tell him you love him." We were eating dinner in a fish restaurant. "Or if you don't love him, tell him you don't."

"Look, Pop," I said now.

"What?"

I was forty-two years old. We were in a hospital and he had tubes in his arms. All kinds of everything: needles, air, tape. I said it again.

"Look, Pop."

Anne and I have seen a counselor, who told me that I had to learn to accept kindness from people. He saw Anne and me together, then Anne alone, then me. Children's toys were scattered on the floor of his office. "You sound as if you don't want to let people near you," he said. "Right?"

"I'm a reasonably happy man," I answered.

I hadn't wanted to see the counselor. Anne and I have been married seven years, and sometimes I think the history of marriage can be written like this: People Want Too Much. Anne and I have suffered no plague; we sleep late two mornings a week; we laugh at most of the same things; we have a decent house in a suburb of Boston, where, after the commuter traffic has eased, a quiet descends and the world is at peace. She writes for a newspaper, and I teach the children of lawyers and insurance men. At times I'm alone, and need to be alone; at times she does too. But I can always count on a moment, sometimes once in a day, sometimes more, when I see her patting down the sheets on the bed, or watering the front window violets, and I am struck by the good fortune of my life.

Still, Anne says I don't feel things.

It comes up at dinner, outside in the yard, in airports as we wait for planes. You don't let yourself feel, she tells me; and I tell her that I think it's a crazy thing, all this talk about feeling. What do the African Bushmen say? They say, Will we eat tomorrow? Will there be rain?

When I was sixteen, sitting in the back seat of a squad car, the policeman stopped in front of our house on Huron Avenue, turned around against the headrest, and asked me if I was sure this was where I lived.

"Yes, sir," I said.

He spoke through a metal grate. "Your daddy owns this house?"

"Yes, sir."

"But for some reason you don't like windows."

He got out and opened my door, and we walked up the porch steps. The swirling lights on the squad car were making crazy patterns in the French panes of the living room bays. He knocked. "What's your daddy do?"

I heard lights snapping on, my mother moving through the house. "He's in business," I said. "But he won't be home now." The policeman wrote something on his notepad. I saw my mother's eye through the glass in the door, and then the locks were being unlatched, one by one, from the top.

When Anne and I came to California to visit, we stayed at my mother's for three days. On her refrigerator door was a calendar with men's names marked on it—dinner dates, theater—and I knew this was done for our benefit. My mother has been alone for fifteen years. She's still thin, and her eyes still water, and I noticed that books were lying open all through the house. Thick paperbacks—*Doctor Zhivago, The Thorn Birds*—in the bathroom and the studio and the bedroom. We never mentioned my father, but at the end of our stay, when we had packed the car for our drive north along the coast, after she'd hugged us both and we'd backed out of the driveway, she came down off the lawn into the street, her arms crossed over her chest, leaned into the window, and said, "You might say hello to your father for me."

We made the drive north on Highway 1. We passed mission towns, fields of butter lettuce, long stretches of pumpkin farms south of San Francisco. It was the first time we were going to see my father with Lorraine. She was a hairdresser. He'd met her a few years after coming north, and one of the first things they'd done together was take a trip around the world. We got postcards from the Nile delta and Bangkok. When I was young, my father had never taken us out of California.

His house in Sausalito was on a cliff above a finger of San Francisco Bay. A new Lincoln stood in the carport. In his bedroom was a teak-framed king-size waterbed, and on the walls were bits of African artwork—opium pipes, metal figurines. Lorraine looked the same age as Anne. One wall of the living room was glass, and after the first night's dinner, while we sat on the leather sofa watching tankers and yachts move under the Golden Gate Bridge, my father put down his Scotch and water, touched his jaw, and said, "Lenny, call Dr. Farmer."

It was his second one. The first had been two years earlier, on the golf course in Monterey, where he'd had to kneel, then sit, then lie down on the fairway.

At dinner the night after I was arrested, my mother introduced her idea. "We're going to try something," she said. She had brought out a chicken casserole, and it was steaming in front of her. "That's what we're going to do. Max, are you listening? This next year, starting tonight, is going to be the year of getting to know us better." She stopped speaking and dished my father some chicken.

"What do you mean?" I asked.

"I mean it will be to a small extent a theme year. Nothing that's going to change every day of our lives, but in this next year I thought we'd all make an attempt to get to know each other better. Especially you, Leonard. Dad and I are going to make a better effort to know you."

"I'm not sure what you mean," said my father.

"All kinds of things, Max. We'll go to movies together, and Lenny can throw a party here at the house. And I personally would like to take a trip, all of us together, to the American Southwest."

"Sounds all right to me," I said.

"And Max," she said, "you can take Lenny with you to play golf. For example." She looked at my father.

"Neither of us would like it," he said.

"Lenny never sees you."

I looked out the window. The trees were turning, dropping their leaves onto the putting green. I didn't care what he said, one way or the other. My mother spooned a chicken thigh onto my plate and covered it with sauce. "All right," my father said. "He can caddie."

"And as preparation for our trip," my mother said, "can you take him on your Sunday rides?"

My father took off his glasses. "The Southwest," he said, wiping the lenses with a napkin, "is exactly like any other part of the country."

Anne had an affair once with a man she met on an assignment. He was young, much younger than either of us—in his late twenties, I would say from the one time I saw him. I saw them because one day on the road home I passed Anne's car in the lot of a Denny's restaurant. I parked around the block and went in to surprise her. I took a table at the back, but from my seat in the corner I didn't realize for several minutes that the youngish-looking woman leaning forward and whispering to the man with a beard was my wife.

I didn't get up and pull the man out with me into the parking lot, or even join them at the table, as I have since thought might have been a good idea. Instead I sat and watched them. I could see that under the table they were holding hands. His back was to me, and I noticed that it was broad, as mine is not. I remember thinking that she probably liked this broadness. Other than that, though, I didn't feel very much. I ordered another cup of coffee just to hear myself talk, but my voice wasn't quavering or fearful. When the waitress left, I took out a napkin and wrote on it, "You are a forty-year-old man with no children and your wife is having an affair." Then I put some money on the table and left the restaurant.

"I think we should see somebody," Anne said to me a few weeks later. It was a Sunday morning, and we were eating breakfast on the porch.

"About what?" I asked.

On a Sunday afternoon when I was sixteen I went out to the garage with a plan my mother had given me. That morning my father had washed the Lincoln. He had detergent-scrubbed the finish and then sun-dried it on Huron Avenue, so that in the workshop light of the garage its highlights shone. The windshield molding, the grille, the chrome side markers, had been cloth-dried to erase water spots. The keys hung from their magnetic sling near the door to the kitchen. I took them out and opened the trunk. Then I hung them up again and sat on the rear quarter panel to consider what to do. It was almost four o'clock. The trunk of my father's car was large enough for a half-dozen suitcases and had been upholstered in a gray medium-pile carpet that was cut to hug the wheel wells and the spare-tire berth. In one corner, fastened down by straps, was his toolbox, and along the back lay the golf bag. In the shadows the yellow dingos of the club socks looked like baby chicks. He was going to come out in a few minutes. I reached in, took off four of the club socks, and made a pillow for my head. Then I stepped into the trunk. The shocks bounced once and stopped. I lay down with my head propped on the quarter panel and my feet resting in the taillight berth, and then I reached up, slammed down the trunk, and was in the dark.

This didn't frighten me. When I was very young, I liked to sleep with the shades drawn and the door closed so that no light entered my room. I used to hold my hand in front of my eyes and see if I could imagine its presence. It was too dark to see anything. I was blind then, lying in my bed, listening for every sound. I used to move my hand back and forth, close to my eyes, until I had the sensation that it was there but had in some way been amputated. I had heard of soldiers who had lost limbs but still felt them attached. Now I held my open hand before my eyes. It was dense black inside the trunk, colorless, without light.

When my father started the car, all the sounds were huge, magnified as if they were inside my own skull. The metal scratched, creaked, slammed when he got in; the bolt of the starter shook all the way through to the trunk; the idle rose and leveled; then the gears changed and the car lurched. I heard the garage door glide up. Then it curled into its housing, bumped once, began descending again. The seams of the trunk lid lightened in the sun. We were in the street now, heading downhill. I lay back and felt the road, listened to the gravel pocking in the wheel wells.

I followed our route in my mind. Left off Huron onto Telscher, where the car bottomed in the rain gulley as we turned, then up the hill to Santa Ana. As we waited for the light, the idle made its change, shifting down, so that below my head I heard the individual piston blasts in the exhaust pipe. Left on Santa Ana, counting the flat stretches where I felt my father tap the brakes, numbering the intersections as we headed west toward the ocean. I heard cars pull up next to us, accelerate, slow down, make turns. Bits of gravel echoed inside the quarter panels. I pulled off more club socks and enlarged my pillow. We slowed down, stopped, and then we accelerated, the soft piston explosions becoming a hiss as we turned onto the Pasadena freeway.

"Dad's rides," my mother had said to me the night before, as I lay in bed, "would be a good way for him to get to know you." It was the first week of the year of getting to know us better. She was sitting at my desk.

"But he won't let me go," I said.

"You're right." She moved some things around on a shelf. The room wasn't quite dark, and I could see the outline of her white blouse. "I talked to Mr. Goldman," she said.

"Mr. Goldman doesn't know me."

"He says you're angry." My mother stood up, and I watched her white blouse move to the window. She pulled back the shade until a triangle of light from the streetlamp fell on my sheets. "Are you angry?"

"I don't know," I said. "I don't think so."

"I don't think so either." She replaced the shade, came over and kissed me on the forehead, and then went out into the hall. In the dark I looked for my hand.

A few minutes later the door opened again. She put her head in. "If he won't let you come," she said, "sneak along."

On the freeway the thermal seams whizzed and popped in my ears. The ride had smoothed out now, as the shocks settled into the high speed, hardly dipping on curves, muffling everything as if we were under water. As far as I could tell, we were still driving west, toward the ocean. I sat halfway up and rested my back against the golf bag. I could see shapes now inside the trunk. When we slowed down and the blinker went on, I attempted bearings, but the sun was the same in all directions and the trunk lid was without shadow. We braked hard. I felt the car leave the freeway. We made turns. We went straight. Then more turns, and as we slowed down and I was stretching out, uncurling my body along the diagonal, we made a sharp right onto gravel and pulled over and stopped.

My father opened the door. The car dipped and rocked, shuddered. The engine clicked. Then the passenger door opened. I waited.

If I heard her voice today, twenty-six years later, I would recognize it.

"Angel," she said.

I heard the weight of their bodies sliding across the back seat, first hers, then his. They weren't three feet away. I curled up, crouched into the low space between the golf bag and the back of the passenger compartment. There were two firm points in the cushion where it was displaced. As I lay there, I went over the voice again in my head: it was nobody I knew. I heard a laugh from her, and then something low from him. I felt the shift of the trunk's false rear, and then, as I lay behind them, I heard the contact: the crinkle of clothing, arms wrapping, and the half-delicate, muscular sounds. It was like hearing a television in the next room. His voice once more, and then the rising of their breath, slow; a minute of this, maybe another; then shifting again, the friction of cloth on the leather seat and the car's soft rocking. "Dad," I whispered. Then rocking again; my father's sudden panting, harder and harder, his half-words. The car shook violently. "Dad," I whispered. I shouted, "Dad!"

The door opened.

His steps kicked up gravel. I heard jingling metal, the sound of the key in the trunk lock. He was standing over me in an explosion of light.

He said, "Put back the club socks."

I did and got out of the car to stand next to him. He rubbed his hands down the front of his shirt.

"What the hell," he said.

"I was in the trunk."

"I know," he said. "What the goddamn."

The year I graduated from college, I found a job teaching junior high school in Boston. The school was a cement building with small windows well up from the street, and dark classrooms in which I spent a lot of time maintaining discipline. In the middle of an afternoon that first winter a boy knocked on my door to tell me I had a phone call. I knew who it was going to be.

"Dad's gone," my mother said.

He'd taken his things in the Lincoln, she told me, and driven away that morning before dawn. On the kitchen table he'd left a note and some cash. "A lot of cash," my mother added, lowering her voice. "Twenty thousand dollars."

I imagined the sheaf of bills on our breakfast table, held down by the ceramic butter dish, the bank notes ruffling in the breeze from the louvered windows that opened onto his green. In the note he said he had gone north and would call her when he'd settled. It was December. I told my mother that I would visit in a week, when school was out for Christmas. I told her to go to her sister's and stay there, and then I said that I was working and had to get back to my class. She didn't say anything on the other end of the line, and in the silence I imagined my father crisscrossing the state of California, driving north, stopping in Palm Springs and Carmel, the Lincoln riding low with the weight.

"Leonard," my mother said, "did you know anything like this was happening?"

During the spring of the year of getting to know us better I caddied for him a few times. On Saturdays he played early in the morning, when the course was mostly empty and the grass was still wet from the night. I learned to fetch the higher irons as the sun rose over the back nine and the ball, on drying ground, rolled farther. He hit skybound approach shots with backspin, chips that bit into the green and stopped. He played in a foursome with three other men, and in the locker room, as they changed their shoes, they told jokes and poked one another in the belly. The lockers were shiny green metal, the floor clean white tiles that clicked under the shoe spikes. Beneath the mirrors were jars of combs in green disinfectant. When I combed my hair with them it stayed in place and smelled like limes.

We were on the course at dawn. At the first fairway the other men dug in their spikes, shifted their weight from leg to leg, dummy-swung at an empty tee while my father lit a cigarette and looked out over the hole. "The big gun," he said to me, or, if it was a par three, "The lady." He stepped on his cigarette. I wiped the head with the club sock before I handed it to him. When he took the club, he felt its balance point, rested it on one finger, and then, in slow motion, he gripped the shaft. Left hand first, then right, the fingers wrapping pinkie to index. Then he leaned down over the ball. On a perfect drive the tee flew straight up in the air and landed in front of his feet.

Over the weekend his heart lost its rhythm for a few seconds. It happened Saturday night, when Anne and I were at the house in Sausalito, and we didn't hear about it until Sunday. "Ventricular fibrillation," the intern said. "Circus movements." The condition was always a danger after a heart attack. He had been given a shock and his heartbeat had returned to normal.

"But I'll be honest with you," the intern said. We were in the hall. He looked down, touched his stethoscope. "It isn't a good sign."

The heart gets bigger as it dies, he told me. Soon it spreads across the x-ray. He brought me with him to a room and showed me strips of paper with the electric tracings: certain formations. The muscle was dying in patches, he said. He said things might get better, they might not.

My mother called that afternoon. "Should I come up?"

"He was a bastard to you," I said.

When Lorraine and Anne were eating dinner, I found the intern again. "I want to know," I said. "Tell me the truth." The intern was tall and thin, sick-looking himself. So were the other doctors I had seen around the place. Everything in that hospital was pale—the walls, the coats, the skin.

He said, "What truth?"

I told him that I'd been reading about heart disease. I'd read about EKGs, knew about the medicines—lidocaine, propranolol. I knew that the lungs filled up with water, that heart failure was death by drowning. I said, "The truth about my father."

The afternoon I had hidden in the trunk, we came home while my mother was cooking dinner. I walked up the path from the garage behind my father, watching the pearls of sweat on his neck. He was whistling a tune. At the door he kissed my mother's cheek. He touched the small of her back. She was cooking vegetables, and the steam had fogged up the kitchen windows and dampened her hair. My father sat down in the chair by the window and opened the newspaper. I thought of the way the trunk rear had shifted when he and the woman had moved into the back of the Lincoln. My mother was smiling.

"Well?" she said.

"What's for dinner?" I asked.

"Well?" she said again.

"It's chicken," I said. "Isn't it?"

"Max, aren't you going to tell me if anything unusual happened today?"

My father didn't look up from the newspaper. "Did anything unusual happen today?" he said. He turned the page, folded it back smartly. "Why don't you ask Lenny?"

She smiled at me.

"I surprised him," I said. Then I turned and looked out the window.

"I have something to tell you," Anne said to me one Sunday morning in the fifth year of our marriage. We were lying in bed. I knew what was coming.

"I already know," I said.

"What do you already know?"

"I know about your lover."

She didn't say anything.

"It's all right," I said.

It was winter. The sky was gray, and although the sun had risen only a few hours earlier, it seemed like late afternoon. I waited for Anne to say something more. We were silent for several minutes. Then she said, "I wanted to hurt you." She got out of bed and began straightening out the bureau. She pulled my sweaters from the drawer and refolded them. She returned all our shoes to the closet. Then she came back to the bed, sat down, and began to cry. Her back was toward me. It shook with her gasps, and I put my hand out and touched her. "It's all right," I said.

"We only saw each other a few times," she answered. "I'd take it back if I could. I'd make it never happen."

"I know you would."

"For some reason I thought I couldn't really hurt you."

She had stopped crying. I looked out the window at the tree branches hung low with snow. It didn't seem I had to say anything.

"I don't know why I thought I couldn't hurt you," she said. "Of course I can hurt you."

"I forgive you."

Her back was still toward me. Outside, a few snowflakes drifted up in the air.

"*Did* I hurt you?"

"Yes, you did. I saw you two in a restaurant."

"Where?"

"At Denny's."

"No," she said. "I mean, where did I hurt you?"

The night he died, Anne stayed awake with me in bed. "Tell me about him," she said.

"What about?"

"Stories. Tell me what it was like growing up, things you did together."

"We didn't do that much," I said. "I caddied for him. He taught me things about golf."

That night I never went to sleep. Lorraine was at a friend's apartment and we were alone in my father's empty house, but we pulled out the sheets anyway, and the two wool blankets, and we lay on the fold-out sofa in the den. I told stories about my father until I couldn't think of any more, and then I talked about my mother until Anne fell asleep.

In the middle of the night I got up and went into the living room. Through the glass I could see lights across the water, the bridges, Belvedere and San Francisco, ships. It was clear outside, and when I walked out to the cement carport the sky was lit with stars. The breeze moved inside my nightclothes. Next to the garage the Lincoln stood half-lit in the porch floodlight. I opened the door and got in. The seats were red leather and smelled of limes and cigarettes. I rolled down the window and took the key from the glove compartment. I thought of writing a note for Anne, but didn't. Instead I coasted down the driveway in neutral and didn't close the door or turn on the lights until the bottom of the hill, or start the engine until I had swung around the corner, so that the house was out of sight and the brine smell of the marina was coming through the open windows of the car. The pistons were almost silent.

I felt urgent, though I had no route in mind. I ran one stop sign, then one red light, and when I reached the ramp onto Highway 101, I squeezed the accelerator and felt the surge of the fuel-injected, computer-sparked V-8. The dash lights glowed. I drove south and crossed over the Golden Gate Bridge at seventy miles an hour, its suspension cables swaying in the wind and the span rocking slowly, ocean to bay. The lanes were narrow. Reflectors zinged when the wheels strayed. If Anne woke, she might come out to the living room and then check for me outside. A light rain began to fall. Drops wet my knees, splattered my cheek. I kept the window open and turned on the radio; the car filled up with wind and music. Brass sounds. Trumpets. Sounds that filled my heart.

The Lincoln drove like a dream. South of San Francisco the road opened up, and in the gulley of a shallow hill I took it up over a hundred. The arrow nosed rightward in the dash. Shapes flattened out. "Dad," I said. The wind sounds changed pitch. I said, "The year of getting to know us." Signposts and power poles were flying by. Only a few cars were on the road, and most moved over before I arrived. In the mirror I could see the faces as I passed. I went through San Mateo, Pacifica, Redwood City, until, underneath a concrete overpass, the radio began pulling in static and I realized that I might die at this speed. I slowed down. At seventy drizzle wandered in the windows again. At fifty-five the scenery stopped moving. In Menlo Park I got off the freeway.

It was dark still, and off the interstate I found myself on a road without streetlights. It entered the center of town and then left again, curving up into shallow hills. The houses were large on either side. They were spaced far apart, three and four stories tall, with white shutters or ornament work that shone in the perimeter of the Lincoln's headlamps. The yards were large, dotted with eucalyptus and laurel. Here and there a light was on. Sometimes I saw faces: someone on an upstairs balcony; a man inside the breakfast room, awake at this hour, peering through the glass to see what car could be passing. I drove slowly, and when I came to a high school with its low buildings and long athletic field I pulled over and stopped.

The drizzle had become mist. I left the headlights on and got out and stood on the grass. I thought, This is the night your father has passed. I looked up at the lightening sky. I said it, "This is the night your father has passed," but I didn't feel what I thought I would. Just the wind on my throat, the chill of the morning. A pickup drove by and flashed its lights at me on the lawn. Then I went to the trunk of the Lincoln, because this was what my father would have done, and I got out the golf bag. It was heavier than I remembered, and the leather was stiff in the cool air. On the damp sod I set up: dimpled white ball, yellow tee. My father would have swung, would have hit drives the length of the football field, high irons that disappeared into the gray sky, but as I stood there I didn't even take the clubs out of the bag. Instead I imagined his stance. I pictured the even weight, the deliberate grip, and after I had stood there for a few moments, I picked up the ball and tee, replaced them in the bag, and drove home to my wife.

The year I was sixteen we never made it to the American Southwest. My mother bought maps anyway, and planned our trip, talking to me about it at night in the dark, taking us in her mind across the Colorado River at the California border, where the water was opal green, into Arizona and along the stretch of desert highway to New Mexico. There, she said, the canyons were a mile deep. The road was lined with sagebrush and a type of cactus, jumping cholla, that launched its spines. Above the desert, where a man could die of dehydration in an afternoon and a morning, the peaks of the Rocky Mountains turned blue with sun and ice.

We didn't ever go. Every weekend my father played golf, and at last, in August, my parents agreed to a compromise. One Sunday morning, before I started the eleventh grade, we drove north in the Lincoln to a state park along the ocean. Above the shore the cliffs were planted with ice plant to resist erosion. Pelicans soared in the thermal currents. My mother had made chicken sandwiches, which we ate on the beach, and after lunch, while I looked at the crabs and swaying fronds in the tide pools, my parents walked to the base of the cliffs. I watched their progress on the shallow dunes. Once when I looked, my father was holding her in his arms and they were kissing.

She bent backward in his hands. I looked into the tide pool where, on the surface, the blue sky, the clouds, the reddish cliffs, were shining. Below them rock crabs scurried between submerged stones. The afternoon my father found me in the trunk, he introduced me to the woman in the back seat. Her name was Christine. She smelled of perfume. The gravel drive where we had parked was behind a warehouse, and after we shook hands through the open window of the car, she got out and went inside. It was low and long, and the metal door slammed behind her. On the drive home, wind blowing all around us in the car, my father and I didn't say much. I watched his hands on the steering wheel. They were big and red-knuckled, the hands of a butcher or a carpenter, and I tried to imagine them on the bend of Christine's back.

Later that afternoon on the beach, while my mother walked along the shore, my father and I climbed a steep trail up the cliffs. From above, where we stood in the carpet of ice plant, we could see the hue of the Pacific change to a more translucent blue—the drop-off and the outline of the shoal where the breakers rose. I tried to see what my father was seeing as he gazed out over the water. He picked up a rock and tossed it over the cliff. "You know," he said without looking at me, "you could be all right on the course." We approached the edge of the palisade, where the ice plant thinned into eroded cuts of sand. "Listen," he said. "We're here on this trip so we can get to know each other a little bit." A hundred yards below us waves broke on the rocks. He lowered his voice. "But I'm not sure about that. Anyway, you don't *have* to get to know me. You know why?"

"Why?" I asked.

"You don't have to get to know me," he said, "because one day you're going to grow up and then you're going to *be* me." He looked at me and then out over the water. "So what I'm going to do is teach you how to hit." He picked up a long stick and put it in my hand. Then he showed me the backswing. "You've got to know one thing to drive a golf ball," he told me, "and that's that the club is part of you." He stood behind me and showed me how to keep the left arm still. "The club is your hand," he said. "It's your bone. It's your whole arm and your skeleton and your heart." Below us on the beach I could see my mother walking the waterline. We took cut after cut, and he taught me to visualize the impact, to sense it. He told me to whittle down the point of energy so that the ball would fly. When I swung he held my head in position. "Don't just watch," he said. "*See.*" I looked. The ice plant was watery-looking and fat, and at the edge of my vision I could see the tips of my father's shoes. I was sixteen years old and waiting for the next thing he would tell me.

QUESTIONS FOR DISCUSSION AND WRITING

1. How does the father's prophecy in the last paragraph—"You don't have to get to know me because one day you're going to grow up and then you're going to *be* me"—reveal the structure of the plot?
2. How is the narrator's description of his wife similar to his characterization of his mother? How does the narrator reveal that he is like his father?
3. How does the father control the setting in the story? How does the Lincoln act as both a setting and a symbol in the story?
4. How is the narrator's credibility challenged by what others—his mother, the two counselors, and his wife—say about him?
5. How many meanings—both literal and metaphorical—are implicit in the title of the story? What is the *year,* who are the *us,* and what does *know* mean?

17

ETHAN CANIN

We are Nighttime Travelers

Where are we going? Where, I might write, is this path leading us? Francine is asleep and I am standing downstairs in the kitchen with the door closed and the light on and a stack of mostly blank paper on the counter in front of me. My dentures are in a glass by the sink. I clean them with a tablet that bubbles in the water, and although they were clean already I just cleaned them again because the bubbles are agreeable and I thought their effervescence might excite me to action. By action, I mean I thought they might excite me to write. But words fail me.

This is a love story. However, its roots are tangled and involve a good bit of my life, and when I recall my life my mood turns sour and I am reminded that no man makes truly proper use of his time. We are blind and small-minded. We are dumb as snails and as frightened, full of vanity and misinformed about the importance of things. I'm an average man, without great deeds except maybe one, and that has been to love my wife.

I have been more or less faithful to Francine since I married her. There has been one transgression—leaning up against a closet wall with a red-haired purchasing agent at a sales meeting once in Minneapolis twenty years ago; but she was buying auto upholstery and I was selling it and in the eyes of judgment this may bear a key weight. Since then, though, I have ambled on this narrow path of life bound to one woman. This is a triumph and a regret. In our current state of affairs it is a regret because in life a man is either on the uphill or on the downhill, and if he isn't procreating he is on the downhill. It is a steep downhill indeed. These days I am tumbling, falling headlong among the scrub oaks and boulders, tearing my knees and abrading all the bony parts of the body. I have given myself to gravity.

Francine and I are married now forty-six years, and I would be a bamboozler to say that I have loved her for any more than half of these. Let us say that for the last year I haven't; let us say this for the last ten, even. Time has made torments of our small differences and tolerance of our passions. This is our state of affairs. Now I stand by myself in our kitchen in the middle of the night; now I lead a secret life. We wake at different hours now, sleep in different corners of the bed. We like different foods and different music, keep our clothing in different drawers, and if it can be said that either of us has aspirations, I believe that they are to a different bliss. Also, she is healthy and I am ill. And as for conversation—that feast of reason, that flow of the soul—our house is silent as the bone yard.

Last week we did talk. "Frank," she said one evening at the table, "there is something I must tell you."

The New York game was on the radio, snow was falling outside, and the pot of tea she had brewed was steaming on the table between us. Her medicine and my medicine were in little paper cups at our places.

"Frank," she said, jiggling her cup, "what I must tell you is that someone was around the house last night."

I tilted my pills onto my hand. "Around the house?"

"Someone was at the window."

On my palm the pills were white, blue, beige, pink: Lasix, Diabinese, Slow-K, Lopressor. "What do you mean?"

She rolled her pills onto the tablecloth and fidgeted with them, made them into a line, then into a circle, then into a line again. I don't know her medicine so well. She's healthy, except for little things. "I mean," she said, "there was someone in the yard last night."

"How do you know?"

"Frank, will you really, please?"

"I'm asking how you know."

"I heard him," she said. She looked down. "I was sitting in the front room and I heard him outside the window."

"You heard him?"

"Yes."

"The front window?"

She got up and went to the sink. This is a trick of hers. At that distance I can't see her face.

"The front window is ten feet off the ground," I said.

"What I know is that there was a man out there last night, right outside the glass." She walked out of the kitchen.

"Let's check," I called after her. I walked into the living room, and when I got there she was looking out the window.

"What is it?"

She was peering out at an angle. All I could see was snow, blue-white.

"Footprints," she said.

I built the house we live in with my two hands. That was forty-nine years ago, when, in my foolishness and crude want of learning, everything I didn't know seemed like a promise. I learned to build a house and then I built one. There are copper fixtures on the pipes, sanded edges on the struts and queen posts. Now, a half-century later, the floors are flat as a billiard table but the man who laid them needs two hands to pick up a woodscrew. This is the diabetes. My feet are gone also. I look down at them and see two black shapes when I walk, things I can't feel. Black clubs. No connection with the ground. If I didn't look, I could go to sleep with my shoes on.

Life takes its toll, and soon the body gives up completely. But it gives up the parts first. This sugar in the blood: God says to me: "Frank Manlius—codger, man of prevarication and half-truth—I shall take your life from you, as from all men. But first—" But first! Clouds in the eyeball, a heart that makes noise, feet cold as uncooked roast. And Francine, beauty that she was—now I see not much more than the dark line of her brow and the intersections of her body: mouth and nose, neck and shoulders. Her smells have changed over the years so that I don't know what's her own anymore and what's powder.

We have two children, but they're gone now too, with children of their own. We have a house, some furniture, small savings to speak of. How Francine spends her day I don't know. This is the sad truth, my confession. I am gone past nightfall. She wakes early with me and is awake when I return, but beyond this I know almost nothing of her life.

I myself spend my days at the aquarium. I've told Francine something else, of course, that I'm part of a volunteer service of retired men, that we spend our days setting young businesses afoot: "Immigrants," I told her early on, "newcomers to the land." I said it was difficult work. In the evenings I could invent stories, but I don't, and Francine doesn't ask.

I am home by nine or ten. Ticket stubs from the aquarium fill my coat pocket. Most of the day I watch the big sea animals—porpoises, sharks, a manatee—turn their saltwater loops. I come late morning and move a chair up close. They are waiting to eat then. Their bodies skim the cool glass, full of strange magnifications. I think, if it is possible, that they are beginning to know me: this man—hunched at the shoulder, cataractic of eye, breathing through water himself—this man who sits and watches. I do not pity them. At lunchtime I buy coffee and sit in one of the hotel lobbies or in the cafeteria next door, and I read poems. Browning, Whitman, Eliot. This is my secret. It is night when I return home. Francine is at the table, four feet across from my seat, the width of two dropleaves. Our medicine is in cups. There have been three Presidents since I held her in my arms.

The cafeteria moves the men along, old or young, who come to get away from the cold. A half-hour for a cup, they let me sit. Then the manager is at my table. He is nothing but polite. I buy a pastry then, something small. He knows me—I have seen him nearly every day for months now—and by his slight limp I know he is a man of mercy. But business is business.

"What are you reading?" he asks me as he wipes the table with a wet cloth. He touches the saltshaker, nudges the napkins in their holder. I know what this means.

"I'll take a cranberry roll," I say. He flicks the cloth and turns back to the counter.

This is what:

> Shall I say, I have gone at dusk through narrow streets
> And watched the smoke that rises from the pipes
> Of lonely men in shirt-sleeves, leaning out of windows?

Through the magnifier glass the words come forward, huge, two by two. With spectacles, everything is twice enlarged. Still, though, I am slow to read it. In a half-hour I am finished, could not read more, even if I bought another roll. The boy at the register greets me, smiles when I reach him. "What are you reading today?" he asks, counting out the change.

The books themselves are small and fit in the inside pockets of my coat. I put one in front of each breast, then walk back to see the fish some more. These are the fish I know: the gafftopsail pompano, sixgill shark, the starry flounder with its upturned eyes, queerly migrated. He rests half-submerged in sand. His scales are platey and flat-hued. Of everything upward he is wary, of the silvery seabass and the bluefin tuna that pass above him in the region of light and open water. For a life he lies on the bottom of the tank. I look at him. His eyes are dull. They are ugly and an aberration. Above us the bony fishes wheel at the tank's corners. I lean forward to the glass. "*Platichthys stellatus,*" I say to him. The caudal fin stirs. Sand moves and resettles, and I see the black and yellow stripes. "Flatfish," I whisper, "we are, you and I, observers of this life."

"A man on our lawn," I say a few nights later in bed.

"Not just that."

I breathe in, breathe out, look up at the ceiling. "What else?"

"When you were out last night he came back."

"He came back."

"Yes."

"What did he do?"

"Looked in at me."

Later, in the early night, when the lights of cars are still passing and the walked dogs still jingle their collar chains out front, I get up quickly from bed and step into the hall. I move fast because this is still possible in short bursts and with concentration. The bed sinks once, then rises. I am on the landing and then downstairs without Francine waking. I stay close to the staircase joists.

In the kitchen I take out my almost blank sheets and set them on the counter. I write standing up because I want to take more than an animal's pose. For me this is futile, but I stand anyway. The page will be blank when I finish. This I know. The dreams I compose are the dreams of others, remembered bits of verse. Songs of greater men than I. In months I have written few more than a hundred words. The pages are stacked, sheets of different sizes.

If I could

one says.

It has never seemed

says another. I stand and shift them in and out. They are mostly blank, sheets from months of nights. But this doesn't bother me. What I have is patience.

Francine knows nothing of the poetry. She's a simple girl, toast and butter. I myself am hardly the man for it: forty years selling (anything—steel piping, heater elements, dried bananas). Didn't read a book except one on sales. Think victory, the book said. Think *sale.* It's a young man's bag of apples, though; young men in pants that nip at the waist. Ten years ago I left the Buick in the company lot and walked home, dye in my hair, cotton rectangles in the shoulders of my coat. Francine was in the house that afternoon also, the way she is now. When I retired we bought a camper and went on a trip. A traveling salesman retires, so he goes on a trip. Forty miles out of town the folly appeared to me, big as a balloon. To Francine, too. "Frank," she said in the middle of a bend, a prophet turning to me, the camper pushing sixty and rocking in the wind, trucks to our left and right big as trains—"Frank," she said, "these roads must be familiar to you."

So we sold the camper at a loss and a man who'd spent forty years at highway speed looked around for something to do before he died. The first poem I read was in a book on a table in a waiting room. My eyeglasses made half-sense of things.

> THESE
> are the desolate, dark weeks

I read

> when nature in its barrenness
> equals the stupidity of man.

Gloom, I thought, and nothing more, but then I reread the words, and suddenly there I was, hunched and wheezing, bald as a trout, and tears were in my eye. I don't know where they came from.

In the morning an officer visits. He has muscles, mustache, skin red from the cold. He leans against the door frame.

"Can you describe him?" he says.

"It's always dark," says Francine.

"Anything about him?"

"I'm an old woman. I can see that he wears glasses."

"What kind of glasses?"

"Black."

"Dark glasses?"

"Black glasses."

"At a particular time?"

"Always when Frank is away."

"Your husband has never been here when he's come?"

"Never."

"I see." He looks at me. This look can mean several things, perhaps that he thinks Francine is imagining. "But never at a particular time?"

"No."

"Well," he says. Outside on the porch his partner is stamping his feet. "Well," he says again. "We'll have a look." He turns, replaces his cap, heads out to the snowy steps. The door closes. I hear him say something outside.

"Last night—" Francine says. She speaks in the dark. "Last night I heard him on the side of the house."

We are in bed. Outside, on the sill, snow has been building since morning.

"You heard the wind."

"Frank." She sits up, switches on the lamp, tilts her head toward the window. Through a ceiling and two walls I can hear the ticking of our kitchen clock.

"I heard him climbing," she says. She has wrapped her arms about her own waist. "He was on the house. I heard him. He went up the drainpipe." She shivers as she says this. "There was no wind. He went up the drainpipe and then I heard him on the porch roof."

"Houses make noise."

"I heard him. There's gravel there."

I imagine the sounds, amplified by hollow walls, rubber heels on timber. I don't say anything. There is an arm's length between us, cold sheet, a space uncrossed since I can remember.

"I have made the mistake in my life of not being interested in enough people," she says then. "If I'd been interested in more people, I wouldn't be alone now."

"Nobody's alone," I say.

"I mean that if I'd made more of an effort with people I would have friends now. I would know the postman and the Giffords and the Kohlers, and we'd be together in this, all of us. We'd sit in each other's living rooms on rainy days and talk about the children. Instead we've kept to ourselves. Now I'm alone."

"You're not alone," I say.

"Yes, I am." She turns the light off and we are in the dark again. "You're alone, too."

My health has gotten worse. It's slow to set in at this age, not the violent shaking grip of death; instead—a slow leak, nothing more. A bicycle tire: rimless, thready, worn treadless already and now losing its fatness. A war of attrition. The tall camels of the spirit steering for the desert. One morning I realized I hadn't been warm in a year.

And there are other things that go, too. For instance, I recall with certainty that it was on the 23rd of April, 1945, that, despite German counteroffensives in the Ardennes, Eisenhower's men reached the Elbe; but I cannot remember whether I have visited the savings and loan this week. Also, I am unable to produce the name of my neighbor, though I greeted him yesterday in the street. And take, for example, this: I am at a loss to explain whole decades of my life. We have children and photographs, and there is an understanding between Francine and me that bears the weight of nothing less than half a century, but when I gather my memories they seem to fill no more than an hour. Where has my life gone?

It has gone partway to shoddy accumulations. In my wallet are credit cards, a license ten years expired, twenty-three dollars in cash. There is a photograph but it depresses me to look at it, and a poem, half-copied and folded into the billfold. The leather is pocked and has taken on the curve of my thigh. The poem is from Walt Whitman. I copy only what I need.

But of all things to do last, poetry is a barren choice. Deciphering other men's riddles while the world is full of procreation and war. A man should go out swinging an axe. Instead, I shall go out in a coffee shop.

But how can any man leave this world with honor? Despite anything he does, it grows corrupt around him. It fills with locks and sirens. A man walks into a store now and the microwaves announce his entry; when he leaves, they make electronic peeks into his coat pockets, his trousers. Who doesn't feel like a thief? I see a policeman now, any policeman, and I feel a fright. And the things I've done wrong in my life haven't been crimes. Crimes of the heart perhaps, but nothing against the state. My soul may turn black but I can wear white trousers at any meeting of men. Have I loved my wife? At one time, yes—in rages and torrents. I've been covered by the pimples of ecstasy and have rooted in the mud of despair; and I've lived for months, for whole years now, as mindless of Francine as a tree of its mosses.

And this is what kills us, this mindlessness. We sit across the tablecloth now with our medicines between us, little balls and oblongs. We sit, sit. This has become our view of each other, a tableboard apart. We sit.

"Again?" I say.

"Last night."

We are at the table. Francine is making a twisting motion with her fingers. She coughs, brushes her cheek with her forearm, stands suddenly so that the table bumps and my medicines move in the cup.

"Francine," I say.

The half-light of dawn is showing me things outside the window: silhouettes, our maple, the eaves of our neighbor's garage. Francine moves and stands against the glass, hugging her shoulders.

"You're not telling me something," I say.

She sits and makes her pills into a circle again, then into a line. Then she is crying.

I come around the table, but she gets up before I reach her and leaves the kitchen. I stand there. In a moment I hear a drawer open in the living room. She moves things around, then shuts it again. When she returns she sits at the other side of the table. "Sit down," she says. She puts two folded sheets of paper onto the table. "I wasn't hiding them," she says.

"What weren't you hiding?"

"These," she says. "He leaves them."

"He leaves them?"

"They say he loves me."

"Francine."

"They're inside the windows in the morning." She picks one up, unfolds it. Then she reads:

> Ah, I remember well (and how can I
> But evermore remember well) when first

She pauses, squint-eyed, working her lips. It is a pause of only faint understanding. Then she continues:

> Our flame began, when scarce we knew what was
> The flame we felt.

When she finishes she refolds the paper precisely. "That's it," she says. "That's one of them."

At the aquarium I sit, circled by glass and, behind it, the senseless eyes of fish. I have never written a word of my own poetry but can recite the verse of others. This is the culmination of a life. *Coryphaena hippurus,* says the plaque on the dolphin's tank, words more beautiful than any of my own. The dolphin circles, circles, approaches with alarming speed, but takes no notice of, if he even sees, my hands. I wave them in front of his tank. What must he think has become of the sea? He turns and his slippery proboscis nudges the glass. I am every part sore from life.

> Ah, silver shrine, here will I take my rest
> After so many hours of toil and quest,
> A famished pilgrim—saved by miracle.

There is nothing noble for either of us here, nothing between us, and no miracles. I am better off drinking coffee. Any fluid refills the blood. The counter boy knows me and later at the café he pours the cup, most of a dollar's worth. Refills are free but my heart hurts if I drink more than one. It hurts no different from a bone, bruised or cracked. This amazes me.

Francine is amazed by other things. She is mystified, thrown beam ends by the romance. She reads me the poems now at breakfast, one by one. I sit. I roll my pills. "Another came last night," she says, and I see her eyebrows rise. "Another this morning." She reads them as if every word is a surprise. Her tongue touches teeth, shows between lips. These lips are dry. She reads:

> Kiss me as if you made believe
> You were not sure, this eve,
> How my face, your flower, had pursed
> Its petals up

That night she shows me the windowsill, second story, rimmed with snow, where she finds the poems. We open the glass. We lean into the air. There is ice below us, sheets of it on the trellis, needles hanging from the drainwork.

"Where do you find them?"

"Outside," she says. "Folded, on the lip."

"In the morning?"

"Always in the morning."

"The police should know about this."

"What will they be able to do?"

I step away from the sill. She leans out again, surveying her lands, which are the yard's-width spit of crusted ice along our neighbor's chain link and the three maples out front, now lost their leaves. She peers as if she expects this man to appear. An icy wind comes inside. "Think," she says. "Think. He could come from anywhere."

One night in February, a month after this began, she asks me to stay awake and stand guard until the morning. It is almost spring. The earth has reappeared in patches. During the day, at the borders of yards and driveways, I see glimpses of brown—though I know I could be mistaken. I come home early that night, before dusk, and when darkness falls I move a chair by the window downstairs. I draw apart the outer curtain and raise the shade. Francine brings me a pot of tea. She turns out the light and pauses next to me, and as she does, her hand on the chair's backbrace, I am so struck by the proximity of elements—of the night, of the teapot's heat, of the sounds of water outside—that I consider speaking.

I want to ask her what has become of us, what has made our breathed air so sorry now, and loveless. But the timing is wrong and in a moment she turns and climbs the stairs. I look out into the night. Later, I hear the closet shut, then our bed creak.

There is nothing to see outside, nothing to hear. This I know. I let hours pass. Behind the window I imagine fish moving down to greet me: broomtail grouper, surfperch, sturgeon with their prehistoric rows of scutes. It is almost possible to see them. The night is full of shapes and bits of light. In it the moon rises, losing the colors of the horizon, so that by early morning it is high and pale. Frost has made a ring around it.

A ringed moon above, and I am thinking back on things. What have I regretted in my life? Plenty of things, mistakes enough to fill the car showroom, then a good deal of the back lot. I've been a man of gains and losses. What gains? My marriage, certainly, though it has been no knee-buckling windfall but more like a split decision in the end, a stock risen a few points since bought. I've certainly enjoyed certain things about the world, too. These are things gone over and over again by the writers and probably enjoyed by everybody who ever lived. Most of them involve air. Early morning air, air after a rainstorm, air through a car window. Sometimes I think the cerebrum is wasted and all we really need is the lower brain, which I've been told is what makes the lungs breathe and the heart beat and what lets us smell pleasant things. What about the poetry? That's another split decision, maybe going the other way if I really made a tally. It's made me melancholy in old age, sad when if I'd stuck with motor homes and the national league standings I don't think I would have been rooting around in regret and doubt at this point. Nothing wrong with sadness, but this is not the real thing—not the death of a child but the feelings of a college student reading *Don Quixote* on a warm afternoon before going out to the lake.

Now, with Francine upstairs, I wait for a night prowler. He will not appear. This I know, but the window glass is ill-blown and makes moving shadows anyway, shapes that change in the wind's rattle. I look out and despite myself am afraid.

Before me, the night unrolls. Now the tree leaves turn yellow in moonshine. By two or three, Francine sleeps, but I get up anyway and change into my coat and hat. The books weigh against my chest. I don gloves, scarf, galoshes. Then I climb the stairs and go into our bedroom, where she is sleeping. On the far side of the bed I see her white hair and beneath the blankets the uneven heave of her chest. I watch the bedcovers rise. She is probably dreaming at this moment. Though we have shared this bed for most of a lifetime I cannot guess what her dreams are about. I step next to her and touch the sheets where they lie across her neck.

"Wake up," I whisper. I touch her cheek, and her eyes open. I know this though I cannot really see them, just the darkness of their sockets.

"Is he there?"

"No."

"Then what's the matter?"

"Nothing's the matter," I say. "But I'd like to go for a walk."

"You've been outside," she says. "You saw him, didn't you?"

"I've been at the window."

"Did you see him?"

"No. There's no one there."

"Then why do you want to walk?" In a moment she is sitting aside the bed, her feet in slippers. "We don't ever walk," she says.

I am warm in all my clothing. "I know we don't," I answer. I turn my arms out, open my hands toward her. "But I would like to. I would like to walk in air that is so new and cold."

She peers up at me. "I haven't been drinking," I say. I bend at the waist, and though my head spins, I lean forward enough so that the effect is of a bow. "Will you come with me?" I whisper. "Will you be queen of this crystal night?" I recover from my bow, and when I look up again she has risen from the bed, and in another moment she has dressed herself in her wool robe and is walking ahead of me to the stairs.

Outside, the ice is treacherous. Snow has begun to fall and our galoshes squeak and slide, but we stay on the plowed walkway long enough to leave our block and enter a part of the neighborhood where I have never been. Ice hangs from the lamps. We pass unfamiliar houses and unfamiliar trees, street signs I have never seen, and as we walk the night begins to change. It is becoming liquor. The snow is banked on either side of the walk, plowed into hillocks at the corners. My hands are warming from the exertion. They are the hands of a younger man now, someone else's fingers in my gloves. They tingle. We take ten minutes to cover a block but as we move through this neighborhood my ardor mounts. A car approaches and I wave, a boatman's salute, because here we are together on these rare and empty seas. We are nighttime travelers. He flashes his headlamps as he passes, and this fills me to the gullet with celebration and bravery. The night sings to us. I am Bluebeard now, Lindbergh, Genghis Khan.

No, I am not.

I am an old man. My blood is dark from hypoxia, my breaths singsong from disease. It is only the frozen night that is splendid. In it we walk, stepping slowly, bent forward. We take steps the length of table forks. Francine holds my elbow.

I have mean secrets and small dreams, no plans greater than where to buy groceries and what rhymes to read next, and by the time we reach our porch again my foolishness has subsided. My knees and elbows ache. They ache with a mortal ache, tired flesh, the cartilage gone sandy with time. I don't have the heart for dreams. We undress in the hallway, ice in the ends of our hair, our coats stiff from cold. Francine turns down the thermostat. Then we go upstairs and she gets into her side of the bed and I get into mine.

It is dark. We lie there for some time, and then, before dawn, I know she is asleep. It is cold in our bedroom. As I listen to her breathing I know my life is coming to an end. I cannot warm myself. What I would like to tell my wife is this:

> What the
> imagination
> seizes
> as beauty must be truth. What holds you
> to what you see of me is
> that grasp alone.

But I do not say anything. Instead I roll in the bed, reach across, and touch her, and because she is surprised she turns to me.

When I kiss her the lips are dry, cracking against mine, unfamiliar as the ocean floor. But then the lips give. They part. I am inside her mouth, and there, still, hidden from the world, as if ruin had forgotten a part, it is wet—Lord! I have the feeling of a miracle. Her tongue comes forward. I do not know myself then, what man I am, who I lie with in embrace. I can barely remember her beauty. She touches my chest and I bite lightly on her lip, spread moisture to her cheek and then kiss there. She makes something like a sigh. "Frank," she says. "Frank." We are lost now in seas and deserts. My hand finds her fingers and grips them, bone and tendon, fragile things.

QUESTIONS FOR DISCUSSION AND WRITING

1. What are the major conflicts in this love story? How are they resolved?
2. How does the reader's view of Frank differ from his characterization of himself? How do the passages he quotes from the poems reveal his true character?
3. Why does Frank feel more at home in the aquarium and the cafeteria than in the house he built with his own hands?
4. What details convince us that we are seeing the story from the perspective of an old man? How does the narrator's voice change during and after the walk?
5. Why does the narrator begin the story with the question "where are we going"? Is the question personal or universal? In what ways does the story answer the question?

18

RAYMOND CARVER

A Small, Good Thing

RAYMOND CARVER (1938–1988) was born in Clatskanie, Oregon, and educated at Humboldt State College (now Humboldt State University, Arcata). After further study at the University of Iowa, Carver worked briefly as an editor for Science Research Associates before accepting several positions as lecturer in creative writing at the University of California, Berkeley, the Writing Workshop at the University of Iowa, and the University of Texas at El Paso. In 1980 he became a Professor of English at Syracuse University. He died in the summer of 1988, at the age of 50, at his home in Port Angeles, Washington. He contributed poems and stories to many literary periodicals and such national magazines as *Esquire* and *Harper's.* His poems are collected in *Near Klamath* (1968), *Winter Insomnia* (1970), and *At Night the Salmon Move* (1976). Carver's stories, which received many awards, are collected in *Will You Please Be Quiet, Please?* (1976), *Furious Seasons* (1977),

What We Talk About When We Talk About Love (1981), _Cathedral_ (1983), _The Stories of Raymond Carver_ (1985), and _Where I'm Calling From,_ completed shortly before his death. In "A Small, Good Thing," reprinted from _Cathedral,_ Carver dramatizes the reactions of a mother and father when their son is struck down by a hit-and-run driver.

Saturday afternoon she drove to the bakery in the shopping center. After looking through a loose-leaf binder with photographs of cakes taped onto the pages, she ordered chocolate, the child's favorite. The cake she chose was decorated with a space ship and launching pad under a sprinkling of white stars, and a planet made of red frosting at the other end. His name, SCOTTY, would be in green letters beneath the planet. The baker, who was an older man with a thick neck, listened without saying anything when she told him the child would be eight years old next Monday. The baker wore a white apron that looked like a smock. Straps cut under his arms, went around in back and then to the front again, where they were secured under his heavy waist. He wiped his hands on his apron as he listened to her. He kept his eyes down on the photographs and let her talk. He let her take her time. He'd just come to work and he'd be there all night, baking, and he was in no real hurry.

She gave the baker her name, Ann Weiss, and her telephone number. The cake would be ready on Monday morning, just out of the oven, in plenty of time for the child's party that afternoon. The baker was not jolly. There were no pleasantries between them, just the minimum exchange of words, the necessary information. He made her feel uncomfortable, and she didn't like that. While he was bent over the counter with the pencil in his hand, she studied his coarse features and wondered if he'd ever done anything else with his life besides be a baker. She was a mother and thirty-three years old, and it seemed to her that everyone, especially someone the baker's age—a man old enough to be her father—must have children who'd gone through this special time of cakes and birthday parties. There must be that between them, she thought. But he was abrupt with her—not rude, just abrupt. She gave up trying to make friends with him. She looked into the back of the bakery and could see a long, heavy wooden table with aluminum pie pans stacked at one end; and beside the table a metal container filled with empty racks. There was an enormous oven. A radio was playing country-Western music.

The baker finished printing the information on the special order card and closed up the binder. He looked at her and said, "Monday morning." She thanked him and drove home.

On Monday morning, the birthday boy was walking to school with another boy. They were passing a bag of potato chips back and forth and the birthday boy was trying to find out what his friend intended to give him for his birthday that afternoon. Without looking, the birthday boy stepped off the curb at an intersection and was immediately knocked down by a car. He fell on his side with his head in the gutter and his legs out in the road. His eyes were closed, but his legs moved back and forth as if he were trying to climb over something. His friend dropped the potato chips and started to cry. The car had gone a hundred feet or so and stopped in the middle of the road. The man in the driver's seat looked back over his shoulder. He waited until the boy got unsteadily to his feet. The boy wobbled a little. He looked dazed, but okay. The driver put the car into gear and drove away.

The birthday boy didn't cry, but he didn't have anything to say about anything either. He wouldn't answer when his friend asked him what it felt like to be hit by a car. He walked home, and his friend went on to school. But after the birthday boy was inside his house and was telling his mother about it—she sitting beside him on the sofa, holding his hands in her lap, saying, "Scotty, honey, are you sure you feel all right, baby?" thinking she would call the doctor anyway—he suddenly lay back on the sofa, closed his eyes, and went limp. When she couldn't wake him up, she hurried to the telephone and called her husband at work. Howard told her to remain calm, remain calm, and then he called an ambulance for the child and left for the hospital himself.

Of course, the birthday party was canceled. The child was in the hospital with a mild concussion and suffering from shock. There'd been vomiting, and his lungs had taken in fluid which needed pumping out that afternoon. Now he simply seemed to be in a very deep sleep—but no coma, Dr. Francis had emphasized, no coma, when he saw the alarm in the parents' eyes. At eleven o'clock that night, when the boy seemed to be resting comfortably enough after the many X-rays and the lab work, and it was just a matter of his waking up and coming around, Howard left the hospital. He and Ann had been at the hospital with the child since that afternoon, and he was going home for a short while to bathe and change clothes. "I'll be back in an hour," he said. She nodded. "It's fine," she said. "I'll be right here." He kissed her on the forehead, and they touched hands. She sat in the chair beside the bed and looked at the child. She was waiting for him to wake up and be all right. Then she could begin to relax.

Howard drove home from the hospital. He took the wet, dark streets very fast, then caught himself and slowed down. Until now, his life had gone smoothly and to his satisfaction—college, marriage, another year of college for the advanced degree in business, a junior partnership in an investment firm. Fatherhood. He was happy and, so far, lucky—he knew that. His parents were still living, his brothers and his sister were established, his friends from college had gone out to take their places in the world. So far, he had kept away from any real harm, from those forces he knew existed and that could cripple or bring down a man if the luck went bad, if things suddenly turned. He pulled into the driveway and parked. His left leg began to tremble. He sat in the car for a minute and tried to deal with the present situation in a rational manner. Scotty had been hit by a car and was in the hospital, but he was going to be all right. Howard closed his eyes and ran his hand over his face. He got out of the car and went up to the front door. The dog was barking inside the house. The telephone rang and rang while he unlocked the door and fumbled for the light switch. He shouldn't have left the hospital, he shouldn't have. "Goddamn it!" he said. He picked up the receiver and said, "I just walked in the door!"

"There's a cake here that wasn't picked up," the voice on the other end of the line said.

"What are you saying?" Howard asked.

"A cake," the voice said. "A sixteen-dollar cake."

Howard held the receiver against his ear, trying to understand. "I don't know anything about a cake," he said. "Jesus, what are you talking about?"

"Don't hand me that," the voice said.

Howard hung up the telephone. He went into the kitchen and poured himself some whiskey. He called the hospital. But the child's condition remained the same; he was still sleeping and nothing had changed there. While water poured into the tub, Howard lathered his face and shaved. He'd just stretched out in the tub and closed his eyes when the telephone rang again. He hauled himself out, grabbed a towel, and hurried through the house, saying, "Stupid, stupid," for having left the hospital. But when he picked up the receiver and shouted, "Hello!" there was no sound at the other end of the line. Then the caller hung up.

He arrived back at the hospital a little after midnight. Ann still sat in the chair beside the bed. She looked up at Howard, and then she looked back at the child. The child's eyes stayed closed, the head was still wrapped in bandages. His breathing was quiet and regular. From an apparatus over the bed hung a bottle of glucose with a tube running from the bottle to the boy's arm.

"How is he?" Howard said. "What's all this?" waving at the glucose and the tube.

"Dr. Francis's orders," she said. "He needs nourishment. He needs to keep up his strength. Why doesn't he wake up, Howard? I don't understand, if he's all right."

Howard put his hand against the back of her head. He ran his fingers through her hair. "He's going to be all right. He'll wake up in a little while. Dr. Francis knows what's what."

After a time, he said, "Maybe you should go home and get some rest. I'll stay here. Just don't put up with this creep who keeps calling. Hang up right away."

"Who's calling?" she asked.

"I don't know who, just somebody with nothing better to do than call up people. You go on now."

She shook her head. "No," she said, "I'm fine."

"Really," he said. "Go home for a while, and then come back and spell me in the morning. It'll be all right. What did Dr. Francis say? He said Scotty's going to be all right. We don't have to worry. He's just sleeping now, that's all."

A nurse pushed the door open. She nodded at them as she went to the bedside. She took the left arm out from under the covers and put her fingers on the wrist, found the pulse, then consulted her watch. In a little while, she put the arm back under the covers and moved to the foot of the bed, where she wrote something on a clipboard attached to the bed.

"How is he?" Ann said. Howard's hand was a weight on her shoulder. She was aware of the pressure from his fingers.

"He's stable," the nurse said. Then she said, "Doctor will be in again shortly. Doctor's back in the hospital. He's making rounds right now."

"I was saying maybe she'd want to go home and get a little rest," Howard said. "After the doctor comes," he said.

"She could do that," the nurse said. "I think you should both feel free to do that, if you wish." The nurse was a big Scandinavian woman with blond hair. There was the trace of an accent in her speech.

"We'll see what the doctor says," Ann said. "I want to talk to the doctor. I don't think he should keep sleeping like this. I don't think that's a good sign." She brought her hand up to her eyes and let her head come forward a little. Howard's grip tightened on her shoulder, and then his hand moved up to her neck, where his fingers began to knead the muscles there.

"Dr. Francis will be here in a few minutes," the nurse said. Then she left the room.

Howard gazed at his son for a time, the small chest quietly rising and falling under the covers. For the first time since the terrible minutes after Ann's telephone call to him at his office, he felt a genuine fear starting in his limbs. He began shaking his head. Scotty was fine, but instead of sleeping at home in his own bed, he was in a hospital bed with bandages around his head and a tube in his arm. But this help was what he needed right now.

Dr. Francis came in and shook hands with Howard, though they'd just seen each other a few hours before. Ann got up from the chair. "Doctor?"

"Ann," he said and nodded. "Let's just first see how he's doing," the doctor said. He moved to the side of the bed and took the boy's pulse. He peeled back one eyelid and then the other. Howard and Ann stood beside the doctor and watched. Then the doctor turned back the covers and listened to the boy's heart and lungs with his stethoscope. He pressed his fingers here and there on the abdomen. When he was finished, he went to the end of the bed and studied the chart. He noted the time, scribbling something on the chart, and then looked at Howard and Ann.

"Doctor, how is he?" Howard said. "What's the matter with him exactly?"

"Why doesn't he wake up?" Ann said.

The doctor was a handsome, big-shouldered man with a tanned face. He wore a three-piece blue suit, a striped tie, and ivory cufflinks. His gray hair was combed along the sides of his head, and he looked as if he had just come from a concert. "He's all right," the doctor said. "Nothing to shout about, he could be better, I think. But he's all right. Still, I wish he'd wake up. He should wake up pretty soon." The doctor looked at the boy again. "We'll know some more in a couple of hours, after the results of a few more tests are in. But he's all right, believe me, except for the hairline fracture of the skull. He does have that."

"Oh, no," Ann said.

"And a bit of a concussion, as I said before. Of course, you know he's in shock," the doctor said. "Sometimes you see this in shock cases. This sleeping."

"But he's out of any real danger?" Howard said. "You said before he's not in a coma. You wouldn't call this a coma, then—would you, doctor?" Howard waited. He looked at the doctor.

"No, I don't want to call it a coma," the doctor said and glanced over at the boy once more. "He's just in a very deep sleep. It's a restorative measure the body is taking on its own. He's out of any real danger, I'd say that for certain, yes. But we'll know more when he wakes up and the other tests are in," the doctor said.

"It's a coma," Ann said. "Of sorts."

"It's not a coma yet, not exactly," the doctor said. "I wouldn't want to call it coma. Not yet, anyway. He's suffered shock. In shock cases, this kind of reaction is common enough; it's a temporary reaction to bodily trauma. Coma. Well, coma is a deep, prolonged unconsciousness, something that could go on for days, or weeks even. Scotty's not in that area, not as far as we can tell. I'm certain his condition will show improvement by morning. I'm betting that it will. We'll know more when he wakes up, which shouldn't be long now. Of course, you may do as you like, stay here or go home for a time. But by all means feel free to leave the hospital for a while if you want. This is not easy, I know." The doctor gazed at the boy again, watching him, and then he turned to Ann and said, "You try not to worry, little mother. Believe me, we're doing all that can be done. It's just a question of a little more time now." He nodded at her, shook hands with Howard again, and then he left the room.

Ann put her hands over the child's forehead. "At least he doesn't have a fever," she said. Then she said, "My God, he feels so cold, though. Howard? Is he supposed to feel like this? Feel his head."

Howard touched the child's temples. His own breathing had slowed. "I think he's supposed to feel this way right now," he said. "He's in shock, remember? That's what the doctor said. The doctor was just in here. He would have said something if Scotty wasn't okay."

Ann stood there a while longer, working her lip with her teeth. Then she moved over to her chair and sat down.

Howard sat in the chair next to her chair. They looked at each other. He wanted to say something else and reassure her, but he was afraid, too. He took her hand and put it in his lap, and this made him feel better, her hand being there. He picked up her hand and squeezed it. Then he just held her hand. They sat like that for a while, watching the boy and not talking. From time to time, he squeezed her hand. Finally, she took her hand away.

"I've been praying," she said.

He nodded.

She said, "I almost thought I'd forgotten how, but it came back to me. All I had to do was close my eyes and say, 'Please God, help us—help Scotty,' and the rest was easy. The words were right there. Maybe if you prayed, too," she said to him.

"I've already prayed," he said. "I prayed this afternoon—yesterday afternoon, I mean—after you called, while I was driving to the hospital. I've been praying," he said.

"That's good," she said. For the first time, she felt they were together in it, this trouble. She realized with a start that, until now, it had only been happening to her and to Scotty. She hadn't let Howard into it, though he was there and needed all along. She felt glad to be his wife.

The same nurse came in and took the boy's pulse again and checked the flow from the bottle hanging above the bed.

In an hour, another doctor came in. He said his name was Parsons, from Radiology. He had a bushy mustache. He was wearing loafers, a Western shirt, and a pair of jeans.

"We're going to take him downstairs for more pictures," he told them. "We need to do some more pictures, and we want to do a scan."

"What's that?" Ann said. "A scan?" She stood between this new doctor and the bed. "I thought you'd already taken all your X-rays."

"I'm afraid we need some more," he said. "Nothing to be alarmed about. We just need some more pictures, and we want to do a brain scan on him."

"My God," Ann said.

"It's perfectly normal procedure in cases like this," this new doctor said. "We just need to find out for sure why he isn't back awake yet. It's normal medical procedure, and nothing to be alarmed about. We'll be taking him down in a few minutes," this doctor said.

In a little while, two orderlies came into the room with a gurney. They were black-haired, dark-complexioned men in white uniforms, and they said a few words to each other in a foreign tongue as they unhooked the boy from the tube and moved him from his bed to the gurney. Then they wheeled him from the room. Howard and Ann got on the same elevator. Ann gazed at the child. She closed her eyes as the elevator began its descent. The orderlies stood at either end of the gurney without saying anything, though once one of the men made a comment to the other in their own language, and the other man nodded slowly in response.

Later that morning, just as the sun was beginning to lighten the windows in the waiting room outside the X-ray department, they brought the boy out and moved him back up to his room. Howard and Ann rode up on the elevator with him once more, and once more they took up their places beside the bed.

They waited all day, but still the boy did not wake up. Occasionally, one of them would leave the room to go downstairs to the cafeteria to drink coffee and then, as if suddenly remembering and feeling guilty, get up from the table and hurry back to the room. Dr. Francis came again that afternoon and examined the boy once more and then left after telling them he was coming along and could wake up at any minute now. Nurses, different nurses from the night before, came in from time to time. Then a young woman from the lab knocked and entered the room. She wore white slacks and a white blouse and carried a little tray of things which she put on the stand beside the bed. Without a word to them, she took blood from the boy's arm. Howard closed his eyes as the woman found the right place on the boy's arm and pushed the needle in.

"I don't understand this," Ann said to the woman.

"Doctor's orders," the young woman said. "I do what I'm told. They say draw that one, I draw. What's wrong with him, anyway?" she said. "He's a sweetie."

"He was hit by a car," Howard said. "A hit-and-run."

The young woman shook her head and looked again at the boy. Then she took her tray and left the room.

"Why won't he wake up?" Ann said. "Howard? I want some answers from these people."

Howard didn't say anything. He sat down again in the chair and crossed one leg over the other. He rubbed his face. He looked at his son and then he settled back in the chair, closed his eyes, and went to sleep.

Ann walked to the window and looked out at the parking lot. It was night, and cars were driving into and out of the parking lot with their lights on. She stood at the window with her hands gripping the sill, and knew in her heart that they were into something now, something hard. She was afraid, and her teeth began to chatter until she tightened her jaws. She saw a big car stop in front of the hospital and someone, a woman in a long coat, get into the car. She wished she were that woman and somebody, anybody, was driving her away from here to somewhere else, a place where she would find Scotty waiting for her when she stepped out of the car, ready to say *Mom* and let her gather him in her arms.

In a little while, Howard woke up. He looked at the boy again. Then he got up from the chair, stretched, and went over to stand beside her at the window. They both stared out at the parking lot. They didn't say anything. But they seemed to feel each other's insides now, as though the worry had made them transparent in a perfectly natural way.

The door opened and Dr. Francis came in. He was wearing a different suit and tie this time. His gray hair was combed along the sides of his head, and he looked as if he had just shaved. He went straight to the bed and examined the boy. "He ought to have come around by now. There's just no good reason for this," he said. "But I can tell you we're all convinced he's out of any danger. We'll just feel better when he wakes up. There's no reason, absolutely none, why he shouldn't come around. Very soon. Oh, he'll have himself a dilly of a headache when he does, you can count on that. But all of his signs are fine. They're as normal as can be."

"It is a coma, then?" Ann said.

The doctor rubbed his smooth cheek. "We'll call it that for the time being, until he wakes up. But you must be worn out. This is hard. I know this is hard. Feel free to go out for a bite," he said. "It would do you good. I'll put a nurse in here while you're gone if you'll feel better about going. Go and have yourselves something to eat."

"I couldn't eat anything," Ann said.

"Do what you need to do, of course," the doctor said. "Anyway, I wanted to tell you that all the signs are good, the tests are negative, nothing showed up at all, and just as soon as he wakes up he'll be over the hill."

"Thank you, doctor," Howard said. He shook hands with the doctor again. The doctor patted Howard's shoulder and went out.

"I suppose one of us should go home and check on things," Howard said. "Slug needs to be fed, for one thing."

"Call one of the neighbors," Ann said. "Call the Morgans. Anyone will feed a dog if you ask them to."

"All right," Howard said. After a while, he said, "Honey, why don't *you* do it? Why don't you go home and check on things, and then come back? It'll do you good. I'll be right here with him. Seriously," he said. "We need to keep up our strength on this. We'll want to be here for a while even after he wakes up."

"Why don't *you* go?" she said. "Feed Slug. Feed yourself."

"I already went," he said. "I was gone for exactly an hour and fifteen minutes. You go home for an hour and freshen up. Then come back."

She tried to think about it, but she was too tired. She closed her eyes and tried to think about it again. After a time, she said, "Maybe I *will* go home for a few minutes. Maybe if I'm not just sitting right here watching him every second, he'll wake up and be all right. You know? Maybe he'll wake up if I'm not here. I'll go home and take a bath and put on clean clothes. I'll feed Slug. Then I'll come back."

"I'll be right here," he said. "You go on home, honey. I'll keep an eye on things here." His eyes were bloodshot and small, as if he'd been drinking for a long time. His clothes were rumpled. His beard had come out again. She touched his face, and then she took her hand back. She understood he wanted to be by himself for a while, not have to talk or share his worry for a time. She picked her purse up from the nightstand, and he helped her into her coat.

"I won't be gone long," she said.

"Just sit and rest for a little while when you get home," he said. "Eat something. Take a bath. After you get out of the bath, just sit for a while and rest. It'll do you a world of good, you'll see. Then come back," he said. "Let's try not to worry. You heard what Dr. Francis said."

She stood in her coat for a minute trying to recall the doctor's exact words, looking for any nuances, any hint of something behind his words other than what he had said. She tried to remember if his expression had changed any when he bent over to examine the child. She remembered the way his features had composed themselves as he rolled back the child's eyelids and then listened to his breathing.

She went to the door, where she turned and looked back. She looked at the child, and then she looked at the father. Howard nodded. She stepped out of the room and pulled the door closed behind her.

She went past the nurses' station and down to the end of the corridor, looking for the elevator. At the end of the corridor, she turned to her right and entered a little waiting room where a Negro family sat in wicker chairs. There was a middle-aged man in a khaki shirt and pants, a baseball cap pushed back on his head. A large woman wearing a house-dress and slippers was slumped in one of the chairs. A teenaged girl in jeans, hair done in dozens of little braids, lay stretched out in one of the chairs smoking a cigarette, her legs crossed at the ankles. The family swung their eyes to Ann as she entered the room. The little table was littered with hamburger wrappers and Styrofoam cups.

"Franklin," the large woman said as she roused herself. "Is it about Franklin?" Her eyes widened. "Tell me now, lady," the woman said. "Is it about Franklin?" She was trying to rise from her chair, but the man had closed his hand over her arm.

"Here, here," he said. "Evelyn."

"I'm sorry," Ann said. "I'm looking for the elevator. My son is in the hospital, and now I can't find the elevator."

"Elevator is down that way, turn left," the man said as he aimed a finger.

The girl drew on her cigarette and stared at Ann. Her eyes were narrowed to slits, and her broad lips parted slowly as she let the smoke escape. The Negro woman let her head fall on her shoulder and looked away from Ann, no longer interested.

"My son was hit by a car," Ann said to the man. She seemed to need to explain herself. "He has a concussion and a little skull fracture, but he's going to be all right. He's in shock now, but it might be some kind of coma, too. That's what really worries us, the coma part. I'm going out for a little while, but my husband is with him. Maybe he'll wake up while I'm gone."

"That's too bad," the man said and shifted in the chair. He shook his head. He looked down at the table, and then he looked back at Ann. She was still standing there. He said, "Our Franklin, he's on the operating table. Somebody cut him. Tried to kill him. There was a fight where he was at. At this party. They say he was just standing and watching. Not bothering nobody. But that don't mean nothing these days. Now he's on the operating table. We're just hoping and praying, that's all we can do now." He gazed at her steadily.

Ann looked at the girl again, who was still watching her, and at the older woman, who kept her head down, but whose eyes were now closed. Ann saw the lips moving silently, making words. She had an urge to ask what those words were. She wanted to talk more with these people who were in the same kind of waiting she was in. She was afraid, and they were afraid. They had that in common. She would have liked to have said something else about the accident, told them more about Scotty, that it had happened on the day of his birthday, Monday, and that he was still unconscious. Yet she didn't know how to begin. She stood looking at them without saying anything more.

She went down the corridor the man had indicated and found the elevator. She waited a minute in front of the closed doors, still wondering if she was doing the right thing. Then she put out her finger and touched the button.

She pulled into the driveway and cut the engine. She closed her eyes and leaned her head against the wheel for a minute. She listened to the ticking sounds the engine made as it began to cool. Then she got out of the car. She could hear the dog barking inside the house. She went to the front door, which was unlocked. She went inside and turned on lights and put on a kettle of water for tea. She opened some dogfood and fed Slug on the back porch. The dog ate in hungry little smacks. It kept running into the kitchen to see that she was going to stay. As she sat down on the sofa with her tea, the telephone rang.

"Yes!" she said as she answered. "Hello!"

"Mrs. Weiss," a man's voice said. It was five o'clock in the morning, and she thought she could hear machinery or equipment of some kind in the background.

"Yes, yes! What is it?" she said. "This is Mrs. Weiss. This is she. What is it please?" She listened to whatever it was in the background. "Is it Scotty, for Christ's sake?"

"Scotty," the man's voice said. "It's about Scotty, yes. It has to do with Scotty, that problem. Have you forgotten about Scotty?" the man said. Then he hung up.

She dialed the hospital's number and asked for the third floor. She demanded information about her son from the nurse who answered the telephone. Then she asked to speak to her husband. It was, she said, an emergency.

She waited, turning the telephone cord in her fingers. She closed her eyes and felt sick at her stomach. She would have to make herself eat. Slug came in from the back porch and lay down near her feet. He wagged his tail. She pulled at his ear while he licked her fingers. Howard was on the line.

"Somebody just called here," she said. She twisted the telephone cord. "He said it was about Scotty," she cried.

"Scotty's fine," Howard told her. "I mean, he's still sleeping. There's been no change. The nurse has been in twice since you've been gone. A nurse or else a doctor. He's all right."

"This man called. He said it was about Scotty," she told him.

"Honey, you rest for a little while, you need the rest. It must be that same caller I had. Just forget it. Come back down here after you've rested. Then we'll have breakfast or something."

"Breakfast," she said. "I don't want any breakfast."

"You know what I mean," he said. "Juice, something. I don't know. I don't know anything, Ann. Jesus, I'm not hungry, either. Ann, it's hard to talk now. I'm standing here at the desk. Dr. Francis is coming again at eight o'clock this morning. He's going to have something to tell us then, something more definite. That's what one of the nurses said. She didn't know any more than that. Ann? Honey, maybe we'll know something more then. At eight o'clock. Come back here before eight. Meanwhile, I'm right here and Scotty's all right. He's still the same," he added.

"I was drinking a cup of tea," she said, "when the telephone rang. They said it was about Scotty. There was a noise in the background. Was there a noise in the background on that call you had, Howard?"

"I don't remember," he said. "Maybe the driver of the car, maybe he's a psychopath and found out about Scotty somehow. But I'm here with him. Just rest like you were going to do. Take a bath and come back by seven or so, and we'll talk to the doctor together when he gets here. It's going to be all right, honey. I'm here, and there are doctors and nurses around. They say his condition is stable."

"I'm scared to death," she said.

She ran water, undressed, and got into the tub. She washed and dried quickly, not taking the time to wash her hair. She put on clean underwear, wool slacks, and a sweater. She went into the living room, where the dog looked up at her and let its tail thump once against the floor. It was just starting to get light outside when she went out to the car.

She drove into the parking lot of the hospital and found a space close to the front door. She felt she was in some obscure way responsible for what had happened to the child. She let her thoughts move to the Negro family. She remembered the name Franklin and the table that was covered with hamburger papers, and the teenaged girl staring at her as she drew on her cigarette. "Don't have children," she told the girl's image as she entered the front door of the hospital. "For God's sake, don't."

She took the elevator up to the third floor with two nurses who were just going on duty. It was Wednesday morning, a few minutes before seven. There was a page for a Dr. Madison as the elevator doors slid open on the third floor. She got off behind the nurses, who turned in the other direction and continued the conversation she had interrupted when she'd gotten into the elevator. She walked down the corridor to the little alcove where the Negro family had been waiting. They were gone now, but the chairs were scattered in such a way that it looked as if people had just jumped up from them the minute before. The tabletop was cluttered with the same cups and papers, the ashtray was filled with cigarette butts.

She stopped at the nurses' station. A nurse was standing behind the counter, brushing her hair and yawning.

"There was a Negro boy in surgery last night," Ann said. "Franklin was his name. His family was in the waiting room. I'd like to inquire about his condition."

A nurse who was sitting at a desk behind the counter looked up from a chart in front of her. The telephone buzzed and she picked up the receiver, but she kept her eyes on Ann.

"He passed away," said the nurse at the counter. The nurse held the hairbrush and kept looking at her. "Are you a friend of the family or what?"

"I met the family last night," Ann said. "My own son is in the hospital. I guess he's in shock. We don't know for sure what's wrong. I just wondered about Franklin, that's all. Thank you." She moved down the corridor. Elevator doors the same color as the walls slid open and a gaunt, bald man in white pants and white canvas shoes pulled a heavy cart off the elevator. She hadn't noticed these doors last night. The man wheeled the cart out into the corridor and stopped in front of the room nearest the elevator and consulted a clipboard. Then he reached down and slid a tray out of the cart. He rapped lightly on the door and entered the room. She could smell the unpleasant odors of warm food as she passed the cart. She hurried on without looking at any of the nurses and pushed open the door to the child's room.

Howard was standing at the window with his hands behind his back. He turned around as she came in.

"How is he?" she said. She went over to the bed. She dropped her purse on the floor beside the nightstand. It seemed to her she had been gone a long time. She touched the child's face. "Howard?"

"Dr. Francis was here a little while ago," Howard said. She looked at him closely and thought his shoulders were bunched a little.

"I thought he wasn't coming until eight o'clock this morning," she said quickly.

"There was another doctor with him. A neurologist."

"A neurologist," she said.

Howard nodded. His shoulders were bunching, she could see that. "What'd they say, Howard? For Christ's sake, what'd they say? What is it?"

"They said they're going to take him down and run more tests on him, Ann. They think they're going to operate, honey. Honey, they *are* going to operate. They can't figure out why he won't wake up. It's more than just shock or concussion, they know that much now. It's in his skull, the fracture, it has something, something to do with that, they think. So they're going to operate. I tried to call you, but I guess you'd already left the house."

"Oh, God," she said. "Oh, please, Howard, please," she said, taking his arms.

"Look!" Howard said. "Scotty! Look, Ann!" He turned her toward the bed.

The boy had opened his eyes, then closed them. He opened them again now. The eyes stared straight ahead for a minute, then moved slowly in his head until they rested on Howard and Ann, then traveled away again.

"Scotty," his mother said, moving to the bed.

"Hey, Scott," his father said. "Hey, son."

They leaned over the bed. Howard took the child's hand in his hands and began to pat and squeeze the hand. Ann bent over the boy and kissed his forehead again and again. She put her hands on either side of his face. "Scotty, honey, it's Mommy and Daddy," she said. "Scotty?"

The boy looked at them, but without any sign of recognition. Then his mouth opened, his eyes scrunched closed, and he howled until he had no more air in his lungs. His face seemed to relax and soften then. His lips parted as his last breath was puffed through his throat and exhaled gently through the clenched teeth.

The doctors called it a hidden occlusion and said it was a one-in-a-million circumstance. Maybe if it could have been detected somehow and surgery undertaken immediately, they could have saved him. But more than likely not. In any case, what would they have been looking for? Nothing had shown up in the tests or in the X-rays.

Dr. Francis was shaken. "I can't tell you how badly I feel. I'm so very sorry, I can't tell you," he said as he led them into the doctors' lounge. There was a doctor sitting in a chair with his legs hooked over the back of another chair, watching an early-morning

TV show. He was wearing a green delivery-room outfit, loose green pants and green blouse, and a green cap that covered his hair. He looked at Howard and Ann and then looked at Dr. Francis. He got to his feet and turned off the set and went out of the room. Dr. Francis guided Ann to the sofa, sat down beside her, and began to talk in a low, consoling voice. At one point, he leaned over and embraced her. She could feel his chest rising and falling evenly against her shoulder. She kept her eyes open and let him hold her. Howard went into the bathroom, but he left the door open. After a violent fit of weeping, he ran water and washed his face. Then he came out and sat down at the little table that held a telephone. He looked at the telephone as though deciding what to do first. He made some calls. After a time, Dr. Francis used the telephone.

"Is there anything else I can do for the moment?" he asked them.

Howard shook his head. Ann stared at Dr. Francis as if unable to comprehend his words.

The doctor walked them to the hospital's front door. People were entering and leaving the hospital. It was eleven o'clock in the morning. Ann was aware of how slowly, almost reluctantly, she moved her feet. It seemed to her that Dr. Francis was making them leave when she felt they should stay, when it would be more the right thing to do to stay. She gazed out into the parking lot and then turned around and looked back at the front of the hospital. She began shaking her head. "No, no," she said. "I can't leave him here, no." She heard herself say that and thought how unfair it was that the only words that came out were the sort of words used on TV shows where people were stunned by violent or sudden deaths. She wanted her words to be her own. "No," she said, and for some reason the memory of the Negro woman's head lolling on the woman's shoulder came to her. "No," she said again.

"I'll be talking to you later in the day," the doctor was saying to Howard. "There are still some things that have to be done, things that have to be cleared up to our satisfaction. Some things that need explaining."

"An autopsy," Howard said.

Dr. Francis nodded.

"I understand," Howard said. Then he said, "Oh, Jesus. No, I don't understand, doctor. I can't, I can't. I just can't."

Dr. Francis put his arm around Howard's shoulders. "I'm sorry. God, how I'm sorry." He let go of Howard's shoulders and held out his hand. Howard looked at the hand, and then he took it. Dr. Francis put his arms around Ann once more. He seemed full of some goodness she didn't understand. She let her head rest on his shoulder, but her eyes stayed open. She kept looking at the hospital. As they drove out of the parking lot, she looked back at the hospital.

At home, she sat on the sofa with her hands in her coat pockets. Howard closed the door to the child's room. He got the coffee-maker going and then he found an empty box. He had thought to pick up some of the child's things that were scattered around the living room. But instead he sat down beside her on the sofa, pushed the box to one side, and leaned forward, arms between his knees. He began to weep. She pulled his head over into her lap and patted his shoulder. "He's gone," she said. She kept patting his shoulder. Over his sobs, she could hear the coffee-maker hissing in the kitchen. "There, there," she said tenderly. "Howard, he's gone. He's gone and now we'll have to get used to that. To being alone."

In a little while, Howard got up and began moving aimlessly around the room with the box, not putting anything into it, but collecting some things together on the floor at one end of the sofa. She continued to sit with her hands in her coat pockets. Howard put the box down and brought coffee into the living room. Later, Ann made calls to relatives. After each call had been placed and the party had answered, Ann would blurt out a few words and cry for a minute. Then she would quietly explain, in a measured voice, what had happened and tell them about arrangements. Howard took the box out to the garage, where he saw the child's bicycle. He dropped the box and sat down on the pavement beside the bicycle. He took hold of the bicycle awkwardly so that it leaned against his chest. He held it, the rubber pedal sticking into his chest. He gave the wheel a turn.

Ann hung up the telephone after talking to her sister. She was looking up another number when the telephone rang. She picked it up on the first ring.

"Hello," she said, and she heard something in the background, a humming noise. "Hello!" she said. "For God's sake," she said. "Who is this? What is it you want?"

"Your Scotty, I got him ready for you," the man's voice said. "Did you forget him?"

"You evil bastard!" she shouted into the receiver. "How can you do this, you evil son of a bitch?"

"Scotty," the man said. "Have you forgotten about Scotty?" Then the man hung up on her.

Howard heard the shouting and came in to find her with her head on her arms over the table, weeping. He picked up the receiver and listened to the dial tone.

Much later, just before midnight, after they had dealt with many things, the telephone rang again.

"You answer it," she said. "Howard, it's him, I know." They were sitting at the kitchen table with coffee in front of them. Howard had a small glass of whiskey beside his cup. He answered on the third ring.

"Hello," he said. "Who is this? Hello! Hello!" The line went dead. "He hung up," Howard said. "Whoever it was."

"It was him," she said. "That bastard. I'd like to kill him," she said. "I'd like to shoot him and watch him kick," she said.

"Ann, my God," he said.

"Could you hear anything?" she said. "In the background? A noise, machinery, something humming?"

"Nothing, really. Nothing like that," he said. "There wasn't much time. I think there was some radio music. Yes, there was a radio going, that's all I could tell. I don't know what in God's name is going on," he said.

She shook her head. "If I could, could get my hands on him." It came to her then. She knew who it was. Scotty, the cake, the telephone number. She pushed the chair away from the table and got up. "Drive me down to the shopping center," she said. "Howard."

"What are you saying?"

"The shopping center. I know who it is who's calling. I know who it is. It's the baker, the son-of-a-bitching baker, Howard. I had him bake a cake for Scotty's birthday.

That's who's calling. That's who has the number and keeps calling us. To harass us about that cake. The baker, that bastard."

They drove down to the shopping center. The sky was clear and stars were out. It was cold, and they ran the heater in the car. They parked in front of the bakery. All of the shops and stores were closed, but there were cars at the far end of the lot in front of the movie theater. The bakery windows were dark, but when they looked through the glass they could see a light in the back room and, now and then, a big man in an apron moving in and out of the white, even light. Through the glass, she could see the display cases and some little tables with chairs. She tried the door. She rapped on the glass. But if the baker heard them, he gave no sign. He didn't look in their direction.

They drove around behind the bakery and parked. They got out of the car. There was a lighted window too high up for them to see inside. A sign near the back door said THE PANTRY BAKERY, SPECIAL ORDERS. She could hear faintly a radio playing inside and something creak—an oven door as it was pulled down? She knocked on the door and waited. Then she knocked again, louder. The radio was turned down and there was a scraping sound now, the distinct sound of something, a drawer, being pulled open and then closed.

Someone unlocked the door and opened it. The baker stood in the light and peered out at them: "I'm closed for business," he said. "What do you want at this hour? It's midnight. Are you drunk or something?"

She stepped into the light that fell through the open door. He blinked his heavy eyelids as he recognized her. "It's you," he said.

"It's me," she said. "Scotty's mother. This is Scotty's father. We'd like to come in."

The baker said, "I'm busy now. I have work to do."

She had stepped inside the doorway anyway. Howard came in behind her. The baker moved back. "It smells like a bakery in here. Doesn't it smell like a bakery in here, Howard?"

"What do you want?" the baker said. "Maybe you want your cake? That's it, you decided you want your cake. You ordered a cake, didn't you?"

"You're pretty smart for a baker," she said. "Howard, this is the man who's been calling us." She clenched her fists. She stared at him fiercely. There was a deep burning inside her, an anger that made her feel larger than herself, larger than either of these men.

"Just a minute here," the baker said. "You want to pick up your three-day-old cake? That it? I don't want to argue with you, lady. There it sits over there, getting stale. I'll give it to you for half of what I quoted you. No. You want it? You can have it. It's no good to me, no good to anyone now. It cost me time and money to make that cake. If you want it, okay, if you don't, that's okay, too. I have to get back to work." He looked at them and rolled his tongue behind his teeth.

"More cakes," she said. She knew she was in control of it, of what was increasing in her. She was calm.

"Lady, I work sixteen hours a day in this place to earn a living," the baker said. He wiped his hands on his apron. "I work night and day in here, trying to make ends meet."

A look crossed Ann's face that made the baker move back and say, "No trouble, now." He reached to the counter and picked up a rolling pin with his right hand and began to tap it against the palm of his other hand. "You want the cake or not? I have to get back to work. Bakers work at night," he said again. His eyes were small, mean-looking, she thought, nearly lost in the bristly flesh around his cheeks. His neck was thick with fat.

"I know bakers work at night," Ann said. "They make phone calls at night, too. You bastard," she said.

The baker continued to tap the rolling pin against his hand. He glanced at Howard. "Careful, careful," he said to Howard.

"My son's dead," she said with a cold, even finality. "He was hit by a car Monday morning. We've been waiting with him until he died. But, of course, you couldn't be expected to know that, could you? Bakers can't know everything—can they, Mr. Baker? But he's dead. He's dead, you bastard!" Just as suddenly as it had welled in her, the anger dwindled, gave way to something else, a dizzy feeling of nausea. She leaned against the wooden table that was sprinkled with flour, put her hands over her face, and began to cry, her shoulders rocking back and forth. "It isn't fair," she said. "It isn't, isn't fair."

Howard put his hand at the small of her back and looked at the baker. "Shame on you," Howard said to him. "Shame."

The baker put the rolling pin back on the counter. He undid his apron and threw it on the counter. He looked at them, and then he shook his head slowly. He pulled a chair out from under the card table that held papers and receipts, an adding machine, and a telephone directory. "Please sit down," he said. "Let me get you a chair," he said to Howard. "Sit down now, please." The baker went into the front of the shop and returned with two little wrought-iron chairs. "Please sit down, you people."

Ann wiped her eyes and looked at the baker. "I wanted to kill you," she said. "I wanted you dead."

The baker had cleared a space for them at the table. He shoved the adding machine to one side, along with the stacks of notepaper and receipts. He pushed the telephone directory onto the floor, where it landed with a thud. Howard and Ann sat down and pulled their chairs up to the table. The baker sat down, too.

"Let me say how sorry I am," the baker said, putting his elbows on the table. "God alone knows how sorry. Listen to me. I'm just a baker. I don't claim to be anything else. Maybe once, maybe years ago, I was a different kind of human being. I've forgotten, I don't know for sure. But I'm not any longer, if I ever was. Now I'm just a baker. That don't excuse my doing what I did, I know. But I'm deeply sorry. I'm sorry for your son, and sorry for my part in this," the baker said. He spread his hands out on the table and turned them over to reveal his palms. "I don't have any children myself, so I can only imagine what you must be feeling. All I can say to you now is that I'm sorry. Forgive me, if you can," the baker said. "I'm not an evil man, I don't think. Not evil, like you said on the phone. You got to understand what it comes down to is I don't know how to act anymore, it would seem. Please," the man said, "let me ask you if you can find it in your hearts to forgive me?"

It was warm inside the bakery. Howard stood up from the table and took off his coat. He helped Ann from her coat. The baker looked at them for a minute and then nodded and got up from the table. He went to the oven and turned off some switches. He found cups and poured coffee from an electric coffee-maker. He put a carton of cream on the table, and a bowl of sugar.

"You probably need to eat something," the baker said. "I hope you'll eat some of my hot rolls. You have to eat and keep going. Eating is a small, good thing in a time like this," he said.

He served them warm cinnamon rolls just out of the oven, the icing still runny. He put butter on the table and knives to spread the butter. Then the baker sat down at the table with them. He waited. He waited until they each took a roll from the platter and began to eat. "It's good to eat something," he said, watching them. "There's more. Eat up. Eat all you want. There's all the rolls in the world in here."

They ate rolls and drank coffee. Ann was suddenly hungry, and the rolls were warm and sweet. She ate three of them, which pleased the baker. Then he began to talk. They listened carefully. Although they were tired and in anguish, they listened to what the baker had to say. They nodded when the baker began to speak of loneliness, and of the sense of doubt and limitation that had come to him in his middle years. He told them what it was like to be childless all these years. To repeat the days with the ovens endlessly full and endlessly empty. The party food, the celebrations he'd worked over. Icing knuckle-deep. The tiny wedding couples stuck into cakes. Hundreds of them, no, thousands by now. Birthdays. Just imagine all those candles burning. He had a necessary trade. He was a baker. He was glad he wasn't a florist. It was better to be feeding people. This was a better smell anytime than flowers.

"Smell this," the baker said, breaking open a dark loaf. "It's a heavy bread, but rich." They smelled it, then he had them taste it. It had the taste of molasses and coarse grains. They listened to him. They ate what they could. They swallowed the dark bread. It was like daylight under the flourescent trays of light. They talked on into the early morning, the high, pale cast of light in the windows, and they did not think of leaving.

QUESTIONS FOR DISCUSSION AND WRITING

1. How do the following scenes contribute to the development of the plot: the opening scene in the bakery, the scene at the hospital with the black family, and the final scene in the bakery?
2. What insight into character is revealed by Howard's associating the accident with the luck upon which his whole life has been based? How is Ann's character revealed through her relationship to Dr. Francis and his choice of words?
3. What details give us a sense of the reality of the hospital, the home, and the bakery?
4. Why does the narrator shift his point of view between Howard and Ann throughout the story? How does his objective approach emphasize their emotional ordeal?
5. In how many different ways does the title of the story suggest its themes? How are the themes developed in Ann and Howard's experience with the baker at the end of the story?

19

WILLA CATHER

Paul's Case

WILLA CATHER (1873–1947) was born in Gore, Virginia, but grew up in Red Cloud, Nebraska, the setting for some of her best-known fiction. After graduating from the University of Nebraska, Cather moved to Pittsburgh, Pennsylvania, working first as a journalist and then as a high-school teacher of English and Latin. During this period she was able to publish some of her poetry and stories in magazines, especially *McClure's.* In 1906 Cather joined the editorial staff of *McClure's,* eventually becoming managing editor. With the successful publication of her first novel, *Alexander's Bridge* (1912), Cather resigned her job to devote full time to her writing. Her next three novels, *O Pioneers!* (1913), *The Song of the Lark* (1915), and *My Antonia* (1918), concern her experience on the Nebraska frontier. In her later novels, Cather abandoned her autobiographical experiences to write about historical material such as the struggles of early Roman Catholic missionaries during the Mexican war in *Death Comes for the Archbishop* (1927) and the lives of settlers in eighteenth-century Quebec in *Shadows on the Rock* (1931). Cather's short stories have been collected in several volumes. "Paul's Case," reprinted from *Youth and the Bright Medusa* (1932), describes a young boy's doomed attempts to fulfill his romantic fantasies.

It was Paul's afternoon to appear before the faculty of the Pittsburgh High School to account for his various misdemeanors. He had been suspended a week ago, and his father had called at the Principal's office and confessed his perplexity about his son. Paul entered the faculty room suave and smiling. His clothes were a trifle outgrown, and the tan velvet on the collar of his open overcoat was frayed and worn; but for all that there was something of a dandy about him, and he wore an opal pin in his neatly knotted black four-in-hand, and a red carnation in his buttonhole. This latter adornment the faculty somehow felt was not properly significant of the contrite spirit befitting a boy under the ban of suspension.

Paul was tall for his age and very thin, with high, cramped shoulders and a narrow chest. His eyes were remarkable for a certain hysterical brilliancy, and he continually used them in a conscious, theatrical sort of way, peculiarly offensive in a boy. The pupils were abnormally large, as though he were addicted to belladonna, but there was a glassy glitter about them which that drug does not produce.

When questioned by the Principal as to why he was there, Paul stated, politely enough, that he wanted to come back to school. This was a lie, but Paul was quite accustomed to lying; found it, indeed, indispensable for overcoming friction. His teachers were asked to state their respective charges against him, which they did with such a rancor and aggrievedness as evinced that this was not a usual case. Disorder and impertinence were among the offenses named, yet each of his instructors felt that it was scarcely possible to put into words the real cause of the trouble, which lay in a sort of hysterically defiant manner of the boy's; in the contempt which they all knew he felt for them, and which he seemingly made not the least effort to conceal. Once, when he had been making a synopsis of a paragraph at the blackboard, his English teacher had stepped to his side and attempted to guide his hand. Paul had started back with a shudder and thrust his hands violently behind him. The astonished woman could scarcely have been more hurt and embarrassed had he struck at her. The insult was so involuntary and definitely personal as to be unforgettable. In one way and another, he had made all his teachers, men and women alike, conscious of the same feeling of physical aversion. In one class he habitually sat with his hand shading his eyes; in another he always looked out of the window during the recitation; in another had made a running commentary on the lecture, with humorous intent.

His teachers felt this afternoon that his whole attitude was symbolized by his shrug and his flippantly red carnation flower, and they fell upon him without mercy, his English teacher leading the pack. He stood through it smiling, his pale lips parted over his white teeth. (His lips were continually twitching, and he had a habit of raising his eyebrows that was contemptuous and irritating to the last degree.) Older boys than Paul had broken down and shed tears under that ordeal, but his set smile did not once desert him, and his only sign of discomfort was the nervous trembling of the fingers that toyed with the buttons of his overcoat, and an occasional jerking of the other hand which held his hat. Paul was always smiling, always glancing about him, seeming to feel that people might be watching him and trying to detect something. This conscious expression, since it was as far as possible from boyish mirthfulness, was usually attributed to insolence or "smartness."

As the inquisition proceeded, one of his instructors repeated an impertinent remark of the boy's, and the Principal asked him whether he thought that a courteous speech to make to a woman. Paul shrugged his shoulders slightly and his eyebrows twitched.

"I don't know," he replied. "I didn't mean to be polite or impolite, either. I guess it's a sort of way I have, of saying things regardless."

The Principal asked him whether he didn't think that a way it would be well to get rid of. Paul grinned and said he guessed so. When he was told that he could go, he bowed gracefully and went out. His bow was like a repetition of the scandalous red carnation.

His teachers were in despair, and his drawing master voiced the feeling of them all when he declared there was something about the boy which none of them understood. He added: "I don't really believe that smile of his comes altogether from insolence; there's something sort of haunted about it. The boy is not strong for one thing. There is something wrong about the fellow."

The drawing master had come to realize that, in looking at Paul, one saw only his white teeth and the forced animation of his eyes. One warm afternoon the boy had gone to sleep at his drawing-board, and his master had noted with amazement what a white, blue-veined face it was; drawn and wrinkled like an old man's about the eyes, the lips twitching even in his sleep.

His teachers left the building dissatisfied and unhappy; humiliated to have felt so vindictive toward a mere boy, to have uttered this feeling in cutting terms, and to have set each other on, as it were, in the gruesome game of intemperate reproach. One of them remembered having seen a miserable street cat set at bay by a ring of tormentors.

As for Paul, he ran down the hill whistling the Soldiers' Chorus from *Faust*, looking behind him now and then to see whether some of his teachers were not there to witness his light-heartedness. As it was now late in the afternoon and Paul was on duty that evening as usher at Carnegie Hall, he decided that he would not go home to supper. When he reached the concert hall, the doors were not yet open. It was chilly outside, and he decided to go up into the picture gallery—always deserted at this hour—where there were some of Raffelli's gay studies of Paris streets and an airy blue Venetian scene or two that always exhilarated him. He was delighted to find no one in the gallery but the old guard, who sat in the corner, a newspaper on his knee, a black patch over one eye and the other closed. Paul possessed himself of the place and walked confidently up and down, whistling under his breath. After a while he sat down before a blue Rico and lost himself. When he bethought him to look at his watch, it was after seven o'clock, and he rose with a start and ran downstairs, making a face at Augustus Caesar, peering out from the cast-room, and an evil gesture at the Venus of Milo as he passed her on the stairway.

When Paul reached the ushers' dressing-room, half a dozen boys were there already, and he began excitedly to tumble into his uniform. It was one of the few that at all approached fitting, and Paul thought it very becoming—though he knew the tight, straight coat accentuated his narrow chest, about which he was exceedingly sensitive. He was always excited while he dressed, twanging all over to the tuning of the strings and the preliminary flourishes of the horns in the music-room; but tonight he seemed quite beside himself, and he teased and plagued the boys until, telling him that he was crazy, they put him down on the floor and sat on him.

Somewhat calmed by his suppression, Paul dashed out to the front of the house to seat the early comers. He was a model usher. Gracious and smiling he ran up and down the aisles. Nothing was too much trouble for him; he carried messages and brought programs as though it were his greatest pleasure in life, and all the people in his section thought him a charming boy, feeling that he remembered and admired them. As the house filled, he grew more and more vivacious and animated, and the color came to his cheeks and lips. It was very much as though this were a great reception and Paul were the host. Just as the musicians came out to take their places, his English teacher arrived with checks for the seats which a prominent manufacturer had taken for the season. She betrayed some embarrassment when she handed Paul the tickets, and a *hauteur* which subsequently made her feel very foolish. Paul was startled for a moment, and had the feeling of wanting to put her out; what business had she here among all these fine people and gay colors? He looked her over and decided that she was not appropriately dressed and must be a fool to sit downstairs in such togs. The tickets had probably been sent to her out of kindness, he reflected, as he put down a seat for her, and she had about as much right to sit there as he had.

When the symphony began, Paul sank into one of the rear seats with a long sigh of relief, and lost himself as he had done before the Rico. It was not that symphonies, as such, meant anything in particular to Paul, but the first sight of the instruments seemed to free some hilarious spirit within him; something that struggled there like the Genius in the bottle found by the Arab fisherman. He felt a sudden zest of life; the lights danced before his eyes and the concert hall blazed into unimaginable splendor. When the soprano soloist came on, Paul forgot even the nastiness of his teacher's being there, and gave himself up to the peculiar intoxication such personages always had for him. The soloist chanced to be a German woman, by no means in her first youth, and the mother of many children; but she wore a satin gown and a tiara, and she had that indefinable air of achievement, that world-shine upon her, which always blinded Paul to any possible defects.

After a concert was over, Paul was often irritable and wretched until he got to sleep—and tonight he was even more than usually restless. He had the feeling of not being able to let down; of its being impossible to give up his delicious excitement which was the only thing that could be called living at all. During the last number he withdrew and, after hastily changing his clothes in the dressing-room, slipped out to the side door where the singer's carriage stood. Here he began pacing rapidly up and down the walk, waiting to see her come out.

Over yonder the Schenley, in its vacant stretch, loomed big and square through the fine rain, the windows of its twelve stories glowing like those of a lighted cardboard house under a Christmas tree. All the actors and singers of any importance stayed there when they were in Pittsburgh, and a number of the big manufacturers of the place lived there in the winter. Paul had often hung about the hotel, watching the people go in and out, longing to enter and leave schoolmasters and dull care behind him forever.

At last the singer came out, accompanied by the conductor, who helped her into her carriage and closed the door with a cordial *auf wiedersehen*—which set Paul to wondering whether she were not an old sweetheart of his. Paul followed the carriage over to the hotel, walking so rapidly as not to be far from the entrance when the singer alighted and disappeared behind the swinging glass doors which were opened by a Negro in a tall hat and a long coat. In the moment that the door was ajar, it seemed to Paul that he, too, entered. He seemed to feel himself go after her up the steps, into the warm, lighted building, into an exotic, a tropical world of shiny, glistening surfaces and basking ease. He reflected upon the mysterious dishes that were brought into the dining-room, the green bottles in buckets of ice, as he had seen them in the supper-party pictures of the Sunday supplement. A quick gust of wind brought the rain down with sudden vehemence, and Paul was startled to find that he was still outside in the slush of the gravel driveway; that his boots were letting in the water and his scanty overcoat was clinging wet about him; that the lights in front of the concert hall were out, and that the rain was driving in sheets between him and the orange glow of the windows above him. There it was, what he wanted—tangibly before him, like the fairy world of a Christmas pantomime; as the rain beat in his face, Paul wondered whether he were destined always to shiver in the black night outside, looking up at it.

He turned and walked reluctantly toward the car tracks. The end had to come sometime; his father in his night-clothes at the top of the stairs, explanations that did not explain, hastily improvised fictions that were forever tripping him up, his upstairs room and its horrible yellow wallpaper, the creaking bureau with the greasy plush collar-box, and over his painted wooden bed the pictures of George Washington and John Calvin, and the framed motto, 'Feed my Lambs,' which had been worked in red worsted by his mother, whom Paul could not remember.

Half an hour later, Paul alighted from the Negley Avenue car and went slowly down one of the side streets off the main thoroughfare. It was a highly respectable street, where all the houses were exactly alike, and where business men of moderate means begot and reared large families of children, all of whom went to Sabbath School and learned the shorter catechism, and were interested in arithmetic; all of whom were as exactly alike as their homes, and of a piece of the monotony in which they lived. Paul never went up Cordelia Street without a shudder of loathing. His home was next to the house of the Cumberland minister. He approached it tonight with the nerveless sense of defeat, the hopeless feeling of sinking back forever into ugliness and commonness that he had always had when he came home. The moment he turned into Cordelia Street he felt the waters close above his head. After each of these orgies of living, he experienced all the physical depression which follows a debauch; the loathing of respectable beds, of common food, of a house permeated by kitchen odors; a shuddering repulsion for the flavorless, colorless mass of every-day existence; a morbid desire for cool things and soft lights and fresh flowers.

The nearer he approached the house, the more absolutely unequal Paul felt to the sight of it all: his ugly sleeping chamber; the old bathroom with the grimy zinc tub, the cracked mirror, the dripping spigots; his father, at the top of the stairs, his hairy legs sticking out from his nightshirt, his feet thrust into carpet slippers. He was so much later than usual that there would certainly be enquiries and reproaches. Paul stopped short before the door. He felt that he could not be accosted by his father tonight; that he could not toss again on that miserable bed. He would not go in. He would tell his father that he had no carfare, and it was raining so hard he had gone home with one of the boys and stayed all night.

Meanwhile, he was wet and cold. He went around to the back of the house and tried one of the basement windows, found it open, and raised it cautiously, and scrambled down the cellar wall to the floor. There he stood, holding his breath, terrified by the noise he had made; but the floor above him was silent, and there was no creak on the stairs. He found a soap-box, and carried it over to the soft ring of light that streamed from the furnace door, and sat down. He was horribly afraid of rats, so he did not try to sleep, but sat looking distrustfully at the dark, still terrified lest he might have awakened his father.

In such reactions, after one of the experiences which made days and nights out of the dreary blanks of the calendar, when his senses were deadened, Paul's head was always singularly clear. Suppose his father had heard him getting in at the window and had come down and shot him for a burglar? Then, again, suppose his father had come down, pistol in hand, and he had cried out in time to save himself, and his father had been horrified to think how nearly he had killed him? Then again, suppose a day should come when his father would remember that night, and wish there had been no warning cry to stay his hand? With this last supposition Paul entertained himself until daybreak.

The following Sunday was fine; the sodden November chill was broken by the last flash of autumnal summer. In the morning Paul had to go to church and Sabbath School, as always. On seasonable Sunday afternoons the burghers of Cordelia Street usually sat out on their front "stoops," and talked to their neighbors on the next stoop, or called to those across the street in neighborly fashion. The men sat placidly on gay cushions placed upon the steps that led down to the sidewalk, while the women, in their Sunday "waists," sat in rockers on the cramped porches, pretending to be greatly at their ease. The children played in the streets; there were so many of them that the place resembled the recreation grounds of a kindergarten. The men on the steps, all in their shirt-sleeves, their vests unbuttoned, sat with their legs well apart, their stomachs comfortably protruding, and talked of the prices of things, or told anecdotes of the sagacity of their various chiefs and overlords. They occasionally looked over the multitude of squabbling children, listened affectionately to their high-pitched, nasal voices, smiling to see their own proclivities reproduced in their offspring, and interspersed their legends of the iron kings with remarks about their sons' progress at school, their grades in arithmetic, and the amounts they had saved in their toy banks.

On this last Sunday of November, Paul sat all afternoon on the lowest step of his "stoop," staring into the street, while his sisters, in their rockers, were talking to the minister's daughters next door about how many shirtwaists they had made in the last week, and how many waffles someone had eaten at the last church supper. When the weather was warm, and his father was in a particularly jovial frame of mind the girls made lemonade, which was always brought out in a red-glass pitcher, ornamented with forget-me-nots in blue enamel. This the girls thought very fine, and the neighbors joked about the suspicious color of the pitcher.

Today Paul's father, on the top step, was talking to a young man who shifted a restless baby from knee to knee. He happened to be the young man who was daily held up to Paul as a model, and after whom it was his father's dearest hope that he would pattern. This young man was of a ruddy complexion, with a compressed, red mouth, and faded, nearsighted eyes, over which he wore thick spectacles, with gold bows that curved about his ears. He was clerk to one of the magnates of a great steel corporation, and was looked upon in Cordelia Street as a young man with a future. There was a story that, some five years ago—he was now barely twenty-six—he had been a trifle "dissipated," but in order to curb his appetites and save the loss of time and strength that a sowing of wild oats might have entailed, he had taken his chief's advice, oft reiterated to his employees, and at twenty-one had married the first woman whom he could persuade to share his fortunes. She happened to be an angular schoolmistress, much older than he, who also wore thick glasses, and who had now borne him four children, all nearsighted like herself.

The young man was relating how his chief, now cruising in the Mediterranean, kept in touch with all the details of the business, arranging his office hours on his yacht just as though he were at home, and "knocking off work enough to keep two stenographers busy." His father told, in turn, the plan his corporation was considering, of putting in an electric railway plant at Cairo. Paul snapped his teeth; he had an awful apprehension that they might spoil it all before he got there. Yet he rather liked to hear these legends of the iron kings, that were told and retold on Sundays and holidays; these stories of palaces in Venice, yachts on the Mediterranean, and high play at Monte Carlo appealed to his fancy, and he was interested in the triumphs of cash-boys who had become famous, though he had no mind for the cash-boy stage.

After supper was over, and he had helped to dry the dishes, Paul nervously asked his father whether he could go to George's to get some help in his geometry, and still more nervously asked for carfare. This latter request he had to repeat, as his father, on principle, did not like to hear requests for money, whether much or little. He asked Paul whether he could not go to some boy who lived nearer, and told him that he ought not to leave his school work until Sunday; but he gave him the dime. He was not a poor man, but he had a worthy ambition to come up in the world. His only reason for allowing Paul to usher was that he thought a boy ought to be earning a little.

Paul bounded upstairs, scrubbed the greasy odor of the dishwater from his hands with the ill-smelling soap he hated, and then shook over his fingers a few drops of violet water from the bottle he kept hidden in his drawer. He left the house with his geometry conspicuously under his arm, and the moment he got out of Cordelia Street and boarded a downtown car, he shook off the lethargy of two deadening days, and began to live again.

The leading juvenile of the permanent stock company which played at one of the downtown theaters was an acquaintance of Paul's and the boy had been invited to drop in at the Sunday-night rehearsals whenever he could. For more than a year Paul had spent every available moment loitering about Charley Edwards's dressing-room. He had won a place among Edwards's following not only because the young actor, who could not afford to employ a dresser, often found him useful, but because he recognized in Paul something akin to what churchmen term "vocation."

It was at the theater and at Carnegie Hall that Paul really lived; the rest was but a sleep and a forgetting. This was Paul's fairy tale, and it had for him all the allurement of a secret love. The moment he inhaled the gassy, painty, dusty odor behind the scenes, he breathed like a prisoner set free, and felt within him the possibility of doing or saying splendid, brilliant things. The moment the cracked orchestra beat out the overture from *Martha*, or jerked at the serenade from *Rigoletto*, all stupid and ugly things slid from him, and his senses were deliciously, yet delicately fired.

Perhaps it was because, in Paul's world, the natural nearly always wore the guise of ugliness, that a certain element of artificiality seemed to him necessary in beauty. Perhaps it was because his experience of life elsewhere was so full of Sabbath-School picnics, petty economies, wholesome advice as to how to succeed in life, and the unescapable odors of cooking, that he found this existence so alluring, these smartly clad men and women so attractive, that he was so moved by these starry apple orchards that bloomed perennially under the limelight. It would be difficult to put it strongly enough how convincingly the stage entrance of the theater was for Paul the actual portal of Romance. Certainly none of the company ever suspected it, least of all Charley Edwards. It was very like the old stories that used to float about London of fabulously rich Jews, who had subterranean halls, with palms, and fountains, and soft lamps and richly appareled women who never saw the disenchanting light of London day. So, in the midst of that smoke-palled city, enamored of figures and grimy oil, Paul had his secret temple, his wishing-carpet, his bit of blue-and-white Mediterranean shore bathed in perpetual sunshine.

Several of Paul's teachers had a theory that his imagination had been perverted by garish fiction; but the truth was he scarcely ever read at all. The books at home were not such as would either tempt or corrupt a youthful mind, and as for reading the novels that some of his friends urged upon him—well, he got what he wanted much more quickly from music; any sort of music, from an orchestra to a barrel-organ. He needed only the spark, the indescribable thrill that made his imagination master of his senses, and he could make plots and pictures enough of his own. It was equally true that he was not stage-struck—not, at any rate, in the usual acceptation of the expression. He had no desire to become an actor, any more than he had to become a musician. He felt no necessity to do any of these things; what he wanted was to see, to be in the atmosphere, float on the wave of it, to be carried out, blue league after league, away from everything.

After a night behind the scenes, Paul found the schoolroom more than ever repulsive; the bare floors and naked walls; the prosy men who never wore frock coats, or violets in their buttonholes; the women with their dull gowns, shrill voices, and pitiful seriousness about prepositions that govern the dative. He could not bear to have the other pupils think, for a moment, that he took these people seriously; he must convey to them that he considered it all trivial, and was there only by way of a joke, anyway. He had autographed pictures of all the members of the stock company which he showed his classmates, telling them the most incredible stories of his familiarity with these people, of his acquaintance with the soloists who came to Carnegie Hall, his suppers with them and the flowers he sent them. When these stories lost their effect, and his audience grew listless, he would bid all the boys goodbye, announcing that he was going to travel for a while; going to Naples, to California, to Egypt. Then, next Monday, he would slip back, conscious and nervously smiling; his sister was ill, and he would have to defer his voyage until spring.

Matters went steadily worse with Paul at school. In the itch to let his instructors know how heartily he despised them, and how thoroughly he was appreciated elsewhere, he mentioned once or twice that he had no time to fool with theorems; adding—with a twitch of the eyebrows and a touch of that nervous bravado which so perplexed them—that he was helping the people down at the stock company; they were old friends of his.

The upshot of the matter was that the Principal went to Paul's father, and Paul was taken out of school and put to work. The manager at Carnegie Hall was told to get another usher in his stead; the doorkeeper at the theater was warned not to admit him to the house; and Charley Edwards remorsefully promised the boy's father not to see him again.

The members of the stock company were vastly amused when some of Paul's stories reached them—especially the women. They were hard-working women, most of them supporting indolent husbands or brothers, and they laughed rather bitterly at having stirred the boy to such fervid and florid inventions. They agreed with the faculty and with his father, that Paul's was a bad case.

The east-bound train was plowing through a January snowstorm; the dull dawn was beginning to show grey when the engine whistled a mile out of Newark. Paul started up from the seat where he had lain curled in uneasy slumber, rubbed the breath-misted window-glass with his hand, and peered out. The snow was whirling in curling eddies above the white bottom lands, and the drifts lay already deep in the fields and along the fences, while here and there the tall dead grass and dried weed stalks protruded black above it. Lights shone from the scattered houses, and a gang of laborers who stood beside the track waved their lanterns.

Paul had slept very little, and he felt grimy and uncomfortable. He had made the all-night journey in a day coach because he was afraid if he took a Pullman he might be seen by some Pittsburgh business man who had noticed him in Denny and Carson's office. When the whistle woke him, he clutched quickly at his breast pocket, glancing about him with an uncertain smile. But the little, clay-bespattered Italians were still sleeping, the slatternly women across the aisle were in open-mouthed oblivion, and even the crumby, crying babies were for the time stilled. Paul settled back to struggle with his impatience as best he could.

When he arrived at the Jersey City station, he hurried through his breakfast, manifestly ill at ease and keeping a sharp eye about him. After he reached the Twenty-Third Street station, he consulted a cabman, and had himself driven to a men's furnishing establishment which was just opening for the day. He spent upward of two hours there, buying with endless reconsidering and great care. His new street suit he put on in the fitting-room; the frock coat and dress clothes he had bundled into the cab with his new shirts. Then he drove to a hatter's and a shoe house. His next errand was at Tiffany's, where he selected silver-mounted brushes and a scarf-pin. He would not wait to have his silver marked, he said. Lastly, he stopped at a trunk shop on Broadway, and had his purchases packed into various traveling-bags.

It was a little after one o'clock when he drove up to the Waldorf, and, after settling with the cabman, went into the office. He registered from Washington; said his mother and father had been abroad, and that he had come down to await the arrival of their steamer. He told his story plausibly and had no trouble, since he offered to pay for them in advance, in engaging his rooms; a sleeping-room, sitting-room, and bath.

Not once, but a hundred times Paul had planned his entry into New York. He had gone over every detail of it with Charley Edwards, and in his scrapbook at home there were pages of description about New York hotels, cut from the Sunday papers.

When he was shown to his sitting-room on the eighth floor, he saw at a glance that everything was as it should be; there was but one detail in his mental picture that the place did not realize, so he rang for the bell-boy and sent him down for flowers. He moved about nervously until the boy returned, putting away his new linen and fingering it delightedly as he did so. When the flowers came, he put them hastily into water, and then tumbled into a hot bath. Presently he came out of his white bathroom, resplendent in his new silk underwear, and playing with the tassels of his red robe. The snow was whirling so fiercely outside his windows that he could scarcely see across the street; but within, the air was deliciously soft and fragrant. He put the violets and jonquils on the taboret beside the couch, and threw himself down with a long sigh, covering himself with a Roman blanket. He was thoroughly tired; he had been in such haste, he had stood up to such a strain, covered so much ground in the last twenty-four hours, that he wanted to think how it had all come about. Lulled by the sound of the wind, the warm air, and the cool fragrance of the flowers, he sank into deep, drowsy retrospection.

It had been wonderfully simple; when they had shut him out of the theater and concert hall, when they had taken away his bone, the whole thing was virtually determined.

The rest was a mere matter of opportunity. The only thing that at all surprised him was his own courage—for he realized well enough that he had always been tormented by fear, a sort of apprehensive dread which, of late years, as the meshes of the lies he had told closed about him, had been pulling the muscles of his body tighter and tighter. Until now, he could not remember a time when he had not been dreading something. Even when he was a little boy, it was always there—behind him, or before, or on either side. There had always been the shadowed corner, the dark place into which he dared not look, but from which something seemed always to be watching him—and Paul had done things that were not pretty to watch, he knew.

But now he had a curious sense of relief, as though he had at last thrown down the gauntlet to the thing in the corner.

Yet it was but a day since he had been sulking in the traces; but yesterday afternoon that he had been sent to the bank with Denny and Carson's deposit, as usual—but this time he was instructed to leave the book to be balanced. There was above two thousand dollars in checks, and nearly a thousand in the banknotes which he had taken from the book and quietly transferred to his pocket. At the bank he had made out a new deposit slip. His nerves had been steady enough to permit of his returning to the office, where he had finished his work and asked for a full day's holiday tomorrow, Saturday, giving a perfectly reasonable pretext. The bank book, he knew, would not be returned before Monday or Tuesday, and his father would be out of town for the next week. From the time he slipped the banknotes into his pocket until he boarded the night train for New York, he had not known a moment's hesitation.

How astonishingly easy it had all been; here he was, the thing done; and this time there would be no awakening, no figure at the top of the stairs. He watched the snowflakes whirling by his window until he fell asleep.

When he awoke, it was four o'clock in the afternoon. He bounded up with a start; one of his precious days gone already! He spent nearly an hour in dressing, watching every stage of his toilet carefully in the mirror. Everything was quite perfect; he was exactly the kind of boy he had always wanted to be.

When he went downstairs, Paul took a carriage and drove up Fifth Avenue toward the Park. The snow had somewhat abated; carriages and tradesmen's wagons were hurrying soundlessly to and fro in the winter twilight; boys in woolen mufflers were shoveling off the doorsteps; the Avenue stages made fine spots of color against the white street. Here and there on the corners whole flower gardens bloomed behind glass windows, against which the snowflakes stuck and melted; violets, roses, carnations, lilies-of-the-valley—somehow vastly more lovely and alluring that they blossomed thus unnaturally in the snow. The Park itself was a wonderful stage winterpiece.

When he returned, the pause of the twilight had ceased, and the tune of the streets had changed. The snow was falling faster, lights streamed from the hotels that reared their many stories fearlessly up into the storm, defying the raging Atlantic winds. A long, black stream of carriages poured down the Avenue, intersected here and there by other streams, tending horizontally. There were a score of cabs about the entrance of his hotel, and his driver had to wait. Boys in livery were running in and out of the awning stretched across the sidewalk, up and down the red velvet carpet laid from the door to the street. Above, about, within it all, was the rumble and roar, the hurry and toss of thousands of human beings as hot for pleasure as himself, and on every side of him towered the glaring affirmation of the omnipotence of wealth.

The boy set his teeth and drew his shoulders together in a spasm of realization; the plot of all dramas, the text of all romances, the nerve-stuff of all sensations was whirling about him like the snowflakes. He burnt like a fagot in a tempest.

When Paul came down to dinner, the music of the orchestra floated up the elevator shaft to greet him. As he stepped into the thronged corridor, he sank back into one of the chairs against the wall to get his breath. The lights, the chatter, the perfumes, the bewildering medley of color—he had, for a moment, the feeling of not being able to stand it. But only for a moment; these were his own people, he told himself. He went slowly about the corridors, through the writing-rooms, smoking-rooms, reception-rooms, as though he were exploring the chambers of an enchanted palace, built and peopled for him alone.

When he reached the dining-room he sat down at a table near a window. The flowers, the white linen, the many-colored wine-glasses, the gay toilettes of the women, the low popping of corks, the undulating repetitions of the "Blue Danube" from the orchestra, all flooded Paul's dream with bewildering radiance. When the roseate tinge of his champagne was added—that cold, precious, bubbling stuff that creamed and foamed in his glass—Paul wondered that there were honest men in the world at all. This was what all the world was fighting for, he reflected; this was what all the struggle was about. He doubted the reality of his past. Had he ever known a place called Cordelia Street, a place where fagged-looking business men boarded the early car? Mere rivets in a machine they seemed to Paul—sickening men, with combings of children's hair always hanging to their coats, and the smell of cooking in their clothes. Cordelia Street—Ah, that belonged to another time and country! Had he not always been thus, had he not sat here night after night, from as far back as he could remember, looking pensively over just such shimmering textures, and slowly twirling the stem of a glass like this one between his thumb and middle finger? He rather thought he had.

He was not in the least abashed or lonely. He had no especial desire to meet or to know any of these people; all he demanded was the right to look on and conjecture, to watch the pageant. The mere stage properties were all he contended for. Nor was he lonely later in the evening, in his loge at the Opera. He was entirely rid of his nervous misgivings, of his forced aggressiveness, of the imperative desire to show himself different from his surroundings. He felt now that his surroundings explained him. Nobody questioned the purple; he had only to wear it passively. He had only to glance down at his dress coat to reassure himself that here it would be impossible for anyone to humiliate him.

He found it hard to leave his beautiful sitting-room to go to bed that night, and sat long watching the raging storm from his turret window. When he went to sleep, it was with the lights turned on in his bedroom; partly because of his old timidity, and partly so that, if he should wake in the night, there would be no wretched moment of doubt, no horrible suspicion of yellow wallpaper, or of Washington and Calvin above his bed.

On Sunday morning the city was practically snowbound. Paul breakfasted late, and in the afternoon he fell in with a wild San Francisco boy, a freshman at Yale, who said he had run down for a "little flyer" over Sunday. The young man offered to show Paul the night side of the town, and the two boys went off together after dinner, not returning to the hotel until seven o'clock the next morning. They had started out in the confiding warmth of a champagne friendship, but their parting in the elevator was singularly cool. The freshman pulled himself together to make his train, and Paul went to bed. He awoke at two o'clock in the afternoon, very thirsty and dizzy, and rang for ice-water, coffee, and the Pittsburgh papers.

On the part of the hotel management, Paul excited no suspicion. There was this to be said for him, that he wore his spoils with dignity and in no way made himself conspicuous. His chief greediness lay in his ears and eyes, and his excesses were not offensive ones. His dearest pleasures were the grey winter twilights in his sitting-room; his quiet enjoyment of his flowers, his clothes, his wide divan, his cigarette, and his sense of power. He could not remember a time when he had felt so at peace with himself. The mere release from the necessity of petty lying, lying every day and every way, restored his self-respect. He had never lied for pleasure, even at school; but to make himself noticed and admired, to assert his difference from other Cordelia Street boys; and he felt a good deal more manly, more honest, even, now that he had no need for boastful pretensions, now that he could, as his actor friends used to say, "dress the part." It was characteristic that remorse did not occur to him. His golden days went by without a shadow, and he made each as perfect as he could.

On the eighth day after his arrival in New York, he found the whole affair exploited in the Pittsburgh papers, exploited with a wealth of detail which indicated that local news of a sensational nature was at a low ebb. The firm of Denny and Carson announced that the boy's father had refunded the full amount of his theft, and that they had no intention of prosecuting. The Cumberland minister had been interviewed, and expressed his hope of yet reclaiming the motherless lad, and Paul's Sabbath-School teacher declared that she would spare no effort to that end. The rumor had reached Pittsburgh that the boy had been seen in a New York hotel, and his father had gone East to find him and bring him home.

Paul had just come in to dress for dinner; he sank into the chair, weak in the knees, and clasped his head in his hands. It was to be worse than jail, even; the tepid waters of Cordelia Street were to close over him finally and forever. The grey monotony stretched before him in hopeless, unrelieved years;—Sabbath School, Young People's Meeting, the yellow-papered room, the damp dish-towels; it all rushed back upon him with sickening vividness. He had the old feeling that the orchestra had suddenly stopped, the sinking sensation that the play was over. The sweat broke out on his face, and he sprang to his feet, looked about him with his white, conscious smile, and winked at himself in the mirror. With something of the childish belief in miracles with which he had so often gone to class, all his lessons unlearned, Paul dressed and dashed whistling down the corridor to the elevator.

He had no sooner entered the dining-room and caught the measure of the music than his remembrance was lightened by his old elastic power of claiming the moment, mounting with it, and finding it all-sufficient. The glare and glitter about him, the mere scenic accessories had again, and for the last time, their old potency. He would show himself that he was game, he would finish the thing splendidly. He doubted, more than ever, the existence of Cordelia Street, and for the first time he drank his wine recklessly. Was he not, after all, one of these fortunate beings? Was he not still himself, and in his own place? He drummed a nervous accompaniment to the music and looked about him, telling himself over and over that it had paid.

He reflected drowsily, to the swell of the violin and the chill sweetness of his wine, that he might have done it more wisely. He might have caught an outbound steamer and been well out of their clutches before now. But the other side of the world had seemed too far away and too uncertain then; he could not have waited for it; his need had been too sharp. If he had to choose over again, he would do the same thing tomorrow. He looked affectionately about the dining-room, now gilded with a soft mist. Ah, it had paid indeed!

Paul was awakened next morning by a painful throbbing in his head and feet. He had thrown himself across the bed without undressing, and had slept with his shoes on. His limbs and hands were lead-heavy, and his tongue and throat were parched. There came upon him one of those fateful attacks of clear-headedness that never occurred except when he was physically exhausted and his nerves hung loose. He lay still and closed his eyes and let the tide of realities wash over him.

His father was in New York; "stopping at some joint or other," he told himself. The memory of successive summers on the front stoop fell upon him like a weight of black water. He had not a hundred dollars left; and he knew now, more than ever, that money was everything, the wall that stood between all he loathed and all he wanted. The thing was winding itself up; he had thought of that on his first glorious day in New York, and had even provided a way to snap the thread. It lay on his dressing-table now; he had got it out last night when he came blindly up from dinner—but the shiny metal hurt his eyes, and he disliked the look of it, anyway.

He rose and moved about with a painful effort, succumbing now and again to attacks of nausea. It was the old depression exaggerated; all the world had become Cordelia Street. Yet somehow he was not afraid of anything, was absolutely calm; perhaps because he had looked into the dark corner at last, and knew. It was bad enough, what he saw there; but somehow not so bad as his long fear of it had been. He saw everything clearly now. He had a feeling that he had made the best of it, that he had lived the sort of life he was meant to live, and for half an hour he sat staring at the revolver. But he told himself that was not the way, so he went downstairs and took a cab to the ferry.

When Paul arrived at Newark, he got off the train and took another cab, directing the driver to follow the Pennsylvania tracks out of town. The snow lay heavy on the roadways and had drifted deep in the open fields. Only here and there the dead grass or dried weed stalks projected, singularly black, above it.

Once well into the country, Paul dismissed the carriage and walked, floundering along the tracks, his mind a medley of irrelevant things. He seemed to hold in his brain an actual picture of everything he had seen that morning. He remembered every feature of both his drivers, the toothless old woman from whom he had bought the red flowers in his coat, the agent from whom he had got his ticket, and all of his fellow-passengers on the ferry. His mind, unable to cope with vital matters near at hand, worked feverishly and deftly at sorting and grouping these images. They made for him a part of the ugliness of the world, of the ache in his head, and the bitter burning on his tongue. He stopped and put a handful of snow into his mouth as he walked, but that, too, seemed hot. When he reached a little hillside, where the tracks ran through a cut some twenty feet below him, he stopped and sat down.

The carnations in his coat were drooping with cold, he noticed; their red glory over. It occurred to him that all the flowers he had seen in the show windows that first night must have gone the same way, long before this. It was only one splendid breath they had, in spite of their brave mockery at the winter outside the glass. It was a losing game in the end, it seemed, this revolt against the homilies by which the world is run. Paul took one of the blossoms carefully from his coat and scooped a little hole in the snow, where he covered it up. Then he dozed awhile, from his weak condition, seeming insensible to the cold.

The sound of an approaching train woke him and he started to his feet, remembering only his resolution, and afraid lest he should be too late. He stood watching the approaching locomotive, his teeth chattering, his lips drawn away from them in a frightened smile; once or twice he glanced nervously sidewise, as though he were being watched. When the right moment came, he jumped. As he fell, the folly of his haste occurred to him with merciless clearness, the vastness of what he had left undone. There flashed through his brain, clearer than ever before, the blue of Adriatic water, the yellow of Algerian sands.

He felt something strike his chest—his body being thrown swiftly through the air, on and on, immeasurably far and fast, while his limbs gently relaxed. Then, because the picture-making mechanism was crushed, the disturbing visions flashed into black, and Paul dropped back into the immense design of things.

QUESTIONS FOR DISCUSSION AND WRITING

1. How does the confrontation between Paul and his teachers set up the major conflicts which develop throughout the story?
2. What external evidence justifies a view of Paul as a "bad case"? How does this exterior view contrast with Cather's portrayal of Paul's interior world?
3. What does Pittsburgh and more particularly Cordelia Street represent for Paul? Why is it important that he escape this setting?
4. Why does Cather choose to tell Paul's story in the third person rather than allowing Paul to tell his own story? How does the story's title help explain Cather's decision?
5. What do carnations symbolize throughout the story? What particular significance do they have for Paul in the conclusion?

20

JOHN CHEEVER

The Swimmer

JOHN CHEEVER (1912–1982) was born in Quincy, Massachusetts, and attended Thayer Academy until he was expelled at the age of seventeen for being, according to his own account, a "quarrelsome, intractable and lousy student." He moved to New York City and began writing, publishing his first story, "Expelled," in *The New Republic* at the age of eighteen. For the next ten years, Cheever published his stories in magazines such as *Collier's, The Atlantic Monthly,* and *The New Yorker.* His first collection of stories, *The Way Some People Live,* was published in 1942. His next collection, *The Enormous Radio and Other Stories* (1953), established his reputation as one of America's most accomplished writers of short fiction. Cheever's first novel, *The Wapshot Chronicle* (1957), and its sequel, *The Wapshot Scandal* (1964), were critically acclaimed, as were subsequent novels such as *Bullet Park* (1969) and *Falconer* (1977). Despite these successes, Cheever will probably be remembered best for his short stories, superbly represented in *The Stories of John Cheever* (1978), which won the Pulitzer Prize. "The Swimmer," reprinted from *The Brigadier and the Golf Widow* (1964), examines the surfaces and realities of affluent suburbia.

It was one of those midsummer Sundays when everyone sits around saying, "I *drank* too much last night." You might have heard it whispered by the parishioners leaving church, heard it from the lips of the priest himself, struggling with his cassock in the *vestiarium,* heard it from the golf links and the tennis courts, heard it from the wildlife preserve where the leader of the Audubon group was suffering from a terrible hangover. "I *drank* too much," said Donald Westerhazy. "We all *drank* too much," said Lucinda Merrill. "It must have been the wine," said Helen Westerhazy. "I *drank* too much of that claret."

This was at the edge of the Westerhazys' pool. The pool, fed by an artesian well with a high iron content, was a pale shade of green. It was a fine day. In the west there was a massive stand of cumulus cloud so like a city seen from a distance—from the bow of an approaching ship—that it might have had a name. Lisbon. Hackensack. The sun was hot. Neddy Merrill sat by the green water, one hand in it, one around a glass of gin. He was a slender man—he seemed to have the especial slenderness of youth—and while he was far from young he had slid down his banister that morning and given the bronze backside of Aphrodite on the hall table a smack, as he jogged toward the smell of coffee in his dining room. He might have been compared to a summer's day, particularly the last hours of one, and while he lacked a tennis racket or a sail bag the impression was definitely one of youth, sport, and clement weather. He had been swimming and now he was breathing deeply, stertorously as if he could gulp into his lungs the components of that moment, the heat of the sun, the intenseness of his pleasure. It all seemed to flow into his chest. His own house stood in Bullet Park, eight miles to the south, where his four beautiful daughters would have had their lunch and might be playing tennis. Then it occurred to him that by taking a dogleg to the southwest he could reach his home by water.

His life was not confining and the delight he took in this observation could not be explained by its suggestion of escape. He seemed to see, with a cartographer's eye, that string of swimming pools, that quasi-subterranean stream that curved across the county. He had made a discovery, a contribution to modern geography; he would name the stream Lucinda after his wife. He was not a practical joker nor was he a fool but he was determinedly original and had a vague and modest idea of himself as a legendary figure. The day was beautiful and it seemed to him that a long swim might enlarge and celebrate its beauty.

He took off a sweater that was hung over his shoulders and dove in. He had an inexplicable contempt for men who did not hurl themselves into pools. He swam a choppy crawl, breathing either with every stroke or every fourth stroke and counting somewhere well in the back of his mind the one-two one-two of a flutter kick. It was not a serviceable stroke for long distances but the domestication of swimming had saddled the sport with some customs and in his part of the world a crawl was customary. To be embraced and sustained by the light green water was less a pleasure, it seemed, than the resumption of a natural condition, and he would have liked to swim without trunks, but this was not possible, considering his project. He hoisted himself up on the far curb—he never used the ladder—and started across the lawn. When Lucinda asked where he was going he said he was going to swim home.

The only maps and charts he had to go by were remembered or imaginary but these were clear enough. First there were the Grahams, the Hammers, the Lears, the Howlands, and the Crosscups. He would cross Ditmar Street to the Bunkers and come, after a short portage, to the Levys, the Welchers, and the public pool in Lancaster. Then there were the Hallorans, the Sachses, the Biswangers, Shirley Adams, the Gilmartins, and the Clydes. The day was lovely, and that he lived in a world so generously supplied with water seemed like a clemency, a beneficence. His heart was high and he ran across the grass. Making his way home by an uncommon route gave him the feeling that he was a pilgrim, an explorer, a man with a destiny, and he knew that he would find friends all along the way; friends would line the banks of the Lucinda River.

He went through a hedge that separated the Westerhazys' land from the Grahams', walked under some flowering apple trees, passed the shed that housed their pump and filter, and came out at the Grahams' pool. "Why, Neddy," Mrs. Graham said, "what a marvelous surprise. I've been trying to get you on the phone all morning. Here, let me get you a drink." He saw then, like an explorer, that the hospitable customs and traditions of the natives would have to be handled with diplomacy if he was ever going to reach his destination. He did not want to mystify or seem rude to the Grahams nor did he have the time to linger there. He swam the length of their pool and joined them in the sun and was rescued, a few minutes later, by the arrival of two carloads of friends from Connecticut. During the uproarious reunions he was able to slip away. He went down by the front of the Grahams' house, stepped over a thorny hedge, and crossed a vacant lot to the Hammers'. Mrs. Hammer, looking up from her roses, saw him swim by although she wasn't quite sure who it was. The Lears heard him splashing past the open windows of their living room. The Howlands and the Crosscups were away. After leaving the Howlands' he crossed Ditmar Street and started for the Bunkers', where he could hear, even at the distance, the noise of a party.

The water refracted the sound of voices and laughter and seemed to suspend it in midair. The Bunkers' pool was on a rise and he climbed some stairs to a terrace where twenty-five or thirty men and women were drinking. The only person in the water was Rusty Towers, who floated there on a rubber raft. Oh, how bonny and lush were the banks of the Lucinda River! Prosperous men and women gathered by the sapphire-colored waters while caterer's men in white coats passed them cold gin. Overhead a red de Haviland trainer was circling around and around and around in the sky with something like the glee of a child in a swing. Ned felt a passing affection for the scene, a tenderness for the gathering, as if it was something he might touch. In the distance he heard thunder. As soon as Enid Bunker saw him she began to scream: "Oh, look who's here! What a marvelous surprise! When Lucinda said that you couldn't come I thought I'd *die*." She made her way to him through the crowd, and when they had finished kissing she led him to the bar, a progress that was slowed by the fact that he stopped to kiss eight or ten other women and shake the hands of as many men. A smiling bartender he had seen at a hundred parties gave him a gin and tonic and he stood by the bar for a moment, anxious not to get stuck in any conversation that would delay his voyage. When he seemed about to be surrounded he dove in and swam close to the side to avoid colliding with Rusty's raft. At the far end of the pool he bypassed the Tomlinsons with a broad smile and jogged up the garden path. The gravel cut his feet but this was the only unpleasantness. The party was confined to the pool, and as he went toward the house he heard the brilliant, watery sound of voices fade, heard the noise of a radio from the Bunkers' kitchen, where someone was listening to a ball game. Sunday afternoon. He made his way through the parked cars and down the grassy border of their driveway to Alewives Lane. He did not want to be seen on the road in his bathing trunks but there was no traffic and he made the short distance to the Levys' driveway, marked with a PRIVATE PROPERTY sign and green tube for *The New York Times*. All the doors and windows of the big house were open but there were no signs of life; not even a dog barked. He went around the side of the house to the pool and saw that the Levys had only recently left. Glasses and bottles and dishes of nuts were on a table at the deep end, where there was a bathhouse or gazebo, hung with Japanese lanterns. After swimming the pool he got himself a glass and poured a drink. It was his fourth or fifth drink and he had swum nearly half the length of the Lucinda River. He felt tired, clean, and pleased at that moment to be alone; pleased with everything.

It would storm. The stand of cumulus cloud—that city—had risen and darkened, and while he sat there he heard the percussiveness of thunder again. The de Haviland trainer was still circling overhead and it seemed to Ned that he could almost hear the pilot laugh with pleasure in the afternoon; but when there was another peal of thunder he took off for home. A train whistle blew and he wondered what time it had gotten to be. Four? Five? He thought of the provincial station at that hour, where a waiter, his tuxedo concealed by a raincoat, a dwarf with some flowers wrapped in newspaper, and a woman who had been crying would be waiting for the local. It was suddenly growing dark; it was that moment when the pin-headed birds seem to organize their song into some acute and knowledgeable recognition of the storm's approach. Then there was a fine noise of rushing water from the crown of an oak at his back, as if a spigot there had been turned. Then the noise of fountains came from the crowns of all the tall trees. Why did he love storms, what was the meaning of his excitement when the door sprang open and the rain wind fled rudely up the stairs, why had the simple task of shutting the windows of an old house seemed fitting and urgent, why did the first watery notes of a storm wind have for him the unmistakable sound of good news, cheer, glad tidings? Then there was an explosion, a smell of cordite, and rain lashed the Japanese lanterns that Mrs. Levy had bought in Kyoto the year before last, or was it the year before that?

He stayed in the Levys' gazebo until the storm had passed. The rain had cooled the air and he shivered. The force of the wind had stripped a maple of its red and yellow leaves and scattered them over the grass and the water. Since it was midsummer the tree must be blighted, and yet he felt a peculiar sadness at this sign of autumn. He braced his shoulders, emptied his glass, and started for the Welchers' pool. This meant crossing the Lindleys' riding ring and he was surprised to find it overgrown with grass and all the jumps dismantled. He wondered if the Lindleys had sold their horses or gone away for the summer and put them out to board. He seemed to remember having heard something about the Lindleys and their horses but the memory was unclear. On he went, barefoot through the wet grass, to the Welchers', where he found their pool was dry.

This breach in his chain of water disappointed him absurdly, and he felt like some explorer who seeks a torrential headwater and finds a dead stream. He was disappointed and mystified. It was common enough to go away for the summer but no one ever drained his pool. The Welchers had definitely gone away. The pool furniture was folded, stacked, and covered with a tarpaulin. The bathhouse was locked. All the windows of the house were shut, and when he went around to the driveway in front he saw a FOR SALE sign nailed to a tree. When had he last heard from the Welchers—when, that is, had he and Lucinda last regretted an invitation to dine with them? It seemed only a week or so ago. Was his memory failing or had he so disciplined it in the repression of unpleasant facts that he had damaged his sense of the truth? Then in the distance he heard the sound of a tennis game. This cheered him, cleared away all his apprehensions and let him regard the overcast sky and the cold air with indifference. This was the day that Neddy Merrill swam across the county. That was the day! He started off then for his most difficult portage.

Had you gone for a Sunday afternoon ride that day you might have seen him, close to naked, standing on the shoulders of Route 424, waiting for a chance to cross. You might have wondered if he was the victim of foul play, had his car broken down, or was he merely a fool. Standing barefoot in the deposits of the highway—beer cans, rags, and blowout patches—exposed to all kinds of ridicule, he seemed pitiful. He had known when he started that this was a part of his journey—it had been on his maps—but confronted with the lines of traffic, worming through the summery light, he found himself unprepared. He was laughed at, jeered at, a beer can was thrown at him, and he had no dignity or humor to bring to the situation. He could have gone back, back to the

Westerhazys', where Lucinda would still be sitting in the sun. He had signed nothing, vowed nothing, pledged nothing, not even to himself. Why, believing as he did, that all human obduracy was susceptible to common sense, was he unable to turn back? Why was he determined to complete his journey even if it meant putting his life in danger? At what point had this prank, this joke, this piece of horseplay become serious? He could not go back, he could not even recall with any clearness the green water at the Westerhazys', the sense of inhaling the day's components, the friendly and relaxed voices saying that they had *drunk* too much. In the space of an hour, more or less, he had covered a distance that made his return impossible.

An old man, tooling down the highway at fifteen miles an hour, let him get to the middle of the road, where there was a grass divider. Here he was exposed to the ridicule of the northbound traffic, but after ten or fifteen minutes he was able to cross. From here he had only a short walk to the Recreation Center at the edge of the village of Lancaster, where there were some handball courts and a public pool.

The effect of the water on voices, the illusion of brilliance and suspense, was the same here as it had been at the Bunkers' but the sounds here were louder, harsher, and more shrill, and as soon as he entered the crowded enclosure he was confronted with regimentation. "ALL SWIMMERS MUST TAKE A SHOWER BEFORE USING THE POOL. ALL SWIMMERS MUST USE THE FOOTBATH. ALL SWIMMERS MUST WEAR THEIR IDENTIFICATION DISKS." He took a shower, washed his feet in a cloudy and bitter solution, and made his way to the edge of the water. It stank of chlorine and looked to him like a sink. A pair of lifeguards in a pair of towers blew police whistles at what seemed to be regular intervals and abused the swimmers through a public address system. Neddy remembered the sapphire water at the Bunkers' with longing and thought that he might contaminate himself—damage his own prosperousness and charm—by swimming in this murk, but he reminded himself that he was an explorer, a pilgrim, and that this was merely a stagnant bend in the Lucinda River. He dove, scowling with distaste, into the chlorine and had to swim with his head above water to avoid collisions, but even so he was bumped into, splashed, and jostled. When he got to the shallow end both lifeguards were shouting at him: "Hey, you, you without the identification disk, get outa the water." He did, but they had no way of pursuing him and he went through the reek of suntan oil and chlorine out through the hurricane fence and passed the handball courts. By crossing the road he entered the wooded part of the Halloran estate. The woods were not cleared and the footing was treacherous and difficult until he reached the lawn and the clipped beech hedge that encircled their pool.

The Hallorans were friends, an elderly couple of enormous wealth who seemed to bask in the suspicion that they might be Communists. They were zealous reformers but they were not Communists, and yet when they were accused, as they sometimes were, of subversion, it seemed to gratify and excite them. Their beech hedge was yellow and he guessed this had been blighted like the Levys' maple. He called hullo, hullo, to warn the Hallorans of his approach, to palliate his invasion of their privacy. The Hallorans, for reasons that had never been explained to him, did not wear bathing suits. No explanations were in order, really. Their nakedness was a detail in their uncompromising zeal for reform and he stepped politely out of his trunks before he went through the opening in the hedge.

Mrs. Halloran, a stout woman with white hair and a serene face, was reading the *Times,* Mr. Halloran was taking beech leaves out of the water with a scoop. They seemed not surprised or displeased to see him. Their pool was perhaps the oldest in the county, a fieldstone rectangle, fed by a brook. It had no filter or pump and its waters were the opaque gold of the stream.

"I'm swimming across the county," Ned said.

"Why, I didn't know one could," exclaimed Mrs. Halloran.

"Well, I've made it from the Westerhazys'," Ned said. "That must be about four miles."

He left his trunks at the deep end, walked to the shallow end, and swam this stretch. As he was pulling himself out of the water he heard Mrs. Halloran say, "We've been *terribly* sorry to hear about all your misfortunes, Neddy."

"My misfortunes?" Ned asked. "I don't know what you mean."

"Why, we heard that you'd sold the house and that your poor children . . ."

"I don't recall having sold the house," Ned said, "and the girls are at home."

"Yes," Mrs. Halloran sighed. "Yes . . ." Her voice filled the air with an unseasonable melancholy and Ned spoke briskly. "Thank you for the swim."

"Well, have a nice trip," said Mrs. Halloran.

Beyond the hedge he pulled on his trunks and fastened them. They were loose and he wondered if, during the space of an afternoon, he could have lost some weight. He was cold and he was tired and the naked Hallorans and their dark water had depressed him. The swim was too much for his strength but how could he have guessed this, sliding down the banister that morning and sitting in the Westerhazys' sun? His arms were lame. His legs felt rubbery and ached at the joints. The worst of it was the cold in his bones and the feeling that he might never be warm again. Leaves were falling down around him and he smelled wood smoke on the wind. Who would be burning wood at this time of year?

He needed a drink. Whiskey would warm him, pick him up, carry him through the last of his journey, refresh his feeling that it was original and valorous to swim across the county. Channel swimmers took brandy. He needed a stimulant. He crossed the lawn in front of the Hallorans' house and went down a little path to where they had built a house for their only daughter, Helen, and her husband, Eric Sachs. The Sachses' pool was small and he found Helen and her husband there.

"Oh, *Neddy,*" Helen said. "Did you lunch at Mother's?"

"Not *really,*" Ned said. "I *did* stop to see your parents." This seemed to be explanation enough. "I'm terribly sorry to break in on you like this but I've taken a chill and I wonder if you'd give me a drink."

"Why, I'd *love* to," Helen said, "but there hasn't been anything in this house to drink since Eric's operation. That was three years ago."

Was he losing his memory, had his gift for concealing painful facts let him forget that he had sold his house, that his children were in trouble, and that his friend had been ill? His eyes slipped from Eric's face to his abdomen, where he saw three pale, sutured scars, two of them at least a foot long. Gone was his naval, and what, Neddy thought, would the roving hand, bed-checking one's gifts at 3 A.M., make of a belly with no navel, no link to birth, this breach in the succession?

"I'm sure you can get a drink at the Biswangers'," Helen said. "They're having an enormous do. You can hear it from here. Listen!"

She raised her head and from across the road, the lawns, the gardens, the woods, the fields, he heard again the brilliant noise of voices over water. "Well, I'll get wet," he said, still feeling that he had no freedom of choice about his means of travel. He dove into the Sachses' cold water and, gasping, close to drowning, made his way from one end of the pool to the other. "Lucinda and I want *terribly* to see you," he said over his shoulder, his face set toward the Biswangers'. "We're sorry it's been so long and we'll call you *very* soon."

He crossed some fields to the Biswangers' and the sounds of revelry there. They would be honored to give him a drink, they would be happy to give him a drink. The Biswangers invited him and Lucinda for dinner four times a year, six weeks in advance. They were always rebuffed and yet they continued to send out their invitations, unwilling to comprehend the rigid and undemocratic realities of their society. They were the sort of people who discussed the price of things at cocktails, exchanged market tips during dinner, and after dinner told dirty stories to mixed company. They did not belong to Neddy's set—they were not even on Lucinda's Christmas-card list. He went toward their pool with feelings of indifference, charity, and some unease, since it seemed to be getting dark and these were the longest days of the year. The party when he joined it was noisy and large. Grace Biswanger was the kind of hostess who asked the optometrist, the veterinarian, the real-estate dealer, and the dentist. No one was swimming and the twilight, reflected on the water of the pool, had a wintry gleam. There was a bar and he started for this. When Grace Biswanger saw him she came toward him, not affectionately as he had every right to expect, but bellicosely.

"Why, this party has everything," she said loudly, "including a gate crasher."

She could not deal him a social blow—there was no question about this and he did not flinch. "As a gate crasher," he asked politely, "do I rate a drink?"

"Suit yourself," she said. "You don't seem to pay much attention to invitations."

She turned her back on him and joined some guests, and he went to the bar and ordered a whiskey. The bartender served him but he served him rudely. His was a world in which the caterer's men kept the social score, and to be rebuffed by a part-time barkeep meant that he had suffered some loss of social esteem. Or perhaps the man was new and uninformed. Then he heard Grace at his back say: "They went for broke overnight—nothing but income—and he showed up drunk one Sunday and asked us to loan him five thousand dollars. . . ." She was always talking about money. It was worse than eating your peas off a knife. He dove into the pool, swam its length and went away.

The next pool on his list, the last but two, belonged to his old mistress, Shirley Adams. If he had suffered any injuries at the Biswangers' they would be cured here. Love—sexual roughhouse in fact—was the supreme elixir, the pain killer, the brightly colored pill that would put the spring back into his step, the joy of life in his heart. They had had an affair last week, last month, last year. He couldn't remember. It was he who had broken it off, his was the upper hand, and he stepped through the gate of the wall that surrounded her pool with nothing so considered as self-confidence. It seemed in a way to be his pool, as the lover, particularly the illicit lover, enjoys the possessions of his mistress with an authority unknown to holy matrimony. She was there, her hair the color of brass, but her figure, at the edge of the lighted, cerulean water, excited in him no profound memories. It had been, he thought, a lighthearted affair, although she had wept when he broke it off. She seemed confused to see him and he wondered if she was still wounded. Would she, God forbid, weep again?

"What do you want?" she asked.

"I'm swimming across the county."

"Good Christ. Will you ever grow up?"

"What's the matter?"

"If you've come here for money," she said, "I won't give you another cent."

"You could give me a drink."

"I could but I won't. I'm not alone."

"Well, I'm on my way."

He dove in and swam the pool, but when he tried to haul himself up onto the curb he found that the strength in his arms and shoulders had gone, and he paddled to the ladder and climbed out. Looking over his shoulder he saw, in the lighted bathhouse, a young man. Going out onto the dark lawn he smelled chrysanthemums or marigolds—some stubborn autumnal fragrance—on the night air, strong as gas. Looking overhead he saw that the stars had come out, but why should he seem to see Andromeda, Cepheus, and Cassiopeia? What had become of the constellations of midsummer? He began to cry.

It was probably the first time in his adult life that he had ever cried, certainly the first time in his life that he had ever felt so miserable, cold, tired, and bewildered. He could not understand the rudeness of the caterer's barkeep or the rudeness of a mistress who had come to him on her knees and showered his trousers with tears. He had swum too long, he had been immersed too long, and his nose and his throat were sore from the water. What he needed then was a drink, some company, and some clean, dry clothes, and while he could have cut directly across the road to his house he went on to the Gilmartins' pool. Here, for the first time in his life, he did not dive but went down the steps into the icy water and swam a hobbled sidestroke that he might have learned as a youth. He staggered with fatigue on his way to the Clydes' and paddled the length of their pool, stopping again and again with his hand on the curb to rest. He climbed up the ladder and wondered if he had the strength to get home. He had done what he wanted, he had swum the county, but he was so stupefied with exhaustion that his triumph seemed vague. Stooped, holding on to the gateposts for support, he turned up the driveway of his own house.

The place was dark. Was it so late that they had all gone to bed? Had Lucinda stayed at the Westerhazys' for supper? Had the girls joined her there or gone someplace else? Hadn't they agreed, as they usually did on Sundays, to regret all their invitations and stay at home? He tried the garage doors to see what cars were in but the doors were locked and rust came off the handles onto his hands. Going toward the house, he saw that the force of the thunderstorm had knocked one of the rain gutters loose. It hung down over the front door like an umbrella rib, but it could be fixed in the morning. The house was locked, and he thought that the stupid cook or the stupid maid must have locked the place up until he remembered that it had been some time since they had employed a maid or a cook. He shouted, pounded on the door, tried to force it with his shoulder, and then, looking in at the windows, saw that the place was empty.

QUESTIONS FOR DISCUSSION AND WRITING

1. How does Cheever's opening paragraph help explain Neddy Merrill's plan to swim across the county?
2. At the beginning of the story, how does Neddy see himself and his pilgrimage? How is he seen by others at different points on his journey? How does Cheever mean for us to see Neddy by the end of the story?
3. How does each pool provide a different kind of setting? In what ways do these settings change as Neddy gets closer to home?
4. What major shift in point of view is marked by the storm?
5. What themes are implied in Cheever's description of this society as "rigid and undemocratic"? Does this world have any redeeming qualities?

21

ANTON CHEKHOV

The Lady with the Dog

TRANSLATED BY CONSTANCE GARNETT

ANTON CHEKHOV (1860–1904) was born in Taganrog, Russia, and studied to be a doctor at the University of Moscow. In 1884, Chekhov completed his medical training and published his first collection of short stories. For a few years he worked as an assistant to a doctor in a small provincial town, but he soon decided to pursue an active literary career. By 1887 Chekhov had written more than six hundred stories and humorous sketches. Although Chekhov dismissed this early work as "thoughtless and frivolous," it won him wide acclaim and enabled him to purchase a small estate near Moscow. During the next decade, Chekhov's work focused on the difficulties of social injustice. It was during this period that Chekhov also began to write for the stage, producing such classic dramas as *The Seagull* (1896), *Uncle Vanya* (1897), and *The Cherry Orchard* (1904). Chekhov's disillusionment, perhaps caused in part by his failing health, permeated his later work. "The Lady with the Dog," the title story of a collection translated into English in 1917, describes the love affair between a cynical older man and an innocent young woman.

It was said that a new person had appeared on the sea-front: a lady with a little dog. Dmitri Dmitritch Gurov, who had by then been a fortnight at Yalta, and so was fairly at home there, had begun to take an interest in new arrivals. Sitting in Verney's pavilion, he saw, walking on the sea-front, a fair-haired young lady of medium height, wearing a *béret;* a white Pomeranian dog was running behind her.

And afterwards he met her in the public gardens and in the square several times a day. She was walking alone, always wearing the same *béret,* and always with the same white dog; no one knew who she was, and every one called her simply "the lady with the dog."

"If she is here alone without a husband or friends, it wouldn't be amiss to make her acquaintance," Gurov reflected.

He was under forty, but he had a daughter already twelve years old, and two sons at school. He had been married young, when he was a student in his second year, and by now his wife seemed half as old again as he. She was a tall, erect woman with dark eyebrows, staid and dignified, and, as she said of herself, intellectual. She read a great deal, used phonetic spelling, called her husband, not Dmitri, but Dimitri, and he secretly considered her unintelligent, narrow, inelegant, was afraid of her, and did not like to be at home. He had begun being unfaithful to her long ago—had been unfaithful to her often, and, probably on that account, almost always spoke ill of women, and when they were talked about in his presence, used to call them "the lower race."

It seemed to him that he had been so schooled by bitter experience that he might call them what he liked, and yet he could not get on for two days together without "the lower race." In the society of men he was bored and not himself, with them he was cold and uncommunicative; but when he was in the company of women he felt free, and knew what to say to them and how to behave; and he was at ease with them even when he was silent. In his appearance, in his character, in his whole nature, there was something attractive and elusive which allured women and disposed them in his favour; he knew that, and some force seemed to draw him, too, to them.

Experience often repeated, truly bitter experience, had taught him long ago that with decent people, especially Moscow people—always slow to move and irresolute—every intimacy, which at first so agreeably diversifies life and appears a light and charming adventure, inevitably grows into a regular problem of extreme intricacy, and in the long run the situation becomes unbearable. But at every fresh meeting with an interesting woman this experience seemed to slip out of his memory, and he was eager for life, and everything seemed simple and amusing.

One evening he was dining in the gardens, and the lady in the *béret* came up slowly to take the next table. Her expression, her gait, her dress, and the way she did her hair told him that she was a lady, that she was married, that she was in Yalta for the first time and alone, and that she was dull there. . . . The stories told of the immorality in such places as Yalta are to a great extent untrue; he despised them, and knew that such stories were for the most part made up by persons who would themselves have been glad to sin if they had been able; but when the lady sat down at the next table three paces from him, he remembered these tales of easy conquests, of trips to the mountains, and the tempting thought of a swift, fleeting love affair, a romance with an unknown woman, whose name he did not know, suddenly took possession of him.

He beckoned coaxingly to the Pomeranian, and when the dog came up to him he shook his finger at it. The Pomeranian growled: Gurov shook his finger at it again.

The lady looked at him and at once dropped her eyes.

"He doesn't bite," she said, and blushed.

"May I give him a bone?" he asked; and when she nodded he asked courteously, "Have you been long in Yalta?"

"Five days."

"And I have already dragged out a fortnight here."

There was a brief silence.

"Time goes fast, and yet it is so dull here!" she said, not looking at him.

"That's only the fashion to say it is dull here. A provincial will live in Belyov or Zhidra and not be dull, and when he comes here it's 'Oh, the dullness! Oh, the dust!' One would think he came from Granada."

She laughed. Then both continued eating in silence, like strangers, but after dinner they walked side by side; and there sprang up between them the light jesting conversation of people who are free and satisfied, to whom it does not matter where they go or what they talk about. They walked and talked of the strange light on the sea: the water was of a soft warm lilac hue, and there was a golden streak from the moon upon it. They talked of how sultry it was after a hot day. Gurov told her that he came from Moscow, that he had taken his degree in Arts, but had a post in a bank; that he had trained as an opera-singer, but had given it up, that he owned two houses in Moscow. . . . And from her he learnt that she had grown up in Petersburg, but had lived in S———since her marriage two years before, that she was staying another month in Yalta, and that her husband, who needed a holiday too, might perhaps come and fetch her. She was not sure whether her husband had a post in a Crown Department or under the Provincial Council—and was amused by her own ignorance. And Gurov learnt, too, that she was called Anna Sergeyevna.

Afterwards he thought about her in his room at the hotel—thought she would certainly meet him next day; it would be sure to happen. As he got into bed he thought how lately she had been a girl at school, doing lessons like his own daughter; he recalled the diffidence, the angularity, that was still manifest in her laugh and her manner of talking with a stranger. This must have been the first time in her life she had been alone in surroundings in which she was followed, looked at, and spoken to merely from a secret motive which she could hardly fail to guess. He recalled her slender, delicate neck, her lovely grey eyes.

"There's something pathetic about her, anyway," he thought, and fell asleep.

2

A week had passed since they had made acquaintance. It was a holiday. It was sultry indoors, while in the street the wind whirled the dust round and round, and blew people's hats off. It was a thirsty day, and Gurov often went into the pavilion, and pressed Anna Sergeyevna to have syrup and water or an ice. One did not know what to do with oneself.

In the evening when the wind had dropped a little, they went out on the groyne to see the steamer come in. There were a great many people walking about the harbour; they had gathered to welcome some one, bringing bouquets. And two peculiarities of a well-dressed Yalta crowd were very conspicuous: the elderly ladies were dressed like young ones, and there were great numbers of generals.

Owing to the roughness of the sea, the steamer arrived late, after the sun had set, and it was a long time turning about before it reached the groyne. Anna Sergeyevna looked through her lorgnette at the steamer and the passengers as though looking for acquaintances, and when she turned to Gurov her eyes were shining. She talked a great deal and asked disconnected questions, forgetting next moment what she had asked; then she dropped her lorgnette in the crush.

The festive crowd began to disperse; it was too dark to see people's faces. The wind had completely dropped, but Gurov and Anna Sergeyevna still stood as though waiting to see some one else come from the steamer. Anna Sergeyevna was silent now, and sniffed the flowers without looking at Gurov.

"The weather is better this evening," he said. "Where shall we go now? Shall we drive somewhere?"

She made no answer.

Then he looked at her intently, and all at once put his arm round her and kissed her on the lips, and breathed in the moisture and the fragrance of the flowers; and he immediately looked round him, anxiously wondering whether any one had seen them.

"Let us go to your hotel," he said softly. And both walked quickly.

The room was close and smelt of the scent she had bought at the Japanese shop. Gurov looked at her and thought: "What different people one meets in the world!" From the past he preserved memories of careless, good-natured women, who loved cheerfully and were grateful to him for the happiness he gave them, however brief it might be; and of women like his wife who loved without any genuine feeling, with superfluous phrases, affectedly, hysterically, with an expression that suggested that it was not love nor passion, but something more significant; and of two or three others, very beautiful, cold women, on whose faces he had caught a glimpse of a rapacious expression—an obstinate desire to snatch from life more than it could give, and these were capricious, unreflecting, domineering, unintelligent women not in their first youth, and when Gurov grew cold to them their beauty excited his hatred, and the lace on their linen seemed to him like scales.

But in this case there was still the diffidence, the angularity of inexperienced youth, an awkward feeling; and there was a sense of consternation as though some one had suddenly knocked at the door. The attitude of Anna Sergeyevna—"the lady with the dog"—to what had happened was somehow peculiar, very grave, as though it were her fall—so it seemed, and it was strange and inappropriate. Her face dropped and faded, and on both sides of it her long hair hung down mournfully; she mused in a dejected attitude like "the woman who was a sinner" in an old-fashioned picture.

"It's wrong," she said. "You will be the first to despise me now."

There was a water-melon on the table. Gurov cut himself a slice and began eating it without haste. There followed at least half an hour of silence.

Anna Sergeyevna was touching; there was about her the purity of a good, simple woman who had seen little of life. The solitary candle burning on the table threw a faint light on her face, yet it was clear that she was very unhappy.

"How could I despise you?" asked Gurov. "You don't know what you are saying."

"God forgive me," she said, and her eyes filled with tears. "It's awful."

"You seem to feel you need to be forgiven."

"Forgiven? No. I am a bad, low woman; I despise myself and I don't attempt to justify myself. It's not my husband but myself I have deceived. And not only just now; I have been deceiving myself for a long time. My husband may be a good, honest man, but he is a flunkey! I don't know what he does there, what his work is, but I know he is a flunkey! I was twenty when I was married to him. I have been tormented by curiosity; I wanted something better. 'There must be a different sort of life,' I said to myself. I wanted to live! To live, to live! . . . I was fired by curiosity . . . you don't understand it, but, I swear to God, I could not control myself; something happened to me: I could not be restrained. I told my husband I was ill, and came here. . . . And here I have been walking about as though I were dazed, like a mad creature; . . . and now I have become a vulgar, contemptible woman whom any one may despise."

Gurov felt bored already, listening to her. He was irritated by the naïve tone, by this remorse, so unexpected and inopportune; but for the tears in her eyes, he might have thought she was jesting or playing a part.

"I don't understand," he said softly. "What is it you want?"

She hid her face on his breast and pressed close to him.

"Believe me, believe me, I beseech you . . ." she said. "I love a pure, honest life, and sin is loathsome to me. I don't know what I am doing. Simple people say: 'The Evil One has beguiled me.' And I may say of myself now that the Evil One has beguiled me."

"Hush, hush! . . ." he muttered.

He looked at her fixed, scared eyes, kissed her, talked softly and affectionately, and by degrees she was comforted, and her gaiety returned; they both began laughing.

Afterwards when they went out there was not a soul on the sea-front. The town with its cypresses had quite a deathlike air, but the sea still broke noisily on the shore; a single barge was rocking on the waves, and a lantern was blinking sleepily on it.

They found a cab and drove to Oreanda.

"I found out your surname in the hall just now: it was written on the board—Von Diderits," said Gurov. "Is your husband a German?"

"No, I believe his grandfather was a German, but he is an Orthodox Russian himself."

At Oreanda they sat on a seat not far from the church, looked down at the sea, and were silent. Yalta was hardly visible through the morning mist; white clouds stood motionless on the mountain-tops. The leaves did not stir on the trees, grasshoppers chirruped, and the monotonous hollow sound of the sea rising up from below, spoke of the peace, of the eternal sleep awaiting us. So it must have sounded when there was no Yalta, no Oreanda here; so it sounds now, and it will sound as indifferently and monotonously when we are all no more. And in this constancy, in this complete indifference to the life and death of each of us, there lies hid, perhaps, a pledge of our eternal salvation, of the unceasing movement of life upon earth, of unceasing progress towards perfection. Sitting beside a young woman who in the dawn seemed so lovely, soothed and spellbound in these magical surroundings—the sea, mountains, clouds, the open sky—Gurov thought how in reality everything is beautiful in this world when one reflects: everything except what we think or do ourselves when we forget our human dignity and the higher aims of our existence.

A man walked up to them—probably a keeper—looked at them and walked away. And this detail seemed mysterious and beautiful, too. They saw a steamer come from Theodosia, with its lights out in the glow of dawn.

"There is dew on the grass," said Anna Sergeyevna, after a silence.

"Yes. It's time to go home."

They went back to the town.

Then they met every day at twelve o'clock on the sea-front, lunched and dined together, went for walks, admired the sea. She complained that she slept badly, that her heart throbbed violently; asked the same questions, troubled now by jealousy and now by the fear that he did not respect her sufficiently. And often in the square or gardens, when there was no one near them, he suddenly drew her to him and kissed her passionately. Complete idleness, these kisses in broad daylight while he looked round in dread of some one's seeing them, the heat, the smell of the sea, and the continual passing to and fro before him of idle, well-dressed, well-fed people, made a new man of him; he told Anna Sergeyevna how beautiful she was, how fascinating. He was impatiently passionate, he would not move a step away from her, while she was often pensive and continually urged him to confess that he did not respect her, did not love her in the least, and thought of her as nothing but a common woman. Rather late almost every evening they drove somewhere out of town, to Oreanda or to the waterfall; and the expedition was always a success, the scenery invariably impressed them as grand and beautiful.

They were expecting her husband to come, but a letter came from him, saying that there was something wrong with his eyes, and he entreated his wife to come home as quickly as possible. Anna Sergeyevna made haste to go.

"It's a good thing I am going away," she said to Gurov. "It's the finger of destiny!"

She went by coach and he went with her. They were driving the whole day. When she had got into a compartment of the express, and when the second bell had rung, she said:

"Let me look at you once more . . . look at you once again. That's right."

She did not shed tears, but was so sad that she seemed ill, and her face was quivering.

"I shall remember you . . . think of you," she said. "God be with you; be happy. Don't remember evil against me. We are parting forever—it must be so, for we ought never to have met. Well, God be with you."

The train moved off rapidly, its lights soon vanished from sight, and a minute later there was no sound of it, as though everything had conspired together to end as quickly as possible that sweet delirium, that madness. Left alone on the platform, and gazing into the dark distance, Gurov listened to the chirrup of the grasshoppers and the hum of the telegraph wires, feeling as though he had only just waked up. And he thought, musing, that there had been another episode or adventure in his life, and it, too, was at an end, and nothing was left of it but a memory. . . . He was moved, sad, and conscious of a slight remorse. This young woman whom he would never meet again had not been happy with him; he was genuinely warm and affectionate with her, but yet in his manner, his tone, and his caresses there had been a shade of light irony, the coarse condescension of a happy man who was, besides, almost twice her age. All the time she had called him kind, exceptional, lofty; obviously he had seemed to her different from what he really was, so he had unintentionally deceived her. . . .

Here at the station was already a scent of autumn; it was a cold evening.

"It's time for me to go north," thought Gurov as he left the platform. "High time!"

3

At home in Moscow everything was in its winter routine; the stoves were heated, and in the morning it was still dark when the children were having breakfast and getting ready for school, and the nurse would light the lamp for a short time. The frosts had begun already. When the first snow has fallen, on the first day of sledge-driving it is pleasant to see the white earth, the white roofs, to draw soft, delicious breath, and the season brings back the days of one's youth. The old limes and birches, white with hoar-frost, have a good-natured expression; they are nearer to one's heart than cypresses and palms, and near them one doesn't want to be thinking of the sea and the mountains.

Gurov was Moscow born; he arrived in Moscow on a fine frosty day, and when he put on his fur coat and warm gloves, and walked along Petrovka, and when on Saturday evening he heard the ringing of the bells, his recent trip and the places he had seen lost all charm for him. Little by little he became absorbed in Moscow life, greedily read three newspapers a day, and declared he did not read the Moscow papers on principle! He already felt a longing to go to restaurants, clubs, dinner-parties, anniversary celebrations and he felt flattered at entertaining distinguished lawyers and artists, and at playing cards with a professor at the doctors' club. He could already eat a whole plateful of salt fish and cabbage. . . .

In another month, he fancied, the image of Anna Sergeyevna would be shrouded in a mist in his memory, and only from time to time would visit him in his dreams with a touching smile as others did. But more than a month passed, real winter had come, and everything was still clear in his memory as though he had parted with Anna Sergeyevna only the day before. And his memories glowed more and more vividly. When in the evening stillness he heard from his study the voices of his children, preparing their lessons, or when he listened to a song or the organ at the restaurant, or the storm howled in the chimney, suddenly everything would rise up in his memory: what had happened on the groyne, and the early morning with the mist on the mountains, and the steamer coming from Theodosia and the kisses. He would pace a long time about his room, remembering it all and smiling; then his memories passed into dreams, and in his fancy the past was mingled with what was to come. Anna Sergeyevna did not visit him in dreams, but followed him about everywhere like a shadow and haunted him. When he shut his eyes he saw her as though she were living before him, and she seemed to him lovelier, younger, tenderer than she was; and he imagined himself finer than he had been in Yalta. In the evenings she peeped out at him from the bookcase, from the fireplace, from the corner—he heard her breathing, the caressing rustle of her dress. In the street he watched the women, looking for some one like her.

He was tormented by an intense desire to confide his memories to some one. But in his home it was impossible to talk of his love, and he had no one outside; he could not talk to his tenants nor to any one at the bank. And what had he to talk to? Had he been in love, then? Had there been anything beautiful, poetical, or edifying or simply interesting in his relations with Anna Sergeyevna? And there was nothing for him but to talk vaguely of love, of woman, and no one guessed what it meant; only his wife twitched her black eyebrows, and said: "The part of a lady-killer does not suit you at all, Dimitri."

One evening, coming out of the doctors' club with an official with whom he had been playing cards, he could not resist saying:

"If only you knew what a fascinating woman I made the acquaintance of in Yalta!"

The official got into his sledge and was driving away, but turned suddenly and shouted:

"Dmitri Dmitritch!"

"What?"

"You were right this evening: the sturgeon was a bit too strong!"

These words, so ordinary, for some reason moved Gurov to indignation, and struck him as degrading and unclean. What savage manners, what people! What senseless nights, what uninteresting, uneventful days! The rage for card-playing, the gluttony, the drunkenness, the continual talk always about the same thing. Useless pursuits and conversations always about the same things absorb the better part of one's time, the better part of one's strength, and in the end there is left a life grovelling and curtailed, worthless and trivial, and there is no escaping or getting away from it—just as though one were in a madhouse or a prison.

Gurov did not sleep all night, and was filled with indignation. And he had a headache all next day. And the next night he slept badly; he sat up in bed, thinking, or paced up and down his room. He was sick of his children, sick of the bank; he had no desire to go anywhere or to talk of anything.

In the holidays in December he prepared for a journey, and told his wife he was going to Petersburg to do something in the interests of a young friend—and he set off for S———. What for? He did not very well know himself. He wanted to see Anna Sergeyevna and to talk with her—to arrange a meeting, if possible.

He reached S———in the morning, and took the best room at the hotel, in which the floor was covered with grey army cloth, and on the table was an inkstand, grey with dust and adorned with a figure on horseback, with its hat and its hand and its head broken off. The hotel porter gave him the necessary information; Von Diderits lived in a house of his own on Old Gontcharny Street—it was not far from the hotel: he was rich and lived in good style, and had his own horses; every one in the town knew him. The porter pronounced the name "Dridirits."

Gurov went without haste to Old Gontcharny Street and found the house. Just opposite the house stretched a long grey fence adorned with nails.

"One would run away from a fence like that," thought Gurov, looking from the fence to the windows of the house and back again.

He considered: to-day was a holiday, and the husband would probably be at home. And in any case it would be tactless to go into the house and upset her. If he were to send her a note it might fall into her husband's hands, and then it might ruin everything. The best thing was to trust to chance. And he kept walking up and down the street by the fence, waiting for the chance. He saw a beggar go in at the gate and dogs fly at him; then an hour later he heard a piano, and the sounds were faint and indistinct. Probably it was Anna Sergeyevna playing. The front door suddenly opened, and an old woman came out, followed by the familiar white Pomeranian. Gurov was on the point of calling to the dog, but his heart began beating violently, and in his excitement he could not remember the dog's name.

He walked up and down, and loathed the grey fence more and more, and by now he thought irritably that Anna Sergeyevna had forgotten him, and was perhaps already amusing herself with some one else, and that that was very natural in a young woman who had nothing to look at from morning till night but that confounded fence. He went back to his hotel room and sat for a long while on the sofa, not knowing what to do, then he had dinner and a long nap.

"How stupid and worrying it is!" he thought when he woke and looked at the dark windows: it was already evening. "Here I've had a good sleep for some reason. What shall I do in the night?"

He sat on the bed, which was covered by a cheap grey blanket, such as one sees in hospitals, and he taunted himself in his vexation:

"So much for the lady with the dog . . . so much for the adventure. . . . You're in a nice fix. . . ."

That morning at the station a poster in large letters had caught his eye. "The Geisha" was to be performed for the first time. He thought of this and went to the theater.

"It's quite possible she may go to the first performance," he thought.

The theatre was full. As in all provincial theatres, there was a fog above the chandelier, the gallery was noisy and restless; in the front row the local dandies were standing up before the beginning of the performance, with their hands behind them; in the Governor's box the Governor's daughter, wearing a boa, was sitting in the front seat, while the Governor himself lurked modestly behind the curtain with only his hands visible; the orchestra was a long time tuning up; the stage curtain swayed. All the time the audience were coming in and taking their seats Gurov looked at them eagerly.

Anna Sergeyevna, too, came in. She sat down in the third row, and when Gurov looked at her his heart contracted, and he understood clearly that for him there was in the whole world no creature so near, so precious, and so important to him; she, this little woman, in no way remarkable, lost in a provincial crowd, with a vulgar lorgnette in her hand, filled his whole life now, was his sorrow and his joy, the one happiness that he now desired for himself, and to the sounds of the inferior orchestra, of the wretched provincial violins, he thought how lovely she was. He thought and dreamed.

A young man with small side-whiskers, tall and stooping, came in with Anna Sergeyevna, and sat down beside her; he bent his head at every step and seemed to be continually bowing. Most likely this was the husband whom at Yalta, in a rush of bitter feeling, she had called a flunkey. And there really was in his long figure, his side-whiskers, and the small bald patch on his head, something of the flunkey's obsequiousness; his smile was sugary, and in his buttonhole there was some badge of distinction like the number on a waiter.

During the first interval the husband went away to smoke; she remained alone in her stall. Gurov, who was sitting in the stalls, too, went up to her and said in a trembling voice, with a forced smile:

"Good-evening."

She glanced at him and turned pale, then glanced again with horror, unable to believe her eyes, and tightly gripped her fan and the lorgnette in her hands, evidently struggling with herself not to faint. Both were silent. She was sitting, he was standing, frightened by her confusion and not venturing to sit down beside her. The violins and the flute began tuning up. He felt suddenly frightened; it seemed as though all the people in the boxes were looking at them. She got up and went quickly to the door; he followed her, and both walked senselessly along passages, and up and down stairs, and figures in legal, scholastic, and civil service uniforms, all wearing badges, flitted before their eyes. They caught glimpses of ladies, of fur coats hanging on pegs; the draughts blew on them, bringing a smell of stale tobacco. And Gurov, whose heart was beating violently, thought:

"Oh, heavens! Why are these people here and this orchestra! . . ."

And at that instant he recalled how when he had seen Anna Sergeyevna off at the station he had thought that everything was over and they would never meet again. But how far they were still from the end!

On the narrow, gloomy staircase over which was written "To the Amphitheatre," she stopped.

"How you have frightened me!" she said, breathing hard, still pale and overwhelmed. "Oh, how you have frightened me! I am half dead. Why have you come? Why?"

"But do understand, Anna, do understand . . ." he said hastily in a low voice. "I entreat you to understand. . . ."

She looked at him with dread, with entreaty, with love; she looked at him intently, to keep his features more distinctly in her memory.

"I am so unhappy," she went on, not heeding him. "I have thought of nothing but you all the time; I live only in the thought of you. And I wanted to forget, to forget you; but why, oh, why, have you come?"

On the landing above them two schoolboys were smoking and looking down, but that was nothing to Gurov; he drew Anna Sergeyevna to him, and began kissing her face, her cheeks, and her hands.

"What are you doing, what are you doing!" she cried in horror, pushing him away. "We are mad. Go away to-day; go away at once. . . . I beseech you by all that is sacred, I implore you. . . . There are people coming this way!"

Some one was coming up the stairs.

"You must go away," Anna Sergeyevna went on in a whisper. "Do you hear, Dmitri Dmitritch? I will come and see you in Moscow. I have never been happy; I am miserable now, and I never, never shall be happy, never! Don't make me suffer still more! I swear I'll come to Moscow. But now let us part. My precious, good, dear one, we must part!"

She pressed his hand and began rapidly going downstairs, looking round at him, and from her eyes he could see that she really was unhappy. Gurov stood for a little while, listened, then, when all sound had died away, he found his coat and left the theatre.

4

And Anna Sergeyevna began coming to see him in Moscow. Once in two or three months she left S———, telling her husband that she was going to consult a doctor about an internal complaint—and her husband believed her, and did not believe her. In Moscow she stayed at the Slaviansky Bazaar hotel, and at once sent a man in a red cap to Gurov. Gurov went to see her, and no one in Moscow knew of it.

Once he was going to see her in this way on a winter morning (the messenger had come the evening before when he was out). With him walked his daughter, whom he wanted to take to school: it was on the way. Snow was falling in big wet flakes.

"It's three degrees above freezing-point, and yet it is snowing," said Gurov to his daughter. "The thaw is only on the surface of the earth; there is quite a different temperature at a greater height in the atmosphere."

"And why are there no thunderstorms in the winter, father?"

He explained that, too. He talked, thinking all the while that he was going to see *her,* and no living soul knew of it, and probably never would know. He had two lives: one, open, seen and known by all who care to know, full of relative truth and of relative falsehood, exactly like the lives of his friends and acquaintances; and another life running its course in secret. And through some strange, perhaps accidental, conjunction of circumstances, everything that was essential, of interest and of value to him, everything in which he was sincere and did not deceive himself, everything that made the kernel of his life, was hidden from other people; and all that was false in him, the sheath in which he hid himself to conceal the truth—such, for instance, as his work in the bank, his discussions at the club, his "lower race," his presence with his wife at anniversary festivities—all that was open. And he judged of others by himself, not believing in what he saw, and always believing that every man had his real, most interesting life under the cover of secrecy and under the cover of night. All personal life rested on secrecy, and possibly it was partly on that account that civilised man was so nervously anxious that personal privacy should be respected.

After leaving his daughter at school, Gurov went on to the Slaviansky Bazaar. He took off his fur coat below, went upstairs, and softly knocked at the door. Anna Sergeyevna, wearing his favourite grey dress, exhausted by the journey and the suspense, had been expecting him since the evening before. She was pale; she looked at him, and did not smile, and he had hardly come in when she fell on his breast. Their kiss was slow and prolonged, as though they had not met for two years.

"Well, how are you getting on there?" he asked. "What news?"

"Wait; I'll tell you directly. . . . I can't talk."

She could not speak; she was crying. She turned away from him, and pressed her handkerchief to her eyes.

"Let her have her cry out. I'll sit down and wait," he thought, and he sat down in an arm-chair.

Then he rang and asked for tea to be brought him, and while he drank his tea she remained standing at the window with her back to him. She was crying from emotion, from the miserable consciousness that their life was so hard for them; they could only meet in secret, hiding themselves from people, like thieves! Was not their life shattered?

"Come, do stop!" he said.

It was evident to him that this love of theirs would not soon be over, that he could not see the end of it. Anna Sergeyevna grew more and more attached to him. She adored him, and it was unthinkable to say to her that it was bound to have an end some day; besides, she would not have believed it!

He went up to her and took her by the shoulders to say something affectionate and cheering, and at that moment he saw himself in the looking-glass.

His hair was already beginning to turn grey. And it seemed strange to him that he had grown so much older, so much plainer during the last few years. The shoulders on which his hands rested were warm and quivering. He felt compassion for this life, still so warm and lovely, but probably already not far from beginning to fade and wither like his own. Why did she love him so much? He always seemed to women different from what he was, and they loved in him not himself, but the man created by their imagination, whom they had been eagerly seeking all their lives; and afterwards, when they noticed their mistake, they loved him all the same. And not one of them had been happy with him. Time passed, he had made their acquaintance, got on with them, parted, but he had never once loved; it was anything you like, but not love.

And only now when his head was grey he had fallen properly, really in love—for the first time in his life.

Anna Sergeyevna and he loved each other like people very close and akin, like husband and wife, like tender friends; it seemed to them that fate itself had meant them for one another, and they could not understand why he had a wife and she a husband; and it was as though they were a pair of birds of passage, caught and forced to live in different cages. They forgave each other for what they were ashamed of in their past, they forgave everything in the present, and felt that this love of theirs had changed them both.

In moments of depression in the past he had comforted himself with any arguments that came into his mind, but now he no longer cared for arguments; he felt profound compassion, he wanted to be sincere and tender. . . .

"Don't cry, my darling," he said. "You've had your cry; that's enough. . . . Let us talk now, let us think of some plan."

Then they spent a long while taking counsel together, talked of how to avoid the necessity for secrecy, for deception, for living in different towns and not seeing each other for long at a time. How could they be free from this intolerable bondage?

"How? How?" he asked, clutching his head. "How?"

And it seemed as though in a little while the solution would be found, and then a new and splendid life would begin; and it was clear to both of them that they had still a long, long road before them, and that the most complicated and difficult part of it was only just beginning.

QUESTIONS FOR DISCUSSION AND WRITING

1. What is the major conflict in each of the four parts of the story? How does Gurov's past experience with "charming adventures" predict the pattern of his adventure with Anna?

2. How does Gurov characterize his wife and the other women he has known? What special, different qualities does he perceive in Anna's character? Would she appear equally irresistible to others? Explain your answer.
3. Why is Yalta an appropriate setting for the affair? How does Yalta compare with the other two settings in the story—Moscow and S———?
4. How does Gurov's point of view toward love change during the course of the story? How does he see himself at Yalta and in the mirror in Moscow?
5. Does Chekhov mean for us to see Gurov as redeemed by his experiences with Anna? Explain your answer.

22

SANDRA CISNEROS

Never Marry a Mexican

SANDRA CISNEROS was born in 1954 in Chicago, Illinois, and spent much of her childhood living in Chicago and Mexico City. A graduate of the University of Iowa Writer's Workshop, she has taught writing at the University of California, Berkeley, and the University of Michigan. She has also taught in the San Antonio Public Schools and worked as Literary Director of the Guadalupe Cultural Arts Center. She has contributed stories and poems to periodicals such as *Imagine, Contact II,* and *Revista Chicano-Riquena.* Her poems appear in *Bad Boys* (1980), *The Rodrigo Poems* (1985), and *My Wicked, Wicked Ways* (1987); her stories are collected in *Woman Hollering Creek* (1991). Cisneros' book for young adults, *The House on Mango Street* (1983), won the American Book Award. "Never Marry a Mexican," reprinted from *Woman Hollering Creek,* reveals the conflicts in a cross-cultural relationship.

Never marry a Mexican, my ma said once and always. She said this because of my father. She said this though she was Mexican too. But she was born here in the U.S., and he was born there, and it's *not* the same, you know.

I'll *never* marry. Not any man. I've known men too intimately. I've witnessed their infidelities, and I've helped them to it. Unzipped and unhooked and agreed to clandestine maneuvers. I've been accomplice, committed premeditated crimes. I'm guilty of having caused deliberate pain to other women. I'm vindictive and cruel, and I'm capable of anything.

I admit, there was a time when all I wanted was to belong to a man. To wear that gold band on my left hand and be worn on his arm like an expensive jewel brilliant in the light of day. Not the sneaking around I did in different bars that all looked the same, red carpets with a black grillwork design, flocked wallpaper, wooden wagon-wheel light fixtures with hurricane lampshades a sick amber color like the drinking glasses you get for free at gas stations.

Dark bars, dark restaurants then. And if not—my apartment, with his toothbrush firmly planted in the toothbrush holder like a flag on the North Pole. The bed so big because he never stayed the whole night. Of course not.

Borrowed. That's how I've had my men. Just the cream skimmed off the top. Just the sweetest part of the fruit, without the bitter skin that daily living with a spouse can rend. They've come to me when they wanted the sweet meat then.

So, no. I've never married and never will. Not because I couldn't, but because I'm too romantic for marriage. Marriage has failed me, you could say. Not a man exists who hasn't disappointed me, whom I could trust to love the way I've loved. It's because I believe too much in marriage that I don't. Better to not marry than live a lie.

Mexican men, forget it. For a long time the men clearing off the tables or chopping meat behind the butcher counter or driving the bus I rode to school every day, those weren't men. Not men I considered as potential lovers. Mexican, Puerto Rican, Cuban, Chilean, Colombian, Panamanian, Salvadorean, Bolivian, Honduran, Argentine, Dominican, Venezuelan, Guatemalan, Ecuadorean, Nicaraguan, Peruvian, Costa Rican, Paraguayan, Uruguayan, I don't care. I never saw them. My mother did this to me.

I guess she did it to spare me and Ximena the pain she went through. Having married a Mexican man at seventeen. Having had to put up with all the grief a Mexican family can put on a girl because she was from *el otro lado,* the other side, and my father had married down by marrying her. If he had married a white woman from *el otro lado,* that would've been different. That would've been marrying up, even if the white girl was poor. But what could be more ridiculous than a Mexican girl who couldn't even speak Spanish, who didn't know enough to set a separate plate for each course at dinner, nor how to fold cloth napkins, nor how to set the silverware.

In my ma's house the plates were always stacked in the center of the table, the knives and forks and spoons standing in a jar, help yourself. All the dishes chipped or cracked and nothing matched. And no tablecloth, ever. And newspapers set on the table whenever my grandpa sliced watermelons, and how embarrassed she would be when her boyfriend, my father, would come over and there were newspapers all over the kitchen floor and table. And my grandpa, big hardworking Mexican man, saying Come, come and eat, and slicing a big wedge of those dark green watermelons, a big slice, he wasn't stingy with food. Never, even during the Depression. Come, come and eat, to whoever came knocking on the back door. Hobos sitting at the dinner table and the children staring and staring. Because my grandfather always made sure they never went without. Flour and rice, by the barrel and by the sack. Potatoes. Big bags of pinto beans. And watermelons, bought three or four at a time, rolled under his bed and brought out when you least expected. My grandpa had survived three wars, one Mexican, two American, and he knew what living without meant. He knew.

My father, on the other hand, did not. True, when he first came to this country he had worked shelling clams, washing dishes, planting hedges, sat on the back of the bus in

Little Rock and had the bus driver shout, You—sit up here, and my father had shrugged sheepishly and said, No speak English.

But he was no economic refugee, no immigrant fleeing a war. My father ran away from home because he was afraid of facing his father after his first-year grades at the university proved he'd spent more time fooling around than studying. He left behind a house in Mexico City that was neither poor nor rich, but thought itself better than both. A boy who would get off a bus when he saw a girl he knew board if he didn't have the money to pay her fare. That was the world my father left behind.

I imagine my father in his *fanfarrón* clothes, because that's what he was, a *fanfarrón*. That's what my mother thought the moment she turned around to the voice that was asking her to dance. A big show-off, she'd say years later. Nothing but a big show-off. But she never said why she married him. My father in his shark-blue suits with the starched handkerchief in the breast pocket, his felt fedora, his tweed topcoat with the big shoulders, and heavy British wing tips with the pin-hole design on the heel and toe. Clothes that cost a lot. Expensive. That's what my father's things said. *Calidad*. Quality.

My father must've found the U.S. Mexicans very strange, so foreign from what he knew at home in Mexico City where the servant served watermelon on a plate with silverware and a cloth napkin, or mangos with their own special prongs. Not like this, eating with your legs wide open in the yard, or in the kitchen hunkered over newspapers. *Come, come and eat*. No, never like this.

How I make my living depends. Sometimes I work as a translator. Sometimes I get paid by the word and sometimes by the hour, depending on the job. I do this in the day, and at night I paint. I'd do anything in the day just so I can keep on painting.

I work as a substitute teacher, too, for the San Antonio Independent School District. And that's worse than translating those travel brochures with their tiny print, believe me. I can't stand kids. Not any age. But it pays the rent.

Any way you look at it, what I do to make a living is a form of prostitution. People say, "A painter? How nice," and want to invite me to their parties, have me decorate the lawn like an exotic orchid for hire. But do they buy art?

I'm amphibious. I'm a person who doesn't belong to any class. The rich like to have me around because they envy my creativity; they know they can't buy *that*. The poor don't mind if I live in their neighborhood because they know I'm poor like they are, even if my education and the way I dress keeps us worlds apart. I don't belong to any class. Not to the poor, whose neighborhood I share. Not to the rich, who come to my exhibitions and buy my work. Not to the middle class from which my sister Ximena and I fled.

When I was young, when I first left home and rented that apartment with my sister and her kids right after her husband left, I thought it would be glamorous to be an artist. I wanted to be like Frida or Tina. I was ready to suffer with my camera and my paint brushes in that awful apartment we rented for $150 each because it had high ceilings and those wonderful glass skylights that convinced us we had to have it. Never mind there was no sink in the bathroom, and a tub that looked like a sarcophagus, and floorboards that didn't meet, and a hallway to scare away the dead. But fourteen-foot ceilings was enough for us to write a check for the deposit right then and there. We thought it all romantic.

You know the place, the one on Zarzamora on top of the barber shop with the Casasola prints of the Mexican Revolution. Neon BIRRIA TEPATITLÁN sign round the corner, two goats knocking their heads together, and all those Mexican bakeries, Las Brisas for *huevos rancheros* and *carnitas* and *barbacoa* on Sundays, and fresh fruit milk shakes, and mango *paletas,* and more signs in Spanish than in English. We thought it was great, great. The barrio looked cute in the daytime, like Sesame Street. Kids hopscotching on the sidewalk, blessed little boogers. And hardware stores that still sold ostrich-feather dusters, and whole families marching out of Our Lady of Guadalupe Church on Sundays, girls in their swirly-whirly dresses and patent-leather shoes, boys in their dress Stacys and shiny shirts.

But nights, that was nothing like what we knew up on the north side. Pistols going off like the wild, wild West, and me and Ximena and the kids huddled in one bed with the lights off listening to it all, saying, Go to sleep, babies, it's just firecrackers. But we knew better. Ximena would say, Clemencia, maybe we should go home. And I'd say, Shit! Because she knew as well as I did there was no home to go home to. Not with our mother. Not with that man she married. After Daddy died, it was like we didn't matter. Like Ma was so busy feeling sorry for herself, I don't know. I'm not like Ximena. I still haven't worked it out after all this time, even though our mother's dead now. My half brothers living in that house that should've been ours, me and Ximena's. But that's—how do you say it?—water under the damn? I can't ever get the sayings right even though I was born in this country. We didn't say shit like that in our house.

Once Daddy was gone, it was like my ma didn't exist, like if she died, too. I used to have a little finch, twisted one of its tiny red legs between the bars of the cage once, who knows how. The leg just dried up and fell off. My bird lived a long time without it, just a little red stump of a leg. He was fine, really. My mother's memory is like that, like if something already dead dried up and fell off, and I stopped missing where she used to be. Like if I never had a mother. And I'm not ashamed to say it either. When she married that white man, and he and his boys moved into my father's house, it was as if she stopped being my mother. Like I never even had one.

Ma always sick and too busy worrying about her own life, she would've sold us to the Devil if she could. "Because I married so young, *mi'ja,*" she'd say. "Because your father, he was so much older than me, and I never had a chance to be young. Honey, try to understand . . ." Then I'd stop listening.

That man she met at work, Owen Lambert, the foreman at the photo-finishing plant, who she was seeing even while my father was sick. Even then. That's what I can't forgive.

When my father was coughing up blood and phlegm in the hospital, half his face frozen, and his tongue so fat he couldn't talk, he looked so small with all those tubes and plastic sacks dangling around him. But what I remember most is the smell, like death was already sitting on his chest. And I remember the doctor scraping the phlegm out of my father's mouth with a white washcloth, and my daddy gagging and I wanted to yell, Stop, you stop that, he's my daddy. Goddamn you. Make him live. Daddy, don't. Not yet, not yet, not yet. And how I couldn't hold myself up, I couldn't hold myself up. Like if they'd beaten me, or pulled my insides out through my nostrils, like if they'd stuffed me with cinnamon and cloves, and I just stood there dry-eyed next to Ximena and my mother, Ximena between us because I wouldn't let her stand next to me. Everyone repeating over and over the Ave Marías and Padre Nuestros. The priest sprinkling holy water, *mundo sin fin, amén.*

Drew, remember when you used to call me your Malinalli? It was a joke, a private game between us, because you looked like a Cortez with that beard of yours. My skin dark against yours. Beautiful, you said. You said I was beautiful, and when you said it, Drew, I was.

My Malinalli, Malinche, my courtesan, you said, and yanked my head back by the braid. Calling me that name in between little gulps of breath and the raw kisses you gave, laughing from that black beard of yours.

Before daybreak, you'd be gone, same as always, before I even knew it. And it was as if I'd imagined you, only the teeth marks on my belly and nipples proving me wrong.

Your skin pale, but your hair blacker than a pirate's. Malinalli, you called me, remember? *Mi doradita.* I liked when you spoke to me in my language. I could love myself and think myself worth loving.

Your son. Does he know how much I had to do with his birth? I was the one who convinced you to let him be born. Did you tell him, while his mother lay on her back laboring his birth, I lay in his mother's bed making love to you.

You're nothing without me. I created you from spit and red dust. And I can snuff you between my finger and thumb if I want to. Blow you to kingdom come. You're just a smudge of paint I chose to birth on canvas. And when I made you over, you were no longer a part of her, you were all mine. The landscape of your body taut as a drum. The heart beneath that hide thrumming and thrumming. Not an inch did I give back.

I paint and repaint you the way I see fit, even now. After all these years. Did you know that? Little fool. You think I went hobbling along with my life, whimpering and whining like some twangy country-and-western when you went back to her. But I've been waiting. Making the world look at you from my eyes. And if that's not power, what is?

Nights I light all the candles in the house, the ones to La Virgen de Guadalupe, the ones to El Niño Fidencio, Don Pedrito Jaramillo, Santo Niño de Atocha, Nuestra Señora de San Juan de los Lagos, and especially, Santa Lucía, with her beautiful eyes on a plate.

Your eyes are beautiful, you said. You said they were the darkest eyes you'd ever seen and kissed each one as if they were capable of miracles. And after you left, I wanted to scoop them out with a spoon, place them on a plate under these blue blue skies, food for the blackbirds.

The boy, your son. The one with the face of that redheaded woman who is your wife. The boy red-freckled like fish food floating on the skin of water. That boy.

I've been waiting patient as a spider all these years, since I was nineteen and he was just an idea hovering in his mother's head, and I'm the one that gave him permission and made it happen, see.

Because your father wanted to leave your mother and live with me. Your mother whining for a child, at least *that.* And he kept saying, Later, we'll see, later. But all along it was me he wanted to be with, it was me, he said.

I want to tell you this evenings when you come to see me. When you're full of talk about what kind of clothes you're going to buy, and what you used to be like when you started high school and what you're like now that you're almost finished. And how everyone knows you as a rocker, and your band, and your new red guitar that you just got because your mother gave you a choice, a guitar or a car, but you don't need a car, do you, because I drive you everywhere. You could be my son if you weren't so light-skinned.

This happened. A long time ago. Before you were born. When you were a moth inside your mother's heart, I was your father's student, yes, just like you're mine now. And your father painted and painted me, because he said, I was his *doradita,* all golden and sun-baked, and that's the kind of woman he likes best, the ones brown as river sand, yes. And he took me under his wing and in his bed, this man, this teacher, your father. I was honored that he'd done me the favor. I was that young.

All I know is I was sleeping with your father the night you were born. In the same bed where you were conceived. I was sleeping with your father and didn't give a damn about that woman, your mother. If she was a brown woman like me, I might've had a harder time living with myself, but since she's not, I don't care. I was there first, always. I've always been there, in the mirror, under his skin, in the blood, before you were born. And he's been here in my heart before I even knew him. Understand? He's always been here. Always. Dissolving like a hibiscus flower, exploding like a rope into dust. I don't care what's right anymore. I don't care about his wife. She's not *my* sister.

And it's not the last time I've slept with a man the night his wife is birthing a baby. Why do I do that, I wonder? Sleep with a man when his wife is giving life, being suckled by a thing with its eyes still shut. Why do that? It's always given me a bit of crazy joy to be able to kill those women like that, without their knowing it. To know I've had their husbands when they were anchored in blue hospital rooms, their guts yanked inside out, the baby sucking their breasts while their husband sucked mine. All this while their ass stitches were still hurting.

Once, drunk on margaritas, I telephoned your father at four in the morning, woke the bitch up. Hello, she chirped. I want to talk to Drew. Just a moment, she said in her most polite drawing-room English. Just a moment. I laughed about that for weeks. What a stupid ass to pass the phone over to the lug asleep beside her. Excuse me, honey, it's for you. When Drew mumbled hello I was laughing so hard I could hardly talk. Drew? That dumb bitch of a wife of yours, I said, and that's all I could manage. That stupid stupid stupid. No Mexican woman would react like that. Excuse me, honey. It cracked me up.

He's got the same kind of skin, the boy. All the blue veins pale and clear just like his mama. Skin like roses in December. Pretty boy. Little clone. Little cells split into you and you and you. Tell me, baby, which part of you is your mother. I try to imagine her lips, her jaw, her long long legs that wrapped themselves around this father who took me to his bed.

This happened. I'm asleep. Or pretend to be. You're watching me, Drew. I feel your weight when you sit on the corner of the bed, dressed and ready to go, but now you're just watching me sleep. Nothing. Not a word. Not a kiss. Just sitting. You're taking me in, under inspection. What do you think already?

I haven't stopped dreaming you. Did you know that? Do you think it's strange? I never tell, though. I keep it to myself like I do all the thoughts I think of you.

After all these years.

I don't want you looking at me. I don't want you taking me in while I'm asleep. I'll open my eyes and frighten you away.

There. What did I tell you? *Drew? What is it?* Nothing. I'd knew you'd say that.

Let's not talk. We're no good at it. With you I'm useless with words. As if somehow I had to learn to speak all over again, as if the words I needed haven't been invented yet. We're cowards. Come back to bed. At least there I feel I have you for a little. For a moment. For a catch of the breath. You let go. You ache and tug. You rip my skin.

You're almost not a man without your clothes. How do I explain it? You're so much a child in my bed. Nothing but a big boy who needs to be held. I won't let anyone hurt you. My pirate. My slender boy of a man.

After all these years.

I didn't imagine it, did I? A Ganges, an eye of the storm. For a little. When we forgot ourselves, you tugged me, I leapt inside you and split you like an apple. Opened for the other to look and not give back. Something wrenched itself loose. Your body doesn't lie. It's not silent like you.

You're nude as a pearl. You've lost your train of smoke. You're tender as rain. If I'd put you in my mouth you'd dissolve like snow.

You were ashamed to be so naked. Pulled back. But I saw you for what you are, when you opened yourself for me. When you were careless and let yourself through. I caught that catch of the breath. I'm not crazy.

When you slept, you tugged me toward you. You sought me in the dark. I didn't sleep. Every cell, every follicle, every nerve, alert. Watching you sigh and roll and turn and hug me closer to you. I didn't sleep. I was taking *you* in that time.

Your mother? Only once. Years after your father and I stopped seeing each other. At an art exhibition. A show on the photographs of Eugène Atget. Those images, I could look at them for hours. I'd taken a group of students with me.

It was your father I saw first. And in that instant I felt as if everyone in the room, all the sepia-toned photographs, my students, the men in business suits, the high-heeled women, the security guards, everyone, could see me for what I was. I had to scurry out, lead my kids to another gallery, but some things destiny has cut out for you.

He caught up with us in the coat-check area, arm in arm with a redheaded Barbie doll in a fur coat. One of those scary Dallas types, hair yanked into a ponytail, big shiny face like the women behind the cosmetic counters at Neiman's. That's what I remember. She must've been with him all along, only I swear I never saw her until that second.

You could tell from a slight hesitancy, only slight because he's too suave to hesitate, that he was nervous. Then he's walking toward me, and I didn't know what to do, just stood there dazed like those animals crossing the road at night when the headlights stun them.

And I don't know why, but all of a sudden I looked at my shoes and felt ashamed at how old they looked. And he comes up to me, my love, your father, in that way of his with that grin that makes me want to beat him, makes me want to make love to him, and he says in the most sincere voice you ever heard, "Ah, Clemencia! *This* is Megan." No introduction could've been meaner. *This* is Megan. Just like that.

I grinned like an idiot and held out my paw—"Hello, Megan"—and smiled too much the way you do when you can't stand someone. Then I got the hell out of there, chattering like a monkey all the ride back with my kids. When I got home I had to lie down with a cold washcloth on my forehead and the TV on. All I could hear throbbing under the washcloth in that deep part behind my eyes: *This* is Megan.

And that's how I fell asleep, with the TV on and every light in the house burning. When I woke up it was something like three in the morning. I shut the lights and TV and went to get some aspirin, and the cats, who'd been asleep with me on the couch, got up too and followed me into the bathroom as if they knew what's what. And then they followed me into bed, where they aren't allowed, but this time I just let them, fleas and all.

This happened, too. I swear I'm not making this up. It's all true. It was the last time I was going to be with your father. We had agreed. All for the best. Surely I could see that, couldn't I? My own good. A good sport. A young girl like me. Hadn't I understood . . . responsibilities. Besides, he could *never* marry *me*. You didn't think . . . ? *Never marry a Mexican. Never marry a Mexican* . . . No, of course not. I see. I see.

We had the house to ourselves for a few days, who knows how. You and your mother had gone somewhere. Was it Christmas? I don't remember.

I remember the leaded-glass lamp with the milk glass above the dining-room table. I made a mental inventory of everything. The Egyptian lotus design on the hinges of the doors. The narrow, dark hall where your father and I had made love once. The four-clawed tub where he had washed my hair and rinsed it with a tin bowl. This window. That counter. The bedroom with its light in the morning, incredibly soft, like the light from a polished dime.

The house was immaculate, as always, not a stray hair anywhere, not a flake of dandruff or a crumpled towel. Even the roses on the dining-room table held their breath. A kind of airless cleanliness that always made me want to sneeze.

Why was I so curious about this woman he lived with? Every time I went to the bathroom, I found myself opening the medicine cabinet, looking at all the things that were hers. Her Estée Lauder lipsticks. Corals and pinks, of course. Her nail polishes—mauve was as brave as she could wear. Her cotton balls and blond hairpins. A pair of bone-colored sheepskin slippers, as clean as the day she'd bought them. On the door hook—a white robe with a MADE IN ITALY label, and a silky nightshirt with pearl buttons. I touched the fabrics. *Calidad*. Quality.

I don't know how to explain what I did next. While your father was busy in the kitchen, I went over to where I'd left my backpack, and took out a bag of gummy bears I'd bought. And while he was banging pots, I went around the house and left a trail of them in places I was sure *she* would find them. One in her lucite makeup organizer. One stuffed inside each bottle of nail polish. I untwisted the expensive lipsticks to their full length and smushed a bear on the top before recapping them. I even put a gummy bear in her diaphragm case in the very center of that luminescent rubber moon.

Why bother? Drew could take the blame. Or he could say it was the cleaning woman's Mexican voodoo. I knew that, too. It didn't matter. I got a strange satisfaction wandering about the house leaving them in places only she would look.

And just as Drew was shouting, "Dinner!" I saw it on the desk. One of those wooden babushka dolls Drew had brought her from his trip to Russia. I know. He'd bought one just like it for me.

I just did what I did, uncapped the doll inside a doll inside a doll, until I got to the very center, the tiniest baby inside all the others, and this I replaced with a gummy bear. And then I put the dolls back, just like I'd found them, one inside the other, inside the other. Except for the baby, which I put inside my pocket. All through dinner I kept reaching in the pocket of my jean jacket. When I touched it, it made me feel good.

On the way home, on the bridge over the *arroyo* on Guadalupe Street, I stopped the car, switched on the emergency blinkers, got out, and dropped the wooden toy into that muddy creek where winos piss and rats swim. The Barbie doll's toy stewing there in that muck. It gave me a feeling like nothing before and since.

Then I drove home and slept like the dead.

These mornings, I fix coffee for me, milk for the boy. I think of that woman, and I can't see a trace of my lover in this boy, as if she conceived him by immaculate conception.

I sleep with this boy, their son. To make the boy love me the way I love his father. To make him want me, hunger, twist in his sleep, as if he'd swallowed glass. I put him in my mouth. Here, little piece of my *corazón*. Boy with hard thighs and just a bit of down and a small hard downy ass like his father's, and that back like a valentine. Come here, *mi cariñito*. Come to *mamita*. Here's a bit of toast.

I can tell from the way he looks at me, I have him in my power. Come, sparrow. I have the patience of eternity. Come to *mamita*. My stupid little bird. I don't move. I don't startle him. I let him nibble. All, all for you. Rub his belly. Stroke him. Before I snap my teeth.

What is it inside me that makes me so crazy at 2 A.M.? I can't blame it on alcohol in my blood when there isn't any. It's something worse. Something that poisons the blood and tips me when the night swells and I feel as if the whole sky were leaning against my brain.

And if I killed someone on a night like this? And if it was *me* I killed instead, I'd be guilty of getting in the line of crossfire, innocent bystander, isn't it a shame. I'd be walking with my head full of images and my back to the guilty. Suicide? I couldn't say. I didn't see it.

Except it's not me who I want to kill. When the gravity of the planets is just right, it all tilts and upsets the visible balance. And that's when it wants to out from my eyes. That's when I get on the telephone, dangerous as a terrorist. There's nothing to do but let it come.

So. What do you think? Are you convinced now I'm as crazy as a tulip or a taxi? As vagrant as a cloud?

Sometimes the sky is so big and I feel so little at night. That's the problem with being a cloud. The sky is so terribly big. Why is it worse at night, when I have such an urge to communicate and no language with which to form the words? Only colors. Pictures. And you know what I have to say isn't always pleasant.

Oh, love, there. I've gone and done it. What good is it? Good or bad, I've done what I had to do and needed to. And you've answered the phone, and startled me away like a bird. And now you're probably swearing under your breath and going back to sleep, with that wife beside you, warm, radiating her own heat, alive under the flannel and down and smelling a bit like milk and hand cream, and that smell familiar and dear to you, oh.

Human beings pass me on the street, and I want to reach out and strum them as if they were guitars. Sometimes all humanity strikes me as lovely. I just want to reach out and stroke someone, and say There, there, it's all right, honey. There, there, there.

QUESTIONS FOR DISCUSSION AND WRITING

1. How do the mother's advice, the encounter in the museum, and the midnight telephone calls mark the stages in the development of the plot?
2. How does the narrator use Spanish terms to describe herself and other characters in the story? How does she characterize Drew's wife?
3. How do the many physical settings in the story—e.g., her parents' home, her apartment, and Drew's house—reveal why the narrator feels "there was no home to go to"?
4. How reliable is the narrator in this story? What evidence can you supply that suggests she is misleading the reader, or that she fails to understand herself and her situation?
5. Why does the narrator feel powerless? What strategies does she use to overcome that powerlessness? By the end of the story, has she "gone and done it"? Explain your answer.

23

JOSEPH CONRAD

Heart of Darkness

JOSEPH CONRAD (1857–1924) was born Josef Teodor Konrad Korzeniowski, in Berdyczew, Poland, the son of a patriot who was exiled to Russia. Conrad spent most of his early adult life in the French mercantile marines, visiting Africa, South America, and Australia, surviving two shipwrecks, and eventually rising to the position of captain. As a commander for British ships in the Orient, Conrad mastered the English language and developed a love for the novels of Charles Dickens. When his health failed, he turned to fiction, writing in his second language, English, and drawing upon

his many experiences at sea. For the next thirty years Conrad wrote stories about physical and psychological journeys. His longer novels include such masterpieces as *Lord Jim* (1900), *Nostromo* (1904), and *Victory* (1915). His shorter works include *The Nigger of the Narcissus* (1898), *Youth* (1903), and *The Secret Sharer* (1912). "Heart of Darkness," reprinted from *Youth,* is based on Conrad's own expedition up the Congo River. The narrator, Marlow, uses the circumstances of the expedition to explore the moral ambiguities of human existence.

The *Nellie,* a cruising yawl, swung to her anchor without a flutter of the sails, and was at rest. The flood had made, the wind was nearly calm, and being bound down the river, the only thing for it was to come to and wait for the turn of the tide.

The sea-reach of the Thames stretched before us like the beginning of an interminable waterway. In the offing the sea and the sky were welded together without a joint, and in the luminous space the tanned sails of the barges drifting up with the tide seemed to stand still in red clusters of canvas sharply peaked, with gleams of varnished spirits. A haze rested on the low shores that ran out to sea in vanishing flatness. The air was dark above Gravesend, and farther back still seemed condensed into a mournful gloom, brooding motionless over the biggest, and the greatest, town on earth.

The Director of Companies was our captain and our host. We four affectionately watched his back as he stood in the bows looking to seaward. On the whole river there was nothing that looked half so nautical. He resembled a pilot, which to a seaman is trustworthiness personified. It was difficult to realize his work was not out there in the luminous estuary, but behind him, within the brooding gloom.

Between us there was, as I have already said somewhere, the bond of the sea. Besides holding our hearts together through long periods of separation, it had the effect of making us tolerant of each other's yarns—and even convictions. The Lawyer—the best of old fellows—had, because of his many years and many virtues, the only cushion on deck, and was lying on the only rug. The Accountant had brought out already a box of dominoes, and was toying architecturally with the bones. Marlow sat cross-legged right aft, leaning against the mizzen-mast. He had sunken cheeks, a yellow complexion, a straight back, an ascetic aspect, and, with his arms dropped, the palms of hands outwards, resembled an idol. The director, satisfied the anchor had good hold, made his way aft and sat down amongst us. We exchanged a few words lazily. Afterwards there was silence on board the yacht. For some reason or other we did not begin that game of dominoes. We felt meditative, and fit for nothing but placid staring. The day was ending in a serenity of still and exquisite brilliance. The water shone pacifically; the sky, without a speck, was a benign immensity of unstained light; the very mist on the Essex marshes was like a gauzy and radiant fabric, hung from the wooded rises inland, and draping the low shores in diaphanous folds. Only the gloom to the west, brooding over the upper reaches, became more sombre every minute, as if angered by the approach of the sun.

And at last, in its curved and imperceptible fall, the sun sank low, and from glowing white changed to a dull red without rays and without heat, as if about to go out suddenly, stricken to death by the touch of that gloom brooding over a crowd of men.

Forthwith a change came over the waters, and the serenity became less brilliant but more profound. The old river in its broad reach rested unruffled at the decline of day, after ages of good service done to the race that peopled its banks, spread out in the tranquil dignity of a waterway leading to the uttermost ends of the earth. We looked at the venerable stream not in the vivid flush of a short day that comes and departs forever, but in the august light of abiding memories. And indeed nothing is easier for a man who has, as the phrase goes, "followed the sea" with reverence and affection, than to evoke the great spirit of the past upon the lower reaches of the Thames. The tidal current runs to and fro in its unceasing service, crowded with memories of men and ships it had borne to the rest of home or to the battles of the sea. It had known and served all the men of whom the nation is proud, from Sir Francis Drake to Sir John Franklin, knights all, titled and untitled—the great knights-errant of the sea. It had borne all the ships whose names are like jewels flashing in the night of time, from the *Golden Hind* returning with her round flanks full of treasure, to be visited by the Queen's Highness and thus pass out of the gigantic tale, to the *Erebus* and *Terror,* bound on other conquests—and that never returned. It had known the ships and the men. They had sailed from Deptford, from Greenwich, from Erith—the adventurers and the settlers; kings' ships and the ships of men on 'Change; captains, admirals, the dark "interlopers" of the Eastern trade, and the commissioned "generals" of East India fleets. Hunters for gold or pursuers of fame, they all had gone out on that stream, bearing the sword, and often the torch, messengers of the might within the land, bearers of a spark from the sacred fire. What greatness had not floated on the ebb of that river into the mystery of an unknown earth! . . . The dreams of men, the seed of commonwealths, the germs of empires.

The sun set; the dusk fell on the stream, and lights began to appear along the shore. The Chapman lighthouse, a three-legged thing erect on a mudflat, shone strongly. Lights of ships moved in the fairway—a great stir of lights going up and going down. And farther west on the upper reaches the place of the monstrous town was still marked ominously on the sky, a brooding gloom in sunshine, a lurid glare under the stars.

"And this also," said Marlow suddenly, "has been one of the dark places of the earth."

He was the only man of us who still "followed the sea." The worst that could be said of him was that he did not represent his class. He was a seaman, but he was a wanderer, too, while most seamen lead, if one may so express it, a sedentary life. Their minds are of the stay-at-home order, and their home is always with them—the ship; and so is their country—the sea. One ship is very much like another, and the sea is always the same. In the immutability of their surroundings the foreign shores, the foreign faces, the changing immensity of life, glide past, veiled not by a sense of mystery but by a slight disdainful ignorance; for there is nothing mysterious to a seaman unless it be the sea itself, which is the mistress of his existence and as inscrutable as Destiny. For the rest, after his hours of work, a casual stroll or a casual spree on shore suffices to unfold for him the secret of a whole continent, and generally he finds the secret not worth knowing. The yarns of seamen have a direct simplicity, the whole meaning of which lies within the shell of a cracked nut. But Marlow was not typical (if his propensity to spin yarns be excepted), and to him the meaning of an episode was not inside like a kernel but outside, enveloping the tale which brought it out only as a glow brings out a haze, in the likeness of one of these misty halos that sometimes are made visible by the spectral illumination of moonshine.

His remark did not seem at all surprising. It was just like Marlow. It was accepted in silence. No one took the trouble to grunt even; and presently he said, very slow—

"I was thinking of very old times, when the Romans first came here, nineteen hundred years ago—the other day. . . . Light came out of this river since—you say Knights? Yes; but it is like a running blaze on a plain, like a flash of lightning in the clouds. We live in the flicker—may it last as long as the old earth keeps rolling! But darkness was here yesterday. Imagine the feelings of a commander of a fine—what d'ye call 'em?—trireme in the Mediterranean, ordered suddenly to the north; run overland across the Gauls in a hurry; put in charge of one of these craft the legionaries—a wonderful lot of handy men they must have been, too—used to build, apparently by the hundred, in a month or two, if we may believe what we read. Imagine him here—the very end of the world, a sea the colour of lead, a sky the colour of smoke, a kind of ship about as rigid as a concertina—and going up this river with stores, or orders, or what you like. Sand-banks, marshes, forests, savages,—precious little to eat fit for a civilized man, nothing but Thames water to drink. No Falernian wine here, no going ashore. Here and there a military camp lost in a wilderness, like a needle in a bundle of hay—cold, fog, tempests, disease, exile, and death,—death skulking in the air, in the water, in the bush. They must have been dying like flies here. Oh, yes—he did it. Did it very well, too, no doubt, and without thinking much about it either, except afterwards to brag of what he had gone through in his time, perhaps. They were men enough to face the darkness. And perhaps he was cheered by keeping his eye on a chance of promotion to the fleet at Ravenna by-and-by, if he had good friends in Rome and survived the awful climate. Or think of a decent young citizen in a toga—perhaps too much dice, you know—coming out here in the train of some prefect, or tax-gatherer, or trader even, to mend his fortunes. Land in a swamp, march through the woods, and in some inland post feel the savagery, the utter savagery, had closed round him,—all that mysterious life of the wilderness that stirs in the forest, in the jungles, in the hearts of wild men. There's no initiation either into such mysteries. He has to live in the midst of the incomprehensible, which is also detestable. And it has a fascination, too, that goes to work upon him. The fascination of the abomination—you know, imagine the growing regrets, the longing to escape, the powerless disgust, the surrender, the hate."

He paused.

"Mind," he began again, lifting one arm from the elbow, the palm of the hand outwards, so that, with his legs folded before him, he had the pose of a Buddha preaching in European clothes and without a lotusflower—"Mind, none of us would feel exactly like this. What saves us is efficiency—the devotion to efficiency. But these chaps were not much account, really. They were no colonists; their administration was merely a squeeze, and nothing more, I suspect. They were conquerors, and for that you want only brute force—nothing to boast of, when you have it, since your strength is just an accident arising from the weakness of others. They grabbed what they could get for the sake of what was to be got. It was just robbery with violence, aggravated murder on a great scale, and men going at it blind—as is very proper for those who tackle a darkness. The conquest of the earth, which mostly means the taking it away from those who have a different complexion or slightly flatter noses than ourselves, is not a pretty thing when you look into it too much. What redeems it is the idea only. An idea at the back of it; not a sentimental pretence but an idea; and an unselfish belief in the idea—something you can set up, and bow down before, and offer a sacrifice to. . . ."

He broke off. Flames glided in the river, small green flames, red flames, white flames, pursuing, overtaking, joining, crossing each other—then separating slowly or hastily. The traffic of the great city went on in the deepening night upon the sleepless river. We looked on, waiting patiently—there was nothing else to do till the end of the flood; but it was only after a long silence, when he said, in a hesitating voice, "I suppose you fellows remember I did once turn fresh-water sailor for a bit," that we knew we were fated, before the ebb began to run, to hear about one of Marlow's inconclusive experiences.

"I don't want to bother you much with what happened to me personally," he began, showing in this remark the weakness of many tellers of tales who seem so often unaware of what their audience would best like to hear; "yet to understand the effect of it on me you ought to know how I got out there, what I saw, how I went up that river to the place where I first met the poor chap. It was the farthest point of navigation and the culminating point of my experience. It seemed somehow to throw a kind of light on everything about me—and into my thoughts. It was sombre enough, too—and pitiful—not extraordinary in any way—not very clear either. No, not very clear. And yet it seemed to throw a kind of light.

"I had then, as you remember, just returned to London after a lot of Indian Ocean, Pacific, China Seas—a regular dose of the East—six years or so, and I was loafing about, hindering you fellows in your work and invading your homes, just as though I had got a heavenly mission to civilize you. It was very fine for a time, but after a bit I did get tired of resting. Then I began to look for a ship—I should think the hardest work on earth. But the ships wouldn't even look at me. And I got tired of that game, too.

"Now when I was a little chap I had a passion for maps. I would look for hours at South America, or Africa, or Australia, and lose myself in all the glories of exploration. At that time there were many blank spaces on the earth, and when I saw one that looked particularly inviting on a map (but they all look that) I would put my finger on it and say, When I grow up I will go there. The North Pole was one of these places, I remember. Well, I haven't been there yet, and shall not try now. The glamour's off. Other places were scattered about the Equator, and in every sort of latitude all over the two hemispheres. I have been in some of them, and . . . well, we won't talk about that. But there was one yet—the biggest, the most blank, so to speak—that I had a hankering after.

"True, by this time it was not a blank space any more. It had got filled since my boyhood with rivers and lakes and names. It had ceased to be a blank space of delightful mystery—a white patch for a boy to dream gloriously over. It had become a place of darkness. But there was in it one river especially, a mighty big river, that you could see on the map, resembling an immense snake uncoiled, with its head in the sea, its body at rest curving afar over a vast country, and its tail lost in the depths of the land. And as I looked at the map of it in a shop-window, it fascinated me as a snake would a bird—a silly little bird. Then I remembered there was a big concern, a Company for trade on that river. Dash it all! I thought to myself, they can't trade without using some kind of craft on that lot of fresh water—steamboats! Why shouldn't I try to get charge of one? I went on along Fleet Street, but could not shake off the idea. The snake had charmed me.

"You understand it was a Continental concern, that Trading society; but I have a lot of relations living on the Continent, because it's cheap and not so nasty as it looks, they say.

"I am sorry to own I began to worry them. This was already a fresh departure for me. I was not used to get things that way, you know. I always went my own road and on my own legs where I had a mind to go. I wouldn't have believed it of myself; but, then—you see—I felt somehow I must get there by hook or by crook. So I worried them. The men said 'My dear fellow,' and did nothing. Then—would you believe it?—I tried the women. I, Charles Marlow, set the women to work—to get a job. Heavens! Well, you see, the notion drove me. I had an aunt, a dear enthusiastic soul. She wrote: 'It will be delightful. I am ready to do anything, anything for you. It is a glorious idea, I know the wife of a very high personage in the Administration, and also a man who has lots of influence with,' etc, etc. She was determined to make no end of fuss to get me appointed skipper of a river steamboat, if such was my fancy.

"I got my appointment—of course; and I got it very quick. It appears the Company had received news that one of their captains had been killed in a scuffle with the natives. This was my chance, and it made me the more anxious to go. It was only months and months afterwards, when I made the attempt to recover what was left of the body, that I heard the original quarrel arose from a misunderstanding about some hens. Yes, two black hens. Fresleven—that was the fellow's name, a Dane—thought himself wronged somehow in the bargain, so he went ashore and started to hammer the chief of the village with a stick. Oh, it didn't surprise me in the least to hear this, and at the same time to be told that Fresleven was the gentlest, quietest creature that ever walked on two legs. No doubt he was; but he had been a couple of years already out there engaged in the noble cause, you know, and he probably felt the need at last of asserting his self-respect in some way. Therefore he whacked the old nigger mercilessly, while a big crowd of his people watched him, thunderstruck, till some man—I was told the chief's son—in desperation at hearing the old chap yell, made a tentative jab with a spear at the white man—and of course it went quite easy between the shoulderblades. Then the whole population cleared into the forest, expecting all kinds of calamities to happen, while, on the other hand, the steamer Fresleven commanded left also in a bad panic, in charge of the engineer, I believe. Afterwards nobody seemed to trouble much about Fresleven's remains, till I got out and stepped into his shoes. I couldn't let it rest, though; but when an opportunity offered at last to meet my predecessor, the grass growing through his ribs was tall enough to hide his bones. They were all there. The supernatural being had not been touched after he fell. And the village was deserted, the huts gaped black, rotting, all askew within the fallen enclosures. A calamity had come to it, sure enough. The people had vanished. Mad terror had scattered them, men, women, and children, through the bush, and they had never returned. What became of the hens I don't know either. I should think the cause of progress got them, anyhow. However, through this glorious affair I got my appointment, before I had fairly begun to hope for it.

"I flew around like mad to get ready, and before forty-eight hours I was crossing the Channel to show myself to my employers, and sign the contract. In a very few hours I arrived in a city that always makes me think of a whited sepulchre. Prejudice no doubt. I had no difficulty in finding the Company's offices. It was the biggest thing in the town, and everybody I met was full of it. They were going to run an over-sea empire, and make no end of coin by trade.

"A narrow and deserted street in deep shadow, high houses, innumerable windows with venetian blinds, a dead silence, grass sprouting between the stones, imposing carriage archways right and left, immense double doors standing ponderously ajar. I slipped through one of these cracks, went up a swept and ungarnished staircase, as arid as a desert, and opened the first door I came to. Two women, one fat and the other slim, sat on straw-bottomed chairs, knitting black wool. The slim one got up and walked straight at me—still knitting with down-cast eyes—and only just as I began to think of getting out of her way, as you would a somnambulist, stood still, and looked up. Her dress was as plain as an umbrella-cover, and she turned round without a word and preceded me into a waiting-room. I gave my name, and looked about. Deal table in the middle, plain chairs all round the walls, on one end a large shining map, marked with all the colours of a rainbow. There was a vast amount of red—good to see at any time, because one knows that some real work is done in there, a deuce of a lot of blue, a little green, smears of orange, and, on the East Coast, a purple patch, to show where the jolly pioneers of progress drink the jolly lager-beer. However, I wasn't going into any of these. I was going into the yellow. Dead in the centre. And the river was there—fascinating—deadly—like a snake. Ough! A door opened, a white-haired secretarial head, but wearing a compassionate expression, appeared, and a skinny forefinger beckoned me into the sanctuary. Its light was dim, and a heavy writing-desk squatted in the middle. From behind that structure came out an impression of pale plumpness in a frock-coat. The great man himself. He was five feet six, I should judge, and had his grip on the handle-end of ever so many millions. He shook hands, I fancy, murmured vaguely, was satisfied with my French. *Bon voyage.*

"In about forty-five seconds I found myself again in the waiting-room with the compassionate secretary, who, full of desolation and sympathy, made me sign some document. I believe I undertook amongst other things not to disclose any trade secrets. Well, I am not going to.

"I began to feel slightly uneasy. You know I am not used to such ceremonies, and there was something ominous in the atmosphere. It was just as though I had been let into some conspiracy—I don't know—something not quite right; and I was glad to get out. In the outer room the two women knitted black wool feverishly. People were arriving, and the younger one was walking back and forth introducing them. The old one sat on her chair. Her flat cloth slippers were propped up on a foot-warmer, and a cat reposed on her lap. She wore a starched white affair on her head, had a wart on one cheek, and silver-rimmed spectacles hung on the tip of her nose. She glanced at me above the glasses. The swift and indifferent placidity of that look troubled me. Two youths with foolish and cheery countenances were being piloted over, and she threw at them the same quick glance of unconcerned wisdom. She seemed to know all about them and about me, too. An eerie feeling came over me. She seemed uncanny and fateful. Often far away there I thought of these two, guarding the door of Darkness, knitting black wool as for a warm pall, one introducing, introducing continuously to the unknown, the other scrutinizing the cheery and foolish faces with unconcerned old eyes. *Ave!* Old knitter of black wool.

Morituri te salutant. Not many of those she looked at ever saw her again—not half, by a long way.

"There was yet a visit to the doctor. 'A simple formality,' assured me the secretary, with an air of taking an immense part in all my sorrows. Accordingly a young chap wearing his hat over the left eyebrow, some clerk I suppose,—there must have been clerks in the business, though the house was as still as a house in a city of the dead—came from somewhere up-stairs, and led me forth. He was shabby and careless, with inkstains on the sleeves of his jacket, and his cravat was large and billowy, under a chin shaped like the toe of an old boot. It was a little too early for the doctor, so I proposed a drink, and thereupon he developed a vein of joviality. As we sat over our vermouths he glorified the Company's business, and by-and-by I expressed casually my surprise at him not going out there. He became very cool and collected all at once. 'I am not such a fool as I look, quoth Plato to his disciples,' he said sententiously, emptied his glass with great resolution, and we rose.

"The old doctor felt my pulse, evidently thinking of something else the while. 'Good, good for there,' he mumbled, and then with a certain eagerness asked me whether I would let him measure my head. Rather surprised, I said Yes, when he produced a thing like calipers and got the dimensions back and front and every way, taking notes carefully. He was an unshaven little man in a threadbare coat like a gaberdine with his feet in slippers, and I thought him a harmless fool. 'I always ask leave, in the interests of science, to measure the crania of those going back out there,' he said. 'And when they come back, too?' I asked. 'Oh. I never see them,' he remarked; 'and, moreover, the changes take place inside, you know.' He smiled, as if at some quiet joke. 'So you are going out there. Famous. Interesting, too.' He gave me a searching glance, and made another note. 'Ever any madness in your family?' he asked, in a matter-of-fact tone. I felt very annoyed. 'Is that question in the interests of science, too?' 'It would be,' he said, without taking notice of my irritation, 'interesting for science to watch the mental changes of individuals, on the spot, but . . .' 'Are you an alienist?' I interrupted. 'Every doctor should be—a little,' answered that original, imperturbably. 'I have a little theory which you Messieurs who go out there must help me to prove. This is my share in the advantages my country shall reap from the possession of such a magnificent dependency. The mere wealth I leave to others. Pardon my questions, but you are the first Englishman coming under my observation . . .' I hastened to assure him I was not in the least typical. 'If I were,' said I, 'I wouldn't be talking like this with you.' 'What you say is rather profound, and probably erroneous,' he said, with a laugh. 'Avoid irritation more than exposure to the sun. Adieu. How do you English say, eh? Goodbye. Ah! Goodbye. Adieu. In the tropics one must before everything keep calm.' . . . He lifted a warning forefinger. . . . '*Du calme, du calme. Adieu.*'

"One thing more remained to do—say good-bye to my excellent aunt. I found her triumphant. I had a cup of tea—that last decent cup of tea for many days—and in a room that most soothingly looked just as you would expect a lady's drawing-room to look, we had a long quiet chat by the fireside. In the course of these confidences it became quite plain to me I had been represented to the wife of the high dignitary, and goodness knows how many more people besides, as an exceptional and gifted creature—a piece of good fortune for the Company—a man you don't get hold of every day. Good heavens! and I was going to take charge of a two-penny-half-penny river-steamboat with a penny whistle attached! It appeared, however, I was also one of the Workers, with a capital—you know. Something like an emissary of light, something like a lower sort of apostle. There had been a lot of such rot let loose in print and talk just about that time, and the excellent woman, living right in the rush of all that humbug, got carried off her feet. She talked about 'weaning those ignorant millions from their horrid ways,' till, upon my words, she made me quite uncomfortable. I ventured to hint that the Company was run for profit.

"'You forget, dear Charlie, that the labourer is worthy of his hire,' she said, brightly. It's queer how out of touch with truth women are. They live in a world of their own, and there had never been anything like it, and never can be. It is too beautiful altogether, and if they were to set it up it would go to pieces before the first sunset. Some confounded fact we men have been living contentedly with ever since the day of creation would start up and knock the whole thing over.

"After this I got embraced, told to wear flannel, be sure to write often, and so on—and I left. In the street—I don't know why—a queer feeling came to me that I was an impostor. Odd thing that I, who used to clear out for any part of the world at twenty-four hours' notice, with less thought than most men give to the crossing of a street, had a moment—I won't say of hesitation, but of startled pause, before this commonplace affair. The best way I can explain it to you is by saying that, for a second or two, I felt as though, instead of going to the centre of a continent, I were about to set off for the centre of the earth.

"I left in a French steamer, and she called in every blamed port they have out there, for, as far as I could see, the sole purpose of landing soldiers and custom-house officers. I watched the coast. Watching a coast as it slips by the ship is like thinking about an enigma. There it is before you—smiling, frowning, inviting, grand, mean, insipid, or savage, and always mute with an air of whispering, Come and find out. This one was almost featureless, as if still in the making, with an aspect of monotonous grimness. The edge of a colossal jungle, so dark-green as to be almost black, fringed with white surf, ran straight, like a ruled line, far, far away along a blue sea whose glitter was blurred by a creeping mist. The sun was fierce, the land seemed to glisten and drip with steam. Here and there grayish-whitish specks showed up clustered inside the white surf, with a flag flying above them perhaps. Settlements some centuries old, and still no bigger than pinheads on the untouched expanse of their background. We pounded along, stopped, landed soldiers; went on, landed custom-house clerks to levy toll in what looked like a God-forsaken wilderness, with a tin shed and a flag-pole lost in it; landed more soldiers—to take care of the custom-house clerks, presumably. Some, I heard, got drowned in the surf; but whether they did or not, nobody seemed particularly to care. They were just flung out there, and on we went. Every day the coast looked the same, as though we had not moved; but we passed various places—trading places—with names like Gran' Bassam, Little Popo; names that seemed to belong to some sordid farce acted in front of a sinister back-cloth. The idleness of a passenger, my isolation amongst all these men with whom I had no point of contact, the oily and languid sea, the uniform sombreness of the coast, seemed to keep me away from the truth of things, within the toil of a mournful and senseless delusion. The voice of the surf heard now and then was a positive pleasure, like the speech of a brother. It was something natural, that had its reason, that had a meaning. Now and then a boat from the shore gave one a momentary contact with reality. It was paddled by black fellows. You could see from afar the white of their eyeballs glistening. They shouted, sang; their bodies streamed with perspiration; they had faces like grotesque masks—these chaps; but they had bone, muscle, a wild vitality, an intense energy of movement, that was as natural and true as the surf along their coast. They wanted no excuse for being there. They were a great comfort to look at. For a time I would feel I belonged still to a world of straight-forward facts; but the feeling would not last long. Something would turn up to scare it away. Once, I remember, we came upon a man-of-war anchored off the coast. There wasn't even a shed there, and she was shelling the bush. It appears the French had one of their wars going on thereabouts. Her ensign dropped limp like a rag; the muzzles of the long six-inch guns stuck out all over the low hull; the greasy, slimy swell swung her up lazily and let her down, swaying her thin masts. In the empty immensity of earth, sky, and water, there she was, incomprehensible, firing into a continent. Pop, would go one of the six-inch guns; a small flame would dart and vanish, a little white smoke would disappear, a tiny projectile would give a feeble screech—and nothing happened. Nothing could happen. There was a touch of insanity in the proceeding, a sense of lugubrious drollery in the sight; and it was not dissipated by somebody on board assuring me earnestly there was a camp of natives—he called them enemies!—hidden out of sight somewhere.

"We gave her letters (I heard the men in that lonely ship were dying of fever at the rate of three a-day) and went on. We called at some more places with farcical names, where the merry dance of death and trade goes on in a still and earthy atmosphere as of an overheated catacomb; all along the formless coast bordered by dangerous surf, as if Nature herself had tried to ward off intruders; in and out of rivers, streams of death in life, whose banks were rotting into mud, whose waters, thickened into slime, invaded the contorted mangroves, that seemed to writhe at us in the extremity of an impotent despair. Nowhere did we stop long enough to get a particularized impression, but the general sense of vague and oppressive wonder grew upon me. It was like a weary pilgrimage amongst hints for nightmares.

"It was upward of thirty days before I saw the mouth of the big river. We anchored off the seat of the government. But my work would not begin till some two hundred miles farther on. So as soon as I could I made a start for a place thirty miles higher up.

"I had my passage on a little sea-going steamer. Her captain was a Swede, and knowing me for a seaman, invited me on the bridge. He was a young man, lean, fair, and morose, with lanky hair and a shuffling gait. As we left the miserable little wharf, he tossed his head contemptuously at the shore. 'Been living there?' he asked. I said, 'Yes.' 'Fine lot these government chaps—are they not?' he went on, speaking English with great precision and considerable bitterness. 'It is funny what some people will do for a few francs a-month. I wonder what becomes of that kind when it goes up country?' I said to him I expected to see that soon. 'So-o-o!' he exclaimed. He shuffled athwart, keeping one eye ahead vigilantly. 'Don't be too sure,' he continued. 'The other day I took up a man who hanged himself on the road. He was a Swede, too.' 'Hanged himself! Why, in God's name?' I cried. He kept on looking out watchfully. 'Who knows? The sun too much for him, or the country perhaps.'

"At last we opened a reach. A rocky cliff appeared, mounds of turned-up earth by the shore, houses on a hill, others with iron roofs, amongst a waste of excavations, or hanging to the declivity. A continuous noise of the rapids above hovered over this scene of inhabited devastation. A lot of people, mostly black and naked, moved about like ants. A jetty projected into the river. A blinding sunlight drowned all this at times in a sudden recrudescence of glare. 'There's your Company's station,' said the Swede, pointing to three wooden barrack-like structures on the rocky slope. 'I will send your things up. Four boxes did you say? So. Farewell.'

"I came upon a boiler wallowing in the grass, then found a path leading up the hill. It turned aside for the boulders, and also for an undersized railway-truck lying there on its back with its wheels in the air. One was off. The thing looked as dead as the carcass of some animal. I came upon more pieces of decaying machinery, a stack of rusty nails. To the left a clump of trees made a shady spot, where dark things seemed to stir feebly. I blinked, the path was steep. A horn tooted to the right, and I saw the black people run. A heavy and dull detonation shook the ground, a puff of smoke came out of the cliff, and that was all. No change appeared on the face of the rock. They were building a railway. The cliff was not in the way or anything; but this objectless blasting was all the work going on.

"A slight clinking behind me made me turn my head. Six black men advanced in a file, toiling up the path. They walked erect and slow, balancing small baskets full of earth on their heads, and the clink kept time with their footsteps. Black rags were wound round their loins, and the short ends behind waggled to and fro like tails. I could see every rib, the joints of their limbs were like knots in a rope; each had an iron collar on his neck, and all were connected together with a chain whose bights swung between them, rhythmically clinking. Another report from the cliff made me think suddenly of that ship of war I had seen firing into a continent. It was the same kind of ominous voice; but these men could by no stretch of imagination be called enemies. They were called criminals, and the outraged law, like the bursting shells, had come to them, an insoluble mystery from the sea. All their meagre breasts panted together, the violently dilated nostrils quivered, the eyes stared stonily up-hill. They passed me within six inches, without a glance, with that complete, deathlike indifference of unhappy savages. Behind this raw matter one of the reclaimed, the product of the new forces at work, strolled despondently, carrying a rifle by its middle. He had a uniform jacket with one button off, and seeing a white man on the path, hoisted his weapon to his shoulder with alacrity. This was simple prudence, white men being so much alike at a distance that he could not tell who I might be. He was speedily reassured, and with a large, white, rascally grin, and a glance at his charge, seemed to take me into partnership in his exalted trust. After all, I also was a part of the great cause of these high and just proceedings.

"Instead of going up, I turned and descended to the left. My idea was to let that chain-gang get out of sight before I climbed the hill. You know I am not particularly tender; I've had to strike and to fend off. I've had to resist and attack sometimes—that's only one way of resisting—without counting the exact cost, according to the demands of such sort of life as I had blundered into. I've seen the devil of violence, and the devil of greed, and the devil of hot desire; but, by all the stars! these were strong, lusty, red-eyed devils, that swayed and drove men—men, I tell you. But as I stood on this hillside, I foresaw that in the blinding sunshine of that land I would become acquainted with a flabby, pretending, weak-eyed devil of a rapacious and pitiless folly. How insidious he could be, too, I was only to find out several months later and a thousand miles farther. For a moment I stood appalled, as though by a warning. Finally I descended the hill, obliquely, towards the trees I had seen.

"I avoided a vast artificial hole somebody had been digging on the slope, the purpose of which I found it impossible to divine. It wasn't a quarry or a sandpit, anyhow. It was just a hole. It might have been connected with the philanthropic desire of giving the criminals something to do. I don't know. Then I nearly fell into a very narrow ravine, almost no more than a scar in the hillside. I discovered that a lot of imported drainage-pipes for a settlement had been tumbled in there. There wasn't one that was not broken. It was a wanton smash-up. At last I got under the trees. My purpose was to stroll into the shade for a moment; but no sooner within than it seemed to me I had stepped into the gloomy circle of some Inferno. The rapids were near, and an uninterrupted, uniform, headlong, rushing noise filled the mournful stillness of the grove, where not a breath stirred, not a leaf moved with a mysterious sound—as though the tearing pace of the launched earth had suddenly become audible.

"Black shapes crouched, lay, sat between the trees leaning against the trunks, clinging to the earth, half coming out, half effaced within the dim light, in all the attitudes of pain, abandonment, and despair. Another mine on the cliff went off, followed by a slight shudder of the soil under my feet. The work was going on. The work! And this was the place where some of the helpers had withdrawn to die.

"They were dying slowly—it was very clear. They were not enemies, they were not criminals, they were nothing earthly now,—nothing but the black shadows of disease and starvation, lying confusedly in the greenish gloom. Brought from all the recesses of the coast in all the legality of time contracts, lost in uncongenial surroundings, fed on unfamiliar food, they sickened, became inefficient, and were then allowed to crawl away and rest. These moribund shapes were free as air—and nearly as thin. I began to distinguish the gleam of the eyes under the trees. Then, glancing down, I saw a face near my hand. The black bones reclined at full length with one shoulder against the tree, and slowly the eyelids rose and the sunken eyes looked up at me, enormous and vacant, a kind of blind, white flicker in the depths of the orbs, which died out slowly. The man seemed young—almost a boy—but you know with them it's hard to tell. I found nothing else to do but to offer him one of my good Swede's ship's biscuits I had in my pocket. The fingers closed slowly on it and held—there was no other movement and no other glance. He had tied a bit of white worsted round his neck—Why? Where did he get it? Was it a badge—an ornament—a charm—a propitiatory act? Was there any idea at all connected with it? It looked startling round his black neck, this bit of white thread from beyond the seas.

"Near the same tree two more bundles of acute angles sat with their legs drawn up. One, with his chin propped on his knees, stared at nothing, in an intolerable and appalling manner: his brother phantom rested its forehead, as if overcome with a great weariness; and all about others were scattered in every pose of contorted collapse, as in some picture of a massacre or a pestilence. While I stood horror-struck, one of these creatures rose to his hands and knees, and went off on all-fours towards the river to drink. He lapped out of his hand, then sat up in the sunlight, crossing his shins in front of him, and after a time let his woolly head fall on his breastbone.

"I didn't want any more loitering in the shade, and I made haste towards the station. When near the buildings I met a white man, in such an unexpected elegance of get-up that in the first moment I took him for a sort of vision. I saw a high starched collar, white cuffs, a light alpaca jacket, snowy trousers, a clear necktie, and varnished boots. No hat. Hair parted, brushed, oiled, under a green-lined parasol held in a big white hand. He was amazing, and had a penholder behind his ear.

"I shook hands with this miracle, and I learned he was the Company's chief accountant, and that all the book-keeping was done at this station. He had come out for a moment, he said, 'to get a breath of fresh air.' The expression sounded wonderfully odd, with its suggestion of sedentary desk-life. I wouldn't have mentioned the fellow to you at all, only it was from his lips that I first heard the name of the man who is so indissolubly connected with the memories of that time. Moreover, I respected the fellow. Yes; I respected his collars, his vast cuffs, his brushed hair. His appearance was certainly that of a hairdresser's dummy; but in the great demoralization of the land he kept up his appearance. That's backbone. His starched collars and got-up shirt-fronts were achievements of character. He had been out nearly three years; and, later, I could not help asking him how he managed to sport such linen. He had just the faintest blush, and said modestly, 'I've been teaching one of the native women about the station. It was difficult. She had a distaste for the work.' Thus this man had verily accomplished something. And he was devoted to his books, which were in apple-pie order.

"Everything else in the station was in a muddle,—heads, things, buildings. Strings of dusty niggers with splay feet arrived and departed; a stream of manufactured goods, rubbishy cottons, beads, and brass-wire set into the depths of darkness, and in return came a precious trickle of ivory.

"I had to wait in the station for ten days—an eternity. I lived in a hut in the yard, but to be out of the chaos I would sometimes get into the accountant's office. It was built of horizontal planks, and so badly put together that, as he bent over his high desk, he was barred from neck to heels with narrow strips of sunlight. There was no need to open the big shutter to see. It was hot there, too; big flies buzzed fiendishly, and did not sting, but stabbed. I sat generally on the floor, while of faultless appearance (and even slightly scented), perching on a high stool, he wrote, he wrote. Sometimes he stood up for exercise. When a trucklebed with a sick man (some invalid agent from upcountry) was put in there, he exhibited a gentle annoyance. 'The groans of this sick person,' he said, 'distract my attention. And without that it is extremely difficult to guard against clerical errors in this climate.'

"One day he remarked, without lifting his head, 'In the interior you will no doubt meet Mr. Kurtz.' On my asking who Mr. Kurtz was, he said he was a first-class agent; and seeing my disappointment at this information, he added slowly, laying down his pen, 'He is a very remarkable person.' Further questions elicited from him that Kurtz was at present in charge of a trading post, a very important one, in the true ivory-country, at 'the very bottom of there. Sends in as much ivory as all the others put together . . .' He began to write again. The sick man was too ill to groan. The flies buzzed in a great peace.

"Suddenly there was a growing murmur of voices and a great tramping of feet. A caravan had come in. A violent babble of uncouth sounds burst out on the other side of the planks. All the carriers were speaking together, and in the midst of the uproar the lamentable voice of the chief agent was heard 'giving it up' tearfully for the twentieth time that day. . . . He rose slowly. 'What a frightful row,' he said. He crossed the room gently to look at the sick man, and returning, said to me, 'He does not hear.' 'What!

Dead?' I asked, startled. 'No, not yet,' he answered, with great composure. Then, alluding with a toss of the head to the tumult in the station-yard. 'When one has got to make correct entries, one comes to hate those savages—hate them to the death.' He remained thoughtful for a moment. 'When you see Mr. Kurtz,' he went on, 'tell him from me that everything here'—he glanced at the desk—'is very satisfactory. I don't like to write him—with those messengers of ours you never know who may get hold of your letter—at that Central Station.' He stared at me for a moment with his mild, bulging eyes. 'Oh, he will go far, very far,' he began again. 'He will be a somebody in the Administration before long. They, above—the Council in Europe, you know—mean him to be.'

"He turned to his work. The noise outside had ceased, and presently in going out I stopped at the door. In the steady buzz of flies the homeward-bound agent was lying flushed and insensible; the other, bent over his books, was making correct entries of perfectly correct transactions; and fifty feet below the doorstep I could see the still tree-tops of the grove of death.

"Next day I left that station at last, with a caravan of sixty men, for a two-hundred-mile tramp.

"No use telling you much about that. Paths, paths, everywhere; a stamped-in network of paths spreading over the empty land, through long grass, through burnt grass, through thickets, down and up chilly ravines, up and down stony hills ablaze with heat; and a solitude, a solitude, nobody, not a hut. The population had cleared out a long time ago. Well, if a lot of mysterious niggers armed with all kinds of fearful weapons suddenly took to travelling on the road between Deal and Gravesend, catching the yokels right and left to carry heavy loads for them, I fancy every farm and cottage thereabouts would get empty very soon. Only here the dwellings were gone, too. Still I passed through several abandoned villages. There's something pathetically childish in the ruins of grass walls. Day after day, with the stamp and shuffle of sixty pairs of bare feet behind me, each pair under a 60-lb. load. Camp, cook, sleep, strike camp, march. Now and then a carrier dead in harness, at rest in the long grass near the path, with an empty water-gourd and his long staff lying by his side. A great silence around and above. Perhaps on some quiet night the tremor of far-off drums, sinking, swelling, a tremor vast, faint; a sound weird, appealing, suggestive, and wild—and perhaps with as profound a meaning as the sound of bells in a Christian country. Once a white man in an unbuttoned uniform, camping on the path with an armed escort of lank Zanzibaris, very hospitable and festive—not to say drunk. Was looking after the upkeep of the road he declared. Can't say I saw any road or any upkeep, unless the body of a middle-aged negro, with a bullet-hole in the forehead, upon which I absolutely stumbled three miles farther on, may be considered as a permanent improvement. I had a white companion, too, not a bad chap, but rather too fleshy and with the exasperating habit of fainting on the hot hillsides, miles away from the least bit of shade and water. Annoying, you know, to hold your own coat like a parasol over a man's head while he is coming-to. I couldn't help asking him once what he meant by coming there at all. 'To make money, of course. What do you think?' he said, scornfully. Then he got fever, and had to be carried in a hammock slung under a pole. As he weighed sixteen stone I had no end of rows with the carriers. They jibbed, ran away, sneaked off with their loads in the night—quite a mutiny. So, one evening, I made a speech in English with gestures, not one of which was lost to the sixty pairs of eyes before me, and the next morning I started the hammock off in front all right. An hour afterwards I came upon the whole concern wrecked in a bush—man, hammock, groans, blankets, horrors. The heavy pole had skinned his poor nose. He was very anxious for me to kill somebody, but there wasn't the shadow of a carrier near. I remember the old doctor,—'It would be interesting for science to watch the mental changes of individuals, on the spot.' I felt I was becoming scientifically interesting. However, all that is to no purpose. On the fifteenth day I came in sight of the big river again, and hobbled into the Central Station. It was on a back water surrounded by scrub and forest, with a pretty border of smelly mud on one side, and on the three others enclosed by a crazy fence of rushes. A neglected gap was all the gate it had, and the first glance at the place was enough to let you see the flabby devil was running that show. White men with long staves in their hands appeared languidly from amongst the buildings, strolling up to take a look at me, and then retired out of sight somewhere. One of them, a stout, excitable chap with black moustaches, informed me with great volubility and many digressions, as soon as I told him who I was, that my steamer was at the bottom of the river. I was thunderstruck. What, how, why? Oh, it was 'all right.' The 'manager himself' was there. All quite correct. 'Everybody had behaved splendidly! splendidly!'—'you must,' he said in agitation, 'go and see the general manager at once. He is waiting!'

"I did not see the real significance of that wreck at once. I fancy I see it now, but I am not sure—not at all. Certainly the affair was too stupid—when I think of it—to be altogether natural. Still . . . But at the moment it presented itself simply as a confounded nuisance. The steamer was sunk. They had started two days before in a sudden hurry up the river with the manager on board, in charge of some volunteer skipper, and before they had been out three hours they tore the bottom out of her on stones, and she sank near the south bank. I asked myself what I was to do there, now my boat was lost. As a matter of fact, I had plenty to do in fishing my command out of the river. I had to set about it the very next day. That, and the repairs when I brought the pieces to the station, took some months.

"My first interview with the manager was curious. He did not ask me to sit down after my twenty-mile walk that morning. He was commonplace in complexion, in feature, in manners, and in voice. He was of middle size and of ordinary build. His eyes, of the usual blue, were perhaps remarkably cold, and he certainly could make his glance fall on one as trenchant and heavy as an axe. But even at these times the rest of his person seemed to disclaim the intention. Otherwise there was only an indefinable, faint expression of his lips, something stealthy—a smile—not a smile—I remember it, but I can't explain. It was unconscious, this smile was, though just after he had said something it got intensified for an instant. It came at the end of his speeches like a seal applied on the words to make the meaning of the commonest phrase appear absolutely inscrutable. He was a common trader, from his youth up employed in these parts—nothing more. He was obeyed, yet he inspired neither love nor fear, nor even respect. He inspired uneasiness. That was it! Uneasiness. Not a definite mistrust—just uneasiness—nothing more. You have no idea how effective such a . . . a . . . faculty can be. He had no genius for organizing, for initiative, or for order even. That was evident in such things as the deplorable state of the station. He had no learning, and no intelligence. His position had come to him—why? Perhaps because he was never ill . . . He had served three terms of three years out there . . . Because triumphant health in the general rout of constitutions is a kind of power in itself. When he went home on leave he rioted on a large scale—pompously. Jack ashore—with a difference—in externals only. This one could gather from his casual talk. He originated nothing, he could keep the routine going—that's all. But he was great. He was great by this little thing that it was impossible to tell what could control such a man. He never gave that secret away. Perhaps there was nothing within him. Such a suspicion made one pause—for out there there were no external checks. Once when various tropical diseases had laid low almost every 'agent' in the station, he was heard to say, 'Men who come out here should have no entrails.' He sealed the utterance with that smile of his, as though it had been a door opening into a darkness he had in his keeping. You fancied you had seen things—but the seal was on. When annoyed at meal-times by the constant quarrels of the white men about precedence, he ordered an immense round table to be made, for which a special house had to be built. This was the station's mess-room. Where he sat was the first place—the rest were nowhere. One felt this to be his unalterable conviction. He was neither civil nor uncivil. He was quiet. He allowed his 'boy'—an overfed young negro from the coast—to treat the white men, under his very eyes, with provoking insolence.

"He began to speak as soon as he saw me. I had been very long on the road. He could not wait. Had to start without me. The up-river stations had to be relieved. There had been so many delays already that he did not know who was dead and who was alive, and how they got on—and so on, and so on. He paid no attention to my explanations, and, playing with a stick of sealing-wax, repeated several times that the situation was 'very grave, very grave.' There were rumours that a very important station was in jeopardy, and its chief, Mr. Kurtz, was ill. Hoped it was not true. Mr. Kurtz was . . . I felt weary and irritable. Hang Kurtz, I thought. I interrupted him by saying I had heard of Mr. Kurtz on the coast. 'Ah! So they talk of him down there,' he murmured to himself. Then he began again, assuring me Mr. Kurtz was the best agent he had, an exceptional man, of the greatest importance to the Company; therefore I could understand his anxiety. He was, he said, 'very, very uneasy.' Certainly he fidgeted on his chair a good deal, exclaimed, 'Ah, Mr. Kurtz!' broke the stick of sealing-wax and seemed dumbfounded by the accident. Next thing he wanted to know 'how long it would take to' . . . I interrupted him again. Being hungry, you know, and kept on my feet, too, I was getting savage. 'How could I tell?' I said. "I hadn't even seen the wreck yet—some months, no doubt.' All this talk seemed to me so futile. 'Some months,' he said. 'Well, let us say three months before we can make a start. Yes. That ought to do the affair.' I flung out of his hut (he lived all alone in a clay hut with a sort of verandah) muttering to myself my opinion of him. He was a chattering idiot. Afterwards I took it back when it was borne in upon me startlingly with what extreme nicety he had estimated the time requisite for the 'affair.'

"I went to work the next day, turning, so to speak, my back on that station. In that way only it seemed to me I could keep my hold on the redeeming facts of life. Still, one must look about sometimes; and then I saw this station, these men strolling aimlessly about in the sunshine of the yard. I asked myself sometimes what it all meant. They wandered here and there with their absurd long staves in their hands, like a lot of faithless pilgrims bewitched inside a rotten fence. The word 'ivory' rang in the air, was whispered, was sighed. You would think they were praying to it. A taint of imbecile rapacity blew through it all, like a whiff from some corpse. By Jove! I've never seen anything so unreal in my life. And outside, the silent wilderness surrounding this cleared speck on the earth struck me as something great and invincible, like evil or truth, waiting patiently for the passing away of this fantastic invasion.

"Oh, these months! Well, never mind. Various things happened. One evening a grass shed full of calico, cotton prints, beads, and I don't know what else, burst into a blaze so suddenly that you would have thought the earth had opened to let an avenging fire consume all that trash. I was smoking my pipe quietly by my dismantled steamer, and saw them all cutting capers in the light, with their arms lifted high, when the stout man with moustaches came tearing down to the river, a tin pail in his hand, assured me that everybody was 'behaving splendidly, splendidly,' dipped about a quart of water and tore back again. I noticed there was a hole in the bottom of his pail.

"I strolled up. There was no hurry. You see the thing had gone off like a box of matches. It had been hopeless from the very first. The flame had leaped high, driven everybody back, lighted up everything—and collapsed. The shed was already a heap of embers glowing fiercely. A nigger was being beaten near by. They said he had caused the fire in some way; be that as it may, he was screeching most horribly. I saw him, later, for several days, sitting in a bit of shade looking very sick and trying to recover himself: afterwards he arose and went out—and the wilderness without a sound took him into its bosom again. As I approached the glow from the dark I found myself at the back of two men, talking. I heard the name of Kurtz pronounced, then the words, 'take advantage of this unfortunate accident.' One of the men was the manager. I wished him a good evening. 'Did you ever see anything like it—eh? it is incredible,' he said, and walked off. The other man remained. He was a first-class agent, young, gentlemanly, a bit reserved, with a forked little beard and a hooked nose. He was stand-offish with the other agents, and they on their side said he was the manager's spy upon them. As to me, I had hardly ever spoken to him before. We got into talk, and by-and-by we strolled away from the hissing ruins. Then he asked me to his room, which was in the main building of the station. He struck a match, and I perceived that this young aristocrat had not only a silver-mounted dressing-case but also a whole candle all to himself. Just at that time the manager was the only man supposed to have any right to candles. Native mats covered the clay walls; a collection of spears, assegais, shields, knives, was hung up in trophies. The business intrusted to this fellow was the making of bricks—so I had been informed; but there wasn't a fragment of a brick anywhere in the station, and he had been there more than a year—waiting. It seems he could not make bricks without something, I don't know what—straw maybe. Anyways, it could not be found there, and as it was not likely to be sent from Europe, it did not appear clear to me what he was waiting for. An act of special creation perhaps. However, they were all waiting—all the sixteen or twenty pilgrims of them—for something; and upon my word it did not seem an uncongenial occupation, from the way they took it, though the only thing that ever came to them was disease—as far as I could see. They beguiled the time by backbiting and intriguing against each other in a foolish kind of way. There was an air of plotting about this station, but nothing came of it, of course. It was as unreal as everything else—as the philanthropic pretence of the whole concern, as their talk, as their government, as their show of work. The only real feeling was a desire to get appointed to a trading-post where ivory was to be had, so that they could earn percentages. They intrigued and slandered and hated each other only on that account,—but as to effectually lifting a little finger—oh, no. By heavens! there is something after all in the world allowing one man to steal a horse while another must not look at a halter. Steal a horse straight out. Very well. He has done it. Perhaps he can ride. But there is a way of looking at a halter that would provoke the most charitable of saints into a kick.

"I had no idea why he wanted to be sociable, but as we chatted in there it suddenly occurred to me the fellow was trying to get at something—in fact, pumping me. He alluded constantly to Europe, to the people I was supposed to know there—putting leading questions as to my acquaintances in the sepulchral city, and so on. His little eyes glittered like mica discs—with curiosity—though he tried to keep up a bit of superciliousness. At first I was astonished, but very soon I became awfully curious to see what he would find out from me. I couldn't possibly imagine what I had in me to make it worth his while. It was very pretty to see how he baffled himself, for in truth my body was full only of chills, and my head had nothing in it but that wretched steamboat business. It was evident he took me for a perfectly shameless prevaricator. At last he got angry, and, to conceal a movement of furious annoyance, he yawned. I rose. Then I noticed a small sketch in oils, on a panel, representing a woman, draped and blindfolded, carrying a lighted torch. The background was sombre—almost black. The movement of the woman was stately, and the effect of the torch-light on the face was sinister.

"It arrested me, and he stood by civilly, holding an empty half-pint champagne bottle (medical comforts) with the candle stuck in it. To my question he said Mr. Kurtz had painted this—in this very station more than a year ago—while waiting for means to go to his trading-post. 'Tell me, pray,' said I, 'who is this Mr. Kurtz?'

" 'The chief of the Inner Station,' he answered in a short tone, looking away. 'Much obliged,' I said, laughing. 'And you are the brickmaker of the Central Station. Everyone knows that.' He was silent for a while. 'He is a prodigy,' he said at last. 'He is an emissary of pity, and science, and progress, and devil knows what else. We want,' he began to declaim suddenly, 'for the guidance of the cause intrusted to us by Europe, so to speak, higher intelligence, wide sympathies, a singleness of purpose.' 'Who says that?' I asked. 'Lots of them,' he replied. 'Some even write that; and so *he* comes here, a special being, as you ought to know.' 'Why ought I to know?' I interrupted, really surprised. He paid no attention. 'Yes. To-day he is chief of the best station, next year he will be assistant-manager, two years more and . . . but I daresay you know what he will be in two years' time. You are of the new gang—the gang of virtue. The same people who sent him specially also recommended you. Oh, don't say no. I've my own eyes to trust.' Light dawned upon me. My dear aunt's influential acquaintances were producing an unexpected effect upon that young man. I nearly burst into a laugh. 'Do you read the Company's confidential correspondence?' I asked. He hadn't a word to say. It was great fun. 'When Mr. Kurtz,' I continued, severely, 'is General Manager, you won't have the opportunity.'

"He blew the candle out suddenly, and we went outside. The moon had risen. Black figures strolled about listlessly, pouring water on the glow, whence proceeded a sound of hissing; steam ascended in the moonlight, the beaten nigger groaned somewhere. 'What a row the brute makes!' said the indefatigable man with the moustaches, appearing near us. 'Serve him right. Transgression—punishment—bang! Pitiless, pitiless. That's the only way. This will prevent all conflagrations for the future. I was just telling the manager . . .' He noticed my companion, and became crestfallen all at once. 'Not in bed yet,' he said, with a kind of servile heartiness; 'it's so natural. Ha! Danger—agitation.' He vanished. I went on to the river-side and the other followed me. I heard a scathing murmur at my ear. 'Heap of muffs—go to.' The pilgrims could be seen in knots gesticulating, discussing. Several had still their staves in their hands. I verily believe they took these sticks to bed with them. Beyond the fence the forest stood up spectrally in the moonlight, and through the dim stir, through the faint sounds of that lamentable courtyard, the silence of the land went home to one's very heart—its mystery, its greatness, the amazing reality of its concealed life. The hurt nigger moaned feebly somewhere near by, and then fetched a deep sigh that made me mend my pace away from there. I felt a hand introducing itself under my arm. 'My dear sir,' said the fellow. 'I don't want to be misunderstood, and especially by you, who will see Mr. Kurtz long before I can have that pleasure. I wouldn't like him to get a false idea of my disposition. . . .'

"I let him run on, this papier-maché Mephistopheles, and it seemed to me that if I tried I could poke my forefinger through him, and would find nothing inside but a little loose dirt, maybe. He, don't you see, had been planning to be assistant-manager by-and-by under the present man, and I could see that the coming of that Kurtz had upset them both not a little. He talked precipitately, and I did not try to stop him. I had my shoulders against the wreck of my steamer, hauled up on the slope like a carcass of some big river animal. The smell of mud, of primeval mud, by Jove! was in my nostrils, the high stillness of primeval forest was before my eyes; there were shiny patches on the black creek. The moon had spread over everything a thin layer of silver—over the rank grass, over the mud, upon the wall of matted vegetation standing higher than the wall of a temple, over the great river I could see through a sombre gap glittering, glittering, as it flowed broadly by without a murmur. All this was great, expectant, mute, while the man jabbered about himself. I wondered whether the stillness on the face of the immensity looking at us two were meant as an appeal or as a menace. What were we who had strayed in here? Could we handle that dumb thing, or would it handle us? I felt how big, how confoundly big, was that thing that couldn't talk, and perhaps was deaf as well. What was in there? I could see a little ivory coming out from there, and I had heard Mr. Kurtz was in there. I had heard enough about it, too—God knows! Yet somehow it didn't bring any image with it—no more than if I had been told an angel or a fiend was in there. I believed it in the same way one of you might believe there are inhabitants in the planet Mars. I knew once a Scotch sailmaker who was certain, dead sure, there were people in Mars. If you asked him for some idea how they looked and behaved, he would get shy and mutter something about 'walking on all-fours.' If you as much as smiled, he would—though a man of sixty—offer to fight you. I would not have gone so far as to fight for Kurtz, but I went for him near enough to a lie. You know I hate, detest, and can't bear a lie, not because I am straighter than the rest of us, but simply because it appalls me. There is a taint of death, a flavour of mortality in lies—which is exactly what I hate and detest in the world—what I want to forget. It makes me miserable and sick, like biting something rotten would do. Temperament, I suppose. Well, I went near enough to it by letting the young fool there believe anything he liked to imagine as to my influence in Europe. I became in an instant as much of a pretence as the rest of the bewitched pilgrims. This simply because I had a notion it somehow would be of help to that Kurtz whom at the time I did not see—you understand. He was just a word for me. I did not see the man in the name any more than you do. Do you see him? Do you see the story? Do you see anything? It seems to me I am trying to tell you a dream—making a vain attempt, because no relation of a dream can convey the dream-sensation, that commingling of absurdity, surprise, and bewilderment in a tremor of struggling revolt, that notion of being captured by the incredible which is of the very essence of dreams. . . ."

He was silent for a while.

". . . No, it is impossible; it is impossible to convey the life-sensation of any given epoch of one's existence—that which makes its truth, its meaning—its subtle and penetrating essence. It is impossible. We live, as we dream—alone. . . ."

He paused again as if reflecting, then added—

"Of course in this you fellows see more than I could then. You see me now, whom you know. . . ."

It had become so pitch dark that we listeners could hardly see one another. For a long time already he, sitting apart, had been no more to us than a voice. There was not a word from anybody. The others might have been asleep, but I was awake. I listened. I listened on the watch for the sentence, for the word, that would give me the clue to the faint uneasiness inspired by this narrative that seemed to shape itself without human lips in the heavy night-air of the river.

". . . Yes—I let him run on," Marlow began again, "and think what he pleased about the powers that were behind me. I did! And there was nothing behind me! There was nothing but that wretched, old, mangled steamboat I was leaning against, while he talked fluently about 'the necessity for every man to get on.' 'And when one comes out here, you conceive, it is not to gaze at the moon.' Mr. Kurtz was a 'universal genius,' but even a genius would find it easier to work with 'adequate tools—intelligent men.' He did not make bricks—why, there was a physical impossibility in the way—as I was well aware; and if he did secretarial work for the manager, it was because 'no sensible man rejects wantonly the confidence of his superiors.' Did I see it? I saw it. What more did I want? What I really wanted was rivets, by heaven! Rivets. To get on with the work—to stop the hole. Rivets I wanted. There were cases of them down at the coast—cases—piled up—burst—split! You kicked a loose rivet at every second step in that station yard on the hillside. Rivets had rolled into the grove of death. You could fill your pockets with rivets for the trouble of stooping down—and there wasn't one rivet to be found where it was wanted. We had plates that would do, but nothing to fasten them with. And every week the messenger, a lone negro, letter-bag on shoulder and staff in hand, left our station for the coast. And several times a week a coast caravan came in with trade goods—ghastly glazed calico that made you shudder only to look at it, glass beads value about a penny a quart, confounded spotted cotton handkerchiefs. And no rivets. Three carriers could have brought all that was wanted to see that steamboat afloat.

"He was becoming confidential now, but I fancy my unresponsive attitude must have exasperated him at last, for he judged it necessary to inform me he feared neither God nor the devil, let alone any mere man. I said I could see that very well, but what I wanted was a certain quantity of rivets—and rivets were what really Mr. Kurtz wanted, if he had only known it. Now letters went to the coast every week. . . . 'My dear sir,' he cried, 'I write from dictation.' I demanded rivets. There was a way—for an intelligent man. He changed his manner; became very cold, and suddenly began to talk about a hippopotamus; wondered whether sleeping on board the steamer (I stuck to my salvage night and day) I wasn't disturbed. There was an old hippo that had the bad habit of getting out on the bank and roaming at night over the station grounds. The pilgrims used to turn out in a body and empty every rifle they could lay hands on at him. Some even had sat up o'nights for him. All this energy was wasted, though. 'That animal has a charmed life,' he said; 'but you can say this only of brutes in this country. No man—you apprehend me?—no man here bears a charmed life.' He stood there for a moment in the moonlight with his delicate hooked nose set a little askew, and his mica eyes glittering without a wink, then, with a curt Good-night, he strode off. I could see he was disturbed and considerably puzzled, which made me feel more hopeful than I had been for days. It was a great comfort to turn from that chap to my influential friend, the battered, twisted, ruined, tin-pot steamboat. I clambered on board. She rang under my feet like an empty Huntley & Palmer biscuit-tin kicked along a gutter; she was nothing so solid in make, and rather less pretty in shape, but I had expended enough hard work on her to make me love her. No influential friend would have served me better. She had given me a chance to come out a bit—to find out what I could do. No, I don't like work. I had rather laze about and think of all the fine things that can be done. I don't like work—no man does—but I like what is in the work,—the chance to find yourself. Your own reality—for yourself, not for others—what no other man can ever know. They can only see the mere show, and never can tell what it really means.

"I was not surprised to see somebody sitting aft, on the deck, with his legs dangling over the mud. You see I rather chummed with the few mechanics there were in that station, whom the other pilgrims naturally despised—on account of their imperfect manners, I suppose. This was the foreman—a boiler-maker by trade—a good worker. He was a lank, bony, yellow-faced man, with big intense eyes. His aspect was worried, and his head was as bald as the palm of my hand; but his hair in falling seemed to have stuck to his chin, and had prospered in the new locality, for his beard hung down to his waist. He was a widower with six young children (he had left them in charge of a sister of his to come out there), and the passion of his life was pigeon-flying. He was an enthusiast and a connoisseur. He would rave about pigeons. After work hours he used sometimes to come over from his hut for a talk about his children and his pigeons; at work, when he had to crawl in the mud under the bottom of the steamboat, he would tie up that beard of his in a kind of white serviette he brought for the purpose. It had loops to go over his ears. In the evening he could be seen squatted on the bank rinsing that wrapper in the creek with great care, then spreading it solemnly on a bush to dry.

"I slapped him on the back and shouted 'We shall have rivets!' He scrambled to his feet exclaiming 'No! Rivets!' as though he couldn't believe his ears. Then in a low voice, 'You . . . eh?' I don't know why we behaved like lunatics. I put my finger to the side of my nose and nodded mysteriously. 'Good for you!' he cried, snapped his fingers above his head, lifting one foot. I tried a jig. We capered on the iron deck. A frightful clatter came out of that hulk, and the virgin forest on the other bank of the creek sent it back in a thundering roll upon the sleeping station. It must have made some of the pilgrims sit up in their hovels. A dark figure obscured the lighted doorway of the manager's hut, vanished, then, a second or so after, the doorway itself vanished, too. We stopped, and the silence driven away by the stamping of our feet flowed back again from the recesses of the land. The great wall of vegetation, an exuberant and entangled mass of trunks, branches, leaves, boughs, festoons, motionless in the moonlight, was like a rioting invasion of soundless life, a rolling wave of plants, piled up, crested, ready to topple over the creek, to sweep every little man of us out of his little existence. And it moved not. A deadened burst of mighty splashes and snorts reached us from afar, as though an ichthyosaurus had been taking a bath of glitter in the great river. 'After all,' said the boiler-maker in a reasonable tone, 'why shouldn't we get the rivets?' Why not, indeed! I did not know of any reason why we shouldn't. 'They'll come in three weeks,' I said, confidently.

"But they didn't. Instead of rivets there came an invasion, an infliction, a visitation. It came in sections during the next three weeks, each section headed by a donkey carrying a white man in new clothes and tan shoes, bowing from that elevation right and left to the impressed pilgrims. A quarrelsome band of footsore sulky niggers trod on the heels of the donkey; a lot of tents, campstools, tin boxes, white cases, brown bales would be shot down in the courtyard, and the air of mystery would deepen a little over the muddle of the station. Five such installments came, with their absurd air of disorderly flight with the loot of innumerable outfit shops and provision stores, that, one would think, they were lugging, after a raid, into the wilderness for equitable division. It was an inextricable mess of things decent in themselves but that human folly made look like spoils of thieving.

"This devoted band called itself the Eldorado Exploring Expedition, and I believe they were sworn to secrecy. Their talk, however, was the talk of sordid buccaneers: it was reckless without hardihood, greedy without audacity, and cruel without courage; there was not an atom of foresight or of serious intention in the whole batch of them, and they did not seem aware these things are wanted for the work of the world. To tear treasure out of the bowels of the land was their desire, with no more moral purpose at the back of it than there is in burglars breaking into a safe. Who paid the expenses of the noble enterprise I don't know; but the uncle of our manager was leader of that lot.

"In exterior he resembled a butcher in a poor neighbourhood, and his eyes had a look of sleepy cunning. He carried his fat paunch with ostentation on his short legs, and during the time his gang infested the station spoke to no one but his nephew. You could see these two roaming about all day long with their heads together in an everlasting confab.

"I had given up worrying myself about the rivets. One's capacity for that kind of folly is more limited than you would suppose. I said Hang!—and let things slide. I had plenty of time for meditation, and now and then I would give some thought to Kurtz. I wasn't very interested in him. No. Still, I was curious to see whether this man, who had come out equipped with moral ideas of some sort, would climb to the top after all and how he would set about his work when there."

2

"One evening as I was lying flat on the deck of my steamboat, I heard voices approaching—and there were the nephew and the uncle strolling along the bank. I laid my head on my arm again, and had nearly lost myself in a doze, when somebody said in my ear, as it were: 'I am as harmless as a little child, but I don't like to be dictated to. Am I the manager—or am I not? I was ordered to send him there. It's incredible.' . . . I became aware that the two were standing on the shore alongside the forepart of the steamboat, just below my head. I did not move; it did not occur to me to move: I was sleepy. 'It *is* unpleasant,' grunted the uncle. 'He has asked the Administration to be sent there,' said the other, 'with the idea of showing what he could do; and I was instructed accordingly. Look at the influence that man must have. Is it not frightful?' They both agreed it was frightful, then made several bizarre remarks: 'Make rain and fine weather—one man—the Council—by the nose'—bits of absurd sentences that got the better of my drowsiness, so that I had pretty near the whole of my wits about me when the uncle said, 'The climate may do away with this difficulty for you. Is he alone there?' 'Yes,' answered the manager; 'he sent his assistant down the river with a note to me in these terms: "Clear this poor devil out of the country, and don't bother sending more of that sort. I had rather be alone than have the kind of men you can dispose of with me." It was more than a year ago. Can you imagine such impudence!' 'Anything since then?' asked the other, hoarsely. 'Ivory,' jerked the nephew; 'lots of it—prime sort—lots—most annoying, from him.' 'And with that?' questioned the heavy rumble. 'Invoice,' was the reply fired out, so to speak. Then silence. They had been talking about Kurtz.

"I was broad awake by this time, but, lying perfectly at ease, remained still, having no inducement to change my position. 'How did that ivory come all this way?' growled the elder man, who seemed very vexed. The other explained that it had come with a fleet of canoes in charge of an English half-caste clerk Kurtz had with him; that Kurtz had apparently intended to return himself, the station being by that time bare of goods and stores, but after coming three hundred miles, had suddenly decided to go back, which he started to do alone in a small dugout with four paddlers, leaving the half-caste to continue down the river with the ivory. The two fellows there seemed astounded at anybody attempting such a thing. They were at a loss for an adequate motive. As to me, I seemed to see Kurtz for the first time. It was a distinct glimpse; the dugout, four paddling savages, and the lone white man turning his back suddenly on the headquarters, on relief, on thoughts of home—perhaps; setting his face towards the depths of the wilderness, towards his empty and desolate station. I did not know the motive. Perhaps he was just simply a fine fellow who stuck to his work for its own sake. His name, you understand, had not been pronounced once. He was 'that man.' The half-caste, who, as far as I could see, had conducted a difficult trip with great prudence and pluck, was invariably alluded to as 'that scoundrel.' The 'scoundrel' had reported that the 'man' had been very ill—had recovered imperfectly. . . . The two below me moved away then a few paces, and strolled back and forth at some little distance. I heard: 'Military post—doctor—two hundred miles—quite alone now—unavoidable, delays—nine months—no news—strange rumours.' They approached again, just as the manager was saying, 'No one, as far as I know, unless a species of wandering trader—a pestilential fellow, snapping ivory from the natives.' Who was it they were talking about now? I gathered in snatches that this was some man supposed to be in Kurtz's district, and of whom the manager did not approve. 'We will not be free from unfair competition till one of these fellows is hanged for an example,' he said. 'Certainly,' grunted the other; 'get him hanged! Why not? Anything—anything can be done in this country. That's what I say; nobody here, you understand, *here,* can endanger your position. And why? You stand the climate—you outlast them all. The danger is in Europe; but there before I left I took care to———' They moved off and whispered, then their voices rose again. 'The extraordinary series of delays is not my fault. I did my best.' The fat man sighed. 'Very sad.' 'And the pestiferous absurdity of his talk,' continued the other; 'he bothered me enough when he was here. "Each station should be like a beacon on the road towards better things, a centre for trade of course, but also for humanizing, improving, instructing." Conceive you—that ass! And he wants to be manager! No, it's———' Here he got choked by excessive indignation, and I lifted my head the least bit. I was surprised to see how near they were—right under me. I could have spat upon their hats. They were looking on the ground, absorbed in thought. The manager was switching his leg with a slender twig: his sagacious relative lifted his head. 'You have been well since you came out this time?' he asked. The other gave a start. 'Who? I? Oh! Like a charm—like a charm. But the rest—oh, my goodness! All sick. They die so quick, too, that I haven't the time to send them out of the country—it's incredible!' 'H'm. Just so,' grunted the uncle. 'Ah! my boy, trust to this—I say, trust to this.' I saw him extend his short flipper of an arm for a gesture that took in the forest, the creek, the mud, the river,—seemed to beckon with a dishonouring flourish before the sunlit face of the land a treacherous appeal to the lurking death, to the hidden evil, to the profound darkness of its heart. It was so startling that I leaped to my feet and looked back at the edge of the forest, as though I had expected an answer of some sort to that black display of confidence. You know the foolish notions that come to one sometimes. The high stillness confronted these two figures with its ominous patience, waiting for the passing away of a fantastic invasion.

"They swore aloud together—out of sheer fright, I believe—then pretending not to know anything of my existence, turned back to the station. The sun was low; and leaning forward side by side, they seemed to be tugging painfully uphill their two ridiculous shadows of unequal length, that trailed behind them slowly over the tall grass without bending a single blade.

"In a few days the Eldorado Expedition went into the patient wilderness, that closed upon it as the sea closes over a diver. Long afterwards the news came that all the donkeys were dead. I know nothing as to the fate of the less valuable animals. They, no doubt, like the rest of us, found what they deserved. I did not inquire. I was then rather excited at the prospect of meeting Kurtz very soon. When I say very soon I mean it comparatively. It was just two months from the day we left the creek when we came to the bank below Kurtz's station.

"Going up that river was like travelling back to the earliest beginnings of the world, when vegetation rioted on the earth and the big trees were kings. An empty stream, a great silence, an impenetrable forest. The air was warm, thick, heavy, sluggish. There was no joy in the brilliance of sunshine. The long stretches of the waterway ran on, deserted, into the gloom of overshadowed distances. On silvery sandbanks hippos and alligators sunned themselves side by side. The broadening waters flowed through a mob of wooded islands; you lost your way on that river as you would in a desert, and butted all day long against shoals, trying to find the channel, till you thought yourself bewitched and cut off for ever from everything you had known once—somewhere—far away—in another existence perhaps. There were moments when one's past came back to one, as it will sometimes when you have not a moment to spare to yourself; but it came in the shape of an unrestful and noisy dream, remembered with wonder amongst the overwhelming realities of this strange world of plants, and water, and silence. And this stillness of life did not in the least resemble a peace. It was the stillness of an implacable force brooding over an inscrutable intention. It looked at you with a vengeful aspect. I got used to it afterwards; I did not see it any more; I had no time. I had to keep guessing at the channel; I had to discern, mostly by inspiration, the signs of hidden banks; I watched for sunken stones; I was learning to clap my teeth smartly before my heart flew out, when I shaved by a fluke some infernal sly old snag that would have ripped the life out of the tin-pot steamboat and drowned all the pilgrims; I had to keep a look-out for the signs of dead wood we could cut up in the night for next day's steaming. When you have to attend to things of that sort, to the mere incidents of the surface, the reality—the reality, I tell you—fades. The inner truth is hidden—luckily, luckily. But I felt it all the same; I felt often its mysterious stillness watching me at my monkey tricks, just as it watches you fellows performing on your respective tight-ropes for—what is it? half a-crown a tumble———"

"Try to be civil, Marlow," growled a voice, and I knew there was at least one listener awake besides myself.

"I beg your pardon. I forgot the heartache which makes up the rest of the price. And indeed what does the price matter, if the trick be well done? You do your tricks very well. And I didn't do badly either, since I managed not to sink that steamboat on my first trip. It's a wonder to me yet. Imagine a blindfolded man set to drive a van over a bad road. I sweated and shivered over that business considerably, I can tell you. After all, for a seaman, to scrape the bottom of the thing that's supposed to float all the time under his care is the unpardonable sin. No one may know of it, but you never forget the thump—eh? A blow on the very heart. You remember it, you dream of it, you wake up at night and think of it—years after—and go hot and cold all over. I don't pretend to say that steamboat floated all the time. More than once she had to wade for a bit, with twenty cannibals splashing around and pushing. We had enlisted some of these chaps on the way for a crew. Fine fellows—cannibals—in their place. They were men one could work with, and I am grateful to them. And, after all, they did not eat each other before my face: they had brought along a provision of hippo-meat which went rotten, and made the mystery of the wilderness stink in my nostrils. Phoo! I can sniff it now. I had the manager on board and three or four pilgrims with their staves—all complete. Sometimes we came upon a station close by the bank, clinging to the skirts of the unknown, and the white men rushing out of a tumbledown hovel, with great gestures of joy and surprise and welcome, seemed very strange—had the appearance of being held there captive by a spell. The word ivory would ring in the air for a while—and on we went again into the silence, along empty reaches, round the still bends, between the high walls of our winding way, reverberating in hollow claps the ponderous beat of the stern-wheel. Trees, trees, millions of trees, massive, immense, running up high; and at their foot, hugging the bank against the stream, crept the little begrimed steamboat, like a sluggish beetle crawling on the floor of a lofty portico. It made you feel very small, very lost, and yet it was not altogether depressing, that feeling. After all, if you were small, the grimy beetle crawled on—which was just what you wanted it to do. Where the pilgrims imagined it crawled to I don't know. To some place where they expected to get something, I bet! For me it crawled towards Kurtz—exclusively; but when the steam-pipes started leaking we crawled very slow. The reaches opened before us and closed behind, as if the forest had stepped leisurely across the water to bar the way for our return. We penetrated deeper and deeper into the heart of darkness. It was very quiet there. At night sometimes the roll of drums behind the curtain of trees would run up the river and remain sustained faintly, as if hovering in the air high over our heads, till the first break of day. Whether it meant war, peace, or prayer we could not tell. The dawns were heralded by the descent of a chill stillness; the wood-cutters slept, their fires burned low; the snapping of a twig would make you start. We were wanderers on prehistoric earth, on an earth that wore the aspect of an unknown planet. We could have fancied ourselves the first of men taking possession of an accursed inheritance, to be subdued at the cost of profound anguish and of excessive toil. But suddenly, as we struggled round a bend, there would be a glimpse of rush walls, of peaked grass-roofs, a burst of yells, a whirl of black limbs, a mass of hands clapping, of feet stamping, of bodies swaying, of eyes rolling, under the droop of heavy and motionless foliage. The steamer toiled along slowly on the edge of a black and incomprehensible frenzy. The prehistoric man was cursing us, praying to us, welcoming us—who could tell? We were cut off from the comprehension of our surroundings; we glided past like phantoms, wondering and secretly appalled, as sane men would be before an enthusiastic outbreak in a madhouse. We could not understand because we were too far and could not remember, because we were travelling in the night of first ages, of those ages that are gone, leaving hardly a sign—and no memories.

"The earth seemed unearthly. We are accustomed to look upon the shackled form of a conquered monster, but there—there you could look at a thing monstrous and free. It was unearthly, and the men were——No, they were not inhuman. Well, you know, that was the worst of it—this suspicion of their not being inhuman. It would come slowly to one. They howled and leaped, and spun, and made horrid faces; but what thrilled you was just the thought of their humanity—like yours—the thought of your remote kinship with this wild and passionate uproar. Ugly. Yes, it was ugly enough; but if you were man enough you would admit to yourself that there was in you just the faintest trace of a response to the terrible frankness of that noise, a dim suspicion of there being a meaning in it which you—you so remote from the night of first ages—could comprehend. And why not? The mind of man is capable of anything—because everything is in it, all the past as well as all the future. What was there after all? Joy, fear, sorrow, devotion, valour, rage—who can tell?—but truth—truth stripped of its cloak of time. Let the fool gape and shudder—the man knows, and can look on without a wink. But he must at least be as much of a man as these on the shore. He must meet that truth with his own true stuff—with his own inborn strength. Principles won't do. Acquisitions, clothes, pretty rags—rags that would fly off at the first good shake. No; you want a deliberate belief. An appeal to me in this fiendish row—is there? Very well; I hear; I admit, but I have a voice, too, and for good or evil mine is the speech that cannot be silenced. Of course, a fool, what with sheer fright and fine sentiments, is always safe. Who's that grunting? You wonder I didn't go ashore for a howl and a dance? Well, no—I didn't. Fine sentiments, you say? Fine sentiments, be hanged! I had not time. I had to mess about with white-lead and strips of woollen blanket helping to put bandages on those leaky steampipes—I tell you. I had to watch the steering, and circumvent those snags, and get the tin-pot along by hook or by crook. There was surface-truth enough in these things to save a wiser man. And between whiles I had to look after the savage who was fireman. He was an improved specimen; he could fire up a vertical boiler. He was there below me, and, upon my word, to look at him was as edifying as seeing a dog in a parody of breeches and a feather hat, walking on his hind-legs. A few months of training had done for that really fine chap. He squinted at the steam-gauge and at the water-gauge with an evident effort of intrepidity—and he had filed teeth, too, the poor devil, and the wool of his pate shaved into queer patterns, and three ornamental scars on each of his cheeks. He ought to have been clapping his hands and stamping his feet on the bank, instead of which he was hard at work, a thrall to strange witchcraft, full of improving knowledge. He was useful because he had been instructed; and what he knew was this—that should the water in that transparent thing disappear, the evil spirit inside the boiler would get angry through the greatness of his thirst, and take a terrible vengeance. So he sweated and fired up and watched the glass fearfully (with an impromptu charm, made of rags, tied to his arm, and a piece of polished bone, as big as a watch, stuck flatways through his lower lip), while the wooded banks slipped past us slowly, the short noise was left behind, the interminable miles of silence—and we crept on, towards Kurtz. But the snags were thick, the water was teacherous and shallow, the boiler seemed indeed to have a sulky devil in it, and thus neither that fireman nor I had any time to peer into our creepy thoughts.

"Some fifty miles below the Inner Station we came upon a hut of reeds, an inclined and melancholy pole, with the unrecognizable tatters of what had been a flag of some sort flying from it, and a neatly stacked wood-pile. This was unexpected. We came to the bank, and on the stack of firewood found a flat piece of board with some faded pencil-writing on it. When deciphered it said: 'Wood for you. Hurry up. Approach cautiously.' There was a signature, but it was illegible—not Kurtz—a much longer word. Hurry up. Where? Up the river? 'Approach cautiously.' We had not done so. But the warning could not have been meant for the place where it could be only found after approach. Something was wrong above. But what—and how much? That was the question. We commented adversely upon the imbecility of that telegraphic style. The bush around said nothing, and would not let us look very far, either. A torn curtain of red twill hung in the doorway of the hut, and flapped sadly in our faces. The dwelling was dismantled; but we could see a white man had lived there not very long ago. There remained a rude table—a plank on two posts; a heap of rubbish reposed in a dark corner, and by the door I picked up a book. It had lost its covers, and the pages had been thumbed into a state of extremely dirty softness; but the back had been lovingly stitched afresh with white cotton thread, which looked clean yet. It was an extraordinary find. Its title was, *An Inquiry into some Points of Seamanship,* by a man Tower, Towson—some such name—Master in his Majesty's Navy. The matter looked dreary reading enough, with illustrative diagrams and repulsive tables of figures, and the copy was sixty years old. I handled this amazing antiquity with the greatest possible tenderness, lest it should dissolve in my hands. Within, Towson or Towser was inquiring earnestly into the breaking strain of ships' chains and tackle, and other such matters. Not a very enthralling book; but at the first glance you could see there a singleness of intention, an honest concern for the right way of going to work, which made these humble pages, thought out so many years ago, luminous with another than a professional light. The simple old sailor, with his talk of chains and purchases, made me forget the jungle and the pilgrims in a delicious sensation of having come upon something unmistakably real. Such a book being there was wonderful enough; but still more astounding were the notes pencilled in the margin, and plainly referring to the text. I couldn't believe my eyes! They were in cipher! Yes, it looked like cipher. Fancy a man lugging with him a book of that description into this nowhere and studying it—and making notes—in cipher at that! It was an extravagant mystery.

"I had been dimly aware for some time of a worrying noise, and when I lifted my eyes I saw the wood-pile was gone, and the manager, aided by all the pilgrims, was shouting at me from the river-side. I slipped the book into my pocket. I assure you to leave off reading was like tearing myself away from the shelter of an old and solid friendship.

"I started the lame engine ahead. 'It must be this miserable trader—this intruder,' exclaimed the manager, looking back malevolently at the place we had left. 'He must be English,' I said. 'It will not save him from getting into trouble if he is not careful,' muttered the manager darkly. I observed with assumed innocence that no man was safe from trouble in this world.

"The current was more rapid now, the steamer seemed at her last gasp, the stern-wheel flopped languidly, and I caught myself listening on tiptoe for the next beat of the boat, for in sober truth I expected the wretched thing to give up every moment. It was like watching the last flickers of a life. But still we crawled. Sometimes I would pick out a tree a little way ahead to measure our progress towards Kurtz by, but I lost it invariably before we got abreast. To keep the eyes so long on one thing was too much for human patience. The manager displayed a beautiful resignation. I fretted and fumed and took to arguing with myself whether or no I would talk openly with Kurtz; but before I could come to any conclusion it occurred to me that my speech or my silence, indeed any action of mine, would be a mere futility. What did it matter what any one knew or ignored? What did it matter who was manager? One gets sometimes such a flash of insight. The essentials of this affair lay deep under the surface, beyond my reach, and beyond my power of meddling.

"Towards the evening of the second day we judged ourselves about eight miles from Kurtz's station. I wanted to push on; but the manager looked grave, and told me the navigation up there was so dangerous that it would be advisable, the sun being very low already, to wait where we were till next morning. Moreover, he pointed out that if the warning to approach cautiously were to be followed, we must approach in daylight—not at dusk, or in the dark. This was sensible enough. Eight miles meant nearly three hours' steaming for us, and I could also see suspicious ripples at the upper end of the reach. Nevertheless, I was annoyed beyond expression at the delay, and most unreasonably, too, since one night more could not matter much after so many months. As we had plenty of wood, and caution was the word, I brought up in the middle of the stream. The reach was narrow, straight, and had high sides like a railway cutting. The dusk came gliding into it long before the sun had set. The current ran smooth and swift, but a dumb immobility sat on the banks. The living trees, lashed together by the creepers and every living bush of the undergrowth, might have been changed into stone, even to the slenderest twig, to the lightest leaf. It was not sleep—it seemed unnatural, like a state of trance. Not the faintest sound of any kind could be heard. You looked on amazed, and began to suspect yourself of being deaf—then the night came suddenly, and struck you blind as well. About three in the morning some large fish leaped, and the loud splash made me jump as though a gun had been fired. When the sun rose there was a white fog, very warm and clammy, and more blinding than the night. It did not shift or drive; it was just there, standing all round you like something solid. At eight or nine, perhaps, it lifted as a shutter lifts. We had a glimpse of the towering multitude of trees, of the immense matted jungle, with the blazing little ball of the sun hanging over it—all perfectly still—and then the white shutter came down again, smoothly, as if sliding in greased grooves. I ordered the chain, which we had begun to heave in, to be paid out again. Before it stopped running with a muffled rattle, a cry, a very loud cry, as of infinite desolation, soared slowly in the opaque air. It ceased. A complaining clamour, modulated in savage discords, filled our ears. The sheer unexpectedness of it made my hair stir under my cap. I don't know how it struck the others; to me it seemed as though the mist itself had screamed, so suddenly, and apparently from all sides at once, did this tumultuous and mournful uproar arise. It culminated in a hurried outbreak of almost intolerably excessive shrieking, which stopped short, leaving us stiffened in a variety of silly attitudes, and obstinately listening to the nearly as appalling and excessive silence. 'Good God! What is the meaning———' stammered at my elbow one of the pilgrims,—a little fat man, with sandy hair and red whiskers, who wore sidespring boots, and pink pyjamas tucked into his socks. Two others remained open-mouthed a whole minute, then dashed into the little cabin, to rush out incontinently and stand darting scared glances, with Winchesters at 'ready' in their hands. What we could see was just the steamer we were on, her outlines blurred as though she had been on the point of dissolving, and a misty strip of water, perhaps two feet broad, around her—and that was all. The rest of the world was nowhere, as far as our eyes and ears were concerned. Just nowhere. Gone, disappeared; swept off without leaving a whisper or a shadow behind.

"I went forward, and ordered the chain to be hauled in short, so as to be ready to trip the anchor and move the steamboat at once if necessary. 'Will they attack?' whispered an awed voice. 'We will be all butchered in this fog,' murmured another. The faces twitched with the strain, the hands trembled slightly, the eyes forgot to wink. It was very curious to see the contrast of expressions of the white men and of the black fellows of our crew, who were as much strangers to that part of the river as we, though their homes were only eight hundred miles away. The whites, of course greatly discomposed, had besides a curious look of being painfully shocked by such an outrageous row. The others had an alert, naturally interested expression; but their faces were essentially quiet, even those of the one or two who grinned as they hauled at the chain. Several exchanged short, grunting phrases, which seemed to settle the matter to their satisfaction. Their headman, a young, broad-chested black, severely draped in dark-blue fringed cloths, with fierce nostrils and his hair all done up artfully in oily ringlets, stood near me. 'Aha!' I said, just for good fellowship's sake. 'Catch 'im,' he snapped, with a bloodshot widening of his eyes and a flash of sharp teeth—'catch 'im. Give 'im to us.' 'To you, eh?' I asked; 'what would you do with them?' 'Eat 'im!' he said, curtly, and, leaning his elbow on the rail, looked out into the fog in a dignified and profoundly pensive attitude. I would no doubt have been properly horrified, had it not occurred to me that he and his chaps must be very hungry: that they must have been growing increasingly hungry for at least this month past. They had been engaged for six months (I don't think a single one of them had any clear idea of time, as we at the end of countless ages have. They still belonged to the beginnings of time—had no inherited experience to teach them as it were), and of course, as long as there was a piece of paper written over in accordance with some farcical law or other made down the river, it didn't enter anybody's head to trouble how they would live. Certainly they had brought with them some rotten hippo-meat, which couldn't have lasted very long, anyway, even if the pilgrims hadn't, in the midst of a shocking hullabaloo, thrown a considerable quantity of it overboard. It looked like a high-handed proceeding; but it was really a case of legitimate self-defence. You can't breathe dead hippo waking, sleeping, and eating, and at the same time keep your precarious grip on existence. Besides that, they had given them every week three pieces of brass wire, each about nine inches long; and the theory was they were to buy their provisions with that currency in river-side villages. You can see how *that* worked. There were either no villages, or the people were hostile, or the director, who like the rest of us fed out of tins, with an occasional old he-goat thrown in, didn't want to stop the steamer for some more or less recondite reason. So, unless they swallowed the wire itself, or made loops of it to snare the fishes with, I don't see what good their extravagant salary could be to them. I must say it was paid with a regularity worthy of a large and honourable trading company. For the rest, the only thing to eat—though it didn't look eatable in the least—I saw in their possession was a few lumps of some stuff like half-cooked dough, of a dirty lavender colour, they kept wrapped in leaves, and now and then swallowed a piece of, but so small that it seemed done more for the looks of the thing than for any serious purpose of sustenance. Why in the name of all the gnawing devils of hunger they didn't go for us—they were thirty to five—and have a good tuck-in for once, amazes me now when I think of it. They were big powerful men, with not much capacity to weigh the consequences, with courage, with strength, even yet, though their skins were no longer glossy and their muscles no longer hard. And I saw that something restraining, one of those human secrets that baffle probability, had come into play there. I looked at them with a swift quickening of interest—not because it occurred to me I might be eaten by them before very long, though I own to you that just then I perceived—in a new light, as it were—how unwholesome the pilgrims looked, and I hoped, yes, I positively hoped, that my aspect was not so—what shall I say?—so—unappetizing: a touch of fantastic vanity which fitted well with the dream-sensation that pervaded all my days at that time. Perhaps I had a little fever, too. One can't live with one's finger everlasting on one's pulse. I had often 'a little fever,' or a little touch of other things—the playful paw-strokes of the wilderness, the preliminary trifling before the more serious onslaught which came in due course. Yes; I looked at them as you would on any human being, with a curiosity of their impulses, motives, capacities, weaknesses, when brought to the test of an inexorable physical necessity. Restraint! What possible restraint? Was it superstition, disgust, patience, fear—or some kind of primitive honour? No fear can stand up to hunger, no patience can wear it out, disgust simply does not exist where hunger is; and as to superstition, beliefs, and what you may call principles, they are less than chaff in a breeze. Don't you know that devilry of lingering starvation, its exasperating torment, its black thoughts, its sombre and brooding ferocity? Well, I do. It takes a man all his inborn strength to fight hunger properly. It's really easier to face bereavement, dishonour, and the perdition of one's soul—than this kind of prolonged hunger. Sad, but true. And these chaps, too, had no earthly reason for any kind of scruple. Restraint! I would just as soon have expected restraint from a hyena prowling amongst the corpses of a battlefield. But there was the fact facing me—the fact dazzling, to be seen, like the foam on the depths of the sea, like a ripple on an unfathomable enigma, a mystery greater—when I thought of it—than the curious, inexplicable note of desperate grief in this savage clamour that had swept by us on the river-bank, behind the blind whiteness of the fog.

"Two pilgrims were quarrelling in hurried whispers as to which bank. 'Left.' 'No, no; how can you? Right, right, of course.' 'It is very serious,' said the manager's voice behind me; 'I would be desolated if anything should happen to Mr. Kurtz before we came up.' I looked at him, and had not the slightest doubt he was sincere. He was just the kind of man who would wish to preserve appearances. That was his restraint. But when he muttered something about going on at once, I did not even take the trouble to answer him. I knew, and he knew, that it was impossible. Were we to let go our hold of the bottom, we would be absolutely in the air—in space. We wouldn't be able to tell where we were going to—whether up or down stream, or across—till we fetched against one bank or the other,—and then we wouldn't know at first which it was. Of course I made no move. I had no mind for a smash-up. You couldn't imagine a more deadly place for a shipwreck. Whether drowned at once or not, we were sure to perish speedily in one way or another. 'I authorize you to take all the risks,' he said, after a short silence. 'I refuse to take any,' I said, shortly; which was just the answer he expected, though its tone might have surprised him. 'Well, I must defer to your judgment. You are captain,' he said, with marked civility. I turned my shoulder to him in sign of my appreciation, and looked into the fog. How long would it last? It was the most hopeless look-out. The approach to this Kurtz grubbing for ivory in the wretched bush was beset by as many dangers as though he had been an enchanted princess sleeping in a fabulous castle. 'Will they attack, do you think?' asked the manager, in a confidential tone.

"I did not think they would attack, for several obvious reasons. The thick fog was one. If they left the bank in their canoes they would get lost in it, as we would be if we attempted to move. Still, I had also judged the jungle of both banks quite impenetrable—and yet eyes were in it, eyes that had seen us. The river-side bushes were certainly very thick; but the undergrowth behind was evidently penetrable. However, during the short lift I had seen no canoes anywhere in the reach—certainly not abreast of the steamer. But what made the idea of attack inconceivable to me was the nature of the noise—of the cries we had heard. They had not the fierce character boding of immediate hostile intention. Unexpected, wild, and violent as they had been, they had given me an irresistible impression of sorrow. The glimpse of the steamboat had for some reason filled those savages with unrestrained grief. The danger, if any, I expounded, was from our proximity to a great human passion let loose. Even extreme grief may ultimately vent itself in violence—but more generally takes the form of apathy. . . .

"You should have seen the pilgrims stare! They had no heart to grin, or even to revile me: but I believe they thought me gone mad—with fright, maybe. I delivered a regular lecture. My dear boys, it was no good bothering. Keep a look-out? Well, you may guess I watched the fog for the signs of lifting as a cat watches a mouse; but for anything else our eyes were of no more use to us than if we had been buried miles deep in a heap of cotton-wool. It felt like it, too—choking, warm, stifling. Besides, all I said, though it sounded extravagant, was absolutely true to fact. What we afterwards alluded to as an attack was really an attempt at repulse. The action was very far from being aggressive—it was not even defensive, in the usual sense: it was undertaken under the stress of desperation, and in its essence was purely protective.

"It developed itself, I should say, two hours after the fog lifted, and its commencement was at a spot, roughly speaking, about a mile and a half below Kurtz's station. We had just floundered and flopped round a bend, when I saw an islet, a mere grassy hummock of bright green, in the middle of the stream. It was the only thing of the kind; but as we opened the reach more, I perceived it was the head of a long sandbank, or rather of a chain of shallow patches stretching down the middle of the river. They were discoloured, just awash, and the whole lot was seen just under the water, exactly as a man's backbone is seen running down the middle of his back under the skin. Now, as far as I did see, I could go to the right or to the left of this. I didn't know either channel, of course. The banks looked pretty well alike, the depth appeared the same; but as I had been informed the station was on the west side, I naturally headed for the western passage.

"No sooner had we fairly entered it than I became aware it was much narrower than I had supposed. To the left of us there was the long uninterrupted shoal, and to the right a high, steep bank heavily overgrown with bushes. Above the bush the trees stood in serried ranks. The twigs overhung the current thickly, and from distance to distance a large limb of some tree projected rigidly over the stream. It was then well on in the afternoon, the face of the forest was gloomy, and a broad strip of shadow had already fallen on the water. In this shadow we steamed up—very slowly, as you may imagine. I sheered her well inshore—the water being deepest near the bank, as the sounding-pole informed me.

"One of my hungry and forebearing friends was sounding in the bows just below me. This steamboat was exactly like a decked scow. On the deck, there were two little teak-wood houses, with doors and windows. The boiler was in the fore-end, and the machinery right astern. Over the whole there was a light roof, supported on stanchions. The funnel projected through that roof, and in front of the funnel a small cabin built of light planks served for a pilot-house. It contained a couch, two camp-stools, a loaded Martini-Henry leaning in one corner, a tiny table, and the steering-wheel. It had a wide door in front and a broad shutter at each side. All these were always thrown open, of course. I spent my days perched up there on the extreme fore-end of that roof, before the door. At night I slept, or tried to, on the couch. An athletic black belonging to some coast tribe, and educated by my poor predecessor, was the helmsman. He sported a pair of brass earrings, wore a blue cloth wrapper from the waist to the ankles, and thought all the world of himself. He was the most unstable kind of fool I had ever seen. He steered with no end of a swagger while you were by; but if he lost sight of you, he became instantly the prey of an abject funk, and would let that cripple of a steamboat get the upper hand of him in a minute.

"I was looking down at the sounding-pole, and feeling much annoyed to see at each try a little more of it stick out of that river, when I saw my poleman give up the business suddenly, and stretch himself flat on the deck, without even taking the trouble to haul his pole in. He kept hold on it though, and it trailed in the water. At the same time the fireman, whom I could also see below me, sat down abruptly before his furnace and ducked his head. I was amazed. Then I had to look at the river mighty quick, because there was a snag in the fairway. Sticks, little sticks, were flying about—thick: they were whizzing before my nose, dropping below me, striking behind me against my pilot-house. All this time the river, the shore, the woods, were very quiet—perfectly quiet. I could only hear the heavy splashing thump of the stern-wheel and the patter of these things. We cleared the snag clumsily. Arrows, by Jove! We were being shot at! I stepped in quickly to close the shutter on the land-side. That fool-helmsman, his hands on the spokes, was lifting his knees high, stamping his feet, champing his mouth, like a reined-in horse. Confound him! And we were staggering within ten feet of the bank. I had to lean right out to swing the heavy shutter, and I saw a face amongst the leaves on the level with my own, looking at me very fierce and steady; and then suddenly, as though a veil had been removed from my eyes, I made out, deep in the tangled gloom, naked breasts, arms, legs, glaring eyes,—the bush was swarming with human limbs in movement, glistening, of bronze colour. The twigs shook, swayed, and rustled, the arrows flew out of them, and then the shutter came to. 'Steer her straight,' I said to the helmsman. He held his head rigid, face forward; but his eyes rolled, he kept on, lifting and setting down his feet gently, his mouth foamed a little. 'Keep quiet!' I said in a fury. I might just as well have ordered a tree not to sway in the wind. I darted out. Below me there was a great scuffle of feet on the iron deck; confused exclamations; a voice screamed, 'Can you turn back?' I caught sight of a V-shaped ripple on the water ahead. What? Another snag! A fusillade burst out under my feet. The pilgrims had opened with their Winchesters and were simply squirting lead into that bush. A deuce of a lot of smoke came up and drove slowly forward. I swore at it. Now I couldn't see the ripple or the snag either. I stood in the doorway, peering, and the arrows came in swarms. They might have been poisoned, but they looked as though they wouldn't kill a cat. The bush began to howl. Our wood-cutters raised a warlike whoop; the report of a rifle just at my back deafened me. I glanced over my shoulder, and the pilot-house was yet full of noise and smoke when I made a dash at the wheel. The fool-nigger had dropped everything, to throw the shutter open and let off that Martini-Henry. He stood before the wide opening, glaring, and I yelled at him to come back, while I straightened the sudden twist out of that steamboat. There was no room to turn even if I had wanted to, the snag was somewhere very near ahead in that confounded smoke, there was no time to lose, so I just crowded her into the bank—right into the bank, where I knew the water was deep.

"We tore slowly along the overhanging bushes in a whirl of broken twigs and flying leaves. The fusillade below stopped short, as I had foreseen it would when the squirts got empty. I threw my head back to a glinting whizz that traversed the pilot-house, in at one shutter-hole and out at the other. Looking past that mad helmsman, who was shaking the empty rifle and yelling at the shore, I saw vague forms of men running bent double, leaping, gliding, distinct, incomplete, evanescent. Something big appeared in the air before the shutter, the rifle went overboard, and the man stepped back swiftly, looked at me over his shoulder in an extraordinary, profound, familiar manner, and fell upon my feet. The side of his head hit the wheel twice, and the end of what appeared a long cane clattered round and knocked over a little camp-stool. It looked as though after wrenching that thing from somebody ashore he had lost his balance in the effort. The thin smoke had blown away, we were clear of the snag, and looking ahead I could see that in another hundred yards or so I would be free to sheer off, away from the bank; but my feet felt so very warm and wet that I had to look down. The man had rolled on his back and stared straight up at me; both his hands clutched that cane. It was the shaft of a spear that, either thrown or lunged through the opening, had caught him in the side just below the ribs; the blade had gone in out of sight, after making a frightful gash; my shoes were full; a pool of blood lay very still, gleaming dark-red under the wheel; his eyes shone with an amazing lustre. The fusillade burst out again. He looked at me anxiously, gripping the spear like something precious, with an air of being afraid I would try to take it away from him. I had to make an effort to free my eyes from his gaze and attend to the steering. With one hand I felt above my head for the line of the steam whistle, and jerked out screech after screech hurriedly. The tumult of angry and warlike yells was checked instantly, and then from the depths of the woods went out such a tremulous and prolonged wail of mournful fear and utter despair as may be imagined to follow the flight of the last hope from the earth. There was a great commotion in the bush; the shower of arrows stopped, a few dropping shots rang out sharply—then silence, in which the languid beat of the stern-wheel came plainly to my ears. I put the helm hard a-star-board at the moment when the pilgrim in pink pyjamas, very hot and agitated, appeared in the doorway. 'The manager sends me———' he began in an official tone, and stopped short. 'Good God!' he said, glaring at the wounded man.

"We two whites stood over him, and his lustrous and inquiring glance enveloped us both. I declare it looked as though he would presently put to us some question in an understandable language; but he died without uttering a sound, without moving a limb, without twitching a muscle. Only in the very last moment, as though in response to some sign we could not see, to some whisper we could not hear, he frowned heavily, and that frown gave to his black death-mask an inconceivably sombre, brooding, and menacing expression. The lustre of inquiring glance faded swiftly into vacant glassiness. 'Can you steer?' I asked the agent eagerly. He looked very dubious; but I made a grab at his arm, and he understood at once I meant him to steer whether or no. I tell you the truth, I was morbidly anxious to change my shoes and socks. 'He is dead,' murmured the fellow, immensely impressed. 'No doubt about it,' said I, tugging like mad at the shoe-laces. 'And by the way, I suppose Mr. Kurtz is dead as well by this time.'

"For the moment that was the dominant thought. There was a sense of extreme disappointment, as though I had found out I had been striving after something altogether without a substance. I couldn't have been more disgusted if I had travelled all this way for the sole purpose of talking with Mr. Kurtz. Talking with. . . . I flung one shoe overboard, and became aware that that was exactly what I had been looking forward to—a talk with Kurtz. I made the strange discovery that I had never imagined him as doing, you know, but as discoursing. I didn't say to myself, 'Now I will never see him,' or 'Now I will never shake him by the hand,' but, 'now I will never hear him.' The man presented himself as a voice. Not of course that I did not connect him with some sort of action. Hadn't I been told in all the tones of jealousy and admiration that he had collected, bartered, swindled, or stolen more ivory than all the other agents together? That was not the point. The point was in his being a gifted creature, and that of all his gifts the one that stood out preëminently, that carried with it a sense of real presence, was his ability to talk, his words—the gift of expression, the bewildering, the illuminating, the most exalted and the most contemptible, the pulsating stream of light, or the deceitful flow from the heart of an impenetrable darkness.

"The other shoe went flying unto the devil-god of that river. I thought, By Jove! It's all over. We are too late; he has vanished—the gift has vanished, by means of some spear, arrow, or club. I will never hear that chap speak after all,—and my sorrow had a startling extravagance of emotion, even such as I had noticed in the howling sorrow of these savages in the bush. I couldn't have felt more of lonely desolation somehow, had I been robbed of a belief or had missed my destiny in life. . . . Why do you sigh in this beastly way, somebody? Absurd? Well, absurd. Good Lord! mustn't a man ever——Here, give me some tobacco." . . .

There was a pause of profound stillness, then a match flared, and Marlow's lean face appeared, worn, hollow, with downward folds and dropped eyelids, with an aspect of concentrated attention; and as he took vigorous draws at his pipe, it seemed to retreat and advance out of the night in the regular flicker of the tiny flame. The match went out.

"Absurd!" he cried. "This is the worst of trying to tell. . . . Here you all are, each moored with two good addresses, like a hulk with two anchors, a butcher round one corner, a policeman round another, excellent appetites, and temperature normal—you hear—normal from year's end to year's end. And you say, Absurd! Absurd be—exploded! Absurd! My dear boys, what can you expect from a man who out of sheer nervousness had just flung overboard a pair of new shoes! Now I think of it, it is amazing I did not shed tears. I am, upon the whole, proud of my fortitude. I was cut to the quick at the idea of having lost the inestimable privilege of listening to the gifted Kurtz. Of course I was wrong. The privilege was waiting for me. Oh, yes, I heard more than enough. And I was right, too. A voice. He was very little more than a voice. And I heard—him—it—this voice—other voices—all of them were so little more than voices—and the memory of that time itself lingers around me, impalpable, like a dying vibration of one immense jabber, silly, atrocious, sordid, savage, or simply mean, without any kind of sense. Voices, voices—even the girl herself—now—"

He was silent for a long time.

"I laid the ghost of his gifts at last with a lie," he began, suddenly. "Girl! What? Did I mention a girl? Oh, she is out of it—completely. They—the women I mean—are out of it—should be out of it. We must help them to stay in that beautiful world of their own, lest ours get worse. Oh, she had to be out of it. You should have heard the disinterred body of Mr. Kurtz saying, 'My Intended.' You would have perceived directly then how completely she was out of it. And the lofty frontal bone of Mr. Kurtz! They say the hair goes on growing sometimes, but this—ah—specimen, was impressively bald. The wilderness had patted him on the head, and, behold, it was like a ball—an ivory ball; it had caressed him, and—lo!—he had withered; it had taken him, loved him, embraced him, got into his veins, consumed his flesh, and sealed his soul to its own by the inconceivable ceremonies of some devilish initiation. He was its spoiled and pampered favourite. Ivory? I should think so. Heaps of it, stacks of it. The old mud shanty was bursting with it. You would think there was not a single tusk left either above or below the ground in the whole country. 'Mostly fossil,' the manager had remarked, disparagingly. It was no more fossil than I am; but they call it fossil when it is dug up. It appears these niggers do bury the tusks sometimes—but evidently they couldn't bury this parcel deep enough to save the gifted Mr. Kurtz from his fate. We filled the steamboat with it, and had to pile a lot on the deck. Thus he could see and enjoy as long as he could see, because the appreciation of this favour had remained with him to the last. You should have heard him say, 'My ivory.' Oh yes, I heard him. 'My Intended, my ivory, my station, my river, my———' everything belonged to him. It made me hold my breath in expectation of hearing the wilderness burst into a prodigious peal of laughter that would shake the fixed stars in their places. Everything belonged to him—but that was a trifle. The thing was to know what he belonged to, how many powers of darkness claimed him for their own. That was the reflection that made you creepy all over. It was impossible—it was not good for one either—trying to imagine. He had taken a high seat amongst the devils of the land—I mean literally. You can't understand. How could you?—with solid pavement under your feet, surrounded by kind neighbours ready to cheer you or to fall on you, stepping delicately between the butcher and the policeman, in the holy terror of scandal and gallows and lunatic asylums—how can you imagine what particular region of the first ages a man's untrammelled feet may take him into by the way of solitude—utter solitude without a policeman—by the way of silence—utter silence, where no warning voice of a kind neighbour can be heard whispering of public opinion? These little things make all the great difference. When they are gone you must fall back upon your own innate strength, upon your own capacity for faithfulness. Of course you may be too much of a fool to go wrong—too dull even to know you are being assaulted by the powers of darkness. I take it, no fool ever made a bargain for his soul with the devil: the fool is too much of a fool, or the devil too much of a devil—I don't know which. Or you may be such a thunderingly exalted creature as to be altogether deaf and blind to anything but heavenly sights and sounds. Then the earth for you is only a standing place—and whether to be like this is your loss or your gain I won't pretend to say. But most of us are neither one nor the other. The earth for us is a place to live in, where we must put up with sights, with sounds, with smells, too, by Jove!—breathe dead hippo, so to speak, and not be contaminated. And there, don't you see? your strength comes in, the faith in your ability for the digging of unostentatious holes to bury the stuff in—your power of devotion, not to yourself, but to an obscure, back-breaking business. And that's difficult enough. Mind, I am not trying to excuse or even explain—I am trying to account to myself for—for—Mr. Kurtz—for the shade of Mr. Kurtz. This initiated wraith from the back of Nowhere honoured me with its amazing confidence before it vanished altogether. This was because it could speak English to me. The original Kurtz had been educated partly in England, and—as he was good enough to say himself—his sympathies were in the right place. His mother was half-English, his father was half-French. All Europe contributed to the making of Kurtz; and by-and-by I learned that, most appropriately, the International Society for the Suppression of Savage Customs had intrusted him with the making of a report, for its future guidance. And he had written it, too. I've seen it. I've read it. It was eloquent, vibrating with eloquence, but too high-strung, I think. Seventeen pages of close writing he had found time for! But this must have been before his—let us say—nerves, went wrong, and caused him to preside at certain midnight dances ending with unspeakable rites, which—as far as I reluctantly gathered from what I heard at various times—were offered up to him—do you understand?—to Mr. Kurtz himself. But it was a beautiful piece of writing. The opening paragraph, however, in the light of later information, strikes me now as ominous. He began with the argument that we whites, from the point of development we had arrived at, 'must necessarily appear to him [savages] in the nature of supernatural beings—we approach them with the might as of a deity,' and so on, and so on. 'By the simple exercise of our will we can exert a power for good practically unbounded,' etc., etc. From that point he soared and took me with him. The peroration was magnificent, though difficult to remember, you know. It gave me the notion of an exotic immensity ruled by an august Benevolence. It made me tingle with enthusiasm. This was the unbounded power of eloquence—of words—of burning noble words. There were no practical hints to interrupt the magic current of phrases, unless a kind of note at the foot of the last page, scrawled evidently much later, in an unsteady hand, may be regarded as the exposition of a method. It was very simple, and at the end of that moving appeal to every altruistic sentiment it blazed at you, luminous and terrifying, like a flash of lightning in a serene sky: 'Exterminate all the brutes!' The curious part was that he had apparently forgotten all about that valuable postscriptum, because, later on, when he in a sense came to himself, he repeatedly entreated me to take good care of 'my pamphlet' (he called it), as it was sure to have in the future a good influence upon his career. I had full information about all these things, and, besides, as it turned out, I was to have the care of his memory. I've done enough for it to give me the indisputable right to lay it, if I choose, for an everlasting rest in the dust-bin of progress, amongst all the sweepings and, figuratively speaking, all the dead cats of civilization. But then, you see, I can't choose. He won't be forgotten. Whatever he was, he was not common. He had the power to charm or frighten rudimentary souls into an aggravated witch-dance in his honour; he could also fill the small souls of the pilgrims with bitter misgivings: he had one devoted friend at least, and he had conquered one soul in the world that was neither rudimentary nor tainted with self-seeking. No; I can't forget him, though I am not prepared to affirm the fellow was exactly worth the life we lost in getting to him. I missed my late helmsman awfully,—I missed him even while his body was still lying in the pilot-house. Perhaps you will think it passing strange this regret for a savage who was no more account than a grain of sand in a black Sahara. Well, don't you see, he had done something, he had steered; for months I had him at my back—a help—an instrument. It was a kind of partnership. He steered for me—I had to look after him, I worried about his deficiencies, and thus a subtle bond had been created, of which I only became aware when it was suddenly broken. And the intimate profundity of that look he gave me when he received his hurt remains to this day in my memory—like a claim of distant kinship affirmed in a supreme moment.

"Poor fool! If he had only left that shutter alone. He had no restraint, no restraint—just like Kurtz—a tree swayed by the wind. As soon as I had put on a dry pair of slippers, I dragged him out, after first jerking the spear out of his side, which operation I confess I performed with my eyes shut tight. His heels leaped together over the little door-step; his shoulders were pressed to my breast; I hugged him from behind desperately. Oh! he was heavy, heavy; heavier than any man on earth, I should imagine. Then without more ado I tipped him overboard. The current snatched him as though he had been a wisp of grass, and I saw the body roll over twice before I lost sight of it for ever. All the pilgrims and the manager were then congregated on the awning-deck about the pilot-house, chattering at each other like a flock of excited magpies, and there was a scandalized murmur at my heartless promptitude. What they wanted to keep that body hanging about for I can't guess. Embalm it, maybe. But I had also heard another, and a very ominous, murmur on the deck below. My friends the wood-cutters were likewise scandalized, and with a better show of reason—though I admit that the reason itself was quite inadmissible. Oh, quite! I had made up my mind that if my late helmsman was to be eaten, the fishes alone should have him. He had been a very second-rate helmsman while alive, but now he was dead he might have become a first-class temptation, and possibly cause some startling trouble. Besides, I was anxious to take the wheel, the man in pink pyjamas showing himself a hopeless duffer at the business.

"This I did directly after the simple funeral was over. We were going half-speed, keeping right in the middle of the stream, and I listened to the talk about me. They had given up Kurtz, they had given up the station; Kurtz was dead, and the station had been burnt—and so on—and so on. The red-haired pilgrim was beside himself with the thought that at least this poor Kurtz had been properly avenged. 'Say! We must have made a glorious slaughter of them in the bush. Eh? What do you think? Say?' He positively danced, the bloodthirsty little gingery beggar. And he had nearly fainted when he saw the wounded man! I could not help saying, 'You made a glorious lot of smoke, anyhow.' I had seen, from the way the tops of the bushes rustled and flew, that almost all the shots had gone too high. You can't hit anything unless you take aim and fire from the shoulder; but these chaps fired from the hip with their eyes shut. The retreat, I maintained—and I was right—was caused by the screeching of the steam-whistle. Upon this they forgot Kurtz, and began to howl at me with indignant protests.

"The manager stood by the wheel murmuring confidentially about the necessity of getting well away down the river before dark at all events, when I saw in the distance a clearing on the river-side and the outlines of some sort of building. 'What's this?' I asked. He clapped his hands in wonder. 'The station!' he cried. I edged in at once, still going half-speed.

"Through my glasses I saw the slope of a hill interspersed with rare trees and perfectly free from undergrowth. A long decaying building on the summit was half buried in the high grass; the large holes in the peaked roof gaped black from afar; the jungle and the woods made a background. There was no enclosure or fence of any kind; but there had been one apparently, for near the house half-a-dozen slim posts remained in a row, roughly trimmed, and with their upper ends ornamented with round carved balls. The rails, or whatever there had been between, had disappeared. Of course the forest surrounded all that. The river-bank was clear, and on the water-side I saw a white man under a hat like a cart-wheel beckoning persistently with his whole arm. Examining the edge of the forest above and below, I was almost certain I could see movements—human forms gliding here and there. I steamed past prudently, then stopped the engines and let her drift down. The man on the shore began to shout, urging us to land, 'We have been attacked,' screamed the manager. 'I know—I know. It's all right,' yelled back the other, as cheerful as you please. 'Come along. It's all right. I am glad.'

"His aspect reminded me of something I had seen—something funny I had seen somewhere. As I manœuvred to get alongside, I was asking myself, 'What does this fellow look like?' Suddenly I got it. He looked like a harlequin. His clothes had been made of some stuff that was brown holland probably, but it was covered with patches all over, with bright patches, blue, red, and yellow,—patches on the back, patches on the front, patches on the elbows, on knees; coloured binding around his jacket, scarlet edging at the bottom of his trousers; and the sunshine made him look extremely gay and wonderfully neat withal, because you could see how beautifully all this patching had been done. A beardless, boyish face, very fair, no features to speak of, nose peeling, little blue eyes, smiles and frowns chasing each other over that open countenance like sunshine and shadow on a wide-swept plain. 'Look out, captain!' he cried; 'there's a snag lodged in here last night.' What! Another snag? I confess I swore shamefully. I had nearly holed my cripple, to finish off that charming trip. The harlequin on the bank turned his little pug-nose up to me. 'You English?' he asked, all smiles. 'Are you?' I shouted from the wheel. The smiles vanished, and he shook his head as if sorry for my disappointment. Then he brightened up. 'Never mind!' he cried, encouragingly. 'Are we in time?' I asked. 'He is up there,' he replied, with a toss of the head up the hill, and becoming gloomy all of a sudden. His face was like the autumn sky, overcast one moment and bright the next.

"When the manager, escorted by the pilgrims, all of them armed to the teeth, had gone to the house this chap came on board. 'I say, I don't like this, these natives are in the bush,' I said. He assured me earnestly it was all right. 'They are simple people,' he added; 'well, I am glad you came. It took me all my time to keep them off.' 'But you said it was all right,' I cried. 'Oh, they meant no harm,' he said; and as I stared he corrected himself, 'Not exactly.' Then vivaciously, 'My faith, your pilot-house wants a clean up!' In the next breath he advised me to keep enough steam on the boiler to blow the whistle in case of any trouble. 'One good screech will do more for you than all your rifles. They are simple people,' he repeated. He rattled away at such a rate he quite overwhelmed me. He seemed to be trying to make up for lots of silence, and actually hinted, laughing, that such was the case. 'Don't you talk with Mr. Kurtz?' I said. 'You don't talk with that man—you listen to him,' he exclaimed with severe exaltation. 'But now———' he waved his arm, and in the twinkling of an eye was in the uttermost depths of despondency. In a moment he came up again with a jump, possessed himself of both my hands, shook them continuously, while he gabbled: 'Brother sailor . . . honour . . . pleasure . . . delight . . . introduce myself . . . Russian . . . son of an arch-priest . . . Government of Tambov . . . What? Tobacco! English tobacco; the excellent English tobacco! Now, that's brotherly. Smoke? Where's a sailor that does not smoke?'

"The pipe soothed him, and gradually I made out he had run away from school, had gone to sea in a Russian ship; ran away again; served some time in English ships; was now reconciled with the arch-priest. He made a point of that. 'But when one is young one must see things, gather experience, ideas; enlarge the mind.' 'Here!' I interrupted. 'You can never tell! Here I met Mr. Kurtz,' he said, youthfully solemn and reproachful. I held my tongue after that. It appears he had persuaded a Dutch trading-house on the coast to fit him out with stores and goods, and had started for the interior with a light heart, and no more idea of what would happen to him than a baby. He had been wandering about that river for nearly two years alone, cut off from everybody and everything. 'I am not so young as I look. I am twenty-five,' he said. 'At first old Van Shuyten would tell me to go to the devil,' he narrated with keen enjoyment; 'but I stuck to him, and talked and talked, till at last he got afraid I would talk the hind-leg off his favourite dog, so he gave me some cheap things and a few guns, and told me he hoped he would never see my face again. Good old Dutchman, Van Shuyten. I've sent him one small lot of ivory a year ago, so that he can't call me a little thief when I get back. I hope he got it. And for the rest I don't care. I had some wood stacked for you. That was my old house. Did you see?'

"I gave him Towson's book. He made as though he would kiss me, but restrained himself. 'The only book I had left, and I thought I had lost it,' he said, looking at it ecstatically. 'So many accidents happen to a man going about alone, you know. Canoes get upset sometimes—and sometimes you've got to clear out so quick when the people get angry.' He thumbed the pages. 'You made notes in Russian?' I asked. He nodded. 'I thought they were written in cipher,' I said. He laughed, then became serious. 'I had lots of trouble to keep these people off,' he said. 'Did they want to kill you?' I asked. 'Oh, no!' he cried, and checked himself. 'Why did they attack us?' I pursued. He hesitated, then said shamefacedly, 'They don't want him to go.' 'Don't they?' I said, curiously. He nodded a nod full of mystery and wisdom. 'I tell you,' he cried, 'this man has enlarged my mind.' He opened his arms wide, staring at me with his little blue eyes that were perfectly round."

3

"I looked at him, lost in astonishment. There he was before me, in motley, as though he had absconded from a troupe of mimes, enthusiastic, fabulous. His very existence was improbable, inexplicable, and altogether bewildering. He was an insoluble problem. It was inconceivable how he had existed, how he had succeeded in getting so far, how he had managed to remain—why he did not instantly disappear. 'I went a little farther,' he said, 'then still a little farther—till I had gone so far that I don't know how I'll ever get back. Never mind. Plenty time. I can manage. You take Kurtz away quick—quick—I tell you.' The glamour of youth enveloped his particoloured rags, his destitution, his loneliness, the essential desolation of his futile wanderings. For months—for years—his life hadn't been worth a day's purchase; and there he was gallantly, thoughtlessly alive, to all appearance indestructible solely by the virtue of his few years and of his unreflecting audacity. I was seduced into something like admiration—like envy. Glamour urged him on, glamour kept him unscathed. He surely wanted nothing from the wilderness but space to breathe in and to push on through. His need was to exist, and to move onwards at the greatest possible risk, and with a maximum of privation. If the absolutely pure, uncalculating, unpractical spirit of adventure had ever ruled a human being, it ruled this bepatched youth. I almost envied him the possession of this modest and clear flame. It seemed to have consumed all thought of self so completely, that even while he was talking to you, you forgot that it was he—the man before your eyes—who had gone through these things. I did not envy him his devotion to Kurtz, though. He had not meditated over it. It came to him, and he accepted it with a sort of eager fatalism. I must say that to me it appeared about the most dangerous thing in every way he had come upon so far.

"They had come together unavoidably, like two ships becalmed near each other, and lay rubbing sides at last. I suppose Kurtz wanted an audience, because on a certain occasion, when encamped in the forest, they had talked all night, or more probably Kurtz had talked. 'We talked of everything,' he said, quite transported at the recollection. 'I forgot there was such a thing as sleep. The night did not seem to last an hour. Everything! Everything! . . . Of love, too.' 'Ah, he talked to you of love!' I said, much amused. 'It isn't what you think,' he cried, almost passionately. 'It was in general. He made me see things—things.'

"He threw his arms up. We were on deck at the time, and the headman of my wood-cutters, lounging nearby, turned upon him his heavy and glittering eyes. I looked around, and I don't know why, but I assure you that never, never before, did this land, this river, this jungle, the very arch of this blazing sky, appear to me so hopeless and so dark, so impenetrable to human thought, so pitiless to human weakness. 'And ever since, you have been with him, of course?' I said.

"On the contrary. It appears their intercourse had been very much broken by various causes. He had, as he informed me proudly, managed to nurse Kurtz through two illnesses (he alluded to it as you would to some risky feat), but as a rule Kurtz wandered alone, far in the depths of the forest. 'Very often coming to this station, I had to wait days and days before he would turn up,' he said. 'Ah, it was worth waiting for!—sometimes.' 'What was he doing? exploring or what?' I asked. 'Oh, yes, of course;' he had discovered lots of villages, a lake, too—he did not know exactly in what direction; it was dangerous to inquire too much—but mostly his expeditions had been for ivory. 'But he had no goods to trade with by that time,' I objected. 'There's a good lot of cartridges left even yet,' he answered, looking away. 'To speak plainly, he raided the country,' I said. He nodded. 'Not alone, surely!' He muttered something about the villages round that lake. 'Kurtz got the tribe to follow him, did he?' I suggested. He fidgeted a little. 'They adored him,' he said. The tone of these words was so extraordinary that I looked at him searchingly. It was curious to see his mingled eagerness and reluctance to speak of Kurtz. The man filled his life, occupied his thoughts, swayed his emotions. 'What can you expect?' he burst out; 'he came to them with thunder and lightning, you know—and they had never seen anything like it—and very terrible. He could be very terrible. You can't judge Mr. Kurtz as you would an ordinary man. No, no, no! Now—just to give you an idea—I don't mind telling you, he wanted to shoot me, too, one day—but I don't judge him.' 'Shoot you!' I cried. 'What for?' 'Well, I had a small lot of ivory the chief of that village near my house gave me. You see I used to shoot game for them. Well, he wanted it, and wouldn't hear reason. He declared he would shoot me unless I gave him the ivory and then cleared out of the country, because he could do so, and had a fancy for it, and there was nothing on earth to prevent him killing whom he jolly well pleased. And it was true, too. I gave him the ivory. What did I care! But I didn't clear out. No, no. I couldn't leave him. I had to be careful, of course, till we got friendly again for a time. He had his second illness then. Afterwards I had to keep out of the way; but I didn't mind. He was living for the most part in those villages on the lake. When he came down to the river, sometimes he would take to me, and sometimes it was better for me to be careful. This man suffered too much. He hated all this, and somehow he couldn't get away. When I had a chance I begged him to try and leave while there was time; I offered to go back with him. And he would say yes, and then he would remain; go off on another ivory hunt; disappear for weeks; forget himself amongst these people—forget himself—you know.' 'Why! he's mad,' I said. He protested indignantly. Mr. Kurtz couldn't be mad. If I had heard him talk, only two days ago, I wouldn't dare hint at such a thing. . . . I had taken up my binoculars while we talked, and was looking at the shore, sweeping the limit of the forest at each side and at the back of the house. The consciousness of there being people in that bush, so silent, so quiet—as silent and quiet as the ruined house on the hill—made me uneasy. There was no sign on the face of nature of this amazing tale that was not so much told as suggested to me in desolate exclamations, completed by shrugs, in interrupted phrases, in hints ending in deep sighs. The woods were unmoved, like a mask—heavy, like the closed door of a prison—they looked with their air of hidden knowledge, of patient expectation, of unapproachable silence. The Russian was explaining to me that it was only lately that Mr. Kurtz had come down to the river, bringing along with him all the fighting men of that lake tribe. He had been absent for several months—getting himself adored, I suppose—and had come down unexpectedly, with the intention to all appearance of making a raid either across the river or down stream. Evidently the appetite for more ivory had got the better of the—what shall I say?—less material aspirations. However he had got much worse suddenly. 'I heard he was laying helpless, and so I came up—took my chance,' said the Russian. 'Oh, he is bad, very bad.' I directed my glass to the house. There were no signs of life, but there was the ruined roof, the long mud wall peeping above the grass, with three little square window-holes, no two of the same size; all this brought within reach of my hand, as it were. And then I made a brusque movement, and one of the remaining posts of that vanished fence leaped up in the field of my glass. You remember I told you I had been struck at the distance by certain attempts at ornamentation, rather remarkable in the ruinous aspect of the place. Now I had suddenly a nearer view, and its first result was to make me throw my head back as if before a blow. Then I went carefully from post to post with my glass, and I saw my mistake. These round knobs were not ornamental but symbolic; they were expressive and puzzling, striking and disturbing—food for thought and also for the vultures if there had been any looking down from the sky; but at all events for such ants as were industrious enough to ascend the pole. They would have been even more impressive, those heads on the stakes, if their faces had not been turned to the house. Only one, the first I had made out, was facing my way. I was not so shocked as you may think. The start back I had given was really nothing but a movement of surprise. I had expected to see a knob of wood there, you know. I returned deliberately to the first I had seen—and there it was, black, dried, sunken, with closed eyelids,—a head that seemed to sleep at the top of that pole, and, with the shrunken dry lips showing a narrow white line of the teeth, was smiling, too, smiling continuously at some endless and jocose dream of that eternal slumber.

"I am not disclosing any trade secrets. In fact, the manager said afterwards that Mr. Kurtz's methods had ruined the district. I have no opinion on that point, but I want you clearly to understand that there was nothing exactly profitable in these heads being there. They only showed that Mr. Kurtz lacked restraint in the gratification of his various lusts, that there was something wanting in him—some small matter which, when the pressing need arose, could not be found under his magnificent eloquence. Whether he knew of this deficiency himself I can't say. I think the knowledge came to him at last—only at the very last. But the wilderness had found him out early, and had taken on him a terrible vengeance for the fantastic invasion. I think it had whispered to him things about himself which he did not know, things of which he had no conception till he took counsel with this great solitude—and the whisper had proved irresistibly fascinating. It echoed loudly within him because he was hollow at the core. . . . I put down the glass, and the head that had appeared near enough to be spoken to seemed at once to have leaped away from me into inaccessible distance.

"The admirer of Mr. Kurtz was a bit crestfallen. In a hurried, indistinct voice he began to assure me he had not dared to take these—say, symbols—down. He was not afraid of the natives; they would not stir till Mr. Kurtz gave the word. His ascendancy was extraordinary. The camps of these people surrounded the place, and the chiefs came every day to see him. They would crawl. . . . 'I don't want to know anything of the ceremonies used when approaching Mr. Kurtz,' I shouted. Curious, this feeling that came over me that such details would be more intolerable than those heads drying on the stakes under Mr. Kurtz's windows. After all, that was only a savage sight, while I seemed at one bound to have been transported into some lightless region of subtle horrors, where pure, uncomplicated savagery was a positive relief, being something that had a right to exist—obviously—in the sunshine. The young man looked at me with surprise. I suppose it did not occur to him that Mr. Kurtz was no idol of mine. He forgot I hadn't heard any of these splendid monologues on, what was it? on love, justice, conduct of life—or what not. If it had come to crawling before Mr. Kurtz, he crawled as much as the veriest savage of them all. I had no idea of the conditions, he said: these heads were the heads of rebels. I shocked him excessively by laughing. Rebels! What would be the next definition I was to hear? There had been enemies, criminals, workers—and these were rebels. Those rebellious heads looked very subdued to me on their sticks. 'You don't know how such a life tries a man like Kurtz,' cried Kurtz's last disciple. 'Well, and you?' I said. 'I! I! I am a simple man. I have no great thoughts. I want nothing from anybody. How can you compare me to? . . .' His feelings were too much for speech, and suddenly he broke down. 'I don't understand,' he groaned. 'I've been doing my best to keep him alive, and that's enough. I had no hand in all this. I have no abilities. There hasn't been a drop of medicine or a mouthful of invalid food for months here. He was shamefully abandoned. A man like this, with such ideas. Shamefully! Shamefully! I—I—haven't slept for the last ten nights. . . .'

"His voice lost itself in the calm of the evening. The long shadows of the forest had slipped down hill while we talked, had gone far beyond the ruined hovel, beyond the symbolic row of stakes. All this was in the gloom, while we down there were yet in the sunshine, and the stretch of the river abreast of the clearing glittered in a still and dazzling splendour, with a murky and overshadowed bend above and below. Not a living soul was seen on the shore. The bushes did not rustle.

"Suddenly round the corner of the house a group of men appeared, as though they had come up from the ground. They waded waist-deep in the grass, in a compact body, bearing an improvised stretcher in their midst. Instantly, in the emptiness of the landscape, a cry arose whose shrillness pierced the still air like a sharp arrow flying straight to the very heart of the land; and, as if by enchantment, streams of human beings—of naked human beings—with spears in their hands, with bows, with shields, with wild glances and savage movements, were poured into the clearing by the dark-faced and pensive forest. The bushes shook, the grass swayed for a time, and then everything stood still in attentive immobility.

"'Now, if he does not say the right thing to them we are all done for,' said the Russian at my elbow. The knot of men with the stretcher had stopped, too, halfway to the steamer, as if petrified. I saw the man on the stretcher sit up, lank and with an uplifted arm, above the shoulders of the bearers. 'Let us hope that the man who can talk so well of love in general will find some particular reason to spare us this time,' I said. I resented bitterly the absurd danger of our situation, as if to be at the mercy of that atrocious phantom had been a dishonouring necessity. I could not hear a sound, but through my glasses I saw the thin arm extended commandingly, the lower jaw moving, the eyes of that apparition shining darkly far in its bony head that nodded with grotesque jerks. Kurtz—Kurtz—that means short in German—don't it? Well, the name was as true as everything else in his life—and death. He looked at least seven feet long. His covering had fallen off, and his body emerged from it pitiful and appalling as from a winding-sheet. I could see the cage of his ribs all astir, the bones of his arm waving. It was as though an animated image of death carved out of old ivory had been shaking its hand with menaces at a motionless crowd of men made of dark and glittering bronze. I saw him open his mouth wide—it gave him a weirdly voracious aspect, as though he had wanted to swallow all the air, all the earth, all the men before him. A deep voice reached me faintly. He must have been shouting. He fell back suddenly. The stretcher shook as the bearers staggered forward again, and almost at the same time I noticed that the crowd of savages was vanishing without any perceptible movement of retreat, as if the forest that had ejected these beings so suddenly had drawn them in again as the breath is drawn in a long aspiration.

"Some of the pilgrims behind the stretcher carried his arms—two shot-guns, a heavy rifle, and a light revolver-carbine—the thunderbolts of that pitiful Jupiter. The manager bent over him murmuring as he walked beside his head. They laid him down in one of the little cabins—just a room for a bedplace and a camp-stool or two, you know. We had brought his belated correspondence, and a lot of torn envelopes and open letters littered his bed. His hand roamed feebly amongst these papers. I was struck by the fire of his eyes and the composed languor of his expression. It was not so much the exhaustion of disease. He did not seem in pain. This shadow looked satiated and calm, as though for the moment it had had its fill of all the emotions.

"He rustled one of the letters, and looking straight in my face said, 'I am glad.' Somebody had been writing to him about me. These special recommendations were turning up again. The volume of tone he emitted without effort, almost without the trouble of moving his lips, amazed me. A voice! a voice! It was grave, profound, vibrating, while the man did not seem capable of a whisper. However, he had enough strength in him—factitious no doubt—to very nearly make an end of us, as you shall hear directly.

"The manager appeared silently in the doorway; I stepped out at once and he drew the curtain after me. The Russian, eyed curiously by the pilgrims, was staring at the shore. I followed the direction of his glance.

"Dark human shapes could be made out in the distance, flitting indistinctly against the gloomy border of the forest, and near the river two bronze figures, leaning on tall spears, stood in the sunlight under fantastic head-dresses of spotted skins, warlike and still in statuesque repose. And from right to left along the lighted shore moved a wild and gorgeous apparition of a woman.

"She walked with measured steps, draped in striped and fringed cloths, treading the earth proudly, with a slight jingle and flash of barbarous ornaments. She carried her head high; her hair was done in the shape of a helmet; she had brass leggings to the knee, brass wire gauntlets to the elbow, a crimson spot on her tawny cheek, innumerable necklaces of glass beads on her neck; bizarre things, charms, gifts of witch-men, that hung about her, glittered and trembled at every step. She must have had the value of several elephant tusks upon her. She was savage and superb, wild-eyed and magnificent; there was something ominous and stately in her deliberate progress. And in the hush that had fallen suddenly upon the whole sorrowful land, the immense wilderness, the colossal body of the fecund and mysterious life seemed to look at her, pensive, as though it had been looking at the image of its own tenebrous and passionate soul.

"She came abreast of the steamer, stood still, and faced us. Her long shadow fell to the water's edge. Her face had a tragic and fierce aspect of wild sorrow and of dumb pain mingled with the fear of some struggling, half-shaped resolve. She stood looking at us without a stir, and like the wilderness itself, with an air of brooding over an inscrutable purpose. A whole minute passed, and then she made a step forward. There was a long jingle, a glint of yellow metal, a sway of fringed draperies, and she stopped as if her heart had failed her. The young fellow by my side growled. The pilgrims murmured at my back. She looked at us all as if her life had depended upon the unswerving steadiness of her glance. Suddenly she opened her bared arms and threw them up rigid above her head, as though in an uncontrollable desire to touch the sky, and at the same time the swift shadows darted out on the earth, swept around on the river, gathering the steamer into a shadowy embrace. A formidable silence hung over the scene.

"She turned away slowly, walked on, following the bank, and passed into the bushes to the left. Once only her eyes gleamed back at us in the dusk of the thickets before she disappeared.

"'If she had offered to come aboard I really think I would have tried to shoot her,' said the man of patches, nervously. 'I had been risking my life every day for the last fortnight to keep her out of the house. She got in one day and kicked up a row about those miserable rags I picked up in the storeroom to mend my clothes with. I wasn't decent. At least it must have been that, for she talked like a fury to Kurtz for an hour, pointing at me now and then. I don't understand the dialect of this tribe. Luckily for me, I fancy Kurtz felt too ill that day to care, or there would have been mischief. I don't understand. . . . No—it's too much for me. Ah, well, it's all over now.'

"At this moment I heard Kurtz's deep voice behind the curtain: 'Save me!—save the ivory, you mean. Don't tell me. Save *me!* Why, I've had to save you. You are interrupting my plans now. Sick! Sick! Not so sick as you would like to believe. Never mind. I'll carry my ideas out yet—I will return. I'll show you what can be done. You with your little peddling notions—you are interfering with me. I will return. I. . . .'

"The manager came out. He did me the honour to take me under the arm and lead me aside. 'He is very low, very low,' he said. He considered it necessary to sigh, but neglected to be consistently sorrowful. 'We have done all we could for him—haven't we? But there is no disguising the fact, Mr. Kurtz has done more harm than good to the Company. He did not see the time was not ripe for vigorous action. Cautiously, cautiously—that's my principle. We must be cautious yet. The district is closed to us for a time. Deplorable! Upon the whole, the trade will suffer, I don't deny there is a remarkable quantity of ivory—mostly fossil. We must save it, at all events—but look how precarious the position is—and why? Because the method is unsound.' 'Do you,' said I, looking at the shore, 'call it "unsound method?"' 'Without doubt,' he exclaimed hotly. 'Don't you?' . . . 'No method at all,' I murmured after a while. 'Exactly,' he exulted. 'I anticipated this. Shows a complete want of judgment. It is my duty to point it out in the proper quarter.' 'Oh,' said I, 'that fellow—what's his name?—the brickmaker, will make a readable report for you.' He appeared confounded for a moment. It seemed to me I had never breathed an atmosphere so vile, and I turned mentally to Kurtz for relief—positively for relief. 'Nevertheless I think Mr. Kurtz is a remarkable man,' I said with emphasis. He started, dropped on me a cold heavy glance, said very quietly, "he *was,*' and turned his back on me. My hour of favour was over; I found myself lumped along with Kurtz as a partisan of methods for which the time was not ripe; I was unsound! Ah! but it was something to have at least a choice of nightmares.

"I had turned to the wilderness really, not to Mr. Kurtz, who, I was ready to admit, was as good as buried. And for a moment it seemed to me as if I also were buried in a vast grave full of unspeakable secrets. I felt an intolerable weight oppressing my breast, the smell of the damp earth, the unseen presence of victorious corruption, the darkness of an impenetrable night. . . . The Russian tapped me on the shoulder. I heard him mumbling and stammering something about 'brother seaman—couldn't conceal—knowledge of matters that would affect Mr. Kurtz's reputation.' I waited. For him evidently Mr. Kurtz was not in his grave; I suspect that for him Mr. Kurtz was one of the immortals. 'Well!' said I at last, 'speak out. As it happens, I am Mr. Kurtz's friend—in a way.'

"He stated with a good deal of formality that had we not been 'of the same profession,' he would have kept the matter to himself without regard to consequences. 'He suspected there was an active ill will towards him on the part of these white men that———' 'You are right,' I said, remembering a certain conversation I had overheard. 'The manager thinks you ought to be hanged.' He showed a concern at this intelligence which amused me at first. 'I had better get out of the way quietly,' he said, earnestly. 'I can do no more for Kurtz now, and they would soon find some excuse. What's to stop them? There's a military post three hundred miles from here.' 'Well, upon my word,' said I, 'perhaps you had better go if you have any friends amongst the savages near by.' 'Plenty,' he said. 'They are simple people—and I want nothing, you know.' He stood biting his lip, then: 'I don't want any harm to happen to these whites here, but of course I was thinking of Mr. Kurtz's reputation—but you are a brother seaman and———' 'All right,' said I, after a time. 'Mr. Kurtz's reputation is safe with me.' I did not know how truly I spoke.

"He informed me, lowering his voice, that it was Kurtz who had ordered the attack to be made on the steamer. 'He hated sometimes the idea of being taken away—and then again. . . . But I don't understand these matters. I am a simple man. He thought it would scare you away—that you would give it up, thinking him dead. I could not stop him. Oh, I had an awful time of it this last month.' 'Very well,' I said. 'He is all right now.' 'Ye-e-es,' he muttered, not very convinced apparently. 'Thanks,' said I; 'I shall keep my eyes open.' 'But quiet—eh?' he urged, anxiously. 'It would be awful for his reputation if anybody here———' I promised a complete discretion with great gravity. 'I have a canoe and three black fellows waiting not very far. I am off. Could you give me a few Martini-Henry cartridges?' I could, and did, with proper secrecy. He helped himself, with a wink at me, to a handful of my tobacco. 'Between sailors—you know—good English tobacco.' At the door of the pilot-house he turned round—'I say, haven't you a pair of shoes you could spare?' He raised one leg. 'Look.' The soles were tied with knotted strings sandal-wise under his bare feet. I rooted out an old pair, at which he looked with admiration before tucking it under his left arm. One of his pockets (bright red) was bulging with cartridges, from the other (dark blue) peeped 'Towson's Inquiry,' etc., etc. He seemed to think himself excellently well equipped for a renewed encounter with the wilderness. 'Ah! I'll never, never meet such a man again. You ought to have heard him recite poetry—his own, too, it was, he told me. Poetry!' He rolled his eyes at the recollection of these delights, 'Oh, he enlarged my mind!' 'Goodbye,' said I. He shook hands and vanished in the night. Sometimes I ask myself whether I had ever really seen him—whether it was possible to meet such a phenomenon! . . .

"When I woke up shortly after midnight his warning came to my mind with its hint of danger that seemed, in the starred darkness, real enough to make me get up for the purpose of having a look round. On the hill a big fire burned, illuminating fitfully a crooked corner of the station-house. One of the agents with a picket of a few of our blacks, armed for the purpose, was keeping guard over the ivory; but deep within the forest, red gleams that wavered, that seemed to sink and rise from the ground amongst confused columnar shapes of intense blackness, showed the exact position of the camp where Mr. Kurtz's adorers were keeping their uneasy vigil. The monotonous beating of a big drum filled the air with muffled shocks and a lingering vibration. A steady droning sound of many men chanting each to himself some weird incantation came out from the black, flat wall of the woods as the humming of bees comes out of a hive, and had a strange narcotic effect upon my half-awake senses. I believe I dozed off leaning over the rail, till an abrupt burst of yells, an overwhelming outbreak of a pent-up and mysterious frenzy, woke me up in a bewildered wonder. It was cut short all at once, and the low droning went on with an effect of audible and soothing silence. I glanced casually into the little cabin. A light was burning within, but Mr. Kurtz was not there.

"I think I would have raised an outcry if I had believed my eyes. But I didn't believe them at first—the thing seemed so impossible. The fact is I was completely unnerved by a sheer blank fright, pure abstract terror, unconnected with any distinct shape of physical danger. What made this emotion so overpowering was—how shall I define it?—the moral shock I received, as if something altogether monstrous, intolerable to thought and odious to the soul, had been thrust upon me unexpectedly. This lasted of course the merest fraction of a second, and then the usual sense of commonplace, deadly danger, the possibility of a sudden onslaught and massacre, or something of the kind, which I saw impending, as positively welcome and composing. It pacified me, in fact, so much, that I did not raise an alarm.

"There was an agent buttoned up inside an ulster and sleeping on a chair on deck within three feet of me. The yells had awakened him; he snored very slightly; I left him to his slumbers and leaped ashore. I did not betray Mr. Kurtz—it was ordered I should never betray him—it was written I should be loyal to the nightmare of my choice. I was anxious to deal with this shadow by myself alone,—and to this day I don't know why I was so jealous of sharing with any one the peculiar blackness of that experience.

"As soon as I got on the bank I saw a trail—a broad trail through the grass. I remember the exultation with which I said to myself, 'He can't walk—he is crawling on all-fours—I've got him.' The grass was wet with dew. I strode rapidly with clenched fists. I fancy I had some vague notion of falling upon him and giving him a drubbing. I don't know. I had some imbecile thoughts. The knitting old woman with the cat obtruded herself upon my memory as a most improper person to be sitting at the other end of such an affair. I saw a row of pilgrims squirting lead in the air out of Winchesters held to the hip. I thought I would never get back to the steamer, and imagined myself living alone and unarmed in the woods to an advanced age. Such silly things—you know. And I remember I confounded the beat of the drum with the beating of my heart, and was pleased at its calm regularity.

"I kept to the track though—then stopped to listen. The night was very clear; a dark blue space, sparkling with dew and starlight, in which black things stood very still. I thought I could see a kind of motion ahead of me. I was strangely cocksure of everything that night. I actually left the track and ran in a wide semicircle (I verily believe chuckling to myself) so as to get in front of that stir, of that motion I had seen—if indeed I had seen anything. I was circumventing Kurtz as though it had been a boyish game.

"I came upon him, and, if he had not heard me coming, I would have fallen over him, too, but he got up in time. He rose, unsteady, long, pale, indistinct, like a vapour exhaled by the earth, and swayed slightly, misty and silent before me; while at my back the fires loomed between the trees, and the murmur of many voices issued from the forest. I had cut him off cleverly; but when actually confronting him I seemed to come to my senses. I saw the danger in its right proportion. It was by no means over yet. Suppose he began to shout? Though he could hardly stand, there was plenty of vigour in his voice. 'Go away—hide yourself,' he said, in that profound tone. It was very awful. I glanced back. We were within thirty yards from the nearest fire. A black figure stood up, strode on long black legs, waving long black arms, across the glow. It had horns—antelope horns, I think—on its head. Some sorcerer, some witch-man, no doubt: it looked fiend-like enough. 'Do you know what you are doing?' I whispered. 'Perfectly,' he answered, raising his voice for that single word: it sounded to me far off and yet loud, like a hail through a speaking-trumpet. If he makes a row we are lost, I thought to myself. This clearly was not a case for fisticuffs, even apart from the very natural aversion I had to beat that Shadow—this wandering and tormented thing. 'You will be lost,' I said—'utterly lost.' One gets sometimes such a flash of inspiration, you know. I did say the right thing, though indeed he could not have been more irretrievably lost than he was at this very moment, when the foundations of our intimacy were being laid—to endure—to endure—even to the end—even beyond.

"'I had immense plans,' he muttered irresolutely. 'Yes,' said I; 'but if you try to shout I'll smash your head with———' There was not a stick or a stone near. 'I will throttle you for good,' I corrected myself. 'I was on the threshold of great things,' he pleaded, in a voice of longing, with a wistfulness of tone that made my blood run cold. 'And now for this stupid scoundrel—' 'Your success in Europe is assured in any case,' I affirmed, steadily. I did not want to have the throttling of him, you understand—and indeed it would have been very little use for any practical purpose. I tried to break the spell—the heavy, mute spell of the wilderness—that seemed to draw him to its pitiless breast by the awakening of forgotten and brutal instincts, by the memory of gratified and monstrous passions. This alone, I was convinced, had driven him out to the edge of the forest, to the bush, towards the gleam of fires, the throb of drums, the drone of weird incantations; this alone had beguiled his unlawful soul beyond the bounds of permitted aspirations. And, don't you see, the terror of the position was not in being knocked on the head—though I had a very lively sense of that danger, too—but in this, that I had to deal with a being to whom I could not appeal in the name of anything high or low. I had, even like the niggers, to invoke him—himself—his own exalted and incredible degradation. There was nothing either above or below him, and I knew it. He had kicked himself loose of the earth. Confound the man! he had kicked the very earth to pieces. He was alone, and I before him did not know whether I stood on the ground or floated in the air. I've been telling you what we said—repeating the phrases we pronounced—but what's the good? They were common everyday words—the familiar, vague sounds exchanged on every waking day of life. But what of that? They had behind them, to my mind, the terrific suggestiveness of words heard in dreams, of phrases spoken in nightmares. Soul! If anybody had ever struggled with a soul, I am the man. And I wasn't arguing with a lunatic either. Believe me or not, his intelligence was perfectly clear—concentrated, it is true, upon himself with horrible intensity, yet clear; and therein was my only chance—barring, of course, the killing him there and then, which wasn't so good, on account of unavoidable noise. But his soul was mad. Being alone in the wilderness, it had looked within itself, and, by heavens! I tell you, it had gone mad. I had—for my sins, I suppose—to go through the ordeal of looking into it myself. No eloquence could have been so withering to one's belief in mankind as his final burst of sincerity. He struggled with himself, too. I saw it,—I heard it. I saw the inconceivable mystery of a soul that knew no restraint, no faith, and no fear, yet struggling blindly with itself. I kept my head pretty well; but when I had him at last stretched on the couch, I wiped my forehead, while my legs shook under me as though I had carried half a ton on my back down that hill. And yet I had only supported him, his bony arm clasped round my neck—and he was not much heavier than a child.

"When next day we left at noon, the crowd, of whose presence behind the curtain of trees I had been acutely conscious all the time, flowed out of the woods again, filled the clearing, covered the slope with a mass of naked, breathing, quivering, bronze bodies. I steamed up a bit, then swung downstream, and two thousand eyes followed the evolutions of the splashing, thumping, fierce river-demon beating the water with its terrible tail and breathing black smoke into the air. In front of the first rank, along the river, three men, plastered with bright red earth from head to foot, strutted to and fro restlessly. When we came abreast again, they faced the river, stamped their feet, nodded their horned heads, swayed their scarlet bodies; they shook towards the fierce river-demon a bunch of black feathers, a mangy skin with a pendent tail—something that looked like a dried gourd; they shouted periodically together strings of amazing words that resembled no sounds of human language; and the deep murmurs of the crowd, interrupted suddenly, were like the responses of some satanic litany.

"We had carried Kurtz into the pilot-house: there was more air there. Lying on the couch, he stared through the open shutter. There was an eddy in the mass of human bodies, and the woman with helmeted head and tawny cheeks rushed out to the very brink of the stream. She put out her hands, shouted something, and all that wild mob took up the shout in a roaring chorus of articulated, rapid breathless utterance.

"'Do you understand this?' I asked.

"He kept on looking out past me with fiery, longing eyes, with a mingled expression of wistfulness and hate. He made no answer, but I saw a smile, a smile of indefinable meaning, appear on his colourless lips that a moment after twitched convulsively. 'Do I not?' he said slowly, gasping, as if the words had been torn out of him by a supernatural power.

"I pulled the string of the whistle, and I did this because I saw the pilgrims on deck getting out their rifles with an air of anticipating a jolly lark. At the sudden screech there was a movement of abject terror through that wedged mass of bodies. 'Don't! don't you frighten them away,' cried someone on deck disconsolately. I pulled the string time after time. They broke and ran, they leaped, they crouched, they swerved, they dodged the flying terror of the sound. The three red chaps had fallen flat, face down on the shore, as though they had been shot dead. Only the barbarous and superb woman did not so much as flinch, and stretched tragically her bare arms after us over the sombre and glittering river.

"And then that imbecile crowd down on the deck started their little fun, and I could see nothing more for smoke.

"The brown current ran swifly out of the heart of darkness, bearing us down toward the sea with twice the speed of our upward progress; and Kurtz's life was running swiftly, too, ebbing, ebbing out of his heart into the sea of inexorable time. The manager was very placid, he had no vital anxieties now, he took us both in with a comprehensive and satisfied glance: the 'affair' had come off as well as could be wished. I saw the time approaching when I would be left alone of the party of 'unsound method.' The pilgrims looked upon me with disfavour. I was, so to speak, numbered with the dead. It is strange how I accepted this unforeseen partnership, this choice of nightmares forced upon me in the tenebrous land invaded by these mean and greedy phantoms.

"Kurtz discoursed. A voice! a voice! It rang deep to the very last. It survived his strength to hide in the magnificent folds of eloquence the barren darkness of his heart. Oh, he struggled! he struggled! The wastes of his weary brain were haunted by shadowy images now—images of wealth and fame revolving obsequiously round his unextinguishable gift of noble and lofty expression. My Intended, my station, my career, my ideas—these were the subjects for the occasional utterances of elevated sentiments. The shade of the original Kurtz frequented the bedside of the hollow sham, whose fate it was to be buried presently in the mould of primeval earth. But both the diabolic love and the unearthly hate of the mysteries it had penetrated fought for the possession of that soul satiated with primitive emotions, avid of lying fame, of sham distinction, of all the appearances of success and power.

"Sometimes he was contemptibly childish. He desired to have kings meet him at railway-stations on his return from some ghastly Nowhere, where he intended to accomplish great things. 'You show them you have in you something that is really profitable, and then there will be no limits to the recognition of your ability,' he would say. 'Of course you must take care of the motives—right motives—always.' The long reaches that were like one and the same reach, monotonous bends that were exactly alike, slipped past the steamer with their multitude of secular trees looking patiently after this grimy fragment of another world, the forerunner of change, of conquest, of trade, of massacres, of blessings. I looked ahead—piloting. 'Close the shutter,' said Kurtz suddenly one day; 'I can't bear to look at this.' I did so. There was a silence. 'Oh, but I will wring your heart yet!' he cried at the invisible wilderness.

"We broke down—as I had expected—and had to lie up for repairs at the head of an island. This delay was the first thing that shook Kurtz's confidence. One morning he gave me a packet of papers and a photograph—the lot tied together with a shoe-string. 'Keep this for me,' he said. 'This noxious fool' (meaning the manager) 'is capable of prying into my boxes when I am not looking.' In the afternoon I saw him. He was lying on his back with closed eyes, and I withdrew quietly, but I heard him mutter, 'Live rightly, die, die . . .' I listened. There was nothing more. Was he rehearsing some speech in his sleep, or was it a fragment of a phrase from some newspaper article? He had been writing for the papers and meant to do so again, 'for the furthering of my ideas. It's a duty.'

"His was an impenetrable darkness. I looked at him as you peer down at a man who is lying at the bottom of a precipice where the sun never shines. But I had not much time to give him, because I was helping the engine-driver to take to pieces the leaky cylinders, to straighten a bent connecting-rod, and in other such matters. I lived in an infernal mess of rust, filings, nuts, bolts, spanners, hammers, ratchet-drills—things I abominate, because I don't get on with them. I tended the little forge we fortunately had aboard; I toiled wearily in a wretched scrap-heap—unless I had the shakes too bad to stand.

"One evening coming in with a candle I was startled to hear him say a little tremulously, 'I am lying here in the dark waiting for death.' The light was within a foot of his eyes. I forced myself to murmur, 'Oh, nonsense!' and stood over him as if transfixed.

"Anything approaching the change that came over his features I have never seen before, and hope never to see again. Oh, I wasn't touched. I was fascinated. It was as though a veil had been rent. I saw on that ivory face the expression of sombre pride, of ruthless power, of craven terror—of an intense and hopeless despair. Did he live his life again in every detail of desire, temptation, and surrender during that supreme moment of complete knowledge? He cried in a whisper at some image, at some vision—he cried out twice, a cry that was no more than a breath—

" 'The horror! The horror!'

"I blew the candle out and left the cabin. The pilgrims were dining in the mess-room, and I took my place opposite the manager, who lifted his eyes to give me a questioning glance, which I successfully ignored. He leaned back, serene, with that peculiar smile of his sealing the unexpressed depths of his meanness. A continuous shower of small flies streamed upon the lamp, upon the cloth, upon our hands and faces. Suddenly the manager's boy put his insolent black head in the doorway, and said in a tone of scathing contempt—

" 'Mistah Kurtz—he dead.'

"All the pilgrims rushed out to see. I remained, and went on with my dinner. I believe I was considered brutally callous. However, I did not eat much. There was a lamp in there—light, don't you know—and outside it was so beastly, beastly dark. I went no more near the remarkable man who had pronounced a judgment upon the adventures of his soul on this earth. The voice was gone. What else had been there? But I am of course aware that next day the pilgrims buried something in a muddy hole.

"And then they very nearly buried me.

"However, as you see, I did not go to join Kurtz there and then. I did not. I remained to dream the nightmare out to the end, and to show my loyalty to Kurtz once more. Destiny. My destiny! Droll thing life is—that mysterious arrangement of merciless logic for a futile purpose. The most you can hope from it is some knowledge of yourself—that comes too late—a crop of unextinguishable regrets. I have wrestled with death. It is the most unexciting contest you can imagine. It takes place in an impalpable grayness, with nothing underfoot, with nothing around, without spectators, without clamour, without glory, without the great desire of victory, without the great fear of defeat, in a sickly atmosphere of tepid scepticism, without much belief in your own right, and still less in that of your adversary. If such is the form of ultimate wisdom, then life is a greater riddle than some of us think it to be. I was within a hair's-breadth of the last opportunity for pronouncement, and I found with humiliation that probably I would have nothing to say. This is the reason why I affirm that Kurtz was a remarkable man. He had something to say. He said it. Since I had peeped over the edge myself, I understand better the meaning of his stare, that could not see the flame of the candle, but was wide enough to embrace the whole universe, piercing enough to penetrate all the hearts that beat in the darkness. He had summed up—he had judged. 'The horror!' He was a remarkable man. After all, this was the expression of some sort of belief; it had candour, it had conviction, it had a vibrating note of revolt in its whisper, it had the appalling face of a glimpsed truth—the strange commingling of desire and hate. And it is not my own extremity I remember best—a vision of grayness without form filled with physical pain, and a careless contempt for the evanescence of all things—even of this pain itself. No! It is his extremity that I seem to have lived through. True, he had made that last stride, he had stepped over the edge, while I had been permitted to draw back my hesitating foot. And perhaps in this is the whole difference; perhaps all the wisdom, and all truth, and all sincerity, are just compressed into that inappreciable moment of time in which we step over the threshold of the invisible. Perhaps! I like to think my summing-up would not have been a word of careless contempt. Better his cry—much better. It was an affirmation, a moral victory paid for by innumerable defeats, by abominable terrors, by abominable satisfactions. But it was a victory! That is why I have remained loyal to Kurtz to the last, and even beyond, when a long time after I heard once more, not his own voice, but the echo of his magnificent eloquence thrown to me from a soul as translucently pure as a cliff of crystal.

"No, they did not bury me, though there is a period of time which I remember mistily, with a shuddering wonder, like a passage through some inconceivable world that had no hope in it and no desire. I found myself in the sepulchral city resenting the sight of people hurrying through the streets to filch a little money from each other, to devour their infamous cookery, to gulp their unwholesome beer, to dream their insignificant and silly dreams. They trespassed upon my thoughts. They were intruders whose knowledge of life was to me an irritating pretence, because I felt so sure they could not possibly know the things I knew. Their bearing, which was simply the bearing of commonplace individuals going about their business in the assurance of perfect safety, was offensive to me like the outrageous flauntings of folly in the face of a danger it is unable to comprehend. I had no particular desire to enlighten them, but I had some difficulty in restraining myself from laughing in their faces, so full of stupid importance. I daresay I was not very well at that time. I tottered about the streets—there were various affairs to settle—grinning bitterly at perfectly respectable persons. I admit my behaviour was inexcusable, but then my temperature was seldom normal in these days. My dear aunt's endeavours to 'nurse up my strength' seemed altogether beside the mark. It was not my strength that wanted nursing, it was my imagination that wanted soothing. I kept the bundle of papers given me by Kurtz, not knowing exactly what to do with it. His mother had died lately, watched over, as I was told, by his Intended. A clean-shaved man, with an official manner and wearing goldrimmed spectacles, called on me one day and made inquiries, at first circuitous, afterwards suavely pressing, about what he was pleased to denominate certain 'documents.' I was not surprised, because I had had two rows with the manager on the subject out there. I had refused to give up the smallest scrap out of that package, and I took the same attitude with the spectacled man. He became darkly menacing at last, and with much heat argued that the Company had the right to every bit of information about its 'territories.' And said he, 'Mr. Kurtz's knowledge of unexplored regions must have been necessarily extensive and peculiar—owing to his great abilities and to the deplorable circumstances in which he had been placed: therefore—' I assured him Mr. Kurtz's knowledge, however extensive, did not bear upon the problems of commerce or administration. He invoked then the name of science. 'It would be an incalculable loss if,' etc., etc. I offered him the report on the 'Suppression of Savage Customs,' with the postscriptum torn off. He took it up eagerly, but ended by sniffing at it with an air of contempt. 'This is not what we had a right to expect,' he remarked. 'Expect nothing else,' I said. 'There are only private letters.' He withdrew upon some threat of legal proceedings, and I saw him no more; but another fellow, calling himself Kurtz's cousin, appeared two days later, and was anxious to hear all the details about his dear relative's last moments. Incidentally he gave me to understand that Kurtz had been essentially a great musician. 'There was the making of an immense success,' said the man, who was an organist, I believe, with lank gray hair flowing over a greasy coat-collar. I had no reason to doubt his statement; and to this day I am unable to say what was Kurtz's profession, whether he ever had any—which was the greatest of his talents. I had taken him for a painter who wrote for the papers, or else for a journalist who could paint—but even the cousin (who took snuff during the interview) could not tell me what he had been—exactly. He was a universal genius—on that point I agreed with the old chap, who thereupon blew his nose noisily into a large cotton handkerchief and withdrew in senile agitation, bearing off some family letters and memoranda without importance. Ultimately a journalist anxious to know something of the fate of his 'dear colleague' turned up. This visitor informed me Kurtz's proper sphere ought to have been politics 'on the popular side.' He had furry straight eyebrows, bristly hair cropped short, an eye-glass on a broad ribbon, and, becoming expansive, confessed his opinion that Kurtz really couldn't write a bit—'but heavens! how that man could talk. He electrified large meetings. He had faith—don't you see?—he had the faith. He could get himself to believe anything—anything. He would have been a splendid leader of an extreme party.' 'What party?' I asked. 'Any party,' answered the other. 'He was an—an—

extremist.' Did I not think so? I assented. Did I know, he asked, with a sudden flash of curiosity, 'what it was that had induced him to go out there?' 'Yes,' said I, and forthwith handed him the famous Report for publication, if he thought fit. He glanced through it hurriedly, mumbling all the time, judged 'it would do,' and took himself off with this plunder.

"Thus I was left at last with a slim packet of letters and the girl's portrait. She struck me as beautiful—I mean she had a beautiful expression. I know that the sunlight can be made to lie, too, yet one felt that no manipulation of light and pose could have conveyed the delicate shade of truthfulness upon those features. She seemed ready to listen without mental reservation, without suspicion, without a thought for herself. I concluded I would go and give her back her portrait and those letters myself. Curiosity? Yes; and also some other feelings perhaps. All that had been Kurtz's had passed out of my hands: his soul, his body, his station, his plans, his ivory, his career. There remained only his memory and his Intended—and I wanted to give that up, too, to the past, in a way—to surrender personally all that remained of him with me to that oblivion which is the last word of our common fate. I don't defend myself. I had no clear perception of what it was I really wanted. Perhaps it was an impulse of unconscious loyalty, or the fulfilment of one of these ironic necessities that lurk in the facts of human existence. I don't know. I can't tell. But I went.

"I thought his memory was like the other memories of the dead that accumulate in every man's life—a vague impress on the brain of shadows that had fallen on it in their swift and final passage; but before the high and ponderous door, between the tall houses of a street as still and decorous as a well-kept alley in a cemetery, I had a vision of him on the stretcher, opening his mouth voraciously, as if to devour all the earth with all its mankind. He lived then before me; he lived as much as he had ever lived—a shadow insatiable of splendid appearances, of frightful realities; a shadow darker than the shadow of the night, and draped nobly in the folds of a gorgeous eloquence. The vision seemed to enter the house with me—the stretcher, the phantom-bearers, the wild crowd of obedient worshippers, the gloom of the forests, the glitter of the reach between the murky bends, the beat of the drum, regular and muffled like the beating of a heart—the heart of a conquering darkness. It was a moment of triumph for the wilderness, an invading and vengeful rush which, it seemed to me, I would have to keep back alone for the salvation of another soul. And the memory of what I had heard him say afar there, with the horned shapes stirring at my back, in the glow of fires, within the patient woods, those broken phrases came back to me, were heard again in their ominous and terrifying simplicity. I remembered his abject pleading, his abject threats, the colossal scale of his vile desires, the meanness, the torment, the tempestuous anguish of his soul. And later on I seemed to see his collected languid manner, when he said one day, 'This lot of ivory now is really mine. The Company did not pay for it. I collected it myself at a very great personal risk. I am afraid they will try to claim it as theirs though. H'm. It is a difficult case. What do you think I ought to do—resist? Eh? I want no more than justice.' . . . He wanted no more than justice—no more than justice. I rang the bell before a mahogany door on the first floor, and while I waited he seemed to stare at me out of the glassy panel—stare with that wide and immense stare embracing, condemning, loathing all the universe. I seemed to hear the whispered cry, 'The horror! The horror!'

"The dusk was falling. I had to wait in a lofty drawing-room with three long windows from floor to ceiling that were like three luminous and bedraped columns. The bent gilt legs and backs of the furniture shone in indistinct curves. The tall marble fireplace had a cold and monumental whiteness. A grand piano stood massively in a corner; with dark gleams on the flat surfaces like a sombre and polished sarcophagus. A high door opened—closed. I rose.

"She came forward, all in black, with a pale head, floating towards me in the dusk. She was in mourning. It was more than a year since his death, more than a year since the news came; she seemed as though she would remember and mourn for ever. She took both my hands in hers and murmured, 'I had heard you were coming.' I noticed she was not very young—I mean not girlish. She had a mature capacity for fidelity, for belief, for suffering. The room seemed to have grown darker, as if all the sad light of the cloudy evening had taken refuge on her forehead. This fair hair, this pale visage, this pure brow, seemed surrounded by an ashy halo from which the dark eyes looked out at me. Their glance was guileless, profound, confident, and trustful. She carried her sorrowful head as though she were proud of that sorrow, as though she would say, I—I alone know how to mourn for him as he deserves. But while we were still shaking hands, such a look of awful desolation came upon her face that I perceived she was one of those creatures that are not the playthings of Time. For her he had died only yesterday. And, by Jove! the impression was so powerful that for me, too, he seemed to have died only yesterday—nay, this very minute. I saw her and him in the same instant of time—his death and her sorrow—I saw her sorrow in the very moment of his death. Do you understand? I saw them together—I heard them together. She had said, with a deep catch of the breath, 'I have survived' while my strained ears seemed to hear distinctly, mingled with her tone of despairing regret, the summing up whisper of his eternal condemnation. I asked myself what I was doing there, with a sensation of panic in my heart as though I had blundered into a place of cruel and absurd mysteries not fit for a human being to behold. She motioned me to a chair. We sat down. I laid the packet gently on the little table, and she put her hand over it. . . . 'You knew him well,' she murmured, after a moment of mourning silence.

"'Intimacy grows quickly out there,' I said. 'I knew him as well as it is possible for one man to know another.'

"'And you admired him,' she said. 'It was impossible to know him and not to admire him. Was it?'

"'He was a remarkable man,' I said, unsteadily. Then before the appealing fixity of her gaze, that seemed to watch for more words on my lips, I went on. 'It was impossible not to———'

"'Love him,' she finished eagerly, silencing me into an appalled dumbness. 'How true! how true! But when you think that no one knew him so well as I! I had all his noble confidence. I knew him best.'

"'You knew him best,' I repeated. And perhaps she did. But with every word spoken the room was growing darker, and only her forehead, smooth and white, remained illumined by the unextinguishable light of belief and love.

"'You were his friend,' she went on. 'His friend,' she repeated, a little louder. 'You must have been, if he had given you this, and sent you to me. I feel I can speak to you—

and oh! I must speak. I want you—you who have heard his last words—to know I have been worthy of him. . . . It is not pride. . . . Yes! I am proud to know I understood him better than any one on earth—he told me so himself. And since his mother died I have had no one—no one—to—to———'

"I listened. The darkness deepened. I was not even sure whether he had given me the right bundle. I rather suspect he wanted me to take care of another batch of his papers which, after his death, I saw the manager examining under the lamp. And the girl talked, easing her pain in the certitude of my sympathy; she talked as thirsty men drink. I had heard that her engagement with Kurtz had been disapproved by her people. He wasn't rich enough or something. And indeed I don't know whether he had not been a pauper all his life. He had given me some reason to infer that it was his impatience of comparative poverty that drove him out there.

"'. . . Who was not his friend who had heard him speak once?' she was saying. 'He drew men towards him by what was best in them.' She looked at me with intensity. 'It is the gift of the great,' she went on, and the sound of her low voice seemed to have the accompaniment of all the other sounds, full of mystery, desolation, and sorrow, I had ever heard—the ripple of the river, the soughing of the trees swayed by the wind, the murmurs of the crowds, the faint ring of incomprehensible words cried from afar, the whisper of a voice speaking from beyond the threshold of an eternal darkness. 'But you have heard him! You know!' she cried.

"'Yes, I know,' I said with something like despair in my heart, but bowing my head before the faith that was in her, before that great and saving illusion that shone with an unearthly glow in the darkness, in the triumphant darkness from which I could not have defended her—from which I could not even defend myself.

"'What a loss to me—to us!'—she corrected herself with beautiful generosity; then added in a murmur, 'To the world.' By the last gleams of twilight I could see the glitter of her eyes, full of tears—of tears that would not fall.

"'I have been very happy—very fortunate—very proud,' she went on. 'Too fortunate. Too happy for a little while. And now I am unhappy for—for life.'

"She stood up; her fair hair seemed to catch all the remaining light in a glimmer of gold. I rose, too.

"'And of all this,' she went on, mournfully, 'of all his promise, and of all his greatness, of his generous mind, of his noble heart, nothing remains—nothing but a memory. You and I———'

"'We shall always remember him,' I said, hastily.

"'No!' she cried. 'It is impossible that all this should be lost—that such a life should be sacrificed to leave nothing—but sorrow. You know what vast plans he had. I knew of them, too—I could not perhaps understand—but others knew of them. Something must remain. His words, at least, have not died.'

"'His words will remain,' I said.

"'And his example,' she whispered to herself. 'Men looked up to him—his goodness shone in every act. His example———'

"'True,' I said; 'his example, too. Yes, his example. I forgot that.'

"'But I do not. I cannot—I cannot believe—not yet. I cannot believe that I shall never see him again, that nobody will see him again, never, never, never.'

"She put out her arms as if after a retreating figure, stretching them back and with clasped pale hands across the fading and narrow sheen of the window. Never see him! I saw him clearly enough then. I shall see this eloquent phantom as long as I live, and I shall see her, too, a tragic and familiar Shade, resembling in this gesture another one, tragic also, and bedecked with powerless charms, stretching bare brown arms over the glitter of the infernal stream, the stream of darkness. She said suddenly very low, 'He died as he lived.'

"'His end,' said I, with dull anger stirring in me, 'was in every way worthy of his life.'

"'And I was not with him,' she murmured. My anger subsided before a feeling of infinite pity.

"'Everything that could be done———' I mumbled.

"'Ah, but I believed in him more than any one on earth—more than his own mother, more than—himself. He needed me! Me! I would have treasured every sigh, every word, every sign, every glance.'

"I felt like a chill grip on my chest. 'Don't,' I said, in a muffled voice.

"'Forgive me. I—I—have mourned so long in silence—in silence. . . . You were with him—to the last? I think of his loneliness. Nobody near to understand him as I would have understood. Perhaps no one to hear. . . .'

"'To the very end,' I said, shakily. 'I heard his very last words. . . .' I stopped in a fright.

"'Repeat them,' she murmured in a heart-broken tone. 'I want—I want—something—something—to—to live with.'

"I was on the point of crying at her, 'Don't you hear them?' The dusk was repeating them in a persistent whisper all around us, in a whisper that seemed to swell menacingly like the first whisper of a rising wind. 'The horror! the horror!'

"'His last word—to live with,' she insisted. 'Don't you understand I loved him—I loved him—I loved him!'

"I pulled myself together and spoke slowly.

"'The last word he pronounced was—your name.'

"I heard a light sigh and then my heart stood still, stopped dead short by an exulting and terrible cry, by the cry of inconceivable triumph and of unspeakable pain. 'I knew it—I was sure!' . . . She knew. She was sure. I heard her weeping; she had hidden her face in her hands. It seemed to me that the house would collapse before I could escape, that the heavens would fall upon my head. But nothing happened. The heavens do not fall for such a trifle. Would they have fallen, I wonder, if I had rendered Kurtz that justice which was his due? Hadn't he said he wanted only justice? But I couldn't. I could not tell her. It would have been too dark—too dark altogether. . . ."

Marlow ceased, and sat apart, indistinct and silent, in the pose of a meditating Buddha. Nobody moved for a time. "We have lost the first of the ebb," said the Director, suddenly. I raised my head. The offing was barred by a black bank of clouds, and the tranquil waterway leading to the uttermost ends of the earth flowed sombre under an overcast sky—seemed to lead into the heart of an immense darkness.

QUESTIONS FOR DISCUSSION AND WRITING

1. What are the most important choices Marlow has to make in the story? How does Marlow's decision to lie to the Intended about Kurtz's last words serve as the climax of the story?
2. What preconception does Marlow form about Kurtz based on the assessment and rumors of others? How does the man Marlow finally meets fulfill or contradict that preconception?
3. What surprising similarities does Marlow discover between the civilized Thames River and the savage Congo? In what sense has the whole world become a dark place for Marlow? What has darkness come to mean to him?
4. How does the first narrator of the story introduce the difference between a typical sea yarn and the kind of story Marlow tells? How does Marlow's statement, "We live, as we dream—alone," explain his difficulty in telling his story to his listeners?
5. What is "the horror, the horror" that Kurtz perceives in the heart of darkness? What restrains Marlow from falling into that horror?

24

STEPHEN CRANE

The Open Boat

A Tale Intended to be after the Fact: Being the Experience of Four Men from the Sunk Steamer Commodore

STEPHEN CRANE (1871–1900) was born in Newark, New Jersey, and spent a term each at Lafayette College and Syracuse University. After this disappointing year, Crane discontinued his university education to work as a free-lance journalist in New York City. More interested in creating moods and examining motives, Crane became disenchanted with routine factual reporting, turning his attention more and more to fiction. His first novel, *Maggie: A Girl of the Streets* (1893), based on his knowledge of New York slum life, was not successful, but his second, *The Red Badge of Courage* (1895), a vivid account of an imaginary episode from the Civil War, won him international acclaim. Crane's newly acquired literary reputation enabled him to travel to various parts of the world as a feature reporter. One such tour of the West, in 1895, produced such memorable stories as "The Blue Hotel" and "The Bride Comes to Yellow Sky." In 1897 Crane was assigned to cover the insurrection in Cuba, but his ship wrecked off the coast of Florida, leading to the adventures he revealed in "The Open Boat." In that same year, Crane covered the Greco-Turkish War,

and in 1898 returned to report on the Spanish-American War in Cuba. After a brief residence in England, Crane checked into a sanatorium in Bodenweiler, Germany, where he died of tuberculosis at the age of twenty-eight. In "The Open Boat," reprinted from *The Open Boat and Other Tales of Adventure* (1898), Crane portrays the human struggle in an indifferent universe. In "The Blue Hotel," reprinted from *The Monster and Other Stories* (1899), Crane describes how chance conspires to fulfill the Swede's prophecy of his fate.

1

None of them knew the colour of the sky. Their eyes glanced level, and were fastened upon the waves that swept toward them. These waves were of the hue of slate, save for the tops, which were of foaming white, and all of the men knew the colours of the sea. The horizon narrowed and widened, and dipped and rose, and at all times its edge was jagged with waves that seemed thrust up in points like rocks.

Many a man ought to have a bathtub larger than the boat which here rode upon the sea. These waves were most wrongfully and barbarously abrupt and tall, and each froth-top was a problem in small-boat navigation.

The cook squatted in the bottom, and looked with both eyes at the six inches of gunwale which separated him from the ocean. His sleeves were rolled over his fat forearms, and the two flaps of his unbuttoned vest dangled as he bent to bail out the boat. Often he said, "Gawd! that was a narrow clip." As he remarked it he invariably gazed eastward over the broken sea.

The oiler, steering with one of the two oars in the boat, sometimes raised himself suddenly to keep clear of water that swirled in over the stern. It was a thin little oar, and it seemed often ready to snap.

The correspondent, pulling at the other oar, watched the waves and wondered why he was there.

The injured captain, lying in the bow, was at this time buried in that profound dejection and indifference which comes, temporarily at least, to even the bravest and most enduring when, willy-nilly, the firm fails, the army loses, the ship goes down. The mind of the master of a vessel is rooted deep in the timbers of her, though he command for a day or a decade; and this captain had on him the stern impression of a scene in the greys of dawn of seven turned faces, and later a stump of a topmast with a white ball on it, that slashed to and fro at the waves, went low and lower, and down. Thereafter there was something strange in his voice. Although steady, it was deep with mourning, and of a quality beyond oration or tears.

"Keep 'er a little more south, Billie," said he.

"A little more south, sir," said the oiler in the stern.

A seat in this boat was not unlike a seat upon a bucking broncho, and by the same token a broncho is not much smaller. The craft pranced and reared and plunged like an animal. As each wave came, and she rose for it, she seemed like a horse making at a fence outrageously high. The manner of her scramble over these walls of water is a mystic thing, and, moreover, at the top of them were ordinarily these problems in white water, the foam racing down from the summit of each wave requiring a new leap, and a leap from the air. Then, after scornfully bumping a crest, she would slide and race and splash down a long incline, and arrive bobbing and nodding in front of the next menace.

A singular disadvantage of the sea lies in the fact that after successfully surmounting one wave you discover that there is another behind it just as important and just as nervously anxious to do something effective in the way of swamping boats. In a ten-foot dinghy one can get an idea of the resources of the sea in the line of waves that is not probable to the average experience which is never at sea in a dinghy. As each slaty wall of water approached, it shut all else from the view of the men in the boat, and it was not difficult to imagine that this particular wave was the final outburst of the ocean, the last effort of the grim water. There was a terrible grace in the move of the waves, and they came in silence, save for the snarling of the crests.

In the wan light the faces of the men must have been grey. Their eyes must have glinted in strange ways as they gazed steadily astern. Viewed from a balcony, the whole thing would doubtless have been weirdly picturesque. But the men in the boat had no time to see it, and if they had had leisure, there were other things to occupy their minds. The sun swung steadily up the sky, and they knew it was broad day because the colour of the sea changed from slate to emerald green streaked with amber lights, and the foam was like tumbling snow. The process of the breaking day was unknown to them. They were aware only of this effect upon the colour of the waves that rolled toward them.

In disjointed sentences the cook and the correspondent argued as to the difference between a life-saving station and a house of refuge. The cook had said: "There's a house of refuge just north of the Mosquito Inlet Light, and as soon as they see us they'll come off in their boat and pick us up."

"As soon as who see us?" said the correspondent.

"The crew," said the cook.

"Houses of refuge don't have crews," said the correspondent. "As I understand them, they are only places where clothes and grub are stored for the benefit of shipwrecked people. They don't carry crews."

"Oh, yes, they do," said the cook.

"No, they don't," said the correspondent.

"Well, we're not there yet, anyhow," said the oiler, in the stern.

"Well," said the cook, "perhaps it's not a house of refuge that I'm thinking of as being near Mosquito Inlet Light; perhaps it's a life-saving station."

"We're not there yet," said the oiler in the stern.

2

As the boat bounced from the top of each wave the wind tore through the hair of the hatless men, and as the craft plopped her stern down again the spray slashed past them. The crest of each of these waves was a hill, from the top of which the men surveyed for a moment a broad tumultuous expanse, shining and wind-riven. It was probably splendid, it was probably glorious, this play of the free sea, wild with lights of emerald and white and amber.

"Bully good thing it's an on-shore wind," said the cook. "If not, where would we be? Wouldn't have a show."

"That's right," said the correspondent.

The busy oiler nodded his assent.

Then the captain, in the bow, chuckled in a way that expressed humour, contempt, tragedy, all in one. "Do you think we've got much of a show now, boys?" said he.

Whereupon the three were silent, save for a trifle of hemming and hawing. To express any particular optimism at this time they felt to be childish and stupid, but they all doubtless possessed this sense of the situation in their minds. A young man thinks doggedly at such times. On the other hand, the ethics of their condition was decidedly against any open suggestion of hopelessness. So they were silent.

"Oh, well," said the captain, soothing his children, "we'll get ashore all right."

But there was that in his tone which made them think; so the oiler quoth, "Yes! if this wind holds."

The cook was bailing, "Yes! if we don't catch hell in the surf."

Canton-flannel gulls flew near and far. Sometimes they sat down on the sea, near patches of brown seaweed that rolled over the waves with a movement like carpets on a line in a gale. The birds sat comfortably in groups, and they were envied by some in the dinghy, for the wrath of the sea was no more to them than it was to a covey of prairie chickens a thousand miles inland. Often they came very close and stared at the men with black bead-like eyes. At these times they were uncanny and sinister in their unblinking scrutiny, and the men hooted angrily at them, telling them to be gone. One came, and evidently decided to alight on the top of the captain's head. The bird flew parallel to the boat and did not circle, but made short sidelong jumps in the air in chicken-fashion. His black eyes were wistfully fixed upon the captain's head. "Ugly brute," said the oiler to the bird. "You look as if you were made with a jackknife." The cook and the correspondent swore darkly at the creature. The captain naturally wished to knock it away with the end of the heavy painter, but he did not dare do it, because anything resembling an emphatic gesture would have capsized this freighted boat; and so, with his open hand, the captain gently and carefully waved the gull away. After it had been discouraged from the pursuit the captain breathed easier on account of his hair, and others breathed easier because the bird struck their minds at this time as being somehow gruesome and ominous.

In the meantime the oiler and the correspondent rowed. And also they rowed. They sat together in the same seat, and each rowed an oar. Then the oiler took both oars; then the correspondent took both oars; then the oiler; then the correspondent. They rowed and they rowed. The very ticklish part of the business was when the time came for the reclining one in the stern to take his turn at the oars. By the very last star of truth, it is easier to steal eggs from under a hen than it was to change seats in the dinghy. First the man in the stern slid his hand along the thwart and moved with care, as if he were of Sèvres. Then the man in the rowing-seat slid his hand along the other thwart. It was all done with the most extraordinary care. As the two sidled past each other, the whole party kept watchful eyes on the coming wave, and the captain cried: "Look out, now! Steady, there!"

The brown mats of seaweed that appeared from time to time were like islands, bits of earth. They were travelling, apparently, neither one way nor the other. They were, to all intents, stationary. They informed the men in the boat that it was making progress slowly toward the land.

The captain, rearing cautiously in the bow after the dinghy soared on a great swell, said that he had seen the lighthouse at Mosquito Inlet. Presently the cook remarked that he had seen it. The correspondent was at the oars then, and for some reason he too wished to look at the lighthouse; but his back was toward the far shore, and the waves were important, and for some time he could not seize an opportunity to turn his head. But at last there came a wave more gentle than the others and when at the crest of it he swiftly scoured the western horizon.

"See it?" said the captain.

"No," said the correspondent, slowly; "I didn't see anything."

"Look again," said the captain. He pointed. "It's exactly in that direction."

At the top of another wave the correspondent did as he was bid, and this time his eyes chanced on a small, still thing on the edge of the swaying horizon. It was precisely like the point of a pin. It took an anxious eye to find a lighthouse so tiny.

"Think we'll make it, Captain?"

"If this wind holds and the boat don't swamp, we can't do much else," said the captain.

The little boat, lifted by each towering sea and splashed viciously by the crests, made progress that in the absence of seaweed was not apparent to those in her. She seemed just a wee thing wallowing, miraculously top up, at the mercy of five oceans. Occasionally a great spread of water, like white flames, swarmed into her.

"Bail her, cook," said the captain, serenely.

"All right, Captain," said the cheerful cook.

3

It would be difficult to describe the subtle brotherhood of men that was here established on the seas. No one said that it was so. No one mentioned it. But it dwelt in the boat, and each man felt it warm him. They were a captain, an oiler, a cook, and a correspondent, and they were friends—friends in a more curiously iron-bound degree than may be common. The hurt captain, lying against the water-jar in the bow, spoke always in a low voice and calmly; but he could never command a more ready and swiftly obedient crew than the motley three of the dinghy. It was more than a mere recognition of what was best for the common safety. There was surely in it a quality that was personal and heart-felt. And after this devotion to the commander of the boat, there was this comradeship, that the correspondent, for instance, who had been taught to be cynical of men, knew even at the time was the best experience of his life. But no one said that it was so. No one mentioned it.

"I wish we had a sail," remarked the captain. "We might try my overcoat on the end of an oar, and give you two boys a chance to rest." So the cook and the correspondent held the mast and spread wide the overcoat; the oiler steered; and the little boat made good way with her new rig. Sometimes the oiler had to scull sharply to keep a sea from breaking into the boat, but otherwise sailing was a success.

Meanwhile the lighthouse had been growing slowly larger. It had now almost assumed colour, and appeared like a little grey shadow on the sky. The man at the oars could not be prevented from turning his head rather often to try for a glimpse of this little grey shadow.

At last, from the top of each wave, the men in the tossing boat could see land. Even as the lighthouse was an upright shadow on the sky, this land seemed but a long black shadow on the sea. It certainly was thinner than paper. "We must be about opposite New Smyrna," said the cook, who had coasted this shore often in schooners. "Captain, by the way, I believe they abandoned that life-saving station there about a year ago."

"Did they?" said the captain.

The wind slowly died away. The cook and the correspondent were not now obliged to slave in order to hold high the oar. But the waves continued their old impetuous swooping at the dinghy, and the little craft, no longer under way, struggled woundily over them. The oiler or the correspondent took the oars again.

Shipwrecks are apropos of nothing. If men could only train for them and have them occur when the men had reached pink condition, there would be less drowning at sea. Of the four in the dinghy none had slept any time worth mentioning for two days and two nights previous to embarking in the dinghy, and in the excitement of clambering about the deck of a foundering ship they had also forgotten to eat heartily.

For these reasons, and for others, neither the oiler nor the correspondent was fond of rowing at this time. The correspondent wondered ingenuously how in the name of all that was sane could there be people who thought it amusing to row a boat. It was not an amusement; it was a diabolical punishment, and even a genius of mental aberrations could never conclude that it was anything but a horror to the muscles and a crime against the back. He mentioned to the boat in general how the amusement of rowing struck him, and the weary-faced oiler smiled in full sympathy. Previously to the foundering, by the way, the oiler had worked a double watch in the engine-room of the ship.

"Take her easy now, boys," said the captain. "Don't spend yourselves. If we have to run a surf you'll need all your strength, because we'll sure have to swim for it. Take your time."

Slowly the land arose from the sea. From a black line it became a line of black and a line of white—trees and sand. Finally the captain said that he could make out a house on the shore. "That's the house of refuge, sure," said the cook. "They'll see us before long, and come out after us."

The distant lighthouse reared high. "The keeper ought to be able to make us out now, if he's looking through a glass," said the captain. "He'll notify the life-saving people."

"None of those other boats could have got ashore to give word of this wreck," said the oiler, in a low voice, "else the life-boat would be out hunting us."

Slowly and beautifully the land loomed out of the sea. The wind came again. It had veered from the north-east to the south-east. Finally a new sound struck the ears of the men in the boat. It was the low thunder of the surf on the shore. "We'll never be able to make the lighthouse now," said the captain. "Swing her head a little more north, Billie."

"A little more north, sir," said the oiler.

Whereupon the little boat turned her nose once more down the wind, and all but the oarsman watched the shore grow. Under the influence of this expansion doubt and direful apprehension were leaving the minds of the men. The management of the boat was still most absorbing, but it could not prevent a quiet cheerfulness. In an hour, perhaps, they would be ashore.

Their backbones had become thoroughly used to balancing in the boat, and they now rode this wild colt of a dinghy like circus men. The correspondent thought that he had been drenched to the skin, but happening to feel in the top pocket of his coat, he found therein eight cigars. Four of them were soaked with sea-water; four were perfectly scatheless. After a search, somebody produced three dry matches; and thereupon the four waifs rode impudently in their little boat and, with an assurance of an impending rescue shining in their eyes, puffed at the big cigars, and judged well and ill of all men. Everybody took a drink of water.

4

"Cook," remarked the captain, "there don't seem to be any signs of life about your house of refuge."

"No," replied the cook. "Funny they don't see us!"

A broad stretch of lowly coast lay before the eyes of the men. It was of low dunes topped with dark vegetation. The roar of the surf was plain, and sometimes they could see the white lip of a wave as it spun up the beach. A tiny house was blocked out black upon the sky. Southward, the slim lighthouse lifted its little grey length.

Tide, wind, and waves were swinging the dinghy northward. "Funny they don't see us," said the men.

The surf's roar was here dulled, but its tone was nevertheless thunderous and mighty. As the boat swam over the great rollers the men sat listening to this roar. "We'll swamp sure," said everybody.

It is fair to say here that there was not a life-saving station within twenty miles in either direction; but the men did not know this fact, and in consequence they made dark and opprobrious remarks concerning the eyesight of the nation's life-savers. Four scowling men sat in the dinghy and surpassed records in the invention of epithets.

"Funny they don't see us."

The light-heartedness of a former time had completely faded. To their sharpened minds it was easy to conjure pictures of all kinds of incompetency and blindness and, indeed, cowardice. There was the shore of the populous land, and it was bitter and bitter to them that from it came no sign.

"Well," said the captain, ultimately, "I suppose we'll have to make a try for ourselves. If we stay out here too long, we'll none of us have strength left to swim after the boat swamps."

And so the oiler, who was at the oars, turned the boat straight for the shore. There was a sudden tightening of muscles.There was some thinking.

"If we don't all get ashore," said the captain—"if we don't all get ashore, I suppose you fellows know where to send news of my finish?"

They then briefly exchanged some addresses and admonitions. As for the reflections of the men, there was a great deal of rage in them. Perchance they might be formulated thus: "If I am going to be drowned—if I am going to be drowned—if I am going to be drowned, why, in the name of the seven mad gods who rule the sea, was I allowed to come thus far and contemplate sand and trees? Was I brought here merely to have my nose dragged away as I was about to nibble the sacred cheese of life? It is preposterous. If this old ninny-woman, Fate, cannot do better than this, she should be deprived of the management of men's fortunes. She is an old hen who knows not her intention. If she has decided to drown me, why did she not do it in the beginning and save me all this trouble? The whole affair is absurd.—But no; she cannot mean to drown me. She dare not drown me. She cannot drown me. Not after all this work." Afterward the man might have had an impulse to shake his fist at the clouds. "Just you drown me, now, and then hear what I call you!"

The billows that came at this time were more formidable. They seemed always just about to break and roll over the little boat in a turmoil of foam. There was a preparatory and long growl in the speech of them. No mind unused to the sea would have concluded that the dinghy could ascend these sheer heights in time. The shore was still afar. The oiler was a wily surfman. "Boys," he said swiftly, "she won't live three minutes more, and we're too far out to swim. Shall I take her to sea again, Captain?"

"Yes; go ahead!" said the captain.

This oiler, by a series of quick miracles and fast and steady oarsmanship, turned the boat in the middle of the surf and took her safely to sea again.

There was a considerable silence as the boat bumped over the furrowed sea to deeper water. Then somebody in gloom spoke: "Well, anyhow, they must have seen us from the shore by now."

The gulls went in slanting flight up the wind toward the grey, desolate east. A squall, marked by dingy clouds and clouds brick-red like smoke from a burning building, appeared from the south-east.

"What do you think of those life-saving people? Ain't they peaches?"

"Funny they haven't seen us."

"Maybe they think we're out here for sport! Maybe they think we're fishin'. Maybe they think we're damned fools."

It was a long afternoon. A changed tide tried to force them southward, but wind and wave said northward. Far ahead, where coast-line, sea, and sky formed their mighty angle, there were little dots which seemed to indicate a city on the shore.

"St. Augustine?"

The captain shook his head. "Too near Mosquito Inlet."

And the oiler rowed, and then the correspondent rowed; then the oiler rowed. It was a weary business. The human back can become the seat of more aches and pains than are registered in books for the composite anatomy of a regiment. It is a limited area, but it can become the theatre of innumerable muscular conflicts, tangles, wrenches, knots, and other comforts.

"Did you ever like to row, Billie?" said the correspondent.

"No," said the oiler; "hang it!"

When one exchanged the rowing-seat for a place in the bottom of the boat, he suffered a bodily depression that caused him to be careless of everything save an obligation to wiggle one finger. There was cold sea-water swashing to and fro in the boat, and he lay in it. His head, pillowed on a thwart, was within an inch of the swirl of a wave-crest, and sometimes a particularly obstreperous sea came inboard and drenched him once more. But these matters did not annoy him. It is almost certain that if the boat had capsized he would have tumbled comfortably out upon the ocean as if he felt sure that it was a great soft mattress.

"Look! There's a man on the shore!"

"Where?"

"There! See 'im? See 'im?"

"Yes, sure! He's walking along."

"Now he's stopped. Look! He's facing us!"

"He's waving at us!"

"So he is! By thunder!"

"Ah, now we're all right! Now we're all right! There'll be a boat out here for us in half an hour."

"He's going on. He's running. He's going up to that house there."

The remote beach seemed lower than the sea, and it required a searching glance to discern the little black figure. The captain saw a floating stick, and they rowed to it. A bath towel was by some weird chance in the boat, and, tying this on the stick, the captain waved it. The oarsman did not dare turn his head, so he was obliged to ask questions.

"What's he doing now?"

"He's standing still again. He's looking, I think.—There he goes again—toward the house.—Now he's stopped again."

"Is he waving at us?"

"No, not now; he was, though."

"Look! There comes another man!"

"He's running."

"Look at him go, would you!"

"Why, he's on a bicycle. Now he's met the other man. They're both waving at us. Look!"

"There comes something up the beach."

"What the devil is that thing?"

"Why, it looks like a boat."

"Why, certainly, it's a boat."

"No; it's on wheels."

"Yes, so it is. Well, that must be the life-boat. They drag them along shore on a wagon."

"That's the life-boat, sure."

"No, by God, it's—it's an omnibus."

"I tell you it's a life-boat."

"It is not! It's an omnibus. I can see it plain. See. One of these big hotel omnibuses."

"By thunder, you're right. It's an omnibus, sure as fate. What do you suppose they are doing with an omnibus? Maybe they are going around collecting the life-crew, hey?"

"That's it, likely. Look! There's a fellow waving a little black flag. He's standing on the steps of the omnibus. There come those other two fellows. Now they're all talking together. Look at the fellow with the flag. Maybe he ain't waving it!"

"That ain't a flag, is it? That's his coat. Why, certainly, that's his coat."

"So it is; it's his coat. He's taken it off and is waving it around his head. But would you look at him swing it!"

"Oh, say, there isn't any life-saving station there. That's just a winter-resort hotel omnibus that has brought over some of the boarders to see us drown."

"What's that idiot with the coat mean? What's he signalling, anyhow?"

"It looks as if he were trying to tell us to go north. There must be a life-saving station up there."

"No; he thinks we're fishing. Just giving us a merry hand. See? Ah, there, Willie!"

"Well, I wish I could make something out of those signals. What do you suppose he means?"

"He don't mean anything; he's just playing."

"Well, if he'd just signal us to try the surf again, or to go to sea and wait, or go north, or go south, or go to hell, there would be some reason in it. But look at him! He just stands there and keeps his coat revolving like a wheel. The ass!"

"There come more people."

"Now there's quite a mob. Look! Isn't that a boat?"

"Where? Oh, I see where you mean. No, that's no boat."

"That fellow is still waving his coat."

"He must think we like to see him do that. Why don't he quit it? It don't mean anything."

"I don't know. I think he is trying to make us go north. It must be that there's a life-saving station there somewhere."

"Say, he ain't tired yet. Look at 'im wave!"

"Wonder how long he can keep that up. He's been revolving his coat ever since he caught sight of us. He's an idiot. Why aren't they getting men to bring a boat out? A fishing boat—one of those big yawls—could come out here all right. Why don't he do something?"

"Oh, it's all right now."

"They'll have a boat out here for us in less than no time, now that they've seen us."

A faint yellow tone came into the sky over the low land. The shadows on the sea slowly deepened. The wind bore coldness with it, and the men began to shiver.

"Holy smoke!" said one, allowing his voice to express his impious mood, "if we keep on monkeying out here! If we've got to flounder out here all night!"

"Oh, we'll never have to stay here all night! Don't you worry. They've seen us now, and it won't be long before they'll come chasing out after us."

The shore grew dusky. The man waving a coat blended gradually into this gloom, and it swallowed in the same manner the omnibus and the group of people. The spray, when it dashed uproariously over the side, made the voyagers shrink and swear like men who were being branded.

"I'd like to catch the chump who waved the coat. I feel like socking him one, just for luck."

"Why? What did he do?"

"Oh, nothing, but then he seemed so damned cheerful."

In the meantime the oiler rowed, and then the correspondent rowed, and then the oiler rowed. Grey-faced and bowed forward, they mechanically, turn by turn, plied the leaden oars. The form of the lighthouse had vanished from the southern horizon, but finally a pale star appeared, just lifting from the sea. The streaked saffron in the west passed before the all-merging darkness, and the sea to the east was black. The land had vanished, and was expressed only by the low and drear thunder of the surf.

"If I am going to be drowned—if I am going to be drowned—if I am going to be drowned, why, in the name of the seven mad gods who rule the sea, was I allowed to come thus far and contemplate sand and trees? Was I brought here merely to have my nose dragged away as I was about to nibble the sacred cheese of life?"

The patient captain, drooped over the water jar, was sometimes obliged to speak to the oarsman.

"Keep her head up! Keep her head up!"

"Keep her head up, sir." The voices were weary and low.

This was surely a quiet evening. All save the oarsman lay heavily and listlessly in the boat's bottom. As for him, his eyes were just capable of noting the tall black waves that swept forward in a most sinister silence, save for an occasional subdued growl of a crest.

The cook's head was on a thwart, and he looked without interest at the water under his nose. He was deep in other scenes. Finally he spoke. "Billie," he murmured, dreamfully, "what kind of pie do you like best?"

5

"Pie!" said the oiler and correspondent, agitatedly. "Don't talk about those things, blast you!"

"Well," said the cook, "I was just thinking about ham sandwiches, and—"

A night on the sea in an open boat is a long night. As darkness settled finally, the shine of the light, lifting from the sea in the south, changed to full gold. On the northern horizon a new light appeared, a small bluish gleam on the edge of the waters. These two lights were the furniture of the world. Otherwise there was nothing but waves.

Two men huddled in the stern, and distances were so magnificent in the dinghy that the rower was enabled to keep his feet partly warm by thrusting them under his companions. Their legs indeed extended far under the rowing-seat until they touched the feet of the captain forward. Sometimes, despite the efforts of the tired oarsman, a wave came piling into the boat, an icy wave of the night, and the chilling water soaked them anew. They would twist their bodies for a moment and groan, and sleep the dead sleep once more, while the water in the boat gurgled about them as the craft rocked.

The plan of the oiler and the correspondent was for one to row until he lost the ability, and then arouse the other from his sea-water couch in the bottom of the boat.

The oiler plied the oars until his head drooped forward and the overpowering sleep blinded him; and he rowed yet afterward. Then he touched a man in the bottom of the boat, and called his name. "Will you spell me for a little while?" he said meekly.

"Sure, Billie," said the correspondent, awaking and dragging himself to a sitting position. They exchanged places carefully, and the oiler, cuddling down in the sea-water at the cook's side, seemed to go to sleep instantly.

The particular violence of the sea had ceased. The waves came without snarling. The obligation of the man at the oars was to keep the boat headed so that the tilt of the rollers would not capsize her, and to preserve her from filling when the crests rushed past. The black waves were silent and hard to be seen in the darkness. Often one was almost upon the boat before the oarsman was aware.

In a low voice the correspondent addressed the captain. He was not sure that the captain was awake, although this iron man seemed to be always awake. "Captain, shall I keep her making for that light north, sir?"

The same steady voice answered him. "Yes. Keep it about two points off the port bow."

The cook had tied a life-belt around himself in order to get even the warmth which this clumsy cork contrivance could donate, and he seemed almost stove-like when a rower, whose teeth invariably chattered wildly as soon as he ceased his labour, dropped down to sleep.

The correspondent, as he rowed, looked down at the two men sleeping underfoot. The cook's arm was around the oiler's shoulders, and, with their fragmentary clothing and haggard faces, they were the babes of the sea—a grotesque rendering of the old babes in the wood.

Later he must have grown stupid at his work, for suddenly there was a growling of water, and a crest came with a roar and a swash into the boat, and it was a wonder that it did not set the cook afloat in his life-belt. The cook continued to sleep, but the oiler sat up, blinking his eyes and shaking with the new cold.

"Oh, I'm awful sorry, Billie," said the correspondent contritely.

"That's all right, old boy," said the oiler, and lay down again and was asleep.

Presently it seemed that even the captain dozed, and the correspondent thought that he was the one man afloat on all the ocean. The wind had a voice as it came over the waves, and it was sadder than the end.

There was a long, loud swishing astern of the boat, and a gleaming trail of phosphorescence, like blue flame, was furrowed on the black waters. It might have been made by a monstrous knife.

Then there came a stillness, while the correspondent breathed with open mouth and looked at the sea.

Suddenly there was another swish and another long flash of bluish light, and this time it was alongside the boat, and might almost have been reached with an oar. The correspondent saw an enormous fin speed like a shadow through the water, hurling the crystalline spray, and leaving the long glowing trail.

The correspondent looked over his shoulder at the captain. His face was hidden, and he seemed to be asleep. He looked at the babes of the sea. They certainly were asleep. So, being bereft of sympathy, he leaned a little way to one side and swore softly into the sea.

But the thing did not then leave the vicinity of the boat. Ahead or astern, on one side or the other, at intervals long or short, fled the long sparkling streak, and there was to be heard the *whirroo* of the dark fin. The speed and power of the thing was greatly to be admired. It cut the water like a gigantic and keen projectile.

The presence of this biding thing did not affect the man with the same horror that it would if he had been a picnicker. He simply looked at the sea dully and swore in an undertone.

Nevertheless, it is true that he did not wish to be alone with the thing. He wished one of his companions to awake by chance and keep him company with it. But the captain hung motionless over the water-jar, and the oiler and the cook in the bottom of the boat were plunged in slumber.

6

"If I am going to be drowned—if I am going to be drowned—if I am going to be drowned, why, in the name of the seven mad gods who rule the sea, was I allowed to come thus far and contemplate sand and trees?"

During this dismal night, it may be remarked that a man would conclude that it was really the intention of the seven mad gods to drown him, despite the abominable injustice of it. For it was certainly an abominable injustice to drown a man who had worked so hard, so hard. The man felt it would be a crime most unnatural. Other people had drowned at sea since galleys swarmed with painted sails, but still—

When it occurs to a man that nature does not regard him as important, and that she feels she would not maim the universe by disposing of him, he at first wishes to throw bricks at the temple, and he hates deeply the fact that there are no bricks and no temples. Any visible expression of nature would surely be pelleted with his jeers.

Then, if there be no tangible thing to hoot, he feels, perhaps, the desire to confront a personification and indulge in pleas, bowed to one knee, and with hands supplicant, saying, "Yes, but I love myself."

A high cold star on a winter's night is the word he feels that she says to him. Thereafter he knows the pathos of his situation.

The men in the dinghy had not discussed these matters, but each had, no doubt, reflected upon them in silence and according to his mind. There was seldom any expression upon their faces save the general one of complete weariness. Speech was devoted to the business of the boat.

To chime the notes of his emotion, a verse mysteriously entered the correspondent's head. He had even forgotten that he had forgotten this verse, but it suddenly was in his mind.

> A soldier of the Legion lay dying in Algiers;
> There was lack of woman's nursing, there was dearth of woman's tears;
> But a comrade stood beside him, and he took that comrade's hand,
> And he said, "I never more shall see my own, my native land."

In his childhood the correspondent had been made acquainted with the fact that a soldier of the Legion lay dying in Algiers, but he had never regarded the fact as important. Myriads of his school-fellows had informed him of the soldier's plight, but the dinning had naturally ended by making him perfectly indifferent. He had never considered it his affair that a soldier of the Legion lay dying in Algiers, nor had it appeared to him as a matter for sorrow. It was less to him than the breaking of a pencil's point.

Now, however, it quaintly came to him as a human, living thing. It was no longer merely a picture of a few throes in the breast of a poet, meanwhile drinking tea and warming his feet at the grate; it was an actuality—stern, mournful, and fine.

The correspondent plainly saw the soldier. He lay on the sand with his feet out straight and still. While his pale left hand was upon his chest in an attempt to thwart the going of his life, the blood came between his fingers. In the far Algerian distance, a city of low square forms was set against a sky that was faint with the last sunset hues. The correspondent, plying the oars and dreaming of the slow and slower movements of the lips of the soldier, was moved by a profound and perfectly impersonal comprehension. He was sorry for the soldier of the Legion who lay dying in Algiers.

The thing which had followed the boat and waited had evidently grown bored at the delay. There was no longer to be heard the slash of the cutwater, and there was no longer the flame of the long trail. The light in the north still glimmered, but it was apparently no nearer to the boat. Sometimes the boom of the surf rang in the correspondent's ears, and he turned the craft seaward then and rowed harder. Southward, some one had evidently built a watch-fire on the beach. It was too low and too far to be seen, but it made a shimmering, roseate reflection upon the bluff in back of it, and this could be discerned from the boat. The wind came stronger, and sometimes a wave suddenly raged out like a mountain cat, and there was to be seen the sheen and sparkle of a broken crest.

The captain, in the bow, moved on his water-jar and sat erect. "Pretty long night," he observed to the correspondent. He looked at the shore. "Those life-saving people take their time."

"Did you see that shark playing around?"

"Yes, I saw him. He was a big fellow, all right."

"Wish I had known you were awake."

Later the correspondent spoke into the bottom of the boat. "Billie!" There was a slow and gradual disentanglement. "Billie, will you spell me?"

"Sure," said the oiler.

As soon as the correspondent touched the cold, comfortable sea-water in the bottom of the boat and had huddled close to the cook's life-belt he was deep in sleep, despite the fact that his teeth played all the popular airs. This sleep was so good to him that it was but a moment before he heard a voice call his name in a tone that demonstrated the last stages of exhaustion. "Will you spell me?"

"Sure, Billie."

The light in the north had mysteriously vanished, but the correspondent took his course from the wide-awake captain.

Later in the night they took the boat farther out to sea, and the captain directed the cook to take one oar at the stern and keep the boat facing the seas. He was to call out if he should hear the thunder of the surf. This plan enabled the oiler and the correspondent to get respite together. "We'll give those boys a chance to get into shape again," said the captain. They curled down and, after a few preliminary chatterings and trembles, slept once more the dead sleep. Neither knew they had bequeathed to the cook the company of another shark, or perhaps the same shark.

As the boat caroused on the waves, spray occasionally bumped over the side and gave them a fresh soaking, but this had no power to break their repose. The ominous slash of the wind and the water affected them as it would have affected mummies.

"Boys," said the cook, with the notes of every reluctance in his voice, "she's drifted in pretty close. I guess one of you had better take her to sea again." The correspondent, aroused, heard the crash of the toppled crests.

As he was rowing, the captain gave him some whiskey-and-water, and this steadied the chills out of him. "If I ever get ashore and anybody shows me even a photograph of an oar—"

At last there was a short conversation.

"Billie!—Billie, will you spell me?"

"Sure," said the oiler.

7

When the correspondent again opened his eyes, the sea and the sky were each of the grey hue of the dawning. Later, carmine and gold was painted upon the waters. The morning appeared finally, in its splendour, with a sky of pure blue, and the sunlight flamed on the tips of the waves.

On the distant dunes were set many little black cottages, and a tall white windmill reared above them. No man, nor dog, nor bicycle appeared on the beach. The cottages might have formed a deserted village.

The voyagers scanned the shore. A conference was held in the boat. "Well," said the captain, "if no help is coming, we might better try a run through the surf right away. If we stay out here much longer we will be too weak to do anything for ourselves at all." The others silently acquiesced in this reasoning. The boat was headed for the beach. The correspondent wondered if none ever ascended the tall wind-tower, and if then they never looked seaward. This tower was a giant, standing with its back to the plight of the ants. It represented in a degree, to the correspondent, the serenity of nature amid the struggles of the individual—nature in the wind, and nature in the vision of men. She did not seem cruel to him then, nor beneficent, nor treacherous, nor wise. But she was indifferent, flatly indifferent. It is, perhaps, plausible that a man in this situation, impressed with the unconcern of the universe, should see the innumerable flaws of his life, and have them taste wickedly in his mind, and wish for another chance. A distinction between right and wrong seems absurdly clear to him, then, in this new ignorance of the grave-edge, and he understands that if he were given another opportunity he would mend his conduct and his words, and be better and brighter during an introduction or at a tea.

"Now, boys," said the captain, "she is going to swamp sure. All we can do is to work her in as far as possible, and then when she swamps, pile out and scramble for the beach. Keep cool now, and don't jump until she swamps sure."

The oiler took the oars. Over his shoulders he scanned the surf. "Captain," he said, "I think I'd better bring her about and keep her head-on to the seas and back her in."

"All right, Billie," said the captain. "Back her in." The oiler swung the boat then, and, seated in the stern, the cook and the correspondent were obliged to look over their shoulders to contemplate the lonely and indifferent shore.

The monstrous inshore rollers heaved the boat high until the men were again enabled to see the white sheets of water scudding up the slanted beach. "We won't get in very close," said the captain. Each time a man could wrest his attention from the rollers, he turned his glance toward the shore, and in the expression of the eyes during this contemplation there was a singular quality. The correspondent, observing the others, knew that they were not afraid, but the full meaning of their glances was shrouded.

As for himself, he was too tired to grapple fundamentally with the fact. He tried to coerce his mind into thinking of it, but the mind was dominated at this time by the muscles, and they did not care. It merely occurred to him that if he should drown it would be a shame.

There were no hurried words, no pallor, no plain agitation. The men simply looked at the shore. "Now, remember to get well clear of the boat when you jump," said the captain.

Seaward the crest of a roller suddenly fell with a thunderous crash, and the long white comber came roaring down upon the boat.

"Steady now," said the captain. The men were silent. They turned their eyes from the shore to the comber and waited. The boat slid up the incline, leaped at the furious top, bounced over it, and swung down the long back of the wave. Some water had been shipped, and the cook bailed it out.

But the next crest crashed also. The tumbling, boiling flood of white water caught the boat and whirled it almost perpendicular. Water swarmed in from all sides. The correspondent had his hands on the gunwale at this time, and when the water entered at that place he swiftly withdrew his fingers, as if he objected to wetting them.

The little boat, drunken with this weight of water, reeled and snuggled deeper into the sea.

"Bail her out, cook! Bail her out!" said the captain.

"All right, Captain," said the cook.

"Now, boys, the next one will do for us sure," said the oiler. "Mind to jump clear of the boat."

The third wave moved forward, huge, furious, implacable. It fairly swallowed the dinghy, and almost simultaneously the men tumbled into the sea. A piece of life-belt had lain in the bottom of the boat, and as the correspondent went overboard he held this to his chest with his left hand.

The January water was icy, and he reflected immediately that it was colder than he had expected to find it off the coast of Florida. This appeared to his dazed mind as a fact important enough to be noted at the time. The coldness of the water was sad; it was tragic. This fact was somehow mixed and confused with his opinion of his own situation, so that it seemed almost a proper reason for tears. The water was cold.

When he came to the surface he was conscious of little but the noisy water. Afterward he saw his companions in the sea. The oiler was ahead in the race. He was swimming strongly and rapidly. Off to the correspondent's left, the cook's great white and corked back bulged out of the water; and in the rear the captain was hanging with his one good hand to the keel of the overturned dinghy.

There is a certain immovable quality to a shore, and the correspondent wondered at it amid the confusion of the sea.

It seemed also very attractive; but the correspondent knew that it was a long journey, and he paddled leisurely. The piece of life-preserver lay under him, and sometimes he whirled down the incline of a wave as if he were on a hand-sled.

But finally he arrived at a place in the sea where travel was beset with difficulty. He did not pause swimming to inquire what manner of current had caught him, but there his progress ceased. The shore was set before him like a bit of scenery on a stage, and he looked at it and understood with his eyes each detail of it.

As the cook passed, much farther to the left, the captain was calling to him. "Turn over on your back, cook! Turn over on your back and use the oar."

"All right, sir." The cook turned on his back, and paddling with an oar, went ahead as if he were a canoe.

Presently the boat also passed to the left of the correspondent, with the captain clinging with one hand to the keel. He would have appeared like a man raising himself to look over a board fence if it were not for the extraordinary gymnastics of the boat. The correspondent marvelled that the captain could still hold to it.

They passed on nearer to shore—the oiler, the cook, the captain—and following them went the water-jar, bouncing gaily over the seas.

The correspondent remained in the grip of this strange new enemy—a current. The shore, with its white slope of sand and its green bluff topped with little silent cottages, was spread like a picture before him. It was very near to him then, but he was impressed as one who, in a gallery, looks at a scene from Brittany or Algiers.

He thought: "I'm going to drown? Can it be possible? Can it be possible? Can it be possible?" Perhaps an individual must consider his own death to be the final phenomenon of nature.

But later a wave perhaps whirled him out of this small deadly current, for he found suddenly that he could again make progress toward the shore. Later still he was aware that the captain, clinging with one hand to the keel of the dinghy, had his face turned away from the shore and toward him, and was calling his name. "Come to the boat! Come to the boat!"

In his struggle to reach the captain and the boat, he reflected that when one gets properly wearied drowning must really be a comfortable arrangement—a cessation of hostilities accompanied by a large degree of relief; and he was glad of it, for the main thing in his mind for some moments had been horror of the temporary agony. He did not wish to be hurt.

Presently he saw a man running along the shore. He was undressing with most remarkable speed. Coat, trousers, shirt, everything flew magically off him.

"Come to the boat!" called the captain.

"All right, Captain." As the correspondent paddled, he saw the captain let himself down to bottom and leave the boat. Then the correspondent performed his own little marvel of the voyage. A large wave caught him and flung him with ease and supreme speed completely over the boat and far beyond it. It struck him even then as an event in gymnastics and a true miracle of the sea. An overturned boat in the surf is not a plaything to a swimming man.

The correspondent arrived in water that reached only to his waist, but his condition did not enable him to stand for more than a moment. Each wave knocked him into a heap, and the undertow pulled at him.

Then he saw the man who had been running and undressing, and undressing and running, come bounding into the water. He dragged ashore the cook, and then waded toward the captain; but the captain waved him away and sent him to the correspondent. He was naked—naked as a tree in winter; but a halo was about his head, and he shone like a saint. He gave a strong pull, and a long drag, and a bully heave at the correspondent's hand. The correspondent, schooled in the minor formulae, said, "Thanks, old man." But suddenly the man cried, "What's that?" He pointed a swift finger. The correspondent said, "Go."

In the shallows, face downward, lay the oiler. His forehead touched sand that was periodically, between each wave, clear of the sea.

The correspondent did not know all that transpired afterward. When he achieved safe ground he fell, striking the sand with each particular part of his body. It was as if he had dropped from a roof, but the thud was grateful to him.

It seems that instantly the beach was populated with men with blankets, clothes, and flasks, and women with coffee-pots and all the remedies sacred to their minds. The welcome of the land to the men from the sea was warm and generous; but a still and dripping shape was carried slowly up the beach, and the land's welcome for it could only be the different and sinister hospitality of the grave.

When it came night, the white waves paced to and fro in the moonlight, and the wind brought the sound of the great sea's voice to the men on the shore, and they felt that they could then be interpreters.

QUESTIONS FOR DISCUSSION AND WRITING

1. This story alternates between extended moments of boredom and intense moments of physical exertion. How do these alternating rhythms sustain the plot? What unifies each of the seven sections of the story?
2. At first, what special quality distinguishes each of the four men in the boat? In what surprising ways do the characters change during the course of the story?

3. How does Crane describe the environment of the open sea? How do the attitudes of the men toward the sea change during the story?
4. Although this story is told from an objective point of view, the correspondent seems to speak for the other men in the boat. How is this essential point of view established in his repeated question: "Why, in the name of the seven mad gods who rule the sea, was I allowed to come thus far and contemplate sand and trees?"
5. What do the verse about "a soldier of the Legion" and the death of the oiler reveal about the nature of existence? How would the three survivors interpret the "sound of the great sea's voice"?

25

STEPHEN CRANE

The Blue Hotel

1

The Palace Hotel at Fort Romper was painted a light blue, a shade that is on the legs of a kind of heron, causing the bird to declare its position against any background. The Palace Hotel, then, was always screaming and howling in a way that made the dazzling winter landscape of Nebraska seem only a grey swampish hush. It stood alone on the prairie, and when the snow was falling the town two hundred yards away was not visible. But when the traveller alighted at the railway station he was obliged to pass the Palace Hotel before he could come upon the company of low clapboard houses which composed Fort Romper, and it was not to be thought that any traveller could pass the Palace Hotel without looking at it. Pat Scully, the proprietor, had proved himself a master of strategy when he chose his paints. It is true that on clear days, when the great transcontinental expresses, long lines of swaying Pullmans, swept through Fort Romper, passengers were overcome at the sight, and the cult that knows the brown-reds and the subdivisions of the dark greens of the East expressed shame, pity, horror, in a laugh. But to the citizens of this prairie town and to the people who would naturally stop there, Pat Scully had performed a feat. With this opulence and splendour, these creeds, classes, egotisms, that streamed through Romper on the rails day after day, they had no colour in common.

As if the displayed delights of such a blue hotel were not sufficiently enticing, it was Scully's habit to go every morning and evening to meet the leisurely trains that stopped at Romper and work his seductions upon any man that he might see wavering, gripsack in hand.

One morning, when a snow-crusted engine dragged its long string of freight cars and its one passenger coach to the station, Scully performed the marvel of catching three men. One was a shaky and quick-eyed Swede, with a great shining cheap valise; one was a tall bronzed cowboy, who was on his way to a ranch near the Dakota line; one was a little silent man from the East, who didn't look it, and didn't announce it. Scully practically made them prisoners. He was so nimble and merry and kindly that each probably felt it would be the height of brutality to try to escape. They trudged off over the creaking board sidewalks in the wake of the eager little Irishman. He wore a heavy fur cap squeezed tightly down on his head. It caused his two red ears to stick out stiffly, as if they were made of tin.

At last, Scully, elaborately, with boisterous hospitality, conducted them through the portals of the blue hotel. The room which they entered was small. It seemed to be merely a proper temple for an enormous stove, which, in the centre, was humming with godlike violence. At various points on its surface the iron had become luminous and glowed yellow from the heat. Beside the stove Scully's son Johnnie was playing High-Five with an old farmer who had whiskers both grey and sandy. They were quarreling. Frequently the old farmer turned his face toward a box of sawdust—coloured brown from tobacco juice—that was behind the stove, and spat with an air of great impatience and irritation. With a loud flourish of words, Scully destroyed the game of cards, and bustled his son upstairs with part of the baggage of the new guests. He himself conducted them to three basins of the coldest water in the world. The cowboy and the Easterner burnished themselves fiery red with this water, until it seemed to be some kind of metal-polish. The Swede, however, merely dipped his fingers gingerly and with trepidation. It was notable that throughout this series of small ceremonies the three travellers were made to feel that Scully was very benevolent. He was conferring great favours upon them. He handed the towel from one to another with an air of philanthropic impulse.

Afterward they went to the first room, and, sitting about the stove, listened to Scully's officious clamour at his daughters, who were preparing the midday meal. They reflected in the silence of experienced men who tread carefully amid new people. Nevertheless, the old farmer, stationary, invincible in his chair near the warmest part of the stove, turned his face from the sawdust-box frequently and addressed a glowing commonplace to the strangers. Usually he was answered in short but adequate sentences by either the cowboy or the Easterner. The Swede said nothing. He seemed to be occupied in making furtive estimates of each man in the room. One might have thought that he had the sense of silly suspicion which comes to guilt. He resembled a badly frightened man.

Later, at dinner, he spoke a little, addressing his conversation entirely to Scully. He volunteered that he had come from New York, where for ten years he had worked as a tailor. These facts seemed to strike Scully as fascinating, and afterward he volunteered that he had lived at Romper for fourteen years. The Swede asked about the crops and the price of labour. He seemed barely to listen to Scully's extended replies. His eyes continued to rove from man to man.

Finally, with a laugh and a wink, he said that some of these Western communities were very dangerous; and after his statement he straightened his legs under the table, tilted his head, and laughed again, loudly. It was plain that the demonstration had no meaning to the others. They looked at him wondering and in silence.

2

As the men trooped heavily back into the front room, the two little windows presented views of a turmoiling sea of snow. The huge arms of the wind were making attempts—mighty, circular, futile—to embrace the flakes as they sped. A gate-post like a still man with a blanched face stood aghast amid this profligate fury. In a hearty voice Scully announced the presence of a blizzard. The guests of the blue hotel, lighting their pipes, assented with grunts of lazy masculine contentment. No island of the sea could be exempt in the degree of this little room with its humming stove. Johnnie, son of Scully, in a tone which defined his opinion of his ability as a card-player, challenged the old farmer of both grey and sandy whiskers to a game of High-Five. The farmer agreed with a contemptuous and bitter scoff. They sat close to the stove, and squared their knees under a wide board. The cowboy and the Easterner watched the game with interest. The Swede remained near the window, aloof, but with a countenance that showed signs of an inexplicable excitement.

The play of Johnnie and the grey-beard was suddenly ended by another quarrel. The old man arose while casting a look of heated scorn at his adversary. He slowly buttoned his coat, and then stalked with fabulous dignity from the room. In the discreet silence of all other men the Swede laughed. His laughter rang somehow childish. Men by this time had begun to look at him askance, as if they wished to inquire what ailed him.

A new game was formed jocosely. The cowboy volunteered to become the partner of Johnnie, and they all then turned to ask the Swede to throw in his lot with the little Easterner. He asked some questions about the game, and, learning that it wore many names, and that he had played it when it was under an alias, he accepted the invitation. He strode toward the men nervously, as if he expected to be assaulted. Finally, seated, he gazed from face to face and laughed shrilly. This laugh was so strange that the Easterner looked up quickly, the cowboy sat intent and with his mouth open, and Johnnie paused, holding the cards with still fingers.

Afterward there was a short silence. Then Johnnie said, "Well, let's get at it. Come on now!" They pulled their chairs forward until their knees were bunched under the board. They began to play, and their interest in the game caused the others to forget the manner of the Swede.

The cowboy was a board-whacker. Each time that he held superior cards he whanged them, one by one, with exceeding force, down upon the improvised table, and took the tricks with a glowing air of prowess and pride that sent thrills of indignation into the hearts of his opponents. A game with a board-whacker in it is sure to become intense. The countenances of the Easterner and the Swede were miserable whenever the cowboy thundered down his aces and kings, while Johnnie, his eyes gleaming with joy, chuckled and chuckled.

Because of the absorbing play none considered the strange ways of the Swede. They paid strict heed to the game. Finally, during a lull caused by a new deal, the Swede suddenly addressed Johnnie: "I suppose there have been a good many men killed in this room." The jaws of the others dropped and they looked at him.

"What in hell are you talking about?" said Johnnie.

The Swede laughed again his blatant laugh, full of a kind of false courage and defiance. "Oh, you know what I mean all right," he answered.

"I'm a liar if I do!" Johnnie protested. The card was halted, and the men stared at the Swede. Johnnie evidently felt that as the son of the proprietor he should make a direct inquiry. "Now, what might you be drivin' at, mister?" he asked. The Swede winked at him. It was a wink full of cunning. His fingers shook on the edge of the board. "Oh, maybe you think I have been to nowheres. Maybe you think I'm a tenderfoot?"

"I don't know nothin' about you," answered Johnnie, "and I don't give a damn where you've been. All I got to say is that I don't know what you're driving at. There hain't never been nobody killed in this room."

The cowboy, who had been steadily gazing at the Swede, then spoke: "What's wrong with you, mister?"

Apparently it seemed to the Swede that he was formidably menaced. He shivered and turned white near the corners of his mouth. He sent an appealing glance in the direction of the little Easterner. During these moments he did not forget to wear his air of advanced pot-valour. "They say they don't know what I mean," he remarked mockingly to the Easterner.

The latter answered after prolonged and cautious reflection. "I don't understand you," he said, impassively.

The Swede made a movement then which announced that he thought he had encountered treachery from the only quarter where he had expected sympathy, if not help. "Oh, I see you are all against me. I see——"

The cowboy was in a state of deep stupefaction. "Say," he cried, as he tumbled the deck violently down upon the board, "say, what are you gittin' at, hey?"

The Swede sprang up with the celerity of a man escaping from a snake on the floor. "I don't want to fight!" he shouted. "I don't want to fight!"

The cowboy stretched his long legs indolently and deliberately. His hands were in his pockets. He spat into the sawdust-box. "Well, who the hell thought you did?" he inquired.

The Swede backed rapidly toward a corner of the room. His hands were out protectingly in front of his chest, but he was making an obvious struggle to control his fright. "Gentlemen," he quavered, "I suppose I am going to be killed before I can leave this house! I suppose I am going to be killed before I can leave this house!" In his eyes was the dying-swan look. Through the windows could be seen the snow turning blue in the shadow of dusk. The wind tore at the house, and some loose thing beat regularly against the clap-boards like a spirit tapping.

A door opened, and Scully himself entered. He paused in surprise as he noted the tragic attitude of the Swede. Then he said, "What's the matter here?"

The Swede answered him swiftly and eagerly: "These men are going to kill me."

"Kill you!" ejaculated Scully. "Kill you! What are you talkin'?"

The Swede made the gesture of a martyr.

Scully wheeled sternly upon his son. "What is this, Johnnie?"

The lad had grown sullen. "Damned if I know," he answered. "I can't make no sense of it." He began to shuffle the cards, fluttering them together with an angry snap. "He says a good many men have been killed in this room, or something like that. And he says he's goin' to be killed here too. I don't know what ails him. He's crazy, I shouldn't wonder."

Scully then looked for explanation to the cowboy, but the cowboy simply shrugged his shoulders.

"Kill you?" said Scully again to the Swede. "Kill you? Man, you're off your nut."

"Oh, I know," burst out the Swede. "I know what will happen. Yes, I'm crazy—yes. Yes, of course, I'm crazy—yes. But I know one thing——" There was a sort of sweat of misery and terror upon his face. "I know I won't get out of here alive."

The cowboy drew a deep breath, as if his mind was passing into the last stages of dissolution. "Well, I'm doggoned," he whispered to himself.

Scully wheeled suddenly and faced his son. "You've been troublin' this man!"

Johnnie's voice was loud with its burden of grievance. "Why, good Gawd, I ain't done nothin' to 'im."

The Swede broke in. "Gentlemen, do not disturb yourselves. I will leave this house. I will go away, because"—he accused them dramatically with his glance—"because I do not want to be killed."

Scully was furious with his son. "Will you tell me what is the matter, you young divil? What's the matter, anyhow? Speak out!"

"Blame it!" cried Johnnie in despair, "don't I tell you I don't know? He—he says we want to kill him, and that's all I know. I can't tell what ails him."

The Swede continued to repeat: "Never mind, Mr. Scully; never mind. I will leave this house. I will go away, because I do not wish to be killed. Yes, of course, I am crazy—yes. But I know one thing! I will go away. I will leave this house. Never mind, Mr. Scully; never mind. I will go away."

"You will not go 'way," said Scully. "You will not go 'way until I hear the reason of this business. If anybody has troubled you I will take care of him. This is my house. You are under my roof, and I will not allow any peaceable man to be troubled here." He cast a terrible eye upon Johnnie, the cowboy, and the Easterner.

"Never mind, Mr. Scully; never mind. I will go away. I do not wish to be killed." The Swede moved toward the door which opened upon the stairs. It was evidently his intention to go at once for his baggage.

"No, no," shouted Scully peremptorily; but the white-faced man slid by him and disappeared. "Now," said Scully severely, "what does this mean?"

Johnnie and the cowboy cried together: "Why, we didn't do nothin' to 'im!"

Scully's eyes were cold. "No," he said, "you didn't?"

Johnnie swore a deep oath. "Why, this is the wildest loon I ever see. We didn't do nothin' at all. We were jest sittin' here playin' cards, and he——"

The father suddenly spoke to the Easterner. "Mr. Blanc," he asked, "what has these boys been doin'?"

The Easterner reflected again. "I didn't see anything wrong at all," he said at last, slowly.

Scully began to howl. "But what does it mean?" He stared ferociously at his son. "I have a mind to lather you for this, me boy."

Johnnie was frantic. "Well, what have I done?" he bawled at his father.

3

"I think you are tongue-tied," said Scully finally to his son, the cowboy, and the Easterner; and at the end of this scornful sentence he left the room.

Upstairs the Swede was swiftly fastening the straps of his great valise. Once his back happened to be half turned toward the door, and, hearing a noise there, he wheeled and sprang up, uttering a loud cry. Scully's wrinkled visage showed grimly in the light of the small lamp he carried. This yellow effulgence, streaming upward, coloured only his prominent features, and left his eyes, for instance, in mysterious shadow. He resembled a murderer.

"Man! man!" he exclaimed, "have you gone daffy?"

"Oh, no! Oh, no!" rejoined the other. "There are people in this world who know pretty nearly as much as you do—understand?"

For a moment they stood gazing at each other. Upon the Swede's deathly pale cheeks were two spots brightly crimson and sharply edged, as if they had been carefully painted. Scully placed the light on the table and sat himself on the edge of the bed. He spoke ruminatively. "By cracky, I never heard of such a thing in my life. It's a complete muddle. I can't, for the soul of me, think how you ever got this idea into your head." Presently he lifted his eyes and asked: "And did you sure think they were going to kill you?"

The Swede scanned the old man as if he wished to see into his mind. "I did," he said at last. He obviously suspected that this answer might precipitate an outbreak. As he pulled on a strap his whole arm shook, the elbow wavering like a bit of paper.

Scully banged his hand impressively on the footboard of the bed. "Why, man, we're goin' to have a line of ilictric street-cars in this town next spring."

"'A line of electric street-cars,'" repeated the Swede, stupidly.

"And," said Scully, "there's a new railroad goin' to be built down from Broken Arm to here. Not to mintion the four churches and the smashin' big brick schoolhouse. Then there's the big factory, too. Why, in two years Romper'll be a met-tro-*pol*-is."

Having finished the preparation of his baggage, the Swede straightened himself. "Mr. Scully," he said, with sudden hardihood, "how much do I owe you?"

"You don't owe me anythin'," said the old man, angrily.

"Yes, I do," retorted the Swede. He took seventy-five cents from his pocket and tendered it to Scully; but the latter snapped his fingers in disdainful refusal. However, it happened that they both stood gazing in a strange fashion at three silver pieces on the Swede's open palm.

"I'll not take your money," said Scully at last. "Not after what's been goin' on here." Then a plan seemed to strike him. "Here," he cried, picking up his lamp and moving toward the door. "Here! Come with me a minute."

"No," said the Swede, in overwhelming alarm.

"Yes," urged the old man. "Come on! I want you to come and see a picter—just across the hall—in my room."

The Swede must have concluded that his hour was come. His jaw dropped and his teeth showed like a dead man's. He ultimately followed Scully across the corridor, but he had the step of one hung in chains.

Scully flashed the light high on the wall of his own chamber. There was revealed a ridiculous photograph of a little girl. She was leaning against a balustrade of gorgeous decoration, and the formidable bang to her hair was prominent. The figure was as graceful as an upright sled-stake, and, withal, it was of the hue of lead. "There," said Scully, tenderly, "that's the picter of my little girl that died. Her name was Carrie. She had the purtiest hair you ever saw! I was that fond of her, she——"

Turning then, he saw that the Swede was not contemplating the picture at all, but, instead, was keeping keen watch on the gloom in the rear.

"Look man!" cried Scully, heartily. "That's the picter of my little gal that died. Her name was Carrie. And then here's the picter of my oldest boy, Michael. He's a lawyer in Lincoln, an' doin' well. I gave that boy a grand eddication, and I'm glad for it now. He's a fine boy. Look at 'im now. Ain't he bold as blazes, him there in Lincoln, an honoured an' respicted gintleman! An honoured and respicted gintleman," concluded Scully with a flourish. And, so saying, he smote the Swede jovially on the back.

The Swede faintly smiled.

"Now," said the old man, "there's only one more thing." He dropped suddenly to the floor and thrust his head beneath the bed. The Swede could hear his muffled voice. "I'd keep it under my piller if it wasn't for that boy Johnnie. Then there's the old woman—— Where is it now? I never put it twice in the same place. Ah, now come out with you!"

Presently he backed clumsily from under the bed, dragging with him an old coat rolled into a bundle. "I've fetched him," he muttered. Kneeling on the floor, he unrolled the coat and extracted from its heart a large yellow-brown whisky-bottle.

His first manœuvre was to hold the bottle up to the light. Reassured, apparently, that nobody had been tampering with it, he thrust it with a generous movement toward the Swede.

The weak-kneed Swede was about to eagerly clutch this element of strength, but he suddenly jerked his hand away and cast a look of horror upon Scully.

"Drink," said the old man affectionately. He had risen to his feet, and now stood facing the Swede.

There was a silence. Then again Scully said: "Drink!"

The Swede laughed wildly. He grabbed the bottle, put it to his mouth; and as his lips curled absurdly around the opening and his throat worked, he kept his glance, burning with hatred, upon the old man's face.

4

After the departure of Scully the three men, with the cardboard still upon their knees, preserved for a long time an astounded silence. Then Johnnie said: "That's the dod-dangedest Swede I ever see."

"He ain't no Swede," said the cowboy scornfully.

"Well, what is he then?" cried Johnnie. "What is he then?"

"It's my opinion," replied the cowboy deliberately, "he's some kind of a Dutchman." It was a venerable custom of the country to entitle as Swedes all light-haired men who spoke with a heavy tongue. In consequence the idea of the cowboy was not without its daring. "Yes, sir," he repeated. "It's my opinion this feller is some kind of a Dutchman."

"Well, he says he's a Swede, anyhow," muttered Johnnie, sulkily. He turned to the Easterner: "What do you think, Mr. Blanc?"

"Oh, I don't know," replied the Easterner.

"Well, what do you think makes him act that way?" asked the cowboy.

"Why, he's frightened." The Easterner knocked his pipe against a rim of the stove. "He's clear frightened out of his boots."

"What at?" cried Johnnie and the cowboy together.

The Easterner reflected over his answer.

"What at?" cried the others again.

"Oh, I don't know, but it seems to me this man has been reading dime novels, and he thinks he's right out in the middle of it—the shootin' and stabbin' and all."

"But," said the cowboy, deeply scandalized, "this ain't Wyoming, ner none of them places. This is Nebrasker."

"Yes," added Johnnie, "an' why don't he wait till he gits *out West?*"

The travelled Easterner laughed. "It isn't different there even—not in these days. But he thinks he's right in the middle of hell."

Johnnie and the cowboy mused along.

"It's awful funny," remarked Johnnie at last.

"Yes," said the cowboy. "This is a queer game. I hope we don't git snowed in, because then we'd have to stand this here man bein' around with us all the time. That wouldn't be no good."

"I wish pop would throw him out," said Johnnie.

Presently they heard a loud stamping on the stairs, accompanied by ringing jokes in the voice of old Scully, and laughter, evidently from the Swede. The men around the stove stared vacantly at each other. "Gosh!" said the cowboy. The door flew open, and old Scully, flushed and anecdotal, came into the room. He was jabbering at the Swede, who followed him, laughing bravely. It was the entry of two roisterers from a banquet hall.

"Come now," said Scully sharply to the three seated men, "move up and give us a chance at the stove." The cowboy and the Easterner obediently sidled their chairs to make room for the new-comers. Johnnie, however, simply arranged himself in a more indolent attitude, and then remained motionless.

"Come! Git over, there," said Scully.

"Plenty of room on the other side of the stove," said Johnnie.

"Do you think we want to sit in the draught?" roared the father.

But the Swede had interposed with a grandeur of confidence. "No, no. Let the boy sit where he likes," he cried in a bullying voice to the father.

"All right! All right!" said Scully, deferentially. The cowboy and the Easterner exchanged glances of wonder.

The five chairs were formed in a crescent about one side of the stove. The Swede began to talk; he talked arrogantly, profanely, angrily. Johnnie, the cowboy, and the Easterner maintained a morose silence, while old Scully appeared to be receptive and eager, breaking in constantly with sympathetic ejaculations.

Finally, the Swede announced that he was thirsty. He moved in his chair, and said that he would go for a drink of water.

"I'll git it for you," cried Scully at once.

"No," said the Swede, contemptuously. "I'll get it for myself." He arose and stalked with the air of an owner off into the executive parts of the hotel.

As soon as the Swede was out of hearing Scully sprang to his feet and whispered intensely to the others: "Upstairs he thought I was tryin' to poison 'im."

"Say," said Johnnie, "this makes me sick. Why don't you throw 'im out in the snow?"

"Why, he's all right now," declared Scully. "It was only that he was from the East, and he thought this was a tough place. That's all. He's all right now."

The cowboy looked with admiration upon the Easterner. "You were straight," he said. "You were on to that there Dutchman."

"Well," said Johnnie to his father, "he may be all right now, but I don't see it. Other time he was scared, but now he's too fresh."

Scully's speech was always a combination of Irish brogue and idiom, Western twang and idiom, and scraps of curiously formal diction taken from the story-books and newspapers. He now hurled a strange mass of language at the head of his son. "What do I keep? What do I keep? What do I keep?" he demanded, in a voice of thunder. He slapped his knee impressively, to indicate that he himself was going to make reply, and that all should heed. "I keep a hotel," he shouted. "A hotel, do you mind? A guest under my roof has sacred privileges. He is to be intimidated by none. Not one word shall he hear that would prijudice him in favour of goin' away. I'll not have it. There's no place in this here town where they can say they iver took in a guest of mine because he was afraid to stay here." He wheeled suddenly upon the cowboy and the Easterner. "Am I right?"

"Yes, Mr. Scully," said the cowboy, "I think you're right."

"Yes, Mr. Scully," said the Easterner, "I think you're right."

5

At six-o'clock supper, the Swede fizzed like a fire-wheel. He sometimes seemed on the point of bursting into riotous song, and in all his madness he was encouraged by old Scully. The Easterner was encased in reserve; the cowboy sat in wide-mouthed amazement, forgetting to eat, while Johnnie wrathily demolished great plates of food. The daughters of the house, when they were obliged to replenish the biscuits, approached as warily as Indians, and, having succeeded in their purpose, fled with ill-concealed trepidation. The Swede domineered the whole feast, and he gave it the appearance of a cruel bacchanal. He seemed to have grown suddenly taller; he gazed, brutally disdainful, into every face. His voice rang through the room. Once when he jabbed out harpoon-fashion with his fork to pinion a biscuit, the weapon nearly impaled the hand of the Easterner, which had been stretched quietly out for the same biscuit.

After supper, as the men filed toward the other room, the Swede smote Scully ruthlessly on the shoulder. "Well, old boy, that was a good, square meal." Johnnie looked hopefully at his father; he knew that shoulder was tender from an old fall; and, indeed, it appeared for a moment as if Scully was going to flame out over the matter, but in the end he smiled a sickly smile and remained silent. The others understood from his manner that he was admitting his responsibility for the Swede's new view-point.

Johnnie, however, addressed his parent in an aside. "Why don't you license somebody to kick you downstairs?" Scully scowled darkly by way of reply.

When they were gathered about the stove, the Swede insisted on another game of High-Five. Scully gently deprecated the plan at first, but the Swede turned a wolfish glare upon him. The old man subsided, and the Swede canvassed the others. In his tone there was always a great threat. The cowboy and the Easterner both remarked indifferently that they would play. Scully said that he would presently have to go to meet the 6:58 train, and so the Swede turned menacingly upon Johnnie. For a moment their glances crossed like blades, and then Johnnie smiled and said, "Yes, I'll play."

They formed a square, with the little board on their knees. The Easterner and the Swede were again partners. As the play went on, it was noticeable that the cowboy was not board-whacking as usual. Meanwhile, Scully, near the lamp, had put on his spectacles and, with an appearance curiously like an old priest, was reading a newspaper. In time he went out to meet the 6:58 train, and, despite his precautions, a gust of polar wind whirled into the room as he opened the door. Besides scattering the cards, it chilled the players to the marrow. The Swede cursed frightfully. When Scully returned, his entrance disturbed a cosy and friendly scene. The Swede again cursed. But presently they were once more intent, their heads bent forward and their hands moving swiftly. The Swede had adopted the fashion of board-whacking.

Scully took up his paper and for a long time remained immersed in matters which were extraordinarily remote from him. The lamp burned badly, and once he stopped to adjust the wick. The newspaper, as he turned from page to page, rustled with a slow and comfortable sound. Then suddenly he heard three terrible words: "You are cheatin'!"

Such scenes often prove that there can be little of dramatic import in environment. Any room can present a tragic front; any room can be comic. This little den was now hideous as a torture-chamber. The new faces of the men themselves had changed it upon the instant. The Swede held a huge fist in front of Johnnie's face, while the latter looked steadily over it into the blazing orbs of his accuser. The Easterner had grown pallid; the cowboy's jaw had dropped in that expression of bovine amazement which was one of his important mannerisms. After the three words, the first sound in the room was made by Scully's paper as it floated forgotten to his feet. His spectacles had also fallen from his nose, but by a clutch he had saved them in air. His hand, grasping the spectacles, now remained posed awkwardly and near his shoulder. He stared at the cardplayers.

Probably the silence was while a second elapsed. Then, if the floor had been suddenly twitched out from under the men they could not have moved quicker. The five had projected themselves headlong toward a common point. It happened that Johnnie, in rising to hurl himself upon the Swede, had stumbled slightly because of his curiously instinctive care for the cards and the board. The loss of the moment allowed time for the arrival of Scully, and also allowed the cowboy time to give the Swede a great push which sent him staggering back. The men found tongue together, and hoarse shouts of rage, appeal, or fear burst from every throat. The cowboy pushed and jostled feverishly at the

Swede, and the Easterner and Scully clung wildly to Johnnie; but through the smoky air, above the swaying bodies of the peace-compellers, the eyes of the two warriors ever sought each other in glances of challenge that were at once hot and steely.

Of course the board had been overturned, and now the whole company of cards was scattered over the floor, where the boots of the men trampled the fat and painted kings and queens as they gazed with their silly eyes at the war that was waging above them.

Scully's voice was dominating the yells. "Stop now! Stop, I say! Stop, now——"

Johnnie, as he struggled to burst through the rank formed by Scully and the Easterner, was crying, "Well, he says I cheated! He says I cheated! I won't allow no man to say I cheated! If he says I cheated, he's a —— ——!"

The cowboy was telling the Swede, "Quit now! Quit, d'ye hear——"

The screams of the Swede never ceased: "He did cheat! I saw him! I saw him——"

As for the Easterner, he was importuning in a voice that was not heeded: "Wait a moment, can't you? Oh, wait a moment. What's the good of a fight over a game of cards? Wait a moment——"

In this tumult no complete sentences were clear. "Cheat"—"Quit"—"He says"—these fragments pierced the uproar and rang out sharply. It was remarkable that, whereas Scully undoubtedly made the most noise, he was the least heard of any of the riotous band.

Then suddenly there was a great cessation. It was as if each man had paused for breath; and although the room was still lighted with the anger of men, it could be seen that there was no danger of immediate conflict, and at once Johnnie, shouldering his way forward, almost succeeded in confronting the Swede. "What did you say I cheated for? What did you say I cheated for? I don't cheat, and I won't let no man say I do!"

The Swede said, "I saw you! I saw you!"

"Well," cried Johnnie, "I'll fight any man what says I cheat!"

"No, you won't," said the cowboy. "Not here."

"Ah, be still, can't you?" said Scully, coming between them.

The quiet was sufficient to allow the Easterner's voice to be heard. He was repeating, "Oh, wait a moment, can't you? What's the good of a fight over a game of cards? Wait a moment!"

Johnnie, his red face appearing above his father's shoulder, hailed the Swede again. "Did you say I cheated?"

The Swede showed his teeth. "Yes."

"Then," said Johnnie, "we must fight."

"Yes, fight," roared the Swede. He was like a demoniac. "Yes, fight! I'll show you what kind of a man I am! I'll show you who you want to fight! Maybe you think I can't fight! Maybe you think I can't! I'll show you, you skin, you card-sharp! Yes, you cheated! You cheated! You cheated!"

"Well, let's go at it, then, mister," said Johnnie, coolly.

The cowboy's brow was beaded with sweat from his efforts in intercepting all sorts of raids. He turned in despair to Scully. "What are you goin' to do now?"

A change had come over the Celtic visage of the old man. He now seemed all eagerness; his eyes glowed.

"We'll let them fight," he answered, stalwartly. "I can't put up with it any longer. I've stood this damned Swede till I'm sick. We'll let them fight."

6

The men prepared to go out of doors. The Easterner was so nervous that he had great difficulty in getting his arms into the sleeves of his new leather coat. As the cowboy drew his fur cap down over his ears his hands trembled. In fact, Johnnie and old Scully were the only ones who displayed no agitation. These preliminaries were conducted without words.

Scully threw open the door. "Well, come on," he said. Instantly a terrific wind caused the flame of the lamp to struggle at its wick, while a puff of black smoke sprang from the chimney-top. The stove was in mid-current of the blast, and its voice swelled to equal the roar of the storm. Some of the scarred and bedabbled cards were caught up from the floor and dashed helplessly against the farther wall. The men lowered their heads and plunged into the tempest as into a sea.

No snow was falling, but great whirls and clouds of flakes, swept up from the ground by the frantic winds, were streaming southward with the speed of bullets. The covered land was blue with the sheen of an unearthly satin, and there was no other hue save where, at the low, black railway station—which seemed incredibly distant—one light gleamed like a tiny jewel. As the men floundered into a thigh-deep drift, it was known that the Swede was bawling out something. Scully went to him, put a hand on his shoulder, and projected an ear. "What's that you say?" he shouted.

"I say," bawled the Swede again, "I won't stand much show against this gang. I know you'll all pitch on me."

Scully smote him reproachfully on the arm. "Tut, man!" he yelled. The wind tore the words from Scully's lips and scattered them far alee.

"You are all a gang of——" boomed the Swede, but the storm also seized the remainder of this sentence.

Immediately turning their backs upon the wind, the men had swung around a corner to the sheltered side of the hotel. It was the function of the little house to preserve here, amid this great devastation of snow, an irregular V-shape of heavily encrusted grass, which crackled beneath the feet. One could imagine the great drifts piled against the windward side. When the party reached the comparative peace of this spot it was found that the Swede was still bellowing.

"Oh, I know what kind of a thing this is! I know you'll all pitch on me. I can't lick you all!"

Scully turned upon him panther-fashion. "You'll not have to whip all of us. You'll have to whip my son Johnnie. An' the man what troubles you durin' that time will have me to dale with."

The arrangements were swiftly made. The two men faced each other, obedient to the harsh commands of Scully, whose face, in the subtly luminous gloom, could be seen set in the austere impersonal lines that are pictured on the countenances of the Roman veterans. The Easterner's teeth were chattering, and he was hopping up and down like a mechanical toy. The cowboy stood rock-like.

The contestants had not stripped off any clothing. Each was in his ordinary attire. Their fists were up, and they eyed each other in a calm that had the elements of leonine cruelty in it.

During this pause, the Easterner's mind, like a film, took lasting impressions of three men—the iron-nerved master of the ceremony; the Swede, pale, motionless, terrible; and Johnnie, serene yet ferocious, brutish yet heroic. The entire prelude had in it a tragedy greater than the tragedy of action, and this aspect was accentuated by the long, mellow cry of the blizzard, as it sped the tumbling and wailing flakes into the black abyss of the south.

"Now!" said Scully.

The two combatants leaped forward and crashed together like bullocks. There was heard the cushioned sound of blows, and of a curse squeezing out from between the tight teeth of one.

As for the spectators, the Easterner's pent-up breath exploded from him with a pop of relief, absolute relief from the tension of the preliminaries. The cowboy bounded into the air with a yowl. Scully was immovable as from supreme amazement and fear at the fury of the fight which he himself had permitted and arranged.

For a time the encounter in the darkness was such a perplexity of flying arms that it presented no more detail than would a swiftly revolving wheel. Occasionally a face, as if illumined by a flash of light, would shine out, ghastly and marked with pink spots. A moment later, the men might have been known as shadows, if it were not for the involuntary utterance of oaths that came from them in whispers.

Suddenly a holocaust of warlike desire caught the cowboy, and he bolted forward with the speed of a broncho. "Go it, Johnnie! Go it! Kill him! Kill him!"

Scully confronted him. "Kape back," he said; and by his glance the cowboy could tell that this man was Johnnie's father.

To the Easterner there was a monotony of unchangeable fighting that was an abomination. This confused mingling was eternal to his sense, which was concentrated in a longing for the end, the priceless end. Once the fighters lurched near him, and as he scrambled hastily backward he heard them breathe like men on the rack.

"Kill him, Johnnie! Kill him! Kill him! Kill him!" The cowboy's face was contorted like one of those agony masks in museums.

"Keep still," said Scully, icily.

Then there was a sudden loud grunt, incomplete, cut short, and Johnnie's body swung away from the Swede and fell with sickening heaviness to the grass. The cowboy was barely in time to prevent the mad Swede from flinging himself upon his prone adversary. "No, you don't," said the cowboy, interposing an arm. "Wait a second."

Scully was at his son's side. "Johnnie! Johnnie, me boy!" His voice had a quality of melancholy tenderness. "Johnnie! Can you go on with it?" He looked anxiously down into the bloody, pulpy face of his son.

There was a moment of silence, and then Johnnie answered in his ordinary voice, "Yes, I—it—yes."

Assisted by his father he struggled to his feet. "Wait a bit now till you git your wind," said the old man.

A few paces away the cowboy was lecturing the Swede. "No, you don't! Wait a second!"

The Easterner was plucking at Scully's sleeve. "Oh, this is enough," he pleaded. "This is enough! Let it go as it stands. This is enough!"

"Bill," said Scully, "git out of the road." The cowboy stepped aside. "Now." The combatants were actuated by a new caution as they advanced toward collision. They glared at each other, and then the Swede aimed a lightning blow that carried with it his entire weight. Johnnie was evidently half stupid from weakness, but he miraculously dodged, and his fist sent the over-balanced Swede sprawling.

The cowboy, Scully, and the Easterner burst into a cheer that was like a chorus of triumphant soldiery, but before its conclusion the Swede had scuffled agilely to his feet and come in berserk abandon at his foe. There was another perplexity of flying arms, and Johnnie's body again swung away and fell, even as a bundle might fall from the roof. The Swede instantly staggered to a little wind-waved tree and leaned upon it, breathing like an engine, while his savage and flamelit eyes roamed from face to face as the men bent over Johnnie. There was a splendour of isolation in his situation at this time which the Easterner felt once when, lifting his eyes from the man on the ground, he beheld that mysterious and lonely figure, waiting.

"Are you any good yet, Johnnie?" asked Scully in a broken voice.

The son gasped and opened his eyes languidly. After a moment he answered, "No—I ain't—any good—any—more." Then, from shame and bodily ill, he began to weep, the tears furrowing down through the blood-stains on his face. "He was too—too—too heavy for me."

Scully straightened and addressed the waiting figure. "Stranger," he said, evenly, "it's all up with our side." Then his voice changed into that vibrant huskiness which is commonly the tone of the most simple and deadly announcements. "Johnnie is whipped."

Without replying, the victor moved off on the route to the front door of the hotel.

The cowboy was formulating new and unspellable blasphemies. The Easterner was startled to find that they were out in a wind that seemed to come direct from the shadowed arctic floes. He heard again the wail of the snow as it was flung to its grave in the south. He knew now that all this time the cold had been sinking into him deeper and deeper, and he wondered that he had not perished. He felt indifferent to the condition of the vanquished man.

"Johnnie, can you walk?" asked Scully.

"Did I hurt—hurt him any?" asked the son.

"Can you walk, boy? Can you walk?"

Johnnie's voice was suddenly strong. There was a robust impatience in it. "I asked you whether I hurt him any!"

"Yes, yes, Johnnie," answered the cowboy, consolingly; "he's hurt a good deal."

They raised him from the ground, and as soon as he was on his feet he went tottering off, rebuffing all attempts at assistance. When the party rounded the corner they were fairly blinded by the pelting of the snow. It burned their faces like fire. The cowboy carried Johnnie through the drift to the door. As they entered, some cards again rose from the floor and beat against the wall.

The Easterner rushed to the stove. He was so profoundly chilled that he almost dared to embrace the glowing iron. The Swede was not in the room. Johnnie sank into a chair and, folding his arms on his knees, buried his face in them. Scully, warming one foot and then the other at a rim of the stove, muttered to himself with Celtic mournfulness. The cowboy had removed his fur cap, and with a dazed and rueful air he was running one hand through his tousled locks. From overhead they could hear the creaking of boards, as the Swede tramped here and there in his room.

The sad quiet was broken by the sudden flinging open of a door that led toward the kitchen. It was instantly followed by an inrush of women. They precipitated themselves upon Johnnie amid a chorus of lamentation. Before they carried their prey off to the kitchen, there to be bathed and harangued with that mixture of sympathy and abuse which is a feat of their sex, the mother straightened herself and fixed old Scully with an eye of stern reproach. "Shame be upon you, Patrick Scully!" she cried. "Your own son, too. Shame be upon you!"

"There, now! Be quiet, now!" said the old man, weakly.

"Shame be upon you, Patrick Scully!" The girls, rallying to this slogan, sniffed disdainfully in the direction of those trembling accomplices, the cowboy and the Easterner. Presently they bore Johnnie away, and left the three men to dismal reflection.

7

"I'd like to fight this here Dutchman myself," said the cowboy, breaking a long silence.

Scully wagged his head sadly. "No, that wouldn't do. It wouldn't be right. It wouldn't be right."

"Well, why wouldn't it?" argued the cowboy. "I don't see no harm in it."

"No," answered Scully, with mournful heroism. "It wouldn't be right. It was Johnnie's fight, and now we mustn't whip the man just because he whipped Johnnie."

"Yes, that's true enough," said the cowboy; "but—he better not get fresh with me, because I couldn't stand no more of it."

"You'll not say a word to him," commanded Scully, and even then they heard the tread of the Swede on the stairs. His entrance was made theatric. He swept the door back with a bang and swaggered to the middle of the room. No one looked at him. "Well," he cried, insolently, at Scully, "I s'pose you'll tell me now how much I owe you!"

The old man remained stolid. "You don't owe me nothin'."

"Huh!" said the Swede, "huh! Don't owe 'im nothin'."

The cowboy addressed the Swede. "Stranger, I don't see how you come to be so gay around here."

Old Scully was instantly alert. "Stop!" he shouted, holding his hand forth, fingers upward. "Bill, you shut up!"

The cowboy spat carelessly into the sawdust-box. "I didn't say a word, did I?" he asked.

"Mr. Scully," called the Swede, "how much do I owe you?" It was seen that he was attired for departure, and that he had his valise in his hand.

"You don't owe me nothin'," repeated Scully in the same imperturbable way.

"Huh!" said the Swede. "I guess you're right. I guess if it was any way at all, you'd owe me somethin'. That's what I guess." He turned to the cowboy. "'Kill him! Kill him! Kill him!'" he mimicked, and then guffawed victoriously. "'Kill him!'" He was convulsed with ironical humour.

But he might have been jeering the dead. The three men were immovable and silent, staring with glassy eyes at the stove.

The Swede opened the door and passed into the storm, giving one derisive glance backward at the still group.

As soon as the door was closed, Scully and the cowboy leaped to their feet and began to curse. They trampled to and fro, waving their arms and smashing into the air with their fists. "Oh, but that was a hard minute!" wailed Scully. "That was a hard minute! Him there leerin' and scoffin'! One bang at his nose was worth forty dollars to me that minute! How did you stand it, Bill?"

"How did I stand it?" cried the cowboy in a quivering voice. "How did I stand it? Oh!"

The old man burst into sudden brogue. "I'd like to take that Swade," he wailed, "and hould 'im down on a shtone flure and bate 'im to a jelly wid a shtick!"

The cowboy groaned in sympathy. "I'd like to git him by the neck and ha-ammer him"—he brought his hand down on a chair with a noise like a pistol-shot—"hammer that there Dutchman until he couldn't tell himself from a dead coyote!"

"I'd bate 'im until he——"

"I'd show *him* some things——"

And then together they raised a yearning, fanatic cry—"Oh-o-oh! if we only could——"

"Yes!"

"Yes!"

"And then I'd——"

"O-o-oh!"

8

The Swede, tightly gripping his valise, tacked across the face of the storm as if he carried sails. He was following a line of little naked, gasping trees which, he knew, must mark the way to the road. His face, fresh from the pounding of Johnnie's fists, felt more pleasure than pain in the wind and the driving snow. A number of square shapes loomed upon him finally, and he knew them as the houses of the main body of the town. He found a street and made travel along it, leaning heavily upon the wind whenever, at a corner, a terrific blast caught him.

He might have been in a deserted village. We picture the world as thick with conquering and elate humanity, but here, with the bugles of the tempest pealing, it was hard to imagine a peopled earth. One viewed the existence of man then as a marvel, and conceded a glamour of wonder to these lice which were caused to cling to a whirling, fire-smitten, ice-locked, disease-stricken, space-lost bulb. The conceit of man was explained by this storm to be the very engine of life. One was a coxcomb not to die in it. However, the Swede found a saloon.

In front of it an indomitable red light was burning, and the snowflakes were made blood-colour as they flew through the circumscribed territory of the lamp's shining. The Swede pushed open the door of the saloon and entered. A sanded expanse was before him, and at the end of it four men sat about a table drinking. Down one side of the room extended a radiant bar, and its guardian was leaning upon his elbows listening to the talk of the men at the table. The Swede dropped his valise upon the floor and, smiling fraternally upon the barkeeper, said, "Gimme some whisky, will you?" The man placed a bottle, a whisky-glass, and a glass of ice-thick water upon the bar. The Swede poured himself an abnormal portion of whisky and drank it in three gulps. "Pretty bad night," remarked the bartender, indifferently. He was making the pretension of blindness which is usually a distinction of his class; but it could have been seen that he was furtively studying the half-erased blood-stains on the face of the Swede. "Bad night," he said again.

"Oh, it's good enough for me," replied the Swede, hardily, as he poured himself some more whisky. The barkeeper took his coin and manœuvred it through its reception by the highly nickelled cash-machine. A bell rang; a card labelled "20 cts." had appeared.

"No," continued the Swede, "this isn't too bad weather. It's good enough for me."

"So?" murmured the barkeeper, languidly.

The copious drams made the Swede's eyes swim, and he breathed a trifle heavier. "Yes, I like this weather. I like it. It suits me." It was apparently his design to impart a deep significance to these words.

"So?" murmured the bartender again. He turned to gaze dreamily at the scroll-like birds and bird-like scrolls which had been drawn with soap upon the mirrors in back of the bar.

"Well, I guess I'll take another drink," said the Swede, presently. "Have something?"

"No, thanks; I'm not drinkin'," answered the bartender. Afterwards he asked, "How did you hurt your face?"

The Swede immediately began to boast loudly. "Why, in a fight. I thumped the soul out of a man down here at Scully's hotel."

The interest of the four men at the table was at last aroused.

"Who was it?" said one.

"Johnnie Scully," blustered the Swede. "Son of the man what runs it. He will be pretty near dead for some weeks, I can tell you. I made a nice thing of him, I did. He couldn't get up. They carried him in the house. Have a drink?"

Instantly the men in some subtle way encased themselves in reserve. "No, thanks," said one. The group was of curious formation. Two were prominent local business men; one was the district attorney; and one was a professional gambler of the kind known as "square." But a scrutiny of the group would not have enabled an observer to pick the gambler from the men of more reputable pursuits. He was, in fact, a man so delicate in manner, when among people of fair class, and so judicious in his choice of victims, that in the strictly masculine part of the town's life he had come to be explicitly trusted and admired. People called him a thoroughbred. The fear and contempt with which his craft was regarded were undoubtedly the reason why his quiet dignity shone conspicuous above the quiet dignity of men who might be merely hatters, billiard-markers, or grocery clerks. Beyond an occasional unwary traveller who came by rail, this gambler was supposed to prey solely upon reckless and senile farmers, who, when flush with good crops, drove into town in all the pride and confidence of an absolutely invulnerable stupidity. Hearing at times in circuitous fashion of the despoilment of such a farmer, the important men of Romper invariably laughed in contempt of the victim, and if they thought of the wolf at all, it was with a kind of pride at the knowledge that he would never dare think of attacking their wisdom and courage. Besides, it was popular that this gambler had a real wife and two real children in a neat cottage in a suburb, where he led an exemplary home life; and when any one even suggested a discrepancy in his character, the crowd immediately vociferated descriptions of this virtuous family circle. Then men who led exemplary home lives, and men who did not lead exemplary home lives, all subsided in a bunch, remarking that there was nothing more to be said.

However, when a restriction was placed upon him—as, for instance, when a strong clique of members of the new Pollywog Club refused to permit him, even as a spectator, to appear in the rooms of the organization—the candour and gentleness with which he accepted the judgment disarmed many of his foes and made his friends more desperately partisan. He invariably distinguished between himself and a respectable Romper man so quickly and frankly that his manner actually appeared to be a continual broadcast compliment.

And one must not forget to declare the fundamental fact of his entire position in Romper. It is irrefutable that in all affairs outside his business, in all matters that occur eternally and commonly between man and man, this thieving card-player was so generous, so just, so moral, that, in a contest, he could have put to flight the consciences of nine tenths of the citizens of Romper.

And so it happened that he was seated in this saloon with the two prominent local merchants and the district attorney.

The Swede continued to drink raw whisky, meanwhile babbling at the barkeeper and trying to induce him to indulge in potations. "Come on. Have a drink. Come on. What—no? Well, have a little one, then. By gawd, I've whipped a man to-night, and I want to celebrate. I whipped him good, too. Gentlemen," the Swede cried to the men at the table, "have a drink?"

"Ssh!" said the barkeeper.

The group at the table, although furtively attentive, had been pretending to be deep in talk, but now a man lifted his eyes toward the Swede and said, shortly, "Thanks. We don't want any more."

At this reply the Swede ruffled out his chest like a rooster. "Well," he exploded, "it seems I can't get anybody to drink with me in this town. Seems so, don't it? Well!"

"Ssh!" said the barkeeper.

"Say," snarled the Swede, "don't you try to shut me up. I won't have it. I'm a gentleman, and I want people to drink with me. And I want 'em to drink with me now. *Now*—do you understand?" He rapped the bar with his knuckles.

Years of experience had calloused the bartender. He merely grew sulky. "I hear you," he answered.

"Well," cried the Swede, "listen hard then. See those men over there? Well, they're going to drink with me, and don't you forget it. Now you watch."

"Hi!" yelled the barkeeper, "this won't do!"

"Why won't it?" demanded the Swede. He stalked over to the table, and by chance laid his hand upon the shoulder of the gambler. "How about this?" he asked wrathfully. "I asked you to drink with me."

The gambler simply twisted his head and spoke over his shoulder. "My friend, I don't know you."

"Oh, hell!" answered the Swede, "come and have a drink."

"Now, my boy," advised the gambler, kindly, "take your hand off my shoulder and go 'way and mind your own business." He was a little, slim man, and it seemed strange to hear him use this tone of heroic patronage to the burly Swede. The other men at the table said nothing.

"What! You won't drink with me, you little dude? I'll make you, then! I'll make you!" The Swede had grasped the gambler frenziedly at the throat, and was dragging him from his chair. The other men sprang up. The barkeeper dashed around the corner of his bar. There was a great tumult, and then was seen a long blade in the hand of the gambler. It shot forward, and a human body, this citadel of virtue, wisdom, power, was pierced as easily as if it had been a melon. The Swede fell with a cry of supreme astonishment.

The prominent merchants and the district attorney must have at once tumbled out of the place backward. The bartender found himself hanging limply to the arm of a chair and gazing into the eyes of a murderer.

"Henry," said the latter, as he wiped his knife on one of the towels that hung beneath the bar rail, "you tell 'em where to find me. I'll be home, waiting for 'em." Then he vanished. A moment afterward the barkeeper was in the street dinning through the storm for help and, moreover, companionship.

The corpse of the Swede, alone in the saloon, had its eyes fixed upon a dreadful legend that dwelt atop of the cash-machine: "This registers the amount of your purchase."

9

Months later, the cowboy was frying pork over the stove of a little ranch near the Dakota line, when there was a quick thud of hoofs outside, and presently the Easterner entered with the letters and the papers.

"Well," said the Easterner at once, "the chap that killed the Swede has got three years. Wasn't much, was it?"

"He has? Three years?" The cowboy poised his pan of pork, while he ruminated upon the news. "Three years. That ain't much."

"No. It was a light sentence," replied the Easterner as he unbuckled his spurs. "Seems there was a good deal of sympathy for him in Romper."

"If the bartender had been any good," observed the cowboy, thoughtfully, "he would have gone in and cracked that there Dutchman on the head with a bottle in the beginnin' of it and stopped all this here murderin'."

"Yes, a thousand things might have happened," said the Easterner, tartly.

The cowboy returned his pan of pork to the fire, but his philosophy continued. "It's funny, ain't it? If he hadn't said Johnnie was cheatin' he'd be alive this minute. He was an awful fool. Game played for fun, too. Not for money. I believe he was crazy."

"I feel sorry for that gambler," said the Easterner.

"Oh, so do I," said the cowboy. "He don't deserve none of it for killin' who he did."

"The Swede might not have been killed if everything had been square."

"Might not have been killed?" exclaimed the cowboy. "Everythin' square? Why, when he said that Johnnie was cheatin' and acted like such a jackass? And then in the saloon he fairly walked up to git hurt?" With these arguments the cowboy browbeat the Easterner and reduced him to rage.

"You're a fool!" cried the Easterner, viciously. "You're a bigger jackass than the Swede by a million majority. Now let me tell you one thing. Let me tell you something. Listen! Johnnie *was* cheating!"

"'Johnnie,'" said the cowboy, blankly. There was a minute of silence, and then he said, robustly, "Why, no. The game was only for fun."

"Fun or not," said the Easterner, "Johnnie was cheating. I saw him. I know it. I saw him. And I refused to stand up and be a man. I let the Swede fight it out alone. And you—you were simply puffing around the place and wanting to fight. And then old Scully himself! We are all in it! This poor gambler isn't even a noun. He is kind of an adverb. Every sin is the result of a collaboration. We, five of us, have collaborated in the murder of this Swede. Usually there are from a dozen to forty women really involved in every murder, but in this case it seems to be only five men—you, I, Johnnie, old Scully; and that fool of an unfortunate gambler came merely as a culmination, the apex of a human movement, and gets all the punishment."

The cowboy, injured and rebellious, cried out blindly into this fog of mysterious theory: "Well, I didn't do anythin', did I?"

QUESTIONS FOR DISCUSSION AND WRITING

1. What is responsible for the Swede's conflict with the other characters? How does the fight reveal the true nature of their conflicts? How does the Swede's conflict with the gambler differ from the earlier conflicts?

2. How do the various characters fulfill or contradict the stereotypes suggested by their names? Why does Crane emphasize in his characterization of the gambler that he is a "square" citizen?

3. How does the powerful storm provide an ironic setting for the human conflicts in the story? What are the differences between the setting of the hotel and the saloon?

4. Why does Crane choose to tell the story from the third-person dominant point of view? How would the story have been different if told by the Swede, by Scully, by the Easterner, or by the cowboy?

5. What does the Easterner mean in the last paragraph when he says, "every sin is the result of a collaboration"? What part does blind chance play in this story?

26

ARTHUR CONAN DOYLE

The Adventure of the Speckled Band

ARTHUR CONAN DOYLE (1859–1930) was born in Edinburgh, Scotland, and was educated at Feldkirch College in Austria and the medical school at Edinburgh University. Doyle practiced medicine for ten years in Southsea, England, but slowly turned his attention to writing short stories. His first major novel, *A Study in Scarlet* (1887), featured the master detective Sherlock Holmes and his admiring assistant, Dr. Watson. For the next forty years Doyle turned out one Holmes story after another for popular magazines. These stories were collected in volumes such as *The Adventures of Sherlock Holmes* (1892), *The Memoirs of Sherlock Holmes* (1894), *The Return of Sherlock Holmes* (1905), and *The Casebook of Sherlock Holmes* (1922). Like his famous creation, Doyle had many interests. He wrote "serious" novels, such as *Micah Clarke* (1889) and *The White Company* (1890), and scholarly studies, such as *The British Campaigns in Europe* (1912); he also worked as a volunteer physician in South Africa during the Boer War. For his bravery in this latter conflict, Doyle was knighted in 1902. In "The Adventure of the Speckled Band," reprinted from *The Adventures of Sherlock Holmes,* Holmes uses his famous powers of reasoning to solve a "fantastic" crime.

On glancing over my notes of the seventy-odd cases in which I have during the last eight years studied the methods of my friend Sherlock Holmes, I find many tragic, some comic, a large number merely strange, but none commonplace; for working as he did rather for the love of his art than for the acquirement of wealth, he refused to associate himself with any investigation which did not tend towards the unusual, and even the fantastic. Of all these varied cases, however, I cannot recall any which presented more singular features than that which was associated with the well-known Surrey family of the Roylotts of Stoke Moran. The events in question occurred in the early days of my association with Holmes, when we were sharing rooms as bachelors in Baker Street. It is possible that I might have placed them upon record before, but a promise of secrecy was made at the time, from which I have only been freed during the last month by the untimely death of the lady to whom the pledge was given. It is perhaps as well that the facts should now come to light, for I have reasons to know that there are widespread rumours as to the death of Dr. Grimesby Roylott which tend to make the matter even more terrible than the truth.

It was early in April in the year '83 that I woke one morning to find Sherlock Holmes standing, fully dressed, by the side of my bed. He was a late riser, as a rule, and as the clock on the mantelpiece showed me that it was only a quarter-past seven, I blinked up at him in some surprise, and perhaps just a little resentment for I was myself regular in my habits.

"Very sorry to knock you up, Watson," said he, "but it's the common lot this morning. Mrs. Hudson has been knocked up, she retorted upon me, and I on you."

"What is it, then—a fire?"

"No; a client. It seems that a young lady has arrived in a considerable state of excitement, who insists upon seeing me. She is waiting now in the sitting-room. Now, when young ladies wander about the metropolis at this hour of the morning, and knock sleepy people up out of their beds, I presume that it is something very pressing which they have to communicate. Should it prove to be an interesting case, you would, I am sure, wish to follow it from the outset. I thought, at any rate, that I should call you and give you the chance."

"My dear fellow, I would not miss it for anything."

I had no keener pleasure than in following Holmes in his professional investigations, and in admiring the rapid deductions, as swift as intuitions, and yet always founded on a logical basis, with which he unravelled the problems which were submitted to him. I rapidly threw on my clothes and was ready in a few minutes to accompany my friend down to the sitting-room. A lady dressed in black and heavily veiled, who had been sitting in the window, rose as we entered.

"Good-morning, madam," said Holmes cheerily. "My name is Sherlock Holmes. This is my intimate friend and associate, Dr. Watson, before whom you can speak as freely as before myself. Ha! I am glad to see that Mrs. Hudson has had the good sense to light the fire. Pray draw up to it, and I shall order you a cup of hot coffee, for I observe that you are shivering."

"It is not cold which makes me shiver," said the woman in a low voice, changing her seat as requested.

"What, then?"

"It is fear, Mr. Holmes. It is terror." She raised her veil as she spoke, and we could see that she was indeed in a pitiable state of agitation, her face all drawn and gray, with restless, frightened eyes, like those of some hunted animal. Her features and figure were those of a woman of thirty, but her hair was shot with premature gray, and her expression was weary and haggard. Sherlock Holmes ran her over with one of his quick, all-comprehensive glances.

"You must not fear," said he soothingly, bending forward and patting her forearm. "We shall soon set matters right, I have no doubt. You have come in by train this morning, I see."

"You know me, then?"

"No, but I observe the second half of a return ticket in the palm of your left glove. You must have started early, and yet you had a good drive in a dog-cart, along heavy roads, before you reached the station."

The lady gave a violent start and stared in bewilderment at my companion.

"There is no mystery, my dear madam," said he, smiling. "The left arm of your jacket is spattered with mud in no less than seven places. The marks are perfectly fresh. There is no vehicle save a dog-cart which throws up mud in that way, and then only when you sit on the left-hand side of the driver."

"Whatever your reasons may be, you are perfectly correct," said she. "I started from home before six, reached Leatherhead at twenty past, and came in by the first train to Waterloo. Sir, I can stand this strain no longer; I shall go mad if it continues. I have no one to turn to—none, save only one, who cares for me, and he, poor fellow, can be of little aid. I have heard of you, Mr. Holmes; I have heard of you from Mrs. Farintosh, whom you helped in the hour of her sore need. It was from her that I had your address. Oh, sir, do you not think that you could help me, too, and at least throw a little light through the dense darkness which surrounds me? At present it is out of my power to reward you for your services, but in a month or six weeks I shall be married, with the control of my own income, and then at least you shall not find me ungrateful."

Holmes turned to his desk and, unlocking it, drew out a small case-book, which he consulted.

"Farintosh," said he. "Ah yes, I recall the case; it was concerned with an opal tiara. I think it was before your time, Watson. I can only say, madam, that I shall be happy to devote the same care to your case as I did to that of your friend. As to reward, my profession is its own reward; but you are at liberty to defray whatever expenses I may be put to, at the time which suits you best. And now I beg that you will lay before us everything that may help us in forming an opinion upon the matter."

"Alas!" replied our visitor, "the very horror of my situation lies in the fact that my fears are so vague, and my suspicions depend so entirely upon small points, which might seem trivial to another, that even he to whom of all others I have a right to look for help and advice looks upon all that I tell him about it as the fancies of a nervous woman. He does not say so, but I can read it from his soothing answers and averted eyes. But I have heard, Mr. Holmes, that you can see deeply into the manifold wickedness of the human heart. You may advise me how to walk amid the dangers which encompass me."

"I am all attention, madam."

"My name is Helen Stoner, and I am living with my stepfather, who is the last survivor of one of the oldest Saxon families in England, the Roylotts of Stoke Moran, on the western border of Surrey."

Holmes nodded his head. "The name is familiar to me," said he.

"The family was at one time among the richest in England, and the estates extended over the borders into Berkshire in the north, and Hampshire in the west. In the last century, however, four successive heirs were of a dissolute and wasteful disposition, and the family ruin was eventually completed by a gambler in the days of the Regency. Nothing was left save a few acres of ground, and the two-hundred-year-old house, which is itself crushed under a heavy mortgage. The last squire dragged out his existence there, living the horrible life of an aristocratic pauper; but his only son, my stepfather, seeing that he must adapt himself to the new conditions, obtained an advance from a relative, which enabled him to take a medical degree and went out to Calcutta, where, by his professional skill and his force of character, he established a large practice. In a fit of anger, however, caused by some robberies which had been perpetrated in the house, he beat his native butler to death and narrowly escaped a capital sentence. As it was, he suffered a long term of imprisonment and afterwards returned to England a morose and disappointed man.

"When Dr. Roylott was in India he married my mother, Mrs. Stoner, the young widow of Major-General Stoner, of the Bengal Artillery. My sister Julia and I were twins, and we were only two years old at the time of my mother's re-marriage. She had a considerable sum of money—not less than £1000 a year—and this she bequeathed to Dr. Roylott entirely while we resided with him, with a provision that a certain annual sum should be allowed to each of us in the event of our marriage. Shortly after our return to England my mother died—she was killed eight years ago in a railway accident near Crewe. Dr. Roylott then abandoned his attempts to establish himself in practice in London and took us to live with him in the old ancestral house at Stoke Moran. The money which my mother had left was enough for our wants, and there seemed to be no obstacle to our happiness.

"But a terrible change came over our stepfather about this time. Instead of making friends and exchanging visits with our neighbours, who had at first been overjoyed to see a Roylott of Stoke Moran back in the family seat, he shut himself up in his house and seldom came out save to indulge in ferocious quarrels with whoever might cross his path. Violence of temper approaching to mania has been hereditary in the men of the family, and in my stepfather's case it had, I believe, been intensified by his long residence in the tropics. A series of disgraceful brawls took place, two of which ended in the police-court, until at last he became the terror of the village, and the folks would fly at his approach, for he is a man of immense strength, and absolutely uncontrollable in his anger.

"Last week he hurled the local blacksmith over a parapet into a stream, and it was only by paying over all the money which I could gather together that I was able to avert another public exposure. He had no friends at all save the wandering gypsies, and he would give these vagabonds leave to encamp upon the few acres of bramble-covered land which represent the family estate, and would accept in return the hospitality of their tents, wandering away with them sometimes for weeks on end. He has a passion also for Indian animals, which are sent over to him by a correspondent, and he has at this moment a cheetah and a baboon, which wander freely over his grounds and are feared by the villagers almost as much as their master.

"You can imagine from what I say that my poor sister Julia and I had no great pleasure in our lives. No servant would stay with us, and for a long time we did all the work of the house. She was but thirty at the time of her death, and yet her hair had already begun to whiten, even as mine has."

"Your sister is dead, then?"

"She died just two years ago, and it is of her death that I wish to speak to you. You can understand that, living the life which I have described, we were little likely to see anyone of our own age and position. We had, however, an aunt, my mother's maiden sister, Miss Honoria Westphail, who lives near Harrow, and we were occasionally allowed to pay short visits at this lady's house. Julia went there at Christmas two years ago, and met there a half-pay major of marines, to whom she became engaged. My stepfather learned of the engagement when my sister returned and offered no objection to the marriage; but within a fortnight of the day which had been fixed for the wedding, the terrible event occurred which has deprived me of my only companion."

Sherlock Holmes had been leaning back in his chair with his eyes closed and his head sunk in a cushion, but he half opened his lids now and glanced across at his visitor.

"Pray be precise as to details," said he.

"It is easy for me to be so, for every event of that dreadful time is seared into my memory. The manorhouse is, as I have already said, very old, and only one wing is now inhabited. The bedrooms in this wing are on the ground floor, the sitting-rooms being in the central block of the buildings. Of these bedrooms the first is Dr. Roylott's, the second my sister's, and the third my own. There is no communication between them, but they all open out into the same corridor. Do I make myself plain?"

"Perfectly so."

"The windows of the three rooms open out upon the lawn. That fatal night Dr. Roylott had gone to his room early, though we knew that he had not retired to rest, for my sister was troubled by the smell of the strong Indian cigar which it was his custom to smoke. She left her room, therefore, and came into mine, where she sat for some time, chatting about her approaching wedding. At eleven o'clock she rose to leave me, but she paused at the door and looked back.

" 'Tell me, Helen,' said she, 'have you ever heard anyone whistle in the dead of the night?'

" 'Never,' said I.

" 'I suppose that you could not possibly whistle, yourself, in your sleep.'

" 'Certainly not. But why?'

" 'Because during the last few nights I have always, about three in the morning, heard a low, clear whistle. I am a light sleeper, and it has awakened me. I cannot tell where it came from—perhaps from the next room, perhaps from the lawn. I thought that I would just ask you whether you had heard it.'

" 'No, I have not. It must be those wretched gypsies in the plantation.'

" 'Very likely. And yet if it were on the lawn, I wonder that you did not hear it also.'

" 'Ah, but I sleep more heavily than you.'

" 'Well, it is of no great consequence, at any rate.' She smiled back at me, closed my door, and a few moments later I heard her key turn in the lock."

"Indeed," said Holmes. "Was it your custom always to lock yourself in at night?"

"Always."

"And why?"

"I think that I mentioned to you that the doctor kept a cheetah and a baboon. We had no feeling of security unless our doors were locked."

"Quite so. Pray proceed with your statement."

"I could not sleep that night. A vague feeling of impending misfortune impressed me. My sister and I, you will recollect, were twins, and you know how subtle are the links which bond two souls which are so closely allied. It was a wild night. The wind was howling outside, and the rain was beating and splashing against the windows. Suddenly, amid all the hubbub of the gale, there burst forth the wild scream of a terrified woman.

I knew that it was my sister's voice. I sprang from my bed, wrapped a shawl around me, and rushed into the corridor. As I opened my door I seemed to hear a low whistle, such as my sister described, and a few moments later a clanging sound, as if a mass of metal had fallen. As I ran down the passage, my sister's door was unlocked, and revolved slowly upon its hinges. I stared at it horror-stricken, not knowing what was about to issue from it. By the light of the corridor-lamp I saw my sister appear at the opening, her face blanched with terror, her hands groping for help, her whole figure swaying to and fro like that of a drunkard. I ran to her and threw my arms around her, but at that moment her knees seemed to give way and she fell to the ground. She writhed as one who is in terrible pain, and her limbs were dreadfully convulsed. At first I thought that she had not recognized me, but as I bent over her she suddenly shrieked out in a voice which I shall never forget, 'Oh, my God! Helen! It was the band! The speckled band!' There was something else which she would fain have said, and she stabbed with her finger into the air in the direction of the doctor's room, but a fresh convulsion seized her and choked her words. I rushed out, calling loudly for my stepfather, and I met him hastening from his room in his dressing-gown. When he reached my sister's side she was unconscious, and though he poured brandy down her throat and sent for medical aid from the village, all efforts were in vain, for she slowly sank and died without having recovered her consciousness. Such was the dreadful end of my beloved sister."

"One moment," said Holmes; "are you sure about this whistle and metallic sound? Could you swear to it?"

"That was what the county coroner asked me at the inquiry. It is my strong impression that I heard it, and yet, among the crash of the gale and the creaking of an old house, I may possibly have been deceived."

"Was your sister dressed?"

"No, she was in her night-dress. In her right hand was found the charred stump of a match, and in her left a match-box."

"Showing that she had struck a light and looked about her when the alarm took place. That is important. And what conclusions did the coroner come to?"

"He investigated the case with great care, for Dr. Roylott's conduct had long been notorious in the county, but he was unable to find any satisfactory cause of death. My evidence showed that the door had been fastened upon the inner side, and the windows were blocked by old-fashioned shutters with broad iron bars, which were secured every night. The walls were carefully sounded, and were shown to be quite solid all round, and the flooring was also thoroughly examined, with the same result. The chimney is wide, but is barred up by four large staples. It is certain, therefore, that my sister was quite alone when she met her end. Besides, there were no marks of any violence upon her."

"How about poison?"

"The doctors examined her for it, but without success."

"What do you think that this unfortunate lady died of, then?"

"It is my belief that she died of pure fear and nervous shock, though what it was that frightened her I cannot imagine."

"Were there gypsies in the plantation at the time?"

"Yes, there are nearly always some there."

"Ah, and what did you gather from this allusion to a band—a speckled band?"

"Sometimes I have thought that it was merely the wild talk of delirium, sometimes that it may have referred to some band of people, perhaps to these very gypsies in the plantation. I do not know whether the spotted handkerchiefs which so many of them wear over their heads might have suggested the strange adjective which she used."

Holmes shook his head like a man who is far from being satisfied.

"These are very deep waters," said he; "pray go on with your narrative."

"Two years have passed since then, and my life has been until lately lonelier than ever. A month ago, however, a dear friend, whom I have known for many years, has done me the honour to ask my hand in marriage. His name is Armitage—Percy Armitage—the second son of Mr. Armitage, of Crane Water, near Reading. My stepfather has offered no opposition to the match, and we are to be married in the course of the spring. Two days ago some repairs were started in the west wing of the building, and my bedroom wall has been pierced, so that I have had to move into the chamber in which my sister died, and to sleep in the very bed in which she slept. Imagine, then, my thrill of terror when last night, as I lay awake, thinking over her terrible fate, I suddenly heard in the silence of the night the low whistle which had been the herald of her own death. I sprang up and lit the lamp, but nothing was to be seen in the room. I was too shaken to go to bed again, however, so I dressed, and as soon as it was daylight I slipped down, got a dog-cart at the Crown Inn, which is opposite, and drove to Leatherhead, from whence I have come on this morning with the one object of seeing you and asking your advice."

"You have done wisely," said my friend. "But have you told me all?"

"Yes, all."

"Miss Roylott, you have not. You are screening your stepfather."

"Why, what do you mean?"

For answer Holmes pushed back the frill of black lace which fringed the hand that lay upon our visitor's knee. Five little livid spots, the marks of four fingers and a thumb, were printed upon the white wrist.

"You have been cruelly used," said Holmes.

The lady coloured deeply and covered over her injured wrist. "He is a hard man," she said, "and perhaps he hardly knows his own strength."

There was a long silence, during which Holmes leaned his chin upon his hands and stared into the crackling fire.

"This is a very deep business," he said at last. "There are a thousand details which I should desire to know before I decide upon our course of action. Yet we have not a moment to lose. If we were to come to Stoke Moran to-day, would it be possible for us to see over these rooms without the knowledge of your stepfather?"

"As it happens, he spoke of coming into town to-day upon some most important business. It is probable that he will be away all day, and that there would be nothing to disturb you. We have a housekeeper now, but she is old and foolish, and I could easily get her out of the way."

"Excellent. You are not averse to this trip, Watson?"

"By no means."

"Then we shall both come. What are you going to do yourself?"

"I have one or two things which I would wish to do now that I am in town. But I shall return by the twelve o'clock train, so as to be there in time for your coming."

"And you may expect us early in the afternoon. I have myself some small business matters to attend to. Will you not wait and breakfast?"

"No, I must go. My heart is lightened already since I have confided my trouble to you. I shall look forward to seeing you again this afternoon." She dropped her thick black veil over her face and glided from the room.

"And what do you think of it all, Watson?" asked Sherlock Holmes, leaning back in his chair.

"It seems to me to be a most dark and sinister business."

"Dark enough and sinister enough."

"Yet if the lady is correct in saying that the flooring and walls are sound, and that the door, window, and chimney are impassable, then her sister must have been undoubtedly alone when she met her mysterious end."

"What becomes, then, of these nocturnal whistles, and what of the very peculiar words of the dying woman?"

"I cannot think."

"When you combine the ideas of whistles at night, the presence of a band of gypsies who are on intimate terms with this old doctor, the fact that we have every reason to believe that the doctor has an interest in preventing his stepdaughter's marriage, the dying allusion to a band, and, finally, the fact that Miss Helen Stoner heard a metallic clang, which might have been caused by one of those metal bars that secured the shutters falling back into its place, I think that there is good ground to think that the mystery may be cleared along those lines."

"But what, then, did the gypsies do?"

"I cannot imagine."

"I see many objections to any such theory."

"And so do I. It is precisely for that reason that we are going to Stoke Moran this day. I want to see whether the objections are fatal, or if they may be explained away. But what in the name of the devil!"

The ejaculation had been drawn from my companion by the fact that our door had been suddenly dashed open, and that a huge man had framed himself in the aperture. His costume was a peculiar mixture of the professional and of the agricultural, having a black top-hat, a long frock-coat, and a pair of high gaiters, with a hunting-crop swinging in his hand. So tall was he that his hat actually brushed the cross-bar of the doorway, and his breadth seemed to span it across from side to side. A large face, seared with a thousand wrinkles burned yellow with the sun, and marked with every evil passion, was turned from one to the other of us, while his deep-set, bile-shot eyes, and his high, thin, fleshless nose, gave him somewhat the resemblance of a fierce old bird of prey.

"Which of you is Holmes?" asked the apparition.

"My name, sir; but you have the advantage of me," said my companion quietly.

"I am Dr. Grimesby Roylott, of Stoke Moran."

"Indeed, Doctor," said Holmes blandly. "Pray take a seat."

"I will do nothing of the kind. My stepdaughter has been here. I have traced her. What has she been saying to you?"

"It is a little cold for the time of the year," said Holmes.

"What has she been saying to you?" screamed the old man furiously.

"But I have heard that the crocuses promise well," continued my companion imperturbably.

"Ha! You put me off, do you?" said our new visitor, taking a step forward and shaking his hunting-crop. "I know you, you scoundrel! I have heard of you before. You are Holmes, the meddler."

My friend smiled.

"Holmes, the busybody!"

His smile broadened.

"Holmes, the Scotland Yard Jack-in-office!"

Holmes chuckled heartily. "Your conversation is most entertaining," said he. "When you go out close the door, for there is a decided draught."

"I will go when I have said my say. Don't you dare meddle with my affairs. I know that Miss Stoner has been here. I traced her! I am a dangerous man to fall foul of! See here." He stepped swiftly forward, seized the poker, and bent it into a curve with his huge brown hands.

"See that you keep yourself out of my grip," he snarled, and hurling the twisted poker into the fireplace he strode out of the room.

"He seems a very amiable person," said Holmes, laughing. "I am not quite so bulky, but if he had remained I might have shown him that my grip was not much more feeble than his own." As he spoke he picked up the steel poker and, with a sudden effort, straightened it out again.

"Fancy his having the insolence to confound me with the official detective force! This incident gives zest to our investigation, however, and I only trust that our little friend will not suffer from her imprudence in allowing this brute to trace her. And now, Watson, we shall order breakfast, and afterwards I shall walk down to Doctors' Commons, where I hope to get some data which may help us in this matter."

It was nearly one o'clock when Sherlock Holmes returned from his excursion. He held in his hand a sheet of blue paper, scrawled over with notes and figures.

"I have seen the will of the deceased wife," said he. "To determine its exact meaning I have been obliged to work out the present prices of the investments with which it is concerned. The total income, which at the time of the wife's death was little short of £1100, is now, through the fall in agricultural prices, not more than £750. Each daughter can claim an income of £250, in case of marriage. It is evident, therefore, that if both girls had married, this beauty would have had a mere pittance, while even one of them would cripple him to a very serious extent. My morning's work has not been wasted, since it has proved that he has the very strongest motives for standing in the way of anything of the sort. And now, Watson, this is too serious for dawdling, especially as the old man is aware that we are interesting ourselves in his affairs; so if you are ready, we shall call a cab and drive to Waterloo. I should be very much obliged if you would slip your revolver in your pocket. An Eley's No. 2 is an excellent argument with gentlemen who can twist steel pokers into knots. That and a tooth-brush are, I think, all that we need."

At Waterloo we were fortunate in catching a train for Leatherhead, where we hired a trap at the station inn and drove for four or five miles through the lovely Surrey lanes. It was a perfect day, with a bright sun and a few fleecy clouds in the heavens. The trees and wayside hedges were just throwing out their first green shoots, and the air was full of the pleasant smell of the moist earth. To me at least there was a strange contrast between the sweet promise of the spring and this sinister quest upon which we were engaged. My companion sat in the front of the trap, his arms folded, his hat pulled down over his eyes, and his chin sunk upon his breast, buried in the deepest thought. Suddenly, however, he started, tapped me on the shoulder, and pointed over the meadows.

"Look there!" said he.

A heavily timbered park stretched up in a gentle slope, thickening into a grove at the highest point. From amid the branches there jutted out the gray gables and high roof-tree of a very old mansion.

"Stoke Moran?" said he.

"Yes, sir, that be the house of Dr. Grimesby Roylott," remarked the driver.

"There is some building going on there," said Holmes; "that is where we are going."

"There's the village," said the driver, pointing to a cluster of roofs some distance to the left; "but if you want to get to the house, you'll find it shorter to get over this stile, and so by the foot-path over the fields. There it is, where the lady is walking."

"And the lady, I fancy, is Miss Stoner," observed Holmes, shading his eyes. "Yes, I think we had better do as you suggest."

We got off, paid our fare, and the trap rattled back on its way to Leatherhead.

"I thought it as well," said Holmes as we climbed the stile, "that this fellow should think we had come here as architects, or on some definite business. It may stop his gossip. Good-afternoon, Miss Stoner. You see that we have been as good as our word."

Our client of the morning had hurried forward to meet us with a face which spoke her joy. "I have been waiting so eagerly for you," she cried, shaking hands with us warmly. "All has turned out splendidly. Dr. Roylott has gone to town, and it is unlikely that he will be back before evening."

"We have had the pleasure of making the doctor's acquaintance," said Holmes, and in a few words he sketched out what had occurred. Miss Stoner turned white to the lips as she listened.

"Good heavens!" she cried, "he has followed me, then."

"So it appears."

"He is so cunning that I never know when I am safe from him. What will he say when he returns?"

"He must guard himself, for he may find that there is someone more cunning than himself upon his track. You must lock yourself up from him to-night. If he is violent, we shall take you away to your aunt's at Harrow. Now, we must make the best use of our time, so kindly take us at once to the rooms which we are to examine."

The building was of gray, lichen-blotched stone, with a high central portion and two curving wings, like the claws of a crab, thrown out on each side. In one of these wings the windows were broken and blocked with wooden boards, while the roof was partly caved in, a picture of ruin. The central portion was in little better repair, but the right-hand block was comparatively modern, and the blinds in the windows, with the blue smoke curling up from the chimneys, showed that this was where the family resided. Some scaffolding had been erected against the end wall, and the stone-work had been broken into, but there were no signs of any workmen at the moment of our visit. Holmes walked slowly up and down the ill-trimmed lawn and examined with deep attention the outsides of the windows.

"This, I take it, belongs to the room in which you used to sleep, the centre one to your sister's, and the one next to the main building to Dr. Roylott's chamber?"

"Exactly so. But I am now sleeping in the middle one."

"Pending the alterations, as I understand. By the way, there does not seem to be any very pressing need for repairs at that end wall."

"There were none. I believe that it was an excuse to move me from my room."

"Ah! that is suggestive. Now, on the other side of this narrow wing runs the corridor from which these three rooms open. There are windows in it, of course?"

"Yes, but very small ones. Too narrow for anyone to pass through."

"As you both locked your doors at night, your rooms were unapproachable from that side. Now, would you have the kindness to go into your room, and bar your shutters?"

Miss Stoner did so, and Holmes, after a careful examination through the open window, endeavoured in every way to force the shutter open, but without success. There was no slit through which a knife could be passed to raise the bar. Then with his lens he tested the hinges, but they were of solid iron, built firmly into the massive masonry. "Hum!" he said, scratching his chin in some perplexity, "my theory certainly presents some difficulties. No one could pass these shutters if they were bolted. Well, we shall see if the inside throws any light upon the matter."

A small side door led into the whitewashed corridor from which the three bedrooms opened. Holmes refused to examine the third chamber, so we passed at once to the second, that in which Miss Stoner was now sleeping, and in which her sister had met with her fate. It was a homely little room, with a low ceiling and a gaping fireplace, after the fashion of old countryhouses. A brown chest of drawers stood in one corner, a narrow white-counterpaned bed in another, and a dressing-table on the left-hand side of the window. These articles, with two small wickerwork chairs, made up all the furniture in the room save for a square of Wilton carpet in the centre. The boards round and the panelling of the walls were of brown, worm-eaten oak, so old and discoloured that it may have dated from the original building of the house. Holmes drew one of the chairs into a corner and sat silent, while his eyes travelled round and round and up and down, taking in every detail of the apartment.

"Where does that bell communicate with?" he asked at last, pointing to a thick bell-rope which hung down beside the bed, the tassel actually lying upon the pillow.

"It goes to the housekeeper's room."

"It looks newer than the other things?"

"Yes, it was only put there a couple of years ago."

"Your sister asked for it, I suppose?"

"No, I never heard of her using it. We used always to get what we wanted for ourselves."

"Indeed, it seemed unnecessary to put so nice a bell-pull there. You will excuse me for a few minutes while I satisfy myself as to this floor." He threw himself down upon his face with his lens in his hand and crawled swiftly backward and forward, examining minutely the cracks between the boards. Then he did the same with the woodwork with which the chamber was panelled. Finally he walked over to the bed and spent some time in staring at it and in running his eye up and down the wall. Finally he took the bell-rope in his hand and gave it a brisk tug.

"Why, it's a dummy," said he.

"Won't it ring?"

"No, it is not even attached to a wire. This is very interesting. You can see now that it is fastened to a hook just above where the little opening for the ventilator is."

"How very absurd! I never noticed that before."

"Very strange!" muttered Holmes, pulling at the rope. "There are one or two very singular points about this room. For example, what a fool a builder must be to open a ventilator into another room, when, with the same trouble, he might have communicated with the outside air!"

"That is also quite modern," said the lady.

"Done about the same time as the bell-rope?" remarked Holmes.

"Yes, there were several little changes carried out about that time."

"They seem to have been of a most interesting character—dummy bell-ropes, and ventilators which do not ventilate. With your permission, Miss Stoner, we shall now carry our researches into the inner apartment."

Dr. Grimesby Roylott's chamber was larger than that of his stepdaughter, but was as plainly furnished. A camp-bed, a small wooden shelf full of books, mostly of a technical character, an armchair beside the bed, a plain wooden chair against the wall, a round table, and a large iron safe were the principal things which met the eye. Holmes walked slowly round and examined each and all of them with the keenest interest.

"What's in here?" he asked, tapping the safe.

"My stepfather's business papers."

"Oh! you have seen inside, then?"

"Only once, some years ago. I remember that it was full of papers."

"There isn't a cat in it, for example?"

"No. What a strange idea!"

"Well, look at this!" He took up a small saucer of milk which stood on the top of it.

"No; we don't keep a cat. But there is a cheetah and a baboon."

"Ah, yes, of course! Well, a cheetah is just a big cat, and yet a saucer of milk does not go very far in satisfying its wants, I daresay. There is one point which I should wish to determine." He squatted down in front of the wooden chair and examined the seat of it with the greatest attention.

"Thank you. That is quite settled," said he, rising and putting his lens in his pocket. "Hello! Here is something interesting!"

The object which had caught his eyes was a small dog leash hung on one corner of the bed. The leash, however, was curled upon itself and tied so as to make a loop of whipcord.

"What do you make of that, Watson?"

"It's a common enough leash. But I don't know why it should be tied."

"That is not quite so common, is it? Ah, me! it's a wicked world, and when a clever man turns his brains to crime it is the worst of all. I think that I have seen enough now, Miss Stoner, and with your permission we shall walk out upon the lawn."

I had never seen my friend's face so grim or his brow so dark as it was when we turned from the scene of this investigation. We had walked several times up and down the lawn, neither Miss Stoner nor myself liking to break in upon his thoughts before he roused himself from his reverie.

"It is very essential, Miss Stoner," said he, "that you should absolutely follow my advice in every respect."

"I shall most certainly do so."

"The matter is too serious for any hesitation. Your life may depend upon your compliance."

"I assure you that I am in your hands."

"In the first place, both my friend and I must spend the night in your room."

Both Miss Stoner and I gazed at him in astonishment.

"Yes, it must be so. Let me explain. I believe that that is the village inn over there?"

"Yes, that is the Crown."

"Very good. Your windows would be visible from there?"

"Certainly."

"You must confine yourself to your room, on pretence of a headache, when your stepfather comes back. Then when you hear him retire for the night, you must open the shutters of your window, undo the hasp, put your lamp there as a signal to us, and then withdraw quietly with everything which you are likely to want into the room which you used to occupy. I have no doubt that, in spite of the repairs, you could manage there for one night."

"Oh, yes, easily."

"The rest you will leave in our hands."

"But what will you do?"

"We shall spend the night in your room, and we shall investigate the cause of this noise which has disturbed you."

"I believe, Mr. Holmes, that you have already made up your mind," said Miss Stoner, laying her hand upon my companion's sleeve.

"Perhaps I have."

"Then, for pity's sake, tell me what was the cause of my sister's death."

"I should prefer to have clearer proofs before I speak."

"You can at least tell me whether my own thought is correct, and if she died from some sudden fright."

"No, I do not think so. I think that there was probably some more tangible cause. And now, Miss Stoner, we must leave you, for if Dr. Roylott returned and saw us our journey would be in vain. Good-bye, and be brave, for if you will do what I have told you you may rest assured that we shall soon drive away the dangers that threaten you."

Sherlock Holmes and I had no difficulty in engaging a bedroom and sitting-room at the Crown Inn. They were on the upper floor, and from our window we could command a view of the avenue gate, and of the inhabited wing of Stoke Moran Manor House. At dusk we saw Dr. Grimesby Roylott drive past, his huge form looming up beside the little figure of the lad who drove him. The boy had some difficulty in undoing the heavy iron gates, and we heard the hoarse roar of the doctor's voice and saw the fury with which he shook his clenched fists at him. The trap drove on, and a few minutes later we saw a sudden light spring up among the trees as the lamp was lit in one of the sitting-rooms.

"Do you know, Watson," said Holmes as we sat together in the gathering darkness, "I have really some scruples as to taking you to-night. There is a distinct element of danger."

"Can I be of assistance?"

"Your presence might be invaluable."

"Then I shall certainly come."

"It is very kind of you."

"You speak of danger. You have evidently seen more in these rooms than was visible to me."

"No, but I fancy that I may have deduced a little more. I imagine that you saw all that I did."

"I saw nothing remarkable save the bell-rope, and what purpose that could answer I confess is more than I can imagine."

"You saw the ventilator, too?"

"Yes, but I do not think that it is such a very unusual thing to have a small opening between two rooms. It was so small that a rat could hardly pass through."

"I knew that we should find a ventilator before ever we came to Stoke Moran."

"My dear Holmes!"

"Oh, yes, I did. You remember in her statement she said that her sister could smell Dr. Roylott's cigar. Now, of course that suggested at once that there must be a communication between the two rooms. It could only be a small one, or it would have been remarked upon at the coroner's inquiry. I deduced a ventilator."

"But what harm can there be in that?"

"Well, there is at least a curious coincidence of dates. A ventilator is made, a cord is hung, and a lady who sleeps in bed dies. Does not that strike you?"

"I cannot as yet see any connection."

"Did you observe anything very peculiar about that bed?"

"No."

"It was clamped to the floor. Did you ever see a bed fastened like that before?"

"I cannot say that I have."

"The lady could not move her bed. It must always be in the same relative position to the ventilator and to the rope—or so we may call it, since it was clearly never meant for a bell-pull."

"Holmes," I cried, "I seem to see dimly what you are hinting at. We are only just in time to prevent some subtle and horrible crime."

"Subtle enough and horrible enough. When a doctor does go wrong he is the first of criminals. He has nerve and he has knowledge. Palmer and Pritchard were among the heads of their profession. This man strikes even deeper, but I think, Watson, that we shall be able to strike deeper still. But we shall have horrors enough before the night is over; for goodness' sake let us have a quiet pipe and turn our minds for a few hours to something more cheerful."

About nine o'clock the light among the trees was extinguished, and all was dark in the direction of the Manor House. Two hours passed slowly away, and then, suddenly, just at the stroke of eleven, a single bright light shone out right in front of us.

"That is our signal," said Holmes, springing to his feet; "it comes from the middle window."

As we passed out he exchanged a few words with the landlord, explaining that we were going on a late visit to an acquaintance, and that it was possible that we might spend the night there. A moment later we were out on the dark road, a chill wind blowing in our faces, and one yellow light twinkling in front of us through the gloom to guide us on our sombre errand.

There was little difficulty in entering the grounds, for unrepaired breaches gaped in the old park wall. Making our way among the trees, we reached the lawn, crossed it, and were about to enter through the window when out from a clump of laurel bushes there darted what seemed to be a hideous and distorted child, who threw itself upon the grass with writhing limbs and then ran swiftly across the lawn into the darkness.

"My God!" I whispered; "did you see it?"

Holmes was for the moment as startled as I. His hand closed like a vise upon my wrist in his agitation. Then he broke into a low laugh and put his lips to my ear.

"It is a nice household," he murmured. "That is the baboon."

I had forgotten the strange pets which the doctor affected. There was a cheetah, too; perhaps we might find it upon our shoulders at any moment. I confess that I felt easier in my mind when, after following Holmes's example and slipping off my shoes, I found myself inside the bedroom. My companion noiselessly closed the shutters, moved the lamp onto the table, and cast his eyes round the room. All was as we had seen it in the daytime. Then creeping up to me and making a trumpet of his hand, he whispered into my ear again so gently that it was all that I could do to distinguish the words:

"The least sound would be fatal to our plans."

I nodded to show that I had heard.

"We must sit without light. He would see it through the ventilator."

I nodded again.

"Do not go asleep; your very life may depend upon it. Have your pistol ready in case we should need it. I will sit on the side of the bed, and you in that chair."

I took out my revolver and laid it on the corner of the table.

Holmes had brought up a long thin cane, and this he placed upon the bed beside him. By it he laid the box of matches and the stump of a candle. Then he turned down the lamp, and we were left in darkness.

How shall I ever forget that dreadful vigil? I could not hear a sound, not even the drawing of a breath, and yet I knew that my companion sat open-eyed, within a few feet of me, in the same state of nervous tension in which I was myself. The shutters cut off the least ray of light, and we waited in absolute darkness. From outside came the occasional cry of a night-bird, and once at our very window a long drawn catlike whine, which told us that the cheetah was indeed at liberty. Far away we could hear the deep tones of the parish clock, which boomed out every quarter of an hour. How long they seemed, those quarters! Twelve struck, and one and two and three, and still we sat waiting silently for whatever might befall.

Suddenly there was the momentary gleam of a light up in the direction of the ventilator, which vanished immediately, but was succeeded by a strong smell of burning oil and heated metal. Someone in the next room had lit a dark-lantern. I heard a gentle sound of movement, and then all was silent once more, though the smell grew stronger. For half an hour I sat with straining ears. Then suddenly another sound became audible—a very gentle, soothing sound, like that of a small jet of steam escaping continually from a kettle. The instant that we heard it, Holmes sprang from the bed, struck a match, and lashed furiously with his cane at the bell-pull.

"You see it, Watson?" he yelled. "You see it?"

But I saw nothing. At the moment when Holmes struck the light I heard a low, clear whistle, but the sudden glare flashing into my weary eyes made it impossible for me to tell what it was at which my friend lashed so savagely. I could, however, see that his face was deadly pale and filled with horror and loathing.

He had ceased to strike and was gazing up at the ventilator when suddenly there broke from the silence of the night the most horrible cry to which I have ever listened. It swelled up louder and louder, a hoarse yell of pain and fear and anger all mingled in the one dreadful shriek. They say that away down in the village, and even in the distant parsonage, that cry raised the sleepers from their beds. It struck cold to our hearts, and I stood gazing at Holmes, and he at me, until the last echoes of it died away into the silence from which it rose.

"What can it mean?" I gasped.

"It means that it is all over," Holmes answered. "And perhaps, after all, it is for the best. Take your pistol, and we will enter Dr. Roylott's room."

With a grave face he lit the lamp and led the way down the corridor. Twice he struck at the chamber door without any reply from within. Then he turned the handle and entered, I at his heels, with the cocked pistol in my hand.

It was a singular sight which met our eyes. On the table stood a dark-lantern with the shutter half open, throwing a brilliant beam of light upon the iron safe, the door of which was ajar. Beside this table, on the wooden chair, sat Dr. Grimesby Roylott, clad in a long gray dressing-gown, his bare ankles protruding beneath, and his feet thrust into red heelless Turkish slippers. Across his lap lay the short stock with the long leash which we had noticed during the day. His chin was cocked upward and his eyes were fixed in a dreadful, rigid stare at the corner of the ceiling. Round his brow he had a peculiar yellow band, with brownish speckles, which seemed to be bound tightly round his head. As we entered he made neither sound nor motion.

"The band! the speckled band!" whispered Holmes.

I took a step forward. In an instant his strange headgear began to move, and there reared itself from among his hair the squat diamond-shaped head and puffed neck of a loathsome serpent.

"It is a swamp adder!" cried Holmes; "the deadliest snake in India. He has died within ten seconds of being bitten. Violence does, in truth, recoil upon the violent, and the schemer falls into the pit which he digs for another. Let us thrust this creature back into its den, and we can then remove Miss Stoner to some place of shelter and let the county police know what has happened."

As he spoke he drew the dog-whip swiftly from the dead man's lap, and throwing the noose round the reptile's neck he drew it from its horrid perch and, carrying it at arm's length, threw it into the iron safe, which he closed upon it.

Such are the true facts of the death of Dr. Grimesby Roylott, of Stoke Moran. It is not necessary that I should prolong a narrative which has already run to too great a length by telling how we broke the sad news to the terrified girl, how we conveyed her by the morning train to the care of her good aunt at Harrow, of how the slow process of official inquiry came to the conclusion that the doctor met his fate while indiscreetly playing with a dangerous pet. The little which I had yet to learn of the case was told me by Sherlock Holmes as we travelled back next day.

"I had," said he, "come to an entirely erroneous conclusion which shows, my dear Watson, how dangerous it always is to reason from insufficient data. The presence of the gypsies, and the use of the word 'band,' which was used by the poor girl, no doubt to explain the appearance which she had caught a hurried glimpse of by the light of her match, were sufficient to put me upon an entirely wrong scent. I can only claim the merit that I instantly reconsidered my position when, however, it became clear to me that whatever danger threatened an occupant of the room could not come either from the window or the door. My attention was speedily drawn, as I have already remarked to you, to this ventilator, and to the bell-rope which hung down to the bed. The discovery that this was a dummy, and that the bed was clamped to the floor, instantly gave rise to the suspicion that the rope was there as a bridge for something passing through the hole and coming to the bed. The idea of a snake instantly occurred to me, and when I coupled it with my knowledge that the doctor was furnished with a supply of creatures from India, I felt that I was probably on the right track. The idea of using a form of poison which could not possibly be discovered by any chemical test was just such a one as would occur to a clever and ruthless man who had had an Eastern training. The rapidity with which such a poison would take effect would also, from his point of view, be an advantage. It would be a sharp-eyed coroner, indeed, who could distinguish the two little dark punctures which would show where the poison fangs had done their work. Then I thought of the whistle. Of course he must recall the snake before the morning light revealed it to the victim. He had trained it, probably by the use of the milk which we saw, to return to him when summoned. He would put it through this ventilator at the hour that he thought best, with the certainty that it would crawl down the rope and land on the bed. It might or might not bite the occupant, perhaps she might escape every night for a week, but sooner or later she must fall a victim.

"I had come to these conclusions before ever I had entered his room. An inspection of his chair showed me that he had been in the habit of standing on it, which of course would be necessary in order that he should reach the ventilator. The sight of the safe, the saucer of milk, and the loop of whipcord were enough to finally dispel any doubts which may have remained. The metallic clang heard by Miss Stoner was obviously caused by her stepfather hastily closing the door of his safe upon its terrible occupant. Having once made up my mind, you know the steps which I took in order to put the matter to the proof. I heard the creature hiss as I have no doubt that you did also, and I instantly lit the light and attacked it."

"With the result of driving it through the ventilator."

"And also with the result of causing it to turn upon its master at the other side. Some of the blows of my cane came home and roused its snakish temper, so that it flew upon the first person it saw. In this way I am no doubt indirectly responsible for Dr. Grimesby Roylott's death, and I cannot say that it is likely to weigh very heavily upon my conscience."

QUESTIONS FOR DISCUSSION AND WRITING

1. How does Dr. Watson's opening comment about Holmes's preference for the unusual and fantastic establish our expectations for the plot? How does Holmes's reticence about his finding prolong the denouement of the story?
2. What special qualities does Dr. Watson admire in Holmes's character? What episodes in the story dramatize these qualities? How does the description of Dr. Grimesby Roylott prepare us for his role in the story?
3. Why is the description of the setting at Stoke Moran Manor House essential to the development and resolution of the story? What specific details in the setting provide the clues and false clues to the solution of the crime?
4. In a detective story, what is the advantage in using a rather unobservant narrator like Dr. Watson?
5. What intellectual assumptions does Holmes make about the world of cause and effect?

27

RALPH ELLISON

Battle Royal

RALPH ELLISON was born in 1914 in Oklahoma City and studied music for three years at Tuskegee Institute in Alabama, a school founded by the black educator Booker T. Washington. In 1936 Ellison went to New York City, met Langston Hughes and Richard Wright, and began working with the Federal Writers Project. In 1942 he became editor of *Negro Quarterly* before serving in the Merchant Marine during World War II. During this period, Ellison published short stories and essays in magazines such as *New Challenge* and *New Masses,* and with the help of several fellowships, began writing his major epic of the black experience in America, *Invisible Man* (1952). The novel was widely acclaimed, winning the 1953 National Book Award and named in a 1965 *Book Week* poll of prominent authors, critics, and editors as "the most distinguished single work published in the last twenty years." Ellison subsequently received a number of fellowships and lectureships, and in 1970 was appointed Albert Schweitzer Professor of Humanities at New York University. Although Ellison published a collection of his essays, *Shadow and Act* in 1964, he has not published another novel and his

stories remain uncollected, though frequently anthologized. "Battle Royal," first published as a short story in 1947, appears in slightly altered form as the opening chapter of *Invisible Man.* The story portrays a young black man's initiation into the rituals of white repression. "King of the Bingo Game," published in *Tomorrow, IV* (1944), documents an older black man's desperate attempt to control his own destiny.

It goes a long way back, some twenty years. All my life I had been looking for something, and everywhere I turned someone tried to tell me what it was. I accepted their answers too, though they were often in contradiction and even self-contradictory. I was naïve. I was looking for myself and asking everyone except myself questions which I, and only I, could answer. It took me a long time and much painful boomeranging of my expectations to achieve a realization everyone else appears to have been born with: That I am nobody but myself. But first I had to discover that I am an invisible man!

And yet I am no freak of nature, nor of history. I was in the cards, other things having been equal (or unequal) eighty-five years ago. I am not ashamed of my grandparents for having been slaves. I am only ashamed of myself for having at one time been ashamed. About eighty-five years ago they were told they were free, united with others of our country in everything pertaining to the common good, and, in everything social, separate like the fingers of the hand. And they believed it. They exulted in it. They stayed in their place, worked hard, and brought up my father to do the same. But my grandfather is the one. He was an odd old guy, my grandfather, and I am told I take after him. It was he who caused the trouble. On his deathbed he called my father to him and said, "Son, after I'm gone I want you to keep up the good fight. I never told you, but our life is a war and I have been a traitor all my born days, a spy in the enemy's country ever since I give up my gun back in the Reconstruction. Live with your head in the lion's mouth. I want you to overcome 'em with yeses, undermine 'em with grins, agree 'em to death and destruction, let 'em swoller you till they vomit or bust wide open." They thought the old man had gone out of his mind. He had been the meekest of men. The younger children were rushed from the room, the shades drawn and the flame of the lamp turned so low that it sputtered on the wick like the old man's breathing. "Learn it to the younguns," he whispered fiercely; then he died.

But my folks were more alarmed over his last words than over his dying. It was as though he had not died at all, his words caused so much anxiety. I was warned emphatically to forget what he had said and, indeed, this is the first time it has been mentioned outside the family circle. It had a tremendous effect upon me, however. I could never be sure of what he meant. Grandfather had been a quiet old man who never made any trouble, yet on his deathbed he had called himself a traitor and a spy, and he had spoken of his meekness as a dangerous activity. It became a constant puzzle which lay unanswered in the back of my mind. And whenever things went well for me I remembered my grandfather and felt guilty and uncomfortable. It was as though I was carrying out his advice in spite of myself. And to make it worse, everyone loved me for it. I was praised by the most lily-white men in town. I was considered an example of desirable conduct—just as my grandfather had been. And what puzzled me was that the old man had defined it as *treachery*. When I was praised for my conduct I felt a guilt that in some way I was doing something that was really against the wishes of the white folks, that if they had understood they would have desired me to act just the opposite, that I should have been sulky and mean, and that that really would have been what they wanted, even though they were fooled and thought they wanted me to act as I did. It made me afraid that some day they would look upon me as a traitor and I would be lost. Still I was more afraid to act any other way because they didn't like that at all. The old man's words were like a curse. On my graduation day I delivered an oration in which I showed that humility was the secret, indeed, the very essence of progress. (Not that I believed this—how could I, remembering my grandfather?—I only believed that it worked.) It was a great success. Everyone praised me and I was invited to give the speech at a gathering of the town's leading white citizens. It was a triumph for the whole community.

It was in the main ballroom of the leading hotel. When I got there I discovered that it was on the occasion of a smoker, and I was told that since I was to be there anyway I might as well take part in the battle royal to be fought by some of my schoolmates as part of the entertainment. The battle royal came first.

All of the town's big shots were there in their tuxedoes, wolfing down the buffet foods, drinking beer and whiskey and smoking black cigars. It was a large room with a high ceiling. Chairs were arranged in neat rows around three sides of a portable boxing ring. The fourth side was clear, revealing a gleaming space of polished floor. I had some misgivings over the battle royal, by the way. Not from a distaste for fighting but because I didn't care too much for the other fellows who were to take part. They were tough guys who seemed to have no grandfather's curse worrying their minds. No one could mistake their toughness. And besides, I suspected that fighting a battle royal might distract from the dignity of my speech. In those pre-invisible days I visualized myself as a potential Booker T. Washington. But the other fellows didn't care too much for me either, and there were nine of them. I felt superior to them in my way, and I didn't like the manner in which we were all crowded together in the servants' elevator. Nor did they like my being there. In fact, as the warmly lighted floors flashed past the elevator we had words over the fact that I, by taking part in the fight, had knocked one of their friends out of a night's work.

We were led out of the elevator through a rococo hall into an anteroom and told to get into our fighting togs. Each of us was issued a pair of boxing gloves and ushered out into the big mirrored hall, which we entered looking cautiously about us and whispering, lest we might accidentally be heard above the noise of the room. It was foggy with cigar smoke. And already the whiskey was taking effect. I was shocked to see some of the most important men of the town quite tipsy. They were all there—bankers, lawyers, judges, doctors, fire chiefs, teachers, merchants. Even one of the more fashionable pastors. Something we could not see was going on up front. A clarinet was vibrating sensuously and the men were standing up and moving eagerly forward. We were a small tight group, clustered together, our bare upper bodies touching and shining with anticipatory sweat; while up front the big shots were becoming increasingly excited over something we still could not see. Suddenly I heard the school superintendent, who had told me to come, yell, "Bring up the shines, gentlemen! Bring up the little shines!"

We were rushed up to the front of the ballroom, where it smelled even more strongly of tobacco and whiskey. Then we were pushed into place. I almost wet my pants. A sea of faces, some hostile, some amused, ringed around us, and in the center, facing us, stood a magnificent blonde—stark naked. There was dead silence. I felt a blast of cold air chill me. I tried to back away, but they were behind me and around me. Some of the boys stood with lowered heads, trembling. I felt a wave of irrational guilt and fear. My teeth chattered, my skin turned to goose flesh, my knees knocked. Yet I was strongly attracted and looked in spite of myself. Had the price of looking been blindness, I would have looked. The hair was yellow like that of a circus kewpie doll, the face heavily powdered and rouged, as though to form an abstract mask, the eyes hollow and smeared a cool blue, the color of a baboon's butt. I felt a desire to spit upon her as my eyes brushed slowly over her body. Her breasts were firm and round as the domes of East Indian temples, and I stood so close as to see the fine skin texture and beads of pearly perspiration glistening like dew around the pink and erected buds of her nipples. I wanted at one and the same time to run from the room, to sink through the floor, or go to her and cover her from my eyes and the eyes of the others with my body; to feel the soft thighs, to caress her and destroy her, to love her and to murder her, to hide from her, and yet to stroke where below the small American flag tattooed upon her belly her thighs formed a capital V. I had a notion that of all in the room she saw only me with her impersonal eyes.

And then she began to dance, a slow sensuous movement; the smoke of a hundred cigars clinging to her like the thinnest of veils. She seemed like a fair bird-girl girdled in veils calling to me from the angry surface of some gray and threatening sea. I was transported. Then I became aware of the clarinet playing and the big shots yelling at us. Some threatened us if we looked and others if we did not. On my right I saw one boy faint. And now a man grabbed a silver pitcher from a table and stepped close as he dashed ice water upon him and stood him up and forced two of us to support him as his head hung and moans issued from his thick bluish lips. Another boy began to plead to go home. He was the largest of the group, wearing dark red fighting trunks much too small to conceal the erection which projected from him as though in answer to the insinuating low-registered moaning of the clarinet. He tried to hide himself with his boxing gloves.

And all the while the blonde continued dancing, smiling faintly at the big shots who watched her with fascination, and faintly smiling at our fear. I noticed a certain merchant who followed her hungrily, his lips loose and drooling. He was a large man who wore diamond studs in a shirtfront which swelled with the ample paunch underneath, and each time the blonde swayed her undulating hips he ran his hand through the thin hair of his bald head and, with his arms upheld, his posture clumsy like that of an intoxicated panda, wound his belly in a slow and obscene grind. This creature was completely hypnotized. The music had quickened. As the dancer flung herself about with a detached expression on her face, the men began reaching out to touch her. I could see their beefy fingers sink into her soft flesh. Some of the others tried to stop them and she began to move around the floor in graceful circles, as they gave chase, slipping and sliding over the polished floor. It was mad. Chairs went crashing, drinks were spilt, as they ran laughing and howling after her. They caught her just as she reached a door, raised her from the floor, and tossed her as college boys are tossed at a hazing, and above her red, fixed-smiling lips I saw the terror and disgust in her eyes, almost like my own terror and that which I saw in some of the other boys. As I watched, they tossed her twice and her soft breasts seemed to flatten against the air and her legs flung wildly as she spun. Some of the more sober ones helped her to escape. And I started off the floor, heading for the anteroom with the rest of the boys.

Some were still crying and in hysteria. But as we tried to leave we were stopped and ordered to get into the ring. There was nothing to do but what we were told. All ten of us climbed under the ropes and allowed ourselves to be blindfolded with broad bands of white cloth. One of the men seemed to feel a bit sympathetic and tried to cheer us up as we stood with our backs against the ropes. Some of us tried to grin. "See that boy over there?" one of the men said. "I want you to run across at the bell and give it to him right in the belly. If you don't get him, I'm going to get you. I don't like his looks." Each of us was told the same. The blindfolds were put on. Yet even then I had been going over my speech. In my mind each word was as bright as a flame. I felt the cloth pressed into place, and frowned so that it would be loosened when I relaxed.

But now I felt a sudden fit of blind terror. I was unused to darkness. It was as though I had suddenly found myself in a dark room filled with poisonous cottonmouths. I could hear the bleary voices yelling insistently for the battle royal to begin.

"Get going in there!"

"Let me at that big nigger!"

I strained to pick up the school superintendent's voice, as though to squeeze some security out of that slightly more familiar sound.

"Let me at those black sonsabitches!" someone yelled.

"No, Jackson, no!" another voice yelled. "Here, somebody, help me hold Jack."

"I want to get at that ginger-colored nigger. Tear him limb from limb," the first voice yelled.

I stood against the ropes trembling. For in those days I was what they called ginger-colored, and he sounded as though he might crunch me between his teeth like a crisp ginger cookie.

Quite a struggle was going on. Chairs were being kicked about and I could hear voices grunting as with terrific effort. I wanted to see, to see more desperately than ever before. But the blindfold was as tight as a thick skin-puckering scab and when I raised my gloved hand to push the layers of white aside a voice yelled, "Oh, no you don't, black bastard! Leave that alone!"

"Ring the bell before Jackson kills him a coon!" someone boomed in the sudden silence. And I heard the bell clang and the sound of the feet scuffling forward.

A glove smacked against my head. I pivoted, striking out stiffly as someone went past, and felt the jar ripple along the length of my arm to my shoulder. Then it seemed as though all nine of the boys had turned upon me at once. Blows pounded me from all sides while I struck out as best I could. So many blows landed upon me that I wondered if I were not the only blindfolded fighter in the ring, or if the man called Jackson hadn't succeeded in getting me after all.

Blindfolded, I could no longer control my motions. I had no dignity. I stumbled about like a baby or a drunken man. The smoke had become thicker and with each new blow it seemed to sear and further restrict my lungs. My saliva became like hot bitter glue.

A glove connected with my head, filling my mouth with warm blood. It was everywhere. I could not tell if the moisture I felt upon my body was sweat or blood. A blow landed hard against the nape of my neck. I felt myself going over, my head hitting the floor. Streaks of blue light filled the black world behind the blindfold. I lay prone, pretending that I was knocked out, but felt myself seized by hands and yanked to my feet. "Get going, black boy! Mix it up!" My arms were like lead, my head smarting from blows. I managed to feel my way to the ropes and held on, trying to catch my breath. A glove landed in my midsection and I went over again, feeling as though the smoke had become a knife jabbed into my guts. Pushed this way and that by the legs milling around me, I finally pulled erect and discovered that I could see the black, sweat-washed forms weaving in the smoky-blue atmosphere like drunken dancers weaving to the rapid drum-like thuds of blows.

Everyone fought hysterically. It was complete anarchy. Everybody fought everybody else. No group fought together for long. Two, three, four, fought one, then turned to fight each other, were themselves attacked. Blows landed below the belt and in the kidney, with the gloves open as well as closed, and with my eye partly opened now there was not so much terror. I moved carefully, avoiding blows, although not too many to attract attention, fighting group to group. The boys groped about like blind, cautious crabs crouching to protect their midsections, their heads pulled in short against their shoulders, their arms stretched nervously before them, with their fists testing the smoke-filled air like the knobbed feelers of hypersensitive snails. In one corner I glimpsed a boy violently punching the air and heard him scream in pain as he smashed his hand against a ring post. For a second I saw him bent over holding his hand, then going down as a blow caught his unprotected head. I played one group against the other, slipping in and throwing a punch then stepping out of range while pushing the others into the melee to take the blows blindly aimed at me. The smoke was agonizing and there were no rounds, no bells at three minute intervals to relieve our exhaustion. The room spun round me, a swirl of lights, smoke, sweating bodies surrounded by tense white faces. I bled from both nose and mouth, the blood spattering upon my chest.

The men kept yelling, "Slug him, black boy! Knock his guts out!"

"Uppercut him! Kill him! Kill that big boy!"

Taking a fake fall, I saw a boy going down heavily beside me as though we were felled by a single blow, saw a sneaker-clad foot shoot into his groin as the two who had knocked him down stumbled upon him. I rolled out of range, feeling a twinge of nausea.

The harder we fought the more threatening the men became. And yet, I had begun to worry about my speech again. How would it go? Would they recognize my ability? What would they give me?

I was fighting automatically when suddenly I noticed that one after another of the boys were leaving the ring. I was surprised, filled with panic, as though I had been left alone with an unknown danger. Then I understood. The boys had arranged it among themselves. It was the custom for the two men left in the ring to slug it out for the winner's prize. I discovered this too late. When the bell sounded two men in tuxedoes leaped into the ring and removed the blindfold. I found myself facing Tatlock, the biggest of the gang. I felt sick at my stomach. Hardly had the bell stopped ringing in my ears than it clanged again and I saw him moving swiftly toward me. Thinking of nothing else to do

I hit him smash on the nose. He kept coming, bringing the rank sharp violence of stale sweat. His face was a black blank of a face, only his eyes alive—with hate of me and aglow with a feverish terror from what had happened to us all. I became anxious. I wanted to deliver my speech and he came at me as though he meant to beat it out of me. I smashed him again and again, taking his blows as they came. Then on a sudden impulse I struck him lightly and we clinched. I whispered, "Fake like I knocked you out, you can have the prize."

"I'll break your behind," he whispered hoarsely.

"For *them*?"

"For *me*, sonafabitch!"

They were yelling for us to break it up and Tatlock spun me half around with a blow, and as a joggled camera sweeps in a reeling scene, I saw the howling red faces crouching tense beneath the cloud of blue-gray smoke. For a moment the world wavered, unraveled, flowed, then my head cleared and Tatlock bounced before me. That fluttering shadow before my eyes was his jabbing left hand. Then falling forward, my head against his damp shoulder, I whispered,

"I'll make it five dollars more."

"Go to hell!"

But his muscles relaxed a trifle beneath my pressure and I breathed, "Seven?"

"Give it to your ma," he said, ripping me beneath the heart.

And while I still held him I butted him and moved away. I felt myself bombarded with punches. I fought back with hopeless desperation. I wanted to deliver my speech more than anything else in the world, because I felt that only these men could judge truly my ability, and now this stupid clown was ruining my chances. I began fighting carefully now, moving in to punch him and out again with my greater speed. A lucky blow to his chin and I had him going too—until I heard a loud voice yell, "I got my money on the big boy."

Hearing this, I almost dropped my guard. I was confused: Should I try to win against the voice out there? Would not this go against my speech, and was not this a moment for humility, for nonresistance? A blow to my head as I danced about sent my right eye popping like a jack-in-the-box and settled my dilemma. The room went red as I fell. It was a dream fall, my body languid and fastidious as to where to land, until the floor became impatient and smashed up to meet me. A moment later I came to. An hypnotic voice said FIVE emphatically. And I lay there, hazily watching a dark red spot of my own blood shaping itself into a butterfly, glistening and soaking into the soiled gray world of the canvas.

When the voice drawled TEN I was lifted up and dragged to a chair. I sat dazed. My eye pained and swelled with each throb of my pounding heart and I wondered if now I would be allowed to speak. I was wringing wet, my mouth still bleeding. We were grouped along the wall now. The other boys ignored me as they congratulated Tatlock and speculated as to how much they would be paid. One boy whimpered over his smashed hand. Looking up front, I saw attendants in white jackets rolling the portable ring away and placing a small square rug in the vacant space surrounded by chairs. Perhaps, I thought, I will stand on the rug to deliver my speech.

Then the M.C. called to us, "Come on up here boys and get your money."

We ran forward to where the men laughed and talked in their chairs, waiting. Everyone seemed friendly now.

"There it is on the rug," the man said. I saw the rug covered with coins of all dimensions and a few crumpled bills. But what excited me, scattered here and there, were the gold pieces.

"Boys, it's all yours," the man said. "You get all you grab."

"That's right, Sambo," a blond man said, winking at me confidentially.

I trembled with excitement, forgetting my pain. I would get the gold and the bills, I thought. I would use both hands. I would throw my body against the boys nearest me to block them from the gold.

"Get down around the rug now," the man commanded, "and don't anyone touch it until I give the signal."

"This ought to be good," I heard.

As told, we got around the square rug on our knees. Slowly the man raised his freckled hand as we followed it upward with our eyes.

I heard, "These niggers look like they're about to pray!"

Then, "Ready," the man said. "Go!"

I lunged for a yellow coin lying on the blue design of the carpet, touching it and sending a surprised shriek to join those around me. I tried frantically to remove my hand but could not let go. A hot, violent force tore through my body, shaking me like a wet rat. The rug was electrified. The hair bristled up on my head as I shook myself free. My muscles jumped, my nerves jangled, writhed. But I saw that this was not stopping the other boys. Laughing in fear and embarrassment, some were holding back and scooping up the coins knocked off by the painful contortions of others. The men roared above us as we struggled.

"Pick it up, goddamnit, pick it up!" someone called like a bass-voiced parrot. "Go on, get it!"

I crawled rapidly around the floor, picking up the coins, trying to avoid the coppers and to get greenbacks and the gold. Ignoring the shock by laughing, as I brushed the coins off quickly, I discovered that I could contain the electricity—a contradiction but it works. Then the men began to push us onto the rug. Laughing embarrassedly, we struggled out of their hands and kept after the coins. We were all wet and slippery and hard to hold. Suddenly I saw a boy lifted into the air, glistening with sweat like a circus seal, and dropped, his wet back landing flush upon the charged rug, heard him yell and saw him literally dance upon his back, his elbows beating a frenzied tattoo upon the floor, his muscles twitching like the flesh of a horse stung by many flies. When he finally rolled off, his face was gray and no one stopped him when he ran from the floor amid booming laughter.

"Get the money," the M.C. called. "That's good hard American cash!"

And we snatched and grabbed, snatched and grabbed. I was careful not to come too close to the rug now, and when I felt the hot whiskey breath descend upon me like a cloud of foul air I reached out and grabbed the leg of a chair. It was occupied and I held on desperately.

"Leggo, nigger! Leggo!"

The huge face wavered down to mine as he tried to push me free. But my body was slippery and he was too drunk. It was Mr. Colcord, who owned a chain of movie houses and "entertainment palaces." Each time he grabbed me I slipped out of his hands. It became a real struggle. I feared the rug more than I did the drunk, so I held on, surprising myself for a moment by trying to topple *him* upon the rug. It was such an enormous idea that I found myself actually carrying it out. I tried not to be obvious, yet when I grabbed his leg, trying to tumble him out of the chair, he raised up roaring with laughter, and, looking at me with soberness dead in the eye, kicked me viciously in the chest. The chair leg flew out of my hand and I felt myself going and rolled. It was as though I had rolled through a bed of hot coals. It seemed a whole century would pass before I would roll free, a century in which I was seared through the deepest levels of my body to the fearful breath within me and the breath seared and heated to the point of explosion. It'll all be over in a flash, I thought as I rolled clear. It'll all be over in a flash.

But not yet, the men on the other side were waiting, red faces swollen as though from apoplexy as they bent forward in their chairs. Seeing their fingers coming toward me I rolled away as a fumbled football rolls off the receiver's fingertips, back into the coals. That time I luckily sent the rug sliding out of place and heard the coins ringing against the floor and the boys scuffling to pick them up and the M.C. calling, "All right, boys, that's all. Go get dressed and get your money."

I was limp as a dish rag. My back felt as though it had been beaten with wires.

When we had dressed the M.C. came in and gave us each five dollars, except Tatlock, who got ten for being the last in the ring. Then he told us to leave. I was not to get a chance to deliver my speech, I thought. I was going out into the dim alley in despair when I was stopped and told to go back. I returned to the ballroom, where the men were pushing back their chairs and gathering in small groups to talk.

The M.C. knocked on a table for quiet. "Gentlemen," he said, "we almost forgot an important part of the program. A most serious part, gentlemen. This boy was brought here to deliver a speech which he made at his graduation yesterday. . . ."

"Bravo!"

"I'm told that he is the smartest boy we've got out there in Greenwood. I'm told that he knows more big words than a pocket-sized dictionary."

Much applause and laughter.

"So now, gentlemen, I want you to give him your attention."

There was still laughter as I faced them, my mouth dry, my eyes throbbing. I began slowly, but evidently my throat was tense, because they began shouting, "Louder! Louder!"

"We of the younger generation extol the wisdom of that great leader and educator," I shouted, "who first spoke these flaming words of wisdom: 'A ship lost at sea for many days suddenly sighted a friendly vessel. From the mast of the unfortunate vessel was seen a signal: "Water, water; we die of thirst!" The answer from the friendly vessel came back: "Cast down your bucket where you are." The captain of the distressed vessel, at last heeding the injunction, cast down his bucket, and it came up full of fresh sparkling water from the mouth of the Amazon River.' And like him I say, and in his words, 'To those of my race who depend upon bettering their condition in a foreign land, or who underestimate the importance of cultivating friendly relations with the Southern white man, who is his next-door neighbor, I would say: "Cast down your bucket where you are"—cast it down in making friends in every manly way of the people of all races by whom we are surrounded. . . .'"

I spoke automatically and with such fervor that I did not realize that the men were still talking and laughing until my dry mouth, filling up with blood from the cut, almost strangled me. I coughed, wanting to stop and go to one of the tall brass, sand-filled spittoons to relieve myself, but a few of the men, especially the superintendent, were listening and I was afraid. So I gulped it down, blood, saliva and all, and continued. (What power of endurance I had during those days! What enthusiasm! What a belief in the rightness of things!) I spoke even louder in spite of the pain. But still they talked and still they laughed, as though deaf with cotton in dirty ears. So I spoke with greater emotional emphasis. I closed my ears and swallowed blood until I was nauseated. The speech seemed a hundred times as long as before, but I could not leave out a single word. All had to be said, each memorized nuance considered, rendered. Nor was that all. Whenever I uttered a word of three or more syllables a group of voices would yell for me to repeat it. I used the phrase "social responsibility" and they yelled:

"What's the word you say, boy?"

"Social responsibility," I said.

"What?"

"Social . . ."

"Louder."

". . . responsibility"

"More!"

"Respon—"

"Repeat!"

"—sibility."

The room filled with the uproar of laughter until, no doubt, distracted by having to gulp down my blood, I made a mistake and yelled a phrase I had often seen denounced in newspaper editorials, heard debated in private.

"Social . . ."

"What?" they yelled.

". . . equality—"

The laughter hung smokelike in the sudden stillness. I opened my eyes, puzzled. Sounds of displeasure filled the room. The M.C. rushed forward. They shouted hostile phrases at me. But I did not understand.

A small dry mustached man in the front row blared out, "Say that slowly, son!"

"What, sir?"

"What you just said!"

"Social responsibility, sir," I said.

"You weren't being smart, were you boy?" he said, not unkindly.

"No, sir!"

"You sure that about 'equality' was a mistake?"

"Oh, yes, sir," I said. "I was swallowing blood."

"Well, you had better speak more slowly so we can understand. We mean to do right by you, but you've got to know your place at all times. All right, now, go on with your speech."

I was afraid. I wanted to leave but I wanted also to speak and I was afraid they'd snatch me down.

"Thank you sir," I said, beginning where I had left off, and having them ignore me as before.

Yet when I finished there was a thunderous applause. I was surprised to see the superintendent come forth with a package wrapped in white tissue paper, and, gesturing for quiet, address the men.

"Gentlemen, you see that I did not overpraise the boy. He makes a good speech and some day he'll lead his people in the proper paths. And I don't have to tell you that this is important in these days and times. This is a good, smart boy, and so to encourage him in the right direction, in the name of the Board of Education I wish to present him a prize in the form of this . . ."

He paused, removing the tissue paper and revealing a gleaming calfskin briefcase.

". . . in the form of this first-class article from Shad Whitmore's shop."

"Boy," he said, addressing me, "take this prize and keep it well. Consider it a badge of office. Prize it. Keep developing as you are and some day it will be filled with important papers that will help shape the destiny of your people."

I was so moved that I could hardly express my thanks. A rope of bloody saliva forming a shape like an undiscovered continent drooled upon the leather and I wiped it quickly away. I felt an importance that I had never dreamed.

"Open it and see what's inside," I was told.

My fingers a-tremble, I complied, smelling fresh leather and finding an official-looking document inside. It was a scholarship to the state college for Negroes. My eyes filled with tears and I ran awkwardly off the floor.

I was overjoyed; I did not even mind when I discovered the gold pieces I had scrambled for were brass pocket tokens advertising a certain make of automobile.

When I reached home everyone was excited. Next day the neighbors came to congratulate me. I even felt safe from grandfather, whose deathbed curse usually spoiled my triumphs. I stood beneath his photograph with my briefcase in hand and smiled triumphantly into his stolid black peasant's face. It was a face that fascinated me. The eyes seemed to follow everywhere I went.

That night I dreamed I was at a circus with him and that he refused to laugh at the clowns no matter what they did. Then later he told me to open my briefcase and read what was inside and I did, finding an official envelope stamped with the state seal; and inside the envelope I found another and another, endlessly, and I thought I would fall of weariness. "Them's years," he said. "Now open that one." And I did and in it I found an engraved stamp containing a short message in letters of gold. "Read it," my grandfather said. "Out loud."

"To Whom It May Concern," I intoned. "Keep This Nigger-Boy Running."

I awoke with the old man's laughter ringing in my ears.

QUESTIONS FOR DISCUSSION AND WRITING

1. How do the dying words of the narrator's grandfather establish the various conflicts in the story? In what sense does the narrator's dream about his grandfather bring those conflicts to a satisfactory conclusion?
2. How does the narrator characterize himself? In what way does he characterize the other participants in the battle royal? How does the behavior of these "leading white citizens" contrast with the behavior expected of men in their social position?
3. What kind of setting does the narrator expect when he is invited to give his speech at "a gathering of the town's leading citizens"? What kind of setting does he discover at the smoker? What does this contrast suggest about the setting promised by his scholarship?
4. How does the opening paragraph of the story establish the point of view of the narrator? What has the narrator presumably learned since the time of the events he is describing? How does this knowledge influence the way he tells his tale?
5. What are the specific events portrayed in the story designed to demonstrate? In what ways do these "rituals" symbolize the relationships between blacks and whites in our culture?

28
RALPH ELLISON
King of the Bingo Game

The woman in front of him was eating roasted peanuts that smelled so good that he could barely contain his hunger. He could not even sleep and wished they'd hurry and begin the bingo game. There, on his right, two fellows were drinking wine out of a bottle wrapped in a paper bag, and he could hear soft gurgling in the dark. His stomach gave a low, gnawing growl. "If this was down South," he thought, "all I'd have to do is lean over and say, 'Lady, gimme a few of those peanuts, please ma'am,' and she'd pass me the bag and never think nothing of it." Or he could ask the fellows for a drink in the same way. Folks down South stuck together that way; they didn't even have to know you. But up here it was different. Ask somebody for something, and they'd think you were crazy. Well, I ain't crazy. I'm just broke, 'cause I got no birth certificate to get a job, and Laura 'bout to die 'cause we got no money for a doctor. But I ain't crazy. And yet a pinpoint of doubt was focused in his mind as he glanced toward the screen and saw the hero stealthily entering a dark room and sending the beam of a flashlight along a wall of bookcases. This is where he finds the trapdoor, he remembered. The man would pass abruptly through the wall and find the girl tied to a bed, her legs and arms spread wide, and her clothing torn to rags. He laughed softly to himself. He had seen the picture three times, and this was one of the best scenes.

On his right the fellow whispered wide-eyed to his companion, "Man, look a-yonder!"

"Damn!"

"Wouldn't I like to have her tied up like that . . ."

"Hey! That fool's letting her loose!"

"Aw, man, he loves her."

"Love or no love!"

The man moved impatiently beside him, and he tried to involve himself in the scene. But Laura was on his mind. Tiring quickly of watching the picture he looked back to where the white beam filtered from the projection room above the balcony. It started small and grew large, specks of dusk dancing in its whiteness as it reached the screen. It was strange how the beam always landed right on the screen and didn't mess up and fall somewhere else. But they had it all fixed. Everything was fixed. Now suppose when they showed that girl with her dress torn the girl started taking off the rest of her clothes, and when the guy came in he didn't untie her but kept her there and went to taking off his own clothes? *That* would be something to see. If a picture got out of hand like that those guys up there would go nuts. Yeah, and there'd be so many folks in here you couldn't find a seat for nine months! A strange sensation played over his skin. He shuddered. Yesterday he'd seen a bedbug on a woman's neck as they walked out into the bright street. But exploring his thigh through a hole in his pocket he found only goose pimples and old scars.

The bottle gurgled again. He closed his eyes. Now a dreamy music was accompanying the film and train whistles were sounding in the distance, and he was a boy again walking along a railroad trestle down South, and seeing the train coming, and running back as fast as he could go, and hearing the whistle blowing, and getting off the trestle to solid ground just in time, with the earth trembling beneath his feet, and feeling relieved as he ran down the cinder-strewn embankment onto the highway, and looking back and seeing with terror that the train had left the track and was following him right down the middle of the street, and all the white people laughing as he ran screaming . . .

"Wake up there, buddy! What the hell do you mean hollering like that? Can't you see we trying to enjoy this here picture?"

He stared at the man with gratitude.

"I'm sorry, old man," he said. "I musta been dreaming."

"Well, here, have a drink. And don't be making no noise like that, damn!"

His hands trembled as he tilted his head. It was not wine, but whiskey. Cold rye whiskey. He took a deep swoller, decided it was better not to take another, and handed the bottle back to its owner.

"Thanks, old man," he said.

Now he felt the cold whiskey breaking a warm path straight through the middle of him, growing hotter and sharper as it moved. He had not eaten all day, and it made him light-headed. The smell of the peanuts stabbed him like a knife, and he got up and found a seat in the middle aisle. But no sooner did he sit than he saw a row of intense-faced young girls, and got up again, thinking, "You chicks musta been Lindy-hopping somewhere." He found a seat several rows ahead as the lights came on, and he saw the screen disappear behind a heavy red and gold curtain; then the curtain rising, and the man with the microphone and a uniformed attendant coming on the stage.

He felt for his bingo cards, smiling. The guy at the door wouldn't like it if he knew about his having *five* cards. Well, not everyone played the bingo game; and even with five cards he didn't have much of a chance. For Laura, though, he had to have faith. He studied the cards, each with its different numerals, punching the free center hole in each and spreading them neatly across his lap; and when the lights faded he sat slouched in his seat so that he could look from his cards to the bingo wheel with but a quick shifting of his eyes.

Ahead, at the end of the darkness, the man with the microphone was pressing a button attached to a long cord and spinning the bingo wheel and calling out the number each time the wheel came to rest. And each time the voice rang out his finger raced over the cards for the number. With five cards he had to move fast. He became nervous; there were too many cards, and the man went too fast with his grating voice. Perhaps he should just select one and throw the others away. But he was afraid. He became warm. Wonder how much Laura's doctor would cost? Damn that, watch the cards! And with despair he heard the man call three in a row which he missed on all five cards. This way he'd never win . . .

When he saw the row of holes punched across the third card, he sat paralyzed and heard the man call three more numbers before he stumbled forward, screaming,

"Bingo! Bingo!"

"Let that fool up there," someone called.

"Get up there, man!"

He stumbled down the aisle and up the steps to the stage into a light so sharp and bright that for a moment it blinded him, and he felt that he had moved into the spell of some strange, mysterious power. Yet it was as familiar as the sun, and he knew it was the perfectly familiar bingo.

The man with the microphone was saying something to the audience as he held out his card. A cold light flashed from the man's finger as the card left his hand. His knees trembled. The man stepped closer, checking the card against the numbers chalked on the board. Suppose he had made a mistake? The pomade on the man's hair made him feel faint, and he backed away. But the man was checking the card over the microphone now, and he had to stay. He stood tense, listening.

"Under the O, forty-four," the man chanted. "Under the I, seven. Under the G, three. Under the B, ninety-six. Under the N, thirteen!"

His breath came easier as the man smiled at the audience.

"Yessir, ladies and gentlemen, he's one of the chosen people!"

The audience rippled with laughter and applause.

"Step right up to the front of the stage."

He moved slowly forward, wishing that the light was not so bright.

"To win tonight's jackpot of $36.90 the wheel must stop between the double zero, understand?"

He nodded, knowing the ritual from the many days and nights he had watched the winners march across the stage to press the button that controlled the spinning wheel and receive the prizes. And now he followed the instructions as though he'd crossed the slippery stage a million prize-winning times.

The man was making some kind of a joke, and he nodded vacantly. So tense had he become that he felt a sudden desire to cry and shook it away. He felt vaguely that his whole life was determined by the bingo wheel; not only that which would happen now that he was at last before it, but all that had gone before, since his birth, and his mother's birth and the birth of his father. It had always been there, even though he had not been aware of it, handing out the unlucky cards and numbers of his days. The feeling persisted, and he started quickly away. I better get down from here before I make a fool of myself, he thought.

"Here, boy," the man called. "You haven't started yet."

Someone laughed as he went hesitantly back.

"Are you all reet?"

He grinned at the man's jive talk, but no words would come, and he knew it was not a convincing grin. For suddenly he knew that he stood on the slippery brink of some terrible embarrassment.

"Where you from boy?" the man asked.

"Down South."

"He's from down South, ladies and gentlemen," the man said. "Where from? Speak right into the mike."

"Rocky Mont," he said. "Rock' Mont, North Car'lina."

"So you decided to come down off that mountain to the U.S.," the man laughed. He felt that the man was making a fool of him, but then something cold was placed in his hand, and the lights were no longer behind him.

Standing before the wheel he felt alone, but that was somehow right, and he remembered his plan. He would give the wheel a short quick twirl. Just a touch of the button. He had watched it many times, and always it came close to double zero when it was short and quick. He steeled himself; the fear had left, and he felt a profound sense of promise, as though he were about to be repaid for all the things he'd suffered all his life. Trembling, he pressed the button. There was a whirl of lights, and in a second he realized with finality that though he wanted to, he could not stop. It was as though he held a high-powered line in his naked hand. His nerves tightened. As the wheel increased its speed it seemed to draw him more and more into its power, as though it held his fate; and with it came a deep need to submit, to whirl, to lose himself in its swirl of color. He could not stop it now, he knew. So let it be.

The button rested snugly in his palm where the man had placed it. And now he became aware of the man beside him, advising him through the microphone, while behind the shadowy audience hummed with noisy voices. He shifted his feet. There was still that feeling of helplessness within him, making part of him desire to turn back, even now that the jackpot was right in his hand. He squeezed the button until his fist ached. Then, like the sudden shriek of a subway whistle, a doubt tore through his head. Suppose he did not spin the wheel long enough? What could he do, and how could he tell? And then he knew, even as he wondered, that as long as he pressed the button, he could control the jackpot. He and only he could determine whether or not it was to be his. Not even the man with the microphone could do anything about it now. He felt drunk. Then, as though he had come down from a high hill into a valley of people, he heard the audience yelling.

"Come down from there, you jerk!"

"Let somebody else have a chance. . . ."

"Ole Jack thinks he done found the end of the rainbow. . . ."

The last voice was not unfriendly, and he turned and smiled dreamily into the yelling mouths. Then he turned his back squarely on them.

"Don't take too long, boy," a voice said.

He nodded. They were yelling behind him. Those folks did not understand what had happened to him. They had been playing the bingo game day and night for years, trying to win rent money or hamburger change. But not one of those wise guys had discovered this wonderful thing. He watched the wheel whirling past the numbers and experienced a burst of exaltation: This is God! This is the really truly God! He said it aloud, "This is God!"

He said it with such absolute conviction that he feared he would fall fainting into the footlights. But the crowd yelled so loud that they could not hear. These fools, he thought. I'm here trying to tell them the most wonderful secret in the world, and they're yelling like they gone crazy. A hand fell upon his shoulder.

"You'll have to make a choice now, boy. You've taken too long."

He brushed the hand violently away.

"Leave me alone, man. I know what I'm doing!"

The man looked surprised and held on to the microphone for support. And because he did not wish to hurt the man's feelings he smiled, realizing with a sudden pang that there was no way of explaining to the man just why he had to stand there pressing the button forever.

"Come here," he called tiredly.

The man approached, rolling the heavy microphone across the stage.

"Anybody can play this bingo game, right?" he said.

"Sure, but . . ."

He smiled, feeling inclined to be patient with this slick looking white man with his blue sport shirt and his sharp gabardine suit.

"That's what I thought," he said. "Anybody can win the jackpot as long as they get the lucky number, right?"

"That's the rule, but after all . . ."

"That's what I thought," he said. "And the big prize goes to the man who knows how to win it?"

The man nodded speechlessly.

"Well then, go on over there and watch me win like I want to. I ain't going to hurt nobody," he said, "and I'll show you how to win. I mean to show the whole world how it's got to be done."

And because he understood, he smiled again to let the man know that he held nothing against him for being white and impatient. Then he refused to see the man any longer and stood pressing the button, the voices of the crowd reaching him like sounds in distant streets. Let them yell. All the Negroes down there were just ashamed because he was black like them. He smiled inwardly, knowing how it was. Most of the time he was ashamed of what Negroes did himself. Well, let them be ashamed for something this time. Like him. He was like a long thin black wire that was being stretched and wound upon the bingo wheel; wound until he wanted to scream; wound, but this time himself controlling the winding and the sadness and the shame, and because he did, Laura would be all right. Suddenly the lights flickered. He staggered backwards. Had something gone wrong? All this noise. Didn't they know that although he controlled the wheel, it also controlled him, and unless he pressed the button forever and forever and ever it would stop, leaving him high and dry, dry and high on this hard high slippery hill and Laura dead? There was only one chance; he had to do whatever the wheel demanded. And gripping the button in despair, he discovered with surprise that it imparted a nervous energy. His spine tingled. He felt a certain power.

Now he faced the raging crowd with defiance, its screams penetrating his eardrums like trumpets shrieking from a juke-box. The vague faces glowing in the bingo lights gave him a sense of himself that he had never known before. He was running the show, by God! They had to read to him, for he was their luck. This is *me*, he thought. Let the bastards yell. Then someone was laughing inside him, and he realized that somehow he had forgotten his own name. It was a sad, lost feeling to lose your name, and a crazy thing to do. That name had been given him by the white man who had owned his grandfather a long time ago down South. But maybe those wise guys knew his name.

"Who am I?" he screamed.

"Hurry up and bingo, you jerk!"

They didn't know either, he thought sadly. They didn't even know their own names, they were all poor nameless bastards. Well, he didn't need that old name; he was reborn. For as long as he pressed the button he was The-man-who-pressed-the-button-who-held-the-prize-who-was-the-King-of-Bingo. That was the way it was, and he'd have to press the button even if nobody understood, even though Laura did not understand.

"Live!" he shouted.

The audience quieted like the dying of a huge fan.

"Live, Laura, baby. I got holt of it now, sugar. Live!"

He screamed it, tears streaming down his face. "I got nobody but you!"

The screams tore from his very guts. He felt as though the rush of blood to his head would burst out in baseball seams of small red droplets, like a head beaten by police clubs. Bending over he saw a trickle of blood splashing the toe of his shoe. With his free hand he searched his head. It was his nose. God, suppose something has gone wrong? He felt that the whole audience had somehow entered him and was stamping its feet in his stomach and he was unable to throw them out. They wanted the prize, that was it. They wanted the secret for themselves. But they'd never get it; he would keep the bingo wheel whirling forever, and Laura would be safe in the wheel. But would she? It had to be, because if she were not safe the wheel would cease to turn; it could not go on. He had to get away, *vomit* all, and his mind formed an image of himself running with Laura in his arms down the tracks of the subway just ahead of an A train, running desperately *vomit* with people screaming for him to come out but knowing no way of leaving the tracks because to stop would bring the train crushing down upon him and to attempt to leave across the other tracks would mean to run into a hot third rail as high as his waist which threw blue sparks that blinded his eyes until he could hardly see.

He heard singing and the audience was clapping its hands.

Shoot the liquor to him, Jim, boy!
Clap-clap-clap
Well a-calla the cop
He's blowing his top!
Shoot the liquor to him, Jim, boy!

Bitter anger grew within him at the singing. They think I'm crazy. Well let 'em laugh. I'll do what I got to do.

He was standing in an attitude of intense listening when he saw that they were watching something on the stage behind him. He felt weak. But when he turned he saw no one. If only his thumb did not ache so. Now they were applauding. And for a moment he thought that the wheel had stopped. But that was impossible, his thumb still pressed the button. Then he saw them. Two men in uniform beckoned from the end of the stage. They were coming toward him, walking in step, slowly, like a tap-dance team returning for a third encore. But their shoulders shot forward, and he backed away, looking wildly about. There was nothing to fight them with. He had only the long black cord which led to a plug somewhere back stage, and he couldn't use that because it operated the bingo wheel. He backed slowly, fixing the men with his eyes as his lips stretched over his teeth in a tight, fixed grin; moved toward the end of the stage and realizing that he couldn't go much further, for suddenly the cord became taut and he couldn't afford to break the cord. But he had to do something. The audience was howling. Suddenly he stopped dead, seeing the men halt, their legs lifted as in an interrupted step of a slow-motion dance. There was nothing to do but run in the other direction and he dashed forward, slipping and sliding. The men fell back, surprised. He struck out violently going past.

"Grab him!"

He ran, but all too quickly the cord tightened, resistingly, and he turned and ran back again. This time he slipped them, and discovered by running in a circle before the wheel he could keep the cord from tightening. But this way he had to flail his arms to keep the men away. Why couldn't they leave a man alone? He ran, circling.

"Ring down the curtain," someone yelled. But they couldn't do that. If they did the wheel flashing from the projection room would be cut off. But they had him before he could tell them so, trying to pry open his fist, and he was wrestling and trying to bring his knees into the fight and holding on to the button, for it was his life. And now he was down, seeing a foot coming down, crushing his wrist cruelly, down, as he saw the wheel whirling serenely above.

"I can't give it up," he screamed. Then quietly, in a confidential tone, "Boys, I really can't give it up."

It landed hard against his head. And in the blank moment they had it away from him, completely now. He fought them trying to pull him up from the stage as he watched the wheel spin slowly to a stop. Without surprise he saw it rest at double-zero.

"You see," he pointed bitterly.

"Sure, boy, sure, it's O.K.," one of the men said smiling.

And seeing the man bow his head to someone he could not see, he felt very, very happy; he would receive what all the winners received.

But as he warmed in the justice of the man's tight smile he did not see the man's slow wink, nor see the bow-legged man behind him step clear of the swiftly descending curtain and set himself for a blow. He only felt the dull pain exploding in his skull, and he knew even as it slipped out of him that his luck had run out on the stage.

QUESTIONS FOR DISCUSSION AND WRITING

1. How do the narrator's thoughts about the plot of the movie prepare us for the resolution of the plot of the story?
2. Why doesn't the character have a name? What does he represent? What is his major motive for all that he does in the story? How does that motive humanize him and thus add pathos to his final defeat?
3. How does the narrator contrast his home in the South with his new home in the North? How does the setting of the movie theater emphasize the central character's isolation?
4. How does the character's point of view toward the big wheel change once he holds the button? What secret does he discover?
5. What is significant about the end of the story? Does the character win? What is ironic about the wheel coming to rest on double-zero?

29

WILLIAM FAULKNER

A Rose for Emily

WILLIAM FAULKNER (1897–1962) was born in New Albany, Mississippi, but soon moved to Oxford, Mississippi, where his father worked as the business manager of the University of Mississippi. Faulkner left high school to work in a local bank and then in 1918 enlisted in the Royal Canadian Air Force, before returning for a brief period to study at the University of Mississippi. During the early twenties, Faulkner began writing poetry and fiction and became acquainted with various members of the literary community in New Orleans, most notably Sherwood Anderson, who encouraged his endeavors. In 1929 Faulkner published *Sartoris,* the first of his novels dealing with the life and legends of Yoknapatawpha, an imaginary county in Mississippi. Although Faulkner wrote novels about this county at an astonishing pace—*The Sound and the Fury* (1929), *As I Lay Dying* (1930), *Light in August* (1932), *Absalom, Absalom* (1936), *The Hamlet* (1940), *Go*

Down, Moses (1942)—and although he published his short stories in such commercially recognized magazines as *The Saturday Evening Post,* his literary reputation during this period was negligible. Faulkner's need for money forced him to accept many off-and-on assignments as a screen writer in Hollywood, working on such films as *To Have and Have Not* and *The Big Sleep.* Faulkner was finally recognized as a major literary talent when he was awarded the Nobel Prize in 1949. He continued to produce novels such as *The Town* (1957), *The Mansion* (1959), and *The Reivers* (1963), and collected many of his stories in a 1950 volume that won the National Book Award. The following stories, reprinted from that volume, deal with various aspects of life in Yoknapatawpha. "A Rose for Emily" is a community's account of the life of one of its oldest citizens. "Barn Burning" describes the complex social and psychological causes that lead the father of a poor family to commit acts of revenge.

1

When Miss Emily Grierson died, our whole town went to her funeral: the men through a sort of respectful affection for a fallen monument, the women mostly out of curiosity to see the inside of her house, which no one save an old manservant—a combined gardener and cook—had seen in at least ten years.

It was a big, squarish frame house that had once been white, decorated with cupolas and spires and scrolled balconies in the heavily lightsome style of the seventies, set on what had once been our most select street. But garages and cotton gins had encroached and obliterated even the august names of that neighborhood; only Miss Emily's house was left, lifting its stubborn and coquettish decay above the cotton wagons and the gasoline pumps—an eyesore among eyesores. And now Miss Emily had gone to join the representatives of those august names where they lay in the cedar-bemused cemetery among the ranked and anonymous graves of Union and Confederate soldiers who fell at the battle of Jefferson.

Alive, Miss Emily had been a tradition, a duty, and a care; a sort of hereditary obligation upon the town, dating from that day in 1894 when Colonel Sartoris, the mayor—he who fathered the edict that no Negro woman should appear on the streets without an apron—remitted her taxes, the dispensation dating from the death of her father on into perpetuity. Not that Miss Emily would have accepted charity. Colonel Sartoris invented an involved tale to the effect that Miss Emily's father had loaned money to the town, which the town, as a matter of business, preferred this way of repaying. Only a man of Colonel Sartoris' generation and thought could have invented it, and only a woman could have believed it.

When the next generation, with its more modern ideas, became mayors and aldermen, this arrangement created some little dissatisfaction. On the first of the year they mailed her a tax notice. February came, and there was no reply. They wrote her a formal letter, asking her to call at the sheriff's office at her convenience. A week later the mayor wrote her himself, offering to call or to send his car for her, and received in reply a note on paper of an archaic shape, in a thin, flowing calligraphy in faded ink, to the effect that she no longer went out at all. The tax notice was also enclosed, without comment.

They called a special meeting of the Board of Aldermen. A deputation waited upon her, knocked at the door through which no visitor had passed since she ceased giving china-painting lessons eight or ten years earlier. They were admitted by the old Negro into a dim hall from which a stairway mounted into still more shadow. It smelled of dust and disuse—a close, dank smell. The Negro led them into the parlor. It was furnished in heavy, leather-covered furniture. When the Negro opened the blinds of one window, they could see that the leather was cracked; and when they sat down, a faint dust rose sluggishly about their thighs, spinning with slow motions in the single sun-ray. On a tarnished gilt easel before the fireplace stood a crayon portrait of Miss Emily's father.

They rose when she entered—a small, fat woman in black, with a thin gold chain descending to her waist and vanishing into her belt, leaning on an ebony cane with a tarnished gold head. Her skeleton was small and spare; perhaps that was why what would have been merely plumpness in another was obesity in her. She looked bloated, like a body long submerged in motionless water, and of that pallid hue. Her eyes, lost in the fatty ridges of her face, looked like two small pieces of coal pressed into a lump of dough as they moved from one face to another while the visitors stated their errand.

She did not ask them to sit. She just stood in the door and listened quietly until the spokesman came to a stumbling halt. Then they could hear the invisible watch ticking at the end of the gold chain.

Her voice was dry and cold. "I have no taxes in Jefferson. Colonel Sartoris explained it to me. Perhaps one of you can gain access to the city records and satisfy yourselves."

"But we have. We are the city authorities, Miss Emily. Didn't you get a notice from the sheriff, signed by him?"

"I received a paper, yes," Miss Emily said. "Perhaps he considers himself the sheriff . . . I have no taxes in Jefferson."

"But there is nothing on the books to show that, you see. We must go by the—"

"See Colonel Sartoris." (Colonel Sartoris had been dead almost ten years.) "I have no taxes in Jefferson. Tobe!" The Negro appeared. "Show these gentlemen out."

2

So she vanquished them, horse and foot, just as she had vanquished their fathers thirty years before about the smell. That was two years after her father's death and a short time after her sweetheart—the one we believed would marry her—had deserted her. After her father's death she went out very little; after her sweetheart went away, people hardly saw her at all. A few of the ladies had the temerity to call, but were not received, and the only sign of life about the place was the Negro man—a young man then—going in and out with a market basket.

"Just as if a man—any man—could keep a kitchen properly," the ladies said; so they were not surprised when the smell developed. It was another link between the gross, teeming world and the high and mighty Griersons.

A neighbor, a woman, complained to the mayor, Judge Stevens, eighty years old.

"But what will you have me do about it, madam?" he said.

"Why, send her word to stop it," the woman said. "Isn't there a law?"

"I'm sure that won't be necessary," Judge Stevens said. "It's probably just a snake or a rat that nigger of hers killed in the yard. I'll speak to him about it."

The next day he received two more complaints, one from a man who came in diffident deprecation. "We really must do something about it, Judge. I'd be the last one in the world to bother Miss Emily, but we've got to do something." That night the Board of Aldermen met—three graybeards and one younger man, a member of the rising generation.

"It's simple enough," he said. "Send her word to have her place cleaned up. Give her a certain time to do it in, and if she don't . . ."

"Dammit, sir," Judge Stevens said, "will you accuse a lady to her face of smelling bad?"

So the next night, after midnight, four men crossed Miss Emily's lawn and slunk about the house like burglars, sniffing along the base of the brickwork and at the cellar openings while one of them performed a regular sowing motion with his hand out of a sack slung from his shoulder. They broke open the cellar door and sprinkled lime there, and in all the outbuildings. As they recrossed the lawn, a window that had been dark was lighted and Miss Emily sat in it, the light behind her, and her upright torso motionless as that of an idol. They crept quietly across the lawn and into the shadow of the locusts that lined the street. After a week or two the smell went away.

That was when people had begun to feel really sorry for her. People in our town, remembering how old lady Wyatt, her great-aunt, had gone completely crazy at last, believed that the Griersons held themselves a little too high for what they really were. None of the young men were quite good enough for Miss Emily and such. We had long thought of them as a tableau, Miss Emily a slender figure in white in the background, her father a spraddled silhouette in the foreground, his back to her and clutching a horsewhip, the two of them framed by the back-flung front door. So when she got to be thirty and was still single, we were not pleased exactly, but vindicated; even with insanity in the family she wouldn't have turned down all of her chances if they had really materialized.

When her father died, it got about that the house was all that was left to her; and in a way, people were glad. At last they could pity Miss Emily. Being left alone, and a pauper, she had become humanized. Now she too would know the old thrill and the old despair of a penny more or less.

The day after his death all the ladies prepared to call at the house and offer condolence and aid, as is our custom. Miss Emily met them at the door, dressed as usual and with no trace of grief on her face. She told them that her father was not dead. She did that for three days, with the ministers calling on her, and the doctors, trying to persuade her to let them dispose of the body. Just as they were about to resort to law and force, she broke down, and they buried her father quickly.

We did not say she was crazy then. We believed she had to do that. We remembered all the young men her father had driven away, and we knew that with nothing left, she would have to cling to that which had robbed her, as people will.

3

She was sick for a long time. When we saw her again, her hair was cut short, making her look like a girl, with a vague resemblance to those angels in colored church windows—sort of tragic and serene.

The town had just let the contracts for paving the sidewalks, and in the summer after her father's death they began the work. The construction company came with niggers and mules and machinery, and a foreman named Homer Barron, a Yankee—a big, dark, ready man, with a big voice and eyes lighter than his face. The little boys would follow in groups to hear him cuss the niggers, and the niggers singing in time to the rise and fall of picks. Pretty soon he knew everybody in town. Whenever you heard a lot of laughing anywhere about the square, Homer Barron would be in the center of the group. Presently we began to see him and Miss Emily on Sunday afternoons driving in the yellow-wheeled buggy and the matched team of bays from the livery stable.

At first we were glad that Miss Emily would have an interest, because the ladies all said, "Of course a Grierson would not think seriously of a Northerner, a day laborer." But there were still others, older people, who said that even grief could not cause a real lady to forget *noblesse oblige*—without calling it *noblesse oblige.* They just said, "Poor Emily. Her kinsfolk should come to her." She had some kin in Alabama; but years ago her father had fallen out with them over the estate of old lady Wyatt, the crazy woman, and there was no communication between the two families. They had not even been represented at the funeral.

And as soon as the old people said, "Poor Emily," the whispering began. "Do you suppose it's really so?" they said to one another. "Of course it is. What else could . . ." This behind their hands; rustling of craned silk and satin behind jalousies closed upon the sun of Sunday afternoon as the thin, swift clop-clop-clop of the matched team passed: "Poor Emily."

She carried her head high enough—even when we believed that she was fallen. It was as if she demanded more than ever the recognition of her dignity as the last Grierson; as if it had wanted that touch of earthiness to reaffirm her imperviousness. Like when she bought the rat poison, the arsenic. That was over a year after they had begun to say "Poor Emily," and while the two female cousins were visiting her.

"I want some poison," she said to the druggist. She was over thirty then, still a slight woman, though thinner than usual, with cold, haughty black eyes in a face the flesh of which was strained across the temples and about the eye-sockets as you imagine a lighthouse-keeper's face ought to look. "I want some poison," she said.

"Yes, Miss Emily. What kind? For rats and such? I'd recom—"

"I want the best you have. I don't care what kind."

The druggist named several. "They'll kill anything up to an elephant. But what you want is—"

"Arsenic," Miss Emily said. "Is that a good one?"

"Is . . . arsenic? Yes, ma'am. But what you want—"

"I want arsenic."

The druggist looked down at her. She looked back at him, erect, her face like a strained flag. "Why, of course," the druggist said. "If that's what you want. But the law requires you to tell what you are going to use it for."

Miss Emily just stared at him, her head tilted back in order to look him eye for eye, until he looked away and went and got the arsenic and wrapped it up. The Negro delivery boy brought her the package; the druggist didn't come back. When she opened the package at home there was written on the box, under the skull and bones: "For rats."

4

So the next day we all said, "She will kill herself"; and we said it would be the best thing. When she had first begun to be seen with Homer Barron, we had said, "She will marry him." Then we said, "She will persuade him yet," because Homer himself had remarked—he liked men, and it was known that he drank with the younger men in the Elks' Club—that he was not a marrying man. Later we said, "Poor Emily" behind the jalousies as they passed on Sunday afternoon in the glittering buggy, Miss Emily with her head high and Homer Barron with his hat cocked and a cigar in his teeth, reins and whip in a yellow glove.

Then some of the ladies began to say that it was a disgrace to the town and a bad example to the young people. The men did not want to interfere, but at last the ladies forced the Baptist minister—Miss Emily's people were Episcopal—to call upon her. He would never divulge what happened during that interview, but he refused to go back again. The next Sunday they again drove about the streets, and the following day the minister's wife wrote to Miss Emily's relations in Alabama.

So she had blood-kin under her roof again and we sat back to watch developments. At first nothing happened. Then we were sure that they were to be married. We learned that Miss Emily had been to the jeweler's and ordered a man's toilet set in silver, with the letters H.B. on each piece. Two days later we learned that she had bought a complete outfit of men's clothing, including a nightshirt, and we said, "They are married." We were really glad. We were glad because the two female cousins were even more Grierson than Miss Emily had ever been.

So we were not surprised when Homer Barron—the streets had been finished some time since—was gone. We were a little disappointed that there was not a public blowing-off, but we believed that he had gone on to prepare for Miss Emily's coming, or to give her a chance to get rid of the cousins. (By that time it was a cabal, and we were all Miss Emily's allies to help circumvent the cousins.) Sure enough, after another week they departed. And, as we had expected all along, within three days Homer Barron was back in town. A neighbor saw the Negro man admit him at the kitchen door at dusk one evening.

And that was the last we saw of Homer Barron. And of Miss Emily for some time. The Negro man went in and out with the market basket, but the front door remained closed. Now and then we would see her at a window for a moment, as the men did that night when they sprinkled the lime, but for almost six months she did not appear on the streets. Then we knew that this was to be expected too; as if that quality of her father which had thwarted her woman's life so many times had been too virulent and too furious to die.

When we next saw Miss Emily, she had grown fat and her hair was turning gray. During the next few years it grew grayer and grayer until it attained an even pepper-and-salt iron-gray, when it ceased turning. Up to the day of her death at seventy-four it was still that vigorous iron-gray, like the hair of an active man.

From that time on her front door remained closed, save for a period of six or seven years, when she was about forty, during which she gave lessons in china-painting. She fitted up a studio in one of the downstairs rooms, where the daughters and granddaughters of Colonel Sartoris' contemporaries were sent to her with the same regularity and in the same spirit that they were sent to church on Sundays with a twenty-five-cent piece for the collection plate. Meanwhile her taxes had been remitted.

Then the newer generation became the backbone and the spirit of the town, and the painting pupils grew up and fell away and did not send their children to her with boxes of color and tedious brushes and pictures cut from the ladies' magazines. The front door closed upon the last one and remained closed for good. When the town got free postal delivery, Miss Emily alone refused to let them fasten the metal numbers above her door and attach a mailbox to it. She would not listen to them.

Daily, monthly, yearly we watched the Negro grow grayer and more stooped, going in and out with the market basket. Each December we sent her a tax notice, which would be returned by the post office a week later, unclaimed. Now and then we would see her in one of the downstairs windows—she had evidently shut up the top floor of the house—like the carven torso of an idol in a niche, looking or not looking at us, we could never tell which. Thus she passed from generation to generation—dear, inescapable, impervious, tranquil, and perverse.

And so she died. Fell ill in the house filled with dust and shadows, with only a doddering Negro man to wait on her. We did not even know she was sick; we had long since given up trying to get any information from the Negro. He talked to no one, probably not even to her, for his voice had grown harsh and rusty, as if from disuse.

She died in one of the downstairs rooms, in a heavy walnut bed with a curtain, her gray head propped on a pillow yellow and moldy with age and lack of sunlight.

5

The Negro met the first of the ladies at the front door and let them in, with their hushed, sibilant voices and their quick, curious glances, and then he disappeared. He walked right through the house and out the back and was not seen again.

The two female cousins came at once. They held the funeral on the second day, with the town coming to look at Miss Emily beneath a mass of bought flowers, with the crayon face of her father musing profoundly above the bier and the ladies sibilant and macabre; and the very old men—some in their brushed Confederate uniforms—on the porch and the lawn, talking of Miss Emily as if she had been a contemporary of theirs, believing that they had danced with her and courted her perhaps, confusing time with its mathematical progression, as the old do, to whom all the past is not a diminishing road but, instead, a huge meadow which no winter ever quite touches, divided from them now by the narrow bottle-neck of the most recent decade of years.

Already we knew that there was one room in that region above stairs which no one had seen in forty years, and which would have to be forced. They waited until Miss Emily was decently in the ground before they opened it.

The violence of breaking down the door seemed to fill this room with pervading dust. A thin, acrid pall as of the tomb seemed to lie everywhere upon this room decked and furnished as for a bridal: upon the valance curtains of faded rose color, upon the rose-shaded lights, upon the dressing table, upon the delicate array of crystal and the man's toilet things backed with tarnished silver, silver so tarnished that the monogram was obscured. Among them lay a collar and tie, as if they had just been removed, which, lifted, left upon the surface a pale crescent in the dust. Upon a chair hung the suit, carefully folded; beneath it the two mute shoes and the discarded socks.

The man himself lay in the bed.

For a long while we just stood there, looking down at the profound and fleshless grin. The body had apparently once lain in the attitude of an embrace, but now the long sleep that outlasts love, that conquers even the grimace of love, had cuckolded him. What was left of him, rotted beneath what was left of the nightshirt, had become inextricable from the bed in which he lay; and upon him and upon the pillow beside him lay that even coating of the patient and biding dust.

Then we noticed that in the second pillow was the indentation of a head. One of us lifted something from it, and leaning forward, that faint and invisible dust dry and acrid in the nostrils, we saw a long strand of iron-gray hair.

QUESTIONS FOR DISCUSSION AND WRITING

1. Why is the story not told in a strictly chronological order? What is the logic in the ordering of events? How does the revelation in part 5 change our attitude toward the information presented in the other parts?
2. How does the town characterize Emily? Why does it both resent and pity her? How does it characterize Homer Barron?
3. How is the setting for this story revealed in the actions of its various citizens? How does the description of Emily's house help us understand her actions?
4. Who is the narrator of the story? How does "the town" gather its information? What will the town never know?
5. What themes are suggested by the title of this story? What does a rose traditionally symbolize? How is that meaning ironically twisted by the situation and characters of the story?

30

WILLIAM FAULKNER

Barn Burning

The store in which the Justice of the Peace's court was sitting smelled of cheese. The boy, crouched on his nail keg at the back of the crowded room, knew he smelled cheese, and more: from where he sat he could see the ranked shelves close-packed with the solid, squat, dynamic shapes of tin cans whose labels his stomach read, not from the lettering which meant nothing to his mind but from the scarlet devils and the silver curve of fish—this, the cheese which he knew he smelled and the hermetic meat which his intestines believed he smelled coming in intermittent gusts momentary and brief between the other constant one, the smell and sense just a little of fear because mostly of despair and grief, the old fierce pull of blood. He could not see the table where the Justice sat and before which his father and his father's enemy (*our enemy* he thought in that despair; *ourn! mine and hisn both! He's my father!*) stood, but he could hear them, the two of them that is, because his father had said no word yet:

"But what proof have you, Mr. Harris?"

"I told you. The hog got into my corn. I caught it up and sent it back to him. He had no fence that would hold it. I told him so, warned him. The next time I put the hog in my pen. When he came to get it I gave him enough wire to patch up his pen. The next time I put the hog up and kept it. I rode down to his house and saw the wire I gave him still rolled on to the spool in his yard. I told him he could have the hog when he paid me a dollar pound fee. That evening a nigger came with the dollar and got the hog. He was a strange nigger. He said, 'He say to tell you wood and hay kin burn.' I said, 'What?' 'That whut he say to tell you,' the nigger said. 'Wood and hay kin burn.' That night my barn burned. I got the stock out but I lost the barn."

"Where is the nigger? Have you got him?"

"He was a strange nigger, I tell you. I don't know what became of him."

"But that's not proof. Don't you see that's not proof?"

"Get that boy up here. He knows." For a moment the boy thought too that the man meant his older brother until Harris said, "Not him. The little one. The boy," and, crouching, small for his age, small and wiry like his father, in patched and faded jeans even too small for him, with straight, uncombed, brown hair and eyes gray and wild as storm scud, he saw the men between himself and the table part and become a lane of grim faces, at the end of which he saw the Justice, a shabby, collarless, graying man in spectacles, beckoning him. He felt no floor under his bare feet; he seemed to walk beneath the palpable weight of the grim turning faces. His father, stiff in his black Sunday coat donned not for the trial but for the moving, did not even look at him. *He aims for me to lie,* he thought, again with that frantic grief and despair. *And I will have to do hit.*

"What's your name, boy?" the Justice said.

"Colonel Sartoris Snopes," the boy whispered.

"Hey?" the Justice said. "Talk louder. Colonel Sartoris? I reckon anybody named for Colonel Sartoris in this country can't help but tell the truth, can they?" The boy said nothing. *Enemy! Enemy!* he thought; for a moment he could not even see, could not see that the Justice's face was kindly nor discern that his voice was troubled when he spoke to the man named Harris: "Do you want me to question this boy?" But he could hear, and during those subsequent long seconds while there was absolutely no sound in the crowded little room save that of quiet and intent breathing it was as if he had swung outward at the end of a grape vine, over a ravine, and at the top of the swing had been caught in a prolonged instant of mesmerized gravity, weightless in time.

"No!" Harris said violently, explosively. "Damnation! Send him out of here!" Now time, the fluid world, rushed beneath him again, the voices coming to him again through the smell of cheese and sealed meat, the fear and despair and the old grief of blood:

"This case is closed. I can't find against you, Snopes, but I can give you advice. Leave this country and don't come back to it."

His father spoke for the first time, his voice cold and harsh, level, without emphasis: "I aim to. I don't figure to stay in a country among people who . . ." he said something unprintable and vile, addressed to no one.

"That'll do," the Justice said. "Take your wagon and get out of this country before dark. Case dismissed."

His father turned, and he followed the stiff black coat, the wiry figure walking a little stiffly from where a Confederate provost's man's musket ball had taken him in the heel on a stolen horse thirty years ago, followed the two backs now, since his older brother had appeared from somewhere in the crowd, no taller than the father but thicker, chewing tobacco steadily, between the two lines of grim-faced men and out of the store and across the worn gallery and down the sagging steps and among the dogs and half-grown boys in the mild May dust, where as he passed a voice hissed:

"Barn burner!"

Again he could not see, whirling; there was a face in a red haze, moonlike, bigger than the full moon, the owner of it half again his size, he leaping in the red haze toward the face, feeling no blow, feeling no shock when his head struck the earth, scrabbling up and leaping again, feeling no blow this time either and tasting no blood, scrabbling up to see the other boy in full flight and himself already leaping into pursuit as his father's hand jerked him back, the harsh, cold voice speaking above him: "Go get in the wagon."

It stood in a grove of locusts and mulberries across the road. His two hulking sisters in their Sunday dresses and his mother and her sister in calico and sunbonnets were already in it, sitting on and among the sorry residue of the dozen and more movings which even the boy could remember—and battered stove, the broken beds and chairs, the clock inlaid with mother-of-pearl, which would not run, stopped at some fourteen minutes past two o'clock of a dead and forgotten day and time, which had been his mother's dowry. She was crying, though when she saw him she drew her sleeve across her face and began to descend from the wagon. "Get back," the father said.

"He's hurt. I got to get some water and wash his . . ."

"Get back in the wagon," his father said. He got in too, over the tail-gate. His father mounted to the seat where the older brother already sat and struck the gaunt mules two savage blows with the peeled willow, but without heat. It was not even sadistic; it was exactly that same quality which in later years would cause his descendants to over-run the engine before putting a motor car into motion, striking and reining back in the same movement. The wagon went on, the store with its quiet crowd of grimly watching men dropped behind; a curve in the road hid it. *Forever* he thought. *Maybe he's done satisfied now, now that he has . . .* stopping himself, not to say it aloud even to himself. His mother's hand touched his shoulder.

"Does hit hurt?" she said.

"Naw," he said. "Hit don't hurt. Lemme be."

"Can't you wipe some of the blood off before hit dries?"

"I'll wash to-night," he said. "Lemme be, I tell you."

The wagon went on. He did not know where they were going. None of them ever did or ever asked, because it was always somewhere, always a house of sorts waiting for them a day or two days or even three days away. Likely his father had already arranged to make a crop on another farm before he . . . Again he had to stop himself. He (the father) always did. There was something about his wolflike independence and even courage when the advantage was at least neutral which impressed strangers, as if they got from his latent ravening ferocity not so much a sense of dependability as a feeling that his ferocious conviction in the rightness of his own actions would be of advantage to all whose interest lay with his.

That night they camped, in a grove of oaks and beeches where a spring ran. The nights were still cool and they had a fire against it, of a rail lifted from a nearby fence and cut into lengths—a small fire, neat, niggard almost, a shrewd fire; such fires were his father's habit and custom always, even in freezing weather. Older, the boy might have remarked this and wondered why not a big one; why should not a man who had not only seen the waste and extravagance of war, but who had in his blood an inherent voracious prodigality with material not his own, have burned everything in sight? Then he might have gone a step farther and thought that that was the reason: that niggard blaze was the living fruit of nights passed during those four years in the woods hiding from all men, blue or gray, with his strings of horses (captured horses, he called them). And older still, he might have divined the true reason: that the element of fire spoke to some deep mainspring of his father's being, as the element of steel or of powder spoke to other men, as the one weapon for the preservation of integrity, else breath were not worth the breathing, and hence to be regarded with respect and used with discretion.

But he did not think this now and he had seen those same niggard blazes all his life. He merely ate his supper beside it and was already half asleep over his iron plate when his father called him, and once more he followed the stiff back, the stiff and ruthless limp, up the slope and on to the starlit road where, turning, he could see his father against the stars but without face or depth—a shape black, flat, and bloodless as though cut from tin in the iron folds of the frockcoat which had not been made for him, the voice harsh like tin and without heat like tin:

"You were fixing to tell him. You would have told him." He didn't answer. His father struck him with the flat of his hand on the side of the head, hard but without heat, exactly as he had struck the two mules at the store, exactly as he would strike either of them with any stick in order to kill a horse fly, his voice still without heat or anger: "You're getting to be a man. You got to learn. You got to learn to stick to your own blood or you ain't going to have any blood to stick to you. Do you think either of them, any man there this morning, would? Don't you know all they wanted was a chance to get at me because they knew I had them beat? Eh?" Later, twenty years later, he was to tell himself, "If I said they wanted only truth, justice, he would have hit me again." But now he said nothing. He was not crying. He just stood there. "Answer me," his father said.

"Yes," he whispered. His father turned.

"Get on to bed. We'll be there to-morrow."

To-morrow they were there. In the early afternoon the wagon stopped before a paintless two-room house identical almost with the dozen others it had stopped before even in the boy's ten years, and again, as on the other dozen occasions, his mother and aunt got down and began to unload the wagon, although his two sisters and his father and brother had not moved.

"Likely hit ain't fitten for hawgs," one of the sisters said.

"Nevertheless, fit it will and you'll hog it and like it," his father said. "Get out of them chairs and help your Ma unload."

The two sisters got down, big, bovine, in a flutter of cheap ribbons; one of them drew from the jumbled wagon bed a battered lantern, the other a worn broom. His father handed the reins to the older son and began to climb stiffly over the wheel. "When they get unloaded, take the team to the barn and feed them." Then he said, and at first the boy thought he was still speaking to his brother: "Come with me."

"Me?" he said.

"Yes," his father said. "You."

"Abner," his mother said. His father paused and looked back—the harsh level stare beneath the shaggy, graying, irascible brows.

"I reckon I'll have a word with the man that aims to begin to-morrow owning me body and soul for the next eight months."

They went back up the road. A week ago—or before last night, that is—he would have asked where they were going, but not now. His father had struck him before last night but never before had he paused afterward to explain why; it was as if the blow and the following calm, outrageous voice still rang, repercussed, divulging nothing to him save the terrible handicap of being young, the light weight of his few years, just heavy enough to prevent his soaring free of the world as it seemed to be ordered but not heavy enough to keep him footed solid in it, to resist it and try to change the course of its events.

Presently he could see the grove of oaks and cedars and the other flowering trees and shrubs where the house would be, though not the house yet. They walked beside a fence massed with honeysuckle and Cherokee roses and came to a gate swinging open between two brick pillars, and now, beyond a sweep of drive, he saw the house for the first time and at that instant he forgot his father and the terror and despair both, and even when he remembered his father again (who had not stopped) the terror and despair did not return. Because, for all the twelve movings, they had sojourned until now in a poor country, a land of small farms and fields and houses, and he had never seen a house like this before. *Hit's big as a courthouse* he thought quietly, with a surge of peace and joy whose reason he could not have thought into words, being too young for that: *They are safe from him. People whose lives are a part of this peace and dignity are beyond his touch, he no more to them than a buzzing wasp: capable of stinging for a little moment but that's all; the spell of this peace and dignity rendering even the barns and stable and cribs which belong to it impervious to the puny flames he might contrive* . . . this, the peace and joy, ebbing for an instant as he looked again at the stiff black back, the stiff and implacable limp of the figure which was not dwarfed by the house, for the reason that it had never looked big anywhere and which now, against the serene columned backdrop, had more than ever that impervious quality of something cut ruthlessly from tin, depthless, as though, sidewise to the sun, it would cast no shadow. Watching him, the boy remarked the absolutely undeviating course which his father held and saw the stiff foot come squarely down in a pile of fresh droppings where a horse had stood in the drive and which his father could have avoided by a simple change of stride. But it ebbed only for a moment, though he could not have thought this into words either, walking on in the spell of the house, which he could even want but without envy, without sorrow, certainly never with that ravening and jealous rage which unknown to him walked in the ironlike black coat before him: *Maybe he will feel it too. Maybe it will even change him now from what maybe he couldn't help but be.*

They crossed the portico. Now he could hear his father's stiff foot as it came down on the boards with clocklike finality, a sound out of all proportion to the displacement of the body it bore and which was not dwarfed either by the white door before it, as though it had attained to a sort of vicious and ravening minimum not to be dwarfed by anything—the flat, wide, black hat, the formal coat of broadcloth which had once been black but which had now that friction-glazed greenish cast of the bodies of old house flies, the lifted sleeve which was too large, the lifted hand like a curled claw. The door opened so promptly that the boy knew the Negro must have been watching them all the time, an old man with neat grizzled hair, in a linen jacket, who stood barring the door with his body, saying, "Wipe yo foots, white man, fo you come in here. Major ain't home nohow."

"Get out of my way, nigger," his father said, without heat too, flinging the door back and the Negro also and entering, his hat still on his head. And now the boy saw the prints of the stiff foot on the doorjamb and saw them appear on the pale rug behind the machinelike deliberation of the foot which seemed to bear (or transmit) twice the weight which the body compassed. The Negro was shouting "Miss Lula! Miss Lula!" somewhere behind them, then the boy, deluged as though by a warm wave by a suave turn of carpeted stairs and a pendant glitter of chandeliers and a mute gleam of gold frames, heard the swift feet and saw her too, a lady—perhaps he had never seen her like before either—in a gray, smooth gown with lace at the throat and an apron tied at the waist and the sleeves turned back, wiping cake or biscuit dough from her hands with a towel as she came up the hall, looking not at his father at all but at the tracks on the blond rug with an expression of incredulous amazement.

"I tried," the Negro cried. "I tole him to . . ."

"Will you please go away?" she said in a shaking voice. "Major de Spain is not at home. Will you please go away?"

His father had not spoken again. He did not speak again. He did not even look at her. He just stood stiff in the center of the rug, in his hat, the shaggy iron-gray brows twitching slightly above the pebble-colored eyes as he appeared to examine the house with brief deliberation. Then with the same deliberation he turned; the boy watched him pivot on the good leg and saw the stiff foot drag round the arc of the turning, leaving a final long and fading smear. His father never looked at it, he never once looked down at the rug. The Negro held the door. It closed behind them, upon the hysteric and indistinguishable woman-wail. His father stopped at the top of the steps and scraped his boot clean on the edge of it. At the gate he stopped again. He stood for a moment, planted stiffly on the stiff foot, looking back at the house. "Pretty and white, ain't it?" he said. "That's sweat. Nigger sweat. Maybe it ain't white enough yet to suit him. Maybe he wants to mix some white sweat with it."

Two hours later the boy was chopping wood behind the house within which his mother and aunt and the two sisters (the mother and aunt, not the two girls, he knew that; even at this distance and muffled by walls the flat loud voices of the two girls emanated an incorrigible idle inertia) were setting up the stove to prepare a meal, when he heard the hooves and saw the linen-clad man on a fine sorrel mare, whom he recognized even before he saw the rolled rug in front of the Negro youth following on a fat bay carriage horse—a suffused, angry face vanishing, still at full gallop, beyond the corner of the house where his father and brother were sitting in the two tilted chairs; and a moment later, almost before he could have put the axe down, he heard the hooves again and watched the sorrel mare go back out of the yard, already galloping again. Then his father began to shout one of the sisters' names, who presently emerged backward from the kitchen door dragging the rolled rug along the ground by one end while the other sister walked behind it.

"If you ain't going to tote, go on and set up the wash pot," the first said.

"You, Sarty!" the second shouted. "Set up the wash pot!" His father appeared at the door, framed against that shabbiness, as he had been against that other bland perfection, impervious to either, the mother's anxious face at his shoulder.

"Go on," the father said. "Pick it up." The two sisters stooped, broad, lethargic; stooping, they presented an incredible expanse of pale cloth and a flutter of tawdry ribbons.

"If I thought enough of a rug to have to git hit all the way from France I wouldn't keep hit where folks coming in would have to tromp on hit," the first said. They raised the rug.

"Abner," the mother said. "Let me do it."

"You go back and git dinner," his father said. "I'll tend to this."

From the woodpile through the rest of the afternoon the boy watched them, the rug spread flat in the dust beside the bubbling wash-pot, the two sisters stooping over it with that profound and lethargic reluctance, while the father stood over them in turn, implacable and grim, driving them though never raising his voice again. He could smell the harsh homemade lye they were using; he saw his mother come to the door once and look toward them with an expression not anxious now but very like despair; he saw his father turn, and he fell to with the axe and saw from the corner of his eye his father raise from the ground a flattish fragment of field stone and examine it and return to the pot, and this time his mother actually spoke: "Abner. Abner. Please don't. Please, Abner."

Then he was done too. It was dusk; the whippoorwills had already begun. He could smell coffee from the room where they would presently eat the cold food remaining from the mid-afternoon meal, though when he entered the house he realized they were having coffee again probably because there was a fire on the hearth, before which the rug now lay spread over the backs of the two chairs. The tracks of his father's foot were gone. Where they had been were now long, water-cloudy scoriations resembling the sporadic course of a lilliputian mowing machine.

It still hung there while they ate the cold food and then went to bed, scattered without order or claim up and down the two rooms, his mother in one bed, where his father would later lie, the older brother in the other, himself, the aunt, and the two sisters on pallets on the floor. But his father was not in bed yet. The last thing the boy remembered was the depthless, harsh silhouette of the hat and coat bending over the rug and it seemed to him that he had not even closed his eyes when the silhouette was standing over him, the fire almost dead behind it, the stiff foot prodding him awake. "Catch up the mule," his father said.

When he returned with the mule his father was standing in the back door, the rolled rug over his shoulder. "Ain't you going to ride?" he said.

"No. Give me your foot."

He bent his knee into his father's hand, the wiry, surprising power flowed smoothly, rising, he rising with it, on to the mule's bare back (they had owned a saddle once; the boy could remember it though not when or where) and with the same effortlessness his father swung the rug up in front of him. Now in the starlight they retraced the afternoon's path, up the dusty road rife with honeysuckle, through the gate and up the black tunnel of the drive to the lightless house, where he sat on the mule and felt the rough warp of the rug drag across his thighs and vanish.

"Don't you want me to help?" he whispered. His father did not answer and now he heard again that stiff foot striking the hollow portico with that wooden and clocklike deliberation, that outrageous overstatement of the weight it carried. The rug, hunched, not flung (the boy could tell that even in the darkness) from his father's shoulder struck the angle of wall and floor with a sound unbelievably loud, thunderous, then the foot again, unhurried and enormous; a light came on in the house and the boy sat, tense, breathing steadily and quietly and just a little fast, though the foot itself did not increase its beat at all, descending the steps now; now the boy could see him.

"Don't you want to ride now?" he whispered. "We kin both ride now," the light within the house altering now, flaring up and sinking. *He's coming down the stairs now,* he thought. He had already ridden the mule up beside the horse block; presently his father was up behind him and he doubled the reins over and slashed the mule across the neck, but before the animal could begin to trot the hard, thin arm came round him, the hard, knotted hand jerking the mule back to a walk.

In the first red rays of the sun they were in the lot, putting plow gear on the mules. This time the sorrel mare was in the lot before he heard it at all, the rider collarless and even bareheaded, trembling, speaking in a shaking voice as the woman in the house had done. His father merely looking up once before stooping again to the hame he was buckling, so that the man on the mare spoke to his stooping back:

"You must realize you have ruined that rug. Wasn't there anybody here, any of your women? . . ." he ceased, shaking, the boy watching him, the older brother leaning now in the stable door, chewing, blinking slowly and steadily at nothing apparently. "It cost a hundred dollars. But you never had a hundred dollars. You never will. So I'm going to charge you twenty bushels of corn against your crop. I'll add it in your contract and when you come to the commissary you can sign it. That won't keep Mrs. de Spain quiet but maybe it will teach you to wipe your feet off before you enter her house again."

Then he was gone. The boy looked at his father, who still had not spoken or even looked up again, who was now adjusting the loggerhead in the hame.

"Pap," he said. His father looked at him—the inscrutable face, the shaggy brows beneath which the gray eyes glinted coldly. Suddenly the boy went toward him, fast, stopping as suddenly. "You done the best you could!" he cried. "If he wanted hit done different why didn't he wait and tell you how? He won't git no twenty bushels! He won't git none! We'll gether hit and hide hit! I kin watch . . ."

"Did you put the cutter back in that straight stock like I told you?"

"No, sir," he said.

"Then go do it."

That was Wednesday. During the rest of that week he worked steadily, at what was within his scope and some which was beyond it, with an industry that did not need to be driven nor even commanded twice; he had this from his mother, with the difference that some at least of what he did he liked to do, such as splitting wood with the half-size axe which his mother and aunt had earned, or saved money somehow, to present him with at Christmas. In company with the two older women (and on one afternoon, even one of the sisters), he built pens for the shoat and the cow which were a part of his father's contract with the landlord, and one afternoon, his father being absent, gone somewhere on one of the mules, he went to the field.

They were running a middle buster now, his brother holding the plow straight while he handled the reins, and walking beside the straining mule, the rich black soil shearing cool and damp against his bare ankles, he thought *Maybe this is the end of it. Maybe even that twenty bushels that seems hard to have to pay for just a rug will be a cheap price for him to stop forever and always from being what he used to be;* thinking, dreaming now, so that his brother had to speak sharply to him to mind the mule: *Maybe he even won't collect the twenty bushels. Maybe it will all add up and balance and vanish—corn, rug, fire; the terror and grief, the being pulled two ways like between two teams of horses—gone, done with for ever and ever.*

Then it was Saturday; he looked up from beneath the mule he was harnessing and saw his father in the black coat and hat. "Not that," his father said. "The wagon gear." And then, two hours later, sitting in the wagon bed behind his father and brother on the seat, the wagon accomplished a final curve, and he saw the weathered paintless store with its tattered tobacco- and patent-medicine posters and the tethered wagons and saddle animals below the gallery. He mounted the gnawed steps behind his father and brother, and there again was the lane of quiet, watching faces for the three of them to walk through. He saw the man in spectacles sitting at the plank table and he did not need to be told this was a Justice of the Peace; he sent one glare of fierce, exultant, partisan defiance at the man in collar and cravat now, whom he had seen but twice before in his life, and that on a galloping horse, who now wore on his face an expression not of rage but of amazed unbelief which the boy could not have known was at the incredible circumstance of being sued by one of his own tenants, and came and stood against his father and cried at the Justice: "He ain't done it! He ain't burnt . . ."

"Go back to the wagon," his father said.

"Burnt?" the Justice said. "Do I understand this rug was burned too?"

"Does anybody here claim it was?" his father said. "Go back to the wagon." But he did not, he merely retreated in the rear of the room, crowded as that other had been, but not to sit down this time, instead, to stand pressing among the motionless bodies, listening to the voices:

"And you claim twenty bushels of corn is too high for the damage you did to the rug?"

"He brought the rug to me and said he wanted the tracks washed out of it. I washed the tracks out and took the rug back to him."

"But you didn't carry the rug back to him in the same condition it was in before you made the tracks on it."

His father did not answer, and now for perhaps half a minute there was no sound at all save that of breathing, the faint, steady suspiration of complete and intent listening.

"You decline to answer that, Mr. Snopes?" Again his father did not answer. "I'm going to find against you, Mr. Snopes. I'm going to find that you were responsible for the injury to Major de Spain's rug and hold you liable for it. But twenty bushels of corn seems a little high for a man in your circumstances to have to pay. Major de Spain claims it cost a hundred dollars. October corn will be worth about fifty cents. I figure that if Major de Spain can stand a ninety-five-dollar loss on something he paid cash for, you can stand a five-dollar loss you haven't earned yet. I hold you in damages to Major de Spain to the amount of ten bushels of corn over and above your contract with him, to be paid to him out of your crop at gathering time. Court adjourned."

It had taken no time hardly, the morning was but half begun. He thought they would return home and perhaps back to the field, since they were late, far behind all other farmers. But instead his father passed on behind the wagon, merely indicating with his hand for the older brother to follow with it, and crossed the road toward the blacksmith shop opposite, pressing on after his father, overtaking him, speaking, whispering up at the harsh, calm face beneath the weathered hat: "He won't git no ten bushels neither. He won't git one. We'll . . ." until his father glanced for an instant down at him, the face absolutely calm, the grizzled eyebrows tangled above the cold eyes, the voice almost pleasant, almost gentle:

"You think so? Well, we'll wait till October anyway."

The matter of the wagon—the setting of a spoke or two and the tightening of the tires—did not take long either, the business of the tires accomplished by driving the wagon into the spring branch behind the shop and letting it stand there, the mules nuzzling into the water from time to time, and the boy on the seat with the idle reins, looking up the slope and through the sooty tunnel of the shed where the slow hammer rang and where his father sat on an upended cypress bolt, easily, either talking or listening, still sitting there when the boy brought the dripping wagon up out of the branch and halted it before the door.

"Take them on to the shade and hitch," his father said. He did so and returned. His father and the smith and a third man squatting on his heels inside the door were talking, about crops and animals; the boy, squatting too in the ammoniac dust and hoof-parings and scales of rust, heard his father tell a long and unhurried story out of the time before the birth of the older brother even when he had been a professional horsetrader. And then his father came up beside him where he stood before a tattered last year's circus poster on the other side of the store, gazing rapt and quiet at the scarlet horses, the incredible poisings and convolutions of tulle and tights and the painted leers of comedians, and said, "It's time to eat."

But not at home. Squatting beside his brother against the front wall, he watched his father emerge from the store and produce from a paper sack a segment of cheese and divide it carefully and deliberately into three with his pocket knife and produce crackers from the same sack. They all three squatted on the gallery and ate, slowly, without talking; then in the store again, they drank from a tin dipper tepid water smelling of the cedar bucket and of living beech trees. And still they did not go home. It was a horse lot this time, a tall rail fence upon and along which men stood and sat and out of which one by one horses were led, to be walked and trotted and then cantered back and forth along the road while the slow swapping and buying went on and the sun began to slant westward, they—the three of them—watching and listening, the older brother with his muddy eyes and his steady, inevitable tobacco, the father commenting now and then on certain of the animals, to no one in particular.

It was after sundown when they reached home. They ate supper by lamplight, then, sitting on the doorstep, the boy watched the night fully accomplish, listening to the whippoorwills and the frogs, when he heard his mother's voice: "Abner! No! No! Oh, God. Oh, God. Abner!" and he rose, whirled, and saw the altered light through the door where a candle stub now burned in a bottle neck on the table and his father, still in the hat and coat, at once formal and burlesque as though dressed carefully for some shabby and ceremonial violence, emptying the reservoir of the lamp back into the five-gallon kerosene can from which it had been filled, while the mother tugged at his arm until he shifted the lamp to the other hand and flung her back, not savagely or vicious, just hard, into the wall, her hands flung out against the wall for balance, her mouth open and in her face the same quality of hopeless despair as had been in her voice. Then his father saw him standing in the door.

"Go to the barn and get that can of oil we were oiling the wagon with," he said. The boy did not move. Then he could speak.

"What . . ." he cried. "What are you . . ."

"Go get that oil," his father said. "Go."

Then he was moving, running, outside the house, toward the stable: this the old habit, the old blood which he had not been permitted to choose for himself, which had been bequeathed him willy nilly and which had run for so long (and who knew where, battening on what of outrage and savagery and lust) before it came to him. *I could keep on*, he thought. *I could run on and on and never look back, never need to see his face again. Only I can't. I can't,* the rusted can in his hand now, the liquid sploshing in it as he ran back to the house and into it, into the sound of his mother's weeping in the next room, and handed the can to his father.

"Ain't you going to even send a nigger?" he cried. "At least you sent a nigger before!"

This time his father didn't strike him. The hand came even faster than the blow had, the same hand which had set the can on the table with almost excruciating care flashing from the can toward him too quick for him to follow it, gripping him by the back of his shirt and on to tiptoe before he had seen it quit the can, the face stooping at him in breathless and frozen ferocity, the cold, dead voice speaking over him to the older brother who leaned against the table, chewing with that steady, curious, sidewise motion of cows:

"Empty the can into the big one and go on. I'll catch up with you."

"Better tie him up to the bedpost," the brother said.

"Do like I told you," the father said. Then the boy was moving, his bunched shirt and the hard, bony hand between his shoulderblades, his toes just touching the floor, across the room and into the other one, past the sisters sitting with spread heavy thighs in the two chairs over the cold hearth, and to where his mother and aunt sat side by side on the bed, the aunt's arms about his mother's shoulders.

"Hold him," the father said. The aunt made a startled movement. "Not you," the father said. "Lennie. Take hold of him. I want to see you do it." His mother took him by the wrist. "You'll hold him better than that. If he gets loose don't you know what he is going to do? He will go up yonder." He jerked his head toward the road. "Maybe I'd better tie him."

"I'll hold him," his mother whispered.

"See you do then." Then his father was gone, the stiff foot heavy and measured upon the boards, ceasing at last.

Then he began to struggle. His mother caught him in both arms, he jerking and wrenching at them. He would be stronger in the end, he knew that. But he had no time to wait for it. "Lemme go!" he cried. "I don't want to have to hit you!"

"Let him go!" the aunt said. "If he don't go, before God, I am going up there myself!"

"Don't you see I can't?" his mother cried. "Sarty! Sarty! No! No! Help me, Lizze!"

Then he was free. His aunt grasped at him but it was too late. He whirled, running, his mother stumbled forward on to her knees behind him, crying to the nearer sister: "Catch him, Net! Catch him!" But that was too late too, the sister (the sisters were twins, born at the same time, yet either of them now gave the impression of being, encompassing as much living meat and volume and weight as any other two of the family) not yet having begun to rise from the chair, her head, face, alone merely turned, presenting to him in the flying instant an astonishing expanse of young female features untroubled by any surprise even, wearing only an expression of bovine interest. Then he was out of the room, out of the house, in the mild dust of the starlit road and the heavy rifeness of honeysuckle, the pale ribbon unspooling with terrific slowness under his running feet, reaching the gate at last and turning in, running, his heart and lungs drumming, on up the drive toward the lighted house, the lighted door. He did not knock, he burst in, sobbing for breath, incapable for the moment of speech; he saw the astonished face of the Negro in the linen jacket without knowing when the Negro had appeared.

"De Spain!" he cried, panted. "Where's . . ." then he saw the white man too emerging from a white door down the hall. "Barn!" he cried. "Barn!"

"What?" the white man said. "Barn?"

"Yes!" the boy cried. "Barn!"

"Catch him!" the white man shouted.

But it was too late this time too. The Negro grasped his shirt, but the entire sleeve, rotten with washing, carried away, and he was out that door too and in the drive again, and had actually never ceased to run even while he was screaming into the white man's face.

Behind him the white man was shouting. "My horse! Fetch my horse!" and he thought for an instant of cutting across the park and climbing the fence into the road, but he did not know the park nor how high the vine-massed fence might be and he dared not risk it. So he ran on down the drive, blood and breath roaring; presently he was in the road again though he could not see it. He could not hear either: the galloping mare was almost upon him before he heard her, and even then he held his course, as if the very urgency of his wild grief and need must in a moment more find him wings, waiting until the ultimate instant to hurl himself aside and into the weed-choked roadside ditch as the horse thundered past and on, for an instant in furious silhouette against the stars, the tranquil early summer night sky which, even before the shape of the horse and rider vanished, stained abruptly and violently upward: a long, swirling roar incredible and soundless, blotting the stars, and he springing up and into the road again, running again, knowing it was too late yet still running even after he heard the shot and, an instant later, two shots, pausing now without knowing he had ceased to run, crying "Pap! Pap!", running again before he knew he had begun to run, stumbling, tripping over something and scrabbling up again without ceasing to run, looking backward over his shoulder at the glares as he got up, running on among the invisible trees, panting, sobbing, "Father! Father!"

At midnight he was sitting on the crest of a hill. He did not know it was midnight and he did not know how far he had come. But there was no glare behind him now and he sat now, his back toward what he had called home for four days anyhow, his face toward the dark woods which he would enter when breath was strong again, small, shaking steadily in the chill darkness, hugging himself into the remainder of this thin, rotten shirt, the grief and despair now no longer terror and fear but just grief and despair. *Father. My father,* he thought. "He was brave!" He cried suddenly, aloud but not loud, no more than a whisper: "He was! He was in the war! He was in Colonel Sartoris' cav'ry!" not knowing that his father had gone to that war a private in the fine old European sense, wearing no uniform, admitting the authority of and giving fidelity to no man or army or flag, going to war as Malbrouck himself did: for booty—it meant nothing and less than nothing to him if it were enemy booty or his own.

The slow constellations wheeled on. It would be dawn and then sun-up after a while and he would be hungry. But that would be to morrow and now he was only cold, and walking would cure that. His breathing was easier now and he decided to get up and go on, and then he found that he had been asleep because he knew it was almost dawn, the night almost over. He could tell that from the whippoorwills. They were everywhere now among the dark trees below him, constant and inflectioned and ceaseless, so that, as the instant for giving over to the day birds drew nearer and nearer, there was no interval at all between them. He got up. He was a little stiff, but walking would cure that too as it would the cold, and soon there would be the sun. He went on down the hill, toward the dark woods within which the liquid silver voices of the birds called unceasing— the rapid and urgent beating of the urgent and quiring heart of the late spring night. He did not look back.

QUESTIONS FOR DISCUSSION AND WRITING

1. How does the opening courtroom scene establish the many conflicts in the story? For example, how does Sarty attempt to clarify the external conflict by calling Harris an enemy? What internal conflict does Sarty feel when he thinks he will have to testify?
2. How does Faulkner characterize the father? Explain how the phrase "barn burner" stereotypes the father in the eyes of the community. In what ways does his fierce independence alter that stereotype?
3. In what ways does the Snopes wagon establish the setting for the story? In what kind of houses do the Snopeses live? How often has the family moved and why? What do the "big houses" seem to represent for the family?
4. What device does Faulkner use to emphasize Sarty's thoughts throughout the story? What does Sarty think about his father? How does his thinking lead to his final decision?
5. What is the difference between the community's definition of justice and the family's definition?

31

F. SCOTT FITZGERALD

Babylon Revisited

F. SCOTT FITZGERALD (1896–1940) was born in St. Paul, Minnesota, and attended Princeton University until he left in 1917 to enlist in the Army. World War I ended before he received an assignment overseas, but while he was stationed at Camp Sheridan in Alabama, he began writing his first novel, *This Side of Paradise* (1920), and fell in love with Zelda Sayre, the belle of Montgomery, Alabama. The financial success of his first novel enabled Scott and Zelda to marry and to begin living the high life of the Jazz Age in New York, Paris, and the French Riviera. Most of their income came from stories published in magazines such as *The Saturday Evening Post* and later collected in volumes such as *Flappers and Philosophers* (1921), *Tales of the Jazz Age* (1922), and *All the Sad Young Men* (1926). His finest novel, *The Great Gatsby* (1925), portrays a man whose search for a romantic dream is rivaled only by Fitzgerald's own quest. His wife's mental breakdown in 1930, together with his ensuing alcoholism and financial difficulties, led to the dissipation of his talents and an early death in Hollywood while working as a screen writer. He wrote about his wife's tragedy in *Tender Is the Night* (1934) and his own in two posthumously published works edited by Edmund Wilson, *The Last Tycoon* (1941)

and *The Crack-Up* (1945). In "Babylon Revisited," reprinted from *Taps at Reveille* (1935), Fitzgerald records the attempts of a broken man to reclaim his child and his honor.

1

And where's Mr. Campbell?" Charlie asked.

"Gone to Switzerland. Mr. Campbell's a pretty sick man, Mr. Wales."

"I'm sorry to hear that. And George Hardt?" Charlie inquired.

"Back in America, gone to work."

"And where is the Snow Bird?"

"He was in here last week. Anyway, his friend, Mr. Schaeffer, is in Paris."

Two familiar names from the long list of a year and a half ago. Charlie scribbled an address in his notebook and tore out the page.

"If you see Mr. Schaeffer, give him this," he said. "It's my brother-in-law's address. I haven't settled on a hotel yet."

He was not really disappointed to find Paris was so empty. But the stillness in the Ritz bar was strange and portentous. It was not an American bar any more—he felt polite in it, and not as if he owned it. It had gone back into France. He felt the stillness from the moment he got out of the taxi and saw the doorman, usually in a frenzy of activity at this hour, gossiping with a *chasseur* by the servants' entrance.

Passing through the corridor, he heard only a single, bored voice in the once-clamorous women's room. When he turned into the bar he traveled the twenty feet of green carpet with his eyes fixed straight ahead by old habit; and then, with his foot firmly on the rail, he turned and surveyed the room, encountering only a single pair of eyes that fluttered up from a newspaper in the corner. Charlie asked for the head barman, Paul, who in the latter days of the bull market had come to work in his own custom-built car—disembarking, however, with due nicety at the nearest corner. But Paul was at his country house today and Alix giving him information.

"No, no more," Charlie said. "I'm going slow these days."

Alix congratulated him: "You were going pretty strong a couple of years ago."

"I'll stick to it all right," Charlie assured him. "I've stuck to it for over a year and a half now."

"How do you find conditions in America?"

"I haven't been to America for months. I'm in business in Prague, representing a couple of concerns there. They don't know about me down there."

Alix smiled.

"Remember the night of George Hardt's bachelor dinner here?" said Charlie. "By the way, what's become of Claude Fessenden?"

Alix lowered his voice confidentially: "He's in Paris, but he doesn't come here any more. Paul doesn't allow it. He ran up a bill of thirty thousand francs, charging all his drinks and his lunches, and usually his dinner, for more than a year. And when Paul finally told him he had to pay, he gave him a bad check."

Alix shook his head sadly.

"I don't understand it, such a dandy fellow. Now he's all bloated up—" He made a plump apple of his hands.

Charlie watched a group of strident queens installing themselves in a corner.

"Nothing affects them," he thought. "Stocks rise and fall, people loaf or work, but they go on forever." The place oppressed him. He called for the dice and shook with Alix for the drink.

"Here for long, Mr. Wales?"

"I'm here for four or five days to see my little girl."

"Oh-h! You have a little girl?"

Outside, the fire-red, gas-blue, ghost-green signs shone smokily through the tranquil rain. It was late afternoon and the streets were in movement; the bistros gleamed. At the corner of the Boulevard des Capucines he took a taxi. The Place de la Concorde moved by in pink majesty; they crossed the logical Seine, and Charlie felt the sudden provincial quality of the Left Bank.

Charlie directed his taxi to the Avenue de l'Opéra, which was out of his way. But he wanted to see the blue hour spread over the magnificent façade, and imagine that the cab horns, playing endlessly the first few bars of *Le Plus que Lent,* were the trumpets of the Second Empire. They were closing the iron grill in front of Brentano's Bookstore, and people were already at dinner behind the trim little bourgeois hedge of Duval's. He had never eaten at a really cheap restaurant in Paris. Five-course dinner, four francs fifty, eighteen cents, wine included. For some odd reason he wished that he had.

As they rolled on to the Left Bank, and he felt its sudden provincialism, he thought, "I spoiled this city for myself. I didn't realize it, but the days came along one after another, and then two years were gone, and everything was gone, and I was gone."

He was thirty-five, and good to look at. The Irish mobility of his face was sobered by a deep wrinkle between his eyes. As he rang his brother-in-law's bell in the Rue Palatine, the wrinkle deepened till it pulled down his brows; he felt a cramping sensation in his belly. From behind the maid who opened the door darted a lovely little girl of nine who shrieked "Daddy!" and flew up, struggling like a fish, into his arms. She pulled his head around by one ear and set her cheek against his.

"My old pie," he said.

"Oh, daddy, daddy, daddy, daddy, dads, dads, dads!"

She drew him into the salon, where the family waited, a boy and a girl his daughter's age, his sister-in-law and her husband. He greeted Marion with his voice pitched carefully to avoid either feigned enthusiasm or dislike, but her response was more frankly tepid, though she minimized her expression of unalterable distrust by directing her regard toward his child. The two men clasped hands in a friendly way and Lincoln Peters rested his for a moment on Charlie's shoulder.

The room was warm and comfortably American. The three children moved intimately about, playing through the yellow oblongs that led to other rooms; the cheer of six o'clock spoke in the eager smacks of the fire and the sounds of French activity in the kitchen. But Charlie did not relax; his heart sat up rigidly in his body and he drew confidence from his daughter, who from time to time came close to him, holding in her arms the doll he had brought.

"Really extremely well," he declared in answer to Lincoln's question. "There's a lot of business there that isn't moving at all, but we're doing even better than ever. In fact, damn well. I'm bringing my sister over from America next month to keep house for me. My income last year was bigger than it was when I had money. You see, the Czechs———"

His boasting was for a specific purpose; but after a moment, seeing a faint restiveness in Lincoln's eye, he changed the subject:

"Those are fine children of yours, well brought up, good manners."

"We think Honoria's a great little girl too."

Marion Peters came back from the kitchen. She was a tall woman with worried eyes, who had once possessed a fresh American loveliness. Charlie had never been sensitive to it and was always surprised when people spoke of how pretty she had been. From the first there had been an instinctive antipathy between them.

"Well, how do you find Honoria?" she asked.

"Wonderful. I was astonished how much she's grown in ten months. All the children are looking well."

"We haven't had a doctor for a year. How do you like being back in Paris?"

"It seems very funny to see so few Americans around."

"I'm delighted," Marion said vehemently. "Now at least you can go into a store without their assuming you're a millionaire. We've suffered like everybody, but on the whole it's a good deal pleasanter."

"But it was nice while it lasted," Charlie said. "We were a sort of royalty, almost infallible, with a sort of magic around us. In the bar this afternoon"—he stumbled, seeing his mistake—"there wasn't a man I knew."

She looked at him keenly. "I should think you'd have had enough of bars."

"I only stayed a minute. I take one drink every afternoon, and no more."

"Don't you want a cocktail before dinner?" Lincoln asked.

"I take only one drink every afternoon, and I've had that."

"I hope you keep to it," said Marion.

Her dislike was evident in the coldness with which she spoke, but Charlie only smiled; he had larger plans. Her very aggressiveness gave him an advantage, and he knew enough to wait. He wanted them to initiate the discussion of what they knew had brought him to Paris.

At dinner he couldn't decide whether Honoria was most like him or her mother. Fortunate if she didn't combine the traits of both that had brought them to disaster. A great wave of protectiveness went over him. He thought he knew what to do for her. He believed in character; he wanted to jump back a whole generation and trust in character again as the eternally valuable element. Everything else wore out.

He left soon after dinner, but not to go home. He was curious to see Paris by night with clearer and more judicious eyes than those of other days. He bought a *strapontin* for the Casino and watched Josephine Baker go through her chocolate arabesques.

After an hour he left and strolled toward Montmartre, up the Rue Pigalle into the Place Blanche. The rain had stopped and there were a few people in evening clothes disembarking from taxis in front of cabarets, and *cocottes* prowling singly or in pairs, and many Negroes. He passed a lighted door from which issued music, and stopped with the sense of familiarity; it was Bricktop's, where he had parted with so many hours and so much money. A few doors farther on he found another ancient rendezvous and incautiously put his head inside. Immediately an eager orchestra burst into sound, a pair of professional dancers leaped to their feet and a maître d'hôtel swooped toward him, crying, "Crowd just arriving, sir!" But he withdrew quickly.

"You have to be damn drunk," he thought.

Zelli's was closed, the bleak and sinister cheap hotels surrounding it were dark; up in the Rue Blanche there was more light and a local, colloquial French crowd. The Poet's Cave had disappeared, but the two great mouths of the Café of Heaven and the Café of Hell still yawned—even devoured, as he watched, the meager contents of a tourist bus—a German, a Japanese, and an American couple who glanced at him with frightened eyes.

So much for the effort and ingenuity of Montmartre. All the catering to vice and waste was on an utterly childish scale, and he suddenly realized the meaning of the word "dissipate"—to dissipate into thin air; to make nothing out of something. In the little hours of the night every move from place to place was an enormous human jump, an increase of paying for the privilege of slower and slower motion.

He remembered thousand-franc notes given to an orchestra for playing a single number, hundred-franc notes tossed to a doorman for calling a cab.

But it hadn't been given for nothing.

It had been given, even the most wildly squandered sum, as an offering to destiny that he might not remember the things most worth remembering, the things that now he would always remember—his child taken from his control, his wife escaped to a grave in Vermont.

In the glare of a *brasserie* a woman spoke to him. He bought her some eggs and coffee, and then, eluding her encouraging stare, gave her a twenty-franc note and took a taxi to his hotel.

2

He woke upon a fine fall day—football weather. The depression of yesterday was gone and he liked the people on the streets. At noon he sat opposite Honoria at Le Grand Vatel, the only restaurant he could think of not reminiscent of champagne dinners and long luncheons that began at two and ended in a blurred and vague twilight.

"Now, how about vegetables? Oughtn't you to have some vegetables?"

"Well, yes."

"Here's *épinards* and *chou-fleur* and carrots and *haricots*."

"I'd like *chou-fleur*."

"Wouldn't you like to have two vegetables?"

"I usually only have one at lunch."

The waiter was pretending to be inordinately fond of children. "*Qu'elle est mignonne la petite! Elle parle exactement comme une française.*"

"How about dessert? Shall we wait and see?"

The waiter disappeared. Honoria looked at her father expectantly.

"What are we going to do?"

"First, we're going to that toy store in the Rue Saint-Honoré and buy you anything you like. And then we're going to the vaudeville at the Empire."

She hesitated. "I like it about the vaudeville, but not the toy store."

"Why not?"

"Well, you brought me this doll." She had it with her. "And I've got lots of things. And we're not rich any more, are we?"

"We never were. But today you are to have anything you want."

"All right," she agreed resignedly.

When there had been her mother and a French nurse he had been inclined to be strict; now he extended himself, reached out for a new tolerance; he must be both parents to her and not shut any of her out of communication.

"I want to get to know you," he said gravely. "First let me introduce myself. My name is Charles J. Wales, of Prague."

"Oh, daddy!" her voice cracked with laughter.

"And who are you, please?" he persisted, and she accepted a role immediately: "Honoria Wales, Rue Palatine, Paris."

"Married or single?"

"No, not married. Single."

He indicated the doll. "But I see you have a child, madame."

Unwilling to disinherit it, she took it to her heart and thought quickly: "Yes, I've been married, but I'm not married now. My husband is dead."

He went on quickly, "And the child's name?"

"Simone. That's after my best friend at school."

"I'm very pleased that you're doing so well at school."

"I'm third this month," she boasted. "Elsie"—that was her cousin—"is only about eighteenth, and Richard is about at the bottom."

"You like Richard and Elsie, don't you?"

"Oh, yes. I like Richard quite well and I like her all right."

Cautiously and casually he asked: "And Aunt Marion and Uncle Lincoln—which do you like best?"

"Oh, Uncle Lincoln, I guess."

He was increasingly aware of her presence. As they came in, a murmur of ". . . adorable" followed them, and now the people at the next table bent all their silences upon her, staring as if she were something no more conscious than a flower.

"Why don't I live with you?" she asked suddenly. "Because mamma's dead?"

"You must stay here and learn more French. It would have been hard for daddy to take care of you so well."

"I don't really need much taking care of any more. I do everything for myself."

Going out of the restaurant, a man and a woman unexpectedly hailed him.

"Well, the old Wales!"

"Hello there, Lorraine. . . . Dunc."

Sudden ghosts out of the past: Duncan Schaeffer, a friend from college. Lorraine Quarrles, a lovely, pale blonde of thirty; one of a crowd who had helped him make months into days in the lavish times of three years ago.

"My husband couldn't come this year," she said, in answer to his question. "We're poor as hell. So he gave me two hundred a month and told me I could do my worst on that. . . . This your little girl?"

"What about coming back and sitting down?" Duncan asked.

"Can't do it." He was glad for an excuse. As always, he felt Lorraine's passionate, provocative attraction, but his own rhythm was different now.

"Well, how about dinner?" she asked.

"I'm not free. Give me your address and let me call you."

"Charlie, I believe you're sober," she said judicially. "I honestly believe he's sober, Dunc. Pinch him and see if he's sober."

Charlie indicated Honoria with his head. They both laughed.

"What's your address?" said Duncan skeptically.

He hesitated, unwilling to give the name of his hotel.

"I'm not settled yet. I'd better call you. We're going to see the vaudeville at the Empire."

"There! That's what I want to do," Lorraine said. "I want to see some clowns and acrobats and jugglers. That's just what we'll do, Dunc."

"We've got to do an errand first," said Charlie. "Perhaps we'll see you there."

"All right, you snob. . . . Good-by, beautiful little girl."

"Good-by."

Honoria bobbed politely.

Somehow, an unwelcome encounter. They liked him because he was functioning, because he was serious; they wanted to see him, because he was stronger than they were now, because they wanted to draw a certain sustenance from his strength.

At the Empire, Honoria proudly refused to sit upon her father's folded coat. She was already an individual with a code of her own, and Charlie was more and more absorbed by the desire of putting a little of himself into her before she crystallized utterly. It was hopeless to try to know her in so short a time.

Between the acts they came upon Duncan and Lorraine in the lobby where the band was playing.

"Have a drink?"

"All right, but not up at the bar. We'll take a table."

"The perfect father."

Listening abstractly to Lorraine, Charlie watched Honoria's eyes leave their table, and he followed them wistfully about the room, wondering what they saw. He met her glance and she smiled.

"I liked that lemonade," she said.

What had she said? What had he expected? Going home in a taxi afterward, he pulled her over until her head rested against his chest.

"Darling, do you ever think about your mother?"

"Yes, sometimes," she answered vaguely.

"I don't want you to forget her. Have you got a picture of her?"

"Yes, I think so. Anyhow, Aunt Marion has. Why don't you want me to forget her?"

"She loved you very much."

"I loved her too."

They were silent for a moment.

"Daddy, I want to come and live with you," she said suddenly.

His heart leaped; he had wanted it to come like this.

"Aren't you perfectly happy?"

"Yes, but I love you better than anybody. And you love me better than anybody, don't you, now that mummy's dead?"

"Of course I do. But you won't always like me best, honey. You'll grow up and meet somebody your own age and go marry him and forget you ever had a daddy."

"Yes, that's true," she agreed tranquilly.

He didn't go in. He was coming back at nine o'clock and he wanted to keep himself fresh and new for the thing he must say then.

"When you're safe inside, just show yourself in that window."

"All right. Good-by, dads, dads, dads, dads."

He waited in the dark street until she appeared, all warm and glowing, in the window above and kissed her fingers out into the night.

3

They were waiting. Marion sat behind the coffee service in a dignified black dinner dress that just faintly suggested mourning. Lincoln was walking up and down with the animation of one who had already been talking. They were as anxious as he was to get into the question. He opened it almost immediately.

"I suppose you know what I want to see you about—why I really came to Paris."

Marion played with the black stars on her necklace and frowned.

"I'm awfully anxious to have a home," he continued. "And I'm awfully anxious to have Honoria in it. I appreciate your taking in Honoria for her mother's sake, but things have changed now"—he hesitated and then continued more forcibly—"changed radically with me, and I want to ask you to reconsider the matter. It would be silly for me to deny that about three years ago I was acting badly———"

Marion looked up at him with hard eyes.

"—but all that's over. As I told you, I haven't had more than a drink a day for over a year, and I take that drink deliberately, so that the idea of alcohol won't get too big in my imagination. You see the idea?"

"No," said Marion succinctly.

"It's a sort of stunt I set myself. It keeps the matter in proportion."

"I get you," said Lincoln. "You don't want to admit it's got any attraction for you."

"Something like that. Sometimes I forget and don't take it. But I try to take it. Anyhow, I couldn't afford to drink in my position. The people I represent are more than satisfied with what I've done, and I'm bringing my sister over from Burlington to keep house for me, and I want awfully to have Honoria too. You know that even when her mother and I weren't getting along well we never let anything that happened touch Honoria. I know she's fond of me and I know I'm able to take care of her and—well, there you are. How do you feel about it?"

He knew that now he would have to take a beating. It would last an hour or two hours, and it would be difficult, but if he modulated his inevitable resentment to the chastened attitude of the reformed sinner, he might win his point in the end.

Keep your temper, he told himself. You don't want to be justifed. You want Honoria.

Lincoln spoke first: "We've been talking it over ever since we got your letter last month. We're happy to have Honoria here. She's a dear little thing, and we're glad to be able to help her, but of course that isn't the question———"

Marion interrupted suddenly. "How long are you going to stay sober, Charlie?" she asked.

"Permanently, I hope."

"How can anybody count on that?"

"You know I never did drink heavily until I gave up business and came over here with nothing to do. Then Helen and I began to run around with———"

"Please leave Helen out of it. I can't bear to hear you talk about her like that."

He stared at her grimly; he had never been certain how fond of each other the sisters were in life.

"My drinking only lasted about a year and a half—from the time we came over until I—collapsed."

"It was time enough."

"It was time enough," he agreed.

"My duty is entirely to Helen," she said. "I try to think what she would have wanted me to do. Frankly, from the night you did that terrible thing you haven't really existed for me. I can't help that. She was my sister."

"Yes."

"When she was dying she asked me to look out for Honoria. If you hadn't been in a sanitarium then, it might have helped matters."

He had no answer.

"I'll never in my life be able to forget the morning when Helen knocked at my door, soaked to the skin and shivering, and said you'd locked her out."

Charlie gripped the sides of the chair. This was more difficult than he expected; he wanted to launch out into a long expostulation and explanation, but he only said: "The night I locked her out—" and she interrupted, "I don't feel up to going over that again."

After a moment's silence Lincoln said: "We're getting off the subject. You want Marion to set aside her legal guardianship and give you Honoria. I think the main point for her is whether she has confidence in you or not."

"I don't blame Marion," Charlie said slowly, "but I think she can have entire confidence in me. I had a good record up to three years ago. Of course, it's within human possibilities I might go wrong any time. But if we wait much longer I'll lose Honoria's childhood and my chance for a home." He shook his head. "I'll simply lose her, don't you see?"

"Yes, I see," said Lincoln.

"Why didn't you think of all this before?" Marion asked.

"I suppose I did, from time to time, but Helen and I were getting along badly. When I consented to the guardianship, I was flat on my back in a sanitarium and the market had cleaned me out. I knew I'd acted badly, and I thought if it would bring any peace to Helen, I'd agree to anything. But now it's different. I'm functioning. I'm behaving damn well, so far as———"

"Please don't swear at me," Marion said.

He looked at her, startled. With each remark the force of her dislike became more and more apparent. She had built up her fear of life into one wall and faced it toward him. This trivial reproof was possibly the result of some trouble with the cook several hours before. Charlie became increasingly alarmed at leaving Honoria in this atmosphere of hostility against himself; sooner or later it would come out, in a word here, a shake of the head there, and some of that distrust would be irrevocably implanted in Honoria. But he pulled his temper down out of his face and shut it up inside him; he had won a point, for Lincoln realized the absurdity of Marion's remark and asked her lightly since when she had objected to the word "damn."

"Another thing," Charlie said: "I'm able to give her certain advantages now. I'm going to take a French governess to Prague with me. I've got a lease on a new apartment———"

He stopped, realizing that he was blundering. They couldn't be expected to accept with equanimity the fact that his income was again twice as large as their own.

"I suppose you can give her more luxuries than we can," said Marion. "When you were throwing away money we were living along watching every ten francs. . . . I suppose you'll start doing it again."

"Oh, no," he said. "I've learned. I worked hard for ten years, you know—until I got lucky in the market, like so many people. Terribly lucky. It won't happen again."

There was a long silence. All of them felt their nerves straining, and for the first time in a year Charlie wanted a drink. He was sure now that Lincoln Peters wanted him to have his child.

Marion shuddered suddenly; part of her saw that Charlie's feet were planted on the earth now, and her own maternal feeling recognized the naturalness of his desire; but she had lived for a long time with a prejudice—a prejudice founded on a curious disbelief in her sister's happiness, which, in the shock of one terrible night, had turned to hatred for him. It had all happened at a point in her life where the discouragement of ill health and adverse circumstances made it necessary for her to believe in tangible villainy and a tangible villain.

"I can't help what I think!" she cried out suddenly. "How much you were responsible for Helen's death, I don't know. It's something you'll have to square with your own conscience."

An electric current of agony surged through him; for a moment he was almost on his feet, an unuttered sound echoing in his throat. He hung on to himself for a moment, another moment.

"Hold on there," said Lincoln uncomfortably. "I never thought you were responsible for that."

"Helen died of heart trouble," Charlie said dully.

"Yes, heart trouble." Marion spoke as if the phrase had another meaning for her.

Then, in the flatness that followed her outburst, she saw him plainly and she knew he had somehow arrived at control over the situation. Glancing at her husband, she found no help from him, and as abruptly as if it were a matter of no importance, she threw up the sponge.

"Do what you like!" she cried, springing up from her chair. "She's your child. I'm not the person to stand in your way. I think if it were my child I'd rather see her—" She managed to check herself. "You two decide it. I can't stand this. I'm sick. I'm going to bed."

She hurried from the room; after a moment Lincoln said:

"This has been a hard day for her. You know how strongly she feels—" His voice was almost apologetic: "When a woman gets an idea in her head."

"Of course."

"It's going to be all right. I think she sees now that you—can provide for the child, and so we can't very well stand in your way or Honoria's way."

"Thank you, Lincoln."

"I'd better go along and see how she is."

"I'm going."

He was still trembling when he reached the street, but a walk down the Rue Bonaparte to the *quais* set him up, and as he crossed the Seine, fresh and new by the *quai* lamps, he felt exultant. But back in his room he couldn't sleep. The image of Helen haunted him. Helen whom he had loved so until they had senselessly begun to abuse each other's love, tear it into shreds. On that terrible February night that Marion remembered so vividly, a slow quarrel had gone on for hours. There was a scene at the Florida, and then he attempted to take her home, and then she kissed young Webb at a table; after that there was what she had hysterically said. When he arrived home alone he turned the key in the lock in wild anger. How could he know she would arrive an hour later alone, that there would be a snow storm in which she wandered about in slippers, too confused to find a taxi? Then the aftermath, her escaping pneumonia by a miracle, and all the attendant horror. They were "reconciled," but that was the beginning of the end, and Marion, who had seen with her own eyes and who imagined it to be one of many scenes from her sister's martyrdom, never forgot.

Going over it again brought Helen nearer, and in the white, soft light that steals upon half sleep near morning he found himself talking to her again. She said that he was perfectly right about Honoria and that she wanted Honoria to be with him. She said she was glad he was being good and doing better. She said a lot of other things—very friendly things—but she was in a swing in a white dress, and swinging faster and faster all the time, so that at the end he could not hear clearly all that she said.

4

He woke up feeling happy. The door of the world was open again. He made plans, vistas, futures for Honoria and himself, but suddenly he grew sad, remembering all the plans he and Helen had made. She had not planned to die. The present was the thing—work to do and someone to love. But not to love too much, for he knew the injury that a father can do to a daughter or a mother to a son by attaching them too closely: afterward, out in the world, the child would seek in the marriage partner the same blind tenderness and, failing probably to find it, turn against love and life.

It was another bright, crisp day. He called Lincoln Peters at the bank where he worked and asked if he could count on taking Honoria when he left for Prague. Lincoln agreed that there was no reason for delay. One thing—the legal guardianship. Marion wanted to retain that a while longer. She was upset by the whole matter, and it would oil things if she felt that the situation was still in her control for another year. Charlie agreed, wanting only the tangible, visible child.

Then the question of a governess. Charlie sat in a gloomy agency and talked to a cross Béarnaise and to a buxom Breton peasant, neither of whom he could have endured. There were others whom he would see tomorrow.

He lunched with Lincoln Peters at Griffons, trying to keep down his exultation.

"There's nothing quite like your own child," Lincoln said. "But you understand how Marion feels too."

"She's forgotten how hard I worked for seven years there," Charlie said. "She just remembers one night."

"There's another thing," Lincoln hesitated. "When you and Helen were tearing around Europe throwing money away, we were just getting along. I didn't touch any of the prosperity because I never got ahead enough to carry anything but my insurance. I think Marion felt there was some kind of injustice in it—you not even working toward the end, and getting richer and richer."

"It went just as quick as it came," said Charlie.

"Yes, a lot of it stayed in the hands of *chasseurs* and saxophone players and maitres d'hôtel—well, the big party's over now. I just said that to explain Marion's feeling about those crazy years. If you drop in about six o'clock tonight before Marion's too tired, we'll settle the details on the spot."

Back at his hotel, Charlie found a *pneumatique* that had been redirected from the Ritz bar, where Charlie had left his address for the purpose of finding a certain man.

> DEAR CHARLIE: You were so strange when we saw you the other day I wondered if I did something to offend you. If so, I'm not conscious of it. In fact, I have thought about you much for the last year, and it's always been in the back of my mind that I might see you if I came over here. We *did* have such good times that crazy spring, like the night you and I stole the butcher's tricycle, and the time we tried to call on the president and you had the old derby rim and the wire cane. Everybody seems so old lately, but I don't feel old a bit. Couldn't we get together some time today for old time's sake? I've got a vile hangover for the moment, but will be feeling better this afternoon and will look for you about five in the sweatshop at the Ritz.
>
> Always devotedly,
> Lorraine

His first feeling was one of awe that he had actually, in his mature years, stolen a tricycle and pedaled Lorraine all over the Étoile between the small hours and dawn. In retrospect it was a nightmare. Locking out Helen didn't fit in with any other act of his life, but the tricycle incident did—it was one of many. How many weeks or months of dissipation to arrive at that condition of utter irresponsibility?

He tried to picture how Lorraine had appeared to him then—very attractive; Helen was unhappy about it, though she said nothing. Yesterday, in the restaurant, Lorraine had seemed trite, blurred, worn away. He emphatically did not want to see her, and he was glad Alix had not given away his hotel address. It was a relief to think, instead, of

Honoria, to think of Sundays spent with her and of saying good morning to her and of knowing she was there in his house at night, drawing her breath in the darkness.

At five he took a taxi and bought presents for all the Peterses—a piquant cloth doll, a box of Roman soldiers, flowers for Marion, big linen handkerchiefs for Lincoln.

He saw, when he arrived in the apartment, that Marion had accepted the inevitable. She greeted him now as though he were a recalcitrant member of the family, rather than a menacing outsider. Honoria had been told she was going; Charlie was glad to see that her tact made her conceal her excessive happiness. Only on his lap did she whisper her delight and the question "When?" before she slipped away with the other children.

He and Marion were alone for a minute in the room, and on an impulse he spoke out boldly:

"Family quarrels are bitter things. They don't go according to any rules. They're not like aches or wounds; they're more like splits in the skin that won't heal because there's not enough material. I wish you and I could be on better terms."

"Some things are hard to forget," she answered. "It's a question of confidence." There was no answer to this and presently she asked, "When do you propose to take her?"

"As soon as I can get a governess. I hoped the day after tomorrow."

"That's impossible. I've got to get her things in shape. Not before Saturday."

He yielded. Coming back into the room, Lincoln offered him a drink.

"I'll take my daily whiskey," he said.

It was warm here, it was a home, people together by a fire. The children felt very safe and important; the mother and father were serious, watchful. They had things to do for the children more important than his visit here. A spoonful of medicine was, after all, more important than the strained relations between Marion and himself. They were not dull people, but they were very much in the grip of life and circumstances. He wondered if he couldn't do something to get Lincoln out of his rut at the bank.

A long peal at the doorbell; the *bonne à tout faire* passed through and went down the corridor. The door opened upon another long ring, and then voices, and the three in the salon looked up expectantly; Richard moved to bring the corridor within his range of vision, and Marion rose. Then the maid came back along the corridor, closely followed by the voices, which developed under the light into Duncan Schaeffer and Lorraine Quarrles.

They were gay, they were hilarious, they were roaring with laughter. For a moment Charlie was astounded; unable to understand how they ferreted out the Peterses' address.

"Ah-h-h!" Duncan wagged his finger roguishly at Charlie, "Ah-h-h!"

They both slid down another cascade of laughter. Anxious and at a loss, Charlie shook hands with them quickly and presented them to Lincoln and Marion. Marion nodded, scarcely speaking. She had drawn back a step toward the fire; her little girl stood beside her, and Marion put an arm about her shoulder.

With growing annoyance at the intrusion, Charlie waited for them to explain themselves. After some concentration Duncan said:

"We came to invite you out to dinner. Lorraine and I insist that all this shishi, cagy business 'bout your address got to stop."

Charlie came closer to them, as if to force them backward down the corridor.

"Sorry, but I can't. Tell me where you'll be and I'll phone you in half an hour."

This made no impression. Lorraine sat down suddenly on the side of a chair, and focusing her eyes on Richard, cried, "Oh, what a nice little boy! Come here, little boy." Richard glanced at his mother, but did not move. With a perceptible shrug of her shoulder, Lorraine turned back to Charlie:

"Come and dine. Sure your cousins won' mine. See you so sel'om. Or solemn."

"I can't," said Charlie sharply. "You two have dinner and I'll phone you."

Her voice became suddenly unpleasant. "All right, we'll go. But I remember once when you hammered on my door at four A.M. I was enough of a good sport to give you a drink. Come on, Dunc."

Still in slow motion, with blurred, angry faces, with uncertain feet, they retired along the corridor.

"Good night," Charlie said.

"Good night!" responded Lorraine emphatically.

When he went back into the salon Marion had not moved, only now her son was standing in the circle of her other arm. Lincoln was still swinging Honoria back and forth like a pendulum from side to side.

"What an outrage!" Charlie broke out. "What an absolute outrage!"

Neither of them answered. Charlie dropped into an armchair, picked up his drink, set it down again and said:

"People I haven't seen for two years having the colossal nerve———"

He broke off. Marion had made the sound "Oh!"in one swift, furious breath, turned her body from him with a jerk and left the room.

Lincoln set down Honoria carefully.

"You children go in and start your soup," he said, and when they obeyed, he said to Charlie:

"Marion's not well and she can't stand shocks. That kind of people make her really physically sick."

"I didn't tell them to come here. They wormed your name out of somebody. They deliberately———"

"Well, it's too bad. It doesn't help matters. Excuse me a minute."

Left alone, Charlie sat tense in his chair. In the next room he could hear the children eating, talking in monosyllables, already oblivious to the scene between their elders. He heard a murmur of conversation from a farther room and then the ticking bell of a telephone receiver picked up, and in a panic he moved to the other side of the room and out of earshot.

In a minute Lincoln came back. "Look here, Charlie. I think we'd better call off dinner for tonight. Marion's in bad shape."

"Is she angry with me?"

"Sort of," he said, almost roughly. "She's not strong and———"

"You mean she's changed her mind about Honoria?"

"She's pretty bitter right now. I don't know. You phone me at the bank tomorrow."

"I wish you'd explain to her I never dreamed these people would come here. I'm just as sore as you are."

"I couldn't explain anything to her now."

Charlie got up. He took his coat and hat and started down the corridor. Then he opened the door of the dining room and said in a strange voice, "Good night, children."

Honoria rose and ran around the table to hug him.

"Good night, sweetheart," he said vaguely, and then trying to make his voice more tender, trying to conciliate something, "Good night, dear children."

5

Charlie went directly to the Ritz bar with the furious idea of finding Lorraine and Duncan, but they were not there, and he realized that in any case there was nothing he could do. He had not touched his drink at the Peters, and now he ordered a whiskey-and-soda. Paul came over to say hello.

"It's a great change," he said sadly. "We do about half the business we did. So many fellows I hear about back in the States lost everything, maybe not in the first crash, but then in the second. Your friend George Hardt lost every cent, I hear. Are you back in the States?"

"No, I'm in business in Prague."

"I heard that you lost a lot in the crash."

"I did," and he added grimly, "but I lost everything I wanted in the boom."

"Selling short."

"Something like that."

Again the memory of those days swept over him like a nightmare—the people they had met traveling; then people who couldn't add a row of figures or speak a coherent sentence. The little man Helen had consented to dance with at the ship's party, who had insulted her ten feet from the table; the women and girls carried screaming with drink or drugs out of public places———

The men who locked their wives out in the snow, because the snow of twenty-nine wasn't real snow. If you didn't want it to be snow, you just paid some money.

He went to the phone and called the Peterses' apartment; Lincoln answered.

"I called up because this thing is on my mind. Has Marion said anything definite?"

"Marion's sick," Lincoln answered shortly. "I know this thing isn't altogether your fault, but I can't have her go to pieces about it. I'm afraid we'll have to let it slide for six months; I can't take the chance of working her up to this state again."

"I see."

"I'm sorry, Charlie."

He went back to his table. His whiskey glass was empty, but he shook his head when Alix looked at it questioningly. There wasn't much he could do now except send Honoria some things; he would send her a lot of things tomorrow. He thought rather angrily that this was just money—he had given so many people money. . . .

"No, no more," he said to another waiter. "What do I owe you?"

He would come back some day; they couldn't make him pay forever. But he wanted his child, and nothing was much good now, beside that fact. He wasn't young any more, with a lot of nice things and dreams to have by himself. He was absolutely sure Helen wouldn't have wanted him to be so alone.

QUESTIONS FOR DISCUSSION AND WRITING

1. How does Fitzgerald present the events that took place before the beginning of the action of this story? Contrast the way Charlie and Marion remember those events.
2. How do the various characters help define Charlie's character? For example, compare and contrast the way Marion, Lorraine, and Honoria portray Charlie's character.
3. What kind of setting is evoked by the word "Babylon"? In what sense does the Ritz bar represent Charlie's former life? How does Prague represent his present life?
4. How does the third-person point of view enable us to raise questions about the accuracy of Charlie's current view of himself? Has he changed as much as he believes he has? Explain your answer.
5. Many of the metaphors in this story are economic. What has Charlie lost? What has he sold short? Can they "make him pay forever"?

32

MARY WILKINS FREEMAN

The Revolt of "Mother"

MARY WILKINS FREEMAN (1852–1930) was born in Randolph, Massachusetts, and was educated at Mt. Holyoke Female Seminary and West Brattleboro Seminary. In the early 1880s she established herself as an author of literature for children with the publication of a collection of poems, *Decorative Plaques* (1883). She soon began publishing adult fiction in magazines such as *Harper's Bazaar* and *Harper's Weekly.* Her best stories, focusing on the endurance and pride of the people in New England, are collected in *A Humble Romance and Other Stories* (1887) and *A New England Nun and Other Stories* (1891). In her best novel, *Pembroke* (1894), Freeman is able to reveal "the pathos in the comedy" of the New England character. "The Revolt of 'Mother,'" reprinted from *A New England Nun,* demonstrates how individual victories can be won over entrenched habits and values.

"Father!"

"What is it?"

"What are them men diggin' over there in the field for?"

There was a sudden dropping and enlarging of the lower part of the old man's face, as if some heavy weight had settled therein; he shut his mouth tight, and went on harnessing the great bay mare. He hustled the collar on to her neck with a jerk.

"Father!"

The old man slapped the saddle upon the mare's back.

"Look here, father, I want to know what them men are diggin' over in the field for, an' I'm goin' to know."

"I wish you'd go into the house, mother, an' 'tend to your own affairs," the old man said then. He ran his words together, and his speech was almost as inarticulate as a growl.

But the woman understood; it was her most native tongue. "I ain't goin' into the house till you tell me what them men are doin' over there in the field," said she.

Then she stood waiting. She was a small woman, short and straight-waisted like a child in her brown cotton gown. Her forehead was mild and benevolent between the smooth curves of gray hair; there were meek downward lines about her nose and mouth; but her eyes, fixed upon the old man, looked as if the meekness had been the result of her own will, never of the will of another.

They were in the barn, standing before the wide open doors. The spring air, full of the smell of growing grass and unseen blossoms, came in their faces. The deep yard in front was littered with farm wagons and piles of wood; on the edges, close to the fence and the house, the grass was a vivid green, and there were some dandelions.

The old man glanced doggedly at his wife as he tightened the last buckles on the harness. She looked as immovable to him as one of the rocks in his pasture-land, bound to the earth with generations of blackberry vines. He slapped the reins over the horse, and started forth from the barn.

"Father!" said she.

The old man pulled up. "What is it?"

"I want to know what them men are diggin' over there in that field for."

"They're diggin' a cellar, I s'pose, if you've got to know."

"A cellar for what?"

"A barn."

"A barn? You ain't goin' to build a barn over there where we was goin' to have a house, father?"

The old man said not another word. He hurried the horse into the farm wagon, and clattered out of the yard, jouncing as sturdily on his seat as a boy.

The woman stood a moment looking after him, then she went out of the barn across a corner of the yard to the house. The house, standing at right angles with the great barn and a long reach of sheds and out-buildings, was infinitesimal compared with them. It was scarcely as commodious for people as the little boxes under the barn eaves were for doves.

A pretty girl's face, pink and delicate as a flower, was looking out of one of the house windows. She was watching three men who were digging over in the field which bounded the yard near the road line. She turned quietly when the woman entered.

"What are they digging for, mother?" said she. "Did he tell you?"

"They're diggin' for—a cellar for a new barn."

"Oh, mother, he ain't going to build another barn?"

"That's what he says."

A boy stood before the kitchen glass combing his hair. He combed slowly and painstakingly, arranging his brown hair in a smooth hillock over his forehead. He did not seem to pay any attention to the conversation.

"Sammy, did you know father was going to build a new barn?" asked the girl.

The boy combed assiduously.

"Sammy!"

He turned, and showed a face like his father's under his smooth crest of hair. "Yes, I s'pose I did," he said, reluctantly.

"How long have you known it?" asked his mother.

" 'Bout three months, I guess."

"Why didn't you tell of it?"

"Didn't think 'twould do no good."

"I don't see what father wants another barn for," said the girl, in her sweet, slow voice. She turned again to the window, and stared out at the digging men in the field. Her tender, sweet face was full of a gentle distress. Her forehead was as bald and innocent as a baby's, with the light hair strained back from it in a row of curl-papers. She was quite large, but her soft curves did not look as if they covered muscles.

Her mother looked sternly at the boy. "Is he goin' to buy more cows?" said she.

The boy did not reply; he was tying his shoes.

"Sammy, I want you to tell me if he's goin' to buy more cows."

"I s'pose he is."

"How many?"

"Four, I guess."

His mother said nothing more. She went into the pantry, and there was a clatter of dishes. The boy got his cap from a nail behind the door, took an old arithmetic from the shelf, and started for school. He was lightly built, but clumsy. He went out of the yard with a curious spring in the hips, that made his loose home-made jacket tilt up in the rear.

The girl went to the sink, and began to wash the dishes that were piled up there. Her mother came promptly out of the pantry, and shoved her aside. "You wipe 'em," said she; "I'll wash. There's a good many this mornin'."

The mother plunged her hands vigorously into the water, the girl wiped the plates slowly and dreamily. "Mother," said she, "don't you think it's too bad father's going to build that new barn, much as we need a decent house to live in?"

Her mother scrubbed a dish fiercely. "You ain't found out yet we're women-folks, Nanny Penn," said she. "You ain't seen enough of men-folks yet to. One of these days you'll find it out, an' then you'll know that we know only what men-folks think we do, so far as any use of it goes, an' how we'd ought to reckon men-folks in with Providence, an' not complain of what they do any more than we do of the weather."

"I don't care; I don't believe George is anything like that, anyhow," said Nanny. Her delicate face flushed pink, her lips pouted softly, as if she were going to cry.

"You wait an' see. I guess George Eastman ain't no better than other men. You hadn't ought to judge father, though. He can't help it, 'cause he don't look at things jest the way we do. An' we've been pretty comfortable here, after all. The roof don't leak—ain't never but once—that's one thing. Father's kept it shingled right up."

"I do wish we had a parlor."

"I guess it won't hurt George Eastman any to come to see you in a nice clean kitchen. I guess a good many girls don't have as good a place as this. Nobody's ever heard me complain."

"I ain't complained either, mother."

"Well, I don't think you'd better, a good father an' a good home as you've got. S'pose your father made you go out an' work for your livin'? Lots of girls have to that ain't no stronger an' better able to than you be."

Sarah Penn washed the frying-pan with a conclusive air. She scrubbed the outside of it as faithfully as the inside. She was a masterly keeper of her box of a house. Her one living-room never seemed to have in it any of the dust which the friction of life with inanimate matter produces. She swept, and there seemed to be no dirt to go before the broom; she cleaned, and one could see no difference. She was like an artist so perfect that he has apparently no art. To-day she got out a mixing bowl and a board, and rolled some pies, and there was no more flour upon her than upon her daughter who was doing finer work. Nanny was to be married in the fall, and she was sewing on some white cambric and embroidery. She sewed industriously while her mother cooked, her soft milk-white hands and wrists showed whiter than her delicate work.

"We must have the stove moved out in the shed before long," said Mrs. Penn. "Talk about not havin' things, it's been a real blessin' to be able to put a stove up in that shed in hot weather. Father did one good thing when he fixed that stove-pipe out there."

Sarah Penn's face as she rolled her pies had that expression of meek vigor which might have characterized one of the New Testament saints. She was making mince-pies. Her husband, Adoniram Penn, liked them better than any other kind. She baked twice a week. Adoniram often liked a piece of pie between meals. She hurried this morning. It had been later than usual when she began, and she wanted to have a pie baked for dinner. However deep a resentment she might be forced to hold against her husband, she would never fail in sedulous attention to his wants.

Nobility of character manifests itself in loop-holes when it is not provided with large doors. Sarah Penn's showed itself to-day in flaky dishes of pastry. So she made the pies faithfully, while across the table she could see, when she glanced up from her work, the sight that rankled in her patient and steadfast soul—the digging of the cellar of the new barn in the place where Adoniram forty years ago had promised her their new house should stand.

The pies were done for dinner. Adoniram and Sammy were home a few minutes after twelve o'clock. The dinner was eaten with serious haste. There was never much conversation at the table in the Penn family. Adoniram asked a blessing, and they ate promptly, then rose up and went about their work.

Sammy went back to school, taking soft sly lopes out of the yard like rabbit. He wanted a game of marbles before school, and feared his father would give him some chores to do. Adoniram hastened to the door and called after him, but he was out of sight.

"I don't see what you let him go for, mother," said he. "I wanted him to help me unload that wood."

Adoniram went to work out in the yard unloading wood from the wagon. Sarah put away the dinner dishes, while Nanny took down her curl-papers and changed her dress. She was going down to the store to buy some more embroidery and thread.

When Nanny was gone, Mrs. Penn went to the door. "Father!" she called.

"Well, what is it!"

"I want to see you jest a minute, father."

"I can't leave this wood nohow. I've got to git it unloaded an' go for a load of gravel afore two o'clock. Sammy had ought to helped me. You hadn't ought to let him go to school so early."

"I want to see you jest a minute."

"I tell ye I can't, nohow, mother."

"Father, you come here." Sarah Penn stood in the door like a queen; she held her head as if it bore a crown; there was that patience which makes authority royal in her voice. Adoniram went.

Mrs. Penn led the way into the kitchen, and pointed to a chair. "Sit down, father," said she; "I've got somethin' I want to say to you."

He sat down heavily; his face was quite stolid, but he looked at her with restive eyes. "Well, what is it, mother?"

"I want to know what you're buildin' that new barn for, father?"

"I ain't got nothin' to say about it."

"It can't be you think you need another barn?"

"I tell ye I ain't got nothin' to say about it, mother; an' I ain't goin' to say nothin'."

"Be you goin' to buy more cows?"

Adoniram did not reply; he shut his mouth tight.

"I know you be, as well as I want to. Now, father, look here"—Sarah Penn had not sat down; she stood before her husband in the humble fashion of a Scripture woman—"I'm goin' to talk real plain to you; I never have sence I married you, but I'm goin' to now. I ain't never complained, an' I ain't goin' to complain now, but I'm goin' to talk plain. You see this room here, father; you look at it well. You see there ain't no carpet on the floor, an' you see the paper is all dirty, an' droppin' off the walls. We ain't had no new paper on it for ten year, an' then I put it on myself, an' it didn't cost but ninepence a roll. You see this room, father; it's all the one I've had to work in an' eat in an' sit in sence we was married. There ain't another woman in the whole town whose husband ain't got half the means you have but what's got better. It's all the room Nanny's got to have her company in; an' there ain't one of her mates but what's got better, an' their fathers not so able as hers is. It's all the room she'll have to be married in. What would you have thought, father, if we had had our weddin' in a room no better than this? I was married in my mother's parlor, with a carpet on the floor, an' stuffed furniture, an' a mahogany card-table. An' this is all the room my daughter will have to be married in. Look here, father!"

Sarah Penn went across the room as though it were a tragic stage. She flung open a door and disclosed a tiny bedroom, only large enough for a bed and bureau, with a path between. "There, father," said she—"there's all the room I've had to sleep in forty year. All my children were born there—the two that died, an' the two that's livin'. I was sick with a fever there."

She stepped to another door and opened it. It led into the small, ill-lighted pantry. "Here," said she, "is all the buttery I've got—every place I've got for my dishes, to set away my victuals in, an' to keep my milk-pans in. Father, I've been takin' care of the milk of six cows in this place, an' now you're goin' to build a new barn, an' keep more cows, an' give me more to do in it."

She threw open another door. A narrow crooked flight of stairs wound upward from it. "There, father," said she, "I want you to look at the stairs that go up to them two unfinished chambers that are all the places our son an' daughter have had to sleep in all their lives. There ain't a prettier girl in town nor a more ladylike one than Nanny, an' that's the place she has to sleep in. It ain't so good as your horse's stall; it ain't so warm an' tight."

Sarah Penn went back and stood before her husband. "Now, father," said she, "I want to know if you think you're doin' right an' accordin' to what you profess. Here, when we was married, forty year ago, you promised me faithful that we should have a new house built in that lot over in the field before the year was out. You said you had money enough, an' you wouldn't ask me to live in no such place as this. It is forty year now, an' you've been makin' more money, an' I've been savin' of it for you ever since, an' you ain't built no house yet. You've built sheds an' cow-houses an' one new barn, an' now you're goin' to build another. Father, I want to know if you think it's right. You're lodgin' your dumb beasts better than you are your own flesh an' blood. I want to know if you think it's right."

"I ain't got nothin' to say."

"You can't say nothin' without ownin' it ain't right, father. An' there's another thing—I ain't complained; I've got along forty year, an' I s'pose I should forty more, if it wa'n't for that—if we don't have another house. Nanny she can't live with us after she's married. She'll have to go somewheres else to live away from us, an' it don't seem as if I could have it so, noways, father. She wa'n't ever strong. She's got considerable color, but there wa'n't never any backbone to her. I've always took the heft of everything off her, an' she ain't fit to keep house an' do everything herself. She'll be all worn out inside of a year. Think of her doin' all the washin' an' ironin' an' bakin' with them soft white hands an' arms, an' sweepin'! I can't have it so, noways, father."

Mrs. Penn's face was burning; her mild eyes gleamed. She had pleaded her little cause like a Webster; she had ranged from severity to pathos; but her opponent employed that obstinate silence which makes eloquence futile with mocking echoes. Adoniram arose clumsily.

"Father, ain't you got nothin' to say?" said Mrs. Penn.

"I've got to go off after that load of gravel. I can't stan' here talkin' all day."

"Father, won't you think it over, an' have a house built there instead of a barn?"

"I ain't got nothin' to say."

Adoniram shuffled out. Mrs. Penn went into her bedroom. When she came out, her eyes were red. She had a roll of unbleached cotton cloth. She spread it out on the kitchen table, and began cutting out some shirts for her husband. The men over in the field had a team to help them this afternoon; she could hear their halloos. She had a scanty pattern for the shirts; she had to plan and piece the sleeves.

Nanny came home with her embroidery, and sat down with her needlework. She had taken down her curl-papers, and there was a soft roll of fair hair like an aureole over her forehead; her face was as delicately fine and clear as porcelain. Suddenly she looked up, and the tender red flamed all over her face and neck. "Mother," said she.

"What say?"

"I've been thinking— I don't see how we're goin' to have any—wedding in this room. I'd be ashamed to have his folks come if we didn't have anybody else."

"Mebbe we can have some new paper before then; I can put it on. I guess you won't have no call to be ashamed of your belongin's."

"We might have the wedding in the new barn," said Nanny, with gentle pettishness. "Why, mother, what makes you look so?"

Mrs. Penn had started, and was staring at her with a curious expression. She turned again to her work, and spread out a pattern carefully on the cloth. "Nothin'," said she.

Presently Adoniram clattered out of the yard in his two-wheeled dump cart, standing as proudly upright as a Roman charioteer. Mrs. Penn opened the door and stood there a minute looking out; the halloos of the men sounded louder.

It seemed to her all through the spring months that she heard nothing but the halloos and the noises of saws and hammers. The new barn grew fast. It was a fine edifice for this little village. Men came on pleasant Sundays, in their meeting suits and clean shirt bosoms, and stood around it admiringly. Mrs. Penn did not speak of it, and Adoniram did not mention it to her, although sometimes, upon a return from inspecting it, he bore himself with injured dignity.

"It's a strange thing how your mother feels about the new barn," he said, confidentially, to Sammy one day.

Sammy only grunted after an odd fashion for a boy; he had learned it from his father.

The barn was all completed ready for use by the third week in July. Adoniram had planned to move his stock in on Wednesday; on Tuesday he received a letter which changed his plans. He came in with it early in the morning. "Sammy's been to the post-office," said he, "an' I've got a letter from Hiram." Hiram was Mrs. Penn's brother, who lived in Vermont.

"Well," said Mrs. Penn, "what does he say about the folks?"

"I guess they're all right. He says he thinks if I come up country right off there's a chance to buy jest the kind of a horse I want." He stared reflectively out of the window at the new barn.

Mrs. Penn was making pies. She went on clapping the rolling-pin into the crust, although she was very pale, and her heart beat loudly.

"I dun' know but what I'd better go," said Adoniram. "I hate to go off jest now, right in the midst of hayin', but the ten-acre lot's cut, an' I guess Rufus an' the others can git along without me three or four days. I can't get a horse round here to suit me, nohow, an' I've got to have another for all that wood-haulin' in the fall. I told Hiram to watch out, an' if he got wind of a good horse to let me know. I guess I'd better go."

"I'll get out your clean shirt an' collar," said Mrs. Penn calmly.

She laid out Adoniram's Sunday suit and his clean clothes on the bed in the little bedroom. She got his shaving-water and razor ready. At last she buttoned on his collar and fastened his black cravat.

Adoniram never wore his collar and cravat except on extra occasions. He held his head high, with a rasped dignity. When he was all ready, with his coat and hat brushed, and a lunch of pie and cheese in a paper bag, he hesitated on the threshold of the door. He looked at his wife, and his manner was defiantly apologetic. "*If* them cows come to-day, Sammy can drive 'em into the new barn," said he; "an' when they bring the hay up, they can pitch it in there."

"Well," replied Mrs. Penn.

Adoniram set his shaven face ahead and started. When he had cleared the doorstep, he turned and looked back with a kind of nervous solemnity. "I shall be back by Saturday if nothin' happens," said he.

"Do be careful, father," returned his wife.

She stood in the door with Nanny at her elbow and watched him out of sight. Her eyes had a strange, doubtful expression in them; her peaceful forehead was contracted. She went in, and about her baking again. Nanny sat sewing. Her wedding-day was drawing nearer, and she was getting pale and thin with her steady sewing. Her mother kept glancing at her.

"Have you got that pain in your side this mornin'?" she asked.

"A little."

Mrs. Penn's face, as she worked, changed, her perplexed forehead smoothed, her eyes were steady, her lips firmly set. She formed a maxim for herself, although incoherently with her unlettered thoughts. "Unsolicited opportunities are the guideposts of the Lord to the new roads of life," she repeated in effect, and she made up her mind to her course of action.

"S'posin' I *had* wrote to Hiram," she muttered once, when she was in the pantry—"s'posin' I had wrote, an' asked him if he knew of any horse? But I didn't, an' father's goin' wa'n't none of my doin'. It looks like a providence." Her voice rang out quite loud at the last.

"What you talkin' about, mother?" called Nanny.

"Nothin'."

Mrs. Penn hurried her baking; at eleven o'clock it was all done. The load of hay from the west field came slowly down the cart track, and drew up at the new barn. Mrs. Penn ran out. "Stop!" she screamed—"stop!"

The men stopped and looked; Sammy upreared from the top of the load, and stared at his mother.

"Stop!" she cried out again. "Don't you put the hay in that barn; put it in the old one."

"Why, he said to put it in here," returned one of the haymakers, wonderingly. He was a young man, a neighbor's son, whom Adoniram hired by the year to help on the farm.

"Don't you put the hay in the new barn; there's room enough in the old one, ain't there?" said Mrs. Penn.

"Room enough," returned the hired man, in his thick, rustic tones. "Didn't need the new barn, nohow, far as room's concerned. Well, I s'pose he changed his mind." He took hold of the horses' bridles.

Mrs. Penn went back to the house. Soon the kitchen windows were darkened, and a fragrance like warm honey came into the room.

Nanny laid down her work. "I thought father wanted them to put the hay into the new barn?" she said, wonderingly.

"It's all right," replied her mother.

Sammy slid down from the load of hay, and came in to see if dinner was ready.

"I ain't goin' to get a regular dinner to-day, as long as father's gone," said his mother. "I've let the fire go out. You can have some bread an' milk an' pie. I thought we could get along." She set out some bowls of milk, some bread, and a pie on the kitchen table. "You'd better eat your dinner now," said she. "You might jest as well get through with it. I want you to help me afterward."

Nanny and Sammy stared at each other. There was something strange in their mother's manner. Mrs. Penn did not eat anything herself. She went into the pantry, and they heard her moving dishes while they ate. Presently she came out with a pile of plates. She got the clothesbasket out of the shed, and packed them in it. Nanny and Sammy watched. She brought out cups and saucers, and put them in with the plates.

"What you goin' to do, mother?" inquired Nanny, in a timid voice. A sense of something unusual made her tremble, as if it were a ghost. Sammy rolled his eyes over his pie.

"You'll see what I'm goin' to do," replied Mrs. Penn. "If you're through, Nanny, I want you to go up-stairs an' pack up your things; an' I want you, Sammy, to help me take down the bed in the bedroom."

"Oh, mother, what for?" gasped Nanny.

"You'll see."

During the next few hours a feat was performed by this simple, pious New England mother which was equal in its way to Wolfe's storming of the Heights of Abraham. It took no more genius and audacity of bravery for Wolfe to cheer his wondering soldiers up those steep precipices, under the sleeping eyes of the enemy, than for Sarah Penn, at the head of her children, to move all their little household goods into the new barn while her husband was away.

Nanny and Sammy followed their mother's instructions without a murmur; indeed, they were overawed. There is a certain uncanny and superhuman quality about all such purely original undertakings as their mother's was to them. Nanny went back and forth with her light loads, and Sammy tugged with sober energy.

At five o'clock in the afternoon the little house in which the Penns had lived for forty years had emptied itself into the new barn.

Every builder builds somewhat for unknown purposes, and is in a measure a prophet. The architect of Adoniram Penn's barn, while he designed it for the comfort of four-footed animals, had planned better than he knew for the comfort of humans. Sarah Penn saw at a glance its possibilities. Those great box-stalls, with quilts hung before them, would make better bedrooms than the one she had occupied for forty years, and there was a tight carriage-room. The harness-room, with its chimney and shelves, would make a kitchen of her dreams. The great middle space would make a parlor, by-and-by, fit for a palace. Up stairs there was as much room as down. With partitions and windows, what a house would there be! Sarah looked at the row of stanchions before the allotted space for cows, and reflected that she would have her front entry there.

At six o'clock the stove was up in the harness-room, the kettle was boiling, and the table set for tea. It looked almost as home-like as the abandoned house across the yard had ever done. The young hired man milked, and Sarah directed him calmly to bring the milk to the new barn. He came gaping, dropping little blots of foam from the brimming pails on the grass. Before the next morning he had spread the story of Adoniram Penn's wife moving into the new barn all over the little village. Men assembled in the store and talked it over, women with shawls over their heads scuttled into each other's houses before their work was done. Any deviation from the ordinary course of life in this quiet town was enough to stop all progress in it. Everybody paused to look at the staid, independent figure on the side track. There was a difference of opinion with regard to her. Some held her to be insane; some, of a lawless and rebellious spirit.

Friday the minister went to see her. It was in the forenoon, and she was at the barn door shelling peas for dinner. She looked up and returned his salutation with dignity, then she went on with her work. She did not invite him in. The saintly expression of her face remained fixed, but there was an angry flush over it.

The minister stood awkwardly before her, and talked. She handled the peas as if they were bullets. At last she looked up, and her eyes showed the spirit that her meek front had covered for a lifetime.

"There ain't no use talkin', Mr. Hersey," said she. "I've thought it all over an' over, an' I believe I'm doin' what's right. I've made it the subject of prayer, an' it's betwixt me an' the Lord an' Adoniram. There ain't no call for nobody else to worry about it."

"Well, of course, if you have brought it to the Lord in prayer, and feel satisfied that you are doing right, Mrs. Penn," said the minister, helplessly. His thin gray-bearded face was pathetic. He was a sickly man; his youthful confidence had cooled; he had to scourge himself up to some of his pastoral duties as relentlessly as a Catholic ascetic, and then he was prostrated by the smart.

"I think it's right jest as much as I think it was right for our forefathers to come over from the old country 'cause they didn't have what belonged to 'em," said Mrs. Penn. She arose. The barn threshold might have been Plymouth Rock from her bearing. "I don't doubt you mean well, Mr. Hersey," said she, "but there are things people hadn't ought to interfere with. I've been a member of the church for over forty year. I've got my own mind an' my own feet, an' I'm goin' to think my own thoughts an' go my own ways, an' nobody but the Lord is goin' to dictate to me unless I've a mind to have him. Won't you come in an' set down? How is Mis' Hersey?"

"She is well, I thank you," replied the minister. He added some more perplexed apologetic remarks; then he retreated.

He could expound the intricacies of every character study in the Scriptures, he was competent to grasp the Pilgrim Fathers and all historical innovators, but Sarah Penn was beyond him. He could deal with primal cases, but parallel ones worsted him. But, after all, although it was aside from his province, he wondered more how Adoniram Penn would deal with his wife than how the Lord would. Everybody shared the wonder. When Adoniram's four new cows arrived, Sarah ordered three to be put in the old barn, the other in the house shed where the cooking-stove had stood. That added to the excitement. It was whispered that all four cows were domiciled in the house.

Towards sunset on Saturday, when Adoniram was expected home, there was a knot of men in the road near the new barn. The hired man had milked, but he still hung around the premises. Sarah Penn had supper all ready. There were brown-bread and baked beans and a custard pie; it was the supper that Adoniram loved on a Saturday night. She had on a clean calico, and she bore herself imperturbably. Nanny and Sammy kept close at her heels. Their eyes were large, and Nanny was full of nervous tremors. Still there was to them more pleasant excitement than anything else. An inborn confidence in their mother over their father asserted itself.

Sammy looked out of the harness-room window. "There he is," he announced, in an awed whisper. He and Nanny peeped around the casing. Mrs. Penn kept on about her work. The children watched Adoniram leave the new horse standing in the drive while he went to the house door. It was fastened. Then he went around to the shed. That door was seldom locked, even when the family was away. The thought how her father would be confronted by the cow flashed upon Nanny. There was a hysterical sob in her throat. Adoniram emerged from the shed and stood looking around in a dazed fashion. His lips moved; he was saying something, but they could not hear what it was. The hired man was peeping around a corner of the old barn, but nobody saw him.

Adoniram took the new horse by the bridle and led him across the yard to the new barn. Nanny and Sammy slunk close to their mother. The barn doors rolled back, and there stood Adoniram, with the long mild face of the great Canadian farm horse looking over his shoulder.

Nanny kept behind her mother, but Sammy stepped suddenly forward, and stood in front of her.

Adoniram stared at the group. "What on airth you all down here for?" said he. "What's the matter over to the house?"

"We've come here to live, father," said Sammy. His shrill voice quavered out bravely.

"What"—Adoniram sniffed—"what is it smells like cookin'?" said he. He stepped forward and looked in the open door of the harness-room. Then he turned to his wife. His old bristling face was pale and frightened. "What on airth does this mean, mother?" he gasped.

"You come in here, father," said Sarah. She led the way into the harness-room and shut the door. "Now, father," said she, "you needn't be scared. I ain't crazy. There ain't nothin' to be upset over. But we've come here to live, an' we're goin' to live here. We've got jest as good a right here as new horses an' cows. The house wa'n't fit for us to live in any longer, an' I made up my mind I wa'n't goin' to stay there. I've done my duty by you forty year, an' I'm goin' to do it now; but I'm goin' to live here. You've got to put in some windows and partitions; an' you'll have to buy some furniture."

"Why, mother!" the old man gasped.

"You'd better take your coat off an' get washed—there's the wash-basin—an' then we'll have supper."

"Why, mother!"

Sammy went past the window, leading the new horse to the old barn. The old man saw him, and shook his head speechlessly. He tried to take off his coat, but his arms seemed to lack the power. His wife helped him. She poured some water into the tin basin, and put in a piece of soap. She got the comb and brush, and smoothed his thin gray hair after he had washed. Then she put the beans, hot bread, and tea on the table. Sammy came in and the family drew up. Adoniram sat looking dazedly at his plate, and they waited.

"Ain't you goin' to ask a blessin', father?" said Sarah.

And the old man bent his head and mumbled.

All through the meal he stopped eating at intervals, and stared furtively at his wife; but he ate well. The home food tasted good to him, and his old frame was too sturdily healthy to be affected by his mind. But after supper he went out, and sat down on the step of the smaller door at the right of the barn, through which he had meant his Jerseys to pass in stately file, but which Sarah designed for her front house door, and he leaned his head on his hands.

After the supper dishes were cleared away and the milkpans washed, Sarah went out to him. The twilight was deepening. There was a clear green glow in the sky. Before them stretched the smooth level of field; in the distance was a cluster of haystacks like the huts of a village; the air was very cool and calm and sweet. The landscape might have been an ideal one of peace.

Sarah bent over and touched her husband on one of this thin, sinewy shoulders. "Father!"

The old man's shoulders heaved: he was weeping.

"Why, don't do so, father," said Sarah.

"I'll—put up the—partitions, an'—everything you—want, mother."

Sarah put her apron up to her face; she was overcome by her own triumph.

Adoniram was like a fortress whose walls had no active resistance, and went down the instant the right besieging tools were used. "Why, mother," he said, hoarsely, "I hadn't no idee you was so set on't as all this comes to."

QUESTIONS FOR DISCUSSION AND WRITING

1. How does the major conflict in the story illustrate a clash of gender roles and expectations?
2. How do the physical descriptions in the first few paragraphs reveal the characters? How does the father's refusal to respond to his wife's questions suggest his sense of power?
3. How does the description of the buildings on the farm reflect the values of the people who live there? To what extent does the community share these values?
4. How does the narrator's use of allusion—e.g., General James Wolfe's "storming the Heights of Abraham"—suggest her distance from the people she writes about?
5. Why is it thematically important that Freeman titles her story "The Revolt of 'Mother'" rather than "The Revolt of Sarah"?

33

ERNEST J. GAINES

The Sky Is Gray

ERNEST J. GAINES was born in 1933 in Oscar, Louisiana, and educated at Valley's Junior College, San Francisco State University, and Stanford University. He has worked as a writer-in-residence at Denison University, Stanford University, and the University of Southwestern Louisiana. Gaines's boyhood experiences growing up in Louisiana provide the setting for many of his novels such as *Of Love and Dust* (1967), *The Autobiography of Miss Jane Pittman* (1971), *A Gathering of Old Men* (1983), and his most recent work, *A Lesson Before Dying* (1993). The best of his short stories are collected in *Bloodline* (1968). "The Sky Is Gray," reprinted from *Bloodline*, documents a young boy's growing awareness of what it means to be a man in a world full of poverty and prejudice.

1

Go'n be coming in a few minutes. Coming round that bend down there full speed. And I'm go'n get out my handkerchief and wave it down, and we go'n get on it and go.

I keep on looking for it, but Mama don't look that way no more. She's looking down the road where we just come from. It's a long old road, and far 's you can see you don't see nothing but gravel. You got dry weeds on both sides, and you got trees on both sides, and fences on both sides, too. And you got cows in the pastures and they standing close together. And when we was coming out here to catch the bus I seen the smoke coming out of the cows's noses.

I look at my mama and I know what she's thinking. I been with Mama so much, just me and her, I know what she's thinking all the time. Right now it's home—Auntie and them. She's thinking if they got enough wood—if she left enough there to keep them warm till we get back. She's thinking if it go'n rain and if any of them go'n have to go out in the rain. She's thinking 'bout the hog—if he go'n get out, and if Ty and Val be able to get him back in. She always worry like that when she leaves the house. She don't worry too much if she leave me there with the smaller ones, 'cause she know I'm go'n look after them and look after Auntie and everything else. I'm the oldest and she say I'm the man.

I look at my mama and I love my mama. She's wearing that black coat and that black hat and she's looking sad. I love my mama and I want put my arm round her and tell her. But I'm not supposed to do that. She say that's weakness and that's crybaby stuff, and she don't want no crybaby round her. She don't want you to be scared, either. 'Cause Ty's scared of ghosts and she's always whipping him. I'm scared of the dark, too, but I make 'tend I ain't. I make 'tend I ain't 'cause I'm the oldest, and I got to set a good sample for the rest. I can't ever be scared and I can't ever cry. And that's why I never said nothing 'bout my teeth. It's been hurting me and hurting me close to a month now, but I never said it. I didn't say it 'cause I didn't want act like a crybaby, and 'cause I know we didn't have enough money to go have it pulled. But, Lord, it been hurting me. And look like it wouldn't start till at night when you was trying to get yourself little sleep. Then soon 's you shut your eyes—ummm-ummm, Lord, look like it go right down to your heartstring.

"Hurting, hanh?" Ty'd say.

I'd shake my head, but I wouldn't open my mouth for nothing. You open your mouth and let that wind in, and it almost kill you.

I'd just lay there and listen to them snore. Ty there, right 'side me, and Auntie and Val over by the fireplace. Val younger than me and Ty, and he sleeps with Auntie. Mama sleeps round the other side with Louis and Walker.

I'd just lay there and listen to them, and listen to that wind out there, and listen to that fire in the fireplace. Sometimes it'd stop long enough to let me get little rest. Sometimes it just hurt, hurt, hurt. Lord, have mercy.

2

Auntie knowed it was hurting me. I didn't tell nobody but Ty, 'cause we buddies and he ain't go'n tell nobody. But some kind of way Auntie found out. When she asked me, I told her no, nothing was wrong. But she knowed it all the time. She told me to mash up a piece of aspirin and wrap it in some cotton and jugg it down in that hole. I did it, but it didn't do no good. It stopped for a little while, and started right back again. Auntie wanted to tell Mama, but I told her, "Uh-uh." 'Cause I knowed we didn't have any money, and it just was go'n make her mad again. So Auntie told Monsieur Bayonne, and Monsieur Bayonne came over to the house and told me to kneel down 'side him on the fireplace. He put his finger in his mouth and made the Sign of the Cross on my jaw. The tip of Monsieur Bayonne's finger is some hard, 'cause he's always playing on that guitar. If we sit outside at night we can always hear Monsieur Bayonne playing on his guitar. Sometimes we leave him out there playing on the guitar.

Monsieur Bayonne made the Sign of the Cross over and over on my jaw, but that didn't do no good. Even when he prayed and told me to pray some, too, that tooth still hurt me.

"How you feeling?" he say.

"Same," I say.

He kept on praying and making the Sign of the Cross and I kept on praying, too.

"Still hurting?" he say.

"Yes, sir."

Monsieur Bayonne mashed harder and harder on my jaw. He mashed so hard he almost pushed me over on Ty. But then he stopped.

"What kind of prayers you praying, boy?" he say.

"Baptist," I say.

"Well, I'll be—no wonder that tooth still killing him. I'm going one way and he pulling the other. Boy, don't you know any Catholic prayers?"

"I know 'Hail Mary,' " I say.

"Then you better start saying it."

"Yes, sir."

He started mashing on my jaw again, and I could hear him praying at the same time. And, sure enough, after while it stopped hurting me.

Me and Ty went outside where Monsieur Bayonne's two hounds was and we started playing with them. "Let's go hunting," Ty say. "All right," I say; and we went on back in the pasture. Soon the hounds got on a trail, and me and Ty followed them all 'cross the pasture and then back in the woods, too. And then they cornered this little old rabbit and killed him, and me and Ty made them get back, and we picked up the rabbit and started on back home. But my tooth had started hurting me again. It was hurting me plenty now, but I wouldn't tell Monsieur Bayonne. That night I didn't sleep a bit, and first thing in the morning Auntie told me to go back and let Monsieur Bayonne pray over me some more. Monsieur Bayonne was in his kitchen making coffee when I got there. Soon 's he seen me he knowed what was wrong.

"All right, kneel down there 'side that stove," he say. "And this time make sure you pray Catholic. I don't know nothing 'bout that Baptist, and I don't want know nothing 'bout him."

3

Last night Mama say, "Tomorrow we going to town."

"It ain't hurting me no more," I say. "I can eat anything on it."

"Tomorrow we going to town," she say.

And after she finished eating, she got up and went to bed. She always go to bed early now. 'Fore Daddy went in the Army, she used to stay up late. All of us sitting out on the gallery or round the fire. But now, look like soon 's she finish eating she go to bed.

This morning when I woke up, her and Auntie was standing 'fore the fireplace. She say: "Enough to get there and get back. Dollar and a half to have it pulled. Twenty-five for me to go, twenty-five for him. Twenty-five for me to come back, twenty-five for him. Fifty cents left. Guess I get little piece of salt meat with that."

"Sure can use it," Auntie say. "White beans and no salt meat ain't white beans."

"I do the best I can," Mama say.

They was quiet after that, and I made 'tend I was still asleep.

"James, hit the floor," Auntie say.

I still made 'tend I was asleep. I didn't want them to know I was listening.

"All right," Auntie say, shaking me by the shoulder. "Come on. Today's the day."

I pushed the cover down to get out, and Ty grabbed it and pulled it back.

"You, too, Ty," Auntie say.

"I ain't getting no teef pulled," Ty say.

"Don't mean it ain't time to get up," Auntie say. "Hit it, Ty."

Ty got up grumbling.

"James, you hurry up and get in your clothes and eat your food," Auntie say. "What time y'all coming back?" she say to Mama.

"That 'leven o'clock bus," Mama say. "Got to get back in that field this evening."

"Get a move on you, James," Auntie say.

I went in the kitchen and washed my face, then I ate my breakfast. I was having bread and syrup. The bread was warm and hard and tasted good. And I tried to make it last a long time.

Ty came back there grumbling and mad at me.

"Got to get up," he say. "I ain't having no teefes pulled. What I got to be getting up for?"

Ty poured some syrup in his pan and got a piece of bread. He didn't wash his hands, neither his face, and I could see that white stuff in his eyes.

"You the one getting your teef pulled," he say. "What I got to get up for. I bet if I was getting a teef pulled, you wouldn't be getting up. Shucks; syrup again. I'm getting tired of this old syrup. Syrup, syrup, syrup. I'm go'n take with the sugar diabetes. I want me some bacon sometime."

"Go out in the field and work and you can have your bacon," Auntie say. She stood in the middle door looking at Ty. "You better be glad you got syrup. Some people ain't got that—hard 's time is."

"Shucks," Ty say. "How can I be strong."

"I don't know too much 'bout your strength," Auntie say; "but I know where you go'n be hot at, you keep that grumbling up. James, get a move on you; your mama waiting."

I ate my last piece of bread and went in the front room. Mama was standing 'fore the fireplace warming her hands. I put on my coat and my cap, and we left the house.

4

I look down there again, but it still ain't coming. I almost say, "It ain't coming yet," but I keep my mouth shut. 'Cause that's something else she don't like. She don't like for you to say something just for nothing. She can see it ain't coming, I can see it ain't coming, so why say it ain't coming. I don't say it, I turn and look at the river that's back of us. It's so cold the smoke's just raising up from the water. I see a bunch of pool-doos not too far out—just on the other side the lilies. I'm wondering if you can eat pool-doos. I ain't too sure, 'cause I ain't never ate none. But I done ate owls and blackbirds, and I done ate redbirds, too. I didn't want kill the redbirds, but she made me kill them. They had two of them back there. One in my trap, one in Ty's trap. Me and Ty was go'n play with them and let them go, but she made me kill them 'cause we needed the food.

"I can't," I say. "I can't."

"Here," she say. "Take it."

"I can't," I say. "I can't. I can't kill him, Mama, please."

"Here," she say. "Take this fork, James."

"Please, Mama, I can't kill him," I say.

I could tell she was go'n hit me. I jerked back, but I didn't jerk back soon enough.

"Take it," she say.

I took it and reached in for him, but he kept on hopping to the back.

"I can't, Mama," I say. The water just kept on running down my face. "I can't," I say.

"Get him out of there," she say.

I reached in for him and he kept on hopping to the back. Then I reached in farther, and he pecked me on the hand.

"I can't, Mama," I say.

She slapped me again.

I reached in again, but he kept on hopping out my way. Then he hopped to one side and I reached there. The fork got him on the leg and I heard his leg pop. I pulled my hand out 'cause I had hurt him.

"Give it here," she say, and jerked the fork out my hand.

She reached in and got the little bird right in the neck. I heard the fork go in his neck, and I heard it go in the ground. She brought him out and helt him right in front of me.

"That's one," she say. She shook him off and gived me the fork. "Get the other one."

"I can't, Mama," I say. "I'll do anything, but don't make me do that."

She went to the corner of the fence and broke the biggest switch over there she could find. I knelt 'side the trap, crying.

"Get him out of there," she say.

"I can't, Mama."

She started hitting me 'cross the back. I went down on the ground, crying.

"Get him," she say.

"Octavia?" Auntie say.

'Cause she had come out of the house and she was standing by the tree looking at us.

"Get him out of there," Mama say.

"Octavia," Auntie say, "explain to him. Explain to him. Just don't beat him. Explain to him."

But she hit me and hit me and hit me.

I'm still young—I ain't no more than eight; but I know now; I know why I had to do it. (They was so little, though. They was so little. I 'member how I picked the feathers off them and cleaned them and helt them over the fire. Then we all ate them. Ain't had but a little bitty piece each, but we all had a little bitty piece, and everybody just looked at me 'cause they was so proud.) Suppose she had to go away? That's why I had to do it. Suppose she had to go away like Daddy went away? Then who was go'n look after us? They had to be somebody left to carry on. I didn't know it then, but I know it now. Auntie and Monsieur Bayonne talked to me and made me see.

5

Time I see it I get out my handkerchief and start waving. It's still 'way down there, but I keep waving anyhow. Then it come up and stop and me and Mama get on. Mama tell me go sit in the back while she pay. I do like she say, and the people look at me. When I pass the little sign that say "White" and "Colored," I start looking for a seat. I just see one of them back there, but I don't take it, 'cause I want my mama to sit down herself. She comes in the back and sit down, and I lean on the seat. They got seats in the front, but I know I can't sit there, 'cause I have to sit back of the sign. Anyhow, I don't want sit there if my mama go'n sit back here.

They got a lady sitting 'side my mama and she looks at me and smiles little bit. I smile back, but I don't open my mouth, 'cause the wind'll get in and make that tooth ache. The lady take out a pack of gum and reach me a slice, but I shake my head. The lady just can't understand why a little boy'll turn down gum, and she reach me a slice again. This time I point to my jaw. The lady understands and smiles little bit, and I smile little bit, but I don't open my mouth, though.

They got a girl sitting 'cross from me. She got on a red overcoat and her hair's plaited in one big plait. First, I make 'tend I don't see her over there, but then I start looking at her little bit. She make 'tend she don't see me, either, but I catch her looking that way. She got a cold, and every now and then she h'ist that little handkerchief to her nose. She ought to blow it, but she don't. Must think she's too much a lady or something.

Every time she h'ist that little handkerchief, the lady 'side her say something in her ear. She shakes her head and lays her hands in her lap again. Then I catch her kind of looking where I'm at. I smile at her little bit. But think she'll smile back? Uh-uh. She just turn up her little old nose and turn her head. Well, I show her both of us can turn us head. I turn mine too and look out at the river.

The river is gray. The sky is gray. They have pool-doos on the water. The water is wavy, and the pool-doos go up and down. The bus go round a turn, and you got plenty trees hiding the river. Then the bus go round another turn, and I can see the river again.

I look toward the front where all the white people sitting. Then I look at that little old gal again. I don't look right at her, 'cause I don't want all them people to know I love her. I just look at her little bit, like I'm looking out that window over there. But she knows I'm looking that way, and she kind of look at me, too. The lady sitting 'side her catch her this time, and she leans over and says something in her ear.

"I don't love him nothing," that little old gal says out loud.

Everybody back there hear her mouth, and all of them look at us and laugh.

"I don't love you, either," I say. "So you don't have to turn up your nose, Miss."

"You the one looking," she say.

"I wasn't looking at you," I say. "I was looking out that window, there."

"Out that window, my foot," she say. "I seen you. Everytime I turned round you was looking at me."

"You must of been looking yourself if you seen me all them times," I say.

"Shucks," she say, "I got me all kind of boyfriends."

"I got girlfriends, too," I say.

"Well, I just don't want you getting your hopes up," she say.

I don't say no more to that little old gal 'cause I don't want have to bust her in the mouth. I lean on the seat where Mama sitting, and I don't even look that way no more. When we get to Bayonne, she jugg her little old tongue out at me. I make 'tend I'm go'n hit her, and she duck down 'side her mama. And all the people laugh at us again.

6

Me and Mama get off and start walking in town. Bayonne is a little bitty town. Baton Rouge is a hundred times bigger than Bayonne. I went to Baton Rouge once—me, Ty, Mama, and Daddy. But that was 'way back yonder, 'fore Daddy went in the Army. I wonder when we go'n see him again. I wonder when. Look like he ain't ever coming back home. . . . Even the pavement all cracked in Bayonne. Got grass shooting right out the sidewalk. Got weeds in the ditch, too; just like they got at home.

It's some cold in Bayonne. Look like it's colder than it is home. The wind blows in my face, and I feel that stuff running down my nose. I sniff. Mama says use that handkerchief. I blow my nose and put it back.

We pass a school and I see them white children playing in the yard. Big old red school, and them children just running and playing. Then we pass a café, and I see a bunch of people in there eating. I wish I was in there 'cause I'm cold. Mama tells me keep my eyes in front where they belong.

We pass stores that's got dummies, and we pass another café, and then we pass a shoe shop, and that bald-head man in there fixing on a shoe. I look at him and I butt into that white lady, and Mama jerks me in front and tells me stay there.

We come up to the courthouse, and I see the flag waving there. This flag ain't like the one we got at school. This one here ain't got but a handful of stars. One at school got a big pile of stars—one for every state. We pass it and we turn and there it is—the dentist office. Me and Mama go in, and they got people sitting everywhere you look. They even got a little boy in there younger than me.

Me and Mama sit on that bench, and a white lady come in there and ask me what my name is. Mama tells her and the white lady goes on back. Then I hear somebody hollering in there. Soon 's that little boy hear him hollering, he starts hollering, too. His mama pats him and pats him, trying to make him hush up, but he ain't thinking 'bout his mama.

The man that was hollering in there comes out holding his jaw. He is a big old man and he's wearing overalls and a jumper.

"Got it, hanh?" another man asks him.

The man shakes his head—don't want open his mouth.

"Man, I thought they was killing you in there," the other man says. "Hollering like a pig under a gate."

The man don't say nothing. He just heads for the door, and the other man follows him.

"John Lee," the white lady says. "John Lee Williams."

The little boy juggs his head down in his mama's lap and holler more now. His mama tells him go with the nurse, but he ain't thinking 'bout his mama. His mama tells him again, but he don't even hear her. His mama picks him up and takes him in there, and even when the white lady shuts the door I can still hear little old John Lee.

"I often wonder why the Lord let a child like that suffer," a lady says to my mama. The lady's sitting right in front of us on another bench. She's got on a white dress and a black sweater. She must be a nurse or something herself, I reckon.

"Not us to question," a man says.

"Sometimes I don't know if we shouldn't," the lady says.

"I know definitely we shouldn't," the man says. The man looks like a preacher. He's big and fat and he's got on a black suit. He's got a gold chain, too.

"Why?" the lady says.

"Why anything?" the preacher says.

"Yes," the lady says. "Why anything?"

"Not us to question," the preacher says.

The lady looks at the preacher a little while and looks at Mama again.

"And look like it's the poor who suffers the most," she says. "I don't understand it."

"Best not to even try," the preacher says. "He works in mysterious ways—wonders to perform."

Right then little John Lee bust out hollering, and everybody turn they head to listen.

"He's not a good dentist," the lady says. "Dr. Robillard is much better. But more expensive. That's why most of the colored people come here. The white people go to Dr. Robillard. Y'all from Bayonne?"

"Down the river," my mama says. And that's all she go'n say, 'cause she don't talk much. But the lady keeps on looking at her, and so she says, "Near Morgan."

"I see," the lady says.

7

"That's the trouble with the black people in this country today," somebody else says. This one here's sitting on the same side me and Mama's sitting, and he is kind of sitting in front of that preacher. He looks like a teacher or somebody that goes to college. He's got on a suit, and he's got a book that he's been reading. "We don't question is exactly our problem," he says. "We should question and question and question—question everything."

The preacher just looks at him a long time. He done put a toothpick or something in his mouth, and he just keeps on turning it and turning it. You can see he don't like that boy with that book.

"Maybe you can explain what you mean," he says.

"I said what I meant," the boy says. "Question everything. Every stripe, every star, every word spoken. Everything."

"It 'pears to me that this young lady and I was talking 'bout God, young man," the preacher says.

"Question Him, too," the boy says.

"Wait," the preacher says. "Wait now."

"You heard me right," the boy says. "His existence as well as everything else. Everything."

The preacher just looks across the room at the boy. You can see he's getting madder and madder. But mad or no mad, the boy ain't thinking 'bout him. He looks at that preacher just 's hard 's the preacher looks at him.

"Is this what they coming to?" the preacher says. "Is this what we educating them for?"

"You're not educating me," the boy says. "I wash dishes at night so that I can go to school in the day. So even the words you spoke need questioning."

The preacher just looks at him and shakes his head.

"When I come in this room and seen you there with your book, I said to myself, 'There's an intelligent man.' How wrong a person can be."

"Show me one reason to believe in the existence of a God," the boys says.

"My heart tells me," the preacher says.

" 'My heart tells me,' " the boys says. " 'My heart tells me.' Sure, 'My heart tells me.' And as long as you listen to what your heart tells you, you will have only what the white man gives you and nothing more. Me, I don't listen to my heart. The purpose of the heart is to pump blood throughout the body, and nothing else."

"Who's your paw, boy?" the preacher says.

"Why?"

"Who is he?"

"He's dead."

"And your mom?"

"She's in Charity Hospital with pneumonia. Half killed herself, working for nothing."

"And 'cause he's dead and she's sick, you mad at the world?"

"I'm not mad at the world. I'm questioning the world. I'm questioning it with cold logic, sir. What do words like Freedom, Liberty, God, White, Colored mean? I want to know. That's why *you* are sending us to school, to read and to ask questions. And because we ask these questions, you call us mad. No sir, it is not us who are mad."

"You keep saying 'us'?"

" 'Us.' Yes—us. I'm not alone."

The preacher just shakes his head. Then he looks at everybody in the room—everybody. Some of the people look down at the floor, keep from looking at him. I kind of look 'way myself, but soon 's I know he done turn his head, I look that way again.

"I'm sorry for you," he says to the boy.

"Why?" the boy says. "Why not be sorry for yourself? Why are you so much better off than I am? Why aren't you sorry for these other people in here? Why not be sorry for the lady who had to drag her child into the dentist office? Why not be sorry for the lady sitting on that bench over there? Be sorry for them. Not for me. Some way or the other I'm going to make it."

"No, I'm sorry for you," the preacher says.

"Of course, of course," the boy says, nodding his head. "You're sorry for me because I rock that pillar you're leaning on."

"You can't ever rock the pillar I'm leaning on, young man. It's stronger than anything man can ever do."

"You believe in God because a man told you to believe in God," the boy says. "A white man told you to believe in God. And why? To keep you ignorant so he can keep his feet on your neck."

"So now we the ignorant?" the preacher says.

"Yes," the boy says. "Yes." And he opens his book again.

The preacher just looks at him sitting there. The boy done forgot all about him. Everybody else make 'tend they done forgot the squabble, too.

Then I see that preacher getting up real slow. Preacher's a great big old man and he got to brace himself to get up. He comes over where the boy is sitting. He just stands there a little while looking down at him, but the boy don't raise his head.

"Get up, boy," preacher says.

The boy looks up at him, then he shuts his book real slow and stands up. Preacher just hauls back and hit him in the face. The boy falls back 'gainst the wall, but he straightens himself up and looks right back at that preacher.

"You forgot the other cheek," he says.

The preacher hauls back and hit him again on the other side. But this time the boy braces himself and don't fall.

"That hasn't changed a thing," he says.

The preacher just looks at the boy. The preacher's breathing real hard like he just run up a big hill. The boy sits down and opens his book again.

"I feel sorry for you," the preacher says. "I never felt so sorry for a man before."

The boy makes 'tend he don't even hear that preacher. He keeps on reading his book. The preacher goes back and gets his hat off the chair.

"Excuse me," he says to us. "I'll come back some other time. Y'all, please excuse me."

And he looks at the boy and goes out the room. The boy h'ist his hand up to his mouth one time to wipe 'way some blood. All the rest of the time he keeps on reading. And nobody else in there say a word.

8

Little John Lee and his mama come out the dentist office, and the nurse calls somebody else in. Then little bit later they come out, and the nurse calls another name. But fast 's she calls somebody in there, somebody else comes in the place where we sitting, and the room stays full.

The people coming in now, all of them wearing big coats. One of them says something 'bout sleeting, another one says he hope not. Another one says he think it ain't nothing but rain. 'Cause, he says, rain can get awful cold this time of year.

All round the room they talking. Some of them talking to people right by them, some of them talking to people clear 'cross the room, some of them talking to anybody'll listen. It's a little bitty room, no bigger than us kitchen, and I can see everybody in there. The little old room's full of smoke, 'cause you got two old men smoking pipes over by that side door. I think I feel my tooth thumping me some, and I hold my breath and wait. I wait and wait, but it don't thump me no more. Thank God for that.

I feel like going to sleep, and I lean back 'gainst the wall. But I'm scared to go to sleep. Scared 'cause the nurse might call my name and I won't hear her. And Mama might go to sleep, too, and she'll be mad if neither one of us heard the nurse.

I look up at Mama. I love my mama. I love my mama. And when cotton come I'm go'n get her a new coat. And I ain't go'n get a black one, either. I think I'm go'n get her a red one.

"They got some books over there," I say. "Want read one of them?"

Mama looks at the books, but she don't answer me.

"You got yourself a little man there," the lady says.

Mama don't say nothing to the lady, but she must've smiled, 'cause I seen the lady smiling back. The lady looks at me a little while, like she's feeling sorry for me.

"You sure got that preacher out here in a hurry," she says to that boy.

The boy looks up at her and looks in his book again. When I grow up I want be just like him. I want clothes like that and I want keep a book with me, too.

"You really don't believe in God?" the lady says.

"No," he says.

"But why?" the lady says.

"Because the wind is pink," he says.

"What?" the lady says.

The boy don't answer her no more. He just reads in his book.

"Talking 'bout the wind is pink," that old lady says. She's sitting on the same bench with the boy and she's trying to look in his face. The boy makes 'tend the old lady ain't even there. He just keeps on reading. "Wind is pink," she says again. "Eh, Lord, what children go'n be saying next?"

The lady 'cross from us bust out laughing.

"That's a good one," she says. "The wind is pink. Yes sir, that's a good one."

"Don't you believe the wind is pink?" the boys says. He keeps his head down in the book.

"Course I believe it, honey," the lady says. "Course I do." She looks at us and winks her eye. "And what color is grass, honey?"

"Grass? Grass is black."

She bust out laughing again. The boy looks at her.

"Don't you believe grass is black?" he says.

The lady quits her laughing and looks at him. Everybody else looking at him, too. The place quiet, quiet

"Grass is green, honey," the lady says. "It was green yesterday, it's green today, and it's go'n be green tomorrow."

"How do you know it's green?"

"I know because I know."

"You don't know it's green," the boy says. "You believe it's green because someone told you it was green. If someone had told you it was black you'd believe it was black."

"It's green," the lady says. "I know green when I see green."

"Prove it's green," the boy says.

"Sure, now," the lady says. "Don't tell me it's coming to that."

"It's coming to just that," the boy says. "Words mean nothing. One means no more than the other."

"That's what it all coming to?" that old lady says. That old lady got on a turban and she got on two sweaters. She got a green sweater under a black sweater. I can see the green sweater 'cause some of the buttons on the other sweater's missing.

"Yes ma'am," the boy says. "Words mean nothing. Action is the only thing. Doing. That's the only thing."

"Other words, you want the Lord to come down here and show Hisself to you?" she says.

"Exactly, ma'am," he says.

"You don't mean that, I'm sure?" she says.

"I do, ma'am," he says.

"Done, Jesus," the old lady says, shaking her head.

"I didn't go 'long with that preacher at first," the other lady says; "but now—I don't know. When a person say the grass is black, he's either a lunatic or something's wrong."

"Prove to me that it's green," the boy says.

"It's green because the people say it's green."

"Those same people say we're citizens of these United States," the boy says.

"I think I'm a citizen," the lady says.

"Citizens have certain rights," the boy says. "Name me one right that you have. One right, granted by the Constitution, that you can exercise in Bayonne."

The lady don't answer him. She just looks at him like she don't know what he's talking 'bout. I know I don't.

"Things changing," she says.

"Things are changing because some black men have begun to think with their brains and not their hearts," the boy says.

"You trying to say these people don't believe in God?"

"I'm sure some of them do. Maybe most of them do. But they don't believe that God is going to touch these white people's hearts and change things tomorrow. Things change through action. By no other way."

Everybody sit quiet and look at the boy. Nobody says a thing. Then the lady 'cross the room from me and Mama just shakes her head.

"Let's hope that not all your generation feel the same way you do," she says.

"Think what you please, it doesn't matter," the boy says. "But it will be men who listen to their heads and not their hearts who will see that your children have a better chance than you had."

"Let's hope they ain't all like you, though," the old lady says. "Done forgot the heart absolutely."

"Yes ma'am, I hope they aren't all like me," the boy says. "Unfortunately, I was born too late to believe in your God. Let's hope that the ones who come after will have your faith—if not in your God, then in something else, something definitely that they can lean on. I haven't anything. For me, the wind is pink, the grass is black."

9

The nurse comes in the room where we all sitting and waiting and says the doctor won't take no more patients till one o'clock this evening. My mama jumps up off the bench and goes up to the white lady.

"Nurse, I have to go back in the field this evening," she says.

"The doctor is treating his last patient now," the nurse says. "One o'clock this evening."

"Can I at least speak to the doctor?" my mama asks.

"I'm his nurse," the lady says.

"My little boy's sick," my mama says. "Right now his tooth almost killing him."

The nurse looks at me. She's trying to make up her mind if to let me come in. I look at her real pitiful. The tooth ain't hurting me at all, but Mama say it is, so I make 'tend for her sake.

"This evening," the nurse says, and goes on back in the office.

"Don't feel 'jected, honey," the lady says to Mama. "I been round them a long time—they take you when they want to. If you was white, that's something else; but we the wrong color."

Mama don't say nothing to the lady, and me and her go outside and stand 'gainst the wall. It's cold out there. I can feel that wind going through my coat. Some of the other people come out of the room and go up the street. Me and Mama stand there a little while and we start walking. I don't know where we going. When we come to the other street we just stand there.

"You don't have to make water, do you?" Mama says.

"No, ma'am," I say.

We go on up the street. Walking real slow. I can tell Mama don't know where she's going. When we come to a store we stand there and look at the dummies. I look at a little boy wearing a brown overcoat. He's got on brown shoes, too. I look at my old shoes and look at his'n again. You wait till summer, I say.

Me and Mama walk away. We come up to another store and we stop and look at them dummies, too. Then we go on again. We pass a café where the white people in there eating. Mama tells me keep my eyes in front where they belong, but I can't help from seeing them people eat. My stomach starts to growling 'cause I'm hungry. When I see people eating, I get hungry; when I see a coat, I get cold.

A man whistles at my mama when we go by a filling station. She makes 'tend she don't even see him. I look back and I feel like hitting him in the mouth. If I was bigger, I say; if I was bigger, you'd see.

We keep on going. I'm getting colder and colder, but I don't say nothing. I feel that stuff running down my nose and I sniff.

"That rag," Mama says.

I get it out and wipe my nose. I'm getting cold all over now—my face, my hands, my feet, everything. We pass another little café, but this'n for white people, too, and we can't go in there, either. So we just walk. I'm so cold now I'm 'bout ready to say it. If I knowed where we was going I wouldn't be so cold, but I don't know where we going. We go, we go, we go. We walk clean out of Bayonne. Then we cross the street and we come back. Same thing I seen when I got off the bus this morning. Same old trees, same old walk, same old weeds, same old cracked pave—same old everything.

I sniff again.

"That rag," Mama says.

I wipe my nose real fast and jugg that handkerchief back in my pocket 'fore my hand gets too cold. I raise my head and I can see David's hardware store. When we come up to it, we go in. I don't know why, but I'm glad.

It's warm in there. It's so warm in there you don't ever want to leave. I look for the heater, and I see it over by them barrels. Three white men standing round the heater talking in Creole. One of them comes over to see what my mama want.

"Got any axe handles?" she says.

Me, Mama and the white man start to the back, but Mama stops me when we come up to the heater. She and the white man go on. I hold my hands over the heater and look at them. They go all the way to the back, and I see the white man pointing to the axe handles 'gainst the wall. Mama takes one of them and shakes it like she's trying to figure how much it weighs. Then she rubs her hand over it from one end to the other end. She turns it over and looks at the other side, then she shakes it again, and shakes her head and puts it back. She gets another one and she does it just like she did the first one, then she shakes her head. Then she gets a brown one and do it that, too. But she don't like this one, either. Then she gets another one, but 'fore she shakes it or anything, she looks at me. Look like she's trying to say something to me, but I don't know what it is. All I know is I done got warm now and I'm feeling right smart better. Mama shakes this axe handle just like she did the others, and shakes her head and says something to the white man. The white man just looks at his pile of axe handles, and when Mama pass him to come to the front, the white man just scratch his head and follows her. She tells me come on and we go on out and start walking again.

We walk and walk, and no time at all I'm cold again. Look like I'm colder now 'cause I can still remember how good it was back there. My stomach growls and I suck it in to keep Mama from hearing it. She's walking right 'side me, and it growls so loud you can hear it a mile. But Mama don't say a word.

10

When we come up to the courthouse, I look at the clock. It's got quarter to twelve. Mean we got another hour and a quarter to be out here in the cold. We go and stand 'side a building. Something hits my cap and I look up at the sky. Sleet's falling.

I look at Mama standing there. I want stand close 'side her, but she don't like that. She say that's crybaby stuff. She say you got to stand for yourself, by yourself.

"Let's go back to that office," she says.

We cross the street. When we get to the dentist office I try to open the door, but I can't. I twist and twist, but I can't. Mama pushes me to the side and she twist the knob, but she can't open the door, either. She turns 'way from the door. I look at her, but I don't move and I don't say nothing. I done seen her like this before and I'm scared of her.

"You hungry?" she says. She says it like she's mad at me, like I'm the cause of everything.

"No, ma'am," I say.

"You want eat and walk back, or you rather don't eat and ride?"

"I ain't hungry," I say.

I ain't just hungry, but I'm cold, too. I'm so hungry and cold I want to cry. And look like I'm getting colder and colder. My feet done got numb. I try to work my toes, but I don't even feel them. Look like I'm go'n die. Look like I'm go'n stand right here and freeze to death. I think 'bout home. I think 'bout Val and Auntie and Ty and Louis and Walker. It's 'bout twelve o'clock and I know they eating dinner now. I can hear Ty making jokes. He done forgot 'bout getting up early this morning and right now he's probably making jokes. Always trying to make somebody laugh. I wish I was right there listening to him. Give anything in the world if I was home round the fire.

"Come on," Mama says.

We start walking again. My feet so numb I can't hardly feel them. We turn the corner and go on back up the street. The clock on the courthouse starts hitting for twelve.

The sleet's coming down plenty now. They hit the pave and bounce like rice. Oh, Lord; oh, Lord, I pray. Don't let me die, don't let me die, don't let me die, Lord.

11

Now I know where we going. We going back of town where the colored people eat. I don't care if I don't eat. I been hungry before. I can stand it. But I can't stand the cold.

I can see we go'n have a long walk. It's 'bout a mile down there. But I don't mind. I know when I get there I'm go'n warm myself. I think I can hold out. My hands numb in my pockets and my feet numb, too, but if I keep moving I can hold out. Just don't stop no more, that's all.

The sky's gray. The sleet keeps on falling. Falling like rain now—plenty, plenty. You can hear it hitting the pave. You can see it bouncing. Sometimes it bounces two times 'fore it settles.

We keep on going. We don't say nothing. We just keep on going, keep on going.

I wonder what Mama's thinking. I hope she ain't mad at me. When summer come I'm go'n pick plenty cotton and get her a coat. I'm go'n get her a red one.

I hope they'd make it summer all the time. I'd be glad if it was summer all the time—but it ain't. We got to have winter, too. Lord, I hate the winter. I guess everybody hate the winter.

I don't sniff this time. I get out my handkerchief and wipe my nose. My hands's so cold I can hardly hold the handkerchief.

I think we getting close, but we ain't there yet. I wonder where everybody is. Can't see a soul but us. Look like we the only two people moving round today. Must be too cold for the rest of the people to move round in.

I can hear my teeth. I hope they don't knock together too hard and make that bad one hurt. Lord, that's all I need, for that bad one to start off.

I hear a church bell somewhere. But today ain't Sunday. They must be ringing for a funeral or something.

I wonder what they doing at home. They must be eating. Monsieur Bayonne might be there with his guitar. One day Ty played with Monsieur Bayonne's guitar and broke one of the strings. Monsieur Bayonne was some mad with Ty. He say Ty wasn't go'n ever 'mount to nothing. Ty can go just like Monsieur Bayonne when he ain't there. Ty can make everybody laugh when he starts to mocking Monsieur Bayonne.

I used to like to be with Mama and Daddy. We used to be happy. But they took him in the Army. Now, nobody happy no more. . . . I be glad when Daddy comes home.

Monsieur Bayonne say it wasn't fair for them to take Daddy and give Mama nothing and give us nothing. Auntie say, "Shhh, Etienne. Don't let them hear you talk like that." Monsieur Bayonne say, "It's God truth. What they giving his children? They have to walk three and a half miles to school hot or cold. That's anything to give for a paw? She's got to work in the field rain or shine just to make ends meet. That's anything to give for a husband?" Auntie say, "Shhh, Etienne, shhh." "Yes, you right," Monsieur Bayonne say. "Best don't say it in front of them now. But one day they go'n find out. One day." "Yes, I suppose so," Auntie say. "Then what, Rose Mary?" Monsieur Bayonne say. "I don't know, Etienne," Auntie say. "All we can do is us job, and leave everything else in His hand. . . ."

We getting closer, now. We getting closer. I can even see the railroad tracks.

We cross the tracks, and now I see the café. Just to get in there, I say. Just to get in there. Already I'm starting to feel little better.

12

We go in. Ahh, it's good. I look for the heater; there 'gainst the wall. One of them little brown ones. I just stand there and hold my hands over it. I can't open my hands too wide 'cause they almost froze.

Mama's standing right 'side me. She done unbuttoned her coat. Smoke rises out of the coat, and the coat smells like a wet dog.

I move to the side so Mama can have more room. She opens out her hands and rubs them together. I rub mine together, too, 'cause this keep them from hurting. If you let them warm too fast, they hurt you sure. But if you let them warm just little bit at a time, and you keep rubbing them, they be all right every time.

They got just two more people in the café. A lady back of the counter, and a man on this side the counter. They been watching us ever since we come in.

Mama gets out the handkerchief and count up the money. Both of us know how much money she's got there. Three dollars. No, she ain't got three dollars, 'cause she had to pay us way up here. She ain't got but two dollars and a half left. Dollar and a half to get my tooth pulled, and fifty cents for us to go back on, and fifty cents worth of salt meat.

She stirs the money round with her finger. Most of the money is change 'cause I can hear it rubbing together. She stirs it and stirs it. Then she looks at the door. It's still sleeting. I can hear it hitting 'gainst the wall like rice.

"I ain't hungry, Mama," I say.

"Got to pay them something for they heat," she says.

She takes a quarter out the handkerchief and ties the handkerchief up again. She looks over her shoulder at the people, but she still don't move. I hope she don't spend the money. I don't want her spending it on me. I'm hungry, I'm almost starving I'm so hungry, but I don't want her spending the money on me.

She flips the quarter over like she's thinking. She's must be thinking 'bout us walking back home. Lord, I sure don't want walk home. If I thought it'd do any good to say something, I'd say it. But Mama makes up her own mind 'bout things.

She turns 'way from the heater right fast, like she better hurry up and spend the quarter 'fore she change her mind. I watch her go toward the counter. The man and the lady look at her, too. She tells the lady something and the lady walks away. The man keeps on looking at her. Her back's turned to the man, and she don't even know he's standing there.

The lady puts some cakes and a glass of milk on the counter. Then she pours up a cup of coffee and sets it 'side the other stuff. Mama pays her for the things and comes on back where I'm standing. She tells me sit down at the table 'gainst the wall.

The milk and the cakes's for me; the coffee's for Mama. I eat slow and I look at her. She's looking outside at the sleet. She's looking real sad. I say to myself, I'm go'n make all this up one day. You see, one day, I'm go'n make all this up. I want say it now; I want tell her how I feel right now; but Mama don't like for us to talk like that.

"I can't eat all this," I say.

They ain't got but just three little old cakes there. I'm so hungry right now, the Lord knows I can eat a hundred times three, but I want my mama to have one.

Mama don't even look my way. She knows I'm hungry, she knows I want it. I let it stay there a little while, then I get it and eat it. I eat just on my front teeth, though, 'cause if cake touch that back tooth I know what'll happen. Thank God it ain't hurt me at all today.

After I finish eating I see the man go to the juke box. He drops a nickel in it, then he just stand there a little while looking at the record. Mama tells me keep my eyes in front where they belong. I turn my head like she say, but then I hear the man coming toward us.

"Dance, pretty?" he says.

Mama gets up to dance with him. But 'fore you know it, she done grabbed the little man in the collar and done heaved him 'side the wall. He hit the wall so hard he stop the juke box from playing.

"Some pimp," the lady back of the counter says. "Some pimp."

The little man jumps up off the floor and starts toward my mama. 'Fore you know it, Mama done sprung open her knife and she's waiting for him.

"Come on," she says. "Come on. I'll gut you from your neighbo to your throat. Come on."

I go up to the little man to hit him, but Mama makes me come and stand 'side her. The little man looks at me and Mama and goes on back to the counter.

"Some pimp," the lady back of the counter says. "Some pimp." She starts laughing and pointing at the little man. "Yes sir, you a pimp, all right. Yes sir-ree."

13

"Fasten that coat, let's go," Mama says.

"You don't have to leave," the lady says.

Mama don't answer the lady, and we right out in the cold again. I'm warm right now—my hands, my ears, my feet—but I know this ain't go'n last too long. It done sleet so much now you got ice everywhere you look.

We cross the railroad tracks, and soon's we do, I get cold. That wind goes through this little old coat like it ain't even there. I got on a shirt and a sweater under the coat, but that wind don't pay them no mind. I look up and I can see we got a long way to go. I wonder if we go'n make it 'fore I get too cold.

We cross over to walk on the sidewalk. They got just one sidewalk back here, and it's over there.

After we go just a little piece, I smell bread cooking. I look, then I see a baker shop. When we get closer, I can smell it more better. I shut my eyes and make 'tend I'm eating. But I keep them shut too long and I butt up 'gainst a telephone post. Mama grabs me and see if I'm hurt. I ain't bleeding or nothing and she turns me loose.

I can feel I'm getting colder and colder, and I look up to see how far we still got to go. Uptown is 'way up yonder. A half mile more, I reckon. I try to think of something. They say think and you won't get cold. I think of that poem, "Annabel Lee." I ain't been to school in so long—this bad weather—I reckon they done passed "Annabel Lee" by now. But passed it or not, I'm sure Miss Walker go'n make me recite it when I get there. That woman don't never forget nothing. I ain't never seen nobody like that in my life.

I'm still getting cold. "Annabel Lee" or no "Annabel Lee," I'm still getting cold. But I can see we getting closer. We getting there gradually.

Soon 's we turn the corner, I see a little old white lady up in front of us. She's the only lady on the street. She's all in black and she's got a long black rag over her head.

"Stop," she says.

Me and Mama stop and look at her. She must be crazy to be out in all this bad weather. Ain't got but a few other people out there, and all of them's men.

"Y'all done ate?" she says.

"Just finish," Mama says.

"Y'all must be cold then?" she says.

"We headed for the dentist," Mama says. "We'll warm up when we get there."

"What dentist?" the old lady says. "Mr. Bassett?"

"Yes, ma'am," Mama says.

"Come on in," the old lady says. "I'll telephone him and tell him y'all coming."

Me and Mama follow the old lady in the store. It's a little bitty store, and it don't have much in there. The old lady takes off her head rag and folds it up.

"Helena?" somebody calls from the back.

"Yes, Alnest?" the old lady says.

"Did you see them?"

"They're here. Standing beside me."

"Good. Now you can stay inside."

The old lady looks at Mama. Mama's waiting to hear what she brought us in here for. I'm waiting for that, too.

'I saw y'all each time you went by," she says. "I came out to catch you, but you were gone."

"We went back of town," Mama says.

"Did you eat?"

"Yes, ma'am."

The old lady looks at Mama a long time, like she's thinking Mama might be just saying that. Mama looks right back at her. The old lady looks at me to see what I have to say. I don't say nothing. I sure ain't going 'gainst my mama.

"There's food in the kitchen," she says to Mama. "I've been keeping it warm."

Mama turns right around and starts for the door.

"Just a minute," the old lady says. Mama stops. "The boy'll have to work for it. It isn't free."

"We don't take no handout," Mama says.

"I'm not handing out anything," the old lady says. "I need my garbage moved to the front. Ernest has a bad cold and can't go out there."

"James'll move it for you," Mama says.

"Not unless you eat," the old lady says. "I'm old, but I have my pride, too, you know."

Mama can see she ain't go'n beat this old lady down, so she just shakes her head.

"All right," the old lady says. "Come into the kitchen."

She leads the way with that rag in her hand. The kitchen is a little bitty little old thing, too. The table and the stove just 'bout fill it up. They got a little room to the side. Somebody in there laying 'cross the bed—'cause I can see one of his feet. Must be the person she was talking to: Ernest or Alnest—something like that.

"Sit down," the old lady says to Mama. "Not you," she says to me. "You have to move the cans."

"Helena?" the man says in the other room.

"Yes, Alnest?" the old lady says.

"Are you going out there again?"

"I must show the boy where the garbage is, Alnest," the old lady says.

"Keep that shawl over your head," the old man says.

"You don't have to remind me, Alnest. Come, boy," the old lady says.

We go out in the yard. Little old back yard ain't no bigger than the store or the kitchen. But it can sleet here just like it can sleet in any big back yard. And 'fore you know it, I'm trembling.

"There," the old lady says, pointing to the cans. I pick up one of the cans and set it right back down. The can's so light, I'm go'n see what's inside of it.

"Here," the old lady says. "Leave that can alone."

I look back at her standing there in the door. She's got that black rag wrapped round her shoulders, and she's pointing one of her little old fingers at me.

"Pick it up and carry it to the front," she says. I go by her with the can, and she's looking at me all the time. I'm sure the can's empty. I'm sure she could've carried it herself—maybe both of them at the same time."Set it on the sidewalk by the door and come back for the other one," she says.

I go and come back, and Mama looks at me when I pass her. I get the other can and take it to the front. It don't feel a bit heavier than that first one. I tell myself I ain't go'n be nobody's fool, and I'm go'n look inside this can to see just what I been hauling. First, I look up the street, then down the street. Nobody coming. Then I look over my shoulder toward the door. That little old lady done slipped up there quiet 's mouse, watching me again. Look like she knowed what I was go'n do.

"Ehh, Lord," she says. "Children, children. Come in here, boy, and go wash your hands."

I follow her in the kitchen. She points toward the bathroom, and I go in there and wash up. Little bitty old bathroom, but it's clean, clean. I don't use any of her towels; I wipe my hands on my pants legs.

When I come back in the kitchen, the old lady done dished up the food. Rice, gravy, meat—and she even got some lettuce and tomato in a saucer. She even got a glass of milk and a piece of cake there, too. It looks so good, I almost start eating 'fore I say my blessing.

"Helena?" the old man says.

"Yes, Alnest?"

"Are they eating?"

"Yes," she says.

"Good," he says. "Now you'll stay inside."

The old lady goes in there where he is and I can hear them talking. I look at Mama. She's eating slow like she's thinking. I wonder what's the matter now. I reckon she's thinking 'bout home.

The old lady comes back in the kitchen.

"I talked to Dr. Bassett's nurse," she says. "Dr. Bassett will take you as soon as you get there."

"Thank you, ma'am," Mama says.

"Perfectly all right," the old lady says. "Which one is it?"

Mama nods toward me. The old lady looks at me real sad. I look sad, too.

"You're not afraid, are you?" she says.

"No, ma'am," I say.

"That's a good boy," the old lady says. "Nothing to be afraid of. Dr. Bassett will not hurt you."

When me and Mama get through eating, we thank the old lady again.

"Helena, are they leaving?" the old man says.

"Yes, Alnest."

"Tell them I say good-bye."

"They can hear you, Alnest."

"Good-bye both mother and son," the old man says. "And may God be with you."

Me and Mama tell the old man good-bye, and we follow the old lady in the front room. Mama opens the door to go out, but she stops and comes back in the store.

"You sell salt meat?" she says.

"Yes."

"Give me two bits worth."

"That isn't very much salt meat," the old lady says.

"That's all I have," Mama says.

The old lady goes back of the counter and cuts a big piece off the chunk. Then she wraps it up and puts it in a paper bag.

"Two bits," she says.

"That looks like awful lot of meat for a quarter," Mama says.

"Two bits," the old lady says. "I've been selling salt meat behind this counter twenty-five years. I think I know what I'm doing."

"You got a scale there," Mama says.

"What?" the old lady says.

"Weigh it," Mama says.

"What?" the old lady says. "Are you telling me how to run my business?"

"Thanks very much for the food," Mama says.

"Just a minute," the old lady says.

"James," Mama says to me. I move toward the door.

"Just one minute, I said," the old lady says.

Me and Mama stop again and look at her. The old lady takes the meat out of the bag and unwraps it and cuts 'bout half of it off. Then she wraps it up again and juggs it back in the bag and gives the bag to Mama. Mama lays the quarter on the counter.

"Your kindness will never be forgotten," she says. "James," she says to me.

We go out, and the old lady comes to the door to look at us. After we go a little piece I look back, and she's still there watching us.

The sleet's coming down heavy, heavy now, and I turn up my coat collar to keep my neck warm. My mama tells me turn it right back down.

"You not a bum," she says. "You a man."

QUESTIONS FOR DISCUSSION AND WRITING

1. How are the conflicts in the story personified in the characters of the preacher, the young man with the book, the pimp, and the old couple?
2. How does the reader's view of the mother's motives and behavior change as the story develops? Why does the narrator want to be like the young man with the book?
3. Why is the winter setting important to the development of the story? What details does Gaines use to document the social context of the story?
4. Is the narrator in this story—James—reliable even though he is only eight years old? Explain your answer. How might the narrator and the reader interpret the events in this story differently?
5. How does the story lead the reader to believe that James will become a man of both reason and faith?

34

GABRIEL GARCIA MARQUEZ

A Very Old Man with Enormous Wings

A TALE FOR CHILDREN

TRANSLATED BY GREGORY RABASSA

GABRIEL GARCIA MARQUEZ was born in 1928 in Aracataca, Colombia, a remote town near the Caribbean seacoast. Although he was brought up in considerable poverty, García Márquez was sent away to school at the age of eight to attend the Liceo Nacional near Bogotá. After his graduation in 1946, he began studying at Bogotá University until the civil war forced the university to close in 1948. García Márquez moved to Cartagena and began his career as a journalist, moving on to Barranquilla in 1950, where he wrote a daily column for *El Heraldo* and lived in a four-story brothel called "The Skyscraper." In 1954 he returned to Bogotá to work as a reporter and film critic for *El Espectador.* After the publication of his first collection of stories, *Leaf Storm and Other Stories* (1955), García Márquez traveled to Europe as a foreign correspondent, but political turmoil at home closed down *El Espectador,* putting him out of work. He spent the next few years in Paris, living in great poverty and writing two short novels, *No One Writes to the Colonel* (1958) and *In Evil Hour* (1961). After living for a time in Havana, he moved to Mexico City to begin a new career as a screen writer. It was during this period that García Márquez wrote his masterpiece, *One Hundred Years of Solitude* (1967). His later works include a collection of short stories, *The Incredible and Sad Story of Innocent Eréndira and Her Heartless Grandmother* (1972), and three novels, *The Autumn of the Patriarch* (1975), *Chronicle of a Death Foretold* (1982), and *The Story of the Shipwrecked Sailor: Who . . .* (1986). In 1982, García Márquez was awarded the Nobel Prize for literature. "A Very Old Man with Enormous Wings," reprinted from *Leaf Storm and Other Stories,* documents the reactions of a community to a strange visitor.

On the third day of rain they had killed so many crabs inside the house that Pelayo had to cross his drenched courtyard and throw them into the sea, because the newborn child had a temperature all night and they thought it was due to the stench. The world had been sad since Tuesday. Sea and sky were a single ash-gray thing and the sands of the beach, which on March nights glimmered like powdered light, had become a stew of mud and rotten shellfish. The light was so weak at noon that when Pelayo was coming back to the house after throwing away the crabs, it was hard for him to see what it was that was moving and groaning in the rear of the courtyard. He had to go very close to see that it was an old man, a very old man, lying face down in the mud, who, in spite of his tremendous efforts, couldn't get up, impeded by his enormous wings.

Frightened by that nightmare, Pelayo ran to get Elisenda, his wife, who was putting compresses on the sick child, and he took her to the rear of the courtyard. They both looked at the fallen body with mute stupor. He was dressed like a ragpicker. There were only a few faded hairs left on his bald skull and very few teeth in his mouth, and his pitiful condition of a drenched great-grandfather had taken away any sense of grandeur he might have had. His huge buzzard wings, dirty and half-plucked, were forever entangled in the mud. They looked at him so long and so closely that Pelayo and Elisenda very soon overcame their surprise and in the end found him familiar. Then they dared speak to him, and he answered in an incomprehensible dialect with a strong sailor's voice. That was how they skipped over the inconvenience of the wings and quite intelligently concluded that he was a lonely castaway from some foreign ship wrecked by the storm. And yet, they called in a neighbor woman who knew everything about life and death to see him, and all she needed was one look to show them their mistake.

"He's an angel," she told them. "He must have been coming for the child, but the poor fellow is so old that the rain knocked him down."

On the following day everyone knew that a flesh-and-blood angel was held captive in Pelayo's house. Against the judgment of the wise neighbor woman, for whom angels in those times were the fugitive survivors of a celestial conspiracy, they did not have the heart to club him to death. Pelayo watched over him all afternoon from the kitchen, armed with his bailiff's club, and before going to bed he dragged him out of the mud and locked him up with the hens in the wire chicken coop. In the middle of the night, when the rain stopped, Pelayo and Elisenda were still killing crabs. A short time afterward the child woke up without a fever and with a desire to eat. Then they felt magnanimous and decided to put the angel on a raft with fresh water and provisions for three days and leave him to his fate on the high seas. But when they went out into the courtyard with the first light of dawn, they found the whole neighborhood in front of the chicken coop having fun with the angel, without the slightest reverence, tossing him things to eat through the openings in the wire as if he weren't a supernatural creature but a circus animal.

Father Gonzaga arrived before seven o'clock, alarmed at the strange news. By that time onlookers less frivolous than those at dawn had already arrived and they were making all kinds of conjectures concerning the captive's future. The simplest among them thought that he should be named mayor of the world. Others of sterner mind felt that he should be promoted to the rank of five-star general in order to win all wars. Some visionaries hoped that he could be put to stud in order to implant on earth a race of winged wise men who could take charge of the universe. But Father Gonzaga, before becoming a priest, had been a robust woodcutter. Standing by the wire, he reviewed his catechism in an instant and asked them to open the door so that he could take a close look at that pitiful man who looked more like a huge decrepit hen among the fascinated chickens. He was lying in a corner drying his open wings in the sunlight among the fruit peels and breakfast leftovers that the early risers had thrown him. Alien to the impertinences of the world, he only lifted his antiquarian eyes and murmured something in his dialect when Father Gonzaga went into the chicken coop and said good morning to him in Latin. The parish priest had his first suspicion of an impostor when he saw that he did not understand the language of God or know how to greet His ministers. Then he noticed that seen close up he was much too human; he had an unbearable smell of the outdoors, the back side of his wings was strewn with parasites and his main feathers had been mistreated by terrestrial winds, and nothing about him measured up to the proud dignity of angels. Then he came out of the chicken coop and in a brief sermon warned the curious against the risks of being ingenuous. He reminded them that the devil had the bad habit of making use of carnival tricks in order to confuse the unwary. He argued that if wings were not the essential element in determining the difference between a hawk and an airplane, they were even less so in the recognition of angels. Nevertheless, he promised to write a letter to his bishop so that the latter would write to his primate so that the latter would write to the Supreme Pontiff in order to get the final verdict from the highest courts.

His prudence fell on sterile hearts. The news of the captive angel spread with such rapidity that after a few hours the courtyard had the bustle of a marketplace and they had to call in troops with fixed bayonets to disperse the mob that was about to knock the house down. Elisenda, her spine all twisted from sweeping up so much marketplace trash, then got the idea of fencing in the yard and charging five cents admission to see the angel.

The curious came from far away. A traveling carnival arrived with a flying acrobat who buzzed over the crowd several times, but no one paid any attention to him because his wings were not those of an angel but, rather, those of a sidereal bat. The most unfortunate invalids on earth came in search of health: a poor woman who since childhood had been counting her heartbeats and had run out of numbers; a Portuguese man who couldn't sleep because the noise of the stars disturbed him; a sleepwalker who got up at night to undo the things he had done while awake; and many others with less serious ailments. In the midst of that shipwreck disorder that made the earth tremble, Pelayo and Elisenda were happy with fatigue, for in less than a week they had crammed their rooms with money and the line of pilgrims waiting their turn to enter still reached beyond the horizon.

The angel was the only one who took no part in his own act. He spent his time trying to get comfortable in his borrowed nest, befuddled by the hellish heat of the oil lamps and sacramental candles that had been placed along the wire. At first they tried to make him eat some mothballs, which, according to the wisdom of the wise neighbor woman, were the food prescribed for angels. But he turned them down, just as he turned down the papal lunches that the penitents brought him, and they never found out whether it was because he was an angel or because he was an old man that in the end he ate nothing but eggplant mush. His only supernatural virtue seemed to be patience. Especially during the first days, when the hens pecked at him, searching for the stellar parasites that proliferated in his wings, and the cripples pulled out feathers to touch their defective parts with, and even the most merciful threw stones at him, trying to get him to rise so they could see him standing. The only time they succeeded in arousing him was when they burned his side with an iron for branding steers, for he had been motionless for so many hours that they thought he was dead. He awoke with a start, ranting in his hermetic language and with tears in his eyes, and he flapped his wings a couple of times, which brought on a whirlwind of chicken dung and lunar dust and a gale of panic that did not seem to be of this world. Although many thought that his reaction had been one not of rage but of pain, from then on they were careful not to annoy him, because the majority understood that his passivity was not that of a hero taking his ease but that of a cataclysm in repose.

Father Gonzaga held back the crowd's frivolity with formulas of maidservant inspiration while awaiting the arrival of a final judgment on the nature of the captive. But the mail from Rome showed no sense of urgency. They spent their time finding out if the prisoner had a navel, if his dialect had any connection with Aramaic, how many times he could fit on the head of a pin, or whether he wasn't just a Norwegian with wings. Those meager letters might have come and gone until the end of time if a providential event had not put an end to the priest's tribulations.

It so happened that during those days, among so many other carnival attractions, there arrived in town the traveling show of the woman who had been changed into a spider for having disobeyed her parents. The admission to see her was not only less than the admission to see the angel, but people were permitted to ask her all manner of questions about her absurd state and to examine her up and down so that no one would ever doubt the truth of her horror. She was a frightful tarantula the size of a ram and with the head of a sad maiden. What was most heart-rending, however, was not her outlandish shape but the sincere affliction with which she recounted the details of her misfortune. While still practically a child she had sneaked out of her parents' house to go to a dance, and while she was coming back through the woods after having danced all night without permission, a fearful thunderclap rent the sky in two and through the crack came the lightning bolt of brimstone that changed her into a spider. Her only nourishment came from the meatballs that charitable souls chose to toss into her mouth. A spectacle like that, full of so much human truth and with such a fearful lesson, was bound to defeat without even trying that of a haughty angel who scarcely deigned to look at mortals. Besides, the few miracles attributed to the angel showed a certain mental disorder, like the blind man who didn't recover his sight but grew three new teeth, or the paralytic who didn't get to walk but almost won the lottery, and the leper whose sores sprouted sunflowers. Those consolation miracles, which were more like mocking fun, had already ruined the angel's reputation when the woman who had been changed into a spider finally crushed him completely. That was how Father Gonzaga was cured forever of his insomnia and Pelayo's courtyard went back to being as empty as during the time it had rained for three days and crabs walked through the bedrooms.

The owners of the house had no reason to lament. With the money they saved they built a two-story mansion with balconies and gardens and high netting so that crabs wouldn't get in during the winter, and with iron bars on the windows so that angels wouldn't get in. Pelayo also set up a rabbit warren close to town and gave up his job as bailiff for good, and Elisenda bought some satin pumps with high heels and many dresses of iridescent silk, the kind worn on Sunday by the most desirable women in those times. The chicken coop was the only thing that didn't receive any attention. If they washed it down with creolin and burned tears of myrrh inside it every so often, it was not in homage to the angel but to drive away the dung heap stench that still hung everywhere like a ghost and was turning the new house into an old one. At first, when the child learned to walk, they were careful that he not get too close to the chicken coop. But then they began to lose their fears and got used to the smell, and before the child got his second teeth he'd gone inside the chicken coop to play, where the wires were falling apart. The angel was no less standoffish with him than with other mortals, but he tolerated the most ingenious infamies with the patience of a dog who had no illusions. They both came down with chicken pox at the same time. The doctor who took care of the child couldn't resist the temptation to listen to the angel's heart, and he found so much whistling in the heart and so many sounds in his kidneys that it seemed impossible for him to be alive. What surprised him most, however, was the logic of his wings. They seemed so natural on that completely human organism that he couldn't understand why other men didn't have them too.

When the child began school it had been some time since the sun and rain had caused the collapse of the chicken coop. The angel went dragging himself about here and there like a stray dying man. They would drive him out of the bedroom with a broom and a moment later find him in the kitchen. He seemed to be in so many places at the same time that they grew to think that he'd been duplicated, that he was reproducing himself all through the house, and the exasperated and unhinged Elisenda shouted that it was awful living in that hell full of angels. He could scarcely eat and his antiquarian eyes had also become so foggy that he went about bumping into posts. All he had left were the bare cannulae of his last feathers. Pelayo threw a blanket over him and extended him the charity of letting him sleep in the shed, and only then did they notice that he had a temperature at night, and was delirious with the tongue twisters of an old Norwegian. That was one of the few times they became alarmed, for they thought he was going to die and not even the wise neighbor woman had been able to tell them what to do with dead angels.

And yet he not only survived his worst winter, but seemed improved with the first sunny days. He remained motionless for several days in the farthest corner of the courtyard, where no one would see him, and at the beginning of December some large, stiff feathers began to grow on his wings, the feathers of a scarecrow, which looked more like another misfortune of decrepitude. But he must have known the reason for those changes, for he was quite careful that no one should notice them, that no one should hear the sea chanteys that he sometimes sang under the stars. One morning Elisenda was cutting some bunches of onions for lunch when a wind that seemed to come from the high seas blew into the kitchen. Then she went to the window and caught the angel in his first attempts at flight. They were so clumsy that his fingernails opened a furrow in the vegetable patch and he was on the point of knocking the shed down with the ungainly flapping that slipped on the light and couldn't get a grip on the air. But he did manage to gain altitude. Elisenda let out a sigh of relief, for herself and for him, when she saw him pass over the last houses, holding himself up in some way with the risky flapping of a senile vulture. She kept watching him even when she was through cutting the onions and she kept on watching until it was no longer possible for her to see him, because then he was no longer an annoyance in her life but an imaginary dot on the horizon of the sea.

QUESTIONS FOR DISCUSSION AND WRITING

1. What expectations does the "angel" produce within the community and surrounding territories? How does the spider woman revise those expectations? What events enable the angel to depart?
2. What is Pelayo's first impression of the old man with wings? How does his impression change once the neighbor woman identifies his visitor as an angel? Why does the priest suspect the angel is an impostor? What single virtue characterizes the angel during the story?
3. How does the opening sentence establish an appropriate setting for the appearance of the angel? What kind of world is represented in a story where people believe in angels, celestial conspiracies, and consolation miracles?
4. How does the subtitle suggest the author's point of view toward the story? To what extent do the various characters in the story exhibit a childlike point of view toward the events they witness?
5. What is the "fearful lesson" of the angel's story? How does it compare with the "human truth" of the spider woman?

35

ELLEN GILCHRIST

Revenge

ELLEN GILCHRIST was born in 1935 in Vicksburg, Mississippi, and educated at Millsaps College and the University of Arkansas. She has worked as a reporter for *Vieux Carré Courier* and as a weekly commentator on National Public Radio's daily "Morning Edition" show. Gilchrist's first major publication was a collection of short stories, *In the Land of Dreamy Dreams* (1981), that focused on adolescents living in New Orleans and the Mississippi Delta. Her first novel, *The Annunciation* (1983), traces the life of a Mississippi girl from an early marriage to a wealthy New Orleans man to her membership in a hippie commune in the Ozarks. Gilchrist's next collection of stories, *Victory Over Japan* (1984), won the American Book Award for Fiction. Her other work includes a book of poems, *The Land Surveyor's Daughter* (1974), and a play, "A Season of Dreams," based on the short stories of Eudora Welty. In "Revenge," reprinted from *In the Land of Dreamy Dreams,* a young girl tests her identity in various settings.

It was the summer of the Broad Jump Pit.

The Broad Jump Pit, how shall I describe it! It was a bright orange rectangle in the middle of a green pasture. It was three feet deep, filled with river sand and sawdust. A real cinder track led up to it, ending where tall poles for pole-vaulting rose forever in the still Delta air.

I am looking through the old binoculars. I am watching Bunky coming at a run down the cinder path, pausing expertly at the jump-off line, then rising into the air, heels stretched far out in front of him, landing in the sawdust. Before the dust has settled Saint John comes running with the tape, calling out measurements in his high, excitable voice.

Next comes my thirteen-year-old brother, Dudley, coming at a brisk jog down the track, the pole-vaulting pole held lightly in his delicate hands, then vaulting, high into the sky. His skinny tanned legs make a last, desperate surge, and he is clear and over.

Think how it looked from my lonely exile atop the chicken house. I was ten years old, the only girl in a house full of cousins. There were six of us, shipped to the Delta for the summer, dumped on my grandmother right in the middle of a world war.

They built this wonder in answer to a V-Mail letter from my father in Europe. The war was going well, my father wrote, within a year the Allies would triumph over the forces of evil, the world would be at peace, and the Olympic torch would again be brought down from its mountain and carried to Zurich or Amsterdam or London or Mexico City, wherever free men lived and worshiped sports. My father had been a participant in an Olympic event when he was young.

Therefore, the letter continued, Dudley and Bunky and Philip and Saint John and Oliver were to begin training. The United States would need athletes now, not soldiers.

They were to train for broad jumping and pole-vaulting and discus throwing, for fifty-, one-hundred-, and four-hundred-yard dashes, for high and low hurdles. The letter included instructions for building the pit, for making pole-vaulting poles out of cane, and for converting ordinary sawhorses into hurdles. It ended with a page of tips for proper eating and admonished Dudley to take good care of me as I was my father's own dear sweet little girl.

The letter came one afternoon. Early the next morning they began construction. Around noon I wandered out to the pasture to see how they were coming along. I picked up a shovel.

"Put that down, Rhoda," Dudley said. "Don't bother us now. We're working."

"I know it," I said. "I'm going to help."

"No, you're not," Bunky said. "This is the Broad Jump Pit. We're starting our training."

"I'm going to do it too," I said. "I'm going to be in training."

"Get out of here now," Dudley said. "This is only for boys, Rhoda. This isn't a game."

"I'm going to dig it if I want to," I said, picking up a shovelful of dirt and throwing it on Philip. On second thought I picked up another shovelful and threw it on Bunky.

"Get out of here, Ratface," Philip yelled at me. "You German spy." He was referring to the initials on my Girl Scout uniform.

"You goddamn niggers," I yelled. "You niggers. I'm digging this if I want to and you can't stop me, you nasty niggers, you Japs, you Jews." I was throwing dirt on everyone now. Dudley grabbed the shovel and wrestled me to the ground. He held my arms down in the coarse grass and peered into my face.

"Rhoda, you're not having anything to do with this Broad Jump Pit. And if you set foot inside this pasture or come around here and touch anything we will break your legs and drown you in the bayou with a crowbar around your neck." He was twisting my leg until it creaked at the joints. "Do you get it, Rhoda? Do you understand me?"

"Let me up," I was screaming, my rage threatening to split open my skull. "Let me up, you goddamn nigger, you Jap, you spy. I'm telling Grannie and you're going to get the worst whipping of your life. And you better quit digging this hole for the horses to fall in. Let me up, let me up. Let me go."

"You've been ruining everything we've thought up all summer," Dudley said, "and you're not setting foot inside this pasture."

In the end they dragged me back to the house, and I ran screaming into the kitchen where Grannie and Calvin, the black man who did the cooking, tried to comfort me, feeding me pound cake and offering to let me help with the mayonnaise.

"You be a sweet girl, Rhoda," my grandmother said, "and this afternoon we'll go over to Eisenglas Plantation to play with Miss Ann Wentzel."

"I don't want to play with Miss Ann Wentzel," I screamed. "I hate Miss Ann Wentzel. She's fat and she calls me a Yankee. She said my socks were ugly."

"Why, Rhoda," my grandmother said. "I'm surprised at you. Miss Ann Wentzel is your own sweet friend. Her momma was your momma's roommate at All Saint's. How can you talk like that?"

"She's a nigger," I screamed. "She's a goddamned nigger German spy."

"Now it's coming. Here comes the temper," Calvin said, rolling his eyes back in their sockets to make me madder. I threw my second fit of the morning, beating my fists into a door frame. My grandmother seized me in soft arms. She led me to a bedroom where I sobbed myself to sleep in a sea of down pillows.

The construction went on for several weeks. As soon as they finished breakfast every morning they started out for the pasture. Wood had to be burned to make cinders, sawdust brought from the sawmill, sand hauled up from the riverbank by wheelbarrow.

When the pit was finished the savage training began. From my several vantage points I watched them. Up and down, up and down they ran, dove, flew, sprinted. Drenched with sweat they wrestled each other to the ground in bitter feuds over distances and times and fractions of inches.

Dudley was their self-appointed leader. He drove them like a demon. They began each morning by running around the edge of the pasture several times, then practicing their hurdles and dashes, then on to discus throwing and calisthenics. Then on to the Broad Jump Pit with its endless challenges.

They even pressed the old mare into service. Saint John was from New Orleans and knew the British ambassador and was thinking of being a polo player. Up and down the pasture he drove the poor old creature, leaning far out of the saddle, swatting a basketball with my grandaddy's cane.

I spied on them from the swing that went out over the bayou, and from the roof of the chicken house, and sometimes from the pasture fence itself, calling out insults or attempts to make them jealous.

"Guess what," I would yell, "I'm going to town to the Chinaman's store." "Guess what, I'm getting to go to the beauty parlor." "Doctor Biggs says you're adopted."

They ignored me. At meals they sat together at one end of the table, making jokes about my temper and my red hair, opening their mouths so I could see their half-chewed food, burping loudly in my direction.

At night they pulled their cots together on the sleeping porch, plotting against me while I slept beneath my grandmother's window, listening to the soft assurance of her snoring.

I began to pray the Japs would win the war, would come marching into Issaquena County and take them prisoners, starving and torturing them, sticking bamboo splinters under their fingernails. I saw myself in the Japanese colonel's office, turning them in, writing their names down, myself being treated like an honored guest, drinking tea from tiny blue cups like the ones the Chinaman had in his store.

They would be outside, tied up with wire. There would be Dudley, begging for mercy. What good to him now his loyal gang, his photographic memory, his trick magnet dogs, his perfect pitch, his camp shorts, his Baby Brownie camera.

I prayed they would get polio, would be consigned forever to iron lungs. I put myself to sleep at night imagining their labored breathing, their five little wheelchairs lined up by the store as I drove by in my father's Packard, my arm around the jacket of his blue uniform, on my way to Hollywood for my screen test.

Meanwhile, I practiced dancing. My grandmother had a black housekeeper named Baby Doll who was a wonderful dancer. In the mornings I followed her around while she dusted, begging for dancing lessons. She was a big woman, as tall as a man, and gave off a dark rich smell, an unforgettable incense, a combination of Evening in Paris and the sweet perfume of the cabins.

Baby Doll wore bright skirts and on her blouses a pin that said REMEMBER, then a real pearl, then HARBOR. She was engaged to a sailor and was going to California to be rich as soon as the war was over.

I would put a stack of heavy, scratched records on the record player, and Baby Doll and I would dance through the parlors to the music of Glenn Miller or Guy Lombardo or Tommy Dorsey.

Sometimes I stood on a stool in front of the fireplace and made up lyrics while Baby Doll acted them out, moving lightly across the old dark rugs, turning and swooping and shaking and gliding.

Outside the summer sun beat down on the Delta, beating down a million volts a minute, feeding the soybeans and cotton and clover, sucking Steele's Bayou up into the clouds, beating down on the road and the store, on the pecans and elms and magnolias, on the men at work in the fields, on the athletes at work in the pasture.

Inside Baby Doll and I would be dancing. Or Guy Lombardo would be playing "Begin the Beguine" and I would be belting out lyrics.

"Oh, let them begin . . . we don't care,
America all . . . ways does its share,
We'll be there with plenty of ammo,
Allies . . . don't ever despair . . ."

Baby Doll thought I was a genius. If I was having an especially creative morning she would go running out to the kitchen and bring anyone she could find to hear me.

"Oh, let them begin any warrr . . ." I would be singing, tapping one foot against the fireplace tiles, waving my arms around like a conductor.

"Uncle Sam will fight
for the underrr . . . doggg.
Never fear, Allies, never fear."

A new record would drop. Baby Doll would swoop me into her fragrant arms, and we would break into an improvisation of Tommy Dorsey's "Boogie-Woogie."

But the Broad Jump Pit would not go away. It loomed in my dreams. If I walked to the store I had to pass the pasture. If I stood on the porch or looked out my grandmother's window, there it was, shimmering in the sunlight, constantly guarded by one of the Olympians.

Things went from bad to worse between me and Dudley. If we so much as passed each other in the hall a fight began. He would hold up his fists and dance around, trying to look like a fighter. When I came flailing at him he would reach underneath my arms and punch me in the stomach.

I considered poisoning him. There was a box of white powder in the toolshed with a skull and crossbones above the label. Several times I took it down and held it in my hands, shuddering at the power it gave me. Only the thought of the electric chair kept me from using it.

Every day Dudley gathered his troops and headed out for the pasture. Every day my hatred grew and festered. Then, just about the time I could stand it no longer, a diversion occurred.

One afternoon about four o'clock an official-looking sedan clattered across the bridge and came roaring down the road to the house.

It was my cousin, Lauralee Manning, wearing her WAVE uniform and smoking Camels in an ivory holder. Lauralee had been widowed at the beginning of the war when her young husband crashed his Navy training plane into the Pacific.

Lauralee dried her tears, joined the WAVES, and went off to avenge his death. I had not seen this paragon since I was a small child, but I had memorized the photograph Miss Onnie Maud, who was Lauralee's mother, kept on her dresser. It was a photograph of Lauralee leaning against the rail of a destroyer.

Not that Lauralee ever went to sea on a destroyer. She was spending the war in Pensacola, Florida, being secretary to an admiral.

Now, out of a clear blue sky, here was Lauralee, home on leave with a two-carat diamond ring and the news that she was getting married.

"You might have called and given some warning," Miss Onnie Maud said, turning Lauralee into a mass of wrinkles with her embraces. "You could have softened the blow with a letter."

"Who's the groom?" my grandmother said. "I only hope he's not a pilot."

"Is he an admiral?" I said, "or a colonel or a major or a commander?"

"My fiancé's not in uniform, Honey," Lauralee said. "He's in real estate. He runs the war-bond effort for the whole state of Florida. Last year he collected half a million dollars."

"In real estate!" Miss Onnie Maud said, gasping. "What religion is he?"

"He's Unitarian," she said. "His name is Donald Marcus. He's best friends with Admiral Semmes, that's how I met him. And he's coming a week from Saturday, and that's all the time we have to get ready for the wedding."

"Unitarian!" Miss Onnie Maud said. "I don't think I've ever met a Unitarian."

"Why isn't he in uniform?" I insisted.

"He has flat feet," Lauralee said gaily. "But you'll love him when you see him."

Later that afternoon Lauralee took me off by myself for a ride in the sedan.

"Your mother is my favorite cousin," she said, touching my face with gentle fingers. "You'll look just like her when you grow up and get your figure."

I moved closer, admiring the brass buttons on her starched uniform and the brisk way she shifted and braked and put in the clutch and accelerated.

We drove down the river road and out to the bootlegger's shack where Lauralee bought a pint of Jack Daniel's and two Cokes. She poured out half of her Coke, filled it with whiskey, and we roared off down the road with the radio playing.

We drove along in the lengthening day. Lauralee was chain-smoking, lighting one Camel after another, tossing the butts out the window, taking sips from her bourbon and Coke. I sat beside her, pretending to smoke a piece of rolled-up paper, making little noises into the mouth of my Coke bottle.

We drove up to a picnic spot on the levee and sat under a tree to look out at the river.

"I miss this old river," she said. "When I'm sad I dream about it licking the tops of the levees."

I didn't know what to say to that. To tell the truth I was afraid to say much of anything to Lauralee. She seemed so splendid. It was enough to be allowed to sit by her on the levee.

"Now, Rhoda," she said, "your mother was matron of honor in my wedding to Buddy, and I want you, her own little daughter, to be maid of honor in my second wedding."

I could hardly believe my ears! While I was trying to think of something to say to this wonderful news I saw that Lauralee was crying, great tears were forming in her blue eyes.

"Under this very tree is where Buddy and I got engaged," she said. Now the tears were really starting to roll, falling all over the front of her uniform. "He gave me my ring right where we're sitting."

"The maid of honor?" I said, patting her shoulder, trying to be of some comfort. "You really mean the maid of honor?"

"Now he's gone from the world," she continued, "and I'm marrying a wonderful man, but that doesn't make it any easier. Oh, Rhoda, they never even found his body, never even found his body."

I was patting her on the head now, afraid she would forget her offer in the midst of her sorrow.

"You mean I get to be the real maid of honor?"

"Oh yes, Rhoda, Honey," she said. "The maid of honor, my only attendant." She blew her nose on a lace-trimmed handkerchief and sat up straighter, taking a drink from the Coke bottle.

"Not only that, but I have decided to let you pick out your own dress. We'll go to Greenville and you can try on every dress at Nell's and Blum's and you can have the one you like the most."

I threw my arms around her, burning with happiness, smelling her whiskey and Camels and the dark Tabu perfume that was her signature. Over her shoulder and through the low branches of the trees the afternoon sun was going down in an orgy of reds and blues and purples and violets, falling from sight, going all the way to China.

Let them keep their nasty Broad Jump Pit I thought. Wait till they hear about this. Wait till they find out I'm maid of honor in a military wedding.

Finding the dress was another matter. Early the next morning Miss Onnie Maud and my grandmother and Lauralee and I set out for Greenville.

As we passed the pasture I hung out the back window making faces at the athletes. This time they only pretended to ignore me. They couldn't ignore this wedding. It was going to be in the parlor instead of the church so they wouldn't even get to be altar boys. They wouldn't get to light a candle.

"I don't know why you care what's going on in that pasture," my grandmother said. "Even if they let you play with them all it would do is make you a lot of ugly muscles."

"Then you'd have big old ugly arms like Weegie Toler," Miss Onnie Maud said. "Lauralee, you remember Weegie Toler, that was a swimmer. Her arms got so big no one would take her to a dance, much less marry her."

"Well, I don't want to get married anyway," I said. "I'm never getting married. I'm going to New York City and be a lawyer."

"Where does she get those ideas?" Miss Onnie Maud said.

"When you get older you'll want to get married," Lauralee said. "Look at how much fun you're having being in my wedding."

"Well, I'm never getting married," I said. "And I'm never having any children. I'm going to New York and be a lawyer and save people from the electric chair."

"It's the movies," Miss Onnie Maud said. "They let her watch anything she likes in Indiana."

We walked into Nell's and Blum's Department Store and took up the largest dressing room. My grandmother and Miss Onnie Maud were seated on brocade chairs and every saleslady in the store came crowding around trying to get in on the wedding.

I refused to even consider the dresses they brought from the "girls'" department.

"I told her she could wear whatever she wanted," Lauralee said, "and I'm keeping my promise."

"Well, she's not wearing green satin or I'm not coming," my grandmother said, indicating the dress I had found on a rack and was clutching against me.

"At least let her try it on," Lauralee said. "Let her see for herself." She zipped me into the green satin. It came down to my ankles and fit around my midsection like a girdle, making my waist seem smaller than my stomach. I admired myself in the mirror. I was almost perfect. I looked exactly like a nightclub singer.

"This one's fine," I said. "This is the one I want."

"It looks marvelous, Rhoda," Lauralee said, "but it's the wrong color for the wedding. Remember I'm wearing blue."

"I believe the child's color-blind," Miss Onnie Maud said. "It runs in her father's family."

"I am not color-blind," I said, reaching behind me and unzipping the dress. "I have twenty-twenty vision."

"Let her try on some more," Lauralee said. "Let her try on everything in the store."

I proceeded to do just that, with the salesladies getting grumpier and grumpier. I tried on a gold gabardine dress with a rhinestone-studded cumberbund. I tried on a pink ballerina-length formal and a lavender voile tea dress and several silk suits. Somehow nothing looked right.

"Maybe we'll have to make her something," my grandmother said.

"But there's no time," Miss Onnie Maud said. "Besides first we'd have to find out what she wants. Rhoda, please tell us what you're looking for."

Their faces all turned to mine, waiting for an answer. But I didn't know the answer.

The dress I wanted was a secret. The dress I wanted was dark and tall and thin as a reed. There was a word for what I wanted, a word I had seen in magazines. But what was that word? I could not remember.

"I want something dark," I said at last. "Something dark and silky."

"Wait right there," the saleslady said. "Wait just a minute." Then, from out of a prewar storage closet she brought a black-watch plaid recital dress with spaghetti straps and a white piqué jacket. It was made of taffeta and rustled when I touched it. There was a label sewn into the collar of the jacket. *Little Miss Sophisticate*, it said. *Sophisticate*, that was the word I was seeking.

I put on the dress and stood triumphant in a sea of ladies and dresses and hangers.

"This is the dress," I said. "This is the dress I'm wearing."

"It's perfect," Lauralee said. "Start hemming it up. She'll be the prettiest maid of honor in the whole world."

All the way home I held the box on my lap thinking about how I would look in the dress. Wait till they see me like this, I was thinking. Wait till they see what I really look like.

I fell in love with the groom. The moment I laid eyes on him I forgot he was flat-footed. He arrived bearing gifts of music and perfume and candy, a warm dark-skinned man with eyes the color of walnuts.

He laughed out loud when he saw me, standing on the porch with my hands on my hips.

"This must be Rhoda," he exclaimed, "the famous red-haired maid of honor." He came running up the steps, gave me a slow, exciting hug, and presented me with a whole album of Xavier Cugat records. I had never owned a record of my own, much less an album.

Before the evening was over I put on a red formal I found in a trunk and did a South American dance for him to Xavier Cugat's "Poinciana." He said he had never seen anything like it in his whole life.

The wedding itself was a disappointment. No one came but the immediate family and there was no aisle to march down and the only music was Onnie Maud playing "Liebestraum."

Dudley and Philip and Saint John and Oliver and Bunky were dressed in long pants and white shirts and ties. They had fresh military crew cuts and looked like a nest of new birds, huddled together on the blue velvet sofa, trying to keep their hands to themselves, trying to figure out how to act at a wedding.

The elderly Episcopal priest read out the ceremony in a gravelly smoker's voice, ruining all the good parts by coughing. He was in a bad mood because Lauralee and Mr. Marcus hadn't found time to come to him for marriage instruction.

Still, I got to hold the bride's flowers while he gave her the ring and stood so close to her during the ceremony I could hear her breathing.

The reception was better. People came from all over the Delta. There were tables with candles set up around the porches and sprays of greenery in every corner. There were gentlemen sweating in linen suits and the record player playing every minute. In the back hall Calvin had set up a real professional bar with tall, permanently frosted glasses and ice and mint and lemons and every kind of whiskey and liqueur in the world.

I stood in the receiving line getting compliments on my dress, then wandered around the room eating cake and letting people hug me. After a while I got bored with that and went out to the back hall and began to fix myself a drink at the bar.

I took one of the frosted glasses and began filling it from different bottles, tasting as I went along. I used plenty of crème de menthe and soon had something that tasted heavenly. I filled the glass with crushed ice, added three straws, and went out to sit on the back steps and cool off.

I was feeling wonderful. A full moon was caught like a kite in the pecan trees across the river. I sipped along on my drink. Then, without planning it, I did something I had never dreamed of doing. I left the porch alone at night. Usually I was in terror of the dark. My grandmother had told me that alligators come out of the bayou to eat children who wander alone at night.

I walked out across the yard, the huge moon giving so much light I almost cast a shadow. When I was nearly to the water's edge I turned and looked back toward the house. It shimmered in the moonlight like a jukebox alive in a meadow, seemed to pulsate with music and laughter and people, beautiful and foreign, not a part of me.

I looked out at the water, then down the road to the pasture. The Broad Jump Pit! There it was, perfect and unguarded. Why had I never thought of doing this before?

I began to run toward the road. I ran as fast as my Mary Jane pumps would allow me. I pulled my dress up around my waist and climbed the fence in one motion, dropping lightly down on the other side. I was sweating heavily, alone with the moon and my wonderful courage.

I knew exactly what to do first. I picked up the pole and hoisted it over my head. It felt solid and balanced and alive. I hoisted it up and down a few times as I had seen Dudley do, getting the feel of it.

Then I laid it ceremoniously down on the ground, reached behind me, and unhooked the plaid formal. I left it lying in a heap on the ground. There I stood, in my cotton underpants, ready to take up pole-vaulting.

I lifted the pole and carried it back to the end of the cinder path. I ran slowly down the path, stuck the pole in the wooden cup, and attempted throwing my body into the air, using it as a lever.

Something was wrong. It was more difficult than it appeared from a distance. I tried again. Nothing happened. I sat down with the pole across my legs to think things over.

Then I remembered something I had watched Dudley doing through the binoculars. He measured down from the end of the pole with his fingers spread wide. That was it, I had to hold it closer to the end.

I tried it again. This time the pole lifted me several feet off the ground. My body sailed across the grass in a neat arc and I landed on my toes. I was a natural!

I do not know how long I was out there, running up and down the cinder path, thrusting my body further and further through space, tossing myself into the pit like a mussel shell thrown across the bayou.

At last I decided I was ready for the real test. I had to vault over a cane barrier. I examined the pegs on the wooden poles and chose one that came up to my shoulder.

I put the barrier pole in place, spit over my left shoulder, and marched back to the end of the path. Suck up your guts, I told myself. It's only a pole. It won't get stuck in your stomach and tear out your insides. It won't kill you.

I stood at the end of the path eyeballing the barrier. Then, above the incessant racket of the crickets, I heard my name being called. Rhoda . . . the voices were calling. Rhoda . . . Rhoda . . . Rhoda . . . Rhoda.

I turned toward the house and saw them coming. Mr. Marcus and Dudley and Bunky and Calvin and Lauralee and what looked like half the wedding. They were climbing the fence, calling my name, and coming to get me. Rhoda . . . they called out. Where on earth have you been? What on earth are you doing?

I hoisted the pole up to my shoulders and began to run down the path, running into the light from the moon. I picked up speed, thrust the pole into the cup, and threw myself into the sky, into the still Delta night. I sailed up and was clear and over the barrier.

I let go of the pole and began my fall, which seemed to last a long time, long time. It was like falling through clear water. I dropped into the sawdust and lay very still, waiting for them to reach me.

Sometimes I think whatever has happened since has been of no real interest to me.

QUESTIONS FOR DISCUSSION AND WRITING

1. How does the letter from the father prompt the conflict in the story? Why doesn't the wedding provide the climax Rhoda had anticipated? Why does Rhoda's successful pole vault provide a resolution?
2. What does the imaginary role that Rhoda projects reveal about her? How does Rhoda's relationship with Lauralee give her a new sense of her own potential?
3. How is the unconscious sexism and racism of the place and the period made obvious throughout the story? Explain how the pole-vaulting serves as a focus for these attitudes.
4. How does the retrospective frame of the story give us a sense of the grim intensity of the child's experience and the humorous observations of the adult narrator?
5. How does the last sentence of the story help us interpret the title?

36

CHARLOTTE PERKINS GILMAN

The Yellow Wallpaper

CHARLOTTE PERKINS GILMAN (1860–1935) was born in Hartford, Connecticut, the daughter of a family related to Lyman Beecher, the abolitionist; Henry Ward Beecher, the preacher; and Harriet Beecher Stowe, the author of *Uncle Tom's Cabin.* After briefly attending the Rhode Island School of Design, Gilman was forced to work as a commercial artist and art teacher because of her financial situation. In 1884 she married Charles Stetson, another artist. After the birth of her daughter the following year, she suffered a nervous breakdown. In 1888 she left her husband and moved with her daughter to Pasadena where she began writing stories, poems, and political tracts. In 1900, she married her cousin George Gilman, and began an active career as a lecturer on feminist and socialist issues. Her best-known work is *Women and Economics* (1898), which makes an appeal for the financial independence of women. In other books, such as *Concerning Children* (1900), *Human Work* (1904), and *The Man-Made World* (1911), she called for a re-examination of the traditional roles assigned to women in our culture. Her fiction includes *What Diantha Did* (1910), *The Crux* (1911), and short stories collected in *The Charlotte Perkins Gilman Reader* (1979). "The Yellow Wallpaper," first published in *The New England Magazine* (January 1892), is a study of a woman driven to madness.

It is very seldom that mere ordinary people like John and myself secure ancestral halls for the summer.

A colonial mansion, a hereditary estate, I would say a haunted house and reach the height of romantic felicity—but that would be asking too much of fate!

Still I will proudly declare that there is something queer about it.

Else, why should it be let so cheaply? And why have stood so long untenanted?

John laughs at me, of course, but one expects that.

John is practical in the extreme. He has no patience with faith, an intense horror of superstition, and he scoffs openly at any talk of things not to be felt and seen and put down in figures.

John is a physician, and *perhaps*—(I would not say it to a living soul, of course, but this is dead paper and a great relief to my mind)—*perhaps* that is one reason I do not get well faster.

You see, he does not believe I am sick! And what can one do?

If a physician of high standing, and one's own husband, assures friends and relatives that there is really nothing the matter with one but temporary nervous depression—a slight hysterical tendency—what is one to do?

My brother is also a physician, and also of high standing, and he says the same thing.

So I take phosphates or phosphites—whichever it is—and tonics, and air and exercise, and journeys, and am absolutely forbidden to "work" until I am well again.

Personally, I disagree with their ideas.

Personally, I believe that congenial work, with excitement and change, would do me good.

But what is one to do?

I did write for a while in spite of them; but it *does* exhaust me a good deal—having to be so sly about it, or else meet with heavy opposition.

I sometimes fancy that in my condition, if I had less opposition and more society and stimulus—but John says the very worst thing I can do is to think about my condition, and I confess it always makes me feel bad.

So I will let it alone and talk about the house.

The most beautiful place! It is quite alone, standing well back from the road, quite three miles from the village. It makes me think of English places that you read about, for there are hedges and walls and gates that lock, and lots of separate little houses for the gardeners and people.

There is a *delicious* garden! I never saw such a garden—large and shady, full of box-bordered paths, and lined with long grape-covered arbors with seats under them.

There were greenhouses, but they are all broken now.

There was some legal trouble, I believe, something about the heirs and co-heirs; anyhow, the place has been empty for years.

That spoils my ghostliness, I am afraid, but I don't care—there is something strange about the house—I can feel it.

I even said so to John one moonlight evening, but he said what I felt was a draught, and shut the window.

I get unreasonably angry with John sometimes. I'm sure I never used to be so sensitive. I think it is due to this nervous condition.

But John says if I feel so I shall neglect proper self-control; so I take pains to control myself—before him, at least, and that makes me very tired.

I don't like our room a bit. I wanted one downstairs that opened onto the piazza and had roses all over the window, and such pretty old-fashioned chintz hangings! But John would not hear of it.

He said there was only one window and not room for two beds, and no near room for him if he took another.

He is very careful and loving, and hardly lets me stir without special direction.

I have a schedule prescription for each hour in the day; he takes all care from me, and so I feel basely ungrateful not to value it more.

He said he came here solely on my account, that I was to have perfect rest and all the air I could get. "Your exercise depends on your strength, my dear," said he, "and your food somewhat on your appetite; but air you can absorb all the time." So we took the nursery at the top of the house.

It is a big, airy room, the whole floor nearly, with windows that look all ways, and air and sunshine galore. It was nursery first, and then playroom and gymnasium, I should judge, for the windows are barred for little children, and there are rings and things in the walls.

The paint and paper look as if a boys' school had used it. It is stripped off—the paper—in great patches all around the head of my bed, about as far as I can reach, and in a great place on the other side of the room low down. I never saw a worse paper in my life. One of those sprawling, flamboyant patterns committing every artistic sin.

It is dull enough to confuse the eye in following, pronounced enough constantly to irritate and provoke study, and when you follow the lame uncertain curves for a little distance they suddenly commit suicide—plunge off at outrageous angles, destroy themselves in unheard-of contradictions.

The color is repellant, almost revolting: a smouldering unclean yellow, strangely faded by the slow-turning sunlight. It is a dull yet lurid orange in some places, a sickly sulphur tint in others.

No wonder the children hated it! I should hate it myself if I had to live in this room long.

There comes John, and I must put this away—he hates to have me write a word.

We have been here two weeks, and I haven't felt like writing before, since that first day.

I am sitting by the window now, up in this atrocious nursery, and there is nothing to hinder my writing as much as I please, save lack of strength.

John is away all day, and even some nights when his cases are serious.

I am glad my case is not serious!

But these nervous troubles are dreadfully depressing.

John does not know how much I really suffer. He knows there is no reason to suffer, and that satisfies him.

Of course it is only nervousness. It does weigh on me so not to do my duty in any way!

I meant to be such a help to John, such a real rest and comfort, and here I am a comparative burden already!

Nobody would believe what an effort it is to do what little I am able—to dress and entertain, and order things.

It is fortunate Mary is so good with the baby. Such a dear baby!

And yet I *cannot* be with him, it makes me so nervous.

I suppose John never was nervous in his life. He laughs at me so about this wallpaper!

At first he meant to repaper the room, but afterward he said that I was letting it get the better of me, and that nothing was worse for a nervous patient than to give way to such fancies.

He said that after the wallpaper was changed it would be the heavy bedstead, and then the barred windows, and then that gate at the end of the stairs, and so on.

"You know the place is doing you good," he said, "and really, dear, I don't care to renovate the house just for a three months' rental."

"Then do let us go downstairs," I said. "There are such pretty rooms there."

Then he took me in his arms and called me a blessed little goose, and said he would go down to the cellar, if I wished, and have it whitewashed into the bargain.

But he is right enough about the beds and windows and things.

It is as airy and comfortable a room as anyone need wish, and, of course, I would not be so silly as to make him uncomfortable just for a whim.

I'm really getting quite fond of the big room, all but that horrid paper.

Out of one window I can see the garden—those mysterious deep-shaded arbors, the riotous old-fashioned flowers, and bushes and gnarly trees.

Out of another I get a lovely view of the bay and a little private wharf belonging to the estate. There is a beautiful shaded lane that runs down there from the house. I always fancy I see people walking in these numerous paths and arbors, but John has cautioned me not to give way to fancy in the least. He says that with my imaginative power and habit of story-making, a nervous weakness like mine is sure to lead to all manner of excited fancies, and that I ought to use my will and good sense to check the tendency. So I try.

I think sometimes that if I were only well enough to write a little it would relieve the press of ideas and rest me.

But I find I get pretty tired when I try.

It is so discouraging not to have any advice and companionship about my work. When I get really well, John says we will ask Cousin Henry and Julia down for a long visit; but he says he would as soon put fireworks in my pillow-case as to let me have those stimulating people about now.

I wish I could get well faster.

But I must not think about that. This paper looks to me as if it *knew* what a vicious influence it had!

There is a recurrent spot where the pattern lolls like a broken neck and two bulbous eyes stare at you upside down.

I get positively angry with the impertinence of it and the everlastingness. Up and down and sideways they crawl, and those absurd unblinking eyes are everywhere. There is one place where two breadths didn't match, the eyes go all up and down the line, one a little higher than the other.

I never saw so much expression in an inanimate thing before, and we all know how much expression they have! I used to lie awake as a child and get more entertainment and terror out of blank walls and plain furniture than most children could find in a toy-store.

I remember what a kindly wink the knobs of our big old bureau used to have, and there was one chair that always seemed like a strong friend.

I used to feel that if any of the other things looked too fierce I could always hop into that chair and be safe.

The furniture in this room is no worse than inharmonious, however, for we had to bring it all from downstairs. I suppose when this was used as a playroom they had to take the nursery things out, and no wonder! I never saw such ravages as the children have made here.

The wallpaper, as I said before, is torn off in spots, and it sticketh closer than a brother—they must have had perseverance as well as hatred.

Then the floor is scratched and gouged and splintered, the plaster itself is dug out here and there, and this great heavy bed, which is all we found in the room, looks as if it had been through the wars.

But I don't mind it a bit—only the paper.

There comes John's sister. Such a dear girl as she is, and so careful of me! I must not let her find me writing.

She is a perfect and enthusiastic housekeeper, and hopes for no better profession. I verily believe she thinks it is the writing which makes me sick!

But I can write when she is out, and see her a long way off from these windows.

There is one that commands the road, a lovely shaded winding road, and one that just looks off over the country. A lovely country, too, full of great elms and velvet meadows.

This wallpaper has a kind of sub-pattern in a different shade, a particularly irritating one, for you can only see it in certain lights, and not clearly then.

But in the places where it isn't faded and where the sun is just so—I can see a strange, provoking, formless sort of figure that seems to skulk about behind that silly and conspicuous front design.

There's sister on the stairs!

Well, the Fourth of July is over! The people are all gone, and I am tired out. John thought it might do me good to see a little company, so we just had Mother and Nellie and the children down for a week.

Of course I didn't do a thing. Jennie sees to everything now.

But it tired me all the same.

John says if I don't pick up faster he shall send me to Weir Mitchell in the fall.

But I don't want to go there at all. I had a friend who was in his hands once, and she says he is just like John and my brother, only more so!

Besides, it is such an undertaking to go so far.

I don't feel as if it was worthwhile to turn my hand over for anything, and I'm getting dreadfully fretful and querulous.

I cry at nothing, and cry most of the time.

Of course I don't when John is here, or anybody else, but when I am alone.

And I am alone a good deal just now. John is kept in town very often by serious cases, and Jennie is good and lets me alone when I want her to.

So I walk a little in the garden or down that lovely lane, sit on the porch under the roses, and lie down up here a good deal.

I'm getting really fond of the room in spite of the wallpaper. Perhaps *because* of the wallpaper.

It dwells in my mind so!

I lie here on this great immovable bed—it is nailed down, I believe—and follow that pattern about by the hour. It is as good as gymnastics, I assure you. I start, we'll say, at the bottom, down in the corner over there where it has not been touched, and I determine for the thousandth time that I *will* follow that pointless pattern to some sort of a conclusion.

I know a little of the principle of design, and I know this thing was not arranged on any laws of radiation, or alternation, or repetition, or symmetry, or anything else that I ever heard of.

It is repeated, of course, by the breadths, but not otherwise.

Looked at in one way, each breadth stands alone; the bloated curves and flourishes—a kind of "debased Romanesque" with delirium tremens go waddling up and down in isolated columns of fatuity.

But, on the other hand, they connect diagonally, and the sprawling outlines run off in great slanting waves of optic horror, like a lot of wallowing sea-weeds in full chase.

The whole thing goes horizontally, too, at least it seems so, and I exhaust myself trying to distinguish the order of its going in that direction.

They have used a horizontal breadth for a frieze, and that adds wonderfully to the confusion.

There is one end of the room where it is almost intact, and there, when the cross-lights fade and the low sun shines directly upon it, I can almost fancy radiation after all—the interminable grotesque seems to form around a common center and rush off in headlong plunges of equal distraction.

It makes me tired to follow it. I will take a nap, I guess.

I don't know why I should write this.

I don't want to.

I don't feel able.

And I know John would think it absurd. But I *must* say what I feel and think in some way—it is such a relief!

But the effort is getting to be greater than the relief.

Half the time now I am awfully lazy, and lie down ever so much. John says I mustn't lose my strength, and has me take cod liver oil and lots of tonics and things, to say nothing of ale and wine and rare meat.

Dear John! He loves me very dearly, and hates to have me sick. I tried to have a real earnest reasonable talk with him the other day, and tell him how I wish he would let me go and make a visit to Cousin Henry and Julia.

But he said I wasn't able to go, nor able to stand it after I got there; and I did not make out a very good case for myself, for I was crying before I had finished.

It is getting to be a great effort for me to think straight. Just this nervous weakness, I suppose.

And dear John gathered me up in his arms, and just carried me upstairs and laid me on the bed, and sat by me and read to me till it tired my head.

He said I was his darling and his comfort and all he had, and that I must take care of myself for his sake, and keep well.

He says no one but myself can help me out of it, that I must use my will and self-control and not let any silly fancies run away with me.

There's one comfort—the baby is well and happy, and does not have to occupy this nursery with the horrid wallpaper.

If we had not used it, that blessed child would have! What a fortunate escape! Why, I wouldn't have a child of mine, an impressionable little thing, live in such a room for worlds.

I never thought of it before, but it is lucky that John kept me here after all; I can stand it so much easier than a baby, you see.

Of course I never mention it to them any more—I am too wise—but I keep watch for it all the same.

There are things in that wallpaper that nobody knows about but me, or ever will.

Behind that outside pattern the dim shapes get clearer every day.

It is always the same shape, only very numerous.

And it is like a woman stooping down and creeping about behind that pattern. I don't like it a bit. I wonder—I began to think—I wish John would take me away from here!

It is so hard to talk with John about my case, because he is so wise, and because he loves me so.

But I tried it last night.

It was moonlight. The moon shines in all around just as the sun does.

I hate to see it sometimes, it creeps so slowly, and always comes in by one window or another.

John was asleep and I hated to waken him, so I kept still and watched the moonlight on that undulating wallpaper till I felt creepy.

The faint figure behind seemed to shake the pattern, just as if she wanted to get out.

I got up softly and went to feel and see if the paper *did* move, and when I came back John was awake.

"What is it, little girl?" he said. "Don't go walking about like that—you'll get cold."

I thought it was a good time to talk, so I told him that I really was not gaining here, and that I wished he would take me away.

"Why, darling!" said he. "Our lease will be up in three weeks, and I can't see how to leave before.

"The repairs are not done at home, and I cannot possibly leave town just now. Of course, if you were in any danger, I could and would, but you really are better, dear, whether you can see it or not. I am a doctor, dear, and I know. You are gaining flesh and color, your appetite is better, I feel really much easier about you."

"I don't weight a bit more," said I, "nor as much; and my appetite may be better in the evening when you are here but it is worse in the morning when you are away!"

"Bless her little heart!" said he with a big hug. "She shall be as sick as she pleases! But now let's improve the shining hours by going to sleep, and talk about it in the morning!"

"And you won't go away?" I asked gloomily.

"Why, how can I, dear? It is only three weeks more and then we will take a nice little trip of a few days while Jennie is getting the house ready. Really, dear, you are better!"

"Better in body perhaps—" I began, and stopped short, for he sat up straight and looked at me with such a stern, reproachful look that I could not say another word.

"My darling," said he, "I beg of you, for my sake and for our child's sake, as well as for your own, that you will never for one instant let that idea enter your mind! There is nothing so dangerous, so fascinating, to a temperament like yours. It is a false and foolish fancy. Can you not trust me as a physician when I tell you so?"

So of course I said no more on that score, and we went to sleep before long. He thought I was asleep first, but I wasn't, and lay there for hours trying to decide whether that front pattern and the back pattern really did move together or separately.

On a pattern like this, by daylight, there is a lack of sequence, a defiance of law, that is a constant irritant to a normal mind.

The color is hideous enough, and unreliable enough, and infuriating enough, but the pattern is torturing.

You think you have mastered it, but just as you get well under way in following, it turns a back-somersault and there you are. It slaps you in the face, knocks you down, and tramples upon you. It is like a bad dream.

The outside pattern is a florid arabesque, reminding one of a fungus. If you can imagine a toadstool in joints, an interminable string of toadstools, budding and sprouting in endless convolutions—why, that is something like it.

That is, sometimes!

There is one marked peculiarity about this paper, a thing nobody seems to notice but myself, and that is that it changes as the light changes.

When the sun shoots in through the east window—I always watch for that first long, straight ray—it changes so quickly that I never can quite believe it.

That is why I watch it always.

By moonlight—the moon shines in all night when there is a moon—I wouldn't know it was the same paper.

At night in any kind of light, in twilight, candlelight, lamplight, and worst of all by moonlight, it becomes bars! The outside pattern, I mean, and the woman behind it is as plain as can be.

I didn't realize for a long time what the thing was that showed behind, that dim sub-pattern, but now I am quite sure it is a woman.

By daylight she is subdued, quiet. I fancy it is the pattern that keeps her so still. It is so puzzling. It keeps me quiet by the hour.

I lie down ever so much now. John says it is good for me, and to sleep all I can.

Indeed he started the habit by making me lie down for an hour after each meal.

It is a very bad habit, I am convinced, for you see, I don't sleep.

And that cultivates deceit, for I don't tell them I'm awake—oh, no!

The fact is I am getting a little afraid of John.

He seems very queer sometimes, and even Jennie has an inexplicable look.

It strikes me occasionally, just as a scientific hypothesis, that perhaps it is the paper!

I have watched John when he did not know I was looking, and come into the room suddenly on the most innocent excuses, and I've caught him several times *looking at the paper*! And Jennie too. I caught Jennie with her hand on it once.

She didn't know I was in the room, and when I asked her in a quiet, a very quiet voice, with the most restrained manner possible, what she was doing with the paper, she turned around as if she had been caught stealing, and looked quite angry—asked me why I should frighten her so!

Then she said that the paper stained everything it touched, that she had found yellow smooches on all my clothes and John's and she wished we would be more careful!

Did not that sound innocent? But I know she was studying that pattern, and I am determined that nobody shall find it out but myself!

Life is very much more exciting now than it used to be. You see, I have something more to expect, to look forward to, to watch. I really do eat better, and am more quiet than I was.

John is so pleased to see me improve! He laughed a little the other day, and said I seemed to be flourishing in spite of my wallpaper.

I turned it off with a laugh. I had no intention of telling him it was *because* of the wallpaper—he would make fun of me. He might even want to take me away.

I don't want to leave now until I have found it out. There is a week more, and I think that will be enough.

I'm feeling so much better!

I don't sleep much at night, for it is so interesting to watch developments; but I sleep a good deal during the daytime.

In the daytime it is tiresome and perplexing.

There are always new shoots on the fungus, and new shades of yellow all over it. I cannot keep count of them, though I have tried conscientiously.

It is the strangest yellow, that wallpaper! It makes me think of all the yellow things I ever saw—not beautiful ones like buttercups, but old, foul, bad yellow things.

But there is something else about that paper—the smell! I noticed it the moment we came into the room, but with so much air and sun it was not bad. Now we have had a week of fog and rain, and whether the windows are open or not, the smell is here.

It creeps all over the house.

I find it hovering in the dining-room, skulking in the parlor, hiding in the hall, lying in wait for me on the stairs.

It gets into my hair.

Even when I go to ride, if I turn my head suddenly and surprise it—there is that smell!

Such a peculiar odor, too! I have spent hours in trying to analyze it, to find what it smelled like.

It is not bad—at first—and very gentle, but quite the subtlest, most enduring odor I ever met.

In this damp weather it is awful. I wake up in the night and find it hanging over me.

It used to disturb me at first. I thought seriously of burning the house—to reach the smell.

But now I am used to it. The only thing I can think of that it is like is the *color* of the paper! A yellow smell.

There is a very funny mark on this wall, low down, near the mopboard. A streak that runs round the room. It goes behind every piece of furniture, except the bed, a long, straight, even *smooch*, as if it had been rubbed over and over.

I wonder how it was done and who did it, and what they did it for. Round and round and round—round and round and round—it makes me dizzy!

I really have discovered something at last.

Through watching so much at night, when it changes so, I have finally found out.

The front pattern *does* move—and no wonder! The woman behind shakes it!

Sometimes I think there are a great many women behind, and sometimes only one, and she crawls around fast, and her crawling shakes it all over.

Then in the very bright spots she keeps still, and in the very shady spots she just takes hold of the bars and shakes them hard.

And she is all the time trying to climb through. But nobody could climb through that pattern—it strangles so; I think that is why it has so many heads.

They get through and then the pattern strangles them off and turns them upside down, and makes their eyes white!

If those heads were covered or taken off it would not be half so bad.

I think that woman gets out in the daytime!

And I'll tell you why—privately—I've seen her!

I can see her out of every one of my windows!

It is the same woman, I know, for she is always creeping, and most women do not creep by daylight.

I see her in that long shaded lane, creeping up and down. I see her in those dark grape arbors, creeping all around the garden.

I see her on that long road under the trees, creeping along, and when a carriage comes she hides under the blackberry vines.

I don't blame her a bit. It must be very humiliating to be caught creeping by daylight!

I always lock the door when I creep by daylight. I can't do it at night, for I know John would suspect something at once.

And John is so queer now that I don't want to irritate him. I wish he would take another room! Besides, I don't want anybody to get that woman out at night but myself.

I often wonder if I could see her out of all the windows at once.

But, turn as fast as I can, I can only see out of one at a time.

And though I always see her, she *may* be able to creep faster than I can turn! I have watched her sometimes away off in the open country, creeping as fast as a cloud shadow in a wind.

If only that top pattern could be gotten off from the under one! I mean to try it, little by little.

I have found out another funny thing, but I shan't tell this time! It does not do to trust people too much.

There are only two more days to get this paper off, and I believe John is beginning to notice. I don't like the look in his eyes.

And I heard him ask Jennie a lot of professional questions about me. She had a very good report to give.

She said I slept a good deal in the daytime.

John knows I don't sleep very well at night, for all I'm so quiet!

He asked me all sorts of questions, too, and pretended to be very loving and kind.

As if I couldn't see through him!

Still, I don't wonder he acts so, sleeping under this paper for three months.

It only interests me, but I feel sure John and Jennie are affected by it.

Hurray! This is the last day, but it is enough. John is to stay in town over night, and won't be out until this evening.

Jennie wanted to sleep with me—the sly thing; but I told her I should undoubtedly rest better for a night all alone.

That was clever, for really I wasn't alone a bit! As soon as it was moonlight and that poor thing began to crawl and shake the pattern, I got up and ran to help her.

I pulled and she shook. I shook and she pulled, and before morning we had peeled off yards of that paper.

A strip about as high as my head and half around the room.

And then when the sun came and that awful pattern began to laugh at me, I declared I would finish it today!

We go away tomorrow, and they are moving all my furniture down again to leave things as they were before.

Jennie looked at the wall in amazement, but I told her merrily that I did it out of pure spite at the vicious thing.

She laughed and said she wouldn't mind doing it herself, but I must not get tired.

How she betrayed herself that time!

But I am here, and no person touches this paper but Me—not *alive*!

She tried to get me out of the room—it was too patent! But I said it was so quiet and empty and clean now that I believed I would lie down again and sleep all I could, and not to wake me even for dinner—I would call when I woke.

So now she is gone, and the servants are gone, and the things are gone, and there is nothing left but that great bedstead nailed down, with the canvas mattress we found on it.

We shall sleep downstairs tonight, and take the boat home tomorrow.

I quite enjoy the room, now it is bare again.

How those children did tear about here!

This bedstead is fairly gnawed!

But I must get to work.

I have locked the door and thrown the key down into the front path.

I don't want to go out, and I don't want to have anybody come in, till John comes.

I want to astonish him.

I've got a rope up here that even Jennie did not find. If that woman does get out, and tries to get away, I can tie her!

But I forgot I could not reach far without anything to stand on!

This bed will *not* move!

I tried to lift and push it until I was lame, and then I got so angry I bit off a little piece at one corner—but it hurt my teeth.

Then I peeled off all the paper I could reach standing on the floor. It sticks horribly and the pattern just enjoys it! All those strangled heads and bulbous eyes and waddling fungus growths just shriek with derision!

I am getting angry enough to do something desperate. To jump out of the window would be admirable exercise, but the bars are too strong even to try.

Besides I wouldn't do it. Of course not. I know well enough that a step like that is improper and might be misconstrued.

I don't like to *look* out of the windows even—there are so many of those creeping women, and they creep so fast.

I wonder if they all come out of that wallpaper as I did?

But I am securely fastened now by my well-hidden rope—you don't get *me* out in the road there!

I suppose I shall have to get back behind the pattern when it comes night, and that is hard!

It is so pleasant to be out in this great room and creep around as I please!

I don't want to go outside. I won't, even if Jennie asks me to.

For outside you have to creep on the ground, and everything is green instead of yellow.

But here I can creep smoothly on the floor, and my shoulder just fits in that long smooch around the wall, so I cannot lose my way.

Why, there's John at the door!

It is no use, young man, you can't open it!

How he does call and pound!

Now he's crying to Jennie for an axe.

It would be a shame to break down that beautiful door!

"John, dear!" said I in the gentlest voice. "The key is down by the front steps, under a plantain leaf!"

That silenced him for a few moments.

Then he said, very quietly indeed, "Open the door, my darling!"

"I can't," said I. "The key is down by the front door under a plantain leaf!" And then I said it again, several times, very gently and slowly, and said it so often that he had to go and see, and he got it of course, and came in. He stopped short by the door.

"What is the matter?" he cried. "For God's sake, what are you doing?"

I kept on creeping just the same, but I looked at him over my shoulder.

"I've got out at last," said I, "in spite of you and Jennie. And I've pulled off most of the paper, so you can't put me back."

Now why should that man have fainted? But he did, and right across my path by the wall, so that I had to creep over him every time!

QUESTIONS FOR DISCUSSION AND WRITING

1. How do the six sections of the story document the gradual deterioration of the narrator's condition? Where does the story reach its climax and conclusion?
2. How reliable is the narrator's characterization of her husband? How does her husband treat her? Describe how their relationship changes during the course of the story.
3. How does the narrator feel initially about the setting for her recuperation? In what way does the increasingly detailed description of the wallpaper produce a tone of mounting horror in the story?
4. What effect does the author achieve by allowing the narrator to tell her own story? What effect does the narrator create by recording her impressions in such brief paragraphs?
5. In what ways does the treatment—rigid confinement and absolute passivity—create the disease? What evidence is there that the husband's love is a destructive rather than a healing force in the life of the narrator?

37

GAIL GODWIN

Dream Children

GAIL GODWIN was born in Birmingham, Alabama, in 1937 and was educated at the University of North Carolina and the University of Iowa. She has worked as a journalist for the Miami *Herald,* as a travel consultant with the United States Embassy in London, and as an English instructor at the University of Iowa, Vassar College, and Columbia University. Godwin's essays and short stories have appeared in magazines such as *Harper's, Esquire, Cosmopolitan, Mademoiselle,* and *Ms.* She has also written librettos for four musical compositions by Robert Starer. Her novels, *The Perfectionists* (1970), *Glass People* (1972), *The Odd Woman* (1974), *Violet Clay* (1978), *A Mother and Two Daughters* (1981), *The Finishing School* (1985), and *Father's Melancholy Daughter* (1991), capture the consciousness of contemporary women. In "Dream Children," the title story from her 1976 collection, Godwin recounts a young woman's attempts to find happiness after she has been victimized by a terrible, freakish mistake.

The worst thing. Such a terrible thing to happen to a young woman. It's a wonder she didn't go mad.

As she went about her errands, a cheerful, neat young woman, a wife, wearing pants with permanent creases and safari jackets and high-necked sweaters that folded chastely just below the line of the small gold hoops she wore in her ears, she imagined people saying this, or thinking it to themselves. But nobody knew. Nobody knew anything, other than that she and her husband had moved here a year ago, as so many couples were moving farther away from the city, the husband commuting, or staying in town during the week—as hers did. There was nobody here, in this quaint, unspoiled village, nestled in the foothills of the mountains, who could have looked at her and guessed that anything out of the ordinary, predictable, auspicious spectrum of things that happen to bright, attractive young women had happened to her. She always returned her books to the local library on time; she bought liquor at the local liquor store only on Friday, before she went to meet her husband's bus from the city. He was something in television, a producer? So many ambitious young couples moving to this Dutch farming village, founded in 1690, to restore ruined fieldstone houses and plant herb gardens and keep their own horses and discover the relief of finding oneself insignificant in Nature for the first time!

A terrible thing. So freakish. If you read it in a story or saw it on TV, you'd say no, this sort of thing could never happen in an American hospital.

DePuy, who owned the Old Patroon farm adjacent to her land, frequently glimpsed her racing her horse in the early morning, when the mists still lay on the fields, sometimes just before the sun came up and there was a frost on everything. "One woodchuck hole and she and that stallion will both have to be put out of their misery," he told his wife. "She's too reckless. I'll bet you her old man doesn't know she goes streaking to hell across the fields like that." Mrs. DePuy nodded, silent, and went about her business. She, too, watched that other woman ride, a woman not much younger than herself, but with an aura of romance—of tragedy, perhaps. The way she looked: like those heroines in English novels who ride off their bad tempers and unrequited love affairs, clenching their thighs against the flanks of spirited horses with murderous red eyes. Mrs. DePuy, who had ridden since the age of three, recognized something beyond recklessness in that elegant young woman, in her crisp checked shirts and her dove-gray jodhpurs. *She has nothing to fear anymore,* thought the farmer's wife, with sure feminine instinct; she both envied and pitied her. "What she needs is children," remarked DePuy.

"A Dry Sack, a Remy Martin, and . . . let's see, a half-gallon of the Chablis, and I think I'd better take a Scotch . . . and the Mouton-Cadet . . . and maybe a dry vermouth." Mrs. Frye, another farmer's wife, who runs the liquor store, asks if her husband is bringing company for the weekend. "He sure is; we couldn't drink all that by ourselves," and the young woman laughs, her lovely teeth exposed, her small gold earrings quivering in the light. "You know, I saw his name—on the television the other night," says Mrs. Frye. "It was at the beginning of that new comedy show, the one with the woman who used to be on another show with her husband and little girl, only they divorced, you know the one?" "Of course I do. It's one of my husband's shows. I'll tell him you watched it." Mrs. Frye puts the bottles in an empty box, carefully inserting wedges of cardboard between them. Through the window of her store she sees her customer's pert bottle-green car, some sort of little foreign car with the engine running, filled with groceries and weekend parcels, and that big silver-blue dog sitting up in the front seat just like a human being. "I think that kind of thing is so sad," says Mrs. Frye; "families breaking up, poor little children having to divide their loyalties." "I couldn't agree more," replies the young woman, nodding gravely. Such a personable, polite girl! "Are you sure you can carry that, dear? I can get Earl from the back. . . ." But the girl has it hoisted on her shoulder in a flash, is airily maneuvering between unopened cartons stacked in the aisle, in her pretty boots. Her perfume lingers in Mrs. Frye's store for a half-hour after she has driven away.

After dinner, her husband and his friends drank brandy. She lay in front of the fire, stroking the dog, and listening to Victoria Darrow, the news commentator, in person. A few minutes ago, they had all watched Victoria on TV. "That's right; thirty-nine!" Victoria now whispered to her. "What? That's kind of you. I'm photogenic, thank God, or I'd have been put out to pasture long before. . . . I look five, maybe seven years younger on the screen . . . but the point I'm getting at is, I went to this doctor and he said, 'If you want to do this thing, you'd better go home today and get started.' He told me—did you know this? Did you know that a woman is born with all the eggs she'll ever have, and when she gets to my age, the ones that are left have been rattling around so long they're a little shopworn; then every time you fly you get an extra dose of radioactivity, so those poor eggs. He told me when a woman over forty comes into his office pregnant, his heart sinks; that's why he quit practicing obstetrics, he said; he could still remember the screams of a woman whose baby he delivered . . . she was having natural childbirth and she kept saying, 'Why won't you let me see it, I insist on seeing it,' and so he had to, and he says he can still hear her screaming."

"Oh, what was—what was wrong with it?"

But she never got the answer. Her husband, white around the lips, was standing over Victoria ominously, offering the Remy Martin bottle. "Vicky, let me pour you some more," he said. And to his wife, "I think Blue Boy needs to go out."

"Yes, yes, of course. Please excuse me, Victoria. I'll just be . . ."

Her husband followed her to the kitchen, his hand on the back of her neck. "Are you okay? That stupid yammering bitch. She and her twenty-six-year-old lover! I wish I'd never brought them, but she's been hinting around the studio for weeks."

"But I like them, I like having them. I'm fine. Please go back. I'll take the dog out and come back. Please . . ."

"All right. If you're sure you're okay." He backed away, hands dangling at his sides. A handsome man, wearing a pink shirt with Guatemalan embroidery. Thick black hair and a face rather boyish, but cunning. Last weekend she had sat beside him, alone in this house, just the two of them, and watched him on television: a documentary, in several parts, in which TV "examines itself." There was his double, sitting in an armchair in his executive office, coolly replying to the questions of Victoria Darrow. "*Do you personally watch all the programs you produce, Mr. McNair?*" She watched the man on the screen, how he moved his lips when he spoke, but kept the rest of his face, his body perfectly still. Funny, she had never noticed this before. He managed to say that he did and did not watch all the programs he produced.

Now, in the kitchen, she looked at him backing away, a little like a renegade in one of his own shows—a desperate man, perhaps, who had just killed somebody and is backing away, hands dangling loosely at his sides, Mr. McNair, her husband. That man on the screen. Once a lover above her in bed. That friend who held her hand in the hospital.

One hand in hers, the other holding the stopwatch. For a brief instant, all the images coalesce and she feels something again. But once outside, under the galaxies of autumn-sharp stars,the intelligent dog at her heels like some smart gray ghost, she is glad to be free of all that. She walks quickly over the damp grass to the barn, to look in on her horse. She understands something: her husband, Victoria Darrow lead double lives that seem perfectly normal to them. But if she told her husband that she, too, is in two lives, he would become alarmed; he would sell this house and make her move back to the city where he could keep an eye on her welfare.

She is discovering people like herself, down through the centuries, all over the world. She scours books with titles like *The Timeless Moment, The Sleeping Prophet, Between Two Worlds, Silent Union: A Record of Unwilled Communication;* collecting evidence, weaving a sort of underworld net of colleagues around her.

A rainy fall day. Too wet to ride. The silver dog asleep beside her in her special alcove, a padded window seat filled with pillows and books. She is looking down on the fields of dried lithrium, and the fir trees beyond, and the mountains gauzy with fog and rain, thinking, in a kind of terror and ecstasy, about all these connections. A book lies face down on her lap. She has just read the following:

> Theodore Dreiser and his friend John Cowper Powys had been dining at Dreiser's place on West Fifty Seventh Street. As Powys made ready to leave and catch his train to the little town up the Hudson, where he was then living, he told Dreiser, "I'll appear before you here, later in the evening."
>
> Dreiser laughed. "Are you going to turn yourself into a ghost, or have you a spare key?" he asked. Powys said he would return "in some form," he didn't know exactly what kind.
>
> After his friend left, Dreiser sat up and read for two hours. Then he looked up and saw Powys standing in the doorway to the living room. It was Powys' features, his tall stature, even the loose tweed garments which he wore. Dreiser rose at once and strode toward the figure, saying, "Well, John, you kept your word. Come on in and tell me how you did it." But the figure vanished when Dreiser came within three feet of it.
>
> Dreiser then went to the telephone and called Powys' house in the country. Powys answered. Dreiser told him what had happened and Powys said, "I told you I'd be there and you oughtn't to be surprised." But he refused to discuss how he had done it, if, indeed, he knew how.

"But don't you get frightened, up here all by yourself, alone with all these creaky sounds?" asked Victoria, the next morning.

"No, I guess I'm used to them," she replied, breaking eggs into a bowl. "I know what each one means. The wood expanding and contracting . . . the wind getting caught between the shutter and the latch . . . Sometimes small animals get lost in the stone walls and scratch around till they find their way out . . . or die."

"Ugh. But don't you imagine things? I would, in a house like this. How old? That's almost three hundred years of lived lives, people suffering and shouting and making love and giving birth, under this roof. . . . You'd think there'd be a few ghosts around."

"I don't know," said her hostess blandly. "I haven't heard any. But of course, I have Blue Boy, so I don't get scared." She whisked the eggs, unable to face Victoria. She and her husband had lain awake last night, embarrassed at the sounds coming from the next room. No ghostly moans, those. "Why can't that bitch control herself, or at least lower her voice," he said angrily. He stroked his wife's arm, both of them pretending not to remember. She had bled for an entire year afterward, until the doctor said they would have to remove everything. "I'm empty," she had said when her husband had tried again, after she was healed. "I'm sorry, I just don't feel anything." Now they lay tenderly together on these weekends, like childhood friends, like effigies on a lovers' tomb, their mutual sorrow like a sword between them. She assumed he had another life, or lives, in town. As she had here. Nobody is just one person, she had learned.

"I'm sure I would imagine things," said Victoria. "I would see things and hear things inside my head much worse than an ordinary murderer or rapist."

The wind caught in the shutter latch . . . a small animal dislodging pieces of fieldstone in its terror, sending them tumbling down the inner walls, from attic to cellar . . . a sound like a child rattling a jar full of marbles, or small stones . . .

"I have so little imagination," she said humbly, warming the butter in the omelet pan. She could feel Victoria Darrow's professional curiosity waning from her dull country life, focusing elsewhere.

Cunning!

As a child of nine, she had gone through a phase of walking in her sleep. One summer night, they found her bed empty, and after an hour's hysterical search they had found her in her nightgown, curled up on the flagstones beside the fishpond. She woke, baffled, in her father's tense clutch, the stars all over the sky, her mother repeating over and over again to the night at large, "Oh, my God, she could have drowned!" They took her to a child psychiatrist, a pretty Austrian woman who spoke to her with the same vocabulary she used on grownups, putting the child instantly at ease. "It is not at all uncommon what you did. I have known so many children who take little night journeys from their beds, and then they awaken and don't know what all the fuss is about! Usually these journeys are quite harmless, because children are surrounded by a magical reality that keeps them safe. Yes, the race of children possesses magically sagacious powers! But the grownups, they tend to forget how it once was for them. They worry, they are afraid of so many things. You do not want your mother and father, who love you so anxiously, to live in fear of you going to live with the fishes." She had giggled at the thought. The woman's steady gray-green eyes were trained on her carefully, suspending her in a kind of bubble. Then she had rejoined her parents, a dutiful "child" again, holding a hand up to each of them. The night journeys had stopped.

A thunderstorm one night last spring. Blue Boy whining in his insulated house below the garage. She had lain there, strangely elated by the nearness of the thunderclaps that tore at the sky, followed by instantaneous flashes of jagged light. Wondering shouldn't she go down and let the dog in; he hated storms. Then dozing off again . . .

She woke. The storm had stopped. The dark air was quiet. Something had changed, some small thing—what? She had to think hard before she found it: the hall light, which she kept burning during the week-nights when she was there alone, had gone out. She reached over and switched the button on her bedside lamp. Nothing. A tree must have fallen and hit a wire, causing the power to go off. This often happened here. No problem. The dog had stopped crying. She felt herself sinking into a delicious, deep reverie, the kind that sometimes came just before morning, as if her being broke slowly into tiny pieces and spread itself over the world. It was a feeling she had not known until she had lived by herself in this house: this weightless though conscious state in which she lay, as if in a warm bath, and yet was able to send her thoughts anywhere, as if her mind contained the entire world.

And as she floated in this silent world, transparent and buoyed upon the dream layers of the mind, she heard a small rattling sound, like pebbles being shaken in a jar. The sound came distinctly from the guest room, a room so chosen by her husband and herself because it was the farthest room from their bedroom on this floor. It lay above what had been the old side of the house, built seventy-five years before the new side, which was completed in 1753. There was a bed in it, and a chair, and some plants in the window. Sometimes on weekends when she could not sleep, she went and read there, or meditated, to keep from waking her husband. It was the room where Victoria Darrow and her young lover would not sleep the following fall, because she would say quietly to her husband, "No . . . not that room. I—I've made up the bed in the other room," "What?" he would want to know. "The one next to ours? Right under our noses?"

She did not lie long listening to this sound before she understood it was one she had never heard in the house before. It had a peculiar regularity to its rhythm; there was nothing accidental about it, nothing influenced by the wind, or the nerves of some lost animal. *K-chunk, k-chunk, k-chunk,* it went. At intervals of exactly a half-minute apart. She still remembered how to time such things, such intervals. She was as good as any stopwatch when it came to timing certain intervals.

K-chunk, k-chunk, k-chunk. That determined regularity. Something willed, something poignantly repeated, as though the repetition was a means of consoling someone in the dark. Her skin began to prickle. Often, lying in such states of weightless reverie, she had practiced the trick of sending herself abroad, into rooms of the house, out into the night to check on Blue Boy, over to the barn to look in on her horse, who slept standing up. Once she had heard a rather frightening noise, as if someone in the basement had turned on a faucet, and so she forced herself to "go down," floating down two sets of stairs into the darkness, only to discover what she had known all the time: the hookup system between the hot-water tank and the pump, which sounded like someone turning on the water.

Now she went through the palpable, prickly darkness, without lights, down the chilly hall in her sleeveless gown, into the guest room. Although there was no light, not even a moon shining through the window, she could make out the shape of the bed and then the chair, the spider plants on the window, and a small dark shape in one corner, on the floor, which she and her husband had painted a light yellow.

K-chunk, k-chunk, k-chunk. The shape moved with the noise.

Now she knew what they meant, that "someone's hair stood on end." It was true. As she forced herself across the borders of a place she had never been, she felt, distinctly, every single hair on her head raise itself a millimeter or so from her scalp.

She knelt down and discovered him. He was kneeling, a little cold and scared, shaking a small jar filled with some kind of pebbles. (She later found out, in a subsequent visit, that they were small colored shells, of a triangular shape, called coquinas: she found them in a picture in a child's nature book at the library.) He was wearing pajamas a little too big for him, obviously hand-me-downs, and he was exactly two years older than the only time she had ever held him in her arms.

The two of them knelt in the corner of the room, taking each other in. His large eyes were the same as before: dark and unblinking. He held the small jar close to him, watching her. He was not afraid, but she knew better than to move too close.

She knelt, the tears streaming down her cheeks, but she made no sound, her eyes fastened on that small form. And then the hall light came on silently, as well as the lamp beside her bed, and with wet cheeks and pounding heart she could not be sure whether or not she had actually been out of the room.

But what did it matter, on the level where they had met? He traveled so much farther than she to reach that room. ("*Yes, the race of children possesses magically sagacious powers!*")

She and her husband sat together on the flowered chintz sofa, watching the last of the series in which TV purportedly examined itself. She said, "Did you ever think that the whole thing is really a miracle? I mean, here we sit, eighty miles away from your studios, and we turn on a little machine and there is Victoria, speaking to us as clearly as she did last weekend when she was in this very room. Why, it's magic, it's time travel and space travel right in front of our eyes, but because it's been 'discovered,' because the world understands that it's only little dots that transmit Victoria electrically to us, it's *all right*. We can bear it. Don't you sometimes wonder about all the miracles that haven't been officially approved yet? I mean, who knows, maybe in a hundred years everybody will take it for granted that they can send an image of themselves around in space by some perfectly natural means available to us now. I mean, when you think about it, what *is* space? What *is* time? Where do the so-called boundaries of each of us begin and end? Can anyone explain it?"

He was drinking Scotch and thinking how they had decided not to renew Victoria Darrow's contract. Somewhere on the edges of his mind hovered an anxious, growing certainty about his wife. At the local grocery store this morning, when he went to pick up a carton of milk and the paper, he had stopped to chat with DePuy. "I don't mean to interfere, but she doesn't know those fields," said the farmer. "Last year we had to shoot a mare, stumbled into one of those holes. . . . It's madness, the way she rides."

And look at her now, her face so pale and shining, speaking of miracles and space travel, almost on the verge of tears. . . .

And last night, his first night up from the city, he had wandered through the house, trying to drink himself into this slower weekend pace, and he had come across a pile of her books, stacked in the alcove where, it was obvious, she lay for hours, escaping into science fiction, and the occult.

Now his own face appeared on the screen. "I want to be fair," he was telling Victoria Darrow. "I want to be objective. . . . Violence has always been part of the human makeup. I don't like it anymore than you do, but there it is. I think it's more a question of whether we want to face things as they are or escape into fantasies of how we would like them to be."

Beside him, his wife uttered a sudden bell-like laugh.

(" . . . *It's madness, the way she rides.*")

He did want to be fair, objective. She had told him again and again that she liked her life here. And he—well, he had to admit he liked his own present setup.

"I am a pragmatist," he was telling Victoria Darrow on the screen. He decided to speak to his wife about her riding and leave her alone about the books. She had the right to some escape, if anyone did. But the titles: *Marvelous Manifestations, The Mind Travellers, A Doctor Looks at Spiritualism, The Other Side* . . . Something revolted in him, he couldn't help it; he felt an actual physical revulsion at this kind of thinking. Still it was better than some other escapes. His friend Barnett, the actor, who said at night he went from room to room, after his wife was asleep, collecting empty glasses. ("Once I found one by the Water Pik, a second on the ledge beside the tub, a third on the back of the john, and a fourth on the floor beside the john. . . .")

He looked sideways at his wife, who was absorbed, it seemed, in watching him on the screen. Her face was tense, alert, animated. She did not look mad. She wore slim gray pants and a loose-knit pullover made of some silvery material, like a knight's chain mail. The lines of her profile were clear and silvery themselves, somehow sexless and pure, like a child's profile. He no longer felt lust when he looked at her, only a sad determination to protect her. He had a mistress in town, whom he loved, but he had explained, right from the beginning, that he considered himself married for the rest of his life. He told this woman the whole story. "And I am implicated in it. I could never leave her." An intelligent, sensitive woman, she had actually wept and said, "Of course not."

He always wore the same pajamas, a shade too big, but always clean. Obviously washed again and again in a machine that went through its cycles frequently. She imagined his "other mother," a harassed woman with several children, short on money, on time, on dreams—all the things she herself had too much of. The family lived, she believed, somewhere in Florida, probably on the west coast. She had worked that out from the little coquina shells: their bright colors, even in moonlight shining through a small window with spider plants in it. His face and arms had been suntanned early in the spring and late into the autumn. They never spoke or touched. She was not sure how much of this he understood. She tried and failed to remember where she herself had gone, in those little night journeys to the fishpond. Perhaps he never remembered afterward, when he woke up, clutching his jar, in a roomful of brothers and sisters. Or with a worried mother or father come to collect him, asleep by the sea. Once she had a very clear dream of the whole family, living in a trailer, with palm trees. But that was a dream; she recognized its difference in quality from those truly magic times when, through his own childish powers, he somehow found a will strong enough, or innocent enough, to project himself upon her still-floating consciousness, as clearly and as believably as her own husband's image on the screen.

There had been six of those times in six months. She dared to look forward to more. So unafraid he was. The last time was the day after Victoria Darrow and her young lover and her own good husband had returned to the city. She had gone farther with the child than ever before. On a starry-clear, cold September Monday, she had coaxed him down the stairs and out of the house with her. He held to the banisters, a child unused to stairs, and yet she knew there was no danger; he floated in his own dream with her. She took him to see Blue Boy. Who disappointed her by whining and backing away in fear. And then to the barn to see the horse. Who perked up his ears and looked interested. There was no touching, of course, no touching or speaking. Later she wondered if horses, then, were more magical than dogs. If dogs were more "realistic." She was glad the family was poor, the mother harassed. They could not afford any expensive child psychiatrist who would hypnotize him out of his night journeys.

He loved her. She knew that. Even if he never remembered her in his other life.

"At last I was beginning to understand what Teilhard de Chardin meant when he said that man's true home is the mind. I understood that when the mystics tell us that the mind is a place, they *don't mean it as a metaphor.* I found these new powers developed with practice. I had to detach myself from my ordinary physical personality. The intelligent part of me had to remain wide awake, and move down into this world of thoughts, dreams and memories. After several such journeyings I understood something else: dream and reality aren't competitors, but reciprocal sources of consciousness." This she read in a "respectable book," by a "respectable man," a scientist, alive and living in England, only a few years older than herself. She looked down at the dog, sleeping on the rug. His lean silvery body actually ran as he slept! Suddenly his muzzle lifted, the savage teeth snapped. Where was he "really" now? Did the dream rabbit in his jaws know it was a dream? There was much to think about, between her trips to the nursery.

Would the boy grow, would she see his body slowly emerging from its child's shape, the arms and legs lengthening, the face thinning out into a man's—like a certain advertisement for bread she had seen on TV where a child grows up, in less than a half-minute of sponsor time, right before the viewer's eyes. Would he grow into a man, grow a beard . . . outgrow the nursery region of his mind where they had been able to meet?

And yet, some daylight part of his mind must have retained an image of her from that single daylight time they had looked into each other's eyes.

The worst thing, such an awful thing to happen to a young woman . . . She was having this natural childbirth, you see, her husband in the delivery room with her, and the pains were coming a half-minute apart, and the doctor had just said, "This is going to be a breeze, Mrs. McNair," and they never knew exactly what went wrong, but all of a sudden the pains stopped and they had to go in after the baby without even time to give her a saddle block or any sort of anesthetic. . . . They must have practically had to tear it out of her . . . the husband fainted. The baby was born dead, and they gave her a heavy sedative to put her out all night.

When she woke the next morning, before she had time to remember what had happened, a nurse suddenly entered the room and laid a baby in her arms. "Here's your little boy," she said cheerfully, and the woman thought, with a profound, religious relief,

So that other nightmare was a dream, and she had the child at her breast feeding him before the nurse realized her mistake and rushed back into the room, but they had to knock the poor woman out with more sedatives before she would let the child go. She was screaming and so was the little baby and they clung to each other till she passed out.

They would have let the nurse go, only it wasn't entirely her fault. The hospital was having a strike at the time; some of the nurses were outside picketing and this nurse had been working straight through for forty-eight hours, and when she was questioned afterward she said she had just mixed up the rooms, and yet, she said, when she had seen the woman and the baby clinging to each other like that, she had undergone a sort of revelation in her almost hallucinatory exhaustion: the nurse said she saw that all children and mothers were interchangeable, that nobody could own anybody or anything, anymore than you could own an idea that happened to be passing through the air and caught on your mind, or anymore than you owned the rosebush that grew in your back yard. There were only mothers and children, she realized; though, afterward, the realization faded.

It was the kind of freakish thing that happens once in a million times, and it's a wonder the poor woman kept her sanity.

In the intervals, longer than those measured by any stopwatch, she waited for him. In what the world accepted as "time," she shopped for groceries, for clothes; she read; she waved from her bottle-green car to Mrs. Frye, trimming the hedge in front of the liquor store, to Mrs. DePuy, hanging out her children's pajamas in the back yard of the old Patroon farm. She rode her horse through the fields of the waning season, letting him have his head; she rode like the wind, a happy, happy woman. She rode faster than fear because she was a woman in a dream, a woman anxiously awaiting her child's sleep. The stallion's hoofs pounded the earth. Oiling his tractor, DePuy resented the foolish woman and almost wished for a woodchuck hole to break that arrogant ride. Wished deep in a violent level of himself he never knew he had. For he was a kind, distracted father and husband, a practical, hard-working man who would never descend deeply into himself. Her body, skimming through time, felt weightless to the horse.

Was she a woman riding a horse and dreaming she was a mother who anxiously awaited her child's sleep; or was she a mother dreaming of herself as a free spirit who could ride her horse like the wind because she had nothing to fear?

I am a happy woman, that's all I know. Who can explain such things?

QUESTIONS FOR DISCUSSION AND WRITING

1. How does Mrs. McNair's reading and her childhood sessions with her psychiatrist help establish the conflict in this story? What justifies the narrator's resolution of this conflict?
2. How do neighbors characterize Mrs. McNair? In what ways does Victoria serve as a direct contrast to her? How does such a contrast help characterize the two women?

3. In what ways do the Dutch farming village and the old house provide an appropriate setting for this story? In particular, how does the guest room provide an appropriate setting for Victoria?
4. Godwin tells this story primarily from the wife's point of view, but occasionally she switches to the point of view of a neighbor or of Mr. McNair. How do they help verify the wife's assumption that everyone lives a double life?
5. In what sense does this story demonstrate that "man's true home is the mind"? What produces Mrs. McNair's sense of complete freedom and joy in the final scene of the story?

38

NADINE GORDIMER

The Train from Rhodesia

NADINE GORDIMER was born in 1923 in Springs, South Africa, and attended private preparatory schools as well as the University of Witwatersrand in Johannesburg. Although Gordimer has held teaching positions at Harvard, Northwestern, Michigan, and Columbia universities, she has devoted most of her time to writing about life in her native South Africa. Her stories have appeared in magazines such as *The New Yorker, Atlantic Monthly, Harper's,* and *Holiday,* and have been collected in several volumes such as *Face to Face* (1949), *The Soft Voice of the Serpent* (1952), *Friday's Footprint* (1960), *Not for Publication* (1965), *Livingstone's Companions* (1971), *A Soldier's Embrace* (1980), and *Something Out There* (1984). Some of her best nonfiction appears in *The Essential Gordimer* (1988). Her novels, widely acclaimed for their sensitive examination of the effects of apartheid on the people of her politically troubled homeland, include *Occasion for Loving* (1963), *The Burgher's Daughter* (1979), and *July's People* (1981). Gordimer was awarded the Nobel Prize for literature in 1991. In "The Train from Rhodesia," reprinted from *The Soft Voice of the Serpent,* Gordimer reveals the social and economic complexities of Africa by documenting the brief coming and going of a train.

The train came out of the red horizon and bore down toward them over the single straight track.

The stationmaster came out of his little brick station with its pointed chalet roof, feeling the creases in his serge uniform in his legs as well. A stir of preparedness rippled through the squatting native vendors waiting in the dust; the face of a carved wooden animal, eternally surprised, stuck out of a sack. The stationmaster's barefoot children wandered over. From the gray mud huts with the untidy heads that stood within a decorated mud wall, chickens, and dogs with their skin stretched like parchment over their bones, followed the piccanins down to the track. The flushed and perspiring west cast a reflection, faint, without heat, upon the station, upon the tin shed marked "Goods," upon the walled kraal, upon the gray tin house of the stationmaster and upon the sand, that lapped all around, from sky to sky, cast little rhythmical cups of shadow, so that the sand became the sea, and closed over the children's black feet softly and without imprint.

The stationmaster's wife sat behind the mesh of her verandah. Above her head the hunk of a sheep's carcass moved slightly, dangling in a current of air.

They waited.

The train called out, along the sky; but there was no answer; and the cry hung on: I'm coming . . . I'm coming . . .

The engine flared out now, big, whisking a dwindling body behind it; the track flared out to let it in.

Creaking, jerking, jostling, gasping, the train filled the station.

Here, let me see that one—the young woman curved her body further out of the corridor window. Missus? smiled the old boy, looking at the creatures he held in his hand. From a piece of string on his gray finger hung a tiny woven basket; he lifted it, questioning. No, no, she urged, leaning down toward him, across the height of the train, toward the man in the piece of old rug; that one, that one, her hand commanded. It was a lion, carved out of soft dry wood that looked like spongecake; heraldic, black and white, with impressionistic detail burnt in. The old man held it up to her still smiling, not from the heart, but at the customer. Between its Vandyke teeth, in the mouth opened in an endless roar too terrible to be heard, it had a black tongue. Look, said the young husband, if you don't mind! And round the neck of the thing, a piece of fur (rat? rabbit? meerkat?); a real mane, majestic, telling you somehow that the artist had delight in the lion.

All up and down the length of the train in the dust the artists sprang, walking bent, like performing animals, the better to exhibit the fantasy held toward the faces on the train. Buck, startled and stiff, staring with round black and white eyes. More lions, standing erect, grappling with strange, thin, elongated warriors who clutched spears and showed no fear in their slits of eyes. How much, they asked from the train, how much?

Give me penny, said the little ones with nothing to sell. The dogs went and sat, quite still, under the dining car, where the train breathed out the smell of meat, cooking with onion.

A man passed beneath the arch of reaching arms meeting gray-black and white in the exchange of money for the staring wooden eyes, the stiff wooden legs sticking up in the air; went along under the voices and the bargaining, interrogating the wheels. Past the dogs; glancing up at the dining car where he could stare at the faces, behind glass, drinking beer, two by two, on either side of a uniform railway vase with its pale dead flower. Right to the end, to the guard's van, where the stationmaster's children had just collected their mother's two loaves of bread; to the engine itself, where the stationmaster and the driver stood talking against the steaming complaint of the resting beast.

The man called out to them, something loud and joking. They turned to laugh, in a twirl of steam. The two children careered over the sand, clutching the bread, and burst through the iron gate and up the path through the garden in which nothing grew.

Passengers drew themselves in at the corridor windows and turned into compartments to fetch money, to call someone to look. Those sitting inside looked up: suddenly different, caged faces, boxed in, cut off, after the contact of outside. There was an orange a piccanin would like. . . . What about that chocolate? It wasn't very nice. . . .

A young girl had collected a handful of the hard kind, that no one liked, out of the chocolate box, and was throwing them to the dogs, over at the dining car. But the hens darted in, and swallowed the chocolates, incredibly quick and accurate, before they had even dropped in the dust, and the dogs, a little bewildered, looked up with their brown eyes, not expecting anything.

—No, leave it, said the girl, don't take it. . .

Too expensive, too much, she shook her head and raised her voice to the old boy, giving up the lion. He held it up where she had handed it to him. No, she said, shaking her head. Three-and-six? insisted her husband, loudly. Yes baas! laughed the boy. *Three-and-six?*—the young man was incredulous. Oh leave it—she said. The young man stopped. Don't you want it? he said, keeping his face closed to the boy. No, never mind, she said, leave it. The old native kept his head on one side, looking at them sideways, holding the lion. Three-and-six, he murmured, as old people repeat things to themselves.

The young woman drew her head in. She went into the coupé and sat down. Out of the window, on the other side, there was nothing; sand and bush; a thorn tree. Back through the open doorway, past the figure of her husband in the corridor, there was the station, the voices, wooden animals waving, running feet. Her eye followed the funny little valance of scrolled wood that outlined the chalet roof of the station; she thought of the lion and smiled. That bit of fur round the neck. But the wooden buck, the hippos, the elephants, the baskets that already bulked out of their brown paper under the seat and on the luggage rack! How will they look at home? Where will you put them? What will they mean away from the places you found them? Away from the unreality of the last few weeks? The man outside. But he is not part of the unreality; he is for good now. Odd . . . somewhere there was an idea that he, that living with him, was part of the holiday, the strange places.

Outside, a bell rang. The stationmaster was leaning against the end of the train, green flag rolled in readiness. A few men who had got down to stretch their legs sprang on to the train, clinging to the observation platforms, or perhaps merely standing on the iron step, holding the rail; but on the train, safe from the one dusty platform, the one tin house, the empty sand.

There was a grunt. The train jerked. Through the glass the beer drinkers looked out, as if they could not see beyond it. Behind the fly-screen, the stationmaster's wife sat facing back at them beneath the darkening hunk of meat.

There was a shout. The flag drooped out. Joints not yet coordinated, the segmented body of the train heaved and bumped back against itself. It began to move; slowly the scrolled chalet moved past it, the yells of the natives, running alongside, jetted up into the air, fell back at different levels. Staring wooden faces waved drunkenly, there, then gone, questioning for the last time at the windows. Here, one-and-six baas!—As one automatically opens a hand to catch a thrown ball, a man fumbled wildly down his pocket, brought up the shilling and sixpence and threw them out; the old native, gasping, his skinny toes splaying the sand, flung the lion.

The piccanins were waving, the dogs stood, tails uncertain, watching the train go: past the mud huts, where a woman turned to look, up from the smoke of the fire, her hand pausing on her hip.

The stationmaster went slowly in under the chalet.

The old native stood, breath blowing out the skin between his ribs, feet tense, balanced in the sand, smiling and shaking his head. In his opened palm, held in the attitude of receiving, was the retrieved shilling and sixpence.

The blind end of the train was being pulled helplessly out of the station.

The young man swung in from the corridor, breathless. He was shaking his head with laughter and triumph. Here! he said. And waggled the lion at her. One-and-six!

What? she said.

He laughed. I was arguing with him for fun, bargaining—when the train had pulled out already, he came tearing after. . . . One-and-six baas! So there's your lion.

She was holding it away from her, the head with the open jaws, the pointed teeth, the black tongue, the wonderful ruff of fur facing her. She was looking at it with an expression of not seeing, of seeing something different. Her face was drawn up, wryly, like the face of a discomforted child. Her mouth lifted nervously at the corner. Very slowly, cautious, she lifted her finger and touched the mane, where it was joined to the wood.

But how could you, she said. He was shocked by the dismay of her face.

Good Lord, he said, what's the matter?

If you wanted the thing, she said, her voice rising and breathing with the shrill impotence of anger, why didn't you buy it in the first place? If you wanted it, why didn't you pay for it? Why didn't you take it decently, when he offered it? Why did you have to wait for him to run after the train with it, and give him one-and-six? One-and-six!

She was pushing it at him, trying to force him to take it. He stood astonished, his hands hanging at his sides.

But you wanted it! You liked it so much?

—It's a beautiful piece of work, she said fiercely, as if to protect it from him.

You liked it so much! You said yourself it was too expensive—

Oh *you*—she said, hopeless and furious. *You*. . . . She threw the lion on to the seat.

He stood looking at her.

She sat down again in the corner and, her face slumped in her hand, stared out of the window. Everything was turning round inside her. One-and-six. One-and-six. One-and-six for the wood and the carving and the sinews of the legs and the switch of the tail. The mouth open like that and the teeth. The black tongue, rolling, like a wave. The mane round the neck. To give one-and-six for that. The heat of shame mounted through her legs and body and sounded in her ears like the sound of sand pouring. Pouring, pouring. She sat there, sick. A weariness, a tastelessness, the discovery of a void made her hands slacken their grip, atrophy emptily, as if the hour was not worth their grasp. She was feeling like this again. She had thought it was something to do with singleness, with being alone and belonging too much to oneself.

She sat there not wanting to move or speak, or to look at anything, even; so that the mood should be associated with nothing, no object, word or sight that might recur and so recall the feeling again. . . . Smuts blew in grittily, settled on her hands. Her back remained at exactly the same angle, turned against the young man sitting with his hands drooping between his sprawled legs, and the lion, fallen on its side in the corner.

The train had cast the station like a skin. It called out to the sky. I'm coming. I'm coming; and again, there was no answer.

QUESTIONS FOR DISCUSSION AND WRITING

1. How does the coming and going of the train serve to structure the plot of the story? What conflicts arise while the train is in the station? To what extent are they resolved?
2. How does Gordimer characterize the buyers and sellers in this story? In what sense are the natives artists? How does their art represent their world? To what extent do the buyers understand what they are buying?
3. How does the opening description of the native village prepare us for the events that are to take place once the train pulls into the station? What details does Gordimer use to contrast the environment inside the train with the external environment?
4. What attracts the young woman to the wooden lion? Why does she object to the manner in which her husband purchased it for her? What is the real source of friction between them?
5. In what ways does this brief story provide a criticism of the social and economic conditions in Africa? How do the attitudes and assumptions of the people on the train account for these contradictions?

39

JIM HARRISON

The Woman Lit by Fireflies

JIM HARRISON was born in 1937 in Grayling, Michigan and educated at Michigan State University. He has taught English at State University of New York at Stony Brook and has written screenplays for Warner Brothers and other film studios. He has contributed poems, stories and reviews to periodicals such as *American Poetry Review, Esquire,* and the *New York Times Book*

Review. Harrison's poetry is collected in volumes such as _Plain Song_ (1945), _Outlyer and Ghazals_ (1971), and _Returning to Earth_ (1977) and his novels include _Wolf: A False Memoir_ (1971), _A Good Day to Die_ (1973), and _Warlock_ (1981). He has also published two collections of novellas, _Legends of the Fall_ (1979) and _The Woman Lit by Fireflies_ (1991). "The Woman Lit by Fireflies," the title story from the latter volume, portrays the complicated events that prompt a woman to flee from her husband.

She had not yet accepted as real the quiver in her stomach and the slight green dot of pain in the middle of her head that signaled an incipient migraine. Her husband on the car seat beside her punched in a tape called "Tracking the Blues" which contained no black music, but rather the witless drone of a weekly financial lecture sent from New York City. This particular tape was seven days stale and had been played three times on their trip, but Donald repeated it to get "fair value" for his money. The tape, not incidentally, replaced Stravinsky's "Histoire du Soldat" from an Iowa City FM station, a piece she always enjoyed.

"Do you mind, darling?" he asked.

"Not at all, dear," she replied, partly because the pain clinic she had attended in Arizona that spring had emphasized giving up resistance to outside phenomena at the possible onset of a migraine under the notion you wanted to starve rather than feed the affliction. For instance, she shouldn't have been driving—sitting with her eyes closed listening to music would have been helpful, but she drove to avoid reading to him, which is what he required when he drove. An additional, insurmountable problem was that his car, an Audi 5000, was low-slung and the early August corn beside Interstate 80 in Iowa presented itself as a dense green wall. She preferred the higher vantage of her own nine-year-old Toyota Land Cruiser, a functional clumsy old machine that she and her beloved friend Zilpha used on their outings, or so they called them, which were somewhat famous in their neighborhood in Bloomfield Hills, a suburb of Detroit.

Clare would be fifty in another week, Donald was fifty-one and eager to get on with life, a matter about which she had mixed feelings. They had just been visiting their daughter Laurel, who at twenty-nine was a veterinarian married to a veterinarian, the both of them ministering to horses and cattle in a clinic outside of Sioux City, Iowa, up near the Nebraska border. The visit had been cut short two days by a quarrel between Laurel and Donald. On the way home they were to spend the weekend with Donald Jr., who at twenty-seven was a commodities market whiz in Chicago.

"I love you, Mom, but I can't understand why you don't leave that asshole," Laurel had said.

"Please, Laurel, he's your father."

"In name only," she had replied, and then they kissed goodbye as they always did, with Clare's heart giving a breathless wrench at separation.

A specific giddiness began to overtake her when she thought of the goodbye. *This is the way, after all, I've spent my life,* she thought. You could not fault Donald for being Donald, any more than you could fault Laurel for being the same as she was at three years, a cantankerous little girl with a sure though general sense of mission, a personality so specific as to be sometimes offensive.

"The overloaded leverages are coming home to roost," Donald brayed so loud she applied the brakes. She quickly reset the cruise control at a modest seventy considering that most cars passed her at that speed. The week before at the club she attempted a witticism about how all the lives saved by the Mothers Against Drunk Driving were being lost to the raising of the speed limit. The luncheon ladies were used to Clare and let the quip pass, but not a new member who found it "dreadfully morbid." Suddenly it occurred to her that Donald didn't feel really good about making money unless others were losing theirs, which made it all, to her mind, a silly game to spend your life on rather than the grave process with which he was totally obsessed.

An ever so slight tremor of head pain made her dismiss the thought about Donald and money as true but banal. She forced her thoughts back to a pleasant morning with Laurel, spent hiking on some bluffs above the Missouri River. Laurel had discovered a rattlesnake that had difficulty getting out of their way because of a huge lump in its belly—no doubt, Laurel said, from swallowing a gopher. They both laughed when Laurel added, "Poor thing, also poor gopher." The laughter was nervous relief. The first hour of their walk had been spent lifting Clare's confusion over a pamphlet an anti-vivisectionist neighbor had given her concerning a doctor down south who, on a defense contract, had shot several thousand cats in the head for research. Laurel habitually defended the scientific community but this one puzzled her, as the brain of a cat was dissimilar enough to that of a human as to make the research appear useless. She did not tell Clare that it would have made more sense to shoot several thousand dogs, or better yet chimpanzees, though the latter were very expensive. The purpose of the research, of course, was to better treat head wounds in soldiers. Then Clare had brought up another item that she had brooded about for two years without mentioning. Laurel had sent her an article from *Orion Nature Quarterly,* by a Spanish fellow, Lopez, called "The Passing Wisdom of Birds," in which the author described Cortez's vengeful burning of the aviaries in Mexico City in the sixteenth century. Clare loved birds and cats and could easily overlook the fact that Cortez had destroyed the city and murdered hundreds of thousands of citizens—that was to be expected—but the burning of Montezuma's aviaries seemed to stand for something far more grotesque and the image of the conflagration passed through her mind daily. So she had asked Laurel, a scant fifteen minutes before they saw the gorged rattlesnake, why she had sent the article, and Laurel had said, "People who love each other try to explain themselves to each other. I wanted you to see again why I work with animals. I can't stand people. Now it's your turn to explain yourself to me." That, as they say, was that, until the poor snake appeared as a convenience, almost a stage prop if it weren't for the immensity of the sky above and the wide, brown Missouri River below them.

Back on Interstate 80 she wondered why they bothered teaching us the things they did—the grandeur, sweep and intricacies of civilization at its best—when there was little enough to do with the knowledge. Clare's criticisms of the human condition were sharp but basically mid-range and items like Cortez and the birds shifted her off balance as did, to a lesser degree, the three thousand holes in the heads of three thousand cats. Now she tried to reduce the growing pain by an act of will, dimming the fluttery green energy to a pinpoint if only for a moment as she had been taught to do in Arizona. There was a sign for a rest stop in ten miles and it was 2:50 which meant she would beat the phone call by a minute. The tape about blue chip stocks had mercifully finished but now Donald was whistling "The Colonel Bogey March" and tapping out the rhythm on the cellular car phone, anticipatory to his daily broker call. His lips pursed and the whistling and tapping stopped as he made a notation in red pencil on the day's *Wall Street Journal.*

"I'm going to have to stop while you phone. I'm not feeling all that well," she said, stiffening at his possible reaction.

"Fine, honey. We've got time to kill." Donald glanced at his watch. "There's room for your nappy in Davenport."

She never understood quite how "nap" became "nappy" but had always judged an inquiry as not quite worthwhile. She looked at him with a longing close to homesickness that the troubled at heart feel for those who treat the world as their lovely private apple. Donald was a passably good man, or so everyone thought, a citizen so apparently solid that, as a club jokester had said, he could throw a successful fund raiser for a crack dealer. A business associate had organized a dinner for ten at a hotel in Davenport, which Donald looked forward to as an orphan would his first circus. He was being especially tender because Clare was the daughter of one of the founding partners of the accounting firm which had branches throughout the Midwest, and the Davenport office was doing especially well. The Davenport people would be thrilled to meet Clare. It would be all bows by the men and curtsies by the ladies. He had even alerted them about Clare's taste in wine which he thought a wasteful vice she had inherited from her mother. Frequently, he noted, the wine on a dinner bill equaled the price of the food, and when he picked up a case of Meursault or Chambertin at the wine store he liked to joke out loud: "Here goes three shares of General Motors." The old clerk at the wine store invariably smiled his mask of a smile knowing it was Clare's money in the first place, a point which would appall Clare herself in that she was so fair-minded as to be frequently rendered immobile.

But not now. She eased the car into the rest stop, slowing to a creep for fear of hitting the children darting in and out of campers and cars in the crowded parking area. Across a green swath semis were parked with the muffled drone of their engines at rest only at destinations. One of the semis held squealing pigs in metal-slatted layers while another was full of silent cattle. Clare got out, taking the leather and canvas Buitoni bag Donald had bought her on their trip to Florence. At the time she could not believe his brusque affability translated so well. They had dined nearly every evening with Italians he had met in his tours of brokerage offices, several times in their homes, allowing Clare a look into the life of Florence never allowed the ordinary tourist. Donald waved at her with the other hand on the phone, antsy to make his daily call. She watched him dial, then walked toward the Iowa Welcome Center and the adjoining bathrooms, her head beginning to thrum in the noisy heat. It occurred to her that the tourists all looked blowzy and fatigued because they were headed back east at the end of their vacations.

When she thought about it later Clare was surprised again by how clear and cool her painful mind had felt. Every human and object, the landscape itself, had the distinct outlines found in a coloring book before the crayons are applied. The green wall of the cornfield behind the Welcome Center became luminous and of surpassing loveliness. She turned and walked back toward Donald in the car but he was in his brokerage trance, his clipped business voice saying, "But what the hell happened to Isomet?"

In the bathroom stall she checked her bag for certain items: Donald Jr.'s Boy Scout compass she used on hikes with Zilpha, a small can of cranberry juice, the addresses of three orphan children she wrote to and helped support in Santo Domingo, Mexico and Costa Rica; in a leather packet was her passport and a copy of the new translation of the *Tao Te Ching* given to her by a counselor at the pain clinic, and at the bottom, and most important, was the tan beret she had bought thirty years before on Rue St.-Jacques and had never worn. As a comparative literature senior at Michigan State she was to spend a year studying in Paris which lasted only three weeks when her father died and the family sent her boyfriend Donald to fetch her home. At the time Donald was her act of rebellion, a left-wing political science major who wore lumberjack shirts, the only son in a working-class family from Flint, who intended to be a writer or labor leader. On dates they read John Dos Passos's *U.S.A.* trilogy aloud to each other. Curiously her father had rather liked Donald, and perhaps this was foresight into the man Donald would become. So each morning for three weeks in her tiny *pension* Clare would look at her beret but was too timid to put it on.

Now in the toilet stall she finally put on the beret and laughed softly to herself. It was so easy. For luck she also slipped on a conch pearl ring Zilpha had given her in March as a remembrance. Among her last words had been "We never got around to the Amazon," a trip they had planned since they were girls when they were convinced they'd discover a pleasanter civilization somewhere in the jungle. Clare took out a Cafergot pill, then put it back, preferring pain-ridden consciousness. She tried to remember something René Char had written, "Blank blank blank the legitimate fruits of daring," but the growing pain blinded her memory. The note itself was simple enough: "I am in a small red car driving east. My husband has been abusing me. Do not believe anything he says. Call my daughter." She added Laurel's number, wrote "To The Police" on the envelope and stuck it to the side of the stall with a postage stamp. She noted that someone had scratched "Bob is cute" with a sharp object on the paint and she smiled with the confusion of female and male.

Behind the Welcome Center a small boy walking the family dog held Clare's bag as she climbed the fence which was more difficult than she anticipated. She wobbled and the wire cut into the soles of her tennis shoes. On the other side she lost a few moments explaining to the boy why he couldn't go along, but then the dog started barking and she hurried off down between two corn rows, toward the interior, wherever that might be.

Within a scant five minutes Clare would have liked to turn around, had turning around not already become so improbable. A hundred yards into the cornfield the beret made her feel silly so she took it off and stuffed it into her bag. The moment the hat came off the pain became so excruciating she fell to her hands and knees and retched up her lunch of iced tea and a club sandwich. The pain was such that she could not balance herself on her hands and knees, but pushed her legs backward until she lay on her stomach. She closed her eyes a moment but the world became bright red and whirling. There was the slightest memory of a pain lesson but it was too abstract to be of much use: the secret was to maintain your equilibrium in the face of incomprehension, as pain, finally, could not be understood.

At eye level she looked at the way the roots of the corn broke up the earth. She tried to let go of her brain which it now seemed would boil over with its brew of knots and hackings, clots, soft lumps against sharp hot stones. She rolled over onto her back. By the time the sun made its way down through the tassels, leaves and stalks, it was weak and liquid. There was a crow call so close it startled her, the bird flapping low over her row, then twisting, darting back for another look, squawking loudly in warning at the intruder, then a third pass up the row out of curiosity. She had never been so close to a crow, she thought, and tried closing her eyes a moment to rehearse crows from the past. The red storm had somewhat subsided and she saw the open mouth of a rooster at her grandmother's, and herself as a child stooping near the rooster as he swelled his throat, craned his neck outward and crowed as if he could not stop himself. As a child she had liked cellars because they frightened her, and now she longed for a cool, black cellar with a rooster for company, for her grandmother's dog whom the rooster pretended to chase though he kept a safe distance, as if he and the dog had agreed upon a reasonable pace for the dog to walk away. Grandfather told her that the rooster felt the whole world was after his hens, and that was all he thought about.

Now she heard a siren, but only gradually understood the sound, from back toward the rest stop. She scrambled to her feet and they moved off quickly down the row as if informed by their own panic. The siren became louder, then stopped abruptly. She continued to run, holding her hands and the bag up against the slapping of the leaves. There was an image of Donald explaining himself to the police, who she hoped would call Laurel despite Donald's usual cagey aplomb. But then Donald passed away with her breathlessness and her flayed brain began to play the rest of the Stravinsky Donald had truncated, then she tripped on a clod of earth and fell sprawling in a bare row where the corn turned direction. Now she was far enough from Route 80 so that she no longer could hear the trucks, only the crows, as the one had become five, and she twisted her neck for a look as they passed over, apparently discussing her. Perhaps the police could see the birds far out in the cornfield and guess that she was there, but she hoped they would believe the "small red car driving east." The sun was warm in the narrow clearing and she moved her upper body into the shade. She drew out the cranberry juice, drank it, then looked at the Boy Scout compass, deciding to head west along the wider row after a rest. She curled up, noting the earth smelled like a damp board after rain, then more heat. She looked at a dirty hand and thought idly with a smile, despite the pain, that for the first time in her life she did not know where her next shower was coming from.

Clare slept for a few minutes but was startled awake by her first dream in several months. She was a girl again, out in her rowboat on Burt Lake, and Dr. Roth was on the dock calling out and asking her why she had died. That was all there was to the dream and then she awoke. The pain had localized toward the right side of her head and within it Dr. Roth continued to call after she woke up. Clare was difficult to push off balance and ignored the phenomenon which was not unlike certain other symptoms of classic migraines. Besides, she liked Dr. Roth very much; he was not only her doctor and confidant, up to a point, but also had been Zilpha's doctor. Dreams are no respecter of time and Dr. Roth couldn't have been more than a child when Clare was a girl in a rowboat. She turned over and thought, at the very least, she had her first dream since Zilpha died, and then two weeks later when Clare's dog died her sleep had become even blacker. The dream wasn't ominous to Clare: death simply didn't hold her interest, but there was the nagging angle of Dr. Roth who Clare at the very moment realized she had been in love with for a brief period.

This recognition jolted her to her feet and she continued to head west, wondering if "maize" and "maze" were somehow connected. She normally walked a great deal because she was essentially claustrophobic and walking made the world appear larger. The fact that the field offered no variation was moot. Dr. Roth's lighthearted question meant something different to her than might appear. Once, when they had a drink after a library board meeting, he had said that most of his patients were already dead, and life herself was merely a technicality that allowed them to get up in the morning to collect a pay-check. They shared this sort of acerbic wit that made them both somewhat mistrusted in what are known as the better circles. The characteristic was harder on Dr. Roth than on Clare because this sharp wit, added to his slowness to write unnecessary prescriptions, limited his practice to those who desired honesty in medicine.

But on another evening after another library board meeting, when they had had to deal with a group of evangelical nitwits who wanted *The Catcher in the Rye* and *Slaughter-house Five* banned from public consumption, Dr. Roth had looked up from his melancholy brandy and said, "You should be careful. You've lived your life with the kind of will that could later cause a lot of problems."

"I know it," she had said. But she didn't know it; the statement only brought forth the familiar feeling of an unpleasant truth.

That was half a year ago and the morning after, when she heard Donald pull out of the driveway she began to weep, an act so strange to her she couldn't pinpoint the event that had made her weep before. A few weeks later both Zilpha and Clare's dog had been diagnosed, Zilpha with lung and the dog with fibroid cancer.

Down toward the end of the row the greenness narrowed and blurred, and then there seemed to be a line of taller greenery. Her pace quickened in wan hope for a change of view, but she slowed down as the pain redeveloped with the swiftness of pace, though luckily enough the pain had moved to the left side of the head where it was more confinable. On the left side Clare could reduce the pain to a diffuse green light, then work consciously on reducing the dimensions of the light. The only side effect was that her sense of time became utterly jumbled, which was vertiginous but preferable to the pain. During one of these seizures, and at this particular state, the best she could do was to remember to feed the dog. Out in the field all that was required was to walk a straight line.

In fact, she thought she was moving within the heart of time. Normally she stood aside and lived on her comments to herself on what was happening to her, but when the pain moved to the left she moved inside herself, and this had the virtue of being novel within the framework of suffering. The pain was always a moment behind her as if she stood on the platform of a caboose watching the world go away. There was a sudden impulse to pray but she found the act embarrassing because, of course, she could *see* herself praying. As a child up near Petoskey on summer vacation her parents had allowed her to go to Daily Vacation Bible School with the maid's daughter. The maid was a mixed-blood Chippewa but her religion was Evangelical. Clare's parents had once discovered their daughter out in the garage praying over a three-legged cat that lived in the neighborhood. This was viewed as highly amusing and became part of a repertoire of "Clare stories" her parents shared with their friends during the rites of the martini hour. Now, to her surprise, this made Clare angry. What was the point of being angry at her parents for something that happened forty years ago, but then what was so funny about a child praying for a three-legged cat? In defiance she dropped to her knees but couldn't think of anything to say so got up again. Dr. Roth should see her now. He liked to think that, all efforts of the glitz media to the contrary, life is Dickensian, and that pathos is invariably the morning's leading news item. Clare with dusty knees and a verbless prayer would, no doubt, amuse him.

It had taken Dr. Roth several years to set Clare straight over the fact that Donald was an anti-Semite, albeit a quiet one. Clare had invited Dr. Roth and his wife to a large dinner party and late in a rather boozy evening Dr. Roth had made an acid but very funny comment about Richard Nixon which everyone had laughed at but Donald, to whom Nixon was an object of reverence. "Golly, but you guys can be smartasses," Donald had said, and the table had become so quiet that Zilpha had plunged courageously ahead with a lame joke. When everyone left Clare was instantly furious, partly at herself for letting the first incident pass. Years before, they had been visiting friends in Palm Beach with the real purpose of the trip being to pick up the dog from other friends. They had all eaten dinner at the Everglades Club and their host had proudly announced that the club was off limits to Jews. Clare had merely said that she found the fact odd just twenty-five years after World War II and let it drop, though the comment put everyone on edge. Before bedtime Donald had said something critical about her dinner behavior, admitting quite pompously that he agreed with the club policy. She had only looked at him and said, "I see." Next morning the joy of picking up the yellow Labrador, who was being given away for littering the pristine lawn with stray coconuts and palm fronds, made her overlook the issue.

Curiously, Dr. Roth was remote and analytical on the subject of anti-Semitism. He had grown up in Ann Arbor in a sheltered academic family, and after medical school had married a Jewish girl from Memphis whose family had been in the country from well before the Civil War. His experience was limited to a number of minor incidents similar to the one with Donald. He tried to tease his way out of Clare's questions by saying that being Jewish couldn't be as bad as being a manic depressive or a woman, and his wife was all three. When Clare insisted, he finally admitted that his own Jewish experience could be likened to her acute migraine, not in the degree of pain but in the utter uncertainty of when something unpleasant was going to occur. The incident could be a small item in the paper, say an inept political statement, or the recent suicide of one of his favorite authors, Primo Levi. The condition of being Jewish bred a perpetual wariness shared by all minorities, and the wariness tended to become an irksome cliché in life unless one was careful. The true burden of awareness had been carried by his parents' generation where the threat was all too specific.

One late afternoon over drinks he said something that disturbed Clare, to the effect that they shared an economic condition that was out of sync, and definitely out of sympathy with ninety-nine point ninety-nine percent of the rest of the world, and they had to walk an extremely narrow line not to die from being rich freaks. He asked how Clare and Donald got their home and she said it had been a wedding gift from her mother. Dr. Roth said his own home had come from his father-in-law on the same occasion, and when had either of them given more than nominal consideration to the purchase of anything—food, clothing, wine, books, cars, vacations? He said he would have gone mad long ago without the single day a week he spent as a volunteer at Detroit Receiving, a hospital that serviced the black ghetto and the poorest whites. Then he noticed a hurt look quickly pass across her face before she could conceal it.

"What about me?" she said.

"Oh, your reading in unpleasant areas and your migraines keep the tips of your toes in the real world."

"That's not very much, is it?"

"It's usually enough. Our sort doesn't need a great deal of consciousness to get by. Most often sending a check will do."

"I'm not leaving this shitheel fern bar on that sour note." She signaled the waiter for another glass of wine. Clare swore on the order of once a year. "This can't be another monkey occasion." She was referring to a benefit ball they had attended, the purpose of which was to raise money for new accommodations for the chimpanzees at the Detroit Zoo. Donald was in Atlanta for a few days and Dr. Roth's wife had entered a manic shopping phase that could best be resolved in New York City. Zilpha had only recently died and Dr. Roth thought it important for Clare to get out of the house. Unfortunately they were seated at a table with two self-important General Motors executives whose wives ignored everyone, and an exhausted neurosurgeon whose wife obviously wanted to be at a zippier table. Despite a normal aversion for talking shop in front of laymen, Dr. Roth and the neurosurgeon began some heavy-hearted joking on the effects of crack cocaine on the nervous system of newborn infants, the neurosurgeon's punch line forcing everyone to drink hard and fast.

"We're going to have to look at Detroit as a vast rookery for psychotics," the man said.

"What's a rookery?" a GM wife asked.

"A breeding ground. Our dominant product is psychosis. It's moved ahead of automobiles."

"That doesn't speak well for the future of the work force," an executive huffed.

"Not unless you're producing worker-tested automatic rifles," Dr. Roth quipped.

That evening had been effectively deadened and in the shitheel fern bar they tried to work themselves out of the hole that they had dug.

"I'm tired. Can't you look in your catalogue of piths and gists?" Dr. Roth was referring to a ledger Clare had started at the university and continued to the present where she recorded passages of literature she cherished. Dr. Roth had been amazed at Clare's ledger, the range was boggling, all recorded in a neat, almost lapidary script, from Aeschylus down to E. M. Cioran, with a preponderance coming from the early modernist period in world literature from 1880 to 1920. Her intended but never finished senior honors thesis was to be on Apollinaire and there were many translated quotes, but her temperament seemed to have been most captured by Rilke. Dr. Roth's own sense of balance had been disturbed when he came across Yeats's notion to the effect that life was a long preparation for something that never occurred.

"My piths and gists don't work since Zilpha and Sammy died." Sammy was the name of the female Labrador. In an instant Clare relived Dr. Roth's stricken look when he had stopped by late one afternoon for a drink and found her and Zilpha listening to the Beethoven "Last Quartets" while Zilpha held the fat, stinking, cancerous Sammy on her lap, smooching with the dog, hugging its bulk to her breast, both of them within a month of death.

"I'm thinking hard," Dr. Roth said. "Let's not come to this place again. It's full of binge shoppers trying to sedate themselves. Now, I know you have an aversion to anything Oriental as being too passive, even though you're utterly passive yourself. A Wayne State University student suffering from obvious malnutrition said it to me. The general notion is that the only use for today is today. The only reality you are ever going to get is the ordinary one you make for yourself. In other words, there's no big breakthrough."

"That's awfully grim. Does that mean there's no Christmas on earth? And what does he do with the information?"

"The 'he' is a 'she.' I gave her ten bucks and made her promise she'd go eat a good meal. Then I loaded her up with vitamin samples. I don't know what she does with this information. I only know she doesn't take care of herself."

"Can I make a donation?" Clare had become nervous.

"Not at the moment. Perhaps later when a donation doesn't mean you're delaying doing something about yourself."

"When you say 'doing something about yourself' it sounds like psychobabble. You know the big section in Borders Bookstore that covers self-improvement."

"Pathology can only be imaginative up to a certain point. If you like, I'll work on the sentence."

Clare found herself nearly at the end of the row and presented with a barrier she hadn't allowed herself to comprehend while thinking about Dr. Roth. It was a dense thicket, apparently as impenetrable as any of the topiary hedges she had seen in England and France. The thicket grew into the cornfield so she couldn't turn right or left. She stepped back twenty feet for a better view and thought she could make out the top of a cottonwood; as her breathing calmed she was sure she heard flowing water, then she remembered that a mile or so before they reached the rest stop there had been a creek or river named after a cow—Guernsey, she thought. Her watch said that had been over two hours ago which didn't seem possible. A creek crossed at seventy miles an hour in a split second doesn't look threatening, but now she felt tears welling up. She had expected a barnyard and farmhouse at the end of the row, and now the compass said that was a possibility only in a southerly direction since north was the interstate. Millions of women merely leave their husbands; why had she fled? She swallowed with difficulty, wishing she had saved some of the cranberry juice, then looked up at the thunderheads, their edges lined with silver from the descending sun. She sat down and made traceries in the dirt with the compass bracket. She had an impulse to discuss the situation with Zilpha but she felt that would further loosen her tenuous grip. Laurel was a better choice.

"Laurel, you little bitch, this is partly your idea. What do I do now?" There was an urge to be angry, cheap, vulgar.

"You could have waited until Davenport and taken a cab to the airport when Dad was in the shower." This was so like Laurel who was matter-of-fact even in the cradle.

"I knew the pain was coming and I lost my good sense." The pain was increasing a bit with the tinge of self-pity so she stiffened up. At the clinic one of the first lessons was never to adopt a "why me?" attitude which might precipitate a collapse.

"You know very well your good sense is bullshit. Remember when I came home from college years ago and said that you act as if you're living three feet from yourself? You were angry but it's true."

"I suppose so, but let's get back to the situation right now. I'm sitting here in the dirt and I don't know what to do. Like most people I'm only prepared for the life I've already lived, none of which included this sort of thing." Clare remained cool with this admission. On all the trips she had made to beautiful places with Zilpha they had never camped out, though twice they had bought a lot of expensive equipment that was donated to the Boy Scouts on return. Laurel and her husband had backpacked everywhere, even in the winter on cross-country skis.

"For Christ's sake, Mother, you're going to have to toughen up. You said you read that book on camping I sent. You're going to have to get some water in your system to avoid hypothermia. You know that from a lifetime of tennis which I always thought was a waste of time. You might have to go back to the rest stop for water."

"I refuse. It looks like it's going to rain. My bag is canvas so maybe I could catch some water."

"It's important that you crawl into that thicket to stay dry. No matter how warm it is now, if you get wet you'll be cold by nightfall. Don't drink any water from that creek unless you find a way to boil it. If you get desperate, don't forget why you're doing this. I'd say you're in for a long night unless you're willing to hoof it back to the interstate. I hope you'll come to spend a few months with us."

"That's kind of you but I have my heart set on Paris."

"That's silly of you. Paris isn't the same as it was thirty years ago. You'll be disappointed."

"I don't care. I've passed through a few times since and I don't care if I'm disappointed."

Clare signed off on the phantom conversation with a wave at the oncoming thunderheads that had begun to rumble. She rechecked the edge of the thicket, noting that there were narrow breaks and holes that raccoon and perhaps deer made. She crawled in a small opening in the greenery and looked upward, seeing enough of the sky to know it would still be wet in a hard rain. She remembered with a smile something she had overheard her gay decorator say on the phone, to the effect that his friend should fasten his seat belt because it was going to be a bumpy night. President Reagan had also liked to quote from the movies. Then she recalled as a child at Thanksgiving time on her grandparents' farm how she liked to make small caves in dried corn that had been stacked in shocks. She felt this memory comprised her first bright idea of the day other than leaving Donald, and she busied herself uprooting the green stalks which came up easily, and which she layered on top of the thicket. It was easy so she erred on the side of excess until, when she crawled into the thicket hole, there was a large area that blocked out the sky. If she hadn't been so thirsty she would have been happy in the choice. She emptied out the bag containing her small purse, compass, address book, the beret, the empty juice can (she didn't want to litter), and the passport. It had been Zilpha's notion that the act of taking your passport with you everywhere added drama to life. She arranged these objects like talismans, then scooted back out and spread the bag's mouth open.

The thunder deepened in its volume and she looked up to see lightning shattering the sky like luminous tree roots. The thunderclap that followed had a sharp edge as if the sky were being torn, and the wind came up suddenly so that the leaves down the row were pale and flapping. Clare backed into her makeshift cave with a feeling that things were well in hand, at least for the moment, but the torrent that followed, brief as it was, cast her behavior in a fresh light. When she gave birth to Laurel that early May so long ago she could hear a cloudburst beyond the walls and windows of the delivery room, and there was a tinge of déjà vu in the present rain. *I had two children and lived with a man nearly thirty years. I don't seem to have a real idea what occurred to me. Maybe nobody does, or just a few.*

The driving rain splattered mud upward and formed puddles in the opening, but she was dry and warm and drowsy, the remnants of pain merely diffuse and endurable. She froze then, startled at the slightest movement to her left, but then saw it was only a cottontail, the same kind of rabbit that made her put chicken wire around her herb garden back home. The rabbit studied Clare from half a dozen feet away, then continued feeding on wild clover shoots, but with its ears alertly erect and its nose trying to determine if Clare presented a danger. Within its ears on the pinkish lobes wood ticks dotted the flesh, gorging on blood. Clare counted seven. She and the rabbit stared at each other so long that Clare didn't notice that the rain had stopped and the water caught by her bag was both being absorbed and draining slowly out. The rabbit's ears stiffened for an instant at the sound of a cock pheasant crowing from the direction of the creek, followed by the sharp clear notes of red-winged blackbirds. There was a new dimension of stillness in all of this and Clare felt somehow heartened that the rabbit didn't feel in danger, much less know what a human was. She stayed absolutely quiet, breathing soundlessly and not even blinking her eyes for fear the rabbit would leave her alone. Laurel should see her now, she thought, well within her body, moving gracefully in the heart of time, but then the rabbit hopped off for reasons of its own. The message was dim but Laurel seemed to be asking a question.

"Mother, what about the water?"

Clare scrambled out, her hands skidding in the fresh mud. "Oh fuck!" she yelled, for the first time in her life. The bag was soaked but nearly empty with scarcely a gulp left down in a corner. She pressed her face into it for fear of losing any of the precious water, which tasted a little of the sunscreen lotion that had leaked there years ago.

How dumb. There was the sense that she was stuck in a children's story of enormous dimensions, one of those old Europeans out of *The Book House: Ramona fled, watching the barbarians destroy the village, hiding herself behind a tree on the edge of the dark forest.* Clare supposed that even if she did make her way back to the rest stop and drop a quarter in the pay phone the world could never repair itself. With a smile she imagined Donald's umbrage when the police asked him if he had abused his wife. And did he know who might own the red car traveling east? It was she who had set fire to the village before running into the dark forest, and now the consequences enlarged themselves as the sun reappeared casting a golden late afternoon light off the tassels. She was a free woman but would gladly have traded anything for a quart of cold water. Donald was also free to go home and soothe his wounds with his Bing Crosby collection that he liked to tell visitors "was known far and wide," at least among other collectors. Clare was not a bully, though, and raised in her mind some of Donald's good points: he was, surprisingly, a relentless lover; he had taken Laurel and Donald Jr. everywhere, from Disneyland to Busch Gardens, the Smithsonian, and the Museum of Natural History in New York (while Clare was at the Whitney), to Detroit Pistons games, to the Lions, to the Red Wings, to their corporate box for the Detroit Tigers, while Clare stayed home and read or went on outings with Zilpha. Donald loved the life outside the mind and slept like a rock, though he had recently surprised her with a first edition of *Tar* to round out her Sherwood Anderson collection. And last Christmas he had managed to find Faulkner's book of poems *A Green Bough,* which, she overheard him telling a friend, cost him "an arm and a leg."

Clare cleaned the drying mud off her hands with a sharp stone and tried not to think of water. Perhaps the beginning of the end had been five years ago just after Donald Jr. had graduated from the University of Michigan. Clare and Zilpha, on whim, had been late additions to a list of matrons who wished to go on a Detroit Institute of Arts tour of the museums of Moscow and Leningrad. Zilpha's visa had come in ten days but Clare's had never arrived despite repeated phone calls from her travel agent to Washington, and they had missed the trip. Zilpha's husband, whom Donald loathed, was a big-time liberal dope lawyer, and through the intercession of a black congressman he discovered that Donald had jinxed the visa with a phone call to a friend in the State Department, the sort of favor that is due a major Republican fund raiser like Donald. When Clare confronted him he had affected a minor breakdown, saying he couldn't have borne up under the strain of his beloved wife's visiting the "evil empire." Untypically, Clare thought of shooting him while he slept, but instead she and Zilpha went off to Costa Rica to visit one of the children whose survival the brochure and a letter said she sponsored. This trip had also made Donald frantic despite the assurances of his State Department friend that Costa Rica was "as safe as Switzerland."

Clare was beginning to feel the mild dizziness brought on by hypothermia, a lightness in the head from her extreme thirst; vomiting plus the long hot walk had pushed her to the edge of tolerance, and though the late afternoon sun was cooling she found it unendurable. Back in her green cave she felt she was due another reassuring message from Laurel when her eyes lit on the cranberry juice can. The camping book said to boil suspicious water for fifteen minutes. Of course. She grabbed the can and scrambled on her hands and knees through the dense thicket toward what she thought of as the distant sound of water, much increased after the cloudburst. Unfortunately the Guernsey was less than twenty feet distant and Clare nearly catapulted down the slick, muddy bank into the sluggish, dark brown water, an inadvertent baptism by immersion, but she came up waist deep and laughing. The world that had been so narrowed by her physical and mental anguish became quite suddenly larger as she filled the cranberry juice can, resisting the strong temptation to drink the water straight.

Half an hour later Clare had the water bubbling away, the can stuck in a small mound of dirt and the fire crackling around it, with the dry grass and reed stalks kindling the dampish sticks found beneath the cottonwood tree. To extend her patience to the advised fifteen minutes she looked at her only book, the *Tao Te Ching,* for a few minutes but she was far too excited about the boiling muddy water to concentrate. The counselor at the pain clinic had told her that if she adapted all the principles of the volume to her life she could very well be cured of her migraines. Dr. Roth had not been sanguine on this prospect, saying that if she were Pope John XXIII or Martin Buber or Saint Theresa she would also be free of the disease. Clare carried the book along, though she had a childish aversion to Orientals, because the translator was the same as that of her favorite volume of Rilke, *The Sonnets to Orpheus.* The aversion had been occasioned by her father's service as a major during World War II, though he never got beyond Washington, D.C. One day Clare stayed home from kindergarten in order to ride along with her mother when she took her dad to the train station. He had been home on leave for only a few days when he was called back to Washington, and both of her parents had wept at the station. After the train pulled away her mother had told her that "he's off to fight Tojo." Clare knew that Tojo chopped the heads off American soldiers and she was terribly frightened at the idea of a headless father.

At the clinic in Arizona she had become friendly with a wheat farmer from Fort Dodge, Kansas, who was suffering a spinal defect, the accompanying spasms of which could strike him to the ground at any time. When they had all been given the *Tao* one evening at dinner he had been irritable, but in the morning he assured Clare that the "secrets" of the book might save them. She was startled at this statement because Frank, the farmer, was critical of their counselor whom he referred to as a "goofy bastard," partly because the counselor wore an earring. Frank had also been outspoken against an Italian from Albany with a bone disease who had told Clare at the dinner table that she had "nice stems." Frank had fairly shouted at the Italian to mind his language. A plump woman from Pasadena had piped up that there was nothing dirty about good legs, and the table had agreed, with Frank leaving in a huff before dessert. After that, despite the heat, Clare had worn slacks rather than hiking shorts.

She carefully eased the can out of the mound of dirt with her handkerchief, managing to burn the tip of a finger which she ignored. Now she had to wait for the water to cool sufficiently and glanced to the west at the setting sun, guessing that she had another hour of daylight. She hoped to do at least three more of the six-ounce cans, plus an extra for the night, before dark, and the sure thought of removing this manic thirst made her feel giddy. It was so utterly ordinary, this thirst, that it returned her solidly to earth, the only concern being for immediate comfort.

"Laurel, I'm doing rather well considering. I was just wondering if there were rattlesnakes around here."

"That's unlikely. They prefer rocky hillsides where they can find rodents. I heard there are a few moccasins in the southern part of the state but they'd be a rarity and you're well up in the middle. The main problem might be mosquitoes."

"I've already noticed that. At what point does the daughter become the mother?"

"You're not ready for that. I bet you still get a few passes."

"Perhaps. I certainly don't want to talk about it to my daughter."

"Back in high school my friends and I used to wonder if you and Zilpha had some boyfriends stashed on your outings. We thought you two were so thrilling."

"Everyone suspected that we might have gentleman friends, and it was fun to let them think so. It used to drive your father a bit crazy, and I'd say, 'But dear, you go on business trips at least once a month and I don't wonder about you.' "

"You never suspected him?"

"I didn't really care."

"Then why did you hold on so long?"

"I had my friends, my books, dogs, garden, my children. Why does a husband have to be the absolute center of a married woman's life?"

"I don't know but they always are. Actually, I know you're the center of his life, with making money a close second."

"Are you suddenly getting warm about your father?"

"No, it was only an observation."

"I'm the center like a prized possession. Remember when I wouldn't go to any more fund raisers after I was introduced as a 'prominent Republican wife,' with no name attached. It seemed to stand for something quite out of focus."

"That was funny, also sad. I'm sure you were sorely missed. Dad always liked to pretend we had more money than we did. I mean, we had plenty so why pretend? Kevin pointed out my trust would have grown as much in a savings account as it did under Dad's care."

"Was Kevin upset?"

"Not at all. It's just Dad always treats him as if as a veterinarian he has his head in the clouds, when if you pull a difficult calf or help a mare drop a foal it's pretty realistic."

"Businessmen would be utterly destroyed if they didn't think they were the most practical men on earth. Lawyers tend to be that way too. Zilpha's husband used to say that a lawyer was society's proctologist. Sadly, that was the only charming thing he ever said."

"You miss her terribly, don't you? And Sammy too?"

"More than I dreamed possible. Strangely, I couldn't have done this if they had still been with me. It was a pleasure to give so much to them because I loved them. Then they were gone and I had to do something. I just tasted my hot water. It's somewhere between truck stop coffee and the average veal glacé in a Detroit restaurant, the kind where they slip in a bouillon cube. I'd better get busy now."

"Keep me posted. Remember, you don't have to spend the night. There's still time to make it back to the highway if you hurry."

"No thanks, dear."

Clare finished her first can of water with pleasure, spitting out a bit of grit that had accumulated at the bottom and setting out for the next. It was similar to weeding her large herb garden because she didn't think about anything except what she was doing, though thoughts might float easily in and out. The difference was that she didn't try to hold on to the thoughts so that the bad ones disappeared on their own accord.

On the third trip, when her thirst was somewhat abated and the sun was beginning to set, she made her way down the riverbank searching for more wood. Just past the single cottonwood tree there was a large branch she tugged away from clinging vines as if she had found the mother lode. If she could keep a small fire going she wouldn't miss a flashlight so much. If you're going to leave your husband, take a flashlight. That was about as sensible as the rules could get for the time being. A movement in the vines startled her and an opossum scurried out, looked at Clare and flopped over in fake death. She had seen this twice before in her garden back home and it was difficult not to draw certain parallels, amusing ones, though if you played dead long enough the act of coming back to life was questionable. Of the seven women who had been in her tennis group (the A class) a decade ago, four had been divorced in the past few years and none of them were doing very well, but then it was so easy to be smug about her own passivity, the way she let the years float gently by, relying on Zilpha's natural ebullience, two long walks a day with Sammy, hours of reading and cooking, the latter more for herself than for Donald who ate everything she cooked him with equal gusto.

Back at the campsite she coaxed the dwindling fire back to life, broke up the branches and put the sticks in a neat pile, stooping there, impatient for the water to boil. There was a reassuring chatter of birds but she guessed there was at most only a half hour of daylight. She put down a layer of corn leaves, then pulled enough dry marsh grass to cover them, to protect her sleep from the ground's dampness. She took off her skirt and blouse, hung them on a stick and held the clothes over the fire to draw out the slight amount of moisture left from her river plunge. It was a balmy night, but with nothing to wrap herself in but her own arms she was sure she would be cold by morning.

It was so strange to stand there nearly naked, feeling the smoke and heat purl up her body, with just enough darkness to make her legs and tummy golden. She felt good enough for the moment not to have to think of herself as an admirable person. If Zilpha had been there she would have been smoking the cigarettes that killed her. It had been her nature to defy everything, just as many intelligent men drink themselves to death. Right up until the last day Zilpha had said she had no regrets about dying, and on the last day she had only joked, "I'm not absolutely sure this is a good idea. Too bad I can't call and let you know." With her husband her eyes had brimmed with tears and she had merely shook her head. It was by common consent the lousiest marriage in the neighborhood and everyone wondered why they bothered to hang on.

Clare stuck her clothes stake in the ground and decided once again to make sense out of the *Tao,* especially a single line Frank had thought was so wonderful. The line was disappointingly sparse: "Thus whoever is stiff and inflexible/is a disciple of death." Frank had said that he'd spent thirty years being angry at the United States Department of Agriculture over grain prices and all of that energy had been wasted, and the anger had vastly accelerated his back problems. Clare and Frank had been talking in the shade of an enormous boulder; hiding, in fact, from the counselor who was being especially captious and unnerving that day, or so they thought. The twelve of them were being led on a "meditation hike" and were supposed to be dispersed in a boulder-strewn valley to sit alone and concentrate on a double-faced question: "Do you want to live?" and, simply enough, "Who dies?" There was also an admonition to keep alert for rattlesnakes. To break up the obvious tedium and anguish of the questions, Frank and Clare, through hand signals, had met behind the boulder for a chat.

"What the hell does that hippie mean? Suicide's not Christian."

"It's not supposed to be something to get angry about," Clare said without a good deal of conviction. "He says that our bodies are quarreling with themselves and that makes them hard to heal. He's not the USDA. They don't wear earrings."

Frank smiled, then developed a stricken look so Clare massaged his back and shoulders. Clare had seen one of his seizures the first day of the clinic and had doubted that she could handle one behind the boulder. He had twisted on the floor of the dining area and at one point his entire weight was supported by his heels and the back of his head, his trunk thrusting upward. Now his back softened from iron to clay under her hands and they embraced for a moment but he began weeping after he kissed her. At the time she wished she had the gumption to seduce him despite the consequences, whatever they might be. After that incident Frank was embarrassed when talking to her, as if he had behaved badly, and she didn't know how to tell him otherwise. At the end of the clinic Frank's wife picked him up and she looked overplump and spiteful to Clare.

Back at the fire Clare felt the warm smoking clothes and decided she wasn't inflexible, at least compared to Donald, but maybe that was one thing wrong with marriage, or smallish social settings, where the comparisons were so limited. Her brother felt he never drank more than his three best friends, but the four of them had all nearly drunk themselves to death, and were at present all leading lights in the AA for the Detroit area. The sheer taffy in self-awareness exhausted her. Saying that you were no more inflexible than your husband was small-minded dogshit, and she laughed out loud. She wanted more life, not *Robert's Rules of Order.* Crossing a fence was certainly a start, a flexible one at that. It occurred to Clare that while Zilpha swore occasionally, and Laurel repeatedly, she had never learned how. "Fuck you, Donald, you jerkoff," she whispered to the gathering dark, but the oath was froth. "Jerkoff" was what the boys who worked at the neighborhood gas station called each other. They always glanced down at her legs while they were doing the windshield. If she was wearing a tennis skirt they did an especially good job at the windshield. Quite suddenly a blush rose to Clare's face as she thought of Zilpha's son Michael. It had been an unforgivable mistake, and constituted her only secret from Zilpha.

"It's okay, Mother. It was the right thing to do."

"No it wasn't. I was never so ashamed of myself. How did you know?"

"Michael told me way back when. I think it was four years ago, right after it happened. He called to say he was going to ask you to run away to New York with him. He wondered if I thought it was a good idea." Laurel and Michael had been close since childhood, an unlikely pair, with Michael as obsessed with art as Laurel was with the life sciences.

"How absurd. It was stupid of me to let it go that far. I must have been sleepwalking." Clare put on her warm, smoky clothes in defense. The clothes felt wonderful against her skin.

"I doubt that. The last thing I ever felt when I was making love was asleep."

"You're simple-minded if you think I'm going to talk to you about it."

"Suit yourself. What I'm trying to say is that your night is going to be long enough without feeling guilty about something so innocent. If you get hungry just roll a couple of ears of that field corn in that wet clay and lay them at the edge of the fire. By the time the clay dries and hardens the corn will be ready. Not great, but better than nothing. I love you. Good night."

"I love you. You didn't tell anyone, did you?"

"Of course not. And I doubt Michael will ever write his memoirs."

"Thanks. Good night."

Clare picked two ears of corn and rolled them in the remains of a mud puddle until they were covered with a thickish layer of clay. It was a messy business and she dried her hands before the fire until she could flake off the clay. Perhaps Laurel was right. She felt guilt because she had pretended she only made love to Michael to get out of an uncomfortable situation, but then Michael was as removed from a rapist as could be imagined. A modest "no" would have pushed him over. Also, it was soon after Donald's nasty interference in her Russian trip, but she recognized that was only a minuscule part of it. In fact, Donald hadn't been given a thought.

"Be honest with yourself," Laurel chimed in from the dark.

"Why? Okay, then. At the moment Michael reminded me of a young English instructor I studied with as a freshman. I knew we both wanted to make love but there were rules against it and besides we were too shy. When I came back as a sophomore I found out he had committed suicide that summer in New York City. Every time I got a crush on someone, they moved to New York. I chose badly."

"Did he leave a note?"

"Not that I know of. Once we had coffee at a cafeteria and he gave me some bad advice. He told me that literature was so rich with possibility that I could safely ignore life itself. I asked him why Pasternak had said that despite all appearances, it took a lot of volume to fill a life. He told me Pasternak's reputation had been discounted by the higher critics. Two of his colleagues passed our table and one of them winked at him as if I were his bimbo."

"Which is what you wanted to be."

"You might say that. When I met your father I made sure he didn't get away."

"I know all about that one. It fails to interest. Anyway, Michael said you only had that single event. As they say, don't sweat it. I made love to him once myself when we were fourteen. We smoked a marijuana cigarette, drank some wine and did it. We decided afterwards that we wouldn't let it ruin our friendship. Actually we fell asleep and Zilpha caught us. She broke out laughing and closed the door."

"So I heard. We didn't come to any conclusions when we discussed it."

"You two never had any secrets, did you?"

"I never told her I made love to her son. It still bothers me."

"Oh, for Christ's sake, Mother. The corn should be roasted by now."

"Good night, dear."

"Keep in touch if you get lonely."

"I will."

Clare tapped the baked clay with her knuckles to no effect, then used a stone to break it. The green shucks steamed on the night air and she waited for them to cool. What had happened one day was that she and Zilpha were supposed to help Michael pack up to move to New York after a morning tennis game. Zilpha looked terrible, having spent the night arguing with her husband, plus she had a summer cold, so Clare volunteered to go solo on the packing chores. She went straight to his studio apartment from the tennis game and found him untypically organized. Michael had given all of his furniture to friends, and he wandered around the apartment stuffing what he called simply his "art" into portfolios, wearing pajamas which was all he ever wore unless it was absolutely necessary to wear clothes. If the trip was to the grocery store or to his mother's house he'd slip a raincoat over the pajamas.

Clare began by disassembling some large unstretched frames. Michael, more than anyone she had ever met, had no abilities outside of his imagination, nor was he interested in any. Michael and his father had given up on each other in his early teens, and he kept his doting mother at an affectionate distance. He developed a few friendships among other burgeoning artists at Cranbrook, and he and Laurel kept close though she went to Country Day, but Michael had been considered pretentious and unlikable in the neighborhood. He had not been at the club since his fourteenth birthday when he took off his clothes and pissed in the fireplace. He was flunked out of Rhode Island School of Design for a total lack of interest, spent a year in Paris and Florence, then came home for a few years in Detroit where his paintings caused a minor rage in the art community. The paintings were a bit of a puzzle to Clare because Michael painted only what he called "the insides of things": animals, engines, clouds, trees, women. For a year or so on his return from Europe Clare and Michael had become close again, just as they were when he was young. She helped him hang his paintings at several galleries, bought not a few of them and had lunch with him at least once a week at a restaurant that indulged him his pajamas. Donald didn't begrudge the time she spent with Michael, never referring to him as anything but "the poor little bugger," though Michael was of average size. Of course he seemed a bit effeminate, but then Donald and his cronies were sure that all men but themselves betrayed gay tendencies, even professional hockey players. This was a mystery to Clare when she listened to their after-dinner jokes. Sadly to her, Michael sensed charity in her continued purchase of paintings and began to keep her at a distance. Only in the last few weeks before his move to New York had they become quite friendly again

That day in the dull, humid heat of a Detroit July Michael surprised her with her favorite wine, a Château d'Yquem, saying that he wished he had swiped it from his father but he had bought it himself. They drank the wine on the floor, her back against the wall, but Michael sprawled in front of her. He told her about a recent adventure with a lovely black girl who had decided he was too crazy and went back to her musician. He was a bit sad about that and said so. The wine was nearly gone and they had lapsed into silence when he looked at her strangely.

"I'm finding you quite exciting," he said.

"I'm the same person I've always been."

"That's not what I mean."

"Michael, I don't believe that. You're teasing me." She blushed deeply, unable to look at his eyes. "You shouldn't tease about such things."

"I'm not teasing."

He put a hand around her ankle and she let a leg straighten out. His other hand covered the crotch of his pajamas where it was obvious that he wasn't teasing. She closed her eyes and said, "Oh, well," with her ears buzzing. He made love to her quickly there on the floor and she was embarrassed at her excitement. Afterwards, they stood in the kitchen apologizing to each other in miserable half sentences, then went back into the main room where she tried to think of a graceful way to pick up her panties on the bare floor. They stood there for a few minutes, then he embraced her strongly and they took off everything and made love for quite a long time, ending with exhaustion, then laughter. He yelped when she put hydrogen peroxide on his raw knees.

The ear of corn was much better than Clare had reason to expect, lacking sweetness but full-flavored. It was now dark but a three-quarter moon was rising, a cream-colored globe barely above the horizon. A full moon would have been too dramatic, she reflected. One of the grandest times ever with her father had been a long walk one night in the summer during a full moon up near their cottage on Burt Lake. They had taken the long way through a virgin oak forest down to a Chippewa graveyard near the lake, and her father, who was inventive for an accountant, made up new variations on the Robin Hood stories. When they reached the white picket fence of the cemetery she clutched his hand tightly as they looked out over the crosses at the sheen of the moon on the lake. At this juncture her father always tried to spook her by saying in a whisper, "Perhaps there'll be a message from the spirit world," but this time when he finished they heard from far out on the lake the tremulous wail of a loon as if it had been arranged. He clutched her hand as hard as she did his, then they laughed at their fright and made unsuccessful loon imitations.

Clare considered saving the second ear for morning, then thought why bother, since she was surrounded by virtually millions of them. The idea that she probably wouldn't have married Donald if her father hadn't died was less interesting at the moment than Robin Hood. Michael had sent her a book of poems called *Roots and Branches* by Robert Duncan, whom she had never heard of; the poems were splendid though difficult, and now she could remember an entire passage she had copied in her ledger:

> Robin Hood in the greenwood outside
> Christendom faces peril as if it were a friend.
> Foremost we admire the outlaw
> who has the strength of his own
> lawfulness. How we loved him
> in childhood and hoped to abide by his code
> that took life as its law!

The day after her lovemaking with Michael she and Zilpha had a final lunch with him, then a trip to the airport. It was an unsuccessful event with the only lighter moments provided by the memory of the time the three of them had packed a picnic basket to search for Michael's car which he had "misplaced" a week before. They had driven all the way to Zug Island near Wyandotte to consult an actual Gypsy fortune teller who, startlingly enough, had pinpointed the lost car within a block of Wayne State University. It seemed terribly funny when they had arrived at the car and found the tires were gone.

At the restaurant Zilpha went off to the bathroom and Michael suggested, half seriously, that they get rid of her and make love in the airport parking lot. Clare became angry and said, "Never again," and Michael paled. He was quite hopeless and she didn't hear from him again for several years until his mother's funeral, where he looked harsh, thin, hardened, which she supposed was part of living in New York. They were both weeping over Zilpha when they embraced, and Michael pinched her bottom and whispered, "I'm willing when you are." She stepped back sensing the kind of humor that arises out of grief, but no, he wasn't kidding.

Clare stirred the fire and wondered if her diminished pile of sticks would last, but then even the slightest of fires would suffice to leaven the balmy night. She feared the dissociation of waking up in the middle of the night to total blackness, though the moon should be a modest compensation. She rearranged the wood where she could reach it from her green cave, and firmed some dirt around her can of water so she wouldn't inadvertently tip it over. She wished she felt a little stronger when she curled up for sleep and thought again of the notion of prayer, but she lacked the solace of a religion that does not depend on ignoring the human condition. When she prayed as a child, God's face in her mind was similar to her father's—the graying hair, the furrowed brow, the essentially kind look that was still not interested in trivialities. Her childhood prayer from Sunday school was simple enough: "Now I lay me down to sleep, I pray the Lord my soul to keep. If I should die before I wake, I pray the Lord my soul to take." Curled there on her bed of leaves and grass, Clare thought this prayer lacked a great deal in terms of reassurance. She didn't want the Lord to take her soul in the night; she wanted to go to Europe without having to listen to Donald's incessant business prattle. In the nave of Notre-Dame he had whispered, "Remind me to make a call," as if he ever forgot. In the Uffizi he couldn't stop saying, "I wonder what this would bring at Parke-Bernet."

The world itself was a marketing possibility. Before he had played his *Tracking the Blues* tape today in the car he had interrupted a favorite Stravinsky passage by saying that local acreage was recovering from the 1985 downturn, though Donald Jr. had said pork bellies had the flutters but would really firm up by Labor Day. A signal announcement had been that the black walnut tree in their backyard was worth seven thousand bucks as furniture veneer, and that walnut tree thieves were circulating the Midwest waiting for the innocent to go on vacation. Curiously enough, Donald didn't mind when she asked him to write a large check for the American Indian College Fund or the NAACP, two of her favorite charities, saying something to the effect that "those folks got the wrong end of the stick," as if all American history had been a business deal. Maybe it was. Donald had tried to hedge at her support of the Nature Conservancy and Greenpeace because he felt the bird watchers and "little old ladies in tennis shoes" were cramping certain resort complexes in northern Michigan that were otherwise good investment potentials. Clare reminded him that if she wasn't already a little old lady in tennis shoes, it could clearly be seen on the horizon.

But how could you blame Donald for so fulsomely taking on the colors of the workaday world? Perhaps the lines were drawn more clearly than she had ever thought, and that was why she lay curled in a thicket staring at the weak light of a cottonwood fire. One autumn afternoon when she was helping her father comb burrs out of the long hair of their English setters she had asked him why the Bible said it was easier for a camel to get through the eye of a needle than for a rich man to enter heaven. He treated the question gravely and said that if all your mind is full of is money you become crazy, and that insane people live in a private hell without even knowing it, and that insane rich people created a hell for a lot of other people without knowing or caring about it. As simplistic as this seemed Clare still essentially believed it. Her father said it and he looked like God, though he had done a lot of bad things to her without knowing it. He couldn't have done them on purpose.

Clare sat up as a lump had begun to form beneath her breastbone at the first indication of certain childhood memories. She put a fresh stick on the fire and watched its brief, feverish blaze. She always read herself to sleep and the absence of this routine was haunting. She would have read the footnotes in the *Tao* if there had been enough light. She studied a book of matches from a truck-stop restaurant in Illinois called R Place where they had stopped for lunch on the way out. The restaurant gave a special award and inscribed the name on a plaque of anyone who could eat a four-pound hamburger. The waitress had told Clare that the meat patty was only a little over three pounds but the bun and all the fixings brought the weight up to an even four. For some reason this disgusted Donald who thought the idea "lowlife." The waitress pointed out a burly trucker on the other side of the room who was on his way to victory. Clare excused herself to wash her hands and passed by the trucker on the way to the bathroom, though the trucker was well out of the way. She paused at the table.

"I hope you manage. It looks wonderful," she said.

"You look pretty damn good yourself. I'd give you a bite but I'd be disqualified."

She waved and passed on, wondering if the man had a wife and what she looked like.

Now she reached out and put her beret on tight for extra comfort. She took off her watch and stowed it in the bag thinking if she kept looking at it time itself would swallow her. It was extraordinary that at one moment she could be thinking of making love to Michael on the floor and at the next she was trying to devise a prayer appropriate to the situation. Back to the basics, she joked: religion, fucking and Dad at the cemetery.

When and if she emerged, her friends and acquaintances back in the neighborhood were bound to prate "nervous breakdown" or "depression" during countless phone calls and lunches. One of the favorite local psychiatrists was an ardent pill pusher in his efforts to remove any socially embarrassing symptoms. The probable cause in her case would be obvious to all—the deaths of Zilpha and Sammy—but her marriage, which was considered to be improbably solid, would not be questioned. The same psychiatrist had offered nothing when she had gone to him, troubled about Donald Jr.'s apparent lack of morals in school. He seduced innocent, homely girls and kept a tally, cheated wherever possible on school work, plagiarized term papers and, as a school leader, made problems for teachers who didn't give him good grades. The psychiatrist had dismissed all of this as Donald Jr.'s effort to take short cuts into his father's world, and when sufficient negative reinforcement came from his "peer group" the behavior would cease. Unfortunately for this theory Donald Jr. continued to be widely admired as charming and capable. His SATs were too mediocre to get him into an Ivy League college, which his father hoped for, but strings were pulled and he was accepted at University of Michigan where he became the president of his fraternity. Donald Jr. had always been impeccably dressed, even for a trip to the 7-Eleven, while Laurel, who had gone to Northwestern, was a slob, drank beer and smoked marijuana, and graduated summa cum laude. She had also been the best student in her class at Michigan State's veterinary school, neither of which honors made more than a cursory dent in her father's consciousness.

There was a rustling in the thicket off to the left and Clare's pulse quickened, but then a barred owl called from the cottonwood and Clare supposed the other creatures were making adjustments to keep out of the owl's way. At one time Donald Jr.'s character had been puzzling because she was blinded by the fact that he had been a much more loving child than Laurel, helping Clare in the garden, arranging his Audubon cards, building bird houses, acting as a deft little "sous chef" when she cooked. It was as if during puberty he woke up, looked around and decided to become a child of his time.

Clare wriggled closer to the opening for a look at the moon and stars, then sat up and stuffed her bag with dry grass for a pillow. This camping had its moments but she was claustrophobic enough to dread tents, elevators and theater lines, and the stars and moon were a tonic after the dark lid of her thicket. There was still the slightest twinge of pain in her left lobe and she monitored the size of the speck of green light. She heard a strain of Monteverdi, then a bar of *The Firebird,* and the light diminished. With Laurel the light was steady but the images of Donald and Donald Jr. increased it. She searched for good memories to control her fear of another attack.

When they were first married and Donald had just entered the firm as an assistant office manager he still wore his lumberjack shirts in the evening and on weekends. He hadn't finished his senior thesis, an essay, ironically enough, on Thorstein Veblen's *Theory of the Leisure Class,* so through the long winter of the pregnancy Clare had actually written most of the thesis. She thought Donald talked brilliantly but didn't write well, while she was shy but wrote well, if a little too carefully. Some of Donald's politically active friends from Michigan State were back in the Detroit area and they all met at least once a week. Donald would regale them with stories about the "bourgeoisie" at work and in the neighborhood near their Birmingham apartment.

Clare's mother had busied herself in her grief by drinking even more than usual and shopping for a perfect home for her daughter. Clare's brother Ted, younger by five years, was in his junior year at Kent, a prep school in Connecticut, his fourth in four years. When her mother had finally found the home, she and Clare had spent a great deal of time overseeing the redecorating. Clare was unconcerned and felt the project was good therapy for her mother. Meanwhile she and Donald and their scrubby friends ate at inexpensive Polish, Italian, Chinese and Greek restaurants, and went to the wonderful movies of those times: all of Bergman, Fellini and the early Antonioni. They marched with other civil rights protesters, hand in hand with blacks, and listened religiously each Sunday morning to the wild-eyed sermons of the Reverend C. L. Franklin, Aretha's father. They actually shook hands with the great man himself, Martin Luther King. He had said to Donald, "Keep up the good work, brother," and Donald had beamed. Like so many others they had been paralyzed with fear by the Cuban missile crisis. Clare had been reading William Faulkner's *The Reivers* when she heard on WJR that President Kennedy had been shot in Dallas. Donald rushed home from work and they wept together, glued to the icy, catatonic replays on television.

One evening, before they had moved into the house, all of their friends had come over for dinner and to listen to blues and jazz records on their new stereo. Donald discoursed on Charlie Parker, Muddy Waters, B. B. King and the primitive discs recorded by Alan Lomax, before carefully putting the needle on the record. Among their favorites were Forest City Joe singing "Chevrolet" and Vera Hall's "Can't You Hear That Wild Ox

Moan." Clare thought that perhaps that evening had been the beginning of the end. Laurel had been sick with a cold, and Clare at the time was a distinctly amateur cook. Hearing of the party, her mother had volunteered to send over a little something from the club. Two waiters showed up at 8 P.M. sharp when the guests were groggy from Gallo burgundy and famished to despair. Clare went into the bathroom, embarrassed to the point of tears when the food arrived. She primped herself, wiped away her tears, blew her nose and emerged when she heard the shouts of joy from the other room. There were only ten of them but her mother had sent over a huge prime rib roast, a Smithfield ham, side dishes including six dozen oysters, a mixed case of French wine and two cases of imported beer. Their friends were utterly thrilled with the food, without a single negative comment. They ate, drank, danced and laughed, and at the bleary end of the party Clare wrapped up ample packages of leftovers for each of the guests.

In the morning they had the first serious argument of their marriage, over, oddly enough, a novel by James Baldwin and a profile of Malcolm X in a Detroit newspaper. A week later they moved into the house and things were never the same again, nor were they meant to be. Despite his jokes about work Donald had become a well-concealed predator, a skilled manipulator, something he had learned as a political activist, and was earning a degree in accounting at night school at the University of Detroit. During the longish evenings alone Clare began reading again and hadn't stopped since. Over the long haul she couldn't have endured Donald without her books, but now the idea of the books without Donald seemed rather nice. Two years after Laurel, who had been nicknamed "Papoose," Donald Jr. was born, and when Donald arrived late at the hospital with three dozen roses he announced, in his first tailored suit, that he had been elected a member of the Detroit Athletic Club. Clare put down the book she was reading, a novel called *The Deer Park* by Norman Mailer, in which there were no deer to be found but lots of intriguing bad behavior. She remembered looking closely at Donald, a long pause where she waited patiently for him to mention the birth of his son.

Clare dozed for a half hour, waking fearfully with a deep chest pain, then smiled because she had rolled over and clenched a fist against her heart, mistaking it for an attack. The fire was down to embers and she decided to use the largest of the sticks in hope that it would last until she slept long and deeply, if ever. She strained above the hiss and sputter of the fire to hear something just on the edge of the audible. There it was again. And again. A dog barking far to the south, she imagined in some barnyard at the outer edge of the arc thrown by a porch light, the dog's body stiffening as it barked at the night as Sammy's body had every single night just before bedtime. It was an unimaginably comforting sound and tears of joy formed in her throat. How wonderful it would have been to have the dog with her, not for protection, as Sammy's bravura was mostly fake, but for companionship. Sammy had been afraid of cats and snakes, but her thunderous bark warned away possible intruders and door-to-door salesmen and the irksome approach of Jehovah's Witnesses. For unclear reasons she like the Federal Express man but loathed the one for UPS. The black furnace repairman once threw her into a fearsome rage which caused Clare to offer an embarrassed apology after she had closed Sammy up in the garage. The black man, who was about her age, looked at her strangely, then offered his hand. It turned out they had been in a civil rights march together well over twenty years before, and the man's little son who had played with Laurel in Hart Plaza now taught high school science in Ypsilanti. When the repairman left it wasn't the happiest occasion because the intervening years acquired the sharpest of focuses. The man had mentioned seeing her name in the *Detroit News* where she had been referred to rather nastily as a "well-heeled liberal environmentalist."

At dinner when she brought up the repairman Donald had become vague and nearly morose for a minute. It had been difficult for him lately as one of his minor saving graces was an abiding concern for probity in government, and the successive scandals in Pentagon procurement, HUD, and the enormity of the savings-and-loan mess disturbed him deeply. She tended to go easy on him on the rare occasions when he became vulnerable, but two summers before, near Bay View in Petoskey, they had come upon a ragged Chippewa selling Korean-made moccasins. Clare had bought several pairs, quipping that the Chippewa apparently didn't own any oil wells, a reference to a Reagan gaff. They usually avoided political discussions, settling for canceling each other's vote at the polls.

Laurel, however, was merciless and could redden Donald's face by saying that she wanted to go to Costa Rica and speak Latin just like Dan Quayle. Laurel was never particularly interested in novels or poetry, and her single misquote was from Yeats, the sense being that while the best lacked all conviction, the worst were full of passionate intensity. That appeared to sum up Laurel's feelings toward the political world. Donald Jr. tended merely to be a more cynical version of his father. Clare herself had come to the point that all the highest hopes of her twenties had dissembled to the degree that she was relegated to writing checks to distant organizations and trying to save the occasional pond, creek or sorry woodlot in Michigan. The heady idealism of the Labor State had died with Walter Reuther, and the prospects for social services and the environment had become dismal in the face of lobbyists' opportunism.

Fortunately, the thought of politics made her sleepy, though sodden might be a better word, she thought. She heard the dog's bark a little more clearly and there was an eerie moment when she thought it might be her own ghost dog, but the image of it barking out its loneliness under the porch light was dominant. The stars and the moon didn't seem quite high enough, and she remembered Donald's chagrin when they added a master bedroom with a sixteen-foot ceiling. Clare couldn't stay in newish hotels where the windows didn't open. She often regretted her mother's gift of a house so soon after they were married. Money tended to derange people when it arrived so abruptly, and the house wasn't, ultimately, fair to Donald. The ceilings were high in Europe but less equitable societies made her nervous after a few weeks. When this was over she intended to live in an apartment or in a smallish house on the far edge of a town. It would be near a woods and farm country. She would find a job in a library or bookstore where she could make herself useful, a sense she had lost since Donald Jr. had gone off to college. The woman who ran the local office for the charity in Costa Rica had said she was an overworked volunteer and that sounded good to Clare. The woman had advised against visiting the child and she was right. The family had been fearful that something might be taken from them, that they were being judged, but they had warmed to Zilpha and the atmosphere had become relaxed in the one-room stucco cottage near Punta Arenas.

Clare traced a finger across the dew gathering on her face. She had learned enough Spanish to translate the thank you notes from the child who was now in her early teens. The parents had been painfully shy but the second child, a boy of seven, was perfectly round and had thought everything about Zilpha was funny. Clare's mother definitely had been a problem drinker and Clare thought again of the nightmares caused by rich, overgenerous alcoholics. The new, homely word "yuppie" had been devised for the grandchildren of the Depression and she wondered how gracefully they would age. Another ugly word was "schmucks." Last Christmas when Donald Jr. came home from Chicago with a rather pretty but vacant girl, he told Clare her "main problem" was that she expected too much from people when they were really only schmucks.

Sleep was too far away for the clumsiest of prayers. She got up, put another stick on the fire and looked at her bed in the brief yellow flare-up. It was the nest of a not very skilled animal, a temporary measure like a deer bed in high grass. She turned and the wider row she had come down a lifetime ago was now aligned with the moon, a darkling path between silvered leaves which a breeze was lightly rustling. It was a path from a children's book of the twenties in the golden age of illustration, lovely, foreboding, irresistible. She decided to walk herself to sleep as she did so often with her dog at home. Donald had bought her a small pistol which she never took along because the presence of a pistol would have changed the nature of the walk. And Sammy, though still frightened by cats, thought she was a grizzly bear after dark. Besides, she was in fine trim, and asked Donald why they'd remained in so otiose a neighborhood if it wasn't the safest in the Detroit area. She could tell he didn't know what "otiose" meant but pretended he did as he watched Pisor, his favorite late-news baritone. *Oh, fuck Donald,* she reminded herself. *I am here because he isn't.*

She set off at a relaxed but steady pace, fixed on the moon as if she were trying to walk to a place directly under it. After a few hundred yards she quickened her gait and felt that delightful sense that her joints had become oiled, and the night air was sweet and drinkable. Dr. Roth liked to say that the overexamined life was not worth living, and that the quasi-upper-class life had become the shabbiest of self-improvement videos. Goddamn but her mind was so exhausted with trying to hold the world together, tired of being the living glue for herself, as if she let go, great pieces of her life would shatter and fall off in mockery of the apocalypse. Or it would simply deflate, letting off its sour air like a punctured rubber ball. She was delighted when she thought she saw the moon move a bit as it must. Time moved the moon. You should be lucky enough to be there when the tree falls in the desert. Dr. Roth, who was fascinated with the history of religions, gave her what he called a "nice Jewish present," *The Unvarnished Gospels,* a new translation by Gaus. The language was so stark and commonplace as to be almost unreadable.

The world is likely commonplace, she thought. There was the amusing memory of the second term of her sophomore year when East Lansing was frozen in dirty ice. She had met a boy in the periodicals room who was reading her favorite literary journal, *Botteghe Oscure,* edited in Rome by Marguerite Caetani. Clare's secret ambition was to be Marguerite Caetani's secretary and meet the French poet René Char, whose long poem "To a Tensed Serenity" was in the latest issue. The boy reading the journal was shabby, condescending, an avowed "beatnik" who smelled strongly of potato chips. She found him exciting though he looked down his pale, mottled nose at her pleated skirt and gray cashmere cardigan. The boy let her sit near him at Kewpee's, a cafeteria favored by the intellectual and artistic types, the latter having the advantage of smelling like paint rather than something else.

She and the boy would sit as close as possible to a table of seniors dominated by a strange-looking young man who, on alternate days, wore army surplus or the kind of suit and Chesterfield coat worn in her hometown. He was more vigorous and arrogant than her suicidal instructor and she and the boy listened raptly as the young man droned on about Rimbaud, Verlaine, Laforgue, Péguy, Alain-Fournier, Camus, Kierkegaard, Yesenin and the "obvious" structure of Joyce's *Finnegans Wake.* He had taken to glancing at her legs now and then and once loudly told a story about fucking a fat, drunken waitress who wore an ankle bracelet which spelled "Herbert." One day the man looked over at her and asked her if she had read Dostoevsky, especially the new translation of his *Notebooks* wherein there was an entry about a girl who, one cold St. Petersburg afternoon, drank a bottle of wine and committed suicide out of boredom. She answered that she hadn't read Dostoevsky but Turgenev's *Sportsman's Sketches* was one of her favorites (it was actually her father's favorite). "That's good," he said, "but read *Fathers and Sons.* I'm actually Bazarov. Get off your pretty ass and read all of Dostoevsky or you'll become a punching bag for some Grosse Pointe fraternity boy." Then the man stood up and announced to his cronies that it was time to get drunk and play pool. On the way out the man paused by her chair and pronounced loudly that she was "edible" which confused her somewhat.

After she said goodbye to the boy she cut a class and went immediately to the campus bookstore and bought all of the Dostoevsky in the Modern Library editions, the Constance Garnett translations. She read *The Idiot, The Gambler, Notes from Underground, The Possessed, Crime and Punishment* and *The Brothers Karamazov.* Her eyes were hot red balls in her head but her life was changed. The great Russian had devoured another piece of her each time she wept over a hero or heroine, a grand conception, the marriage of heaven and hell that was his peculiar genius, and spat her out in bones and gristle. But after she and the beatnik boy had returned on three successive empty days they finally heard the young man had suffered a nervous breakdown and had run off to New York City, leaving a wife and child in married housing. Clare stayed in her room for a week until a dorm counselor escorted her to the campus psychiatric clinic where a sluggish doctor advised her to construct some effective shields against her emotional life, a project at which she proved most successful.

Her skin was moist and her breathing harder as the darkness of the path ahead yielded to a lighter shade of gray. There was a hissing, clicking sound which could have been a flying saucer had she not recognized the sound of irrigation sprinklers from the golf course near their home. The cornfield gave way to another huge field she guessed must be soybeans, the sprinklers tossing water into the moonlight as far as she could see to the east. Off to the north were the soundless lights of trucks and cars on Route 80, with the illusion at that distance that they were traveling slowly, creeping toward Chicago or back west toward Omaha. There was a two-track lane between the soybeans and corn and she walked south for a while, hoping to see the light of a farmhouse. She wanted to hear the dog bark and there was nothing, but she suspected everyone must be asleep by now. She followed a thumping in the ground to a tall thicket of grass and weeds growing up around the main outlet and valve for the irrigation system. She slid in a big puddle but maintained her balance, the water pleasantly icy on her hot feet. Where the main pipe curved up and out of the ground there was a wheel to turn the water off and on, and a large connecting pipe to the field, out of which came a steady gout of water from a bad fitting. Clare cupped her hands, pausing to let their warmth cut the water's icy edge to avoid the onset of a headache. The water was clean and marvelous after the tea-colored sludge from the creek and she stooped there drinking until she felt a little bilious. She slipped off her blouse, skirt, panties and bra, bathing herself slowly with her hands. She did not feel remotely sorry for herself which there had been a trace of earlier. Dr. Roth had a theory that self-pity was the most injurious emotion to mental and physical health. In the small desert town near the pain clinic a trinket store sold T-shirts that read, "The Pain People," which they all bought with irony and humor.

Clare let the breeze dry her off. People used to say "buck naked" and that's what she was, with more than a twinge of desire for Dr. Roth at the moment his image shifted out of the dark in connection with Dostoevsky. She felt quite free to think about making love to him because she knew it would never happen. It would break the etiquette of their affection for each other. For an uncharacteristic few seconds she thought that any farmer would do, or even the trucker who ate the four-pound hamburger, but certainly not Donald, who would not be caught dead out here unless he was bent on buying the farm. She was nearly dry and thinking about nothing in particular except how smooth and strong her body was for her age, when Dr. Roth arrived again. She had told him about the Dostoevsky incident at the bar of the Townsend Hotel and was miffed when he began laughing.

"Life is so unforgiving when you're nineteen," he said.

"And that makes my sad tale funny?"

"If it's not funny by now you might have to shoot yourself. That's what I mean by unforgiving. Actually, if you shoot anyone it should be the psychiatrist. All he did was try to lower the ceilings."

"I suppose he was tired of the anguish of hundreds of nineteen-year-olds."

"Then he should have gotten the fuck out of the business. You have to remain vulnerable to treat the vulnerable."

"I'm not so sure he could have said anything valuable."

"Of course he could. He might have said that neurotic intellectuals can be as dangerous as cheese-brained fraternity boys. He could have said if you really wanted the guy you could have closed the deal before you read all the books, but it probably wouldn't have been a good idea."

"But I didn't know I could have closed the deal."

"That's ladylike bullshit. You knew that on a particular level. I think it's intriguing that you wanted to fuck someone for their mind. I sure could have used that at nineteen." Dr. Roth nearly blushed at this, the first mention of sex between them, albeit abstract.

"I would have been twenty-six at the time, already an old lady for a nineteen-year-old." She was going to let him fry for a moment.

"That's not the way it works. I'd feel more comfortable talking about religion."

"I remember when I wrote about Apollinaire that he said Jesus held the world's high-altitude record. Is that religious enough?"

"It's definitely safer. We always like to think we're on the verge of danger when we're nearly immobile, don't we?"

"I suppose so. It's nice to hear that you think of yourself as no more adventurous than me."

"Now it's my turn to suppose so." He had become strained and distraught. "That's what is finally unforgiving. All of this mythological freedom we grow up on which we usually get to express standing around in a field wearing a baseball mitt. Or sailing a quarter-million-dollar sailboat down the Detroit River hoping the water won't corrode a hole in the bottom."

On the long walk back to her nest Clare remembered that Apollinaire left his wife by merely getting on a train and disappearing, but the idea of her own escape was too obvious to attribute to the poet. The beauty and dread of time was that nothing was forgiven. Not a single minute. The years she had spent in consideration of this act were not only lost, irretrievable, but the recognition of the loss was so naive as to leave her breathless. And she lacked the convenient excuse of children to care for, or the most central excuse of all, poverty. The bondage for most women was not enough money to live on, especially if there were children. And for men there was the perpetual bondage of work and debt, to which was added so frequently a level of spending far beyond their means. In Clare and Donald's class it meant something quite different. Donald had explained several personal bankruptcies after Black Monday. A number of their club members had been making five hundred thousand a year but regularly spent seven hundred. This fact dumfounded Clare whose extravagances were limited to a good bottle of wine a day and rare books. On vacations she like deluxe hotels but flew tourist class, which had always irritated Donald. She liked to send the difference to a charity so that it wasn't a matter of being an unpretentious skinflint.

Her brother Ted always seemed a more elegant version of Donald and tended to avoid seeing her except around the holidays when it was pro forma. He had been to Hazelden in Minnesota three times to dry out, and the last trip was to the Betty Ford which still didn't do the trick. What finally worked was a panel of doctors' absolute guarantee that he'd die within a year if he continued drinking. His three failed marriages and obsession with racing sailboats in the Great Lakes and the Caribbean had diminished his trusts by two-thirds, until he was forced to live quite modestly. Clare had loaned him a great deal of money over the years and this made Donald quarrelsome. Her brother liked to make her feel guilty by repeating that she had inherited all the good genes from their father, while he was stuck with the unstable propensities of their mother. Unfortunately, Dr. Roth had said, that was a possibility. The bottom line, Clare thought, was that her brother had been a bully since he was an infant, and had tended to bully himself into the middle of any misery he could find. To an unimaginable degree he had ruined his life and caused a great deal of pain to his wives and children. He was a living poster child for the evil potential of inherited wealth.

Clare was absurdly happy when she reached her nest, as if returning home from a tiring day. She tended to the remaining embers of the fire, bringing them to life with dry grass and sticks. There was a lightness in her body brought about by the fact that she did not give a flat fuck if she ever saw her brother or Donald again. It was as simple as that. She repeated the phrase "flat fuck" with the avowed intent to take up swearing as a pressure valve. The phrase was used by April, a rotund woman Clare and Zilpha met up near Pellston the October before on an outing. It was at a small county park on a lake, the autumn colors so stridently lovely as to approach banality, with Sammy swimming through the red and yellow leaves on the lake. When Sammy finished swimming she came up to

Clare and waited patiently for Clare to pick the wet maple leaves off her back, then rolled vigorously in the dust and ashes of a campfire site. Zilpha had started a fire in the small Weber grill they traveled with, using the dry split oak that was kept neatly tied in a bundle. From home Clare had brought the salad, the dressing, and a pheasant Donald had shot at a hunting preserve near Holly. The pheasant had looked a bit lean so she had split it in half before daylight that morning, puréed butter, fresh thyme and sage and forced the mixture gently up under the skin while Donald was already barking on the phone in the breakfast nook.

April was driving down the gravel road when she blew a tire with a shotgun sound not fifty yards from them, and Sammy rushed into the woods, remembering the few times she had been used as a bird dog in her youth. April got out of the car with her five-year-old daughter, a chubby miniature of her mother.

"I can't believe this fucking shitass car," April hollered with a volume that brought Sammy running back from the woods.

Zilpha and Clare went to her aid. There was a bald spare tire but no jack among the hundreds of returnable beer cans in the trunk. Zilpha got the jack from the Toyota and swiftly changed the tire which amazed April. Zilpha's husband was a car buff, and before their marriage had ruptured into boredom they had restored a number of old cars together.

"Lady, you could get a job in a flat-fucking garage," April said. She continued to talk, bearing down on the day's problems, with every sentence peppered with phrases polite folks think of as filth. Zilpha and Clare couldn't help but begin to laugh and April said she was sorry but she always talked that way. Meanwhile the child was off throwing a stick into the lake for the dog, her voice pealing out, "Bring it back, you son-of-a-bitch." Clare asked April if she'd like a drink or something to eat. April said she had just had lunch but "I could use a fucking drink to turn the day around."

They sat at the picnic table drinking white wine with Clare getting up now and then to tend the broiling pheasant, watching the child wrestle with the wet dog. April was a local and worked as a barmaid up the road. Her ex-husband was a welder in Detroit but was in jail on assault. She had had his checks garnished but he wasn't getting paid in jail so times were hard. Zilpha took down the information, saying that her husband might be able to look into it. Then April said, "Where do you gals work?" and there was an embarrassed silence.

"We're sort of housewives," Clare said, and April said she had tried that once but it "bored the shit out of me." She liked working in the bar because you could shoot the shit with the customers, and if you got a little horny you could always find someone. Clare had set out a small wheel of Camembert and cut a wedge for the daughter who was eyeing it. The child smelled the cheese, announced loudly that it smelled like poop and ran off again with Sammy. When April left she thanked them profusely, took one more swig from the bottle of wine and said, "You fucking ladies got it all." When she was gone their laughter was mixed with a little melancholy. The pheasant was delicious and Sammy got a chunk of raw shin bone of beef that had been packed for her in a cellophane sack.

That had been their next to last outing before Zilpha's diagnosis had come, right after Thanksgiving. In early December they went off to a spa near Tecate in northern

Sonora, just a few hours south of San Diego. The trip had its moments but the diagnosis was too fresh in mind to try to ignore. After the first day of group exercise they gave up the program in favor of hiking in the mountains, most of the time well off the marked trails.

They had been at the spa together a decade earlier, and since then it had vastly upgraded its facilities, and the clientele had become a bit more hard and glitzy. One evening in the dining hall Zilpha said, "We're all the same here," and it was true. Other than a dozen men there were nearly ninety women, between the ages of forty and sixty, but a concentration around fifty. More than age, the women seemed to be fighting a malaise of fatigue and dissociation, of free-floating anxiety so deeply ingrained as to be invisible to the bearer. The regimen of a vegetarian diet and relentless exercise in a lovely setting far from home, the source of the gray-area angst, worked quite well, and within two days spirits were lifted. It was a break, not a cure, a shifting into a pleasant neutral where the body's exhaustion supplanted the brain's dreary machinations. Unfortunately, given the death sentence of Zilpha, the function of the place was too clearly scribed, so they took refuge in the mountains, packing along water bottles, hard-boiled eggs and oranges, descending in the late afternoon to start a fire in the fireplace and drink a glass of wine before dinner. Clare had been thrilled to discover that their small villa had once been used on a regular basis by Aldous Huxley, one of her earliest reading enthusiasms. Zilpha was a steady reader herself but disliked Huxley's brittle intelligence which reminded her of her husband. At dinner every evening Zilpha would look out over the assembled ladies and whisper, "Don't you wish April was here to sweeten them up?"

One afternoon they were sitting on a boulder halfway up Mount Cuchama when a Pacific front swept in over a distant ridge and within a few minutes they were looking down at the roiling tops of clouds with far less security than is felt in an airplane. They were excited and girlish at the experience, noting the occasional hawk or raven that would pop up through the clouds, circle around, then dive back down into the moving fleece. "These clouds aren't comforting enough for the afterlife," Zilpha said, just before they heard a rattle of stone and a ragged, desperate Mexican man appeared before them. He gestured at his mouth in hunger and they handed down a remaining orange and hard-boiled egg from their perch on the boulder. The man pocketed the food, smiled, bowed and scampered up the steep mountain at an alarming rate, with physical verve that Clare pointed out none of the fitness instructors could have managed. Zilpha became depressed that the man was headed for America and might be disappointed, then she began coughing so they headed down the mountain.

Clare sat before her fire and decided that at last she was ready for sleep. She felt a trace of something new and feared she might be like a patient emerging from an asylum, using a cornstalk as a scepter, and saying, "As of today I'm giving up control of the entire world and all of its inhabitants." A half-dozen fireflies had gathered in the darkness around her green cave, and the tiny beams seemed to trace the convolutions of her thought. Life outside the asylum was not necessarily more pleasant. It could be, but it didn't have to be. She tried to recall what her beloved Camus said about "terrible freedom," that once you decided not to commit suicide, whether physically or figuratively, you assumed the responsibility of freedom. The thought blurred with a firefly's movement past her nose. She curled up fetally, rejected the position and stretched out strenuously on her back until there were bone crackles.

When she woke up a few days before this trip she noted that her feet were getting old, and laughed. She met Dr. Roth downtown for lunch because it was his volunteer day. He looked grim in the foyer of the Caucus Club and she feared a bad morning at the hospital, but it turned out an auto dealer had called to tell him his wife was intent on buying the same car she had bought the day before. The restaurant seemed suddenly inappropriate so they walked down the street and bought two coney islands apiece. Clare admitted she had never eaten one in her life but found the frankfurters covered with onions, mustard and chili quite delicious.

"You just saved a hundred bucks," he said, examining a splotch of mustard on his necktie. Clare had always insisted on the check.

"Too bad they don't sell these out our way."

They ducked into a bar, had a quick beer and removed the mustard from his tie. When they left and began walking again it was by common consent they decided not to be witty.

"What would you think if I left Donald?"

"I'd think you were sane"—his reply was quick—"but that's as much as I'll say. When did this come up?"

"About seven years ago. Why won't you say any more?"

"Because I've seen dozens of divorces in my practice and the act is so utterly intimate that outside advice only confuses the issue. Also, anything I'd say would be an abridgment of your freedom."

"I understand that. I've actually reduced it to an abstract principle." She hesitated, feeling foolish.

"Let's have it. Don't leave me hanging. This will be a first."

"I want to evoke life and he wants to dominate it. Is that too simple?"

"No, I don't think so. I'll have to spend an evening with that one. When are you going to do it?"

"I have no idea."

"Where are you going?"

"I don't know."

"Well I don't believe you don't know. In the ten years we've known each other you've mentioned a number of places you'd like to live. Let's see, there was Flagstaff, Minneapolis, Durango in Colorado, Pendleton in Oregon, and Duluth. And the obvious Paris."

"You have a remarkable memory for my nonsense."

"I've never been to any of them, but when you'd mention a place I'd look it up in the atlas and think it over." He was nervous with this admission and looked at his watch. It was then that she understood that at one time, at least, he had cared for her. They walked on in silence for a few minutes, her heart swelling in her throat. When they reached her car he hugged her and rushed off.

Clare was sinking into the ground, into a point well past sleep, or so she thought, with her body sweet, warm, deadened, giving itself up to the bed of leaves and grass, the green odor transmitting a sense she belonged to the earth as much as any other living thing. *I don't need to change. I'm just this.* Her brain had grown larger, its outer reaches vertiginous, grand, so that she could move within it as if taking an evening walk. She understood that she had been abandoned there by her mother and father, Donald, her children, Sammy and Zilpha, and that only being abandoned by Sammy and her children was natural. Zilpha was torn off the earth, taken away. Donald had disfigured himself beyond recognition and bore no resemblance to the man she in innocence had once been proud to love. Her mother smelled of allspice, martinis. Her ears smelled of gin. *Be careful because they'll always try to put their thing in you, dear. No matter what they say, that's what they're trying to do.* Her father had said, *Clare, look at your mother and don't drink anything stronger than wine,* and she hadn't except an occasional brandy. But when she slept in her birthday tent out by the grape trellis with the English setter, Tess, the dog had growled when her mother covered her in a mink coat, then she heard her mother vomit in the yard. Her legs were so thin and she died a year after him, unable to stand on thin legs still smelling of gin after death, beside him in the cemetery Clare could not bear to visit. Now she would, to say goodbye. As a child puzzled by age she'd say, Why is Dad older? Why does he say, *Take the best bite first?* We went for a drive that took all day from the cottage to a man's farm near Gaylord to get Tess bred. We dropped her off and he didn't want me to see it so we went to town for lunch. Mother was in the hospital so I got to eat French fried potatoes, then we went to see the Hartwick Pines, the biggest trees left, then we went to the wilderness where there were only huge old stumps. He said all but a few white pines five feet thick were cut down. *They're like the buffalo,* but I didn't understand. At Christmas he gave me a silver dog whistle with three small diamonds set in it because I could make the setters mind. Sit, stay, come, heel, slow. I never got to go hunting. My brother hated it. Girls don't hunt, he said. My brother hit the dogs with a stick and got spanked. He would always hit me but Mother said I did the bruises myself to make my brother look naughty. The clock said three and I didn't hear Sammy's breath and I knew she was gone. It was May and the lilacs had just come out. I wore my nightgown and put on my hiking boots. I carried her down the hall and Donald looked out of his bedroom door and I said, *Go back to bed Donald this is my dog.* Out at the end of the garden I began digging and it was more than an hour before the hole was deep enough. I got down in the hole chest deep and could see that dumb bastard Donald staring at me out the kitchen window, then he went away. I lifted Sammy in after I kissed her goodbye and covered her with the dirt, and sat down out of breath. At Zilpha's grave they covered the dirt with a rug of fake grass the color of grass in Easter baskets.

Something brushed against her leg and she bolted upright from the waist in alarm with hundreds of yellow dots whirling about her and above the rabbit that paused beside the dim coals of the fire. The moon made shadows of the rabbit's twitching ears. She scrambled out of the green cave and stood, gulping air in fright, the rabbit shooting back into the thicket. She prayed for her heart to stop thumping and looked up at the moon, and there were fireflies above her. As her heartbeat slowed she still did not want to look down at her body or touch herself because she thought she might be seven again. The fireflies were thicker in some places above the thicket, blinking off and on, whirling toward each other so if you blurred your eyes there were tracers, yellow lines of light everywhere. She thought, *Laurel should see this, Laurel would love this,* and then she was no longer seven.

Clare rebuilt the small fire to break the unearthly mood but the fireflies weren't disturbed. She walked up the row fifty feet, turned and looked back, hoping that she wouldn't see herself standing there. The countless thousands of fireflies stayed just outside and within and above the thicket. Quite suddenly she felt blessed without thinking whether or not she deserved it. She went back to her nest, lay down and wept for a few minutes, then watched a firefly hovering barely a foot above her head. She tried out *Now I lay me down to sleep* despite its failure to reassure. *All souls will be taken, including the souls of fireflies.*

She closed her eyes and felt herself floating in memory from her beginning, as if on a river but more quickly along the surface than what had happened to her. Now she saw when it was she had slept on the ground without covers up at the cottage when she was seven, with Tess curled up in her arms, smelling like a skunk Tess had bothered. In March that year, 1947, there was a serious bout of pneumonia and the doctors had given her too much of the new wonder drug, penicillin. At first she was better, though she hated the hospital and asked her parents daily if she could go home and they kept forgetting to bring along her small ceramic dog. All her joints began to redden and swell and her fever rose precipitously. The doctors diagnosed rheumatoid arthritis, a terrible disease, and then she lapsed into a coma for five days. All that she could remember from the coma was that her grandfather had brought into her hospital room his huge Belgian draft horse mare with the rooster perched on its back. When her grandfather left with the horse and rooster, her grandmother came in leading a black bear with a red leash. Her grandmother said nothing but the bear had sat down beside her and talked in a soothing language, and before the bear said goodbye she put Clare's ceramic dog on the nightstand so it was there when she woke up with a big needle putting juice in her arm. No one was there when she woke up though she thought she still smelled the bear in the room. A specialist from the university said she was allergic to penicillin and the drug had poisoned her system. Her parents were happy she didn't have rheumatoid arthritis (they kept saying it) but Clare felt things were never quite the same again. In her child's mind she felt that they had abandoned her because she had frightened them with her illness, an almost imperceptible withholding of affection that became directed to her little brother, or so she believed. When she got out of the hospital it was nearly time to move up to the summer place, but when they got there she was told she was too ill to go fishing with her father. He kept saying, *Maybe next month.* One evening her parents went to a party down the lake, the babysitter was awful just sitting out on the porch with a boyfriend, and her little brother had purposefully broken the tail off her ceramic dog by hitting it against the fireplace. She stayed up late to show the broken dog to her parents, but they came home a little drunk and spanked her for staying up late. She crawled out the window with Tess and slept under the bushes near the garage where the three-legged cat had visited them. Tess liked cats and tried to lick their fur. Early in the morning she was discovered when Tess started barking at a motorboat, and she was spanked for sleeping outside.

She never did get to go fishing that summer though she happily threw her brother's favorite teddy bear off the dock and stood there a long time until it drowned. Then her mother had to go to the hospital down near Ann Arbor, Mercy Wood, because she drank too much, though her dad said she was just sick. The good trip was to take Tess to Gaylord to find her a "husband." That's what he said though there was no church, just a farm with English setters. Then came the lunch, the big trees and the buffalo stumps.

When Clare awoke again the fireflies were gone. She rummaged in the bag until she found her watch, lit a match and saw it was four A.M., with dawn less than two hours away. She felt drowsy and unafraid so didn't bother to rekindle the fire. It was pleasant to know she had no idea what she was going to do other than wear a beret in Paris on at least a single walk, she hoped on a rainy August afternoon. Barring small children, most women in her neighborhood in broken marriages ran afoul of sheer idleness. Clare knew she was bright enough to make herself useful somewhere, especially when she wouldn't be running the house, which she tended at the moment to look upon as a preposterous imposition put on her by her mother. Her father tended to be naturally morose, taciturn, but the times her mother began drinking again after a supposed cure were hard on him. Once Clare came upon him crying in the den after her mother had fallen down the stairs. She hadn't really injured herself but the family doctor thought it an opportunity for a quick cure. His eyes had also become moist when Clare was dressed up for her first formal dance at fourteen. He had just arrived home from a business trip to New York and stood in the hall with his ponderous briefcase, and as she was leaving, he turned and nodded to her boyfriend standing on the porch, kissed her and said, *This can't be, this is too sudden,* and off she went. The last time was when, despite the pressures of business, he drove her up to East Lansing to enter college. Going to Michigan State was Clare's first act of total defiance against her mother to whom the college was unmentionable. Her mother had insisted on her own alma mater, Smith, and Clare had said, *You're not much of a recommendation, the only thing I've seen you read is Vogue,* and her mother had slapped her for the last time. Clare's favorite teacher had gone to MSU and had set up a program with old professor friends so that after basics Clare would have clear sailing in comparative literature. She envisioned a career that allowed her to read world literature, think about it, and anything beyond that was an irritation. Her father was fairly strict about her spending but gave her free rein with books. Sadly, Clare thought, the only time he truly defended her against her mother was in the choice of a college. But he had become quite upset when he dropped her off at her dorm, and they had talked with an intimacy previously unknown to them about her mother. He nearly begged her to come home as often as possible, if only for his sake. It was an unnerving moment for her, this first time her father was not quite her father but an intimate. Why had he waited until she was eighteen to try to become close, a time when it was no longer achievable, though it might have been later, had he lived? *Oh Father don't worry I'm doing fine,* and then she slept a pure, deep, dreamless sleep.

At first light there were more birds than she had ever heard at one time. It was as if she were *within* the birds, and wrens fluttered skillfully through the branches of the thicket. She heard whippoorwills, mourning doves, the resurgence of the red-winged blackbirds from the marsh beyond the creek. She ran a finger through the dew on her face which was slick as fine oil, and her movement disturbed something beside her. She turned and her heart stopped as a very long, thick, black snake eased himself off into the deeper reaches of the thicket. *Holy Jesus I have slept with a snake.* She laughed as her heart restarted. She gathered up her bag, took a sip of the boiled creek water, which had settled somewhat during the night, and scrambled out into the dawn. If someone would just bring coffee she might stay a few hours more. She began to walk down the row, then turned around, having forgot the cranberry juice can. When she picked it up there was a clear view of her nest, and it reminded her in the first light of a swamp near their cabin where her father said a bear slept. She made a little goodbye bow to the green cave, examined her filthy clothes and set off down the row toward the east where a burnished orange sun was rising. She thought that in the future any place she lived would have to have a clear view of the east.

Two weeks later in a not altogether pleasant room in a small hotel a block off Rue St. Jacques, Clare's view was a scant dozen feet in whatever direction, but the ceiling was high. The room was as close as she could get to the *pension* she had stayed in for three weeks thirty years before, and twenty times as expensive. She had had her walk in an August shower in her beret, without an umbrella, until she was quite wet, and then a coffee and calvados at Café de Flore, where she had overheard an American couple her age asking a waiter where Camus had sat. There are other pilgrims, she thought, without a trace of self-mockery. She read Guillevic and Sarraute in her room, reread Alain-Fournier's *The Wanderer* and planned a train trip into the countryside. In the café where she took her lunch every day she knew she was referred to as "the schoolteacher." This pleased her though it wasn't meant to.

On long walks in the overwarm city she had occasion to think of the cool breezes that came in the evening off Lake Michigan. If she had the whole thing to do over she would have done it differently, but then no one has anything to do over. Down near the end of the corn row a pickup truck passed and she hid as an old man turned off the irrigation for the soybean field which was tinged orange and glistened in the morning sun. She followed the path of the pickup to the back of a barn where there was a field of pigs with small, low-slung sheds in rows, and a smell that would take some time to get used to. She went through a gate into a barnyard where the old man had the hood up on his pickup and was tinkering. A collie mongrel rushed at her, barking, but Clare said a quiet hello and the dog wagged its tail. The old man looked at her without alarm and put his hands in his denim jacket.

"What can I do for you?"

"I've been misplaced. I'd like a cup of coffee."

"If it's coffee you want, we got coffee. You must be the woman we heard about all evening on the radio. You're supposed to be in a red car."

"I spent the night in your field." Her voice began to quiver.

"You had to get loose. The radio said he was beating on you."

The old man led her toward the porch where a very large old woman was standing with her arms crossed. "She looks just like Grandma, doesn't she, Ed?" she said. At the screen door with a tuft of cotton on it to keep away flies the old man nodded in assent.

Ed disappeared into the house and came back with an antique gold-leaf mirror with a photo portrait of a woman framed on the back of it. The woman wore a stiff-necked black dress and had an amazing resemblance to Clare who was momentarily disoriented.

"That picture was took in 1890," said the old woman.

"I suppose I should make some phone calls," Clare said.

Laurel arrived in two hours from Des Moines in a police car with a state trooper who talked farm prices and drank coffee with Ed while Laurel and Clare sat on a porch swing. Laurel had come down from Sioux Falls and spent the night in vigil with Donald in Des Moines. "I never thought you would do it," Laurel kept saying.

"How's Donald?"

"He's unhappy but he'll survive. He told the police you had a nervous breakdown, but I had them call Dr. Roth. You have to tell the trooper that he didn't abuse you within Iowa state lines."

"The poor thing," Clare said, and began to cry.

Clare spent a scant hour talking with Donald in a room at a Best Western motel in Des Moines. There was more than a trace of the vulnerability in him that she once had cherished. He wanted to put off any decision "in depth" until Clare "came to her senses," which is precisely what she thought he'd say. She sat next to her suitcase on the bed near the open window, as always. She couldn't help but notice the day's *Wall Street Journal* and a note pad covered with numbers on the nightstand. He was the same Donald, only paler, and she waited fearfully for some tremor to come, but it didn't. There were a few surprises.

"I can't say I didn't see this coming, but I hoped we'd carry on."

"I don't have anything left to carry on." It was so utterly painful to say it.

"Is it Dr. Roth?" He looked away when he asked this, as if fearing a blow.

"No. Don't be absurd. You were always more than enough."

"What about the house? What about everything, for God's sake?"

"I hope you'll look after everything. I don't care about the house. I want my books, but the house was Mother's idea." She found that she was three feet from her body again, but craving the immediacy of the thicket. What did fireflies do in the daytime? Perhaps Laurel would know.

"I had a good talk with Laurel last night. Per usual she told me what was wrong with me. When she was little she even told me how to shave. She said you were tired of the life you were living and wanted to do something else. Is it as simple as that?"

Clare looked up and saw that he had begun to cry, but it was Donald crying, not her father. She nodded yes, it was as simple as that. She got up and hugged him, and saw herself hugging him in the wall mirror, with a wave of claustrophobia sweeping through her body.

"We'll talk it over in October," she said, because that was what Laurel told her to say.

Laurel was dozing in the car and awoke with a start when her father put Clare's suitcase in the back seat. Laurel got out and began to cry which was so untypical that both Clare and Donald were nonplused, though it seemed Donald might have felt some subdued pleasure. They consoled Laurel, and it occurred to a couple driving up to the entrance that they were seeing a happy, if tearful, reunion.

In Paris at a newsstand Clare bought a *Rand McNally Road Atlas* of America. Due to the strength of the franc many prosperous French were visiting the States. In her room she spent a warm, humid afternoon looking at the locations that interested her, letting the maps bring back Zilpha, and Sammy sitting expectantly in the back seat waiting for a lunch break or a rest-stop stroll. Clare felt a little lost but then she always had, and supposed easily that it was the condition of life. Lying back on the bed, under the whir of the fan on the nightstand, she decided that she felt less lost than before her night in the thicket, and when the afternoon cooled she would write letters to Dr. Roth and Laurel. If it rained, she would wear her beret to dinner.

QUESTIONS FOR DISCUSSION AND WRITING

1. What are the functions of the following episodes in the plot: Clare's affair with Michael; meeting April; burying Sammy; and seeing the old picture of the woman who looks just like Clare?
2. How do Donald and Clare's possessions help define their characters—e.g., Donald's cellular car phone; Clare's bag (and its contents)?
3. Why does Clare feel more at home in the nest she builds in the cornfield in Iowa than in the house her mother purchased for her in the fashionable suburb of Detroit?
4. Why does Clare choose Laurel as her imaginary confidant during her night in the cornfield?
5. How might the story be read as an illustration of "Yeats's notion to the effect that life was a long preparation for something that never occurred"? What has Clare been trying to escape? Does she finally succeed? Explain your answer.

40

NATHANIEL HAWTHORNE

Young Goodman Brown

NATHANIEL HAWTHORNE (1804–1864) was born in Salem, Massachusetts, the descendant of a prominent Puritan family that included a judge at the Salem witchcraft trials. After graduating from Bowdoin College in 1825, Hawthorne returned to Salem to live a life of almost total seclusion for twelve years as he mastered his skills as a writer. His first novel, *Fanshawe* (1828), based on his experiences at Bowdoin, was an embarrassing failure, but he soon published enough stories in magazines to collect his first volume of stories, *Twice-Told Tales* (1837). The volume was a critical but not a

commercial success, so Hawthorne was forced to support himself working in the United States Custom House in Boston. He invested his savings in a communal experiment at Brook Farm, but soon withdrew from the community to marry and take up residence in Concord, Massachusetts, where he rented the "Old Manse," a house built by Ralph Waldo Emerson's grandfather. Another collection of stories, *Mosses from an Old Manse* (1846), was followed by his masterpiece, *The Scarlet Letter* (1850). The sales from this novel allowed him to move to the Berkshires in western Massachusetts, where he wrote two novels—*The House of the Seven Gables* (1851) and *The Blithedale Romance* (1852)—collected another volume of his stories, *The Snow-Image* (1852), and completed a campaign biography, *The Life of Franklin Pierce* (1852). When Pierce was elected president of the United States in 1852, Hawthorne was rewarded with a consulship first in England, and then in Italy. He returned to the United States in 1860 to live in Concord. "Young Goodman Brown," reprinted from *Mosses from an Old Manse,* tells of a young man's journey into the wilderness on a mysterious errand. "The Birthmark," from the same collection, explores the cost of man's attempt to transform earthly beauty into heavenly perfection. "Rappaccini's Daughter," also from *Mosses from an Old Manse,* dramatizes the conflict between love and science.

Young Goodman Brown came forth at sunset into the street at Salem village; but put his head back, after crossing the threshold, to exchange a parting kiss with his young wife. And Faith, as the wife was aptly named, thrust her own pretty head into the street, letting the wind play with the pink ribbons on her cap while she called to Goodman Brown.

"Dearest heart," whispered she, softly and rather sadly, when her lips were close to his ear, "prithee put off your journey until sunrise and sleep in your own bed to-night. A lone woman is troubled with such dreams and such thoughts that she's afeard of herself sometimes. Pray tarry with me this night, dear husband, of all nights in the year."

"My love and my Faith," replied young Goodman Brown, "of all nights in the year, this one night must I tarry away from thee. My journey, as thou callest it, forth and back again, must needs be done 'twixt now and sunrise. What, my sweet, pretty wife, dost thou doubt me already, and we but three months married?"

"Then God bless you!" said Faith, with the pink ribbons; "and may you find all well when you come back."

"Amen!" cried Goodman Brown. "Say thy prayers, dear Faith, and go to bed at dusk, and no harm will come to thee."

So they parted; and the young man pursued his way until, being about to turn the corner by the meeting-house, he looked back and saw the head of Faith still peeping after him with a melancholy air, in spite of her pink ribbons.

"Poor little Faith!" thought he, for his heart smote him. "What a wretch am I to leave her on such an errand! She talks of dreams, too. Methought as she spoke there was trouble in her face, as if a dream had warned her what work is to be done to-night. But no, no; 'twould kill her to think it. Well, she's a blessed angel on earth; and after this one night I'll cling to her skirts and follow her to heaven."

With this excellent resolve for the future, Goodman Brown felt himself justified in making more haste on his present evil purpose. He had taken a dreary road, darkened by all the gloomiest trees of the forest, which barely stood aside to let the narrow path creep through, and closed immediately behind. It was all as lonely as could be; and there is this peculiarity in such a solitude, that the traveller knows not who may be concealed by the innumerable trunks and the thick boughs overhead; so that with lonely footsteps he may yet be passing through an unseen multitude.

"There may be a devilish Indian behind every tree," said Goodman Brown to himself; and he glanced fearfully behind him as he added, "What if the devil himself should be at my very elbow!"

His head being turned back, he passed a crook of the road, and, looking forward again, beheld the figure of a man, in grave and decent attire, seated at the foot of an old tree. He arose at Goodman Brown's approach and walked onward side by side with him.

"You are late, Goodman Brown," said he. "The clock of the Old South was striking as I came through Boston, and that is full fifteen minutes agone."

"Faith kept me back a while," replied the young man, with a tremor in his voice, caused by the sudden appearance of his companion, though not wholly unexpected.

It was now deep dusk in the forest, and deepest in that part of it where these two were journeying. As nearly as could be discerned, the second traveller was about fifty years old, apparently in the same rank of life as Goodman Brown, and bearing a considerable resemblance to him, though perhaps more in expression than features. Still they might have been taken for father and son. And yet, though the elder person was as simply clad as the younger, and as simple in manner too, he had an indescribable air of one who knew the world, and who would not have felt abashed at the governor's dinner table or in King William's court, were it possible that his affairs should call him thither. But the only thing about him that could be fixed upon as remarkable was his staff, which bore the likeness of a great black snake, so curiously wrought that it might almost be seen to twist and wriggle itself like a living serpent. This, of course, must have been an ocular deception, assisted by the uncertain light.

"Come, Goodman Brown," cried his fellow-traveller, "this is a dull pace for the beginning of a journey. Take my staff, if you are so soon weary."

"Friend," said the other, exchanging his slow pace for a full stop, "having kept convenant by meeting thee here, it is my purpose now to return whence I came. I have scruples touching the matter thou wot'st of."

"Sayest thou so?" replied he of the serpent, smiling apart. "Let us walk on, nevertheless, reasoning as we go; and if I convince thee not thou shalt turn back. We are but a little way in the forest yet."

"Too far! too far!" exclaimed the goodman, unconsciously resuming his walk. "My father never went into the woods on such an errand, nor his father before him. We have been a race of honest men and good Christians since the days of the martyrs; and shall I be the first of the name of Brown that ever took this path and kept"—

"Such company, thou wouldst say," observed the elder person, interpreting his pause. "Well said, Goodman Brown! I have been as well acquainted with your family as with ever a one among the Puritans; and that's no trifle to say. I helped your grandfather, the constable, when he lashed the Quaker woman so smartly through the streets of Salem; and it was I that brought your father a pitch-pine knot, kindled at my own hearth, to set fire to an Indian village, in King Philip's war. They were my good friends, both; and many a pleasant walk have we had along this path, and returned merrily after midnight. I would fain be friends with you for their sake."

"If it be as thou sayest," replied Goodman Brown, "I marvel they never spoke of these matters; or, verily, I marvel not, seeing that the least rumor of the sort would have driven them from New England. We are a people of prayer, and good works to boot, and abide no such wickedness."

"Wickedness or not," said the traveller with the twisted staff, "I have a very general acquaintance here in New England. The deacons of many a church have drunk the communion wine with me; the selectmen of divers towns make me their chairman; and a majority of the Great and General Court are firm supporters of my interest. The governor and I, too— But these are state secrets."

"Can this be so?" cried Goodman Brown, with a stare of amazement at his undisturbed companion. "Howbeit, I have nothing to do with the governor and council; they have their own ways, and are no rule for a simple husbandman like me. But, were I to go on with thee, how should I meet the eye of that good old man, our minister, at Salem village? Oh, his voice would make me tremble both Sabbath day and lecture day."

Thus far the elder traveller had listened with due gravity; but now burst into a fit of irrepressible mirth, shaking himself so violently that his snake-like staff actually seemed to wriggle in sympathy.

"Ha! ha! ha!" shouted he again and again; then composing himself, "Well, go on, Goodman Brown, go on; but, prithee, don't kill me with laughing."

"Well, then, to end the matter at once," said Goodman Brown, considerably nettled, "there is my wife, Faith. It would break her dear little heart; and I'd rather break my own."

"Nay, if that be the case," answered the other, "e'en go thy ways, Goodman Brown. I would not for twenty old women like the one hobbling before us that Faith should come to any harm."

As he spoke he pointed his staff at a female figure on the path, in whom Goodman Brown recognized a very pious and exemplary dame, who had taught him his catechism in youth, and was still his moral and spiritual adviser, jointly with the minister and Deacon Gookin.

"A marvel, truly, that Goody Cloyse should be so far in the wilderness at nightfall," said he. "But with your leave, friend, I shall take a cut through the woods until we have left this Christian woman behind. Being a stranger to you, she might ask whom I was consorting with and whither I was going."

"Be it so," said his fellow-traveller. "Betake you to the woods, and let me keep the path."

Accordingly the young man turned aside, but took care to watch his companion, who advanced softly along the road until he had come within a staff's length of the old dame. She, meanwhile, was making the best of her way, with singular speed for so aged a woman, and mumbling some indistinct words—a prayer, doubtless—as she went. The traveller put forth his staff and touched her withered neck with what seemed the serpent's tail.

"The devil!" screamed the pious old lady.

"Then Goody Cloyse knows her old friend?" observed the traveller, confronting her and leaning on his writhing stick.

"Ah, forsooth, and is it your worship indeed?" cried the good dame. "Yes, truly is it, and in the very image of my old gossip, Goodman Brown, the grandfather of the silly fellow that now is. But—would your worship believe it?—my broomstick hath strangely disappeared, stolen, as I suspect, by that unhanged witch, Goody Cory, and that, too, when I was all anointed with the juice of smallage, and cinquefoil, and wolf's bane"—

"Mingled with fine wheat and the fat of a new-born babe," said the shape of old Goodman Brown.

"Oh, your worship knows the recipe," cried the old lady, cackling aloud. "So, as I was saying, being all ready for the meeting, and no horse to ride on, I made up my mind to foot it, for they tell me there is a nice young man to be taken into communion tonight. But now your good worship will lend me your arm, and we shall be there in a twinkling."

"That can hardly be," answered her friend. "I may not spare you my arm, Goody Cloyse; but here is my staff, if you will."

So saying, he threw it down at her feet, where, perhaps, it assumed life, being one of the rods which its owner had formerly lent to the Egyptian magi. Of this fact, however, Goodman Brown can not take cognizance. He had cast up his eyes in astonishment, and, looking down again, beheld neither Goody Cloyse nor the serpentine staff, but his fellow-traveller alone, who waited for him as calmly as if nothing had happened.

"That old woman taught me my catechism," said the young man; and there was a world of meaning in this simple comment.

They continued to walk onward, while the elder traveller exhorted his companion to make good speed and persevere in the path, discoursing so aptly that his arguments seemed rather to spring up in the bosom of his auditor than to be suggested by himself. As they went, he plucked a branch of maple to serve for a walking stick, and began to strip it of the twigs and little boughs, which were wet with evening dew. The moment his fingers touched them they became strangely withered and dried up as with a week's sunshine. Thus the pair proceeded, at a good free pace, until suddenly, in a gloomy hollow of the road, Goodman Brown sat himself down on the stump of a tree and refused to go any farther.

"Friend," said he, stubbornly, "my mind is made up. Not another step will I budge on this errand. What if a wretched old woman do choose to go to the devil when I thought she was going to heaven: is that any reason why I should quit my dear Faith and go after her?"

"You will think better of this by and by," said his acquaintance, composedly. "Sit here and rest yourself a while; and when you feel like moving again, there is my staff to help you along."

Without words, he threw his companion the maple stick, and was as speedily out of sight as if he had vanished into the deepening gloom. The young man sat a few moments by the roadside, applauding himself greatly, and thinking with how clear a conscience he should meet the minister in his morning walk, nor shrink from the eye of good old Deacon Gookin. And what calm sleep would be his that very night, which was to have been spent so wickedly, but so purely and sweetly now, in the arms of Faith! Amidst these pleasant and praiseworthy meditations, Goodman Brown heard the tramp of horses along the road, and deemed it advisable to conceal himself within the verge of the forest, conscious of the guilty purpose that had brought him thither, though now so happily turned from it.

On came the hoof tramps and the voices of the riders, two grave old voices, conversing soberly as they drew near. These mingled sounds appeared to pass along the road, within a few yards of the young man's hiding-place; but, owing doubtless to the depth of the gloom at that particular spot, neither the travellers nor their steeds were visible. Though their figures brushed the small boughs by the wayside, it could not be seen that they intercepted, even for a moment; the faint gleam from the strip of bright sky athwart which they must have passed. Goodman Brown alternately crouched and stood on tiptoe, pulling aside the branches and thrusting forth his head as far as he durst without discerning so much as a shadow. It vexed him the more, because he could have sworn, were such a thing possible, that he recognized the voices of the minister and Deacon Gookin, jogging along quietly, as they were wont to do, when bound to some ordination or ecclesiastical council. While yet within hearing one of the riders stopped to pluck a switch.

"Of the two, reverend sir," said the voice like the deacon's, "I had rather miss an ordination dinner than to-night's meeting. They tell me that some of our community are to be here from Falmouth and beyond, and others from Connecticut and Rhode Island besides several of Indian powwows, who, after their fashion, know almost as much deviltry as the best of us. Moreover, there is a goodly young woman to be taken into communion."

"Mighty well, Deacon Gookin!" replied the solemn old tones of the minister. "Spur up, or we shall be late. Nothing can be done you know until I get on the ground."

The hoofs clattered again; and the voices, talking so strangely in the empty air, passed on through the forest, where no church had ever been gathered or solitary Christian prayed. Whither, then, could these holy men be journeying so deep into the heathen wilderness? Young Goodman Brown caught hold of a tree for support, being ready to sink down on the ground, faint and overburdened with the heavy sickness of his heart. He looked up to the sky, doubting whether there really was a heaven above him. Yet there was the blue arch, and the stars brightening in it.

"With heaven above and Faith below, I will yet stand firm against the devil!" cried Goodman Brown.

While he still gazed upward into the deep arch of the firmament and had lifted his hands to pray, a cloud, though no wind was stirring, hurried across the zenith and hid the brightening stars. The blue sky was still visible, except directly overhead, where this black mass of cloud was sweeping swiftly northward. Aloft in the air, as if from the depths of the cloud, came a confused and doubtful sound of voices. Once the listener fancied that he could distinguish the accents of townspeople of his own, men, and women, both pious and ungodly, many of whom he had met at the communion table, and had seen others rioting at the tavern. The next moment, so indistinct were the sounds, he doubted whether he had heard aught but the murmur of the old forest, whispering without a wind. Then came a stronger swell of those familiar tones, heard daily in the sunshine at Salem village, but never until now from a cloud of night. There was one voice of a young woman uttering lamentations, yet with an uncertain sorrow, and entreating for some favor, which perhaps, it would grieve her to obtain; and all the unseen multitude, both saints and sinners, seemed to encourage her onward.

"Faith!" shouted Goodman Brown, in a voice of agony and desperation; and the echoes of the forest mocked him, crying, "Faith! Faith!" as if bewildered wretches were seeking her all through the wilderness.

The cry of grief, rage, and terror was yet piercing the night, when the unhappy husband held his breath for a response. There was a scream, drowned immediately in a loud murmur of voices, fading into far-off laughter, as the dark cloud swept away, leaving the clear and silent sky above Goodman Brown. But something fluttered lightly down through the air and caught on the branch of a tree. The young man seized it, and beheld a pink ribbon.

"My Faith is gone!" cried he, after one stupefied moment. "There is no good on earth; and sin is but a name. Come, devil; for to thee is this world given."

And, maddened with despair, so that he laughed loud and long, did Goodman Brown grasp his staff and set forth again, at such a rate that he seemed to fly along the forest path rather than to walk or run. The road grew wilder and drearier and more faintly traced, and vanished at length, leaving him in the heart of the dark wilderness, still rushing onward with the instinct that guides mortal man to evil. The whole forest was peopled with frightful sounds—the creaking of the trees, the howling of wild beasts, and the yells of Indians; while sometimes the wind tolled like a distant church bell, and sometimes gave a broad roar around the traveller, as if all Nature were laughing him to scorn. But he was himself the chief horror of the scene, and shrank not from its other horrors.

"Ha! ha! ha!" roared Goodman Brown when the wind laughed at him. "Let us hear which will laugh loudest. Think not to frighten me with your deviltry. Come witch, come wizard, come Indian powwow, come devil himself, and here comes Goodman Brown. You may as well fear him as he fear you."

In truth, all through the haunted forest there could be nothing more frightful than the figure of Goodman Brown. On he flew among the black pines, brandishing his staff with frenzied gestures, now giving vent to an inspiration of horrid blasphemy, and now shouting forth such laughter as set all the echoes of the forest laughing like demons around him. The fiend in his own shape is less hideous than when he rages in the breast of man. Thus sped the demoniac on his course, until, quivering among the trees, he saw a red light before him, as when the felled trunks and branches of a clearing have been set on fire, and throw up their lurid blaze against the sky, at the hour of midnight. He paused, in a lull of the tempest that had driven him onward, and heard the swell of what seemed a hymn, rolling solemnly from a distance with the weight of many voices. He knew the tune; it was a familiar one in the choir of the village meeting-house. The verse died heavily away, and was lengthened by a chorus, not of human voices, but of all the sounds of the benighted wilderness pealing in awful harmony together. Goodman Brown cried out, and his cry was lost to his own ear by its unison with the cry of the desert.

In the interval of silence he stole forward until the light glared full upon his eyes. At one extremity of an open space, hemmed in by the dark wall of the forest, arose a rock, bearing some rude, natural resemblance either to an altar or a pulpit, and surrounded by four blazing pines, their tops aflame, their stems untouched, like candles at an evening meeting. The mass of foliage that had overgrown the summit of the rock was all on fire, blazing into the night and fitfully illuminating the whole field. Each pendant twig and leafy festoon was in a blaze. As the red light arose and fell, a numerous congregation alternately shone forth, then disappeared in shadow, and again grew, as it were, out of the darkness, peopling the heart of the solitary woods at once.

"A grave and dark-clad company," quoth Goodman Brown.

In truth they were such. Among them, quivering to and fro between gloom and splendor, appeared faces that would be seen next day at the council board of the province, and others which, Sabbath after Sabbath, looked devoutly heavenward, and benignantly over the crowded pews, from the holiest pulpits in the land. Some affirm that the lady of the governor was there. At least there were high dames well known to her, and wives of honored husbands, and widows, a great multitude, and ancient maidens, all of excellent repute, and fair young girls, who trembled lest their mothers should espy them. Either the sudden gleams of light flashing over the obscure field bedazzled Goodman Brown, or he recognized a score of the church members of Salem village famous for their special sanctity. Good old Deacon Gookin had arrived, and waited at the skirts of that venerable saint, his revered pastor. But, irreverently consorting with these grave, reputable, and pious people, these elders of the church, these chaste dames and dewy virgins, there were men of dissolute lives and women of spotted fame, wretches given over to all mean and filthy vice, and suspected even of horrid crimes. It was strange to see that the good shrank not from the wicked, nor were the sinners abashed by the saints. Scattered also among their pale-faced enemies were the Indian priests, or powwows, who had often scared their native forest with more hideous incantations than any known to English witchcraft.

"But where is Faith?" thought Goodman Brown; and, as hope came into his heart, he trembled.

Another verse of the hymn arose, a slow and mournful strain, such as the pious love, but joined to words which expressed all that our nature can conceive of sin, and darkly hinted at far more. Unfathomable to mere mortals is the lore of fiends. Verse after verse was sung; and still the chorus of the desert swelled between like the deepest tone of a mighty organ; and with the final peal of that dreadful anthem there came a sound, as if the roaring wind, the rushing streams, the howling beasts, and every other voice of the unconcerted wilderness were mingling and according with the voice of guilty man in homage to the prince of all. The four blazing pines threw up a loftier flame, and obscurely discovered shapes and visages of horror on the smoke wreaths above the impious assembly. At the same moment the fire on the rock shot redly forth and formed a glowing arch above its base, where now appeared a figure. With reverence be it spoken, the figure bore no slight similitude, both in garb and manner, to some grave divine of the New England churches.

"Bring forth the converts!" cried a voice that echoed through the field and rolled into the forest.

At the word, Goodman Brown stepped forth from the shadow of the trees and approached the congregation, with whom he felt a loathful brotherhood by the sympathy of all that was wicked in his heart. He could have well-nigh sworn that the shape of his own dead father beckoned him to advance, looking downward from a smoke wreath, while a woman, with dim features of despair, threw out her hand to warn him back. Was it his mother? But he had no power to retreat one step, nor to resist, even in thought, when the minister and good old Deacon Gookin seized his arms and led him to the blazing rock. Thither came also the slender form of a veiled female, led between Goody Cloyse, that pious teacher of the catechism, and Martha Carrier, who had received the devil's promise to be queen of hell. A rampant hag was she. And there stood the proselytes beneath the canopy of fire.

"Welcome, my children," said the dark figure, "to the communion of your race. Ye have found thus young your nature and your destiny. My children, look behind you!"

They turned; and flashing forth, as it were, in a sheet of flame, the fiend worshippers were seen; the smile of welcome gleamed darkly on every visage.

"There," resumed the sable form, "are all whom ye have reverenced from youth. Ye deemed them holier than yourself, and shrank from your own sins, contrasting it with their lives of righteousness and prayerful aspirations heavenward. Yet here are they all in my worshipping assembly. This night it shall be granted you to know their secret deeds: how hoary-bearded elders of the church have whispered wanton words to the young maids of their households; how many a woman, eager for widows' weeds, has given her husband a drink at bedtime and let him sleep his last sleep in her bosom; how beardless youths have made haste to inherit their fathers' wealth, and how fair damsels—blush not, sweet ones—have dug little graves in the garden, and bidden me, the sole guest to an infant's funeral. By the sympathy of your human hearts for sin ye shall scent out all the places—whether in church, bed-chamber, street, field, or forest—where crime has been committed, and shall exult to behold the whole earth one stain of guilt, one mighty blood spot. Far more than this. It shall be yours to penetrate, in every bosom, the deep mystery of sin, the fountain of all wicked arts, and which inexhaustibly supplies more evil impulses than human power—than my power at its utmost—can make manifest in deeds. And now, my children, look upon each other."

They did so; and, by the blaze of the hell-kindled torches, the wretched man beheld his Faith, and the wife her husband, trembling before that unhallowed altar.

"Lo, there ye stand, my children," said the figure, in a deep and solemn tone, almost sad with its despairing awfulness, as if his once angelic nature could yet mourn for our miserable race. "Depending upon one another's hearts, ye had still hoped that virtue were not all a dream. Now are ye undeceived. Evil is the nature of mankind. Evil must be your only happiness. Welcome again, my children, to the communion of your race."

"Welcome," repeated the fiend worshippers, in one cry of despair and triumph.

And there they stood, the only pair, as it seemed, who were yet hesitating on the verge of wickedness in this dark world. A basin was hollowed, naturally, in the rock. Did it contain water, reddened by the lurid light? or was it blood? or, perchance, a liquid flame? Herein did the shape of evil dip his hand and prepare to lay the mark of baptism upon their foreheads, that they might be partakers of the mystery of sin, more conscious of the secret guilt of others, both in deed and thought, than they could now be of their own. The husband cast one look at his pale wife, and Faith at him. What polluted wretches would the next glance show them to each other, shuddering alike at what they disclosed and what they saw!

"Faith! Faith!" cried the husband, "look up to heaven, and resist the wicked one."

Whether Faith obeyed he knew not. Hardly had he spoken when he found himself amid calm night and solitude, listening to a roar of the wind which died heavily away through the forest. He staggered against the rock, and felt it chill and damp; while a hanging twig, that had been all on fire, besprinkled his cheek with the coldest dew.

The next morning young Goodman Brown came slowly into the street of Salem village, staring around him like a bewildered man. The good old minister was taking a walk along the graveyard to get an appetite for breakfast and meditate his sermon, and bestowed a blessing, as he passed, on Goodman Brown. He shrank from the venerable saint as if to avoid an anathema. Old Deacon Gookin was at domestic worship, and the holy words of his prayer were heard through the open window. "What God does the wizard pray to?" quoth Goodman Brown. Goody Cloyse, that excellent old Christian, stood in the early sunshine at her own lattice, catechizing a little girl who had brought her a pint of morning's milk. Goodman Brown snatched away the child as from the grasp of the fiend himself. Turning the corner by the meeting-house, he spied the head of Faith, with the pink ribbons, gazing anxiously forth, and bursting into such joy at sight of him that she skipped along the street and almost kissed her husband before the whole village. But Goodman Brown looked sternly and sadly into her face, and passed on without a greeting.

Had Goodman Brown fallen asleep in the forest and only dreamed a wild dream of a witch-meeting?

Be it so if you will; but, alas! it was a dream of evil omen for young Goodman Brown. A stern, a sad, a darkly meditative, a distrustful, if not a desperate man did he become from the night of that fearful dream. On the Sabbath day, when the congregation were singing a holy psalm, he could not listen because an anthem of sin rushed loudly upon his ears and drowned all the blessed strain. When the minister spoke from the pulpit with power and fervid eloquence, and, with his hand on the open Bible, of the sacred truths of our religion, and of saint-like lives and triumphant death and of future bliss or misery unutterable, then did Goodman Brown turn pale, dreading lest the roof should thunder down upon the gray blasphemer and his hearers. Often, waking suddenly at midnight, he shrank from the bosom of Faith; and at morning or eventide, when the family knelt down at prayer, he scowled and muttered to himself, and gazed sternly at his wife, and turned away. And when he had lived long, and was borne to his grave a hoary corpse, followed by Faith, an aged woman, and children and grandchildren, a goodly procession, besides neighbors not a few, they carved no hopeful verse upon his tombstone, for his dying hour was gloom.

QUESTIONS FOR DISCUSSION AND WRITING

1. What is significant about the order in which Brown meets the people in the woods? What is the greatest danger he faces? Does the denouement suggest that he has escaped that danger? Explain your answer.
2. In what ways do the names *Young Goodman Brown* and *Faith* characterize the young couple? How does Hawthorne's assertion that "the fiend in his own shape is less hideous than when he rages in the breast of man" characterize the devil?
3. Why is the forest an appropriate setting for Brown's journey? How does Brown perceive the setting of the town? How does that perception change after his night in the woods?

4. How does Hawthorne's omniscient point of view help establish the dreamlike quality of the story? Does it finally matter, from Brown's point of view, whether he attended or merely dreamed about the meeting of the witches?

5. What is the theme of the devil's sermon? In what sense do the final three paragraphs of the story demonstrate that the devil was right?

41

NATHANIEL HAWTHORNE
The Birthmark

In the latter part of the last century there lived a man of science, an eminent proficient in every branch of natural philosophy, who not long before our story opens had made experience of a spiritual affinity more attractive than any chemical one. He had left his laboratory to the care of an assistant, cleared his fine countenance from the furnace smoke, washed the stain of acids from his fingers, and persuaded a beautiful woman to become his wife. In those days when the comparatively recent discovery of electricity and other kindred mysteries of Nature seemed to open paths into the region of miracle, it was not unusual for the love of science to rival the love of woman in its depth and absorbing energy. The higher intellect, the imagination, the spirit, and even the heart might all find their congenial aliment in pursuits which, as some of their ardent votaries believed, would ascend from one step of powerful intelligence to another, until the philosopher should lay his hand on the secret of creative force and perhaps make new worlds for himself. We know not whether Aylmer possessed this degree of faith in man's ultimate control over Nature. He had devoted himself, however, too unreservedly to scientific studies ever to be weaned from them by any second passion. His love for his young wife might prove the stronger of the two; but it could only be by intertwining itself with his love of science, and uniting the strength of the latter to his own.

Such a union accordingly took place, and was attended with truly remarkable consequences and a deeply impressive moral. One day, very soon after their marriage, Aylmer sat gazing at his wife with a trouble in his countenance that grew stronger until he spoke.

"Georgiana," said he, "has it never occurred to you that the mark upon your cheek might be removed?"

"No, indeed," said she, smiling; but perceiving the seriousness of his manner, she blushed deeply. "To tell you the truth it has been so often called a charm that I was simple enough to imagine it might be so."

"Ah, upon another face perhaps it might," replied her husband; "but never on yours. No, dearest Georgiana, you came so nearly perfect from the hand of Nature that this slightest possible defect, which we hestitate whether to term a defect or a beauty, shocks me, as being the visible mark of earthly imperfection."

"Shocks you, my husband!" cried Georgiana, deeply hurt; at first reddening with momentary anger, but then bursting into tears. "Then why did you take me from my mother's side? You cannot love what shocks you!"

To explain this conversation it must be mentioned that in the centre of Georgiana's left cheek there was a singular mark, deeply interwoven, as it were, with the texture and substance of her face. In the usual state of her complexion—a healthy though delicate bloom—the mark wore a tint of deeper crimson, which imperfectly defined its shape amid the surrounding rosiness. When she blushed it gradually became more indistinct, and finally vanished amid the triumphant rush of blood that bathed the whole cheek with its brilliant glow. But if any shifting motion caused her to turn pale there was the mark again, a crimson stain upon the snow, in which Aylmer sometimes deemed an almost fearful distinctness. Its shape bore not a little similarity to the human hand, though of the smallest pygmy size. Georgiana's loves were wont to say that some fairy at her birth hour had laid her tiny hand upon the infant's cheek, and left this impress there in token of the magic endowments that were to give her such sway over all hearts. Many a desperate swain would have risked life for the privilege of pressing his lips to the mysterious hand. It must not be concealed, however, that the impression wrought by this fairy sign manual varied exceedingly, according to the difference of temperament in the beholders. Some fastidious persons—but they were exclusively of her own sex—affirmed that the bloody hand, as they chose to call it, quite destroyed the effect of Georgiana's beauty, and rendered her countenance even hideous. But it would be as reasonable to say that one of those small blue stains which sometimes occur in the purest statuary marble would convert the Eve of Powers to a monster. Masculine observers, if the birthmark did not heighten their admiration, contented themselves with wishing it away, that the world might possess one living specimen of ideal loveliness without the semblance of a flaw. After his marriage—for he thought little or nothing of the matter before—Aylmer discovered that this was the case with himself.

Had she been less beautiful—if Envy's self could have found aught else to sneer at—he might have felt his affection heightened by the prettiness of this mimic hand, now vaguely portrayed, now lost, now stealing forth again and glimmering to and fro with every pulse of emotion that throbbed within her heart; but seeing her otherwise so perfect, he found this one defect grow more and more intolerable with every moment of their united lives. It was the fatal flaw of humanity which Nature, in one shape or another, stamps ineffaceably on all her productions, either to imply that they are temporary and finite, or that their perfection must be wrought by toil and pain. The crimson hand expressed the ineludible grip in which mortality clutches the highest and purest of earthly mould, degrading them into kindred with the lowest, and even with the very brutes, like whom their visible frames return to dust. In this manner, selecting it as the symbol of his wife's liability to sin, sorrow, decay, and death, Aylmer's sombre imagination was not long in rendering the birthmark a frightful object, causing him more trouble and horror than ever Georgiana's beauty, whether of soul or sense, had given him delight.

At all the seasons which should have been their happiest, he invariably and without intending it, nay, in spite of a purpose to the contrary, reverted to this one disastrous topic. Trifling as it at first appeared, it so connected itself with innumerable trains of thought and modes of feeling that it became the central point of all. With the morning twilight Aylmer opened his eyes upon his wife's face and recognized the symbol of imperfection; and when they sat together at the evening hearth his eyes wandered stealthily to her cheek, and beheld, flickering with the blaze of the wood fire, the spectral hand that wrote mortality where he would fain have worshipped. Georgiana soon learned to shudder at his gaze. It needed but a glance with the peculiar expression that his face often wore to change the roses of her cheek into a deathlike paleness, amid which the crimson hand was brought strongly out, like bas-relief of ruby on the whitest marble.

Late one night when the lights were growing dim, so as hardly to betray the stain on the poor wife's cheek, she herself, for the first time, voluntarily took up the subject.

"Do you remember, my dear Aylmer," said she, with a feeble attempt at a smile, "have you any recollection of a dream last night about this odious hand?"

"None! none whatever!" replied Aylmer, starting; but then he added, in a dry, cold tone, affected for the sake of concealing the real depth of his emotion, "I might well dream of it; for before I fell asleep it had taken a pretty firm hold of my fancy."

"And you did dream of it?" continued Georgiana, hastily; for she dreaded lest a gush of tears should interrupt what she had to say. "A terrible dream! I wonder that you can forget it. Is it possible to forget this one expression?—'It is in her heart now; we must have it out!' Reflect, my husband; for by all means I would have you recall that dream."

The mind is in a sad state when Sleep, the all-involving, cannot confine her spectres within the dim region of her sway, but suffers them to break forth, affrighting this actual life with secrets that perchance belong to a deeper one. Aylmer now remembered his dream. He had fancied himself with his servant Aminadab, attempting an operation for the removal of the birthmark; but the deeper went the knife, the deeper sank the hand, until at length its tiny grasp appeared to have caught hold of Georgiana's heart; whence, however, her husband was inexorably resolved to cut or wrench it away.

When the dream had shaped itself perfectly in his memory, Aylmer sat in his wife's presence with a guilty feeling. Truth often finds its way to the mind close muffled in robes of sleep, and then speaks with uncompromising directness of matters in regard to which we practise an unconscious self-deception during our waking moments. Until now he had not been aware of the tyrannizing influence acquired by one idea over his mind, and of the lengths which he might find in his heart to go for the sake of giving himself peace.

"Aylmer," resumed Georgiana, solemnly, "I know not what may be the cost to both of us to rid me of this fatal birthmark. Perhaps its removal may cause cureless deformity; or it may be the stain goes as deep as life itself. Again: do we know that there is a possibility, on any terms, of unclasping the firm grip of this little hand which was laid upon me before I came into the world?"

"Dearest Georgiana, I have spent much thought upon the subject," hastily interrupted Aylmer. "I am convinced of the perfect practicability of its removal."

"If there be the remotest possibility of it," continued Georgiana, "let the attempt be made at whatever risk. Danger is nothing to me; for life, while this hateful mark makes me the object of your horror and disgust—life is a burden which I would fling down with joy. Either remove this dreadful hand, or take my wretched life! You have deep science. All the world bears witness of it. You have achieved great wonders. Cannot you remove this little, little mark, which I cover with the tips of two small fingers? Is this beyond your power, for the sake of your own peace, and to save your poor wife from madness?"

"Noblest, dearest, tenderest wife," cried Aylmer, rapturously, "doubt not my power. I have already given this matter the deepest thought—thought which might almost have enlightened me to create a being less perfect than yourself. Georgiana, you have led deeper than ever into the heart of science. I feel myself fully competent to render this dear cheek as faultless as its fellow; and then, most beloved, what will be my triumph when I shall have corrected what Nature left imperfect in her fairest work! Even Pygmalion, when his scupltured woman assumed life, felt not greater ecstasy than mine will be."

"It is resolved, then," said Georgiana, faintly smiling. "And, Aylmer, spare me not, though you should find the birthmark take refuge in my heart at last."

Her husband tenderly kissed her cheek—her right cheek—not that which bore the impress of the crimson hand.

The next day Aylmer apprised his wife of a plan that he had formed whereby he might have opportunity for the intense thought and constant watchfulness which the proposed operation would require; while Georgiana, likewise, would enjoy the perfect repose essential to its success. They were to seclude themselves in the extensive apartments occupied by Aylmer as a laboratory, and where, during his toilsome youth, he had made discoveries in the elemental powers of Nature that had roused the admiration of all the learned societies in Europe. Seated calmly in this laboratory, the pale philosopher had investigated the secrets of the highest cloud region and of the profoundest mines; he had satisfied himself of the causes that kindled and kept alive the fires of the volcano; and had explained the mystery of the fountains, and how it is that they gush forth, some so bright and pure, and others with such rich medicinal virtues, from the dark bosom of the earth. Here, too, at an earlier period, he had studied the wonders of the human frame, and attempted to fathom the very process by which Nature assimilates all her precious influences from earth and air, and from the spiritual world, to create and foster man, her masterpiece. The latter pursuit, however, Aylmer had long laid aside in unwilling recognition of the truth—against which all seekers sooner or later stumble—that our great creative Mother, while she amuses us with apparently working in the broadest sunshine, is yet severely careful to keep her own secrets, and, in spite of her pretended openness, shows us nothing but results. She permits us, indeed, to mar, but seldom to mend, and, like a jealous patentee, on no account to make. Now, however, Aylmer resumed these half-forgotten investigations; not, of course, with such hopes or wishes as first suggested them; but because they involved much physiological truth and lay in the path of his proposed scheme for the treatment of Georgiana.

As he led her over the threshold of the laboratory, Georgiana was cold and tremulous. Aylmer looked cheerfully into her face, with intent to reassure her, but was so startled with the intense glow of the birthmark upon the whiteness of her cheek that he could not restrain a strong convulsive shudder. His wife fainted.

"Aminadab! Aminadab!" shouted Aylmer, stamping violently on the floor.

Forthwith there issued from an inner apartment a man of low stature, but bulky frame, with shaggy hair hanging about his visage, which was grimed with the vapors of the furnace. This personage had been Aylmer's underworker during his whole scientific career, and was admirably fitted for that office by his great mechanical readiness, and the skill with which, while incapable of comprehending a single principle, he executed all the details of his master's experiments. With his vast strength, his shaggy hair, his smoky aspect, and the indescribable earthiness that incrusted him, he seemed to represent man's physical nature; while Aylmer's slender figure, and pale, intellectual face, were no less apt a type of the spiritual element.

"Throw open the door of the boudoir, Aminadab," said Aylmer, "and burn a pastil."

"Yes, master," answered Aminadab, looking intently at the lifeless form of Georgiana; and then he muttered to himself, "If she were my wife, I'd never part with that birthmark."

When Georgiana recovered consciousness she found herself breathing an atmosphere of penetrating fragrance, the gentle potency of which had recalled her from her deathlike faintness. The scene around her looked like enchantment. Aylmer had converted those smoky, dingy, sombre rooms, where he had spent his brightest years in recondite pursuits, into a series of beautiful apartments not unfit to be the secluded abode of a lovely woman. The walls were hung with gorgeous curtains, which imparted the combination of grandeur and grace that no other species of adornment can achieve; and as they fell from the ceiling to the floor, their rich and ponderous folds, concealing all angles and straight lines, appeared to shut in the scene from infinite space. For aught Georgiana knew, it might be a pavilion among the clouds. And Aylmer, excluding the sunshine, which would have interfered with his chemical processes, had supplied its place with perfumed lamps, emitting flames of various hue, but all uniting in a soft, impurpled radiance. He now knelt by his wife's side, watching her earnestly, but without alarm; for he was confident in his science, and felt that he could draw a magic circle round her within which no evil might intrude.

"Where am I? Ah, I remember," said Georgiana, faintly; and she placed her hand over her cheek to hide the terrible mark from her husband's eyes.

"Fear not, dearest!"exclaimed he. "Do not shrink from me! Believe me, Georgiana, I even rejoice in this single imperfection, since it will be such a rapture to remove it."

"Oh, spare me!" sadly replied his wife. "Pray do not look at it again. I never can forget that convulsive shudder."

In order to soothe Georgiana, and, as it were, to release her mind from the burden of actual things, Aylmer now put in practice some of the light and playful secrets which science had taught him among its profounder lore. Airy figures, absolutely bodiless ideas, and forms of unsubstantial beauty came and danced before her, imprinting their momentary footsteps on beams of light. Though she had some indistinct idea of the method of these optical phenomena, still the illusion was almost perfect enough to warrant the belief that her husband possessed sway over the spiritual world. Then again, when she felt a wish to look forth from her seclusion, immediately, as if her thoughts were answered, the procession of external existence flitted across a screen. The scenery and the figures of actual life were perfectly represented, but with that bewitching, yet indescribable difference which always makes a picture, an image, or a shadow so much more attractive than the original. When wearied of this Aylmer bade her cast her eyes upon a vessel containing a quantity of earth. She did so, with little interest at first; but was soon startled to perceive the germ of a plant shooting upward from the soil. Then came the slender stalk; the leaves gradually unfolded themselves; and amid them was a perfect and lovely flower.

"It is magical!" cried Georgiana. "I dare not touch it."

"Nay, pluck it," answered Aylmer,—"pluck it, and inhale its brief perfume while you may. The flower will wither in a few moments and leave nothing save its brown seed vessels; but thence may be perpetuated a race as ephemeral as itself."

But Georgiana had no sooner touched the flower than the whole plant suffered a blight, its leaves turning coal-black as if by the agency of fire.

"There was too powerful a stimulus," said Aylmer, thoughtfully.

To make up for this abortive experiment, he proposed to take her portrait by a scientific process of his own invention. It was to be effected by rays of light striking upon a polished plate of metal. Georgiana assented; but, on looking at the result, was affrighted to find the features of the portrait blurred and indefinable; while the minute figure of a hand appeared where the cheek should have been. Aylmer snatched the metallic plate and threw it into a jar of corrosive acid.

Soon, however, he forgot these mortifying failures. In the intervals of study and chemical experiment he came to her flushed and exhausted, but seemed invigorated by her presence, and spoke in glowing language of the resources of his art. He gave a history of the long dynasty of the alchemists, who spent so many ages in quest of the universal solvent by which the golden principle might be elicited from all things vile and base. Aylmer appeared to believe that, by the plainest scientific logic, it was altogether within the limits of possibility to discover this long-sought medium; "but," he added, "a philosopher who should go deep enough to acquire the power would attain too lofty a wisdom to stoop to the exercise of it." Not less singular were his opinions in regard to the elixir vitæ. He more than intimated that it was at his option to concoct a liquid that should prolong life for years, perhaps interminably; but that it would produce a discord in Nature which all the world, and chiefly the quaffer of the immortal nostrum, would find cause to curse.

"Aylmer, are you in earnest?" asked Georgiana, looking at him with amazement and fear. "It is terrible to possess such power, or even to dream of possessing it."

"Oh, do not tremble, my love," said her husband. "I would not wrong either you or myself by working such inharmonious effects upon our lives; but I would have you consider how trifling, in comparison, is the skill requisite to remove this little hand."

At the mention of the birthmark, Georgiana, as usual, shrank as if a redhot iron had touched her cheek.

Again Aylmer applied himself to his labors. She could hear his voice in the distant furnace room giving directions to Aminadab, whose harsh, uncouth, misshapen tones were audible in response, more like the grunt or growl of a brute than human speech. After hours of absence, Aylmer reappeared and proposed that she should now examine his cabinet of chemical products and natural treasures of the earth. Among the former he showed her a small vial, in which, he remarked, was contained a gentle yet most powerful fragrance, capable of impregnating all the breezes that blow across a kingdom. They were of inestimable value, the contents of that little vial; and, as he said so, he threw some of the perfume into the air and filled the room with piercing and invigorating delight.

"And what is this?" asked Georgiana, pointing to a small crystal globe containing a gold-colored liquid. "It is so beautiful to the eye that I could imagine it the elixir of life."

"In one sense it is," replied Aylmer; "or, rather, the elixir of immortality. It is the most precious poison that ever was concocted in this world. By its aid I could apportion the lifetime of any mortal at whom you might point your finger. The strength of the dose would determine whether he were to linger out years, or drop dead in the midst of a breath. No king on his guarded throne could keep his life if I, in my private station, should deem that the welfare of millions justified me in depriving him of it."

"Why do you keep such a terrific drug?" inquired Georgiana in horror.

"Do not mistrust me, dearest," said her husband, smiling; "its virtuous potency is yet greater than its harmful one. But see! here is a powerful cosmetic. With a few drops of this in a vase of water, freckles may be washed away as easily as the hands are cleansed. A stronger infusion would take the blood out of the cheek, and leave the rosiest beauty a pale ghost."

"Is it with this lotion that you intend to bathe my cheek?" asked Georgiana anxiously.

"Oh, no," hastily replied her husband; "this is merely superficial. Your case demands a remedy that shall go deeper."

In his interviews with Georgiana, Aylmer generally made minute inquiries as to her sensations and whether the confinement of the rooms and the temperature of the atmosphere agreed with her. These questions had such a particular drift that Georgiana began to conjecture that she was already subjected to certain physical influences, either breathed in with the fragrant air or taken with her food. She fancied likewise, but it might be altogether fancy, that there was a stirring up of her system—a strange, indefinite sensation creeping through her veins, and tingling, half painfully, half pleasurably, at her heart. Still, whenever she dared to look into the mirror, there she beheld herself pale as a white rose and with the crimson birthmark stamped upon her cheek. Not even Aylmer now hated it so much as she.

To dispel the tedium of the hours which her husband found it necessary to devote to the processes of combination and analysis, Georgiana turned over the volumes of his scientific library. In many dark old tomes she met with chapters full of romance and poetry. They were the work of philosophers of the middle ages, such as Albertus Magnus, Cornelius Agrippa, Paracelsus, and the famous friar who created the prophetic Brazen Head. All these antique naturalists stood in advance of their centuries, yet were imbued with some of their credulity, and therefore were believed, and perhaps imagined themselves to have acquired from the investigation of Nature a power above Nature, and from physics a sway over the spiritual world. Hardly less curious and imaginative were the early volumes of the Transactions of the Royal Society, in which the members, knowing little of the limits of natural possibility, were continually recording wonders or proposing methods whereby wonders might be wrought.

But to Georgiana the most engrossing volume was a large folio from her husband's own hand, in which he had recorded every experiment of his scientific career, its original aim, the methods adopted for its development, and its final success or failure, with the circumstances to which either event was attributable. The book, in truth, was both the history and emblem of his ardent, ambitious, imaginative, yet practical and laborious life.

He handled physical details as if there were nothing beyond them; yet spiritualized them all, and redeemed himself from materialism by his strong and eager aspiration towards the infinite. In his grasp the veriest clod of earth assumed a soul. Georgiana, as she read, reverenced Aylmer and loved him more profoundly than ever, but with a less entire dependence on his judgment than heretofore. Much as he had accomplished, she could not but observe that his most splendid successes were almost invariably failures, if compared with the ideal at which he aimed. His brightest diamonds were the merest pebbles, and felt to be so by himself, in comparison with the inestimable gems which lay hidden beyond his reach. The volume, rich with achievements that had won renown for its author, was yet as melancholy a record as ever mortal hand had penned. It was the sad confession and continual exemplification of the shortcomings of the composite man, the spirit burdened with clay and working in matter, and of the despair that assails the higher nature at finding itself so miserably thwarted by the earthly part. Perhaps every man of genius in whatever sphere might recognize the image of his own experience in Aylmer's journal.

So deeply did these reflections affect Georgiana that she laid her face upon the open volume and burst into tears. In this situation she was found by her husband.

"It is dangerous to read in a sorcerer's books," said he with a smile, though his countenance was uneasy and displeased. "Georgiana, there are pages in that volume which I can scarcely glance over and keep my senses. Take heed lest it prove as detrimental to you."

"It has made me worship you more than ever," said she.

"Ah, wait for this one success," rejoined he, "then worship me if you will. I shall deem myself hardly unworthy of it. But come, I have sought you for the luxury of your voice. Sing to me, dearest."

So she poured out the liquid music of her voice to quench the thirst of his spirit. He then took his leave with a boyish exuberance of gayety, assuring her that her seclusion would endure but a little longer, and that the result was already certain. Scarcely had he departed when Georgiana felt irresistibly impelled to follow him. She had forgotten to inform Aylmer of a symptom which for two or three hours past had begun to excite her attention. It was a sensation in the fatal birthmark, not painful, but which induced a restlessness throughout her system. Hastening after her husband, she intruded for the first time into the laboratory.

The first thing that struck her eye was the furnace, that hot and feverish worker, with the intense glow of its fire, which by the quantities of soot clustered above it seemed to have been burning for ages. There was a distilling apparatus in full operation. Around the room were retorts, tubes, cylinders, crucibles, and other apparatus of chemical research. An electrical machine stood ready for immediate use. The atmosphere felt oppressively close, and was tainted with gaseous odors which had been tormented forth by the processes of science. The severe and homely simplicity of the apartment, with its naked walls and brick pavement, looked strange, accustomed as Georgiana had become to the fantastic elegance of her boudoir. But what chiefly, indeed almost solely, drew her attention, was the aspect of Aylmer himself.

He was pale as death, anxious and absorbed, and hung over the furnace as if it depended upon his utmost watchfulness whether the liquid which it was distilling should be the draught of immortal happiness or misery. How different from the sanguine and joyous mien that he had assumed for Georgiana's encouragement!

"Carefully now, Aminadab; carefully, thou human machine; carefully, thou man of clay!" muttered Aylmer, more to himself than his assistant. "Now if there be a thought too much or too little, it is all over."

"Ho! ho!" mumbled Aminadab. "Look, master! look!"

Aylmer raised his eyes hastily, and at first reddened, then grew paler than ever, on beholding Georgiana. He rushed towards her and seized her arm with a grip that left the print of his fingers upon it.

"Why do you come hither? Have you no trust in your husband?" cried he, impetuously. "Would you throw the blight of that fatal birthmark over my labors? It is not well done. Go, prying woman, go!"

"Nay, Aylmer," said Georgiana with the firmness of which she possessed no stinted endowment, "it is not you that have a right to complain. You mistrust your wife; you have concealed the anxiety with which you watch the development of this experiment. Think not so unworthily of me, my husband. Tell me all the risk we run, and fear not that I shall shrink; for my share in it is far less than your own."

"No, no, Georgiana!" said Aylmer, impatiently; "it must not be."

"I submit," replied she calmly. "And, Aylmer, I shall quaff whatever draught you bring me; but it will be on the same principle that would induce me to take a dose of poison if offered by your hand."

"My noble wife," said Aylmer, deeply moved, "I knew not the height and depth of your nature until now. Nothing shall be concealed. Know, then, that this crimson hand, superficial as it seems, has clutched its grasp into your being with a strength of which I had no previous conception. I have already administered agents powerful enough to do aught except to change your entire physical system. Only one thing remains to be tried. If that fails us we are ruined."

"Why did you hesitate to tell me this?" asked she.

"Because, Georgiana," said Aylmer, in a low voice, "there is danger."

"Danger? There is but one danger—that this horrible stigma shall be left upon my cheek!" cried Georgiana. "Remove it, remove it, whatever be the cost, or we shall both go mad!"

"Heaven knows your words are too true," said Aylmer, sadly. "And now, dearest, return to your boudoir. In a little while all will be tested."

He conducted her back and took leave of her with a solemn tenderness which spoke far more than his words how much was now at stake. After his departure, Georgiana became rapt in musings. She considered the character of Aylmer, and did it completer justice than at any previous moment. Her heart exulted, while it trembled, at his honorable love—so pure and lofty that it would accept nothing less than perfection nor miserably make itself contented with an earthlier nature than he had dreamed of. She felt how much more precious was such a sentiment than that meaner kind which would have borne with the imperfection for her sake, and have been guilty of treason to holy love by degrading its perfect idea to the level of the actual; and with her whole spirit she prayed that, for a single moment, she might satisfy his highest and deepest conception. Longer than one moment she well knew it could not be; for his spirit was ever on the march, ever ascending, and each instant required something that was beyond the scope of the instant before.

The sound of her husband's footsteps aroused her. He bore a crystal goblet containing a liquor colorless as water, but bright enough to be the draught of immortality. Aylmer was pale; but it seemed rather the consequence of a highly-wrought state of mind and tension of spirit than fear or doubt.

"The concoction of the draught has been perfect," said he, in answer to Georgiana's look. "Unless all my science have deceived me, it cannot fail."

"Save on your account, my dearest Aylmer," observed his wife, "I might wish to put off this birthmark of mortality by relinquishing mortality itself in preference to any other mode. Life is but a sad possession to those who have attained precisely the degree of moral advancement at which I stand. Were I weaker and blinder it might be happiness. Were I stronger, it might be endured hopefully. But being what I find myself, methinks I am of all mortals the most fit to die."

"You are fit for heaven without tasting death!" replied her husband. "But why do we speak of dying? The draught cannot fail. Behold its effect upon this plant."

On the window seat there stood a geranium diseased with yellow blotches, which had overspread all its leaves. Aylmer poured a small quantity of the liquid upon the soil in which it grew. In a little time, when the roots of the plant had taken up the moisture, the unsightly blotches began to be extinguished in a living verdure.

"There needed no proof," said Georgiana, quietly. "Give me the goblet. I joyfully stake all upon your word."

"Drink, then, thou lofty creature!" exclaimed Aylmer, with fervid admiration. "There is no taint of imperfection on thy spirit. Thy sensible frame, too, shall soon be all perfect."

She quaffed the liquid and returned the goblet to his hand.

"It is grateful," said she with a placid smile. "Methinks it is like water from a heavenly fountain; for it contains I know not what of unobtrusive fragrance and deliciousness. It allays a feverish thirst that had parched me for many days. Now, dearest, let me sleep. My earthly senses are closing over my spirit like the leaves around the heart of a rose at sunset."

She spoke the last words with a gentle reluctance, as if it required almost more energy than she could command to pronounce the faint and lingering syllables. Scarcely had they loitered through her lips ere she was lost in slumber. Aylmer sat by her side, watching her aspect with the emotions proper to a man the whole value of whose existence was involved in the process now to be tested. Mingled with this mood, however, was the philosophic investigation characteristic of the man of science. Not the minutest symptom escaped him. A heightened flush of the cheek, a slight irregularity of breath, a quiver of the eyelid, a hardly perceptible tremor through the frame—such were the details which, as the moments passed, he wrote down in his folio volume. Intense thought had set its stamp upon every previous page of that volume, but the thoughts of years were all concentrated upon the last.

While thus employed, he failed not to gaze often at the fatal hand, and not without a shudder. Yet once, by a strange and unaccountable impulse, he pressed it with his lips. His spirit recoiled, however, in the very act; and Georgiana, out of the midst of her deep sleep, moved uneasily and murmured as if in remonstrance. Again Aylmer resumed his watch. Nor was it without avail. The crimson hand, which at first had been strongly visible upon the marble paleness of Georgiana's cheek, now grew more faintly outlined. She remained not less pale than ever; but the birthmark, with every breath that came and went, lost somewhat of its former distinctness. Its presence had been awful; its departure was more awful still. Watch the stain of the rainbow fading out the sky, and you will know how the mysterious symbol passed away.

"By Heaven! it is well-nigh gone!" said Aylmer to himself, in almost irrepressible ecstasy. "I can scarcely trace it now. Success! success! And now it is like the faintest rose color. The lightest flush of blood across her cheek would overcome it. But she is so pale!"

He drew aside the window curtain and suffered the light of natural day to fall into the room and rest upon her cheek. At the same time he heard a gross, hoarse chuckle, which he had long known as his servant Aminadab's expression of delight.

"Ah, clod! ah, earthly mass!" cried Aylmer, laughing in a sort of frenzy, "you have served me well! Matter and spirit—earth and heaven—have both done their part in this! Laugh, thing of the senses! You have earned the right to laugh."

These exclamations broke Georgiana's sleep. She slowly unclosed her eyes and gazed into the mirror which her husband had arranged for that purpose. A faint smile flitted over her lips when she recognized how barely perceptible was now that crimson hand which had once blazed forth with such disastrous brilliancy as to scare away all their happiness. But then her eyes sought Aylmer's face with a trouble and anxiety that he could by no means account for.

"My poor Aylmer!" murmured she.

"Poor? Nay, richest, happiest, most favored!" exclaimed he. "My peerless bride, it is successful! You are perfect!"

"My poor Aylmer," she repeated, with a more than human tenderness, "you have aimed loftily; you have done nobly. Do not repent that with so high and pure a feeling, you have rejected the best the earth could offer. Aylmer, dearest Aylmer, I am dying!"

Alas! it was too true! the fatal hand had grappled with the mystery of life, and was the bond by which an angelic spirit kept itself in union with a mortal frame. As the last crimson tint of the birthmark—that sole token of human imperfection—faded from her cheek, the parting breath of the now perfect woman passed into the atmosphere, and her soul, lingering a moment near her husband, took its heavenward flight. Then a hoarse, chuckling laugh was heard again! Thus ever does the gross fatality of earth exult in its invariable triumph over the immortal essence which, in this dim sphere of half development, demands the completeness of a higher state. Yet, had Aylmer reached a profounder wisdom, he need not thus have flung away the happiness which would have woven his mortal life of the selfsame texture with the celestial. The momentary circumstance was too strong for him; he failed to look beyond the shadowy scope of time, and, living once for all in eternity, to find the perfect future in the present.

QUESTIONS FOR DISCUSSION AND WRITING

1. In what sense does the story represent a conflict between the love of science and the love of a woman? How does Aylmer's dream foreshadow the resolution of that conflict?

2. How do Georgiana's, Aylmer's, and Aminadab's reactions to the birthmark help to characterize them? In what sense does each character represent one of the following functions—head, heart, and body? Explain your answer.
3. What is the significant difference between Georgiana's chamber and Aylmer's laboratory? Why can't the experiment be conducted in a more ordinary or natural setting?
4. How does Hawthorne use the opening and closing paragraphs of the story to establish his point of view toward the events he narrates?
5. What do Aylmer's journals suggest about man's attempt to solve the mysteries of nature? What does Hawthorne think Aylmer has learned as the result of his attempt to erase his wife's birthmark?

42

NATHANIEL HAWTHORNE

Rappaccini's Daughter

FROM THE WRITINGS OF AUBEPINE

We do not remember to have seen any translated specimens of the productions of M. de l'Aubépine; a fact the less to be wondered at, as his very name is unknown to many of his own countrymen, as well as to the student of foreign literature. As a writer, he seems to occupy an unfortunate position between the Transcendentalists (who, under one name or another, have their share in all the current literature of the world), and the great body of pen-and-ink men who address the intellect and sympathies of the multitude. If not too refined, at all events too remote, too shadowy and unsubstantial in his modes of development, to suit the taste of the latter class, and yet too popular to satisfy the spiritual or metaphysical requisitions of the former, he must necessarily find himself without an audience; except here and there an individual, or possibly an isolated clique. His writings, to do them justice, are not altogether destitute of fancy and originality; they might have won him greater reputation but for an inveterate love of allegory, which is apt to invest his plots and characters with the aspect of scenery and people in the clouds, and to steal away the human warmth out of his conceptions. His fictions are sometimes historical, sometimes of the present day, and sometimes, so far as can be discovered, have little or no reference either to time or space. In any case, he generally contents himself with a very slight embroidery of outward manners,—the faintest possible counterfeit of real life,—and endeavors to create an interest by some less obvious peculiarity of the subject. Occasionally, a breath of nature, a rain-drop of pathos and tenderness, or a gleam of humor, will find its way into the midst of his fantastic imagery, and make us feel as if, after all, we were yet within the limits of our native earth. We will only add to this very cursory notice, that M. de l'Aubépine's productions, if the reader chance to take them in precisely the proper point of view, may amuse a leisure hour as well as those of a brighter man; if otherwise, they can hardly fail to look excessively like nonsense.

Our author is voluminous; he continues to write and publish with as much praiseworthy and indefatigable prolixity, as if his efforts were crowned with the brilliant success that so justly attends those of Eugene Sue. His first appearance was by a collection of stories, in a long series of volumes, entitled "*Contes deux fois racontées.*" The titles of some of his more recent works (we quote from memory) are as follows:—"*Le Voyage Céleste à Chemin de Fer,*" 3 tom. 1838. "*Le nouveau Père Adam et la nouvelle Mère Eve,*" 2 tom. 1839. "*Roderic; ou le Serpent à l'estomac,*" 2 tom. 1840. "*Le Culte du Feu,*" a folio volume of ponderous research into the religion and ritual of the old Persian Ghebers, published in 1841. "*La Soirée du Chateau en Espagne,*" 1 tom. 8vo. 1842; and "*L'Artiste du Beau; ou le Papillon Mécanique,*" 5 tom. 4to. 1843. Our somewhat wearisome perusal of this startling catalogue of volumes has left behind it a certain personal affection and sympathy, though by no means admiration, for M. de l'Aubépine; and we would fain do the little in our power towards introducing him favorably to the American public. The ensuing tale is a translation of his "*Beatrice; ou la Belle Empoisonneuse,*" recently published in "*La Revue Anti-Aristocratique.*" This journal, edited by the Comte de Bearhaven, has, for some years past, led the defence of liberal principles and popular rights, with a faithfulness and ability worthy of all praise.

A young man, named Giovanni Guasconti, came, very long ago, from the more southern region of Italy, to pursue his studies at the University of Padua. Giovanni, who had but a scanty supply of gold ducats in his pocket, took lodgings in a high and gloomy chamber of an old edifice, which looked not unworthy to have been the palace of a Paduan noble, and which, in fact, exhibited over its entrance the armorial bearings of a family long since extinct. The young stranger, who was not unstudied in the great poem of his country, recollected that one of the ancestors of this family, and perhaps an occupant of this very mansion, had been pictured by Dante as a partaker of the immortal agonies of his Inferno. These reminiscences and associations, together with the tendency to heart-break natural to a young man for the first time out of his native sphere, caused Giovanni to sigh heavily, as he looked around the desolate and ill-furnished apartment.

"Holy Virgin, Signor," cried old dame Lisabetta, who, won by the youth's remarkable beauty of person, was kindly endeavoring to give the chamber a habitable air, "what a sigh was that to come out of a young man's heart! Do you find this old mansion gloomy? For the love of heaven, then, put your head out of the window, and you will see as bright sunshine as you have left in Naples."

Guasconti mechanically did as the old woman advised, but could not quite agree with her that the Paduan sunshine was as cheerful as that of southern Italy. Such as it was, however, it fell upon a garden beneath the window, and expended its fostering influences on a variety of plants, which seemed to have been cultivated with exceeding care.

"Does this garden belong to the house?" asked Giovanni.

"Heaven forbid, Signor!—unless it were fruitful of better pot-herbs than any that grow there now," answered old Lisabetta. "No; that garden is cultivated by the own hands of Signor Giacomo Rappaccini, the famous Doctor, who, I warrant him, has been heard of as far as Naples. It is said that he distils these plants into medicines that are as potent as a charm. Oftentimes you may see the Signor Doctor at work, and perchance the Signora his daughter, too, gathering the strange flowers that grow in the garden."

The old woman had now done what she could for the aspect of the chamber, and, commending the young man to the protection of the saints, took her departure.

Giovanni still found no better occupation than to look down into the garden beneath his window. From its appearance, he judged it to be one of those botanic gardens, which were of earlier date in Padua than elsewhere in Italy, or in the world. Or, not improbably, it might once have been the pleasure-place of an opulent family; for there was the ruin of a marble fountain in the centre, sculptured with rare art, but so wofully shattered that it was impossible to trace the original design from the chaos of remaining fragments. The water, however, continued to gush and sparkle into the sunbeams as cheerfully as ever. A little gurgling sound ascended to the young man's window, and made him feel as if the fountain were an immortal spirit, that sung its song unceasingly, and without heeding the vicissitudes around it; while one century embodied it in marble, and another scattered the perishable garniture on the soil. All about the pool into which the water subsided, grew various plants, that seemed to require a plentiful supply of moisture for the nourishment of gigantic leaves, and, in some instances, flowers gorgeously magnificent. There was one shrub in particular, set in a marble vase in the midst of the pool, that bore a profusion of purple blossoms, each of which had the lustre and richness of a gem; and the whole together made a show so resplendent that it seemed enough to illuminate the garden, even had there been no sunshine. Every portion of the soil was peopled with plants and herbs, which, if less beautiful, still bore tokens of assiduous care; as if all had their individual virtues, known to the scientific mind that fostered them. Some were placed in urns, rich with old carving, and others in common garden-pots; some crept serpent-like along the ground, or climbed on high, using whatever means of ascent was offered them. One plant had wreathed itself round a statue of Vertumnus, which was thus quite veiled and shrouded in a drapery of hanging foliage, so happily arranged that it might have served a sculptor for a study.

While Giovanni stood at the window, he heard a rustling behind a screen of leaves, and became aware that a person was at work in the garden. His figure soon emerged into view, and showed itself to be that of no common laborer, but a tall, emaciated, sallow, and sickly-looking man, dressed in a scholar's garb of black. He was beyond the middle term of life, with grey hair, a thin grey beard, and a face singularly marked with intellect and cultivation, but which could never, even in his more youthful days, have expressed much warmth of heart.

Nothing could exceed the intentness with which this scientific gardener examined every shrub which grew in his path; it seemed as if he was looking into their inmost nature, making observations in regard to their creative essence, and discovering why one leaf grew in this shape, and another in that, and wherefore such and such flowers differed among themselves in hue and perfume. Nevertheless, in spite of this deep intelligence on his part, there was no approach to intimacy between himself and these vegetable existences. On the contrary, he avoided their actual touch, or the direct inhaling of their odors, with a caution that impressed Giovanni most disagreeably; for the man's demeanor was that of one walking among malignant influences, such as savage beasts, or deadly snakes, or evil spirits, which, should he allow them one moment of license, would wreak upon him some terrible fatality. It was strangely frightful to the young man's imagination, to see this air of insecurity in a person cultivating a garden, that most simple and innocent of human toils, and which had been alike the joy and labor of the unfallen parents of the race. Was this garden, then, the Eden of the present world?—and this man, with such a perception of harm in what his own hands caused to grow, was he the Adam?

The distrustful gardener, while plucking away the dead leaves or pruning the too luxuriant growth of the shrubs, defended his hands with a pair of thick gloves. Nor were these his only armor. When, in his walk through the garden, he came to the magnificent plant that hung its purple gems beside the marble fountain, he placed a kind of mask over his mouth and nostrils, as if all this beauty did but conceal a deadlier malice. But finding his task still too dangerous, he drew back, removed the mask, and called loudly, but in the infirm voice of a person affected with inward disease:

"Beatrice!—Beatrice!"

"Here am I, my father! What would you?" cried a rich and youthful voice from the window of the opposite house; a voice as rich as a tropical sunset, and which made Giovanni, though he knew not why, think of deep hues of purple or crimson, and of perfumes heavily delectable.—"Are you in the garden?"

"Yes, Beatrice," answered the gardener, "and I need your help."

Soon there emerged from under a sculptured portal the figure of a young girl, arrayed with as much richness of taste as the most splendid of the flowers, beautiful as the day, and with a bloom so deep and vivid that one shade more would have been too much. She looked redundant with life, health, and energy; all of which attributes were bound down and compressed, as it were, and girdled tensely, in their luxuriance, by her virgin zone. Yet Giovanni's fancy must have grown morbid, while he looked down into the garden; for the impression which the fair stranger made upon him was as if here were another flower, the human sister of those vegetable ones, as beautiful as they—more beautiful than the richest of them—but still to be touched only with a glove, nor to be approached without a mask. As Beatrice came down the garden path, it was observable that she handled and inhaled the odor of several of the plants, which her father had most sedulously avoided.

"Here, Beatrice," said the latter,—"see how many needful offices require to be done to our chief treasure. Yet, shattered as I am, my life might pay the penalty of approaching it so closely as circumstances demand. Henceforth, I fear, this plant must be consigned to your sole charge."

"And gladly will I undertake it," cried again the rich tones of the young lady, as she bent towards the magnificent plant, and opened her arms as if to embrace it. "Yes, my sister, my splendor, it shall be Beatrice's task to nurse and serve thee; and thou shalt reward her with thy kisses and perfumed breath, which to her is as the breath of life!"

Then, with all the tenderness in her manner that was so strikingly expressed in her words, she busied herself with such attentions as the plant seemed to require; and Giovanni, at his lofty window, rubbed his eyes, and almost doubted whether it were a girl tending her favorite flower, or one sister performing the duties of affection to another. The scene soon terminated. Whether Doctor Rappaccini had finished his labors in the garden, or that his watchful eye had caught the stranger's face, he now took his daughter's arm and retired. Night was already closing in; oppressive exhalations seemed to proceed from the plants, and steal upward past the open window; and Giovanni, closing the lattice, went to his couch, and dreamed of a rich flower and beautiful girl. Flower and maiden were different and yet the same, and fraught with some strange peril in either shape.

But there is an influence in the light of morning that tends to rectify whatever errors of fancy, or even of judgment, we may have incurred during the sun's decline, or among the shadows of the night, or in the less wholesome glow of moonshine. Giovanni's first movement on starting from sleep, was to throw open the window, and gaze down into the garden which his dreams had made so fertile of mysteries. He was surprised, and a little ashamed, to find how real and matter-of-fact an affair it proved to be, in the first rays of the sun, which gilded the dewdrops that hung upon leaf and blossom, and, while giving a brighter beauty to each rare flower, brought everything within the limits of ordinary experience. The young man rejoiced, that, in the heart of the barren city, he had the privilege of overlooking this spot of lovely and luxuriant vegetation. It would serve, he said to himself, as a symbolic language, to keep him in communion with Nature. Neither the sickly and thought-worn Doctor Giacomo Rappaccini, it is true, nor his brilliant daughter, were now visible; so that Giovanni could not determine how much of the singularity which he attributed to both, was due to their own qualities, and how much to his wonder-working fancy. But he was inclined to take a most rational view of the whole matter.

In the course of the day, he paid his respects to Signor Pietro Baglioni, professor of medicine in the University, a physician of eminent repute, to whom Giovanni had brought a letter of introduction. The Professor was an elderly personage, apparently of genial nature, and habits that might almost be called jovial; he kept the young man to dinner, and made himself very agreeable by the freedom and liveliness of his conversation, especially when warmed by a flask or two of Tuscan wine. Giovanni, conceiving that men of science, inhabitants of the same city, must needs be on familiar terms with one another, took an opportunity to mention the name of Doctor Rappaccini. But the Professor did not respond with so much cordiality as he had anticipated.

"Ill would it become a teacher of the divine art of medicine," said Professor Pietro Baglioni, in answer to a question of Giovanni, "to withhold due and well-considered praise of a physician so eminently skilled as Rappaccini. But, on the other hand, I should answer it but scantily to my conscience, were I to permit a worthy youth like yourself, Signor Giovanni, the son of an ancient friend, to imbibe erroneous ideas respecting a man who might hereafter chance to hold your life and death in his hands. The truth is, our worshipful Doctor Rappaccini has as much science as any member of the faculty—with perhaps one single exception—in Padua, or all Italy. But there are certain grave objections to his professional character."

"And what are they?" asked the young man.

"Has my friend Giovanni any disease of body or heart, that he is so inquisitive about physicians?" said the Professor, with a smile. "But as for Rappaccini, it is said of him—and I, who know the man well, can answer for its truth—that he cares infinitely more for science than for mankind. His patients are interesting to him only as subjects for some new experiment. He would sacrifice human life, his own among the rest, or whatever else was dearest to him, for the sake of adding so much as a grain of mustard-seed to the great heap of his accumulated knowledge."

"Methinks he is an awful man, indeed," remarked Guasconti, mentally recalling the cold and purely intellectual aspect of Rappaccini. "And yet, worshipful Professor, is it not a noble spirit? Are there many men capable of so spiritual a love of science?"

"God forbid," answered the Professor, somewhat testily—"at least, unless they take sounder views of the healing art than those adopted by Rappaccini. It is his theory, that all medicinal virtues are comprised within those substances which we term vegetable poisons. These he cultivates with his own hands, and is said even to have produced new varieties of poison, more horribly deleterious than Nature, without the assistance of this learned person, would ever have plagued the world withal. That the Signor Doctor does less mischief than might be expected, with such dangerous substances, is undeniable. Now and then, it must be owned, he has effected—or seemed to effect—a marvellous cure. But, to tell you my private mind, Signor Giovanni, he should receive little credit for such instances of success—they being probably the work of chance—but should be held strictly accountable for his failures, which may justly be considered his own work."

The youth might have taken Baglioni's opinions with many grains of allowance, had he known that there was a professional warfare of long continuance between him and Doctor Rappaccini, in which the latter was generally thought to have gained the advantage. If the reader be inclined to judge for himself, we refer him to certain black-letter tracts on both sides, preserved in the medical department of the University of Padua.

"I know not, most learned Professor," returned Giovanni, after musing on what had been said of Rappaccini's exclusive zeal for science—"I know not how dearly this physician may love his art; but surely there is one object more dear to him. He has a daughter."

"Aha!" cried the Professor with a laugh. "So now our friend Giovanni's secret is out. You have heard of this daughter, whom all the young men in Padua are wild about, though not half a dozen have ever had the good hap to see her face. I know little of the Signora Beatrice, save that Rappaccini is said to have instructed her deeply in his science, and that, young and beautiful as fame reports her, she is already qualified to fill a professor's chair. Perchance her father destines her for mine! Other absurd rumors there be, not worth talking about, or listening to. So now, Signor Giovanni, drink off your glass of Lacryma."

Guasconti returned to his lodgings somewhat heated with the wine he had quaffed, and which caused his brain to swim with strange fantasies in reference to Doctor Rappaccini and the beautiful Beatrice. On his way, happening to pass by a florist's, he bought a fresh bouquet of flowers.

Ascending to his chamber, he seated himself near the window, but within the shadow thrown by the depth of the wall, so that he could look down into the garden with little risk of being discovered. All beneath his eye was a solitude. The strange plants were basking in the sunshine, and now and then nodding gently to one another, as if in acknowledgment of sympathy and kindred. In the midst, by the shattered fountain, grew the magnificent shrub, with its purple gems clustering all over it; they glowed in the air, and gleamed back again out of the depths of the pool, which thus seemed to overflow with colored radiance from the rich reflection that was steeped in it. At first, as we have said, the garden was a solitude. Soon, however,—as Giovanni had half-hoped, half-feared, would be the case,—a figure appeared beneath the antique sculptured portal, and came down between the rows of plants, inhaling their various perfumes, as if she were one of those beings of old classic fable, that lived upon sweet odors. On again beholding Beatrice, the young man was even startled to perceive how much her beauty exceeded his recollection of it; so brilliant, so vivid was its character, that she glowed amid the sunlight, and, as Giovanni whispered to himself, positively illuminated the more shadowy intervals of the garden path. Her face being now more revealed than on the former occasion, he was struck by its expression of simplicity and sweetness; qualities that had not entered into his idea of her character, and which made him ask anew, what manner of mortal she might be. Nor did he fail again to observe, or imagine, an analogy between the beautiful girl and the gorgeous shrub that hung its gem-like flowers over the fountain; a resemblance which Beatrice seemed to have indulged a fantastic humor in heightening, both by the arrangement of her dress and the selection of its hues.

Approaching the shrub, she threw open her arms, as with a passionate ardor, and drew its branches into an intimate embrace; so intimate, that her features were hidden in its leafy bosom, and her glistening ringlets all intermingled with the flowers.

"Give me thy breath, my sister," exclaimed Beatrice; "for I am faint with common air! And give me this flower of thine, which I separate with gentlest fingers from the stem, and place it close beside my heart."

With these words, the beautiful daughter of Rappaccini plucked one of the richest blossoms of the shrub, and was about to fasten it in her bosom. But now, unless Giovanni's draughts of wine had bewildered his senses, a singular incident occurred. A small orange-colored reptile, of the lizard or chameleon species, chanced to be creeping along the path, just at the feet of Beatrice. It appeared to Giovanni—but, at the distance from which he gazed, he could scarcely have seen anything so minute—it appeared to him, however, that a drop or two of moisture from the broken stem of the flower descended upon the lizard's head. For an instant, the reptile contorted itself violently, and then lay motionless in the sunshine. Beatrice observed this remarkable phenomenon, and crossed herself, sadly, but without surprise; nor did she therefore hesitate to arrange the fatal flower in her bosom. There it blushed, and almost glimmered with the dazzling effect of a precious stone, adding to her dress and aspect the one appropriate charm, which nothing else in the world could have supplied. But Giovanni, out of the shadow of his window, bent forward and shrank back, and murmured and trembled.

"Am I awake? Have I my senses?" said he to himself. "What is this being?—beautiful, shall I call her?—or inexpressibly terrible?"

Beatrice now strayed carelessly through the garden, approaching closer beneath Giovanni's window, so that he was compelled to thrust his head quite out of its concealment in order to gratify the intense and painful curiosity which she excited. At this moment, there came a beautiful insect over the garden wall; it had perhaps wandered through the city and found no flowers nor verdure among those antique haunts of men, until the heavy perfumes of Doctor Rappaccini's shrubs had lured it from afar. Without alighting on the flowers, this winged brightness seemed to be attracted by Beatrice, and lingered in the air and fluttered about her head. Now, here it could not be but that Giovanni Guasconti's eyes deceived him. Be that as it might, he fancied that while Beatrice was gazing at the insect with childish delight, it grew faint and fell at her feet;—its bright wings shivered; it was dead—from no cause that he could discern, unless it were the atmosphere of her breath. Again Beatrice crossed herself and sighed heavily, as she bent over the dead insect.

An impulsive movement of Giovanni drew her eyes to the window. There she beheld the beautiful head of the young man—rather a Grecian than an Italian head, with fair, regular features, and a glistening of gold among his ringlets—gazing down upon her like a being that hovered in mid-air. Scarcely knowing what he did, Giovanni threw down the bouquet which he had hitherto held in his hand.

"Signora," said he, "there are pure and healthful flowers. Wear them for the sake of Giovanni Guasconti!"

"Thanks, Signor," replied Beatrice, with her rich voice, that came forth as it were like a gush of music; and with a mirthful expression half childish and half woman-like. "I accept your gift, and would fain recompense it with this precious purple flower; but if I toss it into the air, it will not reach you. So Signor Guasconti must even content himself with my thanks."

She lifted the bouquet from the ground, and then as if inwardly ashamed at having stepped aside from her maidenly reserve to respond to a stranger's greeting, passed swiftly homeward through the garden. But, few as the moments were, it seemed to Giovanni when she was on the point of vanishing beneath the sculptured portal, that his beautiful bouquet was already beginning to wither in her grasp. It was an idle thought; there could be no possibility of distinguishing a faded flower from a fresh one at so great a distance.

For many days after this incident, the young man avoided the window that looked into Doctor Rappaccini's garden, as if something ugly and monstrous would have blasted his eye-sight, had he been betrayed into a glance. He felt conscious of having put himself, to a certain extent, within the influence of an unintelligible power, by the communication which he had opened with Beatrice. The wisest course would have been, if his heart were in any real danger, to quit his lodgings and Padua itself, at once; the next wiser, to have accustomed himself, as far as possible, to the familiar and day-light view of Beatrice; thus bringing her rigidly and systematically within the limits of ordinary experience. Least of all, while avoiding her sight, ought Giovanni to have remained so near this extraordinary being, that the proximity and possibility even of intercourse, should give a kind of substance and reality to the wild vagaries which his imagination ran riot continually in producing. Guasconti had not a deep heart—or at all events, its depths were not sounded now—but he had a quick fancy, and an ardent southern temperament, which rose every instant to a higher fever-pitch. Whether or no Beatrice possessed those terrible attributes—that fatal breath—the affinity with those so beautiful and deadly flowers—which were indicated by what Giovanni had witnessed, she had at least instilled a fierce and subtle poison into his system. It was not love, although her rich beauty was a madness to him; nor horror, even while he fancied her spirit to be imbued with the same baneful essence that seemed to pervade her physical frame; but a wild offspring of both love and horror that had each parent in it, and burned like one and shivered like the other. Giovanni knew not what to dread; still less did he know what to hope; yet hope and dread kept a continual warfare in his breast, alternately vanquishing one another and starting up afresh to renew the contest. Blessed are all simple emotions, be they dark or bright! It is the lurid intermixture of the two that produces the illuminating blaze of the infernal regions.

Sometimes he endeavored to assuage the fever of his spirit by a rapid walk through the streets of Padua, or beyond its gates; his footsteps kept time with the throbbings of his brain, so that the walk was apt to accelerate itself to a race. One day, he found himself arrested; his arm was seized by a portly personage who had turned back on recognizing the young man, and expended much breath in overtaking him.

"Signor Giovanni!—stay, my young friend!" cried he. "Have you forgotten me? That might well be the case, if I were as much altered as yourself."

It was Baglioni, whom Giovanni had avoided, ever since their first meeting, from a doubt that the Professor's sagacity would look too deeply into his secrets. Endeavoring to recover himself, he stared forth wildly from his inner world into the outer one, and spoke like a man in a dream:

"Yes; I am Giovanni Guasconti. You are Professor Pietro Baglioni. Now let me pass!"

"Not yet—not yet, Signor Giovanni Guasconti," said the Professor, smiling, but at the same time scrutinizing the youth with an earnest glance—"What; did I grow up side by side with your father, and shall his son pass me like a stranger, in these old streets of Padua? Stand still, Signor Giovanni; for we must have a word or two, before we part."

"Speedily, then, most worshipful Professor, speedily!" said Giovanni, with feverish impatience. "Does not your worship see that I am in haste?"

Now, while he was speaking, there came a man in black along the street, stooping and moving feebly, like a person in inferior health. His face was all overspread with a most sickly and sallow hue, but yet so pervaded with an expression of piercing and active intellect, that an observer might easily have overlooked the merely physical attributes, and have seen only this wonderful energy. As he passed, this person exchanged a cold and distant salutation with Baglioni, but fixed his eyes upon Giovanni with an intentness that seemed to bring out whatever was within him worthy of notice. Nevertheless, there was a peculiar quietness in the look, as if taking merely a speculative, not a human, interest in the young man.

"It is Doctor Rappaccini!" whispered the Professor, when the stranger had passed—"Has he ever seen your face before?"

"Not that I know," answered Giovanni, starting at the name.

"He *has* seen you!—he must have seen you!" said Baglioni, hastily. "For some purpose or other, this man of science is making a study of you. I know that look of his! It is the same that coldly illuminates his face, as he bends over a bird, a mouse, or a butterfly, which, in pursuance of some experiment, he has killed by the perfume of a flower;—a look as deep as Nature itself, but without Nature's warmth of love. Signor Giovanni, I will stake my life upon it, you are the subject of one of Rappaccini's experiments!"

"Will you make a fool of me?" cried Giovanni, passionately. "*That,* Signor Professor, were an untoward experiment."

"Patience, patience!" replied the imperturbable Professor.—"I tell thee, my poor Giovanni, that Rappaccini has a scientific interest in thee. Thou hast fallen into fearful hands! And the Signora Beatrice? What part does she act in this mystery?"

But Guasconti, finding Baglioni's pertinacity intolerable, here broke away, and was gone before the Professor could again seize his arm. He looked after the young man intently, and shook his head.

"This must not be," said Baglioni to himself. "The youth is the son of my old friend, and shall not come to any harm from which the arcana of medical science can preserve him. Besides, it is too insufferable an impertinence in Rappaccini, thus to snatch the lad out of my own hands, as I may say, and make use of him for his infernal experiments. This daughter of his! It shall be looked to. Perchance, most learned Rappaccini, I may foil you where you little dream of it!"

Meanwhile, Giovanni had pursued a circuitous route, and at length found himself at the door of his lodgings. As he crossed the threshold, he was met by old Lisabetta, who smirked and smiled, and was evidently desirous to attract his attention; vainly, however, as the ebullition of his feelings had momentarily subsided into a cold and dull vacuity. He turned his eyes full upon the withered face that was puckering itself into a smile, but seemed to behold it not. The old dame, therefore, laid her grasp upon his cloak.

"Signor!—Signor!" whispered she, still with a smile over the whole breadth of her visage, so that it looked not unlike a grotesque carving in wood, darkened by centuries—"Listen, Signor! There is a private entrance into the garden!"

"What do you say?" exclaimed Giovanni, turning quickly about, as if an inanimate thing should start into feverish life—"A private entrance into Doctor Rappaccini's garden!"

"Hush! hush!—not so loud!" whispered Lisabetta, putting her hand over his mouth. "Yes; into the worshipful Doctor's garden, where you may see all his fine shrubbery. Many a young man in Padua would give gold to be admitted among those flowers."

Giovanni put a piece of gold into her hand.

"Show me the way," said he.

A surmise, probably excited by his conversation with Baglioni, crossed his mind, that this interposition of old Lisabetta might perchance be connected with the intrigue, whatever were its nature, in which the Professor seemed to suppose that Doctor Rappaccini was involving him. But such a suspicion, though it disturbed Giovanni, was inadequate to restrain him. The instant that he was aware of the possibility of approaching Beatrice, it seemed an absolute necessity of his existence to do so. It mattered not whether she were angel or demon; he was irrevocably within her sphere, and must obey the law that whirled him onward, in ever lessening circles, towards a result which he did not attempt to foreshadow. And yet, strange to say, there came across him a sudden doubt, whether this intense interest on his part were not delusory—whether it were really of so deep and positive a nature as to justify him in now thrusting himself into an incalculable position—whether it were not merely the fantasy of a young man's brain, only slightly, or not at all, connected with his heart!

He paused—hesitated—turned half about—but again went on. His withered guide led him along several obscure passages, and finally undid a door, through which, as it was opened, there came the sight and sound of rustling leaves, with the broken sunshine glimmering among them. Giovanni stepped forth, and forcing himself through the entanglement of a shrub that wreathed its tendrils over the hidden entrance, he stood beneath his own window, in the open area of Doctor Rappaccini's garden.

How often is it the case, that, when impossibilities have come to pass, and dreams have condensed their misty substance into tangible realities, we find ourselves calm, and even coldly self-possessed, amid circumstances which it would have been a delirium of joy or agony to anticipate! Fate delights to thwart us thus. Passion will choose his own time to rush upon the scene, and lingers sluggishly behind, when an appropriate adjustment of events would seem to summon his appearance. So was it now with Giovanni. Day after day, his pulses had throbbed with feverish blood, at the improbable idea of an interview with Beatrice, and of standing with her, face to face, in this very garden, basking in the Oriental sunshine of her beauty, and snatching from her full gaze the mystery which he deemed the riddle of his own existence. But now there was a singular and untimely equanimity within his breast. He threw a glance around the garden to discover if Beatrice or her father were present, and perceiving that he was alone, began a critical observation of the plants.

The aspect of one and all of them dissatisfied him; their gorgeousness seemed fierce, passionate, and even unnatural. There was hardly an individual shrub which a wanderer, straying by himself through a forest, would not have been startled to find growing wild, as if an unearthly face had glared at him out of the thicket. Several, also, would have shocked a delicate instinct by an appearance of artificialness, indicating that there had been such commixture, and, as it were, adultery of various vegetable species, that the production was no longer of God's making, but the monstrous offspring of man's depraved fancy, glowing with only an evil mockery of beauty. They were probably the result of experiment, which, in one or two cases, had succeeded in mingling plants individually lovely into a compound possessing the questionable and ominous character that distinguished the whole growth of the garden. In fine, Giovanni recognized but two or three plants in the collection, and those of a kind that he well knew to be poisonous. While busy with these contemplations, he heard the rustling of a silken garment, and turning, beheld Beatrice emerging from beneath the sculptured portal.

Giovanni had not considered with himself what should be his deportment; whether he should apologize for his intrusion into the garden, or assume that he was there with the privity, at least, if not by the desire, of Doctor Rappaccini or his daughter. But Beatrice's manner placed him at his ease, though leaving him still in doubt by what agency he had gained admittance. She came lightly along the path, and met him near the broken fountain. There was surprise in her face, but brightened by a simple and kind expression of pleasure.

"You are a connoisseur in flowers, Signor," said Beatrice with a smile, alluding to the bouquet which he had flung her from the window. "It is no marvel, therefore, if the sight of my father's rare collection has tempted you to take a nearer view. If he were here, he could tell you many strange and interesting facts as to the nature and habits of these shrubs, for he has spent a life-time in such studies, and this garden is his world."

"And yourself, lady"—observed Giovanni—"if fame says true—you, likewise, are deeply skilled in the virtues indicated by these rich blossoms, and these spicy perfumes. Would you deign to be my instructress, I should prove an apter scholar than if taught by Signor Rappaccini himself."

"Are there such idle rumors?" asked Beatrice, with the music of a pleasant laugh. "Do people say that I am skilled in my father's science of plants? What a jest is there! No; though I have grown up among these flowers, I know no more of them than their hues and perfume; and sometimes, methinks I would fain rid myself of even that small knowledge. There are many flowers here, and those not the least brilliant, that shock and offend me, when they meet my eye. But, pray, Signor, do not believe these stories about my science. Believe nothing of me save what you see with your own eyes."

"And must I believe all that I have seen with my own eyes?" asked Giovanni pointedly, while the recollection of former scenes made him shrink. "No, Signora, you demand too little of me. Bid me believe nothing, save what comes from your own lips."

It would appear that Beatrice understood him. There came a deep flush to her cheek; but she looked full into Giovanni's eyes, and responded to his gaze of uneasy suspicion with a queen-like haughtiness.

"I do so bid you, Signor!" she replied. "Forget whatever you may have fancied in regard to me. If true to the outward senses, still it may be false in its essence. But the words of Beatrice Rappaccini's lips are true from the depths of the heart outward. Those you may believe!"

A fervor glowed in her whole aspect, and beamed upon Giovanni's consciousness like the light of truth itself. But while she spoke, there was a fragrance in the atmosphere around her, rich and delightful, though evanescent, yet which the young man, from an indefinable reluctance, scarcely dared to draw into his lungs. It might be the odor of the flowers. Could it be Beatrice's breath, which thus embalmed her words with a strange richness, as if by steeping them in her heart? A faintness passed like a shadow over Giovanni, and flitted away; he seemed to gaze through the beautiful girl's eyes into her transparent soul, and felt no more doubt or fear.

The tinge of passion that had colored Beatrice's manner vanished; she became gay, and appeared to derive a pure delight from her communion with the youth, not unlike what the maiden of a lonely island might have felt, conversing with a voyager from the civilized world. Evidently her experience of life had been confined within the limits of that garden. She talked now about matters as simple as the daylight or summer-clouds, and now asked questions in reference to the city, or Giovanni's distant home, his friends, his mother, and his sisters; questions indicating such seclusion, and such lack of familiarity with modes and forms, that Giovanni responded as if to an infant. Her spirit gushed out before him like a fresh rill, that was just catching its first glimpse of the sunlight, and wondering at the reflections of earth and sky which were flung into its bosom. There came thoughts, too, from a deep source, and fantasies of a gemlike brilliancy, as if diamonds and rubies sparkled upward among the bubbles of the fountain. Ever and anon, there gleamed across the young man's mind a sense of wonder, that he should be walking side by side with the being who had so wrought upon his imagination—whom he had idealized in such hues of terror—in whom he had positively witnessed such manifestations of dreadful attributes—that he should be conversing with Beatrice like a brother, and should find her so human and so maiden-like. But such reflections were only momentary; the effect of her character was too real, not to make itself familiar at once.

In this free intercourse, they had strayed through the garden, and now, after many turns among its avenues, were come to the shattered fountain, beside which grew the magnificent shrub with its treasury of glowing blossoms. A fragrance was diffused from it, which Giovanni recognized as identical with that which he had attributed to Beatrice's breath, but incomparably more powerful. As her eyes fell upon it, Giovanni beheld her press her hand to her bosom, as if her heart were throbbing suddenly and painfully.

"For the first time in my life," murmured she, addressing the shrub, "I had forgotten thee!"

"I remember, Signora," said Giovanni, "that you once promised to reward me with one of these living gems for the bouquet, which I had the happy boldness to fling to your feet. Permit me now to pluck it as a memorial of this interview."

He made a step towards the shrub, with extended hand. But Beatrice darted forward, uttering a shriek that went through his heart like a dagger. She caught his hand, and drew it back with the whole force of her slender figure. Giovanni felt her touch thrilling through his fibres.

"Touch it not!" exclaimed she, in a voice of agony. "Not for thy life! It is fatal!"

Then, hiding her face, she fled from him, and vanished beneath the sculptured portal. As Giovanni followed her with his eyes, he beheld the emaciated figure and pale intelligence of Doctor Rappaccini, who had been watching the scene, he knew not how long, within the shadow of the entrance.

No sooner was Guasconti alone in his chamber, than the image of Beatrice came back to his passionate musings, invested with all the witchery that had been gathering around it ever since his first glimpse of her, and now likewise imbued with a tender warmth of girlish womanhood. She was human: her nature was endowed with all gentle and feminine qualities; she was worthiest to be worshipped; she was capable, surely, on her part, of the height and heroism of love. Those tokens, which he had hitherto considered as proofs of a frightful peculiarity in her physical and moral system, were now either forgotten, or, by the subtle sophistry of passion, transmuted into a golden crown of enchantment, rendering Beatrice the more admirable, by so much as she was the more unique. Whatever had looked ugly, was now beautiful; or, if incapable of such a change, it stole away and hid itself among those shapeless half-ideas, which throng the dim region beyond the daylight of our perfect consciousness. Thus did he spend the night, nor fell asleep, until the dawn had begun to awake the slumbering flowers in Doctor Rappaccini's garden, whither Giovanni's dreams doubtless led him. Up rose the sun in his due season, and flinging his beams upon the young man's eyelids, awoke him to a sense of pain. When thoroughly aroused, he became sensible of a burning and tingling agony in his hand—in his right hand—the very hand which Beatrice had grasped in her own, when he was on the point of plucking one of the gem-like flowers. On the back of that hand there was now a purple print, like that of four small fingers, and the likeness of a slender thumb upon his wrist.

Oh, how stubbornly does love—or even that cunning semblance of love which flourishes in the imagination, but strikes no depth of root into the heart—how stubbornly does it hold its faith, until the moment come, when it is doomed to vanish into thin mist! Giovanni wrapt a handkerchief about his hand, and wondered what evil thing had stung him, and soon forgot his pain in a reverie of Beatrice.

After the first interview, a second was in the inevitable course of what we call fate. A third; a fourth; and a meeting with Beatrice in the garden was no longer an incident in Giovanni's daily life, but the whole space in which he might be said to live; for the anticipation and memory of that ecstatic hour made up the remainder. Nor was it otherwise with the daughter of Rappaccini. She watched for the youth's appearance, and flew to his side with confidence as unreserved as if they had been playmates from early infancy—as if they were such playmates still. If, by any unwonted chance, he failed to come at the appointed moment, she stood beneath the window, and sent up the rich sweetness of her tones to float around him in his chamber, and echo and reverberate throughout his heart—"Giovanni! Giovanni! Why tarriest thou? Come down!"—And down he hastened into that Eden of poisonous flowers.

But, with all this intimate familiarity, there was still a reserve in Beatrice's demeanor, so rigidly and invariably sustained, that the idea of infringing it scarcely occurred to his imagination. By all appreciable signs, they loved; they had looked love, with eyes that conveyed the holy secret from the depths of one soul into the depths of the other, as if it were too sacred to be whispered by the way; they had even spoken love, in those gushes of passion when their spirits darted forth in articulated breath, like tongues of long-hidden flame; and yet there had been no seal of lips, no clasp of hands, nor any slightest caresses, such as love claims and hallows. He had never touched one of the gleaming ringlets of her hair; her garment—so marked was the physical barrier between them—had never been waved against him by a breeze. On the few occasions when Giovanni had seemed tempted to overstep the limit, Beatrice grew so sad, so stern, and withal wore such a look of desolate separation, shuddering at itself, that not a spoken word was requisite to repel him. At such times, he was startled at the horrible suspicions that rose, monster-like, out of the caverns of his heart, and stared him in the face; his love grew thin and faint as the morning-mist; his doubts alone had substance. But when Beatrice's face brightened again, after the momentary shadow, she was transformed at once from the mysterious, questionable being, whom he had watched with so much awe and horror; she was now the beautiful and unsophisticated girl, whom he felt that his spirit knew with a certainty beyond all other knowledge.

A considerable time had now passed since Giovanni's last meeting with Baglioni. One morning, however, he was disagreeably surprised by a visit from the Professor, whom he had scarcely thought of for whole weeks, and would willingly have forgotten still longer. Given up, as he had long been, to a pervading excitement, he could tolerate no companions, except upon condition of their perfect sympathy with his present state of feeling. Such sympathy was not to be expected from Professor Baglioni.

The visitor chatted carelessly, for a few moments, about the gossip of the city and the University, and then took up another topic.

"I have been reading an old classic author lately," said he, "and met with a story that strangely interested me. Possibly you may remember it. It is of an Indian prince, who sent a beautiful woman as a present to Alexander the Great. She was as lovely as the dawn, and gorgeous as the sunset; but what especially distinguished her was a certain rich perfume in her breath—richer than a garden of Persian roses. Alexander, as was natural to a youthful conqueror, fell in love at first sight with this magnificent stranger. But a certain sage physician, happening to be present, discovered a terrible secret in regard to her."

"And what was that?" asked Giovanni, turning his eyes downward to avoid those of the Professor.

"That this lovely woman," continued Baglioni, with emphasis, "had been nourished with poisons from her birth upward, until her whole nature was so imbued with them, that she herself had become the deadliest poison in existence. Poison was her element of life. With that rich perfume of her breath, she blasted the very air. Her love would have been poison!—her embrace death! Is not this a marvelous tale?"

"A childish fable," answered Giovanni, nervously starting from his chair. "I marvel how your worship finds time to read such nonsense, among your graver studies."

"By the bye," said the Professor, looking uneasily about him, "what singular fragrance is this in your apartment? Is it the perfume of your gloves? It is faint, but delicious, and yet, after all, by no means agreeable. Were I to breathe it long, methinks it would make me ill. It is like the breath of a flower—but I see no flowers in the chamber."

"Nor are there any," replied Giovanni, who had turned pale as the Professor spoke; "nor, I think, is there any fragrance, except in your worship's imagination. Odors, being a sort of element combined of the sensual and the spiritual, are apt to deceive us in this manner. The recollection of a perfume—the bare idea of it—may easily be mistaken for a present reality."

"Aye; but my sober imagination does not often play such tricks," said Baglioni; "and were I to fancy any kind of odor, it would be that of some vile apothecary drug, wherewith my fingers are likely enough to be imbued. Our worshipful friend Rappaccini, as I have heard, tinctures his medicaments with odors richer than those of Araby. Doubtless, likewise, the fair and learned Signora Beatrice would minister to her patients with draughts as sweet as a maiden's breath. But wo to him that sips them!"

Giovanni's face evinced many contending emotions. The tone in which the Professor alluded to the pure and lovely daughter of Rappaccini was a torture to his soul; and yet, the intimation of a view of her character, opposite to his own, gave instantaneous distinctness to a thousand dim suspicions, which now grinned at him like so many demons. But he strove hard to quell them, and to respond to Baglioni with a true lover's perfect faith.

"Signor Professor," said he, "you were my father's friend—perchance, too, it is your purpose to act a friendly part towards his son. I would fain feel nothing towards you, save respect and deference. But I pray you to observe, Signor, that there is one subject on which we must not speak. You know not the Signora Beatrice. You cannot, therefore, estimate the wrong—the blasphemy, I may even say—that is offered to her character by a light or injurious word."

"Giovanni!—my poor Giovanni!" answered the Professor, with a calm expression of pity, "I know this wretched girl far better than yourself. You shall hear the truth in respect to the poisoner Rappaccini, and his poisonous daughter. Yes; poisonous as she is beautiful! Listen; for even should you do violence to my grey hairs, it shall not silence me. That old fable of the Indian woman has become a truth, by the deep and deadly science of Rappaccini, and in the person of the lovely Beatrice!"

Giovanni groaned and hid his face.

"Her father," continued Baglioni, "was not restrained by natural affection from offering up his child, in this horrible manner, as the victim of his insane zeal for science. For—let us do him justice—he is as true a man of science as ever distilled his own heart in an alembic. What, then, will be your fate? Beyond a doubt, you are selected as the material of some new experiment. Perhaps the result is to be death—perhaps a fate more awful still! Rappaccini, with what he calls the interest of science before his eyes, will hesitate at nothing."

"It is a dream!" muttered Giovanni to himself, "surely it is a dream!"

"But," resumed the Professor, "be of good cheer, son of my friend! It is not yet too late for the rescue. Possibly, we may even succeed in bringing back this miserable child within the limits of ordinary nature, from which her father's madness has estranged her. Behold this little silver vase! It was wrought by the hands of the renowned Benvenuto Cellini, and is well worthy to be a love-gift to the fairest dame in Italy. But its contents are invaluable. One little sip of this antidote would have rendered the most virulent poisons of the Borgias innocuous. Doubt not that it will be as efficacious against those of Rappaccini. Bestow the vase, and the precious liquid within it, on your Beatrice, and hopefully await the result."

Baglioni laid a small exquisitely wrought silver phial on the table, and withdrew, leaving what he had said to produce its effect upon the young man's mind.

"We will thwart Rappaccini yet!" thought he, chuckling to himself, as he descended the stairs. "But, let us confess the truth of him, he is a wonderful man!—a wonderful man indeed! A vile empiric, however, in his practice, and therefore not to be tolerated by those who respect the good old rules of the medical profession!"

Throughout Giovanni's whole acquaintance with Beatrice, he had occasionally, as we have said, been haunted by dark surmises as to her character. Yet, so thoroughly had she made herself felt by him as a simple, natural, most affectionate and guileless creature, that the image now held up by Professor Baglioni, looked as strange and incredible, as if it were not in accordance with his own original conception. True, there were ugly recollections connected with his first glimpses of the beautiful girl; he could not quite forget the bouquet that withered in her grasp, and the insect that perished amid the sunny air, by no ostensible agency, save the fragrance of her breath. These incidents, however, dissolving in the pure light of her character, had no longer the efficacy of facts, but were acknowledged as mistaken fantasies, by whatever testimony of the senses they might appear to be substantiated. There is something truer and more real, than what we can see with the eyes, and touch with the finger. On such better evidence, had Giovanni founded his confidence in Beatrice, though rather by the necessary force of her high attributes, than by any deep and generous faith, on his part. But, now, his spirit was incapable of sustaining itself at the height to which the early enthusiasm of passion had exalted it; he fell down, grovelling among earthly doubts, and defiled therewith the pure whiteness of Beatrice's image. Not that he gave her up; he did but distrust. He resolved to institute some decisive test that should satisfy him, once for all, whether there were those dreadful peculiarities in her physical nature, which could not be supposed to exist without some corresponding monstrosity of soul. His eyes, gazing down afar, might have deceived him as to the lizard, the insect, and the flowers. But if he could witness, at the distance of a few paces, the sudden blight of one fresh and healthful flower in Beatrice's hand, there would be room for no further question. With this idea, he hastened to the florist's, and purchased a bouquet that was still gemmed with the morning dewdrops.

It was now the customary hour of his daily interview with Beatrice. Before descending into the garden, Giovanni failed not to look at his figure in the mirror; a vanity to be expected in a beautiful young man, yet, as displaying itself at that troubled and feverish moment, the token of a certain shallowness of feeling and insincerity of character. He did gaze, however, and said to himself, that his features had never before possessed so rich a grace, nor his eyes such vivacity, nor his cheeks so warm a hue of superabundant life.

"At least," thought he, "her poison has not yet insinuated itself into my system. I am no flower to perish in her grasp!"

With that thought, he turned his eyes on the bouquet, which he had never once laid aside from his hand. A thrill of indefinable horror shot through his frame, on perceiving that those dewy flowers were already beginning to droop; they wore the aspect of things that had been fresh and lovely, yesterday. Giovanni grew white as marble, and stood motionless before the mirror, staring at his own reflection there, as at the likeness of something frightful. He remembered Baglioni's remark about the fragrance that seemed to pervade the chamber. It must have been the poison in his breath! Then he shuddered—shuddered at himself! Recovering from his stupor, he began to watch, with curious eye, a spider that was busily at work, hanging its web from the antique cornice of the apartment, crossing and re-crossing the artful system of interwoven lines, as vigorous and active a spider as ever dangled from an old ceiling. Giovanni bent towards the insect, and emitted a deep, long breath. The spider suddenly ceased its toil; the web vibrated with a tremor originating in the body of the small artisan. Again Giovanni sent forth a breath, deeper, longer, and imbued with a venomous feeling out of his heart; he knew not whether he were wicked or only desperate. The spider made a convulsive gripe with his limbs, and hung dead across the window.

"Accursed! Accursed!" muttered Giovanni, addressing himself. "Hast thou grown so poisonous, that this deadly insect perishes by thy breath?"

At that moment, a rich, sweet voice came floating up from the garden:—

"Giovanni! Giovanni! It is past the hour! Why tarriest thou! Come down!"

"Yes," muttered Giovanni again. "She is the only being whom my breath may not slay! Would that it might!"

He rushed down, and in an instant, was standing before the bright and loving eyes of Beatrice. A moment ago, his wrath and despair had been so fierce that he could have desired nothing so much as to wither her by a glance. But, with her actual presence, there came influences which had too real an existence to be at once shaken off; recollections of the delicate and benign power of her feminine nature, which had so often enveloped him in a religious calm; recollections of many a holy and passionate outgush of her heart, when the pure fountain had been unsealed from its depths, and made visible in its transparency to his mental eye; recollections which, had Giovanni known how to estimate them, would have assured him that all this ugly mystery was but an earthly illusion, and that, whatever mist of evil might seem to have gathered over her, the real Beatrice was a heavenly angel. Incapable as he was of such high faith, still her presence had not utterly lost its magic. Giovanni's rage was quelled into an aspect of sullen insensibility. Beatrice, with a quick spiritual sense, immediately felt that there was a gulf of blackness between them, which neither he nor she could pass. They walked on together, sad and silent, and came thus to the marble fountain, and to its pool of water on the ground, in the midst of which grew the shrub that bore gem-like blossoms. Giovanni was affrighted at the eager enjoyment—the appetite, as it were—with which he found himself inhaling the fragrance of the flowers.

"Beatrice," asked he abruptly, "whence came this shrub?"

"My father created it," answered she, with simplicity.

"Created it! created it!" repeated Giovanni. "What mean you, Beatrice?"

"He is a man fearfully acquainted with the secrets of nature," replied Beatrice; "and, at the hour when I first drew breath, this plant sprang from the soil, the offspring of his science, of his intellect, while I was but his earthly child. Approach it not!" continued she, observing with terror that Giovanni was drawing nearer to the shrub. "It has qualities that you little dream of. But I, dearest Giovanni—I grew up and blossomed with the plant, and was nourished with its breath. It was my sister, and I loved it with a human affection: for—alas! hast thou not suspected it? there was an awful doom."

Here Giovanni frowned so darkly upon her that Beatrice paused and trembled. But her faith in his tenderness reassured her, and made her blush that she had doubted for an instant.

"There was an awful doom," she continued,—"the effect of my father's fatal love of science—which estranged me from all society of my kind. Until Heaven sent thee, dearest Giovanni, Oh! how lonely was thy poor Beatrice!"

"Was it a hard doom?" asked Giovanni, fixing his eyes upon her.

"Only of late have I known how hard it was," answered she tenderly. "Oh, yes; but my heart was torpid, and therefore quiet."

Giovanni's rage broke forth from his sullen gloom like a lightning-flash out of a dark cloud.

"Accursed one!" cried he, with venomous scorn and anger. "And finding thy solitude wearisome, thou hast severed me, likewise, from all the warmth of life, and enticed me into thy region of unspeakable horror!"

"Giovanni!" exclaimed Beatrice, turning her large bright eyes upon his face. The force of his words had not found its way into her mind; she was merely thunder-struck.

"Yes, poisonous thing!" repeated Giovanni, beside himself with passion. "Thou hast done it! Thou hast blasted me! Thou hast filled my veins with poison! Thou hast made me as hateful, as ugly, as loathsome and deadly a creature as thyself,—a world's wonder of hideous monstrosity! Now—if our breath be happily as fatal to ourselves as to all others—let us join our lips in one kiss of unutterable hatred, and so die!"

"What has befallen me?" murmured Beatrice, with a low moan out of her heart. "Holy Virgin pity me, a poor heartbroken child!"

"Thou! Dost thou pray?" cried Giovanni, still with the same fiendish scorn. "Thy very prayers, as they come from thy lips, taint the atmosphere with death. Yes, yes; let us pray! Let us to church, and dip our fingers in the holy water at the portal! They that come after us will perish as by a pestilence. Let us sign crosses in the air! It will be scattering curses abroad in the likeness of holy symbols!"

"Giovanni," said Beatrice calmly, for her grief was beyond passion, "why dost thou join thyself with me thus in those terrible words? I, it is true, am the horrible thing thou namest me. But thou!—what hast thou to do, save with one other shudder at my hideous misery, to go forth out of the garden and mingle with thy race, and forget that there ever crawled on earth such a monster as poor Beatrice?"

"Dost thou pretend ignorance?" asked Giovanni, scowling upon her. "Behold! This power have I gained from the pure daughter of Rappaccini!"

There was a swarm of summer-insects flitting through the air, in search of the food promised by the flower-odors of the fatal garden. They circled round Giovanni's head, and were evidently attracted towards him by the same influence which had drawn them, for an instant, within the sphere of several of the shrubs. He sent forth a breath among them, and smiled bitterly at Beatrice, as at least a score of the insects fell dead upon the ground.

"I see it! I see it!" shrieked Beatrice. "It is my father's fatal science! No, no, Giovanni; it was not I! Never, never! I dreamed only to love thee, and be with thee a little time, and so to let thee pass away, leaving but thine image in mine heart. For, Giovanni—believe it—though my body be nourished with poison, my spirit is God's creature, and craves love as its daily food. But my father!—he has united us in this fearful sympathy. Yes; spurn me!—tread upon me!—kill me! Oh, what is death, after such words as thine? But it was not I! Not for a world of bliss would I have done it!"

Giovanni's passion had exhausted itself in its outburst from his lips. There now came across him a sense, mournful, and not without tenderness, of the intimate and peculiar relationship between Beatrice and himself. They stood, as it were, in an utter solitude, which would be made none the less solitary by the densest throng of human life. Ought not, then, the desert of humanity around them to press this insulated pair closer together? If they should be cruel to one another, who was there to be kind to them? Besides, thought Giovanni, might there not still be a hope of his returning within the limits of ordinary nature, and leading Beatrice—the redeemed Beatrice—by the hand? Oh, weak, and selfish, and unworthy spirit, that could dream of an earthly union and earthly happiness as possible, after such deep love had been so bitterly wronged as was Beatrice's love by Giovanni's blighting words! No, no; there could be no such hope. She must pass heavily, with that broken heart, across the borders of Time—she must bathe her hurts in some fount of Paradise, and forget her grief in the light of immortality—and *there* be well!

But Giovanni did not know it.

"Dear Beatrice," said he, approaching her, while she shrank away, as always at his approach, but now with a different impulse—"dearest Beatrice, our fate is not yet so desperate. Behold! There is a medicine, potent, as a wise physician has assured me, and almost divine in its efficacy. It is composed of ingredients the most opposite to those by which thy awful father has brought this calamity upon thee and me. It is distilled of blessed herbs. Shall we not quaff it together, and thus be purified from evil?"

"Give it me!" said Beatrice, extending her hand to receive the little silver phial which Giovanni took from his bosom. She added, with a peculiar emphasis: "I will drink—but do thou await the result."

She put Baglioni's antidote to her lips; and, at the same moment, the figure of Rappaccini emerged from the portal, and came slowly towards the marble fountain. As he drew near, the pale man of science seemed to gaze with a triumphant expression at the beautiful youth and maiden, as might an artist who should spend his life in achieving a picture or a group of statuary, and finally be satisfied with his success. He paused—his bent form grew erect with conscious power, he spread out his hands over them, in the attitude of a father imploring a blessing upon his children. But those were the same hands that had thrown poison into the stream of their lives! Giovanni trembled. Beatrice shuddered nervously, and pressed her hand upon her heart.

"My daughter," said Rappaccini, "thou art no longer lonely in the world! Pluck one of those precious gems from thy sister shrub, and bid thy bridegroom wear it in his bosom. It will not harm him now! My science, and the sympathy between thee and him, have so wrought within his system, that he now stands apart from common men, as thou dost, daughter of my pride and triumph, from ordinary women. Pass on, then, through the world, most dear to one another, and dreadful to all besides!"

"My father," said Beatrice, feebly—and still, as she spoke, she kept her hand upon her heart—"wherefore didst thou inflict this miserable doom upon thy child?"

"Miserable!" exclaimed Rappaccini. "What mean you, foolish girl? Dost thou deem it misery to be endowed with marvellous gifts, against which no power nor strength could avail an enemy? Misery, to be able to quell the mightiest with a breath? Misery, to be as terrible as thou art beautiful? Wouldst thou, then, have preferred the condition of a weak woman, exposed to all evil, and capable of none?"

"I would fain have been loved, not feared," murmured Beatrice, sinking down upon the ground—"But now it matters not; I am going, father, where the evil, which thou hast striven to mingle with my being, will pass away like a dream—like the fragrance of these poisonous flowers, which will no longer taint my breath among the flowers of Eden. Farewell, Giovanni! Thy words of hatred are like lead within my heart—but they, too, will fall away as I ascend. Oh, was there not, from the first, more poison in thy nature than in mine?"

To Beatrice—so radically had her earthly part been wrought upon by Rappaccini's skill—as poison had been life, so the powerful antidote was death. And thus the poor victim of man's ingenuity and of thwarted nature, and of the fatality that attends all such efforts of perverted wisdom, perished there, at the feet of her father and Giovanni. Just at that moment, Professor Pietro Baglioni looked forth from the window, and called loudly, in a tone of triumph mixed with horror, to the thunder-stricken man of science:

"Rappaccini! Rappaccini! And is *this* the upshot of your experiment?"

QUESTIONS FOR DISCUSSION AND WRITING

1. How do Baglioni's appearances mark important stages in the development of the plot?
2. What qualities do the male characters in the story have in common? In what ways is Beatrice like the flower she calls "sister"?
3. How does the Italian setting make possible the rich allusiveness of this story—as in the references to Roman gods, Dante, and Beatrice?
4. How would you characterize the attitude of the narrator toward the story he tells? How do the first two paragraphs establish the qualities of this narrator?
5. Because the narrator confesses to an "inveterate love of allegory," the reader expects a moral truth to emerge from the narrative. How would you state the moral truth in the story?

43

ERNEST HEMINGWAY

The Short Happy Life of Francis Macomber

ERNEST HEMINGWAY (1899–1961) was born in Oak Park, Illinois, but spent most of his summers in upper Michigan where he developed his skills in hunting and fishing. After high school, Hemingway worked as a journalist for the Kansas City *Star* until the outbreak of World War I. He then served as an ambulance driver, first in France and then in Italy, where he was seriously wounded. After the war, Hemingway lived in Paris, working as a foreign correspondent for the Toronto *Star* and writing the stories and novels that eventually earned him the 1954 Nobel Prize and a legendary place in American literature. His novels include *The Sun Also Rises* (1926), *A Farewell to Arms* (1929), *For Whom the Bell Tolls* (1940), and his Pulitzer Prize novel, *The Old Man and the Sea* (1953). On July 2, 1961, Hemingway, plagued by the sense that his health and literary ability were failing, used his favorite shotgun to take his life. Hemingway was fascinated by war, sports, bullfighting, and other moments of extreme adventure that provided men with the opportunity to perform acts of courage with grace and poise. "The Short Happy Life of Francis Macomber," reprinted from *The Short Stories of Ernest Hemingway* (1938), recounts one such brief moment.

It was now lunch time and they were all sitting under the double green fly of the dining tent pretending that nothing had happened.

"Will you have lime juice or lemon squash?" Macomber asked.

"I'll have a gimlet," Robert Wilson told him.

"I'll have a gimlet too. I need something," Macomber's wife said.

"I suppose it's the thing to do," Macomber agreed. "Tell him to make three gimlets."

The mess boy had started them already, lifting the bottles out of the canvas cooling bags that sweated wet in the wind that blew through the trees that shaded the tents.

"What had I ought to give them?" Macomber asked.

"A quid would be plenty," Wilson told him. "You don't want to spoil them."

"Will the headman distribute it?"

"Absolutely."

Francis Macomber had, half an hour before, been carried to his tent from the edge of the camp in triumph on the arms and shoulders of the cook, the personal boys, the skinner and the porters. The gunbearers had taken no part in the demonstration. When the native boys put him down at the door of his tent, he had shaken all their hands, received their congratulations, and then gone into the tent and sat on the bed until his wife came in. She did not speak to him when she came in and he left the tent at once to wash his face and hands in the portable wash basin outside and go over to the dining tent to sit in a comfortable canvas chair in the breeze and the shade.

"You've got your lion," Robert Wilson said to him, "and a damned fine one too."

Mrs. Macomber looked at Wilson quickly. She was an extremely handsome and well-kept woman of the beauty and social position which had, five years before, commanded five thousand dollars as the price of endorsing, with photographs, a beauty product which she had never used. She had been married to Francis Macomber for eleven years.

"He is a good lion, isn't he?" Macomber said. His wife looked at him now. She looked at both these men as though she had never seen them before.

One, Wilson, the white hunter, she knew she had never truly seen before. He was about middle height with sandy hair, a stubby mustache, a very red face and extremely cold blue eyes with faint white wrinkles at the corners that grooved merrily when he smiled. He smiled at her now and she looked away from his face at the way his shoulders sloped in the loose tunic he wore with the four big cartridges held in loops where the left breast pocket should have been, at his big brown hands, his old slacks, his very dirty boots and back to his red face again. She noticed where the baked red of his face stopped in a white line that marked the circle left by his Stetson hat that hung now from one of the pegs of the tent pole.

"Well, here's to the lion," Robert Wilson said. He smiled at her again and, not smiling, she looked curiously at her husband.

Francis Macomber was very tall, very well built if you did not mind that length of bone, dark, his hair cropped like an oarsman, rather thin-lipped, and was considered handsome. He was dressed in the same sort of safari clothes that Wilson wore except that his were new, he was thirty-five years old, kept himself very fit, was good at court games, had a number of big-game fishing records, and had just shown himself, very publicly, to be a coward.

"Here's to the lion," he said. "I can't ever thank you for what you did."

Margaret, his wife, looked away from him and back to Wilson.

"Let's not talk about the lion," she said.

Wilson looked over at her without smiling and now she smiled at him.

"It's been a very strange day," she said. "Hadn't you ought to put your hat on even under the canvas at noon? You told me that, you know."

"Might put it on," said Wilson.

"You know you have a very red face, Mr. Wilson," she told him and smiled again.

"Drink," said Wilson.

"I don't think so," she said. "Francis drinks a great deal, but his face is never red."

"It's red today," Macomber tried a joke.

"No," said Margaret. "It's mine that's red today. But Mr. Wilson's is always red."

"Must be racial," said Wilson. "I say, you wouldn't like to drop my beauty as a topic, would you?"

"I've just started on it."

"Let's chuck it," said Wilson.

"Conversation is going to be so difficult," Margaret said.

"Don't be silly, Margot," her husband said.

"No difficulty," Wilson said. "Got a damn fine lion."

Margot looked at them both and they both saw that she was going to cry. Wilson had seen it coming for a long time and he dreaded it. Macomber was past dreading it.

"I wish it hadn't happened. Oh, I wish it hadn't happened," she said and started for her tent. She made no noise of crying but they could see that her shoulders were shaking under the rose-colored, sun-proofed shirt she wore.

"Women upset," said Wilson to the tall man. "Amounts to nothing. Strain on the nerves and one thing'n another."

"No," said Macomber. "I suppose that I rate that for the rest of my life now."

"Nonsense. Let's have a spot of the giant killer," said Wilson. "Forget the whole thing. Nothing to it anyway."

"We might try," said Macomber. "I won't forget what you did for me though."

"Nothing," said Wilson. "All nonsense."

So they sat there in the shade where the camp was pitched under some wide-topped acacia trees with a boulder-strewn cliff behind them, and a stretch of grass that ran to the bank of a boulder-filled stream in front with forest beyond it, and drank their just-cool lime drinks and avoided one another's eyes while the boys set the table for lunch. Wilson could tell that the boys all knew about it now and when he saw Macomber's personal boy looking curiously at his master while he was putting dishes on the table he snapped at him in Swahili. The boy turned away with his face blank.

"What were you telling him?" Macomber asked.

"Nothing. Told him to look alive or I'd see he got about fifteen of the best."

"What's that? Lashes?"

"It's quite illegal," Wilson said. "You're supposed to fine them."

"Do you still have them whipped?"

"Oh, yes. They could raise a row if they chose to complain. But they don't. They prefer it to the fines."

"How strange!" said Macomber.

"Not strange, really," Wilson said. "Which would you rather do? Take a good birching or lose your pay?"

Then he felt embarrassed at asking it and before Macomber could answer he went on, "We all take a beating every day, you know, one way or another."

This was no better. "Good God," he thought. "I am a diplomat, aren't I?"

"Yes, we take a beating," said Macomber, still not looking at him. "I'm awfully sorry about that lion business. It doesn't have to go any further, does it? I mean no one will hear about it, will they?"

"You mean will I tell it at the Mathaiga Club?" Wilson looked at him now coldly. He had not expected this. So he's a bloody four-letter man as well as a bloody coward, he thought. I rather liked him too until today. But how is one to know about an American?

"No," said Wilson. "I'm a professional hunter. We never talk about our clients. You can be quite easy on that. It's supposed to be bad form to ask us not to talk though."

He had decided now that to break would be much easier. He would eat, then, by himself and could read a book with his meals. They would eat by themselves. He would see them through the safari on a very formal basis—what was it the French called it?

Distinguished consideration—and it would be a damn sight easier than having to go through this emotional trash. He'd insult him and make a good clean break. Then he could read a book with his meals and he'd still be drinking their whisky. That was the phrase for it when a safari went bad. You ran into another white hunter and you asked, "How is everything going?" and he answered, "Oh, I'm still drinking their whisky," and you knew everything had gone to pot.

"I'm sorry," Macomber said and looked at him with his American face that would stay adolescent until it became middle-aged, and Wilson noted his crew-cropped hair, fine eyes only faintly shifty, good nose, thin lips and handsome jaw. "I'm sorry I didn't realize that. There are lots of things I don't know."

So what could he do, Wilson thought. He was all ready to break it off quickly and neatly and here the beggar was apologizing after he had just insulted him. He made one more attempt. "Don't worry about me talking," he said. "I have a living to make. You know in Africa no woman ever misses her lion and no white man ever bolts."

"I bolted like a rabbit," Macomber said.

Now what in hell were you going to do about a man who talked like that, Wilson wondered.

Wilson looked at Macomber with his flat, blue, machine-gunner's eyes and the other smiled back at him. He had a pleasant smile if you did not notice how his eyes showed when he was hurt.

"Maybe I can fix it up on buffalo," he said. "We're after them next, aren't we?"

"In the morning if you like," Wilson told him. Perhaps he had been wrong. This was certainly the way to take it. You most certainly could not tell a damned thing about an American. He was all for Macomber again. If you could forget the morning. But, of course, you couldn't. The morning had been about as bad as they come.

"Here comes the Memsahib," he said. She was walking over from her tent looking refreshed and cheerful and quite lovely. She had a very perfect oval face, so perfect that you expected her to be stupid. But she wasn't stupid, Wilson thought, no, not stupid.

"How is the beautiful red-faced Mr. Wilson? Are you feeling better, Francis, my pearl?"

"Oh, much," said Macomber.

"I've dropped the whole thing," she said, sitting down at the table. "What importance is there to whether Francis is any good at killing lions? That's not his trade. That's Mr. Wilson's trade. Mr. Wilson is really very impressive killing anything. You do kill anything, don't you?"

"Oh, anything," said Wilson. "Simply anything." They are, he thought, the hardest in the world; the hardest, the cruelest, the most predatory and the most attractive and their men have softened or gone to pieces nervously as they have hardened. Or is it that they pick men they can handle? They can't know that much at the age they marry, he thought. He was grateful that he had gone through his education on American women before now because this was a very attractive one.

"We're going after buff in the morning," he told her.

"I'm coming," she said.

"No, you're not."

"Oh, yes, I am. Mayn't I, Francis?"

"Why not stay in camp?"

"Not for anything," she said. "I wouldn't miss something like today for anything."

When she left, Wilson was thinking, when she went off to cry, she seemed a hell of a fine woman. She seemed to understand, to realize, to be hurt for him and for herself and to know how things really stood. She is away for twenty minutes and now she is back, simply enamelled in that American female cruelty. They are the damnedest women. Really the damnedest.

"We'll put on another show for you tomorrow," Francis Macomber said.

"You're not coming," Wilson said.

"You're very mistaken," she told him. "And I want *so* to see you perform again. You were lovely this morning. That is if blowing things' heads off is lovely."

"Here's the lunch," said Wilson. "You're very merry, aren't you?"

"Why not? I didn't come out here to be dull."

"Well, it hasn't been dull," Wilson said. He could see the boulders in the river and the high bank beyond with the trees and he remembered the morning.

"Oh, no," she said. "It's been charming. And tomorrow. You don't know how I look forward to tomorrow."

"That's eland he's offering you," Wilson said.

"They're the big cowy things that jump like hares, aren't they?"

"I suppose that describes them," Wilson said.

"It's very good meat," Macomber said.

"Didn't you shoot it, Francis?" she asked.

"Yes."

"They're not dangerous, are they?"

"Only if they fall on you," Wilson told her.

"I'm so glad."

"Why not let up on the bitchery just a little, Margot," Macomber said, cutting the eland steak and putting some mashed potato, gravy and carrot on the down-turned fork that tined through the piece of meat.

"I suppose I could," she said, "since you put it so prettily."

"Tonight we'll have champagne for the lion," Wilson said. "It's a bit too hot at noon."

"Oh, the lion," Margot said. "I'd forgotten the lion!"

So, Robert Wilson thought to himself, she *is* giving him a ride, isn't she? Or do you suppose that's her idea of putting up a good show? How should a woman act when she discovers her husband is a bloody coward? She's damn cruel but they're all cruel. They govern, of course, and to govern one has to be cruel sometimes. Still, I've seen enough of their damn terrorism.

"Have some more eland," he said to her politely.

That afternoon, late, Wilson and Macomber went out in the motor car with the native driver and the two gun-bearers. Mrs. Macomber stayed in the camp. It was too hot to go out, she said, and she was going with them in the early morning. As they drove off Wilson saw her standing under the big tree, looking pretty rather than beautiful in her faintly rosy khaki, her dark hair drawn back off her forehead and gathered in a knot low on her neck, her face as fresh, he thought, as though she were in England. She waved to them as the car went off through the swale of high grass and curved around through the trees into the small hills of orchard bush.

In the orchard bush they found a herd of impala, and leaving the car they stalked one old ram with long, wide-spread horns and Macomber killed it with a very creditable shot that knocked the buck down at a good two hundred yards and sent the herd off bounding wildly and leaping over one another's backs in long, leg-drawn-up leaps as unbelievable and as floating as those one makes sometimes in dreams.

"That was a good shot," Wilson said. "They're a small target."

"Is it a worthwhile head?" Macomber asked.

"It's excellent," Wilson told him. "You shoot like that and you'll have no trouble."

"Do you think we'll find buffalo tomorrow?"

"There's a good chance of it. They feed out early in the morning and with luck we may catch them in the open."

"I'd like to clear away that lion business," Macomber said. "It's not very pleasant to have your wife see you do something like that."

I should think it would be even more unpleasant to do it, Wilson thought, wife or no wife, or to talk about it having done it. But he said, "I wouldn't think about that any more. Anyone could be upset by his first lion. That's all over."

But that night after dinner and a whisky and soda by the fire before going to bed, as Francis Macomber lay on his cot with the mosquito bar over him and listened to the night noises, it was not all over. It was neither all over nor was it beginning. It was there exactly as it happened with some parts of it indelibly emphasized and he was miserably ashamed at it. But more than shame he felt cold, hollow fear in him. The fear was still there like a cold slimy hollow in all the emptiness where once his confidence had been and it made him feel sick. It was still there with him now.

It had started the night before when he had wakened and heard the lion roaring somewhere up along the river. It was a deep sound and at the end there were sort of coughing grunts that made him seem just outside the tent, and when Francis Macomber woke in the night to hear it he was afraid. He could hear his wife breathing quietly, asleep. There was no one to tell he was afraid, nor to be afraid with him, and lying alone, he did not know the Somali proverb that says a brave man is always frightened three times by a lion; when he first sees his track, when he first hears him roar and when he first confronts him. Then while they were eating breakfast by lantern light out in the dining tent, before the sun was up, the lion roared again and Francis thought he was just at the edge of camp.

"Sounds like an old-timer," Robert Wilson said, looking up from his kippers and coffee. "Listen to him cough."

"Is he very close?"

"A mile or so up the stream."

"Will we see him?"

"We'll have a look."

"Does his roaring carry that far? It sounds as though he were right in camp."

"Carries a hell of a long way," said Robert Wilson. "It's strange the way it carries. Hope he's a shootable cat. The boys said there was a very big one about here."

"If I get a shot, where should I hit him," Macomber asked, "to stop him?"

"In the shoulders," Wilson said. "In the neck if you can make it. Shoot for bone. Break him down."

"I hope I can place it properly," Macomber said.

"You shoot very well," Wilson told him. "Take your time. Make sure of him. The first one in is the one that counts."

"What range will it be?"

"Can't tell. Lion has something to say about that. Won't shoot unless it's close enough so you can make sure."

"At under a hundred yards?" Macomber asked.

Wilson looked at him quickly.

"Hundred's about right. Might have to take him a bit under. Shouldn't chance a shot at much over that. A hundred's a decent range. You can hit him wherever you want at that. Here comes the Memsahib."

"Good morning," she said. "Are you going after that lion?"

"As soon as you deal with your breakfast," Wilson said. "How are you feeling?"

"Marvellous," she said. "I'm very excited."

"I'll just go and see that everything is ready." Wilson went off. As he left the lion roared again.

"Noisy beggar," Wilson said. "We'll put a stop to that."

"What's the matter, Francis?" his wife asked him.

"Nothing," Macomber said.

"Yes, there is," she said. "What are you upset about?"

"Nothing," he said.

"Tell me," she looked at him. "Don't you feel well?"

"It's that damned roaring," he said. "It's been going on all night, you know."

"Why didn't you wake me?" she said. "I'd love to have heard it."

"I've got to kill the damned thing," Macomber said, miserably.

"Well, that's what you're out here for, isn't it?"

"Yes. But I'm nervous. Hearing the thing roar gets on my nerves."

"Well then, as Wilson said, kill him and stop his roaring."

"Yes, darling," said Francis Macomber. "It sounds easy, doesn't it?"

"You're not afraid, are you?"

"Of course not. But I'm nervous from hearing him roar all night."

"You'll kill him marvellously," she said. "I know you will. I'm awfully anxious to see it."

"Finish your breakfast and we'll be starting."

"It's not light yet," she said. "This is a ridiculous hour."

Just then the lion roared in a deep-chested moaning, suddenly guttural, ascending vibration that seemed to shake the air and ended in a sigh and a heavy, deep-chested grunt.

"He sounds almost here," Macomber's wife said.

"My God," said Macomber. "I hate that damned noise."

"It's very impressive."

"Impressive. It's frightful."

Robert Wilson came up then carrying his short, ugly, shockingly big-bored .505 Gibbs and grinning.

"Come on," he said. "Your gun-bearer has your Springfield and the big gun. Everything's in the car. Have you solids?"

"Yes."

"I'm ready," Mrs. Macomber said.

"Must make him stop that racket," Wilson said. "You get in front. The Memsahib can sit back here with me."

They climbed into the motor car and, in the gray first daylight, moved off up the river through the trees. Macomber opened the breech of his rifle and saw he had metal-cased bullets; shut the bolt and put the rifle on safety. He saw his hand was trembling. He felt in his pocket for more cartridges and moved his fingers over the cartridges in the loops of his tunic front. He turned back to where Wilson sat in the rear seat of the doorless, box-bodied motor car beside his wife, them both grinning with excitement, and Wilson leaned forward and whispered,

"See the birds dropping. Means the old boy has left his kill."

On the far bank of the stream Macomber could see, above the trees, vultures circling and plummeting down.

"Chances are he'll come to drink along here," Wilson whispered. "Before he goes to lay up. Keep an eye out."

They were driving slowly along the high bank of the stream which here cut deeply to its boulder-filled bed, and they wound in and out through big trees as they drove. Macomber was watching the opposite bank when he felt Wilson take hold of his arm. The car stopped.

"There he is," he heard the whisper. "Ahead and to the right. Get out and take him. He's a marvellous lion."

Macomber saw the lion now. He was standing almost broadside, his great head up and turned toward them. The early morning breeze that blew toward them was just stirring his dark mane, and the lion looked huge, silhouetted on the rise of bank in the gray morning light, his shoulders heavy, his barrel of a body bulking smoothly.

"How far is he?" asked Macomber, raising his rifle.

"About seventy-five. Get out and take him."

"Why not shoot from where I am?"

"You don't shoot them from cars," he heard Wilson saying in his ear. "Get out. He's not going to stay there all day."

Macomber stepped out of the curved opening at the side of the front seat, onto the step and down onto the ground. The lion still stood looking majestically and coolly toward this object that his eyes only showed in silhouette, bulking like some super-rhino. There was no man smell carried toward him and he watched the object, moving his great head a little from side to side. Then watching the object, not afraid, but hesitating before going down the bank to drink with such a thing opposite him, he saw a man figure detach itself from it and he turned his heavy head and swung away toward the cover of the trees as he heard a cracking crash and felt the slam of a .30–06 220-grain solid bullet that bit his flank and ripped in sudden hot scalding nausea through his stomach. He trotted, heavy, big-footed, swinging wounded full-bellied, through the trees toward the tall grass and cover, and the crash came again to go past him ripping the air apart. Then it crashed again and he felt the blow as it hit his lower ribs and ripped on through, blood sudden hot and frothy in his mouth, and he galloped toward the high grass where he could crouch and not be seen and make them bring the crashing thing close enough so he could make a rush and get the man that held it.

Macomber had not thought how the lion felt as he got out of the car. He only knew his hands were shaking and as he walked away from the car it was almost impossible for him to make his legs move. They were stiff in the thighs, but he could feel the muscles fluttering. He raised the rifle, sighted on the junction of the lion's head and shoulders and pulled the trigger. Nothing happened though he pulled until he thought his finger would break. Then he knew he had the safety on and as he lowered the rifle to move the safety over he moved another frozen pace forward, and the lion seeing his silhouette now clear of the silhouette of the car, turned and started off at a trot, and, as Macomber fired, he heard a whunk that meant that the bullet was home; but the lion kept on going. Macomber shot again and everyone saw the bullet throw a spout of dirt beyond the trotting lion. He shot again, remembering to lower his aim, and they all heard the bullet hit, and the lion went into a gallop and was in the tall grass before he had the bolt pushed forward.

Macomber stood there feeling sick at his stomach, his hands that held the Springfield still cocked, shaking, and his wife and Robert Wilson were standing by him. Beside him too were the two gunbearers chattering in Wakamba.

"I hit him," Macomber said. "I hit him twice."

"You gut-shot him and you hit him somewhere forward," Wilson said without enthusiasm. The gun-bearers looked very grave. They were silent now.

"You may have killed him," Wilson went on. "We'll have to wait a while before we go in to find out."

"What do you mean?"

"Let him get sick before we follow him up."

"Oh," said Macomber.

"He's a hell of a fine lion," Wilson said cheerfully. "He's gotten into a bad place though."

"Why is it bad?"

"Can't see him until you're on him."

"Oh," said Macomber.

"Come on," said Wilson. "The Memsahib can stay here in the car. We'll go to have a look at the blood spoor."

"Stay here, Margot," Macomber said to his wife. His mouth was very dry and it was hard for him to talk.

"Why?" she asked.

"Wilson says to."

"We're going to have a look," Wilson said. "You stay here. You can see even better from here."

"All right."

Wilson spoke in Swahili to the driver. He nodded and said, "Yes, Bwana."

Then they went down the steep bank and across the stream, climbing over and around the boulders and up the other bank, pulling up by some projecting roots, and along it until they found where the lion had been trotting when Macomber first shot. There was dark blood on the short grass that the gun-bearers pointed out with grass stems, and that ran away behind the river bank trees.

"What do we do?" asked Macomber.

"Not much choice," said Wilson. "We can't bring the car over. Bank's too steep. We'll let him stiffen up a bit and then you and I'll go in and have a look for him."

"Can't we set the grass on fire?" Macomber asked.

"Too green."

"Can't we send beaters?"

Wilson looked at him appraisingly. "Of course we can," he said. "But it's just a touch murderous. You see we know the lion's wounded. You can drive an unwounded lion—he'll move on ahead of a noise—but a wounded lion's going to charge. You can't see him until you're right on him. He'll make himself perfectly flat in cover you wouldn't think would hide a hare. You can't very well send boys in there to that sort of a show. Somebody bound to get mauled."

"What about the gun-bearers?"

"Oh, they'll go with us. It's their *shauri*. You see, they signed on for it. They don't look too happy though, do they?"

"I don't want to go in there," said Macomber. It was out before he knew he'd said it.

"Neither do I," said Wilson very cheerily. "Really no choice though." Then, as an afterthought, he glanced at Macomber and saw suddenly how he was trembling and the pitiful look on his face.

"You don't have to go in, of course," he said. "That's what I'm hired for, you know. That's why I'm so expensive."

"You mean you'd go in by yourself? Why not leave him there?"

Robert Wilson, whose entire occupation had been with the lion and the problem he presented, and who had not been thinking about Macomber except to note that he was rather windy, suddenly felt as though he had opened the wrong door in a hotel and seen something shameful.

"What do you mean?"

"Why not just leave him?"

"You mean pretend to ourselves he hasn't been hit?"

"No. Just drop it."

"It isn't done."

"Why not?"

"For one thing, he's certain to be suffering. For another, some one else might run onto him."

"I see."

"But you don't have to have anything to do with it."

"I'd like to," Macomber said. "I'm just scared, you know."

"I'll go ahead when we go in," Wilson said, "with Kongoni tracking. You keep behind me and a little to one side. Chances are we'll hear him growl. If we see him we'll both shoot. Don't worry about anything. I'll keep you backed up. As a matter of fact, you know, perhaps you'd better not go. It might be much better. Why don't you go over and join the Memsahib while I just get it over with?"

"No, I want to go."

"All right," said Wilson. "But don't go in if you don't want to. This is my *shauri* now, you know."

"I want to go," said Macomber.

They sat under a tree and smoked.

"Want to go back and speak to the Memsahib while we're waiting?" Wilson asked.

"No."

"I'll just step back and tell her to be patient."

"Good," said Macomber. He sat there, sweating under his arms, his mouth dry, his stomach hollow feeling, wanting to find courage to tell Wilson to go on and finish off the lion without him. He could not know that Wilson was furious because he had not noticed the state he was in earlier and sent him back to his wife. While he sat there Wilson came up. "I have your big gun," he said. "Take it. We've given him time, I think. Come on."

Macomber took the big gun and Wilson said:

"Keep behind me and about five yards to the right and do exactly as I tell you." Then he spoke in Swahili to the two gun-bearers, who looked the picture of gloom.

"Let's go," he said.

"Could I have a drink of water?" Macomber asked. Wilson spoke to the older gun-bearer, who wore a canteen on his belt, and the man unbuckled it, unscrewed the top and handed it to Macomber, who took it noticing how heavy it seemed and how hairy and shoddy the felt covering was in his hand. He raised it to drink and looked ahead at the high grass with the flat-topped trees behind it. A breeze was blowing toward them and the grass rippled gently in the wind. He looked at the gun-bearer and he could see the gun-bearer was suffering too with fear.

Thirty-five yards into the grass the big lion lay flattened out along the ground. His ears were back and his only movement was a slight twitching up and down of his long, black-tufted tail. He had turned at bay as soon as he had reached this cover and he was sick with the wound through his full belly, and weakening with the wound through his lungs that brought a thin foamy red to his mouth each time he breathed. His flanks were wet and hot and flies were on the little openings the solid bullets had made in his tawny hide, and his big yellow eyes, narrowed with hate, looked straight ahead, only blinking when the pain came as he breathed, and his claws dug in the soft baked earth. All of him, pain, sickness, hatred and all of his remaining strength, was tightening into an absolute concentration for a rush. He could hear the men talking and he waited, gathering all of himself into this preparation for a charge as soon as the men would come into the grass. As he heard their voices his tail stiffened to twitch up and down, and, as they came into the edge of the grass, he made a coughing grunt and charged.

Kongoni, the old gun-bearer, in the lead watching the blood spoor, Wilson watching the grass for any movement, his big gun ready, the second gun-bearer looking ahead and listening, Macomber close to Wilson, his rifle cocked, they had just moved into the grass when Macomber heard the blood-choked coughing grunt, and saw the swishing rush in the grass. The next thing he knew he was running; running wildly, in panic in the open, running toward the stream.

He heard the *ca-ra-wong!* of Wilson's big rifle, and again in a second crashing *carawong!* and turning saw the lion, horrible-looking now, with half his head seeming to be gone, crawling toward Wilson in the edge of the tall grass while the red-faced man worked the bolt of the short ugly rifle and aimed carefully as another blasting *carawong!* came from the muzzle, and crawling, heavy, yellow bulk of the lion stiffened and the huge, mutilated head slid forward and Macomber, standing by himself in the clearing where he had run, holding a loaded rifle, while two black men and a white man looked back at him in contempt, knew the lion was dead. He came toward Wilson, his tallness all seeming a naked reproach, and Wilson looked at him and said:

"Want to take pictures?"

"No," he said.

That was all any one had said until they reached the motor car. Then Wilson had said:

"Hell of a fine lion. Boys will skin him out. We might as well stay here in the shade."

Macomber's wife had not looked at him nor he at her and he had sat by her in the back seat with Wilson sitting in the front seat. Once he had reached over and taken his wife's hand without looking at her and she had removed her hand from his. Looking across the stream to where the gun-bearers were skinning out the lion he could see that she had been able to see the whole thing. While they sat there his wife had reached forward and put her hand on Wilson's shoulder. He turned and she had leaned forward over the low seat and kissed him on the mouth.

"Oh, I say," said Wilson, going redder than his natural baked color.

"Mr. Robert Wilson," she said. "The beautiful red-faced Mr. Robert Wilson."

Then she sat down beside Macomber again and looked away across the stream to where the lion lay, with uplifted, white-muscled, tendon-marked naked forearms, and white bloating belly, as the black men fleshed away the skin. Finally the gun-bearers brought the skin over, wet and heavy, and climbed in behind with it, rolling it up before they got in, and the motor car started. No one had said anything more until they were back in camp.

That was the story of the lion. Macomber did not know how the lion had felt before he started his rush, nor during it when the unbelievable smash of the .505 with a muzzle velocity of two tons had hit him in the mouth, nor what kept him coming after that, when the second ripping crash had smashed his hind quarters and he had come crawling on toward the crashing, blasting thing that had destroyed him. Wilson knew something about it and only expressed it by saying, "Damned fine lion," but Macomber did not know how Wilson felt about things either. He did not know how his wife felt except that she was through with him.

His wife had been through with him before but it never lasted. He was very wealthy, and would be much wealthier, and he knew she would not leave him ever now. That was one of the few things that he really knew. He knew about that, about motorcycles—that was earliest—about motor cars, about duck-shooting, about fishing, trout, salmon and big-sea, and sex in books, many books, too many books, about all court games, about dogs, not much about horses, about hanging on to his money, about most of the other things his world dealt in, and about his wife not leaving him. His wife had been a great beauty and she was still a great beauty in Africa, but she was not a great enough beauty any more at home to be able to leave him and better herself and she knew it and he knew it. She had missed the chance to leave him and he knew it. If he had been better with women she would probably have started to worry about him getting another new, beautiful wife; but she knew too much about him to worry about him either. Also, he had always had a great tolerance which seemed the nicest thing about him if it were not the most sinister.

All in all they were known as a comparatively happily married couple, one of those whose disruption is often rumored but never occurs, and as the society columnist put it, they were adding more than a spice of *adventure* to their much envied and ever-enduring *Romance* by a *Safari* in what was known as *Darkest Africa* until the Martin Johnsons lighted it on so many silver screens where they were pursuing *Old Simba* the lion, the buffalo, *Tembo* the elephant and as well collecting specimens for the Museum of Natural History. This same columnist had reported them *on the verge* at least three times in the past and they had been. But they always made it up. They had a sound basis of union. Margot was too beautiful for Macomber to divorce her and Macomber had too much money for Margot ever to leave him.

It was now about three o'clock in the morning and Francis Macomber, who had been asleep a little while after he had stopped thinking about the lion, wakened and then slept again, woke suddenly, frightened in a dream of the bloody-headed lion standing over him, and listening while his heart pounded, he realized that his wife was not in the other cot in the tent. He lay awake with that knowledge for two hours.

At the end of that time his wife came into the tent, lifted her mosquito bar and crawled cozily into bed.

"Where have you been?" Macomber asked in the darkness.

"Hello," she said. "Are you awake?"

"Where have you been?"

"I just went out to get a breath of air."

"You did, like hell."

"What do you want me to say, darling?"

"Where have you been?"

"Out to get a breath of air."

"That's a new name for it. You *are* a bitch."

"Well, you're a coward."

"All right," he said. "What of it?"

"Nothing as far as I'm concerned. But please let's not talk, darling, because I'm very sleepy."

"You think that I'll take anything."

"I know you will, sweet."

"Well, I won't."

"Please, darling, let's not talk, I'm so very sleepy."

"There wasn't going to be any of that. You promised there wouldn't be."

"Well, there is now," she said sweetly.

"You said if we made this trip that there would be none of that. You promised."

"Yes, darling. That's the way I meant it to be. But the trip was spoiled yesterday. We don't have to talk about it, do we?"

"You don't wait long when you have an advantage, do you?"

"Please let's not talk. I'm so sleepy, darling."

"I'm going to talk."

"Don't mind me then, because I'm going to sleep." And she did.

At breakfast they were all three at the table before daylight and Francis Macomber found that, of all the many men that he had hated, he hated Robert Wilson the most.

"Sleep well?" Wilson asked in his throaty voice, filling a pipe.

"Did you?"

"Topping," the white hunter told him.

You bastard, thought Macomber, you insolent bastard.

So she woke him when she came in, Wilson thought, looking at them both with his flat, cold eyes. Well, why doesn't he keep his wife where she belongs? What does he think I am, a bloody plaster saint? Let him keep her where she belongs. It's his own fault.

"Do you think we'll find buffalo?" Margot asked, pushing away a dish of apricots.

"Chance of it," Wilson said and smiled at her. "Why don't you stay in camp?"

"Not for anything," she told him.

"Why not order her to stay in camp?" Wilson said to Macomber.

"You order her," said Macomber coldly.

"Let's not have any ordering, nor," turning to Macomber, "any silliness, Francis," Margot said quite pleasantly.

"Are you ready to start?" Macomber asked.

"Any time," Wilson told him. "Do you want the Memsahib to go?"

"Does it make any difference whether I do or not?"

The hell with it, thought Robert Wilson. The utter complete hell with it. So this is what it's going to be like. Well, this is what it's going to be like, then.

"Makes no difference," he said.

"You're sure you wouldn't like to stay in camp with her yourself and let me go out and hunt the buffalo?" Macomber asked.

"Can't do that," said Wilson. "Wouldn't talk rot if I were you."

"I'm not talking rot. I'm disgusted."

"Bad word, disgusted."

"Francis, will you please try to speak sensibly?" his wife said.

"I speak too damned sensibly," Macomber said. "Did you ever eat such filthy food?"

"Something wrong with the food?" asked Wilson quietly.

"No more than with everything else."

"I'd pull yourself together, laddybuck," Wilson said very quietly. "There's a boy waits at table that understands a little English."

"The hell with him."

Wilson stood up and puffing on his pipe strolled away, speaking a few words in Swahili to one of the gun-bearers who was standing waiting for him. Macomber and his wife sat on at the table. He was staring at his coffee cup.

"If you make a scene I'll leave you, darling," Margot said quietly.

"No, you won't."

"You can try it and see."

"You won't leave me."

"No," she said. "I won't leave you and you'll behave yourself."

"Behave myself? That's a way to talk. Behave myself."

"Yes. Behave yourself."

"Why don't *you* try behaving?"

"I've tried it so long. So very long."

"I hate that red-faced swine," Macomber said. "I loathe the sight of him."

"He's really *very* nice."

"Oh, *shut up,*" Macomber almost shouted. Just then the car came up and stopped in front of the dining tent and the driver and the two gun-bearers got out. Wilson walked over and looked at the husband and wife sitting there at the table.

"Going shooting?" he asked.

"Yes," said Macomber, standing up. "Yes."

"Better bring a woolly. It will be cool in the car," Wilson said.

"I'll get my leather jacket," Margot said.

"The boy has it," Wilson told her. He climbed into the front with the driver and Francis Macomber and his wife sat, not speaking, in the back seat.

Hope the silly beggar doesn't take a notion to blow the back of my head off, Wilson thought to himself. Women *are* a nuisance on safari.

The car was grinding down to cross the river at a pebbly ford in the gray daylight and then climbed, angling up the steep bank, where Wilson had ordered a way shovelled out the day before so they could reach the parklike wooded rolling country on the far side.

It was a good morning, Wilson thought. There was a heavy dew and as the wheels went through the grass and low bushes he could smell the odor of the crushed fronds. It was an odor like verbena and he liked this early morning smell of the dew, the crushed bracken and the look of the tree trunks showing black through the early morning mist, as the car made its way through the untracked, parklike country. He had put the two in the back seat out of his mind now and was thinking about buffalo. The buffalo that he was after stayed in the daytime in a thick swamp where it was impossible to get a shot, but in the night they fed out into an open stretch of country and if he could come between them and their swamp with the car, Macomber would have a good chance at them in the open. He did not want to hunt buff with Macomber in thick cover. He did not want to hunt buff or anything else with Macomber at all, but he was a professional hunter and he had hunted with some rare ones in his time. If they got buff today there would only be rhino to come and the poor man would have gone through his dangerous game and things might pick up. He'd have nothing more to do with the woman and Macomber would get over that too. He must have gone through plenty of that before by the look of things. Poor beggar. He must have a way of getting over it. Well, it was the poor sod's own bloody fault.

He, Robert Wilson, carried a double size cot on safari to accommodate any windfalls he might receive. He had hunted for a certain clientele, the international, fast, sporting set, where the women did not feel they were getting their money's worth unless they had shared that cot with the white hunter. He despised them when he was away from them although he liked some of them well enough at the time, but he made his living by them; and their standards were his standards as long as they were hiring him.

They were his standards in all except the shooting. He had his own standards about the killing and they could live up to them or get some one else to hunt them. He knew, too, that they all respected him for this. This Macomber was an odd one though. Damned if he wasn't. Now the wife. Well, the wife. Yes, the wife. Hm, the wife. Well he'd dropped all that. He looked around at them. Macomber sat grim and furious. Margot smiled at him. She looked younger today, more innocent and fresher and not so professionally beautiful. What's in her heart God knows, Wilson thought. She hadn't talked much last night. At that it was a pleasure to see her.

The motor car climbed up a slight rise and went on through the trees and then out into a grassy prairie-like opening and kept in the shelter of the trees along the edge, the driver going slowly and Wilson looking carefully out across the prairie and all along its far side. He stopped the car and studied the opening with his field glasses. Then he motioned to the driver to go on and the car moved slowly along, the driver avoiding wart-hog holes and driving around the mud castles ants had built. Then, looking across the opening, Wilson suddenly turned and said,

"By God, there they are!"

And looking where he pointed, while the car jumped forward and Wilson spoke in rapid Swahili to the driver, Macomber saw three huge, black animals looking almost cylindrical in their long heaviness, like big black tank cars, moving at a gallop across the far edge of the open prairie. They moved at a stiff-necked, stiff-bodied gallop and he could see the upswept wide black horns on their heads as they galloped heads out; the heads not moving.

"They're three old bulls," Wilson said. "We'll cut them off before they get to the swamp."

The car was going a wild forty-five miles an hour across the open and as Macomber watched, the buffalo got bigger and bigger until he could see the gray, hairless, scabby look of one huge bull and how his neck was a part of his shoulders and the shiny black of his horns as he galloped a little behind the others that were strung out in that steady plunging gait; and then, the car swaying as though it had just jumped a road, they drew up close and he could see the plunging hugeness of the bull, and the dust in his sparsely haired hide, the side boss of horn and his outstretched, wide-nostrilled muzzle, and he was raising his rifle when Wilson shouted, "Not from the car, you fool!" and he had no fear, only hatred of Wilson, while the brakes clamped on and the car skidded, plowing sideways to an almost stop and Wilson was out on one side and he on the other, stumbling as his feet hit the still speeding-by of the earth, and then he was shooting at the bull as he moved away, hearing the bullets whunk into him, emptying his rifle at him as he moved steadily away, finally remembering to get his shots forward into the shoulder, and as he fumbled to re-load, he saw the bull was down. Down on his knees, his big head tossing, and seeing the other two still galloping he shot at the leader and hit him. He shot again and missed and heard the *carawonging* roar as Wilson shot and saw the leading bull slide forward onto his nose.

"Get the other," Wilson said. "Now you're shooting!"

But the other bull was moving steadily at the same gallop and he missed, throwing a spout of dirt, and Wilson missed and the dust rose in a cloud and Wilson shouted, "Come on. He's too far!" and grabbed his arm and they were in the car again, Macomber and Wilson hanging on the sides and rocketing swayingly over the uneven ground, drawing up on the steady, plunging, heavy-necked, straight-moving gallop of the bull.

They were behind him and Macomber was filling his rifle, dropping shells onto the ground, jamming it, clearing the jam, then they were almost up with the bull when Wilson yelled "Stop," and the car skidded so that it almost swung over and Macomber fell forward onto his feet, slammed his bolt forward and fired as far forward as he could aim into the galloping, rounded black back, aimed and shot again, then again, then again, and the bullets, all of them hitting, had no effect on the buffalo that he could see. Then Wilson shot, the roar deafening him, and he could see the bull stagger. Macomber shot again, aiming carefully, and down he came, onto his knees.

"All right," Wilson said. "Nice work. That's the three."

Macomber felt a drunken elation.

"How many times did you shoot?" he asked.

"Just three," Wilson said. "You killed the first bull. The biggest one. I helped you finish the other two. Afraid they might have got into cover. You had them killed. I was just mopping up a little. You shot damn well."

"Let's go to the car," said Macomber. "I want a drink."

"Got to finish off that buff first," Wilson told him. The buffalo was on his knees and he jerked his head furiously and bellowed in pigeyed, roaring rage as they came toward him.

"Watch he doesn't get up," Wilson said. Then, "Get a little broadside and take him in the neck just behind the ear."

Macomber aimed carefully at the center of the huge, jerking, rage-driven neck and shot. At the shot the head dropped forward.

"That does it," said Wilson. "Got the spine. They're a hell of a looking thing, aren't they?"

"Let's get the drink," said Macomber. In his life he had never felt so good.

In the car Macomber's wife sat very white faced. "You were marvellous, darling," she said to Macomber. "What a ride."

"Was it rough?" Wilson asked.

"It was frightful. I've never been more frightened in my life."

"Let's all have a drink," Macomber said.

"By all means," said Wilson. "Give it to the Memsahib." She drank the neat whisky from the flask and shuddered a little when she swallowed. She handed the flask to Macomber who handed it to Wilson.

"It was frightfully exciting," she said. "It's given me a dreadful headache. I didn't know you were allowed to shoot them from cars though."

"No one shot from cars," said Wilson coldly.

"I mean chase them from cars."

"Wouldn't ordinarily," Wilson said. "Seemed sporting enough to me though while we were doing it. Taking more chance driving that way across the plain full of holes and one thing and another than hunting on foot. Buffalo could have charged us each time we shot if he liked. Gave him every chance. Wouldn't mention it to any one though. It's illegal if that's what you mean."

"It seemed very unfair to me," Margot said, "chasing those big helpless things in a motor car."

"Did it?" said Wilson.

"What would happen if they heard about it in Nairobi?"

"I'd lose my license for one thing. Other unpleasantnesses," Wilson said, taking a drink from the flask. "I'd be out of business."

"Really?"

"Yes, really."

"Well," said Macomber, and he smiled for the first time all day. "Now she has something on you."

"You have such a pretty way of putting things, Francis," Margot Macomber said. Wilson looked at them both. If a four-letter man marries a five-letter woman, he was thinking, what number of letters would their children be? What he said was, "We lost a gun-bearer. Did you notice it?"

"My God, no," Macomber said.

"Here he comes," Wilson said. "He's all right. He must have fallen off when we left the first bull."

Approaching them was the middle-aged gun-bearer, limping along in his knitted cap, khaki tunic, shorts and rubber sandals, gloomy-faced and disgusted looking. As he came up he called out to Wilson in Swahili and they all saw the change in the white hunter's face.

"What does he say?" asked Margot.

"He says the first bull got up and went into the bush," Wilson said with no expression in his voice.

"Oh," said Macomber blankly.

"Then it's going to be just like the lion," said Margot, full of anticipation.

"It's not going to be a damned bit like the lion," Wilson told her. "Did you want another drink, Macomber?"

"Thanks, yes," Macomber said. He expected the feeling he had had about the lion to come back but it did not. For the first time in his life he really felt wholly without fear. Instead of fear he had a feeling of definite elation.

"We'll go and have a look at the second bull," Wilson said. "I'll tell the driver to put the car in the shade."

"What are you going to do?" asked Margaret Macomber.

"Take a look at the buff," Wilson said.

"I'll come."

"Come along."

The three of them walked over to where the second buffalo bulked blackly in the open, head forward on the grass, the massive horns swung wide.

"He's a very good head," Wilson said. "That's close to a fifty-inch spread."

Macomber was looking at him with delight.

"He's hateful looking," said Margot. "Can't we go into the shade?"

"Of course," Wilson said. "Look," he said to Macomber, and pointed. "See that patch of bush?"

"Yes."

"That's where the first bull went in. The gun-bearer said when he fell off the bull was down. He was watching us helling along and the other two buff galloping. When he looked up there was the bull up and looking at him. Gun-bearer ran like hell and the bull went off slowly into that bush."

"Can we go in after him now?" asked Macomber eagerly.

Wilson looked at him appraisingly. Damned if this isn't a strange one, he thought. Yesterday he's scared sick and today he's a ruddy fire eater.

"No, we'll give him a while."

"Let's please go into the shade," Margot said. Her face was white and she looked ill.

They made their way to the car where it stood under a single, wide-spreading tree and all climbed in.

"Chances are he's dead in there," Wilson remarked. "After a little we'll have a look."

Macomber felt a wild unreasonable happiness that he had never known before.

"By God, that was a chase," he said. "I've never felt any such feeling. Wasn't it marvellous, Margot?"

"I hated it."

"Why?"

"I hated it," she said bitterly. "I loathed it."

"You know I don't think I'd ever be afraid of anything again," Macomber said to Wilson. "Something happened in me after we first saw the buff and started after him. Like a dam bursting. It was pure excitement."

"Cleans out your liver," said Wilson. "Damn funny things happen to people."

Macomber's face was shining. "You know something did happen to me," he said. "I feel absolutely different."

His wife said nothing and eyed him strangely. She was sitting far back in the seat and Macomber was sitting forward talking to Wilson who turned sideways talking over the back of the front seat.

"You know, I'd like to try another lion," Macomber said. "I'm really not afraid of them now. After all, what can they do to you?"

"That's it," said Wilson. "Worst one can do is kill you. How does it go? Shakespeare. Damned good. See if I can remember. Oh, damned good. Used to quote it to myself at one time. Let's see. 'By my troth, I care not; a man can die but once; we owe God a death and let it go which way it will he that dies this year is quit for the next.' Damned fine, eh?"

He was very embarrassed, having brought out this thing he had lived by, but he had seen men come of age before and it always moved him. It was not a matter of their twenty-first birthday.

It had taken a strange chance of hunting, a sudden precipitation into action without opportunity for worrying beforehand, to bring this about with Macomber, but regardless of how it had happened it had most certainly happened. Look at the beggar now, Wilson thought. It's that some of them stay little boys so long, Wilson thought. Sometimes all their lives. Their figures stay boyish when they're fifty. The great American boy-men. Damned strange people. But he liked this Macomber now. Damned strange fellow. Probably meant the end of cuckoldry too. Well, that would be a damned good thing. Damned good thing. Beggar had probably been afraid all his life. Don't know what started it. But over now. Hadn't had time to be afraid with the buff. That and being angry too. Motor car too. Motor cars made it familiar. Be a damn fire eater now. He'd seen it in the war work the same way. More of a change than any loss of virginity. Fear gone like an operation. Something else grew in its place. Main thing a man had. Made him into a man. Women knew it too. No bloody fear.

From the far corner of the seat Margaret Macomber looked at the two of them. There was no change in Wilson. She saw Wilson as she had seen him the day before when she had first realized what his great talent was. But she saw the change in Francis Macomber now.

"Do you have that feeling of happiness about what's going to happen?" Macomber asked, still exploring his new wealth.

"You're not supposed to mention it," Wilson said, looking in the other's face. "Much more fashionable to say you're scared. Mind you, you'll be scared too, plenty of times."

"But you *have* a feeling of happiness about action to come?"

"Yes," said Wilson. "There's that. Doesn't do to talk too much about all this. Talk the whole thing away. No pleasure in anything if you mouth it up too much."

"You're both talking rot," said Margot. "Just because you've chased some helpless animals in a motor car you talk like heroes."

"Sorry," said Wilson. "I have been gassing too much." She's worried about it already, he thought.

"If you don't know what we're talking about why not keep out of it?" Macomber asked his wife.

"You've gotten awfully brave, awfully suddenly," his wife said contemptuously, but her contempt was not secure. She was very afraid of something.

Macomber laughed, a very natural hearty laugh. "You know I *have,*" he said. "I really have."

"Isn't it sort of late?" Margot said bitterly. Because she had done the best she could for many years back and the way they were together now was no one person's fault.

"Not for me," said Macomber.

Margot said nothing but sat back in the corner of the seat.

"Do you think we've given him time enough?" Macomber asked Wilson cheerfully.

"We might have a look," Wilson said. "Have you any solids left?"

"The gun-bearer has some."

Wilson called in Swahili and the older gun-bearer, who was skinning out one of the heads, straightened up, pulled a box of solids out of his pocket and brought them over to Macomber, who filled his magazine and put the remaining shells in his pocket.

"You might as well shoot the Springfield," Wilson said. "You're used to it. We'll leave the Mannlicher in the car with the Memsahib. Your gun-bearer can carry your heavy gun. I've this damned cannon. Now let me tell you about them." He had saved this until the last because he did not want to worry Macomber. "When a buff comes he comes with his head high and thrust straight out. The boss of the horns covers any sort of a brain shot. The only shot is straight into the nose. The only other shot is into his chest or, if you're to one side, into the neck or the shoulders. After they've been hit once they take a hell of a lot of killing. Don't try anything fancy. Take the easiest shot there is. They've finished skinning out that head now. Should we get started?"

He called to the gun-bearers, who came up wiping their hands, and the older one got into the back.

"I'll only take Kongoni," Wilson said. "The other can watch to keep the birds away."

As the car moved slowly across the open space toward the island of brushy trees that ran in a tongue of foliage along a dry water course that cut the open swale, Macomber felt his heart pounding and his mouth was dry again, but it was excitement, not fear.

"Here's where he went in," Wilson said. Then to the gun-bearer in Swahili, "Take the blood spoor."

The car was parallel to the patch of bush. Macomber, Wilson and the gun-bearer got down. Macomber, looking back, saw his wife, with the rifle by her side, looking at him. He waved to her and she did not wave back.

The brush was very thick ahead and the ground was dry. The middle-aged gun-bearer was sweating heavily and Wilson had his hat down over his eyes and his red neck showed just ahead of Macomber. Suddenly the gun-bearer said something in Swahili to Wilson and ran forward.

"He's dead in there," Wilson said. "Good work," and he turned to grip Macomber's hand and as they shook hands, grinning at each other, the gun-bearer shouted wildly and they saw him coming out of the brush sideways, fast as a crab, and the bull coming, nose out, mouth tight closed, blood dripping, massive head straight out, coming in a charge, his little pig eyes bloodshot as he looked at them. Wilson, who was ahead was kneeling shooting, and Macomber, as he fired, unhearing his shot in the roaring of Wilson's gun, saw fragments like slate burst from the huge boss of the horns, and the head jerked, he shot again at the wide nostrils and saw the horns jolt again and fragments fly, and he did not see Wilson now and, aiming carefully, shot again with the buffalo's huge bulk almost on him and his rifle almost level with the on-coming head, nose out, and he could see the little wicked eyes and the head started to lower and he felt a sudden white-hot, blinding flash explode inside his head and that was all he ever felt.

Wilson had ducked to one side to get in a shoulder shot. Macomber had stood solid and shot for the nose, shooting a touch high each time and hitting the heavy horns, splintering and chipping them like hitting a slate roof, and Mrs. Macomber, in the car, had shot at the buffalo with the 6.5 Mannlicher as it seemed about to gore Macomber and had hit her husband about two inches up and a little to one side of the base of his skull.

Francis Macomber lay now, face down, not two yards from where the buffalo lay on his side and his wife knelt over him with Wilson beside her.

"I wouldn't turn him over," Wilson said.

The woman was crying hysterically.

"I'd get back in the car," Wilson said. "Where's the rifle?"

She shook her head, her face contorted. The gun-bearer picked up the rifle.

"Leave it as it is," said Wilson. Then, "Go get Abdulla so that he may witness the manner of the accident."

He knelt down, took a handkerchief from his pocket, and spread it over Francis Macomber's crew-cropped head where it lay. The blood sank into the dry, loose earth.

Wilson stood up and saw the buffalo on his side, his legs out, his thinly-haired belly crawling with ticks. "Hell of a good bull," his brain registered automatically. "A good fifty inches, or better. Better." He called to the driver and told him to spread a blanket over the body and stay by it. Then he walked over to the motor car where the woman sat crying in the corner.

"That was a pretty thing to do," he said in a toneless voice. "He *would* have left you too."

"Stop it," she said.

"Of course, it's an accident," he said. "I know that."

"Stop it," she said.

"Don't worry," he said. "There will be a certain amount of unpleasantness but I will have some photographs taken that will be very useful at the inquest. There's the testimony of the gun-bearers and the driver too. You're perfectly all right."

"Stop it," she said.

"There's a hell of a lot to be done," he said. "And I'll have to send a truck off to the lake to wireless for a plane to take the three of us into Nairobi. Why didn't you poison him? That's what they do in England."

"Stop it. Stop it. Stop it," the woman cried.

Wilson looked at her with his flat blue eyes.

"I'm through now," he said. "I was a little angry. I'd begun to like your husband."

"Oh, please stop it," she said. "Please, please stop it."

"That's better," Wilson said. "Please is much better. Now I'll stop."

QUESTIONS FOR DISCUSSION AND WRITING

1. What effect does Hemingway create by beginning his story "after" the event that brought Macomber his dishonor? How does this opening create suspense for the flashback that recounts those events? Compare and contrast the beginning, middle, and end of the hunt for the lion and buffalo.

2. How does the opening scene help characterize Macomber, his wife, and Wilson? How do Macomber's and his wife's actions toward each other reveal their relationship? In what way does Wilson characterize Macomber and his wife? What does Wilson's phrase "still drinking their whisky" suggest about his ethics as a man and as a hunter?

3. In what ways does Hemingway evoke the sights and sounds of a jungle safari? What specific settings—such as the campsite or the high grass—help shape the action of the story?

4. Why does Hemingway tell parts of his story from Macomber's, Wilson's, and the lion's point of view, but rarely from Mrs. Macomber's point of view? Since we don't know what she is thinking, how do we explain her final action?

5. How does the title announce the theme of the story? How does the quote from Shakespeare summarize this theme?

44

SHIRLEY JACKSON

The Lottery

SHIRLEY JACKSON (1919–1965) was born in San Francisco and was educated at the University of Rochester and Syracuse University. In 1940 she married author and critic Stanley Edgar

Hyman and settled in North Bennington, Vermont, where Hyman was on the faculty of Bennington College. Jackson published her first novel, *The Road Through the Wall,* in 1948, the same year she published her controversial first story "The Lottery" in *The New Yorker.* Jackson continued to publish novels that dealt with bizarre, gothic, and mythic elements such as *Hangsaman* (1951), *The Haunting of Hill House* (1959), and *We Have Always Lived in the Castle* (1962). But she could also write easily and with humor about family life, as in *Life Among the Savages* (1953), and produce fascinating stories for children, such as *9 Magic Wishes* (1963). Despite a productive writing career in which many of her novels and stories were adapted for stage and screen, Jackson's most famous story remains her first. "The Lottery," reprinted from *The Lottery; or, The Adventures of James Harris,* presents a community's annual reenactment of a mysterious ritual.

The morning of June 27th was clear and sunny, with the fresh warmth of a full-summer day; the flowers were blossoming profusely and the grass was richly green. The people of the village began to gather in the square, between the post office and the bank, around ten o'clock; in some towns there were so many people that the lottery took two days and had to be started on June 26th, but in this village, where there were only about three hundred people, the whole lottery took less than two hours, so it could begin at ten o'clock in the morning and still be through in time to allow the villagers to get home for noon dinner.

The children assembled first, of course. School was recently over for the summer, and the feeling of liberty sat uneasily on most of them; they tended to gather together quietly for a while before they broke into boisterous play, and their talk was still of the classroom and the teacher, of books and reprimands. Bobby Martin had already stuffed his pockets full of stones, and the other boys soon followed his example, selecting the smoothest and roundest stones; Bobby and Harry Jones and Dickie Delacroix—the villagers pronounced this name "Dellacroy"—eventually made a great pile of stones in one corner of the square and guarded it against the raids of the other boys. The girls stood aside, talking among themselves, looking over their shoulders at the boys, and the very small children rolled in the dust or clung to the hands of their older brothers or sisters.

Soon the men began to gather, surveying their own children, speaking of planting and rain, tractors and taxes. They stood together, away from the pile of stones in the corner, and their jokes were quiet and they smiled rather than laughed. The women, wearing faded house dresses and sweaters, came shortly after their menfolk. They greeted one another and exchanged bits of gossip as they went to join their husbands. Soon the women, standing by their husbands, began to call to their children, and the children came reluctantly, having to be called four or five times. Bobby Martin ducked under his mother's grasping hand and ran, laughing, back to the pile of stones. His father spoke up sharply, and Bobby came quickly and took his place between his father and his oldest brother.

The lottery was conducted—as were the square dances, the teenage club, the Halloween program—by Mr. Summers, who had time and energy to devote to civic activities.

He was a round-faced, jovial man and he ran the coal business, and people were sorry for him, because he had no children and his wife was a scold. When he arrived in the square, carrying the black wooden box, there was a murmur of conversation among the villagers, and he waved and called, "Little late today, folks." The postmaster, Mr. Graves, followed him, carrying a three-legged stool, and the stool was put in the center of the square and Mr. Summers set the black box down on it. The villagers kept their distance, leaving a space between themselves and the stool, and when Mr. Summers said, "Some of you fellows want to give me a hand?" there was a hesitation before two men, Mr. Martin and his oldest son, Baxter, came forward to hold the box steady on the stool while Mr. Summers stirred up the papers inside it.

The original paraphernalia for the lottery had been lost long ago, and the black box now resting on the stool had been put into use even before Old Man Warner, the oldest man in town, was born. Mr. Summers spoke frequently to the villagers about making a new box, but no one liked to upset even as much tradition as was represented by the black box. There was a story that the present box had been made with some pieces of the box that had preceded it, the one that had been constructed when the first people settled down to make a village here. Every year, after the lottery, Mr. Summers began talking again about a new box, but every year the subject was allowed to fade off without anything's being done. The black box grew shabbier each year; by now it was no longer completely black but splintered badly along one side to show the original wood color, and in some places faded or stained.

Mr. Martin and his oldest son, Baxter, held the black box securely on the stool until Mr. Summers had stirred the papers thoroughly with his hand. Because so much of the ritual had been forgotten or discarded, Mr. Summers had been successful in having slips of paper substituted for the chips of wood that had been used for generations. Chips of wood, Mr. Summers had argued, had been all very well when the village was tiny, but now that the population was more than three hundred and likely to keep on growing, it was necessary to use something that would fit more easily into the black box. The night before the lottery, Mr. Summers and Mr. Graves made up the slips of paper and put them in the box, and it was then taken to the safe of Mr. Summers's coal company and locked up until Mr. Summers was ready to take it to the square next morning. The rest of the year, the box was put away, sometimes one place, sometimes another; it had spent one year in Mr. Graves's barn and another year underfoot in the post office, and sometimes it was set on a shelf in the Martin grocery and left there.

There was a great deal of fussing to be done before Mr. Summers declared the lottery open. There were the lists to make up—of heads of families, heads of households in each family, members of each household in each family. There was the proper swearing-in of Mr. Summers by the postmaster, as the official of the lottery; at one time, some people remembered, there had been a recital of some sort, performed by the official of the lottery, a perfunctory, tuneless chant that had been rattled off duly each year; some people believed that the official of the lottery used to stand just so when he said or sang it, others believed that he was supposed to walk among the people, but years and years ago this part of the ritual had been allowed to lapse. There had been, also, a ritual salute, which the official of the lottery had had to use in addressing each person who came up to draw from the box, but this also had changed with time, until now it was felt necessary only for the official to speak to each person approaching. Mr. Summers was very good at all this; in his clean white shirt and blue jeans, with one hand resting carelessly on the black box, he seemed very proper and important as he talked interminably to Mr. Graves and the Martins.

Just as Mr. Summers finally left off talking and turned to the assembled villagers, Mrs. Hutchinson came hurriedly along the path to the square, her sweater thrown over her shoulders, and slid into place in the back of the crowd. "Clean forgot what day it was," she said to Mrs. Delacroix, who stood next to her, and they both laughed softly. "Thought my old man was out back stacking wood," Mrs. Hutchinson went on, "and then I looked out the window and the kids was gone, and then I remembered it was the twenty-seventh and came a-running." She dried her hands on her apron, and Mrs. Delacroix said, "You're in time, though. They're still talking away up there."

Mrs. Hutchinson craned her neck to see through the crowd and found her husband and children standing near the front. She tapped Mrs. Delacroix on the arm as a farewell and began to make her way through the crowd. The people separated good-humoredly to let her through; two or three people said, in voices just loud enough to be heard across the crowd, "Here comes your Missus, Hutchinson," and "Bill, she made it after all." Mrs. Hutchinson reached her husband, and Mr. Summers, who had been waiting, said cheerfully, "Thought we were going to have to get on without you, Tessie." Mrs. Hutchinson said, grinning, "Wouldn't have me leave m'dishes in the sink, now, would you, Joe?" and soft laughter ran through the crowd as the people stirred back into position after Mrs. Hutchinson's arrival.

"Well, now," Mr. Summers said soberly, "guess we better get started, get this over with, so's we can go back to work. Anybody ain't here?"

"Dunbar," several people said. "Dunbar, Dunbar."

Mr. Summers consulted his list. "Clyde Dunbar," he said. "That's right. He's broke his leg, hasn't he? Who's drawing for him?"

"Me, I guess," a woman said, and Mr. Summers turned to look at her. "Wife draws for her husband," Mr. Summers said. "Don't you have a grown boy to do it for you, Janey?" Although Mr. Summers and everyone else in the village knew the answer perfectly well, it was the business of the official of the lottery to ask such questions formally. Mr. Summers waited with an expression of polite interest while Mrs. Dunbar answered.

"Horace's not but sixteen yet," Mrs. Dunbar said regretfully. "Guess I gotta fill in for the old man this year."

"Right," Mr. Summers said. He made a note on the list he was holding. Then he asked, "Watson boy drawing this year?"

A tall boy in the crowd raised his hand. "Here," he said. "I'm drawing for m'mother and me." He blinked his eyes nervously and ducked his head as several voices in the crowd said things like "Good fellow, Jack," and "Glad to see your mother's got a man to do it."

"Well," Mr. Summers said, "guess that's everyone. Old Man Warner make it?"

"Here," a voice said, and Mr. Summers nodded.

A sudden hush fell on the crowd as Mr. Summers cleared his throat and looked at the list. "All ready?" he called. "Now, I'll read the names—heads of families first—and the men come up and take a paper out of the box. Keep the paper folded in your hand without looking at it until everyone has had a turn. Everything clear?"

The people had done it so many times that they only half-listened to the directions; most of them were quiet, wetting their lips, not looking around. Then Mr. Summers raised one hand high and said, "Adams." A man disengaged himself from the crowd and came forward. "Hi, Steve," Mr. Summers said, and Mr. Adams said, "Hi, Joe." They grinned at one another humorlessly and nervously. Then Mr. Adams reached into the black box and took out a folded paper. He held it firmly by one corner as he turned and went hastily back to his place in the crowd, where he stood a little apart from his family, not looking down at his hand.

"Allen," Mr. Summers said. "Anderson. . . . Bentham."

"Seems like there's no time at all between lotteries any more," Mrs. Delacroix said to Mrs. Graves in the back row. "Seems like we got through with the last one only last week."

"Time sure goes fast," Mrs. Graves said.

"Clark. . . . Delacroix."

"There goes my old man," Mrs. Delacroix said. She held her breath while her husband went forward.

"Dunbar," Mr. Summers said, and Mrs. Dunbar went steadily to the box while one of the women said, "Go on, Janey," and another said, "There she goes."

"We're next," Mrs. Graves said. She watched while Mr. Graves came around from the side of the box, greeted Mr. Summers gravely, and selected a slip of paper from the box. By now, all through the crowd there were men holding the small folded papers in their large hands, turning them over and over nervously. Mrs. Dunbar and her two sons stood together, Mrs. Dunbar holding the slip of paper.

"Harburt. . . . Hutchinson."

"Get up there, Bill," Mrs. Hutchinson said, and the people near her laughed.

"Jones."

"They do say," Mr. Adams said to Old Man Warner, who stood next to him, "that over in the north village they're talking of giving up the lottery."

Old Man Warner snorted. "Pack of crazy fools," he said. "Listening to the young folks, nothing's good enough for *them*. Next thing you know, they'll be wanting to go back to living in caves, nobody work any more, live *that* way for a while. Used to be a saying about 'Lottery in June, corn be heavy soon.' First thing you know, we'd all be eating stewed chickweed and acorns. There's *always* been a lottery," he added petulantly. "Bad enough to see young Joe Summers up there joking with everybody."

"Some places have already quit lotteries," Mrs. Adams said.

"Nothing but trouble in *that*," Old Man Warner said stoutly. "Pack of young fools."

"Martin." And Bobby Martin watched his father go forward. "Overdyke. . . . Percy."

"I wish they'd hurry," Mrs. Dunbar said to her older son. "I wish they'd hurry."

"They're almost through," her son said.

"You get ready to run tell Dad," Mrs. Dunbar said.

Mr. Summers called his own name and then stepped forward precisely and selected a slip from the box. Then he called, "Warner."

"Seventy-seventh year I been in the lottery," Old Man Warner said as he went through the crowd. "Seventy-seventh time."

"Watson." The tall boy came awkwardly through the crowd. Someone said, "Don't be nervous, Jack," and Mr. Summers said, "Take your time, son."

"Zanini."

After that, there was a long pause, a breathless pause, until Mr. Summers, holding his slip of paper in the air, said, "All right, fellows." For a minute, no one moved, and then all the slips of paper were opened. Suddenly, all the women began to speak at once, saying, "Who is it?," "Who's got it?," "Is it the Dunbars?," "Is it the Watsons?" Then the voices began to say, "It's Hutchinson. It's Bill," "Bill Hutchinson's got it."

"Go tell your father," Mrs. Dunbar said to her older son.

People began to look around to see the Hutchinsons. Bill Hutchinson was standing quiet, staring down at the paper in his hand. Suddenly, Tessie Hutchinson shouted to Mr. Summers, "You didn't give him time enough to take any paper he wanted. I saw you. It wasn't fair!"

"Be a good sport, Tessie," Mrs. Delacroix called, and Mrs. Graves said, "All of us took the same chance."

"Shut up, Tessie," Bill Hutchinson said.

"Well, everyone," Mr. Summers said, "that was done pretty fast, and now we've got to be hurrying a little more to get done in time." He consulted his next list. "Bill," he said, "you draw for the Hutchinson family. You got any other households in the Hutchinsons?"

"There's Don and Eva," Mrs. Hutchinson yelled. "Make *them* take their chance!"

"Daughters draw with their husbands' families, Tessie," Mr. Summers said gently. "You know that as well as anyone else."

"It wasn't *fair,*" Tessie said.

"I guess not, Joe," Bill Hutchinson said regretfully. "My daughter draws with her husband's family, that's only fair. And I've got no other family except the kids."

"Then, as far as drawing for families is concerned, it's you," Mr. Summers said in explanation, "and as far as drawing for households is concerned, that's you, too. Right?"

"Right," Bill Hutchinson said.

"How many kids, Bill?" Mr. Summers asked formally.

"Three," Bill Hutchinson said. "There's Bill, Jr., and Nancy, and little Dave. And Tessie and me."

"All right, then," Mr. Summers said. "Harry, you got their tickets back?"

Mr. Graves nodded and held up the slips of paper. "Put them in the box, then," Mr. Summers directed. "Take Bill's and put it in."

"I think we ought to start over," Mrs. Hutchinson said, as quietly as she could. "I tell you it wasn't *fair.* You didn't give him time enough to choose. *Every*body saw that."

Mr. Graves had selected the five slips and put them in the box, and he dropped all the papers but those onto the ground, where the breeze caught them and lifted them off.

"Listen, everybody," Mrs. Hutchinson was saying to the people around her.

"Ready, Bill?" Mr. Summers asked, and Bill Hutchinson, with one quick glance around at his wife and children, nodded.

"Remember," Mr. Summers said, "take the slips and keep them folded until each person has taken one. Harry, you help little Dave." Mr. Graves took the hand of the little boy, who came willingly with him up to the box. "Take a paper out of the box, Davy,"

Mr. Summers said. Davy put his hand into the box and laughed. "Take just *one* paper," Mr. Summers said. "Harry, you hold it for him." Mr. Graves took the child's hand and removed the folded paper from the tight fist and held it while little Dave stood next to him and looked up at him wonderingly.

"Nancy next," Mr. Summers said. Nancy was twelve, and her school friends breathed heavily as she went forward, switching her skirt, and took a slip daintily from the box. "Bill, Jr.," Mr. Summers said, and Billy, his face red and his feet overlarge, nearly knocked the box over as he got a paper out. "Tessie," Mr. Summers said. She hesitated for a minute, looking around defiantly, and then set her lips and went up to the box. She snatched a paper out and held it behind her.

"Bill," Mr. Summers said, and Bill Hutchinson reached into the box and felt around, bringing his hand out at last with the slip of paper in it.

The crowd was quiet. A girl whispered, "I hope it's not Nancy," and the sound of the whisper reached the edges of the crowd.

"It's not the way it used to be," Old Man Warner said clearly. "People ain't the way they used to be."

"All right," Mr. Summers said. "Open the papers. Harry, you open little Dave's."

Mr. Graves opened the slip of paper and there was a general sigh through the crowd as he held it up and everyone could see that it was blank. Nancy and Bill, Jr., opened theirs at the same time, and both beamed and laughed, turning around to the crowd and holding their slips of paper above their heads.

"Tessie," Mr. Summers said. There was a pause, and then Mr. Summers looked at Bill Hutchinson, and Bill unfolded his paper and showed it. It was blank.

"It's Tessie," Mr. Summers said, and his voice was hushed. "Show us her paper, Bill."

Bill Hutchinson went over to his wife and forced the slip of paper out of her hand. It had a black spot on it, the black spot Mr. Summers had made the night before with the heavy pencil in the coal-company office. Bill Hutchinson held it up, and there was a stir in the crowd.

"All right, folks," Mr. Summers said. "Let's finish quickly."

Although the villagers had forgotten the ritual and lost the original black box, they still remembered to use stones. The pile of stones the boys had made earlier was ready; there were stones on the ground with the blowing scraps of paper that had come out of the box. Mrs. Delacroix selected a stone so large she had to pick it up with both hands and turned to Mrs. Dunbar. "Come on," she said. "Hurry up."

Mrs. Dunbar had small stones in both hands, and she said, gasping for breath, "I can't run at all. You'll have to go ahead and I'll catch up with you."

The children had stones already, and someone gave little Davy Hutchinson a few pebbles.

Tessie Hutchinson was in the center of a cleared space by now, and she held her hands out desperately as the villagers moved in on her. "It isn't fair," she said. A stone hit her on the side of the head.

Old Man Warner was saying, "Come on, come on, everyone." Steve Adams was in the front of the crowd of villagers, with Mrs. Graves beside him.

"It ain't fair, it isn't right," Mrs. Hutchinson screamed, and then they were upon her.

QUESTIONS FOR DISCUSSION AND WRITING

1. What are the first signs that something sinister lurks beneath the surface of this story? How does the end of the story alter our perception of the events of the day?
2. How does our first view of Tessie help to establish her character? To what extent is her final protest justified? How do the other characters portray themselves by their attitudes toward the ritual?
3. Why is Jackson purposely vague about where this story takes place? What do the characters in this particular community say about the way the lottery is practiced in nearby communities?
4. How does the objective point of view of the story help contribute to its festive tone? How is that tone reversed at the conclusion of the story?
5. Compare and contrast the lottery with other social or religious rituals. Why do communities honor the traditions of such rituals? How do they feel about individuals who rebel against them?

45

SARAH ORNE JEWETT

A White Heron

SARAH ORNE JEWETT (1849–1909) was born in South Berwick, Maine, the daughter of a country doctor. Although she attended Berwick Academy, Jewett's real education came from reading and accompanying her father as he called on sick people in the remote countryside. Prompted in part by the example of Harriet Beecher Stowe's novel about Maine, *The Pearl of Orr's Island* (1862), Jewett began writing sketches and stories about her native region. At the age of nineteen, she published her first story, "Mr. Bruce," in *The Atlantic Monthly*. Her editor, William Dean Howells, encouraged her to publish *Deephaven,* a collection of her stories, in 1877. Her friendship with Anne Fields, her publisher's wife, brought her frequently to Boston and resulted in extensive European travel. However, she always returned to her native town where she wrote books such as the biography of her father, *A Country Doctor* (1884), novels such as *A Marsh Island* (1886), and numerous short stories, the best of which were collected in volumes such as *A White Heron* (1886) and *The Country of the Pointed Firs* (1896). "A White Heron," the title story from her 1886 collection, tells of a young girl's choice between the treasures she can buy with money and the treasures she is given by nature.

1

The woods were already filled with shadows one June evening, just before eight o'clock, though a bright sunset still glimmered faintly among the trunks of the trees. A little girl was driving home her cow, a plodding, dilatory, provoking creature in her behavior, but a valued companion for all that. They were going away from the western light, and striking deep into the dark woods, but their feet were familiar with the path, and it was no matter whether their eyes could see it or not.

There was hardly a night the summer through when the old cow could be found waiting at the pasture bars; on the contrary, it was her greatest pleasure to hide herself away among the high huckleberry bushes, and though she wore a loud bell she had made the discovery that if one stood perfectly still it would not ring. So Sylvia had to hunt for her until she found her, and call Co'! Co'! with never an answering Moo, until her childish patience was quite spent. If the creature had not given good milk and plenty of it, the case would have seemed very different to her owners. Besides, Sylvia had all the time there was, and very little use to make of it. Sometimes in pleasant weather it was a consolation to look upon the cow's pranks as an intelligent attempt to play hide and seek, and as the child had no playmates she lent herself to this amusement with a good deal of zest. Though this chase had been so long that the wary animal herself had given an unusual signal of her whereabouts, Sylvia had only laughed when she came upon Mistress Moolly at the swamp-side, and urged her affectionately homeward with a twig of birch leaves. The old cow was not inclined to wander farther, she even turned in the right direction for once as they left the pasture, and stepped along the road at a good pace. She was quite ready to be milked now, and seldom stopped to browse. Sylvia wondered what her grandmother would say because they were so late. It was a great while since she had left home at half past five o'clock, but everybody knew the difficulty of making this errand a short one. Mrs. Tilley had chased the horned torment too many summer evenings herself to blame any one else for lingering, and was only thankful as she waited that she had Sylvia, nowadays, to give such valuable assistance. The good woman suspected that Sylvia loitered occasionally on her own account; there never was such a child for straying about out-of-doors since the world was made! Everybody said that it was a good change for a little maid who had tried to grow for eight years in a crowded manufacturing town, but, as for Sylvia herself, it seemed as if she never had been alive at all before she came to live at the farm. She thought often with wistful compassion of a wretched dry geranium that belonged to a town neighbor.

"'Afraid of folks,'" old Mrs. Tilley said to herself, with a smile, after she had made the unlikely choice of Sylvia from her daughter's houseful of children, and was returning to the farm. "'Afraid of folks,' they said! I guess she won't be troubled no great with 'em up to the old place!" When they reached the door of the lonely house and stopped to unlock it, and the cat came to purr loudly, and rub against them, a deserted pussy, indeed, but fat with young robins, Sylvia whispered that this was a beautiful place to live in, and she never should wish to go home.

The companions followed the shady wood-road, the cow taking slow steps, and the child very fast ones. The cow stopped long at the brook to drink, as if the pasture were not half a swamp, and Sylvia stood still and waited, letting her bare feet cool themselves in the shoal water, while the great twilight moths struck softly against her. She waded on through the brook as the cow moved away, and listened to the thrushes with a heart that beat fast with pleasure. There was a stirring in the great boughs overhead. They were full of little birds and beasts that seemed to be wide-awake, and going about their world, or else saying good-night to each other in sleepy twitters. Sylvia herself felt sleepy as she walked along. However, it was not much farther to the house, and the air was soft and sweet. She was not often in the woods so late as this, and it made her feel as if she were a part of the gray shadows and the moving leaves. She was just thinking how long it seemed since she first came to the farm a year ago, and wondering if everything went on in the noisy town just the same as when she was there; the thought of the great red-faced boy who used to chase and frighten her made her hurry along the path to escape from the shadow of the trees.

Suddenly this little woods-girl is horror-stricken to hear a clear whistle not very far away. Not a bird's whistle, which would have a sort of friendliness, but a boy's whistle, determined, and somewhat aggressive. Sylvia left the cow to whatever sad fate might await her, and stepped discreetly aside into the bushes, but she was just too late. The enemy had discovered her, and called out in a very cheerful and persuasive tone, "Halloa, little girl, how far is it to the road?" and trembling Sylvia answered almost inaudibly, "A good ways."

She did not dare to look boldly at the tall young man, who carried a gun over his shoulder, but she came out of her bush and again followed the cow, while he walked alongside.

"I have been hunting for some birds," the stranger said kindly, "and I have lost my way, and need a friend very much. Don't be afraid," he added gallantly. "Speak up and tell me what your name is, and whether you think I can spend the night at your house, and go out gunning early in the morning."

Sylvia was more alarmed than before. Would not her grandmother consider her much to blame? But who could have foreseen such an accident as this? It did not appear to be her fault, and she hung her head as if the stem of it were broken, but managed to answer, "Sylvy," with much effort when her companion again asked her name.

Mrs. Tilley was standing in the doorway when the trio came into view. The cow gave a loud moo by way of explanation.

"Yes, you'd better speak up for yourself, you old trial! Where'd she tucked herself away this time, Sylvy?" Sylvia kept an awed silence; she knew by instinct that her grandmother did not comprehend the gravity of the situation. She must be mistaking the stranger for one of the farmer-lads of the region.

The young man stood his gun beside the door, and dropped a heavy game-bag beside it; then he bade Mrs. Tilley good-evening, and repeated his wayfarer's story, and asked if he could have a night's lodging.

"Put me anywhere you like," he said. "I must be off early in the morning, before day; but I am very hungry, indeed. You can give me some milk at any rate, that's plain."

"Dear sakes, yes," responded the hostess, whose long slumbering hospitality seemed to be easily awakened. "You might fare better if you went out on the main road a mile or so, but you're welcome to what we've got. I'll milk right off, and you make yourself at home. You can sleep on husks or feathers," she proffered graciously. "I raised them all myself. There's good pasturing for geese just below here towards the ma'sh. Now step round and set a plate for the gentleman, Sylvy!" And Sylvia promptly stepped. She was glad to have something to do, and she was hungry herself.

It was a surprise to find so clean and comfortable a dwelling in this New England wilderness. The young man had known the horrors of its most primitive housekeeping, and the dreary squalor of that level of society which does not rebel at the companionship of hens. This was the best thrift of an old-fashioned farmstead, though on such a small scale that it seemed like a hermitage. He listened eagerly to the old woman's quaint talk, he watched Sylvia's pale face and shining gray eyes with ever growing enthusiasm, and insisted that this was the best supper he had eaten for a month; then, afterward, the new-made friends sat down in the doorway together while the moon came up.

Soon it would be berry-time, and Sylvia was a great help at picking. The cow was a good milker, though a plaguy thing to keep track of, the hostess gossiped frankly, adding presently that she had buried four children, so that Sylvia's mother, and a son (who might be dead) in California were all the children she had left. "Dan, my boy, was a great hand to go gunning," she explained sadly. "I never wanted for pa'tridges or gray squer'ls while he was to home. He's been a great wand'rer, I expect, and he's no hand to write letters. There, I don't blame him, I'd ha' seen the world myself if it had been so I could.

"Sylvia takes after him," the grandmother continued affectionately, after a minute's pause. "There ain't a foot o'ground she don't know her way over, and the wild creatur's counts her one o'themselves. Squer'ls she'll tame to come an' feed right out o' her hands, and all sorts o'birds. Last winter she got the jay-birds to bangeing here, and I believe she'd 'a' scanted herself of her own meals to have plenty to throw out amongst 'em, if I hadn't kep' watch. Anything but crows, I tell her, I'm willin' to help support—though Dan he went an' tamed one o' them that did seem to have reason same as folks. It was round here a good spell after he went away. Dan an' his father they didn't hitch—but he never held up his head ag'in after Dan had dared him an' gone off."

The guest did not notice this hint of family sorrows in his eager interest in something else.

"So Sylvy knows all about birds, does she?" he exclaimed, as he looked round at the little girl who sat, very demure but increasingly sleepy, in the moonlight. "I am making a collection of birds myself. I have been at it ever since I was a boy." (Mrs. Tilley smiled.) "There are two or three very rare ones I have been hunting for these five years. I mean to get them on my own ground if they can be found."

"Do you cage 'em up?" asked Mrs. Tilley doubtfully, in response to this enthusiastic announcement.

"Oh, no, they're stuffed and preserved, dozens and dozens of them," said the ornithologist, "and I have shot or snared every one myself. I caught a glimpse of a white heron three miles from here on Saturday, and I have followed it in this direction. They have never been found in this district at all. The little white heron, it is," and he turned again to look at Sylvia with the hope of discovering that the rare bird was one of her acquaintances.

But Sylvia was watching a hop-toad in the narrow footpath.

"You would know the heron if you saw it," the stranger continued eagerly. "A queer tall white bird with soft feathers and long thin legs. And it would have a nest perhaps in the top of a high tree, made of sticks, something like a hawk's nest."

Sylvia's heart gave a wild beat; she knew that strange white bird, and had once stolen softly near where it stood in some bright green swamp grass, away over at the other side of the woods. There was an open place where the sunshine always seemed strangely yellow and hot, where tall, nodding rushes grew, and her grandmother had warned her that she might sink in the soft black mud underneath and never be heard of more. Not far beyond were the salt marshes and beyond those was the sea, the sea which Sylvia wondered and dreamed about, but never had looked upon, though its great voice could often be heard above the noise of the woods on stormy nights.

"I can't think of anything I should like so much as to find that heron's nest," the handsome stranger was saying. "I would give ten dollars to anybody who could show it to me," he added desperately, "and I mean to spend my whole vacation hunting for it if need be. Perhaps it was only migrating, or had been chased out of its own region by some bird of prey."

Mrs. Tilley gave amazed attention to all this, but Sylvia still watched the toad, not divining, as she might have done at some calmer time, that the creature wished to get to its hole under the doorstep, and was much hindered by the unusual spectators at that hour of the evening. No amount of thought, that night, could decide how many wished-for treasures the ten dollars, so lightly spoken of, would buy.

The next day the young sportsman hovered about the woods, and Sylvia kept him company, having lost her first fear of the friendly lad, who proved to be most kind and sympathetic. He told her many things about the birds and what they knew and where they lived and what they did with themselves. And he gave her a jack-knife, which she thought as great a treasure as if she were a desert-islander. All day long he did not once make her troubled or afraid except when he brought down some unsuspecting singing creature from its bough. Sylvia would have liked him vastly better without his gun; she could not understand why he killed the very birds he seemed to like so much. But as the day waned, Sylvia still watched the young man with loving admiration. She had never seen anybody so charming and delightful; the woman's heart, asleep in the child, was vaguely thrilled by a dream of love. Some premonition of that great power stirred and swayed these young foresters who traversed the solemn woodlands with soft-footed silent care. They stopped to listen to a bird's song; they pressed forward again eagerly, parting the branches—speaking to each other rarely and in whispers; the young man going first and Sylvia following, fascinated, a few steps behind, with her gray eyes dark with excitement.

She grieved because the longed-for white heron was elusive, but she did not lead the guest, she only followed, and there was no such thing as speaking first. The sound of her own unquestioned voice would have terrified her—it was hard enough to answer yes or no when there was need of that. At last evening began to fall, and they drove the cow home together, and Sylvia smiled with pleasure when they came to the place where she heard the whistle and was afraid only the night before.

2

Half a mile from home, at the farther edge of the woods, where the land was highest, a great pine-tree stood, the last of its generation. Whether it was left for a boundary mark, or for what reason, no one could say; the woodchoppers who had felled its mates were dead and gone long ago, and a whole forest of sturdy trees, pines and oaks and maples, had grown again. But the stately head of this old pine towered above them all and made a landmark for sea and shore miles and miles away. Sylvia knew it well. She had always believed that whoever climbed to the top of it could see the ocean; and the little girl had often laid her hand on the great rough trunk and looked up wistfully at those dark boughs that the wind always stirred, no matter how hot and still the air might be below. Now she thought of the tree with a new excitement, for why, if one climbed it at break of day, could not one see all the world, and easily discover whence the white heron flew, and mark the place, and find the hidden nest?

What a spirit of adventure, what wild ambition! What fancied triumph and delight and glory for the later morning when she could make known the secret! It was almost too real and too great for the childish heart to bear.

All night the door of the little house stood open, and the whippoorwills came and sang upon the very step. The young sportsman and his old hostess were sound asleep, but Sylvia's great design kept her broad awake and watching. She forgot to think of sleep. The short summer night seemed as long as the winter darkness, and at last when the whippoorwills ceased, and she was afraid the morning would after all come too soon, she stole out of the house and followed the pasture path through the woods, hastening toward the open ground beyond, listening with a sense of comfort and companionship to the drowsy twitter of a half-awakened bird, whose perch she had jarred in passing. Alas, if the great wave of human interest which flooded for the first time this dull little life should sweep away the satisfactions of an existence heart to heart with nature and the dumb life of the forest!

There was the huge tree asleep yet in the paling moonlight, and small and hopeful Sylvia began with utmost bravery to mount to the top of it, with tingling, eager blood coursing the channels of her whole frame, with her bare feet and fingers, that pinched and held like bird's claws to the monstrous ladder reaching up, up, almost to the sky itself. First she must mount the white oak tree that grew alongside, where she was almost lost among the dark branches and the green leaves heavy and wet with dew; a bird fluttered off its nest, and a red squirrel ran to and fro and scolded pettishly at the harmless house-breaker. Sylvia felt her way easily. She had often climbed there, and knew that higher still one of the oak's upper branches chafed against the pine trunk, just where its lower boughs were set close together. There, when she made the dangerous pass from one tree to the other, the great enterprise would really begin.

She crept out along the swaying oak limb at last, and took the daring step across into the old pine-tree. The way was harder than she thought; she must reach far and hold fast, the sharp dry twigs caught and held her and scratched her like angry talons, the pitch made her thin little fingers clumsy and stiff as she went round and round the tree's great stem, higher and higher upward. The sparrows and robins in the woods below were beginning to wake and twitter to the dawn, yet it seemed much lighter there aloft in the pine-tree, and the child knew that she must hurry if her project were to be of any use.

The tree seemed to lengthen itself out as she went up, and to reach farther and farther upward. It was like a great main-mast to the voyaging earth; it must truly have been amazed that morning through all its ponderous frame as it felt this determined spark of human spirit creeping and climbing from higher branch to branch. Who knows how steadily the least twigs held themselves to advantage this light, weak creature on her way! The old pine must have loved his new dependent. More than all the hawks, and bats, and moths, and even the sweet-voiced thrushes, was the brave, beating heart of the solitary gray-eyed child. And the tree stood still and held away the winds that June morning while the dawn grew bright in the east.

Sylvia's face was like a pale star, if one had seen it from the ground, when the last thorny bough was past, and she stood trembling and tired but wholly triumphant, high in the tree-top. Yes, there was the sea with the dawning sun making a golden dazzle over it, and toward that glorious east flew two hawks with slow-moving pinions. How low they looked in the air from that height when before one had only seen them far up, and dark against the blue sky. Their gray feathers were as soft as moths; they seemed only a little way from the tree, and Sylvia felt as if she too could go flying away among the clouds. Westward, the woodlands and farms reached miles and miles into the distance; here and there were church steeples, and white villages; truly it was a vast and awesome world.

The birds sang louder and louder. At last the sun came up bewilderingly bright. Sylvia could see the white sails of ships out at sea, and the clouds that were purple and rose-colored and yellow at first began to fade away. Where was the white heron's nest in the sea of green branches, and was this wonderful sight and pageant of the world the only reward for having climbed to such a giddy height? Now look down again, Sylvia, where the green marsh is set among the shining birches and dark hemlocks; there where you saw the white heron once you will see him again; look, look! a white spot of him like a single floating feather comes up from the dead hemlock and grows larger, and rises, and comes close at last, and goes by the landmark pine with a steady sweep of wing and outstretched slender neck and crested head. And wait! wait! do not move a foot or a finger, little girl, do not send an arrow of light and consciousness from your two eager eyes, for the heron has perched on a pine bough not far beyond yours, and cries back to his mate on the nest, and plumes his feathers for the new day!

The child gives a long sigh a minute later when a company of shouting cat-birds comes also to the tree, and vexed by their fluttering and lawlessness the solemn heron goes away. She knows his secret now, the wild, light, slender bird that floats and wavers, and goes back like an arrow presently to his home in the green world beneath. Then Sylvia, well satisfied, makes her perilous way down again, not daring to look far below the branch she stands on, ready to cry sometimes because her fingers ache and her lamed feet slip. Wondering over and over again what the stranger would say to her, and what he would think when she told him how to find his way straight to the heron's nest.

"Sylvy, Sylvy!" called the busy old grandmother again and again, but nobody answered, and the small husk bed was empty, and Sylvia had disappeared.

The guest waked from a dream, and remembering his day's pleasure hurried to dress himself that it might sooner begin. He was sure from the way the shy little girl looked once or twice yesterday that she had at least seen the white heron, and now she must really be persuaded to tell. Here she comes now, paler than ever, and her worn old frock is torn and tattered, and smeared with pine pitch. The grandmother and the sportsman stand in the door together and question her, and the splendid moment has come to speak of the dead hemlock-tree by the green marsh.

But Sylvia does not speak after all, though the old grandmother fretfully rebukes her, and the young man's kind appealing eyes are looking straight in her own. He can make them rich with money; he has promised it, and they are poor now. He is so well worth making happy, and he waits to hear the story she can tell.

No, she must keep silence! What is it that suddenly forbids her and makes her dumb? Has she been nine years growing, and now, when the great world for the first time puts out a hand to her, must she thrust it aside for a bird's sake? The murmur of the pine's green branches is in her ears, she remembers how the white heron came flying through the golden air and how they watched the sea and the morning together, and Sylvia cannot speak, she cannot tell the heron's secret and give its life away.

Dear loyalty, that suffered a sharp pang as the guest went away disappointed later in the day, that could have served and followed him and loved him as a dog loves! Many a night Sylvia heard the echo of his whistle haunting the pasture path as she came home with the loitering cow. She forgot even her sorrow at the sharp report of his gun and the piteous sight of thrushes and sparrows dropping silent to the ground, their songs hushed and their pretty feathers stained and wet with blood. Were the birds better friends than their hunter might have been—who can tell? Whatever treasures were lost to her, woodlands and summer-time, remember! Bring your gifts and graces and tell your secrets to this lonely country child!

QUESTIONS FOR DISCUSSION AND WRITING

1. What is the major conflict Sylvia must resolve in the story? What motive prompts her to climb the pine tree? What decision does she make once she has made the climb?
2. How do Sylvia's mother and grandmother describe her? How does Sylvia characterize herself? Why is she attracted to the young man with the gun?
3. How does the rural setting for this story help shape Sylvia's attitudes and values? For example, why does she feel that "she never had been alive at all before she came to live on the farm"?
4. Although most of the story is told from Sylvia's point of view, the author shifts perspective several times. What kind of information does Jewett convey from these other perspectives?
5. In what sense does the last paragraph state the theme of the story? How would the omission of this paragraph change the story? Explain your answer.

46

CHARLES JOHNSON

Moving Pictures

CHARLES JOHNSON was born in 1948 in Evanston, Illinois, and educated at Southern Illinois University and the State University of New York at Stony Brook. He worked as a cartoonist and reporter for the *Chicago Tribune* and as a member of the art staff at *St. Louis Proud* before accepting a position as professor of English at the University of Washington, Seattle. Under the tutelage of the late author John Gardner, Johnson published his first novel, *Faith and the Good Thing* (1974), a humorous folktale of a Southern black girl's trip to Chicago. Johnson's second novel, *Oxherding Tale* (1982), a modern, comic, philosophical slave narrative, tells of a young herdsman's search for his rebellious ox. Johnson has also written for two collections of drawings, *Black Humor* (1970) and *Half-Past Nation Time* (1972); written numerous scripts for PBS, most notably "Charlie's Pad" (1970) and "Booker" (1983); and published a collection of short stories, *The Sorcerer's Apprentice* (1986). His third novel, *Middle Passage* (1990), won the National Book Award for fiction. "Moving Pictures," reprinted from *The Sorcerer's Apprentice,* documents the costs of engaging in collaborative, creative work.

You sit in the Neptune Theater waiting for the thin, overhead lights to dim with a sense of respect, perhaps even reverence, for American movie houses are, as everyone knows, the new cathedrals, their stories better remembered than legends, totems, or mythologies, their directors more popular than novelists, more influential than saints—enough people, you've been told, have seen the James Bond adventures to fill the entire country of Argentina. Perhaps you have written this movie. Perhaps not. Regardless, you come to it as everyone does, as a seeker groping in the darkness for light, hoping something magical will be beamed from above, and no matter how bad this matinee is, or silly, something deep and maybe even too dangerous to talk loudly about will indeed happen to you and the others, before this drama reels to its last transparent frame.

Naturally, you have left your life outside the door. Like any life, it's a messy thing, hardly as orderly as art, what some call life in the fast lane: the Sanka and sugar-doughnut breakfasts, bumper-to-bumper traffic downtown, the business lunches, and a breakneck schedule not to get ahead but simply to stay in one place, which is peculiar, because you grew up in the sixties speeding on methadone and despising all this, knowing your Age (Aquarian) was made for finer stuff. But no matter. Outside, across town, you have put away for ninety minutes the tedious, repetitive job that is, obviously, beneath your talents, sensitivity, and education (a degree in English), the once beautiful woman—or wife—a former model (local), college dancer, or semiprofessional actress named Megan or Daphne, who has grown tired of you, or you of her, and talks now of legal separation and finding herself, the children from a former, frighteningly brief marriage whom you don't want to lose, the mortgage, alimony, IRS audit, the aging, gin-fattened face that once favored a rock star's but now frowns back at you in the bathroom mirror, the young woman at work born in 1960 and unable to recall John Kennedy who, after the Christmas party, took you to bed in her spacious downtown loft, perhaps out of pity because your mother, God bless her, died and left you with $1,000 in debt before you could get the old family house clear—all that shelved, mercifully, as the film starts, first that frosty mountaintop ringed by stars, or a lion roaring, or floodlights bathing the tips of buildings in a Hollywood skyline: stable trademarks in a world of flux, you think, surefire signs that whatever follows—tragedy or farce—is made by people who are accomplished dream merchants. Perhaps more: masters of vision, geniuses of the epistemological Murphy.

If you have written this film, which is possible, you look for your name in the credits, and probably frown at the names of the Crew, each recalling some disaster during the production, first at the studio, then later on location for five weeks in Oklahoma cow towns during the winter, which was worse than living on the moon, the days boiling and nights so cold. Nevertheless, you'd seen it as a miracle, an act of God when the director, having read your novel, called, offering you the project—a historical romance—then walked you patiently through the first eight drafts, suspicious of you at first (there was real money riding on this; it wasn't poetry), of your dreary, novelistic pretensions to Deep Profundity, and you equally suspicious of him, his background in sitcoms, obsession with "keeping it sexy," and love of Laurel and Hardy films. For this you wrote a dissertation on Derrida? Yet you'd listened. He was right, in the end. He was good, you admitted, grudgingly. He knew, as you—with your liberal arts degree—didn't, the meaning of Entertainment. You'd learned. With his help, you got good, too. You gloated. And lost friends. "A movie?" said your poet friends. "That's wonderful, it's happening for you," and then they avoided you as if you had AIDS. What *was* happening was this:

You'd shelved the novel, the Big Book, for bucks monitored by the Writers Guild (West), threw yourself into fast-and-dirty scripts, the instant gratification of quick deadlines and fat checks because the Book, with its complexity and promise of critical praise, the Book, with its long-distance demands and no financial reward whatsoever, was impossible, and besides, you didn't have it anymore, not really, the gift for narrative or language, while the scripts were easy, like writing shorthand, and soon—way sooner than you thought—the films, with their life span shorter than a mayfly's, were all you could do. It's a living, you said. Nothing lasts forever. And you pushed on.

The credits crawl up against a montage of Oklahoma farm life, and in this you read a story, too, even before the film begins. For the audience, the actors are stars, the new Olympians, but oh, you know them, this one—the male lead—whose range is boundless, who could be a Brando, but who hadn't seen work in two years before this role and survived by doing voice-overs for a cartoon villain in *The Smurfs;* that one—the female supporting role—who can play the full scale of emotions, but whose last memorable performance was a commercial for Rolaids, all of them; all, including you, fighting for life in a city where the air is so corrupt joggers spit black after a two-mile run; failing, trying desperately to keep up the front of doing-well, these actors, treating you shabbily sometimes because your salary was bigger than theirs, even larger than the producer's, though he wasn't exactly hurting—no, he was richer than a medieval king, a complex man of remarkable charm and cunning, someone both to admire for his Horatio Alger orphan-boy success and to fear for his worship at the altar of power. You won't forget the evening he asked you to his home after a long conference, served you scotch, and then, from inside a drawer in his desk removed an envelope, dumped its contents out, and you saw maybe fifty snapshots of beautiful, naked women on his bed—all of them second-rate actresses, though the female supporting role was there, too—and he watched you closely for your reaction, sipping his drink, smiling, then asked, "You ever sleep with a woman like that?" No, you hadn't. And no, you didn't trust him either. You didn't turn your back. But, then again, nobody in this business did, and in some ways he was, you knew, better than most.

You'd compromised, given up ground, won a few artistic points, but generally you agreed to the producer's ideas—it *was* his show—and then the small army of badly paid performers and production people took over, you trailing behind them in Oklahoma, trying to look writerly, wearing a Panama hat, holding your notepad ready for re-writes, surviving the tedium of eight or nine takes for difficult scenes, the fights, fallings-out, bad catered food, and midnight affairs, watching your script change at each level of interpretation—director, actor—until it was unrecognizable, a new thing entirely, a celebration of the Crew. Not you. Does anyone suspect how bad this thing really looked in rough cut? How miraculous it is that its rags of shots, conflicting ideas, and scraps of footage actually cohere? You sneak a look around at the audience, the faces lit by the glow of the screen. No one suspects. You've managed to fool them again, you old fox.

No matter whether the film is yours or not, it pulls you in, reels in your perception like a trout. On the narrow screen, the story begins with an establishing wide shot of an Oklahoma farm, then in close-up shows the face of a big, tow-headed, brown-freckled boy named Bret, and finally settles on a two-shot of Bret and his blond, bosomy girl friend, Bess. No margin for failure in a formula like that. In the opening funeral scene at a tiny whitewashed church, camera favors Bret, whose father has died. Our hero must seek his fortune in the city. Bess just hates to see him go. Dissolve to cemetery gate. As they leave the cemetery, and the coffin is lowered, she squeezes his hand, and something inside you shivers, the sense of ruin you felt at your own mother's funeral, the irreversible feeling of abandonment. There was no girl with you, but you wished to heaven there had been, the one named Sondra you knew in high school who wouldn't see you for squat, preferring basketball players to weird little wimps and geeks, which is pretty much what you were back then, a washout to those who knew you, but you give all that to Bret and Bess, the pain of parental loss, the hopeless, quiet love never to be, which thickens the screen so thoroughly that when Bess kisses Bret, your nose is clogged with tears and mucus, and then you have your handkerchief out, honking shamelessly, your eyes streaming, locked—even you—in a cycle of emotion (yours) which their images have borrowed, intensified, then given back to you, not because the images or sensations are sad, but because, at bottom, all you have known these last few minutes are the workings of your own nervous system. That is all you have ever known. You yourself have been supplying the grief and satisfaction all along, from within. But even that is not the true magic of film.

As Bret rides away, you remember sitting in the studio's tiny editing room amidst reels of film hanging like stockings in a bathroom, the editor, a fat, friendly man named Coates, tolerating your curiosity, letting you peer into his viewer as he patched the first reel together, figuring he owed you, a semifamous scriptwriter, that much. Each frame, you recall, was a single frozen image, like an individual thought, complete in itself, with no connection to the others, as if time stood still; but then the frames came faster as the viewer sped up, chasing each other, surging forward and creating a linear, continuous motion that outstripped your perception, and presto: a sensuously rich world erupted and took such nerve-knocking reality that you shielded your eyes when the harpsichord music came up and Bret stepped into a darkened Oklahoma shed seen only from his point of view—oh, yes, at times even your body responded, the sweat glands swaling, but it was lunchtime then and Coates wanted to go to the cafeteria for coffee and clicked off his viewer; the images flipped less quickly, slowed finally to a stop, the drama disappearing again into frames, and you saw, pulling on your coat, the nerve racking, heart-thumping vision for what it really was: the illusion of speed.

But is even that the magic of film? Sitting back in your seat, aware of your right leg falling asleep, you think so, for the film has no capacity to fool you anymore. You do not give it your feelings to transfigure. All that you see with godlike detachment are your own decisions, the lines that were dropped, and the microphone just visible in a corner of one scene. Nevertheless, it's gratifying to see the audience laugh out loud at the funny parts, and blubber when Bret rides home at last to marry Bess (actually, they hated each other on the set), believing, as you can't, in a dream spun from accelerated imagery. It almost makes a man feel superior, like knowing how Uri Geller bends all those spoons.

And then it is done, the theater emptying, the hour and a half of illusion over. You file out with the others, amazed by how so much can be projected onto the tabula rasa of the Big Screen—grief, passion, fire, death—yet it remains, in the end, untouched. Dragging on your overcoat, the images still an afterglow in your thoughts, you step outside to the street. It takes your eyes, still in low gear, a moment to adjust to the light of late afternoon, traffic noise, and the things around you as you walk to your Fiat, feeling good, the objects on the street as flat and dimensionless at first as props on a stage. And then you stop.

The Fiat, you notice, has been broken into. The glove compartment has been rifled, and this is where you keep a checkbook, an extra key to the house, and where—you remember—you put the report due tomorrow at nine sharp. The glove compartment, how does it look? Like a part of your body, yes? A wound? From it spills a crumpled photo of your wife, who has asked you to move out so she can have the house, and another one of the children, who haven't the faintest idea how empty you feel getting up every morning to finance their lives at a job that is a ghastly joke, given your talents, where you can't slow down and at least four competitors stand waiting for you to step aside, fall on your face, or die, and the injustice of all this, what you see in the narrow range of radiation you call vision, in the velocity of thought, is necessary and sufficient—as some logicians say—to bring your fists down again and again on the Fiat's roof. You climb inside, sit, furiously cranking the starter, then swear and lower your forehead to the steering wheel, which is, as anyone in Hollywood can tell you, conduct unbecoming a triple-threat talent like yourself: producer, star, and director in the longest, most fabulous show of all.

QUESTIONS FOR DISCUSSION AND WRITING

1. In what unusual way does the narrator provide the exposition for this story? How does the narrator's discovery that his car has been broken into bring to a climax the various conflicts in the story?
2. What evidence is there to support the narrator's view that he has compromised his talent? How does he characterize the director's, the actors', the producer's and the editors' roles in this compromise?
3. How does the narrator create a sense that the movie house is more than a place of entertainment? How does the setting on location differ from the setting in the book and the one created in the film?
4. Why does the narrator shift the second person point of view? How does the "you" shift in meaning throughout the story?
5. What are the different meanings suggested by the title? In what ways does the last sentence in the story suggest that movies provide an escape from and an intensification of reality?

47

JAMES JOYCE

Araby

JAMES JOYCE (1882–1941) was born in Dublin, Ireland, and was given a strict Jesuit education at schools such as Belvedere College in Dublin. During his last year at Belvedere, Joyce began to reject his Catholic faith, choosing instead to study modern languages at University College, Dublin. Joyce's literary hero was playwright Henrik Ibsen, whose plays embodied a theme that intrigued Joyce: the cost of individual rebellion in the face of community conformity. So that he could read and write about Ibsen's plays, Joyce taught himself Norwegian. In 1902, Joyce left home, religion, and country to spend the rest of his life as an exile in Europe. He lived briefly in Paris, Trieste, and Zurich, teaching school and writing stories about the various forms of intellectual paralysis he perceived in his homeland. Joyce published these stories, *Dubliners,* in 1914 and then, in 1916, produced a semi-autobiographical account of his own development as a writer, *A Portrait of the Artist as a Young Man.* In 1920 Joyce moved back to Paris, where he found

support and sympathy for the literary innovations in his masterpiece, *Ulysses* (1922). Complex and uncompromising in its language, the book created such a public controversy that it was banned in America until a high court cleared the way for its publication in 1933. Ignored and often misunderstood, Joyce spent the remaining years of his life working on his final experimental epic, *Finnegans Wake* (1939). "Araby" and "The Dead" are both reprinted from *Dubliners.* The first story tells of a young boy's disappointment and the second of an older man's disillusionment.

North Richmond Street, being blind, was a quiet street except at the hour when the Christian Brothers' School set the boys free. An uninhabited house of two storeys stood at the blind end, detached from its neighbours in a square ground. The other houses of the street, conscious of decent lives within them, gazed at one another with brown imperturbable faces.

The former tenant of our house, a priest, had died in the back drawing-room. Air, musty from having been long enclosed, hung in all the rooms, and the waste room behind the kitchen was littered with old useless papers. Among these I found a few paper-covered books, the pages of which were curled and damp: *The Abbot,* by Walter Scott, *The Devout Communicant* and *The Memoirs of Vidocq*. I liked the last best because its leaves were yellow. The wild garden behind the house contained a central apple-tree and a few straggling bushes under one of which I found the late tenant's rusty bicycle-pump. He had been a very charitable priest; in his will he had left all his money to institutions and the furniture of his house to his sister.

When the short days of winter came dusk fell before we had well eaten our dinners. When we met in the street the houses had grown sombre. The space of sky above us was the colour of ever-changing violet and towards it the lamps of the street lifted their feeble lanterns. The cold air stung us and we played till our bodies glowed. Our shouts echoed in the silent street. The career of our play brought us through the dark muddy lanes behind the houses where we ran the gauntlet of the rough tribes from the cottages, to the back doors of the dark dripping gardens where odours arose from the ashpits, to the dark odorous stables where a coachman smoothed and combed the horse or shook music from the buckled harness. When we returned to the street light from the kitchen windows had filled the areas. If my uncle was seen turning the corner we hid in the shadow until we had seen him safely housed. Or if Mangan's sister came out on the doorstep to call her brother in to his tea we watched her from our shadow peer up and down the street. We waited to see whether she would remain or go in and, if she remained, we left our shadow and walked up to Mangan's steps resignedly. She was waiting for us, her figure defined by the light from the half-opened door. Her brother always teased her before he obeyed and I stood by the railings looking at her. Her dress swung as she moved her body and the soft rope of her hair tossed from side to side.

Every morning I lay on the floor in the front parlour watching her door. The blind was pulled down to within an inch of the sash so that I could not be seen. When she came out on the doorstep my heart leaped. I ran to the hall, seized my books and followed her. I kept her brown figure always in my eye, and, when we came near the point at which our ways diverged, I quickened my pace and passed her. This happened morning after morning. I had never spoken to her, except for a few casual words, and yet her name was like a summons to all my foolish blood.

Her image accompanied me even in places the most hostile to romance. On Saturday evenings when my aunt went marketing I had to go to carry some of the parcels. We walked through the flaring streets, jostled by drunken men and bargaining women, amid the curses of labourers, the shrill litanies of shop-boys who stood on guard by the barrels of pigs' cheeks, the nasal chanting of street-singers, who sang a *come-all-you* about O'Donovan Rossa, or a ballad about the troubles in our native land. These noises converged in a single sensation of life for me: I imagined that I bore my chalice safely through a throng of foes. Her name sprang to my lips at moments in strange prayers and praises which I myself did not understand. My eyes were often full of tears (I could not tell why) and at times a flood from my heart seemed to pour itself out into my bosom. I thought little of the future. I did not know whether I would ever speak to her or not or, if I spoke to her, how I could tell her of my confused adoration. But my body was like a harp and her words and gestures were like fingers running upon the wires.

One evening I went into the back drawing-room in which the priest had died. It was a dark rainy evening and there was no sound in the house. Through one of the broken panes I heard the rain impinge upon the earth, the fine incessant needles of water playing in the sodden beds. Some distant lamp or lighted window gleamed below me. I was thankful that I could see so little. All my senses seemed to desire to veil themselves and, feeling that I was about to slip from them, I pressed the palms of my hands together until they trembled, murmuring: "*O love! O love!*" many times.

At last she spoke to me. When she addressed the first words to me I was so confused that I did not know what to answer. She asked me was I going to *Araby*. I forgot whether I answered yes or no. It would be a splendid bazaar, she said she would love to go.

"And why can't you?" I asked.

While she spoke she turned a silver bracelet round and round her wrist. She could not go, she said, because there would be a retreat that week in her convent. Her brother and two other boys were fighting for their caps and I was alone at the railings. She held one of the spikes, bowing her head towards me. The light from the lamp opposite our door caught the white curve of her neck, lit up her hair that rested there and, falling, lit up the hand upon the railing. It fell over one side of her dress and caught the white border of a petticoat, just visible as she stood at ease.

"It's well for you," she said.

"If I go," I said, "I will bring you something."

What innumerable follies laid waste my waking and sleeping thoughts after that evening! I wished to annihilate the tedious intervening days. I chafed against the work of school. At night in my bedroom and by day in the classroom her image came between me and the page I strove to read. The syllables of the word *Araby* were called to me through the silence in which my soul luxuriated and cast an Eastern enchantment over me. I asked for leave to go to the bazaar on Saturday night. My aunt was surprised and hoped it was not some Freemason affair. I answered few questions in class. I watched my master's face pass from amiability to sternness; he hoped I was not beginning to idle. I could not call my wandering thoughts together. I had hardly any patience with the serious work of life which, now that it stood between me and my desire, seemed to me child's play, ugly monotonous child's play.

On Saturday morning I reminded my uncle that I wished to go to the bazaar in the evening. He was fussing at the hallstand, looking for the hat-brush, and answered curtly:

"Yes, boy, I know."

As he was in the hall I could not go into the front parlour and lie at the window. I left the house in bad humour and walked slowly towards the school. The air was pitilessly raw and already my heart misgave me.

When I came home to dinner my uncle had not yet been home. Still it was early. I sat staring at the clock for some time and, when its ticking began to irritate me, I left the room. I mounted the staircase and gained the upper part of the house. The high cold empty gloomy rooms liberated me and I went from room to room singing. From the front window I saw my companions playing below in the street. Their cries reached me weakened and indistinct and, leaning my forehead against the cool glass, I looked over at the dark house where she lived. I may have stood there for an hour, seeing nothing but the brown-clad figure cast by my imagination, touched discreetly by the lamplight at the curved neck, at the hand upon the railing and at the border below the dress.

When I came downstairs again I found Mrs. Mercer sitting at the fire. She was an old garrulous woman, a pawnbroker's widow, who collected used stamps for some pious purpose. I had to endure the gossip of the tea-table. The meal was prolonged beyond an hour and still my uncle did not come. Mrs. Mercer stood up to go: she was sorry she couldn't wait any longer, but it was after eight o'clock and she did not like to be out late, as the night air was bad for her. When she had gone I began to walk up and down the room, clenching my fists. My aunt said:

"I'm afraid you may put off your bazaar for this night of Our Lord."

At nine o'clock I heard my uncle's latchkey in the halldoor. I heard him talking to himself and heard the hallstand rocking when it had received the weight of his overcoat. I could interpret these signs. When he was midway through his dinner I asked him to give me the money to go to the bazaar. He had forgotten.

"The people are in bed and after their first sleep now," he said.

I did not smile. My aunt said to him energetically:

"Can't you give him the money and let him go? You've kept him late enough as it is."

My uncle said he was very sorry he had forgotten. He said he believed in the old saying: "All work and no play makes Jack a dull boy." He asked me where I was going and, when I had told him a second time he asked me did I know *The Arab's Farewell to his Steed*. When I left the kitchen he was about to recite the opening lines of the piece to my aunt.

I held a florin tightly in my hand as I strode down Buckingham Street towards the station. The sight of the streets thronged with buyers and glaring with gas recalled to me the purpose of my journey. I took my seat in a third-class carriage of a deserted train. After an intolerable delay the train moved out of the station slowly. It crept onward among ruinous houses and over the twinkling river. At Westland Row Station a crowd of people pressed to the carriage doors; but the porters moved them back, saying that it was a special train for the bazaar. I remained alone in the bare carriage. In a few minutes the train drew up beside an improvised wooden platform. I passed out on to the road and saw by the lighted dial of a clock that it was ten minutes to ten. In front of me was a large building which displayed the magical name.

I could not find any sixpenny entrance and, fearing that the bazaar would be closed, I passed in quickly through a turnstile, handing a shilling to a weary-looking man. I found myself in a big hall girdled at half its height by a gallery. Nearly all the stalls were closed and the greater part of the hall was in darkness. I recognised a silence like that which pervades a church after a service. I walked into the centre of the bazaar timidly. A few people were gathered about the stalls which were still open. Before a curtain, over which the words *Café Chantant* were written in coloured lamps, two men were counting money on a salver. I listened to the fall of the coins.

Remembering with difficulty why I had come I went over to one of the stalls and examined porcelain vases and flowered tea-sets. At the door of the stall a young lady was talking and laughing with two young gentlemen. I remarked their English accents and listened vaguely to their conversation.

"Oh, I never said such a thing!"

"Oh, but you did!"

"Oh, but I didn't!"

"Didn't she say that?"

"Yes. I heard her."

"Oh, there's a . . . fib!"

Observing me the young lady came over and asked me did I wish to buy anything. The tone of her voice was not encouraging; she seemed to have spoken to me out of a sense of duty. I looked humbly at the great jars that stood like eastern guards at either side of the dark entrance to the stall and murmured:

"No, thank you."

The young lady changed the position of one of the vases and went back to the two young men. They began to talk of the same subject. Once or twice the young lady glanced at me over her shoulder.

I lingered before her stall, though I knew my stay was useless, to make my interest in her wares seem the more real. Then I turned away slowly and walked down the middle of the bazaar. I allowed the two pennies to fall against the sixpence in my pocket. I heard a voice call from one end of the gallery that the light was out. The upper part of the hall was now completely dark.

Gazing up into the darkness I saw myself as a creature driven and derided by vanity; and my eyes burned with anguish and anger.

QUESTIONS FOR DISCUSSION AND WRITING

1. What does the narrator hope to accomplish by going to the bazaar? How does his uncle momentarily complicate his purpose? What prevents the boy from accomplishing his purpose once he arrives at the bazaar?

2. How does the narrator use external details to characterize Mangan's sister? What qualities or ideas does she seem to represent? For example, what does he mean by "I imagined that I bore my chalice safely through a throng of foes?"

3. In what ways does the setting of North Richmond Street help establish the tone of the story? How does the narrator perceive the priest's house, the market, and the bazaar?
4. To what extent does the narrator understand the motives for his actions? What revision in his point of view does he acknowledge in the last paragraph of the story?
5. How does the story reveal the connection between the boy's sexual awakening and his yearning for idealized romance?

48
JAMES JOYCE
The Dead

Lily, the caretaker's daughter, was literally run off her feet. Hardly had she brought one gentleman into the little pantry behind the office on the ground floor and helped him off with his overcoat than the wheezy hall-door bell clanged again and she had to scamper along the bare hallway to let in another guest. It was well for her she had not to attend to the ladies also. But Miss Kate and Miss Julia had thought of that and had converted the bathroom upstairs into a ladies' dressing-room. Miss Kate and Miss Julia were there, gossiping and laughing and fussing, walking after each other to the head of the stairs, peering down over the banisters and calling down to Lily to ask her who had come.

It was always a great affair, the Misses Morkan's annual dance. Everybody who knew them came to it, members of the family, old friends of the family, the members of Julia's choir, any of Kate's pupils that were grown up enough and even some of Mary Jane's pupils too. Never once had it fallen flat. For years and years it had gone off in splendid style as long as anyone could remember; ever since Kate and Julia, after the death of their brother Pat, had left the house in Stoney Batter and taken Mary Jane, their only niece, to live with them in the dark gaunt house on Usher's Island, the upper part of which they had rented from Mr. Fulham, the cornfactor on the ground floor. That was a good thirty years ago if it was a day. Mary Jane, who was then a little girl in short clothes, was now the main prop of the household for she had the organ in Haddington Road. She had been through the Academy and gave a pupils' concert every year in the upper room of the Antient Concert Rooms. Many of her pupils belonged to better-class families on the Kingstown and Dalkey line. Old as they were, her aunts also did their share. Julia, though she was quite grey, was still the leading soprano in Adam and Eve's, and Kate, being too feeble to go about much, gave music lessons to beginners on the old square piano in the back room. Lily, the caretaker's daughter, did housemaid's work for them. Though their life was modest they believed in eating well; the best of everything: diamond-bone sirloins, three-shilling tea, and the best bottled stout. But Lily seldom made a mistake in the orders so that she got on well with her three mistresses. They were fussy, that was all. But the only thing they would not stand was back answers.

Of course they had good reason to be fussy on such a night. And then it was long after ten o'clock and yet there was no sign of Gabriel and his wife. Besides they were dreadfully afraid that Freddy Malins might turn up screwed. They would not wish for worlds that any of Mary Jane's pupils should see him under the influence; and when he was like that it was sometimes very hard to manage him. Freddy Malins always came late but they wondered what could be keeping Gabriel: and that was what brought them every two minutes to the banisters to ask Lily had Gabriel or Freddy come.

—O, Mr. Conroy, said Lily to Gabriel when she opened the door for him, Miss Kate and Miss Julia thought you were never coming. Good-night, Mrs. Conroy.

—I'll engage they did, said Gabriel, but they forgot that my wife here takes three mortal hours to dress herself.

He stood on the mat, scraping the snow from his goloshes, while Lily led his wife to the foot of the stairs and called out:

—Miss Kate, here's Mrs. Conroy.

Kate and Julia came toddling down the dark stairs at once. Both of them kissed Gabriel's wife, said she must be perished alive and asked was Gabriel with her.

—Here I am as right as the mail, Aunt Kate! Go on up. I'll follow, called out Gabriel from the dark.

He continued scraping his feet vigorously while the three women went upstairs, laughing, to the ladies' dressing-room. A light fringe of snow lay like a cape on the shoulders of his overcoat and like toecaps on the toes of his goloshes; and, as the buttons of his overcoat slipped with a squeaking noise through the snow-stiffened frieze, a cold fragrant air from out-of-doors escaped from crevices and folds.

—It is snowing again, Mr. Conroy? asked Lily.

She had preceded him into the pantry to help him off with his overcoat. Gabriel smiled at the three syllables she had given his surname and glanced at her. She was a slim, growing girl, pale in complexion and with hay-coloured hair. The gas in the pantry made her look still paler. Gabriel had known her when she was a child and used to sit on the lowest step nursing a rag doll.

—Yes, Lily, he answered, and I think we're in for a night of it.

He looked up at the pantry ceiling, which was shaking with the stamping and shuffling of feet on the floor above, listened for a moment to the piano and then glanced at the girl, who was folding his overcoat carefully at the end of a shelf.

—Tell me, Lily, he said in a friendly tone, do you still go to school?

—O no, sir, she answered. I'm done schooling this year and more.

—O, then, said Gabriel gaily. I suppose we'll be going to your wedding one of these fine days with your young man, eh?

The girl glanced back at him over her shoulder and said with great bitterness:

—The men that is now is only all palaver and what they can get out of you.

Gabriel coloured as if he felt he had made a mistake and, without looking at her, kicked off his goloshes and flicked actively with his muffler at his patent-leather shoes.

He was a stout tallish young man. The high colour of his cheeks pushed upwards even to his forehead where it scattered itself in a few formless patches of pale red; and on his hairless face there scintillated restlessly the polished lenses and the bright gilt rims of the glasses which screened his delicate and restless eyes. His glossy black hair was parted in the middle and brushed in a long curve behind his ears where it curled slightly beneath the groove left by his hat.

When he had flicked lustre into his shoes he stood up and pulled his waistcoat down more tightly on his plump body. Then he took a coin rapidly from his pocket.

—O Lily, he said, thrusting it into her hands, it's Christmastime, isn't it? Just . . . here's a little. . . .

He walked rapidly towards the door.

—O no, sir! cried the girl, following him. Really sir, I wouldn't take it.

—Christmas-time! Christmas-time! said Gabriel, almost trotting to the stairs and waving his hand to her in deprecation.

The girl, seeing that he had gained the stairs, called out after him:

—Well, thank you, sir.

He waited outside the drawing-room door until the waltz should finish, listening to the skirts that swept against it and to the shuffling of feet. He was still discomposed by the girl's bitter and sudden retort. It had cast a gloom over him which he tried to dispel by arranging his cuffs and the bows of his tie. Then he took from his waistcoat pocket a little paper and glanced at the headings he had made for his speech. He was undecided about the lines from Robert Browning for he feared they would be above the heads of his hearers. Some quotation that they could recognise from Shakespeare or from the Melodies would be better. The indelicate clacking of the men's heels and the shuffling of their soles reminded him that their grade of culture differed from his. He would only make himself ridiculous by quoting poetry to them which they could not understand. They would think that he was airing his superior education. He would fail with them just as he had failed with the girl in the pantry. He had taken up a wrong tone. His whole speech was a mistake from first to last, an utter failure.

Just then his aunts and his wife came out of the ladies' dressing-room. His aunts were two small plainly dressed old women. Aunt Julia was an inch or so the taller. Her hair, drawn low over the tops of her ears, was grey; and grey also, with darker shadows, was her large flaccid face. Though she was stout in build and stood erect her slow eyes and parted lips gave her the appearance of a woman who did not know where she was or where she was going. Aunt Kate was more vivacious. Her face, healthier than her sister's, was all puckers and creases, like a shrivelled red apple, and her hair, braided in the same old-fashioned way, had not lost its ripe nut colour.

They both kissed Gabriel frankly. He was their favorite nephew, the son of their dead elder sister, Ellen, who had married T. J. Conroy of the Port and Docks.

—Gretta tells me you're not going to take a cab back to Monkstown to-night, Gabriel, said Aunt Kate.

—No, said Gabriel, turning to his wife, we had quite enough of that last year, hadn't we? Don't you remember, Aunt Kate, what a cold Gretta got out of it? Cab windows rattling all the way, and the east wind blowing in after we passed Merrion. Very jolly it was. Gretta caught a dreadful cold.

Aunt Kate frowned severely and nodded her head at every word.

—Quite right, Gabriel, quite right, she said. You can't be too careful.

—But as for Gretta there, said Gabriel, she'd walk home in the snow if she were let.

Mrs. Conroy laughed.

—Don't mind him, Aunt Kate, she said. He's really an awful bother, what with green shades for Tom's eyes at night and making him do the dumb-bells, and forcing Eva to eat the stirabout. The poor child! And she simply hates the sight of it! . . . O, but you'll never guess what he makes me wear now!

She broke out into a peal of laughter and glanced at her husband, whose admiring and happy eyes had been wandering from her dress to her face and hair. The two aunts laughed heartily too, for Gabriel's solicitude was a standing joke with them.

—Goloshes! said Mrs. Conroy. That's the latest. Whenever it's wet underfoot I must put on my goloshes. To-night even he wanted me to put them on, but I wouldn't. The next thing he'll buy me will be a diving suit.

Gabriel laughed nervously and patted his tie reassuringly while Aunt Kate nearly doubled herself, so heartily did she enjoy the joke. The smile soon faded from Aunt Julia's face and her mirthless eyes were directed towards her nephew's face. After a pause she asked:

—And what are goloshes, Gabriel?

—Goloshes, Julia! exclaimed her sister. Goodness me, don't you know what goloshes are? You wear them over your . . . over your boots, Gretta, isn't it?

—Yes, said Mrs. Conroy. Guttapercha things. We both have a pair now. Gabriel says everyone wears them on the continent.

—O, on the continent, murmured Aunt Julia, nodding her head slowly.

Gabriel knitted his brows and said, as if he were slightly angered:

—It's nothing very wonderful but Gretta thinks it very funny because she says the word reminds her of Christy Minstrels.

—But tell me, Gabriel, said Aunt Kate, with brisk tact. Of course, you've seen about the room. Gretta was saying . . .

—O, the room is all right, replied Gabriel. I've taken one in the Gresham.

—To be sure, said Aunt Kate, by far the best thing to do. And the children, Gretta, you're not anxious about them?

—O, for one night, said Mrs. Conroy. Besides, Bessie will look after them.

—To be sure, said Aunt Kate again. What a comfort it is to have a girl like that, one you can depend on! There's that Lily, I'm sure I don't know what has come over her lately. She's not the girl she was at all.

Gabriel was about to ask his aunt some questions on this point but she broke off suddenly to gaze after her sister who had wandered down the stairs and was craning her neck over the banisters.

—Now, I ask you, she said, almost testily, where is Julia going? Julia! Julia! Where are you going?

Julia, who had gone halfway down one flight, came back and announced blandly:

—Here's Freddy.

At the same moment a clapping of hands and a final flourish of the pianist told that the waltz had ended. The drawing-room door was opened from within and some couples came out. Aunt Kate drew Gabriel aside hurriedly and whispered into his ear:

—Slip down, Gabriel, like a good fellow and see if he's all right, and don't let him up if he's screwed. I'm sure he's screwed. I'm sure he is.

Gabriel went to the stairs and listened over the banisters. He could hear two persons talking in the pantry. Then he recognised Freddy Malins' laugh. He went down the stairs noisily.

—It's such a relief, said Aunt Kate to Mrs. Conroy, that Gabriel is here. I always feel easier in my mind when he's here. . . . Julia, there's Miss Daly and Miss Power will take some refreshment. Thanks for your beautiful waltz, Miss Daly. It made lovely time.

A tall wizen-faced man, with a stiff grizzled moustache and swarthy skin, who was passing out with his partner said:

—And may we have some refreshment, too, Miss Morkan?

—Julia, said Aunt Kate summarily, and here's Mr. Browne and Miss Furlong. Take them in, Julia, with Miss Daly and Miss Power.

—I'm the man for the ladies, said Mr. Browne, pursing his lips until his moustache bristled and smiling in all his wrinkles. You know, Miss Morkan, the reason they are so fond of me is—

He did not finish his sentence, but, seeing that Aunt Kate was out of earshot, at once led the three young ladies into the back room. The middle of the room was occupied by two square tables placed end to end, and on these Aunt Julia and the caretaker were straightening and smoothing a large cloth. On the sideboard were arrayed dishes and plates, and glasses and bundles of knives and forks and spoons. The top of the closed square piano served also as a sideboard for viands and sweets. At a smaller sideboard in one corner two young men were standing, drinking hop-bitters.

Mr. Browne led his charges thither and invited them all, in jest, to some ladies' punch, hot, strong and sweet. As they said they never took anything strong he opened three bottles of lemonade for them. Then he asked one of the young men to move aside, and, taking hold of the decanter, filled out for himself a goodly measure of whisky. The young man eyed him respectfully while he took a trial sip.

—God help me, he said, smiling, it's the doctor's orders.

His wizened face broke into a broader smile, and the three young ladies laughed in musical echo to his pleasantry, swaying their bodies to and fro, with nervous jerks of their shoulders. The boldest said:

—O, now, Mr. Browne, I'm sure the doctor never ordered anything of the kind.

Mr. Browne took another sip of his whisky and said, with sidling mimicry:

—Well, you see, I'm like the famous Mrs. Cassidy, who is reported to have said: *Now, Mary Grimes, if I don't take it, make me take it, for I feel I want it.*

His hot face had leaned forward a little too confidentially and he had assumed a very low Dublin accent so that the young ladies, with one instinct, received his speech in silence. Miss Furlong, who was one of Mary Jane's pupils, asked Miss Daly what was the name of the pretty waltz she had played; and Mr. Browne, seeing that he was ignored, turned promptly to the two young men who were more appreciative.

A red-faced young woman, dressed in pansy, came into the room, excitedly clapping her hands and crying:

—Quadrilles! Quadrilles!

Close on her heels came Aunt Kate, crying:

—Two gentlemen and three ladies, Mary Jane!

—O, here's Mr. Bergin and Mr. Kerrigan, said Mary Jane. Mr. Kerrigan, will you take Miss Power? Miss Furlong, may I get you a partner, Mr. Bergin. O, that'll just do now.

—Three ladies, Mary Jane, said Aunt Kate.

The two young gentlemen asked the ladies if they might have the pleasure, and Mary Jane turned to Miss Daly.

—O, Miss Daly, you're really awfully good, after playing for the last two dances, but really we're so short of ladies to-night.

—I don't mind in the least, Miss Morkan.

—But I've a nice partner for you, Mr. Bartell D'Arcy, the tenor. I'll get him to sing later on. All Dublin is raving about him.

—Lovely voice, lovely voice! said Aunt Kate.

As the piano had twice begun the prelude to the first figure Mary Jane led her recruits quickly from the room. They had hardly gone when Aunt Julia wandered slowly into the room, looking behind her at something.

—What is the matter, Julia? asked Aunt Kate anxiously. Who is it?

Julia, who was carrying in a column of table-napkins turned to her sister and said, simply, as if the question had surprised her:

—It's only Freddy, Kate, and Gabriel with him.

In fact right behind her Gabriel could be seen piloting Freddy Malins across the landing. The latter, a young man of forty, was of Gabriel's size and build, with very round shoulders. His face was fleshy and pallid, touched with colour only at the thick hanging lobes of his ears and at the wide wings of his nose. He had coarse features, a blunt nose, a convex and receding brow, tumid and protruded lips. His heavy-lidded eyes and the disorder of his scanty hair made him look sleepy. He was laughing heartily in a high key at a story which he had been telling Gabriel on the stairs and at the same time rubbing the knuckles of his left fist backwards and forwards into his left eye.

—Good-evening, Freddy, said Aunt Julia.

Freddy Malins bade the Misses Morkan good-evening in what seemed an offhand fashion by reason of the habitual catch in his voice and then, seeing that Mr. Browne was grinning at him from the sideboard, crossed the room on rather shaky legs and began to repeat in an undertone the story he had just told to Gabriel.

—He's not so bad, is he? said Aunt Kate to Gabriel.

Gabriel's brows were dark but he raised them quickly and answered:

—O no, hardly noticeable.

—Now, isn't he a terrible fellow! she said. And his poor mother made him take the pledge on New Year's Eve. But come on, Gabriel, into the drawing-room.

Before leaving the room with Gabriel she signalled to Mr. Browne by frowning and shaking her forefinger in warning to and fro. Mr. Browne nodded in answer and, when she had gone, said to Freddy Malins:

—Now, then, Teddy, I'm going to fill you out a good glass of lemonade just to buck you up.

Freddy Malins, who was nearing the climax of his story, waved the offer aside impatiently but Mr. Browne, having first called Freddy Malins' attention to a disarray in his dress, filled out and handed him a full glass of lemonade. Freddy Malins' left hand accepted the glass mechanically, his right hand being engaged in the mechanical readjustment of his dress. Mr. Browne, whose face was once more wrinkling with mirth, poured out for himself a glass of whisky while Freddy Malins exploded, before he had well reached the climax of his story, in a kink of high-pitched bronchitic laughter and, setting down his untasted and overflowing glass, began to rub the knuckles of his left fist backwards and forwards into his left eye, repeating words of his last phrase as well as his fit of laughter would allow him.

Gabriel could not listen while Mary Jane was playing her Academy piece, full of runs and difficult passages, to the hushed drawing-room. He liked music but the piece she was playing had no melody for him and he doubted whether it had any melody for the other listeners, though they begged Mary Jane to play something. Four young men, who had come from the refreshment-room to stand in the doorway at the sound of the piano, had gone away quietly in couples after a few minutes. The only persons who seemed to follow the music were Mary Jane herself, her hands racing along the key-board or lifted from it at the pauses like those of a priestess in momentary imprecation, and Aunt Kate standing at her elbow to turn the page.

Gabriel's eyes, irritated by the floor, which glittered with beeswax under the heavy chandelier, wandered to the wall above the piano. A picture of the balcony scene in *Romeo and Juliet* hung there and beside it was a picture of the two murdered princes in the Tower which Aunt Julia had worked in red, blue and brown wools when she was a girl. Probably in the school they had gone to as girls that kind of work had been taught, for one year his mother had worked for him as a birthday present a waistcoat of purple tabinet, with little foxes' heads upon it, lined with brown satin and having round mulberry buttons. It was strange that his mother had had no musical talent though Aunt Kate used to call her the brains carrier of the Morkan family. Both she and Julia had always seemed a little proud of their serious and matronly sister. Her photograph stood before the pierglass. She held an open book on her knees and was pointing out something in it to Constantine who, dressed in a man-o'-war suit, lay at her feet. It was she who had chosen the names for her sons for she was very sensible of the dignity of family life. Thanks to her, Constantine was now senior curate in Balbriggan and, thanks to her, Gabriel himself had taken his degree in the Royal University. A shadow passed over his face as he remembered her sullen opposition to his marriage. Some slighting phrases she had used still rankled in his memory; she had once spoken of Gretta as being country cute and that was not true of Gretta at all. It was Gretta who had nursed her during all her last long illness in their house at Monkstown.

He knew that Mary Jane must be near the end of her piece for she was playing again the opening melody with runs of scales after every bar and while he waited for the end the resentment died down in his heart. The piece ended with a trill of octaves in the treble and a final deep octave in the bass. Great applause greeted Mary Jane as, blushing and rolling up her music nervously, she escaped from the room. The most vigorous clapping came from the four young men in the doorway who had gone away to the refreshment-room at the beginning of the piece but had come back when the piano had stopped.

Lancers were arranged. Gabriel found himself partnered with Miss Ivors. She was a frank-mannered talkative young lady, with a freckled face and prominent brown eyes. She did not wear a low-cut bodice and the large brooch which was fixed in the front of her collar bore on it an Irish device.

When they had taken their places she said abruptly:

—I have a crow to pluck with you.

—With me? said Gabriel.

She nodded her head gravely.

—What is it? asked Gabriel, smiling at her solemn manner.

—Who is G. C.? answered Miss Ivors, turning her eyes upon him.

Gabriel coloured and was about to knit his brows, as if he did not understand, when she said bluntly:

—O, innocent Amy! I have found out that you write for *The Daily Express*. Now, aren't you ashamed of yourself?

—Why should I be ashamed of myself? asked Gabriel, blinking his eyes and trying to smile.

—Well, I'm ashamed of you, said Miss Ivors frankly. To say you'd write for a rag like that. I didn't think you were a West Briton.

A look of perplexity appeared on Gabriel's face. It was true that he wrote a literary column every Wednesday in *The Daily Express*, for which he was paid fifteen shillings. But that did not make him a West Briton surely. The books he received for review were almost more welcome than the paltry cheque. He loved to feel the covers and turn over the pages of newly printed books. Nearly every day when his teaching in the college was ended he used to wander down the quays to the second-hall booksellers, to Hickey's on Bachelor's Walk, to Webb's or Massey's on Aston's Quay, or to O'Clohissey's in the by-street. He did not know how to meet her charge. He wanted to say that literature was above politics. But they were friends of many years' standing and their careers had been parallel, first at the University and then as teachers: he could not risk a grandiose phrase with her. He continued blinking his eyes and trying to smile and murmured lamely that he saw nothing political in writing reviews of books.

When their turn to cross had come he was still perplexed and inattentive. Miss Ivors promptly took his hand in a warm grasp and said in a soft friendly voice:

—Of course, I was only joking. Come, we cross now.

When they were together again she spoke of the University question, and Gabriel felt more at ease. A friend of hers had shown her his review of Browning's poems. That was how she had found out the secret: but she liked the review immensely. Then she said suddenly:

—O, Mr. Conroy, will you come for an excursion to the Aran Isles this summer? We're going to stay there a whole month. It will be splendid out in the Atlantic. You ought to come. Mr. Clancy is coming, and Mr. Kilkelly and Kathleen Kearney. It would be splendid for Gretta too if she'd come. She's from Connacht, isn't she?

—Her people are, said Gabriel shortly.

—But you will come, won't you? said Miss Ivors, laying her warm hand eagerly on his arm.

—The fact is, said Gabriel, I have already arranged to go—

—Go where? asked Miss Ivors.

—Well, you know, every year I go for a cycling tour with some fellows and so—

—But where? asked Miss Ivors.

—Well, we usually go to France or Belgium or perhaps Germany, said Gabriel awkwardly.

—And why do you go to France and Belgium, said Miss Ivors, instead of visiting your own land?

—Well, said Gabriel, it's partly to keep in touch with the languages and partly for a change.

—And haven't you your own language to keep in touch with—Irish? asked Miss Ivors.

—Well, said Gabriel, if it comes to that, you know, Irish is not my language.

Their neighbours had turned to listen to the cross-examination. Gabriel glanced right and left nervously and tried to keep his good humour under the ordeal which was making a blush invade his forehead.

—And haven't you your own land to visit, continued Miss Ivors, that you know nothing of, your own people, and your own country?

—O, to tell you the truth, retorted Gabriel suddenly, I'm sick of my own country, sick of it!

—Why? asked Miss Ivors.

Gabriel did not answer for his retort had heated him.

—Why? repeated Miss Ivors.

They had to go visiting together and, as he had not answered her, Miss Ivors said warmly:

—Of course, you've no answer.

Gabriel tried to cover his agitation by taking part in the dance with great energy. He avoided her eyes for he had seen a sour expression on her face. But when they met in the long chain he was surprised to feel his hand firmly pressed. She looked at him from under her brows for a moment quizzically until he smiled. Then, just as the chain was about to start again, she stood on tiptoe and whispered into his ear:

—West Briton!

When the lancers were over Gabriel went away to a remote corner of the room where Freddy Malins' mother was sitting. She was a stout feeble old woman with white hair. Her voice had a catch in it like her son's and she stuttered slightly. She had been told that Freddy had come and that he was nearly all right. Gabriel asked her whether she had had a good crossing. She lived with her married daughter in Glasgow and came to Dublin on a visit once a year. She answered placidly that she had had a beautiful crossing and that the captain had been most attentive to her. She spoke also of the beautiful house her daughter kept in Glasgow, and of all the nice friends they had there. While her tongue rambled on Gabriel tried to banish from his mind all memory of the unpleasant incident with Miss Ivors. Of course the girl or woman, or whatever she was, was an enthusiast but there was a time for all things. Perhaps he ought not to have answered her like that. But she had no right to call him a West Briton before people, even in joke. She had tried to make him ridiculous before people, heckling him and staring at him with her rabbit's eyes.

He saw his wife making her way towards him through the waltzing couples. When she reached him she said into his ear:

—Gabriel, Aunt Kate wants to know won't you carve the goose as usual. Miss Daly will carve the ham and I'll do the pudding.

—All right, said Gabriel.

—She's sending in the younger ones first as soon as this waltz is over so that we'll have the table to ourselves.

—Were you dancing? asked Gabriel.

—Of course I was. Didn't you see me? What words had you with Molly Ivors?

—No words. Why? Did she say so?

—Something like that. I'm trying to get that Mr. D'Arcy to sing. He's full of conceit, I think.

—There were no words, said Gabriel moodily, only she wanted me to go for a trip to the west of Ireland and I said I wouldn't.

His wife clasped her hands excitedly and gave a little jump.

—O, do go, Gabriel, she cried. I'd love to see Galway again.

—You can go if you like, said Gabriel coldly.

She looked at him for a moment, then turned to Mrs. Malins and said:

—There's a nice husband for you, Mrs. Malins.

While she was threading her way back across the room Mrs. Malins, without adverting to the interruption, went on to tell Gabriel what beautiful places there were in Scotland and beautiful scenery. Her son-in-law brought them every year to the lakes and they used to go fishing. Her son-in-law was a splendid fisher. One day he caught a fish, a beautiful big big fish, and the man in the hotel boiled it for their dinner.

Gabriel hardly heard what she said. Now that supper was coming near he began to think again about his speech and about the quotation. When he saw Freddy Malins coming across the room to visit his mother Gabriel left the chair free for him and retired into the embrasure of the window. The room had already cleared and from the back room came the clatter of plates and knives. Those who still remained in the drawing-room seemed tired of dancing and were conversing quietly in little groups. Gabriel's warm trembling fingers tapped the cold pane of the window. How cool it must be outside! How pleasant it would be to walk out alone, first along by the river and then through the park! The snow would be lying on the branches of the trees and forming a bright cap on the top of the Wellington Monument. How much more pleasant it would be there than at the supper-table!

He ran over the headings of his speech: Irish hospitality, sad memories, the Three Graces, Paris, the quotation from Browning. He repeated to himself a phrase he had written in his review: *One feels that one is listening to a thought-tormented music.* Miss Ivors had praised the review. Was she sincere? Had she really any life of her own behind all her propagandism? There had never been any ill-feeling between them until that night. It unnerved him to think that she would be at the supper-table, looking up at him while he spoke with her critical quizzing eyes. Perhaps she would not be sorry to see him fail in his speech. An idea came into his mind and gave him courage. He would say, alluding to Aunt Kate and Aunt Julia: *Ladies and Gentlemen, the generation which is now on the wane among us may have had its faults but for my part I think it had certain qualities of hospitality, of humor, of humanity, which the new and very serious and hypereducated generation that is growing up around us seems to me to lack.* Very good: that was one for Miss Ivors. What did he care that his aunts were only two ignorant old women?

A murmur in the room attracted his attention. Mr. Browne was advancing from the door, gallantly escorting Aunt Julia, who leaned upon his arm, smiling and hanging her head. An irregular musketry of applause escorted her also as far as the piano and then, as Mary Jane seated herself on the stool, and Aunt Julia, no longer smiling, half turned so as to pitch her voice fairly into the room, gradually ceased. Gabriel recognized the prelude. It was that of an old song of Aunt Julia's—*Arrayed for the Bridal.* Her voice, strong and clear in tone, attacked with great spirit the runs which embellish the air and though she sang very rapidly she did not miss even the smallest of the grace notes. To follow the voice, without looking at the singer's face, was to feel and share the excitement of swift and secure flight. Gabriel applauded loudly with all the others at the close of the song and loud applause was borne in from the invisible supper-table. It sounded so genuine that a little colour struggled into Aunt Julia's face as she bent to replace in the music-stand the old leather-bound song-book that had her initials on the cover. Freddy Malins, who had listened with his head perched sideways to hear her better, was still applauding when everyone else had ceased and talking animatedly to his mother who nodded her head gravely and slowly in acquiescence. At last, when he could clap no more, he stood up suddenly and hurried across the room to Aunt Julia whose hand he seized and held in both his hands, shaking it when words failed him or the catch in his voice proved too much for him.

—I was just telling my mother, he said, I never heard you sing so well, never. No, I never heard your voice so good as it is to-night. Now! Would you believe that now? That's the truth. Upon my word and honour that's the truth. I never heard your voice sound so fresh and so . . . so clear and fresh, never.

Aunt Julia smiled broadly and murmured something about compliments as she released her hand from his grasp. Mr. Browne extended his open hand towards her and said to those who were near in the manner of a showman introducing a prodigy to an audience:

—Miss Julia Morkan, my latest discovery!

He was laughing very heartily at this himself when Freddy Malins turned to him and said:

—Well, Browne, if you're serious you might make a worse discovery. All I can say is I never heard her sing half so well as I am coming here. And that's the honest truth.

—Neither did I, said Mr. Browne. I think her voice has greatly improved.

Aunt Julia shrugged her shoulders and said with meek pride:

—Thirty years ago I hadn't a bad voice as voices go.

—I often told Julia, said Aunt Kate emphatically, that she was simply thrown away in that choir. But she never would be said by me.

She turned as if to appeal to the good sense of the others against a refractory child while Aunt Julia gazed in front of her, a vague smile of reminiscence playing on her face.

—No, continued Aunt Kate, she wouldn't be said or led by anyone, slaving there in that choir night and day, night and day. Six o'clock on Christmas morning! And all for what?

—Well, isn't it for the honour of God, Aunt Kate? asked Mary Jane, twisting round on the piano-stool and smiling.

Aunt Kate turned fiercely on her niece and said:

—I know all about the honour of God, Mary Jane, but I think it's not at all honourable for the pope to turn out the women out of the choirs that have slaved there all their lives and put little whipper-snappers of boys over their heads. I suppose it is for the good of the Church if the pope does it. But it's not just, Mary Jane, and it's not right.

She had worked herself into a passion and would have continued in defence of her sister for it was a sore subject with her but Mary Jane, seeing that all the dancers had come back, intervened pacifically:

—Now, Aunt Kate, you're giving scandal to Mr. Browne who is of the other persuasion.

Aunt Kate turned to Mr. Browne, who was grinning at this allusion to his religion, and said hastily:

—O, I don't question the pope's being right. I'm only a stupid old woman and I wouldn't presume to do such a thing. But there's such a thing as common everyday politeness and gratitude. And if I were in Julia's place I'd tell that Father Healy straight up to his face . . .

—And besides, Aunt Kate, said Mary Jane, we really are all hungry and when we are hungry we are all very quarrelsome.

—And when we are thirsty we are also quarrelsome, added Mr. Browne.

—So that we had better go to supper, said Mary Jane, and finish the discussion afterwards.

On the landing outside the drawing-room Gabriel found his wife and Mary Jane trying to persuade Miss Ivors to stay for supper. But Miss Ivors, who had put on her hat and was buttoning her cloak, would not stay. She did not feel in the least hungry and she had already overstayed her time.

—But only for ten minutes, Molly, said Mrs. Conroy. That won't delay you.

—To take a pick itself, said Mary Jane, after all your dancing.

—I really couldn't, said Miss Ivors.

—I am afraid you didn't enjoy yourself at all, said Mary Jane hopelessly.

—Ever so much, I assure you, said Miss Ivors, but you really must let me run off now.

—But how can you get home? asked Mrs. Conroy.

—O, it's only two steps up the quay.

Gabriel hesitated a moment and said:

—If you will allow me, Miss Ivors, I'll see you home if you really are obliged to go.

But Miss Ivors broke away from them.

—I won't hear of it, she cried. For goodness sake go in to your suppers and don't mind me. I'm quite well able to take care of myself.

—Well, you're the comical girl, Molly, said Mrs. Conroy frankly.

—*Beannacht libh,* cried Miss Ivors, with a laugh, as she ran down the staircase.

Mary Jane gazed after her, a moody puzzled expression on her face, while Mrs. Conroy leaned over the banisters to listen for the hall-door. Gabriel asked himself was he the cause of her abrupt departure. But she did not seem to be in ill humour: she had gone away laughing. He stared blankly down the staircase.

At that moment Aunt Kate came toddling out of the supper-room, almost wringing her hands in despair.

—Where is Gabriel? she cried. Where on earth is Gabriel? There's everyone waiting in there, stage to let, and nobody to carve the goose!

—Here I am, Aunt Kate! cried Gabriel, with sudden animation, ready to carve a flock of geese, if necessary.

A fat brown goose lay at one end of the table and at the other end, on a bed of creased paper strewn with sprigs of parsley, lay a great ham, stripped of its outer skin and peppered over with crust crumbs, a neat paper frill round its shin and beside this was a round of spiced beef. Between these rival ends ran parallel lines of side-dishes: two little minsters of jelly, red and yellow; a shallow dish full of blocks of blancmange and red jam, a large green leaf-shaped dish with a stalk-shaped handle, on which lay bunches of purple raisins and peeled almonds, a companion dish on which lay a solid rectangle of Smyrna figs, a dish of custard topped with grated nutmeg, a small bowl full of chocolates and sweets wrapped in gold and silver papers and a glass vase in which stood some tall celery stalks. In the centre of the table there stood, as sentries to a fruit-stand which upheld a pyramid of oranges and American apples, two squat old-fashioned decanters of cut glass, one containing port and the other dark sherry. On the closed square piano a pudding in a huge yellow dish lay in waiting and behind it were three squads of bottles of stout and ale and minerals, drawn up according to the colours of their uniforms, the first two black, with brown and red labels, the third and smallest squad white, with transverse green sashes.

Gabriel took his seat boldly at the head of the table and, having looked to the edge of the carver, plunged his fork firmly into the goose. He felt quite at ease now for he was an expert carver and liked nothing better than to find himself at the head of a well-laden table.

—Miss Furlong, what shall I send you? he asked. A wing or a slice of the breast?

—Just a small slice of the breast.

—Miss Higgins, what for you?

—O, anything at all, Mr. Conroy.

While Gabriel and Miss Daly exchanged plates of goose and plates of ham and spiced beef Lily went from guest to guest with a dish of hot floury potatoes wrapped in a white napkin. This was Mary Jane's idea and she had also suggested apple sauce for the goose but Aunt Kate had said that plain roast goose without apple sauce had always been good enough for her and she hoped she might never eat worse. Mary Jane waited on her pupils and saw that they got the best slices and Aunt Kate and Aunt Julia opened and carried across from the piano bottles of stout and ale for the gentlemen and bottles of minerals for the ladies. There was a great deal of confusion and laughter and noise, the noise of orders and counter-orders, of knives and forks, of corks and glass-stoppers. Gabriel began to carve second helpings as soon as he had finished the first round without serving himself. Everyone protested loudly so that he compromised by taking a long draught of stout for he had found the carving hot work. Mary Jane settled down quietly to her supper but Aunt Kate and Aunt Julia were still toddling round the table, walking on each other's heels, getting in each other's way and giving each other unheeded orders. Mr. Browne begged of them to sit down and eat their suppers and so did Gabriel but they said there was time enough so that, at last, Freddy Malins stood up and, capturing Aunt Kate, plumped her down on her chair amid general laughter.

When everyone had been well served Gabriel said, smiling:

—Now, if anyone wants a little more of what vulgar people call stuffing let him or her speak.

A chorus of voices invited him to begin his own supper and Lily came forward with three potatoes which she had reserved for him.

—Very well, said Gabriel amiably, as he took another preparatory draught, kindly forget my existence, ladies and gentlemen, for a few minutes.

He set to his supper and took no part in the conversation with which the table covered Lily's removal of the plates. The subject of talk was the opera company which was then at the Theatre Royal. Mr. Bartell D'Arcy, the tenor, a dark-complexioned young man with a smart moustache, praised very highly the leading contralto of the company but Miss Furlong thought she had a rather vulgar style of production. Freddy Malins said there was a negro chieftain singing in the second part of the Gaiety pantomime who had one of the finest tenor voices he had ever heard.

—Have you heard him? he asked Mr. Bartell D'Arcy across the table.

—No, answered Mr. Bartell D'Arcy carelessly.

—Because, Freddy Malins explained, now I'd be curious to hear your opinion of him. I think he has a grand voice.

—It takes Teddy to find out the really good things, said Mr. Browne familiarly to the table.

—And why couldn't he have a voice too? asked Freddy Malins sharply. Is it because he's only a black?

Nobody answered this question and Mary Jane led the table back to the legitimate opera. One of her pupils had given her a pass for *Mignon*. Of course it was very fine, she said, but it made her think of poor Georgina Burns. Mr. Browne could go back farther still, to the old Italian companies that used to come to Dublin—Tietjens, Ilma de Murzka, Campanini, the great Trebelli, Giuglini, Ravelli, Aramburo. Those were the days, he said, when there was something like singing to be heard in Dublin. He told too of how the top gallery of the old Royal used to be packed night after night, of how one night an Italian tenor had sung five encores to *Let Me Like a Soldier Fall,* introducing a high C every time, and of how the gallery boys would sometimes in their enthusiasm unyoke the horses from the carriage of some great *prima donna* and pull her themselves through the streets to her hotel. Why did they never play the grand old operas now, he asked, *Dinorah, Lucrezia Borgia?* Because they could not get the voices to sing them: that was why.

—O, well, said Mr. Bartell D'Arcy, I presume there are as good singers to-day as there were then.

—Where are they? asked Mr. Browne defiantly.

—In London, Paris, Milan, said Mr. Bartell D'Arcy warmly. I suppose Caruso, for example, is quite as good, if not better than any of the men you have mentioned.

—Maybe so, said Mr. Browne. But I may tell you I doubt it strongly.

—O, I'd give anything to hear Caruso sing, said Mary Jane.

—For me, said Aunt Kate, who had been picking a bone, there was only one tenor. To please me, I mean. But I suppose none of you ever heard of him.

—Who was he, Miss Morkan? asked Mr. Bartell D'Arcy politely.

—His name, said Aunt Kate, was Parkinson. I heard him when he was in his prime and I think he had then the purest tenor voice that was ever put into a man's throat.

—Strange, said Mr. Bartell D'Arcy. I never even heard of him.

—Yes, yes, Miss Morkan is right, said Mr. Browne. I remember hearing of old Parkinson but he's too far back for me.

—A beautiful pure sweet mellow English tenor, said Aunt Kate with enthusiasm.

Gabriel having finished, the huge pudding was transferred to the table. The clatter of forks and spoons began again. Gabriel's wife served out spoonfuls of the pudding and passed the plates down the table. Midway down they were held up by Mary Jane, who replenished them with raspberry or orange jelly or with blancmange and jam. The pudding was of Aunt Julia's making and she received praises for it from all quarters. She herself said that it was not quite brown enough.

—Well, I hope, Miss Morkan, said Mr. Browne, that I'm brown enough for you because, you know, I'm all brown.

All the gentlemen, except Gabriel, ate some of the pudding out of compliment to Aunt Julia. As Gabriel never ate sweets the celery had been left for him. Freddy Malins also took a stalk of celery and ate it with his pudding. He had been told that celery was a capital thing for the blood and he was just then under doctor's care. Mrs. Malins, who had been silent all through the supper, said that her son was going down to Mount Melleray in a week or so. The table then spoke of Mount Melleray, how bracing the air was down there, how hospitable the monks were and how they never asked for a penny-piece from their guests.

—And you do mean to say, asked Mr. Browne incredulously, that a chap can go down there and put up there as if it were a hotel and live on the fat of the land and then come away without paying a farthing?

—O, most people give some donation to the monastery when they leave, said Mary Jane.

—I wish we had an institution like that in our Church, said Mr. Browne candidly.

He was astonished to hear that the monks never spoke, got up at two in the morning and slept in their coffins. He asked what they did it for.

—That's the rule of the order, said Aunt Kate firmly.

—Yes, but why? asked Mr. Browne.

Aunt Kate repeated that it was the rule, that was all. Mr. Browne still seemed not to understand. Freddy Malins explained to him as best he could, that the monks were trying to make up for the sins committed by all the sinners in the outside world. The explanation was not very clear for Mr. Browne grinned and said:

—I like that idea very much but wouldn't a comfortable spring bed do them as well as a coffin?

—The coffin, said Mary Jane, is to remind them of their last end.

As the subject had grown lugubrious it was buried in a silence of the table during which Mrs. Malins could be heard saying to her neighbour in an indistinct undertone:

—They are very good men, the monks, very pious men.

The raisins and almonds and figs and apples and oranges and chocolates and sweets were now passed about the table and Aunt Julia invited all the guests to have either port or sherry. At first Mr. Bartell D'Arcy refused to take either but one of his neighbours nudged him and whispered something to him upon which he allowed his glass to be filled. Gradually as the last glasses were being filled the conversation ceased. A pause followed, broken only by the noise of the wine and by unsettlings of chairs. The Misses Morkan, all three, looked down at the tablecloth. Someone coughed once or twice and then a few gentlemen patted the table gently as a signal for silence. The silence came and Gabriel pushed back his chair and stood up.

The patting at once grew louder in encouragement and then ceased altogether. Gabriel leaned his ten trembling fingers on the tablecloth and smiled nervously at the company. Meeting a row of upturned faces he raised his eyes to the chandelier. The piano was playing a waltz tune and he could hear the skirts sweeping against the drawing-room door. People, perhaps, were standing in the snow on the quay outside, gazing up at the lighted windows and listening to the waltz music. The air was pure there. In the distance lay the park where the trees were weighted with snow. The Wellington Monument wore a gleaming cap of snow that flashed westward over the white field of Fifteen Acres.

He began:

—Ladies and Gentlemen.

—It has fallen to my lot this evening, as in years past, to perform a very pleasing task but a task for which I am afraid my poor powers as a speaker are all too inadequate.

—No, no! said Mr. Browne.

—But, however that may be, I can only ask you to-night to take the will for the deed and to lend me your attention for a few moments while I endeavour to express to you in words what my feelings are on this occasion.

—Ladies and Gentlemen. It is not the first time that we have gathered together under this hospitable roof, around this hospitable board. It is not the first time that we have been the recipients—or perhaps, I had better say, the victims—of the hospitality of certain good ladies.

He made a circle in the air with his arm and paused. Everyone laughed or smiled at Aunt Kate and Aunt Julia and Mary Jane who all turned crimson with pleasure. Gabriel went on more boldly:

—I feel more strongly with every recurring year that our country has no tradition which does it so much honour and which it should guard so jealously as that of its hospitality. It is a tradition that is unique as far as my experience goes (and I have visited not a few places abroad) among the modern nations. Some would say, perhaps, that with us it is rather a failing than anything to be boasted of. But granted even that, it is, to my mind, a princely failing, and one that I trust will long be cultivated among us. Of one thing, at least, I am sure. As long as this one roof shelters the good ladies aforesaid—and I wish from my heart it may do so for many and many a long year to come—the tradition of genuine warm-hearted courteous Irish hospitality, which our forefathers have handed down to us and which we in turn must hand down to our descendants, is still alive among us.

A hearty murmur of assent ran round the table. It shot through Gabriel's mind that Miss Ivors was not there and that she had gone away discourteously: and he said with confidence in himself:

—Ladies and Gentlemen.

—A new generation is growing up in our midst, a generation actuated by new ideas and new principles. It is serious and enthusiastic for these new ideas and its enthusiasm, even when it is misdirected, is, I believe, in the main sincere. But we are living in a sceptical and, if I may use the phrase, a thought-tormented age: and sometimes I fear that this new generation, educated or hypereducated as it is, will lack those qualities of humanity, of hospitality, of kindly humour which belonged to an older day. Listening tonight to the names of all those great singers of the past it seemed to me, I must confess, that we were living in a less spacious age. Those days might, without exaggeration, be called spacious days: and if they are gone beyond recall let us hope, at least, that in gatherings such as this we shall still speak of them with pride and affection, still cherish in our hearts the memory of those dead and gone great ones whose fame the world will not willingly let die.

—Hear, hear! said Mr. Browne loudly.

—But yet, continued Gabriel, his voice falling into a softer inflection, there are always in gatherings such as this sadder thoughts that will recur to our minds: thoughts of the past, of youth, of changes, of absent faces that we miss here tonight. Our path through life is strewn with many such sad memories: and were we to brood upon them always we could not find the heart to go on bravely with our work among the living. We have all of us living duties and living affections which claim, and rightly claim, our strenuous endeavours.

—Therefore, I will not linger on the past. I will not let any gloomy moralising intrude upon us here to-night. Here we are gathered together for a brief moment from the bustle and rush of our everyday routine. We are met here as friends, in the spirit of good-fellowship, as colleagues, also to a certain extent, in the true spirit of *camaraderie,* and as the guests of—what shall I call them?—the Three Graces of the Dublin musical world.

The table burst into applause and laughter at this sally. Aunt Julia vainly asked each of her neighbours in turn to tell her what Gabriel had said.

—He says we are the Three Graces, Aunt Julia, said Mary Jane.

Aunt Julia did not understand but she looked up, smiling, at Gabriel, who continued in the same vein:

—Ladies and Gentlemen.

—I will not attempt to play to-night the part that Paris played on another occasion. I will not attempt to choose between them. The task would be an invidious one and one beyond my poor powers. For when I view them in turn, whether it be our chief hostess herself, whose good heart, whose too good heart, has become a byword with all who know her, or her sister, who seems to be gifted with perennial youth and whose singing must have been a surprise and a revelation to us all to-night, or, last but not least, when I consider our youngest hostess, talented, cheerful, hard-working and the best of nieces, I confess, Ladies and Gentlemen, that I do not know to which of them I should award the prize.

Gabriel glanced down at his aunts and, seeing the large smile on Aunt Julia's face and the tears which had risen to Aunt Kate's eyes, hastened to his close. He raised his glass of port gallantly, while every member of the company fingered a glass expectantly, and said loudly:

—Let us toast them all three together. Let us drink to their health, wealth, long life, happiness and prosperity and may they long continue to hold the proud and self-won position which they hold in their profession and the position of honour and affection which they hold in our hearts.

All the guests stood up, glass in hand, and, turning towards the three seated ladies, sang in unison, with Mr. Browne as leader:

For they are jolly gay fellows,
For they are jolly gay fellows,
For they are jolly gay fellows,
Which nobody can deny.

Aunt Kate was making frank use of her handkerchief and even Aunt Julia seemed moved. Freddy Malins beat time with his pudding-fork and the singers turned towards one another, as if in melodious conference, while they sang, with emphasis:

Unless he tells a lie,
Unless he tells a lie.

Then, turning once more towards their hostesses, they sang:

For they are jolly gay fellows,
For they are jolly gay fellows,
For they are jolly gay fellows,
Which nobody can deny

The acclamation which followed was taken up beyond the door of the supper-room by many of the other guests and renewed time after time, Freddy Malins acting as officer with his fork on high.

The piercing morning air came into the hall where they were standing so that Aunt Kate said:

—Close the door, somebody. Mrs. Malins will get her death of cold.

—Browne is out there, Aunt Kate, said Mary Jane.

—Browne is everywhere, said Aunt Kate, lowering her voice.

Mary Jane laughed at her tone.

—Really, she said archly, he is very attentive.

—He has been laid on here like the gas, said Aunt Kate in the same tone, all during the Christmas.

She laughed herself this time good-humouredly and then added quickly:

—But tell him to come in, Mary Jane, and close the door. I hope to goodness he didn't hear me.

At that moment the hall-door was opened and Mr. Browne came in from the doorstep, laughing as if his heart would break. He was dressed in a long green overcoat with mock astrakhan cuffs and collar and wore on his head an oval fur cap. He pointed down the snow-covered quay from where the sound of shrill prolonged whistling was borne in.

—Teddy will have all the cabs in Dublin out, he said.

Gabriel advanced from the little pantry behind the office, struggling into his overcoat and, looking round the hall, said:

—Gretta not down yet?

—She's getting on her things, Gabriel, said Aunt Kate.

—Who's playing up there? asked Gabriel.

—Nobody. They're all gone.

—O no, Aunt Kate, said Mary Jane. Bartell D'Arcy and Miss O'Callaghan aren't gone yet.

—Somebody is strumming at the piano, anyhow, said Gabriel.

Mary Jane glanced at Gabriel and Mr. Browne and said with a shiver:

—It makes me feel cold to look at you two gentlemen muffled up like that. I wouldn't like to face your journey home at this hour.

—I'd like nothing better this minute, said Mr. Browne stoutly, than a rattling fine walk in the country or a fast drive with a good spanking goer between the shafts.

—We used to have a very good horse and trap at home, said Aunt Julia sadly.

—The never-to-be-forgotten Johnny, said Mary Jane, laughing.

Aunt Kate and Gabriel laughed too.

—Why, what was wonderful about Johnny? asked Mr. Browne.

—The late lamented Patrick Morkan, our grandfather, that is, explained Gabriel, commonly known in his later years as the old gentleman, with a glue-boiler.

—O, now, Gabriel, said Aunt Kate, laughing, he had a starch mill.

—Well, glue or starch, said Gabriel, the old gentleman had a horse by the name of Johnny. And Johnny used to work in the old gentleman's mill, walking round and round in order to drive the mill. That was all very well; but now comes the tragic part about Johnny. One fine day the old gentleman thought he'd like to drive out with the quality to a military review in the park.

—The Lord have mercy on his soul, said Aunt Kate compassionately.

—Amen, said Gabriel. So the old gentleman, as I said, harnessed Johnny and put on his very best tall hat and his very best stock collar and drove out in grand style from his ancestral mansion somewhere near Back Lane, I think.

Everyone laughed, even Mrs. Malins, at Gabriel's manner and Aunt Kate said:

—O now, Gabriel, he didn't live in Back Lane, really. Only the mill was there.

—Out from the mansion of his forefathers, continued Gabriel, he drove with Johnny. And everything went on beautifully until Johnny came in sight of King Billy's statue: and whether he fell in love with the horse King Billy sits on or whether he thought he was back again in the mill, anyhow he began to walk round the statue.

Gabriel paced in a circle round the hall in his goloshes amid the laughter of the others.

—Round and round he went, said Gabriel, and the old gentleman, who was a very pompous old gentleman, was highly indignant. *Go on, sir! What do you mean, sir? Johnny! Johnny! Most extraordinary conduct! Can't understand the horse!*

The peals of laughter which followed Gabriel's imitation of the incident were interrupted by a resounding knock at the hall-door. Mary Jane ran to open it and let in Freddy Malins. Freddy Malins, with his hat well back on his head and his shoulders humped with cold, was puffing and steaming after his exertions.

—I could only get one cab, he said.

—O, we'll find another along the quay, said Gabriel.

—Yes, said Aunt Kate. Better not keep Mrs. Malins standing in the draught.

Mrs. Malins was helped down the front steps by her son and Mr. Browne and, after many manœuvres, hoisted into the cab. Freddy Malins clambered in after her and spent a long time settling her on the seat, Mr. Browne helped him with advice. At last she was settled comfortably and Freddy Malins invited Mr. Browne into the cab. There was a good deal of confused talk, and then Mr. Browne got into the cab. The cabman settled his rug over his knees, and bent down for the address. The confusion grew greater and the cabman was directed differently by Freddy Malins and Mr. Browne, each of whom had his head out through a window of the cab. The difficulty was to know where to drop Mr. Browne along the route and Aunt Kate, Aunt Julia and Mary Jane helped the discussion from the doorstep with cross-directions and contradictions and abundance of laughter. As for Freddy Malins he was speechless with laughter. He popped his head in and out of the window every moment, to the great danger of his hat, and told his mother how the discussion was progressing till at last Mr. Browne shouted to the bewildered cabman above the din of everybody's laughter:

—Do you know Trinity College?

—Yes, sir, said the cabman.

—Well, drive bang up against Trinity College gates, said Mr. Browne, and then we'll tell you where to go. You understand now?

—Yes, sir, said the cabman.

—Make like a bird for Trinity College.

—Right, sir, cried the cabman.

The horse was whipped up and the cab rattled off along the quay amid a chorus of laughter and adieus.

Gabriel had not gone to the door with the others. He was in a dark part of the hall gazing up the staircase. A woman was standing near the top of the first flight, in the shadow also. He could not see her face but he could see the terracotta and salmonpink panels of her skirt which the shadow made appear black and white. It was his wife. She was leaning on the banisters, listening to something. Gabriel was surprised at her stillness and strained his ear to listen also. But he could hear little save the noise of laughter and dispute on the front steps, a few chords struck on the piano and a few notes of a man's voice singing.

He stood still in the gloom of the hall, trying to catch the air that the voice was singing and gazing up at his wife. There was grace and mystery in her attitude as if she were a symbol of something. He asked himself what is a woman standing on the stairs in the shadow, listening to distant music, a symbol of. If he were a painter he would paint her in that attitude. Her blue felt hat would show off the bronze of her hair against the darkness and the dark panels of her skirt would show off the light ones. *Distant Music* he would call the picture if he were a painter.

The hall-door was closed; and Aunt Kate, Aunt Julia and Mary Jane came down the hall, still laughing.

—Well, isn't Freddy terrible? said Mary Jane. He's really terrible.

Gabriel said nothing but pointed up the stairs towards where his wife was standing. Now that the hall-door was closed the voice and the piano could be heard more clearly. Gabriel held up his hand for them to be silent. The song seemed to be in the old Irish tonality and the singer seemed uncertain both of his words and of his voice. The voice, made plaintive by distance and by the singer's hoarseness, faintly illuminated the cadence of the air with words expressing grief:

O, the rain falls on my heavy locks
And the dew wets my skin,
My babe lies cold . . .

—O, exclaimed Mary Jane. It's Bartell D'Arcy singing and he wouldn't sing all the night. O, I'll get him to sing a song before he goes.

—O do, Mary Jane, said Aunt Kate.

Mary Jane brushed past the others and ran to the staircase but before she reached it the singing stopped and the piano was closed abruptly.

—O, what a pity! she cried. Is he coming down, Gretta?

Gabriel heard his wife answer yes and saw her come down towards them. A few steps behind her were Mr. Bartell D'Arcy and Miss O'Callaghan.

—O, Mr. D'Arcy, cried Mary Jane, it's downright mean of you to break off like that when we were all in raptures listening to you.

—I have been at him all the evening, said Miss O'Callaghan, and Mrs. Conroy too and he told us he had a dreadful cold and couldn't sing.

—O, Mr. D'Arcy, said Aunt Kate, now that was a great fib to tell.

—Can't you see that I'm as hoarse as a crow? said Mr. D'Arcy roughly.

He went into the pantry hastily and put on his overcoat. The others, taken aback by his rude speech, could find nothing to say. Aunt Kate wrinkled her brows and made signs to the others to drop the subject. Mr. D'Arcy stood swathing his neck carefully and frowning.

—It's the weather, said Aunt Julia, after a pause.

—Yes, everybody has colds, said Aunt Kate readily, everybody.

—They say, said Mary Jane, we haven't had snow like it for thirty years; and I read this morning in the newspapers that the snow is general all over Ireland.

—I love the look of snow, said Aunt Julia sadly.

—So do I, said Miss O'Callaghan. I think Christmas is never really Christmas unless we have the snow on the ground.

—But poor Mr. D'Arcy doesn't like the snow, said Aunt Kate, smiling.

Mr. D'Arcy came from the pantry, fully swathed and buttoned, and in a repentant tone told them the history of his cold. Everyone gave him advice and said it was a great pity and urged him to be very careful of his throat in the night air. Gabriel watched his wife who did not join in the conversation. She was standing right under the dusty fanlight and the flame of the gas lit up the rich bronze of her hair which he had seen her drying at the fire few days before. She was in the same attitude and seemed unaware of the talk about her. At last she turned towards them and Gabriel saw that there was colour on her cheeks and that her eyes were shining. A sudden tide of joy went leaping out of his heart.

—Mr. D'Arcy, she said, what is the name of that song you were singing?

—It's called *The Lass of Aughrim,* said Mr. D'Arcy, but I couldn't remember it properly. Why? Do you know it?

—*The Lass of Aughrim,* she repeated. I couldn't think of the name.

—It's a very nice air, said Mary Jane. I'm sorry you were not in voice to-night.

—Now, Mary Jane, said Aunt Kate, don't annoy Mr. D'Arcy. I won't have him annoyed.

Seeing that all were ready to start she shepherded them to the door where good-night was said:

—Well, good-night, Aunt Kate, and thanks for the pleasant evening.

—Good-night, Gabriel. Good-night, Gretta!

—Good-night, Aunt Kate, and thanks ever so much. Good-night, Aunt Julia.

—O, good-night, Gretta, I didn't see you.

—Good-night, Mr. D'Arcy. Good-night, Miss O'Callaghan.

—Good-night, Miss Morkan.

—Good-night, again.

—Good-night, all. Safe home.

—Good-night. Good-night.

The morning was still dark. A dull yellow light brooded over the houses and the river; and the sky seemed to be descending. It was slushy underfoot; and only streaks and patches of snow lay on the roofs, on the parapets of the quay and on the area railings. The lamps were still burning redly in the murky air and, across the river, the palace of the Four Courts stood out menacingly against the heavy sky.

She was walking on before him with Mr. Bartell D'Arcy, her shoes in a brown parcel tucked under one arm and her hands holding her skirt up from the slush. She had no longer any grace of attitude but Gabriel's eyes were still bright with happiness. The blood went bounding along his veins; and the thoughts went rioting through his brain, proud, joyful, tender, valorous.

She was walking on before him so lightly and so erect that he longed to run after her noiselessly, catch her by the shoulders and say something foolish and affectionate into her ear. She seemed to him so frail that he longed to defend her against something and then to be alone with her. Moments of their secret life together burst like stars upon his memory. A heliotrope envelope was lying beside his breakfast-cup and he was caressing it with his hand. Birds were twittering in the ivy and the sunny web of the curtain was shimmering along the floor: he could not eat for happiness. They were standing on the crowded platform and he was placing a ticket inside the warm palm of her glove. He was standing with her in the cold, looking in through a grated window at a man making bottles in a roaring furnace. It was very cold. Her face, fragrant in the cold air, was quite close to his; and suddenly she called out to the man at the furnace:

—Is the fire hot, sir?

But the man could not hear her with the noise of the furnace. It was just as well. He might have answered rudely.

A wave of yet more tender joy escaped from his heart and went coursing in warm flood along his arteries. Like the tender fires of stars moments of their life together, that no one knew of or would ever know of, broke upon and illumined his memory. He longed to recall to her those moments, to make her forget the years of their dull existence together and remember only their moments of ecstasy. For the years, he felt, had not quenched his soul or hers. Their children, his writing, her household cares had not quenched all their souls' tender fire. In one letter that he had written to her then he had said: *Why is it that words like these seem to me so dull and cold? Is it because there is no word tender enough to be your name?*

Like distant music these words that he had written years before were borne towards him from the past. He longed to be alone with her. When the others had gone away, when he and she were in their room in the hotel, then they would be alone together. He would call her softly:

—Gretta!

Perhaps she would not hear at once: she would be undressing. Then something in his voice would strike her. She would turn and look at him.

At the corner of Winetavern Street they met a cab. He was glad of its rattling noise as it saved him from conversation. She was looking out of the window and seemed tired. The others spoke only a few words, pointing out some building or street. The horse galloped along wearily under the murky morning sky, dragging his old rattling box after his heels, and Gabriel was again in a cab with her, galloping to catch the boat, galloping to their honeymoon.

As the cab drove across O'Connel Bridge Miss O'Callaghan said:

—They say you never cross O'Connel Bridge without seeing a white horse.

—I see a white man this time, said Gabriel.

—Where? asked Mr. Bartell D'Arcy.

Gabriel pointed to the statue, on which lay patches of snow. Then he nodded familiarly to it and waved his hand.

—Good-night, Dan, he said gaily.

When the cab drew up before the hotel Gabriel jumped out and, in spite of Mr. Bartell D'Arcy's protest, paid the driver. He gave the man a shilling over his fare. The man saluted and said:

—A prosperous New Year to you, sir.

—The same to you, said Gabriel cordially.

She leaned for a moment on his arm in getting out of the cab and while standing at the curbstone, bidding the others good-night. She leaned lightly on his arm, as lightly as when she had danced with him a few hours before. He had felt proud and happy then, happy that she was his, proud of her grace and wifely carriage. But now, after the kindling again of so many memories, the first touch of her body, musical and strange and perfumed, sent through him a keen pang of lust. Under cover of her silence he pressed her arm closely to his side; and, as they stood at the hotel door, he felt that they had escaped from their lives and duties, escaped from home and friends and run away together with wild and radiant hearts to a new adventure.

An old man was dozing in a great hooded chair in the hall. He lit a candle in the office and went before them to the stairs. They followed him in silence, their feet falling in soft thuds on the thickly carpeted stairs. She mounted the stairs behind the porter, her head bowed in the ascent, her frail shoulders curved as with a burden, her skirt girt tightly about her. He could have flung his arms about her hips and held her still for his arms were trembling with desire to seize her and only the stress of his nails against the palms of his hands held the wild impulse of his body in check. The porter halted on the stairs to settle his guttering candle. They halted too on the steps below him. In the silence Gabriel could hear the falling of the molten wax into the tray and the thumping of his own heart against his ribs.

The porter led them along a corridor and opened a door. Then he set his unstable candle down on a toilet-table and asked at what hour they were to be called in the morning.

—Eight, said Gabriel.

The porter pointed to the tap of the electric-light and began a muttered apology but Gabriel cut him short.

—We don't want any light. We have light enough from the street. And I say, he added, pointing to the candle, you might remove that handsome article, like a good man.

The porter took up his candle again, but slowly for he was surprised by such a novel idea. Then he mumbled good-night and went out. Gabriel shot the lock to.

A ghostly light from the street lamp lay in a long shaft from one window to the door. Gabriel threw his overcoat and hat on a couch and crossed the room towards the window. He looked down into the street in order that his emotion might calm a little. Then he turned and leaned against a chest of drawers with his back to the light. She had taken off her hat and cloak and was standing before a large swinging mirror, unhooking her waist. Gabriel paused for a few moments, watching her, and then said:

—Gretta!

She turned away from the mirror slowly and walked along the shaft of light towards him. Her face looked so serious and weary that the words would not pass Gabriel's lips No, it was not the moment yet.

—You looked tired, he said.

—I am a little, she answered.

—You don't feel ill or weak?

—No, tired: that's all.

She went on to the window and stood there, looking out. Gabriel waited again and then, fearing that diffidence was about to conquer him, he said abruptly:

—By the way, Gretta!

—What is it?

—You know that poor fellow Malins? he said quickly.

—Yes. What about him?

—Well, poor fellow, he's a decent sort of chap after all, continued Gabriel in a false voice. He gave me back that sovereign I lent him and I didn't expect it really. It's a pity he wouldn't keep away from that Browne, because he's not a bad fellow at heart.

He was trembling now with annoyance. Why did she seem so abstracted? He did not know how he could begin. Was she annoyed, too, about something? If she would only turn to him or come to him of her own accord! To take her as she was would be brutal. No, he must see some ardour in her eyes first. He longed to be master of her strange mood.

—When did you lend him the pound? she asked, after a pause.

Gabriel strove to restrain himself from breaking out into brutal language about the sottish Malins and his pound. He longed to cry to her from his soul, to crush her body against his, to overmaster her. But he said:

—O, at Christmas, when he opened that little Christmas-card shop in Henry Street.

He was in such a fever of rage and desire that he did not hear her come from the window. She stood before him for an instant, looking at him strangely. Then, suddenly raising herself on tiptoe and resting her hands lightly on his shoulders, she kissed him.

—You are a very generous person, Gabriel, she said.

Gabriel, trembling with delight at her sudden kiss and at the quaintness of her phrase, put his hands on her hair and began smoothing it back, scarcely touching it with his fingers. The washing had made it fine and brilliant. His heart was brimming over with happiness. Just when he was wishing for it she had come to him of her own accord. Perhaps her thoughts had been running with his. Perhaps she had felt the impetuous desire that was in him and then the yielding mood had come upon her. Now that she had fallen to him so easily he wondered why he had been so diffident.

He stood, holding her head between his hands. Then, slipping one arm swiftly about her body and drawing her towards him, he said softly:

—Gretta dear, what are you thinking about?

She did not answer nor yield wholly to his arm. He said again, softly:

—Tell me what it is, Gretta. I think I know what is the matter. Do I know?

She did not answer at once. Then she said in an outburst of tears:

—O, I am thinking about that song, *The Lass of Aughrim.*

She broke loose from him and ran to the bed and, throwing her arms across the bed-rail, hid her face. Gabriel stood stock-still for a moment in astonishment and then followed her. As he passed in the way of the cheval-glass he caught sight of himself in full length, his broad, well-filled shirt-front, the face whose expression always puzzled him when he saw it in a mirror and his glimmering gilt-rimmed eyeglasses. He halted a few paces from her and said:

—What about the song? Why does that make you cry?

She raised her head from her arms and dried her eyes with the back of her hand like a child. A kinder note than he had intended went into his voice.

—Why, Gretta? he asked.

—I am thinking about a person long ago who used to sing that song.

—And who was the person long ago? asked Gabriel, smiling.

—It was a person I used to know in Galway when I was living with my grandmother, she said.

The smile passed away from Gabriel's face. A dull anger began to gather again at the back of his mind and the dull fires of his lust began to glow angrily in his veins.

—Someone you were in love with? he asked ironically.

—It was a young boy I used to know, she answered, named Michael Furey. He used to sing that song. *The Lass of Aughrim.* He was very delicate.

Gabriel was silent. He did not wish her to think that he was interested in this delicate boy.

—I can see him so plainly, she said after a moment. Such eyes as he had: big dark eyes! And such an expression in them—an expression!

—O then, you were in love with him? said Gabriel.

—I used to go out walking with him, she said, when I was in Galway.

A thought flew across Gabriel's mind.

—Perhaps that was why you wanted to go to Galway with that Ivors girl? he said coldly.

She looked at him and asked in surprise:

—What for?

Her eyes made Gabriel feel awkward. He shrugged his shoulders and said:

—How do I know? To see him perhaps.

She looked away from him along the shaft of light towards the window in silence.

—He is dead, she said at length. He died when he was only seventeen. Isn't it a terrible thing to die so young as that?

—What was he? asked Gabriel, still ironically.

—He was in the gasworks, she said.

Gabriel felt humiliated by the failure of his irony and by the evocation of this figure from the dead, a boy in the gasworks. While he had been full of memories of their secret life together, full of tenderness and joy and desire, she had been comparing him in her mind with another. A shameful consciousness of his own person assailed him. He saw himself as a ludicrous figure, acting as a pennyboy for his aunts, a nervous well-meaning sentimentalist, orating to vulgarians and idealising his own clownish lusts, the pitiable fatuous fellow he had caught a glimpse of in the mirror. Instinctively he turned his back more to the light lest she might see the shame that burned upon his forehead.

He tried to keep up his tone of cold interrogation but his voice when he spoke was humble and indifferent.

—I suppose you were in love with this Michael Furey, Gretta, he said.

—I was great with him at that time, she said.

Her voice was veiled and sad. Gabriel, feeling now how vain it would be to try to lead her whither he had purposed, caressed one of her hands and said, also sadly:

—And what did he die of so young, Gretta? Consumption, was it?

—I think he died for me, she answered.

A vague terror seized Gabriel at this answer as if, at that hour when he had hoped to triumph, some impalpable and vindictive being was coming against him, gathering forces against him in its vague world. But he shook himself free of it with an effort of reason and continued to caress her hand. He did not question her again for he felt that she would tell him of herself. Her hand was warm and moist: it did not respond to his touch but he continued to caress it just as he had caressed her first letter to him that spring morning.

—It was in the winter, she said, about the beginning of the winter when I was going to leave my grandmother's and come up here to the convent. And he was ill at the time in his lodgings in Galway and wouldn't be let out and his people in Oughterard were written to. He was in decline, they said, or something like that. I never knew rightly.

She paused for a moment and sighed.

—Poor fellow, she said. He was very fond of me and he was such a gentle boy. We used to go out together, walking, you know, Gabriel, like they way they do in the country. He was going to study singing only for his health. He had a very good voice, poor Michael Furey.

—Well; and then? asked Gabriel.

—And then when it came to the time for me to leave Galway and come up to the convent he was much worse and I wouldn't be let see him so I wrote a letter saying I was going up to Dublin and would be back in the summer and hoping he would be better then.

She paused for a moment to get her voice under control and then went on:

—Then the night before I left I was in my grandmother's house in Nun's Island, packing up, and I heard gravel thrown up against the window. The window was so wet I couldn't see so I ran downstairs as I was and slipped out the back into the garden and there was the poor fellow at the end of the garden, shivering.

—And did you not tell him to go back? asked Gabriel.

—I implored of him to go home at once and told him he would get his death in the rain. But he said he did not want to live. I can see his eyes as well! He was standing at the end of the wall where there was a tree.

—And did he go home? asked Gabriel.

—Yes, he went home. And when I was only a week in the convent he died and he was buried in Oughterard where his people came from. O, the day I heard that, that he was dead!

She stopped, choking with sobs, and, overcome by emotion, flung herself face downward on the bed, sobbing in the quilt. Gabriel held her hand for a moment longer, irresolutely, and then, shy of intruding on her grief, let it fall gently and walked quietly to the window.

She was fast asleep.

Gabriel, leaning on his elbow, looked for a few moments unresentfully on her tangled hair and half-open mouth, listening to her deep-drawn breath. So she had had that romance in her life: a man had died for her sake. It hardly pained him now to think how poor a part he, her husband, had played in her life. He watched her while she slept as though he and she had never lived together as man and wife. His curious eyes rested long upon her face and on her hair: and, as he thought of what she must have been then, in that time of her first girlish beauty, a strange friendly pity for her entered his soul. He did not like to say even to himself that her face was no longer beautiful but he knew that it was no longer the face for which Michael Furey had braved death.

Perhaps she had not told him all the story. His eyes moved to the chair over which she had thrown some of her clothes. A petticoat string dangled to the floor. One boot stood upright, its limp upper fallen down: the fellow of it lay upon its side. He wondered at his riot of emotions of an hour before. From what had it proceeded? From his aunt's supper, from his own foolish speech, from the wine and dancing, the merrymaking when saying good-night in the hall, the pleasure of the walk along the river in the snow. Poor Aunt Julia! She, too, would soon be a shade with the shade of Patrick Morkan and his horse. He had caught that haggard look upon her face for a moment when she was singing *Arrayed for the Bridal.* Soon, perhaps, he would be sitting in that same drawing-room, dressed in black, his silk hat on his knees. The blinds would be drawn down and Aunt Kate would be sitting beside him, crying and blowing her nose and telling him how Julia had died. He would cast about in his mind for some words that might console her, and would find only lame and useless ones. Yes, yes: that would happen very soon.

The air of the room chilled his shoulders. He stretched himself cautiously along under the sheets and lay down beside his wife. One by one they were all becoming shades. Better pass boldly into that other world, in the full glory of some passion, than fade and wither dismally with age. He thought of how she who lay beside him had locked in her heart for so many years that image of her lover's eyes when he had told her that he did not wish to live.

Generous tears filled Gabriel's eyes. He had never felt like that himself towards any woman but he knew that such a feeling must be love. The tears gathered more thickly in his eyes and in the partial darkness he imagined he saw the form of a young man standing under a dripping tree. Other forms were near. His soul had approached that region where dwell the vast hosts of the dead. He was conscious of, but could not apprehend, their wayward and flickering existence. His own identity was fading out into a grey impalpable world: the solid world itself which these dead had one time reared and lived in was dissolving and dwindling.

A few light taps upon the pane made him turn to the window. It had begun to snow again. He watched sleepily the flakes, silver and dark, falling obliquely against the lamp-light. The time had come for him to set out on his journey westward. Yes, the newspapers were right: snow was general all over Ireland. It was falling on every part of the dark central plain, on the treeless hills, falling softly upon the Bog of Allen and, farther westward, softly falling into the dark mutinous Shannon waves. It was falling, too, upon every part of the lonely churchyard on the hill where Michael Furey lay buried. It lay thickly drifted on the crooked crosses and headstones, on the spears of the little gate, on the barren thorns. His soul swooned slowly as he heard the snow falling faintly through the universe and faintly falling, like the descent of their last end, upon all the living and the dead.

QUESTIONS FOR DISCUSSION AND WRITING

1. How does the opening scene prepare for Gabriel's entrance? What minor conflicts does he encounter throughout the evening? How do those conflicts reach a climax in the hotel room?

2. How do the various people at the party characterize Gabriel? What does he think of himself? How does he see himself in the mirror at the hotel room?

3. Why does Joyce spend so much time describing the conversation and activities at the annual dance? How does this setting compare with the setting in the garden at Galway, where Michael Furey comes to see Gretta?

4. How does Gabriel's point of view toward himself change during the course of the evening? What does he learn about himself once he hears the story of Michael Furey?

5. What events during the evening—especially Gabriel's speech and D'Arcy's song—establish the contrast between the romantic past and "living duties and affections"? How do Gabriel's final observations about the falling snow reveal his new awareness?

49

FRANZ KAFKA

A Hunger Artist

FRANZ KAFKA (1883–1924) was born in Prague, Czechoslovakia, and educated at Karl Ferdinand University, where he earned a doctorate in jurisprudence. Rather than work as an attorney, he accepted a position as a civil service lawyer investigating workers' insurance claims. During the day, Kafka tried to fit into the mundane life of a civil servant, and at night, he wrote his dreamlike stories and novels about alienation, exile, fear, and failure. During his lifetime, Kafka published two short novels, *The Metamorphosis* (1915) and *In the Penal Colony* (1919), and two collections of stories, *The Country Doctor* (1919) and *The Hunger Artist* (1924). In 1924, Kafka died of tuberculosis in Berlin, leaving instructions with his literary executor, Max Brod, to destroy his published work and all his remaining manuscripts. Because he did not share Kafka's evaluation of this work, Brod disregarded his friend's request. In the next three years, Brod published three novels that brought Kafka posthumous fame as one of our century's great writers: *The Trial* (1925), *The Castle* (1926), and *Amerika* (1927). In the subsequent years his stories have been collected in *The Great Wall of China* (1933), *A Franz Kafka Miscellany* (1940), and *The Complete Stories* (1976). "A Hunger Artist," "The Metamorphosis," and "In the Penal Colony," all reprinted from *The Penal Colony* (1948), are bizarre, symbolic tales. The first recounts the demise of the public's appreciation for professional fasting. The second records a family's reaction to the discovery of a son's transformation into an insect. The third dramatizes a terrifying method for inflicting punishment.

During these last decades the interest in professional fasting has markedly diminished. It used to pay very well to stage such great performances under one's own management, but today that is quite impossible. We live in a different world now. At one time the whole town took a lively interest in the hunger artist; from day to day of his fast the excitement mounted; everybody wanted to see him at least once a day; there were people who bought season tickets for the last few days and sat from morning till night in front of his small barred cage; even in the nighttime there were visiting hours, when the whole effect was heightened by torch flares; on fine days the cage was set out in the open air, and then it was the children's special treat to see the hunger artist; for their elders he was often just a joke that happened to be in fashion, but the children stood open-mouthed, holding each other's hands for greater security, marveling at him as he sat there pallid in black tights, with his ribs sticking out so prominently, not even on a seat but down among straw on the ground, sometimes giving a courteous nod, answering questions with a constrained smile, or perhaps stretching an arm through the bars so that one might feel how thin it was, and then again withdrawing deep into himself, paying no attention to anyone or anything, not even to the all-important striking of the clock that was the only piece of furniture in his cage, but merely staring into vacancy with half shut eyes, now and then taking a sip from a tiny glass of water to moisten his lips.

Beside casual onlookers there were also relays of permanent watchers selected by the public, usually butchers, strangely enough, and it was their task to watch the hunger artist day and night, three of them at a time, in case he should have some secret recourse to nourishment. This was nothing but a formality, instituted to reassure the masses, for the initiates knew well enough that during his fast the artist would never in any circumstances, not even under forcible compulsion, swallow the smallest morsel of food; the honor of his profession forbade it. Not every watcher, of course, was capable of understanding this; there were often groups of night watchers who were very lax in carrying out their duties and deliberately huddled together in a retired corner to play cards with great absorption, obviously intending to give the hunger artist the chance of a little refreshment, which they supposed he could draw from some private hoard. Nothing annoyed the artist more than such watchers; they made him miserable; they made his fast seem unendurable; sometimes he mastered his feebleness sufficiently to sing during their watch for as long as he could keep going, to show them how unjust their suspicions were. But that was of little use; they only wondered at his cleverness in being able to fill his mouth even while singing. Much more of his taste were the watchers who sat close up to the bars, who were not content with the dim night lighting of the hall but focused him in the full glare of the electric pocket torch given them by the impresario. The harsh light did not trouble him at all, in any case he could never sleep properly, and he could always drowse a little, whatever the light, at any hour, even when the hall was thronged with noisy onlookers. He was quite happy at the prospect of spending a sleepless night with such watchers; he was ready to exchange jokes with them, to tell them stories out of his nomadic life, anything at all to keep them awake and demonstrate to them again that he had no eatables in his cage and that he was fasting as not one of them could fast. But his happiest moment was when the morning came and an enormous breakfast was brought them, at his expense, on which they flung themselves with the keen appetite of healthy men after a weary night of wakefulness. Of course there were people who argued that this breakfast was an unfair attempt to bribe the watchers, but that was going rather too far, and when they were invited to take on a night's vigil without a breakfast, merely for the sake of the cause, they made themselves scarce, although they stuck stubbornly to their suspicions.

Such suspicions, anyhow, were a necessary accompaniment to the profession of fasting. No one could possibly watch the hunger artist continuously, day and night, and so no one could produce first-hand evidence that the fast had really been rigorous and continuous; only the artist himself could know that, he was therefore bound to be the sole completely satisfied spectator of his own fast. Yet for other reasons he was never satisfied; it was not perhaps mere fasting that had brought him to such skeleton thinness that many people had regretfully to keep away from his exhibitions, because the sight of him was too much for them, perhaps it was dissatisfaction with himself that had worn him down. For he alone knew, what no other initiate knew, how easy it was to fast. It was the easiest thing in the world. He made no secret of this, yet people did not believe him, at the best they set him down as modest; most of them, however, thought he was out for publicity or else was some kind of cheat who found it easy to fast because he had discovered a way of making it easy, and then had the impudence to admit the fact, more or less. He had to put up with all that, and in the course of time had got used to it, but his inner dissatisfaction always rankled, and never yet, after any term of fasting—this must be granted to his credit—had he left the cage of his own free will. The longest period of fasting was fixed by his impresario at forty days, beyond that term he was not allowed to go, not even in great cities, and there was good reason for it, too. Experience had proved that for about forty days the interest of the public could be stimulated by a steadily increasing pressure of advertisement, but after that the town began to lose interest, sympathetic support began notably to fall off; there were of course local variations as between one town and another or one country and another, but as a general rule forty days marked the limit. So on the fortieth day the flower bedecked cage was opened, enthusiastic spectators filled the hall, a military band played, two doctors entered the cage to measure the results of the fast, which were announced through a megaphone, and finally two young ladies appeared, blissful at having been selected for the honor, to help the hunger artist down the few steps leading to a small table on which was spread a carefully chosen invalid repast. And at this very moment the artist always turned stubborn. True, he would entrust his bony arms to the outstretched helping hands of the ladies bending over him but stand up he would not. Why stop fasting at this particular moment, after forty days of it? He had held out for a long time, an illimitably long time; why stop now, when he was in his best fasting form, or rather, not yet quite in his best fasting form? Why should he be cheated of the fame he would get for fasting longer, for being not only the record hunger artist of all time, which presumably he was already, but for beating his own record by a performance beyond human imagination, since he felt that there were no limits to his capacity for fasting? His public pretended to admire him so much, why should it have so little patience with him; if he could endure fasting longer, why shouldn't the public endure it? Besides, he was tired, he was comfortable sitting in the straw, and now he was supposed to lift himself to his full height and go down to a meal the very thought of which gave him a nausea that only the presence of the ladies kept him from betraying, and even that with an effort. And he looked up into the eyes of the ladies who were apparently so friendly and in reality so cruel, and shook his head, which felt too heavy on its strengthless neck. But then there happened yet again what always happened. The impresario came forward, without a word—for the band made speech impossible—lifted his arms in the air above the artist, as if inviting Heaven to look down upon its creature here in the straw, this suffering martyr, which indeed he was, although in quite another sense; grasped him round the emaciated waist, with exaggerated caution, so that the frail condition he was in might be appreciated; and committed him to the care of the blenching ladies, not without secretly giving him a shaking so that his legs and body tottered and swayed. The artist now submitted completely; his head lolled on his breast as if it had landed there by chance; his body was hollowed out; his legs in a spasm of self-preservation clung close to each other at the knees, yet scraped on the ground as if it were not really solid ground, as if they were only trying to find solid ground; and the whole weight of his body, a feather-weight after all, relapsed onto one of the ladies, who, looking round for help and panting a little—this post of honor was not at all what she had expected it to be—first stretched her neck as far as she could to keep her face at least free from contact with the artist, when finding this impossible, and her more fortunate companion not coming to her aid but merely holding extended on her own trembling hand the little bunch of knucklebones that was the artist's, to the great delight of the spectators burst into tears and had to be replaced by an attendant who had long been stationed in readiness. Then came the food, a little of which the impresario managed to get between the artist's lips, while he sat in a kind of half-fainting trance, to the accompaniment of cheerful patter designed to distract the public's attention from the artist's condition; after that, a toast was drunk to the public, supposedly prompted by a whisper from the artist in the impresario's ear; the band confirmed it with a mighty flourish, the spectators melted away, and no one had any cause to be dissatisfied with the proceedings, no one except the hunger artist himself, he only, as always.

So he lived for many years, with small regular intervals of recuperation, in visible glory, honored by the world, yet in spite of that troubled in spirit, and all the more troubled because no one would take his trouble seriously. What comfort could he possibly need? What more could he possibly wish for? And if some good-natured person, feeling sorry for him, tried to console him by pointing out that his melancholy was probably caused by fasting; it could happen, especially when he had been fasting for some time, that he reacted with an outburst of fury and to the general alarm began to shake the bars of his cage like a wild animal. Yet the impresario had a way of punishing these outbreaks which he rather enjoyed putting into operation. He would apologize publicly for the artist's behavior, which was only to be excused, he admitted, because of the irritability caused by fasting; a condition hardly to be understood by well-fed people; then by natural transition he went on to mention the artist's equally incomprehensible boast that he could fast for much longer than he was doing; he praised the high ambition, the good will, the great self-denial undoubtedly implicit in such a statement; and then quite simply countered it by bringing out photographs, which were also on sale to the public, showing the artist on the fortieth day of a fast lying in bed almost dead from exhaustion. This perversion of the truth, familiar to the artist though it was, always unnerved him afresh and proved too much for him. What was a consequence of the premature ending of his fast was here presented as the cause of it! To fight against this lack of understanding, against a whole world of nonunderstanding, was impossible. Time and again in good faith he stood by the bars listening to the impresario, but as soon as the photographs appeared he always let go and sank with a groan back on to his straw, and the reassured public could once more come close and gaze at him.

A few years later when the witnesses of such scenes called them to mind, they often failed to understand themselves at all. For meanwhile the aforementioned change in public interest had set in; it seemed to happen almost overnight; there may have been profound causes for it, but who was going to bother about that; at any rate the pampered hunger artist suddenly found himself deserted one fine day by the amusement seekers, who were streaming past him to other more favored attractions. For the last time the impresario hurried him over half Europe to discover whether the old interest might still survive here and there; all in vain; everywhere, as if by secret agreement, a positive revulsion from professional fasting was in evidence. Of course it could not really have sprung up so suddenly as all that, and many premonitory symptoms which had not been sufficiently remarked or suppressed during the rush and glitter of success now came retrospectively to mind, but it was now too late to take any countermeasures. Fasting would surely come into fashion again at some future date, yet that was no comfort for those living in the present. What, then, was the hunger artist to do? He had been applauded by thousands in his time and could hardly come down to showing himself in a street booth at village fairs, and as for adopting another profession, he was not only too old for that but too frantically devoted to fasting. So he took leave of the impresario, his partner in an unparalleled career, and hired himself to a large circus; in order to spare his own feelings he avoided reading the conditions of his contract.

A large circus with its enormous traffic in replacing and recruiting men, animals and apparatus can always find a use for people at any time, even for a hunger artist, provided of course that he does not ask too much, and in this particular case anyhow it was not only the artist who was taken on but his famous and long-known name as well, indeed considering the peculiar nature of his performance, which was not impaired by advancing age, it could not be objected that there was an artist past his prime, no longer at the height of his professional skill, seeking a refuge in some quiet corner of a circus; on the contrary, the hunger artist averred that he could fast as well as ever, which was entirely credible; he even alleged that if he were allowed to fast as he liked, and this was at once promised him without more ado, he could astound the world by establishing a record never yet achieved, a statement which certainly provoked a smile among the other professionals, since it left out of account the change in public opinion, which the hunger artist in his zeal conveniently forgot.

He had not, however, actually lost his sense of the real situation and took it as a matter of course that he and his cage should be stationed, not in the middle of the ring as a main attraction, but outside, near the animal cages, on a site that was after all easily accessible. Large and gaily painted placards made a frame for the cage and announced what was to be seen inside it. When the public came thronging out in the intervals to see the animals, they could hardly avoid passing the hunger artist's cage and stopping there for a moment; perhaps they might even have stayed longer had not those pressing behind them in the narrow gangway, who did not understand why they should be held up on their way toward the excitements of the menagerie, made it impossible for anyone to stand gazing quietly for any length of time. And that was the reason why the hunger artist, who had of course been looking forward to these visiting hours as the main achievement of his life, began instead to shrink from them. At first he could hardly wait for the intervals; it was exhilarating to watch the crowds come streaming his way, until only too soon—not even the most obstinate self-deception, clung to almost consciously, could hold out against the fact—the conviction was borne in upon him that these people, most of them, to judge from their actions, again and again, without exception, were all on their way to the menagerie. And the first sight of them from the distance remained the best. For when they reached his cage he was at once deafened by the storm of shouting and abuse that arose from the two contending factions, which renewed themselves continuously, of those who wanted to stop and stare at him—he soon began to dislike them more than the others—not out of real interest but only out of obstinate self-assertiveness, and those who wanted to go straight on to the animals. When the first great rush was past, the stragglers came along, and these, whom nothing could have prevented from stopping to look at him as long as they had breath, raced past with long strides, hardly even glancing at him, in their haste to get to the menagerie in time. And all too rarely did it happen that he had a stroke of luck, when some father of a family fetched up before him with his children, pointed a finger at the hunger artist and explained at length what the phenomenon meant, telling stories of earlier years when he himself had watched similar but much more thrilling performances, and the children, still rather uncomprehending, since neither inside nor outside school had they been sufficiently prepared for this lesson—what did they care about fasting?—yet showed by the brightness of their intent eyes that new and better times might be coming. Perhaps, said the hunger artist to himself many a time, things would be a little better if his cage were set not quite so near the menagerie. That made it too easy for people to make their choice, to say nothing of what he suffered from the stench of the menagerie, the animals' restlessness by night, the carrying past of raw lumps of flesh for the beasts of prey, the roaring at feeding times, which depressed him continually. But he did not dare to lodge a complaint with the management; after all, he had the animals to thank for the troops of people who passed his cage, among whom there might always be one here and there to take an interest in him, and who could tell where they might seclude him if he called attention to his existence and thereby to the fact that, strictly speaking, he was only an impediment on the way to the menagerie.

A small impediment, to be sure, one that grew steadily less. People grew familiar with the strange idea that they could be expected, in times like these, to take an interest in a hunger artist, and with this familiarity the verdict went out against him. He might fast as much as he could, and he did so; but nothing could save him now, people passed him by. Just try to explain to anyone the art of fasting! Anyone who has no feeling for it cannot be made to understand it. The fine placards grew dirty and illegible, they were torn down; the little notice board telling the number of fast days achieved, which at first was changed carefully every day, had long stayed at the same figure, for after the first few weeks even this small task seemed pointless to the staff; and so the artist simply fasted on and on, as he had once dreamed of doing, and it was no trouble to him, just as he had always foretold, but no one counted the days, no one, not even the artist himself, knew what records he was already breaking, and his heart grew heavy. And when once in a time some leisurely passer-by stopped, made merry over the old figure on the board and spoke of swindling, that was in its way the stupidest lie ever invented by indifference and inborn malice, since it was not the hunger artist who was cheating; he was working honestly, but the world was cheating him of his reward.

Many more days went by, however, and that too came to an end. An overseer's eye fell on the cage one day and asked the attendants why this perfectly good cage should be left standing there unused with dirty straw inside; nobody knew, until one man, helped out by the notice board, remembered about the hunger artist. They poked into the straw with sticks and found him in it. "Are you still fasting?" asked the overseer. "When on earth do you mean to stop?" "Forgive me, everybody," whispered the hunger artist; only the overseer, who had his ear to the bars, understood him. "Of course," said the overseer, and tapped his forehead with a finger to let the attendants know what state the man was in, "we forgive you." "I always wanted you to admire my fasting," said the hunger artist. "We do admire it," said the overseer, affably. "But you shouldn't admire it," said the hunger artist. "Well, then we don't admire it," said the overseer, "but why shouldn't we admire it?" "Because I have to fast, I can't help it," said the hunger artist. "What a fellow you are," said the overseer, "and why can't you help it?" "Because," said the hunger artist, lifting his head a little and speaking, with his lips pursed, as if for a kiss, right into the overseer's ear, so that no syllable might be lost, "because I couldn't find the food I liked. If I had found it, believe me, I should have made no fuss and stuffed myself like you or anyone else." These were his last words, but in his dimming eyes remained the firm though no longer proud persuasion that he was still continuing to fast.

"Well, clear this out now!" said the overseer, and they buried the hunger artist, straw and all. Into the cage they put a young panther. Even the most insensitive felt it refreshing to see this wild creature leaping around the cage that had so long been dreary. The panther was all right. The food he liked was brought him without hesitation by the attendants; he seemed not even to miss his freedom; his noble body, furnished almost to the bursting point with all that it needed, seemed to carry freedom around with it too; somewhere in his jaws it seemed to lurk; and the joy of life streamed with such ardent passion from his throat that for the onlookers it was not easy to stand the shock of it. But they braced themselves, crowded round the cage, and did not want ever to move away.

QUESTIONS FOR DISCUSSION AND WRITING

1. What is the principal conflict in the story? Why does the public change its attitude toward the drama of this conflict?
2. How do the various members of the community view the hunger artist? Why is he always dissatisfied with their opinion of him? How does he envision his own professionalism?
3. Why does Kafka avoid identifying the precise setting for this story? How does the position of the cage—town square, menagerie—record the change in public fashion about the hunger artist?
4. How does the point of view of the story affect our attitude toward the events in the story? Why does the hunger artist object to his impresario's point of view toward his performance?
5. How might this story be interpreted symbolically? For example, what does the panther symbolize? By contrast, what does the hunger artist possess that makes him an artist?

50

FRANZ KAFKA

The Metamorphosis

TRANSLATED BY EDWIN AND WILLA MUIR

1

As Gregor Samsa awoke one morning from uneasy dreams he found himself transformed in his bed into a gigantic insect. He was lying on his hard, as it were armor-plated, back and when he lifted his head a little he could see his dome-like brown belly divided into stiff arched segments on top of which the bed quilt could hardly keep in position and was about to slide off completely. His numerous legs, which were pitifully thin compared to the rest of his bulk, waved helplessly before his eyes.

What has happened to me? he thought. It was no dream. His room, a regular human bedroom, only rather too small, lay quiet between the four familiar walls. Above the table on which a collection of cloth samples was unpacked and spread out—Samsa was a commercial traveler—hung the picture which he had recently cut out of an illustrated magazine and put into a pretty gilt frame. It showed a lady, with a fur cap on and a fur stole, sitting upright and holding out to the spectator a huge fur muff into which the whole of her forearm had vanished!

Gregor's eyes turned next to the window, and the overcast sky—one could hear rain drops beating on the window gutter—made him quite melancholy. What about sleeping a little longer and forgetting all this nonsense, he thought, but it could not be done, for he was accustomed to sleep on his right side and in his present condition he could not turn himself over. However violently he forced himself towards his right side he always rolled on to his back again. He tried it at least a hundred times, shutting his eyes to keep from seeing his struggling legs, and only desisted when he began to feel in his side a faint dull ache he had never experienced before.

Oh God, he thought, what an exhausting job I've picked on! Traveling about day in, day out. It's much more irritating work than doing the actual business in the office, and on top of that there's the trouble of constant traveling, of worrying about train connections, the bed and irregular meals, casual acquaintances that are always new and never become intimate friends. The devil take it all! He felt a slight itching up on his belly; slowly pushed himself on his back nearer to the top of the bed so that he could lift his head more easily; identified the itching place which was surrounded by many small white spots the nature of which he could not understand and made to touch it with a leg, but drew the leg back immediately, for the contact made a cold shiver run through him.

He slid down again into his former position. This getting up early, he thought, makes one quite stupid. A man needs his sleep. Other commercials live like harem women. For instance, when I come back to the hotel of a morning to write up the orders I've got, these others are only sitting down to breakfast. Let me just try that with my chief; I'd be sacked on the spot. Anyhow, that might be quite a good thing for me, who can tell? If I didn't have to hold my hand because of my parents I'd have given notice long ago, I'd have gone to the chief and told him exactly what I think of him. That would knock him endways from his desk! It's a queer way of doing, too, this sitting on high at a desk and talking down to employees, especially when they have to come quite near because the chief is hard of hearing. Well, there's still hope; once I've saved enough money to pay back my parents' debts to him—that should take another five or six years—I'll do it without fail. I'll cut myself completely loose then. For the moment, though, I'd better get up, since my train goes at five.

He looked at the alarm clock ticking on the chest. Heavenly Father! he thought. It was half-past six o'clock and the hands were quietly moving on, it was even past the half-hour, it was getting on toward a quarter to seven. Had the alarm clock not gone off? From the bed one could see that it had been properly set for four o'clock; of course it must have gone off. Yes, but was it possible to sleep quietly through that ear-splitting noise? Well, he had not slept quietly, yet apparently all the more soundly for that. But what was he to do now? The next train went at seven o'clock; to catch that he would need to hurry like mad and his samples weren't even packed up, and he himself wasn't feeling particularly fresh and active. And even if he did catch the train he wouldn't avoid a row with the chief, since the firm's porter would have been waiting for the five o'clock train and would have long since reported his failure to turn up. The porter was a creature of the chief's, spineless and stupid. Well, supposing he were to say he was sick? But that would be most unpleasant and would look suspicious, since during his five years' employment he had not been ill once. The chief himself would be sure to come with the sick-insurance doctor, would reproach his parents with their son's laziness and would cut all excuses short by referring to the insurance doctor, who of course regarded all mankind as perfectly healthy malingerers. And would he be so far wrong on this occasion? Gregor really felt quite well, apart from a drowsiness that was utterly superfluous after such a long sleep, and he was even unusually hungry.

As all this was running through his mind at top speed without his being able to decide to leave his bed—the alarm clock had just struck a quarter to seven—there came a cautious tap at the door behind the head of his bed. "Gregor," said a voice—it was his mother's—"it's a quarter to seven. Hadn't you a train to catch?" That gentle voice! Gregor had a shock as he heard his own voice answering hers, unmistakably his own voice, it was true, but with a persistent horrible twittering squeak behind it like an undertone, that left the words in their clear shape only for the first moment and then rose up reverberating round them to destroy their sense, so that one could not be sure one had heard them rightly. Gregor wanted to answer at length and explain everything, but in the circumstances he confined himself to saying: "Yes, yes, thank you, Mother, I'm getting up now." The wooden door between them must have kept the change in his voice from being noticeable outside, for his mother contented herself with this statement and shuffled away. Yet this brief exchange of words had made the other members of the family aware that Gregor was still in the house, as they had not expected, and at one of the side doors his father was already knocking, gently, yet with his fist. "Gregor, Gregor," he called, "what's the matter with you?" And after a little while he called again in a deeper voice: "Gregor!

Gregor!" At the other side door his sister was saying in a low, plaintive tone: "Gregor? Aren't you well? Are you needing anything?" He answered them both at once: "I'm just ready," and did his best to make his voice sound as normal as possible by enunciating the words very clearly and leaving long pauses between them. So his father went back to his breakfast, but his sister whispered: "Gregor, open the door, do." However, he was not thinking of opening the door, and felt thankful for the prudent habit he had acquired in traveling of locking all doors during the night, even at home.

His immediate intention was to get up quietly without being disturbed, to put on his clothes and above all eat his breakfast, and only then to consider what else was to be done, since in bed, he was well aware, his meditations would come to no sensible conclusion. He remembered that often enough in bed he had felt small aches and pains, probably caused by awkward postures, which had proved purely imaginary once he got up, and he looked forward eagerly to seeing this morning's delusions gradually fall away. That the change in his voice was nothing but the precursor of a severe chill, a standing ailment of commercial travelers, he had not the least possible doubt.

To get rid of the quilt was quite easy; he had only to inflate himself a little and it fell off by itself. But the next move was difficult, especially because he was so uncommonly broad. He would have needed arms and hands to hoist himself up; instead he had only the numerous little legs which never stopped waving in all directions and which he could not control in the least. When he tried to bend one of them it was the first to stretch itself straight; and did he succeed at last in making it do what he wanted, all the other legs meanwhile waved the more wildly in a high degree of unpleasant agitation. "But what's the use of lying idle in bed," said Gregor to himself.

He thought that he might get out of bed with the lower part of his body first, but this lower part, which he had not yet seen and of which he could form no clear conception, proved too difficult to move; it shifted so slowly; and when finally, almost wild with annoyance, he gathered his forces together and thrust out recklessly, he had miscalculated the direction and bumped heavily against the lower end of the bed, and the stinging pain he felt informed him that precisely this lower part of his body was at the moment probably the most sensitive.

So he tried to get the top part of himself out first, and cautiously moved his head towards the edge of the bed. That proved easy enough, and despite its breadth and mass the bulk of his body at last slowly followed the movement of his head. Still, when he finally got his head free over the edge of the bed he felt too scared to go on advancing, for after all if he let himself fall in this way it would take a miracle to keep his head from being injured. And at all costs he must not lose consciousness now, precisely now; he would rather stay in bed.

But when after a repetition of the same efforts he lay in his former position again, sighing, and watching his little legs struggling against each other more wildly than ever, if that were possible, and saw no way of bringing any order into this arbitrary confusion, he told himself again that it was impossible to stay in bed and that the most sensible course was to risk everything for the smallest hope of getting away from it. At the same time he did not forget meanwhile to remind himself that cool reflection, the coolest possible, was much better than desperate resolves. In such moments he focused his eyes as sharply as possible on the window, but, unfortunately, the prospect of the morning fog, which muffled even the other side of the narrow street, brought him little encouragement and comfort. "Seven o'clock already," he said to himself when the alarm clock chimed again, "seven o'clock already and still such a thick fog." And for a little while he lay quiet, breathing lightly, as if perhaps expecting such complete repose to restore all things to their real and normal condition.

But then he said to himself: "Before it strikes a quarter past seven I must be quite out of this bed, without fail. Anyhow, by that time someone will have come from the office to ask for me, since it opens before seven." And he set himself to rocking his whole body at once in a regular rhythm, with the idea of swinging it out of the bed. If he tipped himself out in that way he could keep his head from injury by lifting it at an acute angle when he fell. His back seemed to be hard and was not likely to suffer from a fall on the carpet. His biggest worry was the loud crash he would not be able to help making, which would probably cause anxiety, if not terror, behind all the doors. Still, he must take the risk.

When he was already half out of the bed—the new method was more a game than an effort, for he needed only to hitch himself across by rocking to and fro—it struck him how simple it would be if he could get help. Two strong people—he thought of his father and the servant girl—would be amply sufficient; they would only have to thrust their arms under his convex back, lever him out of the bed, bend down with their burden and then be patient enough to let him turn himself right over on to the floor, where it was to be hoped his legs would then find their proper function. Well, ignoring the fact that the doors were all locked, ought he really to call for help? In spite of his misery he could not suppress a smile at the very idea of it.

He had got so far that he could barely keep his equilibrium when he rocked himself strongly, and he would have to nerve himself very soon for the final decision since in five minutes' time it would be a quarter past seven—when the front doorbell rang. "That's someone from the office," he said to himself, and grew almost rigid, while his little legs only jigged about all the faster. For a moment everything stayed quiet. "They're not going to open the door," said Gregor to himself, catching at some kind of irrational hope. But then of course the servant girl went as usual to the door with her heavy tread and opened it. Gregor needed only to hear the first good morning of the visitor to know immediately who it was—the chief clerk himself. What a fate, to be condemned to work for a firm where the smallest omission at once gave rise to the gravest suspicion! Were all employees in a body nothing but scoundrels, was there not among them one single loyal devoted man who, had he wasted only an hour or so of the firm's time in a morning, was so tormented by conscience as to be driven out of his mind and actually incapable of leaving his bed? Wouldn't it really have been sufficient to send an apprentice to inquire—if any inquiry were necessary at all—did the chief clerk himself have to come and thus indicate to the entire family, an innocent family, that this suspicious circumstance could be investigated by no one less versed in affairs than himself? And more through the agitation caused by these reflections than through any act of will Gregor swung himself out of bed with all his strength. There was a loud thump, but it was not really a crash. His fall was broken to some extent by the carpet, his back, too, was less stiff than he thought, and so there was merely a dull thud, not so very startling. Only he had not lifted his head carefully enough and had hit it; he turned it and rubbed it on the carpet in pain and irritation.

"That was something falling down in there," said the chief clerk in the next room to the left. Gregor tried to suppose to himself that something like what had happened to him today might some day happen to the chief clerk; one really could not deny that it was possible. But as if in brusque reply to this supposition the chief clerk took a couple of firm steps in the next-door room and his patent leather boots creaked. From the right-hand room his sister was whispering to inform him of the situation: "Gregor, the chief clerk's here." "I know," muttered Gregor to himself; but he didn't dare to make his voice loud enough for his sister to hear it.

"Gregor," said his father now from the left-hand room, "the chief clerk has come and wants to know why you didn't catch the early train. We don't know what to say to him. Besides, he wants to talk to you in person. So open the door, please. He will be good enough to excuse the untidiness of your room." "Good morning, Mr. Samsa," the chief clerk was calling amiably meanwhile. "He's not well," said his mother to the visitor, while his father was still speaking through the door, "he's not well, sir, believe me. What else would make him miss a train! The boy thinks about nothing but his work. It makes me almost cross the way he never goes out in the evenings; he's been here the last eight days and has stayed at home every single evening. He just sits there quietly at the table reading a newspaper or looking through railway timetables. The only amusement he gets is doing fretwork. For instance, he spent two or three evenings cutting out a little picture frame; you would be surprised to see how pretty it is; it's hanging in his room; you'll see it in a minute when Gregor opens the door. I must say I'm glad you've come, sir; we should never have got him to unlock the door by ourselves; he's so obstinate; and I'm sure he's unwell, though he wouldn't have it to be so this morning." "I'm just coming," said Gregor slowly and carefully, not moving an inch for fear of losing one word of the conversation. "I can't think of any other explanation, madam," said the chief clerk, "I hope it's nothing serious. Although on the other hand I must say that we men of business—fortunately or unfortunately—very often simply have to ignore any slight indisposition, since business must be attended to." "Well, can the chief clerk come in now?" asked Gregor's father impatiently, again knocking on the door. "No," said Gregor. In the left-hand room a painful silence followed this refusal, in the right-hand room his sister began to sob.

Why didn't his sister join the others? She was probably newly out of bed and hadn't even begun to put on her clothes yet. Well, why was she crying? Because he wouldn't get up and let the chief clerk in, because he was in danger of losing his job, and because the chief would begin dunning his parents again for the old debts? Surely these were things one didn't need to worry about for the present. Gregor was still at home and not in the least thinking of deserting the family. At the moment, true, he was lying on the carpet and no one who knew the condition he was in could seriously expect him to admit the chief clerk. But for such a small discourtesy, which could plausibly be explained away somehow later on, Gregor could hardly be dismissed on the spot. And it seemed to Gregor that it would be much more sensible to leave him in peace for the present than to trouble him with tears and entreaties. Still, of course, their uncertainty bewildered them all and excused their behavior.

"Mr. Samsa," the chief clerk called now in a louder voice, "what's the matter with you? Here you are, barricading yourself in your room, giving only 'yes' and 'no' for answers, causing your parents a lot of unnecessary trouble and neglecting—I mention this only in passing—neglecting your business duties in an incredible fashion. I am speaking here in the name of your parents and of your chief, and I beg you quite seriously to give me an immediate and precise explanation. You amaze me, you amaze me. I thought you were a quiet, dependable person, and now all at once you seem bent on making a disgraceful exhibition of yourself. The chief did hint to me early this morning a possible explanation for your disappearance—with reference to the cash payments that were entrusted to you recently—but I almost pledged my solemn word of honor that this could not be so. But now that I see how incredibly obstinate you are, I no longer have the slightest desire to take your part at all. And your position in the firm is not so unassailable. I came with the intention of telling you all this in private, but since you are wasting my time so needlessly I don't see why your parents shouldn't hear it too. For some time past your work has been most unsatisfactory; this is not the season of the year for a business boom, of course, we admit that, but a season of the year for doing no business at all, that does not exist, Mr. Samsa, must not exist."

"But, sir," cried Gregor, beside himself and in his agitation forgetting everything else, "I'm just going to open the door this very minute. A slight illness, an attack of giddiness, has kept me from getting up. I'm still lying in bed. But I feel all right again. I'm getting out of bed now. Just give me a moment or two longer! I'm not quite so well as I thought. But I'm all right, really. How a thing like that can suddenly strike one down! Only last night I was quite well, my parents can tell you, or rather I did have a slight presentiment. I must have showed some sign of it. Why didn't I report it at the office! But one always thinks that an indisposition can be got over without staying in the house. Oh sir, do spare my parents! All that you're reproaching me with now has no foundation; no one has ever said a word to me about it. Perhaps you haven't looked at the last orders I sent in. Anyhow, I can still catch the eight o'clock train, I'm much the better for my few hours' rest. Don't let me detain you here sir; I'll be attending to business very soon, and do be good enough to tell the chief so and to make my excuses to him!"

And while all this was tumbling out pell-mell and Gregor hardly knew what he was saying, he had reached the chest quite easily, perhaps because of the practice he had had in bed, and was now trying to lever himself upright by means of it. He meant actually to open the door, actually to show himself and speak to the chief clerk; he was eager to find out what the others, after all their insistence, would say at the sight of him. If they were horrified then the responsibility was no longer his and he could stay quiet. But if they took it calmly, then he had no reason either to be upset, and could really get to the station for the eight o'clock train if he hurried. At first he slipped down a few times from the polished surface of the chest, but at length with a last heave he stood upright; he paid no more attention to the pains in the lower part of his body, however they smarted. Then he let himself fall against the back of a nearby chair, and clung with his little legs to the edges of it. That brought him into control of himself again and he stopped speaking, for now he could listen to what the chief clerk was saying.

"Did you understand a word of it?" the chief clerk was asking; "surely he can't be trying to make fools of us?" "Oh dear," cried his mother, in tears, "perhaps he's terribly ill and we're tormenting him. Grete! Grete!" she called out then. "Yes Mother?" called his sister from the other side. They were calling to each other across Gregor's room. "You must go this minute for the doctor. Gregor is ill. Go for the doctor, quick. Did you hear how he was speaking?" "That was no human voice," said the chief clerk in a voice noticeably low beside the shrillness of the mother's. "Anna! Anna!" his father was calling through the hall to the kitchen, clapping his hands, "get a locksmith at once!" And the two girls were already running through the hall with a swish of skirts—how could his sister have got dressed so quickly?—and were tearing the front door open. There was no sound of its closing again; they had evidently left it open, as one does in houses where some great misfortune has happened.

But Gregor was now much calmer. The words he uttered were no longer understandable, apparently, although they seemed clear enough to him, even clearer than before, perhaps because his ear had grown accustomed to the sound of them. Yet at any rate people now believed that something was wrong with him, and were ready to help him. The positive certainty with which these first measures had been taken comforted him. He felt himself drawn once more into the human circle and hoped for great and remarkable results from both the doctor and the locksmith, without really distinguishing precisely between them. To make his voice as clear as possible for the decisive conversation that was now imminent he coughed a little, as quietly as he could, of course, since this noise too might not sound like a human cough for all he was able to judge. In the next room meanwhile there was complete silence. Perhaps his parents were sitting at the table with the chief clerk, whispering, perhaps they were all leaning against the door and listening.

Slowly Gregor pushed the chair towards the door, then let go of it, caught hold of the door for support—the soles at the end of his little legs were somewhat sticky—and rested against it for a moment after his efforts. Then he set himself to turning the key in the lock with his mouth. It seemed, unhappily, that he hadn't really any teeth—what could he grip the key with?—but on the other hand his jaws were certainly very strong; with their help he did manage to set the key in motion, heedless of the fact that he was undoubtedly damaging them somewhere, since a brown fluid issued from his mouth, flowed over the key and dripped on the floor. "Just listen to that," said the chief clerk next door; "he's turning the key." That was a great encouragement to Gregor; but they should all have shouted encouragement to him, his father and mother too: "Go on, Gregor," they should have called out, "keep going, hold on to that key!" And in the belief that they were all following his efforts intently, he clenched his jaws recklessly on the key with all the force at his command. As the turning of the key progressed he circled round the lock, holding on now with his mouth, pushing on the key, as required, or pulling it down again with all the weight of his body. The louder click of the finally yielding lock literally quickened Gregor. With a deep breath of relief he said to himself: "So I didn't need the locksmith," and laid his head on the handle to open the door wide.

Since he had to pull the door towards him, he was still invisible when it was really wide open. He had to edge himself very slowly round the near half of the double door, and to do it very carefully if he was not to fall plump upon his back just on the threshold. He was still carrying out this difficult manoeuvre, with no time to observe anything else, when he heard the chief clerk utter a loud "Oh!"—it sounded like a gust of wind—and now he could see the man, standing as he was nearest to the door, clapping one hand before his open mouth and slowly backing away as if driven by some invisible steady pressure. His mother—in spite of the chief clerk's being there her hair was still undone and sticking up in all directions—first clasped her hands and looked at his father, then took two steps towards Gregor and fell on the floor among her outspread skirts, her face quite hidden on her breast. His father knotted his fist with a fierce expression on his face as if he meant to knock Gregor back into the room, then looked uncertainly round the living room, covered his eyes with his hands and wept till his great chest heaved.

Gregor did not go now into the living room, but leaned against the inside of the firmly shut wing of the door, so that only half his body was visible and his head above it bending sideways to look at the others. The light had meanwhile strengthened; on the other side of the street one could see clearly a section of the endlessly long, dark gray building opposite—it was a hospital—abruptly punctuated by its row of regular windows; the rain was still falling, but only in large singly discernible and literally singly splashing drops. The breakfast dishes were set out on the table lavishly, for breakfast was the most important meal of the day to Gregor's father, who lingered it out for hours over various newspapers. Right opposite Gregor on the wall hung a photograph of himself on military service, as a lieutenant, hand on sword, a carefree smile on his face, inviting one to respect his uniform and military bearing. The door leading to the hall was open, and one could see that the front door stood open too, showing the landing beyond and the beginning of the stairs going down.

"Well," said Gregor, knowing perfectly that he was the only one who had retained any composure, "I'll put my clothes on at once, pack up my samples and start off. Will you only let me go? You see, sir, I'm not obstinate, and I'm willing to work; traveling is a hard life, but I couldn't live without it. Where are you going, sir? To the office? Yes? Will you give a true account of all this? One can be temporarily incapacitated, but that's just the moment for remembering former services and bearing in mind that later on, when the incapacity has been got over, one will certainly work with all the more industry and concentration. I'm loyally bound to serve the chief, you know that very well. Besides, I have to provide for my parents and my sister. I'm in great difficulties, but I'll get out of them again. Don't make things any worse for me than they are. Stand up for me in the firm. Travelers are not popular there, I know. People think they earn sacks of money and just have a good time. A prejudice there's no particular reason for revising. But you, sir, have a more comprehensive view of affairs than the rest of the staff, yes, let me tell you in confidence, a more comprehensive view than the chief himself, who, being the owner, lets his judgment easily be swayed against one of his employees. And you know very well that the traveler, who is never seen in the office almost the whole year round, can so easily fall a victim to gossip and ill luck and unfounded complaints, which he mostly knows nothing about, except when he comes back exhausted from his rounds, and only then suffers in person from their evil consequences, which he can no longer trace back to the original causes. Sir, sir, don't go away without a word to me to show that you think me in the right at least to some extent!"

But at Gregor's very first words the chief clerk had already backed away and only stared at him with parted lips over one twitching shoulder. And while Gregor was speaking he did not stand still one moment but stole away towards the door, without taking his eyes off Gregor, yet only an inch at a time, as if obeying some secret injunction to leave the room. He was already at the hall, and the suddenness with which he took his last step out of the living room would have made one believe he had burned the sole of his foot.

Once in the hall he stretched his right arm before him towards the staircase, as if some supernatural power were waiting there to deliver him.

Gregor perceived that the chief clerk must on no account be allowed to go away in this frame of mind if his position in the firm were not to be endangered to the utmost. His parents did not understand this so well; they had convinced themselves in the course of years that Gregor was settled for life in this firm, and besides they were so occupied with their immediate troubles that all foresight had forsaken them. Yet Gregor had this foresight. The chief clerk must be detained, soothed, persuaded and finally won over; the whole future of Gregor and his family depended on it! If only his sister had been there! She was intelligent; she had begun to cry while Gregor was still lying quietly on his back. And no doubt the chief clerk, so partial to ladies, would have been guided by her; she would have shut the door of the flat and in the hall talked him out of this horror. But she was not there, and Gregor would have to handle the situation himself. And without remembering that he was still unaware what powers of movement he possessed, without even remembering that his words in all possibility, indeed in all likelihood, would again be unintelligible, he let go the wing of the door, pushed himself through the opening, started to walk towards the chief clerk, who was already ridiculously clinging with both hands to the railing on the landing; but immediately, as he was feeling for a support, he fell down with a little cry upon all his numerous legs. Hardly was he down when he experienced for the first time this morning a sense of physical comfort; his legs had firm ground under them; they were completely obedient, as he noted with joy; they even strove to carry him forward in whatever direction he chose; and he was inclined to believe that a final relief from all his sufferings was at hand. But in the same moment as he found himself on the floor, rocking with suppressed eagerness to move, not far from his mother, indeed just in front of her, she, who had seemed so completely crushed, sprang all at once to her feet, her arms and fingers outspread, cried: "Help, for God's sake, help!" bent her head down as if to see Gregor better, yet on the contrary kept backing senselessly away; had quite forgotten that the laden table stood behind her; sat upon it hastily, as if in absence of mind, when she bumped into it; and seemed altogether unaware that the big coffee pot beside her was upset and pouring coffee in a flood over the carpet.

"Mother, Mother," said Gregor in a low voice, and looked up at her. The chief clerk, for the moment, had quite slipped from his mind; instead he could not resist snapping his jaws together at the sight of the steaming coffee. That made his mother scream again, she fled from the table and fell into the arms of his father, who hastened to catch her. But Gregor had now no time to spare for his parents; the chief clerk was already on the stairs; with his chin on the banisters he was taking one last backward look. Gregor made a spring, to be as sure as possible of overtaking him; the chief clerk must have divined his intention, for he leaped down several steps and vanished; he was still yelling "Ugh!" and it echoed through the whole staircase.

Unfortunately, the flight of the chief clerk seemed completely to upset Gregor's father, who had remained relatively calm until now, for instead of running after the man himself, or at least not hindering Gregor in his pursuit, he seized in his right hand the walking stick which the chief clerk had left behind on a chair, together with a hat and greatcoat, snatched in his left hand a large newspaper from the table and began stamping his feet and flourishing the stick and the newspaper to drive Gregor back into his room.

No entreaty of Gregor's availed, indeed no entreaty was even understood; however humbly he bent his head his father only stamped on the floor the more loudly. Behind his father his mother had torn open a window, despite the cold weather, and was leaning far out of it with her face in her hands. A strong draught set in from the street to the staircase, the window curtain blew in, the newspapers on the table fluttered, stray pages whisked over the floor. Pitilessly Gregor's father drove him back, hissing and crying "Shoo!" like a savage. But Gregor was quite unpracticed in walking backwards, it really was a slow business. If he only had a chance to turn round he could get back to his room at once, but he was afraid of exasperating his father by the slowness of such a rotation and at any moment the stick in his father's hand might hit him a fatal blow on the back or on the head. In the end, however, nothing else was left for him to do since to his horror he observed that in moving backwards he could not even control the direction he took; and so, keeping an anxious eye on his father all the time over his shoulder, he began to turn round as quickly as he could, which was in reality very slowly. Perhaps his father noted his good intentions, for he did not interfere except every now and then to help him in the manoeuvre from a distance with the point of the stick. If only he would have stopped making that unbearable hissing noise! It made Gregor quite lose his head. He had turned almost completely round when the hissing noise so distracted him that he even turned a little the wrong way again. But when at last his head was fortunately right in front of the doorway, it appeared that his body was too broad simply to get through the opening. His father, of course, in his present mood was far from thinking of such a thing as opening the other half of the door, to let Gregor have enough space. He had merely the fixed idea of driving Gregor back into his room as quickly as possible. He would have never suffered Gregor to make the circumstantial preparations for standing up on end and perhaps slipping his way through the door. Maybe he was now making more noise than ever to urge Gregor forward, as if no obstacle impeded him; to Gregor, anyhow, the noise in his rear sounded no longer like the voice of one single father; this was really no joke, and Gregor thrust himself—come what might—into the doorway. One side of his body rose up, he was tilted at an angle in the doorway, his flank was quite bruised, horrid blotches stained the white door, soon he was stuck fast and, left to himself could not have moved at all, his legs on one side fluttered trembling in the air, those on the other were crushed painfully to the door—when from behind his father gave him a strong push which was literally a deliverance and he flew far into the room, bleeding freely. The door was slammed behind him with the stick, and then at last there was silence.

2

Not until it was twilight did Gregor awake out of a deep sleep, more like a swoon than a sleep. He would certainly have waked up of his own accord not much later, for he felt himself sufficiently rested and well-slept, but it seemed to him as if a fleeting step and a cautious shutting of the door leading into the hall had aroused him. The electric lights in the street cast a pale sheen here and there on the ceiling and the upper surfaces of the furniture, but down below, where he lay, it was dark. Slowly, awkwardly trying out his feelers, which he now first learned to appreciate, he pushed his way to the door to see what had been happening there. His left side felt like one single long, unpleasantly tense scar, and he had actually to limp on his two rows of legs. One little leg, moreover, had been severely damaged in the course of that morning's events—it was almost a miracle that only one had been damaged—and trailed uselessly behind him.

He had reached the door before he discovered what had really drawn him to it: the smell of food. For there stood a basin filled with fresh milk in which floated little sops of white bread. He could almost have laughed with joy, since he was now still hungrier than in the morning, and dipped his head almost over the eyes straight into the milk. But soon in disappointment he withdrew it again; not only did he find it difficult to feed because of his tender left side—and he could only feed with the palpitating collaboration of his whole body—he did not like the milk either, although milk had been his favorite drink and that was certainly why his sister had set it there for him, indeed it was almost with repulsion that he turned away from the basin and crawled back to the middle of the room.

He could see through the crack of the door that the gas was turned on in the living room, but while usually at this time his father made a habit of reading the afternoon newspaper in a loud voice to his mother and occasionally to his sister as well, not a sound was now to be heard. Well, perhaps his father had recently given up this habit of reading aloud, which his sister had mentioned so often in conversation and in her letters. But there was the same silence all around, although the flat was certainly not empty of occupants. "What a quiet life our family has been leading," said Gregor to himself, and as he sat there motionless staring into the darkness he felt great pride in the fact that he had been able to provide such a life for his parents and sister in such a fine flat. But what if all the quiet, the comfort, the contentment were now to end in horror? To keep himself from being lost in such thoughts Gregor took refuge in movement and crawled up and down the room.

Once during the long evening one of the side doors was opened a little and quickly shut again, later the other side door too; someone had apparently wanted to come in and then thought better of it. Gregor now stationed himself immediately before the living-room door, determined to persuade any hesitating visitor to come in or at least to discover who it might be; but the door was not opened again and he waited in vain. In the early morning, when the doors were locked, they had all wanted to come in; now that he had opened one door and the other had apparently been opened during the day, no one came in and even the keys were on the other side of the doors.

It was late at night before the gas went out in the living room, and Gregor could easily tell that his parents and his sister had all stayed awake until then, for he could clearly hear the three of them stealing away on tiptoe. No one was likely to visit him, not until the morning, that was certain; so he had plenty of time to meditate at his leisure on how he was to arrange his life afresh. But the lofty, empty room in which he had to lie flat on the floor filled him with an apprehension he could not account for, since it had been his very own room for the past five years—and with a half-unconscious action, not without a slight feeling of shame, he scuttled under the sofa, where he felt comfortable at once, although his back was a little cramped and he could not lift his head up, and his only regret was that his body was too broad to get the whole of it under the sofa.

He stayed there all night, spending the time partly in a light slumber, from which his hunger kept waking him up with a start, and partly in worrying and sketching vague hopes, which all led to the same conclusion, that he must lie low for the present and, by exercising patience and the utmost consideration, help the family to bear the inconvenience he was bound to cause them in his present condition.

Very early in the morning, it was still almost night, Gregor had the chance to test the strength of his new resolutions, for his sister, nearly fully dressed, opened the door from the hall and peered in. She did not see him at once, yet when she caught sight of him under the sofa—well, he had to be somewhere, he couldn't have flown away, could he?—she was so startled that without being able to help it she slammed the door shut again. But as if regretting her behavior she opened the door again immediately and came in on tiptoe, as if she were visiting an invalid or even a stranger. Gregor had pushed his head forward to the very edge of the sofa and watched her. Would she notice that he had left the milk standing, and not for lack of hunger, and would she bring in some other kind of food more to his taste? If she did not do it of her own accord, he would rather starve than draw her attention to the fact, although he felt a wild impulse to dart out from under the sofa, throw himself at her feet and beg her for something to eat. But his sister at once noticed, with surprise, that the basin was still full, except for a little milk that had been spilt all around it. She lifted it immediately, not with her bare hands, true, but with a cloth and carried it away. Gregor was wildly curious to know what she would bring instead, and made various speculations about it. Yet what she actually did next, in the goodness of her heart, he could never have guessed at. To find out what he liked she brought him a whole selection of food, all set out on an old newspaper. There were old, half-decayed vegetables, bones from last night's supper covered with a white sauce that had thickened; some raisins and almonds; a piece of cheese that Gregor would have called uneatable two days ago; a dry roll of bread, a buttered roll, and a roll both buttered and salted. Besides all that, she set down again the same basin, into which she had poured some water, and which was apparently to be reserved for his exclusive use. And with fine tact, knowing that Gregor would not eat in her presence, she withdrew quickly and even turned the key, to let him understand that he could take his ease as much as he liked. Gregor's legs all whizzed towards the food. His wounds must have healed completely, moreover, for he felt no disability, which amazed him and made him reflect how more than a month ago he had cut one finger a little with a knife and had still suffered pain from the wound only the day before yesterday. Am I less sensitive now? he thought, and sucked greedily at the cheese, which above all the other edibles attracted him at once and strongly. One after another and with tears of satisfaction in his eyes he quickly devoured the cheese, the vegetables and the sauce; the fresh food, on the other hand, had no charms for him, he could not even stand the smell of it and actually dragged away to some little distance the things he could eat. He had long finished his meal and was only lying lazily on the same spot when his sister turned the key slowly as a sign for him to retreat. That roused him at once, although he was nearly asleep, and he hurried under the sofa again. But it took considerable self-control for him to stay under the sofa, even for the short time his sister was in the room, since the large meal had swollen his body somewhat and he was so cramped he could hardly breathe. Slight attacks of breathlessness afflicted him and his eyes were starting a little out of his head as he watched his unsuspecting sister sweeping together with a broom not only the remains of what he had eaten but even the things he had not touched, as if these were now of no use to anyone, and hastily shoveling it all into a bucket, which she covered with a wooden lid and carried away. Hardly had she turned her back when Gregor came from under the sofa and stretched and puffed himself out.

In this manner Gregor was fed, once in the early morning while his parents and the servant girl were still asleep, and a second time after they had all had their midday dinner, for then his parents took a short nap and the servant girl could be sent out on some errand or other by his sister. Not that they would have wanted him to starve, of course, but perhaps they could not have borne to know more about his feeding than from hearsay, perhaps too his sister wanted to spare them such little anxieties wherever possible, since they had quite enough to bear as it was.

Under what pretext the doctor and the locksmith had been got rid of on that first morning Gregor could not discover, for since what he said was not understood by the others it never struck any of them, not even his sister, that he could understand what they said, and so whenever his sister came into his room he had to content himself with hearing her utter only a sigh now and then and an occasional appeal to the saints. Later on, when she had got a little used to the situation—of course she could never get completely used to it—she sometimes threw out a remark which was kindly meant or could be so interpreted. "Well, he liked his dinner today," she would say when Gregor had made a good clearance of his food; and when he had not eaten, which gradually happened more and more often, she would say almost sadly: "Everything's been left standing again."

But although Gregor could get no news directly, he overheard a lot from the neighboring rooms, and as soon as voices were audible, he would run to the door of the room concerned and press his whole body against it. In the first few days especially there was no conversation that did not refer to him somehow, even if only indirectly. For two whole days there were family consultations at every mealtime about what should be done; but also between meals the same subject was discussed, for there were always at least two members of the family at home, since no one wanted to be alone in the flat and to leave it quite empty was unthinkable. And on the very first of these days the household cook—it was not quite clear what and how much she knew of the situation—went down on her knees to his mother and begged leave to go, and when she departed, a quarter of an hour later, gave thanks for her dismissal with tears in her eyes as if for the greatest benefit that could have been conferred on her, and without any prompting swore a solemn oath that she would never say a single word to anyone about what had happened.

Now Gregor's sister had to cook too, helping her mother; true, the cooking did not amount to much, for they ate scarcely anything. Gregor was always hearing one of the family vainly urging another to eat and getting no answer but: "Thanks, I've had all I want," or something similar. Perhaps they drank nothing either. Time and again his sister kept asking his father if he wouldn't like some beer and offered kindly to go and fetch it herself, and when he made no answer suggested that she could ask the concierge to fetch it, so that he need feel no sense of obligation, but then a round "No" came from his father and no more was said about it.

In the course of that very first day Gregor's father explained the family's financial position and prospects to both his mother and his sister. Now and then he rose from the table to get some voucher or memorandum out of the small safe he had rescued from the collapse of his business five years earlier. One could hear him opening the complicated lock and rustling papers out and shutting it again. This statement made by his father was the first cheerful information Gregor had heard since his imprisonment. He had been of the opinion that nothing at all was left over from his father's business, at least his father had never said anything to the contrary, and of course he had not asked him directly. At that time Gregor's sole desire was to do his utmost to help the family to forget as soon as possible the catastrophe which had overwhelmed the business and thrown them all into a state of complete despair. And so he had set to work with unusual ardor and almost overnight had become a commercial traveler instead of a little clerk, with of course much greater chances of earning money, and his success was immediately translated into good round coin which he could lay on the table for his amazed and happy family. These had been fine times, and they had never recurred, at least not with the same sense of glory, although later on Gregor had earned so much money that he was able to meet the expenses of the whole household and did so. They had simply got used to it, both the family and Gregor; the money was gratefully accepted and gladly given, but there was no special uprush of warm feeling. With his sister alone had he remained intimate, and it was a secret plan of his that she, who loved music, unlike himself, and could play movingly on the violin, should be sent next year to study at the Conservatorium, despite the great expense that would entail, which must be made up in some other way. During his brief visits home the Conservatorium was often mentioned in the talks he had with his sister, but always merely as a beautiful dream which could never come true, and his parents discouraged even these innocent references to it; yet Gregor had made up his mind firmly about it and meant to announce the fact with due solemnity on Christmas Day.

Such were the thoughts, completely futile in his present condition, that went through his head as he stood clinging upright to the door and listening. Sometimes out of sheer weariness he had to give up listening and let his head fall negligently against the door, but he always had to pull himself together again at once, for even the slight sound his head made was audible next door and brought all conversation to a stop. "What can he be doing now?" his father would say after a while, obviously turning towards the door, and only then would the interrupted conversation gradually be set going again.

Gregor was now informed as amply as he could wish—for his father tended to repeat himself in his explanations, partly because it was a long time since he had handled such matters and partly because his mother could not always grasp things at once—that a certain amount of investments, a very small amount it was true, had survived the wreck of their fortunes and had even increased a little because the dividends had not been touched meanwhile. And besides that, the money Gregor brought home every month—he had kept only a few dollars for himself—had never been quite used up and now amounted to a small capital sum. Behind the door Gregor nodded his head eagerly, rejoiced at this evidence of unexpected thrift and foresight. True, he could really have paid off some more of his father's debts to the chief with this extra money, and so brought much nearer the day on which he could quit his job, but doubtless it was better the way his father had arranged it.

Yet this capital was by no means sufficient to let the family live on the interest of it; for one year, perhaps, or at the most two, they could live on the principal, that was all. It was simply a sum that ought not to be touched and should be kept for a rainy day; money for living expenses would have to be earned. Now his father was still hale enough but an old man, and he had done no work for the past five years and could not be expected to do much; during these five years, the first years of leisure in his laborious though unsuccessful life, he had grown rather fat and become sluggish. And Gregor's old mother, how was she to earn a living with her asthma, which troubled her even when she walked through the flat, and kept her lying on a sofa every other day panting for breath beside an open window? And was his sister to earn her bread, she who was still a child of seventeen and whose life hitherto had been so pleasant, consisting as it did in dressing herself nicely, sleeping long, helping in the housekeeping, going out to a few modest entertainments and above all playing the violin? At first whenever the need for earning money was mentioned Gregor let go his hold on the door and threw himself down on the cool leather sofa beside it, he felt so hot with shame and grief.

Often he just lay there the long nights through without sleeping at all, scrabbling for hours on the leather. Or he nerved himself to the great effort of pushing an armchair to the window, then crawled up over the window sill and, braced against the chair, leaned against the window panes, obviously in some recollection of the sense of freedom that looking out of a window always used to give him. For in reality day by day things that were even a little way off were growing dimmer to his sight; the hospital across the street, which he used to execrate for being all too often before his eyes, was not quite beyond his range of vision, and if he had not known that he lived in Charlotte Street, a quiet street but still a city street, he might have believed that his window gave on a desert waste where gray sky and gray land blended indistinguishably into each other. His quick-witted sister only needed to observe twice that the armchair stood by the window; after that whenever she had tidied the room she always pushed the chair back to the same place at the window and even left the inner casements open.

If he could have spoken to her and thanked her for all she had to do for him, he could have borne her ministrations better; as it was, they oppressed him. She certainly tried to make as light as possible of whatever was disagreeable in her task, and as time went on she succeeded, of course, more and more, but time brought more enlightenment to Gregor too. The very way she came in distressed him. Hardly was she in the room when she rushed to the window, without even taking time to shut the door, careful as she was usually to shield the sight of Gregor's room from the others, and as if she were almost suffocating tore the casements open with hasty fingers, standing then in the open draught for a while even in the bitterest cold and drawing deep breaths. This noisy scurry of hers upset Gregor twice a day; he would crouch trembling under the sofa all the time, knowing quite well that she would certainly have spared him such a disturbance had she found it at all possible to stay in his presence without opening the window.

On one occasion, about a month after Gregor's metamorphosis, when there was surely no reason for her to be still startled at his appearance, she came a little earlier than usual and found him gazing out of the window, quite motionless, and thus well placed to look like a bogey. Gregor would not have been surprised had she not come in at all, for she could not immediately open the window while he was there, but not only did she retreat, she jumped back as if in alarm and banged the door shut; a stranger might well have thought that he had been lying in wait for her there meaning to bite her. Of course he hid himself under the sofa at once, but he had to wait until midday before she came again, and she seemed more ill at ease than usual. This made him realize how repulsive the sight of him still was to her, and that it was bound to go on being repulsive, and what an effort it must cost her not to run away even from the sight of the small portion of his body that stuck out from under the sofa. In order to spare her that, therefore, one day he carried a sheet on his back to the sofa—it cost him four hours' labor—and arranged it there in such a way as to hide him completely, so that even if she were to bend down she could not see him. Had she considered the sheet unnecessary, she would certainly have stripped it off the sofa again, for it was clear enough that this curtaining and confining of himself was not likely to conduce Gregor's comfort, but she left it where it was, and Gregor even fancied that he caught a thankful glance from her eye when he lifted the sheet carefully a very little with his head to see how she was taking the new arrangement.

For the first fortnight his parents could not bring themselves to the point of entering his room, and he often heard them expressing their appreciation of his sister's activities, whereas formerly they had frequently scolded her for being as they thought a somewhat useless daughter. But now, both of them often waited outside the door, his father and his mother, while his sister tidied his room, and as soon as she came out she had to tell them exactly how things were in the room, what Gregor had eaten, how he had conducted himself this time and whether there was not perhaps some slight improvement in his condition. His mother, moreover, began relatively soon to want to visit him, but his father and sister dissuaded her at first with arguments which Gregor listened to very attentively and altogether approved. Later, however, she had to be held back by main force, and when she cried out: "Do let me in to Gregor, he is my unfortunate son! Can't you understand that I must go to him?" Gregor thought that it might be well to have her come in, not every day, of course, but perhaps once a week; she understood things, after all, much better than his sister, who was only a child despite the efforts she was making and had perhaps taken on so difficult a task merely out of childish thoughtlessness.

Gregor's desire to see his mother was soon fulfilled. During the daytime he did not want to show himself at the window, out of consideration for his parents, but he could not crawl very far around the few square yards of floor space he had, nor could he bear lying quietly at rest all during the night, while he was fast losing any interest he had ever taken in food, so that for mere recreation he had formed the habit of crawling crisscross over the walls and ceiling. He especially enjoyed hanging suspended from the ceiling; it was much better than lying on the floor. One could breathe more freely; one's body swung and rocked lightly; and in the almost blissful absorption induced by this suspension it could happen to his own surprise that he let go and fell plump on the floor. Yet he now had his body much better under control than formerly, and even such a big fall did him no harm. His sister at once remarked the new distraction Gregor had found for himself—he left traces behind him of the sticky stuff on his soles wherever he crawled—and she got the idea in her head of giving him as wide a field as possible to crawl in and of removing the pieces of furniture that hindered him, above all the chest of drawers and the writing desk. But that was more than she could manage all by herself; she did not dare ask her father to help her; and as for the servant girl, a young creature of sixteen who had had the courage to stay on after the cook's departure, she could not be asked to help, for she had begged as an especial favor that she might keep the kitchen door locked and open it only on a definite summons; so there was nothing left but to apply to her mother at an hour when her father was out. And the old lady did come, with exclamations of joyful eagerness, which, however, died away at the door of Gregor's room. Gregor's sister, of course, went in first, to see that everything was in order before letting his mother enter. In great haste Gregor pulled the sheet lower and tucked it more in folds so that it really looked as if it had been thrown accidentally over the sofa. And this time he did not peer out from under it; he renounced the pleasure of seeing his mother on this occasion and was only glad that she had come at all. "Come in, he's out of sight," said his sister, obviously leading her mother by the hand. Gregor could now hear the two women struggling to shift the heavy old chest from its place, and his sister claiming the greater part of the labor for herself, without listening to the admonitions of her mother who feared she might overstrain herself. It took a long time. After at least a quarter of an hour's tugging his mother objected that the chest had better be left where it was, for in the first place it was too heavy and could never be got out before his father came home, and standing in the middle of the room like that it would only hamper Gregor's movements, while in the second place it was not at all certain that removing the furniture would be doing a service to Gregor. She was inclined to think to the contrary; the sight of the naked walls made her own heart heavy; and why shouldn't Gregor have the same feeling, considering that he had been used to his furniture for so long and might feel forlorn without it. "And doesn't it look," she concluded in a low voice—in fact she had been almost whispering all the time as if to avoid letting Gregor, whose exact whereabouts she did not know, hear even the tones of her voice, for she was convinced that he could not understand her words—"doesn't it look as if we were showing him, by taking away his furniture, that we have given up hope of his ever getting better and are just leaving him coldly to himself? I think it would be best to keep his room exactly as it has always been, so that when he comes back to us he will find everything unchanged and be able all the more easily to forget what has happened in between."

On hearing these words from his mother Gregor realized that the lack of all direct human speech for the past two months together with the monotony of family life must have confused his mind, otherwise he could not account for the fact that he had quite earnestly looked forward to having his room emptied of furnishing. Did he really want his warm room, so comfortably fitted with old family furniture, to be turned into a naked den in which he would certainly be able to crawl unhampered in all directions but at the price of shedding simultaneously all recollection of his human background? He had indeed been so near the brink of forgetfulness that only the voice of his mother, which he had not heard for so long, had drawn him back from it. Nothing should be taken out of his room; everything must stay as it was; he could not dispense with the good influence of the furniture on his state of mind; and even if the furniture did hamper him in his senseless crawling round and round, that was no drawback but a great advantage.

Unfortunately his sister was of the contrary opinion; she had grown accustomed, and not without reason, to consider herself an expert in Gregor's affairs as against her parents, and so her mother's advice was now enough to make her determined on the removal not only of the chest and the writing desk, which had been her first intention, but of all the furniture except the indispensable sofa. This determination was not, of course, merely the outcome of childish recalcitrance and of the self-confidence she had recently developed so unexpectedly and at such cost; she had in fact perceived that Gregor needed a lot of space to crawl about in, while on the other hand he never used the furniture at all, so far as could be seen. Another factor might have been also the enthusiastic temperament of an adolescent girl, which seeks to indulge itself on every opportunity and which now tempted Grete to exaggerate the horror of her brother's circumstances in order that she might do all the more for him. In a room where Gregor lorded it all alone over empty walls no one save herself was likely ever to set foot.

And so she was not to be moved from her resolve by her mother who seemed moreover to be ill at ease in Gregor's room and therefore unsure of herself, was soon reduced to silence and helped her daughter as best she could to push the chest outside. Now, Gregor could do without the chest, if need be, but the writing desk he must retain. As soon as the two women had got the chest out of his room, groaning as they pushed it, Gregor stuck his head out from under the sofa to see how he might intervene as kindly and cautiously as possible. But as bad luck would have it, his mother was the first to return, leaving Grete clasping the chest in the room next door where she was trying to shift it all by herself, without of course moving it from the spot. His mother however was not accustomed to the sight of him, it might sicken her and so in alarm Gregor backed quickly to the other end of the sofa, yet could not prevent the sheet from swaying a little in front. That was enough to put her on the alert. She paused, stood still for a moment and then went back to Grete.

Although Gregor kept reassuring himself that nothing out of the way was happening, but only a few bits of furniture were being changed round, he soon had to admit that all this trotting to and fro of the two women, their little ejaculations and the scraping of furniture along the floor affected him like a vast disturbance coming from all sides at once, and however much he tucked in his head and legs and cowered to the very floor he was bound to confess that he would not be able to stand it for long. They were clearing his room out; taking away everything he loved; the chest in which he kept his fret saw and other tools was already dragged off; they were now loosening the writing desk which had almost sunk into the floor, the desk at which he had done all his homework when he was at the commercial academy, at the grammar school before that, and yes, even at the primary school—he had no more time to waste in weighing the good intentions of the two women, whose existence he had by now almost forgotten, for they were so exhausted that they were laboring in silence and nothing could be heard but the heavy scuffling of their feet.

And so he rushed out—the women were just leaning against the writing desk in the next room to give themselves a breather—and four times changed his direction, since he really did not know what to rescue first, then on the wall opposite, which was already otherwise cleared, he was struck by the picture of the lady muffled in so much fur and quickly crawled up to it and pressed himself to the glass, which was a good surface to hold on to and comforted his hot belly. This picture at least, which was entirely hidden beneath him, was going to be removed by nobody. He turned his head towards the door of the living room so as to observe the women when they came back.

They had not allowed themselves much of a rest and were already coming; Grete had twined her arm round her mother and was almost supporting her. "Well, what shall we take now?" said Grete, looking round. Her eyes met Gregor's from the wall. She kept her composure, presumably because of her mother, bent her head down to her mother, to keep her from looking up, and said, although in a fluttering, unpremeditated voice:

"Come, hadn't we better go back to the living room for a moment?" Her intentions were clear enough to Gregor, she wanted to bestow her mother in safety and then chase him down from the wall. Well, just let her try it! He clung to his picture and would not give it up. He would rather fly in Grete's face.

But Grete's words had succeeded in disquieting her mother, who took a step to one side, caught sight of the huge brown mass on the flowered wallpaper, and before she was really conscious that what she saw was Gregor screamed in a loud, hoarse voice: "Oh God, oh God!" fell with outspread arms over the sofa as if giving up and did not move. "Gregor!" cried his sister, shaking her fist and glaring at him. This was the first time she had directly addressed him since his metamorphosis. She ran into the next room for some aromatic essence with which to rouse her mother from her fainting fit. Gregor wanted to help too—there was still time to rescue the picture—but he was stuck fast to the glass and had to tear himself loose; he then ran after his sister into the next room as if he could advise her, as he used to do; but then had to stand helplessly behind her; she meanwhile searched among various small bottles and when she turned round started in alarm at the sight of him; one bottle fell on the floor and broke; a splinter of glass cut Gregor's face and some kind of corrosive medicine splashed him; without pausing a moment longer Grete gathered up all the bottles she could carry and ran to her mother with them; she banged the door shut with her foot. Gregor was now cut off from his mother, who was perhaps nearly dying because of him; he dared not open the door for fear of frightening away his sister, who had to stay with her mother; there was nothing he could do but wait; and harassed by self-reproach and worry he began now to crawl to and fro, over everything, walls, furniture and ceiling, and finally in his despair, when the whole room seemed to be reeling round him, fell down on to the middle of the big table.

A little while elapsed, Gregor was still lying there feebly and all around was quiet, perhaps that was a good omen. Then the doorbell rang. The servant girl was of course locked in her kitchen, and Grete would have to open the door. It was his father. "What's been happening?" were his first words; Grete's face must have told him everything. Grete answered in a muffled voice, apparently hiding her head on his breast: "Mother has been fainting, but she's better now. Gregor's broken loose." "Just what I expected," said his father, "just what I've been telling you, but you women would never listen." It was clear to Gregor that his father had taken the worst interpretation of Grete's all too brief statement and was assuming that Gregor had been guilty of some violent act. Therefore Gregor must now try to propitiate his father, since he had neither time nor means for an explanation. And so he fled to the door of his own room and crouched against it, to let his father see as soon as he came in from the hall that his son had the good intention of getting back into his room immediately and that it was not necessary to drive him there, but that if only the door were opened he would disappear at once.

Yet his father was not in the mood to perceive such fine distinctions. "Ah!" he cried as soon as he appeared, in a tone which sounded at once angry and exultant. Gregor drew his head back from the door and lifted it to look at his father. Truly, this was not the father he had imagined to himself; admittedly he had been too absorbed of late in his new recreation of crawling over the ceiling to take the same interest as before in what was happening elsewhere in the flat, and he ought really to be prepared for some changes. And yet, and yet, could that be his father? The man who used to lie wearily sunk in bed whenever Gregor set out on a business journey; who welcomed him back of an evening lying in a long chair in a dressing gown; who could not really rise to his feet but only lifted his arms in greeting, and on the rare occasions when he did go out with his family, on one or two Sundays a year and on high holidays, walked between Gregor and his mother, who were slow walkers anyhow, even more slowly than they did, muffled in his old greatcoat, shuffling laboriously forward with the help of his crook-handled stick which he set down most cautiously at every step and, whenever he wanted to say anything, nearly always came to a full stop and gathered his escort around him? Now he was standing there in fine shape; dressed in a smart blue uniform with gold buttons, such as bank messengers wear; his strong double chin bulged over the stiff high collar of his jacket; from under his bushy eyebrows his black eyes darted fresh and penetrating glances; his one-time tangled white hair had been combed flat on either side of a shining and carefully exact parting. He pitched his cap, which bore a gold monogram, probably the badge of some bank, in a wide sweep across the whole room on to a sofa and with the tail-ends of his jacket thrown back, his hands in his trousers pockets, advanced with a grim visage towards Gregor. Likely enough he did not himself know what he meant to do; at any rate he lifted his feet uncommonly high, and Gregor was dumbfounded at the enormous size of his shoe soles. But Gregor could not risk standing up to him, aware as he had been from the very first day of his new life that his father believed only the severest measures suitable for dealing with him. And so he ran before his father, stopping when he stopped and scuttling forward again when his father made any kind of move. In this way they circled the room several times without anything decisive happening, indeed the whole operation did not even look like a pursuit because it was carried out so slowly. And so Gregor did not leave the floor, for he feared that his father might take as a piece of peculiar wickedness any excursion of his over the walls or the ceiling. All the same, he could not stay this course much longer, for while his father took one step he had to carry out a whole series of movements. He was already beginning to feel breathless, just as in his former life his lungs had not been very dependable. As he was staggering along, trying to concentrate his energy on running, hardly keeping his eyes open; in his dazed state never even thinking of any other escape than simply going forward; and having almost forgotten that the walls were free to him, which in this room were well provided with finely carved pieces of furniture full of knobs and crevices—suddenly something lightly flung landed close behind him and rolled before him. It was an apple; a second apple followed immediately; Gregor came to a stop in alarm; there was no point in running on, for his father was determined to bombard him. He had filled his pockets with fruit from the dish on the sideboard and was now shying apple after apple, without taking particularly good aim for the moment. The small red apples rolled about the floor as if magnetized and cannoned into each other. An apple thrown without much force grazed Gregor's back and glanced off harmlessly. But another following immediately landed right on his back and sank in; Gregor wanted to drag himself forward, as if this startling, incredible pain could be left behind him; but he felt as if nailed to the spot and flattened himself out in a complete derangement of all his senses. With his last conscious look he saw the door of his room being torn open and his mother rushing out ahead of his screaming sister, in her underbodice, for her daughter had loosened her clothing to let her breathe more freely and recover from her swoon, he saw his mother rushing towards his father, leaving one after another behind her on the floor her loosened petticoats, stumbling over her petticoats straight to his father and embracing him, in complete union with him—but here Gregor's sight began to fail—with her hands clasped round his father's neck as she begged for her son's life.

3

The serious injury done to Gregor, which disabled him for more than a month—the apple went on sticking in his body as a visible reminder, since no one ventured to remove it—seemed to have made even his father recollect that Gregor was a member of the family, despite his present unfortunate and repulsive shape, and ought not to be treated as an enemy, that, on the contrary, family duty required the suppression of disgust and the exercise of patience, nothing but patience.

And although his injury had impaired, probably for ever, his power of movement, and for the time being it took him long, long minutes to creep across his room like an old invalid—there was no question now of crawling up the wall—yet in his own opinion he was sufficiently compensated for this worsening of his condition by the fact that towards evening the living-room door, which he used to watch intently for an hour or two beforehand, was always thrown open, so that lying in the darkness of his room, invisible to the family, he could see them all at the lamp-lit table and listen to their talk, by general consent as it were, very different from his earlier eavesdropping.

True, their intercourse lacked the lively character of former times, which he had always called to mind with a certain wistfulness in the small hotel bedrooms where he had been wont to throw himself down, tired out, on damp bedding. They were now mostly very silent. Soon after supper his father would fall asleep in his armchair; his mother and sister would admonish each other to be silent; his mother, bending low over the lamp, stitched at fine sewing for an underwear firm, his sister, who had taken a job as a salesgirl, was learning shorthand and French in the evenings on the chance of bettering herself. Sometimes his father woke up, and as if quite unaware that he had been sleeping said to his mother: "What a lot of sewing you're doing today!" and at once fell asleep again, while the two women exchanged a tired smile.

With a kind of mulishness his father persisted in keeping his uniform on even in the house; his dressing gown hung uselessly on its peg and he slept fully dressed where he sat, as if he were ready for service at any moment and even here only at the beck and call of his superior. As a result, his uniform, which was not brand-new to start with, began to look dirty, despite all the loving care of the mother and sister to keep it clean, and Gregor often spent whole evenings gazing at the many greasy spots on the garment, gleaming with gold buttons always in a high state of polish, in which the old man sat sleeping in extreme discomfort and yet quite peacefully.

As soon as the clock struck ten his mother tried to rouse his father with gentle words and to persuade him after that to get into bed, for sitting there he could not have a proper sleep and that was what he needed most, since he had to go to duty at six. But with the mulishness that had obsessed him since he became a bank messenger he always insisted on staying longer at the table, although he regularly fell asleep again and in the end only with the greatest trouble could be got out of his armchair and into his bed. However insistently Gregor's mother and sister kept urging him with gentle reminders, he would go on slowly shaking his head for a quarter of an hour, keeping his eyes shut, and refuse to get to his feet. The mother plucked at his sleeve, whispering endearments in his ear, the sister left her lessons to come to her mother's help, but Gregor's father was not to be caught. He would only sink down deeper in his chair. Not until the two women hoisted him up by the armpits did he open his eyes and look at them both, one after the other, usually with the remark: "This is a life. This is the peace and quiet of my old age." And leaning on the two of them he would heave himself up, with difficulty, as if he were a great burden to himself, suffer them to lead him as far as the door and then wave them off and go on alone, while the mother abandoned her needlework and the sister her pen in order to run after him and help him farther.

Who could find time, in this overworked and tired-out family, to bother about Gregor more than was absolutely needful? The household was reduced more and more; the servant girl was turned off; a gigantic bony charwoman with white hair flying round her head came in morning and evening to do the rough work; everything else was done by Gregor's mother, as well as great piles of sewing. Even various family ornaments, which his mother and sister used to wear with pride at parties and celebrations, had to be sold, as Gregor discovered of an evening from hearing them all discuss the prices obtained. But what they lamented most was the fact that they could not leave the flat which was much too big for their present circumstances, because they could not think of any way to shift Gregor. Yet Gregor saw well enough that consideration for him was not the main difficulty preventing the removal, for they could have easily shifted him in some suitable box with a few air holes in it; what really kept them from moving into another flat was rather their own complete hopelessness and the belief that they had been singled out for a misfortune such as had never happened to any of their relations or acquaintances. They fulfilled to the uttermost all that the world demands of poor people, the father fetched breakfast for the small clerks in the bank, the mother devoted her energy to making underwear for strangers, the sister trotted to and fro behind the counter at the behest of customers, but more than this they had not the strength to do. And the wound in Gregor's back began to nag at him afresh when his mother and sister, after getting his father into bed, came back again, left their work lying, drew close to each and sat cheek by cheek; when his mother, pointing towards his room said: "Shut that door now, Grete," and he was left again in darkness, while next door the women mingled their tears or perhaps sat dry-eyed staring at the table.

Gregor hardly slept at all by night or by day. He was often haunted by the idea that next time the door opened he would take the family's affairs in hand again just as he used to do; once more, after his long interval, there appeared in his thoughts the figures of the chief and the chief clerk, the commercial travelers and the apprentices, the porter who was so dull-witted, two or three friends in other firms, a chambermaid in one of the rural hotels, a sweet and fleeting memory, a cashier in a milliner's shop, whom he had wooed earnestly but too slowly—they all appeared, together with strangers or people he had quite forgotten, but instead of helping him and his family they were one and all unapproachable and he was glad when they vanished. At other times he would not be in the mood to bother about his family, he was only filled with rage at the way they were neglecting him, and although he had no clear idea of what he might care to eat he would make plans for getting into the larder to take the food that was after all his due, even if he were not hungry. His sister no longer took thought to bring him what might especially please him, but in the morning and at noon before she went to business hurriedly pushed into his room with her foot any food that was available, and in the evening cleared it out again with one sweep of the broom, heedless of whether it had been merely tasted, or—as most frequently happened—left untouched. The cleaning of his room, which she now did always in the evenings, could not have been more hastily done. Streaks of dirt stretched along the walls, here and there lay balls of dust and filth. At first Gregor used to station himself in some particularly filthy corner when his sister arrived, in order to reproach her with it, so to speak. But he could have sat there for weeks without getting her to make any improvements; she could see the dirt as well as he did, but she had simply made up her mind to leave it alone. And yet, with a touchiness that was new to her, which seemed anyhow to have infected the whole family, she jealously guarded her claim to be the sole caretaker of Gregor's room. His mother once subjected his room to a thorough cleaning, which was achieved only by means of several buckets of water—all this dampness of course upset Gregor too and he lay widespread, sulky and motionless on the sofa—but she was well punished for it. Hardly had his sister noticed the changed aspect of his room that evening than she rushed in high dudgeon into the living room and, despite the imploringly raised hands of her mother, burst into a storm of weeping, while her parents—her father had of course been startled out of his chair—looked on at first in helpless amazement; then they too began to go into action; the father reproached the mother on his right for not having left the cleaning of Gregor's room to his sister; shrieked at the sister on his left that never again was she to be allowed to clean Gregor's room; while the mother tried to pull the father into his bedroom, since he was beyond himself with agitation; the sister, shaken with sobs, then beat upon the table with her small fists; and Gregor hissed loudly with rage because not one of them thought of shutting the door to spare him such a spectacle and so much noise.

Still, even if the sister, exhausted by her daily work, had grown tired of looking after Gregor as she did formerly, there was no need for his mother's intervention or for Gregor's being neglected at all. The charwoman was there. This old widow, whose strong bony frame had enabled her to survive the worst a long life could offer, by no means recoiled from Gregor. Without being in the least curious she had once by chance opened the door of his room and at the sight of Gregor, who, taken by surprise, began to rush to and fro although no one was chasing him, merely stood there with her arms folded. From that time she never failed to open his door a little for a moment, morning and evening, to have a look at him. At first she even used to call him to her, with words which apparently she took to be friendly; such as: "Come along, then, you old dung beetle!" or "Look at the old dung beetle, then!" To such allocutions Gregor made no answer, but stayed motionless where he was, as if the door had never been opened. Instead of being allowed to disturb him so senselessly whenever the whim took her, she should rather have been ordered to clean out his room daily, that charwoman! Once, early in the morning—heavy rain was lashing on the windowpanes, perhaps a sign that spring was on the way—Gregor was so exasperated when she began addressing him again that he ran for her, as if to attack her, although slowly and feebly enough. But the charwoman instead of showing fright merely lifted high a chair that happened to be beside the door, and as she stood there with her mouth wide open it was clear that she meant to shut it only when she brought the chair down on Gregor's back. "So you're not coming any nearer?" she asked, as Gregor turned away again, and quietly put the chair back into the corner.

Gregor was now eating hardly anything. Only when he happened to pass the food laid out for him did he take a bit of something in his mouth as a pastime, kept it there for an hour at a time and usually spat it out again. At first he thought it was chagrin over the state of his room that prevented him from eating, yet he soon got used to the various changes in his room. It had become a habit in the family to push into his room things there was no room for elsewhere, and there were plenty of these now, since one of the rooms had been let to three lodgers. These serious gentlemen—all three of them with full beards, as Gregor once observed through a crack in the door—had a passion for order, not only in their own room but, since they were now members of the household, in all its arrangements, especially in the kitchen. Superfluous, not to say dirty, objects they could not bear. Besides, they had brought with them most of the furnishings they needed. For this reason many things could be dispensed with that it was no use trying to sell but should not be thrown away either. All of them found their way into Gregor's room. The ash can likewise and the kitchen garbage can. Anything that was not needed for the moment was simply flung into Gregor's room by the charwoman, who did everything in a hurry; fortunately Gregor usually saw only the object, whatever it was, and the hand that held it. Perhaps she intended to take the things away again as time and opportunity offered, or to collect them until she could throw them all out in a heap, but in fact they just lay wherever she happened to throw them, except when Gregor pushed his way through the junk heap and shifted it somewhat, at first out of necessity, because he had not room enough to crawl, but later with increasing enjoyment, although after such excursions, being sad and weary to death, he would lie motionless for hours. And since the lodgers often ate their supper at home in the common living room, the living-room door stayed shut many an evening, yet Gregor reconciled himself quite easily to the shutting of the door, for often enough on evenings when it was opened he had disregarded it entirely and lain in the darkest corner of his room, quite unnoticed by the family. But on one occasion the charwoman left the door open a little and it stayed ajar even when the lodgers came in for supper and the lamp was lit. They sat themselves at the top end of the table where formerly Gregor and his father and mother had eaten their meals, unfolded their napkins and took knife and fork in hand. At once his mother appeared in the doorway with a dish of meat and close behind her his sister with a dish of potatoes piled high. The food steamed with a thick vapor. The lodgers bent over the food set before them as if to scrutinize it before eating, in fact the man in the middle, who seemed to pass for an authority with the other two, cut a piece of meat as it lay on the dish, obviously to discover if it were tender or should be sent back to the kitchen. He showed satisfaction, and Gregor's mother and sister, who had been watching anxiously, breathed freely and began to smile.

The family itself took its meals in the kitchen. None the less, Gregor's father came into the living room before going into the kitchen and with one prolonged bow, cap in hand, made a round of the table. The lodgers all stood up and murmured something in their beards. When they were alone again they ate their food in almost complete silence.

It seemed remarkable to Gregor that among the various noises coming from the table he could always distinguish the sound of their masticating teeth, as if this were a sign to Gregor that one needed teeth in order to eat, and that with toothless jaws even of the finest make one could do nothing. "I'm hungry enough," said Gregor sadly to himself, "but not for that kind of food. How these lodgers are stuffing themselves, and here am I dying of starvation!"

On that very evening—during the whole of his time there Gregor could not remember ever having heard the violin—the sound of violin-playing came from the kitchen. The lodgers had already finished their supper, the one in the middle had brought out a newspaper and given the other two a page apiece, and now they were leaning back at ease reading and smoking. When the violin began to play they pricked up their ears, got to their feet, and went on tiptoe to the hall door where they stood huddled together. Their movements must have been heard in the kitchen, for Gregor's father called out: "Is the violin-playing disturbing you gentlemen? It can be stopped at once." "On the contrary," said the middle lodger, "could not Fräulein Samsa come and play in this room, beside us, where it is much more convenient and comfortable?" "Oh certainly," cried Gregor's father, as if he were the violin-player. The lodgers came back into the living room and waited. Presently Gregor's father arrived with the music stand, his mother carrying the music and his sister with the violin. His sister quietly made everything ready to start playing; his parents, who had never let rooms before and so had an exaggerated idea of the courtesy due to lodgers, did not venture to sit down on their own chairs; his father leaned against the door, the right hand thrust between two buttons of his livery coat, which was formerly buttoned up; but his mother was offered a chair by one of the lodgers and, since she left the chair just where he had happened to put it, sat down in a corner to one side.

Gregor's sister began to play; the father and mother, from either side, intently watched the movements of her hands. Gregor, attracted by the playing, ventured to move forward a little until his head was actually inside the living room. He felt hardly any surprise at his growing lack of consideration for the others; there had been a time when he prided himself on being considerate. And yet just on this occasion he had more reason than ever to hide himself, since owing to the amount of dust which lay thick in his room and rose into the air at the slightest movement, he too was covered with dust; fluff and hair and remnants of food trailed with him, caught on his back and along his sides; his indifference to everything was much too great for him to turn on his back and scrape himself clean on the carpet, as once he had done several times a day. And in spite of his condition, no shame deterred him from advancing a little over the spotless floor of the living room.

To be sure, no one was aware of him. The family was entirely absorbed in the violin-playing; the lodgers, however, who first of all had stationed themselves, hands in pockets, much too close behind the music stand so that they could all have read the music, which must have bothered his sister, had soon retreated to the window, half-whispering with downbent heads, and stayed there while his father turned an anxious eye on them. Indeed, they were making it more than obvious that they had been disappointed in their expectation of hearing good or enjoyable violin-playing, that they had had more than enough of the performance and only out of courtesy suffered a continued disturbance of their peace. From the way they all kept blowing the smoke of their cigars high in the air through nose and mouth one could divine their irritation. And yet Gregor's sister was playing so beautifully. Her face leaned sideways, intently and sadly her eyes followed the notes of music. Gregor crawled a little farther forward and lowered his head to the ground so that it might be possible for his eyes to meet hers. Was he an animal, that music had such an effect upon him? He felt as if the way were opening before him to the unknown nourishment he craved. He was determined to push forward till he reached his sister, to pull at her skirt and so let her know that she was to come into his room with her violin, for no one here appreciated her playing as he would appreciate it. He would never let her out of his room, at least, not so long as he lived; his frightful appearance would become, for the first time, useful to him; he would watch all the doors of his room at once and spit at intruders; but his sister should need no constraint, she should stay with him of her own free will; she should sit beside him on the sofa, bend down her ear to him and hear him confide that he had had the firm intention of sending her to the Conservatorium, and that, but for his mishap, last Christmas—surely Christmas was long past?—he would have announced it to everybody without allowing a single objection. After this confession his sister would be so touched that she would burst into tears, and Gregor would then raise himself to her shoulder and kiss her on the neck, which, now that she went to business, she kept free of any ribbon or collar.

"Mr. Samsa!" cried the middle lodger, to Gregor's father, and pointed, without wasting any more words, at Gregor, now working himself slowly forwards. The violin fell silent, the middle lodger first smiled to his friends with a shake of the head and then looked at Gregor again. Instead of driving Gregor out, his father seemed to think it more needful to begin by soothing down the lodgers, although they were not at all agitated and apparently found Gregor more entertaining than the violin-playing. He hurried towards them and, spreading out his arms, tried to urge them back into their own room and at the same time to block their view of Gregor. They now began to be really a little angry, one could not tell whether because of the old man's behavior or because it just dawned on them that all unwittingly they had such a neighbor as Gregor next door. They demanded explanations of his father, they waved their arms like him, tugged uneasily at their beards, and only with reluctance backed towards their room. Meanwhile Gregor's sister, who stood there as if lost when her playing was so abruptly broken off, came to life again, pulled herself together all at once after standing for a while holding violin and bow in nervelessly hanging hands and staring at her music, pushed her violin into the lap of her mother, who was still sitting in her chair fighting asthmatically for breath, and ran into the lodgers' room to which they were now being shepherded by her father rather more quickly than before. One could see the pillows and blankets on the beds flying under her accustomed fingers and being laid in order. Before the lodgers had actually reached their room she had finished making the beds and slipped out.

The old man seemed once more to be so possessed by his mulish self-assertiveness that he was forgetting all the respect he should show to his lodgers. He kept driving them on and driving them on until in the very door of the bedroom the middle lodger stamped his foot loudly on the floor and so brought him to a halt. "I beg to announce," said the lodger, lifting one hand and looking also at Gregor's mother and sister, "that because of the disgusting conditions prevailing in this household and family"—here he spat on the floor with emphatic brevity—"I give you notice on the spot. Naturally I won't pay you a penny for the days I have lived here, on the contrary I shall consider bringing an action for damages against you, based on claims—believe me—that will be easily susceptible of proof." He ceased and stared straight in front of him, as if he expected something. In fact his two friends at once rushed into the breach with these words: "And we too give notice on the spot." On that he seized the door-handle and shut the door with a slam.

Gregor's father, groping with his hands, staggered forward and fell into his chair; it looked as if he were stretching himself there for his ordinary evening nap, but the marked jerkings of his head, which was as if uncontrollable, showed that he was far from asleep. Gregor had simply stayed quietly all the time on the spot where the lodgers had espied him. Disappointment at the failure of his plan, perhaps also the weakness arising from extreme hunger, made it impossible for him to move. He feared, with a fair degree of certainty, that at any moment the general tension would discharge itself in a combined attack upon him, and he lay waiting. He did not react even to the noise made by the violin as it fell off his mother's lap from under her trembling fingers and gave out a resonant note.

"My dear parents," said his sister, slapping her hand on the table by way of introduction, "things can't go on like this. Perhaps you don't realize that, but I do. I won't utter my brother's name in the presence of this creature, and so all I say is: we must try to get rid of it. We've tried to look after it and to put up with it as far as is humanly possible, and I don't think anyone could reproach us in the slightest."

"She is more than right," said Gregor's father to himself. His mother, who was still choking for lack of breath, began to cough hollowly into her hand with a wild look in her eyes.

His sister rushed over to her and held her forehead. His father's thoughts seemed to have lost their vagueness at Grete's words, he sat more upright, fingering his service cap that lay among the plates still lying on the table from the lodgers' supper, and from time to time looked at the still form of Gregor.

"We must try to get rid of it," his sister now said explicitly to her father, since her mother was coughing too much to hear a word, "it will be the death of both of you, I can see that coming. When one has to work as hard as we do, all of us, one can't stand this continual torment at home on top of it. At least I can't stand it any longer." And she burst into such a passion of sobbing that her tears dropped on her mother's face, where she wiped them off mechanically.

"My dear," said the old man sympathetically, and with evident understanding, "but what can we do?"

Gregor's sister merely shrugged her shoulders to indicate the feeling of helplessness that had now overmastered her during her weeping fit, in contrast to her former confidence.

"If he could understand us," said her father, half questioningly; Grete, still sobbing, vehemently waved a hand to show how unthinkable that was.

"If he could understand us," repeated the old man, shutting his eyes to consider his daughter's conviction that understanding was impossible, "then perhaps we might come to some agreement with him. But as it is—"

"He must go," cried Gregor's sister, "that's the only solution, Father. You must just try to get rid of the idea that this is Gregor. The fact that we've believed it for so long is the root of all our trouble. But how can it be Gregor? If this were Gregor, he would have realized long ago that human beings can't live with such a creature, and he'd have gone away on his own accord. Then we wouldn't have any brother, but we'd be able to go on living and keep his memory in honor. As it is, this creature persecutes us, drives away our lodgers, obviously wants the whole apartment to himself and would have us all sleep in the gutter. Just look, Father," she shrieked all at once, "he's at it again!" And in an access of panic that was quite incomprehensible to Gregor she even quitted her mother, literally thrusting the chair from her as if she would rather sacrifice her mother than stay so near to Gregor, and rushed behind her father, who also rose up, being simply upset by her agitation, and half-spread his arms out as if to protect her.

Yet Gregor had not the slightest intention of frightening anyone, far less his sister. He had only begun to turn round in order to crawl back to his room, but it was certainly a startling operation to watch, since because of his disabled condition he could not execute the difficult turning movements except by lifting his head and then bracing it against the floor over and over again. He paused and looked round. His good intentions seemed to have been recognized; the alarm had only been momentary. Now they were all watching him in melancholy silence. His mother lay in her chair, her legs stiffly outstretched and pressed together, her eyes almost closing for sheer weariness; his father and his sister were sitting beside each other, his sister's arm around the old man's neck.

Perhaps I can go on turning round now, thought Gregor, and began his labors again. He could not stop himself from panting with the effort, and had to pause now and then to take breath. Nor did anyone harass him, he was left entirely to himself. When he had completed the turn-round he began at once to crawl straight back. He was amazed at the distance separating him from his room and could not understand how in his weak state he had managed to accomplish the same journey so recently, almost without remarking it. Intent on crawling as fast as possible, he barely noticed that not a single word, not an ejaculation from his family, interfered with his progress. Only when he was already in the doorway did he turn his head round, not completely, for his neck muscles were getting stiff, but enough to see that nothing had changed behind him except that his sister had risen to her feet. His last glance fell on his mother, who was not quite overcome by sleep.

Hardly was he well inside his room when the door was hastily pushed shut, bolted and locked. The sudden noise in his rear startled him so much that his little legs gave beneath him. It was his sister who had shown such haste. She had been standing ready waiting and had made a light spring forward. Gregor had not even heard her coming, and she cried "At last!" to her parents as she turned the key in the lock.

"And what now?" said Gregor to himself, looking round in the darkness. Soon he made the discovery that he was now unable to stir a limb. This did not surprise him, rather it seemed unnatural that he should ever actually have been able to move on these feeble little legs. Otherwise he felt relatively comfortable. True, his whole body was aching, but it seemed that the pain was gradually growing less and would finally pass away. The rotting apple in his back and the inflamed area round it, all covered with soft dust, already hardly troubled him. He thought of his family with tenderness and love. The decision that he must disappear was one that he held to even more strongly than his sister, if that were possible. In this state of vacant and peaceful meditation he remained until the tower clock struck three in the morning. The first broadening of light in the world outside the window entered his consciousness once more. Then his head sank to the floor of its own accord and from his nostrils came the last faint flicker of his breath.

When the charwoman arrived early in the morning—what between her strength and her impatience she slammed all the doors so loudly, never mind how often she had been begged not to do so, that no one in the whole apartment could enjoy any quiet sleep after her arrival—she noticed nothing unusual as she took her customary peep into Gregor's room. She though he was lying motionless on purpose, pretending to be in the sulks; she credited him with every kind of intelligence. Since she happened to have the long-handled broom in her hand she tried to tickle him up with it from the doorway. When that too produced no reaction she felt provoked and poked at him a little harder, and only when she had pushed him along the floor without meeting any resistance was her attention aroused. It did not take her long to establish the truth of the matter, and her eyes widened, she let out a whistle, yet did not waste much time over it but tore open the door of the Samsas' bedroom and yelled into the darkness at the top of her voice: "Just look at this, it's dead; it's lying here dead and done for!"

Mr. and Mrs. Samsa started up in their double bed and before they realized the nature of the charwoman's announcement had some difficulty in overcoming the shock of it. But then they got out of bed quickly, one on either side, Mr. Samsa throwing a blanket over his shoulders, Mrs. Samsa in nothing but her nightgown; in this array they entered Gregor's room. Meanwhile the door of the living room opened, too, where Grete had been sleeping since the advent of the lodgers; she was completely dressed as if she had not been to bed, which seemed to be confirmed also by the paleness of her face. "Dead?" said Mrs. Samsa, looking questioningly at the charwoman, although she could have investigated for herself, and the fact was obvious enough without investigation. "I should say so," said the charwoman, proving her words by pushing Gregor's corpse a long way to one side with her broomstick. Mrs. Samsa made a movement as if to stop her, but checked it. "Well," said Mr. Samsa, "now thanks be to God." He crossed himself, and the three women followed his example. Grete, whose eyes never left the corpse, said: "Just see how thin he was. It's such a long time since he's eaten anything. The food came out again just as it went in." Indeed, Gregor's body was completely flat and dry, as could only now be seen when it was no longer supported by the legs and nothing prevented one from looking closely at it.

"Come in beside us, Grete, for a little while," said Mrs. Samsa with a tremulous smile, and Grete, not without looking back at the corpse, followed her parents into their bedroom. The charwoman shut the door and opened the window wide. Although it was so early in the morning a certain softness was perceptible in the fresh air. After all, it was already the end of March.

The three lodgers emerged from their room and were surprised to see no breakfast; they had been forgotten. "Where's our breakfast?" said the middle lodger peevishly to the charwoman. But she put her finger to her lips and hastily, without a word, indicated by gestures that they should go into Gregor's room. They did so and stood, their hands in the pockets of their somewhat shabby coats, around Gregor's corpse in the room where it was now fully light.

At that the door of the Samsas' bedroom opened and Mr. Samsa appeared in his uniform, his wife on one arm, his daughter on the other. They all looked a little as if they had been crying; from time to time Grete hid her face on her father's arm.

"Leave my house at once!" said Mr. Samsa, and pointed to the door without disengaging himself from the women. "What do you mean by that?" said the middle lodger, taken somewhat aback, with a feeble smile. The two others put their hands behind them and kept rubbing them together, as if in gleeful expectation of a fine set-to in which they were bound to come off the winners. "I mean just what I say," answered Mr. Samsa, and advanced in a straight line with his two companions towards the lodger. He stood his ground at first quietly, looking at the floor as if his thoughts were taking a new pattern in his head. "Then let us go, by all means," he said and looked up at Mr. Samsa as if in a sudden access of humility he were expecting some renewed sanction for this decision. Mr. Samsa merely nodded briefly once or twice with meaning eyes. Upon that the lodger really did go with long strides into the hall, his two friends had been listening and had quite stopped rubbing their hands for some moments and now went scuttling after him as if afraid that Mr. Samsa might get into the hall before them and cut them off from their leader. In the hall they all three took their hats from the rack, their sticks from the umbrella stand, bowed in silence and quitted the apartment. With a suspiciousness which proved quite unfounded Mr. Samsa and the two women followed them out to the landing; leaning over the banister they watched the three figures slowly but surely going down the long stairs, vanishing from sight at a certain turn of the staircase on every floor and coming into view again after a moment or so; the more they dwindled, the more the Samsa family's interest in them dwindled, and when a butcher's boy met them and passed them on the stairs coming up proudly with a tray on his head, Mr. Samsa and the two women soon left the landing and as if a burden had been lifted from them went back into their apartment.

They decided to spend this day in resting and going for a stroll; they had not only deserved such a respite from work, but absolutely needed it. And so they sat down at the table and wrote three notes of excuse, Mr. Samsa to his board of management, Mrs. Samsa to her employer and Grete to the head of her firm. While they were writing, the charwoman came in to say that she was going now, since her morning's work was finished. At first they only nodded without looking up, but as she kept hovering there they eyed her irritably. "Well?" said Mr. Samsa. The charwoman stood grinning in the doorway as if she had good news to impart to the family but meant not to say a word unless properly questioned. The small ostrich feather standing upright on her hat, which had annoyed Mr. Samsa ever since she was engaged, was waving gaily in all directions. "Well, what is it then?" asked Mrs. Samsa, who obtained more respect from the charwoman than the others. "Oh," said the charwoman, giggling so amiably that she could not at once continue, "just this, you don't need to bother about how to get rid of the thing next door. It's been seen to already." Mrs. Samsa and Grete bent over their letters again, as if preoccupied; Mr. Samsa, who perceived that she was eager to begin describing it all in detail, stopped her with a decisive hand. But since she was not allowed to tell her story, she remembered the great hurry she was in, being obviously deeply huffed: "Bye, everybody," she said, whirling off violently, and departed with a frightful slamming of doors.

"She'll be given notice tonight," said Mr. Samsa, but neither from his wife nor his daughter did he get any answer, for the charwoman seemed to have shattered again the composure they had barely achieved. They rose, went to the window and stayed there, clasping each other tight. Mr. Samsa turned in his chair to look at them and quietly observed them for a little. Then he called out: "Come along, now, do. Let bygones be bygones. And you might have some consideration for me." The two of them complied at once, hastened to him, caressed him and quickly finished their letters.

Then they all three left the apartment together, which was more than they had done for months, and went by tram into the open country outside the town. The tram, in which they were the only passengers, was filled with warm sunshine. Leaning comfortably back in their seats they canvassed their prospects for the future, and it appeared on closer inspection that these were not at all bad, for the jobs they had got, which so far they had never really discussed with each other, were all three admirable and likely to lead to better things later on. The greatest immediate improvement in their condition would of course arise from moving to another house; they wanted to take a smaller and cheaper but also better situated and more easily run apartment than the one they had, which Gregor had selected. While they were thus conversing, it struck both Mr. and Mrs. Samsa, almost at the same moment, as they became aware of their daughter's increasing vicacity, that in spite of all the sorrow of recent times, which had made her cheeks pale, she had bloomed into a pretty girl with a good figure. They grew quieter and half unconsciously exchanged glances of complete agreement, having come to the conclusion that it would soon be time to find a good husband for her. And it was like a confirmation of their new dreams and excellent intentions that at the end of their journey their daughter sprang to her feet first and stretched her young body.

QUESTIONS FOR DISCUSSION AND WRITING

1. The story is divided into three parts. What conflict seems to be at the center of each section? How are these conflicts finally resolved?
2. How does Gregor characterize his relationship to his family before his metamorphosis? How do the members of his family characterize themselves by their reaction to his metamorphosis?
3. How does the setting of the apartment, and especially Gregor's room, symbolize the nature of the action of the story? For example, how do the sister, the mother, and the charwoman take care of Gregor's room?
4. What is the effect of telling this story largely from Gregor's point of view? How does he feel about what has happened to him? How do his feelings affect the tone of the story?
5. How would you state the theme of this story? In what ways does Gregor's metamorphosis remind you of other events—such as a serious illness—that may affect the actions and aspirations of a family?

51

FRANZ KAFKA

In the Penal Colony

It's a remarkable piece of apparatus," said the officer to the explorer and surveyed with a certain air of admiration the apparatus which was after all quite familiar to him. The explorer seemed to have accepted merely out of politeness the Commandant's invitation to witness the execution of a soldier condemned to death for disobedience and insulting behavior to a superior. Nor did the colony itself betray much interest in this execution. At least, in the small sandy valley, a deep hollow surrounded on all sides by naked crags, there was no one present save the officer, the explorer, the condemned man, who was a stupid-looking wide-mouthed creature with bewildered hair and face, and the soldier who held the heavy chain controlling the small chains locked on the prisoner's ankles, wrists and neck, chains which were themselves attached to each other by communicating links. In any case, the condemned man looked so like a submissive dog that one might have thought he could be left to run free on the surrounding hills and would only need to be whistled for when the execution was due to begin.

The explorer did not much care about the apparatus and walked up and down behind the prisoner with almost visible indifference while the officer made the last adjustments, now creeping beneath the structure, which was bedded deep in the earth, now climbing a ladder to inspect its upper parts. These were tasks that might well have been left to a mechanic, but the officer performed them with great zeal, whether because he was a devoted admirer of the apparatus or because of other reasons the work could be entrusted to no one else. "Ready now!" he called at last and climbed down from the ladder. He looked uncommonly limp, breathed with his mouth wide open and had tucked two fine ladies' handkerchiefs under the collar of his uniform. "These uniforms are too heavy for the tropics, surely," said the explorer, instead of making some inquiry about the apparatus, as the officer had expected. "Of course," said the officer, washing his oily and greasy hands in a bucket of water that stood ready, "but they mean home to us; we don't want to forget about home. Now just have a look at this machine," he added at once, simultaneously drying his hands on a towel and indicating the apparatus. "Up till now a few things still had to be set by hand, but from this moment it works all by itself." The explorer nodded and followed him. The officer, anxious to secure himself against all contingencies, said: "Things sometimes go wrong, of course; I hope that nothing goes wrong today, but we have to allow for the possibility. The machinery should go on working continuously for twelve hours. But if anything does go wrong it will only be some small matter that can be set right at once."

"Won't you take a seat?" he asked finally, drawing a cane chair out from among a heap of them and offering it to the explorer, who could not refuse it. He was now sitting at the edge of a pit, into which he glanced for a fleeting moment. It was not very deep. On one side of the pit the excavated soil had been piled up in a rampart, on the other side of it stood the apparatus. "I don't know," said the officer, "if the Commandant has already explained this apparatus to you." The explorer waved one hand vaguely; the officer asked for nothing better, since now he could explain the apparatus himself. "This apparatus," he said, taking hold of a crank handle and leaning against it, "was invented by our former Commandant. I assisted at the very earliest experiments and had a share in all the work until its completion. But the credit of inventing it belongs to him alone. Have you ever heard of our former Commandant? No? Well, it isn't saying too much if I tell you that the organization of the whole penal colony is his work. We who were his friends knew even before he died that the organization of the colony was so perfect that his successor, even with a thousand new schemes in his head, would find it impossible to alter anything, at least for many years to come. And our prophecy has come true; the new Commandant has had to acknowledge its truth. A pity you never met the old Commandant!—But," the officer interrupted himself, "I am rambling on, and here stands his apparatus before us. It consists, as you see, of three parts. In the course of time each of these parts has acquired a kind of popular nickname. The lower one is called the 'Bed,' the upper one the 'Designer,' and this one here in the middle that moves up and down is called the 'Harrow.'" "The Harrow?" asked the explorer. He had not been listening very attentively, the glare of the sun in the shadeless valley was altogether too strong, it was difficult to collect one's thoughts. All the more did he admire the officer, who in spite of his tight-fitting full-dress uniform coat, amply befrogged and weighed down by epaulettes, was pursuing his subject with such enthusiasm and, besides talking, was still tightening a screw here and there with a spanner. As for the soldier, he seemed to be in much the same condition as the explorer. He had wound the prisoner's chain round both his wrists, propped himself on his rifle, let his head hang and was paying no attention to anything. That did not surprise the explorer, for the officer was speaking French, and certainly neither the soldier nor the prisoner understood a word of French. It was all the more remarkable, therefore, that the prisoner was none the less making an effort to follow the officer's explanations. With a kind of drowsy persistence he directed his gaze wherever the officer pointed a finger, and at the interruption of the explorer's question he, too, as well as the officer, looked round.

"Yes, the Harrow," said the officer, "a good name for it. The needles are set in like the teeth of a harrow and the whole thing works something like a harrow, although its action is limited to one place and contrived with much more artistic skill. Anyhow, you'll soon understand it. On the Bed here the condemned man is laid—I'm going to describe the apparatus first before I set it in motion. Then you'll be able to follow the proceedings better. Besides, one of the cog wheels in the Designer is badly worn; it creaks a lot when it's working; you can hardly hear yourself speak; spare parts, unfortunately, are difficult to get here.—Well, here is the Bed, as I told you. It is completely covered with a layer of cotton wool; you'll find out why later. On this cotton wool the condemned man is laid, face down, quite naked, of course; here are straps for the hands, here for the feet, and here for the neck, to bind him fast. Here at the head of the bed, where the man, as I said, first lays down his face, is this little gag of felt, which can be easily regulated to go straight into his mouth. It is meant to keep him from screaming and biting his tongue. Of course the man is forced to take the felt into his mouth, for otherwise his neck would be broken by the strap." "Is that cotton wool?" asked the explorer, bending forward. "Yes, certainly," said the officer, with a smile, "feel it for yourself." He took the explorer's hand and guided it over the bed. "It's specially prepared cotton wool, that's why it looks so different; I'll tell you presently what it's for." The explorer already felt a dawning interest in the apparatus; he sheltered his eyes from the sun with one hand and gazed up at the structure. It was a huge affair. The Bed and the Designer were of the same size and looked like two dark wooden chests. The Designer hung about two meters above the Bed; each of them was bound at the corners with four rods of brass that almost flashed out rays in the sunlight. Between the chests shuttled the Harrow on a ribbon of steel.

The officer had scarcely noticed the explorer's previous indifference, but he was now well aware of his dawning interest; so he stopped explaining in order to leave a space of time for quiet observation. The condemned man imitated the explorer; since he could not use a hand to shelter his eyes he gazed upwards without shade.

"Well, the man lies down," said the explorer, leaning back in his chair and crossing his legs.

"Yes," said the officer, pushing his cap back a little and passing one hand over his heated face, "now listen! Both the Bed and the Designer have an electric battery each; the Bed needs one for itself, the Designer for the Harrow. As soon as the man is strapped down, the Bed is set in motion. It quivers in minute, very rapid vibrations, both from side to side and up and down. You will have seen similar apparatus in hospitals; but in our Bed the movements are all precisely calculated; you see, they have to correspond very exactly to the movements of the Harrow. And the Harrow is the instrument for the actual execution of the sentence."

"And how does the sentence run?" asked the explorer.

"You don't know that either?" said the officer in amazement, and bit his lips. "Forgive me if my explanations seem rather incoherent. I do beg your pardon. You see, the Commandant always used to do the explaining; but the new Commandant shirks this duty; yet that such an important visitor"—the explorer tried to deprecate the honor with both hands, the officer, however, insisted—"that such an important visitor should not even be told about the kind of sentence we pass is a new development, which—" He was just on the point of using strong language but checked himself and said only: "I was not informed, it is not my fault. In any case, I am certainly the best person to explain our procedure, since I have here"—he patted his breast pocket—"the relevant drawings made by our former Commandant."

"The Commandant's own drawings?" asked the explorer. "Did he combine everything in himself, then? Was he soldier, judge, mechanic, chemist and draughtsman?"

"Indeed he was," said the officer, nodding assent, with a remote, glassy look. Then he inspected his hands critically; they did not seem clean enough to him for touching the drawings; so he went over to the bucket and washed them again. Then he drew out a small leather wallet and said: "Our sentence does not sound severe. Whatever commandment the prisoner has disobeyed is written upon his body by the Harrow. This prisoner, for instance"—the officer indicated the man—"will have written on his body: HONOR THY SUPERIORS!"

The explorer glanced at the man; he stood, as the officer pointed him out, with bent head, apparently listening with all his ears in an effort to catch what was being said. Yet the movement of his blubber lips, closely pressed together, showed clearly that he could not understand a word. Many questions were troubling the explorer, but at the sight of the prisoner he asked only: "Does he know his sentence?" "No," said the officer, eager to go on with his exposition, but the explorer interrupted him: "He doesn't know the sentence that has been passed on him?" "No," said the officer again, pausing a moment as if to let the explorer elaborate his question, and then said: "There would be no point in telling him. He'll learn it on his body." The explorer intended to make no answer, but he felt the prisoner's gaze turned on him; it seemed to ask if he approved such ongoings. So he bent forward again, having already leaned back in his chair, and put another question: "But surely he knows that he has been sentenced?" "Nor that either," said the officer, smiling at the explorer as if expecting him to make further surprising remarks. "No," said the explorer, wiping his forehead, "then he can't know either whether his defense was effective?" "He has had no chance of putting up a defense," said the officer, turning his eyes away as if speaking to himself and so sparing the explorer the shame of hearing self-evident matters explained. "But he must have had some chance of defending himself," said the explorer, and rose from his seat.

The officer realized that he was in danger of having his exposition of the apparatus held up for a long time; so he went up to the explorer, took him by the arm, waved a hand towards the condemned man, who was standing very straight now that he had so obviously become the center of attention—the soldier had also given the chain a jerk—and said: "This is how the matter stands. I have been appointed judge in this penal colony. Despite my youth. For I was the former Commandant's assistant in all penal matters and know more about the apparatus than anyone. My guiding principle is this: Guilt is never to be doubted. Other courts cannot follow that principle, for they consist of several opinions and have higher courts to scrutinize them. That is not the case here, or at least, it was not the case in the former Commandant's time. The new man has certainly shown some inclination to interfere with my judgments, but so far I have succeeded in fending him off and will go on succeeding. You wanted to have the case explained; it is quite simple, like all of them. A captain reported to me this morning that this man, who had been assigned to him as a servant and sleeps before his door, had been asleep on duty. It is his duty, you see, to get up every time the hour strikes and salute the captain's door. Not an exacting duty, and very necessary, since he has to be a sentry as well as a servant, and must be alert in both functions. Last night the captain wanted to see if the man was doing his duty. He opened the door as the clock struck two and there was his man curled up asleep. He took his riding whip and lashed him across the face. Instead of getting up and begging pardon, the man caught hold of his master's legs, shook him and cried: 'Throw that whip away or I'll eat you alive.'—That's the evidence. The captain came to me an hour ago, I wrote down his statement and appended the sentence to it. Then I had the man put in chains. That was all quite simple. If I had first called the man before me and interrogated him, things would have got into a confused tangle. He would have told lies, and had I exposed these lies he would have backed them up with more lies, and so on and so forth. As it is, I've got him and I won't let him go.—Is that quite clear now? But we're wasting time, the execution should be beginning and I haven't finished explaining the apparatus yet." He pressed the explorer back into his chair, went up again to the apparatus and began: "As you see, the shape of the Harrow corresponds to the human form; here is the harrow for the torso, here are the harrows for the legs. For the head there is only this one small spike. Is that quite clear?" He bent amiably forward towards the explorer, eager to provide the most comprehensive explanations.

The explorer considered the Harrow with a frown. The explanation of the judicial procedure had not satisfied him. He had to remind himself that this was in any case a penal colony where extraordinary measures were needed and that military discipline must be enforced to the last. He also felt that some hope might be set on the new Commandant, who was apparently of a mind to bring in, although gradually, a new kind of procedure which the officer's narrow mind was incapable of understanding. This train of thought prompted his next question: "Will the Commandant attend the execution?" "It is not certain," said the officer, wincing at the direct question, and his friendly expression darkened. "That is just why we have to lose no time. Much as I dislike it, I shall have to cut my explanations short. But of course tomorrow, when the apparatus has been cleaned—its one drawback is that it gets so messy—I can recapitulate all the details. For the present, then, only the essentials.—When the man lies down on the Bed and it begins to vibrate, the Harrow is lowered onto his body. It regulates itself automatically so that the needles barely touch his skin; once contact is made the steel ribbon stiffens immediately into a rigid band. And then the performance begins. An ignorant onlooker would see no difference between one punishment and another. The Harrow appears to do its work with uniform regularity. As it quivers, its points pierce the skin of the body which is itself quivering from the vibration of the Bed. So that the actual progress of the sentence can be watched, the Harrow is made of glass. Getting the needles fixed in the glass was a technical problem, but after many experiments we overcame the difficulty. No trouble was too great for us to take, you see. And now anyone can look through the glass and watch the inscription taking form on the body. Wouldn't you care to come a little nearer and have a look at the needles?"

The explorer got up slowly, walked across and bent over the Harrow. "You see," said the officer, "there are two kinds of needles arranged in multiple patterns. Each long needle has a short one beside it. The long needle does the writing, and the short needle sprays a jet of water to wash away the blood and keep the inscription clear. Blood and water together are then conducted here through small runnels into this main runnel and down a waste pipe into the pit." With his finger the officer traced the exact course taken by the blood and water. To make the picture as vivid as possible he held both hands below the outlet of the waste pipe as if to catch the outflow, and when he did this the explorer drew back his head and feeling behind him with one hand sought to return to his chair. To his horror he found that the condemned man too had obeyed the officer's invitation to examine the Harrow at close quarters and had followed him. He had pulled forward the sleepy soldier with the chain and was bending over the glass. One could see that his uncertain eyes were trying to perceive what the two gentlemen had been looking at, but since he had not understood the explanation he could not make head or tail of it. He was peering this way and that way. He kept running his eyes along the glass. The explorer wanted to drive him away, since what he was doing was probably culpable. But the officer firmly restrained the explorer with one hand and with the other took a clod of earth from the rampart and threw it at the soldier. He opened his eyes with a jerk, saw what the condemned man had dared to do, let his rifle fall, dug his heels into the ground, dragged his prisoner back so that he stumbled and fell immediately, and then stood looking down at him, watching him struggling and rattling in his chains. "Set him on his feet!" yelled the officer, for he noticed that the explorer's attention was being too much distracted by the prisoner. In fact he was even leaning right across the Harrow, without taking any notice of it, intent only on finding out what was happening to the prisoner. "Be careful with him!" cried the officer again. He ran round the apparatus, himself caught the condemned man under the shoulders and with the soldier's help got him up on his feet, which kept slithering from under him.

"Now I know all about it," said the explorer as the officer came back to him. "All except the most important thing," he answered, seizing the explorer's arm and pointing upwards: "In the Designer are all the cogwheels that control the movements of the Harrow, and this machinery is regulated according to the inscription demanded by the sentence. I am still using the guiding plans drawn by the former Commandant. Here they are"—he extracted some sheets from the leather wallet—"but I'm sorry I can't let you handle them, they are my most precious possessions. Just take a seat and I'll hold them in front of you like this, then you'll be able to see everything quite well." He spread out the first sheet of paper. The explorer would have liked to say something appreciative, but all he could see was a labyrinth of lines crossing and re-crossing each other, which covered the paper so thickly that it was difficult to discern the blank spaces between them. "Read it," said the officer. "I can't," said the explorer. "Yet it's clear enough," said the officer. "It's very ingenious," said the explorer evasively, "but I can't make it out." "Yes," said the officer with a laugh, putting the paper away again, "it's no calligraphy for school children. It needs to be studied closely. I'm quite sure that in the end you would understand it too. Of course the script can't be a simple one; it's not supposed to kill a man straight off, but only after an interval of, on an average, twelve hours; the turning point is reckoned to come at the sixth hour. So there have to be lots and lots of flourishes around the actual script; the script itself runs round the body only in a narrow girdle; the rest of the body is reserved for the embellishments. Can you appreciate now the work accomplished by the Harrow and the whole apparatus?—Just watch it!" He ran up the ladder, turned a wheel, called down: "Look out, keep to one side!" and everything started working. If the wheel had not creaked, it would have been marvelous. The officer, as if surprised by the noise of the wheel, shook his fist at it, then spread out his arms in excuse to the explorer and climbed down rapidly to peer at the working of the machine from below. Something perceptible to no one save himself was still not in order; he clambered up again, did something with both hands in the interior of the Designer, then slid down one of the rods, instead of using the ladder, so as to get down quicker, and with the full force of his lungs, to make himself heard at all in the noise, yelled in the explorer's ear: "Can you follow it? The Harrow is beginning to write; when it finishes the first draft of the inscription on the man's back, the layer of cotton wool begins to roll and slowly turns the body over, to give the Harrow fresh space for writing. Meanwhile the raw part that has been written on lies on the cotton wool, which is specially prepared to staunch the bleeding and so makes all ready for a new deepening of the script. Then these teeth at the edge of the Harrow, as the body turns further round, tear the cotton wool away from the wounds, throw it into the pit, and there is more work for the Harrow. So it keeps on writing deeper and deeper for the whole twelve hours. The first six hours the condemned man stays alive almost as before, he suffers only pain. After two hours the felt gag is taken away, for he has no longer strength to scream. Here, into this electrically heated basin at the head of the bed, some warm rice pap is poured, from which the man, if he feels like it, can take as much as his tongue can lap. Not one of them ever misses the chance. I can remember none, and my experience is extensive. Only about the sixth hour does the man lose all desire to eat. I usually kneel down here at that moment and observe what happens. The man rarely swallows his last mouthful, he only rolls it round his mouth and spits it out into the pit. I have to duck just then or he would spit it in my face. But how quiet he grows at just about the sixth hour! Enlightenment comes to the most dull-witted. It begins around the eyes. From there it radiates. A moment that might tempt one to get under the Harrow oneself. Nothing more happens than that the man begins to understand the inscription, he purses his mouth as if he were listening. You have seen how difficult it is to decipher the script with one's eyes; but our man deciphers it with his wounds. To be sure, that is a hard task; he needs six hours to accomplish it. By that time the Harrow has pierced him quite through and casts him into the pit, where he pitches down upon the blood and water and the cotton wool. Then the judgment has been fulfilled, and we, the soldier and I, bury him."

The explorer had inclined his ear to the officer and with his hands in his jacket pockets watched the machine at work. The condemned man watched it too, but uncomprehendingly. He bent forward a little and was intent on the moving needles when the soldier, at a sign from the officer, slashed through his shirt and trousers from behind with a knife, so that they fell off; he tried to catch at his falling clothes to cover his nakedness, but the soldier lifted him into the air and shook the last remnants from him. The officer stopped the machine, and in the sudden silence the condemned man was laid under the Harrow. The chains were loosened and the straps fastened on instead; in the first moment that seemed almost a relief to the prisoner. And now the Harrow was adjusted a little lower, since he was a thin man. When the needle points touched him a shudder ran over his skin; while the soldier was busy strapping his right hand, he flung out his left hand blindly; but it happened to be in the direction towards where the explorer was standing. The officer kept watching the explorer sideways, as if seeking to read from his face the impression made on him by the execution, which had been at least cursorily explained to him.

The wrist strap broke; probably the soldier had drawn it too tight. The officer had to intervene, the soldier held up the broken piece of strap to show him. So the officer went over to him and said, his face still turned towards the explorer: "This is a very complex machine, it can't be helped that things are breaking or giving way here and there; but one must not thereby allow oneself to be diverted in one's general judgment. In any case, this strap is easily made good; I shall simply use a chain; the delicacy of the vibrations for the right arm will of course be a little impaired." And while he fastened the chains, he added: "The resources for maintaining the machine are now very much reduced. Under the former Commandant I had free access to a sum of money set aside entirely for this purpose. There was a store, too, in which spare parts were kept for repairs of all kinds. I confess I have been almost prodigal with them, I mean in the past, not now as the new Commandant pretends, always looking for an excuse to attack our old way of doing things. Now he has taken charge of the machine money himself, and if I send for a new strap they ask for the broken old strap as evidence, and the new strap takes ten days to appear and then is of shoddy material and not much good. But how I am supposed to work the machine without a strap, that's something nobody bothers about."

The explorer thought to himself: It's always a ticklish matter to intervene decisively in other people's affairs. He was neither a member of the penal colony nor a citizen of the state to which it belonged. Were he to denounce this execution or actually try to stop it, they could say to him: You are a foreigner, mind your own business. He could make no answer to that, unless he were to add that he was amazed at himself in this connection, for he traveled only as an observer, with no intention at all of altering other people's methods of administering justice. Yet here he found himself strongly tempted. The injustice of the procedure and the inhumanity of the execution were undeniable. No one could suppose that he had any selfish interest in the matter, for the condemned man was a complete stranger, not a fellow countryman or even at all sympathetic to him. The explorer himself had recommendations from high quarters, had been received here with great courtesy, and the very fact that he had been invited to attend the execution seemed to suggest that his views would be welcome. And this was all the more likely since the Commandant, as he had heard only too plainly, was no upholder of the procedure and maintained an attitude almost of hostility to the officer.

At that moment the explorer heard the officer cry out in rage. He had just, with considerable difficulty, forced the felt gag into the condemned man's mouth when the man in an irresistible access of nausea shut his eyes and vomited. Hastily the officer snatched him away from the gag and tried to hold his head over the pit; but it was too late, the vomit was running all over the machine. "It's all the fault of that Commandant!" cried the officer, senselessly shaking the brass rods in front, "the machine is befouled like a pigsty." With trembling hands he indicated to the explorer what had happened. "Have I not tried for hours at a time to get the Commandant to understand that the prisoner must fast for a whole day before the execution. But our new, mild doctrine thinks otherwise. The Commandant's ladies stuff the man with sugar candy before he's led off. He has lived on stinking fish his whole life long and now he has to eat sugar candy! But it could still be possible, I should have nothing to say against it, but why won't they get me a new felt gag, which I have been begging for the last three months. How should a man not feel sick when he takes a felt gag into his mouth which more than a hundred men have already slobbered and gnawed in their dying moments?"

The condemned man had laid his head down and looked peaceful, the soldier was busy trying to clean the machine with the prisoner's shirt. The officer advanced towards the explorer, who in some vague presentiment fell back a pace, but the officer seized him by the hand, and drew him to one side. "I should like to exchange a few words with you in confidence," he said, "may I?" "Of course," said the explorer, and listened with downcast eyes.

"This procedure and method of execution, which you are now having the opportunity to admire, has at the moment no longer any open adherents in our colony. I am its sole advocate, and at the same time the sole advocate of the old Commandant's tradition. I can no longer reckon on any further extension of the method, it takes all my energy to maintain it as it is. During the old Commandant's lifetime the colony was full of his adherents; his strength of conviction I still have in some measure, but not an atom of his power; consequently the adherents have skulked out of sight, there are still many of them but none of them will admit it. If you were to go into the teahouse today, on execution day, and listen to what is being said, you would perhaps hear only ambiguous remarks. These would all be made by adherents, but under the present Commandant and his present doctrines they are of no use to me. And now I ask you: because of this Commandant and the women who influence him, is such a piece of work, the work of a lifetime"—he pointed to the machine—"to perish? Ought one to let that happen? Even if one has only come as a stranger to our island for a few days? But there's no time to lose, an attack of some kind is impending on my function as judge; conferences are already being held in the Commandant's office from which I am excluded; even your coming here today seems to me a significant move; they are cowards and use you as a screen, you, a stranger.—How different an execution was in the old days! A whole day before the ceremony the valley was packed with people; they all came only to look on; early in the morning the Commandant appeared with his ladies; fanfares roused the whole camp; I reported that everything was in readiness; the assembled company—no high official dared to absent himself—arranged itself round the machine; this pile of cane chairs is a miserable survival from that epoch. The machine was freshly cleaned and glittering, I got new spare parts for almost every execution. Before hundreds of spectators—all of them standing on tiptoe as far as the heights there—the condemned man was laid under the Harrow by the Commandant himself. What is left today for a common soldier to do was then my task, the task of the presiding judge, and was an honor for me. And then the execution began! No discordant noise spoilt the working of the machine. Many did not care to watch it but lay with closed eyes in the sand; they all knew: Now Justice is being done. In the silence one heard nothing but the condemned man's sighs, half muffled by the felt gag. Nowadays the machine can no longer wring from anyone a sigh louder than the felt gag can stifle; but in those days the writing needles let drop an acid fluid, which we're no longer permitted to use. Well, and then came the sixth hour! It was impossible to grant all the requests to be allowed to watch it from near by. The Commandant in his wisdom ordained that the children should have the preference; I, of course, because of my office had the privilege of always being at hand; often enough I would be squatting there with a small child in either arm. How we all absorbed the look of transfiguration on the face of the sufferer, how we bathed our cheeks in the radiance of that justice, achieved at last and fading so quickly! What times these were, my comrade!" The officer had obviously forgotten whom he was addressing; he had embraced the explorer and laid his head on his shoulder. The explorer was deeply embarrassed, impatiently he stared over the officer's head. The soldier had finished his cleaning job and was now pouring rice pap from a pot into the basin. As soon as the condemned man, who seemed to have recovered entirely, noticed this action he began to reach for the rice with his tongue. The soldier kept pushing him away, since the rice pap was certainly meant for a later hour, yet it was just as unfitting that the soldier himself should thrust his dirty hands into the basin and eat out of it before the other's avid face.

The officer quickly pulled himself together. "I didn't want to upset you," he said, "I know it is impossible to make those days credible now. Anyhow, the machine is still working and it is still effective in itself. It is effective in itself even though it stands alone in this valley. And the corpse still falls at the last into the pit with an incomprehensibly gentle wafting motion, even although there are no hundreds of people swarming round like flies as formerly. In those days we had to put a strong fence round the pit, it has long since been torn down."

The explorer wanted to withdraw his face from the officer and looked round him at random. The officer thought he was surveying the valley's desolation; so he seized him by the hands, turned him round to meet his eyes, and asked: "Do you realize the shame of it?"

But the explorer said nothing. The officer left him alone for a little; with legs apart, hands on hips, he stood very still, gazing at the ground. Then he smiled encouragingly at the explorer and said: "I was quite near you yesterday when the Commandant gave you the invitation. I heard him giving it. I know the Commandant. I divined at once what he was after. Although he is powerful enough to take measures against me, he doesn't dare to do it yet, he certainly means to use your verdict against me, the verdict of an illustrious foreigner. He has calculated it carefully: this is your second day on the island, you did not know the old Commandant and his ways, you are conditioned by European ways of thought, perhaps you object on principle to capital punishment in general and to such mechanical instruments of death in particular, besides you will see that the execution has no support from the public, a shabby ceremony—carried out with a machine already somewhat old and worn—now, taking all that into consideration, would it not be likely (so thinks the Commandant) that you might disapprove of my methods? And if you disapprove, you wouldn't conceal the fact (I'm still speaking from the Commandant's point of view), for you are a man to feel confidence in your own well-tried conclusions. True, you have seen and learned to appreciate the peculiarities of many peoples, and so you would not be likely to take a strong line against our proceedings, as you might do in your own country. But the Commandant has no need of that. A casual, even an unguarded remark will be enough. It doesn't even need to represent what you really think, so long as it can be used speciously to serve his purpose. He will try to prompt you with sly questions, of that I am certain. And his ladies will sit around you and prick up their ears; you might be saying something like this: 'In our country we have a different criminal procedure,' or 'In our country the prisoner is interrogated before he is sentenced,' or 'We haven't used torture since the Middle Ages.' All these statements are as true as they seem natural to you, harmless remarks that pass no judgment on my methods. But how would the Commandant react to them? I can see him, our good Commandant, pushing his chair away immediately and rushing on to the balcony, I can see his ladies streaming out after him, I can hear his voice—the ladies call it a voice of thunder—well, and this is what he says: 'A famous Western investigator, sent out to study criminal procedure in all the countries of the world, has just said that our old tradition of administering justice is inhumane. Such a verdict from such a personality makes it impossible for me to countenance these methods any longer. Therefore from this very day I ordain . . .' and so on. You may want to interpose that you never said any such thing, that you never called my methods inhumane, on the contrary your profound experience leads you to believe they are most humane and most in consonance with human dignity, and you admire the machine greatly—but it will be too late; you won't even get onto the balcony, crowded as it will be with ladies; you may try to draw attention to yourself; you may want to scream out; but a lady's hand will close your lips—and I and the work of the old Commandant will be done for."

The explorer had to suppress a smile; so easy, then, was the task he had felt to be so difficult. He said evasively: "You overestimate my influence; the Commandant has read my letters of recommendation, he knows that I am no expert in criminal procedure. If I were to give an opinion, it would be as a private individual, an opinion no more influential than that of any ordinary person, and in any case much less influential than that of the Commandant, who, I am given to understand, has very extensive powers in this penal colony. If his attitude to your procedure is as definitely hostile as you believe, then I fear the end of your tradition is at hand, even without any humble assistance from me."

Had it dawned on the officer at last? No, he still did not understand. He shook his head emphatically, glanced briefly round at the condemned man and the soldier, who both flinched away from the rice, came close up to the explorer and without looking at his face but fixing his eye on some spot on his coat said in a lower voice than before: "You don't know the Commandant; you feel yourself—forgive the expression—a kind of outsider so far as all of us are concerned; yet, believe me, your influence cannot be rated too highly. I was simply delighted when I heard that you were to attend the execution all by yourself. The Commandant arranged it to aim a blow at me, but I shall turn it to my advantage. Without being distracted by lying whispers and contemptuous glances—which could not have been avoided had a crowd of people attended the execution—you have heard my explanations, seen the machine and are now in course of watching the execution. You have doubtless already formed your own judgment; if you still have some small uncertainties the sight of the execution will resolve them. And now I make this request to you: help me against the Commandant!"

The explorer would not let him go on. "How could I do that," he cried, "it's quite impossible. I can neither help nor hinder you."

"Yes, you can," the officer said. The explorer saw with a certain apprehension that the officer had clenched his fists. "Yes, you can," repeated the officer, still more insistently. "I have a plan that is bound to succeed. You believe your influence is insufficient. I know that it is sufficient. But even granted that you are right, is it not necessary, for the sake of preserving this tradition, to try even what might prove insufficient? Listen to my plan, then. The first thing necessary for you to carry it out is to be as reticent as possible today regarding your verdict on these proceedings. Unless you are asked a direct question you must say nothing at all; but what you do say must be brief and general; let it be remarked that you would prefer not to discuss the matter, that you are out of patience with it, that if you are to let yourself go you would use strong language. I don't ask you to tell any lies; by no means; you should only give curt answers, such as: 'Yes, I saw the execution,' or 'Yes, I had it explained to me.' Just that, nothing more. There are grounds enough for any impatience you betray, although not such as will occur to the Commandant. Of course, he will mistake your meaning and interpret it to please himself. That's what my plan depends on. Tomorrow in the Commandant's office there is to be a large conference of all the high administrative officials, the Commandant presiding. Of course the Commandant is the kind of man to have turned these conferences into public spectacles. He has had a gallery built that is always packed with spectators. I am compelled to take part in the conferences, but they make me sick with disgust. Now, whatever happens, you will certainly be invited to this conference; if you behave today as I suggest the invitation will become an urgent request. But if for some mysterious reason you're not invited, you'll have to ask for an invitation; there's no doubt of your getting it then. So tomorrow you're sitting in the Commandant's box with the ladies. He keeps looking up to make sure you're there. After various trivial and ridiculous matters, brought in merely to impress the audience—mostly harbor works, nothing but harbor works!—our judicial procedure comes up for discussion too. If the Commandant doesn't introduce it, or not soon enough, I'll see that it's mentioned. I'll stand up and report that today's execution has taken place. Quite briefly, only a statement. Such a statement is not usual, but I shall make it. The Commandant thanks me, as always, with an amiable smile, and then he can't restrain himself, he seizes the excellent opportunity. 'It has just been reported,' he will say, or words to that effect, 'that an execution has taken place. I should like merely to add that this execution was witnessed by the famous explorer who has, as you all know, honored our colony so greatly by his visit to us. His presence at today's session of our conference also contributes to the importance of this occasion. Should we not now ask the famous explorer to give us his verdict on our traditional mode of execution and the procedure that leads up to it?' Of course there is loud applause, general agreement, I am more insistent than anyone. The Commandant bows to you and says: 'Then in the name of the assembled company, I put the question to you.' And now you advance to the front of the box. Lay your hands where everyone can see them, or the ladies will catch them and press your fingers.—And then at last you can speak out. I don't know how I'm going to endure the tension of waiting for that moment. Don't put any restraint on yourself when you make your speech, publish the truth aloud, lean over the front of the box, shout, yes indeed, shout your verdict, your unshakable conviction, at the Commandant. Yet perhaps you wouldn't care to do that, it's not in keeping with your character, in your country perhaps people do these things differently, well, that's all right too, that will be quite as effective, don't even stand up, just say a few words, even in a whisper, so that only the officials beneath you will hear them, that will be quite enough, you don't even need to mention the lack of public support for the execution, the creaking wheel, the broken strap, the filthy gag of felt, no, I'll take all that upon me, and, believe me, if my indictment doesn't drive him out of the conference hall, it will force him to his knees to make the acknowledgment: Old Commandant, I humble myself before you.—That is my plan; will you help me to carry it out? But of course you are willing, what is more, you must." And the officer seized the explorer by both arms and gazed, breathing heavily, into his face. He had shouted the last sentence so loudly that even the soldier and the condemned man were startled into attending; they had not understood a word but they stopped eating and looked over at the explorer, chewing their previous mouthfuls.

From the very beginning the explorer had no doubt about what answer he must give; in his lifetime he had experienced too much to have an uncertainty here; he was fundamentally honorable and unafraid. And yet now, facing the soldier and the condemned man, he did hesitate, for as long as it took to draw one breath. At last, however, he said, as he had to: "No." The officer blinked several times but did not turn his eyes away. "Would you like me to explain?" asked the explorer. The officer nodded wordlessly. "I do not approve of your procedure," said the explorer then, "even before you took me into your confidence—of course I shall never in any circumstances betray your confidence—I was already wondering whether it would be my duty to intervene and whether my intervention would have the slightest chance of success. I realized to whom I ought to turn: to the Commandant, of course. You have made that fact even clearer, but without having strengthened my resolution; on the contrary, your sincere conviction has touched me, even though it cannot influence my judgment."

The officer remained mute, turned to the machine, caught hold of a brass rod, and then, leaning back a little, gazed at the Designer as if to assure himself that all was in order. The soldier and the condemned man seemed to have come to some understanding; the condemned man was making signs to the soldier, difficult though his movements were because of the tight straps; the soldier was bending down to him; the condemned man whispered something and the soldier nodded.

The explorer followed the officer and said: "You don't know yet what I mean to do. I shall tell the Commandant what I think of the procedure, certainly, but not at a public conference, only in private; nor shall I stay here long enough to attend any conference; I am going away early tomorrow morning, or at least embarking on my ship."

It did not look as if the officer had been listening. "So you did not find the procedure convincing," he said to himself and smiled, as an old man smiles at childish nonsense and yet pursues his own meditations behind the smile.

"Then the time has come," he said at last, and suddenly looked at the explorer with bright eyes that held some challenge, some appeal for co-operation. "The time for what?" asked the explorer uneasily, but got no answer.

"You are free," said the officer to the condemned man in the native tongue. The man did not believe it at first. "Yes, you are set free," said the officer. For the first time the condemned man's face woke to real animation. Was it true? Was it only a caprice of the officer's, that might change again? Had the foreign explorer begged him off? What was it? One could read these questions on his face. But not for long. Whatever it might be, he wanted to be really free if he might, and he began to struggle so far as the Harrow permitted him.

"You'll burst my straps," cried the officer, "lie still! We'll soon loosen them." And signing the soldier to help him, he set about doing so. The condemned man laughed wordlessly to himself, now he turned his face left towards the officer, now right towards the soldier, nor did he forget the explorer.

"Draw him out," ordered the officer. Because of the Harrow this had to be done with some care. The condemned man had already torn himself a little in the back through his impatience.

From now on, however, the officer paid hardly any attention to him. He went up to the explorer, pulled out the small leather wallet again, turned over the papers in it, found the one he wanted and showed it to the explorer. "Read it," he said. "I can't," said the explorer, "I told you before that I can't make out these scripts." "Try taking a close look at it," said the officer and came quite near to the explorer so that they might read it together. But when even that proved useless, he outlined the script with his little finger, holding it high above the paper as if the surface dared not be sullied by touch, in order to help the explorer to follow the script in that way. The explorer did make an effort, meaning to please the officer in this respect at least, but he was quite unable to follow. Now the officer began to spell it, letter by letter, and then read out the words. "'BE JUST!' is what is written there," he said, "surely you can read it now." The explorer bent so close to the paper that the officer feared he might touch it and drew it farther away; the explorer made no remark, yet it was clear that he still could not decipher it. "'BE JUST!' is what is written there," said the officer once more. "Maybe," said the explorer, "I am prepared to believe you." "Well, then," said the officer, at least partly satisfied, and climbed up the ladder with the paper; very carefully he laid it inside the Designer and seemed to be changing the disposition of all the cogwheels; it was a troublesome piece of work and must have involved wheels that were extremely small, for sometimes the officer's head vanished altogether from sight inside the Designer, so precisely did he have to regulate the machinery.

The explorer, down below, watched the labor uninterruptedly, his neck grew stiff and his eyes smarted from the glare of sunshine over the sky. The soldier and the condemned man were now busy together. The man's shirt and trousers, which were already lying in the pit, were fished out by the point of the soldier's bayonet. The shirt was abominably dirty and its owner washed it in the bucket of water. When he put on the shirt and trousers both he and the soldier could not help guffawing, for the garments were of course slit up behind. Perhaps the condemned man felt it incumbent on him to amuse the soldier, he turned round and round in his slashed garments before the soldier, who squatted on the ground beating his knees with mirth. All the same, they presently controlled their mirth out of respect for the gentlemen.

When the officer had at length finished his task aloft, he surveyed the machinery in all its details once more, with a smile, but this time shut the lid of the Designer, which had stayed open till now, climbed down, looked into the pit and then at the condemned man, noting with satisfaction that the clothing had been taken out, then went over to wash his hands in the water bucket, perceived too late that it was disgustingly dirty, was unhappy because he could not wash his hands, in the end thrust them into the sand—this alternative did not please him, but he had to put up with it—then stood upright and began to unbutton his uniform jacket. As he did this, the two ladies' handkerchiefs he had tucked under his collar fell into his hands. "Here are your handkerchiefs," he said, and threw them to the condemned man. And to the explorer he said in explanation: "A gift from the ladies."

In spite of the obvious haste with which he was discarding first his uniform jacket and then all his clothing, he handled each garment with loving care, he even ran his fingers caressingly over the silver lace on the jacket and shook a tassel into place. This loving care was certainly out of keeping with the fact that as soon as he had a garment off he flung it at once with a kind of unwilling jerk into the pit. The last thing left to him was his short sword with the sword belt. He drew it out of the scabbard, broke it, then gathered all together, the bits of the sword, the scabbard and the belt, and flung them so violently down that they clattered into the pit.

Now he stood naked there. The explorer bit his lips and said nothing. He knew very well what was going to happen, but he had no right to obstruct the officer in anything. If the judicial procedure which the officer cherished were really so near its end—possibly as a result of his own intervention, as to which he felt himself pledged—then the officer was doing the right thing; in his place the explorer would not have acted otherwise.

The soldier and the condemned man did not understand at first what was happening, at first they were not even looking on. The condemned man was gleeful at having got the handkerchiefs back, but he was not allowed to enjoy them for long, since the soldier snatched them with a sudden, unexpected grab. Now the condemned man in turn was trying to twitch them from under the belt where the soldier had tucked them, but the soldier was on his guard. So they were wrestling, half in jest. Only when the officer stood quite naked was their attention caught. The condemned man especially seemed struck with the notion that some great change was impending. What had happened to him was now going to happen to the officer. Perhaps even to the very end. Apparently the foreign explorer had given the order for it. So this was revenge. Although he himself had not suffered to the end, he was to be revenged to the end. A broad, silent grin now appeared on his face and stayed there all the rest of the time.

The officer, however, had turned to the machine. It had been clear enough previously that he undestood the machine well, but now it was almost staggering to see how he managed it and how it obeyed him. His hand had only to approach the Harrow for it to rise and sink several times till it was adjusted to the right position for receiving him; he touched only the edge of the Bed and already it was vibrating; the felt gag came to meet his mouth, one could see that the officer was really reluctant to take it but he shrank from it only a moment, soon he submitted and received it. Everything was ready, only the straps hung down at the sides, yet they were obviously unnecessary, the officer did not need to be fastened down. Then the condemned man noticed the loose straps, in his opinion the execution was incomplete unless the straps were buckled, he gestured eagerly to the soldier and they ran together to strap the officer down. The latter had already stretched out one foot to push the lever that started the Designer; he saw the two men coming up; so he drew his foot back and let himself be buckled in. But now he could not reach the lever; neither the soldier nor the condemned man would be able to find it, and the explorer was determined not to lift a finger. It was not necessary; as soon as the straps were fastened the machine began to work; the Bed vibrated, the needles flickered above the skin, the Harrow rose and fell. The explorer had been staring at it quite a while before he remembered that a wheel in the Designer should have been creaking; but everything was quiet, not even the slightest hum could be heard.

Because it was working so silently the machine simply escaped one's attention. The explorer observed the soldier and the condemned man. The latter was the more animated of the two, everything in the machine interested him, now he was bending down and now stretching up on tiptoe, his forefinger was extended all the time pointing out details to the soldier. This annoyed the explorer. He was resolved to stay till the end, but he could not bear the sight of these two. "Go back home," he said. The soldier would have been willing enough, but the condemned man took the order as a punishment. With clasped hands he implored to be allowed to stay, and when the explorer shook his head and would not relent, he even went down on his knees. The explorer saw that it was no use merely giving orders, he was on the point of going over and driving them away. At that moment he heard a noise above him in the Designer. He looked up. Was that cogwheel going to make trouble after all? But it was something quite different. Slowly the lid of the Designer rose up and then clicked wide open. The teeth of a cogwheel showed themselves and rose higher, soon the whole wheel was visible, it was as if some enormous force were squeezing the Designer so that there was no longer room for the wheel, the wheel moved up till it came to the very edge of the Designer, fell down, rolled along the sand a little on its rim and then lay flat. But a second wheel was already rising after it, followed by many others, large and small and indistinguishably minute, the same thing happened to all of them, at every moment one imagined the Designer must now really be empty, but another complex of numerous wheels was already rising into sight, falling down, trundling along the sand and lying flat. This phenomenon made the condemned man completely forget the explorer's command, the cogwheels fascinated him, he was always trying to catch one and at the same time urging the soldier to help, but always drew back his hand in alarm, for another wheel always came hopping along which, at least on its first advance, scared him off.

The explorer, on the other hand, felt greatly troubled; the machine was obviously going to pieces; its silent working was a delusion; he had a feeling that he must now stand by the officer, since the officer was no longer able to look after himself. But while the tumbling cogwheels absorbed his whole attention he had forgotten to keep an eye on the rest of the machine; now that the last cogwheel had left the Designer, however, he bent over the Harrow and had a new and still more unpleasant surprise. The Harrow was not writing, it was only jabbing, and the bed was not turning the body over but only bringing it up quivering against the needles. The explorer wanted to do something, if possible, to bring the whole machine to a standstill, for this was no exquisite torture such as the officer desired, this was plain murder. He stretched out his hands. But at that moment the Harrow rose with the body spitted on it and moved to the side, as it usually did only when the twelfth hour had come. Blood was flowing in a hundred streams, not mingled with water, the water jets too had failed to function. And now the last action failed to fulfill itself, the body did not drop off the long needles, streaming with blood it went on hanging over the pit without falling into it. The Harrow tried to move back to its old position, but as if it had itself noticed that it had not yet got rid of its burden it stuck after all where it was, over the pit. "Come and help!" cried the explorer to the other two, and himself seized the officer's feet. He wanted to push against the feet while the others seized the head from the opposite side and so the officer might be slowly eased off the needles. But the other two could not make up their minds to come; the condemned man actually turned away; the explorer had to go over to them and force them into position at the officer's head. And here, almost against his will, he had to look at the face of the corpse. It was as it had been in life; no sign was visible of the promised redemption; what the others had found in the machine the officer had not found; the lips were firmly pressed together, the eyes were open, with the same expression as in life, the look was calm and convinced, through the forehead went the point of the great iron spike.

As the explorer, with the soldier and the condemned man behind him, reached the first houses of the colony, the soldier pointed to one of them and said: "This is the teahouse."

In the ground floor of the house was a deep, low, cavernous space, its walls and ceiling blackened with smoke. It was open to the road all along its length. Although this teahouse was very little different from the other houses of the colony, which were all very dilapidated, even up to the Commandant's palatial headquarters, it made on the explorer the impression of a historic tradition of some kind, and he felt the power of past days. He went near to it, followed by his companions, right up between the empty tables which stood in the street before it, and breathed the cool, heavy air that came from the interior.

"The old man's buried here," said the soldier, "the priest wouldn't let him lie in the churchyard. Nobody knew where to bury him for a while, but in the end they buried him here. The officer never told you about that, for sure, because of course that's what he was most ashamed of. He even tried several times to dig the old man up by night, but he was always chased away." "Where is the grave?" asked the explorer, who found it impossible to believe the soldier. At once both of them, the soldier and the condemned man, ran before him pointing with outstretched hands in the direction where the grave should be. They led the explorer right up to the back wall, where guests were sitting at a few tables. They were apparently dock laborers, strong men with short, glistening, full black beards. None had a jacket, their shirts were torn, they were poor, humble creatures. As the explorer drew near, some of them got up, pressed close to the wall, and stared at him. "It's a foreigner," ran the whisper around him, "he wants to see the grave." They pushed one of the tables aside, and under it there was really a gravestone. It was a simple stone, low enough to be covered by a table. There was an inscription on it in very small letters, the explorer had to kneel down to read it. This was what it said: "Here rests the old Commandant. His adherents, who now must be nameless, have dug this grave and set up this stone. There is a prophecy that after a certain number of years the Commandant will rise again and lead his adherents from this house to recover the colony. Have faith and wait!" When the explorer had read this and risen to his feet he saw all the bystanders around him smiling, as if they too had read the inscription, had found it ridiculous and were expecting him to agree with them. The explorer ignored this, distributed a few coins among them, waiting till the table was pushed over the grave again, quitted the teahouse and made for the harbor.

The soldier and the condemned man had found some acquaintances in the teahouse, who detained them. But they must have soon shaken them off, for the explorer was only halfway down the long flight of steps leading to the boats when they came rushing after him. Probably they wanted to force him at the last minute to take them with him. While he was bargaining below with a ferryman to row him to the steamer, the two of them came headlong down the steps, in silence, for they did not dare to shout. But by the time they reached the foot of the steps the explorer was already in the boat, and the ferryman was just casting off from the shore. They could have jumped into the boat, but the explorer lifted a heavy knotted rope from the floor boards, threatened them with it and so kept them from attempting the leap.

QUESTIONS FOR DISCUSSION AND WRITING

1. How does the officer's explanation of the apparatus establish the conflicts in the story? When does the turning point occur in the story? How do the explorer's actions in the teahouse provide an ironic conclusion to the story?
2. What is the officer's motivation in the story? How does he contrast the policies of the old and new Commandant? In what ways does the explorer finally exchange roles with the officer?
3. How does the story reveal that all the characters are aliens in this setting? Why does the apparatus seem more important than the characters?

4. How does the flatly objective point of view intrigue and horrify the reader? How is this point of view explained by the explorer's admission that "he traveled only as an observer"?

5. What are the religious implications in the story concerning guilt, revelation through suffering, atonement, and redemption? What thematic point is made when the apparatus malfunctions and murders the officer?

52

D. H. LAWRENCE

The Rocking-Horse Winner

DAVID HERBERT LAWRENCE (1885–1930) was born in Eastwood, a coal mining town in the industrial midlands of England, and studied for two years at Nottingham University, where he obtained his teaching certificate. From 1909 to 1912, he worked as a school teacher at Croydon in south London, began writing romantic love poetry, and published three novels, *The White Peacock* (1911), *The Trespasser* (1912), and *Sons and Lovers* (1913). The last novel, largely autobiographical, was extremely successful, thus enabling Lawrence to give up his teaching position and to turn his full attention to writing. It was during this period that he met his wife, Frieda von Richthofen Weekley, the daughter of a Prussian nobleman. Although his marriage initiated one of Lawrence's most creative periods—*The Rainbow* (1915) and *Women in Love* (1920)—it also produced personal and political problems, many of the latter caused by Frieda's suspected ties to Germany during World War I. The Lawrences left England in 1919, traveling to Italy, Ceylon, Australia, Tahiti, Mexico, and finally New Mexico, where they settled on a primitive ranch near Taos. Lawrence's fiction during this period includes *Aaron's Rod* (1922), *Kangaroo* (1923), *The Plumed Serpent* (1926), and concludes with his most controversial novel, *Lady Chatterley's Lover* (1928). Lawrence returned to England briefly before moving to Vence on the French Riviera where he died of tuberculosis. His ashes were eventually returned to Taos. "The Rocking-Horse Winner," reprinted from the third volume of *The Complete Stories of D. H. Lawrence* (1934), tells of a young boy's attempt to win his mother's love. "The Horse Dealer's Daughter," reprinted from the second volume of *The Complete Stories* (1922), presents a young doctor's reluctant discovery of love. "Odour of Chrysanthemums," reprinted from the same volume, dramatizes a woman's response to family tragedy.

There was a woman who was beautiful, who started with all the advantages, yet she had no luck. She married for love, and the love turned to dust. She had bonny children, yet she felt they had been thrust upon her, and she could not love them. They looked at her coldly, as if they were finding fault with her. And hurriedly she felt she must cover up some fault in herself. Yet what it was that she must cover up she never knew. Nevertheless, when her children were present, she always felt the centre of her heart go hard. This troubled her, and in her manner she was all the more gentle and anxious for her children, as if she loved them very much. Only she herself knew that at the centre of her heart was a hard little place that could not feel love, no, not for anybody. Everybody else said of her: "She is such a good mother. She adores her children." Only she herself, and her children themselves, knew it was not so. They read it in each other's eyes.

There were a boy and two little girls. They lived in a pleasant house, with a garden, and they had discreet servants, and felt themselves superior to anyone in the neighbourhood.

Although they lived in style, they felt always an anxiety in the house. There was never enough money. The mother had a small income, and the father had a small income, but not nearly enough for the social position which they had to keep up. The father went into town to some office. But though he had good prospects, these prospects never materialised. There was always the grinding sense of the shortage of money, though the style was always kept up.

At last the mother said: "I will see if *I* can't make something." But she did not know where to begin. She racked her brains, and tried this thing and the other, but could not find anything successful. The failure made deep lines come into her face. Her children were growing up, they would have to go to school. There must be more money, there must be more money. The father, who was always very handsome and expensive in his tastes, seemed as if he never *would* be able to do anything worth doing. And the mother, who had a great belief in herself, did not succeed any better, and her tastes were just as expensive.

And so the house came to be haunted by the unspoken phrase: *There must be more money! There must be more money!* The children could hear it all the time, though nobody said it aloud. They heard it at Christmas, when the expensive and splendid toys filled the nursery. Behind the shining modern rocking-horse, behind the smart doll's house, a voice would start whispering: "There *must* be more money! There *must* be more money!" And the children would stop playing, to listen for a moment. They would look into each other's eyes, to see if they had all heard. And each one saw in the eyes of the other two that they too had heard. "There *must* be more money! There *must* be more money!"

It came whispering from the springs of the still-swaying rocking-horse, and even the horse, bending his wooden, champing head, heard it. The big doll, sitting so pink and smirking in her new pram, could hear it quite plainly, and seemed to be smirking all the more self-consciously because of it. The foolish puppy, too, that took the place of the teddy-bear, he was looking so extraordinarily foolish for no other reason but that he heard the secret whisper all over the house: "There *must* be more money!"

Yet nobody ever said it aloud. The whisper was everywhere, and therefore no one spoke it. Just as no one ever says: "We are breathing!" in spite of the fact that breath is coming and going all the time.

"Mother," said the boy Paul one day, "why don't we keep a car of our own? Why do we always use uncle's, or else a taxi?"

"Because we're the poor members of the family," said the mother.

"But why *are* we, mother?"

"Well—I suppose," she said slowly and bitterly, "it's because your father has no luck."

The boy was silent for some time.

"Is luck money, mother?" he asked, rather timidly.

"No, Paul. Not quite. It's what causes you to have money."

"Oh!" said Paul vaguely. "I thought when Uncle Oscar said *filthy lucker,* it meant money."

"*Filthy lucre* does mean money," said the mother. "But it's lucre, not luck."

"Oh!" said the boy. "Then what *is* luck, mother?"

"It's what causes you to have money. If you're lucky you have money. That's why it's better to be born lucky than rich. If you're rich, you may lose your money. But if you're lucky, you will always get more money."

"Oh! Will you? And is father not lucky?"

"Very unlucky, I should say," she said bitterly.

The boy watched her with unsure eyes.

"Why?" he asked.

"I don't know. Nobody ever knows why one person is lucky and another unlucky."

"Don't they? Nobody at all? Does *nobody* know?"

"Perhaps God. But He never tells."

"He ought to, then. And aren't you lucky either, mother?"

"I can't be, if I married an unlucky husband."

"But by yourself, aren't you?"

"I used to think I was, before I married. Now I think I am very unlucky indeed."

"Why?"

"Well—never mind! Perhaps I'm not really," she said.

The child looked at her to see if she meant it. But he saw, by the lines of her mouth, that she was only trying to hide something from him.

"Well, anyhow," he said stoutly, "I'm a lucky person."

"Why?" said his mother, with a sudden laugh.

He stared at her. He didn't even know why he had said it.

"God told me," he asserted, brazening it out.

"I hope He did, dear!" she said, again with a laugh, but rather bitter.

"He did, mother!"

"Excellent!" said the mother, using one of her husband's exclamations.

The boy saw she did not believe him; or rather, that she paid no attention to his assertion. This angered him somewhat, and made him want to compel her attention.

He went off by himself, vaguely, in a childish way, seeking for the clue to "luck." Absorbed, taking no heed of other people, he went about with a sort of stealth, seeking inwardly for luck. He wanted luck, he wanted it, he wanted it. When the two girls were playing dolls in the nursery, he would sit on his big rocking-horse, charging madly into space, with a frenzy that made the little girls peer at him uneasily. Wildly the horse careered, the waving dark hair of the boy tossed, his eyes had a strange glare in them. The little girls dared not speak to him.

When he had ridden to the end of his mad little journey, he climbed down and stood in front of his rocking-horse, staring fixedly into its lowered face. Its red mouth was slightly open, its big eye was wide and glassy-bright.

"Now!" he would silently command the snorting steed. "Now, take me to where there is luck! Now take me!"

And he would slash the horse on the neck with the little whip he had asked Uncle Oscar for. He *knew* the horse could take him to where there was luck, if only he forced it. So he would mount again and start on his furious ride, hoping at last to get there. He knew he could get there.

"You'll break your horse, Paul!" said the nurse.

"He's always riding like that! I wish he'd leave off!" said his elder sister Joan.

But he only glared down on them in silence. Nurse gave him up. She could make nothing of him. Anyhow, he was growing beyond her.

One day his mother and his Uncle Oscar came in when he was on one of his furious rides. He did not speak to them.

"Hallo, you young jockey! Riding a winner?" said his uncle.

"Aren't you growing too big for a rocking-horse? You're not a very little boy any longer, you know," said his mother.

But Paul only gave a blue glare from his big, rather close-set eyes. He would speak to nobody when he was in full tilt. His mother watched him with an anxious expression on her face.

At last he suddenly stopped forcing his horse into the mechanical gallop and slid down.

"Well, I got there!" he announced fiercely, his blue eyes still flaring, and his sturdy long legs straddling apart.

"Where did you get to?" asked his mother.

"Where I wanted to go," he flared back at her.

"That's right, son!" said Uncle Oscar. "Don't you stop till you get there. What's the horse's name?"

"He doesn't have a name," said the boy.

"Gets on without all right?" asked the uncle.

"Well, he has different names. He was called Sansovino last week."

"Sansovino, eh? Won the Ascot. How did you know this name?"

"He always talks about horse-races with Bassett," said Joan.

The uncle was delighted to find that his small nephew was posted with all the racing news. Bassett, the young gardener, who had been wounded in the left foot in the war and had got his present job through Oscar Cresswell, whose batman he had been, was a perfect blade of the "turf." He lived in the racing events, and the small boy lived with him.

Oscar Cresswell got it all from Bassett.

"Master Paul comes and asks me, so I can't do more than tell him, sir," said Bassett, his face terribly serious, as if he were speaking of religious matters.

"And does he ever put anything on a horse he fancies?"

"Well—I don't want to give him away—he's a young sport, a fine sport, sir. Would you mind asking him yourself? He sort of takes a pleasure in it, and perhaps he'd feel I was giving him away, sir, if you don't mind."

Bassett was serious as a church.

The uncle went back to his nephew and took him off for a ride in the car.

"Say, Paul, old man, do you ever put anything on a horse?" the uncle asked.

The boy watched the handsome man closely.

"Why, do you think I oughtn't to?" he parried.

"Not a bit of it! I thought perhaps you might give me a tip for the Lincoln."

The car sped on into the country, going down to Uncle Oscar's place in Hampshire.

"Honour bright?" said the nephew.

"Honour bright, son!" said the uncle.

"Well, then, Daffodil."

"Daffodil! I doubt it, sonny. What about Mirza?"

"I only know the winner," said the boy. "That's Daffodil."

"Daffodil, eh?"

There was a pause. Daffodil was an obscure horse comparatively.

"Uncle!"

"Yes, son?"

"You won't let it go any further, will you? I promised Bassett."

"Bassett be damned, old man! What's he got to do with it?"

"We're partners. We've been partners from the first. Uncle, he lent me my first five shillings, which I lost. I promised him, honour bright, it was only between me and him; only you gave me that ten-shilling note I started winning with, so I thought you were lucky. You won't let it go any further, will you?"

The boy gazed at his uncle from those big, hot, blue eyes, set rather close together. The uncle stirred and laughed uneasily.

"Right you are, son! I'll keep your tip private. Daffodil, eh? How much are you putting on him?"

"All except twenty pounds," said the boy. "I keep that in reserve."

The uncle thought it a good joke.

"You keep twenty pounds in reserve, do you, you young romancer? What are you betting, then?"

"I'm betting three hundred," said the boy gravely. "But it's between you and me, Uncle Oscar! Honour bright?"

The uncle burst into a roar of laughter.

"It's between you and me all right, you young Nat Gould," he said, laughing. "But where's your three hundred?"

"Bassett keeps it for me. We're partners."

"You are, are you! And what is Bassett putting on Daffodil?"

"He won't go quite as high as I do, I expect. Perhaps he'll go a hundred and fifty."

"What, pennies?" laughed the uncle.

"Pounds," said the child, with a surprised look at his uncle. "Bassett keeps a bigger reserve than I do."

Between wonder and amusement Uncle Oscar was silent. He pursued the matter no further, but he determined to take his nephew with him to the Lincoln races.

"Now, son," he said, "I'm putting twenty on Mirza, and I'll put five on for you on any horse you fancy. What's your pick?"

"Daffodil, uncle."

"No, not the fiver on Daffodil!"

"I should if it was my own fiver," said the child.

"Good! Good! Right you are! A fiver for me and a fiver for you on Daffodil."

The child had never been to a race-meeting before, and his eyes were blue fire. He pursed his mouth tight and watched. A Frenchman just in front had put his money on Lancelot. Wild with excitement, he flayed his arms up and down, yelling *"Lancelot! Lancelot!"* in his French accent.

Daffodil came in first, Lancelot second, Mirza third. The child, flushed and with eyes blazing, was curiously serene. His uncle brought him four five-pound notes, four to one.

"What am I to do with these?" he cried, waving them before the boy's eyes.

"I suppose we'll talk to Bassett," said the boy. "I expect I have fifteen hundred now; and twenty in reserve; and this twenty."

His uncle studied him for some moments.

"Look here, son!" he said. "You're not serious about Bassett and that fifteen hundred, are you?"

"Yes, I am. But it's between you and me, uncle. Honour bright?"

"Honour bright all right, son! But I must talk to Bassett."

"If you'd like to be a partner, uncle, with Bassett and me, we could all be partners. Only, you'd have to promise, honour bright, uncle, not to let it go beyond us three. Bassett and I are lucky, and you must be lucky, because it was your ten shillings I started winning with. . . ."

Uncle Oscar took both Bassett and Paul into Richmond Park for an afternoon, and there they talked.

"It's like this, you see, sir," Bassett said. "Master Paul would get me talking about racing events, spinning yarns, you know, sir. And he was always keen on knowing if I'd made or if I'd lost. It's about a year since, now, that I put five shillings on Blush of Dawn for him; and we lost. Then the luck turned, with that ten shillings he had from you: that we put on Singhalese. And since that time, it's been pretty steady, all things considering. What do you say, Master Paul?"

"We're all right when we're sure," said Paul. "It's when we're not quite sure that we go down."

"Oh, but we're careful then," said Bassett.

"But when are you *sure*?" smiled Uncle Oscar.

"It's Master Paul, sir," said Bassett in a secret, religious voice. "It's as if he had it from heaven. Like Daffodil, now, for the Lincoln. That was as sure as eggs."

"Did you put anything on Daffodil?" asked Oscar Cresswell.

"Yes, sir. I made my bet."

"And my nephew?"

Bassett was obstinately silent, looking at Paul.

"I made twelve hundred, didn't I, Bassett? I told uncle I was putting three hundred on Daffodil."

"That's right," said Bassett, nodding.

"But where's the money?" asked the uncle.

"I keep it safe locked up, sir. Master Paul he can have it any minute he likes to ask for it."

"What, fifteen hundred pounds?"

"And twenty! And *forty,* that is, with the twenty he made on the course."

"It's amazing!" said the uncle.

"If Master Paul offers you to be partners, sir, I would, if I were you: if you'll excuse me," said Bassett.

Oscar Cresswell thought about it.

"I'll see the money," he said.

They drove home again, and, sure enough, Bassett came round to the garden-house with fifteen hundred pounds in notes. The twenty pounds reserve was left with Joe Glee, in the Turf Commission deposit.

"You see, it's all right, uncle, when I'm *sure*! Then we go strong, for all we're worth. Don't we, Bassett?"

"We do that, Master Paul."

"And when are you sure?" said the uncle, laughing.

"Oh, well, sometimes I'm *absolutely* sure, like about Daffodil," said the boy; "and sometimes I have an idea; and sometimes I haven't even an idea, have I, Bassett? Then we're careful, because we mostly go down."

"You do, do you! And when you're sure, like about Daffodil, what makes you sure, sonny?"

"Oh, well, I don't know," said the boy uneasily. "I'm sure, you know, uncle; that's all."

"It's as if he had it from heaven, sir," Bassett reiterated.

"I should say so!" said the uncle.

But he became a partner. And when the Leger was coming on Paul was "sure" about Lively Spark, which was a quite inconsiderable horse. The boy insisted on putting a thousand on the horse, Bassett went for five hundred, and Oscar Cresswell two hundred. Lively Spark came in first, and the betting had been ten to one against him. Paul had made ten thousand.

"You see," he said, "I was absolutely sure of him."

Even Oscar Cresswell had cleared two thousand.

"Look here, son," he said, "this sort of thing makes me nervous."

"It needn't, uncle! Perhaps I shan't be sure again for a long time."

"But what are you going to do with your money?" asked the uncle.

"Of course," said the boy, "I started it for mother. She said she had no luck, because father is unlucky, so I thought if *I* was lucky, it might stop whispering."

"What might stop whispering?"

"Our house. I *hate* our house for whispering."

"What does it whisper?"

"Why—why"—the boy fidgeted—"why, I don't know. But it's always short of money, you know, uncle."

"I know it, son, I know it."

"You know people send mother writs, don't you, uncle?"

"I'm afraid I do," said the uncle.

"And then the house whispers, like people laughing at you behind your back. It's awful, that is! I thought if I was lucky——"

"You might stop it," added the uncle.

The boy watched him with big blue eyes, that had an uncanny cold fire in them, and he said never a word.

"Well, then!" said the uncle. "What are we doing?"

"I shouldn't like mother to know I was lucky," said the boy.

"Why not, son?"

"She'd stop me."

"I don't think she would."

"Oh!"—and the boy writhed in an odd way—"I *don't* want her to know, uncle."

"All right, son! We'll manage it without her knowing."

They managed it very easily. Paul, at the other's suggestion, handed over five thousand pounds to his uncle, who deposited it with the family lawyer, who was then to inform Paul's mother that a relative had put five thousand pounds into his hands, which sum was to be paid out a thousand pounds at a time, on the mother's birthday, for the next five years.

"So she'll have a birthday present of a thousand pounds for five successive years," said Uncle Oscar. "I hope it won't make it all the harder for her later."

Paul's mother had her birthday in November. The house had been "whispering" worse than ever lately, and, even in spite of his luck, Paul could not bear up against it. He was very anxious to see the effect of the birthday letter, telling his mother about the thousand pounds.

When there were no visitors, Paul now took his meals with his parents, as he was beyond the nursery control. His mother went into town nearly every day. She had discovered that she had an odd knack of sketching furs and dress materials, so she worked secretly in the studio of a friend who was the chief "artist" for the leading drapers. She drew the figures of ladies in furs and ladies in silk and sequins for the newspaper advertisements. This young woman artist earned several thousand pounds a year, but Paul's mother only made several hundred, and she was again dissatisfied. She so wanted to be first in something, and she did not succeed, even in making sketches for drapery advertisements.

She was down to breakfast on the morning of her birthday. Paul watched her face as she read her letters. He knew the lawyer's letter. As his mother read it, her face hardened and became more expressionless. Then a cold, determined look came on her mouth. She hid the letter under the pile of others, and said not a word about it.

"Didn't you have anything nice in the post for your birthday, mother?" said Paul.

"Quite moderately nice," she said, her voice cold and absent.

She went away to town without saying more.

But in the afternoon Uncle Oscar appeared. He said Paul's mother had had a long interview with the lawyer, asking if the whole five thousand could not be advanced at once, as she was in debt.

"What do you think, uncle?" said the boy.

"I leave it to you, son."

"Oh, let her have it, then! We can get some more with the other," said the boy.

"A bird in the hand is worth two in the bush, laddie!" said Uncle Oscar.

"But I'm sure to *know* for the Grand National; or the Lincolnshire; or else the Derby. I'm sure to know for *one* of them," said Paul.

So Uncle Oscar signed the agreement, and Paul's mother touched the whole five thousand. Then something very curious happened. The voices in the house suddenly went mad, like a chorus of frogs on a spring evening. There were certain new furnishings, and Paul had a tutor. He was *really* going to Eton, his father's school, in the following autumn. There were flowers in the winter, and a blossoming of the luxury Paul's mother had been used to. And yet the voices in the house, behind the sprays of mimosa and almond blossom, and from under the piles of iridescent cushions, simply trilled and screamed in a sort of ecstacy: "There *must* be more money! Oh-h-h; there *must* be more money. Oh, now, now-w! Now-w-w—there *must* be more money!—more than ever! More than ever!"

It frightened Paul terribly. He studied away at his Latin and Greek with his tutor. But his intense hours were spent with Bassett. The Grand National had gone by: he had not "known," and had lost a hundred pounds. Summer was at hand. He was in agony for the Lincoln. But even for the Lincoln he didn't "know," and he lost fifty pounds. He became wild-eyed and strange, as if something were going to explode in him.

"Let it alone, son! Don't you bother about it!" urged Uncle Oscar. But it was as if the boy couldn't really hear what his uncle was saying.

"I've got to know for the Derby! I've got to know for the Derby!" the child reiterated, his big blue eyes blazing with a sort of madness.

His mother noticed how overwrought he was.

"You'd better go to the seaside. Wouldn't you like to go now to the seaside, instead of waiting? I think you'd better," she said, looking down at him anxiously, her heart curiously heavy because of him.

But the child lifted his uncanny blue eyes.

"I couldn't possibly go before the Derby, mother!" he said. "I couldn't possibly!"

"Why not?" she said, her voice becoming heavy when she was opposed. "Why not? You can still go from the seaside to see the Derby with your Uncle Oscar, if that's what you wish. No need for you to wait here. Besides, I think you care too much about these races. It's a bad sign. My family has been a gambling family, and you won't know till you grow up how much damage it has done. But it has done damage. I shall have to send Bassett away, and ask Uncle Oscar not to talk racing to you, unless you promise to be reasonable about it: go away to the seaside and forget it. You're all nerves!"

"I'll do what you like, mother, so long as you don't send me away till after the Derby," the boy said.

"Send you away from where? Just from this house?"

"Yes," he said, gazing at her.

"Why, you curious child, what makes you care about this house so much, suddenly? I never knew you loved it."

He gazed at her without speaking. He had a secret within a secret, something he had not divulged, even to Bassett or to his Uncle Oscar.

But his mother, after standing undecided and a little bit sullen for some moments, said:

"Very well, then! Don't go to the seaside till after the Derby, if you don't wish it. But promise me you won't let your nerves go to pieces. Promise you won't think so much about horse-racing and *events,* as you call them!"

"Oh no," said the boy casually. "I won't think much about them, mother. You needn't worry. I wouldn't worry, mother, if I were you."

"If you were me and I were you," said his mother, "I wonder what we *should* do!"

"But you know you needn't worry, mother, don't you?" the boy repeated.

"I should be awfully glad to know it," she said wearily.

"Oh, well, you *can,* you know. I mean, you *ought* to know you needn't worry," he insisted.

"Ought I? Then I'll see about it," she said.

Paul's secret of secrets was his wooden horse, that which had no name. Since he was emancipated from a nurse and a nursery-governess, he had had his rocking-horse removed to his own bedroom at the top of the house.

"Surely you're too big for a rocking-horse!" his mother had remonstrated.

"Well, you see, mother, till I can have a *real* horse, I like to have *some* sort of animal about," had been his quaint answer.

"Do you feel he keeps you company?" she laughed.

"Oh yes! He's very good, he always keeps me company, when I'm there," said Paul.

So the horse, rather shabby, stood in an arrested prance in the boy's bedroom.

The Derby was drawing near, and the boy grew more and more tense. He hardly heard what was spoken to him, he was very frail, and his eyes were really uncanny. His mother had sudden strange seizures of uneasiness about him. Sometimes, for half an hour, she would feel a sudden anxiety about him that was almost anguish. She wanted to rush to him at once, and know he was safe.

Two nights before the Derby, she was at a big party in town, when one of her rushes of anxiety about her boy, her first-born, gripped her heart till she could hardly speak. She fought with the feeling, might and main, for she believed in common sense. But it was too strong. She had to leave the dance and go downstairs to telephone to the country. The children's nursery-governess was terribly surprised and startled at being rung up in the night.

"Are the children all right, Miss Wilmot?"

"Oh yes, they are quite all right."

"Master Paul? Is he all right?"

"He went to bed as right as a trivet. Shall I run up and look at him?"

"No," said Paul's mother reluctantly. "No! Don't trouble. It's all right. Don't sit up. We shall be home fairly soon." She did not want her son's privacy intruded upon.

"Very good," said the governess.

It was about one o'clock when Paul's mother and father drove up to their house. All was still. Paul's mother went to her room and slipped off her white fur cloak. She had told her maid not to wait up for her. She heard her husband downstairs, mixing a whisky and soda.

And then, because of the strange anxiety at her heart, she stole upstairs to her son's room. Noiselessly she went along the upper corridor. Was there a faint noise? What was it?

She stood, with arrested muscles, outside his door, listening. There was a strange, heavy, and yet not loud noise. Her heart stood still. It was a soundless noise, yet rushing and powerful. Something huge, in violent, hushed motion. What was it? What in God's name was it? She ought to know. She felt that she knew the noise. She knew what it was.

Yet she could not place it. She couldn't say what it was. And on and on it went, like a madness.

Softly, frozen with anxiety and fear, she turned the doorhandle.

The room was dark. Yet in the space near the window, she heard and saw something plunging to and fro. She gazed in fear and amazement.

Then suddenly she switched on the light, and saw her son, in his green pyjamas, madly surging on the rocking-horse. The blaze of light suddenly lit him up, as he urged the wooden horse, and lit her up, as she stood, blonde, in her dress of pale green and crystal, in the doorway.

"Paul!" she cried. "Whatever are you doing?"

"It's Malabar!" he screamed in a powerful, strange voice. "It's Malabar!"

His eyes blazed at her for one strange and senseless second, as he ceased urging his wooden horse. Then he fell with a crash to the ground, and she, all her tormented motherhood flooding upon her, rushed to gather him up.

But he was unconscious, and unconscious he remained, with some brain-fever. He talked and tossed, and his mother sat stonily by his side.

"Malabar! It's Malabar! Bassett, Bassett, I *know*! It's Malabar!"

So the child cried, trying to get up and urge the rocking-horse that gave him his inspiration.

"What does he mean by Malabar?" asked the heart-frozen mother.

"I don't know," said the father stonily.

"What does he mean by Malabar?" she asked her brother Oscar.

"It's one of the horses running for the Derby," was the answer.

And, in spite of himself, Oscar Cresswell spoke to Bassett, and himself put a thousand on Malabar: at fourteen to one.

The third day of the illness was critical: they were waiting for a change. The boy, with his rather long, curly hair, was tossing ceaselessly on the pillow. He neither slept nor regained consciousness, and his eyes were like blue stones. His mother sat, feeling her heart had gone, turned actually into a stone.

In the evening, Oscar Cresswell did not come, but Bassett sent a message, saying could he come up for one moment, just one moment? Paul's mother was very angry at the intrusion, but on second thoughts she agreed. The boy was the same. Perhaps Bassett might bring him to consciousness.

The gardener, a shortish fellow with a little brown moustache and sharp little brown eyes, tiptoed into the room, touched his imaginary cap to Paul's mother, and stole to the bedside, staring with glittering, smallish eyes at the tossing, dying child.

"Master Paul!" he whispered. "Master Paul! Malabar came in first all right, a clean win. I did as you told me. You've made over seventy thousand pounds, you have; you've got over eighty thousand. Malabar came in all right, Master Paul."

"Malabar! Malabar! Did I say Malabar, mother? Did I say Malabar? Do you think I'm lucky, mother? I knew Malabar, didn't I? Over eighty thousand pounds! I call that lucky, don't you, mother? Over eighty thousand pounds? I knew, didn't I know I knew? Malabar came in all right. If I ride my horse till I'm sure, then I tell you, Bassett, you can go as high as you like. Did you go for all you were worth, Bassett?"

"I went a thousand on it, Master Paul."

"I never told you, mother, that if I can ride my horse, and *get there,* then I'm absolutely sure—oh, absolutely! Mother, did I ever tell you? I *am* lucky!"

"No, you never did," said his mother.

But the boy died in the night.

And even as he lay dead, his mother heard her brother's voice saying to her: "My God, Hester, you're eighty-odd thousand to the good, and a poor devil of a son to the bad. But, poor devil, poor devil, he's best gone out of a life where he rides his rocking-horse to find a winner."

QUESTIONS FOR DISCUSSION AND WRITING

1. How does the opening paragraph establish the context for the action of the story? How does Paul's birthday gift to his mother bring the story to its climax? How do Uncle Oscar's final words resolve the conflicts in the plot?
2. How does Lawrence characterize Paul's mother and father? How does Paul characterize himself? What qualities does Uncle Oscar possess that prompt Paul to include him as a partner?
3. In what sense is the house haunted? How does it provide the setting necessary for Paul's knowledge? Where does Paul's rocking horse take him?
4. What would have been the effect of allowing Paul to tell his own story? Compare and contrast the mother's and Uncle Oscar's point of view toward Paul.
5. What does this story reveal about luck? What does Paul hope to win when he wins?

53
D. H. LAWRENCE
The Horse Dealer's Daughter

Well, Mabel, and what are you going to do with yourself?" asked Joe, with foolish flippancy. He felt quite safe himself. Without listening for an answer, he turned aside, worked a grain of tobacco to the tip of his tongue, and spat it out. He did not care about anything, since he felt safe himself.

The three brothers and the sister sat round the desolate breakfast table, attempting some sort of desultory consultation. The morning's post had given the final tap to the family fortune, and all was over. The dreary dining-room itself, with its heavy mahogany furniture, looked as if it were waiting to be done away with.

But the consultation amounted to nothing. There was a strange air of ineffectuality about the three men, as they sprawled at table, smoking and reflecting vaguely on their own condition. The girl was alone, a rather short, sullen-looking young woman of twenty-seven. She did not share the same life as her brothers. She would have been good-looking, save for the impassive fixity of her face, "bull-dog," as her brothers called it.

There was a confused tramping of horses' feet outside. The three men all sprawled round in their chairs to watch. Beyond the dark hollybushes that separated the strip of lawn from the high-road, they could see a cavalcade of shire horses swinging out of their own yard, being taken for exercise. This was the last time. These were the last horses that would go through their hands. The young men watched with critical, callous looks. They were all frightened at the collapse of their lives, and the sense of disaster in which they were involved left them no inner freedom.

Yet they were three fine, well-set fellows enough. Joe, the eldest, was a man of thirty-three, broad and handsome in a hot, flushed way. His face was red, he twisted his black moustache over a thick finger, his eyes were shallow and restless. He had a sensual way of uncovering his teeth when he laughed, and his bearing was stupid. Now he watched the horses with a glazed look of helplessness in his eyes, a certain stupor of downfall.

The great draught-horses swung past. They were tied head to tail, four of them, and they heaved along to where a lane branched off from the highroad, planting their great hoofs floutingly in the fine black mud, swinging their great rounded haunches sumptuously, and trotting a few sudden steps as they were led into the lane, round the corner. Every movement showed a massive, slumbrous strength, and stupidity which held them in subjection. The groom at the head looked back, jerking the leading rope. And the cavalcade moved out of sight up the lane, the tail of the last horse bobbed up tight and stiff, held out taut from the swinging great haunches as they rocked behind the hedges in a motion like sleep.

Joe watched with glazed hopeless eyes. The horses were almost like his own body to him. He felt he was done for now. Luckily he was engaged to a woman as old as himself, and therefore her father, who was steward of a neighbouring estate, would provide him with a job. He would marry and go into harness. His life was over, he would be a subject animal now.

He turned uneasily aside, the retreating steps of the horses echoing in his ears. Then, with foolish restlessness, he reached for the scraps of bacon-rind from the plates, and making a faint whistling sound, flung them to the terrier that lay against the fender. He watched the dog swallow them, and waited till the creature looked into his eyes. Then a faint grin came on his face, and in a high, foolish voice he said:

"You won't get much more bacon, shall you, you little bitch?"

The dog faintly and dismally wagged its tail, then lowered its haunches, circled round, and lay down again.

There was another helpless silence at the table. Joe sprawled uneasily in his seat, not willing to go till the family conclave was dissolved. Fred Henry, the second brother, was erect, clean-limbed, alert. He had watched the passing of the horses with more *sang-froid*. If he was an animal, like Joe, he was an animal which controls, not one which is controlled. He was master of any horse, and he carried himself with a well-tempered air of mastery. But he was not master of the situations of life. He pushed his coarse brown moustache upwards, off his lips, and glanced irritably at his sister, who sat impassive and inscrutable.

"You'll go and stop with Lucy for a bit, shan't you?" he asked. The girl did not answer.

"I don't see what else you can do," persisted Fred Henry.

"Go as a skivvy," Joe interpolated laconically.

The girl did not move a muscle.

"If I was her, I should go in for training for a nurse," said Malcolm, the youngest of them all. He was the baby of the family, a young man of twenty-two, with a fresh, jaunty *museau*.

But Mabel did not take any notice of him. They had talked at her and round her for so many years, that she hardly heard them at all.

The marble clock on the mantelpiece softly chimed the half-hour, the dog rose uneasily from the hearthrug and looked at the party at the breakfast table. But still they sat on in ineffectual conclave.

"Oh, all right," said Joe suddenly, apropos of nothing. "I'll get a move on."

He pushed back his chair, straddled his knees with a downward jerk, to get them free, in horsey fashion, and went to the fire. Still he did not go out of the room; he was curious to know what the others would do or say. He began to charge his pipe, looking down at the dog and saying, in a high, affected voice:

"Going wi' me? Going wi' me are ter? Tha'rt goin' further than tha counts on just now, dost hear?"

The dog faintly wagged its tail, the man stuck out his jaw and covered his pipe with his hands, and puffed intently, losing himself in the tobacco, looking down all the while at the dog with an absent brown eye. The dog looked up at him in mournful distrust. Joe stood with his knees stuck out, in real horsey fashion.

"Have you had a letter from Lucy?" Fred Henry asked of his sister.

"Last week," came the neutral reply.

"And what does she say?"

There was no answer.

"Does she *ask* you to go and stop there?" persisted Fred Henry.

"She says I can if I like."

"Well, then, you'd better. Tell her you'll come on Monday."

This was received in silence.

"That's what you'll do then, is it?" said Fred Henry, in some exasperation.

But she made no answer. There was a silence of futility and irritation in the room. Malcolm grinned fatuously.

"You'll have to make up your mind between now and next Wednesday," said Joe loudly, "or else find yourself lodgings on the kerbstone."

The face of the young woman darkened, but she sat on immutable.

"Here's Jack Fergusson!" exclaimed Malcolm, who was looking aimlessly out of the window.

"Where?" exclaimed Joe, loudly.

"Just gone past."

"Coming in?"

Malcolm craned his neck to see the gate.

"Yes," he said.

There was a silence. Mabel sat on like one condemned, at the head of the table. Then a whistle was heard from the kitchen. The dog got up and barked sharply. Joe opened the door and shouted:

"Come on."

After a moment a young man entered. He was muffled up in overcoat and a purple woollen scarf, and his tweed cap, which he did not remove, was pulled down on his head. He was of medium height, his face was rather long and pale, his eyes looked tired.

"Hello, Jack! Well, Jack!" exclaimed Malcolm and Joe. Fred Henry merely said, "Jack."

"What's doing?" asked the newcomer, evidently addressing Fred Henry.

"Same. We've got to be out by Wednesday. Got a cold?"

"I have—got it bad, too."

"Why don't you stop in?"

"*Me* stop in? When I can't stand on my legs, perhaps I shall have a chance." The young man spoke huskily. He had a slight Scotch accent.

"It's a knock-out, isn't it?" said Joe, boisterously, "if a doctor goes round croaking with a cold. Looks bad for the patients, doesn't it?"

The young doctor looked at him slowly.

"Anything the matter with *you,* then?" he asked sarcastically.

"Not as I know of. Damn your eyes, I hope not. Why?"

"I thought you were very concerned about the patients, wondered if you might be one yourself."

"Damn it, no, I've never been patient to no flaming doctor, and hope I never shall be," returned Joe.

At this point Mabel rose from the table, and they all seemed to become aware of her existence. She began putting the dishes together. The young doctor looked at her, but did not address her. He had not greeted her. She went out of the room with the tray, her face impassive and unchanged.

"When are you off then, all of you?" asked the doctor.

"I'm catching the eleven-forty," replied Malcolm. "Are you goin' down wi' th' trap, Joe?"

"Yes, I've told you I am going down wi' th' trap, haven't I?"

"We'd better be getting her in then. So long, Jack, if I don't see you before I go," said Malcolm, shaking hands.

He went out, followed by Joe, who seemed to have his tail between his legs.

"Well, this is the devil's own," exclaimed the doctor, when he was left alone with Fred Henry. "Going before Wednesday, are you?"

"That's the orders," replied the other.

"Where, to Northampton?"

"That's it."

"The devil!" exclaimed Fergusson, with quiet chagrin.

And there was silence between the two.

"All settled up, are you?" asked Fergusson.

"About."

There was another pause.

"Well, I shall miss yer, Freddy, boy," said the young doctor.

"And I shall miss thee, Jack," returned the other.

"Miss you like hell," mused the doctor.

Fred Henry turned aside. There was nothing to say. Mabel came in again, to finish clearing the table.

"What are *you* to do, then, Miss Pervin?" asked Fergusson. "Going to your sister's, are you?"

Mabel looked at him with her steady, dangerous eyes, that always made him uncomfortable, unsettling his superficial ease.

"No," she said.

"Well, what in the name of fortune are *you* going to do? Say what you mean to do," cried Fred Henry, with futile intensity.

But she only averted her head, and continued her work. She folded the white tablecloth, and put on the chenile cloth.

"The sulkiest bitch that ever trod!" muttered her brother.

But she finished her task with perfectly impassive face, the young doctor watching her interestedly all the while. Then she went out.

Fred Henry stared after her, clenching his lips, his blue eyes fixing in sharp antagonism, as he made a grimace of sour exasperation.

"You could bray her into bits, and that's all you'd get out of her," he said in a small, narrowed tone.

The doctor smiled faintly.

"What's she *going* to do, then?" he asked.

"Strike me if I know!" returned the other.

There was a pause. Then the doctor stirred.

"I'll be seeing you to-night, shall I?" he said to his friend.

"Ay—where's it to be? Are we going over to Jessdale?"

"I don't know. I've got such a cold on me. I'll come round to the Moon and Stars, anyway."

"Let Lizzie and May miss their night for once, eh?"

"That's it—if I feel as I do now."

"All's one—"

The two young men went through the passage and down to the back door together. The house was large, but it was servantless now, and desolate. At the back was a small bricked house-yard, and beyond that a big square, gravelled fine and red, and having stables on two sides. Sloping, dank, winter-dark fields stretched away on the open sides.

But the stables were empty. Joseph Pervin, the father of the family, had been a man of no education, who had become a fairly large horse dealer. The stables had been full of horses, there was a great turmoil and come-and-go of horses and of dealers and grooms. Then the kitchen was full of servants. But of late things had declined. The old man had married a second time, to retrieve his fortunes. Now he was dead and everything was gone to the dogs, there was nothing but debt and threatening.

For months, Mabel had been servantless in the big house, keeping the home together in penury for her ineffectual brothers. She had kept house for ten years. But previously it was with unstinted means. Then, however brutal and coarse everything was, the sense of money had kept her proud, confident. The men might be foul-mouthed, the women in the kitchen might have bad reputations, her brothers might have illegitimate children. But so long as there was money, the girl felt herself established and brutally proud, reserved.

No company came to the house, save dealers and coarse men. Mabel had no associates of her own sex, after her sister went away. But she did not mind. She went regularly to church, she attended to her father. And she lived in the memory of her mother, who had died when she was fourteen, and whom she had loved. She had loved her father, too, in a different way, depending upon him, and feeling secure in him, until at the age of fifty-four he married again. And then she had set hard against him. Now he had died and left them all hopelessly in debt.

She had suffered badly during the period of poverty. Nothing, however, could shake the curious sullen, animal pride that dominated each member of the family. Now, for Mabel, the end had come. Still she would not cast about her. She would follow her own way just the same. She would always hold the keys of her own situation. Mindless and persistent, she endured from day to day. What should she think? Why should she answer anybody? It was enough that this was the end and there was no way out. She need not pass any more darkly along the main street of the small town, avoiding every eye. She need not demean herself any more, going into the shops and buying the cheapest food. This was at an end. She thought of nobody, not even of herself. Mindless and persistent, she seemed in a sort of ecstasy to be coming nearer to her fulfilment, her own glorification, approaching her dead mother, who was glorified.

In the afternoon she took a little bag, with shears and sponge and a small scrubbing brush, and went out. It was a grey, wintry day, with saddened, dark green fields and an atmosphere blackened by the smoke of foundries not far off. She went quickly, darkly along the causeway, heeding nobody, through the town to the churchyard.

There she always felt secure, as if no one could see her, although as a matter of fact she was exposed to the stare of every one who passed along under the churchyard wall. Nevertheless, once under the shadow of the great looming church, among the graves, she felt immune from the world, reserved within the thick churchyard wall as in another country.

Carefully she clipped the grass from the grave, and arranged the pinky white, small chrysanthemums in the tin cross. When this was done, she took an empty jar from a neighbouring grave, brought water, and carefully, most scrupulously sponged the marble head-stone and the coping-stone.

It gave her sincere satisfaction to do this. She felt in immediate contact with the world of her mother. She took minute pains, went through the park in a state bordering on pure happiness, as if in performing this task she came into a subtle, intimate connection with her mother. For the life she followed here in the world was far less real than the world of death she inherited from her mother.

The doctor's house was just by the church. Fergusson, being a mere hired assistant, was slave to the country-side. As he hurried now to attend to the out-patients in the surgery, glancing across the graveyard with his quick eye, he saw the girl at her task at the grave. She seemed so intent and remote, it was like looking into another world. Some mystical element was touched in him. He slowed down as he walked, watching her as if spell-bound.

She lifted her eyes, feeling him looking. Their eyes met. And each looked away again at once, each feeling, in some way, found out by the other. He lifted his cap and passed on down the road. There remained distinct in his consciousness, like a vision, the memory of her face, lifted from the tombstone in the churchyard, and looking at him with slow, large, portentous eyes. It *was* portentous, her face. It seemed to mesmerize him. There was a heavy power in her eyes which laid hold of his whole being, as if he had drunk some powerful drug. He had been feeling weak and done before. Now the life came back into him, he felt delivered from his own fretted, daily self.

He finished his duties at the surgery as quickly as might be, hastily filling up the bottle of the waiting people with cheap drugs. Then, in perpetual haste, he set off again to visit several cases in another part of his round, before tea-time. At all times he preferred to walk if he could, not particularly when he was not well. He fancied the motion restored him.

The afternoon was falling. It was grey, deadened, and wintry, with a slow, moist, heavy coldness sinking in and deadening all the faculties. But why should he think or notice? He hastily climbed the hill and turned across the dark green fields, following the black cinder-track. In the distance, across a shallow dip in the country, the small town was clustered like smouldering ash, a tower, a spire, a heap of low, raw, extinct houses. And on the nearest fringe of the town, sloping into the dip, was Oldmeadow, the Pervins' house. He could see the stables and the outbuildings distinctly, as they lay towards him on the slope. Well, he would not go there many more times! Another resource would be lost to him, another place gone: the only company he cared for in the alien, ugly little town he was losing. Nothing but work, drudgery, constant hastening from dwelling to dwelling among the colliers and the ironworkers. It wore him out, but at the same time he had a craving for it. It was a stimulant to him to be in the homes of the working people, moving as it were through the innermost body of their life. His nerves were excited and gratified. He could come so near, into the very lives of the rough, inarticulate, powerfully emotional men and women. He grumbled, he said he hated the hellish hole. But as a matter of fact it excited him, the contact with the rough, strongly-feeling people was a stimulant applied direct to his nerves.

Below Oldmeadow, in the green, shallow, soddened hollow of fields lay a square, deep pond. Roving across the landscape, the doctor's quick eye detected a figure in black passing through the gate of the field, down towards the pond. He looked again. It would be Mabel Pervin. His mind suddenly became alive and attentive.

Why was she going down there? He pulled up on the path on the slope above, and stood staring. He could just make sure of the small black figure moving in the hollow of the failing day. He seemed to see her in the midst of such obscurity, that he was like a clairvoyant, seeing rather with the mind's eye than with ordinary sight. Yet he could see her positively enough, whilst he kept his eye attentive. He felt, if he looked away from her, in the thick, ugly falling dusk, he would lose her altogether.

He followed her minutely as she moved, direct and intent, like something transmitted rather than stirring in voluntary activity, straight down the field towards the pond. There she stood on the bank for a moment. She never raised her head. Then she waded slowly into the water.

He stood motionless as the small black figure walked slowly and deliberately towards the centre of the pond, very slowly, gradually moving deeper into the motionless water, and still moving forward as the water got up to her breast. Then he could see her no more in the dusk of the dead afternoon.

"There!" he exclaimed. "Would you believe it?"

And he hastened straight down, running over the wet, soddened fields, pushing through the hedges, down into the depression of callous wintry obscurity. It took him several minutes to come to the pond. He stood on the bank, breathing heavily. He could see nothing. His eyes seemed to penetrate the dead water. Yes, perhaps that was the dark shadow of her black clothing beneath the surface of the water.

He slowly ventured into the pond. The bottom was deep, soft clay, he sank in, and the water clasped dead cold round his legs. As he stirred he could smell the cold, rotten clay that fouled up into the water. It was objectionable in his lungs. Still, repelled and yet not heeding, he moved deeper into the pond. The cold water rose over his thighs, over his loins, upon his abdomen. The lower part of his body was all sunk in the hideous cold element. And the bottom was so deeply soft and uncertain, he was afraid of pitching with his mouth underneath. He could not swim, and was afraid.

He crouched a little, spreading his hands under the water and moving them round, trying to feel for her. The dead cold pond swayed upon his chest. He moved again, a little deeper, and again, with his hands underneath, he felt all around the water. And he touched her clothing. But it evaded his fingers. He made a desperate effort to grasp it.

And so doing he lost his balance and went under, horribly, suffocating in the foul earthy water, struggling madly for a few moments. At last, after what seemed an eternity, he got his footing, rose again into the air and looked around. He gasped, and knew he was in the world. Then he looked at the water. She had risen near him. He grasped her clothing, and drawing her nearer, turned to take his way to land again.

He went very slowly, carefully, absorbed in the slow progress. He rose higher, climbing out of the pond. The water was now only about his legs; he was thankful, full of relief to be out of the clutches of the pond. He lifted her and staggered on to the bank, out of the horror of wet, grey clay.

He laid her down on the bank. She was quite unconscious and running with water. He made the water come from her mouth, he worked to restore her. He did not have to work very long before he could feel the breathing begin again in her; she was breathing naturally. He worked a little longer. He could feel her live beneath his hands; she was coming back. He wiped her face, wrapped her in his overcoat, looked round into the dim, dark grey world, then lifted her and staggered down the bank and across the fields.

It seemed an unthinkably long way, and his burden so heavy he felt he would never get to the house. But at last he was in the stable-yard, and then in the house-yard. He opened the door and went into the house. In the kitchen he laid her down on the hearth-rug, and called. The house was empty. But the fire was burning in the grate.

Then again he kneeled to attend to her. She was breathing regularly, her eyes were wide open and as if conscious, but there seemed something missing in her look. She was conscious in herself, but unconscious of her surroundings.

He ran upstairs, took blankets from a bed, and put them before the fire to warm. Then he removed her saturated, earth-smelling clothing, rubbed her dry with a towel, and wrapped her naked in the blankets. Then he went into the dining-room, to look for spirits. There was a little whiskey. He drank a gulp himself, and put some into her mouth.

The effect was instantaneous. She looked full into his face, as if she had been seeing him for some time, and yet had only just become conscious of him.

"Dr. Fergusson?" she said.

"What?" he answered.

He was divesting himself of his coat, intending to find some dry clothing upstairs. He could not bear the smell of the dead, clayey water, and he was mortally afraid for his own health.

"What did I do?" she asked.

"Walked into the pond," he replied. He had begun to shudder like one sick, and could hardly attend to her. Her eyes remained full on him, he seemed to be going dark in his mind, looking back at her helplessly. The shuddering became quieter in him, his life came back in him, dark and unknowing, but strong again.

"Was I out of my mind?" she asked, while her eyes were fixed on him all the time.

"Maybe, for the moment," he replied. He felt quiet, because his strength had come back. The strange fretful strain had left him.

"Am I out of my mind now?" she asked.

"Are you?" he reflected a moment. "No," he answered truthfully. "I don't see that you are." He turned his face aside. He was afraid now, because he felt dazed, and felt dimly that her power was stronger than his, in this issue. And she continued to look at him fixedly all the time. "Can you tell me where I shall find some dry things to put on?" he asked.

"Did you dive into the pond for me?" she asked.

"No," he answered. "I walked in. But I went in overhead as well."

There was a silence for a moment. He hesitated. He very much wanted to go upstairs to get into dry clothing. But there was another desire in him. And she seemed to hold him. His will seemed to have gone to sleep, and left him, standing there slack before her. But he felt warm inside himself. He did not shudder at all, though his clothes were sodden on him.

"Why did you?" she asked.

"Because I didn't want you to do such a foolish thing," he said.

"It wasn't foolish," she said, still gazing at him as she lay on the floor, with a sofa cushion under her head. "It was the right thing to do. *I* knew best, then."

"I'll go and shift these wet things," he said. But still he had not the power to move out of her presence, until she sent him. It was as if she had the life of his body in her hands, and he could not extricate himself. Or perhaps he did not want to.

Suddenly she sat up. Then she became aware of her own immediate condition. She felt the blankets about her, she knew her own limbs. For a moment it seemed as if her reason were going. She looked round, with wild eyes, as if seeking something. He stood still with fear. She saw her clothing lying scattered.

"Who undressed me?" she asked, her eyes resting full and inevitable on his face.

"I did," he replied, "to bring you round."

For some moments she sat and gazed at him awfully, her lips parted.

"Do you love me, then?" she asked.

He only stood and stared at her, fascinated. His soul seemed to melt.

She shuffled forward on her knees, and put her arms around him, round his legs, as he stood there, pressing her breasts against his knees and thighs, clutching him with strange, convulsive certainty, pressing his thighs against her, drawing him to her face, her throat, as she looked up at him with flaring, humble eyes of transfiguration, triumphant in first possession.

"You love me," she murmured, in strange transport, yearning and triumphant and confident. "You love me. I know you love me, I know."

And she was passionately kissing his knees, through the wet clothing, passionately and indiscriminately kissing his knees, his legs, as if unaware of everything.

He looked down at the tangled wet hair, the wild, bare, animal shoulders. He was amazed, bewildered, and afraid. He had never thought of loving her. He had never wanted to love her. When he rescued her and restored her, he was a doctor, and she was a patient. He had had no single personal thought of her. Nay, this introduction of the personal element was very distasteful to him, a violation of his professional honour. It was horrible to have her there embracing his knees. It was horrible. He revolted from it, violently. And yet—and yet—he had not the power to break away.

She looked at him again, with the same supplication of powerful love, and that same transcendent, frightening light of triumph. In view of the delicate flame which seemed to come from her face like a light, he was powerless. And yet he had never intended to love her. He had never intended. And something stubborn in him could not give way.

"You love me," she repeated, in a murmur of deep rhapsodic assurance. "You love me."

Her hands were drawing him, drawing him down to her. He was afraid, even a little horrified. For he had, really, no intention of loving her. Yet her hands were drawing him towards her. He put out his hand quickly to steady himself, and grasped her bare shoulder. A flame seemed to burn the hand that grasped her soft shoulder. He had no intention of loving her: his whole will was against his yielding. It was horrible. And yet wonderful was the touch of her shoulders, beautiful the shining of her face. Was she perhaps mad? He had a horror of yielding to her. Yet something in him ached also.

He had been staring away at the door, away from her. But his hand remained on her shoulder. She had gone suddenly very still. He looked down at her. Her eyes were now wide with fear, and doubt, the light was dying from her face, a shadow of terrible greyness was returning. He could not bear the touch of her eyes' question upon him, and the look of death behind the question.

With an inward groan he gave way, and let his heart yield towards her. A sudden gentle smile came on his face. And her eyes, which never left his face, slowly, slowly filled with tears. He watched the strange water rise in her eyes, like some slow fountain coming up. And his heart seemed to burn and melt away in his breast.

He could not bear to look at her any more. He dropped on his knees and caught her head with his arms and pressed her face against his throat. She was very still. His heart, which seemed to have broken, was burning with a kind of agony in his breast. And he felt her slow, hot tears wetting his throat. But he could not move.

He felt the hot tears wet his neck and the hollows of his neck, and he remained motionless, suspended through one of man's eternities. Only now it had become indispensable to him to have her face pressed close to him; he could never let her go again. He could never let her head go away from the close clutch of his arm. He wanted to remain like that for ever, with his heart hurting him in a pain that was also life to him. Without knowing, he was looking down on her damp, soft brown hair.

Then, as it were suddenly, he smelt the horrid stagnant smell of that water. And at the same moment she drew away from him and looked at him. Her eyes were wistful and unfathomable. He was afraid of them, and he fell to kissing her, not knowing what he was doing. He wanted her eyes not to have that terrible, wistful, unfathomable look.

When she turned her face to him again, a faint delicate flush was glowing, and there was again dawning that terrible shining of joy in her eyes, which really terrified him, and yet which he now wanted to see, because he feared the look of doubt still more.

"You love me?" she said, rather faltering.

"Yes." The word cost him a painful effort. Not because it wasn't true. But because it was too newly true, the *saying* seemed to tear open again his newly-torn heart. And he hardly wanted it to be true, even now.

She lifted her face to him, and he bent forward and kissed her on the mouth, gently, with the one kiss that is an eternal pledge. And as he kissed her his heart strained again in his breast. He never intended to love her. But now it was over. He had crossed over the gulf to her, and all that he had left behind had shrivelled and become void.

After the kiss, her eyes again slowly filled with tears. She sat still, away from him, with her face drooped aside, and her hands folded in her lap. The tears fell very slowly. There was complete silence. He too sat there motionless and silent on the hearthrug. The strange pain of his heart that was broken seemed to consume him. That he should love her? That this was love! That he should be ripped open in this way! Him, a doctor! How they would all jeer if they knew! It was agony to him to think they might know.

In the curious naked pain of the thought he looked again to her. She was sitting there drooped into a muse. He saw a tear fall, and his heart flared hot. He saw for the first time that one of her shoulders was quite uncovered, one arm bare, he could see one of her small breasts; dimly, because it had become almost dark in the room.

"Why are you crying?" he asked, in an altered voice.

She looked at him, and behind her tears the consciousness of her situation for the first time brought a dark look of shame to her eyes.

"I'm not crying, really," she said, watching him half frightened.

He reached his hand, and softly closed it on her bare arm.

"I love you! I love you!" he said in a soft, low vibrating voice, unlike himself.

She shrank, and dropped her head. The soft, penetrating grip of his hand on her arm distressed her. She looked up at him.

"I want to go," she said. "I want to go and get you some dry things."

"Why?" he said. "I'm all right."

"But I want to go," she said. "And I want you to change your things."

He released her arm, and she wrapped herself in the blanket, looking at him rather frightened. And still she did not rise.

"Kiss me," she said wistfully.

He kissed her, but briefly, half in anger.

Then, after a second, she rose nervously, all mixed up in the blanket. He watched her in her confusion, as she tried to extricate herself and wrap herself up so that she could walk. He watched her relentlessly, as she knew. And as she went, the blanket trailing, and as he saw a glimpse of her feet and her white leg, he tried to remember her as she was when he had wrapped her in the blanket. But then he didn't want to remember, because she had been nothing to him then, and his nature revolted from remembering her as she was when she was nothing to him.

A tumbling, muffled noise from within the dark house startled him. Then he heard her voice:—"There are clothes." He rose and went to the foot of the stairs, and gathered up the garments she had thrown down. Then he came back to the fire, to rub himself down and dress. He grinned at his own appearance when he had finished.

The fire was sinking, so he put on coal. The house was now quite dark, save for the light of a street-lamp that shone in faintly from beyond the holly trees. He lit the gas with matches he found on the mantelpiece. Then he emptied the pockets of his own clothes, and threw all his wet things in a heap into the scullery. After which he gathered up her sodden clothes, gently, and put them in a separate heap on the copper-top in the scullery.

It was six o'clock on the clock. His own watch had stopped. He ought to go back to the surgery. He waited, and still she did not come down. So he went to the foot of the stairs and called:

"I shall have to go."

Almost immediately he heard her coming down. She had on her best dress of black voile, and her hair was tidy, but still damp. She looked at him—and in spite of herself, smiled.

"I don't like you in those clothes," she said.

"Do I look a sight?" he answered.

They were shy of one another.

"I'll make you some tea," she said.

"No, I must go."

"Must you?" And she looked at him again with the wide, strained, doubtful eyes. And again, from the pain of his breast, he knew he loved her. He went and bent to kiss her, gently, passionately, with his heart's painful kiss.

"And my hair smells so horrible," she murmured in distraction. "And I'm so awful, I'm so awful! Oh, no, I'm too awful." And she broke into bitter, heartbroken sobbing. "You can't want to love me, I'm horrible."

"Don't be silly, don't be silly," he said, trying to comfort her, kissing her, holding her in his arms. "I want you, I want to marry you, we're going to be married, quickly, quickly—tomorrow if I can."

But she only sobbed terribly, and cried:

"I feel awful. I feel awful. I feel I'm horrible to you."

"No, I want you, I want you," was all he answered, blindly, with that terrible intonation which frightened her almost more than her horror lest he should *not* want her.

QUESTIONS FOR DISCUSSION AND WRITING

1. How does the question that opens the story lead to the first major crisis in the plot? How does Dr. Fergusson's heroism produce the second crisis? To what extent does his decision to marry Mabel resolve that crisis?
2. How are the children of the horse dealer like the animals they manage? What animal qualities does Mabel possess? How does Dr. Fergusson respond to those qualities?
3. How does the setting control the fate of the characters? How does their father's death deprive each child of "inner freedom"? Why does Dr. Fergusson feel like a "slave to the countryside"?
4. Why does Lawrence shift the point of view in the story from the brothers to Mabel to Dr. Fergusson? How does Dr. Fergusson's point of view toward his other patients help explain his attitude toward Mabel?
5. What does this story reveal about the relationship between men and women? What aspect of Dr. Fergusson's personality resists Mabel's love? What new aspect of his personality does he discover with Mabel?

54

D. H. LAWRENCE

Odour of Chrysanthemums

1

The small locomotive engine, Number 4, came clanking, stumbling down from Selston with seven full wagons. It appeared round the corner with loud threats of speed, but the colt that it startled from among the gorse, which still flickered indistinctly in the raw afternoon, out-distanced it at a canter. A woman, walking up the railway line to Underwood, drew back into the hedge, held her basket aside, and watched the footplate of the engine advancing. The trucks thumped heavily past, one by one, with slow inevitable movement, as she stood insignificantly trapped between the jolting black wagons and the hedge; then they curved away towards the coppice where the withered oak leaves dropped noiselessly, while the birds, pulling at the scarlet hips beside the track, made off into the dusk that had already crept into the spinney. In the open, the smoke from the engine sank and cleaved to the rough grass. The fields were dreary and forsaken, and in the marshy strip that led to the whimsey, a reedy pit-pond, the fowls had already abandoned their run among the alders, to roost in the tarred fowl-house. The pit-bank loomed up beyond the pond, flames like red sores licking its ashy sides, in the afternoon's stagnant light. Just beyond rose the tapering chimneys and the clumsy black headstocks of Brinsley Colliery. The two wheels were spinning fast up against the sky, and the winding engine rapped out its little spasms. The miners were being turned up.

The engine whistled as it came into the wide bay of railway lines beside the colliery, where rows of trucks stood in harbour.

Miners, single, trailing and in groups, passed like shadows diverging home. At the edge of the ribbed level of sidings squat a low cottage, three steps down from the cinder track. A large bony vine clutched at the house, as if to claw down the tiled roof. Round the bricked yard grew a few wintry primroses. Beyond, the long garden sloped down to a bush-covered brook course. There were some twiggy apple trees, winter-crack trees, and ragged cabbages. Beside the path hung dishevelled pink chrysanthemums, like pink cloths hung on bushes. A woman came stooping out of the felt-covered fowl-house, half-way down the garden. She closed and padlocked the door, then drew herself erect, having brushed some bits from her white apron.

She was a tall woman of imperious mien, handsome, with definite black eyebrows. Her smooth black hair was parted exactly. For a few moments she stood steadily watching the miners as they passed along the railway: then she turned towards the brook course. Her face was calm and set, her mouth was closed with disillusionment. After a moment she called:

"John!" There was no answer. She waited, and then said distinctly:

"Where are you?"

"Here!" replied a child's sulky voice from among the bushes. The woman looked piercingly through the dusk.

"Are you at that brook?" she asked sternly.

For answer the child showed himself before the raspberry-canes that rose like whips. He was a small, sturdy boy of five. He stood quite still, defiantly.

"Oh!" said the mother, conciliated. "I thought you were down at that wet brook—and you remember what I told you———"

The boy did not move or answer.

"Come, come on in," she said more gently, "it's getting dark. There's your grandfather's engine coming down the line!"

The lad advanced slowly, with resentful, taciturn movement. He was dressed in trousers and waistcoat of cloth that was too thick and hard for the size of the garments. They were evidently cut down from a man's clothes.

As they went slowly towards the house he tore at the ragged wisps of chrysanthemums and dropped the petals in handfuls among the path.

"Don't do that—it does look nasty," said his mother. He refrained, and she, suddenly pitiful, broke off a twig with three or four wan flowers and held them against her face. When mother and son reached the yard her hand hesitated, and instead of laying the flower aside, she pushed it in her apron-band. The mother and son stood at the foot of the three steps looking across the bay of lines at the passing home of the miners. The trundle of the small train was imminent. Suddenly the engine loomed past the house and came to a stop opposite the gate.

The engine-driver, a short man with round grey beard, leaned out of the cab high above the woman.

"Have you got a cup of tea?" he said in a cheery, hearty fashion.

It was her father. She went in, saying she would mash. Directly, she returned.

"I didn't come to see you on Sunday," began the little grey-bearded man.

"I didn't expect you," said his daughter.

The engine-driver winced; then, reassuming his cheery, airy manner, he said:

"Oh, have you heard then? Well, and what do you think———?"

"I think it is soon enough," she replied.

At her brief censure the little man made an impatient gesture, and said coaxingly, yet with dangerous coldness:

"Well, what's a man to do? It's no sort of life for a man of my years, to sit at my own hearth like a stranger. And if I'm going to marry again it may as well be soon as late—what does it matter to anybody?"

The woman did not reply, but turned and went into the house. The man in the engine-cab stood assertive, till she returned with a cup of tea and a piece of bread and butter on a plate. She went up the steps and stood near the footplate of the hissing engine.

"You needn't 'a' brought me bread an' butter," said her father. "But a cup of tea"—he sipped appreciatively—"it's very nice." He sipped for a moment or two, then: "I hear as Walter's got another bout on," he said.

"When hasn't he?" said the woman bitterly.

"I heerd tell of him in the 'Lord Nelson' braggin' as he was going to spend that b———afore he went: half a sovereign that was."

"When?" asked the woman.

"A' Sat'day night—I know that's true."

"Very likely," she laughed bitterly. "He gives me twenty-three shillings."

"Aye, it's a nice thing, when a man can do nothing with his money but make a beast of himself!" said the grey-whiskered man. The woman turned her head away. Her father swallowed the last of his tea and handed her the cup.

"Aye," he sighed, wiping his mouth. "It's a settler, it is———"

He put his hand on the lever. The little engine strained and groaned, and the train rumbled towards the crossing. The woman again looked across the metals. Darkness was settling over the spaces of the railway and trucks: the miners, in grey sombre groups, were still passing home. The winding engine pulsed hurriedly, with brief pauses. Elizabeth

Bates looked at the dreary flow of men, then she went indoors. Her husband did not come.

The kitchen was small and full of firelight; red coals piled glowing up the chimney mouth. All the life of the room seemed in the white, warm hearth and the steel fender reflecting the red fire. The cloth was laid for tea; cups glinted in the shadows. At the back, where the lowest stairs protruded into the room, the boy sat struggling with a knife and a piece of white wood. He was almost hidden in the shadow. It was half-past four. They had but to await the father's coming to begin tea. As the mother watched her son's sullen little struggle with the wood, she saw herself in his silence and pertinacity; she saw the father in her child's indifference to all but himself. She seemed to be occupied by her husband. He had probably gone past his home, slunk past his own door, to drink before he came in, while his dinner spoiled and wasted in waiting. She glanced at the clock, then took the potatoes to strain them in the yard. The garden and fields beyond the brook were closed in uncertain darkness. When she rose with the saucepan, leaving the drain steaming into the night behind her, she saw the yellow lamps were lit along the high road that went up the hill away beyond the space of the railway lines and the field.

Then again she watched the men trooping home, fewer now and fewer.

Indoors the fire was sinking and the room was dark red. The woman put her saucepan on the hob, and set a batter-pudding near the mouth of the oven. Then she stood unmoving. Directly, gratefully, came quick young steps to the door. Someone hung on the latch a moment, then a little girl entered and began pulling off her outdoor things, dragging a mass of curls, just ripening from gold to brown, over her eyes with her hat.

Her mother chid her for coming late from school, and said she would have to keep her at home the dark winter days.

"Why, mother, it's hardly a bit dark yet. The lamp's not lighted, and my father's not home."

"No, he isn't. But it's a quarter to five! Did you see anything of him?"

The child became serious. She looked at her mother with large, wistful blue eyes.

"No, mother, I've never seen him. Why? Has he come up an' gone past, to Old Brinsley? He hasn't, mother, 'cos I never saw him."

"He'd watch that," said the mother bitterly, "he'd take care as you didn't see him. But you may depend upon it, he's seated in the 'Prince o' Wales.' He wouldn't be this late."

The girl looked at her mother piteously.

"Let's have our teas, mother, should we?" said she.

The mother called John to table. She opened the door once more and looked out across the darkness of the lines. All was deserted: she could not hear the winding-engines.

"Perhaps," she said to herself, "he's stopped to get some ripping done."

They sat down to tea. John, at the end of the table near the door, was almost lost in the darkness. Their faces were hidden from each other. The girl crouched against the fender slowly moving a thick piece of bread before the fire. The lad, his face a dusky mark on the shadow, sat watching her who was transfigured in the red glow.

"I do think it's beautiful to look in the fire," said the child.

"Do you?" said her mother. "Why?"

"It's so red, and full of little caves—and it feels so nice, and you can fair smell it."

"It'll want mending directly," replied her mother, "and then if your father comes he'll carry on and say there never is a fire when a man comes home sweating from the pit. A public-house is always warm enough."

There was silence till the boy said complainingly: "Make haste, our Annie."

"Well, I am doing! I can't make the fire do it no faster, can I?"

"She keeps wafflin' it about so's to make 'er slow," grumbled the boy.

"Don't have such an evil imagination, child," replied the mother.

Soon the room was busy in the darkness with the crisp sound of crunching. The mother ate very little. She drank her tea determinedly, and sat thinking. When she rose her anger was evident in the stern unbending of her head. She looked at the pudding in the fender, and broke out:

"It is a scandalous thing as a man can't even come home to his dinner! If it's crozzled up to a cinder I don't see why I should care. Past his very door he goes to get to a public-house, and here I sit with his dinner waiting for him———"

She went out. As she dropped piece after piece of coal on the red fire, the shadows fell on the walls, till the room was almost in total darkness.

"I canna see," grumbled the invisible John. In spite of herself, the mother laughed.

"You know the way to your mouth," she said. She set the dust-pan outside the door. When she came again like a shadow on the hearth, the lad repeated, complaining sulkily:

"I canna see."

"Good gracious!" cried the mother irritably, "you're as bad as your father if it's a bit dusk!"

Nevertheless, she took a paper spill from a sheaf on the mantelpiece and proceeded to light the lamp that hung from the ceiling in the middle of the room. As she reached up, her figure displayed itself just rounding with maternity.

"Oh, mother———!" exclaimed the girl.

"What?" said the woman, suspended in the act of putting the lamp-glass over the flame. The copper reflector shone handsomely on her, as she stood with uplifted arm, turning to face her daughter.

"You've got a flower in your apron!" said the child, in a little rapture at this unusual event.

"Goodness me!" exclaimed the woman, relieved. "One would think the house was afire." She replaced the glass and waited a moment before turning up the wick. A pale shadow was seen floating vaguely on the floor.

"Let me smell!" said the child, still rapturously, coming forward and putting her face to her mother's waist.

"Go along, silly!" said the mother, turning up the lamp. The light revealed their suspense so that the woman felt it almost unbearable. Annie was still bending at her waist. Irritably, the mother took the flowers out from her apron-band.

"Oh, mother—don't take them out!" Annie cried, catching her hand and trying to replace the sprig.

"Such nonsense!" said the mother, turning away. The child put the pale chrysanthemums to her lips, murmuring:

"Don't they smell beautiful!"

Her mother gave a short laugh.

"No," she said, "not to me. It was chrysanthemums when I married him, and chrysanthemums when you were born, and the first time they ever brought him home drunk, he'd got brown chrysanthemums in his button-hole."

She looked at the children. Their eyes and their parted lips were wondering. The mother sat rocking in silence for some time. Then she looked at the clock.

"Twenty minutes to six!" In a tone of fine bitter carelessness she continued: "Eh, he'll not come now till they bring him. There he'll stick! But he needn't come rolling in here in his pit-dirt, for *I* won't wash him. He can lie on the floor———Eh, what a fool I've been, what a fool! And this is what I came here for, to this dirty hole, rats and all, for him to slink past his very door. Twice last week—he's begun now———"

She silenced herself, and rose to clear the table.

While for an hour or more the children played, subduedly intent, fertile of imagination, united in fear of the mother's wrath, and in dread of their father's home-coming, Mrs. Bates sat in her rocking-chair making a 'singlet' of thick cream-coloured flannel, which gave a dull wounded sound as she tore off the grey edge. She worked at her sewing with energy, listening to the children, and her anger wearied itself, lay down to rest, opening its eyes from time to time and steadily watching, its ears raised to listen. Sometimes even her anger quailed and shrank, and the mother suspended her sewing, tracing the footsteps that thudded along the sleepers outside; she would lift her head sharply to bid the children 'hush', but she recovered herself in time, and the footsteps went past the gate, and the children were not flung out of their play-world.

But at last Annie sighed, and gave in. She glanced at her wagon of slippers, and loathed the game. She turned plaintively to her mother.

"Mother!"—but she was inarticulate.

John crept out like a frog from under the sofa. His mother glanced up.

"Yes," she said, "just look at those shirt-sleeves!"

The boy held them out to survey them, saying nothing. Then somebody called in a hoarse voice away down the line, and suspense bristled in the room, till two people had gone by outside, talking.

"It is time for bed," said the mother.

"My father hasn't come," wailed Annie plaintively. But her mother was primed with courage.

"Never mind. They'll bring him when he does come—like a log." She meant there would be no scene. "And he may sleep on the floor till he wakes himself. I know he'll not go to work to-morrow after this!"

The children had their hands and faces wiped with a flannel. They were very quiet. When they had put on their nightdresses, they said their prayers, the boy mumbling. The mother looked down at them, at the brown silken bush of intertwining curls in the nape of the girl's neck, at the little black head of the lad, and her heart burst with anger at their father, who caused all three such distress. The children hid their faces in her skirts for comfort.

When Mrs. Bates came down, the room was strangely empty, with a tension of expectancy. She took up her sewing and stitched for some time without raising her head. Meantime her anger was tinged with fear.

2

The clock struck eight and she rose suddenly, dropping her sewing on her chair. She went to the stair-foot door, opened it, listening. Then she went out, locking the door behind her.

Something scuffled in the yard, and she started, though she knew it was only the rats with which the place was over-run. The night was very dark. In the great bay of railway lines, bulked with trucks, there was no trace of light, only away back she could see a few yellow lamps at the pit-top, and the red smear of the burning pit-bank on the night. She hurried along the edge of the track, then, crossing the converging lines, came to the stile by the white gates, whence she emerged on the road. Then the fear which had led her shrank. People were walking up to New Brinsley; she saw the lights in the houses; twenty yards farther on were the broad windows of the 'Prince of Wales', very warm and bright, and the loud voices of men could be heard distinctly. What a fool she had been to imagine that anything had happened to him! He was merely drinking over there at the 'Prince of Wales'. She faltered. She had never yet been to fetch him, and she never would go. So she continued her walk towards the long straggling line of houses, standing back on the highway. She entered a passage between the dwellings.

"Mr. Rigley?—Yes! Did you want him? No, he's not in at this minute."

The raw-boned woman leaned forward from her dark scullery and peered at the other, upon whom fell a dim light through the blind of the kitchen window.

"Is it Mrs. Bates?" she asked in a tone tinged with respect.

"Yes. I wondered if your Master was at home. Mine hasn't come yet."

"'Asn't 'e! Oh, Jack's been 'ome an' 'ad 'is dinner an' gone out. 'E's just gone for 'alf an hour afore bed-time. Did you call at the 'Prince of Wales'?"

"No———"

"No, you didn't like———! It's not very nice." The other woman was indulgent. There was an awkward pause. "Jack never said nothink about—about your Master," she said.

"No!—I expect he's stuck in there!"

Elizabeth Bates said this bitterly, and with recklessness. She knew that the woman across the yard was standing at her door listening, but she did not care. As she turned:

"Stop a minute! I'll just go an' ask Jack if 'e knows anythink," said Mrs. Rigley.

"Oh no—I wouldn't like to put———!"

"Yes, I will, if you'll just step inside an' see as th' childer doesn't come downstairs and set theirselves afire."

Elizabeth Bates, murmuring a remonstrance, stepped inside. The other woman apologised for the state of the room.

The kitchen needed apology. There were little frocks and trousers and childish undergarments on the squab and on the floor, and a litter of playthings everywhere. On the black American cloth of the table were pieces of bread and cake, crusts, slops, and a teapot with cold tea.

"Eh, ours is just as bad," said Elizabeth Bates, looking at the woman, not at the house. Mrs. Rigley put a shawl over her head and hurried out, saying:

"I shanna be a minute."

The other sat, noting with faint disapproval the general untidiness of the room. Then she fell to counting the shoes of various sizes scattered over the floor. There were twelve. She sighed and said to herself: "No wonder!"—glancing at the litter. There came the scratching of two pairs of feet on the yard, and the Rigleys entered. Elizabeth Bates rose. Rigley was a big man, with very large bones. His head looked particularly bony. Across his temple was a blue scar, caused by a wound got in the pit, a wound in which the coal-dust remained blue like tattooing.

"'Asna 'e come whoam yit?" asked the man, without any form of greeting, but with deference and sympathy. "I couldna say wheer he is—'e's non ower theer!"—he jerked his head to signify the 'Prince of Wales'.

"'E's 'appen gone up to th' 'Yew'," said Mrs. Rigley.

There was another pause. Rigley had evidently something to get off his mind:

"Ah left 'im finishin' a stint," he began. "Loose-all 'ad bin gone about ten minutes when we com'n away, an' I shouted: 'Are ter comin', Walt?' an' 'e said: 'Go on, Ah shanna be but a'ef a minnit,' so we com'n ter th' bottom, me an' Bowers, thinkin' as 'e wor just behint, an' 'ud come up i' th' next bantle———"

He stood perplexed, as if answering a charge of deserting his mate. Elizabeth Bates, now again certain of disaster, hastened to reassure him:

"I expect 'e's gone up to th' 'Yew Tree', as you say. It's not the first time. I've fretted myself into a fever before now. He'll come home when they carry him."

"Ay, isn't it too bad!" deplored the other woman.

"I'll just step up to Dick's an' see if 'e *is* theer," offered the man, afraid of appearing alarmed, afraid of taking liberties.

"Oh, I wouldn't think of bothering you that far," said Elizabeth Bates, with emphasis, but he knew she was glad of his offer.

As they stumbled up the entry, Elizabeth Bates heard Rigley's wife run across the yard and open her neighbour's door. At this, suddenly all the blood in her body seemed to switch away from her heart.

"Mind!" warned Rigley. "Ah've said many a time as Ah'd fill up them ruts in this entry, sumb'dy 'll be breakin' their legs yit."

She recovered herself and walked quickly along with the miner.

"I don't like leaving the children in bed, and nobody in the house," she said.

"No, you dunna!" he replied courteously. They were soon at the gate of the cottage.

"Well, I shanna be many minnits. Dunna you be frettin' now, 'e'll be all right," said the butty.

"Thank you very much, Mr. Rigley," she replied.

"You're welcome!" he stammered, moving away. "I shanna be many minnits."

The house was quiet. Elizabeth Bates took off her hat and shawl, and rolled back the rug. When she had finished, she sat down. It was a few minutes past nine. She was startled by the rapid chuff of the winding-engine at the pit, and the sharp whirr of the brakes on the rope as it descended. Again she felt the painful sweep of her blood, and she put her hand to her side, saying aloud: "Good gracious!—it's only the nine o'clock deputy going down," rebuking herself.

She sat still, listening. Half an hour of this, and she was wearied out.

"What am I working myself up like this for?" she said pitiably to herself, "I s'll only be doing myself some damage."

She took out her sewing again.

At a quarter to ten there were footsteps. One person! She watched for the door to open. It was an elderly woman, in a black bonnet and a black woollen shawl—his mother. She was about sixty years old, pale, with blue eyes, and her face all wrinkled and lamentable. She shut the door and turned to her daughter-in-law peevishly.

"Eh, Lizzie, whatever shall we do, whatever shall we do!" she cried.

Elizabeth drew back a little, sharply.

"What is it, mother?" she said.

The elder woman seated herself on the sofa.

"I don't know, child, I can't tell you!"—she shook her head slowly. Elizabeth sat watching her, anxious and vexed.

"I don't know," replied the grandmother, sighing very deeply. "There's no end to my troubles, there isn't. The things I've gone through, I'm sure it's enough———!" She wept without wiping her eyes, the tears running.

"But, mother," interrupted Elizabeth, "what do you mean? What is it?"

The grandmother slowly wiped her eyes. The fountains of her tears were stopped by Elizabeth's directness. She wiped her eyes slowly.

"Poor child! Eh, you poor thing!" she moaned. "I don't know what we're going to do, I don't—and you as you are—it's a thing, it is indeed!"

Elizabeth waited.

"Is he dead?" she asked, and at the words her heart swung violently, though she felt a slight flush of shame at the ultimate extravagance of the question. Her words sufficiently frightened the old lady, almost brought her to herself.

"Don't say so, Elizabeth! We'll hope it's not as bad as that; no, may the Lord spare us that, Elizabeth. Jack Rigley came just as I was sittin' down to a glass afore going to bed, an' 'e said: ''Appen you'll go down th' line, Mrs. Bates. Walt's had an accident. 'Appen you'll go an' sit wi' 'er till we can get him home.' I hadn't time to ask him a word afore he was gone. An' I put my bonnet on an' come straight down, Lizzie. I thought to myself: 'Eh, that poor blessed child, if anybody should come an' tell her of a sudden, there's no knowin' what'll 'appen to 'er.' You mustn't let it upset you, Lizzie—or you know what to expect. How long is it, six months—or is it five, Lizzie? Ay!"—the old woman shook her head—"time slips on, it slips on! Ay!"

Elizabeth's thoughts were busy elsewhere. If he was killed—would she be able to manage on the little pension and what she could earn?—she counted up rapidly. If he was hurt—they wouldn't take him to the hospital—how tiresome he would be to nurse!—but perhaps she'd be able to get him away from the drink and his hateful ways. She would—while he was ill. The tears offered to come to her eyes at the picture. But what sentimental luxury was this she was beginning? She turned to consider the children. At any rate she was absolutely necessary for them. They were her business.

"Ay!" repeated the old woman, "it seems but a week or two since he brought me his first wages. Ay—he was a good lad, Elizabeth, he was, in his way. I don't know why he got to be such a trouble, I don't. He was a happy lad at home, only full of spirits. But there's no mistake he's been a handful of trouble, he has! I hope the Lord'll spare him to mend his ways. I hope so, I hope so. You've had a sight o' trouble with him, Elizabeth, you have indeed. But he was a jolly enough lad wi' me, he was, I can assure you. I don't know how it is. . . ."

The old woman continued to muse aloud, a monotonous irritating sound, while Elizabeth thought concentratedly, startled once, when she heard the winding-engine chuff quickly, and the brakes skirr with a shriek. Then she heard the engine more slowly, and the brakes made no sound. The old woman did not notice. Elizabeth waited in suspense. The mother-in-law talked, with lapses into silence.

"But he wasn't your son, Lizzie, an' it makes a difference. Whatever he was, I remember him when he was little, an' I learned to understand him and to make allowances. You've got to make allowances for them———"

It was half-past ten, and the old woman was saying: "But it's trouble from beginning to end; you're never too old for trouble, never too old for that———" when the gate banged back, and there were heavy feet on the steps.

"I'll go, Lizzie, let me go," cried the old woman, rising. But Elizabeth was at the door. It was a man in pit-clothes.

"They're bringin' 'im, Missis," he said. Elizabeth's heart halted a moment. Then it surged on again, almost suffocating her.

"Is he—is it bad?" she asked.

The man turned away, looking at the darkness:

"The doctor says 'e'd been dead hours. 'E saw 'im i' th' lamp-cabin."

The old woman, who stood just behind Elizabeth, dropped into a chair, and folded her hands, crying: "Oh, my boy, my boy!"

"Hush!" said Elizabeth, with a sharp twitch of a frown. "Be still, mother, don't waken th' children: I wouldn't have them down for anything!"

The old woman moaned softly, rocking herself. The man was drawing away. Elizabeth took a step forward.

"How was it?" she asked.

"Well, I couldn't say for sure," the man replied, very ill at ease. "'E wor finishin' a stint an' th' butties 'ad gone, an' a lot o' stuff come down atop 'n 'im."

"And crushed him?" cried the widow, with a shudder.

"No," said the man, "it fell at th' back of 'im. 'E wor under th' face, an' it niver touched 'im. It shut 'im in. It seems 'e wor smothered."

Elizabeth shrank back. She heard the old woman behind her cry:

"What?—what did 'e say it was?"

The man replied, more loudly: "'E wor smothered!"

Then the old woman wailed aloud, and this relieved Elizabeth.

"Oh, mother," she said, putting her hand on the old woman, "don't waken th' children, don't waken th' children."

She wept a little, unknowing, while the old mother rocked herself and moaned. Elizabeth remembered that they were bringing him home, and she must be ready. "They'll lay him in the parlour," she said to herself, standing a moment pale and perplexed.

Then she lighted a candle and went into the tiny room. The air was cold and damp, but she could not make a fire, there was no fireplace. She set down the candle and looked round. The candlelight glittered on the lustre-glasses, on the two vases that held some of the pink chrysanthemums, and on the dark mahogany. There was a cold, deathly smell of chrysanthemums in the room. Elizabeth stood looking at the flowers. She turned away, and calculated whether there would be room to lay him on the floor, between the couch and the chiffonier. She pushed the chairs aside. There would be room to lay him down and to step round him. Then she fetched the old red tablecloth, and another old cloth, spreading them down to save her bit of carpet. She shivered on leaving the parlour; so, from the dresser drawer she took a clean shirt and put it at the fire to air. All the time her mother-in-law was rocking herself in the chair and moaning.

"You'll have to move from there, mother," said Elizabeth. "They'll be bringing him in. Come in the rocker."

The old mother rose mechanically, and seated herself by the fire, continuing to lament. Elizabeth went into the pantry for another candle, and there, in the little pent-house under the naked tiles, she heard them coming. She stood still in the pantry doorway, listening. She heard them pass the end of the house, and come awkwardly down the three steps, a jumble of shuffling footsteps and muttering voices. The old woman was silent. The men were in the yard.

Then Elizabeth heard Matthews, the manager of the pit, say: "You go in first, Jim. Mind!"

The door came open, and the two women saw a collier backing into the room, holding one end of a stretcher, on which they could see the nailed pit-boots of the dead man. The two carriers halted, the man at the head stooping to the lintel of the door.

"Wheer will you have him?" asked the manager, a short, white-bearded man.

Elizabeth roused herself and came from the pantry carrying the unlighted candle.

"In the parlour," she said.

"In there, Jim!" pointed the manager, and the carriers backed round into the tiny room. The coat with which they had covered the body fell off as they awkwardly turned through the two doorways, and the women saw their man, naked to the waist, lying stripped for work. The old woman began to moan in a low voice of horror.

"Lay th' stretcher at th' side," snapped the manager, "an' put 'im on th' cloths. Mind now, mind! Look you now——!"

One of the men had knocked off a vase of chrysanthemums. He stared awkwardly, then they set down the stretcher. Elizabeth did not look at her husband. As soon as she could get in the room, she went and picked up the broken vase and the flowers.

"Wait a minute!" she said.

The three men waited in silence while she mopped up the water with a duster.

"Eh, what a job, what a job, to be sure!" the manager was saying, rubbing his brow with trouble and perplexity. "Never knew such a thing in my life, never! He'd no business to ha' been left. I never knew such a thing in my life! Fell over him clean as a whistle, an' shut him in. Not four foot of space, there wasn't—yet it scarce bruised him."

He looked down at the dead man, lying prone, half naked, all grimed with coal-dust.

"''Sphyxiated', the doctor said. It *is* the most terrible job I've ever known. Seems as if it was done o' purpose. Clean over him, an' shut 'im in, like a mouse-trap"—he made a sharp, descending gesture with his hand.

The colliers standing by jerked aside their heads in hopeless comment.

The horror of the thing bristled upon them all.

Then they heard the girl's voice upstairs calling shrilly: "Mother, mother—who is it? Mother, who is it?"

Elizabeth hurried to the foot of the stairs and opened the door:

"Go to sleep!" she commanded sharply. "What are you shouting about? Go to sleep at once—there's nothing———"

Then she began to mount the stairs. They could hear her on the boards, and on the plaster floor of the little bedroom. They could hear her distinctly:

"What's the matter now?—what's the matter with you, silly thing?"—her voice was much agitated, with an unreal gentleness.

"I thought it was some men come," said the plaintive voice of the child. "Has he come?"

"Yes, they've brought him. There's nothing to make a fuss about. Go to sleep now, like a good child."

They could hear her voice in the bedroom, they waited whilst she covered the children under the bedclothes.

"Is he drunk?" asked the girl, timidly, faintly.

"No! No—he's not! He—he's asleep."

"Is he asleep downstairs?"

"Yes—and don't make a noise."

There was silence for a moment, then the men heard the frightened child again:

"What's that noise?"

"It's nothing, I tell you, what are you bothering for?"

The noise was the grandmother moaning. She was oblivious of everything, sitting on her chair rocking and moaning. The manager put his hand on her arm and bade her "Sh—sh!!"

The old woman opened her eyes and looked at him. She was shocked by this interruption, and seemed to wonder.

"What time is it?" the plaintive thin voice of the child, sinking back unhappily into sleep, asked this last question.

"Ten o'clock," answered the mother more softly. Then she must have bent down and kissed the children.

Matthews beckoned to the men to come away. They put on their caps and took up the stretcher. Stepping over the body, they tiptoed out of the house. None of them spoke till they were far from the wakeful children.

When Elizabeth came down she found her mother alone on the parlour floor, leaning over the dead man, the tears dropping on him.

"We must lay him out," the wife said. She put on the kettle, then returning knelt at the feet, and began to unfasten the knotted leather laces. The room was clammy and dim with only one candle, so that she had to bend her face almost to the floor. At last she got off the heavy boots and put them away.

"You must help me now," she whispered to the old woman. Together they stripped the man.

When they arose, saw him lying in the naïve dignity of death, the women stood arrested in fear and respect. For a few moments they remained still, looking down, the old mother whimpering. Elizabeth felt countermanded. She saw him, how utterly inviolable he lay in himself. She had nothing to do with him. She could not accept it. Stooping, she laid her hand on him, in claim. He was still warm, for the mine was hot where he had died. His mother had his face between her hands, and was murmuring incoherently. The old tears fell in succession as drops from wet leaves; the mother was not weeping, merely her tears flowed. Elizabeth embraced the body of her husband, with cheek and lips. She seemed to be listening, inquiring, trying to get some connection. But she could not. She was driven away. He was impregnable.

She rose, went into the kitchen, where she poured warm water into a bowl, brought soap and flannel and a soft towel.

"I must wash him," she said.

Then the old mother rose stiffly, and watched Elizabeth as she carefully washed his face, carefully brushing the big blond moustache from his mouth with the flannel. She was afraid with a bottomless fear, so she ministered to him. The old woman, jealous, said:

"Let me wipe him!"—and she kneeled on the other side drying slowly as Elizabeth washed, her big black bonnet sometimes brushing the dark head of her daughter-in-law. They worked thus in silence for a long time. They never forgot it was death, and the touch of the man's dead body gave them strange emotions, different in each of the women; a great dread possessed them both, the mother felt the lie was given to her womb, she was denied; the wife felt the utter isolation of the human soul, the child within her was a weight apart from her.

At last it was finished. He was a man of handsome body, and his face showed no traces of drink. He was blond, full-fleshed, with fine limbs. But he was dead.

"Bless him," whispered his mother, looking always at his face, and speaking out of sheer terror. "Dear lad—bless him!" She spoke in a faint, sibilant ecstasy of fear and mother love.

Elizabeth sank down again to the floor, and put her face against his neck, and trembled and shuddered. But she had to draw away again. He was dead, and her living flesh had no place against his. A great dread and weariness held her: she was so unavailing. Her life was gone like this.

"White as milk he is, clear as a twelve-month baby, bless him, the darling!" the old mother murmured to herself. "Not a mark on him, clear and clean and white, beautiful as ever a child was made," she murmured with pride. Elizabeth kept her face hidden.

"He went peaceful, Lizzie—peaceful as sleep. Isn't he beautiful, the lamb? Ay—he must ha' made his peace, Lizzie. 'Appen he made it all right, Lizzie, shut in there. He'd have time. He wouldn't look like this if he hadn't made his peace. The lamb, the dear lamb. Eh, but he had a hearty laugh. I loved to hear it. He had the heartiest laugh, Lizzie, as a lad———"

Elizabeth looked up. The man's mouth was fallen back, slightly open under the cover of the moustache. The eyes, half shut, did not show glazed in the obscurity. Life with its smoky burning gone from him, had left him apart and utterly alien to her. And she knew what a stranger he was to her. In her womb was ice of fear, because of this separate stranger with whom she had been living as one flesh. Was this what it all meant—utter, intact separateness, obscured by heat of living? In dread she turned her face away. The fact was too deadly. There had been nothing between them, and yet they had come together, exchanging their nakedness repeatedly. Each time he had taken her, they had been two isolated beings, far apart as now. He was no more responsible than she. The child was like ice in her womb. For as she looked at the dead man, her mind, cold and detached, said clearly: "Who am I? What have I been doing? I have been fighting a husband who did not exist. *He* existed all the time. What wrong have I done? What was that I have been living with? There lies the reality, this man." And her soul died in her for fear: she knew she had never seen him, he had never seen her, they had met in the dark and had fought in the dark, not knowing whom they met nor whom they fought. And now she saw, and turned silent in seeing. For she had been wrong. She had said he was something he was not; she had felt familiar with him. Whereas he was apart all the while, living as she never lived, feeling as she never felt.

In fear and shame she looked at his naked body, that she had known falsely. And he was the father of her children. Her soul was torn from her body and stood apart. She looked at his naked body and was ashamed, as if she had denied it. After all, it was itself. It seemed awful to her. She looked at his face, and she turned her own face to the wall. For his look was other than hers, his way was not her way. She had denied him what he was—she saw it now. She had refused him as himself. And this had been her life, and his life. She was grateful to death, which restored the truth. And she knew she was not dead.

And all the while her heart was bursting with grief and pity for him. What had he suffered? What stretch of horror for this helpless man! She was rigid with agony. She had not been able to help him. He had been cruelly injured, this naked man, this other being, and she could make no reparation. There were the children—but the children belonged to life. This dead man had nothing to do with them. He and she were only channels through which life had flowed to issue in the children. She was a mother—but how awful she knew it now to have been a wife. And he, dead now, how awful he must have felt it to be a husband. She felt that in the next world he would be a stranger to her. If they met there, in the beyond, they would only be ashamed of what had been before. The children had come, for some mysterious reason, out of both of them. But the children did not unite them. Now he was dead, she knew how eternally he was apart from her, how eternally he had nothing more to do with her. She saw this episode of her life closed. They had denied each other in life. Now he had withdrawn. An anguish came over her. It was finished then: it had become hopeless between them long before he died. Yet he had been her husband. But how little!

"Have you got his shirt, 'Lizabeth?"

Elizabeth turned without answering, though she strove to weep and behave as her mother-in-law expected. But she could not, she was silenced. She went into the kitchen and returned with the garment.

"It is aired," she said, grasping the cotton shirt here and there to try. She was almost ashamed to handle him; what right had she or anyone to lay hands on him; but her touch was humble on his body. It was hard work to clothe him. He was so heavy and inert. A terrible dread gripped her all the while: that he could be so heavy and utterly inert, unresponsive, apart. The horror of the distance between them was almost too much for her—it was so infinite a gap she must look across.

At last it was finished. They covered him with a sheet and left him lying, with his face bound. And she fastened the door of the little parlour, lest the children should see what was lying there. Then, with peace sunk heavy on her heart, she went about making tidy the kitchen. She knew she submitted to life, which was her immediate master. But from death, her ultimate master, she winced with fear and shame.

QUESTIONS FOR DISCUSSION AND WRITING

1. How does Lawrence establish the sense of time passing in the story? How does this element enhance the climax in the plot?
2. How does Lawrence reveal Elizabeth's character in her external actions with other characters—her father, daughter, son, and neighbors? In what sense do these external actions reveal her inner nature?
3. How do the connotative words in the first three paragraphs establish both the setting and tone for this story?
4. How do Lawrence's references to the main character as *Mother* and then *Elizabeth* mark a shift in the point of view in the story?
5. How does Elizabeth make chrysanthemums a unifying symbol in the story? In light of the scene with the corpse, how would you interpret the last two sentences of the story?

55

URSULA K. LE GUIN

The Ones Who Walk Away from Omelas[1]

URSULA K. LE GUIN was born in 1929 in Berkeley, California, and educated at Radcliffe College and Columbia University. In 1952 she obtained a Fulbright Fellowship to study in Paris, where she met her husband, historian Charles A. Le Guin. In the mid-fifties, she worked as a part-time writing instructor at Mercer University and the University of Idaho before moving to Portland, Oregon, where she was able to pursue a full-time career as a writer. She published her first novel, *Rocannon's World,* in 1964 and established herself as a leading writer of science fiction and fantasy. Le Guin has contributed short stories, essays, and reviews to numerous science fiction, scholarly, and popular journals, such as *Fantastic, Western Humanities Review,* and *The New Yorker.* Her novels include *The Left Hand of Darkness* (1969), *The Lathe of Heaven* (1970), and her "Earthsea" trilogy: *The Wizard of Earthsea* (1968),

1. The author says the name comes from "a road sign: Salem (Oregon) backwards. . . . Salem equals schelomo equals salaam equals Peace. Melas. O melas. Omelas. Homme hélas." The last phrase equals "Man, alas."

***The Tombs of Atuan* (1971), and *The Farthest Shore* (1972). The last volume was selected for a National Book Award. Le Guin's short fiction, which has won numerous prizes, is collected in *The Wind's Twelve Quarters* (1975) and *Orsinian Tales* (1976). Her more recent work includes *The Beginning Place* (1980) and *Hard Words and Other Poems* (1981). "The Ones Who Walk Away from Omelas," reprinted from *The Wind's Twelve Quarters,* depicts an idyllic community where the conditions for happiness are "strict and absolute."**

With a clamor of bells that set the swallows soaring, the Festival of Summer came to the city Omelas, bright-towered by the sea. The rigging of the boats in harbor sparkled with flags. In the streets between houses with red roofs and painted walls, between old moss-grown gardens and under avenues of trees, past great parks and public buildings, processions moved. Some were decorous: old people in long stiff robes of mauve and gray, grave master workmen, quiet, merry women carrying their babies and chatting as they walked. In other streets the music beat faster, a shimmering of gong and tambourine, and the people went dancing, the procession was a dance. Children dodged in and out, their high calls rising like the swallows' crossing flights over the music and the singing. All the processions wound towards the north side of the city, where on the great water-meadow called the Green Fields boys and girls, naked in the bright air, with mud-stained feet and ankles and long, lithe arms, exercised their restive horses before the race. The horses wore no gear at all but a halter without bit. Their manes were braided with streamers of silver, gold, and green. They flared their nostrils and pranced and boasted to one another; they were vastly excited, the horse being the only animal who has adopted our ceremonies as his own. Far off to the north and west the mountains stood up half encircling Omelas on her bay. The air of morning was so clear that the snow still crowning the Eighteen Peaks burned with white-gold fire across the miles of sunlit air, under the dark blue of the sky. There was just enough wind to make the banners that marked the racecourse snap and flutter now and then. In the silence of the broad green meadows one could hear the music winding through the city streets, farther and nearer and ever approaching, a cheerful faint sweetness of the air from time to time trembled and gathered together and broke out into the great joyous clanging of the bells.

Joyous! How is one to tell about joy? How describe the citizens of Omelas?

They were not simple folk, you see, though they were happy. But we do not say the words of cheer much any more. All smiles have become archaic. Given a description such as this one tends to make certain assumptions. Given a description such as this one tends to look next for the King, mounted on a splendid stallion and surrounded by his noble knights, or perhaps in a golden litter borne by great-muscled slaves. But there was no king. They did not use swords, or keep slaves. They were not barbarians. I do not know the rules and laws of their society, but I suspect that they were singularly few. As they did without monarchy and slavery, so they also got on without the stock exchange, the advertisement, the secret police, and the bomb. Yet I repeat that these were not simple folk, not dulcet shepherds, noble savages, bland utopians. They were not less complex than us. The trouble is that we have a bad habit, encouraged by pedants and sophisticates, of considering happiness as something rather stupid. Only pain is intellectual, only evil interesting. This is the treason of the artist: a refusal to admit the banality of evil and the terrible boredom of pain. If you can't lick 'em, join 'em. If it hurts, repeat it. But to praise despair is to condemn delight, to embrace violence is to lose hold of everything else. We have almost lost hold; we can no longer describe a happy man, nor make any celebration of joy. How can I tell you about the people of Omelas? They were not naïve and happy children—though their children were, in fact, happy. They were mature, intelligent, passionate adults whose lives were not wretched. O miracle! but I wish I could describe it better. I wish I could convince you. Omelas sounds in my words like a city in a fairy tale, long ago and far away, once upon a time. Perhaps it would be best if you imagined it as your own fancy bids, assuming it will rise to the occasion, for certainly I cannot suit you all. For instance, how about technology? I think that there would be no cars or helicopters in and above the streets; this follows from the fact that the people of Omelas are happy people. Happiness is based on a just discrimination of what is necessary, what is neither necessary nor destructive, and what is destructive. In the middle category, however—that of the unnecessary but undestructive, that of comfort, luxury, exuberance, etc.—they could perfectly well have central heating, subway trains, washing machines, and all kinds of marvelous devices not yet invented here, floating light-sources, fuelless power, a cure for the common cold. Or they could have none of that: it doesn't matter. As you like it. I incline to think that people from towns up and down the coast have been coming in to Omelas during the last days before the Festival on very fast little trains and double-decked trams, and that the train station of Omelas is actually the handsomest building in town, though plainer than the magnificent Farmers' Market. But even granted trains, I fear that Omelas so far strikes some of you as goody-goody. Smiles, bells, parades, horses, bleh. If so, please add an orgy. If an orgy would help, don't hesitate. Let us not, however, have temples from which issue beautiful nude priests and priestesses already half in ecstasy and ready to copulate with any man or woman, lover or stranger, who desires union with the deep godhead of the blood, although that was my first idea. But really it would be better not to have any temples in Omelas—at least, not manned temples. Religion yes, clergy no. Surely the beautiful nudes can just wander about, offering themselves like divine soufflés to the hunger of the needy and the rapture of the flesh. Let them join the processions. Let tambourines be struck above the copulations, and the glory of desire be proclaimed upon the gongs, and (a not unimportant point) let the offspring of these delightful rituals be beloved and looked after by all. One thing I know there is none of in Omelas is guilt. But what else should there be? I thought at first there were no drugs, but that is puritanical. For those who like it, the faint insistent sweetness of *drooz* may perfume the ways of the city, *drooz* which first brings a great lightness and brilliance to the mind and limbs, and then after some hours a dreamy languor, and wonderful visions at last of the very arcana and inmost secrets of the Universe, as well as exciting the pleasure of sex beyond all belief; and it is not habit-forming. For more modest tastes I think there ought to be beer. What else, what else belongs in the joyous city? The sense of victory, surely, the celebration of courage. But as we did without clergy, let us do without soldiers. The joy built upon successful slaughter is not the right kind of joy; it will not do; it is fearful and it is trivial. A boundless and generous contentment, a magnanimous triumph felt not against some outer enemy but in communion with the finest and fairest in the souls of all men everywhere and the splendor of the world's summer: this is what swells the hearts of the people of Omelas, and the victory they celebrate is that of life. I really don't think many of them need to take *drooz*.

Most of the processions have reached the Green Fields by now. A marvelous smell of cooking goes forth from the red and blue tents of the provisioners. The faces of small children are amiably sticky; in the benign gray beard of a man a couple of crumbs of rich pastry are entangled. The youths and girls have mounted their horses and are beginning to group around the starting line of the course. An old woman, small, fat, and laughing, is passing out flowers from a basket, and tall young men wear her flowers in their shining hair. A child of nine or ten sits at the edge of the crowd, alone, playing on a wooden flute. People pause to listen, and they smile, but they do not speak to him, for he never ceases playing and never sees them, his dark eyes wholly rapt in the sweet, thin magic of the tune.

He finishes, and slowly lowers his hands holding the wooden flute.

As if that little private silence were the signal, all at once a trumpet sounds from the pavilion near the starting line: imperious, melancholy, piercing. The horses rear on their slender legs, and some of them neigh in answer. Sober-faced, the young riders stroke the horses' necks and soothe them, whispering. "Quiet, quiet, there my beauty, my hope. . . ." They begin to form in rank along the starting line. The crowds along the racecourse are like a field of grass and flowers in the wind. The Festival of Summer has begun.

Do you believe? Do you accept the festival, the city, the joy? No? Then let me describe one more thing.

In a basement under one of the beautiful public buildings of Omelas, or perhaps in the cellar of one of its spacious private homes, there is a room. It has one locked door, and no window. A little light seeps in dustily between cracks in the boards, secondhand from a cobwebbed window somewhere across the cellar. In one corner of the little room a couple of mops, with stiff, clotted, foul-smelling heads, stand near a rusty bucket. The floor is dirt, a little damp to the touch, as cellar dirt usually is. The room is about three paces long and two wide: a mere broom closet or disused tool room. In the room a child is sitting. It could be a boy or a girl. It looks about six, but actually is nearly ten. It is feeble-minded. Perhaps it was born defective, or perhaps it has become imbecile through fear, malnutrition, and neglect. It picks its nose and occasionally fumbles vaguely with its toes or genitals, as it sits hunched in the corner farthest from the bucket and the two mops. It is afraid of the mops. It finds them horrible. It shuts its eyes, but it knows the mops are still standing there; and the door is locked; and nobody will come. The door is always locked; and nobody ever comes, except that sometimes—the child has no understanding of time or interval—sometimes the door rattles terribly and opens, and a person, or several people, are there. One of them may come in and kick the child to make it stand up. The others never come close, but peer in at it with frightened, disgusted eyes. The food bowl and the water jug are hastily filled, the door is locked; the eyes disappear. The people at the door never say anything, but the child, who has not always lived in the tool room, and can remember sunlight and its mother's voice, sometimes speaks. "I will be good," it says. "Please let me out. I will be good!" They never answer. The child used to scream for help at night, and cry a good deal, but now it only makes a kind of whining, "eh-haa, eh-haa," and it speaks less and less often. It is so thin there are no calves to its legs; its belly protrudes; it lives on a half-bowl of corn meal and grease a day. It is naked. Its buttocks and thighs are a mass of festered sores, as it sits in its own excrement continually.

They all know it is there, all the people of Omelas. Some of them have come to see it, others are content merely to know it is there. They all know that it has to be there. Some of them understand why, and some do not, but they all understand that their happiness, the beauty of their city, the tenderness of their friendships, the health of their children, the wisdom of their scholars, the skill of their makers, even the abundance of their harvest and the kindly weathers of their skies, depend wholly on this child's abominable misery.

This is usually explained to children when they are between eight and twelve, whenever they seem capable of understanding; and most of those who come to see the child are young people, though often enough an adult comes, or comes back, to see the child. No matter how well the matter has been explained to them, these young spectators are always shocked and sickened at the sight. They feel disgust, which they had thought themselves superior to. They feel anger, outrage, impotence, despite all the explanations. They would like to do something for the child. But there is nothing they can do. If the child were brought up into the sunlight out of that vile place, if it were cleaned and fed and comforted, that would be a good thing, indeed; but if it were done, in that day and hour all the prosperity and beauty and delight of Omelas would wither and be destroyed. Those are the terms. To exchange all the goodness and grace of every life in Omelas for that single, small improvement: to throw away the happiness of thousands for the chance of the happiness of one: that would be to let guilt within the walls indeed.

The terms are strict and absolute; there may not even be a kind word spoken to the child.

Often the young people go home in tears, or in a tearless rage, when they have seen the child and faced this terrible paradox. They may brood over it for weeks or years. But as time goes on they begin to realize that even if the child could be released, it would not get much good of its freedom: a little vague pleasure of warmth and food, no doubt, but little more. It is too degraded and imbecile to know any real joy. It has been afraid too long ever to be free of fear. Its habits are too uncouth for it to respond to humane treatment. Indeed, after so long it would probably be wretched without walls about it to protect it, and darkness for its eyes, and its own excrement to sit in. Their tears at the bitter injustice dry when they begin to perceive the terrible justice of reality, and to accept it. Yet it is their tears and anger, the trying of their generosity and the acceptance of their helplessness, which are perhaps the true source of the splendor of their lives. Theirs is no vapid, irresponsible happiness. They know that they, like the child, are not free. They know compassion. It is the existence of the child, and their knowledge of its existence, that makes possible the nobility of their architecture, the poignancy of their music, the profundity of their science. It is because of the child that they are so gentle with children. They know that if the wretched one were not there sniveling in the dark, the other one, the flute-player, could make no joyful music as the young riders line up in their beauty for the race in the sunlight of the first morning of summer.

Now do you believe in them? Are they not more credible? But there is one more thing to tell, and this is quite incredible.

At times one of the adolescent girls or boys who go to see the child does not go home to weep or rage, does not, in fact, go home at all. Sometimes also a man or woman much older falls silent for a day or two, and then leaves home. These people go out into the street, and walk down the street alone. They keep walking, and walk straight out of the city of Omelas, through the beautiful gates. They keep walking across the farmlands of Omelas. Each one goes alone, youth or girl, man or woman. Night falls; the traveler must pass down village streets, between the houses with yellow-lit windows, and on out into the darkness of the fields. Each alone, they go west or north, towards the mountains. They go on. They leave Omelas, they walk ahead into the darkness, and they do not come back. The place they go towards is a place even less imaginable to most of us than the city of happiness. I cannot describe it at all. It is possible that it does not exist. But they seem to know where they are going, the ones who walk away from Omelas.

QUESTIONS FOR DISCUSSION AND WRITING

1. How do the questions posed by the author establish the plot of the story? Do the author's answers to these questions provide sufficient information to resolve the conflicts in the story?
2. How does the author characterize the citizens of Omelas? How does their happiness depend on the child in the cellar? How does the author characterize "the ones who walk away from Omelas"?
3. To what extent is Omelas a real place? Why does the narrator present herself as uncertain about the various features of the world she creates? What does she mean when she says "perhaps it would be best if you imagined it as your fancy bids"?
4. How would you characterize the identity of the narrator? What is her relationship to Omelas? Why is she so concerned that you *believe* in and *accept* the credibility of Omelas?
5. What does this story reveal about the condition of happiness? What prompts "pedants and sophisticates" to consider happiness as something stupid? What prompts some to reject the happiness of Omelas?

56

DORIS LESSING

A Woman on a Roof

DORIS LESSING was born in 1919 in Kermanshah, Persia, and was raised on a remote tobacco farm in Southern Rhodesia. She attended a Catholic convent in Salisbury for a few years, but dropped out because of eye trouble and returned to her family's farm to complete her education through independent reading. In

1937 Lessing returned to Salisbury, where she worked as a part-time secretary and became involved in radical politics. By the time she left Africa for England in 1949, she had been married and divorced twice. In 1950 Lessing published her first novel, *The Grass Is Singing,* about the psychological and social causes of violence in South Africa. Her other early works also drew on her African experience: *Martha's Quest* (1952), *Five* (1953), and *A Proper Marriage* (1954). In 1956 Lessing returned to Rhodesia to write *Going Home* (1957) but was prohibited from entering South Africa because of her liberal racial views. In 1962 she published *The Golden Notebook,* a novel that combined her interest in social commentary and psychological analysis. Lessing's later novels have moved increasingly away from realism toward fantasy as she has worked out certain psychological theories in *Briefing for a Descent into Hell* (1971) or explored the realm of science fiction in *Canopus in Argos: Archives* (1981). Her recent work includes *The Diaries of Jane Somers* (1984) and *The Good Terrorist* (1985). "A Woman on a Roof," reprinted from *A Man and Two Women* (1963), reports the attempts of three workers trying to come to terms with their fantasies about a woman sunbather.

It was during the week of hot sun, that June.

Three men were at work on the roof, where the leads got so hot they had the idea of throwing water on to cool them. But the water steamed, then sizzled; and they made jokes about getting an egg from some woman in the flats under them, to poach it for their dinner. By two it was not possible to touch the guttering they were replacing, and they speculated about what workmen did in regularly hot countries. Perhaps they should borrow kitchen gloves with the egg? They were all a bit dizzy, not used to the heat; and they shed their coats and stood side by side squeezing themselves into a foot-wide patch of shade against a chimney, careful to keep their feet in the thick socks and boots out of the sun. There was a fine view across several acres of roofs. Not far off a man sat in a deck chair reading the newspaper. Then they saw her, between chimneys, about fifty yards away. She lay face down on a brown blanket. They could see the top part of her: black hair, a flushed solid back, arms spread out.

"She's stark naked," said Stanley, sounding annoyed.

Harry, the oldest, a man of about forty-five, said: "Looks like it."

Young Tom, seventeen, said nothing, but he was excited and grinning.

Stanley said: "Someone'll report her if she doesn't watch out."

"She thinks no one can see," said Tom, craning his head all ways to see more.

At this point the woman, still lying prone, brought her two hands up behind her shoulders with the ends of her scarf in them, tied it behind her back, and sat up. She wore a red scarf tied around her breasts and brief red bikini pants. This being the first day of the sun she was white, flushing red. She sat smoking, and did not look up when Stanley let out a wolf whistle. Harry said: "Small things amuse small minds," leading the way back to their part of the roof, but it was scorching. Harry said: "Wait, I'm going to rig up some shade," and disappeared down the skylight into the building. Now that he'd gone, Stanley and Tom went to the farthest point they could to peer at the woman. She had moved, and all they could see were two pink legs stretched on the blanket. They whistled and shouted but the legs did not move. Harry came back with a blanket and shouted: "Come on, then." He sounded irritated with them. They clambered back to him and he said to Stanley: "What about your missus?" Stanley was newly married, about three months. Stanley said, jeering: "What about my missus?"—preserving his independence. Tom said nothing, but his mind was full of the nearly naked woman. Harry slung the blanket, which he had borrowed from a friendly woman downstairs, from the stem of a television aerial to a row of chimney-pots. This shade fell across the piece of gutter they had to replace. But the shade kept moving, they had to adjust the blanket, and not much progress was made. At last some of the heat left the roof, and they worked fast, making up for lost time. First Stanley, then Tom, made a trip to the end of the roof to see the woman. "She's on her back," Stanley said, adding a jest which made Tom snicker, and the older man smiled tolerantly. Tom's report was that she hadn't moved, but it was a lie. He wanted to keep what he had seen to himself: he had caught her in the act of rolling down the little red pants over her hips, till they were no more than a small triangle. She was on her back, fully visible, glistening with oil.

Next morning, as soon as they came up, they went to look. She was already there, face down, arms spread out, naked except for the little red pants. She had turned brown in the night. Yesterday she was a scarlet-and-white woman, today she was a brown woman. Stanley let out a whistle. She lifted her head, startled, as if she'd been asleep, and looked straight over at them. The sun was in her eyes, she blinked and stared, then she dropped her head again. At this gesture of indifference, they all three, Stanley, Tom and old Harry, let out whistles and yells. Harry was doing it in parody of the younger men, making fun of them, but he was also angry. They were all angry because of her utter indifference to the three men watching her.

"Bitch," said Stanley.

"She should ask us over," said Tom, snickering.

Harry recovered himself and reminded Stanley: "If she's married, her old man wouldn't like that."

"Christ," said Stanley virtuously, "if my wife lay about like that, for everyone to see, I'd soon stop her."

Harry said, smiling: "How do you know, perhaps she's sunning herself at this very moment?"

"Not a chance, not on our roof." The safety of his wife put Stanley into a good humor, and they went to work. But today it was hotter than yesterday; and several times one or the other suggested they should tell Matthew, the foreman, and ask to leave the roof until the heat wave was over. But they didn't. There was work to be done in the basement of the big block of flats, but up here they felt free, on a different level from ordinary humanity shut in the streets or the buildings. A lot more people came out on to the roofs that day, for an hour at midday. Some married couples sat side by side in deck chairs, the women's legs stockingless and scarlet, the men in vests with reddening shoulders.

The woman stayed on her blanket, turning herself over and over. She ignored them, no matter what they did. When Harry went off to fetch more screws, Stanley said: "Come on." Her roof belonged to a different system of roofs, separated from theirs at one point by about twenty feet. It meant a scrambling climb from one level to another, edging along parapets, clinging to chimneys, while their big boots slipped and slithered, but at last they stood on a small square projecting roof looking straight down at her, close. She sat smoking, reading a book. Tom thought she looked like a poster, or a magazine cover, with the blue sky behind her and her legs stretched out. Behind her a great crane at work on a new building in Oxford Street swung its black arm across roofs in a great arc. Tom imagined himself at work on the crane, adjusting the arm to swing over and pick her up and swing her back across the sky to drop her near him.

They whistled. She looked up at them, cool and remote, then went on reading. Again, they were furious. Or, rather, Stanley was. His sun-heated face was screwed into a rage as he whistled again and again, trying to make her look up. Young Tom stopped whistling. He stood beside Stanley, excited, grinning; but he felt as if he were saying to the woman: Don't associate me with *him,* for his grin was apologetic. Last night he had thought of the unknown woman before he slept, and she had been tender with him. This tenderness he was remembering as he shifted his feet by the jeering, whistling Stanley, and watched the indifferent, healthy brown woman a few feet off, with the gap that plunged to the street between them. Tom thought it was romantic, it was like being high on two hilltops. But there was a shout from Harry, and they clambered back. Stanley's face was hard, really angry. The boy kept looking at him and wondered why he hated the woman so much, for by now he loved her.

They played their little games with the blanket, trying to trap shade to work under; but again it was not until nearly four that they could work seriously, and they were exhausted, all three of them. They were grumbling about the weather by now. Stanley was in a thoroughly bad humor. When they made their routine trip to see the woman before they packed up for the day, she was apparently asleep, face down, her back all naked save for the scarlet triangle on her buttocks. "I've got a good mind to report her to the police," said Stanley, and Harry said: "What's eating you? What harm's she doing?"

"I tell you, if she was my wife!"

"But she isn't is she?" Tom knew that Harry, like himself, was uneasy at Stanley's reaction. He was normally a sharp young man, quick at his work, making a lot of jokes, good company.

"Perhaps it will be cooler tomorrow," said Harry.

But it wasn't; it was hotter, if anything, and the weather forecast said the good weather would last. As soon as they were on the roof, Harry went over to see if the woman was there, and Tom knew it was to prevent Stanley going, to put off his bad humor. Harry had grownup children, a boy the same age as Tom, and the youth trusted and looked up to him.

Harry came back and said: "She's not there."

"I bet her old man put his foot down," said Stanley, and Harry and Tom caught each other's eyes and smiled behind the young married man's back.

Harry suggested they should get permission to work in the basement, and they did, that day. But before packing up Stanley said: "Let's have a breath of fresh air." Again Harry and Tom smiled at each other as they followed Stanley up to the roof, Tom in the devout conviction that he was there to protect the woman from Stanley. It was about five-thirty, and a calm, full sunlight lay over the roofs. The great crane still swung its black arm from Oxford Street to above their heads. She was not there. Then there was a flutter of white from behind a parapet, and she stood up, in a belted, white dressing-gown. She had been there all day, probably, but on a different patch of roof, to hide from them. Stanley did not whistle; he said nothing, but watched the woman bend to collect papers, books, cigarettes, then fold the blanket over her arm. Tom was thinking: If they weren't here, I'd go over and say . . . what? But he knew from his nightly dreams of her that she was kind and friendly. Perhaps she would ask him down to her flat? Perhaps . . . He stood watching her disappear down the skylight. As she went, Stanley let out a shrill derisive yell; she started, and it seemed as if she nearly fell. She clutched to save herself, they could hear things falling. She looked straight at them, angry. Harry said, facetiously: "Better be careful on those slippery ladders, love." Tom knew he said it to save her from Stanley, but she could not know it. She vanished, frowning. Tom was full of a secret delight, because he knew her anger was for the others, not for him.

"Roll on some rain," said Stanley, bitter, looking at the blue evening sky.

Next day was cloudless, and they decided to finish the work in the basement. They felt excluded, shut in the grey cement basement fitting pipes, from the holiday atmosphere of London in a heat wave. At lunchtime they came up for some air, but while the married couples, and the men in shirt-sleeves or vests, were there, she was not there, either on her usual patch of roof or where she had been yesterday. They all, even Harry, clambered about, between chimney-pots, over parapets, the hot leads stinging their fingers. There was not a sign of her. They took off their shirts and vests and exposed their chests, feeling their feet sweaty and hot. They did not mention the woman. But Tom felt alone again. Last night she had him into her flat: it was big and had fitted white carpets and a bed with a padded white leather head-board. She wore a black filmy negligée and her kindness to Tom thickened his throat as he remembered it. He felt she had betrayed him by not being there.

And again after work they climbed up, but still there was nothing to be seen of her. Stanley kept repeating that if it was as hot as this tomorrow he wasn't going to work and that's all there was to it. But they were all there next day. By ten the temperature was in the middle seventies, and it was eighty long before noon. Harry went to the foreman to say it was impossible to work on the leads in that heat; but the foreman said there was nothing else he could put them on, and they'd have to. At midday they stood, silent, watching the skylight on her roof open, and then she slowly emerged in her white gown, holding a bundle of blanket. She looked at them, gravely, then went to the part of the roof where she was hidden from them. Tom was pleased. He felt she was more his when the other men couldn't see her. They had taken off their shirts and vests, but now they put them back again, for they felt the sun bruising their flesh. "She must have the hide of a rhino," said Stanley, tugging at guttering and swearing. They stopped work, and sat in the shade, moving around behind chimney stacks. A woman came to water a yellow window box opposite them. She was middle-aged, wearing a flowered summer dress. Stanley said to her: "We need a drink more than them." She smiled and said: "Better drop down to the pub quick, it'll be closing in a minute." They exchanged pleasantries, and she left them with a smile and a wave.

"Not like Lady Godiva," said Stanley. "She can give us a bit of a chat and a smile."

"You didn't whistle at *her,*" said Tom, reproving.

"Listen to him," said Stanley, "you didn't whistle, then?"

But the boy felt as if he hadn't whistled, as if only Harry and Stanley had. He was making plans, when it was time to knock off work, to get left behind and somehow make his way over to the woman. The weather report said the hot spell was due to break, so he had to move quickly. But there was no chance of being left. The other two decided to knock off work at four, because they were exhausted. As they went down, Tom quickly climbed a parapet and hoisted himself higher by pulling his weight up a chimney. He caught a glimpse of her lying on her back, her knees up, eyes closed, a brown woman lolling in the sun. He slipped and clattered down, as Stanley looked for information: "She's gone down," he said. He felt as if he had protected her from Stanley, and that she must be grateful to him. He could feel the bond between the woman and himself.

Next day, they stood around on the landing below the roof, reluctant to climb up into the heat. The woman who had lent Harry the blanket came out and offered them a cup of tea. They accepted gratefully, and sat around Mrs. Pritchett's kitchen an hour or so, chatting. She was married to an airline pilot. A smart blonde, of about thirty, she had an eye for the handsome sharp-faced Stanley; and the two teased each other while Harry sat in a corner, watching, indulgent, though his expression reminded Stanley that he was married. And young Tom felt envious of Stanley's ease in badinage; felt, too, that Stanley's getting off with Mrs. Pritchett left his romance with the woman on the roof safe and intact.

"I thought they said the heat wave'd break," said Stanley, sullen, as the time approached when they really would have to climb up into the sunlight.

"You don't like it, then?" asked Mrs. Pritchett.

"All right for some," said Stanley. "Nothing to do but lie about as if it was a beach up there. Do you ever go up?"

"Went up once," said Mrs. Pritchett. "But it's a dirty place up there, and it's too hot."

"Quite right too," said Stanley.

Then they went up, leaving the cool neat little flat and the friendly Mrs. Pritchett.

As soon as they were up they saw her. The three men looked at her, resentful at her ease in this punishing sun. Then Harry said, because of the expression on Stanley's face: "Come on, we've got to pretend to work, at least."

They had to wrench another length of guttering that ran beside a parapet out of its bed, so that they could replace it. Stanley took it in his two hands, tugged, swore, stood up. "Fuck it," he said, and sat down under a chimney. He lit a cigarette. "Fuck them," he said. "What do they think we are, lizards? I've got blisters all over my hands." Then he jumped up and climbed over the roofs and stood with his back to them. He put his fingers either side of his mouth and let out a shrill whistle. Tom and Harry squatted, not looking at each other, watching him. They could just see the woman's head, the beginnings of her brown shoulders. Stanley whistled again. Then he began stamping with his feet, and whistled and yelled and screamed at the woman, his face getting scarlet. He seemed quite mad, as he stamped and whistled, while the woman did not move, she did not move a muscle.

"Barmy," said Tom.

"Yes," said Harry, disapproving.

Suddenly the older man came to a decision. It was, Tom knew, to save some sort of scandal or real trouble over the woman. Harry stood up and began packing tools into a length of oily cloth. "Stanley," he said, commanding. At first Stanley took no notice, but Harry said: "Stanley, we're packing it in, I'll tell Matthew."

Stanley came back, cheeks mottled, eyes glaring.

"Can't go on like this," said Harry. "It'll break in a day or so. I'm going to tell Matthew we've got sunstroke, and if he doesn't like, it's too bad." Even Harry sounded aggrieved, Tom noted. The small, competent man, the family man with his grey hair, who was never at a loss, sounded really off balance. "Come on," he said, angry. He fitted himself into the open square in the roof, and went down, watching his feet on the ladder. Then Stanley went, with not a glance at the woman. Then Tom, who, his throat beating with excitement, silently promised her on a backward glance: Wait for me, wait, I'm coming.

On the pavement Stanley said: "I'm going home." He looked white now, so perhaps he really did have sunstroke. Harry went off to find the foreman, who was at work on the plumbing of some flats down the street. Tom slipped back, not into the building they had been working on, but the building on whose roof the woman lay. He went straight up, no one stopping him. The skylight stood open, with an iron ladder leading up. He emerged on to the roof a couple of yards from her. She sat up, pushing back her black hair with both hands. The scarf across her breasts bound them tight, and brown flesh bulged around it. Her legs were brown and smooth. She stared at him in silence. The boy stood grinning, foolish, claiming the tenderness he expected from her.

"What do you want?" she asked.

"I . . . I came to . . . make your acquaintance," he stammered, grinning, pleading with her.

They looked at each other, the slight, scarlet-faced excited boy, and the serious, nearly naked woman. Then, without a word, she lay down on her brown blanket, ignoring him.

"You like the sun, do you?" he enquired of her glistening back.

Not a word. He felt panic, thinking of how she had held him in her arms, stroked his hair, brought him where he sat, lordly, in her bed, a glass of some exhilarating liquor he had never tasted in life. He felt that if he knelt down, stroked her shoulders, her hair, she would turn and clasp him in her arms.

He said: "The sun's all right for you, isn't it?"

She raised her head, set her chin on two small fists. "Go away," she said. He did not move. "Listen," she said, in a slow reasonable voice, where anger was kept in check, though with difficulty; looking at him, her face weary with anger, "if you get a kick out of seeing women in bikinis, why don't you take a sixpenny bus ride to the Lido? You'd see dozens of them, without all this mountaineering."

She hadn't understood him. He felt her unfairness pale him. He stammered: "But I like you, I've been watching you and . . ."

"Thanks," she said, and dropped her face again, turned away from him.

She lay there. He stood there. She said nothing. She had simply shut him out. He stood, saying nothing at all, for some minutes. He thought: She'll have to say something if I stay. But the minutes went past, with no sign of them in her, except in the tension of her back, her thighs, her arms—the tension of waiting for him to go.

He looked up at the sky, where the sun seemed to spin in heat; and over the roofs where he and his mates had been earlier. He could see the heat quivering where they had worked. And they expect us to work in these conditions! he thought, filled with righteous indignation. The woman hadn't moved. A bit of hot wind blew her black hair softly; it shone, and was iridescent. He remembered how he had stroked it last night.

Resentment of her at last moved him off and away down the ladder, through the building, into the street. He got drunk then, in hatred of her.

Next day when he woke the sky was grey. He looked at the wet grey and thought, vicious: Well, that's fixed you, hasn't it now? That's fixed you good and proper.

The three men were at work early on the cool leads, surrounded by damp drizzling roofs where no one came to sun themselves, black roofs, slimy with rain. Because it was cool now, they would finish the job that day, if they hurried.

QUESTIONS FOR DISCUSSION AND WRITING

1. How does the conflict between the three workers and the woman change during six days of good weather? How does Stanley's yell bring this conflict to a crisis? How does the rain resolve the conflict?
2. How does each man characterize himself by his attitude toward the woman on the roof? For example, why does Stanley approve of the woman who waters the window box? Why does Tom think he is different from the others? Why does Harry ask his foreman if they can work somewhere else?
3. Is this a story about setting or a story about character? For example, how does the sun affect the workers' ability to do their job? Why do the workers resent the woman's leisure in the sun?
4. Although the point of view is omniscient, the story is told from the workers' point of view. What evidence in the story suggests that the woman is changing her point of view toward the men who are watching her?
5. What does the woman symbolize for each man? How does the gap in the roof enrich the significance of each of these symbols? What does Tom discover about the woman and himself when he is able to gain access to her roof?

57

JACK LONDON

To Build a Fire

JACK LONDON (1876–1916) was born in San Francisco and attended Oakland High School and the University of California, Berkeley. London's formal education was intermittent and brief. At fourteen, he bought a sloop and became an oyster pirate, raiding the oyster beds in San Francisco Bay. At seventeen, he joined a sealing expedition that took him to Japan and Siberia. When London returned, he tramped throughout the United States, joining Coxey's Army of unemployed workers in its march on Washington and becoming a member of the Socialist Labor Party. In 1897, at the age of twenty-one, London joined the gold rush to the Klondike. Although he was unsuccessful as a miner, London decided to write about his experiences in the Yukon—publishing his first short story, "To the Man on the Trail," in *Overland Monthly* in 1899. He published his first collection of stories, *Son of the Wolf,* in 1900 and his first novel, *The Call of the Wild,* in 1903. The latter became an instant best seller, making London the highest-paid writer of his time. During the remaining years of his life, he produced almost fifty volumes of prose. As a journalist, London covered the Russian-Japanese War, the San Francisco earthquake, and the Mexican Revolution. His later works include *The Sea Wolf* (1904), *White Fang* (1906), *The Iron Heel* (1908), and *Martin Eden* (1909). The last book, largely autobiographical, chronicles London's literary success, disenchantment with socialism, and thoughts about suicide. "To Build a Fire," reprinted from *Lost Face* (1910), tells the story of one man's struggle for survival in an indifferent universe.

Day had broken cold and grey, exceedingly cold and grey, when the man turned aside from the main Yukon trail and climbed the high earth-bank, where a dim and little-travelled trail led eastward through the fat spruce timberland. It was a steep bank, and he paused for breath at the top, excusing the act to himself by looking at his watch. It was nine o'clock. There was no sun nor hint of sun, though there was not a cloud in the sky. It was a clear day, and yet there seemed an intangible pall over the face of things, a subtle gloom that made the day dark, and that was due to the absence of sun. This fact did not worry the man. He was used to the lack of sun. It had been days since he had seen the sun, and he knew that a few more days must pass before that cheerful orb, due south, would just peep above the skyline and dip immediately from view.

The man flung a look back along the way he had come. The Yukon lay a mile wide and hidden under three feet of ice. On top of this ice were as many feet of snow. It was all pure white, rolling in gentle undulations where the ice jams of the freeze-up had formed. North and south, as far as his eye could see, it was unbroken white, save for a dark hairline that curved and twisted from around the spruce-covered island to the south, and that curved and twisted away into the north, where it disappeared behind another spruce-covered island. This dark hairline was the trail—the main trail—that led south five hundred miles to the Chilcoot Pass, Dyea, and salt water; and that led north seventy miles to Dawson, and still on to the north a thousand miles to Nulato, and finally to St. Michael, on Bering Sea, a thousand miles and half a thousand more.

But all this—the mysterious, far-reaching hairline trail, the absence of sun from the sky, the tremendous cold, and the strangeness and weirdness of it all—made no impression on the man. It was not because he was long used to it. He was a newcomer in the land, a *chechaquo*, and this was his first winter. The trouble with him was that he was without imagination. He was quick and alert in the things of life, but only in the things, and not in the significances. Fifty degrees below zero meant eighty-odd degrees of frost. Such fact impressed him as being cold and uncomfortable, and that was all. It did not lead him to meditate upon his frailty as a creature of temperature, and upon man's frailty in general, able only to live within certain narrow limits of heat and cold; and from there on it did not lead him to the conjectural field of immortality and man's place in the universe. Fifty degrees below zero stood for a bite of frost that hurt and that must be guarded against by the use of mittens, ear flaps, warm moccasins, and thick socks. Fifty degrees below zero. That there should be anything more to it than that was a thought that never entered his head.

As he turned to go on, he spat speculatively. There was a sharp explosive crackle that startled him. He spat again. And again, in the air, before it could fall to the snow, the spittle crackled. He knew that at fifty below spittle crackled on the snow, but this spittle had crackled in the air. Undoubtedly it was colder than fifty below—how much colder he did not know. But the temperature did not matter. He was bound for the old claim on the left fork of Henderson Creek, where the boys were already. They had come over across the divide from the Indian Creek country, while he had come the roundabout way to take a look at the possibilities of getting out logs in the spring from the islands in the Yukon. He would be in to camp by six o'clock; a bit after dark, it was true, but the boys would be there, a fire would be going, and a hot supper would be ready. As for lunch, he pressed his hand against the protruding bundle under his jacket. It was also under his shirt, wrapped up in a handkerchief and lying against the naked skin. It was the only way to keep the biscuits from freezing. He smiled agreeably to himself as he thought of those biscuits, each cut open and sopped in bacon grease, and each enclosing a generous slice of fried bacon.

He plunged in among the big spruce trees. The trail was faint. A foot of snow had fallen since the last sled had passed over, and he was glad he was without a sled, travelling light. In fact, he carried nothing but the lunch wrapped in the handkerchief. He was surprised, however, at the cold. It certainly was cold, he concluded, as he rubbed his numb nose and cheekbones with his mittened hand. He was a warm-whiskered man, but the hair on his face did not protect the high cheekbones and the eager nose that thrust itself aggressively into the frosty air.

At the man's heels trotted a dog, a big native husky, the proper wolf dog, grey-coated and without any visible or temperamental difference from its brother, the wild wolf. The animal was depressed by the tremendous cold. It knew that it was no time for travelling. Its instinct told it a truer tale than was told to the man by the man's judgment. In reality, it was not merely colder than fifty below zero; it was colder than sixty below, than seventy below. It was seventy-five below zero. Since the freezing point is thirty-two above zero, it meant that one hundred and seven degrees of frost obtained. The dog did not know anything about thermometers. Possibly in its brain there was no sharp consciousness of a condition of very cold such as was in the man's brain. But the brute had its instinct. It experienced a vague but menacing apprehension that subdued it and made it slink along at the man's heels, and that made it question eagerly every unwonted movement of the man as if expecting him to go into camp and to seek shelter somewhere and build a fire. The dog had learned fire, and it wanted fire, or else to burrow under the snow and cuddle its warmth away from the air.

The frozen moisture of its breathing had settled on its fur in a fine powder of frost, and especially were its jowls, muzzle, and eyelashes whitened by its crystalled breath. The man's red beard and moustache were likewise frosted, but more solidly, the deposit taking the form of ice and increasing with every warm, moist breath he exhaled. Also, the man was chewing tobacco, and the muzzle of ice held his lips so rigidly that he was unable to clear his chin when he expelled the juice. The result was that a crystal beard of the colour and solidity of amber was increasing its length on his chin. If he fell down it would shatter itself, like glass, into brittle fragments. But he did not mind the appendage. It was the penalty all tobacco chewers paid in that country, and he had been out before in two cold snaps. They had not been so cold as this, he knew, but by the spirit thermometer at Sixty Mile he knew they had been registered at fifty below and at fifty-five.

He held on through the level stretch of woods for several miles, crossed a wide flat of nigger heads, and dropped down a bank to the frozen bed of a small stream. This was Henderson Creek, and he knew he was ten miles from the forks. He looked at his watch. It was ten o'clock. He was making four miles an hour, and he calculated that he would arrive at the forks at half-past twelve. He decided to celebrate that event by eating his lunch there.

The dog dropped in again at his heels, with a tail drooping discouragement, as the man swung along the creek bed. The furrow of the old sled trail was plainly visible, but a dozen inches of snow covered up the marks of the last runners. In a month no man had come up or down that silent creek. The man held steadily on. He was not much given to thinking, and just then particularly he had nothing to think about save that he would eat lunch at the forks and that at six o'clock he would be in camp with the boys. There was nobody to talk to; and, had there been, speech would have been impossible because of the ice muzzle on his mouth. So he continued monotonously to chew tobacco and to increase the length of his amber beard.

Once in a while the thought reiterated itself that it was very cold and that he had never experienced such cold. As he walked along he rubbed his cheekbones and nose with the back of his mittened hand. He did this automatically, now and again changing hands. But, rub as he would, the instant he stopped his cheekbones went numb, and the following instant the end of his nose went numb. He was sure to frost his cheeks; he knew that, and experienced a pang of regret that he had not devised a nose strap of the sort Bud wore in cold snaps. Such a strap passed across the cheeks, as well, and saved them. But it didn't matter much, after all. What were frosted cheeks? A bit painful, that was all; they were never serious.

Empty as the man's mind was of thoughts, he was keenly observant, and he noticed the changes in the creeks, the curves and bends and timber jams, and always he sharply noted where he placed his feet. Once, coming round a bend, he shied abruptly, like a startled horse, curved away from the place where he had been walking, and retreated several paces back along the trail. The creek he knew was frozen clear to the bottom—no creek could contain water in that arctic winter—but he knew also that there were springs that bubbled out from the hillsides and ran along under the snow and on top of the ice of the creek. He knew that the coldest snaps never froze these springs, and he knew likewise their danger. They were traps. They hid pools of water under the snow that might be three inches deep, or three feet. Sometimes a skin of ice half an inch thick covered them, and in turn was covered by snow. Sometimes there were alternate layers of water and ice skin, so that when one broke through he kept on breaking through for a while, sometimes wetting himself to the waist.

That was why he had shied in such a panic. He had felt the give under his feet and heard the crackle of a snow-hidden ice skin. And to get his feet wet in such a temperature meant trouble and danger. At the very least it meant delay, for he would be forced to stop and build a fire, and under its protection to bare his feet while he dried his socks and moccasins. He stood and studied the creek bed and its banks, and decided that the flow of water came from the right. He reflected awhile, rubbing his nose and cheeks, then skirted to the left, stepping gingerly and testing the footing for each step. Once clear of the danger, he took a fresh chew of tobacco and swung along at his four-mile gait.

In the course of the next two hours he came upon several similar traps. Usually the snow above the hidden pools had a sunken, candied appearance that advertised the danger. Once again, however, he had a close call; and once, suspecting danger, he compelled the dog to go on in front. The dog did not want to go. It hung back until the man shoved it forward, and then it went quickly across the white, unbroken surface. Suddenly it broke through, floundered to one side, and got away to firmer footing. It had wet its forefeet and legs, and almost immediately the water that clung to it turned to ice. It made quick efforts to lick the ice off its legs, then dropped down in the snow and began to bite out the ice that had formed between the toes. This was a matter of instinct. To permit the ice to remain would mean sore feet. It did not know this. It merely obeyed the mysterious prompting that arose from the deep crypts of its being. But the man knew, having achieved a judgment on the subject, and he removed the mitten from his right hand and helped to tear out the ice particles. He did not expose his fingers more than a minute, and was astonished at the swift numbness that smote them. It certainly was cold. He pulled on the mitten hastily, and beat the hand savagely across his chest.

At twelve o'clock the day was at its brightest. Yet the sun was too far south on its winter journey to clear the horizon. The bulge of the earth intervened between it and

Henderson Creek, where the man walked under a clear sky at noon and cast no shadow. At half-past twelve, to the minute, he arrived at the forks of the creek. He was pleased at the speed he had made. If he kept it up, he would certainly be with the boys by six. He unbuttoned his jacket and shirt and drew forth his lunch. The action consumed no more than a quarter of a minute, yet in that brief moment the numbness laid hold of the exposed fingers. He did not put the mitten on, but, instead, struck the fingers a dozen sharp smashes against his leg. Then he sat down on a snow-covered log to eat. The sting that followed upon the striking of his fingers against his leg ceased so quickly that he was startled. He had had no chance to take a bit of biscuit. He struck the fingers repeatedly and returned them to the mitten, baring the other hand for the purpose of eating. He tried to take a mouthful, but the ice muzzle prevented. He had forgotten to build a fire and thaw out. He chuckled at his foolishness, and as he chuckled he noted the numbness creeping into the exposed fingers. Also, he noted that the stinging which had first come to his toes when he sat down was already passing away. He wondered whether the toes were warm or numb. He moved them inside the moccasins and decided that they were numb.

He pulled the mitten on hurriedly and stood up. He was a bit frightened. He stamped up and down until the stinging returned into the feet. It certainly was cold, was his thought. That man from Sulphur Creek had spoken the truth when telling how cold it sometimes got in the country. And he had laughed at him at the time! That showed one must not be too sure of things. There was no mistake about it, it *was* cold. He strode up and down, stamping his feet and threshing his arms, until reassured by the returning warmth. Then he got out matches and proceeded to make a fire. From the undergrowth, where high water of the previous spring had lodged a supply of seasoned twigs, he got his firewood. Working carefully from a small beginning, he soon had a roaring fire, over which he thawed the ice from his face and in the protection of which he ate his biscuits. For the moment the cold of space was outwitted. The dog took satisfaction in the fire, stretching out close enough for warmth and far enough away to escape being singed.

When the man had finished, he filled his pipe and took his comfortable time over a smoke. Then he pulled on his mittens, settled the ear-flaps of his cap firmly about his ears, and took the creek trail up the left fork. The dog was disappointed and yearned back towards the fire. This man did not know cold. Possibly all the generations of his ancestry had been ignorant of cold, of real cold, of cold one hundred and seven degrees below freezing point. But the dog knew; all its ancestry knew, and it had inherited the knowledge. And it knew that it was not good to walk abroad in such fearful cold. It was the time to lie snug in a hole in the snow and wait for a curtain of cloud to be drawn across the face of outer space whence this cold came. On the other hand, there was no keen intimacy between the dog and the man. The one was the toil slave of the other, and the only caresses it had ever received were the caresses of the whip lash and of harsh and menacing throat sounds that threatened the whip lash. So the dog made no effort to communicate its apprehension to the man. It was not concerned in the welfare of the man; it was for its own sake that it yearned back towards the fire. But the man whistled, and spoke to it with the sound of whip lashes, and the dog swung in at the man's heels and followed after.

The man took a chew of tobacco and proceeded to start a new amber beard. Also, his moist breath quickly powdered with white his moustache, eyebrows, and lashes. There did not seem to be so many springs on the left fork of the Henderson, and for half an hour the man saw no signs of any. And then it happened. At a place where there were no signs, where the soft, unbroken snow seemed to advertise solidity beneath, the man broke through. It was not deep. He wet himself half-way to the knees before he floundered out to the firm crust.

He was angry, and cursed his luck aloud. He had hoped to get into camp with the boys at six o'clock, and this would delay him an hour, for he would have to build a fire and dry out his footgear. This was imperative at that low temperature—he knew that much; and he turned aside to the bank, which he climbed. On top, tangled in the underbrush about the trunks of several small spruce trees, was a high-water deposit of dry firewood—sticks and twigs, principally, but also larger portions of seasoned branches and fine, dry, last year's grasses. He threw down several large pieces on top of the snow. This served for a foundation and prevented the young flame from drowning itself in the snow it otherwise would melt. The flame he got by touching a match to a small shred of birch bark that he took from his pocket. This burned even more readily than paper. Placing it on the foundation, he fed the young flame with wisps of dry grass and with the tiniest dry twigs.

He worked slowly and carefully, keenly aware of his danger. Gradually, as the flame grew stronger, he increased the size of the twigs with which he fed it. He squatted in the snow pulling the twigs out from their entanglement in the brush and feeding directly to the flame. He knew there must be no failure. When it is seventy-five below zero, a man must not fail in his first attempt to build a fire—that is, if his feet are wet. If his feet are dry, and he fails, he can run along the trail for half a mile and restore his circulation. But the circulation of wet and freezing feet cannot be restored by running when it is seventy-five below. No matter how fast he runs, the wet feet will freeze the harder.

All this the man knew. The old-timer on Sulphur Creek had told him about it the previous fall, and now he was appreciating the advice. Already all sensation had gone out of his feet. To build the fire he had been forced to remove his mittens, and the fingers had quickly gone numb. His pace of four miles an hour had kept his heart pumping blood to the surface of his body and to all the extremities. But the instant he stopped, the action of the pump eased down. The cold of space smote the unprotected tip of the planet, and he, being on that unprotected tip, received the full force of the blow. The blood of his body recoiled before it. The blood was alive, like the dog, and like the dog it wanted to hide away and cover itself up from the fearful cold. So long as he walked four miles an hour, he pumped that blood, willy-nilly, to the surface; but now it ebbed away and sank down into the recesses of his body. The extremities were the first to feel its absence. His wet feet froze faster, and his exposed fingers numbed the faster, though they had not yet begun to freeze. Nose and cheeks were already freezing, while the skin of all his body chilled as it lost its blood.

But he was safe. Toes and nose and cheeks would be only touched by the frost, for the fire was beginning to burn with strength. He was feeding it with twigs the size of his finger. In another minute he would be able to feed it with branches the size of his wrist, and then he could remove his wet footgear, and, while it dried, he could keep his naked feet warm by the fire, rubbing them at first, of course, with snow. The fire was a success. He was safe. He remembered the advice of the old-timer on Sulphur Creek, and smiled. The old-timer had been very serious in laying down the law that no man must travel alone in the Klondike after fifty below. Well, here he was; he had had the accident; he was alone; and he had saved himself. Those old-timers were rather womanish, some of them, he thought. All a man had to do was to keep his head, and he was all right. Any man who was a man could travel alone. But it was surprising, the rapidity with which his cheeks and nose were freezing. And he had not thought his fingers could go lifeless in so short a time. Lifeless they were, for he could scarcely make them move together to grip a twig, and they seemed remote from his body and from him. When he touched a twig, he had to look and see whether or not he had hold of it. The wires were pretty well down between him and his finger ends.

All of which counted for little. There was the fire, snapping and crackling and promising life with every dancing flame. He started to untie his moccasins. They were coated with ice; the thick German socks were like sheaths of iron halfway to the knees; and the moccasin strings were like rods of steel all twisted and knotted as by some conflagration. For a moment he tugged with his numb fingers, then, realizing the folly of it, he drew his sheath knife.

But before he could cut the strings, it happened. It was his own fault, or, rather, his mistake. He should not have built the fire under the spruce tree. He should have built it in the open. But it had been easier to pull the twigs from the brush and drop them directly on the fire. Now the tree under which he had done this carried a weight of snow on its boughs. No wind had blown for weeks, and each bough was fully freighted. Each time he had pulled a twig he had communicated a slight agitation to the tree—an imperceptible agitation, so far as he was concerned, but an agitation sufficient to bring about the disaster. High up in the tree one bough capsized its load of snow. This fell on the boughs beneath, capsizing them. This process continued, spreading out and involving the whole tree. It grew like an avalanche, and it descended without warning upon the man and the fire, and the fire was blotted out! Where it had burned was a mantle of fresh and disordered snow.

The man was shocked. It was as though he had just heard his own sentence of death. For a moment he sat and stared at the spot where the fire had been. Then he grew very calm. Perhaps the old-timer on Sulphur Creek was right. If he had only had a trail mate he would have been in no danger now. The trail mate could have built the fire. Well, it was up to him to build the fire over again, and this second time there must be no failure. Even if he succeeded, he would most likely lose some toes. His feet must be badly frozen by now, and there would be some time before the second fire was ready.

Such were his thoughts, but he did not sit and think them. He was busy all the time they were passing through his mind. He had made a new foundation for a fire, this time in the open, where no treacherous tree could blot it out. Next he gathered dry grasses and tiny twigs from the high-water flotsam. He could not bring his fingers together to pull them out, but he was able to gather them by the handful. In this way he got many rotten twigs and bits of green moss that were undesirable, but it was the best he could do. He worked methodically, even collecting an armful of the larger branches to be used later when the fire gathered strength. And all the while the dog sat and watched him, a certain yearning wistfulness in its eyes, it looked upon him as the fire provider, and the fire was slow in coming.

When all was ready, the man reached in his pocket for a second piece of birch bark. He knew the bark was there, and, though he could not feel it with his fingers, he could hear its crisp rustling as he fumbled for it. Try as he would, he could not clutch hold of it. And all the time, in his consciousness, was the knowledge that each instant his feet were freezing. This thought tended to put him in a panic, but he fought against it and kept calm. He pulled on his mittens with his teeth, and threshed his arms back and forth, beating his hands with all his might against his sides. He did this sitting down, and he stood up to do it; and all the while the dog sat in the snow, its wolf brush of a tail curled around warmly over its forefeet, its sharp wolf ears pricked forward intently as it watched the man. And the man, as he beat and threshed with his arms and hands, felt a great surge of envy as he regarded the creature that was warm and secure in its natural covering.

After a time he was aware of the first faraway signals of sensation in his beaten fingers. The faint tingling grew stronger till it evolved into a stinging ache that was excruciating, but which the man hailed with satisfaction. He stripped the mitten from his right hand and fetched forth the birch bark. The exposed fingers were quickly going numb again. Next he brought out his bunch of sulphur matches. But the tremendous cold had already driven the life out of his fingers. In his effort to separate one match from the others, the whole bunch fell in the snow. He tried to pick it out of the snow, but failed. The dead fingers could neither touch nor clutch. He was very careful. He drove the thought of his freezing feet, and nose, and cheeks, out of his mind, devoting his whole soul to the matches. He watched, using the sense of vision in place of that of touch, and when he saw his fingers on each side the bunch, he closed them—that is, he willed to close them, for the wires were down, and the fingers did not obey. He pulled the mitten on the right hand, and beat it fiercely against the knee. Then with both mittened hands, he scooped the bunch of matches, along with much snow, into his lap. Yet he was no better off.

After some manipulation he managed to get the bunch between the heels of his mittened hands. In this fashion he carried it to his mouth. The ice crackled and snapped when by a violent effort he opened his mouth. He drew the lower jaw in, curled the upper lip out of the way, and scraped the bunch with his upper teeth in order to separate a match. He succeeded in getting one, which he dropped on his lap. He was no better off. He could not pick it up. Then he devised a way. He picked it up in his teeth and scratched it on his leg. Twenty times he scratched before he succeeded in lighting it. As it flamed he held it with his teeth to the birth bark. But the burning brimstone went up his nostrils and into his lungs, causing him to cough spasmodically. The match fell into the snow and went out.

The old-timer on Sulphur Creek was right, he thought in the moment of controlled despair that ensued: after fifty below, a man should travel with a partner. He beat his hands, but failed in exciting any sensation. Suddenly he bared both hands, removing the mittens with his teeth. He caught the whole bunch between the heels of his hands. His arm muscles not being frozen enabled him to press the hand heels tightly against the matches. Then he scratched the bunch along his leg. It flared into flame, seventy sulphur matches at once! There was no wind to blow them out. He kept his head to one side to escape the strangling fumes, and held the blazing bunch to the birch bark. As he so held it, he became aware of sensation in his hand. His flesh was burning. He could smell it. Deep down below the surface he could feel it. The sensation developed into pain that grew acute. And still he endured it, holding the flame of the matches clumsily to the bark that would not light readily because his own burning hands were in the way, absorbing most of the flame.

At last, when he could endure no more, he jerked his hands apart. The blazing matches fell sizzling into the snow, but the birch bark was alight. He began laying dry grasses and tiniest twigs on the flame. He could not pick and choose, for he had to lift the fuel between the heels of his hands. Small pieces of rotten wood and green moss clung to the twigs, and he bit them off as well as he could with his teeth. He cherished the flame carefully and awkwardly. It meant life, and it must not perish. The withdrawal of blood from the surface of his body now made him begin to shiver, and he grew more awkward. A large piece of green moss fell squarely on the little fire. He tried to poke it out with his fingers, but his shivering frame made him poke too far, and he disrupted the nucleus of the little fire, the burning grasses and tiny twigs separating and scattering. He tried to poke them together again, but in spite of the tenseness of the effort, his shivering got away with him, and the twigs were hopelessly scattered. Each twig gushed a puff of smoke and went out. The fire provider had failed. As he looked apathetically about him, his eyes chanced on the dog, sitting across the ruins of the fire from him, in the snow, making restless, hunching movements, slightly lifting one forefoot and then the other, shifting its weight back and forth on them with wistful eagerness.

The sight of the dog put a wild idea into his head. He remembered the tale of the man, caught in a blizzard, who killed a steer and crawled inside the carcass, and so was saved. He would kill the dog and bury his hands in the warm body until the numbness went out of them. Then he could build another fire. He spoke to the dog, calling it to him; but in his voice was a strange note of fear that frightened the animal, who had never known the man to speak in such a way before. Something was the matter, and its suspicious nature sensed danger—it knew not what danger, but somewhere, somehow, in its brain arose an apprehension of the man. It flattened its ears down at the sound of the man's voice, and its restless, hunching movements and the liftings and shiftings of its forefeet became more pronounced; but it would not come to the man. He got on his hands and knees and crawled toward the dog. This unusual posture again excited suspicion, and the animal sidled mincingly away.

The man sat up in the snow for a moment and struggled for calmness. Then he pulled on his mittens, by means of his teeth, and got upon his feet. He glanced down at first in order to assure himself that he was really standing up, for the absence of sensation in his feet left him unrelated to the earth. His erect position in itself started to drive the webs of suspicion from the dog's mind; and when he spoke peremptorily, with the sound of whip lashes in his voice, the dog rendered its customary allegiance and came to him. As it came within reaching distance, the man lost his control. His arms flashed out to the dog, and he experienced genuine surprise when he discovered that his hands could not clutch, that there was neither bend nor feeling in the fingers. He had forgotten for the moment that they were frozen and that they were freezing more and more. All this happened quickly, and before the animal could get away, he encircled its body with his arms. He sat down in the snow, and in his fashion held the dog, while it snarled and whined and struggled.

But it was all he could do, hold its body encircled in his arms and sit there. He realized he could not kill the dog. There was no way to do it. With his helpless hands he could neither draw nor hold his sheath knife nor throttle the animal. He released it, and it plunged wildly away, with tail between its legs, and still snarling. It halted forty feet away and surveyed him curiously, with ears pricked forward.

The man looked down at his hands in order to locate them, and found them hanging on the ends of his arms. It struck him as curious that one should have to use his eyes in order to find out where his hands were. He began threshing his arms back and forth, beating the mittened hands against his sides. He did this for five minutes, violently, and his heart pumped enough blood up to the surface to put a stop to his shivering. But no sensation was aroused in the hands. He had an impression that they hung like weights on the ends of his arms, but when he tried to run the impression down, he could not find it.

A certain fear of death, dull and oppressive, came to him. This fear quickly became poignant as he realized that it was no longer a mere matter of freezing his fingers and toes, or of losing his hands and feet, but that it was a matter of life and death with the chances against him. This threw him into a panic, and he turned and ran up the creek bed along the old, dim trail. The dog joined in behind him and kept up with him. He ran blindly, without intention, in fear such as he had never known in his life. Slowly, as he ploughed and floundered through the snow, he began to see things again—the banks of the creek, the old timber jams, the leafless aspens, and the sky. The running made him feel better. He did not shiver. Maybe, if he ran on, his feet would thaw out; and, anyway, if he ran far enough, he would reach camp and the boys. Without doubt he would lose some fingers and toes and some of his face; but the boys would take care of him, and save the rest of him when he got there. And at the same time there was another thought in his mind that said he would never get to the camp and the boys; that it was too many miles away, that the freezing had too great a start on him, and that he would soon be stiff and dead. This thought he kept in the background and refused to consider. Sometimes it pushed itself forward and demanded to be heard, but he thrust it back and strove to think of other things.

It struck him as curious that he could run at all on feet so frozen that he could not feel them when they struck the earth and took the weight of his body. He seemed to himself to skim along above the surface, and to have no connection with the earth. Somewhere he had once seen a winged Mercury, and he wondered if Mercury felt as he felt when skimming over the earth.

His theory of running until he reached camp and the boys had one flaw in it: he lacked the endurance. Several times he stumbled, and finally he tottered, crumpled up, and fell. When he tried to rise, he failed. He must sit and rest, he decided, and next time he would merely walk and keep on going. As he sat and regained his breath, he noted that he was feeling quite warm and comfortable. He was not shivering, and it even seemed that a warm glow had come to his chest and trunk. And yet, when he touched his nose or cheeks, there was no sensation. Running would not thaw them out. Nor would it thaw out his hands and feet. Then the thought came to him that the frozen portions of his body must be extending. He tried to keep this thought down, to forget it, to think of something else; he was aware of the panicky feeling that it caused, and he was afraid of the panic. But the thought asserted itself, and persisted, until it produced a vision of his body totally frozen. This was too much, and he made another wild run along the trail. Once he slowed down to a walk, but the thought of the freezing extending itself made him run again.

And all the time the dog ran with him, at his heels. When he fell down a second time, it curled its tail over its forefeet and sat in front of him, facing him, curiously eager and intent. The warmth and security of the animal angered him, and he cursed it till it flattened down its ears appeasingly. This time the shivering came more quickly upon the man. He was losing in his battle with the frost. It was creeping into his body from all sides. The thought of it drove him on, but he ran no more than a hundred feet, when he staggered and pitched headlong. It was his last panic. When he had recovered his breath and control, he sat up and entertained in his mind the conception of meeting death with dignity. However, the conception did not come to him in such terms. His idea of it was that he had been making a fool of himself, running around like a chicken with its head cut off—such was the simile that occurred to him. Well, he was bound to freeze anyway, and he might as well take it decently. With this new-found peace of mind came the first glimmerings of drowsiness. A good idea, he thought, to sleep off to death. It was like taking an anaesthetic. Freezing was not so bad as people thought. There were lots worse ways to die.

He pictured the boys finding his body next day. Suddenly he found himself with them, coming along the trail looking for himself. And, still with them, he came around a turn in the trail and found himself lying in the snow. He did not belong with himself any more, for even then he was out of himself, standing with the boys and looking at himself in the snow. It certainly was cold, was his thought. When he got back to the States he could tell the folks what real cold was. He drifted on from this to a vision of the old-timer on Sulphur Creek. He could see him quite clearly, warm and comfortable, and smoking a pipe.

'You were right, old hoss; you were right,' the man mumbled to the old-timer of Sulphur Creek.

Then the man drowsed off into what seemed to him the most comfortable and satisfying sleep he had ever known. The dog sat facing him and waiting. The brief day drew to a close in a long, slow twilight. There were no signs of a fire to be made, and, besides, never in the dog's experience had it known a man to sit like that in the snow and make no fire. As the twilight drew on, its eager yearning for the fire mastered it, and with a great lifting and shifting of forefeet, it whined softly, then flattened its ears down in anticipation of being chidden by the man. But the man remained silent. Later the dog whined loudly. And still later it crept close to the man and caught the scent of death. This made the animal bristle and back away. A little longer it delayed, howling under the stars that leaped and danced and shone brightly in the cold sky. Then it turned and trotted up the trail in the direction of the camp it knew, where were the other food providers and fire providers.

QUESTIONS FOR DISCUSSION AND WRITING

1. What external and internal conflicts does the man face on his journey? How does each of the three fires he attempts to build bring those conflicts to a climax?
2. What is significant about London's characterization of the nameless protagonist as a man "without imagination"? How does the protagonist characterize himself? How does he compare himself to the "old timer"?
3. In what sense is the setting a trap? What specific traps is the man able to avoid? What prevents him from avoiding all the traps?
4. How does the man's point of view toward his own judgment change during the course of his journey? What is the dog's point of view toward the man and his decisions?
5. How do London's statements about man's place in the universe establish the theme of this story? How does the story advance this theme by illustrating the relationship of caution, courage, and foolishness?

58

CARSON McCULLERS

A Tree, a Rock, a Cloud

CARSON McCULLERS (1917–1967) was born in Columbus, Georgia. After graduating from high school, she worked briefly as a reporter for the Columbus *Enquirer* before going to New York to study at the Juilliard School of Music. In New York, McCullers changed her mind and enrolled in writing courses at Columbia University and New York University. In 1940, at the age of twenty-three, she published her first novel, *The Heart Is a Lonely Hunter,* a book that attracted wide critical attention as the newest example of Southern gothic fiction. After her second novel, *Reflections in a Golden Eye* (1941), McCullers began contributing stories to magazines such as *Vogue, The New Yorker,* and *Mademoiselle.* Her third novel, *The Member of the Wedding* (1946), was later adapted for a play and a film, the stage version winning both the New York Critics Circle and Donaldson awards. As a young adult, McCullers suffered a series of strokes and by the age of thirty-one her entire left side was paralyzed. Although writing became an ordeal, she continued to compose and dictate her work, such as the novel *Clock Without Hands* (1961), until she died of a brain hemorrhage at the age of fifty. Her short stories are collected in *The Ballad of the Sad Café* (1951), *The Mortgaged Heart* (1971), and *Collected Stories* (1973). "A Tree, a Rock, a Cloud," reprinted from *The Ballad of the Sad Café,* is the story of an old man whose experience has forced him to develop a science of love.

It was raining that morning, and still very dark. When the boy reached the streetcar café he had almost finished his route and he went in for a cup of coffee. The place was an all-night café owned by a bitter and stingy man called Leo. After the raw, empty street, the café seemed friendly and bright: along the counter there were a couple of soldiers, three spinners from the cotton mill, and in a corner a man who sat hunched over with his nose and half his face down in a beer mug. The boy wore a helmet such as aviators wear. When he went into the café he unbuckled the chin strap and raised the right flap up over his pink little ear; often as he drank his coffee someone would speak to him in a friendly way. But this morning Leo did not look into his face and none of the men were talking. He paid and was leaving the café when a voice called out to him:

"Son! Hey Son!"

He turned back and the man in the corner was crooking his finger and nodding to him. He had brought his face out of the beer mug and he seemed suddenly very happy. The man was long and pale, with a big nose and faded orange hair.

"Hey Son!"

The boy went toward him. He was an undersized boy of about twelve, with one shoulder drawn higher than the other because of the weight of the paper sack. His face was shallow, freckled, and his eyes were round child eyes.

"Yeah Mister?"

The man laid one hand on the paper boy's shoulders, then grasped the boy's chin and turned his face slowly from one side to the other. The boy shrank back uneasily.

"Say! What's the big idea?"

The boy's voice was shrill; inside the café it was suddenly very quiet.

The man said slowly, "I love you."

All along the counter the men laughed. The boy, who had scowled and sidled away, did not know what to do. He looked over the counter at Leo, and Leo watched him with a weary, brittle jeer. The boy tried to laugh also. But the man was serious and sad.

"I did not mean to tease you, Son," he said. "Sit down and have a beer with me. There is something I have to explain."

Cautiously, out of the corner of his eye, the paper boy questioned the men along the counter to see what he should do. But they had gone back to their beer or their breakfast and did not notice him. Leo put a cup of coffee on the counter and a little jug of cream.

"He is a minor," Leo said.

The paper boy slid himself up onto the stool. His ear beneath the upturned flap of the helmet was very small and red. The man was nodding at him soberly. "It is important," he said. Then he reached in his hip pocket and brought out something which he held up in the palm of his hand for the boy to see.

"Look very carefully," he said.

The boy stared, but there was nothing to look at very carefully. The man held in his big, grimy palm a photograph. It was the face of a woman, but blurred, so that only the hat and the dress she was wearing stood out clearly.

"See?" the man asked.

The boy nodded and the man placed another picture in his palm. The woman was standing on a beach in a bathing suit. The suit made her stomach very big, and that was the main thing you noticed.

"Got a good look?" He leaned over closer and finally asked: "You ever seen her before?"

The boy sat motionless, staring slantwise at the man. "Not so I know of."

"Very well." The man blew on the photographs and put them back into his pocket. "That was my wife."

"Dead?" the boy asked.

Slowly the man shook his head. He pursed his lips as though about to whistle and answered in a long-drawn way: "Nuuu—" he said. "I will explain."

The beer on the counter before the man was in a large brown mug. He did not pick it up to drink. Instead he bent down and, putting his face over the rim, he rested there for a moment. Then with both hands he tilted the mug and sipped.

"Some night you'll go to sleep with your big nose in a mug and drown," said Leo. "Prominent transient drowns in beer. That would be a cute death."

The paper boy tried to signal to Leo. While the man was not looking he screwed up his face and worked his mouth to question soundlessly: "Drunk?" But Leo only raised his eyebrows and turned away to put some pink strips of bacon on the grill. The man pushed the mug away from him, straightened himself, and folded his loose crooked hands on the counter. His face was sad as he looked at the paper boy. He did not blink, but from time to time the lids closed down with delicate gravity over his pale green eyes. It was nearing dawn and the boy shifted the weight of the paper sack.

"I am talking about love," the man said. "With me it is a science."

The boy half slid down from the stool. But the man raised his forefinger, and there was something about him that held the boy and would not let him go away.

"Twelve years ago I married the woman in the photograph. She was my wife for one year, nine months, three days, and two nights. I loved her. Yes. . . ." He tightened his blurred, rambling voice and said again: "I loved her. I thought also that she loved me. I was a railroad engineer. She had all home comforts and luxuries. It never crept into my brain that she was not satisfied. But do you know what happened?"

"Mgneeow!" said Leo.

The man did not take his eyes from the boy's face. "She left me. I came in one night and the house was empty and she was gone. She left me."

"With a fellow?" the boy asked.

Gently the man placed his palm down on the counter. "Why naturally, Son. A woman does not run off like that alone."

The café was quiet, the soft rain black and endless in the street outside. Leo pressed down the frying bacon with the prongs of his long fork. "So you have been chasing the floozie for eleven years. You frazzled old rascal!"

For the first time the man glanced at Leo. "Please don't be vulgar. Besides, I was not speaking to you." He turned back to the boy and said in a trusting and secretive undertone, "Let's not pay any attention to him. O.K.?"

The paper boy nodded doubtfully.

"It was like this," the man continued. "I am a person who feels many things. All of my life one thing after another has impressed me. Moonlight. The leg of a pretty girl. One thing after another. But the point is that when I had enjoyed anything there was a peculiar sensation as though it was laying around loose in me. Nothing seemed to finish itself up or fit in with the other things. Women? I had my portion of them. The same. Afterwards laying around loose in me. I was a man who had never loved."

Very slowly he closed his eyelids, and the gesture was like a curtain drawn at the end of a scene in a play. When he spoke again his voice was excited and the words came fast—the lobes of his large, loose ears seemed to tremble.

"Then I met this woman. I was fifty-one years old and she always said she was thirty. I met her at a filling station and we were married within three days. And do you know what it was like? I just can't tell you. All I had ever felt was gathered together around this woman. Nothing lay around loose in me any more but was finished up by her."

The man stopped suddenly and stroked his long nose. His voice sank down to a steady and reproachful undertone: "I'm not explaining this right. What happened was this. There were these beautiful feelings and loose little pleasures inside me. And this woman was something like an assembly line for my soul. I run these little pieces of myself through her and I come out complete. Now do you follow me?"

"What was her name?" the boy asked.

"Oh," he said. "I called her Dodo. But that is immaterial."

"Did you try to make her come back?"

The man did not seem to hear. "Under the circumstances you can imagine how I felt when she left me."

Leo took the bacon from the grill and folded two strips of it between a bun. He had a gray face, with slitted eyes, and a pinched nose saddled by faint blue shadows. One of the mill workers signaled for more coffee and Leo poured it. He did not give refills on coffee free. The spinner ate breakfast there every morning, but the better Leo knew his customers the stingier he treated them. He nibbled his own bun as though he grudged it to himself.

"And you never got hold of her again?"

The boy did not know what to think of the man, and his child's face was uncertain with mingled curiosity and doubt. He was new on the paper route; it was still strange to him to be out in the town in the black, queer early morning.

"Yes," the man said. "I took a number of steps to get her back. I went around trying to locate her. I went to Tulsa where she had folks. And to Mobile. I went to every town she had ever mentioned to me, and I hunted down every man she had formerly been connected with. Tulsa, Atlanta, Chicago, Cheehaw, Memphis. . . . For the better part of two years I chased around the country trying to lay hold of her."

"But the pair of them had vanished from the face of the earth!" said Leo.

"Don't listen to him," the man said confidentially. "And also just forget those two years. They are not important. What matters is that around the third year a curious thing began to happen to me."

"What?" the boy asked.

The man leaned down and tilted his mug to take a sip of beer. But as he hovered over the mug his nostrils fluttered slightly; he sniffled the staleness of the beer and did not drink. "Love is a curious thing to begin with. At first I thought only of getting her back. It was a kind of mania. But then as time went on I tried to remember her. But do you know what happened?"

"No," the boy said.

"When I laid myself down on a bed and tried to think about her my mind became a blank. I couldn't see her. I would take out her pictures and look. No good. Nothing doing. A blank. Can you imagine it?"

"Say, Mac!" Leo called down the counter. "Can you imagine this bozo's mind a blank!"

Slowly, as though fanning away flies, the man waved his hand. His green eyes were concentrated and fixed on the shallow little face of the paper boy.

"But a sudden piece of glass on a sidewalk. Or a nickel tune in a music box. A shadow on a wall at night. And I would remember. It might happen in a street and I would cry or bang my head against a lamppost. You follow me?"

"A piece of glass . . ." the boy said.

"Anything. I would walk around and I had no power of how and when to remember her. You think you can put up a kind of shield. But remembering don't come to a man face forward—it corners around sideways. I was at the mercy of everything I saw and heard. Suddenly instead of me combing the countryside to find her she began to chase me around in my very soul. *She* chasing *me,* mind you! and in my soul."

The boy asked finally: "What part of the country were you in then?"

"Ooh," the man groaned. "I was a sick mortal. It was like smallpox. I confess, Son, that I boozed. I fornicated. I committed any sin that suddenly appealed to me. I am loath to confess it but I will do so. When I recall that period it is all curdled in my mind, it was so terrible."

The man leaned his head down and tapped his forehead on the counter. For a few seconds he stayed bowed over in this position, the back of his stringy neck covered with orange furze, his hands with their long warped fingers held palm to palm in an attitude of prayer. Then the man straightened himself; he was smiling and suddenly his face was bright and tremulous and old.

"It was in the fifth year that it happened," he said. "And with it I started my science."

Leo's mouth jerked with a pale, quick grin. "Well none of we boys are getting any younger," he said. Then with sudden anger he balled up a dishcloth he was holding and threw it down hard on the floor. "You draggle-tailed old Romeo!"

"What happened?" the boy asked.

The old man's voice was high and clear: "Peace," he answered.

"Huh?"

"It is hard to explain scientifically, Son," he said. "I guess the logical explanation is that she and I had fleed around from each other for so long that finally we just got tangled up together and lay down and quit. Peace. A queer and beautiful blankness. It was spring in Portland and the rain came every afternoon. All evening I just stayed there on my bed in the dark. And that is how the science come to me."

The windows in the streetcar were pale blue with light. The two soldiers paid for their beers and opened the door—one of the soldiers combed his hair and wiped off his muddy puttees before they went outside. The three mill workers bent silently over their breakfasts. Leo's clock was ticking on the wall.

"It is this. And listen carefully. I meditated on love and reasoned it out. I realized what is wrong with us. Men fall in love for the first time. And what do they fall in love with?"

The boy's soft mouth was partly open and he did not answer.

"A woman," the old man said. "Without science, with nothing to go by, they undertake the most dangerous and sacred experience in God's earth. They fall in love with a woman. Is that correct, Son?"

"Yeah," the boy said faintly.

"They start at the wrong end of love. They begin at the climax. Can you wonder it is so miserable? Do you know how men should love?"

The old man reached over and grasped the boy by the collar of his leather jacket. He gave him a gentle little shake and his green eyes gazed down unblinking and grave.

"Son, do you know how love should be begun?"

The boy sat small and listening and still. Slowly he shook his head. The old man leaned closer and whispered:

"A tree. A rock. A cloud."

It was still raining outside in the street: a mild, gray, endless rain. The mill whistle blew for the six o'clock shift and the three spinners paid and went away. There was no one in the café but Leo, the old man, and the little paper boy.

"The weather was like this in Portland," he said. "At the time my science was begun. I meditated and I started very cautious. I would pick up something from the street and take it home with me. I bought a goldfish and I concentrated on the goldfish and I loved it. I graduated from one thing to another. Day by day I was getting this technique. On the road from Portland to San Diego—"

"Aw shut up!" screamed Leo suddenly. "Shut up! Shut up!"

The old man still held the collar of the boy's jacket; he was trembling and his face was earnest and bright and wild. "For six years now I have gone around by myself and built up my science. And now I am a master. Son, I can love anything. No longer do I have to think about it even. I see a street full of people and a beautiful light comes in me. I watch a bird in the sky. Or I meet a traveler on the road. Everything, Son. And anybody. All strangers and all loved! Do you realize what a science like mine can mean?"

The boy held himself stiffly, his hands curled tight around the counter edge. Finally he asked: "Did you ever really find that lady?"

"What? What say, Son?"

"I mean," the boy asked timidly. "Have you fallen in love with a woman again?"

The old man loosened his grasp on the boy's collar. He turned away and for the first time his green eyes had a vague and scattered look. He lifted the mug from the counter, drank down the yellow beer. His head was shaking slowly from side to side. Then finally he answered: "No, Son. You see that is the last step in my science. I go cautious. And I am not quite ready yet."

"Well!" said Leo. "Well well well!"

The old man stood in the open doorway. "Remember," he said. Framed there in the gray damp light of the early morning he looked shrunken and seedy and frail. But his smile was bright. "Remember I love you," he said with a last nod. And the door closed quietly behind him.

The boy did not speak for a long time. He pulled down the bangs on his forehead and slid his grimy little forefinger around the rim of his empty cup. Then without looking at Leo he finally asked:

"Was he drunk?"

"No," said Leo shortly.

The boy raised his clear voice higher. "Then was he a dope fiend?"

"No."

The boy looked up at Leo, and his flat little face was desperate, his voice urgent and shrill. "Was he crazy? Do you think he was a lunatic?" The paper boy's voice dropped suddenly with doubt. "Leo? Or not?"

But Leo would not answer him. Leo had run a night café for fourteen years, and he held himself to be a critic of craziness. There were the town characters and also the transients who roamed in from the night. He knew the manias of all of them. But he did not want to satisfy the questions of the waiting child. He tightened his pale face and was silent.

So the boy pulled down the right flap of his helmet and as he turned to leave he made the only comment that seemed safe to him, the only remark that could not be laughed down and despised:

"He sure has done a lot of traveling."

QUESTIONS FOR DISCUSSION AND WRITING

1. How does the man's confession that he loves the boy introduce the conflict in the story? What four stages has the man passed through on his way to resolving this conflict?
2. What does the young boy think of the man at the bar? What does Leo think of the man? How does his initial reaction to the man help characterize Leo's part in the story?
3. Why is the all-night café an appropriate setting for this story? How does McCullers connect the world outside the café with the little world inside it? How do Leo and the other people in the café provide a comic counterpoint to the man's serious story?
4. How does McCullers' decision to tell this story from the limited omniscient point of view help establish the ambiguities in the story? In what manner is Leo's final point of view revealed by his refusal to answer the boy's question?
5. How does the title of the story symbolize the man's science of love? Has the man really developed a science of love or has he merely developed a rationalization that allows him to live with his loss? Explain your answer.

59

DENNIS McFARLAND

Nothing to Ask For

DENNIS McFARLAND was born in 1950 in Mobile, Alabama, and was educated at Brooklyn College and Goddard College. He has taught at Stanford University, where he served as a Wallace E. Stegner Fellow, and at Emerson College in Boston, Massachusetts.

He has published his short stories in magazines such as *Sequoia, Mademoiselle, Vogue,* and *The New Yorker.* His novel, *The Music Room* (1990), describes how a privileged family, rich in talent and promise, is overwhelmed by alcoholism. "Nothing to Ask For," reprinted from *The New Yorker,* documents how two friends—one gay, one straight—confront the devastating effects of AIDS.

Inside Mack's apartment, a concentrator—a medical machine that looks like an elaborate stereo speaker on casters—sits behind an orange swivel chair, making its rhythmic, percussive noise like ocean waves, taking in normal filthy air, humidifying it, and filtering out everything but the oxygen, which it sends through clear plastic tubing to Mack's nostrils. He sits on the couch, as usual, channel grazing, the remote-control button under his thumb, and he appears to be scrutinizing the short segments of what he sees on the TV screen with Zen-like patience. He has planted one foot on the bevelled edge of the long oak coffee table, and he dangles one leg—thinner at the thigh than my wrist—over the other. In the sharp valley of his lap, Eberhardt, his old long-haired dachshund, lies sleeping. The table is covered with two dozen medicine bottles, though Mack has now taken himself off all drugs except cough syrup and something for heartburn. Also, stacks of books and pamphlets—though he has lost the ability to read—on how to heal yourself, on Buddhism, on Hinduism, on dying. In one pamphlet there's a long list that includes most human ailments, the personality traits and character flaws that cause these ailments, and the affirmations that need to be said in order to overcome them. According to this well-intentioned misguidedness, most disease is caused by self-hatred, or rejection of reality, and almost anything can be cured by learning to love yourself—which is accomplished by saying, aloud and often, "I love myself." Next to these books are pamphlets and Xeroxed articles describing more unorthodox remedies—herbal brews, ultrasound, lemon juice, urine, even penicillin. And, in a ceramic dish next to these, a small, waxy envelope that contains "ash"—a very fine, gray-white, spiritually enhancing powder materialized out of thin air by Swami Lahiri Baba.

As I change the plastic liner inside Mack's trash can, into which he throws his millions of Kleenex, I block his view of the TV screen—which he endures serenely, his head perfectly still, eyes unaverted. "Do you remember old Dorothy Hughes?" he asks me. "What do you suppose ever happened to her?"

"I don't know," I say. "I saw her years ago on the nude beach at San Gregorio. With some black guy who was down by the surf doing cartwheels. She pretended she didn't know me."

"I don't blame her," says Mack, making bug-eyes. "I wouldn't like to be seen with any grownup who does cartwheels, would you?"

"No," I say.

Then he asks, "Was everybody we knew back then crazy?"

What Mack means by "back then" is our college days, in Santa Cruz, when we judged almost everything in terms of how freshly it rejected the status quo: the famous professor who began his twentieth-century-philosophy class by tossing pink rubber dildos in through the classroom window; Antonioni and Luis Buñuel screened each weekend in the dormitory basement; the artichokes in the student garden, left on their stalks and allowed to open and become what they truly were—enormous, purple-hearted flowers.

There were no paving-stone quadrangles or venerable colonnades—our campus was the redwood forest, the buildings nestled among the trees, invisible one from the other—and when we emerged from the woods at the end of the school day, what we saw was nothing more or less than the sun setting over the Pacific. We lived with thirteen other students, in a rented Victorian mansion on West Cliff Drive, and at night the yellow beacon from the nearby lighthouse invaded our attic windows; we drifted to sleep listening to the barking of seals. On weekends we had serious softball games in the vacant field next to the house—us against a team of tattooed, long-haired townies—and afterward, keyed up, tired and sweating, Mack and I walked the north shore to a place where we could watch the waves pound into the rocks and send up sun-ignited columns of water twenty-five and thirty feet tall. Though most of what we initiated "back then" now seems to have been faddish and wrongheaded, our friendship was exceptionally sane and has endured for twenty years. It endured the melodramatic confusion of Dorothy Hughes, our beautiful short-stop—I loved her, but she loved Mack. It endured the subsequent revelation that Mack was gay—any tension on that count managed by him with remarks about what a homely bastard I was. It endured his fury and frustration over my low-bottom alcoholism, and my sometimes raging (and *en*raging) process of getting clean and sober. And it has endured the onlooking fisheyes of his long string of lovers and my two wives. Neither of us had a biological brother—that could account for something—but at recent moments when I have felt most frightened, now that Mack is so ill, I've thought that we persisted simply because we couldn't let go of the sense of *thoroughness* our friendship gave us; we constantly reported to each other on our separate lives, as if we knew that by doing so we were getting more from life than we would ever have been entitled to individually.

In answer to his question—was everybody crazy back then—I say, "Yes, I think so."

He laughs, then coughs. When he coughs these days—which is often—he goes on coughing until a viscous, bloody fluid comes up, which he catches in a Kleenex and tosses into the trash can. Earlier, his doctors could drain his lungs with a needle through his back—last time they collected an entire litre from one lung—but now that Mack has developed the cancer, there are tumors that break up the fluid into many small isolated pockets, too many to drain. Radiation or chemotherapy would kill him; he's too weak even for a flu shot. Later today, he will go to the hospital for another bronchoscopy; they want to see if there's anything they can do to help him, though they have already told him there isn't. His medical care comes in the form of visiting nurses, physical therapists, and a curious duo at the hospital: one doctor who is young, affectionate, and incompetent but who comforts and consoles, hugs and holds hands; another—old, rude, brash, and expert—who says things like "You might as well face it. You're going to die. Get your papers in order." In fact, they've given Mack two weeks to two months, and it has now been ten weeks.

"Oh, my God," cries Lester, Mack's lover, opening the screen door, entering the room, and looking around. "I don't recognize this hovel. And what's that wonderful smell?"

This morning, while Lester was out, I vacuumed and generally straightened up. Their apartment is on the ground floor of a building like all the buildings in this Southern California neighborhood—a two-story motel-like structure of white stucco and steel railings. Outside the door are an X-rated hibiscus (blood red, with its jutting, yellow powder-tipped stamen), a plastic macaw on a swing, two enormous yuccas; inside, carpet, and plainness. The wonderful smell is the turkey I'm roasting; Mack can't eat anything before the bronchoscopy, but I figure it will be here for them when they return from the hospital, and they can eat off it for the rest of the week.

Lester, a South Carolina boy in his late twenties, is sick, too—twice he has nearly died of pneumonia—but he's in a healthy period now. He's tall, thin, and bearded, a devotee of the writings of Shirley MacLaine—an unlikely guru, if you ask me, but my wife, Marilyn, tells me I'm too judgmental. Probably she is right.

The dog, Eberhardt, has woken up and waddles sleepily over to where Lester stands. Lester extends his arm toward Mack, two envelopes in his hand, and after a moment's pause Mack reaches for them. It's partly this typical hesitation of Mack's—a slowing of the mind, actually—that makes him appear serene, contemplative these days. Occasionally, he really does get confused, which terrifies him. But I can't help thinking that something in there has sharpened as well—maybe a kind of simplification. Now he stares at the top envelope for a full minute, as Lester and I watch him. This is something we do: we watch him. "Oh-h-h," he says, at last. "A letter from my mother."

"And one from Lucy, too," says Lester. "Isn't that nice?"

"I guess," says Mack. Then: "Well, yes. It is."

"You want me to open them?" I ask.

"Would you?" he says, handing them to me. "Read 'em to me, too."

They are only cards, with short notes inside, both from Des Moines. Mack's mother says it just makes her *sick* that he's sick, wants to know if there's anything he needs. Lucy, the sister, is gushy, misremembers a few things from the past, says she's writing instead of calling because she knows she will cry if she tries to talk. Lucy, who refused to let Mack enter her house at Christmastime one year—actually left him on the stoop in sub-zero cold—until he removed the gold earring from his ear. Mack's mother, who waited until after the funeral last year to let Mack know that his father had died; Mack's obvious illness at the funeral would have been an embarrassment.

But they've come around, Mack has told me in the face of my anger.

I said better late than never.

And Mack, all forgiveness, all humility, said that's exactly right: much better.

"Mrs. Mears is having a craft sale today," Lester says. Mrs. Mears, an elderly neighbor, lives out back in a cottage with her husband. "You guys want to go?"

Eberhardt, hearing "go," begins leaping at Lester's shins, but when we look at Mack, his eyelids are at half-mast—he's half asleep.

We watch him for a moment, and I say, "Maybe in a little while, Lester."

Lester sits on the edge of his bed reading the newspaper, which lies flat on the spread in front of him. He has his own TV in his room, and a VCR. On the dresser, movies whose cases show men in studded black leather jockstraps, with gloves to match—dungeon masters of startling handsomeness. On the floor, a stack of gay magazines. Somewhere on the cover of each of these magazines the word "macho" appears; and inside some of them, in the personal ads, men, meaning to attract others, refer to themselves as pigs. "Don't putz," Lester says to me as I straighten some things on top of the dresser. "Enough already."

I wonder where he picked up "putz"—surely not in South Carolina. I say, "You need to get somebody in. To help. You need to arrange it now. What if you were suddenly to get sick again?"

"I know," he says. "He's gotten to be quite a handful, hasn't he? Is he still asleep?"

"Yes," I answer. "Yes and yes."

The phone rings and Lester reaches for it. As soon as he begins to speak I can tell, from his tone, that it's my four-year-old on the line. After a moment, Lester says, "Kit," smiling, and hands me the phone, then returns to his newspaper.

I sit on the other side of the bed, and after I say hello, Kit says, "We need some milk."

"O.K.," I say. "Milk. What are you up to this morning?"

"Being angry mostly," she says.

"Oh?" I say. "Why?"

"Mommy and I are not getting along very well."

"That's too bad," I say. "I hope you won't stay angry for long."

"We won't," she says. "We're going to make up in a minute."

"Good," I say.

"When are you coming home?"

"In a little while."

"After my nap?"

"Yes," I say. "Right after your nap."

"Is Mack very sick?"

She already knows the answer, of course. "Yes," I say.

"Is he going to die?"

This one, too. "Most likely," I say. "He's that sick."

"Bye," she says suddenly—her sense of closure always takes me by surprise—and I say, "Don't stay angry for long, O.K.?"

"You already said that," she says, rightly, and I wait for a moment, half expecting Marilyn to come onto the line; ordinarily she would, and hearing her voice right now would do me good. After another moment, though, there's the click.

Marilyn is back in school, earning a Ph.D. in religious studies. I teach sixth grade, and because I'm faculty adviser for the little magazine the sixth graders put out each year, I stay late many afternoons. Marilyn wanted me home this Saturday morning. "You're at work all week," she said, "and then you're over there on Saturday. Is that fair?"

I told her I didn't know—which was the honest truth. Then, in a possibly dramatic way, I told her that fairness was not my favorite subject these days, given that my best friend was dying.

We were in our kitchen, and through the window I could see Kit playing with a neighbor's cat in the back yard. Marilyn turned on the hot water in the kitchen sink and stood still while the steam rose into her face. "It's become a question of where you belong," she said at last. "I think you're too involved."

For this I had no answer, except to say, "I agree"—which wasn't really an answer, since I had no intention of staying home, or becoming less involved, or changing anything.

Now Lester and I can hear Mack's scraping cough in the next room. We are silent until he stops. "By the way," Lester says at last, taking the telephone receiver out of my hand, "have you noticed that he *listens* now?"

"I know," I say. "He told me he'd finally entered his listening period."

"Yeah," says Lester, "as if it's the natural progression. You blab your whole life away, ignoring other people, and then right before you die you start to listen."

The slight bitterness in Lester's tone makes me feel shaky inside. It's true that Mack was always a better talker than a listener, but I suddenly feel that I'm walking a thin wire, and that anything like collusion would throw me off balance. All I know for sure is that I don't want to hear any more. Maybe Lester reads this in my face, because what he says next sounds like an explanation: he tells me that his poor old backwoods mother was nearly deaf when he was growing up, that she relied almost entirely on reading lips. "All she had to do when she wanted to turn me off," he says, "was to just turn her back on me. Simple," he says, making a little circle with his finger. "No more Lester."

"That's terrible," I say.

"I was a terrible coward," he says. "Can you imagine Kit letting you get away with something like that? She'd bite your kneecaps."

"Still," I say, "that's terrible."

Lester shrugs his shoulders, and after another moment I say, "I'm going to the Kmart. Mack needs a padded toilet seat. You want anything?"

"Yeah," he says. "But they don't sell it at Kmart."

"What is it?" I ask.

"It's a *joke,* Dan, for Chrissake," he says. "Honestly, I think you've completely lost your sense of humor."

When I think about this, it seems true.

"Are you coming back?" he asks.

"Right back," I answer. "If you think of it, baste the turkey."

"How could I not think of it?" he says, sniffing the air.

In the living room, Mack is lying with his eyes open now, staring blankly at the TV. At the moment, a shop-at-home show is on, but he changes channels, and an announcer says, "When we return, we'll talk about tree pruning," and Mack changes the channel again. He looks at me, nods thoughtfully, and says, "Tree pruning. Interesting. It's just like the way they put a limit on your credit card, so you don't spend too much."

"I don't understand," I say.

"Oh, you know," he says. "Pruning the trees. Didn't the man just say something about pruning trees?" He sits up and adjusts the plastic tube in one nostril.

"Yes," I say.

"Well, it's like the credit cards. The limit they put on the credit cards is . . ." He stops talking and looks straight into my eyes, frightened. "It doesn't make any sense, does it?" he says. "Jesus Christ. I'm not making sense."

Way out east on University, there is a video arcade every half mile or so. Adult peepshows. Also a McDonald's, and the rest. Taverns—the kind that are open at eight in the morning—with clever names: Tobacco Rhoda's, the Cruz Inn. Bodegas that smell of cat piss and are really fronts for numbers games. Huge discount stores. Lester, who is an expert in these matters, has told me that all these places feed on addicts. "What do you think—those peepshows stay in business on the strength of the occasional customer? No way. It's a steady clientele of people in there every day, for hours at a time, dropping in quarters. That whole strip of road is *made* for addicts. And all the strips like it. That's what America's all about, you know. You got your alcoholics in the bars. Your food addicts sucking it up at Jack-in-the-Box—you ever go in one of those places and count the fat people? You got your sex addicts in the peepshows. Your shopping addicts at the Kmart. Your gamblers running numbers in the bodegas and your junkies in the alley-ways. We're all nothing but a bunch of addicts. The whole fucking addicted country."

In the arcades, says Lester, the videos show myriad combinations and arrangements of men and women, men and men, women and women. Some show older men being serviced by eager, selfless young women who seem to live for one thing only, who can't get enough. Some of these women have put their hair into pigtails and shaved themselves—they're supposed to look like children. Inside the peepshow booths there's semen on the floor. And in the old days, there were glory holes cut into the wooden walls between some of the booths, so, if it pleased you, you could communicate with your neighbor. Not anymore. Mack and Lester tell me that some things have changed. The holes have been boarded up. In the public men's rooms you no longer read, scribbled in the stalls, "All faggots should die." You read, "All faggots should die of AIDS." Mack rails against the moratorium on fetal-tissue research, the most promising avenue for a cure. "If it was Legionnaires dying, we wouldn't have any moratorium," he says. And he often talks about Africa, where governments impede efforts to teach villagers about condoms: a social worker, attempting to explain their use, isn't allowed to remove the condoms from their foil packets; in another country, with a slightly more liberal government, a field nurse stretches a condom over his hand, to show how it works, and later villagers are found wearing the condoms like mittens, thinking this will protect them from disease. Lester laughs at these stories but shakes his head. In our own country, something called "family values" has emerged with clarity. "*Whose* family?" Mack wants to know, holding out his hands palms upward. "I mean we *all* come from families, don't we? The dizziest queen comes from a family. The axe-murderer. Even Dan *Quayle* comes from a family of some kind."

But Mack and Lester are dying, Mack first. As I steer my pickup into the parking lot at the Kmart, I almost clip the front fender of a big, deep-throated Chevy that's leaving. I have startled the driver, a young Chicano boy with four kids in the back seat, and he flips me the bird—aggressively, his arm out the window—but I feel protected today by my sense of purpose: I have come to buy a padded toilet seat for my friend.

When he was younger, Mack wanted to be a cultural anthropologist, but he was slow to break in after we were out of graduate school—never landed anything more than a low-paying position assisting someone else, nothing more than a student's job, really. Eventually, he began driving a tour bus in San Diego, which not only provided a steady income but suited him so well that in time he was managing the line and began to refer to the position not as his job but as his calling. He said that San Diego was like a pretty blond boy without too many brains. He knew just how to play up its cultural assets while allowing its beauty to speak for itself. He said he liked being "at the controls." But he had to quit work over a year ago, and now his hands have become so shaky that he can no longer even manage a pen and paper.

When I get back to the apartment from my trip to the Kmart, Mack asks me to take down a letter for him to an old high-school buddy back in Des Moines, a country-and-Western singer who has sent him a couple of her latest recordings. "*Whenever I met a new doctor or nurse,*" he dictates, "*I always asked them whether they believed in miracles.*"

Mack sits up a bit straighter and rearranges the pillows behind his back on the couch. "What did I just say?" he asks me.

"'I always asked them whether they believed in miracles.'"

"Yes," he says, and continues. "*And if they said no, I told them I wanted to see someone else. I didn't want them treating me. Back then, I was hoping for a miracle, which seemed reasonable.* Do you think this is too detailed?" he asks me.

"No," I say. "I think it's fine."

"I don't want to depress her."

"Go on," I say.

"*But now I have lung cancer,*" he continues. "*So now I need not one but two miracles. That doesn't seem as possible somehow.* Wait. Did you write 'possible' yet?"

"No," I say. "'That doesn't seem as . . .'"

"Reasonable," he says. "Didn't I say 'reasonable' before?"

"Yes," I say. "'That doesn't seem as reasonable somehow.'"

"Yes," he says. "How does that sound?"

"It sounds fine, Mack. It's not for publication, you know."

"It's not?" he says, feigning astonishment. "I thought it was: 'Letters of an AIDS Victim.'" He says this in a spooky voice and makes his bug-eyes. Since his head is a perfect skull, the whole effect really is a little spooky.

"What else?" I say.

"*Thank you for your nice letter,*" he continues, "*and for the tapes.*" He begins coughing—a horrible, rasping seizure. Mack has told me that he has lost all fear; he said he realized this a few weeks ago, on the skyride at the zoo. But when the coughing sets in, when it seems that it may never stop, I think I see terror in his eyes: he begins tapping his breastbone with the fingers of one hand, as if he's trying to wake up his lungs, prod them to do their appointed work. Finally he does stop, and he sits for a moment in silence, in thought. Then he dictates: "*It makes me very happy that you are so successful.*"

At Mrs. Mears' craft sale, in the alley behind her cottage, she has set up several card tables: Scores of plastic dolls with hand-knitted dresses, shoes, and hats. Handmade doll furniture. Christmas ornaments. A whole box of knitted bonnets and scarves for dolls. Also, some baked goods. Now, while Lester holds Eberhardt, Mrs. Mears, wearing a large straw hat and sunglasses, outfits the dachshund in one of the bonnets and scarves. "There now," she says. "Have you ever seen anything so *precious?* I'm going to get my camera."

Mack sits in a folding chair by one of the tables; next to him sits Mr. Mears, also in a folding chair. The two men look very much alike, though Mr. Mears is not nearly as emaciated as Mack. And of course Mr. Mears is eighty-seven. Mack, on the calendar, is not quite forty. I notice that Mack's shoelaces are untied, and I kneel to tie them. "The thing about reincarnation," he's saying to Mr. Mears, "is that you can't remember anything and you don't recognize anybody."

"Consciously," says Lester, butting in. "*Sub*consciously you do."

"Subconsciously," says Mack. "What's the point? I'm not the least bit interested."

Mr. Mears removes his houndstooth-check cap and scratches his bald, freckled head. "I'm not, either," he says with great resignation.

As Mrs. Mears returns with the camera, she says, "Put him over there, in Mack's lap."

"It doesn't matter whether you're interested or not," says Lester, dropping Eberhardt into Mack's lap.

"Give me good old-fashioned Heaven and Hell," says Mr. Mears.

"I should think you would've had enough of that already," says Lester.

Mr. Mears gives Lester a suspicious look, then gazes down at his own knees. "Then give me nothing," he says finally.

I stand up and step aside just in time for Mrs. Mears to snap the picture. "Did you ever *see* anything?" she says, all sunshades and yellow teeth, but as she heads back toward the cottage door, her face is immediately serious. She takes me by the arm and pulls me along, reaching for something from one of the tables—a doll's bed, white with a red strawberry painted on the headboard. "For your little girl," she says aloud. Then she whispers, "You better get him out of the sun, don't you think? He doesn't look so good."

But when I turn again, I see that Lester is already helping Mack out of his chair. "Here—let me," says Mrs. Mears, reaching an arm toward them, and she escorts Mack up the narrow, shaded sidewalk, back toward the apartment building. Lester moves alongside me and says, "Dan, do you think you could give Mack his bath this afternoon? I'd like to take Eberhardt for a walk."

"Of course," I say, quickly.

But a while later—after I have drawn the bath, after I've taken a large beach towel out of the linen closet, refolded it into a thick square, and put it into the water to serve as a cushion for Mack to sit on in the tub; when I'm holding the towel under, against some resistance, waiting for the bubbles to stop surfacing, and there's something horrible about it, like drowning a small animal—I think Lester has tricked me into this task of bathing Mack, and the saliva in my mouth suddenly seems to taste of Scotch, which I have not actually tasted in nine years.

There is no time to consider any of this, however, for in a moment Mack enters the bathroom, trailing his tubes behind him, and says, "Are you ready for my Auschwitz look?"

"I've seen it before," I say.

And it's true. I have, a few times, helping him with his shirt and pants after Lester has bathed him and gotten him into his underwear. But that doesn't feel like preparation. The sight of him naked is like a powerful, scary drug: you forget between trips, remember only when you start to come on to it again. I help him off with his clothes now and guide him into the tub and gently onto the underwater towel. "That's nice," he says, and I begin soaping the hollows of his shoulders, the hard washboard of his back. This is not human skin as we know it but something already dead—so dry, dense, and pleasantly brown as to appear manufactured. I soap the cage of his chest, his stomach—the hard, depressed abdomen of a greyhound—the steep vaults of his armpits, his legs, his feet. Oddly, his hands and feet appear almost normal, even a bit swollen. At last I give him the slippery bar of soap. "Your turn," I say.

"My poor cock," he says as he begins to wash himself.

When he's done, I rinse him all over with the hand spray attached to the faucet. I lather the feathery white wisps of his hair—we have to remove the plastic oxygen tubes for this—then rinse again. "You know," he says, "I know it's irrational, but I feel kind of turned off to sex."

The apparent understatement of this almost takes my breath away. "There are more important things," I say.

"Oh, I know," he says. "I just hope Lester's not too unhappy." Then, after a moment, he says, "You know, Dan, it's only logical that they've all given up on me. And I've accepted it mostly. But I still have days when I think I should at least be given a chance."

"You can ask them for anything you want, Mack," I say.

"I know," he says. "That's the problem—there's nothing to ask for."

"Mack," I say. "I think I understand what you meant this morning about the tree pruning and the credit cards."

"You do?"

"Well, I think your mind just shifted into metaphor. Because I can see that pruning trees is like imposing a limit—just like the limit on the credit cards."

Mack is silent, pondering this. "Maybe," he says at last, hesitantly—a moment of disappointment for us both.

I get him out and hooked up to the oxygen again, dry him off, and begin dressing him. Somehow I get the oxygen tubes trapped between his legs and the elastic waistband of his sweatpants—no big deal, but I suddenly feel panicky—and I have to take them off his face again to set them to rights. After he's safely back on the living-room couch and I've returned to the bathroom, I hear him: low, painful-sounding groans. "Are you all right?" I call from the hallway.

"Oh, yes," he says, "I'm just moaning. It's one of the few pleasures I have left."

The bathtub is coated with a crust of dead skin, which I wash away with the sprayer. Then I find a screwdriver and go to work on the toilet seat. After I get the old one off, I need to scrub around the area where the plastic screws were. I've sprinkled Ajax all around the rim of the bowl and found the scrub brush when Lester appears at the bathroom door, back with Eberhardt from their walk. "Oh, Dan, really," he says. "You go too far. Down on your knees now, scrubbing our toilet."

"Lester, leave me alone," I say.

"Well, it's true," he says. "You really do."

"Maybe I'm working out my survivor's guilt," I say, "if you don't mind."

"You mean because your best buddy's dying and you're not?"

"Yes," I say. "It's very common."

He parks one hip on the edge of the sink. And after a moment he says this: "Danny boy, if you feel guilty about surviving . . . that's not irreversible, you know. I could fix that."

We are both stunned. He looks at me. In another moment, there are tears in his eyes. He quickly closes the bathroom door, moves to the tub and turns on the water, sits on the side, and bursts into sobs. "I'm sorry," he says. "I'm so sorry."

"Forget it," I say.

He begins to compose himself almost at once. "This is what Jane Alexander did when she played Eleanor Roosevelt," he says. "Do you remember? When she needed to cry she'd go in the bathroom and turn on the water, so nobody could hear her. Remember?"

In the pickup, on the way to the hospital, Lester—in the middle, between Mack and me—says, "Maybe after they're down there you could doze off, but on the *way* down, they want you awake." He's explaining the bronchoscopy to me—the insertion of the tube down the windpipe—with which he is personally familiar: "They reach certain points on the way down where they have to ask you to swallow."

"*He's* not having the test, is he?" Mack says, looking confused.

"No, of course not," says Lester.

"Didn't you just say to him that he had to swallow?"

"I meant *anyone,* Mack," says Lester.

"Oh," says Mack. "Oh, yeah."

"The general 'you,'" Lester says to me. "He keeps forgetting little things like that."

Mack shakes his head, then points at his temple with one finger. "My mind," he says.

Mack is on tank oxygen now, which comes with a small caddy. I push the caddy, behind him, and Lester assists him along the short walk from the curb to the hospital's front door and the elevators. Nine years ago, it was Mack who drove *me* to a different wing of this same hospital—against my drunken, slobbery will—to dry out. And as I watch him struggle up the low inclined ramp toward the glass-and-steel doors, I recall the single irrefutable thing he said to me in the car on the way. "You stink," he said. "You've puked and probably pissed your pants and you *stink,*" he said—my loyal, articulate, and best friend, saving my life, and causing me to cry like a baby.

Inside the clinic upstairs, the nurse, a sour young blond woman in a sky-blue uniform who looks terribly overworked, says to Mack, "You know better than to be late."

We are five minutes late to the second. Mack looks at her incredulously. He stands with one hand on the handle of the oxygen-tank caddy. He straightens up, perfectly erect—the indignant, shockingly skeletal posture of a man fasting to the death for some holy principle. He gives the nurse the bug-eyes, and says, "And you know better than to keep me waiting every time I come over here for some goddam procedure. But get over yourself: shit happens."

He turns and winks at me.

Though I've offered to return for them afterward, Lester has insisted on taking a taxi, so I will leave them here and drive back home, where again I'll try—successfully, this time—to explain to my wife how all this feels to me, and where, a few minutes later, I'll stand outside the door to my daughter's room, comforted by the music of her small high voice as she consoles her dolls.

Now the nurse gets Mack into a wheelchair and leaves us in the middle of the reception area; then, from the proper position at her desk, she calls Mack's name, and says he may proceed to the laboratory.

"Dan," Mack says, stretching his spotted, broomstick arms toward me. "Old pal. Do you remember the Christmas we drove out to Des Moines on the motorcycle?"

We did go to Des Moines together, one very snowy Christmas—but of course we didn't go on any motorcycle, not in December.

"We had fun," I say and put my arms around him, awkwardly, since he is sitting.

"Help me up," he whispers—confidentially—and I begin to lift him.

QUESTIONS FOR DISCUSSION AND WRITING

1. How do the following scenes provide the structure for the plot: Mack's rejection by his family; the narrator's quarrel with his wife; the narrator's encounter with Lester in the bathroom; and Mack's confrontation with the nurse?
2. What ways does the narrator characterize Mack so that he appears more than simply a victim? How does the narrator reveal his character through his attitude toward friendship?
3. How do the University of California, Santa Cruz; Mack's apartment; the strip East on University; and the hospital form the literal and symbolic settings for the story?
4. Why does McFarland choose a straight rather than gay narrator for this story? What are the advantages of selecting a narrator who does not appear to analyze his feelings?
5. In what sense is Lester's assessment of the various addictions on the strip a fair assessment of American life? How does Mack interpret the phrase "family values"?

60

JAMES ALAN McPHERSON

The Silver Bullet

JAMES ALAN McPHERSON was born in 1943 in Savannah, Georgia, and educated at Morris Brown College, Harvard University, and the University of Iowa. He has taught writing at the University of California, Santa Cruz; Morgan State University; and the University of Iowa. His fiction, focusing on the plight of urban characters, mainly black, has appeared in *The Atlantic Monthly* and *Esquire.* He has also edited a work of nonfiction, *Railroad: Trains and Train People in American Culture* (1976). His stories have been collected in two volumes, *Hue and Cry: Short Stories* (1969) and *Elbow Room: Stories* (1977). The latter volume won the Pulitzer Prize in 1978. "The Silver Bullet," reprinted from *Elbow Room,* recounts a young boy's attempt to prove himself in the bewildering, but often comic world of urban violence.

When Willis Davis tried to join up with the Henry Street guys, they told him that first he had to knock over Slick's Bar and Grill to show them what kind of stuff he had. Actually, they needed the money for the stocking of new equipment to be used in a pending reprisal against the Conchos over on the West Side. News of a Concho spring offensive was in the wind. But they did not tell Willis this. They told him they had heard he had no stuff. Willis protested, saying that he was ready to prove himself in any way but this one. He said that everyone knew Slick was in the rackets and that was why his bar had never been hit. As a matter of fact, he did not know this for certain, but he did not really want to do the job. Also, no one could remember having seen Slick around the neighborhood for the past three years.

"Slick ain't in no rackets!" Dewey Bivins had screamed at Willis. "You just tryin' to get outta it on a *humble!* Slick died of TB over in Jersey two years ago. And don't come tellin' me you don't know that." Dewey was recognized as the war lord of the group, and there were many stories circulating, some dating several years back, about the number of dedicated Concho assassins who were out to get him. Some said that at least two of the Concho membership had taken a blood oath and waited at night in the darker areas of Henry Street for Dewey to pass. Others maintained that the Concho leadership, fearing disproportionate retaliations, had given orders that Dewey, of all the Henry Street guys, should go unmolested. Dewey himself argued that at least four guys were looking for him, day and night, and liked it known that he walked the streets unarmed, all the time. In fact, each time he was seen walking, his reputation grew. People feared him, respected his dash, his temper, the way he cocked his purple beret to the side. The little fellows in the neighborhood imitated his swagger. He was a dangerous enemy, but a powerful associate. So Willis decided to give it a try.

But first he went around to see Curtis Carter, hoping to get him to go along. Carter wanted no part of it. "I know for a fact that Slick ain't dead," he pointed out. "You'd be a fool to mess with his establishment."

"Aah, *bull*shit!" Willis replied. "When was the last time you seen Slick? There's another guy runnin' the joint now." But his voice was not as convincing as he wanted it to be. And Carter was not moved, not even when Willis suggested that this job could lead to a closer association for both of them with the Henry Street guys.

Carter was not impressed. "If Slick takes after you," he said, "how can them guys help you run any faster than you'll have to run by yourself?" Willis did not like to think about that possibility, so he called Carter a ball-less son of a bitch and announced that he would do it alone.

But now that he was forced to do it alone, Willis began to really wonder about Slick's connections with the rackets. He remembered hearing stories about Slick in the old days. These stories frightened him. And even with Slick gone for good, the bar might still be covered. He wanted to ask around about it, but was afraid of calling attention to himself. Instead, he made several brief trips into the place to check out the lay of the land. The bar opened sometime between eleven and twelve o'clock, when Alphaeus Jones, the bartender, came in; but it did no real business, aside from the winos, until well after three. He figured that two o'clock would be the best time. By then the more excitable winos would have come and gone and the small trickle of people who went in for the advertised home-cooked lunch would have died away. Alphaeus Jones took his own lunch around one-thirty or two, sitting on the stool at the end of the counter, just in case any customer entered. And the cook, Bertha Roy, whom Willis recognized as a neighbor of his aunt's in the projects over on Gilman, left the place around that same time to carry bag lunches to the ladies at Martha's Beauty Salon down the block. This kept her out of the place for at least half an hour. He did not want Bertha to see him, so he decided the best time would be the minute she left with the lunches.

Again he went to Curtis Carter, begging for help. Curtis worked in an auto-parts warehouse about four blocks away from Slick's. Willis told him that the job would be muchsofter if they could pull it off together and then make a run back to the warehouse to hide out until after dark. But Curtis still did not want any part of the operation. He made a long speech in which he stressed the importance of independent actions, offering several of his own observations on the dependability of the Henry Street guys; and then disclosed, by way of example, that he already had a nice steady income produced by ripping off, from the stockroom, new accessories and mended parts, which he sold to a garage over on the West Side. "There ain't no fair percentage in group actions," he concluded, the righteousness of a self-made man oiling his words. Willis called him a mild-fed jive and said that he was after bigger stuff. Curtis checked his temper and wished him luck.

The following afternoon, Willis waited across the street, leaning against the window of a barbershop and smoking a cigarette, until he saw Bertha Roy come out the door with the lunch bags. When he was sure that she was not going to turn around and go back, he threw the cigarette into the gutter and crossed over, trying to work up a casual amble. But his knees were much too close together. He pushed through the door, sweeping with his eyes the few tables against the wall on his left. The place was empty. Alphaeus Jones, a balding, honey-colored man with a shiny forehead, looked up from his lunch. A blob of mustard from the fish sandwich he was eating clung to the corner of his mouth. "What you want?" he asked, chewing.

Willis moved closer to the end of the bar and licked his lips. "What you got?" he asked.

Jones raised his left arm and motioned to where the sunlight glittered through the green and brown and white bottles on the shelves behind him. With his other hand, he raised the fish sandwich and took another bite. Willis licked his lips again. Then he shook his head, trying hard to work the amble up into his voice. "Naw, man," he said, his voice even but still a bit too high, "I mean what you got in the register?" And he made a fist with his right hand inside the pocket of his jacket.

Jones eyed him, sucking his teeth. Then he said, "A silver bullet." And looking up into the space above Willis's head, he lifted the sandwich again in his right hand. But just before it reached his mouth, he looked Willis directly in the face and asked, impatience hurrying his voice on, "You want it, Roscoe?"

"It ain't for *me,*" Willis said very fast.

"Ain't for nobody else. You the first fool to come in here for years. You want it now, or later?"

Willis thought it over. Then ever so slowly, he took his right hand out of his jacket pocket and laid both hands, fingers spread, on the bar.

Jones sucked his teeth again. "You done decided?" he asked.

"A beer," Willis said.

When he reported to the Henry Street boys what had happened, Dewey said: "You a silver-bullet lie!" The other guys crowded around him. They were in the storage basement at 1322 Henry. There was no door. "Chimney" Sutton, high on stuff, stood by the stairs leading up to the first floor, smashing his fist into his open palm. Besides needing the money for the coming offensive, they did not like to have an initiate seem so humble in his failures. "First you come with that mess about Slick," Dewey said. "Now you say old Jones bluffed you outta there on a bullshit tip." He paced the floor, making swift turns on his heels and jabbing an accusing brown finger at Willis, who slumped in a green metal chair with his head bowed. Sutton kept slamming his fist. The others—Harvey Gomez and Clyde Kelley—watched Willis with stone faces. "I know what your problem is," Dewey continued. "You just wanna get in the club without payin' no dues. You didn't never go in there in the first place."

"That ain't true," Willis protested, his hands spread out over his face. "I'll pay. You guys know how bad I wanna get in. But there wasn't no sense in takin' a chance like that. A guy would have to be crazy to call a bluff like that," he said, peering through his fingers at Dewey. "I tell you, his hands was under the counter."

"Aah, get off my case!" Dewey shouted. He jerked his head toward the stairs where Chimney Sutton was standing, still pounding his fist. Willis slid off the chair and eased across the room. Sutton was about to grab him when he saw Dewey wave his hand down in a gesture of disgust. Sutton moved a few inches away from the bottom step. Willis got out of the basement.

He hurried away from Henry Street, thinking it through. He still wanted to get into the organization. He felt that a man should belong to something representative. He was not against people going to work or joining churches or unions if these things represented them. But he wanted something more. And the Henry Street guys were not really bad, he thought. The papers just made them out to be that way. Several of them were family men. Dewey himself had been a family man at one time; that showed that they respected the family as an organization. But this by itself was not enough. There was not enough respect in it. And after a while you realized that something more was needed. Willis was not sure of what that thing was, but he knew that he had to try for it.

In the late afternoon, he went back around to the warehouse to see Curtis Carter. It was near closing time, but Curtis was still sorting greasy valves and mufflers into separate piles on the floor. His blue overalls were dirty and rust-stained. When Curtis saw him come in, he motioned him over to the john in the rear of the shop, where McElrath, the manager, could not hear them. "You do it?" Curtis asked, his voice hollow with suppressed excitement.

"No."

Curtis grinned. He seemed relieved. His mouth was smeared with black grease from his hands. "Couldn't get up the balls by yourself, huh?"

Willis told him about the silver bullet.

Curtis laughed aloud and said, "That's some more jive. Jones wouldn't never shoot nobody in there. In the afternoon they wouldn't have no more than fifty dollars in the register, anyhow. You think he wanna get in the news for somethin' like that?"

Now Willis felt bad. He knew that, from all angles, Curtis was right. He could see that Curtis knew it, too. He began to feel cheated, tricked, a laughingstock. "What can I do now?" he asked. "The guys are gonna be hard on me 'cause I didn't deliver."

"I told you so in the first place," Curtis said. "Now you go'n get it, no matter whichaway you turn. Don't think that old Jones go'n keep his mouth shut about what happen today."

"What can I do?" Willis asked, his lowered voice begging support.

"Get yourself some protection," Curtis said. "Maybe try a new approach."

"Like what?"

Curtis, still with the air of an objective adviser, told him about some guys with a new approach. They were over on the West Side. He offered no names but gave Willis the address of an office that, he suggested, might be friendly to Willis's situation.

On Wednesday morning, Willis took the bus over to the office. Once he had located it, he began to suspect that he might have been given the wrong address. This office had the suggestion of real business about it, with large red lettering on the window that read: W. SMITH ENTERPRISES. When Willis entered, he saw two new hardwood desks and tall gray file cabinets on each side of the small room. On the floor was a thin, bright red, wall-to-wall carpet; and behind one of the desks sat a man who wore a full beard, with a matching red shirt and wide tie. The man was watching him and looking very mad about something. Willis approached the desk, holding out his hand as he introduced himself. The man ignored the hand and continued to look very mad. The new hand-carved nameplate on the desk said that his name was R. V. Felton. He was the only person in the office, so Willis had to wait until Felton was through surveying him. Finally, still not seeming to focus on the physical presence before him, the man named Felton asked: "What you want?"

Willis said what he had been told to say: "I got a problem in community relations."

R. V. Felton looked even madder. His cheeks puffed out. His nose widened as he sat erect in the brown leather chair. Then, as if some switch had been clicked on, he began to speak. "Well, brother," he said, "that's our concern here. This office is committed to problems vis-à-vis the community. That's our only concern: an interest in the mobility of the community." His voice as he talked seemed tightly controlled and soft, but his hands suddenly came alive, almost on their own, it seemed to Willis, and began to make grandiose patterns in the air. The index finger of his right hand pumped up and down, now striking the flat palm of his left hand, now jabbing out at Willis. The hands made spirals, sharp, quick cutting motions, limber pirouettes, even while the fingers maintained independent movements. "There are profound problems that relate to community structure that have to be challenged through the appropriate agency," he continued. "We have friends downtown and friends in the community who see the dynamics of our organization, vis-à-vis the community, as the only legitimate and viable group to operate in this sphere. They support us," he said, his eyes wandering, his hands working furiously now, "we support the community dynamic, and together we all know what's going down. That's our dynamic. Dig it?" And he fixed a superior eye on Willis's face.

"Yeah," Willis said.

Now R. V. Felton relaxed in the chair and lifted a pencil from the new brown holder at the edge of his desk. "Now, brother," he said, "suppose you articulate the specifics of your problem."

At one-thirty that same afternoon, Willis, with R. V. Felton behind him, walked into Slick's Bar and Grill. Bertha Roy was back in the kitchen, preparing the bag lunches; at the end table in the far-left corner of the room, a single customer was getting drunk. Jones was pulling his own lunch out of the kitchen window with his back to the door. When he turned and saw that it was Willis standing by the bar, he smiled and asked, "A born fool, hey?"

R. V., looking especially mean, came up to the bar and stood beside Willis. Jones sighed, laid the plate on the bar, and dropped both hands out of sight. "How much this place earn in a week?" R. V. demanded. He had puffed out his cheeks and chest, so that he now looked like a bearded Buddha.

"We eat steady," Jones told him, still smiling.

Bertha Roy looked out at them from the kitchen, her sweating face screwed up in puzzlement.

R. V. sighed, intimating ruffled patience. "A fat mouth make a soft ass, brother," he said to Jones.

"What you boys want?" Bertha called from the kitchen. Her voice sounded like a bark.

"Tend your pots, momma," R. V. called to her. Then he said to Jones: "How much?"

"You better get on out," Jones told him.

Willis, standing beside R. V., tried to look as mad. But his cheeks could not hold as much air, and without a beard, he did not look as imposing.

"Now, listen here, brother," R. V. said to Jones. "As of this minute, I declare this joint nationalized. Every dollar come in here, the community get back twenty-five cents, less three cents for tax. Every plate of food pass over that counter, the community get ten percent of the profit, less two cents tax. Paying-up time is Friday mornings, before noon. You can play ball or close down now."

"Can I ask who go'n do the collecting for the community?" Jones asked, his voice humble.

R. V. snapped his fingers twice. Willis moved in closer to the bar. "This here's our certified community collector vis-à-vis this bar," R. V. announced. "Treat him nice. And when he come in here on Friday mornings, you *smile*."

"Why wait for Friday?" Jones asked. "I'll smile right now." And he raised his hands from under the bar. He was holding a twelve-gauge shotgun. "See how wide my jaws are?" he asked. "I'm smiling so much my ass is tight. Now, what about yours?" And he lifted the gun and backed off for range.

"Let's go, man," Willis said to R. V. He was already moving toward the door.

But R. V. did not move. He held up one long finger and began to wave it at Jones. "A bad move, brother," he said.

"Why don't you boys go on home!" Bertha Roy called from behind Jones. "You oughta be *shame* of yourselfs!"

"Bertha, you don't have to tell them nothin'," Jones said over his shoulder. "They'll be goin' home soon enough."

Willis was already at the door. He did not mind being the first one out, but then, he did not want to leave without R. V. "Let's go, man," he called from the door.

"Tomorrow's Thursday," R. V. said to Jones, ignoring Willis. "We'll be in to inspect the books. And remember, if you get any ideas about disrupting the progress of our dynamic here, there'll be some action, vis-à-vis you." Then he turned sharply and walked toward Willis at the door.

The drunk over in the corner lifted his head from the table and peered after them.

"You boys need a good whippin'," Bertha Roy called.

Jones just watched them go, smiling to himself.

That night, Willis went into Stanley's pool hall and told Dewey Bivins what had happened. He explained that since R. V. Felton and his organization had taken over, there would be a guaranteed cut of 12 percent for him, Willis, every Friday. And since he had decided to join up with the Henry Street guys, rather than with R. V., this would mean a weekly income of from twenty to thirty dollars for the gang. He said that he envisioned new uniforms for the guys, better equipment and a growing slush fund for more speedy bail bonding. But Dewey did not seem to share his enthusiasm. He laid his cue on the table, frowned, and asked, "Who is these guys, anyhow? They don't live round here. This here's *our* territory."

Willis tried to explain, as concretely as possible, the purposes of the organization. And though he made a brave effort to repeat, word for word, the speech that R. V. had given him, he could tell that without the hand movements, it sounded uninspiring. In fact, Dewey said as much even before Willis had finished. "That's bullshit!" he said, his face going tight. "They ain't go'n pull that kind of shit round here. Any naturalizin' that's done, *we'll* be doin' it!"

"Nationalization," said Willis.

"And we'll be doin' it, not them phonies."

"But then I'll be in trouble," Willis explained. "These guys have already taken over the job. If I let you take it from them, they'll be after *me*."

"That's your problem," Dewey said, his eyes showing a single-mindedness. "You wanna be with them or us? Remember, we live round here. If you join up with them, the West Side ain't go'n be far enough away for you to move." He allowed a potent pause to intervene, then asked, "Know what I mean?"

Willis knew.

The following morning, he waited outside the barbershop across the street from Slick's. He smoked, walked up and down the block several times, then got into a throw-to-the-wall game with the boy who worked in the shop. He lost seventeen cents, and then quit. The boy went back into the shop, shaking the coins in his pocket. Willis waited some more. He had planned to go in with the group that arrived first; but as the wait became longer and longer, he began to consider going in alone and apologizing to Jones for the whole thing. He decided against this, however, when he saw Bertha Roy leaving to deliver the lunch bags. The place seemed unsafe with her gone.

Finally, a little after two, R. V. Felton and another fellow drove up in a dark blue Ford. R. V., behind the wheel, was wearing green sunshades. He double-parked and kept the motor running while his man got out and went into Slick's. Willis crossed over and leaned against the car. R. V. was looking especially mean. He looked at his reflection in the rearview mirror, and then looked at it in the side mirror. Willis waited patiently. Finally, R. V. said, "We talked it over. Six percent for you."

"You said twelve!" Willis protested.

"Six," R. V. said. "This here's a small dynamic. Besides, I had to cut Aubrey in on your share. You'll get twelve, maybe more, when you line up some more of these blights on the community."

"I don't wanna get involve no more," Willis said.

"I figured that. That's why it's six."

Willis was about to make further protests when Aubrey came back to the car. He opened the door on the curb side, leaned in, and said, "R. V., you better come on in, man. That dude done pull that heat agin."

"Aah, fuck!" R. V. said. But he got out of the car, pushing Willis aside, and followed Aubrey into the bar. Willis entered behind them.

Jones was standing behind the bar, holding the shotgun.

"You want some trouble, brother?" R. V. asked.

"There ain't go'n be no trouble," Jones said.

"Then let's have them books."

"We don't keep no books," Jones said.

"A strange dynamic," R. V. said, pulling on his beard. "Most strange."

Jones cradled the gun butt against the bend of his right arm. "And here's somethin' stranger," he said. "If I was to blast your ass to kingdom come, there wouldn't be no cops come through that door for at least six hours. And when they come, they might take me down, but in the end, I'd get me a medal."

Now R. V.'s lips curled into a confident grin. He shook his head several times. "Let me run something down for you, brother," he said. "First of all, we are a nonprofit community-based grass-roots organization, totally responsive to the needs of the community. Second"—and here he again brought his fingers into play—"we think the community would be very interested in the articulation of the *total* proceeds of this joint vis-à-vis the *average* income level for this area. Third, you don't want to mess with us. We got the support of college students."

"Do tell," Jones said. "Well, I ain't never been to college myself, but I can count to ten. And if you punks ain't down the block when I finish, that street out there is gonna be full of hamburger meat." He braced his shoulder and lifted the gun. "And one last thing."

"You better say it quick, then," R. V. told him.

"I'm already way past five."

Willis, backing off during the exchange, had the door almost open when it suddenly rammed into his back. Before he could turn around, Dewey Bivins and Chimney Sutton pushed him aside and stepped into the room. As Sutton pushed the door shut again and leaned his back against it, Willis glimpsed Bertha Roy, her face a frightened blur, moving quickly past the window and away down the block. He turned around. Dewey, a tight fist pressed into each hip, stood surveying the room. Both he and Sutton were in full uniform, with purple berets and coffee-colored imitation-leather jackets. Dewey swung his gaze around to Willis, his eyes flashing back fire. Alphaeus Jones, still in the same spot behind the bar, held the gun a bit higher.

"Who are these dudes?" R. V. asked Willis.

Willis, trying to avoid Dewey's eyes, said nothing.

"Who the hell are *you?*" Dewey asked.

"Nine," Jones said.

Willis was still trying for the door. But Sutton moved up behind him, forcing Willis to edge almost to the center of the room.

Dewey walked closer to R. V. "Where's the money?" he demanded.

R. V. began to stroke his beard again. He looked more puzzled than mad. "Brother," he said, "there's some weird vibrations in here. What we need now is some unity. Think of the ramifications that would evolve from our working together. This here's a large community. The funds from this one joint is pure chicken shit compared to the total proceeds we could plow back into community organizations by combining our individual efforts into one dynamic and profound creative approach."

"Yeah?" asked Dewey, his head cocked to the side.

R. V. nodded, looking less puzzled. "Our organization, for example, is a legitimate relevant grass-roots community group," he said, making hyphens with his fingers. "We have been able to study the ramifications of these here bloodsucking community facilities. We have the dynamic. You have the manpower. Together we can begin a nationalization process—"

"You a naturalizin' lie!" Dewey screamed. "*We* the only group operate round here. You better take that bullshit over to the *Conchos.*"

"Let's git 'em," Chimney hissed, moving forward and pounding on his fist.

Jones grinned and raised the gun.

The room tensed. Chimney and Dewey stood close together, almost back to back. Similarly, Aubrey inched closer to R. V and both stood facing Chimney and Dewey, their backs to Jones. Eyes narrowed, hands began to move toward pockets, fingers twitched. Dewey turned to Willis, standing near the door. "Which side *you* on?" he asked through his teeth. Without answering, Willis began to move toward the center of the room.

"Hey, Alphee!" someone said.

They all looked. A man was coming through the door. "Hey, Alphee," he began again, seemingly unaware of the fury he had temporarily aborted, "a cop out there writin' a ticket on that car that's double-parked. The owner in here?" He walked past the group and over to the bar, his face betraying no curiosity.

"Could be," Jones told him, now lowering the gun. "But you know how these big-time businessmen can fix tickets."

The man smiled, then, in the same loud voice, asked, "What you doin' with that gun, Alphee?"

"Fixin' to swat some flies," Jones answered.

Now the man turned and looked at the five in the middle of the room. "Them?" he asked, nodding his head as he surveyed the faces.

Jones smiled. "That's right."

The man smiled, too. He was dressed in a deep green suit and starched white shirt open at the collar. "Which one's the big businessman, Alphee?" he asked, a suggestion of amusement tugging one corner of his mouth.

"You got me," Jones said.

"Is it you?" the man asked R. V. "You the only one in here don't look like a bum."

"Lemme take 'em, R. V.," Aubrey said.

But R. V. didn't answer. He was obviously in deep thought.

Dewey and Chimney began to look troubled. Willis's mind was racing. He looked out the window. The cop was standing with his left foot on the bumper of the car, writing. He began to wish that Bertha Roy would come back or that the cop would finish quickly and then go away.

"Now, a *real* businessman," the man was saying to no one in particular, "he would own him at least six cops, a city councilman, one and a half judges and a personal letter from the mayor. He wouldn't have to worry about one little old cop writin' a ticket." He paused and the smile left his face. "You own anything like that?" he asked R. V.

"Let's go, man," R. V. said to Aubrey in a low voice.

The man walked over and slapped R. V. across the face. "You own anything like that?" he asked again, his voice suddenly dropping the hint of amusement.

R. V. stiffened and drew back his fists. The man slapped him again. "What you wanna do that for?" R. V. whimpered.

"Floor the mother!" Dewey said. "He come in here tryin' to take over."

The man turned to Jones. "Who's that?" he asked.

"Some of them punks that hang out on Henry Street."

"Get out," the man said to Dewey.

"For what?" Dewey asked. "We on *your* side."

"No, you ain't," the man said. "Now, get out before I change my mind."

Dewey and Chimney headed for the door. Willis followed them.

"Not you," the man called after Willis. "You with these other businessmen, ain't you?"

Dewey turned at the door. "Yeah," he said, malice in his voice, "he ain't wearin' our uniform."

"I told you to get out," the man called.

"You go'n let him talk that way?" Chimney asked Dewey.

"Shut up!" Dewey hissed at him, an unfamiliar fear in his eyes.

Willis watched them go out the door. He felt trapped. Now there was only Bertha to hope for. Through the window, he could see that the cop had already left the car. Turning to the room, he saw R. V. and Aubrey standing unnaturally straight, like mechanical toys. R. V.'s lips were pushed out, but now the mean look was gone and R. V. was sulking like a little boy. The man stood at the bar, seemingly engaged in some private conversation with Jones. But after a few seconds, he turned to R. V. again. "Alphee, here, says I should just let you fellows go. He got a good heart and don't want to see you boys in any more trouble." Then he hit R. V. again, this time a quick, hard blow with his fist. R. V. screamed as the knuckles thudded into his face. "Waste him, Aubrey!" he moaned, his face turning deep brown.

But Aubrey did not move. He was looking past the man. Willis looked, too, and saw Jones holding the shotgun again and smiling. "Ten," Jones said.

R. V.'s head fell. He backed off, roughly pushing Aubrey aside. "You go'n be sorry you done that," he muttered, fighting to contain his rage. "We got—"

"Give the boys a beer before they go, Alphee," the man said.

"Let 'em pay," Jones said, following R. V. with the gun.

The man smiled. "Just a regular businessman, huh?"

"We don't want nothin' from here," Aubrey said. R. V. was standing behind him, nursing his face. He didn't say anything.

"Then take that dummy out of here," Jones ordered.

R. V. and Aubrey slowly moved toward the door. Again, Willis followed.

"Not him," Jones said. "He been in here three times already. I want to make sure he don't come back."

Willis stopped. The two others went on out, R. V. pausing only long enough at the door to say, "You ain't seen the last of our dynamic," and to shake his fist vengefully.

"Punks," Jones said.

Now Willis stood alone, frightened and frozen, eager to be going, too. He faced the man. "I didn't know," he said, his voice little more than a tremble.

"Know what?" the man asked in a softer tone.

"That this place was covered by the rackets."

The man laughed. He closed his eyes and kept the laugh suppressed in his throat. He laughed this way for almost a minute. "You hustlers kill me," he said at last. "All that big talk and you still think a black man can't have no balls without being in the rackets."

"I didn't know," Willis said again.

"Aah, *go on* and get out!" Jones said.

"Let him have a beer, Alphee," the man said, still containing his laughter.

"No," Jones said. "Go and get out. You give me a pain."

"They just young," the man told Jones.

"The hell with that," Jones said.

Willis moved toward the door. Any moment he expected them to call him back. But all he could hear as he moved was the jerking laughter coming up from deep inside the man as he made low comments to Jones. When he was going out the door, he heard Jones say, "Sure, I was young. But I ain't never been no *fool*."

Willis ran down the block. As he passed Martha's Beauty Salon, Bertha Roy saw him and raced to the door. "You!" she called after him. Willis turned. Bertha's face was stern and her eyes flashed. "Your momma oughta give you a good whippin'," she said.

Willis pretended he had not heard and ran faster down the block.

QUESTIONS FOR DISCUSSION AND WRITING

1. How does Willis's need to show "his stuff" affect the reader's expectations at the beginning of the story? In what ways is the last scene an anti-climax?
2. What do the following characters represent for Willis: Dewey, Curtis, R.V., Jones, and Bertha? How does his attitude toward these characters change by the end of the story?
3. What does the story assume about the reader's knowledge of urban violence? How does the concept of territory define the setting for the plot?
4. To what extent does the reader accept Willis's interpretation of the events as they occur? Does the reader share Willis's surprise at the outcome of these events? Explain your answer.
5. What does the story reveal about the source of individual and group power?

61

BERNARD MALAMUD

The Magic Barrel

BERNARD MALAMUD (1914–1986) was born in Brooklyn, New York, and educated at the City College of New York and Columbia University. During the 1940s, he worked as a clerk for the Bureau of the Census and as an evening high school teacher in New York City. From 1949 until 1961, Malamud taught writing at Oregon State University, where he began publishing his short stories and novels. His work from this period includes three novels—*The Natural* (1952), *The Assistant* (1957), and *A New Life* (1961)—and a collection of short stories—*The Magic Barrel* (1958), which won the National Book Award. In 1961, Malamud accepted a teaching position at Bennington College, Vermont. He continued to produce major novels such as *The Fixer* (1966), which was awarded a Pulitzer Prize, *The Tenants* (1971), and *Dublin's Lives* (1979). His later short stories, published first in magazines such as *Partisan Review, Harper's Bazaar,* and *The New Yorker,* have been collected in *Idiots First* (1963), *Pictures of Fidelman* (1969), *Rembrandt's Hat* (1973), and, most recently, *The Stories of Bernard Malamud* (1983). "The Magic Barrel," the title story from Malamud's most famous collection, tells of a young rabbinical student's attempt to find love through a marriage broker.

Not long ago there lived in uptown New York, in a small, almost meager room, though crowded with books, Leo Finkle, a rabbinical student in the Yeshivah University. Finkle, after six years of study, was to be ordained in June and had been advised by an acquaintance that he might find it easier to win himself a congregation if he were married. Since he had no present prospects of marriage, after two tormented days of turning it over in his mind, he called in Pinye Salzman, a marriage broker whose two-line advertisement he had read in the *Forward*.

The matchmaker appeared one night out of the dark fourth-floor hallway of the graystone rooming house where Finkle lived, grasping a black, strapped portfolio that had been worn thin with use. Salzman, who had been long in the business, was of slight but dignified build, wearing an old hat, and an overcoat too short and tight for him. He smelled frankly of fish, which he loved to eat, and although he was missing a few teeth, his presence was not displeasing, because of an amiable manner curiously contrasted with mournful eyes. His voice, his lips, his wisp of beard, his bony fingers were animated, but give him a moment of repose and his mild blue eyes revealed a depth of sadness, a characteristic that put Leo a little at ease although the situation, for him, was inherently tense.

He at once informed Salzman why he had asked him to come, explaining that his home was in Cleveland, and that but for his parents, who had married comparatively late in life, he was alone in the world. He had for six years devoted himself almost entirely to his studies, as a result of which, understandably, he had found himself without time for a social life and the company of young women. Therefore he thought it the better part of trial and error—of embarrassing fumbling—to call in an experienced person to advise him on these matters. He remarked in passing that the function of the marriage broker was ancient and honorable, highly approved in the Jewish community, because it made practical the necessary without hindering joy. Moreover, his own parents had been brought together by a matchmaker. They had made, if not a financially profitable marriage—since neither had possessed any worldly goods to speak of—at least a successful one in the sense of their everlasting devotion to each other. Salzman listened in embarrassed surprise, sensing a sort of apology. Later, however, he experienced a glow of pride in his work, an emotion that had left him years ago, and he heartily approved of Finkle.

The two went to their business. Leo had led Salzman to the only clear place in the room, a table near a window that overlooked the lamp-lit city. He seated himself at the matchmaker's side but facing him, attempting by an act of will to suppress the unpleasant tickle in his throat. Salzman eagerly unstrapped his portfolio and removed a loose rubber band from a thin packet of much-handled cards. As he flipped through them, a gesture and sound that physically hurt Leo, the student pretended not to see and gazed steadfastly out the window. Although it was still February, winter was on its last legs, signs of which he had for the first time in years begun to notice. He now observed the round white moon, moving high in the sky through a cloud menagerie, and watched with half-open mouth as it penetrated a huge hen, and dropped out of her like an egg laying itself. Salzman, though pretending through eyeglasses he had just slipped on, to be engaged in scanning the writing on the cards, stole occasional glances at the young man's distinguished face, noting with pleasure the long, severe scholar's nose, brown eyes heavy with learning, sensitive yet ascetic lips, and a certain, almost hollow quality of the dark cheeks. He gazed around at shelves upon shelves of books and let out a soft, contented sigh.

When Leo's eyes fell upon the cards, he counted six spread out in Salzman's hand.

"So few?" he asked in disappointment.

"You wouldn't believe me how much cards I got in my office," Salzman replied. "The drawers are already filled to the top, so I keep them now in a barrel, but is every girl good for a new rabbi?"

Leo blushed at this, regretting all he had revealed of himself in a curriculum vitae he had sent to Salzman. He had thought it best to acquaint him with his strict standards and specifications, but in having done so, felt he had told the marriage broker more than was absolutely necessary.

He hesitantly inquired, "Do you keep photographs of your clients on file?"

"First comes family, amount of dowry, also what kind promises," Salzman replied, unbuttoning his tight coat and settling himself in the chair. "After comes pictures, rabbi."

"Call me Mr. Finkle. I'm not yet a rabbi."

Salzman said he would, but instead called him doctor, which he changed to rabbi when Leo was not listening too attentively.

Salzman adjusted his horn-rimmed spectacles, gently cleared his throat and read in an eager voice the contents of the top card:

"Sophie P. Twenty-four years. Widow one year. No children. Educated high school and two years college. Father promises eight thousand dollars. Has wonderful wholesale business. Also real estate. On the mother's side comes teachers, also one actor. Well known on Second Avenue."

Leo gazed up in surprise. "Did you say a widow?"

"A widow don't mean spoiled, rabbi. She lived with her husband maybe four months. He was a sick boy she made a mistake to marry him."

"Marrying a widow has never entered my mind."

"This is because you have no experience. A widow, especially if she is young and healthy like this girl, is a wonderful person to marry. She will be thankful to you the rest of her life. Believe me, if I was looking now for a bride, I would marry a widow."

Leo reflected, then shook his head.

Salzman hunched his shoulders in an almost imperceptible gesture of disappointment. He placed the card down on the wooden table and began to read another:

"Lily H. High school teacher. Regular. Not a substitute. Has savings and new Dodge car. Lived in Paris one year. Father is successful dentist thirty-five years. Interested in professional man. Well Americanized family. Wonderful opportunity."

"I knew her personally," said Salzman. "I wish you could see this girl. She is a doll. Also very intelligent. All day you could talk to her about books and theater and what not. She also knows current events."

"I don't believe you mentioned her age?"

"Her age?" Salzman said, raising his brows. "Her age is thirty-two years."

Leo said after a while, "I'm afraid that seems a little too old."

Salzman let out a laugh. "So how old are you, rabbi?"

"Twenty-seven."

"So what is the difference, tell me, between twenty-seven and thirty-two? My own wife is seven years older than me. So what did I suffer?—Nothing. If Rothschild's daughter wants to marry you, would you say on account her age, no?"

"Yes," Leo said dryly.

Salzman shook off the no in the yes. "Five years don't mean a thing. I give you my word that when you will live with her for one week, you will forget her age. What does it mean five years—that she lived more and knows more than somebody who is younger? On this girl, God bless you, years are not wasted. Each one that it comes makes better the bargain."

"What subject does she teach in high school?"

"Languages. If you heard the way she speaks French, you will think it is music. I am in the business twenty-five years, and I recommend her with my whole heart. Believe me, I know what I'm talking, rabbi."

"What's on the next card?" Leo said abruptly.

Salzman reluctantly turned up the third card:

"Ruth K. Nineteen years. Honor student. Father offers thirteen thousand cash to the right bridegroom. He is a medical doctor. Stomach specialist with marvelous practice. Brother in law owns own garment business. Particular people."

Salzman looked as if he had read his trump card.

"Did you say nineteen?" Leo said with interest.

"On the dot."

"Is she attractive?" He blushed. "Pretty?"

Salzman kissed his finger tips. "A little doll. On this I give you my word. Let me call the father tonight and you will see what means pretty."

But Leo was troubled. "You're sure she's that young?"

"This I am positive. The father will show you the birth certificate."

"Are you positive there isn't something wrong with her?" Leo insisted.

"Who says there is wrong?"

"I don't understand why an American girl her age should go to a marriage broker."

A smile spread over Salzman's face.

"So for the same reason you went, she comes."

Leo flushed. "I am pressed for time."

Salzman, realizing he had been tactless, quickly explained. "The father came, not her. He wants she should have the best, so he looks around himself. When we will locate the right boy he will introduce him and encourage. This makes a better marriage than if a young girl without experience takes for herself. I don't have to tell you this."

"But don't you think this young girl believes in love?" Leo spoke uneasily.

Salzman was about to guffaw but caught himself and said soberly, "Love comes with the right person, not before."

Leo parted dry lips but did not speak. Noticing that Salzman had snatched a glance at the next card, he cleverly asked, "How is her health?"

"Perfect," Salzman said, breathing with difficulty. "Of course, she is a little lame on her right foot from an auto accident that it happened to her when she was twelve years, but nobody notices on account she is so brilliant and also beautiful."

Leo got up heavily and went to the window. He felt curiously bitter and upbraided himself for having called in the marriage broker. Finally, he shook his head.

"Why not?" Salzman persisted, the pitch of his voice rising.

"Because I detest stomach specialists."

"So what do you care what is his business? After you marry her do you need him? Who says he must come every Friday night in your house?"

Ashamed of the way the talk was going, Leo dismissed Salzman, who went home with heavy, melancholy eyes.

Though he had felt only relief at the marriage broker's departure, Leo was in low spirits the next day. He explained it as arising from Salzman's failure to produce a suitable bride for him. He did not care for his type of clientele. But when Leo found himself hesitating whether to seek out another matchmaker, one more polished than Pinye, he wondered if it could be—his protestations to the contrary, and although he honored his father and mother—that he did not, in essence, care for the matchmaking institution? This thought he quickly put out of mind yet found himself still upset. All day he ran around in the woods—missed an important appointment, forgot to give out his laundry, walked out of a Broadway cafeteria without paying and had to run back with the ticket in his hand; had even not recognized his landlady in the street when she passed with a friend and courteously called out, "A good evening to you, Doctor Finkle." By nightfall, however, he had regained sufficient calm to sink his nose into a book and there found peace from his thoughts.

Almost at once there came a knock on the door. Before Leo could say enter, Salzman, commercial cupid, was standing in the room. His face was gray and meager, his expression hungry, and he looked as if he would expire on his feet. Yet the marriage broker managed, by some trick of the muscles, to display a broad smile.

"So good evening. I am invited?"

Leo nodded, disturbed to see him again, yet unwilling to ask the man to leave.

Beaming still, Salzman laid his portfolio on the table. "Rabbi, I got for you tonight good news."

"I've asked you not to call me rabbi. I'm still a student."

"Your worries are finished. I have for you a first-class bride."

"Leave me in peace concerning this project." Leo pretended lack of interest.

"The world will dance at your wedding."

"Please, Mr. Salzman, no more."

"But first must come back my strength," Salzman said weakly. He fumbled with the portfolio straps and took out of the leather case an oily paper bag, from which he extracted a hard, seeded roll and a small, smoked white fish. With a quick motion of his hand he stripped the fish out of its skin and began ravenously to chew. "All day in a rush," he muttered.

Leo watched him eat.

"A sliced tomato you have maybe?" Salzman hesitantly inquired.

"No."

The marriage broker shut his eyes and ate. When he had finished he carefully cleaned up the crumbs and rolled up the remains of the fish, in the paper bag. His spectacled eyes roamed the room until he discovered, amid some piles of books, a one-burner gas stove. Lifting his hat he humbly asked, "A glass tea you got, rabbi?"

Conscience-stricken, Leo rose and brewed the tea. He served it with a chunk of lemon and two cubes of lump sugar, delighting Salzman.

After he had drunk his tea, Salzman's strength and good spirits were restored.

"So tell me, rabbi," he said amiably, "you considered some more the three clients I mentioned yesterday?"

"There was no need to consider."

"Why not?"

"None of them suits me."

"What then suits you?"

Leo let it pass because he could only give a confused answer.

Without waiting for a reply, Salzman asked, "You remember this girl I talked to you—the high school teacher?"

"Age thirty-two?"

But, surprisingly, Salzman's face lit in a smile. "Age twenty-nine."

Leo shot him a look. "Reduced from thirty-two?"

"A mistake," Salzman avowed. "I talked today with the dentist. He took me to his safety deposit box and showed me the birth certificate. She was twenty-nine years last August. They made her a party in the mountains where she went for her vacation. When her father spoke to me the first time I forgot to write the age and I told you thirty-two, but now I remember this was a different client, a widow."

"The same one you told me about? I thought she was twenty-four?"

"A different. Am I responsible that the world is filled with widows?"

"No, but I'm not interested in them, nor for that matter, in school teachers."

Salzman pulled his clasped hands to his breast. Looking at the ceiling he devoutly exclaimed, "Yiddishe kinder, what can I say to somebody that he is not interested in high school teachers? So what then you are interested?"

Leo flushed but controlled himself.

"In what else will you be interested," Salzman went on, "if you not interested in this fine girl that she speaks four languages and has personally in the bank ten thousand dollars? Also her father guarantees further twelve thousand. Also she has a new car, wonderful clothes, talks on all subjects, and she will give you a first-class home and children. How near do we come in our life to paradise?"

"If she's so wonderful, why wasn't she married ten years ago?"

"Why?" Salzman with a heavy laugh. "—Why? Because she is *partikiler.* This is why. She wants the *best.*"

Leo was silent, amused at how he had entangled himself. But Salzman had aroused his interest in Lily H., and he began seriously to consider calling on her. When the marriage broker observed how intently Leo's mind was at work on the facts he had supplied, he felt certain they would soon come to an agreement.

Late Saturday afternoon, conscious of Salzman, Leo Finkle walked with Lily Hirschorn along Riverside Drive. He walked briskly and erectly, wearing with distinction the black fedora he had that morning taken with trepidation out of the dusty hat box on his closet shelf, and the heavy black Saturday coat he had thoroughly whisked clean. Leo also owned a walking stick, a present from a distant relative, but quickly put temptation aside and did not use it. Lily, petite and not unpretty, had on something signifying the approach of spring. She was au courant, animatedly, with all sorts of subjects, and he weighed her words and found her surprisingly sound—score another for Salzman, whom he uneasily sensed to be somewhere around, hiding perhaps high in a tree along the street, flashing the lady signals with a pocket mirror; or perhaps a cloven-hoofed Pan, piping nuptial ditties as he danced his invisible way before them, strewing wild buds on the walk and purple grapes in their path, symbolizing fruit of a union, though there was of course still none.

Lily startled Leo by remarking, "I was thinking of Mr. Salzman, a curious figure, wouldn't you say?"

Not certain what to answer, he nodded.

She bravely went on, blushing, "I for one am grateful for his introducing us. Aren't you?"

He courteously replied, "I am."

"I mean," she said with a little laugh—and it was all in good taste, or at least gave the effect of being not in bad—"do you mind that we came together so?"

He was not displeased with her honesty, recognizing that she meant to set the relationship aright, and understanding that it took a certain amount of experience in life, and courage, to want to do it quite that way. One had to have some sort of past to make that kind of beginning.

He said that he did not mind. Salzman's function was traditional and honorable—valuable for what it might achieve, which, he pointed out, was frequently nothing.

Lily agreed with a sigh. They walked on for a while and she said after a long silence, again with a nervous laugh, "Would you mind if I asked you something a little bit personal? Frankly, I find the subject fascinating." Although Leo shrugged, she went on half embarrassedly, "How was it that you came to your calling? I mean was it a sudden passionate inspiration?"

Leo, after a time, slowly replied, "I was always interested in the Law."

"You saw revealed in it the presence of the Highest?"

He nodded and changed the subject. "I understand that you spent a little time in Paris, Miss Hirschorn?"

"Oh, did Mr. Salzman tell you, Rabbi Finkle?" Leo winced but she went on, "It was ages ago and almost forgotten. I remember I had to return for my sister's wedding."

And Lily would not be put off. "When," she asked in a trembly voice, "did you become enamoured of God?"

He stared at her. Then it came to him that she was talking not about Leo Finkle, but of a total stranger, some mystical figure, perhaps even passionate prophet that Salzman had dreamed up for her—no relation to the living or dead. Leo trembled with rage and weakness. The trickster had obviously sold her a bill of goods, just as he had him, who'd expected to become acquainted with a young lady of twenty-nine, only to behold, the moment he laid eyes upon her strained and anxious face, a woman past thirty-five and aging rapidly. Only his self control had kept him this long in her presence.

"I am not," he said gravely, "a talented religious person," and in seeking words to go on, found himself possessed by shame and fear. "I think," he said in a strained manner, "that I came to God not because I loved Him, but because I did not."

This confession he spoke harshly because its unexpectedness shook him.

Lily wilted. Leo saw a profusion of loaves of bread go flying like ducks high over his head, not unlike the winged loaves by which he had counted himself to sleep last night. Mercifully, then, it snowed, which he would not put past Salzman's machinations.

He was infuriated with the marriage broker and swore he would throw him out of the room the minute he reappeared. But Salzman did not come that night, and when Leo's anger had subsided, an unaccountable despair grew in its place. At first he thought this was caused by his disappointment in Lily, but before long it became evident that he had involved himself with Salzman without a true knowledge of his own intent. He gradually realized—with an emptiness that seized him with six hands—that he had called in the broker to find him a bride because he was incapable of doing it himself. This terrifying insight he had derived as a result of his meeting and conversation with Lily Hirschorn. Her probing questions had somehow irritated him into revealing—to himself more than her—the true nature of his relationship to God, and from that it had come upon him, with shocking force, that apart from his parents, he had never loved anyone. Or perhaps it went the other way, that he did not love God so well as he might, because he had not loved man. It seemed to Leo that his whole life stood starkly revealed and he saw himself for the first time as he truly was—unloved and loveless. This bitter but somehow not fully unexpected revelation brought him to a point of panic, controlled only by extraordinary effort. He covered his face with his hands and cried.

The week that followed was the worst of his life. He did not eat and lost weight. His beard darkened and grew ragged. He stopped attending seminars and almost never opened a book. He seriously considered leaving the Yeshivah, although he was deeply troubled at the thought of the loss of all his years of study—saw them like pages torn from a book, strewn over the city—and at the devastating effect of this decision upon his parents. But he had lived without knowledge of himself, and never in the Five Books and all the Commentaries—mea culpa—had the truth been revealed to him. He did not know where to turn, and in all this desolating loneliness there was no *to whom,* although he often thought of Lily but not once could bring himself to go downstairs and make the call. He became touchy and irritable, especially with his landlady, who asked him all manner of personal questions; on the other hand, sensing his own disagreeableness, he waylaid her on the stairs and apologized abjectly, until mortified, she ran from him. Out of this, however, he drew the consolation that he was a Jew and that a Jew suffered. But gradually, as the long and terrible week drew to a close, he regained his composure and some idea of purpose in life: to go on as planned. Although he was imperfect, the ideal was not. As for his quest of a bride, the thought of continuing afflicted him with anxiety and heartburn, yet perhaps with this new knowledge of himself he would be more successful than in the past. Perhaps love would now come to him and a bride to that love. And for this sanctified seeking who needed a Salzman?

The marriage broker, a skeleton with haunted eyes, returned that very night. He looked, withal, the picture of frustrated expectancy—as if he had steadfastly waited the week at Miss Lily Hirschorn's side for a telephone call that never came.

Casually coughing, Salzman came immediately to the point: "So how did you like her?"

Leo's anger rose and he could not refrain from chiding the matchmaker: "Why did you lie to me, Salzman?"

Salzman's pale face went dead white, the world had snowed on him.

"Did you not state that she was twenty-nine?" Leo insisted.

"I give you my word—"

"She was thirty-five, if a day. *At least* thirty-five."

"Of this don't be too sure. Her father told me—"

"Never mind. The worst of it was that you lied to her."

"How did I lie to her, tell me?"

"You told her things about me that weren't true. You made me out to be more, consequently less than I am. She had in mind a totally different person, a sort of semi-mystical Wonder Rabbi."

"All I said, you was a religious man."

"I can imagine."

Salzman sighed. "This is my weakness that I have," he confessed. "My wife says to me I shouldn't be a salesman, but when I have two fine people that they would be wonderful to be married, I am so happy that I talk too much." He smiled wanly. "This is why Salzman is a poor man."

Leo's anger left him. "Well, Salzman, I'm afraid that's all."

The marriage broker fastened hungry eyes on him.

"You don't want any more a bride?"

"I do," said Leo, "but I have decided to seek her in a different way. I am no longer interested in an arranged marriage. To be frank, I now admit the necessity of premarital love. That is, I want to be in love with the one I marry."

"Love?" said Salzman, astounded. After a moment he remarked, "For us, our love is our life, not for the ladies. In the ghetto they—"

"I know, I know," said Leo. "I've thought of it often. Love, I have said to myself, should be a by-product of living and worship rather than its own end. Yet for myself I find it necessary to establish the level of my need and fulfill it."

Salzman shrugged but answered, "Listen, rabbi, if you want love, this I can find for you also. I have such beautiful clients that you will love them the minute your eyes will see them."

Leo smiled unhappily. "I'm afraid you don't understand."

But Salzman hastily unstrapped his portfolio and withdrew a manila packet from it.

"Pictures," he said, quickly laying the envelope on the table.

Leo called after him to take the pictures away, but as if on the wings of the wind, Salzman had disappeared.

March came. Leo had returned to his regular routine. Although he felt not quite himself yet—lacked energy—he was making plans for a more active social life. Of course it would cost something, but he was an expert in cutting corners; and when there were no corners left he would make circles rounder. All the while Salzman's pictures had laid on the table, gathering dust. Occasionally as Leo sat studying, or enjoying a cup of tea, his eyes fell on the manila envelope, but he never opened it.

The days went by and no social life to speak of developed with a member of the opposite sex—it was difficult, given the circumstances of his situation. One morning Leo toiled up the stairs to his room and stared out the window at the city. Although the day was bright his view of it was dark. For some time he watched the people in the street below hurrying along and then turned with a heavy heart to his little room. On the table was the packet. With a sudden relentless gesture he tore it open. For a half-hour he stood by the table in a state of excitement, examining the photographs of the ladies Salzman had included. Finally, with a deep sigh he put them down. There were six, of varying degrees of attractiveness, but look at them long enough and they all became Lily Hirschorn: all past their prime, all starved behind bright smiles, not a true personality in the lot. Life, despite their frantic yoohooings, had passed them by; they were pictures in a brief case that stank of fish. After a while, however, as Leo attempted to return the photographs into the envelope, he found in it another, a snapshot of the type taken by a machine for a quarter. He gazed at it a moment and let out a cry.

Her face deeply moved him. Why, he could at first not say. It gave him the impression of youth—spring flowers, yet age—a sense of having been used to the bone, wasted; this came from the eyes, which were hauntingly familiar, yet absolutely strange. He had a vivid impression that he had met her before, but try as he might he could not place her although he could almost recall her name, as if he had read it in her own handwriting. No, this couldn't be; he would have remembered her. It was not, he affirmed, that she had an extraordinary beauty—no, though her face was attractive enough; it was that *something* about her moved him. Feature for feature, even some of the ladies of the photographs could do better; but she leaped forth to his heart—had *lived,* or wanted to—more than just wanted, perhaps regretted how she had lived—had somehow deeply suffered: it could be seen in the depths of those reluctant eyes, and from the way the light enclosed and shone from her, and within her, opening realms of possibility: this was her own. Her he desired. His head ached and eyes narrowed with the intensity of his gazing, then as if an obscure fog had blown up in the mind, he experienced fear of her and was aware that he had received an impression, somehow, of evil. He shuddered, saying softly, it is thus with us all. Leo brewed some tea in a small pot and sat sipping it without sugar, to calm himself. But before he had finished drinking, again with excitement he examined the face and found it good: good for Leo Finkle. Only such a one could understand him and help him seek whatever he was seeking. She might, perhaps, love him. How she had happened to be among the discards in Salzman's barrel he could never guess, but he knew he must urgently go find her.

Leo rushed downstairs, grabbed up the Bronx telephone book, and searched for Salzman's home address. He was not listed, nor was his office. Neither was he in the Manhattan book. But Leo remembered having written down the address on a slip of paper after he had read Salzman's advertisement in the "personals" column of the *Forward.* He ran up to his room and tore through his papers, without luck. It was exasperating. Just when he needed the matchmaker he was nowhere to be found. Fortunately Leo remembered to look in his wallet. There on a card he found his name written and a Bronx address. No phone number was listed, the reason—Leo now recalled—he had originally communicated with Salzman by letter. He got on his coat, put a hat on over his skull cap and hurried to the subway station. All the way to the far end of the Bronx he sat on the edge of his seat. He was more than once tempted to take out the picture and see if the girl's face was as he remembered it, but he refrained, allowing the snapshot to remain in his inside coat pocket, content to have her so close. When the train pulled into the station he was waiting at the door and bolted out. He quickly located the street Salzman had advertised.

The building he sought was less than a block from the subway, but it was not an office building, nor even a loft, nor a store in which one could rent office space. It was a very old tenement house. Leo found Salzman's name in pencil on a soiled tag under the bell and climbed three dark flights to his apartment. When he knocked, the door was opened by a thin, asthmatic, gray-haired woman, in felt slippers.

"Yes?" she said, expecting nothing. She listened without listening. He could have sworn he had seen her, too, before but knew it was an illusion.

"Salzman—does he live here? Pinye Salzman," he said, "the matchmaker?"

She stared at him a long minute. "Of course."

He felt embarrassed. "Is he in?"

"No." Her mouth, though left open, offered nothing more.

"The matter is urgent. Can you tell me where his office is?"

"In the air." She pointed upward.

"You mean he has no office?" Leo asked.

"In his socks."

He peered into the apartment. It was sunless and dingy, one large room divided by a half-open curtain, beyond which he could see a sagging metal bed. The near side of the room was crowded with rickety chairs, old bureaus, a three-legged table, racks of cooking utensils, and all the apparatus of a kitchen. But there was no sign of Salzman or his magic barrel, probably also a figment of the imagination. An odor of frying fish made Leo weak to the knees.

"Where is he?" he insisted. "I've got to see your husband."

At length she answered, "So who knows where he is? Every time he thinks a new thought he runs to a different place. Go home, he will find you."

"Tell him Leo Finkle."

She gave no sign she had heard.

He walked downstairs, depressed.

But Salzman, breathless, stood waiting at his door.

Leo was astounded and overjoyed. "How did you get here before me?"

"I rushed."

"Come inside."

They entered. Leo fixed tea, and a sardine sandwich for Salzman. As they were drinking he reached behind him for the packet of pictures and handed them to the marriage broker.

Salzman put down his glass and said expectantly, "You found somebody you like?"

"Not among these."

The marriage broker turned away.

"Here is the one I want." Leo held forth the snapshot.

Salzman slipped on his glasses and took the picture into his trembling hand. He turned ghastly and let out a groan.

"What's the matter?" cried Leo.

"Excuse me. Was an accident this picture. She isn't for you."

Salzman frantically shoved the manila packet into his portfolio. He thrust the snapshot into his pocket and fled down the stairs.

Leo, after momentary paralysis, gave chase and cornered the marriage broker in the vestibule. The landlady made hysterical outcries but neither of them listened.

"Give me back the picture, Salzman."

"No." The pain in his eyes was terrible.

"Tell me who she is then."

"This I can't tell you. Excuse me."

He made to depart, but Leo, forgetting himself, seized the matchmaker by his tight coat and shook him frenziedly.

"Please," sighed Salzman. "*Please.*"

Leo ashamedly let him go. "Tell me who she is," he begged. "It's very important for me to know."

"She is not for you. She is a wild one—wild, without shame. This is not a bride for a rabbi."

"What do you mean wild?"

"Like an animal. Like a dog. For her to be poor was a sin. This is why to me she is dead now."

"In God's name, what do you mean?"

"Her I can't introduce to you," Salzman cried.

"Why are you so excited?"

"Why, he asks," Salzman said, bursting into tears. "This is my baby, my Stella, she should burn in hell."

Leo hurried up to bed and hid under the covers. Under the covers he thought his life through. Although he soon fell asleep he could not sleep her out of his mind. He woke, beating his breast. Though he prayed to be rid of her, his prayers went unanswered. Through days of torment he endlessly struggled not to love her; fearing success, he escaped it. He then concluded to convert her to goodness, himself to God. The idea alternately nauseated and exalted him.

He perhaps did not know that he had come to a final decision until he encountered Salzman in a Broadway cafeteria. He was sitting alone at a rear table, sucking the bony remains of a fish. The marriage broker appeared haggard, and transparent to the point of vanishing.

Salzman looked up at first without recognizing him. Leo had grown a pointed beard and his eyes were weighted with wisdom.

"Salzman," he said, "love has at last come to my heart."

"Who can love from a picture?" mocked the marriage broker.

"It is not impossible."

"If you can love her, then you can love anybody. Let me show you some new clients that they just sent me their photographs. One is a little doll."

"Just her I want," Leo murmured.

"Don't be a fool, doctor. Don't bother with her."

"Put me in touch with her, Salzman," Leo said humbly. "Perhaps I can be of service."

Salzman had stopped eating and Leo understood with emotion that it was now arranged.

Leaving the cafeteria, he was, however, afflicted by a tormenting suspicion that Salzman had planned it all to happen this way.

Leo was informed by letter that she would meet him on a certain corner, and she was there one spring night, waiting under a street lamp. He appeared, carrying a small bouquet of violets and rosebuds. Stella stood by the lamp post, smoking. She wore white with red shoes, which fitted his expectations, although in a troubled moment he had imagined the dress red, and only the shoes white. She waited uneasily and shyly. From afar he saw that her eyes—clearly her father's—were filled with desperate innocence. He pictured, in her, his own redemption. Violins and lit candles revolved in the sky. Leo ran forward with flowers outthrust.

Around the corner, Salzman, leaning against a wall, chanted prayers for the dead.

QUESTIONS FOR DISCUSSION AND WRITING

1. What is the basic conflict that motivates Leo to seek out the services of a marriage broker? How does his meeting with Lily bring that conflict to a climax? In what way is his meeting with Stella designed to resolve that conflict?
2. How does Salzman characterize himself by the way he describes the three possible prospects? How does Leo reveal his own character by his reaction to these descriptions?

3. Why does Leo believe in the tradition of the marriage broker? Why is it appropriate that Salzman's office is in the air? How do Salzman's magical comings and goings suggest that there is something of the trickster about him?
4. What does Leo learn about himself during his conversation with Lily? What does he suspect about Salzman after their conversation about Stella?
5. What does this story suggest about the nature of love, suffering, and happiness? Why is Leo attracted to Stella's picture? What is ambiguous about her appearance when he meets her? Why is Salzman nearby chanting the prayers for the dead?

62

KATHERINE MANSFIELD

Her First Ball

KATHERINE MANSFIELD (1888–1923) was born in Wellington, New Zealand, but came to England to study music at Queen's College in London. In 1908, after a brief trip home to New Zealand, Mansfield returned to London where, with the help of her friends D. H. Lawrence and Aldous Huxley, she embarked on a literary career. A disastrous marriage and an unplanned pregnancy forced Mansfield to retreat to a German convent. After suffering a miscarriage, Mansfield began writing stories and sketches, which were published as *In a German Pension* (1911). In 1910 she returned to London where she contributed stories to *New Age* and met editor and critic John Middleton Murry, whom she married in 1918. During this period she published many of her stories in two magazines edited by Murry, *Rhythm* and *Blue Review*. In 1916 she began writing a series of stories based on her life in New Zealand. The first of these, *Prelude* (1918), was included in *Bliss and Other Stories* (1920). Mansfield's other best-known collections are *The Garden Party and Other Stories* (1922) and *The Dove's Nest and Other Stories* (1923). In 1918 Mansfield contracted tuberculosis and began seeking cures at health spas throughout southern Europe. She stopped writing in 1922 and died the next year at the age of thirty-five. "Her First Ball," reprinted from *The Short Stories of Katherine Mansfield* (1937), is the story of a young country girl's introduction to "the beginning of everything."

Exactly when the ball began Leila would have found it hard to say. Perhaps her first real partner was the cab. It did not matter that she shared the cab with the Sheridan girls and their brother. She sat back in her own little corner of it, and the bolster on which her hand rested felt like the sleeve of an unknown young man's dress suit; and away they bowled, past waltzing lampposts and houses and fences and trees.

"Have you really never been to a ball before, Leila? But, my child, how too weird—" cried the Sheridan girls.

"Our nearest neighbor was fifteen miles," said Leila softly, gently opening and shutting her fan.

Oh, dear, how hard it was to be indifferent like the others! She tried not to smile too much; she tried not to care. But every single thing was so new and exciting . . . Meg's tuberoses, Jose's long loop of amber, Laura's little dark head, pushing above her white fur like a flower through snow. She would remember for ever. It even gave her a pang to see her cousin Laurie throw away the wisps of tissue paper he pulled from the fastening of his new gloves. She would like to have kept those wisps as a keepsake, as a remembrance. Laurie leaned forward and put his hand on Laura's knee.

"Look here, darling," he said. "The third and the ninth as usual. Twig?"

Oh, how marvellous to have a brother! In her excitement Leila felt that if there had been time, if it hadn't been impossible, she couldn't have helped crying because she was an only child, and no brother had ever said "Twig?" to her; no sister would ever say, as Meg said to Jose that moment, "I've never known your hair go up more successfully than it has tonight!"

But, of course, there was no time. They were at the drill hall already; there were cabs in front of them and cabs behind. The road was bright on either side with moving fan-like lights, and on the pavement gay couples seemed to float through the air; little satin shoes chased each other like birds.

"Hold on to me, Leila; you'll get lost," said Laura.

"Come on, girls, let's make a dash for it," said Laurie.

Leila put two fingers on Laura's pink velvet cloak, and they were somehow lifted past the big gold lantern, carried along the passage, and pushed into the little room marked "Ladies." Here the crowd was so great there was hardly space to take off their things; the noise was deafening. Two benches on either side were stacked high with wraps. Two old women in white aprons ran up and down tossing fresh armfuls. And everybody was pressing forward trying to get at the little dressing table and mirror at the far end.

A great quivering jet of gas lighted the ladies' room. It couldn't wait; it was dancing already. When the door opened again and there came a burst of tuning from the drill hall, it leaped almost to the ceiling.

Dark girls, fair girls were patting their hair, tying ribbons again, tucking handkerchiefs down the front of their bodices, smoothing marble-white gloves. And because they were all laughing it seemed to Leila that they were all lovely.

"Aren't there any invisible hairpins?" cried a voice. "How most extraordinary! I can't see a single invisible hairpin."

"Powder my back, there's a darling," cried some one else.

"But I must have a needle and cotton. I've torn simply miles and miles of the frill," wailed a third.

Then, "Pass them along, pass them along!" The straw basket of programs was tossed from arm to arm. Darling little pink-and-silver programs, with pink pencils and fluffy tassels. Leila's fingers shook as she took one out of the basket. She wanted to ask someone,

"Am I meant to have one too?" but she had just time to read: "Waltz 3. *Two, Two in a Canoe.* Polka 4. *Making the Feathers Fly,*" when Meg cried, "Ready, Leila?" and they pressed their way through the crush in the passage towards the big double doors of the drill hall.

Dancing had not begun yet, but the band had stopped tuning, and the noise was so great it seemed that when it did begin to play it would never be heard. Leila, pressing close to Meg, looking over Meg's shoulder, felt that even the little quivering colored flags strung across the ceiling were talking. She quite forgot to be shy; she forgot how in the middle of dressing she had sat down on the bed with one shoe off and one shoe on and begged her mother to ring up her cousins and say she couldn't go after all. And the rush of longing she had had to be sitting on the veranda of their forsaken upcountry home, listening to the baby owls crying "More pork" in the moonlight, was changed to a rush of joy so sweet that it was hard to bear alone. She clutched her fan, and, gazing at the gleaming, golden floor, the azaleas, the lanterns, the stage at one end with its red carpet and gilt chairs and the band in a corner, she thought breathlessly, "How heavenly; how simply heavenly!"

All the girls stood grouped together at one side of the doors, the men at the other, and the chaperones in dark dresses, smiling rather foolishly, walked with little careful steps over the polished floor towards the stage.

"This is my little country cousin Leila. Be nice to her. Find her partners; she's under my wing," said Meg, going up to one girl after another.

Strange faces smiled at Leila—sweetly, vaguely. Strange voices answered, "Of course, my dear." But Leila felt the girls didn't really see her. They were looking towards the men. Why didn't the men begin? What were they waiting for? There they stood, smoothing their gloves, patting their glossy hair and smiling among themselves. Then, quite suddenly, as if they had only just made up their minds that that was what they had to do, the men came gliding over the parquet. There was a joyful flutter among the girls. A tall, fair man flew up to Meg, seized her program, scribbled something; Meg passed him on to Leila. "May I have the pleasure?" He ducked and smiled. There came a dark man wearing an eyeglass, then cousin Laurie with a friend, and Laura with a little freckled fellow whose tie was crooked. Then quite an old man—fat, with a big bald patch on his head—took her program and murmured, "Let me see, let me see!" And he was a long time comparing his program, which looked black with names, with hers. It seemed to give him so much trouble that Leila was ashamed. "Oh, please don't bother," she said eagerly. But instead of replying the fat man wrote something, glanced at her again. "Do I remember this bright little face?" he said softly. "Is it known to me of yore?" At that moment the band began playing; the fat man disappeared. He was tossed away on a great wave of music that came flying over the gleaming floor, breaking the groups up into couples, scattering them, sending them spinning. . . .

Leila had learned to dance at boarding school. Every Saturday afternoon the boarders were hurried off to a little corrugated iron mission hall where Miss Eccles (of London) held her "select" classes. But the difference between that dusty-smelling hall—with calico texts on the walls, the poor terrified little woman in a brown velvet toque with rabbit's ears thumping the cold piano, Miss Eccles poking the girls' feet with her long white wand—and this was so tremendous that Leila was sure if her partner didn't come and she had to listen to that marvelous music and to watch the others sliding, gliding over the golden floor, she would die at least, or faint, or lift her arms and fly out of one of those dark windows that showed the stars.

"Ours, I think—" Some one bowed, smiled, and offered her his arm; she hadn't to die after all. Some one's hand pressed her waist, and she floated away like a flower that is tossed into a pool.

"Quite a good floor, isn't it?" drawled a faint voice close to her ear.

"I think it's most beautifully slippery," said Leila.

"Pardon!" The faint voice sounded surprised. Leila said it again. And there was a tiny pause before the voice echoed, "Oh, quite!" and she was swung round again.

He steered so beautifully. That was the great difference between dancing with girls and men, Leila decided. Girls banged into each other, and stamped on each other's feet; the girl who was gentleman always clutched you so.

The azaleas were separate flowers no longer; they were pink and white flags streaming by.

"Were you at the Bells' last week?" the voice came again. It sounded tired. Leila wondered whether she ought to ask him if he would like to stop.

"No, this is my first dance," said she.

Her partner gave a little gasping laugh. "Oh, I say," he protested.

"Yes, it is really the first dance I've ever been to." Leila was most fervent. It was such a relief to be able to tell somebody. "You see, I've lived in the country all my life up until now. . . ."

At that moment the music stopped, and they went to sit on two chairs against the wall. Leila tucked her pink satin feet under and fanned herself, while she blissfully watched the other couples passing and disappearing through the swing doors.

"Enjoying yourself, Leila?" asked Jose, nodding her golden head.

Laura passed and gave her the faintest little wink; it made Leila wonder for a moment whether she was quite grown up after all. Certainly her partner did not say very much. He coughed, tucked his handkerchief away, pulled down his waistcoat, took a minute thread off his sleeve. But it didn't matter. Almost immediately the band started, and her second partner seemed to spring from the ceiling.

"Floor's not bad," said the new voice. Did one always begin with the floor? And then, "Were you at the Neaves' on Tuesday?" And again Leila explained. Perhaps it was a little strange that her partners were not more interested. For it was thrilling. Her first ball! She was only at the beginning of everything. It seemed to her that she had never known what the night was like before. Up till now it had been dark, silent, beautiful very often—oh, yes—but mournful somehow. Solemn. And now it would never be like that again—it had opened dazzling bright.

"Care for an ice?" said her partner. And they went through the swing doors, down the passage, to the supper room. Her cheeks burned, she was fearfully thirsty. How sweet the ices looked on little glass plates, and how cold the frosted spoon was, iced too! And when they came back to the hall there was the fat man waiting for her by the door. It gave her quite a shock again to see how old he was; he ought to have been on the stage with the fathers and mothers. And when Leila compared him with her other partners he looked shabby. His waistcoat was creased, there was a button off his glove, his coat looked as if it was dusty with French chalk.

"Come along, little lady," said the fat man. He scarcely troubled to clasp her, and they moved away so gently, it was more like walking than dancing. But he said not a word about the floor. "Your first dance, isn't it?" he murmured.

"How *did* you know?"

"Ah," said the fat man, "that's what it is to be old!" He wheezed faintly as he steered her past an awkward couple. "You see, I've been doing this kind of thing for the last thirty years."

"Thirty years?" cried Leila. Twelve years before she was born!

"It hardly bears thinking about, does it?" said the fat man gloomily. Leila looked at his bald head, and she felt quite sorry for him.

"I think it's marvelous to be still going on," she said kindly.

"Kind little lady," said the fat man, and he pressed her a little closer, and hummed a bar of the waltz. "Of course," he said, "you can't hope to last anything like as long as that. No-o," said the fat man, "long before that you'll be sitting up there on the stage, looking on, in your nice black velvet. And these pretty arms will have turned into little short fat ones, and you'll beat time with such a different kind of fan—a black bony one." The fat man seemed to shudder. "And you'll smile away like the poor old dears up there, and point to your daughter, and tell the elderly lady next to you how some dreadful man tried to kiss her at the club ball. And your heart will ache, ache"—the fat man squeezed her closer still, as if he really was sorry for that poor heart—"because no one wants to kiss you now. And you'll say how unpleasant these polished floors are to walk on, how dangerous they are. Eh, Mademoiselle Twinkletoes?" said the fat man softly.

Leila gave a light little laugh, but she did not feel like laughing. Was it—could it all be true? It sounded terribly true. Was this first ball only the beginning of her last ball after all? At that the music seemed to change; it sounded sad, sad it rose upon a great sigh. Oh, how quickly things changed! Why didn't happiness last for ever? For ever wasn't a bit too long.

"I want to stop," she said in a breathless voice. The fat man led her to the door.

"No," she said, "I won't go outside. I won't sit down. I'll just stand here, thank you." She leaned against the wall, tapping with her foot, pulling up her gloves and trying to smile. But deep inside her a little girl threw her pinafore over her head and sobbed. Why had he spoiled it all?

"I say, you know," said the fat man, "you mustn't take me seriously, little lady."

"As if I should!" said Leila, tossing her small dark head and sucking her underlip. . . .

Again the couples paraded. The swing doors opened and shut. Now new music was given out by the bandmaster. But Leila didn't want to dance any more. She wanted to be home, or sitting on the veranda listening to those baby owls. When she looked through the dark windows at the stars, they had long beams like wings. . . .

But presently a soft, melting, ravishing tune began, and a young man with curly hair bowed before her. She would have to dance, out of politeness, until she could find Meg. Very stiffly she walked into the middle; very haughtily she put her hand on his sleeve. But in one minute, in one turn, her feet glided, glided. The lights, the azaleas, the dresses, the pink faces, the velvet chairs, all became one beautiful flying wheel. And when her next partner bumped her into the fat man and he said, "Par*don,*" she smiled at him more radiantly than ever. She didn't even recognize him again.

QUESTIONS FOR DISCUSSION AND WRITING

1. How does the scene in the cab establish Leila's difference from the others going to the ball? How does the fat man momentarily spoil the ball for her? How is she able to resolve her disappointment?
2. How does Meg's phrase "my little country cousin" characterize Leila? What does Leila think of the people she meets at the ball—especially her young partners? How does she describe the fat man?
3. How does Leila describe the difference between life in the country and life in the city? For example, how does she compare the setting of Miss Eccles's "select" dance classes and the drill hall?
4. What is Leila's point of view toward the evening? How does the conversation of her friends and dancing partners suggest that Leila has overestimated the glamour of the ball? How does her point of view toward the night change after her dance with the fat man?
5. How is the fat man's statement about time supported by other events in the evening? How did he know it was her first ball? Why does she refuse to believe that it is only the beginning of her last ball?

63

BOBBIE ANN MASON

Shiloh

BOBBIE ANN MASON was born in 1940 in Mayfield, Kentucky, and educated at the University of Kentucky, the State University of New York at Binghamton, and the University of Connecticut. In the 1960s Mason worked as a writer for various fan magazines, including *Movie Stars, Movie Life,* and *T.V. Star Parade.* After several years of writing about such teen idols as Fabian and Annette Funicello, Mason decided to return to graduate school to study literature, writing her doctoral dissertation on Nabokov. After graduate school, she immersed herself in popular culture once again by reading children's books such as the Nancy Drew series. In 1972 Mason accepted a teaching position at Mansfield State College in Pennsylvania. In 1974 she published her first book, *Nabokov's Garden: A Study of Ada,* and in 1975 her second, *The Girl*

Sleuth: A Feminist Guide to the Bobbsey Twins, Nancy Drew and Their Sisters. **Mason has contributed most of her short stories to *The New Yorker.* Her recent work includes two novels, *In Country* (1985) and *Spence and Lila* (1988), and a collection of stories, *Love Life: Stories* (1989). "Shiloh," reprinted from *Shiloh and Other Stories* (1982), describes the marriage of a disabled truck driver and his wife.**

Leroy Moffitt's wife, Norma Jean, is working on her pectorals. She lifts three-pound dumbbells to warm up, then progresses to a twenty-pound barbell. Standing with her legs apart, she reminds Leroy of Wonder Woman.

"I'd give anything if I could just get these muscles to where they're real hard," says Norma Jean. "Feel this arm. It's not as hard as the other one."

"That's 'cause you're right-handed," says Leroy, dodging as she swings the barbell in an arc.

"Do you think so?"

"Sure."

Leroy is a truckdriver. He injured his leg in a highway accident four months ago, and his physical therapy, which involves weights and a pulley, prompted Norma Jean to try building herself up. Now she is attending a body-building class. Leroy has been collecting temporary disability since his tractor-trailer jackknifed in Missouri, badly twisting his left leg in its socket. He has a steel pin in his hip. He will probably not be able to drive his rig again. It sits in the backyard, like a gigantic bird that has flown home to roost. Leroy has been home in Kentucky for three months, and his leg is almost healed, but the accident frightened him and he does not want to drive any more long hauls. He is not sure what to do next. In the meantime, he makes things from craft kits. He started by building a miniature log cabin from notched Popsicle sticks. He varnished it and placed it on the TV set, where it remains. It reminds him of a rustic Nativity scene. Then he tried string art (sailing ships on black velvet), a macramé owl kit, a snap-together B-17 Flying Fortress, and a lamp made out of a model truck, with a light fixture screwed in the top of the cab. At first the kits were diversions, something to kill time, but now he is thinking about building a full-scale log house from a kit. It would be considerably cheaper than building a regular house, and besides, Leroy has grown to appreciate how things are put together. He has begun to realize that in all the years he was on the road he never took time to examine anything. He was always flying past scenery.

"They won't let you build a log cabin in any of the new subdivisions," Norma Jean tells him.

"They will if I tell them it's for you," he says, teasing her. Ever since they were married, he has promised Norma Jean he would build her a new home one day. They have always rented, and the house they live in is small and nondescript. It does not even feel like a home, Leroy realizes now.

Norma Jean works at the Rexall drugstore, and she has acquired an amazing amount of information about cosmetics. When she explains to Leroy the three stages of complexion care, involving creams, toners, and moisturizers, he thinks happily of other petroleum products—axle grease, diesel fuel. This is a connection between him and Norma Jean. Since he has been home, he has felt unusually tender about his wife and guilty over his long absences. But he can't tell what she feels about him. Norma Jean has never complained about his traveling; she has never made hurt remarks, like calling his truck a "widow-maker." He is reasonably certain she has been faithful to him, but he wishes she would celebrate his permanent home-coming more happily. Norma Jean is often startled to find Leroy at home, and he thinks she seems a little disappointed about it. Perhaps he reminds her too much of the early days of their marriage, before he went on the road. They had a child who died as an infant, years ago. They never speak about their memories of Randy, which have almost faded, but now that Leroy is home all the time, they sometimes feel awkward around each other, and Leroy wonders if one of them should mention the child. He has the feeling that they are waking up out of a dream together—that they must create a new marriage, start afresh. They are lucky they are still married. Leroy has read that for most people losing a child destroys the marriage—or else he heard this on *Donahue*. He can't always remember where he learns things anymore.

At Christmas, Leroy bought an electric organ for Norma Jean. She used to play the piano when she was in high school. "It don't leave you," she told him once. "It's like riding a bicycle."

The new instrument had so many keys and buttons that she was bewildered by it at first. She touched the keys tentatively, pushed some buttons, then pecked out "Chopsticks." It came out in an amplified fox-trot rhythm, with marimba sounds.

"It's an orchestra!" she cried.

The organ had a pecan-look finish and eighteen preset chords, with optional flute, violin, trumpet, clarinet, and banjo accompaniments. Norma Jean mastered the organ almost immediately. At first she played Christmas songs. Then she bought *The Sixties Songbook* and learned every tune in it, adding variations to each with the rows of brightly colored buttons.

"I didn't like these old songs back then," she said. "But I have this crazy feeling I missed something."

"You didn't miss a thing," said Leroy.

Leroy likes to lie on the couch and smoke a joint and listen to Norma Jean play "Can't Take My Eyes Off You" and "I'll Be Back." He is back again. After fifteen years on the road, he is finally settling down with the woman he loves. She is still pretty. Her skin is flawless. Her frosted curls resemble pencil trimmings.

Now that Leroy has come home to stay, he notices how much the town has changed. Subdivisions are spreading across western Kentucky like an oil slick. The sign at the edge of town says "Pop: 11,500"—only seven hundred more than it said twenty years before. Leroy can't figure out who is living in all the new houses. The farmers who used to gather around the courthouse square on Saturday afternoons to play checkers and spit tobacco juice have gone. It has been years since Leroy has thought about the farmers, and they have disappeared without his noticing.

Leroy meets a kid named Stevie Hamilton in the parking lot at the new shopping center. While they pretend to be strangers meeting over a stalled car, Stevie tosses an ounce of marijuana under the front seat of Leroy's car. Stevie is wearing orange jogging shoes and a T-shirt that says CHATTAHOOCHEE SUPER-RAT. His father is a prominent doctor who lives in one of the expensive subdivisions in a new white-columned brick house that looks like a funeral parlor. In the phone book under his name there is a separate number, with the listing "Teenagers."

"Where do you get this stuff?" asks Leroy. "From your pappy?"

"That's for me to know and you to find out," Stevie says. He is slit-eyed and skinny.

"What else you got?"

"What you interested in?"

"Nothing special. Just wondered."

Leroy used to take speed on the road. Now he has to go slowly. He needs to be mellow. He leans back against the car and says, "I'm aiming to build me a log house, soon as I get time. My wife, though, I don't think she likes the idea."

"Well, let me know when you want me again," Stevie says. He has a cigarette in his cupped palm, as though sheltering it from the wind. He takes a long drag, then stomps it on the asphalt and slouches away.

Stevie's father was two years ahead of Leroy in high school. Leroy is thirty-four. He married Norma Jean when they were both eighteen, and their child Randy was born a few months later, but he died at the age of four months and three days. He would be about Stevie's age now. Norma Jean and Leroy were at the drive-in, watching a double feature (*Dr. Strangelove* and *Lover Come Back*), and the baby was sleeping in the back seat. When the first movie ended, the baby was dead. It was the sudden infant death syndrome. Leroy remembers handing Randy to a nurse at the emergency room, as though he were offering her a large doll as a present. A dead baby feels like a sack of flour. "It just happens sometimes," said the doctor, in what Leroy always recalls as a nonchalant tone. Leroy can hardly remember the child anymore, but he still sees vividly a scene from *Dr. Strangelove* in which the President of the United States was talking in a folksy voice on the hot line to the Soviet premier about the bomber accidentally headed toward Russia. He was in the War Room, and the world map was lit up. Leroy remembers Norma Jean standing catatonically beside him in the hospital and himself thinking: Who is this strange girl? He had forgotten who she was. Now scientists are saying that crib death is caused by a virus. Nobody knows anything, Leroy thinks. The answers are always changing.

When Leroy gets home from the shopping center, Norma Jean's mother, Mabel Beasley, is there. Until this year, Leroy has not realized how much time she spends with Norma Jean. When she visits, she inspects the closets and then the plants, informing Norma Jean when a plant is droopy or yellow. Mabel calls the plants "flowers," although there are never any blooms. She always notices if Norma Jean's laundry is piling up. Mabel is a short, overweight woman whose tight, brown-dyed curls look more like a wig than the actual wig she sometimes wears. Today she has brought Norma Jean an off-white dust ruffle she made for the bed; Mabel works in a custom-upholstery shop.

"This is the tenth one I made this year," Mabel says. "I got started and couldn't stop."

"It's real pretty," says Norma Jean.

"Now we can hide things under the bed," says Leroy, who gets along with his mother-in-law primarily by joking with her. Mabel has never really forgiven him for disgracing her by getting Norma Jean pregnant. When the baby died, she said that fate was mocking her.

"What's that thing?" Mabel says to Leroy in a loud voice, pointing to a tangle of yarn on a piece of canvas.

Leroy holds it up for Mabel to see. "It's my needlepoint," he explains. "This is a *Star Trek* pillow cover."

"That's what a woman would do," says Mabel. "Great day in the morning!"

"All the big football players on TV do it," he says.

"Why, Leroy, you're always trying to fool me. I don't believe you for one minute. You don't know what to do with yourself—that's the whole trouble. Sewing!"

"I'm aiming to build us a log house," says Leroy. "Soon as my plans come."

"Like *heck* you are," says Norma Jean. She takes Leroy's needlepoint and shoves it into a drawer. "You have to find a job first. Nobody can afford to build now anyway."

Mabel straightens her girdle and says, "I still think before you get tied down y'all ought to take a little run to Shiloh."

"One of these days, Mama," Norma Jean says impatiently.

Mabel is talking about Shiloh, Tennessee. For the past few years, she has been urging Leroy and Norma Jean to visit the Civil War battleground there. Mabel went there on her honeymoon—the only real trip she ever took. Her husband died of a perforated ulcer when Norma Jean was ten, but Mabel, who was accepted into the United Daughters of the Confederacy in 1975, is still preoccupied with going back to Shiloh.

"I've been to kingdom come and back in that truck out yonder," Leroy says to Mabel, "but we never yet set foot in that battleground. Ain't that something? How did I miss it?"

"It's not even that far," Mabel says.

After Mabel leaves, Norma Jean reads to Leroy from a list she has made. "Things you could do," she announces. "You could get a job as a guard at Union Carbide, where they'd let you set on a stool. You could get on at the lumberyard. You could do a little carpenter work, if you want to build so bad. You could—"

"I can't do something where I'd have to stand up all day."

"You ought to try standing up all day behind a cosmetics counter. It's amazing that I have strong feet, coming from two parents that never had strong feet at all." At the moment Norma Jean is holding on to the kitchen counter, raising her knees one at a time as she talks. She is wearing two-pound ankle weights.

"Don't worry," says Leroy. "I'll do something."

"You could truck calves to slaughter for somebody. You wouldn't have to drive any big old truck for that."

"I'm going to build you this house," says Leroy. "I want to make you a real home."

"I don't want to live in any log cabin."

"It's not a cabin. It's a house."

"I don't care. It looks like a cabin."

"You and me together could lift those logs. It's just like lifting weights."

Norma Jean doesn't answer. Under her breath, she is counting. Now she is marching through the kitchen. She is doing goose steps.

Before his accident, when Leroy came home he used to stay in the house with Norma Jean, watching TV in bed and playing cards. She would cook fried chicken, picnic ham, chocolate pie—all his favorites. Now he is home alone much of the time. In the mornings, Norma Jean disappears, leaving a cooling place in the bed. She eats a cereal called Body Buddies, and she leaves the bowl on the table, with the soggy tan balls floating in a milk puddle. He sees things about Norma Jean that he never realized before. When she chops onions, she stares off into a corner, as if she can't bear to look. She puts on her house slippers almost precisely at nine o'clock every evening and nudges her jogging shoes under the couch. She saves bread heels for the birds. Leroy watches the birds at the feeder. He notices the peculiar way goldfinches fly past the window. They close their wings, then fall, then spread their wings to catch and lift themselves. He wonders if they close their eyes when they fall. Norma Jean closes her eyes when they are in bed. She wants the lights turned out. Even then, he is sure she closes her eyes.

He goes for long drives around town. He tends to drive a car rather carelessly. Power steering and an automatic shift make a car feel so small and inconsequential that his body is hardly involved in the driving process. His injured leg stretches out comfortably. Once or twice he has almost hit something, but even the prospect of an accident seems minor in a car. He cruises the new subdivisions, feeling like a criminal rehearsing for a robbery. Norma Jean is probably right about a log house being inappropriate here in the new subdivisions. All the houses look grand and complicated. They depress him.

One day when Leroy comes home from a drive he finds Norma Jean in tears. She is in the kitchen making a potato and mushroom-soup casserole, with grated-cheese topping. She is crying because her mother caught her smoking.

"I didn't hear her coming. I was standing here puffing away pretty as you please," Norma Jean says, wiping her eyes.

"I knew it would happen sooner or later," says Leroy, putting his arm around her.

"She don't know the meaning of the word 'knock,'" says Norma Jean. "It's a wonder she hadn't caught me years ago."

"Think of it this way," Leroy says. "What if she caught me with a joint?"

"You better not let her!" Norma Jean shrieks. "I'm warning you, Leroy Moffitt!"

"I'm just kidding. Here, play me a tune. That'll help you relax."

Norma Jean puts the casserole in the oven and sets the timer. Then she plays a ragtime tune, with horns and banjo, as Leroy lights up a joint and lies on the couch, laughing to himself about Mabel's catching him at it. He thinks of Stevie Hamilton—a doctor's son pushing grass. Everything is funny. The whole town seems crazy and small. He is reminded of Virgil Mathis, a boastful policeman Leroy used to shoot pool with. Virgil recently led a drug bust in a back room at a bowling alley, where he seized ten thousand dollars' worth of marijuana. The newspaper had a picture of him holding up the bags of grass and grinning widely. Right now, Leroy can imagine Virgil breaking down the door and arresting him with a lungful of smoke. Virgil would probably have been alerted to the scene because of all the racket Norma Jean is making. Now she sounds like a hard-rock band. Norma Jean is terrific. When she switches to a Latin-rhythm version of "Sunshine Superman," Leroy hums along. Norma Jean's foot goes up and down, up and down.

"Well, what do you think?" Leroy says, when Norma Jean pauses to search through her music.

"What do I think about what?"

His mind had gone blank. Then he says, "I'll sell my rig and build us a house." That wasn't what he wanted to say. He wanted to know what she thought—what she *really* thought—about them.

"Don't start in on that again," says Norma Jean. She begins playing "Who'll Be the Next in Line?"

Leroy used to tell hitchhikers his whole life story—about his travels, his hometown, the baby. He would end with a question: "Well, what do you think?" It was just a rhetorical question. In time, he had the feeling that he'd been telling the same story over and over to the same hitchhikers. He quit talking to hitchhikers when he realized how his voice sounded—whining and self-pitying, like some teenage-tragedy song. Now Leroy has the sudden impulse to tell Norma Jean about himself, as if he had just met her. They have known each other so long they have forgotten a lot about each other. They could become reacquainted. But when the oven timer goes off and she runs to the kitchen, he forgets why he wants to do this.

The next day, Mabel drops by. It is Saturday and Norma Jean is cleaning. Leroy is studying the plans of his log house, which have finally come in the mail. He has them spread out on the table—big sheets of stiff blue paper, with diagrams and numbers printed in white. While Norma Jean runs the vacuum, Mabel drinks coffee. She sets her coffee cup on a blueprint.

"I'm just waiting for time to pass," she says to Leroy, drumming her fingers on the table.

As soon as Norma Jean switches off the vacuum, Mabel says in a loud voice, "Did you hear about the datsun dog that killed the baby?"

Norma Jean says, "The word is 'dachshund.'"

"They put the dog on trial. It chewed the baby's legs off. The mother was in the next room all the time." She raises her voice. "They thought it was neglect."

Norma Jean is holding her ears. Leroy manages to open the refrigerator and get some Diet Pepsi to offer Mabel. Mabel still has some coffee and she waves away the Pepsi.

"Datsuns are like that," Mabel says. "They're jealous dogs. They'll tear a place to pieces if you don't keep an eye on them."

"You better watch out what you're saying, Mabel," says Leroy.

"Well, facts is facts."

Leroy looks out the window at his rig. It is like a huge piece of furniture gathering dust in the backyard. Pretty soon it will be an antique. He hears the vacuum cleaner. Norma Jean seems to be cleaning the living room rug again.

Later, she says to Leroy, "She just said that about the baby because she caught me smoking. She's trying to pay me back."

"What are you talking about?" Leroy says, nervously shuffling blueprints.

"You know good and well," Norma Jean says. She is sitting in a kitchen chair with her feet up and her arms wrapped around her knees. She looks small and helpless. She says, "The very idea, her bringing up a subject like that! Saying it was neglect."

"She didn't mean that," Leroy says.

"She might not have *thought* she meant it. She always says things like that. You don't know how she goes on."

"But she didn't really mean it. She was just talking."

Leroy opens a king-sized bottle of beer and pours it into two glasses, dividing it carefully. He hands a glass to Norma Jean and she takes it from him mechanically. For a long time, they sit by the kitchen window watching the birds at the feeder.

Something is happening. Norma Jean is going to night school. She has graduated from her six-week body-building course and now she is taking an adult-education course in composition at Paducah Community College. She spends her evenings outlining paragraphs.

"First you have a topic sentence," she explains to Leroy. "Then you divide it up. Your secondary topic has to be connected to your primary topic."

To Leroy, this sounds intimidating. "I never was any good in English," he says.

"It makes a lot of sense."

"What are you doing this for, anyhow?"

She shrugs. "It's something to do." She stands up and lifts her dumbbells a few times.

"Driving a rig, nobody cared about my English."

"I'm not criticizing your English."

Norma Jean used to say, "If I lose ten minutes' sleep, I just drag all day." Now she stays up late, writing compositions. She got a B on her first paper—a how-to-theme on soup-based casseroles. Recently Norma Jean has been cooking unusual foods—tacos, lasagna, Bombay chicken. She doesn't play the organ anymore, though her second paper was called "Why Music Is Important to Me." She sits at the kitchen table, concentrating on her outlines, while Leroy plays with his log house plans, practicing with a set of Lincoln Logs. The thought of getting a truckload of notched, numbered logs scares him, and he wants to be prepared. As he and Norma Jean work together at the kitchen table, Leroy has the hopeful thought that they are sharing something, but he knows he is a fool to think this. Norma Jean is miles away. He knows he is going to lose her. Like Mabel, he is just waiting for time to pass.

One day, Mabel is there before Norma Jean gets home from work, and Leroy finds himself confiding in her. Mabel, he realizes, must know Norma Jean better than he does.

"I don't know what's got into that girl," Mabel says. "She used to go to bed with the chickens. Now you say she's up all hours. Plus her a-smoking. I like to died."

"I want to make her this beautiful home," Leroy says, indicating the Lincoln Logs. "I don't think she even wants it. Maybe she was happier with me gone."

"She don't know what to make of you, coming home like this."

"Is that it?"

Mabel takes the roof off his Lincoln Log cabin. "You couldn't get *me* in a log cabin," she says. "I was raised in one. It's no picnic, let me tell you."

"They're different now," says Leroy.

"I tell you what," Mabel says, smiling oddly at Leroy.

"What?"

"Take her on down to Shiloh. Y'all need to get out together, stir a little. Her brain's all balled up over them books."

Leroy can see traces of Norma Jean's features in her mother's face. Mabel's worn face has the texture of crinkled cotton, but suddenly she looks pretty. It occurs to Leroy that Mabel has been hinting all along that she wants them to take her with them to Shiloh.

"Let's all go to Shiloh," he says. "You and me and her. Come Sunday."

Mabel throws up her hand in protest. "Oh, no, not me. Young folks want to be by theirselves."

When Norma Jean comes in with groceries, Leroy says excitedly, "Your mama here's been dying to go to Shiloh for thirty-five years. It's about time we went, don't you think?"

"I'm not going to butt in on anybody's second honeymoon," Mabel says.

"Who's going on a honeymoon, for Christ's sake?" Norma Jean says loudly.

"I never raised no daughter of mine to talk that-a-way," Mabel says.

"You ain't seen nothing yet," says Norma Jean. She starts putting away boxes and cans, slamming cabinet doors.

"There's a log cabin at Shiloh," Mabel says. "It was there during the battle. There's bullet holes in it."

"When are you going to *shut up* about Shiloh, Mama?" asks Norma Jean.

"I always thought Shiloh was the prettiest place, so full of history," Mabel goes on. "I just hoped y'all could see it once before I die, so you could tell me about it." Later, she whispers to Leroy, "You do what I said. A little change is what she needs."

"Your name means 'the king,'" Norma Jean says to Leroy that evening. He is trying to get her to go to Shiloh, and she is reading a book about another century.

"Well, I reckon I ought to be right proud."

"I guess so."

"Am I still king around here?"

Norma Jean flexes her biceps and feels them for hardness. "I'm not fooling around with anybody, if that's what you mean," she says.

"Would you tell me if you were?"

"I don't know."

"What does *your* name mean?"

"It was Marilyn Monroe's real name."

"No kidding!"

"Norma comes from the Normans. They were invaders," she says. She closes her book and looks hard at Leroy. "I'll go to Shiloh with you if you'll stop staring at me."

On Sunday, Norma Jean packs a picnic and they go to Shiloh. To Leroy's relief, Mabel says she does not want to come with them. Norma Jean drives, and Leroy, sitting beside her, feels like some boring hitchhiker she has picked up. He tries some conversation, but she answers him in monosyllables. At Shiloh, she drives aimlessly through the park, past bluffs and trails and steep ravines. Shiloh is an immense place, and Leroy cannot see it as a battleground. It is not what he expected. He thought it would look like a golf course. Monuments are everywhere, showing through the thick clusters of trees. Norma Jean passes the log cabin Mabel mentioned. It is surrounded by tourists looking for bullet holes.

"That's not the kind of log house I've got in mind," says Leroy apologetically.

"I know *that*."

"This is a pretty place. Your mama was right."

"It's O.K.," says Norma Jean. "Well, we've seen it. I hope she's satisfied."

They burst out laughing together.

At the park museum, a movie on Shiloh is shown every half hour, but they decide that they don't want to see it. They buy a souvenir Confederate flag for Mabel, and then they find a picnic spot near the cemetery. Norma Jean has brought a picnic cooler, with pimiento sandwiches, soft drinks, and Yodels. Leroy eats a sandwich and then smokes a joint, hiding it behind the picnic cooler. Norma Jean has quit smoking altogether. She is picking cake crumbs from the cellophane wrapper, like a fussy bird.

Leroy says, "So the boys in gray ended up in Corinth. The Union soldiers zapped 'em finally. April 7, 1862."

They both know that he doesn't know any history. He is just talking about some of the historical plaques they have read. He feels awkward, like a boy on a date with an older girl. They are still just making conversation.

"Corinth is where Mama eloped to," says Norma Jean.

They sit in silence and stare at the cemetery for the Union dead and, beyond, at a tall cluster of trees. Campers are parked nearby, bumper to bumper, and small children in bright clothing are cavorting and squealing. Norma Jean wads up the cake wrapper and squeezes it tightly in her hand. Without looking at Leroy, she says, "I want to leave you."

Leroy takes a bottle of Coke out of the cooler and flips off the cap. He holds the bottle poised near his mouth but cannot remember to take a drink. Finally he says, "No, you don't."

"Yes, I do."

"I won't let you."

"You can't stop me."

"Don't do me that way."

Leroy knows Norma Jean will have her own way. "Didn't I promise to be home from now on?" he says.

"In some ways, a woman prefers a man who wanders," says Norma Jean. "That sounds crazy, I know."

"You're not crazy."

Leroy remembers to drink from his Coke. Then he says, "Yes, you *are* crazy. You and me could start all over again. Right back at the beginning."

"We *have* started all over again," says Norma Jean. "And this is how it turned out."

"What did I do wrong?"

"Nothing."

"Is this one of those women's lib things?" Leroy asks.

"Don't be funny."

The cemetery, a green slope dotted with white markers, looks like a subdivision site. Leroy is trying to comprehend that his marriage is breaking up, but for some reason he is wondering about white slabs in a graveyard.

"Everything was fine till Mama caught me smoking," says Norma Jean, standing up. "That's set something off."

"What are you talking about?"

"She won't leave me alone—*you* won't leave me alone." Norma Jean seems to be crying, but she is looking away from him. "I feel eighteen again. I can't face that all over again." She starts walking away. "No, it *wasn't* fine. I don't know what I'm saying. Forget it."

Leroy takes a lungful of smoke and closes his eyes as Norma Jean's words sink in. He tries to focus on the fact that thirty-five hundred soldiers died on the grounds around him. He can only think of that war as a board game with plastic soldiers. Leroy almost smiles, as he compares the Confederates' daring attack on the Union camps and Virgil Mathis's raid on the bowling alley. General Grant, drunk and furious, shoved the

Southerners back to Corinth, where Mabel and Jet Beasley were married years later, when Mabel was still thin and good-looking. The next day, Mabel and Jet visited the battleground, and then Norma Jean was born, and then she married Leroy and they had a baby, which they lost, and now Leroy and Norma Jean are here at the same battleground. Leroy knows he is leaving out a lot. He is leaving out the insides of history. History was always just names and dates to him. It occurs to him that building a house out of logs is similarly empty—too simple. And the real inner workings of a marriage, like most of history, have escaped him. Now he sees that building a log house is the dumbest idea he could have had. It was clumsy of him to think Norma Jean would want a log house. It was a crazy idea. He'll have to think of something else, quickly. He will wad the blueprints into tight balls and fling them into the lake. Then he'll get moving again. He opens his eyes. Norma Jean has moved away and is walking through the cemetery, following a serpentine brick path.

Leroy gets up to follow his wife, but his good leg is asleep and his bad leg still hurts him. Norma Jean is far away, walking rapidly toward the bluff by the river, and he tries to hobble toward her. Some children run past him, screaming noisily. Norma Jean has reached the bluff, and she is looking out over the Tennessee River. Now she turns toward Leroy and waves her arms. Is she beckoning to him? She seems to be doing an exercise for her chest muscles. The sky is unusually pale—the color of the dust ruffle Mabel made for their bed.

QUESTIONS FOR DISCUSSION AND WRITING

1. How does Leroy's accident produce new conflicts in his marriage? What old conflicts have he and Norma Jean failed to resolve? How does the trip to Shiloh clarify these conflicts?

2. How do Leroy's diversions with craft kits establish his character? How do Norma Jean's body building, organ playing, and night school establish her character? What effect does Mabel have on her children?

3. Now that he is no longer on the road, what details does Leroy notice about his home and community? What does he hope to accomplish by building a log cabin? Why is the Shiloh battleground—and, in particular, the log cabin filled with bullet holes—an appropriate setting for the conclusion of the story?

4. In what sense is this story, told from Leroy's point of view, similar to the stories he used to tell hitchhikers in his rig? What specific evidence prompts him to suggest that something is happening to his marriage?

5. What does Leroy learn about "the insides of history" at Shiloh? How does this lesson pertain to Leroy and Norma Jean's life? What have they "swept under" the dust ruffle made for their bed?

64

GUY DE MAUPASSANT

The Necklace

GUY DE MAUPASSANT (1850–1893) was born near the seacoast town of Dieppe in Normandy, France. He was educated first at a seminary near Yvetot, then in Le Havre and Rouen, where he was supposed to study law. A rebellious and unhappy student, Maupassant gave up his education to serve in the Franco-Prussian war (1870–1871). Upon his return to civilian life, Maupassant moved to Paris, where he worked at the Marine Ministry and the Ministry of Education. It was during this period that he came to know the famous writers living in Paris—Turgenev, Edmond Goncourt, Zola, and particularly Flaubert. Through the assistance of his mother, Maupassant studied with Flaubert, submitting his stories to the master's exacting standards. In 1880, a few months after the death of his mentor, Maupassant published his first story, "Boule de Suif" ("Ball of Fat") in an anthology edited by Zola. Maupassant was an immediate sensation and his dramatic success encouraged him to write six novels and over three hundred stories during the next ten years. His most important novels are *A Woman's Life* (1883), *Bel-Ami* (1885), and *Pierre et Jean* (1888). His most famous short stories are collected in *La Maison Tellier* (1881), *Mademoiselle Fifi* (1882), *Contes de la Bécasse* (1883), *Contes et Nouvelles* (1885), and *L'Inutile Beauté* (1890). In 1888, Maupassant began to show signs of mental illness, probably the result of venereal disease. After he attempted suicide in 1892, he was committed to an asylum where he died in 1893. "The Necklace," reprinted from his *Complete Short Stories* (1903), recounts the cost of a woman's desire to be admired.

She was one of those pretty and charming girls born, as though fate had blundered over her, into a family of artisans. She had no marriage portion, no expectations, no means of getting known, understood, loved, and wedded by a man of wealth and distinction; and she let herself be married off to a little clerk in the Ministry of Education.

Her tastes were simple because she had never been able to afford any other, but she was as unhappy as though she had married beneath her; for women have no caste or class, their beauty, grace, and charm serving them for birth or family. Their natural delicacy, their instinctive elegance, their nimbleness of wit, are their only mark of rank, and put the slum girl on a level with the highest lady in the land.

She suffered endlessly, feeling herself born for every delicacy and luxury. She suffered from the poorness of her house, from its mean walls, worn chairs, and ugly curtains. All these things, of which other women of her class would not even have been aware, tormented and insulted her. The sight of the little Breton girl who came to do the work in her little house aroused heart-broken regrets and hopeless dreams in her mind. She imagined silent antechambers, heavy with Oriental tapestries, lit by torches in lofty bronze sockets, with two tall footmen in knee-breeches sleeping in large arm-chairs, overcome by the heavy warmth of the stove. She imagined vast saloons hung with antique silks, exquisite pieces of furniture supporting priceless ornaments, and small, charming, perfumed rooms, created just for little parties of intimate friends, men who were famous and sought after, whose homage roused every other woman's envious longings.

When she sat down for dinner at the round table covered with a three-days-old cloth, opposite her husband, who took the cover off the soup-tureen, exclaiming delightedly: "Aha! Scotch broth! What could be better?" she imagined delicate meals, gleaming silver, tapestries peopling the walls with folk of a past age and strange birds in faery forests; she imagined delicate food served in marvelous dishes, murmured gallantries, listened to with an inscrutable smile as one trifled with the rosy flesh of trout or wings of asparagus chicken.

She had no clothes, no jewels, nothing. And these were the only things she loved; she felt that she was made for them. She had longed so eagerly to charm, to be desired, to be wildly attractive and sought after.

She had a rich friend, an old school friend whom she refused to visit, because she suffered so keenly when she returned home. She would weep whole days, with grief, regret, despair, and misery.

One evening her husband came home with an exultant air, holding a large envelope in his hand.

"Here's something for you," he said.

Swiftly she tore the paper and drew out a printed card on which were these words:

> "The Minister of Education and Madame Ramponneau request the pleasure of the company of Monsieur and Madame Loisel at the Ministry on the evening of Monday, January the 18th."

Instead of being delighted, as her husband hoped, she flung the invitation petulantly across the table, murmuring:

"What do you want me to do with this?"

"Why, darling, I thought you'd be pleased. You never go out, and this is a great occasion. I had tremendous trouble to get it. Every one wants one; it's very select, and very few go to the clerks. You'll see all the really big people there."

She looked at him out of furious eyes, and said impatiently:

"And what do you suppose I am to wear to such an affair?"

He had not thought about it; he stammered:

"Why, the dress you go to the threatre in. It looks very nice, to me. . . ."

He stopped, stupefied and utterly at a loss when he saw that his wife was beginning to cry. Two large tears ran slowly down from the corners of her eyes towards the corners of her mouth.

"What's the matter with you? What's the matter with you?" he faltered.

But with a violent effort she overcame her grief and replied in a calm voice, wiping her wet cheeks:

"Nothing. Only I haven't a dress and so I can't go to this party. Give your invitation to some friend of yours whose wife will be turned out better than I shall."

He was heart-broken.

"Look here, Mathilde," he persisted. "What would be the cost of a suitable dress, which you could use on other occasions as well, something very simple?"

She thought for several seconds, reckoning up prices and also wondering for how large a sum she could ask without bringing upon herself an immediate refusal and an exclamation of horror from the careful-minded clerk.

At last she replied with some hesitation:

"I don't know exactly, but I think I could do it on four hundred francs."

He grew slightly pale, for this was exactly the amount he had been saving for a gun, intending to get a little shooting next summer on the plain of Nanterre with some friends who went lark-shooting there on Sundays.

Nevertheless he said: "Very well. I'll give you four hundred francs. But try and get a really nice dress with the money."

The day of the party drew near, and Madame Loisel seemed sad, uneasy and anxious. Her dress was ready, however. One evening her husband said to her:

"What's the matter with you? You've been very odd for the last three days."

"I'm utterly miserable at not having any jewels, not a single stone, to wear," she replied. "I shall look absolutely no one. I would almost rather not go to the party."

"Wear flowers," he said. "They're very smart at this time of the year. For ten francs you could get two or three gorgeous roses."

She was not convinced.

"No . . . there's nothing so humiliating as looking poor in the middle of a lot of rich women."

"How stupid you are!" exclaimed her husband. "Go and see Madame Forestier and ask her to lend you some jewels. You know her quite well enough for that."

She uttered a cry of delight.

"That's true. I never thought of it."

Next day she went to see her friend and told her trouble.

Madame Forestier went to her dressing-table, took up a large box, brought it to Madame Loisel, opened it, and said:

"Choose, my dear."

First she saw some bracelets, then a pearl necklace, then a Venetian cross in gold and gems, of exquisite workmanship. She tried the effect of the jewels before the mirror, hesitating, unable to make her mind to leave them, to give them up. She kept on asking:

"Haven't you anything else?"

"Yes. Look for yourself. I don't know what you would like best."

Suddenly she discovered, in a black satin case, a superb diamond necklace; her heart began to beat covetously. Her hands trembled as she lifted it. She fastened it round her neck, upon her high dress, and remained in ecstasy at sight of herself.

Then, with hesitation, she asked in anguish:

"Could you lend me this, just this alone?"

"Yes, of course."

She flung herself on her friend's breast, embraced her frenziedly, and went away with her treasure.

The day of the party arrived. Madame Loisel was a success. She was the prettiest woman present, elegant, graceful, smiling, and quite above herself with happiness. All the men stared at her, inquired her name, and asked to be introduced to her. All the Under-Secretaries of State were eager to waltz with her. The Minister noticed her.

She danced madly, ecstatically, drunk with pleasure, with no thought for anything, in the triumph of her beauty, in the pride of her success, in a cloud of happiness made up of this universal homage and admiration, of the desires she had aroused, of the completeness of a victory so dear to her feminine heart.

She left about four o'clock in the morning. Since midnight her husband had been dozing in a deserted little room, in company with three other men whose wives were having a good time.

He threw over her shoulders the garments he had brought for them to go home in, modest everyday clothes, whose poverty clashed with the beauty of the ball-dress. She was conscious of this and was anxious to hurry away, so that she should not be noticed by the other women putting on their costly furs.

Loisel restrained her.

"Wait a little. You'll catch cold in the open. I'm going to fetch a cab."

But she did not listen to him and rapidly descended the staircase. When they were out in the street they could not find a cab; they began to look for one, shouting at the drivers whom they saw passing in the distance.

They walked down towards the Seine, desperate and shivering. At last they found on the quay one of those old night-prowling carriages which are only to be seen in Paris after dark, as though they were ashamed of their shabbiness in the daylight.

It brought them to their door in the Rue des Martyrs, and sadly they walked up to their own apartment. It was the end, for her. As for him, he was thinking that he must be at the office at ten.

She took off the garments in which she had wrapped her shoulders, so as to see herself in all her glory before the mirror. But suddenly she uttered a cry. The necklace was no longer round her neck!

"What's the matter with you?" asked her husband, already half undressed.

She turned towards him in the utmost distress.

"I . . . I . . . I've no longer got Madame Forestier's necklace. . . ."

He started with astonishment.

"What! . . . Impossible!"

They searched in the folds of her dress, in the folds of the coat, in the pockets, everywhere. They could not find it.

"Are you sure that you still had it on when you came away from the ball?" he asked.

"Yes, I touched it in the hall at the Ministry."

"But if you had lost it in the street, we should have heard it fall."

"Yes. Probably we should. Did you take the number of the cab?"

"No. You didn't notice it, did you?"

"No."

They stared at one another, dumbfounded. At last Loisel put on his clothes again.

"I'll go over all the ground we walked," he said, "and see if I can't find it."

And he went out. She remained in her evening clothes, lacking strength to get into bed, huddled on a chair, without volition or power of thought.

Her husband returned about seven. He found nothing.

He went to the police station, to the newspapers, to offer a reward, to the cab companies, everywhere that a ray of hope impelled him.

She waited all day long, in the same state of bewilderment at this fearful catastrophe.

Loisel came home at night, his face lined and pale; he had discovered nothing.

"You must write to your friend," he said, "and tell her that you've broken the clasp of her necklace and are getting it mended. That will give us time to look about us."

She wrote at his dictation.

By the end of a week they had lost all hope.

Loisel, who had aged five years, declared:

"We must see about replacing the diamonds."

Next day they took the box which had held the necklace and went to the jewellers whose name was inside. He consulted his books.

"It was not I who sold this necklace, Madame; I must have merely supplied the clasp."

Then they went from jeweller to jeweller, searching for another necklace like the first, consulting their memories, both ill with remorse and anguish of mind.

In a shop at the Palais-Royal they found a string of diamonds which seemed to them exactly like the one they were looking for. It was worth forty thousand francs. They were allowed to have it for thirty-six thousand.

They begged the jeweller not to sell it for three days. And they arranged matters on the understanding that it would be taken back for thirty-four thousand francs, if the first one were found before the end of February.

Loisel possessed eighteen thousand francs left to him by his father. He intended to borrow the rest.

He did borrow it, getting a thousand from one man, five hundred from another, five louis here, three louis there. He gave notes of hand, entered into ruinous agreements, did business with usurers and the whole tribe of money-lenders. He mortgaged the whole remaining years of his existence, risked his signature without even knowing if he could honour it and, appalled at the agonising face of the future, at the black misery about to fall upon him, at the prospect of every possible physical privation and moral torture, he went to get the new necklace and put down upon the jeweller's counter thirty-six thousand francs.

When Madame Loisel took back the necklace to Madame Forestier, the latter said to her in a chilly voice:

"You ought to have brought it back sooner; I might have needed it."

She did not, as her friend had feared, open the case. If she had noticed the substitution, what would she have thought? What would she have said? Would she not have taken her for a thief?

Madame Loisel came to know the ghastly life of abject poverty. From the very first she played her part heroically. This fearful debt must be paid off. She would pay it. The servant was dismissed. They changed their flat; they took a garret under the roof.

She came to know the heavy work of the house, the hateful duties of the kitchen. She washed the plates, wearing out her pink nails on the coarse pottery and the bottoms of pans. She washed the dirty linen, the shirts and dish-clothes, and hung them out to dry on a string; every morning she took the dustbin down into the street and carried up the water, stopping on each landing to get her breath. And, clad like a poor woman, she went to the fruiterer, to the grocer, to the butcher, a basket on her arm, haggling, insulted, fighting for every wretched halfpenny of her money.

Every month notes had to be paid off, others renewed, time gained.

Her husband worked in the evenings at putting straight a merchant's accounts, and often at night he did copying at two-pence-halfpenny a page.

And this life lasted ten years.

At the end of ten years everything was paid off, everything, the usurer's charges, the accumulation of superimposed interest.

Madame Loisel looked old now. She had become like all the other strong, hard, coarse women of poor households. Her hair was badly done, her skirts were awry, her hands were red. She spoke in a shrill voice, and the water slopped all over the floor when she scrubbed it. But sometimes, when her husband was at the office, she sat down by the window and thought of that evening long ago, of the ball at which she had been so beautiful and so much admired.

What would have happened if she had never lost those jewels. Who knows? Who knows? How strange life is, how fickle! How little is needed to ruin or to save!

One Sunday, as she had gone for a walk along the Champs-Élysées to freshen herself after the labours of the week, she caught sight suddenly of a woman who was taking a child out for a walk. It was Madame Forestier, still young, still beautiful, still attractive.

Madame Loisel was conscious of some emotion. Should she speak to her? Yes, certainly. And now that she had paid, she would tell her all. Why not?

She went up to her.

"Good morning, Jeanne."

The other did not recognise her, and was surprised at being thus familiarly addressed by a poor woman.

"But . . . Madame . . ." she stammered. "I don't know . . . you must be making a mistake."

"No . . . I am Mathilde Loisel."

Her friend uttered a cry.

"Oh! . . . my poor Mathilde, how you have changed! . . ."

"Yes, I've had some hard times since I saw you last; and many sorrows . . . and all on your account."

"On my account! . . . How was that?"

"You remember the diamond necklace you lent me for the ball at the Ministry?"

"Yes. Well?"

"Well, I lost it."

"How could you? Why, you brought it back."

"I brought you another one just like it. And for the last ten years we have been paying for it. You realise it wasn't easy for me; we had no money. . . . Well, it's paid for at last, and I'm glad indeed."

Madame Forestier had halted.

"You say you bought a diamond necklace to replace mine?"

"Yes. You hadn't noticed it? They were very much alike."

And she smiled in proud and innocent happiness.

Madame Forestier, deeply moved, took her two hands.

"Oh, my poor Mathilde! But mine was imitation. It was worth at the very most five hundred francs! . . ."

QUESTIONS FOR DISCUSSION AND WRITING

1. How do the opening paragraphs of the story establish the conflict between Mme. Loisel and her condition? How does the party momentarily resolve that conflict? How does the lost necklace reestablish the conflict?
2. How does the narrator regard Mme. Loisel's values and attitudes? How does the party confirm Mme. Loisel's conception of herself? How do the events that follow change her character?
3. What specific features of her environment "torment" and "insult" her? What kind of setting does she imagine is appropriate to her? What kind of environment must she endure for ten years to repay the cost of one night of pleasure?
4. What is the narrator's point of view toward the events he describes? How might this story have been altered if Maupassant had told it from the husband's point of view?
5. How does the ending of the story contribute to its theme? How does the "false" necklace serve to symbolize Mme. Loisel's life?

65

HERMAN MELVILLE

Bartleby the Scrivener

HERMAN MELVILLE (1819–1891) was born in New York City, the son of a merchant who went bankrupt in 1830. Two years later his father died, and Melville was forced to withdraw from school, working briefly as a farm laborer, a bank messenger, a clerk in his brother's store, and after two additional years of education, an elementary school teacher. In 1839, Melville escaped the boredom of the schoolroom for life at sea, traveling to Liverpool as a merchant seaman. On his return, Melville tried to find employment writing documents for lawyers. But in 1841 he gave up his ambition to be a legal scrivener and shipped out to the South Pacific, where during the next four years he jumped ship, lived among the cannibals, took part in a mutiny, worked as a harpooner,

and found his way home on the American naval frigate *United States*. Melville began writing about his adventures in novels such as *Typee* (1846), *Omoo* (1847), and *Redburn* (1849). These early books established Melville's reputation as a popular adventure writer—as "the man who lived among the cannibals"—but that reputation soon declined when he began publishing more philosophical books such as *Mardi* (1849) and his masterpiece, *Moby Dick* (1851). Although his work continued to receive enthusiastic criticism from fellow writers such as Nathaniel Hawthorne, Melville's later novels—including *Pierre* (1852) and *The Confidence Man* (1857)—were commercial failures. He drifted from one job to another, finally acquiring the position of collector of customs at New York harbor. During this period, Melville wrote a long poetic account of a pilgrimage to the Holy Land, *Clarel* (1876), which was virtually ignored by the critics. Believing his work was a public failure, Melville became bitter and eventually died in obscurity. In the 1920s, Melville's reputation was restored and another masterpiece, *Billy Budd* (1924), was discovered in his literary effects. "Bartleby the Scrivener: A Story of Wall Street," reprinted from *Piazza Tales* (1856), recounts a good and earnest man's attempt to understand another man's "passive resistance."

I am a rather elderly man. The nature of my avocations, for the last thirty years, has brought me into more than ordinary contact with what would seem an interesting and somewhat singular set of men, of whom, as yet, nothing, that I know of, has ever been written—I mean, the law-copyists, or scriveners. I have known very many of them, professionally and privately, and, if I pleased, could relate divers histories, at which good-natured gentlemen might smile, and sentimental souls might weep. But I waive the biographies of all other scriveners, for a few passages in the life of Bartleby, who was a scrivener, the strangest I ever saw, or heard of. While, of other law-copyists, I might write the complete life, of Bartleby nothing of that sort can be done. I believe that no materials exist for a full and satisfactory biography of this man. It is an irreparable loss to literature. Bartleby was one of those beings of whom nothing is ascertainable, except from the original sources, and, in his case, those are very small. What my own astonished eyes saw of Bartleby, *that* is all I know of him, except, indeed, one vague report, which will appear in the sequel.

Ere introducing the scrivener, as he first appeared to me, it is fit I make some mention of myself, my employees, my business, my chambers, and general surroundings; because some such description is indispensable to an adequate understanding of the chief character about to be presented. Imprimis: I am a man who, from his youth upwards, has been filled with a profound conviction that the easiest way of life is the best. Hence, though I belong to a profession proverbially energetic and nervous, even to turbulence, at times, yet nothing of that sort have I ever suffered to invade my peace. I am one of those unambitious lawyers who never addresses a jury, or in any way draws down public applause; but, in the cool tranquillity of a snug retreat, do a snug business among rich men's bonds, and mortgages, and title-deeds. All who know me, consider me an eminently *safe* man. The late John Jacob Astor, a personage little given to poetic enthusiasm, had no hesitation in pronouncing my first grand point to be prudence; my next, method. I do not speak it in vanity, but simply record the fact, that I was not unemployed in my profession by the late John Jacob Astor; a name which, I admit, I love to repeat; for it hath a rounded and orbicular sound to it, and rings like unto bullion. I will freely add, that I was not insensible to the late John Jacob Astor's good opinion.

Some time prior to the period at which this little history begins, my avocations had been largely increased. The good old office, now extinct in the State of New York, of a Master in Chancery, had been conferred upon me. It was not a very arduous office, but very pleasantly remunerative. I seldom lose my temper; much more seldom indulge in dangerous indignation at wrongs and outrages; but, I must be permitted to be rash here, and declare that I consider the sudden and violent abrogation of the office of Master in Chancery, by the new Constitution, as a—premature act; inasmuch as I had counted upon a life-lease of the profits, whereas I only received those of a few short years. But this is by the way.

My chambers were up stairs, at No.——Wall Street. At one end, they looked upon the white wall of the interior of a spacious sky-light shaft, penetrating the building from top to bottom.

This view might have been considered rather tame than otherwise, deficient in what landscape painters call "life." But, if so, the view from the other end of my chambers offered, at least, a contrast, if nothing more. In that direction, my windows commanded an unobstructed view of a lofty brick wall, black by age and everlasting shade; which wall required no spyglass to bring out its lurking beauties, but, for the benefit of all near-sighted spectators, was pushed up to within ten feet of my window panes. Owing to the great height of the surrounding buildings, and my chambers being on the second floor, the interval between this wall and mine not a little resembled a huge square cistern.

At the period just preceding the advent of Bartleby, I had two persons as copyists in my employment, and a promising lad as an office-boy. First, Turkey; second, Nippers; third, Ginger Nut. These may seem names, the like of which are not usually found in the Directory. In truth, they were nicknames, mutually conferred upon each other by my three clerks, and were deemed expressive of their respective persons or characters. Turkey was a short, pursy Englishman, of about my own age—that is, somewhere not far from sixty. In the morning, one might say, his face was of a fine florid hue, but after twelve o'clock, meridian—his dinner hour—it blazed like a grate full of Christmas coals; and continued blazing—but, as it were, with a gradual wane—till six o'clock P.M., or thereabouts; after which, I saw no more of the proprietor of the face, which, gaining its meridian with the sun, seemed to set with it, to rise, culminate, and decline the following day, with the like regularity and undiminished glory. There are many singular coincidences I have known in the course of my life, not the least among which was the fact, that, exactly when Turkey displayed his fullest beams from his red and radiant countenance, just then, too, at that critical moment, began the daily period when I considered his business capacities as seriously disturbed for the remainder of the twenty-four hours. Not that he was absolutely idle, or averse to business, then; far from it. The difficulty was, he was apt to be altogether too energetic. There was a strange, inflamed, flurried, flighty recklessness of activity about him. He would be incautious in dipping his pen into his inkstand. All his blots upon my documents were dropped there after twelve o'clock meridian. Indeed, not only would he be reckless, and sadly given to making blots in the afternoon, but, some days, he went further, and was rather noisy. At such times, too, his face flamed with augmented blazonry, as if cannel coal had been heaped on anthracite. He made an unpleasant racket with his chair; spilled his sand-box; in mending his pens, impatiently split them all to pieces, and threw them on the floor in a sudden passion; stood up, and leaned over his table, boxing his papers about in a most indecorous manner, very sad to behold in an elderly man like him. Nevertheless, as he was in many ways a most valuable person to me, and all the time before twelve o'clock meridian, was the quickest, steadiest creature, too, accomplishing a great deal of work in a style not easily to be matched—for these reasons, I was willing to overlook his eccentricities, though, indeed, occasionally, I remonstrated with him. I did this very gently, however, because, though the civilest, nay, the blandest and most reverential of men in the morning, yet, in the afternoon, he was disposed, upon provocation, to be slightly rash with his tongue—in fact, insolent. Now, valuing his morning services as I did, and resolved not to lose them—yet, at the same time, made uncomfortable by his inflamed ways after twelve o'clock—and being a man of peace, unwilling by my admonitions to call forth unseemly retorts from him, I took upon me, one Saturday noon (he was always worse on Saturdays) to hint to him, very kindly, that, perhaps, now that he was growing old, it might be well to abridge his labors; in short, he need not come to my chambers after twelve o'clock, but, dinner over, had best go home to his lodgings, and rest himself till tea-time. But no; he insisted upon his afternoon devotions. His countenance became intolerably fervid, as he oratorically assured me—gesticulating with a long ruler at the other end of the room—that if his services in the morning were useful, how indispensable, then, in the afternoon?

"With submission, sir," said Turkey, on this occasion, "I consider myself your right-hand man. In the morning I but marshal and deploy my columns; but in the afternoon I put myself at their head, and gallantly charge the foe, thus"—and he made a violent thrust with the ruler.

"But the blots, Turkey," intimated I.

"True; but, with submission, sir, behold these hairs! I am getting old. Surely, sir, a blot or two of a warm afternoon is not to be severely urged against gray hairs. Old age—even if it blot the page—is honorable. With submission, sir, we *both* are getting old."

This appeal to my fellow-feeling was hardly to be resisted. At all events, I saw that go he would not. So, I made up my mind to let him stay, resolving, nevertheless, to see to it that, during the afternoon, he had to do with my less important papers.

Nippers, the second on my list, was a whiskered, sallow, and upon the whole, rather piratical-looking young man, of about five and twenty. I always deemed him the victim of two evil powers—ambition and indigestion. The ambition was evinced by a certain impatience of the duties of a mere copyist, an unwarrantable usurpation of strictly professional affairs, such as the original drawing up of legal documents. The indigestion seemed betokened in an occasional nervous testiness and grinning irritability, causing the teeth to audibly grind together over mistakes committed in copying; unnecessary maledictions, hissed, rather than spoken, in the heat of business; and especially by a continual discontent with the height of the table where he worked. Though of a very ingenious, mechanical turn, Nippers could never get this table to suit him. He put chips under it, blocks of various sorts, bits of pasteboard, and at last went so far as to attempt an exquisite adjustment, by final pieces of folded blotting-paper. But no invention would answer. If, for the sake of easing his back, he brought the table lid at a sharp angle well up towards his chin, and wrote there like a man using the steep roof of a Dutch house for his desk, then he declared that it stopped the circulation in his arms. If now he lowered the table to his waistbands, and stooped over it in writing, then there was a sore aching in his back. In short, the truth of the matter was, Nippers knew not what he wanted. Or, if he wanted anything, it was to be rid of a scrivener's table altogether. Among the manifestations of his diseased ambition was a fondness he had for receiving visits from certain ambiguous-looking fellows in seedy coats, whom he called his clients. Indeed, I was aware that not only was he, at times, considerable of a ward-politician, but he occasionally did a little business at the Justices' courts, and was not unknown on the steps of the Tombs. I have good reason to believe, however, that one individual who called upon him at my chambers, and who, with a grand air, he insisted was his client, was no other than a dun, and the alleged title-deed, a bill. But, with all his failings, and the annoyances he caused me, Nippers, like his compatriot Turkey, was a very useful man to me; wrote a neat, swift hand; and, when he chose, was not deficient in a gentlemanly sort of deportment. Added to this, he always dressed in a gentlemanly sort of way; and so, incidentally, reflected credit upon my chambers. Whereas, with respect to Turkey, I had much ado to keep him from being a reproach to me. His clothes were apt to look oily, and smell of eating-houses. He wore his pantaloons very loose and baggy in summer. His coats were execrable; his hat not to be handled. But while the hat was a thing of indifference to me, inasmuch as his natural civility and deference, as a dependent Englishman, always led him to doff it the moment he entered the room, yet his coat was another matter. Concerning his coats, I reasoned with him; but with no effect. The truth was, I suppose, that a man with so small an income could not afford to sport such a lustrous face and a lustrous coat at one and the same time. As Nippers once observed, Turkey's money went chiefly for red ink. One winter day, I presented Turkey with a highly respectable-looking coat of my own—a padded gray coat, of a most comfortable warmth, and which buttoned straight up from the knee to the neck. I thought Turkey would appreciate the favor, and abate his rashness and obstreperousness of afternoons. But no; I verily believe that buttoning himself up in so downy and blanket-like a coat had a pernicious effect upon him—upon the same principle that too much oats are bad for horses. In fact, precisely as a rash, restive horse is said to feel his oats, so Turkey felt his coat. It made him insolent. He was a man whom prosperity harmed.

Though, concerning the self-indulgent habits of Turkey, I had my own private surmises, yet, touching Nippers, I was well persuaded that, whatever might be his faults in other respects, he was, at least, a temperate young man. But, indeed, nature herself seemed to have been his vintner, and, at his birth, charged him so thoroughly with an irritable, brandy-like disposition, that all subsequent potations were needless. When I consider how, amid the stillness of my chambers, Nippers would sometimes impatiently rise from his seat, and stooping over his table, spread his arms wide apart, seize the whole desk, and move it, and jerk it, with a grim, grinding motion on the floor, as if the table were a perverse voluntary agent and vexing him, I plainly perceive that, for Nippers, brandy-and-water were altogether superfluous.

It was fortunate for me that, owing to its peculiar cause—indigestion—the irritability and consequent nervousness of Nippers were mainly observable in the morning, while in the afternoon he was comparatively mild. So that, Turkey's paroxysms only coming on about twelve o'clock, I never had to do with their eccentricities at one time. Their fits relieved each other, like guards. When Nippers's was on, Turkey's was off; and *vice versa*. This was a good natural arrangement, under the circumstances.

Ginger Nut, the third on my list, was a lad, some twelve years old. His father was a car-man, ambitious of seeing his son on the bench instead of a cart, before he died. So he sent him to my office, as student at law, errand-boy, cleaner and sweeper, at the rate of one dollar a week. He had a little desk to himself; but he did not use it much. Upon inspection, the drawer exhibited a great array of shells of various sorts of nuts. Indeed, to this quick-witted youth, the whole noble science of the law was contained in a nutshell. Not the least among the employments of Ginger Nut, as well as one which he discharged with the most alacrity, was his duty as cake and apple purveyor for Turkey and Nippers. Copying law-papers being proverbially a dry, husky sort of business, my two scriveners were fain to moisten their mouths very often with Spitzenbergs, to be had at the numerous stalls nigh the Custom House and Post Office. Also, they sent Ginger Nut very frequently for that peculiar cake—small, flat, round, and very spicy—after which he had been named by them. Of a cold morning, when business was but dull, Turkey would gobble up scores of these cakes, as if they were mere wafers—indeed, they sell them at the rate of six or eight for a penny—the scrape of his pen blending with the crunching of the crisp particles in his mouth. Rashest of all the fiery afternoon blunders and flurried rashnesses of Turkey, was his once moistening a ginger-cake between his lips, and clapping it on to a mortgage, for a seal. I came within an ace of dismissing him then. But he mollified me by making an oriental bow, and saying—

"With submission, sir, it was generous of me to find you in stationery on my own account."

Now my original business—that of a conveyancer and title hunter, and drawer-up of recondite documents of all sorts—was considerably increased by receiving the master's office. There was now great work for scriveners. Not only must I push the clerks already with me, but I must have additional help.

In answer to my advertisement, a motionless young man one morning stood upon my office threshold, the door being open, for it was summer. I can see that figure now—pallidly neat, pitiably respectable, incurably forlorn! It was Bartleby.

After a few words touching his qualifications, I engaged him, glad to have among my corps of copyists a man of so singularly sedate an aspect, which I thought might operate beneficially upon the flighty temper of Turkey, and the fiery one of Nippers.

I should have stated before that ground glass folding-doors divided my premises into two parts, one of which was occupied by my scriveners, the other by myself. According to my humor, I threw open these doors, or closed them. I resolved to assign Bartleby a corner by the folding-doors, but on my side of them, so as to have this quiet man within easy call, in case any trifling thing was to be done. I placed his desk close up to a small side-window in that part of the room, a window which originally had afforded a lateral view of certain grimy backyards and bricks, but which, owing to subsequent erections, commanded at present no view at all, though it gave some light. Within three feet of the panes was a wall, and the light came down from far above, between two lofty buildings, as from a very small opening in a dome. Still further to a satisfactory arrangement, I procured a high green folding screen, which might entirely isolate Bartleby from my sight, though not remove him from my voice. And thus, in a manner, privacy and society were conjoined.

At first, Bartleby did an extraordinary quantity of writing. As if long famishing for something to copy, he seemed to gorge himself on my documents. There was no pause for digestion. He ran a day and night line, copying by sun-light and by candle-light. I should have been quite delighted with his application, had he been cheerfully industrious. But he wrote on silently, palely, mechanically.

It is, of course, an indispensable part of a scrivener's business to verify the accuracy of his copy, word by word. Where there are two or more scriveners in an office, they assist each other in this examination, one reading from the copy, the other holding the original. It is a very dull, wearisome, and lethargic affair. I can readily imagine that, to some sanguine temperaments, it would be altogether intolerable. For example, I cannot credit that the mettlesome poet, Byron, would have contentedly sat down with Bartleby to examine a law document of, say five hundred pages, closely written in a crimpy hand.

Now and then, in the haste of business, it had been my habit to assist in comparing some brief document myself, calling Turkey or Nippers for this purpose. One object I had, in placing Bartleby so handy to me behind the screen, was to avail myself of his services on such trivial occasions. It was on the third day, I think, of his being with me, and before any necessity had arisen for having his own writing examined, that, being much hurried to complete a small affair I had in hand, I abruptly called to Bartleby. In my haste and natural expectancy of instant compliance, I sat with my head bent over the original on my desk, and my right hand sideways, and somewhat nervously extended with the copy, so that, immediately upon emerging from his retreat, Bartleby might snatch it and proceed to business without the least delay.

In this very attitude did I sit when I called to him, rapidly stating what it was I wanted him to do—namely, to examine a small paper with me. Imagine my surprise, nay, my consternation, when, without moving from his privacy, Bartleby, in a singularly mild, firm voice, replied, "I would prefer not to."

I sat awhile in perfect silence, rallying my stunned faculties. Immediately it occurred to me that my ears had deceived me, or Bartleby had entirely misunderstood my meaning. I repeated my request in the clearest tone I could assume; but in quite as clear a one came the previous reply, "I would prefer not to."

"Prefer not to," echoed I, rising in high excitement, and crossing the room with a stride. "What do you mean? Are you moon-struck? I want you to help me compare this sheet here—take it," and I thrust it towards him.

"I would prefer not to," said he.

I looked at him steadfastly. His face was leanly composed; his gray eye dimly calm. Not a wrinkle of agitation rippled him. Had there been the least uneasiness, anger, impatience, or impertinence in his manner; in other words, had there been any thing ordinarily human about him, doubtless I should have violently dismissed him from the premises. But as it was, I should have as soon thought of turning my pale plaster-of-paris bust of Cicero out of doors. I stood gazing at him awhile, as he went on with his own writing, and then reseated myself at my desk. This is very strange, thought I. What had one best do? But my business hurried me. I concluded to forget the matter for the present, reserving it for my future leisure. So calling Nippers from the other room, the paper was speedily examined.

A few days after this, Bartleby concluded four lengthy documents, being quadruplicates of a week's testimony taken before me in my High Court of Chancery. It became necessary to examine them. It was an important suit, and great accuracy was imperative. Having all things arranged, I called Turkey, Nippers, and Ginger Nut from the next room, meaning to place the four copies in the hands of my four clerks, while I should read from the original. Accordingly, Turkey, Nippers, and Ginger Nut had taken their seats in a row, each with his document in his hand, when I called to Bartleby to join this interesting group.

"Bartleby! quick, I am waiting."

I heard a slow scrape of his chair legs on the uncarpeted floor, and soon he appeared standing at the entrance of his hermitage.

"What is wanted?" said he, mildly.

"The copies, the copies," said I, hurriedly. "We are going to examine them. There—" and I held towards him the fourth quadruplicate.

"I would prefer not to," he said, and gently disappeared behind the screen.

For a few moments I was turned into a pillar of salt, standing at the head of my seated column of clerks. Recovering myself, I advanced towards the screen, and demanded the reason for such extraordinary conduct.

"*Why* do you refuse?"

"I would prefer not to."

With any other man I should have flown outright into a dreadful passion, scorned all further words, and thrust him ignominiously from my presence. But there was something about Bartleby that not only strangely disarmed me, but in a wonderful manner, touched and disconcerted me. I began to reason with him.

"These are your own copies we are about to examine. It is labor saving to you, because one examination will answer for your four papers. It is common usage. Every copyist is bound to help examine his copy. Is it not so? Will you not speak? Answer!"

"I prefer not to," he replied in a flutelike tone. It seemed to me that, while I had been addressing him, he carefully revolved every statement that I made; fully comprehended the meaning; could not gainsay the irresistable conclusion; but, at the same time, some paramount consideration prevailed with him to reply as he did.

"You are decided, then, not to comply with my request—a request made according to common usage and common sense?"

He briefly gave me to understand, that on that point my judgment was sound. Yes: his decision was irreversible.

It is not seldom the case that, when a man is browbeaten in some unprecedented and violently unreasonable way, he begins to stagger in his own plainest faith. He begins, as it were, vaguely to surmise that, wonderful as it may be, all the justice and all the reason is on the other side. Accordingly, if any disinterested persons are present, he turns to them for some reinforcement of his own faltering mind.

"Turkey," said I, "what do you think of this? Am I not right?"

"With submission, sir," said Turkey, in his blandest tone, "I think that you are."

"Nippers," said I, "what do *you* think of it?"

"I think I should kick him out of the office."

(The reader, of nice perceptions, will here perceive that, it being morning, Turkey's answer is couched in polite and tranquil terms, but Nippers replies in ill-tempered ones. Or, to repeat a previous sentence, Nippers's ugly mood was on duty, and Turkey's off.)

"Ginger Nut," said I, willing to enlist the smallest suffrage in my behalf, "what do *you* think of it?"

"I think, sir, he's a little *luny*," replied Ginger Nut, with a grin.

"You hear what they say," said I, turning towards the screen, "come forth and do your duty."

But he vouchsafed no reply. I pondered a moment in sore perplexity. But once more business hurried me. I determined again to postpone the consideration of this dilemma to my future leisure. With a little trouble we made out to examine the papers without Bartleby, though at every page or two Turkey deferentially dropped his opinion, that this proceeding was quite out of the common; while Nippers, twitching in his chair with a dyspeptic nervousness, ground out, between his set teeth, occasional hissing maledictions against the stubborn oaf behind the screen. And for his (Nippers's) part, this was the first and the last time he would do another man's business without pay.

Meanwhile Bartleby sat in his hermitage, oblivious to everything but his own peculiar business there.

Some days passed, the scrivener being employed upon another lengthy work. His late remarkable conduct led me to regard his ways narrowly. I observed that he never went to dinner; indeed, that he never went anywhere. As yet I had never, of my personal knowledge, known him to be outside of my office. He was a perpetual sentry in the corner. At about eleven o'clock though, in the morning, I noticed that Ginger Nut would advance toward the opening in Bartleby's screen, as if silently beckoned thither by a gesture invisible to me where I sat. The boy would then leave the office, jingling a few pence, and reappear with a handful of ginger-nuts, which he delivered in the hermitage, receiving two of the cakes for his trouble.

He lives, then, on ginger-nuts, thought I; never eats a dinner, properly speaking; he must be a vegetarian, then; but no; he never eats even vegetables; he eats nothing but ginger-nuts. My mind then ran on in reveries concerning the probable effects upon the human constitution of living entirely on ginger-nuts. Ginger-nuts are so called, because they contain ginger as one of their peculiar constituents, and the final flavoring one. Now, what was ginger? A hot, spicy thing. Was Bartleby hot and spicy? Not at all. Ginger, then, had no effect upon Bartleby. Probably he preferred it should have none.

Nothing so aggravates an earnest person as a passive resistance. If the individual so resisted be of a not inhumane temper, and the resisting one perfectly harmless in his passivity, then, in the better moods of the former, he will endeavor charitably to construe to his imagination what proves impossible to be solved by his judgment. Even so, for the most part, I regarded Bartleby and his ways. Poor fellow! thought I, he means no mischief; it is plain he intends no insolence; his aspect sufficiently evinces that his eccentricities are involuntary. He is useful to me. I can get along with him. If I turn him away, the chances are he will fall in with some less-indulgent employer, and then he will be rudely treated, and perhaps driven forth miserably to starve. Yes. Here I can cheaply purchase a delicious self-approval. To befriend Bartleby; to humor him in his strange willfulness, will cost me little or nothing, while I lay up in my soul what will eventually prove a sweet morsel for my conscience. But this mood was not invariable with me. The passiveness of Bartleby sometimes irritated me. I felt strangely goaded on to encounter him in new opposition—to elicit some angry spark from him answerable to my own. But, indeed, I might as well have essayed to strike fire with my knuckles against a bit of Windsor soap. But one afternoon the evil impulse in me mastered me, and the following little scene ensued:

"Bartleby," said I, "when those papers are all copied, I will compare them with you."

"I would prefer not to."

"How? Surely you do not mean to persist in that mulish vagary?"

No answer.

I threw open the folding-doors near by, and, turning upon Turkey and Nippers, exclaimed:

"Bartleby a second time says, he won't examine his papers. What do you think of it, Turkey?"

It was afternoon, be it remembered. Turkey sat glowing like a brass boiler; his bald head steaming; his hands reeling among his blotted papers.

"Think of it?" roared Turkey; "I think I'll just step behind his screen, and black his eyes for him!"

So saying, Turkey rose to his feet and threw his arms into a pugilistic position. He was hurrying away to make good his promise, when I detained him, alarmed at the effect of incautiously rousing Turkey's combativeness after dinner.

"Sit down, Turkey," said I, "and hear what Nippers has to say. What do you think of it, Nippers? Would I not be justified in immediately dismissing Bartleby?"

"Excuse me, that is for you to decide, sir. I think his conduct quite unusual, and, indeed, unjust, as regards Turkey and myself. But it may only be a passing whim."

"Ah," exclaimed I, "you have strangely changed your mind, then—you speak very gently of him now."

"All beer," cried Turkey: "gentleness is effects of beer—Nippers and I dined together to-day. You see how gentle *I* am, sir. Shall I go and black his eyes?"

"You refer to Bartleby, I suppose. No, not to-day, Turkey," I replied; "pray, put up your fists."

I closed the doors, and again advanced towards Bartleby. I felt additional incentives tempting me to my fate. I burned to be rebelled against again. I remembered that Bartleby never left the office.

"Bartleby," said I, "Ginger Nut is away; just step around to the Post Office, won't you? (it was but a three minutes' walk), and see if there is anything for me."

"I would prefer not to."

"You *will* not?"

"I *prefer* not."

I staggered to my desk, and sat there in a deep study. My blind inveteracy returned. Was there any other thing in which I could procure myself to be ignominiously repulsed by this lean, penniless wight?—my hired clerk? What added thing is there, perfectly reasonable, that he will be sure to refuse to do? "Bartleby!"

No answer.

"Bartleby," in a louder tone.

No answer.

"Bartleby," I roared.

Like a very ghost, agreeably to the laws of magical invocation, at the third summons, he appeared at the entrance of his hermitage.

"Go to the next room, and tell Nippers to come to me."

"I prefer not to," he respectfully and slowly said and mildly disappeared.

"Very good, Bartleby," said I, in a quiet sort of serenely-severe, self-possessed tone, intimating the unalterable purpose of some terrible retribution very close at hand. At the moment I half intended something of the kind. But upon the whole, as it was drawing towards my dinner-hour, I thought it best to put on my hat and walk home for the day, suffering much from perplexity and distress of mind.

Shall I acknowledge it? The conclusion of this whole business was, that it soon became a fixed fact of my chambers, that a pale young scrivener, by the name of Bartleby, had a desk there; that he copied for me at the usual rate of four cents a folio (one hundred words); but he was permanently exempt from examining the work done by him, that duty being transferred to Turkey and Nippers, out of compliment, doubtless, to their superior acuteness; moreover, said Bartleby was never, on any account, to be dispatched on the most trivial errand of any sort; and that even if entreated to take upon him such a matter, it was generally understood that he would "prefer not to"—in other words, he would refuse point blank.

As days passed on, I became considerably reconciled to Bartleby; his steadiness, his freedom from all dissipation, his incessant industry (except when he chose to throw himself into a standing revery behind his screen), his great stillness, his unalterableness of demeanor under all circumstances, made him a valuable acquisition. One prime thing was this—*he was always there*—first thing in the morning, continually through the day, and the last at night. I had a singular confidence in his honesty. I felt my most precious papers perfectly safe in his hands. Sometimes, to be sure, I could not, for the very soul of me, avoid falling into sudden spasmodic passions with him. For it was exceedingly difficult to bear in mind all the time those strange peculiarities, privileges, and unheard of exemptions, forming the tacit stipulations on Bartleby's part under which he remained in my office. Now and then, in the eagerness of dispatching pressing business, I would inadvertently summon Bartleby, in a short, rapid tone, to put his finger, say, on the incipient tie of a bit of red tape with which I was about compressing some papers. Of course, from behind the screen the usual answer, "I prefer not to," was sure to come; and then, how could a human creature, with the common infirmities of our nature, refrain from bitterly exclaiming upon such perverseness—such unreasonableness. However, every added repulse of this sort which I received only tended to lessen the probability of my repeating the inadvertence.

Here it must be said, that according to the custom of most legal gentlemen occupying chambers in densely-populated law buildings, there were several keys to my door. One was kept by a woman residing in the attic, which person weekly scrubbed and daily swept and dusted my apartments. Another was kept by Turkey for convenience sake. The third I sometimes carried in my own pocket. The fourth I knew not who had.

Now, one Sunday morning I happened to go to Trinity Church, to hear a celebrated preacher, and finding myself rather early on the ground I thought I would walk around to my chambers for a while. Luckily I had my key with me; but upon applying it to the lock, I found it resisted by something inserted from inside. Quite surprised, I called out; when to my consternation a key was turned from within; and thrusting his lean visage at me, and holding the door ajar, the apparition of Bartleby appeared, in his shirt sleeves, and otherwise in a strangely tattered *déshabillé,* saying quietly that he was sorry, but he was deeply engaged just then, and—preferred not admitting me at present. In a brief word or two, he moreover added, that perhaps I had better walk around the block two or three times, and by that time he would probably have concluded his affairs.

Now, the utterly unsurmised appearance of Bartleby, tenanting my law-chambers on a Sunday morning, with his cadaverously gentlemanly *nonchalance,* yet withal firm and self-possessed, had such a strange effect upon me, that incontinently I slunk away from my own door, and did as desired. But not without sundry twinges of impotent rebellion against the mild effrontery of this unaccountable scrivener. Indeed, it was his wonderful mildness chiefly, which not only disarmed me, but unmanned me as it were. For I consider that one, for the time, is somehow unmanned when he tranquilly permits his hired clerk to dictate to him, and order him away from his own premises. Furthermore, I was full of uneasiness as to what Bartleby could possibly be doing in my office in his shirt sleeves, and in an otherwise dismantled condition of a Sunday morning. Was anything amiss going on? Nay, that was out of the question. It was not to be thought of for a moment that Bartleby was an immoral person. But what could he be doing there?—copying? Nay again, whatever might be his eccentricities, Bartleby was an eminently decorous person. He would be the last man to sit down to his desk in any state approaching to nudity. Besides, it was Sunday; and there was something about Bartleby that forbade the supposition that he would by any secular occupation violate the proprieties of the day.

Nevertheless, my mind was not pacified; and full of a restless curiosity, at last I returned to the door. Without hindrance, I inserted my key, opened it, and entered. Bartleby was not to be seen. I looked round anxiously, peeped behind his screen; but it was very plain that he was gone. Upon more closely examining the place, I surmised that for an indefinite period Bartleby must have eaten, dressed, and slept in my office, and that, too, without plate, mirror, or bed. The cushioned seat of a rickety old sofa in one corner bore the faint impress of a lean, reclining form. Rolled away under his desk, I found a blanket; under the empty grate, a blacking box and brush; on a chair, a tin basin, with soap and a ragged towel; in a newspaper a few crumbs of ginger-nuts and a morsel of cheese. Yes, thought I, it is evident enough that Bartleby has been making his home here, keeping bachelor's hall all by himself. Immediately then the thought came sweeping across me, what miserable friendlessness and loneliness are here revealed! His poverty is great; but his solitude, how horrible! Think of it. Of a Sunday, Wall Street is deserted as Petra; and every night of every day it is an emptiness. This building, too, which of week-days hums with industry and life, at nightfall echoes with sheer vacancy, and all through Sunday is forlorn. And here Bartleby makes his home; sole spectator of a solitude which he has seen all populous—a sort of innocent and transformed Marius brooding among the ruins of Carthage!

For the first time in my life a feeling of over-powering stinging melancholy seized me. Before, I had never experienced aught but a not unpleasing sadness. The bond of a common humanity now drew me irresistibly to gloom. A fraternal melancholy! for both I and Bartleby were sons of Adam. I remembered the bright silks and sparkling faces I had seen that day, in gala trim, swan-like sailing down the Mississippi of Broadway; and I contrasted them with the pallid copyist, and thought to myself, Ah, happiness courts the light, so we deem the world is gay; but misery hides aloof, so we deem that misery there is none. These sad fancyings—chimeras, doubtless, of a sick and silly brain—led on to other and more special thoughts, concerning the eccentricities of Bartleby. Presentiments of strange discoveries hovered round me. The scrivener's pale form appeared to me laid out, among uncaring strangers, in its shivering winding sheet.

Suddenly, I was attracted by Bartleby's closed desk, the key in open sight left in the lock.

I mean no mischief, seek the gratification of no heartless curiosity, thought I; besides, the desk is mine, and its contents, too, so I will make bold to look within. Everything was methodically arranged, the papers smoothly placed. The pigeon holes were deep, and removing the files of documents, I groped into their recesses. Presently I felt something there, and dragged it out. It was an old bandana handkerchief, heavy and knotted. I opened it, and saw it was a savings bank.

I now recalled all the quiet mysteries which I had noted in the man. I remembered that he never spoke but to answer; that, though at intervals he had considerable time to himself, yet I had never seen him reading—no, not even a newspaper; that for long periods he would stand looking out, at his pale window behind the screen, upon the dead brick wall; I was quite sure he never visited any refectory or eating house; while his pale face clearly indicated that he never drank beer like Turkey, or tea and coffee even, like other men; that he never went anywhere in particular that I could learn; never went out for a walk, unless, indeed, that was the case at present; that he had declined telling who he was, or whence he came, or whether he had any relatives in the world; that though so thin and pale, he never complained of ill health. And more than all, I remembered a certain unconscious air of pallid—how shall I call it?—of pallid haughtiness, say, or rather an austere reserve about him, which had positively awed me into tame compliance with his eccentricities, when I had feared to ask him to do the slightest incidental thing for me, even though I might know, from his long-continued motionlessness, that behind his screen he must be standing in one of those dead-wall reveries of his.

Revolving all these things, and coupling them with the recently discovered fact, that he made my office his constant abiding place and home, and not forgetful of his morbid moodiness; revolving all these things, a prudential feeling began to steal over me. My first emotions had been those of pure melancholy and sincerest pity; but just in proportion as the forlornness of Bartleby grew and grew to my imagination, did that same melancholy merge into fear, that pity into repulsion. So true it is, and so terrible, too, that up to a certain point the thought or sight of misery enlists our best affections; but, in certain special cases, beyond that point it does not go. They err who would assert that invariably this is owing to the inherent selfishness of the human heart. It rather proceeds from a certain hopelessness of remedying excessive and organic ill. To a sensitive being, pity is not seldom pain. And when at last it is perceived that such pity cannot lead to effectual succor, common sense bids the soul be rid of it. What I saw that morning persuaded me that the scrivener was the victim of innate and incurable disorder, I might give alms to his body; but his body did not pain him; it was his soul that suffered, and his soul I could not reach.

I did not accomplish the purpose of going to Trinity Church that morning. Somehow, the things I had seen disqualified me for the time from churchgoing. I walked homeward, thinking what I would do with Bartleby. Finally, I resolved upon this—I would put certain calm questions to him the next morning, touching his history, etc., and if he declined to answer them openly and unreservedly (and I supposed he would prefer not), then to give him a twenty dollar bill over and above whatever I might owe him, and tell him his services were no longer required; but that if in any other way I could assist him, I would be happy to do so, especially if he desired to return to his native place, wherever that might be, I would willingly help to defray the expenses. Moreover, if after reaching home, he found himself at any time in want of aid, a letter from him would be sure of a reply.

The next morning came.

"Bartleby," said I, gently calling to him behind his screen.

No reply.

"Bartleby," said I, in a still gentler tone, "come here; I am not going to ask you to do anything you would prefer not to do—I simply wish to speak to you."

Upon this he noiselessly slid into view.

"Will you tell me, Bartleby, where you were born?"

"I would prefer not to."

"Will you tell me *anything* about yourself?"

"I would prefer not to."

"But what reasonable objection can you have to speak to me? I feel friendly towards you."

He did not look at me while I spoke, but kept his glance fixed upon my bust of Cicero, which, as I then sat, was directly behind me, some six inches above my head.

"What is your answer, Bartleby," said I, after waiting a considerable time for a reply, during which his countenance remained immovable, only there was the faintest conceivable tremor of the white attenuated mouth.

"At present I prefer to give no answer," he said, and retired into his hermitage.

It was rather weak in me I confess, but his manner, on this occasion, nettled me. Not only did there seem to lurk in it a certain calm disdain, but his perverseness seemed ungrateful, considering the undeniable good usage and indulgence he had received from me.

Again I sat ruminating what I should do. Mortified as I was at his behavior, and resolved as I had been to dismiss him when I entered my office, nevertheless I strangely felt something superstitious knocking at my heart, and forbidding me to carry out my purpose, and denouncing me for a villain if I dared to breathe one bitter word against this forlornest of mankind. At last, familiarly drawing my chair behind his screen, I sat down and said: "Bartleby, never mind, then, about revealing your history; but let me entreat you, as a friend, to comply as far as may be with the usages of this office. Say now, you will help me to examine papers to-morrow or next day; in short, say now, that in a day or two you will begin to be a little reasonable:—say so, Bartleby."

"At present I would prefer not to be a little reasonable," was his mildly cadaverous reply.

Just then the folding-doors opened, and Nippers approached. He seemed suffering from an unusually bad night's rest, induced by severer indigestion than common. He overheard those final words of Bartleby.

"*Prefer not,* eh?" gritted Nippers—"I'd *prefer* him, if I were you, sir," addressing me—"I'd *prefer* him; I'd give him preferences, the stubborn mule! What is it, sir, pray, that he *prefers* not to do now?"

Bartleby moved not a limb.

"Mr. Nippers," said I, "I'd prefer that you would withdraw at present."

Somehow, of late, I had got into the way of involuntarily using this word "prefer" upon all sorts of not exactly suitable occasions. And I trembled to think that my contact with the scrivener had already and seriously affected me in a mental way. And what further and deeper aberration might it not yet produce? This apprehension had not been without efficacy in determining me to summary measures.

As Nippers, looking very sour and sulky, was departing, Turkey blandly and deferentially approached.

"With submission, sir," said he, "yesterday I was thinking about Bartleby here, and I think that if he would but prefer to take a quart of good ale every day, it would do much towards mending him, and enabling him to assist in examining his papers."

"So you have got the word, too," said I, slightly excited.

"With submission, what word, sir?" asked Turkey, respectfully crowding himself into the contracted space behind the screen, and by so doing, making me jostle the scrivener. "What word, sir?"

"I would prefer to be left alone here," said Bartleby, as if offended at being mobbed in his privacy.

"*That's* the word, Turkey," said I—"*that's* it."

"Oh, *prefer*? oh yes—queer word. I never use it myself. But, sir, as I was saying, if he would but prefer—"

"Turkey," interrupted I, "you will please withdraw."

"Oh certainly, sir, if you prefer that I should."

As he opened the folding-door to retire, Nippers at his desk caught a glimpse of me, and asked whether I would prefer to have a certain paper copied on blue paper or white. He did not in the least roguishly accent the word prefer. It was plain that it involuntarily rolled from his tongue. I thought to myself, surely I must get rid of a demented man, who already has in some degree turned the tongues, if not the heads of myself and clerks. But I thought it prudent not to break the dismission at once.

The next day I noticed that Bartleby did nothing but stand at his window in his dead-wall revery. Upon asking him why he did not write, he said that he had decided upon doing no more writing.

"Why, how now? What next?" exclaimed I, "do no more writing?"

"No more."

"And what is the reason?"

"Do you not see the reason for yourself?" he indifferently replied.

I looked steadfastly at him, and perceived that his eyes looked dull and glazed. Instantly it occurred to me, that his unexampled diligence in copying by his dim window for the first few weeks of his stay with me might have temporarily impaired his vision.

I was touched. I said something in condolence with him. I hinted that of course he did wisely in abstaining from writing for a while; and urged him to embrace that opportunity of taking wholesome exercise in the open air. This, however, he did not do. A few days after this, my other clerks being absent, and being in a great hurry to dispatch certain letters by the mail, I thought that, having nothing else earthly to do, Bartleby would surely be less inflexible than usual, and carry these letters to the post-office. But he blankly declined. So, much to my inconvenience, I went myself.

Still added days went by. Whether Bartleby's eyes improved or not, I could not say. To all appearance I thought they did. But when I asked him if they did, he vouchsafed no answer. At all events, he would do no copying. At last, in reply to my urgings, he informed me that he had permanently given up copying.

"What!" exclaimed I; "suppose your eyes should get entirely well—better than ever before—would you not copy then?"

"I have given up copying," he answered, and slid aside.

He remained as ever, a fixture in my chamber. Nay—if that were possible—he became still more of a fixture than before. What was to be done? He would do nothing in the office; why should he stay there? In plain fact, he had now become a millstone to me, not only useless as a necklace, but afflictive to bear. Yet I was sorry for him. I speak less than truth when I say that, on his own account, he occasioned me uneasiness. If he would but have named a single relative or friend, I would instantly have written, and urged their taking the poor fellow away to some convenient retreat. But he seemed alone, absolutely alone in the universe. A bit of wreck in the mid Atlantic. At length, necessities connected with my business tyrannized over all other considerations. Decently as I could, I told Bartleby that in six days time he must unconditionally leave the office. I warned him to take measures, in the interval, for procuring some other abode. I offered to assist him in his endeavor, if he himself would but take the first step towards a removal. "And when you finally quit me, Bartleby," added I, "I shall see that you go not away entirely unprovided. Six days from this hour, remember."

At the expiration of that period, I peeped behind the screen, and lo! Bartleby was there.

I buttoned up my coat, balanced myself; advanced slowly towards him, touched his shoulder, and said, "The time has come; you must quit this place; I am sorry for you; here is money; but you must go."

"I would prefer not," he replied, with his back still towards me.

"You *must*."

He remained silent.

Now I had an unbounded confidence in this man's common honesty. He had frequently restored to me sixpences and shillings carelessly dropped upon the floor, for I am apt to be very reckless in such shirt-button affairs. The proceeding, then, which followed will not be deemed extraordinary.

"Bartleby," said I, "I owe you twelve dollars on account; here are thirty-two; the odd twenty are yours—Will you take it?" and I handed the bills towards him.

But he made no motion.

"I will leave them here, then," putting them under a weight on the table. Then taking my hat and cane and going to the door, I tranquilly turned and added—"After you have removed your things from these offices, Bartleby, you will of course lock the door—since every one is now gone for the day but you—and if you please, slip your key underneath the mat, so that I may have it in the morning. I shall not see you again; so good-by to you. If, hereafter, in your new place of abode, I can be of any service to you, do not fail to advise me by letter. Good-by, Bartleby, and fare you well."

But he answered not a word; like the last column of some ruined temple, he remained standing mute and solitary in the middle of the otherwise deserted room.

As I walked home in a pensive mood, my vanity got the better of my pity. I could not but highly plume myself on my masterly management in getting rid of Bartleby. Masterly I call it, and such it must appear to any dispassionate thinker. The beauty of my procedure seemed to consist in its perfect quietness. There was no vulgar bullying, no bravado of any sort, no choleric hectoring, and striding to and fro across the apartment, jerking out vehement commands for Bartleby to bundle himself off with his beggarly traps. Nothing of the kind. Without loudly bidding Bartleby depart—as an inferior genius might have done—I *assumed* the ground that depart he must; and upon that assumption built all I had to say. The more I thought over my procedure, the more I was charmed with it. Nevertheless, next morning, upon awakening, I had my doubts—I had somehow slept off the fumes of vanity. One of the coolest and wisest hours a man has, is just after he awakes in the morning. My procedure seemed as sagacious as ever—but only in theory. How it would prove in practice—there was the rub. It was truly a beautiful thought to have assumed Bartleby's departure; but, after all, that assumption was simply my own, and none of Bartleby's. The great point was, not whether I had assumed that he would quit me, but whether he would prefer so to do. He was more a man of preferences than assumptions.

After breakfast, I walked down town, arguing the probabilities *pro* and *con*. One moment I thought it would prove a miserable failure, and Bartleby would be found all alive at my office as usual; the next moment it seemed certain that I should find his chair empty. And so I kept veering about. At the corner of Broadway and Canal Street, I saw quite an excited group of people standing in earnest conversation.

"I'll take odds he doesn't," said a voice as I passed.

"Doesn't go?—done!" said I; "put up your money."

I was instinctively putting my hand in my pocket to produce my own, when I remembered that this was an election day. The words I had overheard bore no reference to Bartleby, but to the success or non-success of some candidate for the mayoralty. In my intent frame of mind, I had, as it were, imagined that all Broadway shared in my excitement, and were debating the same question with me. I passed on, very thankful that the uproar of the street screened my momentary absent-mindedness.

As I had intended, I was earlier than usual at my office door. I stood listening for a moment. All was still. He must be gone. I tried the knob. The door was locked. Yes, my procedure had worked to a charm; he indeed must be vanished. Yet a certain melancholy mixed with this: I was almost sorry for my brilliant success. I was fumbling under the door mat for the key, which Bartleby was to have left there for me, when accidentally my knee knocked against a panel, producing a summoning sound, and in response a voice came to me from within—"Not yet; I am occupied."

It was Bartleby.

I was thunderstruck. For an instant I stood like the man who, pipe in mouth, was killed one cloudless afternoon long ago in Virginia, by summer lightning; at his own warm open window he was killed, and remained leaning out there upon the dreamy afternoon, till some one touched him, when he fell.

"Not gone!" I murmured at last. But again obeying that wondrous ascendancy which the inscrutable scrivener had over me, and from which ascendancy, for all my chafing, I could not completely escape, I slowly went down stairs and out into the street, and while walking round the block, considered what I should next do in this unheard-of perplexity. Turn the man out by an actual thrusting I could not; to drive him away by calling him hard names would not do; calling in the police was an unpleasant idea; and yet, permit him to enjoy his cadaverous triumph over me—this, too, I could not think of. What was to be done? or, if nothing could be done, was there anything further that I could *assume* in the matter? Yes, as before I had prospectively assumed that Bartleby would depart, so now I might retrospectively assume that departed he was. In the legitimate carrying out of this assumption, I might enter my office in a great hurry, and pretending not to see Bartleby at all, walk straight against him as if he were air. Such a proceeding would in a singular degree have the appearance of a home-thrust. It was hardly possible that Bartleby could withstand such an application of the doctrine of assumptions. But upon second thoughts the success of the plan seemed rather dubious. I resolved to argue the matter over with him again.

"Bartleby," said I, entering the office, with a quietly severe expression, "I am seriously displeased. I am pained, Bartleby. I had thought better of you. I had imagined you of such a gentlemanly organization, that in any delicate dilemma a slight hint would suffice—in short, an assumption. But it appears I am deceived. Why," I added, unaffectedly starting, "you have not even touched that money yet," pointing to it, just where I had left it the evening previous.

He answered nothing.

"Will you, or will you not, quit me?" I now demanded in a sudden passion, advancing close to him.

"I would prefer *not* to quit you," he replied, gently emphasizing the *not.*

"What earthly right have you to stay here? Do you pay any rent? Do you pay my taxes? Or is this property yours?"

He answered nothing.

"Are you ready to go on and write now? Are your eyes recovered? Could you copy a small paper for me this morning? or help examine a few lines? or step round to the post-office? In a word, will you do anything at all, to give a coloring to your refusal to depart the premises?"

He silently retired into his hermitage.

I was now in such a state of nervous resentment that I thought it but prudent to check myself at present from further demonstrations. Bartleby and I were alone. I remembered the tragedy of the unfortunate Adams and the still more unfortunate Colt in the solitary office of the latter; and how poor Colt, being dreadfully incensed by Adams, and imprudently permitting himself to get wildly excited, was at unawares hurried into his fatal act—an act which certainly no man could possibly deplore more than the actor himself. Often it had occurred to me in my ponderings upon the subject, that had that altercation taken place in the public street, or at a private residence, it would not have terminated as it did. It was the circumstance of being alone in a solitary office, up stairs, of a building entirely unhallowed by humanizing domestic associations—an uncarpeted office, doubtless, of a dusty, haggard sort of appearance—this it must have been, which greatly helped to enhance the irritable desperation of the hapless Colt.

But when this old Adam of resentment rose in me and tempted me concerning Bartleby, I grappled him and threw him. How? Why, simply by recalling the divine injunction: "A new commandment give I unto you, that ye love one another." Yes, this it was that saved me. Aside from higher considerations, charity often operates as a vastly wise and prudent principle—a great safeguard to its possessor. Men have committed murder for jealousy's sake, and anger's sake, and hatred's sake, and selfishness' sake, and spiritual pride's sake; but no man that ever I heard of, ever committed a diabolical murder for sweet charity's sake. Mere self-interest, then, if no better motive can be enlisted, should, especially with high-tempered men, prompt all beings to charity and philanthropy. At any rate, upon the occasion in question, I strove to drown my exasperated feelings towards the scrivener by benevolently construing his conduct. Poor fellow, poor fellow! thought I, he don't mean anything; and besides, he has seen hard times, and ought to be indulged.

I endeavored, also, immediately to occupy myself, and at the same time to comfort my despondency. I tried to fancy, that in the course of the morning, at such time as might prove agreeable to him, Bartleby, of his own free accord, would emerge from his hermitage and take up some decided line of march in the direction of the door. But no. Half-past twelve o'clock came; Turkey began to glow in the face, overturn his inkstand, and become generally obstreperous; Nippers abated down into quietude and courtesy; Ginger Nut munched his noon apple; and Bartleby remained standing at his window in one of his profoundest dead-wall reveries. Will it be credited? Ought I to acknowledge it? That afternoon I left the office without saying one further word to him.

Some days now passed, during which, at leisure intervals I looked a little into "Edwards on the Will," and "Priestly on Necessity." Under the circumstances, those books induced a salutary feeling. Gradually I slid into the persuasion that these troubles of mine, touching the scrivener, had been all predestinated from eternity, and Bartleby was billeted upon me for some mysterious purpose of an all-wise Providence, which it was not for a mere mortal like me to fathom. Yes, Bartleby, stay there behind your screen, thought I; I shall persecute you no more; you are harmless and noiseless as any of these old chairs; in short, I never feel so private as when I know you are here. At last I see it, I feel it; I penetrate to the predestinated purpose of my life. I am content. Others may have loftier parts to enact; but my mission in this world, Bartleby, is to furnish you with office-room for such period as you may see fit to remain.

I believe that this wise and blessed frame of mind would have continued with me, had it not been for the unsolicited and uncharitable remarks obtruded upon me by my professional friends who visited the rooms. But thus it often is, that the constant friction of illiberal minds wears out at last the best resolves of the more generous. Though to be sure, when I reflected upon it, it was not strange that people entering my office should be struck by the peculiar aspect of the unaccountable Bartleby, and so be tempted to throw out some sinister observations concerning him. Sometimes an attorney, having business with me, and calling at my office, and finding no one but the scrivener there, would undertake to obtain some sort of precise information from him touching my whereabouts; but without heeding his idle talk, Bartleby would remain standing immovable in the middle of the room. So after contemplating him in that position for a time, the attorney would depart, no wiser than he came.

Also, when a reference was going on, and the room full of lawyers and witnesses, and business driving fast, some deeply-occupied legal gentleman present, seeing Bartleby wholly unemployed, would request him to run round to his (the legal gentleman's) office and fetch some papers for him. Thereupon, Bartleby would tranquilly decline, and yet remain idle as before. Then the lawyer would give a great stare, and turn to me. And what could I say? At last I was made aware that all through the circle of my professional acquaintance, a whisper of wonder was running round, having reference to the strange creature I kept at my office. This worried me very much. And as the idea came upon me of his possibly turning out a long-lived man, and keep occupying my chambers, and denying my authority; and perplexing my visitors; and scandalizing my professional reputation; and casting a general gloom over the premises; keeping soul and body together to the last upon his savings (for doubtless he spent but half a dime a day), and in the end perhaps outlive me, and claim possession of my office by right of his perpetual occupancy: as all these dark anticipations crowded upon me more and more, and my friends continually intruded their relentless remarks upon the apparition in my room; a great change was wrought in me. I resolved to gather all my faculties together, and forever rid me of this intolerable incubus.

Ere revolving any complicated project, however, adapted to this end, I first simply suggested to Bartleby the propriety of his permanent departure. In a calm and serious tone, I commended the idea to his careful and mature consideration. But, having taken three days to meditate upon it, he apprised me, that his original determination remained the same; in short, that he still preferred to abide with me.

What shall I do? I now said to myself, buttoning up my coat to the last button. What shall I do? what ought I to do? what does conscience say I *should* do with this man, or, rather, ghost? Rid myself of him, I must; go, he shall. But how? You will not thrust him, the poor, pale, passive mortal—you will not thrust such a helpless creature out of your door? you will not dishonor yourself by such cruelty? No, I will not, I cannot do that. Rather would I let him live and die here, and then mason up his remains in the wall. What, then, will you do? For all your coaxing, he will not budge. Bribes he leaves under your own paper-weight on your table; in short, it is quite plain that he prefers to cling to you.

Then something severe, something unusual must be done. What! surely you will not have him collared by a constable, and commit his innocent pallor to the common jail? And upon what ground could you procure such a thing to be done?—a vagrant, is he? What! he a vagrant, a wanderer, who refuses to budge? It is because he will *not* be a vagrant, then, that you seek to count him *as* a vagrant. That is too absurd. No visible means of support: there I have him. Wrong again: for indubitably he *does* support himself, and that is the only unanswerable proof that any man can show of his possessing the means so to do. No more, then. Since he will not quit me, I must quit him. I will change my offices; I will move elsewhere, and give him fair notice, that if I find him on my new premises I will then proceed against him as a common trespasser.

Acting accordingly, next day I thus addressed him: "I find these chambers too far from the City Hall; the air is unwholesome. In a word, I propose to remove my offices next week, and shall no longer require your services. I tell you this now, in order that you may seek another place."

He made no reply; and nothing more was said.

On the appointed day I engaged carts and men, proceeded to my chambers, and, having but little furniture, everything was removed in a few hours. Throughout, the scrivener remained standing behind the screen, which I directed to be removed the last thing. It was withdrawn; and, being folded up like a huge folio, left him the motionless occupant of a naked room. I stood in the entry watching him a moment, while something from within me upbraided me.

I re-entered, with my hand in my pocket—and—and my heart in my mouth.

"Good-by, Bartleby; I am going—good-by, and God some way bless you; and take that," slipping something in his hand. But it dropped upon the floor, and then—strange to say—I tore myself from him whom I had so longed to be rid of.

Established in my new quarters, for a day or two I kept the door locked, and started at every footfall in the passages. When I returned to my rooms, after any little absence, I would pause at the threshold for an instant, and attentively listen, ere applying my key. But these fears were needless. Bartleby never came nigh me.

I thought all was going well, when a perturbed-looking stranger visited me, inquiring whether I was the person who had recently occupied rooms at No.——Wall Street.

Full of forebodings, I replied that I was.

"Then, sir," said the stranger, who proved a lawyer, "you are responsible for the man you left there. He refuses to do any copying; he refuses to do anything; he says he prefers not to; and he refuses to quit the premises."

"I am very sorry, sir," said I, with assumed tranquillity, but an inward tremor, "but, really, the man you allude to is nothing to me—he is no relation or apprentice of mine, that you should hold me responsible for him."

"In mercy's name, who is he?"

"I certainly cannot inform you. I know nothing about him. Formerly I employed him as a copyist; but he has done nothing for me now for some time past."

"I shall settle him, then—good morning, sir."

Several days passed, and I heard nothing more; and, though I often felt a charitable prompting to call at the place and see poor Bartleby, yet a certain squeamishness, of I know not what, withheld me.

All is over with him, by this time, thought I, at last, when, through another week, no further intelligence reached me. But, coming to my room the day after, I found several persons waiting at my door in a high state of nervous excitement.

"That's the man—here he comes," cried the foremost one, whom I recognized as the lawyer who had previously called upon me alone.

"You must take him away, sir, at once," cried a portly person among them, advancing upon me, and whom I knew to be the landlord of No. ——Wall Street. "These gentlemen, my tenants, cannot stand it any longer; Mr. B—," pointing to the lawyer, "has turned him out of his room, and he now persists in haunting the building generally, sitting upon the banisters of the stairs by day, and sleeping in the entry by night. Everybody is concerned; clients are leaving the offices; some fears are entertained of a mob; something you must do, and that without delay."

Aghast at this torrent, I fell back before it, and would fain have locked myself in my new quarters. In vain I persisted that Bartleby was nothing to me—no more than to any one else. In vain—I was the last person known to have anything to do with him, and they held me to the terrible account. Fearful, then, of being exposed in the papers (as one person present obscurely threatened), I considered the matter, and, at length, said, that if the lawyer would give me a confidential interview with the scrivener, in his (the lawyer's) own room, I would, that afternoon, strive my best to rid them of the nuisance they complained of.

Going up stairs to my old haunt, there was Bartleby silently sitting upon the banister at the landing.

"What are you doing here, Bartleby?" said I.

"Sitting upon the banister," he mildly replied.

I motioned him into the lawyer's room, who then left us.

"Bartleby," said I, "are you aware that you are the cause of great tribulation to me, by persisting in occupying the entry after being dismissed from the office?"

No answer.

"Now one of two things must take place. Either you must do something, or something must be done to you. Now what sort of business would you like to engage in? Would you like to re-engage in copying for some one?"

"No; I would prefer not to make any change."

"Would you like a clerkship in a dry-goods store?"

"There is too much confinement about that. No, I would not like a clerkship; but I am not particular."

"Too much confinement," I cried, "why you keep yourself confined all the time!"

"I would prefer not to take a clerkship," he rejoined, as if to settle that little item at once.

"How would a bar-tender's business suit you? There is no trying of the eyesight in that."

"I would not like it at all; though, as I said before, I am not particular."

His unwonted wordiness inspirited me. I returned to the charge.

"Well, then, would you like to travel through the country collecting bills for the merchants? That would improve your health."

"No, I would prefer to be doing something else."

"How, then, would going as a companion to Europe, to entertain some young gentleman with your conversation—how would that suit you?"

"Not at all. It does not strike me that there is anything definite about that. I like to be stationary. But I am not particular."

"Stationary you shall be, then," I cried, now losing all patience, and, for the first time in all my exasperating connection with him, fairly flying into a passion. "If you do not go away from these premises before night, I shall feel bound—indeed, I *am* bound—to—to—to quit the premises myself!" I rather absurdly concluded, knowing not with what possible threat to try to frighten his immobility into compliance. Despairing of all further efforts, I was precipitately leaving him, when a final thought occurred to me—one which had not been wholly unindulged before.

"Bartleby," said I, in the kindest tone I could assume under such exciting circumstances, "will you go home with me now—not to my office, but my dwelling—and remain there till we can conclude upon some convenient arrangement for you at our leisure? Come, let us start now, right away."

"No: at present I would prefer not to make any change at all."

I answered nothing; but, effectually dodging every one by the suddenness and rapidity of my flight, rushed from the building, ran up Wall Street towards Broadway, and, jumping into the first omnibus, was soon removed from pursuit. As soon as tranquillity returned, I distinctly perceived that I had now done all that I possibly could, both in respect to the demands of the landlord and his tenants, and with regard to my own desire and sense of duty, to benefit Bartleby, and shield him from rude persecution. I now strove to be entirely care-free and quiescent; and my conscience justified me in the attempt; though, indeed, it was not so successful as I could have wished. So fearful was I of being again hunted out by the incensed landlord and his exasperated tenants, that, surrendering my business to Nippers, for a few days, I drove about the upper part of the town and through the suburbs, in my rockaway; crossed over to Jersey City and Hoboken, and paid fugitive visits to Manhattanville and Astoria. In fact, I almost lived in my rockaway for the time.

When again I entered my office, lo, a note from the landlord lay upon the desk. I opened it with trembling hands. It informed me that the writer had sent to the police, and had Bartleby removed to the Tombs as a vagrant. Moreover, since I knew more about him than any one else, he wished me to appear at that place, and make a suitable statement of the facts. These tidings had a conflicting effect upon me. At first I was indignant; but, at last, almost approved. The landlord's energetic, summary disposition, had led him to adopt a procedure which I do not think I would have decided upon myself; and yet, as a last resort, under such peculiar circumstances, it seemed the only plan.

As I afterwards learned, the poor scrivener, when told that he must be conducted to the Tombs, offered not the slightest obstacle, but, in his pale, unmoving way, silently acquiesced.

Some of the compassionate and curious bystanders joined the party; and headed by one of the constables arm in arm with Bartleby, the silent procession filed its way through all the noise, and heat, and joy of the roaring thoroughfares at noon.

The same day I received the note, I went to the Tombs, or, to speak more properly, the Halls of Justice. Seeking the right officer, I stated the purpose of my call, and was informed that the individual I described was, indeed, within. I then assured the functionary that Bartleby was a perfectly honest man, and greatly to be compassionated, however unaccountably eccentric. I narrated all I knew, and closed by suggesting the idea of letting him remain in as indulgent confinement as possible, till something less harsh might be done—though, indeed, I hardly knew what. At all events, if nothing else could be decided upon, the alms-house must receive him. I then begged to have an interview.

Being under no disgraceful charge, and quite serene and harmless in all his ways, they had permitted him freely to wander about the prison, and, especially, in the inclosed grass-platted yards thereof. And so I found him there, standing all alone in the quietest of the yards, his face towards a high wall, while all around, from the narrow slits of the jail windows, I thought I saw peering out upon him the eyes of murderers and thieves.

"Bartleby!"

"I know you," he said, without looking round—"and I want nothing to say to you."

"It was not I that brought you here, Bartleby," said I, keenly pained at his implied suspicion. "And to you, this should not be so vile a place. Nothing reproachful attaches to you by being here. And see, it is not so sad a place as one might think. Look, there is the sky, and here is the grass."

"I know where I am," he replied, but would say nothing more, and so I left him.

As I entered the corridor again, a broad meat-like man, in an apron, accosted me, and, jerking his thumb over his shoulder, said—"Is that your friend?"

"Yes."

"Does he want to starve? If he does, let him live on the prison fare, that's all."

"Who are you?" asked I, not knowing what to make of such an unofficially speaking person in such a place.

"I am the grub-man. Such gentlemen as have friends here, hire me to provide them with something good to eat."

"Is this so?" said I, turning to the turnkey.

He said it was.

"Well, then," said I, slipping some silver into the grub-man's hands (for so they called him), "I want you to give particular attention to my friend there; let him have the best dinner you can get. And you must be as polite to him as possible."

"Introduce me, will you?" said the grub-man, looking at me with an expression which seemed to say he was all impatience for an opportunity to give a specimen of his breeding.

Thinking it would prove of benefit to the scrivener, I acquiesced; and, asking the grub-man his name, went up with him to Bartleby.

"Bartleby, this is a friend; you will find him very useful to you."

"Your sarvant, sir, your sarvant," said the grub-man, making a low salutation behind his apron. "Hope you find it pleasant here, sir; nice grounds—cool apartments—hope you'll stay with us sometime—try to make it agreeable. What will you have for dinner to-day?

"I prefer not to dine to-day," said Bartleby, turning away. "It would disagree with me; I am unused to dinners." So saying, he slowly moved to the other side of the inclosure, and took up a position fronting the dead-wall.

"How's this?" said the grub-man, addressing me with a stare of astonishment. "He's odd, ain't he?"

"I think he is a little deranged," said I, sadly.

"Deranged? deranged is it? Well, now, upon my word, I thought that friend of yourn was a gentleman forger; they are always pale and genteel-like, them forgers. I can't help pity 'em—can't help it, sir. Did you know Monroe Edwards?" he added, touchingly, and paused. Then, laying his hand piteously on my shoulder, sighed, "he died of consumption at Sing-Sing. So you weren't acquainted with Monroe?"

"No, I was never socially acquainted with any forgers. But I cannot stop longer. Look to my friend yonder. You will not lose by it. I will see you again."

Some few days after this, I again obtained admission to the Tombs, and went through the corridors in quest of Bartleby; but without finding him.

"I saw him coming from his cell not long ago," said a turnkey, "may be he's gone to loiter in the yards."

So I went in that direction.

"Are you looking for the silent man?" said another turnkey, passing me. "Yonder he lies—sleeping in the yard there. 'Tis not twenty minutes since I saw him lie down."

The yard was entirely quiet. It was not accessible to the common prisoners. The surrounding walls of amazing thickness, kept off all sounds behind them. The Egyptian character of the masonry weighed upon me with its gloom. But a soft imprisoned turf grew under foot. The heart of the eternal pyramids, it seemed, wherein, by some strange magic, through the clefts, grass-seed, dropped by birds, had sprung.

Strangely huddled at the base of the wall, his knees drawn up, and lying on his side, his head touching the cold stones, I saw the wasted Bartleby. But nothing stirred. I paused; then went close up to him; stooped over, and saw that his dim eyes were open; otherwise he seemed profoundly sleeping. Something prompted me to touch him. I felt his hand, when a tingling shiver ran up my arm and down my spine to my feet.

The round face of the grub-man peered upon me now. "His dinner is ready. Won't he dine to-day, either? Or does he live without dining?"

"Lives without dining," said I, and closed the eyes.

"Eh!—He's asleep, ain't he?"

"With kings and counselors," murmured I.

There would seem little need for proceeding further in this history. Imagination will readily supply the meagre recital of poor Bartleby's interment. But, ere parting with the reader, let me say, that if this little narrative has sufficiently interested him, to awaken curiosity as to who Bartleby was, and what manner of life he led prior to the present narrator's making his acquaintance, I can only reply, that in such curiosity I fully share, but am wholly unable to gratify it. Yet here I hardly know whether I should divulge one little item of rumor, which came to my ear a few months after the scrivener's decease. Upon what basis it rested, I could never ascertain; and hence, how true it is I cannot now tell. But, inasmuch as this vague report has not been without a certain suggestive interest to me, however said, it may prove the same with some others; and so I will briefly mention it. The report was this: that Bartleby had been a subordinate clerk in the Dead Letter Office at Washington, from which he had been suddenly removed by a change in the administration. When I think over this rumor, hardly can I express the emotions which seize me. Dead letters! does it not sound like dead men? Conceive a man by nature and misfortune prone to a pallid hopelessness, can any business seem more fitted to heighten it than that of continually handling these dead letters, and assorting them for the flames? For by the cart-load they are annually burned. Some times from out the folded paper the pale clerk takes a ring—the finger it was meant for, perhaps, moulders in the grave; a bank-note sent in swiftest charity—he whom it would relieve, nor eats nor hungers any more; pardon for those who died despairing; hope for those who died unhoping; good tidings for those who died stifled by unrelieved calamities. On errands of life, these letters speed to death.

Ah, Bartleby! Ah, humanity!

QUESTIONS FOR DISCUSSION AND WRITING

1. What are the stages in Bartleby's gradual withdrawal from human contact? What kind of conflicts does Bartleby's presence create for the narrator and his friends? How does the rumor of Bartleby's previous employment at the Dead Letter Office suggest a resolution for the story?
2. How does the narrator characterize his three employees—Turkey, Nippers, and Ginger Nut? What does he know about the external aspects of Bartleby's character? What does he fail to understand about the internal aspects of Bartleby's character?
3. How does the narrator describe the setting for his story? How does this atmosphere gradually change as a result of Bartleby's presence? How does the subtitle, "A Story of Wall Street," characterize this atmosphere?
4. How does the narrator's admission that he is an "eminently safe" man help establish his point of view toward the events of the story? In what ways does his point of view change as a result of his association with Bartleby?
5. How does this story define the words pity, charity, responsibility? What is the "common bond" the narrator feels toward Bartleby? Why does he abandon him? What is the meaning of his last words, "Ah, Bartleby! Ah, humanity!"?

66

YUKIO MISHIMA

Patriotism

YUKIO MISHIMA (1925–1970), the pen name for Kimitake Hiraoka, was born in Tokyo, Japan, to a family of Samurai nobility, a tradition that combined spiritual dedication and the martial arts. As a young man, Mishima was convinced that he would die for the Emperor during World War II, but he failed the army physical. His rejection caused him great personal dishonor, and he dedicated himself to building up his frail physique. At the end of the war, Mishima studied law at Tokyo University and worked briefly as a civil servant in the Finance Ministry. In 1949 Mishima published his

first novel, *Confessions of a Mask,* a chronicle of his life from early childhood through the war. The success of this book allowed Mishima to pursue his writing full time, composing an astonishing number of poems, stories, and plays. He rejected the Western influences on postwar Japan, preferring the classic traditions of Japanese literature, as evidenced in his modernized versions of the Noh plays. The best-known English translations of his work include *The Temple of the Golden Pavilion* (1959), *The Sailor Who Fell from Grace with the Sea* (1965), and his masterful tetralogy, *The Sea of Fertility* (1975). In 1968 Mishima founded a private army, the Shield Society, with the intent of returning Japan to the Samurai tradition. In 1970, Mishima and four of his followers captured the headquarters of Japan's Eastern Ground Self-Defense Forces. When his demands went unheeded, he committed suicide according to the ritual of *seppuku,* a ceremony reserved for the Samurai warrior. "Patriotism," reprinted from *Death in Midsummer and Other Stories* (1966), realistically portrays a domestic version of this ancient ritual.

1

On the twenty-eighth of February, 1936 (on the third day, that is, of the February 26 Incident), Lieutenant Shinji Takeyama of the Konoe Transport Battalion—profoundly disturbed by the knowledge that his closest colleagues had been with the mutineers from the beginning, and indignant at the imminent prospect of Imperial troops attacking Imperial troops—took his officer's sword and ceremonially disemboweled himself in the eight-mat room of his private residence in the sixth block of Aoba-chō, in Yotsuya Ward. His wife, Reiko, followed him, stabbing herself to death. The lieutenant's farewell note consisted of one sentence: "Long live the Imperial Forces." His wife's, after apologies for her unfilial conduct in thus preceding her parents to the grave, concluded: "The day which, for a soldier's wife, had to come, has come. . . ." The last moments of this heroic and dedicated couple were such as to make the gods themselves weep. The lieutenant's age, it should be noted, was thirty-one, his wife's twenty-three; and it was not half a year since the celebration of their marriage.

2

Those who saw the bride and bridegroom in the commemorative photograph—perhaps no less than those actually present at the lieutenant's wedding—had exclaimed in wonder at the bearing of this handsome couple. The lieutenant, majestic in military uniform, stood protectively beside his bride, his right hand resting upon his sword, his officer's cap held at his left side. His expression was severe, and his dark brows and wide-gazing eyes well conveyed the clear integrity of youth. For the beauty of the bride in her white over-robe no comparisons were adequate. In the eyes, round beneath soft brows, in the slender, finely shaped nose, and in the full lips, there was both sensuousness and refinement. One hand, emerging shyly from a sleeve of the over-robe, held a fan, and the tips of the fingers, clustering delicately, were like the bud of a moonflower.

After the suicide, people would take out this photograph and examine it, and sadly reflect that too often there was a curse on these seemingly flawless unions. Perhaps it was no more than imagination, but looking at the picture after the tragedy it almost seemed as if the two young people before the gold-lacquered screen were gazing, each with equal clarity, at the deaths which lay before them.

Thanks to the good offices of their go-between, Lieutenant General Ozeki, they had been able to set themselves up in a new home at Aoba-chō in Yotsuya. "New home" is perhaps misleading. It was an old three-room rented house backing onto a small garden. As neither the six- nor the four-and-a-half-mat room downstairs was favored by the sun, they used the upstairs eight-mat room as both bedroom and guest room. There was no maid, so Reiko was left alone to guard the house in her husband's absence.

The honeymoon trip was dispensed with on the grounds that these were times of national emergency. The two of them had spent the first night of their marriage at this house. Before going to bed, Shinji, sitting erect on the floor with his sword laid before him, had bestowed upon his wife a soldierly lecture. A woman who had become the wife of a soldier should know and resolutely accept that her husband's death might come at any moment. It could be tomorrow. It could be the day after. But, no matter when it came—he asked—was she steadfast in her resolve to accept it? Reiko rose to her feet, pulled open a drawer of the cabinet, and took out what was the most prized of her new possessions, the dagger her mother had given her. Returning to her place, she laid the dagger without a word on the mat before her, just as her husband had laid his sword. A silent understanding was achieved at once, and the lieutenant never again sought to test his wife's resolve.

In the first few months of her marriage Reiko's beauty grew daily more radiant, shining serene like the moon after rain.

As both were possessed of young, vigorous bodies, their relationship was passionate. Nor was this merely a matter of the night. On more than one occasion, returning home straight from maneuvers, and begrudging even the time it took to remove his mud-splashed uniform, the lieutenant had pushed his wife to the floor almost as soon as he had entered the house. Reiko was equally ardent in her response. For a little more or a little less than a month, from the first night of their marriage Reiko knew happiness, and the lieutenant, seeing this, was happy too.

Reiko's body was white and pure, and her swelling breasts conveyed a firm and chaste refusal; but, upon consent, those breasts were lavish with their intimate, welcoming warmth. Even in bed these two were frighteningly and awesomely serious. In the very midst of wild, intoxicating passion, their hearts were sober and serious.

By day the lieutenant would think of his wife in the brief rest periods between training; and all day long, at home, Reiko would recall the image of her husband. Even when apart, however, they had only to look at the wedding photograph for their happiness to be once more confirmed. Reiko felt not the slightest surprise that a man who had been a complete stranger until a few months ago should now have become the sun about which her whole world revolved.

All these things had a moral basis, and were in accordance with the Education Rescript's injunction that "husband and wife should be harmonious." Not once did Reiko contradict her husband, nor did the lieutenant ever find reason to scold his wife. On the god shelf below the stairway, alongside the tablet from the Great Ise Shrine, were set photographs of their Imperial Majesties, and regularly every morning, before leaving for duty, the lieutenant would stand with his wife at this hallowed place and together they would bow their heads low. The offering water was renewed each morning, and the sacred sprig of *sasaki* was always green and fresh. Their lives were lived beneath the solemn protection of the gods and were filled with an intense happiness which set every fiber in their bodies trembling.

3

Although Lord Privy Seal Saitō's house was in their neighborhood, neither of them heard any noise of gunfire on the morning of February 26. It was a bugle, sounding muster in the dim, snowy dawn, when the ten-minute tragedy had already ended, which first disrupted the lieutenant's slumbers. Leaping at once from his bed, and without speaking a word, the lieutenant donned his uniform, buckled on the sword held ready for him by his wife, and hurried swiftly out into the snow-covered streets of the still darkened morning. He did not return until the evening of the twenty-eighth.

Later, from the radio news, Reiko learned the full extent of this sudden eruption of violence. Her life throughout the subsequent two days was lived alone, in complete tranquility and behind locked doors.

In the lieutenant's face, as he hurried silently out into the snowy morning, Reiko had read the determination to die. If her husband did not return, her own decision was made: she too would die. Quietly she attended to the disposition of her personal possessions. She chose her sets of visiting kimonos as keepsakes for friends of her schooldays, and she wrote a name and address on the stiff paper wrapping in which each was folded. Constantly admonished by her husband never to think of the morrow, Reiko had not even kept a diary and was now denied the pleasure of assiduously rereading her record of the happiness of the past few months and consigning each page to the fire as she did so. Ranged across the top of the radio were a small china dog, a rabbit, a squirrel, a bear, a fox. There were also a small vase and a water pitcher. These comprised Reiko's one and only collection. But it would hardly do, she imagined, to give such things as keepsakes. Nor again would it be quite proper to ask specifically for them to be included in the coffin. It seemed to Reiko, as these thoughts passed through her mind, that the expressions on the small animals' faces grew even more lost and forlorn.

Reiko took the squirrel in her hand and looked at it. And then, her thoughts turning to a realm far beyond these childlike affections, she gazed up into the distance at the great sunlike principle which her husband embodied. She was ready, and happy, to be hurtled along to her destruction in that gleaming sun chariot—but now, for these few moments of solitude, she allowed herself to luxuriate in this innocent attachment to trifles. The time when she had genuinely loved these things, however, was long past. Now she merely loved the memory of having once loved them, and their place in her heart had been filled by more intense passions, by a more frenzied happiness. . . . For Reiko had never, even to herself, thought of those soaring joys of the flesh as a mere pleasure. The February cold, and the icy touch of the china squirrel, had numbed Reiko's slender fingers; yet, even so, in her lower limbs, beneath the ordered repetition of the pattern which crossed the skirt of her trim *meisen* kimono, she could feel now, as she thought of the lieutenant's powerful arms reaching out toward her, a hot moistness of the flesh which defied the snows.

She was not in the least afraid of the death hovering in her mind. Waiting alone at home, Reiko firmly believed that everything her husband was feeling or thinking now, his anguish and distress, was leading her—just as surely as the power in his flesh—to a welcome death. She felt as if her body could melt away with ease and be transformed to the merest fraction of her husband's thought.

Listening to the frequent announcements on the radio, she heard the names of several of her husband's colleagues mentioned among those of the insurgents. This was news of death. She followed the developments closely, wondering anxiously, as the situation became daily more irrevocable, why no Imperial ordinance was sent down, and watching what had at first been taken as a movement to restore the nation's honor come gradually to be branded with the infamous name of mutiny. There was no communication from the regiment. At any moment, it seemed, fighting might commence in the city streets, where the remains of the snow still lay.

Toward sundown on the twenty-eighth Reiko was startled by a furious pounding on the front door. She hurried downstairs. As she pulled with fumbling fingers at the bolt, the shape dimly outlined beyond the frosted-glass panel made no sound, but she knew it was her husband. Reiko had never known the bolt on the sliding door to be so stiff. Still it resisted. The door just would not open.

In a moment, almost before she knew she had succeeded, the lieutenant was standing before her on the cement floor inside the porch, muffled in a khaki greatcoat, his top boots heavy with slush from the street. Closing the door behind him, he returned the bolt once more to its socket. With what significance, Reiko did not understand.

"Welcome home."

Reiko bowed deeply, but her husband made no response. As he had already unfastened his sword and was about to remove his greatcoat, Reiko moved around behind to assist. The coat, which was cold and damp and had lost the odor of horse dung it normally exuded when exposed to the sun, weighed heavily upon her arm. Draping it across a hanger, and cradling the sword and leather belt in her sleeves, she waited while her husband removed his top boots and then followed behind him into the "living room." This was the six-mat room downstairs.

Seen in the clear light from the lamp, her husband's face, covered with a heavy growth of bristle, was almost unrecognizably wasted and thin. The cheeks were hollow, their luster and resilience gone. In his normal good spirits he would have changed into old clothes as soon as he was home and have pressed her to get supper at once, but now he sat before the table still in his uniform, his head drooping dejectedly. Reiko refrained from asking whether she should prepare the supper.

After an interval the lieutenant spoke.

"I knew nothing. They hadn't asked me to join. Perhaps out of consideration, because I was newly married. Kanō, and Homma too, Yamaguchi."

Reiko recalled momentarily the faces of high-spirited young officers, friends of her husband, who had come to the house occasionally as guests.

"There may be an Imperial ordinance sent down tomorrow. They'll be posted as rebels, I imagine. I shall be in command of a unit with orders to attack them. . . . I can't do it. It's impossible to do a thing like that."

He spoke again.

"They've taken me off guard duty, and I have permission to return home for one night. Tomorrow morning, without question, I must leave to join the attack. I can't do it, Reiko."

Reiko sat erect with lowered eyes. She understood clearly that her husband had spoken of his death. The lieutenant was resolved. Each word, being rooted in death, emerged sharply and with powerful significance against this dark, unmovable background. Although the lieutenant was speaking of his dilemma, already there was no room in his mind for vacillation.

However, there was a clarity, like the clarity of a stream fed from melting snows, in the silence which rested between them. Sitting in his own home after the long two-day ordeal, and looking across at the face of his beautiful wife, the lieutenant was for the first time experiencing true peace of mind. For he had at once known, though she said nothing, that his wife divined the resolve which lay beneath his words.

"Well, then . . ." The lieutenant's eyes opened wide. Despite his exhaustion they were strong and clear, and now for the first time they looked straight into the eyes of his wife. "Tonight I shall cut my stomach."

Reiko did not flinch.

Her round eyes showed tension, as taut as the clang of a bell.

"I am ready," she said. "I ask permission to accompany you."

The lieutenant felt almost mesmerized by the strength in those eyes. His words flowed swiftly and easily, like the utterances of a man in delirium, and it was beyond his understanding how permission in a matter of such weight could be expressed so casually.

"Good. We'll go together. But I want you as a witness, first, for my own suicide. Agreed?"

When this was said a sudden release of abundant happiness welled up in both their hearts. Reiko was deeply affected by the greatness of her husband's trust in her. It was vital for the lieutenant, whatever else might happen, that there should be no irregularity in his death. For that reason there had to be a witness. The fact that he had chosen his wife for this was the first mark of his trust. The second, and even greater mark, was that though he had pledged that they should die together he did not intend to kill his wife first—he had deferred her death to a time when he would no longer be there to verify it. If the lieutenant had been a suspicious husband, he would doubtless, as in the usual suicide pact, have chosen to kill his wife first.

When Reiko said, "I ask permission to accompany you," the lieutenant felt these words to be the final fruit of the education which he had himself given his wife, starting on the first night of their marriage, and which had schooled her, when the moment came, to say what had to be said without a shadow of hesitation. This flattered the lieutenant's opinion of himself as a self-reliant man. He was not so romantic or conceited as to imagine that the words were spoken spontaneously, out of love for her husband.

With happiness welling almost too abundantly in their hearts, they could not help smiling at each other. Reiko felt as if she had returned to her wedding night.

Before her eyes was neither pain nor death. She seemed to see only a free and limitless expanse opening out into vast distances.

"The water is hot. Will you take your bath now?"

"Ah yes, of course."

"And supper . . . ?"

The words were delivered in such level, domestic tones that the lieutenant came near to thinking, for the fraction of a second, that everything had been a hallucination.

"I don't think we'll need supper. But perhaps you could warm some sake?"

"As you wish."

As Reiko rose and took a *tanzen* gown from the cabinet for after the bath, she purposely directed her husband's attention to the open drawer. The lieutenant rose, crossed to the cabinet, and looked inside. From the ordered array of paper wrappings he read, one by one, the addresses of the keepsakes. There was no grief in the lieutenant's response to this demonstration of heroic resolve. His heart was filled with tenderness. Like a husband who is proudly shown the childish purchases of a young wife, the lieutenant, overwhelmed by affection, lovingly embraced his wife from behind and implanted a kiss upon her neck.

Reiko felt the roughness of the lieutenant's unshaven skin against her neck. This sensation, more than being just a thing of this world, was for Reiko almost the world itself, but now—with the feeling that it was soon to be lost forever—it had freshness beyond all her experience. Each moment had its own vital strength, and the senses in every corner of her body were reawakened. Accepting her husband's caresses from behind, Reiko raised herself on the tips of her toes, letting the vitality seep through her entire body.

"First the bath, and then, after some sake . . . lay out the bedding upstairs, will you?"

The lieutenant whispered the words into his wife's ear. Reiko silently nodded.

Flinging off his uniform, the lieutenant went to the bath. To faint background noises of slopping water Reiko tended the charcoal brazier in the living room and began the preparations for warming the sake.

Taking the *tanzen,* a sash, and some underclothes, she went to the bathroom to ask how the water was. In the midst of a coiling cloud of steam the lieutenant was sitting cross-legged on the floor, shaving, and she could dimly discern the rippling movements of the muscles on his damp, powerful back as they responded to the movement of his arms.

There was nothing to suggest a time of any special significance. Reiko, going busily about her tasks, was preparing side dishes from odds and ends in stock. Her hands did not tremble. If anything, she managed even more efficiently and smoothly than usually. From time to time, it is true, there was a strange throbbing deep within her breast. Like distant lightning, it had a moment of sharp intensity and then vanished without trace. Apart from that, nothing was in any way out of the ordinary.

The lieutenant, shaving in the bathroom, felt his warmed body miraculously healed at last of the desperate tiredness of the days of indecision and filled—in spite of the death which lay ahead—with pleasurable anticipation. The sound of his wife going about her work came to him faintly. A healthy physical craving, submerged for two days, reasserted itself.

The lieutenant was confident there had been no impurity in that joy they had experienced when resolving upon death. They had both sensed at that moment—though not, of course, in any clear and conscious way—that those permissible pleasures which they shared in private were once more beneath the protection of Righteousness and Divine Power, and of a complete and unassailable morality. On looking into each other's eyes and discovering there an honorable death, they had felt themselves safe once more behind steel walls which none could destroy, encased in an impenetrable armor of Beauty and Truth. Thus, so far from seeing any inconsistency or conflict between the urges of his flesh and the sincerity of his patriotism, the lieutenant was even able to regard the two as parts of the same thing.

Thrusting his face close to the dark, cracked, misted wall mirror, the lieutenant shaved himself with great care. This would be his death face. There must be no unsightly blemishes. The clean-shaven face gleamed once more with a youthful luster, seeming to brighten the darkness of the mirror. There was a certain elegance, he even felt, in the association of death with this radiantly healthy face.

Just as it looked now, this would become his death face! Already, in fact, it had half departed from the lieutenant's personal possession and had become the bust above a dead soldier's memorial. As an experiment he closed his eyes tight. Everything was wrapped in blackness, and he was no longer a living, seeing creature.

Returning from the bath, the traces of the shave glowing faintly blue beneath his smooth cheeks, he seated himself beside the now well-kindled charcoal brazier. Busy though Reiko was, he noticed, she had found time lightly to touch up her face. Her cheeks were gay and her lips moist. There was no shadow of sadness to be seen. Truly, the lieutenant felt, as he saw this mark of his young wife's passionate nature, he had chosen the wife he ought to have chosen.

As soon as the lieutenant had drained his sake cup he offered it to Reiko. Reiko had never before tasted sake, but she accepted without hesitation and sipped timidly.

"Come here," the lieutenant said.

Reiko moved to her husband's side and was embraced as she leaned backward across his lap. Her breast was in violent commotion, as if sadness, joy, and the potent sake were mingling and reacting within her. The lieutenant looked down into his wife's face. It was the last face he would see in this world, the last face he would see of his wife. The lieutenant scrutinized the face minutely, with the eyes of a traveler bidding farewell to splendid vistas which he will never revisit. It was a face he could not tire of looking at—the features regular yet not cold, the lips lightly closed with a soft strength. The lieutenant kissed those lips, unthinkingly. And suddenly, though there was not the slightest distortion of the face into the unsightliness of sobbing, he noticed that tears were welling slowly from beneath the long lashes of the closed eyes and brimming over into a glistening stream.

When, a little later, the lieutenant urged that they should move to the upstairs bedroom, his wife replied that she would follow after taking a bath. Climbing the stairs alone to the bedroom, where the air was already warmed by the gas heater, the lieutenant lay down on the bedding with arms outstretched and legs apart. Even the time at which he lay waiting for his wife to join him was no later and no earlier than usual.

He folded his hands beneath his head and gazed at the dark boards of the ceiling in the dimness beyond the range of the standard lamp. Was it death he was now waiting for? Or a wild ecstasy of the senses? The two seemed to overlap, almost as if the object of this bodily desire was death itself. But, however that might be, it was certain that never before had the lieutenant tasted such total freedom.

There was the sound of a car outside the window. He could hear the screech of its tires skidding in the snow piled at the side of the street. The sound of its horn re-echoed from near-by walls. . . . Listening to these noises he had the feeling that this house rose like a solitary island in the ocean of a society going as restlessly about its business as ever. All around, vastly and untidily, stretched the country for which he grieved. He was to give his life for it. But would that great country, with which he was prepared to remonstrate to the extent of destroying himself, take the slightest heed of his death? He did not know; and it did not matter. He was a battlefield without glory, a battlefield where none could display deeds of valor: it was the front line of the spirit.

Reiko's footsteps sounded on the stairway. The steep stairs in this old house creaked badly. There were fond memories in that creaking, and many a time, while waiting in bed, the lieutenant had listened to its welcome sound. At the thought that he would hear it no more he listened with intense concentration, striving for every corner of every moment of this precious time to be filled with the sound of those soft footfalls on the creaking stairway. The moments seemed transformed to jewels, sparkling with inner light.

Reiko wore a Nagoya sash about the waist of her *yukata,* but as the lieutenant reached toward it, its redness sobered by the dimness of the light, Reiko's hand moved to his assistance and the sash fell away, slithering swiftly to the floor. As she stood before him, still in her *yukata,* the lieutenant inserted his hands through the side slits beneath each sleeve, intending to embrace her as she was; but at the touch of his finger tips upon the warm naked flesh, and as the armpits closed gently about his hands, his whole body was suddenly aflame.

In a few moments the two lay naked before the glowing gas heater.

Neither spoke the thought, but their hearts, their bodies, and their pounding breasts blazed with the knowledge that this was the very last time. It was as if the words "The Last Time" were spelled out, in invisible brushstrokes, across every inch of their bodies.

The lieutenant drew his wife close and kissed her vehemently. As their tongues explored each other's mouths, reaching out into the smooth, moist interior, they felt as if the still-unknown agonies of death had tempered their senses to the keenness of red-hot steel. The agonies they could not yet feel, the distant pains of death, had refined their awareness of pleasure.

"This is the last time I shall see your body," said the lieutenant. "Let me look at it closely." And, tilting the shade on the lampstand to one side, he directed the rays along the full length of Reiko's outstretched form.

Reiko lay still with her eyes closed. The light from the low lamp clearly revealed the majestic sweep of her white flesh. The lieutenant, not without a touch of egocentricity, rejoiced that he would never see this beauty crumble in death.

At his leisure, the lieutenant allowed the unforgettable spectacle to engrave itself upon his mind. With one hand he fondled the hair, with the other he softly stroked the magnificent face, implanting kisses here and there where his eyes lingered. The quiet coldness of the high, tapering forehead, the closed eyes with their long lashes beneath faintly etched brows, the set of the finely shaped nose, the gleam of teeth glimpsed between full, regular lips, the soft cheeks and the small, wise chin . . . these things conjured up in the lieutenant's mind the vision of a truly radiant death face, and again and again he pressed his lips tight against the white throat—where Reiko's own hand was soon to strike—and the throat reddened faintly beneath his kisses. Returning to the mouth he laid his lips against it with the gentlest of pressures, and moved them rhythmically over Reiko's with the light rolling motion of a small boat. If he closed his eyes, the world became a rocking cradle.

Wherever the lieutenant's eyes moved his lips faithfully followed. The high, swelling breasts, surmounted by nipples like the buds of a wild cherry, hardened as the lieutenant's lips closed about them. The arms flowed smoothly downward from each side of the breast, tapering toward the wrists, yet losing nothing of their roundness or symmetry, and at their tips were those delicate fingers which had held the fan at the wedding ceremony. One by one, as the lieutenant kissed them, the fingers withdrew behind their neighbor as if in shame. . . . The natural hollow curving between the bosom and the stomach carried in its lines a suggestion not only of softness but of resilient strength, and while it gave forewarning of the rich curves spreading outward from here to the hips it had, in itself, an appearance only of restraint and proper discipline. The whiteness and richness of the stomach and hips was like milk brimming in a great bowl, and the sharply shadowed dip of the navel could have been the fresh impress of a raindrop, fallen there that very moment. Where the shadows gathered more thickly, hair clustered, gentle and sensitive, and as the agitation mounted in the now no longer passive body there hung over this region a scent like the smoldering of fragrant blossoms, growing steadily more pervasive.

At length, in a tremulous voice, Reiko spoke.

"Show me. . . . Let me look too, for the last time."

Never before had he heard from his wife's lips so strong and unequivocal a request. It was as if something which her modesty had wished to keep hidden to the end had suddenly burst its bonds of constraint. The lieutenant obediently lay back and surrendered himself to his wife. Lithely she raised her white, trembling body, and—burning with an innocent desire to return to her husband what he had done for her—placed two white fingers on the lieutenant's eyes, which gazed fixedly up at her, and gently stroked them shut.

Suddenly overwhelmed by tenderness, her cheeks flushed by a dizzying uprush of emotion, Reiko threw her arms about the lieutenant's close-cropped head. The bristly hairs rubbed painfully against her breast, the prominent nose was cold as it dug into her flesh and his breath was hot. Relaxing her embrace, she gazed down at her husband's masculine face. The severe brows, the closed eyes, the splendid bridge of the nose, the shapely lips drawn firmly together . . . the blue, clean-shaven cheeks reflecting the light and gleaming smoothly. Reiko kissed each of these. She kissed the broad nape of the neck, the strong, erect shoulders, the powerful chest with its twin circles like shields and its russet nipples. In the armpits, deeply shadowed by the ample flesh of the shoulders and chest, a sweet and melancholy odor emanated from the growth of hair, and in the sweetness of this odor was contained, somehow, the essence of young death. The lieutenant's naked skin glowed like a field of barley, and everywhere the muscles showed in sharp relief, converging on the lower abdomen about the small, unassuming navel. Gazing at the youthful, firm stomach, modestly covered by a vigorous growth of hair, Reiko thought of it as it was soon to be, cruelly cut by the sword, and she laid her head upon it, sobbing in pity, and bathed it with kisses.

At the touch of his wife's tears upon his stomach the lieutenant felt ready to endure with courage the cruelest agonies of his suicide.

What ecstasies they experienced after these tender exchanges may well be imagined. The lieutenant raised himself and enfolded his wife in a powerful embrace, her body now limp with exhaustion after her grief and tears. Passionately they held their faces close, rubbing cheek against cheek. Reiko's body was trembling. Their breasts, moist with sweat, were tightly joined, and every inch of the young and beautiful bodies had become so much one with the other that it seemed impossible there should ever again be a separation. Reiko cried out. From the heights they plunged into the abyss, and from the abyss they took wing and soared once more to dizzying heights. The lieutenant panted like the regimental standard-bearer on a route march. . . . As one cycle ended, almost immediately a new wave of passion would be generated, and together—with no trace of fatigue—they would climb again in a single breathless movement to the very summit.

4

When the lieutenant at last turned away, it was not from weariness. For one thing, he was anxious not to undermine the considerable strength he would need in carrying out his suicide. For another, he would have been sorry to mar the sweetness of these last memories by overindulgence.

Since the lieutenant had clearly desisted, Reiko too, with her usual compliance, followed his example. The two lay naked on their backs, with fingers interlaced, staring fixedly at the dark ceiling. The room was warm from the heater, and even when the sweat had ceased to pour from their bodies they felt no cold. Outside, in the hushed night, the sounds of passing traffic had ceased. Even the noise of the trains and streetcars around Yotsuya station did not penetrate this far. After echoing through the region bounded by the moat, they were lost in the heavily wooded park fronting the broad driveway before Akasaka Palace. It was hard to believe in the tension gripping this whole quarter, where the two factions of the bitterly divided Imperial Army now confronted each other, poised for battle.

Savoring the warmth glowing within themselves, they lay still and recalled the ecstasies they had just known. Each moment of the experience was relived. They remembered the taste of kisses which had never wearied, the touch of naked flesh, episode after episode of dizzying bliss. But already, from the dark boards of the ceiling, the face of death was peering down. These joys had been final, and their bodies would never know them again. Not that joy of this intensity—and the same thought had occurred to them both—was ever likely to be re-experienced, even if they should live on to old age.

The feel of their fingers intertwined—this too would soon be lost. Even the wood-grain patterns they now gazed at on the dark ceiling boards would be taken from them. They could feel death edging in, nearer and nearer. There could be no hesitation now. They must have the courage to reach out to death themselves, and to seize it.

"Well, let's make our preparations," said the lieutenant. The note of determination in the words was unmistakable, but at the same time Reiko had never heard her husband's voice so warm and tender.

After they had risen, a variety of tasks awaited them.

The lieutenant, who had never once before helped with the bedding, now cheerfully slid back the door of the closet, lifted the mattress across the room by himself, and stowed it away inside.

Reiko turned off the gas heater and put away the lamp standard. During the lieutenant's absence she had arranged this room carefully, sweeping and dusting it to a fresh cleanness, and now—if one overlooked the rosewood table drawn into one corner—the eight-mat room gave all the appearance of a reception room ready to welcome an important guest.

"We've seen some drinking here, haven't we? With Kanō and Homma and Noguchi . . ."

"Yes, they were great drinkers, all of them."

"We'll be meeting them before long, in the other world. They'll tease us, I imagine, when they find I've brought you with me.

Descending the stairs, the lieutenant turned to look back into this calm, clean room, now brightly illuminated by the ceiling lamp. There floated across his mind the faces of the young officers who had drunk there, and laughed, and innocently bragged. He had never dreamed then that he would one day cut open his stomach in this room.

In the two rooms downstairs husband and wife busied themselves smoothly and serenely with their respective preparations. The lieutenant went to the toilet, and then to the bathroom to wash. Meanwhile Reiko folded away her husband's padded robe, placed his uniform tunic, his trousers, and a newly cut bleached loincloth in the bathroom, and set out sheets of paper on the living room table for the farewell notes. Then she removed the lid from the writing box and began rubbing ink from the ink tablet. She had already decided upon the wording of her own note.

Reiko's fingers pressed hard upon the cold gilt letters of the ink tablet, and the water in the shallow well at once darkened, as if a black cloud had spread across it. She stopped thinking that this repeated action, the pressure from her fingers, this rise and fall of faint sound, was all and solely for death. It was a routine domestic task, a simple paring away of time until death should finally stand before her. But somehow, in the increasingly smooth motion of the tablet rubbing on the stone, and in the scent from the thickening ink, there was unspeakable darkness.

Neat in his uniform, which he now wore next to his skin, the lieutenant emerged from the bathroom. Without a word he seated himself at the table, bolt upright, took a brush in his hand, and stared undecidedly at the paper before him.

Reiko took a white silk kimono with her and entered the bathroom. When she reappeared in the living room, clad in the white kimono and with her face lightly made up, the farewell note lay completed on the table beneath the lamp. The thick black brushstrokes said simply:

"Long Live the Imperial Forces—Army Lieutenant Takeyama Shinji."

While Reiko sat opposite him writing her own note, the lieutenant gazed in silence, intensely serious, at the controlled movement of his wife's pale fingers as they manipulated the brush.

With their respective notes in their hands—the lieutenant's sword strapped to his side, Reiko's small dagger thrust into the sash of her white kimono—the two of them stood before the god shelf and silently prayed. Then they put out all the downstairs lights. As he mounted the stairs the lieutenant turned his head and gazed back at the striking, white-clad figure of his wife, climbing behind him, with lowered eyes, from the darkness beneath.

The farewell notes were laid side by side in the alcove of the upstairs room. They wondered whether they ought not to remove the hanging scroll, but since it had been written by their go-between, Lieutenant General Ozeki, and consisted, moreover, of two Chinese characters signifying "Sincerity," they left it where it was. Even if it were to become stained with splashes of blood, they felt that the lieutenant general would understand.

The lieutenant, sitting erect with his back to the alcove, laid his sword on the floor before him.

Reiko sat facing him, a mat's width away. With the rest of her so severely white the touch of rouge on her lips seemed remarkably seductive.

Across the dividing mat they gazed intently into each other's eyes. The lieutenant's sword lay before his knees. Seeing it, Reiko recalled their first night and was overwhelmed with sadness. The lieutenant spoke, in a hoarse voice:

"As I have no second to help me I shall cut deep. It may look unpleasant, but please do not panic. Death of any sort is a fearful thing to watch. You must not be discouraged by what you see. Is that all right?"

"Yes."

Reiko nodded deeply.

Looking at the slender white figure of his wife the lieutenant experienced a bizarre excitement. What he was about to perform was an act in his public capacity as a soldier, something he had never previously shown his wife. It called for a resolution equal to the courage to enter battle; it was a death of no less degree and quality than death in the front line. It was his conduct on the battlefield that he was now to display.

Momentarily the thought led the lieutenant to a strange fantasy. A lonely death on the battlefield, a death beneath the eyes of his beautiful wife . . . in the sensation that he was now to die in these two dimensions, realizing an impossible union of them both, there was sweetness beyond words. This must be the very pinnacle of good fortune, he thought. To have every moment of his death observed by those beautiful eyes—it was like being borne to death on a gentle, fragrant breeze. There was some special favor here. He did not understand precisely what it was, but it was a domain unknown to others: a dispensation granted to no one else had been permitted to himself. In the radiant, bride-like figure of his white-robed wife the lieutenant seemed to see a vision of all those things he had loved and for which he was to lay down his life—the Imperial Household, the Nation, the Army Flag. All these, no less than the wife who sat before him, were presences observing him closely with clear and never-faltering eyes.

Reiko too was gazing intently at her husband, so soon to die, and she thought that never in this world had she seen anything so beautiful. The lieutenant always looked well in uniform, but now, as he contemplated death with severe brows and firmly closed lips, he revealed what was perhaps masculine beauty at its most superb.

"It's time to go," the lieutenant said at last.

Reiko bent her body low to the mat in a deep bow. She could not raise her face. She did not wish to spoil her make-up with tears, but the tears could not be held back.

When at length she looked up she saw hazily through the tears that her husband had wound a white bandage around the blade of his now unsheathed sword, leaving five or six inches of naked steel showing at the point.

Resting the sword in its cloth wrapping on the mat before him, the lieutenant rose from his knees, resettled himself cross-legged, and unfastened the hooks of his uniform collar. His eyes no longer saw his wife. Slowly, one by one, he undid the flat brass buttons. The dusky brown chest was revealed, and then the stomach. He unclasped his belt and undid the buttons of his trousers. The pure whiteness of the thickly coiled loincloth showed itself. The lieutenant pushed the cloth down with both hands, further to ease his stomach, and then reached for the white-bandaged blade of his sword. With his left hand he massaged his abdomen, glancing downward as he did so.

To reassure himself on the sharpness of his sword's cutting edge the lieutenant folded back the left trouser flap, exposing a little of his thigh, and lightly drew the blade across the skin. Blood welled up in the wound at once, and several streaks of red trickled downward, glistening in the strong light.

It was the first time Reiko had ever seen her husband's blood, and she felt a violent throbbing in her chest. She looked at her husband's face. The lieutenant was looking at the blood with calm appraisal. For a moment—though thinking at the same time that it was hollow comfort—Reiko experienced a sense of relief.

The lieutenant's eyes fixed his wife with an intense, hawk-like stare. Moving the sword around to his front, he raised himself slightly on his hips and let the upper half of his body lean over the sword point. That he was mustering his whole strength was apparent from the angry tension of the uniform at his shoulders. The lieutenant aimed to strike deep into the left of his stomach. His sharp cry pierced the silence of the room.

Despite the effort he had himself put into the blow, the lieutenant had the impression that someone else had struck the side of his stomach agonizingly with a thick rod of iron. For a second or so his head reeled and he had no idea what had happened. The five or six inches of naked point had vanished completely into his flesh, and the white bandage, gripped in his clenched fist, pressed directly against his stomach.

He returned to consciousness. The blade had certainly pierced the wall of the stomach, he thought. His breathing was difficult, his chest thumped violently, and in some far deep region, which he could hardly believe was a part of himself, a fearful and excruciating pain came welling up as if the ground had split open to disgorge a boiling stream of molten rock. The pain came suddenly nearer, with terrifying speed. The lieutenant bit his lower lip and stifled an instinctive moan.

Was this *seppuku*?—he was thinking. It was a sensation of utter chaos, as if the sky had fallen on his head and the world was reeling drunkenly. His will power and courage, which had seemed so robust before he made the incision, had now dwindled to something like a single hairlike thread of steel, and he was assailed by the uneasy feeling that he must advance along this thread, clinging to it with desperation. His clenched fist had grown moist. Looking down, he saw that both his hand and the cloth about the blade were drenched in blood. His loincloth too was dyed a deep red. It struck him as incredible that, amidst this terrible agony, things which could be seen could still be seen, and existing things existed still.

The moment the lieutenant thrust the sword into his left side and she saw the deathly pallor fall across his face, like an abruptly lowered curtain, Reiko had to struggle to prevent herself from rushing to his side. That was the duty her husband had laid upon her. Opposite her, a mat's space away, she could clearly see her husband biting his lip to stifle the pain. The pain was there, with absolute certainty, before her eyes. And Reiko had no means of rescuing him from it.

The sweat glistened on her husband's forehead. The lieutenant closed his eyes, and then opened them again, as if experimenting. The eyes had lost their luster, and seemed innocent and empty like the eyes of a small animal.

The agony before Reiko's eyes burned as strong as the summer sun, utterly remote from the grief which seemed to be tearing herself apart within. The pain grew steadily in stature, stretching upward. Reiko felt that her husband had already become a man in a separate world, a man whose whole being had been resolved into pain, a prisoner in a cage of pain where no hand could reach out to him. But Reiko felt no pain at all. Her grief was not pain. As she thought about this, Reiko began to feel as if someone had raised a cruel wall of glass high between herself and her husband.

Ever since her marriage her husband's existence had been her own existence, and every breath of his had been a breath drawn by herself. But now, while her husband's existence in pain was a vivid reality, Reiko could find in this grief of hers no certain proof at all of her own existence.

With only his right hand on the sword the lieutenant began to cut sideways across his stomach. But as the blade became entangled with the entrails it was pushed constantly outward by their soft resilience; and the lieutenant realized that it would be necessary, as he cut, to use both hands to keep the point pressed deep into his stomach. He pulled the blade across. It did not cut as easily as he had expected. He directed the strength of his whole body into his right hand and pulled again. There was a cut of three or four inches.

The pain spread slowly outward from the inner depths until the whole stomach reverberated. It was like the wild clanging of a bell. Or like a thousand bells which jangled simultaneously at every breath he breathed and every throb of his pulse, rocking his whole being. The lieutenant could no longer stop himself from moaning. But by now the blade had cut its way through to below the navel, and when he noticed this he felt a sense of satisfaction, and a renewal of courage.

The volume of blood had steadily increased, and now it spurted from the wound as if propelled by the beat of the pulse. The mat before the lieutenant was drenched red with splattered blood, and more blood overflowed onto it from pools which gathered in the folds of the lieutenant's khaki trousers. A spot, like a bird, came flying across to Reiko and settled on the lap of her white silk kimono.

By the time the lieutenant had at last drawn the sword across the right side of his stomach, the blade was already cutting shallow and had revealed its naked tip, slippery with blood and grease. But, suddenly stricken by a fit of vomiting, the lieutenant cried out hoarsely. The vomiting made the fierce pain fiercer still, and the stomach, which had thus far remained firm and compact, now abruptly heaved, opening wide its wound, and the entrails burst through, as if the wound too were vomiting. Seemingly ignorant of their master's suffering, the entrails gave an impression of robust health and almost disagreeable vitality as they slipped smoothly out and spilled over into the crotch. The lieutenant's head dropped, his shoulders heaved, his eyes opened to narrow slits, and a thin trickle of saliva dribbled from his mouth. The gold markings on his epaulettes caught the light and glinted.

Blood was scattered everywhere. The lieutenant was soaked in it to his knees, and he sat now in a crumpled and listless posture, one hand on the floor. A raw smell filled the room. The lieutenant, his head drooping, retched repeatedly, and the movement showed vividly in his shoulders. The blade of the sword, now pushed back by the entrails and exposed to its tip, was still in the lieutenant's right hand.

It would be difficult to imagine a more heroic sight than that of the lieutenant at this moment, as he mustered his strength and flung back his head. The movement was performed with sudden violence, and the back of his head struck with a sharp crack against the alcove pillar. Reiko had been sitting until now with her face lowered, gazing in fascination at the tide of blood advancing toward her knees, but the sound took her by surprise and she looked up.

The lieutenant's face was not the face of a living man. The eyes were hollow, the skin parched, the once so lustrous cheeks and lips the color of dried mud. The right hand alone was moving. Laboriously gripping the sword, it hovered shakily in the air like the hand of a marionette and strove to direct the point at the base of the lieutenant's throat. Reiko watched her husband make this last, most heart-rending, futile exertion. Glistening with blood and grease, the point was thrust at the throat again and again. And each time it missed its aim. The strength to guide it was no longer there. The straying point struck the collar and the collar badges. Although its hooks had been unfastened, the stiff military collar had closed together again and was protecting the throat.

Reiko could bear the sight no longer. She tried to go to her husband's help, but she could not stand. She moved through the blood on her knees, and her white skirts grew deep red. Moving to the rear of her husband, she helped no more than by loosening the collar. The quivering blade at last contacted the naked flesh of the throat. At that moment Reiko's impression was that she herself had propelled her husband forward; but that was not the case. It was a movement planned by the lieutenant himself, his last exertion of strength. Abruptly he threw his body at the blade, and the blade pierced his neck, emerging at the nape. There was a tremendous spurt of blood and the lieutenant lay still, cold blue-tinged steel protruding from his neck at the back.

5

Slowly, her socks slippery with blood, Reiko descended the stairway. The upstairs room was now completely still.

Switching on the ground-floor lights, she checked the gas jet and the main gas plug and poured water over the smoldering, half-buried charcoal in the brazier. She stood before the upright mirror in the four-and-a-half-mat room and held up her skirts. The bloodstains made it seem as if a bold, vivid pattern was printed across the lower half of her white kimono. When she sat down before the mirror, she was conscious of the dampness and coldness of her husband's blood in the region of her thighs, and she shivered. Then, for a long while, she lingered over her toilet preparations. She applied the rouge generously to her cheeks, and her lips too she painted heavily. This was no longer make-up to please her husband. It was make-up for the world which she would leave behind, and there was a touch of the magnificent and the spectacular in her brushwork. When she rose, the mat before the mirror was wet with blood. Reiko was not concerned about this.

Returning from the toilet, Reiko stood finally on the cement floor of the porchway. When her husband had bolted the door here last night it had been in preparation for death. For a while she stood immersed in the consideration of a simple problem. Should she now leave the bolt drawn? If she were to lock the door, it could be that the neighbors might not notice their suicide for several days. Reiko did not relish the thought of their two corpses putrifying before discovery. After all, it seemed, it would be best to leave it open. . . . She released the bolt, and also drew open the frosted-glass door a fraction. . . . At once a chill wind blew in. There was no sign of anyone in the midnight streets, and stars glittered ice-cold through the trees in the large house opposite.

Leaving the door as it was, Reiko mounted the stairs. She had walked here and there for some time and her socks were no longer slippery. About halfway up, her nostrils were already assailed by a peculiar smell.

The lieutenant was lying on his face in a sea of blood. The point protruding from his neck seemed to have grown even more prominent than before. Reiko walked heedlessly across the blood. Sitting beside the lieutenant's corpse, she stared intently at the face, which lay on one cheek on the mat. The eyes were opened wide, as if the lieutenant's attention had been attracted by something. She raised the head, folding it in her sleeve, wiped the blood from the lips, and bestowed a last kiss.

Then she rose and took from the closet a new white blanket and a waist cord. To prevent any derangement of her skirts, she wrapped the blanket about her waist and bound it there firmly with the cord.

Reiko sat herself on a spot about one foot distant from the lieutenant's body. Drawing the dagger from her sash, she examined its dully gleaming blade intently, and held it to her tongue. The taste of the polished steel was slightly sweet.

Reiko did not linger. When she thought how the pain which had previously opened such a gulf between herself and her dying husband was now to become a part of her own experience, she saw before her only the joy of herself entering a realm her husband had already made his own. In her husband's agonized face there had been something inexplicable which she was seeing for the first time. Now she would solve the riddle. Reiko sensed that at last she too would be able to taste the true bitterness and sweetness of that great moral principle in which her husband believed. What had until now been tasted only faintly through her husband's example she was about to savor directly with her own tongue.

Reiko rested the point of the blade against the base of her throat. She thrust hard. The wound was only shallow. Her head blazed, and her hands shook uncontrollably. She gave the blade a strong pull sideways. A warm substance flooded into her mouth, and everything before her reddened, in a vision of spouting blood. She gathered her strength and plunged the point of the blade deep into her throat.

QUESTIONS FOR DISCUSSION AND WRITING

1. What questions does Mishima raise by summarizing the "facts" of the story in the first paragraph? How does Shinji's "soldierly lecture" on his wedding night help answer some of

those questions? How does Reiko's little dagger foreshadow how she will respond to the potential crisis Shinji has explained?

2. How do Shinji and Reiko's suicide notes help to establish their characters? What other aspects of their character do they reveal in their last night of lovemaking?

3. Why is the couple's home an appropriate place for their joint suicide? What effect will their deaths have on the outside world? Why does Shinji still insist that his act was "on the front line of the spirit"?

4. The first two parts of the story are told from an objective point of view. The rest of the story, though still omniscient, is told from Reiko's point of view. How do her attitude and emotions influence her role as "witness"?

5. What kind of "patriotism" is exhibited by this "heroic and dedicated couple"? Does Mishima show us that their act is beautiful and meaningful, not merely a gory ritual? Explain your answer.

67

ALICE MUNRO

How I Met My Husband

ALICE MUNRO was born in 1931 in Wingham, Ontario, attended the University of Western Ontario, and moved to Victoria, British Columbia, where she founded a bookstore with her husband, James Munro. In the 1950s she began publishing stories based on the experiences and traditions of the farmers and townspeople of southwestern Ontario. These stories were collected in *Dance of the Happy Shades* (1968), which won the Governor General's Literary Award, the highest award for Canadian writers. Munro's novel *Lives of Girls and Women* (1971) won the Canadian Booksellers Award. Since 1972 Munro has lived with her second husband in the small town of Clinton, Ontario. Her recent short-story collections—*Something I've Been Meaning to Tell You* (1974), *Who Do You Think You Are?* (1978), *The Moons of Jupiter* (1983), and *The Prayers of Love* (1986)—characterize the problems of women with high aspirations trapped by the values and customs of Canadian provincialism. In 1979 Munro published *The Beggar Maid,* which also won the Governor General's Literary Award. This novel, much like her first, uses two central characters to establish the continuity among several groups of tales. In "How I Met My Husband," reprinted from *Something I've Been Meaning to Tell You,* a woman remembers her first experience of intimacy and romance.

We heard the plane come over at noon, roaring through the radio news, and we were sure it was going to hit the house, so we all ran out into the yard. We saw it come in over the treetops, all red and silver, the first close-up plane I ever saw. Mrs. Peebles screamed.

"Crash landing," their little boy said. Joey was his name.

"It's okay," said Dr. Peebles. "He knows what he's doing." Dr. Peebles was only an animal doctor, but had a calming way of talking, like any doctor.

This was my first job—working for Dr. and Mrs. Peebles, who had bought an old house out on the Fifth Line, about five miles out of town. It was just when the trend was starting of town people buying up old farms, not to work them but to live on them.

We watched the plane land across the road, where the fairgrounds used to be. It did make a good landing field, nice and level for the old race track, and the barns and display sheds torn down now for scrap lumber so there was nothing in the way. Even the old grandstand bays had burned.

"All right," said Mrs. Peebles, snappy as she always was when she got over her nerves. "Let's go back in the house. Let's not stand here gawking like a set of farmers."

She didn't say that to hurt my feelings. It never occurred to her.

I was just setting the dessert down when Loretta Bird arrived, out of breath, at the screen door.

"I thought it was going to crash into the house and kill youse all!"

She lived on the next place and the Peebleses thought she was a countrywoman, they didn't know the difference. She and her husband didn't farm, he worked on the roads and had a bad name for drinking. They had seven children and couldn't get credit at the HiWay Grocery. The Peebleses made her welcome, not knowing any better, as I say, and offered her dessert.

Dessert was never anything to write home about, at their place. A dish of Jell-O or sliced bananas or fruit out of a tin. "Have a house without a pie, be ashamed until you die," my mother used to say, but Mrs. Peebles operated differently.

Loretta Bird saw me getting the can of peaches.

"Oh, never mind," she said. "I haven't got the right kind of a stomach to trust what comes out of those tins, I can only eat home canning."

I could have slapped her. I bet she never put down fruit in her life.

"I know what he's landed here for," she said. "He's got permission to use the fairgrounds and take people up for rides. It costs a dollar. It's the same fellow who was over at Palmerston last week and was up the lakeshore before that. I wouldn't go up, if you paid me."

"I'd jump at the chance," Dr. Peebles said. "I'd like to see this neighborhood from the air."

Mrs. Peebles said she would just as soon see it from the ground. Joey said he wanted to go and Heather did, too. Joey was nine and Heather was seven.

"Would you, Edie?" Heather said.

I said I didn't know. I was scared, but I never admitted that, especially in front of children I was taking care of.

"People are going to be coming out here in their cars raising dust and trampling your property, if I was you I would complain," Loretta said. She hooked her legs around the chair rung and I knew we were in for a lengthy visit. After Dr. Peebles went back to his office or out on his next call and Mrs. Peebles went for her nap, she would hang around me while I was trying to do the dishes. She would pass remarks about the Peebleses in their own house.

"She wouldn't find time to lay down in the middle of the day, if she had seven kids like I got."

She asked me did they fight and did they keep things in the dresser drawer not to have babies with. She said it was a sin if they did. I pretended I didn't know what she was talking about.

I was fifteen and away from home for the first time. My parents had made the effort and sent me to high school for a year, but I didn't like it. I was shy of strangers and the work was hard, they didn't make it nice for you or explain the way they do now. At the end of the year the averages were published in the paper, and mine came out at the very bottom, 37 percent. My father said that's enough and I didn't blame him. The last thing I wanted, anyway, was to go on and end up teaching school. It happened the very day the paper came out with my disgrace in it, Dr. Peebles was staying at our place for dinner, having just helped one of our cows have twins, and he said I looked smart to him and his wife was looking for a girl to help. He said she felt tied down, with the two children, out in the country. I guess she would, my mother said, being polite, though I could tell from her face she was wondering what on earth it would be like to have only two children and no barn work, and then to be complaining.

When I went home I would describe to them the work I had to do, and it made everybody laugh. Mrs. Peebles had an automatic washer and dryer, the first I ever saw. I have had those in my own home for such a long time now it's hard to remember how much of a miracle it was to me, not having to struggle with the wringer and hang up and haul down. Let alone not having to heat water. Then there was practically no baking. Mrs. Peebles said she couldn't make pie crust, the most amazing thing I ever heard a woman admit. I could, of course, and I could make light biscuits and a white cake and dark cake, but they didn't want it, she said they watched their figures. The only thing I didn't like about working there, in fact, was feeling half hungry a lot of the time. I used to bring back a box of doughnuts made out at home, and hide them under my bed. The children found out, and I didn't mind sharing, but I thought I better bind them to secrecy.

The day after the plane landed Mrs. Peebles put both children in the car and drove over to Chesley, to get their hair cut. There was a good woman then at Chesley for doing hair. She got hers done at the same place, Mrs. Peebles did, and that meant they would be gone a good while. She had to pick a day Dr. Peebles wasn't going out into the country, she didn't have her own car. Cars were still in short supply then, after the war.

I loved being left in the house alone, to do my work at leisure. The kitchen was all white and bright yellow, with fluorescent lights. That was before they ever thought of making the appliances all different colors and doing the cupboards like dark old wood and hiding the lighting. I loved light. I loved the double sink. So would anybody new-come from washing dishes in a dishpan with a rag-plugged hole on an oilcloth-covered table by light of a coal-oil lamp. I kept everything shining.

The bathroom too. I had a bath in there once a week. They wouldn't have minded if I took one oftener, but to me it seemed like asking too much, or maybe risking making it less wonderful. The basin and the tub and the toilet were all pink, and there were glass doors with flamingoes painted on them, to shut off the tub. The light had a rosy cast and the mat sank under your feet like snow, except that it was warm. The mirror was three-way. With the mirror all steamed up and the air like a perfume cloud, from things I was allowed to use, I stood up on the side of the tub and admired myself naked, from three directions. Sometimes I thought about the way we lived out at home and the way we lived here and how one way was so hard to imagine when you were living the other way. But I thought it was still a lot easier, living the way we lived at home, to picture something like this, the painted flamingoes and the warmth and the soft mat, than it was anybody knowing only things like this to picture how it was the other way. And why was that?

I was through my jobs in no time, and had the vegetables peeled for supper and sitting in cold water besides. Then I went into Mrs. Peebles' bedroom. I had been in there plenty of times, cleaning, and I always took a good look in her closet, at the clothes she had hanging there. I wouldn't have looked in her drawers, but a closet is open to anybody. That's a lie. I would have looked in drawers, but I would have felt worse doing it and been more scared she could tell.

Some clothes in her closet she wore all the time, I was quite familiar with them. Others she never put on, they were pushed to the back. I was disappointed to see no wedding dress. But there was one long dress I could just see the skirt of, and I was hungering to see the rest. Now I took note of where it hung and lifted it out. It was satin, a lovely weight on my arm, light bluish-green in color, almost silvery. It had a fitted, pointed waist and a full skirt and an off-the-shoulder fold hiding the little sleeves.

Next thing was easy. I got out of my own things and slipped it on. I was slimmer at fifteen than anybody would believe who knows me now and the fit was beautiful. I didn't, of course, have a strapless bra on, which was what it needed, I just had to slide my straps down my arms under the material. Then I tried pinning up my hair, to get the effect. One thing led to another. I put on rouge and lipstick and eyebrow pencil from her dresser. The heat of the day and the weight of the satin and all the excitement made me thirsty, and I went out to the kitchen, got-up as I was, to get a glass of ginger ale with ice cubes from the refrigerator. The Peebleses drank ginger ale, or fruit drinks, all day, like water, and I was getting so I did too. Also there was no limit on ice cubes, which I was so fond of I would even put them in a glass of milk.

I turned from putting the ice tray back and saw a man watching me through the screen. It was the luckiest thing in the world I didn't spill the ginger ale down the front of me then and there.

"I never meant to scare you. I knocked but you were getting the ice out, you didn't hear me."

I couldn't see what he looked like, he was dark the way somebody is pressed up against a screen door with the bright daylight behind them. I only knew he wasn't from around here.

"I'm from the plane over there. My name is Chris Watters and what I was wondering was if I could use that pump."

There was a pump in the yard. That was the way the people used to get their water. Now I noticed he was carrying a pail.

"You're welcome," I said. "I can get it from the tap and save you pumping." I guess I wanted him to know we had piped water, didn't pump ourselves.

"I don't mind the exercise." He didn't move, though, and finally he said, "Were you going to a dance?"

Seeing a stranger there had made me entirely forget how I was dressed.

"Or is that the way ladies around here generally get dressed up in the afternoon?"

I didn't know how to joke back then. I was too embarrassed.

"You live here? Are you the lady of the house?"

"I'm the hired girl."

Some people change when they find that out, their whole way of looking at you and speaking to you changes, but his didn't.

"Well, I just wanted to tell you you look very nice. I was so surprised when I looked in the door and saw you. Just because you looked so nice and beautiful."

I wasn't even old enough then to realize how out of the common it is, for a man to say something like that to a woman, or somebody he is treating like a woman. For a man to say a word like *beautiful.* I wasn't old enough to realize or to say anything back, or in fact to do anything but wish he would go away. Not that I didn't like him, but just that it upset me so, having him look at me, and me trying to think of something to say.

He must have understood. He said good-bye, and thanked me, and went and started filling his pail from the pump. I stood behind the Venetian blinds in the dining room, watching him. When he had gone, I went into the bedroom and took the dress off and put it back in the same place. I dressed in my own clothes and took my hair down and washed my face, wiping it on Kleenex, which I threw in the wastebasket.

The Peebleses asked me what kind of man he was. Young, middle-aged, short, tall? I couldn't say.

"Good-looking?" Dr. Peebles teased me.

I couldn't think a thing but that he would be coming to get his water again, he would be talking to Dr. or Mrs. Peebles, making friends with them, and he would mention seeing me that first afternoon, dressed up. Why not mention it? He would think it was funny. And no idea of the trouble it would get me into.

After supper the Peebleses drove into town to go to a movie. She wanted to go somewhere with her hair fresh done. I sat in my bright kitchen wondering what to do, knowing I would never sleep. Mrs. Peebles might not fire me, when she found out, but it would give her a different feeling about me altogether. This was the first place I ever worked but I already had picked up things about the way people feel when you are working for them. They like to think you aren't curious. Not just that you aren't dishonest, that isn't enough. They like to feel you don't notice things, that you don't think or wonder about anything but what they liked to eat and how they liked things ironed, and so on. I don't mean they weren't kind to me, because they were. They had me eat my meals with them (to tell the truth I expected to, I didn't know there were families who don't) and sometimes they took me along in the car. But all the same.

I went up and checked on the children being asleep and then I went out. I had to do it. I crossed the road and went in the old fairgrounds gate. The plane looked unnatural sitting there, and shining with the moon. Off at the far side of the fairgrounds, where the bush was taking over, I saw his tent.

He was sitting outside it smoking a cigarette. He saw me coming.

"Hello, were you looking for a plane ride? I don't start taking people up till tomorrow." Then he looked again and said, "Oh, it's you. I didn't know you without your long dress on."

My heart was knocking away, my tongue was dried up. I had to say something. But I couldn't. My throat was closed and I was like a deaf-and-dumb.

"Did you want a ride? Sit down. Have a cigarette."

I couldn't even shake my head to say no, so he gave me one.

"Put it in your mouth or I can't light it. It's a good thing I'm used to shy ladies."

I did. It wasn't the first time I had smoked a cigarette, actually. My girl friend out home, Muriel Lowe, used to steal them from her brother.

"Look at your hand shaking. Did you just want to have a chat, or what?"

In one burst I said, "I wisht you wouldn't say anything about that dress."

"What dress? Oh, the long dress."

"It's Mrs. Peebles'."

"Whose? Oh, the lady you work for? Is that it? She wasn't home so you got dressed up in her dress, eh? You got dressed up and played queen. I don't blame you. You're not smoking the cigarette right. Don't just puff. Draw it in. Did anybody ever show you how to inhale? Are you scared I'll tell on you? Is that it?"

I was so ashamed at having to ask him to connive this way I couldn't nod. I just looked at him and he saw *yes*.

"Well I won't. I won't in the slightest way mention it or embarrass you. I give you my word of honor."

Then he changed the subject, to help me out, seeing I couldn't even thank him.

"What do you think of this sign?"

It was a board sign lying practically at my feet.

SEE THE WORLD FROM THE SKY. ADULTS $1.00, CHILDREN 50¢. QUALIFIED PILOT.

"My old sign was getting pretty beat up, I thought I'd make a new one. That's what I've been doing with my time today."

The lettering wasn't all that handsome, I thought. I could have done a better one in half an hour.

"I'm not an expert at sign making."

"It's very good," I said.

"I don't need it for publicity, word of mouth is usually enough. I turned away two carloads tonight. I felt like taking it easy. I didn't tell them ladies were dropping in to visit me."

Now I remembered the children and I was scared again, in case one of them had waked up and called me and I wasn't there.

"Do you have to go so soon?"

I remembered some manners. "Thank you for the cigarette."

"Don't forget. You have my word of honor."

I tore off across the fairgrounds, scared I'd see the car heading home from town. My sense of time was mixed up, I didn't know how long I'd been out of the house. But it was all right, it wasn't late, the children were asleep. I got in bed myself and lay thinking what a lucky end to the day, after all, and among things to be grateful for I could be grateful Loretta Bird hadn't been the one who caught me.

The yard and borders didn't get trampled, it wasn't as bad as that. All the same it seemed very public, around the house. The sign was on the fairgrounds gate. People came mostly after supper but a good many in the afternoon, too. The Bird children all came without fifty cents between them and hung on the gate. We got used to the excitement of the plane coming in and taking off, it wasn't excitement anymore. I never went over, after that one time, but would see him when he came to get his water. I would be out on the steps doing sitting-down work, like preparing vegetables, if I could.

"Why don't you come over? I'll take you up in my plane."

"I'm saving my money," I said, because I couldn't think of anything else.

"For what? For getting married?"

I shook my head.

"I'll take you up for free if you come sometime when it's slack. I thought you would come, and have another cigarette."

I made a face to hush him, because you never could tell when the children would be sneaking around the porch, or Mrs. Peebles herself listening in the house. Sometimes she came out and had a conversation with him. He told her things he hadn't bothered to tell me. But then I hadn't thought to ask. He told her he had been in the war, that was where he learned to fly a plane, and now he couldn't settle down to ordinary life, this was what he liked. She said she couldn't imagine anybody liking such a thing. Though sometimes, she said, she was almost bored enough to try anything herself, she wasn't brought up to living in the country. It's all my husband's idea, she said. This was news to me.

"Maybe you ought to give flying lessons," she said.

"Would you take them?"

She just laughed.

Sunday was a busy flying day in spite of it being preached against from two pulpits. We were all sitting out watching. Joey and Heather were over on the fence with the Bird kids. Their father had said they could go, after their mother saying all week they couldn't.

A car came down the road past the parked cars and pulled up right in the drive. It was Loretta Bird who got out, all importance, and on the driver's side another woman got out, more sedately. She was wearing sunglasses.

"This is a lady looking for the man that flies the plane," Loretta Bird said. "I heard her inquire in the hotel coffee shop where I was having a Coke and I brought her out."

"I'm sorry to bother you," the lady said. "I'm Alice Kelling, Mr. Watter's fiancée."

This Alice Kelling had on a pair of brown and white checked slacks and a yellow top. Her bust looked to me rather low and bumpy. She had a worried face. Her hair had had a permanent, but had grown out, and she wore a yellow band to keep it off her face. Nothing in the least pretty or even young-looking about her. But you could tell from how she talked she was from the city, or educated, or both.

Dr. Peebles stood up and introduced himself and his wife and me and asked her to be seated.

"He's up in the air right now, but you're welcome to sit and wait. He gets his water here and he hasn't been yet. He'll probably take his break about five."

"That is him, then?" said Alice Kelling, wrinkling and straining at the sky.

"He's not in the habit of running out on you, taking a different name?" Dr. Peebles laughed. He was the one, not his wife, to offer iced tea. Then she sent me into the kitchen to fix it. She smiled. She was wearing sunglasses too.

"He never mentioned his fiancée," she said.

I loved fixing iced tea with lots of ice and slices of lemon in tall glasses. I ought to have mentioned before, Dr. Peebles was an abstainer, at least around the house, or I wouldn't have been allowed to take the place. I had to fix a glass for Loretta Bird too, though it galled me, and when I went out she had settled in my lawn chair, leaving me the steps.

"I knew you was a nurse when I first heard you in that coffee shop."

"How would you know a thing like that?"

"I get my hunches about people. Was that how you met him, nursing?"

"Chris? Well yes. Yes, it was."

"Oh, were you overseas?" said Mrs. Peebles.

"No, it was before he went overseas. I nursed him when he was stationed at Centralia and had a ruptured appendix. We got engaged and then he went overseas. My, this is refreshing, after a long drive."

"He'll be glad to see you," Dr. Peebles said. "It's a rackety kind of life, isn't it, not staying one place long enough to really make friends."

"Youse've had a long engagement," Loretta Bird said.

Alice Kelling passed that over. "I was going to get a room at the hotel, but when I was offered directions I came on out. Do you think I could phone them?"

"No need," Dr. Peebles said. "You're five miles away from him if you stay at the hotel. Here, you're right across the road. Stay with us. We've got rooms on rooms, look at this big house."

Asking people to stay, just like that, is certainly a country thing, and maybe seemed natural to him now, but not to Mrs. Peebles, from the way she said, oh yes, we have plenty of room. Or to Alice Kelling, who kept protesting, but let herself be worn down. I got the feeling it was a temptation to her, to be that close. I was trying for a look at her ring. Her nails were painted red, her fingers were freckled and wrinkled. It was a tiny stone. Muriel Lowe's cousin had one twice as big.

Chris came to get his water, late in the afternoon just as Dr. Peebles had predicted. He must have recognized the car from a way off. He came smiling.

"Here I am chasing after you to see what you're up to," called Alice Kelling. She got up and went to meet him and they kissed, just touched, in front of us.

"You're going to spend a lot on gas that way," Chris said.

Dr. Peebles invited Chris to stay for supper, since he had already put up the sign that said: NO MORE RIDES TILL 7 P.M. Mrs. Peebles wanted it served in the yard, in spite of the bugs. One thing strange to anybody from the country is this eating outside. I had made a potato salad earlier and she had made a jellied salad, that was one thing she could do, so it was just a matter of getting those out, and some sliced meat and cucumbers and fresh leaf lettuce. Loretta Bird hung around for some time saying, "Oh, well, I guess I better get home to those yappers," and, "It's so nice just sitting here, I sure hate to get up," but nobody invited her, I was relieved to see, and finally she had to go.

That night after rides were finished Alice Kelling and Chris went off somewhere in her car. I lay awake till they got back. When I saw the car lights sweep my ceiling I got up to look down on them through the slats of my blind. I don't know what I thought I was going to see. Muriel Lowe and I used to sleep on her front veranda and watch her sister and her sister's boy friend saying good night. Afterward we couldn't get to sleep, for longing for somebody to kiss us and rub up against us and we would talk about suppose you were out in a boat with a boy and he wouldn't bring you in to shore unless you did it, or what if somebody got you trapped in a barn, you would have to, wouldn't you, it wouldn't be your fault. Muriel said her two girl cousins used to try with a toilet paper roll that one of them was a boy. We wouldn't do anything like that; just lay and wondered.

All that happened was that Chris got out of the car on one side and she got out on the other and they walked off separately—him toward the fairgrounds and her toward the house. I got back in bed and imagined about me coming home with him, not like that.

Next morning Alice Kelling got up late and I fixed a grapefruit for her the way I had learned and Mrs. Peebles sat down with her to visit and have another cup of coffee. Mrs. Peebles seemed pleased enough now, having company. Alice Kelling said she guessed she better get used to putting in a day just watching Chris take off and come down, and Mrs. Peebles said she didn't know if she should suggest it because Alice Kelling was the one with the car, but the lake was only twenty-five miles away and what a good day for a picnic.

Alice Kelling took her up on the idea and by eleven o'clock they were in the car, with Joey and Heather and a sandwich lunch I had made. The only thing was that Chris hadn't come down, and she wanted to tell him where they were going.

"Edie'll go over and tell him," Mrs. Peebles said. "There's no problem."

Alice Kelling wrinkled her face and agreed.

"Be sure and tell him we'll be back by five!"

I didn't see that he would be concerned about knowing this right away, and I thought of him eating whatever he ate over there, alone, cooking on his camp stove, so I got to work and mixed up a crumb cake and baked it, in between the other work I had to do; then, when it was a bit cooled, wrapped it in a tea towel. I didn't do anything to myself but take off my apron and comb my hair. I would like to have put some makeup on, but I was too afraid it would remind him of the way he first saw me, and that would humiliate me all over again.

He had come and put another sign on the gate: NO RIDES THIS P.M. APOLOGIES. I worried that he wasn't feeling well. No sign of him outside and the tent flap was down. I knocked on the pole.

"Come in," he said, in a voice that would just as soon have said *Stay out.*

I lifted the flap.

"Oh, it's you. I'm sorry. I didn't know it was you."

He had been just sitting on the side of the bed, smoking. Why not at least sit and smoke in the fresh air?

"I brought a cake and hope you're not sick," I said.

"Why would I be sick? Oh—that sign. That's all right. I'm just tired of talking to people. I don't mean you. Have a seat." He pinned back the tent flap. "Get some fresh air in here."

I sat on the edge of the bed, there was no place else. It was one of those fold-up cots, really: I remembered and gave him his fiancée's message.

He ate some of the cake. "Good."

"Put the rest away for when you're hungry later."

"I'll tell you a secret. I won't be around here much longer."

"Are you getting married?"

"Ha ha. What time did you say they'd be back?"

"Five o'clock."

"Well, by that time this place will have seen the last of me. A plane can get further than a car." He unwrapped the cake and ate another piece of it, absent-mindedly.

"Now you'll be thirsty."

"There's some water in the pail."

"It won't be very cold. I could bring some fresh. I could bring some ice from the refrigerator."

"No," he said. "I don't want you to go. I want a nice long time of saying good-bye to you."

He put the cake away carefully and sat beside me and started those little kisses, so soft, I can't ever let myself think about them, such kindness in his face and lovely kisses, all over my eyelids and neck and ears, all over, then me kissing back as well as I could (I had only kissed a boy on a dare before, and kissed my own arms for practice) and we lay back on the cot and pressed together, just gently, and he did some other things, not bad things or not in a bad way. It was lovely in the tent, that smell of grass and hot tent cloth with the sun beating down on it, and he said, "I wouldn't do you any harm for the world." Once, when he had rolled on top of me and we were sort of rocking together on the cot, he said softly, "Oh, no," and freed himself and jumped up and got the water pail. He splashed some of it on his neck and face, and the little bit left, on me lying there.

"That's to cool us off, miss."

When we said good-bye I wasn't at all sad, because he held my face and said "I'm going to write you a letter. I'll tell you where I am and maybe you can come and see me. Would you like that? Okay then. You wait." I was really glad I think to get away from him, it was like he was piling presents on me I couldn't get the pleasure of till I considered them alone.

No consternation at first about the plane being gone. They thought he had taken somebody up, and I didn't enlighten them. Dr. Peebles had phoned he had to go to the country, so there was just us having supper, and then Loretta Bird thrusting her head in the door and saying, "I see he's took off."

"What?" said Alice Kelling, and pushed back her chair.

"The kids come and told me this afternoon he was taking down his tent. Did he think he'd run through all the business there was around here? He didn't take off without letting you know, did he?"

"He'll send me word," Alice Kelling said. "He'll probably phone tonight. He's terribly restless, since the war."

"Edie, he didn't mention to you, did he?" Mrs. Peebles said. "When you took over the message?"

"Yes," I said. So far so true.

"Well why didn't you say?" All of them were looking at me. "Did he say where he was going?"

"He said he might try Bayfield," I said. What made me tell such a lie? I didn't intend it.

"Bayfield, how far is that?" said Alice Kelling.

Mrs. Peebles said, "Thirty, thirty-five miles."

"That's not far. Oh, well, that's really not far at all. It's on the lake, isn't it?"

You'd think I'd be ashamed of myself, setting her on the wrong track. I did it to give him more time, whatever time he needed. I lied for him, and also, I have to admit, for me. Women should stick together and not do things like that. I see that now, but didn't then. I never thought of myself as being in any way like her, or coming to the same troubles, ever.

She hadn't taken her eyes off me. I thought she suspected my lie.

"When did he mention this to you?"

"Earlier."

"When you were over at the plane?"

"Yes."

"You must've stayed and had a chat." She smiled at me, not a nice smile. "You must've stayed and had a little visit with him."

"I took a cake," I said, thinking that telling some truth could spare me telling the rest.

"We didn't have a cake," said Mrs. Peebles rather sharply.

"I baked one."

Alice Kelling said, "That was very friendly of you."

"Did you get permission?" said Loretta Bird. "You never know what these girls'll do next," she said. "It's not they mean harm so much, as they're ignorant."

"The cake is neither here nor there," Mrs. Peebles broke in. "Edie, I wasn't aware you knew Chris that well."

I didn't know what to say.

"I'm not surprised," Alice Kelling said in a high voice. "I knew by the look of her as soon as I saw her. We get them at the hospital all the time." She looked hard at me with her stretched smile. "Having their babies. We have to put them in a special ward because of their diseases. Little country tramps. Fourteen and fifteen years old. You should see the babies they have, too."

"There was a bad woman here in town had a baby that pus was running out of its eyes," Loretta Bird put in.

"Wait a minute," said Mrs. Peebles. "What is this talk? Edie. What about you and Mr. Watters? Were you intimate with him?"

"Yes," I said. I was thinking of us lying on the cot and kissing, wasn't that intimate? And I would never deny it.

They were all one minute quiet, even Loretta Bird.

"Well," said Mrs. Peebles. "I am surprised. I think I need a cigarette. This is the first of any such tendencies I've seen in her," she said, speaking to Alice Kelling, but Alice Kelling was looking at me.

"Loose little bitch." Tears ran down her face. "Loose little bitch, aren't you? I knew as soon as I saw you. Men despise girls like you. He just made use of you and went off, you know that, don't you? Girls like you are just nothing, they're just public conveniences, just filthy little rags!"

"Oh, now," said Mrs. Peebles.

"Filthy," Alice Kelling sobbed. "Filthy little rag!"

"Don't get yourself upset," Loretta Bird said. She was swollen up with pleasure at being in on this scene. "Men are all the same."

"Edie, I'm very surprised," Mrs. Peebles said, "I thought your parents were so strict. You don't want to have a baby, do you?"

I'm still ashamed of what happened next. I lost control, just like a six-year-old, I started howling. "You don't get a baby from just doing that!"

"You see. Some of them are that ignorant," Loretta Bird said.

But Mrs. Peebles jumped up and caught my arms and shook me.

"Calm down. Don't get hysterical. Calm down. Stop crying. Listen to me. Listen. I'm wondering, if you know what being intimate means. Now tell me. What did you think it meant?"

"Kissing," I howled.

She let go. "Oh, Edie. Stop it. Don't be silly. It's all right. It's all a misunderstanding. Being intimate means a lot more than that. Oh, I *wondered*."

"She's trying to cover up, now," said Alice Kelling. "Yes. She's not so stupid. She sees she got herself in trouble."

"I believe her," Mrs. Peebles said. "This is an awful scene."

"Well there is one way to find out," said Alice Kelling, getting up. "After all, I am a nurse."

Mrs. Peebles drew a breath and said, "No. No. Go to your room, Edie. And stop that noise. This is too disgusting."

I heard the car start in a little while. I tried to stop crying, pulling back each wave as it started over me. Finally I succeeded, and lay heaving on the bed.

Mrs. Peebles came and stood in the doorway.

"She's gone," she said. "That Bird woman too. Of course, you know you should never have gone near that man and that is the cause of all this trouble. I have a headache. As soon as you can, go and wash your face in cold water and get at the dishes and we will not say any more about this."

Nor we didn't. I didn't figure out till years later the extent of what I had been saved from. Mrs. Peebles was not very friendly to me afterward, but she was fair. Not very friendly is the wrong way of describing what she was. She had never been very friendly. It was just that now she had to see me all the time and it got on her nerves, a little.

As for me, I put it all out of my mind like a bad dream and concentrated on waiting for my letter. The mail came every day except Sunday, between one-thirty and two in the afternoon, a good time for me because Mrs. Peebles was always having her nap. I would get the kitchen all cleaned and then go up the mailbox and sit in the grass, waiting. I was perfectly happy, waiting, I forgot all about Alice Kelling and her misery and awful talk and Mrs. Peebles and her chilliness and the embarrassment of whether she had told

Dr. Peebles and the face of Loretta Bird, getting her fill of other people's troubles. I was always smiling when the mailman got there, and continued smiling even after he gave me the mail and I saw today wasn't the day. The mailman was a Carmichael. I knew by his face because there are a lot of Carmichaels living out by us and so many of them have a sort of sticking-out top lip. So I asked his name (he was a young man, shy, but good-humored, anybody could ask him anything) and then I said, "I knew by your face!" He was pleased by that and always glad to see me and got a little less shy. "You've got the smile I've been waiting on all day!" he used to holler out the car window.

It never crossed my mind for a long time a letter might not come. I believed in it coming just like I believed the sun would rise in the morning. I just put off my hope from day to day, and there was the goldenrod out around the mailbox and the children gone back to school, and the leaves turning, and I was wearing a sweater when I went to wait. One day walking back with the hydro bill stuck in my hand, that was all, looking across at the fairgrounds with the full-blown milkweed and dark teasels, so much like fall, it just struck me: *No letter was ever going to come.* It was an impossible idea to get used to. No, not impossible. If I thought about Chris's face when he said he was going to write to me, it was impossible, but if I forgot that and thought about the actual tin mailbox, empty, it was plain and true. I kept on going to meet the mail, but my heart was heavy now like a lump of lead. I only smiled because I thought of the mailman counting on it, and he didn't have an easy life, with the winter driving ahead.

Till it came to me one day there were women doing this with their lives, all over. There were women just waiting and waiting by mailboxes for one letter or another. I imagined me making this journey day after day and year after year, and my hair starting to go gray, and I thought, I was never made to go on like that. So I stopped meeting the mail. If there were women all through life waiting, and women busy and not waiting, I knew which I had to be. Even though there might be things the second kind of women have to pass up and never know about, it still is better.

I was surprised when the mailman phoned the Peebleses' place in the evening and asked for me. He said he missed me. He asked if I would like to go to Goderich, where some well-known movie was on, I forgot now what. So I said yes, and I went out with him for two years and he asked me to marry him, and we were engaged a year more while I got my things together, and then we did marry. He always tells the children the story of how I went after him by sitting by the mailbox every day, and naturally I laugh and let him, because I like for people to think what pleases them and makes them happy.

QUESTIONS FOR DISCUSSION AND WRITING

1. How does the pilot complicate the established routine of Edie's work at the Peebles's farm? How does Alice's arrival bring that complication to a crisis? How does the mailman provide a satisfactory resolution to the crisis?
2. How does Edie characterize the three other women in the story—Mrs. Peebles, Loretta Bird, and Alice Kelling? How does she distinguish herself from these women? How do the three women characterize Edie?

3. What assumptions does Edie make about country life and city life? In what ways does the Peebles's farm house contradict those assumptions?
4. Although the point of view in this story is first person, it is told retrospectively, some years after the events take place. How does this perspective affect the way Edie sees herself as a fifteen-year-old girl? How does Edie's husband tell the story of how they met?
5. In what way does the title provide a satisfactory explanation of the story's theme? Why, from Edie's point of view, will Carmichael make a better husband than Chris?

68

JOYCE CAROL OATES

Where Are You Going, Where Have You Been?

JOYCE CAROL OATES was born in 1938 in Lockport, New York, and educated at Syracuse University and the University of Wisconsin. Even as an undergraduate, Oates was a prolific writer, winning the 1959 *Mademoiselle* college fiction award for her short story "In the Old World." While she was a graduate student, Oates published stories in magazines such as *Cosmopolitan, Prairie Schooner,* and *The Literary Review*. She accepted her first teaching assignment at the University of Detroit and then moved to the University of Windsor in Ontario, where she taught and wrote for twelve years. Since 1978 she has been a member of the faculty at Princeton University. By any standards, Oates's literary productivity has been astonishing. By 1982 she had published almost forty books, including over a dozen novels and about one hundred short stories. She has also written several volumes of literary criticism, such as *New Haven, New Earth: The Visionary Experience in Literature* (1974), a study of Henry James, Virginia Woolf, D. H. Lawrence, Franz Kafka, and Flannery O'Connor, authors who, like Oates, try to fuse the materialistic and symbolic worlds. Oates's best-known novels include *A Garden of Earthly Delights* (1967), *Them* (1969)—which won the National Book Award, *Wonderland* (1971), *Do with Me What You Will* (1973), *Childwold* (1976), *Angel of Light* (1981), *A Bloodsmoor Romance* (1982), *You Must Remember This* (1987), and *Black Water* (1992). Her short stories have been published in a wide range of magazines and collected in volumes such as *By the North Gate* (1963), *The Wheel of Love* (1970), *Marriages and Infidelities* (1972), *Nightside* (1977), *A Sentimental Education* (1980), and *Last*

Days (1984). "Where Are You Going, Where Have You Been?" is reprinted from _The Wheel of Love,_ and describes a girl's terrifying encounter with a demonic figure from a drive-in restaurant. "The Lady with the Pet Dog," reprinted from _Marriages and Infidelities,_ describes a woman's attempt to redefine herself in a romantic affair.

Her name was Connie. She was fifteen and she had a quick nervous giggling habit of craning her neck to glance into mirrors or checking other people's faces to make sure her own was all right. Her mother, who noticed everything and knew everything and who hadn't much reason any longer to look at her own face, always scolded Connie about it. "Stop gawking at yourself, who are you? You think you're so pretty?" she would say. Connie would raise her eyebrows at these familiar complaints and look right through her mother, into a shadowy vision of herself as she was right at that moment: she knew she was pretty and that was everything. Her mother had been pretty once too, if you could believe those old snapshots in the album, but now her looks were gone and that was why she was always after Connie.

"Why don't you keep your room clean like your sister? How've you got your hair fixed—what the hell stinks? Hair spray? You don't see your sister using that junk."

Her sister June was twenty-four and still lived at home. She was a secretary in the high school Connie attended, and if that wasn't bad enough—with her in the same building—she was so plain and chunky and steady that Connie had to hear her praised all the time by her mother and her mother's sisters. June did this, June did that, she saved money and helped clean the house and cooked and Connie couldn't do a thing, her mind was all filled with trashy daydreams. Their father was away at work most of the time and when he came home he wanted supper and he read the newspaper at supper and after supper he went to bed. He didn't bother talking much to them, but around his bent head Connie's mother kept picking at her until Connie wished her mother were dead and she herself were dead and it were all over. "She makes me want to throw up sometimes," she complained to her friends. She had a high, breathless, amused voice which made everything she said sound a little forced, whether it was sincere or not.

There was one good thing: June went places with girlfriends of hers, girls who were just as plain and steady as she, and so when Connie wanted to do that her mother had no objections. The father of Connie's best girlfriend drove the girls the three miles to town and left them off at a shopping plaza, so that they could walk through the stores or go to a movie, and when he came to pick them up again at eleven he never bothered to ask what they had done.

They must have been familiar sights, walking around that shopping plaza in their shorts and flat ballerina slippers that always scuffed the sidewalk, with charm bracelets jingling on their thin wrists; they would lean together to whisper and laugh secretly if someone passed by who amused or interested them. Connie had long dark blond hair that drew anyone's eye to it, and she wore part of it pulled up on her head and puffed out and the rest of it she let fall down her back. She wore a pullover jersey blouse that looked one way when she was at home and another way when she was away from home. Everything about her had two sides to it, one for home and one for anywhere that was not home: her walk that could be childlike and bobbing, or languid enough to make anyone think she was hearing music in her head, her mouth which was pale and smirking most of the time, but bright and pink on these evenings out, her laugh which was cynical and drawling at home—"Ha, ha, very funny"—but high-pitched and nervous anywhere else, like the jingling of the charms on her bracelet.

Sometimes they did go shopping or to a movie. But sometimes they went across the highway, ducking fast across the busy road, to a drive-in restaurant where older kids hung out. The restaurant was shaped like a big bottle, though squatter than a real bottle, and on its cap was a revolving figure of a grinning boy who held a hamburger aloft. One night in midsummer they ran across, breathless with daring, and right away someone leaned out a car window and invited them over, but it was just a boy from high school they didn't like. It made them feel good to be able to ignore him. They went up through the maze of parked and cruising cars to the bright-lit, fly-infested restaurant, their faces pleased and expectant as if they were entering a sacred building that loomed out of the night to give them what haven and what blessing they yearned for. They sat at the counter and crossed their legs at the ankles, their thin shoulders rigid with excitement, and listened to the music that made everything so good: the music was always in the background like music at a church service, it was something to depend upon.

A boy named Eddie came in to talk with them. He sat backward on his stool, turning himself jerkily around in semicircles and then stopping and turning again, and after a while he asked Connie if she would like something to eat. She said she did and so she tapped her friend's arm on her way out—her friend pulled her face up into a brave droll look—and Connie said she would meet her at eleven, across the way. "I just hate to leave her like that,"Connie said earnestly, but the boy said that she wouldn't be alone for long. So they went out to his car and on the way Connie couldn't help but let her eyes wander over the windshields and faces all around her, her face gleaming with a joy that had nothing to do with Eddie or even this place; it might have been the music. She drew her shoulders up and sucked in her breath with the pure pleasure of being alive, and just at that moment she happened to glance at a face just a few feet from hers. It was a boy with shaggy black hair, in a convertible jalopy painted gold. He stared at her and then his lips widened into a grin. Connie slit her eyes at him and turned away, but she couldn't help glancing back and there he was still watching her. He wagged a finger and laughed and said, "Gonna get you, baby," and Connie turned away again without Eddie noticing anything.

She spent three hours with him, at the restaurant where they ate hamburgers and drank Cokes in wax cups that were always sweating, and then down an alley a mile or so away, and when he left her off at five to eleven only the movie house was still open at the plaza. Her girlfriend was there, talking with a boy. When Connie came up the two girls smiled at each other and Connie said, "How was the movie?" and the girl said, "*You* should know." They rode off with the girl's father, sleepy and pleased, and Connie couldn't help but look at the darkened shopping plaza with its big empty parking lot and its signs that were faded and ghostly now, and over at the drive-in restaurant where cars were still circling tirelessly. She couldn't hear the music at this distance.

Next morning June asked her how the movie was and Connie said, "So-so."

She and that girl and occasionally another girl went out several times a week that way, and the rest of the time Connie spent around the house—it was summer vacation—getting in her mother's way and thinking, dreaming, about the boys she met. But all the boys fell back and dissolved into a single face that was not even a face, but an idea, a feeling, mixed up with the urgent insistent pounding of the music and the humid night air of July. Connie's mother kept dragging her back to the daylight by finding things for her to do or saying, suddenly, "What's this about the Pettinger girl?"

And Connie would say nervously, "Oh, her. That dope." She always drew thick clear lines between herself and such girls, and her mother was simple and kindly enough to believe her. Her mother was so simple, Connie thought, that it was maybe cruel to fool her so much. Her mother went scuffling around the house in old bedroom slippers and complained over the telephone to one sister about the other, then the other called up and the two of them complained about the third one. If June's name was mentioned her mother's tone was approving, and if Connie's name was mentioned it was disapproving. This did not really mean she disliked Connie and actually Connie thought that her mother preferred her to June because she was prettier, but the two of them kept up a pretense of exasperation, a sense that they were tugging and struggling over something of little value to either of them. Sometimes, over coffee, they were almost friends, but something would come up—some vexation that was like a fly buzzing suddenly around their heads—and their faces went hard with contempt.

One Sunday Connie got up at eleven—none of them bothered with church—and washed her hair so that it could dry all day long, in the sun. Her parents and sister were going to a barbecue at an aunt's house and Connie said no, she wasn't interested, rolling her eyes to let her mother know just what she thought of it. "Stay home alone then," her mother said sharply. Connie sat out back in a lawn chair and watched them drive away, her father quiet and bald, hunched around so that he could back the car out, her mother with a look that was still angry and not at all softened through the windshield, and in the back seat poor old June all dressed up as if she didn't know what a barbecue was, with all the running yelling kids and the flies. Connie sat with her eyes closed in the sun, dreaming and dazed with the warmth about her as if this were a kind of love, the caresses of love, and her mind slipped over onto thoughts of the boy she had been with the night before and how nice he had been, how sweet it always was, not the way someone like June would suppose but sweet, gentle, the way it was in movies and promised in songs; and when she opened her eyes she hardly knew where she was, the back yard ran off into weeds and a fence line of trees and behind it the sky was perfectly blue and still. The asbestos "ranch house" that was now three years old startled her—it looked small. She shook her head as if to get awake.

It was too hot. She went inside the house and turned on the radio to drown out the quiet. She sat on the edge of her bed, barefoot, and listened for an hour and a half to a program called XYZ Sunday Jamboree, record after record of hard, fast, shrieking songs she sang along with, interspersed by exclamations from "Bobby King": "An' look here you girls at Napoleon's—Son and Charley want you to pay real close attention to this song coming up!"

And Connie paid close attention herself, bathed in a glow of slow-pulsed joy that seemed to rise mysteriously out of the music itself and lay languidly about the airless little room, breathed in and breathed out with each gentle rise and fall of her chest.

After a while she heard a car coming up the drive. She sat up at once, startled, because it couldn't be her father so soon. The gravel kept crunching all the way in from the road—the driveway was long—and Connie ran to the window. It was a car she didn't know. It was an open jalopy, painted a bright gold that caught the sunlight opaquely. Her heart began to pound and her fingers snatched at her hair, checking it, and she whispered "Christ, Christ," wondering how bad she looked. The car came to a stop at the side door and the horn sounded four short taps as if this were a signal Connie knew.

She went into the kitchen and approached the door slowly, then hung out the screen door, her bare toes curling down off the step. There were two boys in the car and now she recognized the driver: he had shaggy, shabby black hair that looked crazy as a wig and he was grinning at her.

"I ain't late, am I?" he said.

"Who the hell do you think you are?" Connie said.

"Toldja I'd be out, didn't I?"

"I don't even know who you are."

She spoke sullenly, careful to show no interest or pleasure, and he spoke in a fast bright monotone. Connie looked past him to the other boy, taking her time. He had fair brown hair, with a lock that fell onto his forehead. His sideburns gave him a fierce, embarrassed look, but so far he hadn't even bothered to glance at her. Both boys wore sunglasses. The driver's glasses were metallic and mirrored everything in miniature.

"You wanta come for a ride?" he said.

Connie smirked and let her hair fall loose over one shoulder.

"Don'tcha like my car? New paint job," he said. "Hey."

"What?"

"You're cute."

She pretended to fidget, chasing flies away from the door.

"Don'tcha believe me, or what?" he said.

"Look, I don't even know who you are," Connie said in disgust.

"Hey, Ellie's got a radio, see. Mine's broken down." He lifted his friend's arm and showed her the little transistor the boy was holding, and now Connie began to hear the music. It was the same program that was playing inside the house.

"Bobby King?" she said.

"I listen to him all the time. I think he's great."

"He's kind of great," Connie said reluctantly.

"Listen, that guy's *great*. He knows where the action is."

Connie blushed a little, because the glasses made it impossible for her to see just what this boy was looking at. She couldn't decide if she liked him or if he was just a jerk, and so she dawdled in the doorway and wouldn't come down or go back inside. She said, "What's all that stuff painted on your car?"

"Can'tcha read it?" He opened the door very carefully, as if he was afraid it might fall off. He slid out just as carefully, planting his feet firmly on the ground, the tiny metallic world in his glasses slowing down like gelatine hardening and in the midst of it Connie's bright green blouse. "This here is my name, to begin with," he said. ARNOLD FRIEND was written in tarlike black letters on the side, with a drawing of a round grinning face that reminded Connie of a pumpkin, except it wore sunglasses. "I wanta introduce myself, I'm Arnold Friend and that's my real name and I'm gonna be your friend, honey, and inside the car's Ellie Oscar, he's kinda shy." Ellie brought his transistor radio up to his shoulder and balanced it there. "Now these numbers are a secret code, honey," Arnold Friend explained. He read off the numbers 33, 19, 17 and raised his eyebrows at her to see what she thought of that, but she didn't think much of it. The left rear fender had been smashed and around it was written, on the gleaming gold background: DONE BY CRAZY WOMAN DRIVER. Connie had to laugh at that. Arnold Friend was pleased at her laughter and looked up at her. "Around the other side's a lot more—you wanta come and see them?"

"No."

"Why not?"

"Why should I?"

"Don'tcha wanta see what's on the car? Don'tcha wanta go for a ride?"

"I don't know."

"Why not?"

"I got things to do."

"Like what?"

"Things."

He laughed as if she had said something funny. He slapped his thighs. He was standing in a strange way, leaning back against the car as if he were balancing himself. He wasn't tall, only an inch or so taller than she would be if she came down to him. Connie liked the way he was dressed, which was the way all of them dressed; tight faded jeans stuffed into black, scuffed boots, a belt that pulled his waist in and showed how lean he was, and a white pullover shirt that was a little soiled and showed the hard small muscles of his arms and shoulders. He looked as if he probably did hard work, lifting and carrying things. Even his neck looked muscular. And his face was a familiar face, somehow: the jaw and chin and cheeks slightly darkened, because he hadn't shaved for a day or two, and the nose long and hawklike, sniffing as if she were a treat he was going to gobble up and it was all a joke.

"Connie, you ain't telling the truth. This is your day set aside for a ride with me and you know it," he said, still laughing. The way he straightened and recovered from his fit of laughing showed that it had been all fake.

"How do you know what my name is?" she said suspiciously.

"It's Connie."

"Maybe and maybe not."

"I know my Connie," he said, wagging his finger. Now she remembered him even better, back at the restaurant, and her cheeks warmed at the thought of how she sucked in her breath just at the moment she passed him—how she must have looked at him. And he had remembered her. "Ellie and I come out here especially for you," he said. "Ellie can sit in back. How about it?"

"Where?"

"Where what?"

"Where're we going?"

He looked at her. He took off the sunglasses and she saw how pale the skin around his eyes was, like holes that were not in shadow but instead in light. His eyes were like chips of broken glass that catch the light in an amiable way. He smiled. It was as if the idea of going for a ride somewhere, to some place, was a new idea to him.

"Just for a ride, Connie sweetheart."

"I never said my name was Connie," she said.

"But I know what it is. I know your name and all about you, lots of things," Arnold Friend said. He had not moved yet but stood still leaning back against the side of his jalopy. "I took a special interest in you, such a pretty girl, and found out all about you—like I know your parents and sister are gone somewhere and I know where and how long they're going to be gone, and I know who you were with last night, and your best girlfriend's name is Betty. Right?"

He spoke in a simple lilting voice, exactly as if he were reciting the words to a song. His smile assured her that everything was fine. In the car Ellie turned up the volume on his radio and did not bother to look around at them.

"Ellie can sit in the back seat," Arnold Friend said. He indicated his friend with a casual jerk of his chin, as if Ellie did not count and she should not bother with him.

"How'd you find out all that stuff?" Connie said.

"Listen: Betty Schultz and Tony Fitch and Jimmy Pettinger and Nancy Pettinger," he said, in a chant. "Raymond Stanley and Bob Hutter—"

"Do you know all those kids?"

"I know everybody."

"Look, you're kidding. You're not from around here."

"Sure."

"But—how come we never saw you before?"

"Sure you saw me before," he said. He looked down at his boots, as if he were a little offended. "You just don't remember."

"I guess I'd remember you," Connie said.

"Yeah?" He looked up at this, beaming. He was pleased. He began to mark time with the music from Ellie's radio, tapping his fists lightly together. Connie looked away from his smile to the car, which was painted so bright it almost hurt her eyes to look at it. She looked at that name, ARNOLD FRIEND. And up at the front fender was an expression that was familiar—MAN THE FLYING SAUCERS. It was an expression kids had used the year before, but didn't use this year. She looked at it for a while as if the words meant something to her that she did not yet know.

"What're you thinking about? Huh?" Arnold Friend demanded. "Not worried about your hair blowing around in the car, are you?"

"No."

"Think I maybe can't drive good?"

"How do I know?"

"You're a hard girl to handle. How come?" he said. "Don't you know I'm your friend? Didn't you see me put my sign in the air when you walked by?"

"What sign?"

"My sign." And he drew an X in the air, leaning out toward her. They were maybe ten feet apart. After his hand fell back to his side the X was still in the air, almost visible. Connie let the screen door close and stood perfectly still inside it, listening to the music from her radio and the boy's blend together. She stared at Arnold Friend. He stood there so stiffly relaxed, pretending to be relaxed, with one hand idly on the door handle as if he were keeping himself up that way and had no intention of ever moving again. She recognized most things about him, the tight jeans that showed his thighs and buttocks and the greasy leather boots and the tight shirt, and even that slippery friendly smile of his, that sleepy dreamy smile that all the boys used to get across ideas they didn't want to put into words. She recognized all this and also the singsong way he talked, slightly mocking, kidding, but serious and a little melancholy, and she recognized the way he tapped one fist against the other in homage of the perpetual music behind him. But all these things did not come together.

She said suddenly, "Hey, how old are you?"

His smile faded. She could see then that he wasn't a kid, he was much older—thirty, maybe more. At this knowledge her heart began to pound faster.

"That's a crazy thing to ask. Can'tcha see I'm your own age?"

"Like hell you are."

"Or maybe a coupla years older. I'm eighteen."

"Eighteen?" she said doubtfully.

He grinned to reassure her and lines appeared at the corners of his mouth. His teeth were big and white. He grinned so broadly his eyes became slits and she saw how thick the lashes were, thick and black as if painted with a black tarlike material. Then he seemed to become embarrassed, abruptly, and looked over his shoulder at Ellie. "*Him,* he's crazy," he said. "Ain't he a riot, he's a nut, a real character." Ellie was still listening to the music. His sunglasses told nothing about what he was thinking. He wore a bright orange shirt unbuttoned halfway to show his chest, which was a pale, bluish chest and not muscular like Arnold Friend's. His shirt collar was turned up all around and the very tips of the collar pointed out past his chin as if they were protecting him. He was pressing the transistor radio up against his ear and sat there in a kind of daze, right in the sun.

"He's kinda strange," Connie said.

"Hey, she says you're kinda strange! Kinda strange!" Arnold Friend cried. He pounded on the car to get Ellie's attention. Ellie turned for the first time and Connie saw with shock that he wasn't a kid either—he had a fair, hairless face, cheeks reddened slightly as if the veins grew too close to the surface of his skin, the face of a forty-year-old baby. Connie felt a wave of dizziness rise in her at this sight and she stared at him as if waiting for something to change the shock of the moment, make it all right again. Ellie's lips kept shaping words, mumbling along with the words blasting in his ear.

"Maybe you two better go away," Connie said faintly.

"What? How come?" Arnold Friend cried. "We come out here to take you for a ride. It's Sunday." He had the voice of the man on the radio now. It was the same voice, Connie thought. "Don'tcha know it's Sunday all day and honey, no matter who you were with last night today you're with Arnold Friend and don't you forget it!—Maybe you better step out here," he said, and this last was in a different voice. It was a little flatter, as if the heat was finally getting to him.

"No. I got things to do."

"Hey."

"You two better leave."

"We ain't leaving until you come with us."

"Like hell I am—"

"Connie, don't fool around with me. I mean, I mean, don't fool *around,*" he said, shaking his head. He laughed incredulously. He placed his sunglasses on top of his head, carefully, as if he were indeed wearing a wig, and brought the stems down behind his ears. Connie stared at him, another wave of dizziness and fear rising in her so that for a moment he wasn't even in focus but was just a blur, standing there against his gold car, and she had the idea that he had driven up the driveway all right but had come from nowhere before that and belonged nowhere and that everything about him and even about the music that was so familiar to her was only half real.

"If my father comes and sees you—"

"He ain't coming. He's at a barbecue."

"How do you know that?"

"Aunt Tillie's. Right now they're—uh—they're drinking. Sitting around," he said vaguely, squinting as if he were staring all the way to town and over to Aunt Tillie's back yard. Then the vision seemed to get clear and he nodded energetically. "Yeah. Sitting around. There's your sister in a blue dress, huh? And high heels, the poor sad bitch—nothing like you, sweetheart! And your mother's helping some fat woman with the corn, they're cleaning the corn—husking the corn—"

"What fat woman?" Connie cried.

"How do I know what fat woman, I don't know every goddam fat woman in the world!" Arnold laughed.

"Oh, that's Mrs. Hornby . . . Who invited her?" Connie said. She felt a little lightheaded. Her breath was coming quickly.

"She's too fat. I don't like them fat. I like them the way you are, honey," he said, smiling sleepily at her. They stared at each other for a while, through the screen door. He said softly, "Now what you're going to do is this: you're going to come out that door. You're going to sit up front with me and Ellie's going to sit in the back, the hell with Ellie, right? This isn't Ellie's date. You're my date. I'm your lover, honey."

"What? You're crazy—"

"Yes, I'm your lover. You don't know what that is, but you will," he said. "I know that too. I know all about you. But look: it's real nice and you couldn't ask for nobody better than me, or more polite. I always keep my word. I'll tell you how it is, I'm always nice at first, the first time. I'll hold you so tight you won't think you have to try to get away or pretend anything because you'll know you can't. And I'll come inside you where it's all secret and you'll give in to me and you'll love me—"

"Shut up! You're crazy!" Connie said. She backed away from the door. She put her hands against her ears as if she'd heard something terrible, something not meant for her. "People don't talk like that, you're crazy," she muttered. Her heart was almost too big now for her chest and its pumping made sweat break out all over her. She looked out to see Arnold Friend pause and then take a step toward the porch lurching. He almost fell. But, like a clever drunken man, he managed to catch his balance. He wobbled in his high boots and grabbed hold of one of the porch posts.

"Honey?" he said. "You still listening?"

"Get the hell out of here!"

"Be nice, honey. Listen."

"I'm going to call the police—"

He wobbled again and out of the side of his mouth came a fast spat curse, an aside not meant for her to hear. But even this "Christ!" sounded forced. Then he began to smile again. She watched this smile come, awkward as if he were smiling from inside a mask. His whole face was a mask, she thought wildly, tanned down onto his throat but then running out as if he had plastered makeup on his face but had forgotten about his throat.

"Honey—? Listen, here's how it is. I always tell the truth and I promise you this: I ain't coming in that house after you."

"You better not! I'm going to call the police if you—if you don't—"

"Honey," he said, talking right through her voice, "honey, I'm not coming in there but you are coming out here. You know why?"

She was panting. The kitchen looked like a place she had never seen before, some room she had run inside but which wasn't good enough, wasn't going to help her. The kitchen window had never had a curtain, after three years, and there were dishes in the sink for her to do—probably—and if you ran your hand across the table you'd probably feel something sticky there.

"You listening, honey? Hey?"

"—going to call the police—"

"Soon as you touch the phone I don't need to keep my promise and can come inside. You won't want that."

She rushed forward and tried to lock the door. Her fingers were shaking. "But why lock it," Arnold Friend said gently, talking right into her face. "It's just a screen door. It's just nothing." One of his boots was at a strange angle, as if his foot wasn't in it. It pointed out to the left, bent at the ankle. "I mean, anybody can break through a screen door and glass and wood and iron or anything else if he needs to, anybody at all and specially Arnold Friend. If the place got lit up with a fire honey you'd come runnin' out into my arms, right into my arms an' safe at home—like you knew I was your lover and'd stopped fooling around. I don't mind a nice shy girl but I don't like no fooling around." Part of those words were spoken with a slight rhythmic lilt, and Connie somehow recognized them—the echo of a song from last year, about a girl rushing into her boyfriend's arms and coming home again—

Connie stood barefoot on the linoleum floor, staring at him. "What do you want?" she whispered.

"I want you," he said.

"What?"

"Seen you that night and thought, that's the one, yes sir. I never needed to look any more."

"But my father's coming back. He's coming to get me. I had to wash my hair first—" She spoke in a dry, rapid voice, hardly raising it for him to hear.

"No, your Daddy is not coming and yes, you had to wash your hair and you washed it for me. It's nice and shining and all for me, I thank you, sweetheart," he said, with a mock bow, but again he almost lost his balance. He had to bend and adjust his boots. Evidently his feet did not go all the way down; the boots must have been stuffed with something so that he would seem taller. Connie stared out at him and behind him Ellie in the car, who seemed to be looking off toward Connie's right into nothing. This Ellie said, pulling the words out of the air one after another as if he were just discovering them, "You want me to pull out the phone?"

"Shut your mouth and keep it shut," Arnold Friend said, his face red from bending over or maybe from embarrassment because Connie had seen his boots. "This ain't none of your business."

"What—what are you doing? What do you want?" Connie said. "If I call the police they'll get you, they'll arrest you—"

"Promise was not to come in unless you touch that phone, and I'll keep that promise," he said. He resumed his erect position and tried to force his shoulders back. He sounded like a hero in a movie, declaring something important. He spoke too loudly and it was as if he were speaking to someone behind Connie."I ain't made plans for coming in that house where I don't belong but just for you to come out to me, the way you should. Don't you know who I am?"

"You're crazy," she whispered. She backed away from the door but did not want to go into another part of the house, as if this would give him permission to come through the door. "What do you . . . You're crazy, you . . ."

"Huh? What're you saying, honey?"

Her eyes darted everywhere in the kitchen. She could not remember what it was, this room.

"This is how it is, honey; you come out and we'll drive away, have a nice ride. But if you don't come out we're gonna wait till your people come home and then they're all going to get it."

"You want that telephone pulled out?" Ellie said. He held the radio away from his ear and grimaced, as if without the radio the air was too much for him.

"I toldja shut up, Ellie," Arnold Friend said, "you're deaf, get a hearing aid, right? Fix yourself up. This little girl's no trouble and's gonna be nice to me, so Ellie keep to yourself, this ain't your date—right? Don't hem in on me. Don't hog. Don't crush. Don't bird dog. Don't trail me," he said in a rapid meaningless voice, as if he were running through all the expressions he'd learned but was no longer sure which one of them was in style, then rushing on to new ones, making them up with his eyes closed, "Don't crawl under my fence, don't squeeze in my chipmunk hole, don't sniff my glue, suck my popsicle, keep your own greasy fingers on yourself!" He shaded his eyes and peered in at Connie, who was backed against the kitchen table. "Don't mind him honey he's just a creep. He's a dope. Right? I'm the boy for you and like I said you come out here nice like a lady and give me your hand, and nobody else gets hurt, I mean, your nice old bald-headed daddy and your mummy and your sister in her high heels. Because listen: why bring them in this?"

"Leave me alone," Connie whispered.

"Hey, you know that old woman down the road, the one with the chickens and stuff—you know her?"

"She's dead!"

"Dead? What? You know her?" Arnold Friend said.

"She's dead—"

"Don't you like her?"

"She dead—she's—she isn't here any more—"

"But don't you like her, I mean, you got something against her? Some grudge or something?" Then his voice dipped as if he were conscious of a rudeness. He touched the sunglasses perched on top of his head as if to make sure they were still there. "Now you be a good girl."

"What are you going to do?"

"Just two things, or maybe three," Arnold Friend said. "But I promise it won't last long and you'll like me the way you get to like people you're close to. You will. It's all over for you here, so come on out. You don't want your people in any trouble, do you?"

She turned and bumped against a chair or something, hurting her leg, but she ran into the back room and picked up the telephone. Something roared in her ear, a tiny roaring, and she was so sick with fear that she could do nothing but listen to it—the telephone was clammy and very heavy and her fingers groped down to the dial but were too weak to touch it. She began to scream into the phone, into the roaring. She cried out, she cried for her mother, she felt her breath start jerking back and forth in her lungs as if it were something Arnold Friend were stabbing her with again and again with no tenderness. A noisy sorrowful wailing rose all about her and she was locked inside it the way she was locked inside this house.

After a while she could hear again. She was sitting on the floor with her wet back against the wall.

Arnold Friend was saying from the door, "That's a good girl. Put the phone back."

She kicked the phone away from her.

"No, honey. Pick it up. Put it back right."

She picked it up and put it back. The dial tone stopped.

"That's a good girl. Now you come outside."

She was hollow with what had been fear, but what was now just an emptiness. All that screaming had blasted it out of her. She sat, one leg cramped under her, and deep inside her brain was something like a pinpoint of light that kept going and would not let her relax. She thought, I'm not going to see my mother again. She thought, I'm not going to sleep in my bed again. Her bright green blouse was all wet.

Arnold Friend said, in a gentle-loud voice that was like a stage voice, "The place where you came from ain't there any more, and where you had in mind to go is canceled out. This place you are now—inside your daddy's house—is nothing but a cardboard box I can knock down any time. You know that and always did know it. You hear me?"

She thought, I have got to think. I have to know what to do.

"We'll go out to a nice field, out in the country here where it smells so nice and it's sunny," Arnold Friend said. "I'll have my arms tight around you so you won't need to try to get away and I'll show you what love is like, what it does. The hell with this house! It looks solid all right," he said. He ran a fingernail down the screen and the noise did not make Connie shiver, as it would have the day before. "Now put your hand on your heart, honey. Feel that? That feels solid too, but we know better, be nice to me, be sweet like you can because what else is there for a girl like you but to be sweet and pretty and give in?—and get away before her people come back?"

She felt her pounding heart. Her hand seemed to enclose it. She thought for the first time in her life that it was nothing that was hers, that belonged to her, but just a pounding, living thing inside this body that wasn't really hers either.

"You don't want them to get hurt," Arnold Friend went on. "Now get up, honey. Get up all by yourself."

She stood.

"Now turn this way. That's right. Come over here to me—Ellie, put that away, didn't I tell you? You dope. You miserable creepy dope," Arnold Friend said. His words were not angry but only part of an incantation. The incantation was kindly. "Now come out through the kitchen to me honey, and let's see a smile, try it, you're a brave sweet little girl and now they're eating corn and hot dogs cooked to bursting over an outdoor fire, and they don't know one thing about you and never did and honey you're better than them because not a one of them would have done this for you."

Connie felt the linoleum under her feet; it was cool. She brushed her hair back out of her eyes. Arnold Friend let go of the post tentatively and opened his arms for her, his elbows pointing in toward each other and his wrists limp, to show that this was an embarrassed embrace and a little mocking, he didn't want to make her self-conscious.

She put out her hand against the screen. She watched herself push the door slowly open as if she were safe back somewhere in the other doorway, watching this body and this head of long hair moving out into the sunlight where Arnold Friend waited.

"My sweet little blue-eyed girl," he said, in a half-sung sigh that had nothing to do with her brown eyes but was taken up just the same by the vast sunlit reaches of the land behind him and on all sides of him, so much land that Connie had never seen before and did not recognize except to know that she was going to it.

QUESTIONS FOR DISCUSSION AND WRITING

1. How do Connie's trashy daydreams lead inevitably to her meeting with a person such as Arnold Friend? What "promise" does Arnold make to Connie? How does Connie's attempt to call for help bring the plot to its climax?
2. How does the opening paragraph of the story establish Connie's character? How does Arnold's car embody his personality? How does Connie's perception of Arnold change once she realizes that he is not a kid?
3. Why is the drive-in restaurant an appropriate place for Connie's first encounter with Arnold? How does the screen door of Connie's house suggest the precariousness of her situation?
4. How does Connie's recognition that "everything about her had two sides to it" clarify her point of view toward Arnold? How does the author use the music on Ellie's radio to underscore Connie's increasing sense of terror?
5. How does the title of the story comment on its theme? What prompts Connie to go with Arnold to the land that she "had never seen before"?

69

JOYCE CAROL OATES

The Lady with the Pet Dog

1

Strangers parted as if to make way for him.

There he stood. He was there in the aisle, a few yards away, watching her.

She leaned forward at once in her seat, her hand jerked up to her face as if to ward off a blow—but then the crowd in the aisle hid him, he was gone. She pressed both hands against her cheeks. He was not there, she had imagined him.

"My God," she whispered.

She was alone. Her husband had gone out to the foyer to make a telephone call; it was intermission at the concert, a Thursday evening.

Now she saw him again, clearly. He was standing there. He was staring at her. Her blood rocked in her body, draining out of her head . . . she was going to faint. . . . They stared at each other. They gave no sign of recognition. Only when he took a step forward did she shake her head *no—no—keep away.* It was not possible.

When her husband returned, she was staring at the place in the aisle where her lover had been standing. Her husband leaned forward to interrupt that stare.

"What's wrong?" he said. "Are you sick?"

Panic rose in her in long shuddering waves. She tried to get to her feet, panicked at the thought of fainting here, and her husband took hold of her. She stood like an aged woman, clutching the seat before her.

At home he helped her up the stairs and she lay down. Her head was like a large piece of crockery that had to be held still, it was so heavy. She was still panicked. She felt it in the shallows of her face, behind her knees, in the pit of her stomach. It sickened her, it made her think of mucus, of something thick and gray congested inside her, stuck to her, that was herself and yet not herself—a poison.

She lay with her knees drawn up toward her chest, her eyes hotly open, while her husband spoke to her. She imagined that other man saying, *Why did you run away from me?* Her husband was saying other words. She tried to listen to them. He was going to call the doctor, he said, and she tried to sit up. "No, I'm all right now," she said quickly. The panic was like lead inside her, so thickly congested. How slow love was to drain out of her, how fluid and sticky it was inside her head!

Her husband believed her. No doctor. No threat. Grateful, she drew her husband down to her. They embraced, not comfortably. For years now they had not been comfortable together, in their intimacy and at a distance, and now they struggled gently as if the paces of this dance were too rigorous for them. It was something they might have known once, but had now outgrown. The panic in her thickened at this double betrayal:

she drew her husband to her, she caressed him wildly, she shut her eyes to think about that other man.

A crowd of men and women parting, unexpectedly, and there he stood—there he stood—she kept seeing him, and yet her vision blotched at the memory. It had been finished between them, six months before, but he had come out here . . . and she had escaped him, now she was lying in her husband's arms, in his embrace, her face pressed against his. It was a kind of sleep, this love-making. She felt herself falling asleep, her body falling from her. Her eyes shut.

"I love you," her husband said fiercely, angrily.

She shut her eyes and thought of that other man, as if betraying him would give her life a center.

"Did I hurt you? Are you—?" her husband whispered.

Always this hot flashing of shame between them, the shame of her husband's near failure, the clumsiness of his love—

"You didn't hurt me," she said.

2

They had said good-by six months before. He drove her from Nantucket, where they had met, to Albany, New York, where she visited her sister. The hours of intimacy in the car had sealed something between them, a vow of silence and impersonality: she recalled the movement of the highways, the passing of other cars, the natural rhythms of the day hypnotizing her toward sleep while he drove. She trusted him, she could sleep in his presence. Yet she could not really fall asleep in spite of her exhaustion, and she kept jerking awake, frightened, to discover that nothing had changed—still the stranger who was driving her to Albany, still the highway, the sky, the antiseptic odor of the rented car, the sense of a rhythm behind the rhythm of the air that might unleash itself at any second. Everywhere on this highway, at this moment, there were men and women driving together, bonded together—what did that mean, to be together? What did it mean to enter into a bond with another person?

No, she did not really trust him; she did not really trust men. He would glance at her with his small cautious smile and she felt a declaration of shame between them.

Shame.

In her head she rehearsed conversations. She said bitterly, "You'll be relieved when we get to Albany. Relieved to get rid of me." They had spent so many days talking, confessing too much, driven to a pitch of childish excitement, laughing together on the beach, breaking into that pose of laughter that seems to eradicate the soul, so many days of this that the silence of the trip was like the silence of a hospital—all these surface noises, these rattles and hums, but an interior silence, a befuddlement. She said to him in her imagination, "One of us should die." Then she leaned over to touch him. She caressed the back of his neck. She said, aloud, "Would you like me to drive for a while?"

They stopped at a picnic area where other cars were stopped—couples, families—and walked together, smiling at their good luck. He put his arm around her shoulders and she sensed how they were in a posture together, a man and a woman forming a posture, a figure, that someone might sketch and show to them. She said slowly, "I don't want to go back. . . ."

Silence. She looked up at him. His face was heavy with her words, as if she had pulled at his skin with her fingers. Children ran nearby and distracted him—yes, he was a father too, his children ran like that, they tugged at his skin with their light, busy fingers.

"Are you so unhappy?" he said.

"I'm not unhappy, back there. I'm nothing. There's nothing to me," she said.

They stared at each other. The sensation between them was intense, exhausting. She thought that this man was her savior, that he had come to her at a time in her life when her life demanded completion, an end, a permanent fixing of all that was troubled and shifting and deadly. And yet it was absurd to think this. No person could save another. So she drew back from him and released him.

A few hours later they stopped at a gas station in a small city. She went to the women's rest room, having to ask the attendant for a key, and when she came back her eye jumped nervously onto the rented car—why? did she think he might have driven off without her?—onto the man, her friend, standing in conversation with the young attendant. Her friend was as old as her husband, over forty, with lanky, sloping shoulders, a full body, his hair thick, a dark, burnished brown, a festive color that made her eye twitch a little—and his hands were always moving, always those rapid conversational circles, going nowhere, gestures that were at once a little aggressive and apologetic.

She put her hand on his arm, a claim. He turned to her and smiled and she felt that she loved him, that everything in her life had forced her to this moment and that she had no choice about it.

They sat in the car for two hours, in Albany, in the parking lot of a Howard Johnson's restaurant, talking, trying to figure out their past. There was no future. They concentrated on the past, the several days behind them, lit up with a hot, dazzling August sun, like explosions that already belonged to other people, to strangers. Her face was faintly reflected in the green-tinted curve of the windshield, but she could not have recognized that face. She began to cry; she told herself: *I am not here, this will pass, this is nothing.* Still, she could not stop crying. The muscles of her face were springy, like a child's, unpredictable muscles. He stroked her arms, her shoulders, trying to comfort her. "This is so hard . . . this is impossible . . ." he said. She felt panic for the world outside this car, all that was not herself and this man, and at the same time she understood that she was free of him, as people are free of other people, she would leave him soon, safely, and within a few days he would have fallen into the past, the impersonal past. . . .

"I'm so ashamed of myself!" she said finally.

She returned to her husband and saw that another woman, a shadow-woman, had taken her place—noiseless and convincing, like a dancer performing certain difficult steps. Her husband folded her in his arms and talked to her of his own loneliness, his worries about his business, his health, his mother, kept tranquilized and mute in a nursing home, and her spirit detached itself from her and drifted about the rooms of the large house she lived in with her husband, a shadow-woman delicate and imprecise. There was no boundary to her, no edge. Alone, she took hot baths and sat exhausted in the steaming water, wondering at her perpetual exhaustion. All that winter she noticed the limp, languid weight of her arms, her veins bulging slightly with the pressure of her extreme weariness. *This is fate,* she thought, to be here and not there, to be one person and not another, a certain man's wife and not the wife of another man. The long, slow pain of this certainty rose in her, but it never became clear, it was baffling and imprecise. She could not be serious about it; she kept congratulating herself on her own good luck, to have escaped so easily, to have freed herself. So much love had gone into the first several years of her marriage that there wasn't much left, now, for another man. . . . She was certain of that. But the bath water made her dizzy, all that perpetual heat, and one day in January she drew a razor blade lightly across the inside of her arm, near the elbow, to see what would happen.

Afterward she wrapped a small towel around it, to stop the bleeding. The towel soaked through. She wrapped a bath towel around that and walked through the empty rooms of her home, lightheaded, hardly aware of the stubborn seeping of blood. There was no boundary to her in this house, no precise limit. She could flow out like her own blood and come to no end.

She sat for a while on a blue love seat, her mind empty. Her husband telephoned her when he would be staying late at the plant. He talked to her always about his plans, his problems, his business friends, his future. It was obvious that he had a future. As he spoke she nodded to encourage him, and her heartbeat quickened with the memory of her own, personal shame, the shame of this man's particular, private wife. One evening at dinner he leaned forward and put his head in his arms and fell asleep, like a child. She sat at the table with him for a while, watching him. His hair had gone gray, almost white, at the temples—no one would guess that he was so quick, so careful a man, still fairly young about the eyes. She put her hand on his head, lightly, as if to prove to herself that he was real. He slept, exhausted.

One evening they went to a concert and she looked up to see her lover there, in the crowded aisle, in this city, watching her. He was standing there, with his overcoat on, watching her. She went cold. That morning the telephone had rung while her husband was still home, and she had heard him answer it, heard him hang up—it must have been a wrong number—and when the telephone rang again, at 9:30, she had been afraid to answer it. She had left home to be out of the range of that ringing, but now, in this public place, in this busy auditorium, she found herself staring at that man, unable to make any sign to him, any gesture of recognition. . . .

He would have come to her but she shook her head. *No. Stay away.*

Her husband helped her out of the row of seats, saying, "Excuse us, please. Excuse us," so that strangers got to their feet, quickly, alarmed, to let them pass. Was that woman about to faint? What was wrong?

At home she felt the blood drain slowly back into her head. Her husband embraced her hips, pressing his face against her, in that silence that belonged to the earliest days of their marriage. She thought, *He will drive it out of me.* He made love to her and she was back in the auditorium again, sitting alone, now that the concert was over. The stage was empty; the heavy velvet curtains had not been drawn; the musicians' chairs were empty, everything was silent and expectant; in the aisle her lover stood and smiled at her—Her husband was impatient. He was apart from her, working on her, operating on her; and then, stricken, he whispered, "Did I hurt you?"

The telephone rang the next morning. Dully, sluggishly, she answered it. She recognized his voice at once—that "Anna?" with its lifting of the second syllable, questioning and apologetic and making its claim—"Yes, what do you want?" she said.

"Just to see you. Please—"

"I can't."

"Anna, I'm sorry, I didn't mean to upset you—"

"I can't see you."

"Just for a few minutes—I have to talk to you—"

"But why, why now? Why now?" she said.

She heard her voice rising, but she could not stop it. He began to talk again, drowning her out. She remembered his rapid conversation. She remembered his gestures, the witty energetic circling of his hands.

"Please don't hang up!" he cried.

"I can't—I don't want to go through it again—"

"I'm not going to hurt you. Just tell me how you are."

"Everything is the same."

"Everything is the same with me."

She looked up at the ceiling, shyly. "Your wife? Your children?"

"The same."

"Your son?"

"He's fine—"

"I'm glad to hear that. I—"

"Is it still the same with you, your marriage? Tell me what you feel. What are you thinking?"

"I don't know. . . ."

She remembered his intense, eager words, the movement of his hands, that impatient precise fixing of the air by his hands, the jabbing of his fingers.

"Do you love me?" he said.

She could not answer.

"I'll come over to see you," he said.

"No," she said.

What will come next, what will happen?

Flesh hardening on his body, aging. Shrinking. He will grow old, but not soft like her husband. They are two different types: he is nervous, lean, energetic, wise. She will grow thinner, as the tension radiates out from her backbone, wearing down her flesh. Her collarbones will jut out of her skin. Her husband, caressing her in their bed, will discover that she is another woman—she is not there with him—instead she is rising in an elevator in a downtown hotel, carrying a book as a prop, or walking quickly away from that hotel, her head bent and filled with secrets. Love, what to do with it? . . . Useless as moths' wings, as moths' fluttering. . . . She feels the flutterings of silky, crazy wings in her chest.

He flew out to visit her every several weeks, staying at a different hotel each time. He telephoned her, and she drove down to park in an underground garage at the very center of the city.

She lay in his arms while her husband talked to her, miles away, one body fading into another. He will grow old, his body will change, she thought, pressing her cheek against the back of one of these men. If it was her lover, they were in a hotel room: always the propped-up little booklet describing the hotel's many services, with color photographs of its cocktail lounge and dining room and coffee shop. Grow old, leave me, die, go back to your neurotic wife and your sad, ordinary children, she thought, but still her eyes closed gratefully against his skin and she felt how complete their silence was, how they had come to rest in each other.

"Tell me about your life here. The people who love you," he said, as he always did.

One afternoon they lay together for four hours. It was her birthday and she was intoxicated with her good fortune, this prize of the afternoon, this man in her arms! She was a little giddy, she talked too much. She told him about her parents, about her husband. . . . "They were all people I believed in, but it turned out wrong. Now, I believe in you. . . ." He laughed as if shocked by her words. She did not understand. Then she understood. "But I believe truly in you. I can't think of myself without you," she said. . . . He spoke of his wife, her ambitions, her intelligence, her use of the children against him, her use of his younger son's blindness, all of his words gentle and hypnotic and convincing in the late afternoon peace of this hotel room . . . and she felt the terror of laughter, threatening laughter. Their words, like their bodies, were aging.

She dressed quickly in the bathroom, drawing her long hair up around the back of her head, fixing it as always, anxious that everything be the same. Her face was slightly raw, from his face. The rubbing of his skin. Her eyes were too bright, wearily bright. Her hair was blond but not so blond as it had been that summer in the white Nantucket air.

She ran water and splashed it on her face. She blinked at the water. Blind. Drowning. She thought with satisfaction that soon, soon, he would be back home, in that house on Long Island she had never seen, with that woman she had never seen, sitting on the edge of another bed, putting on his shoes. She wanted nothing except to be free of him. Why not be free? *Oh,* she thought suddenly, *I will follow you back and kill you. You and her and the little boy. What is there to stop me?*

She left him. Everyone on the street pitied her, that look of absolute zero.

3

A man and a child, approaching her. The sharp acrid smell of fish. The crashing of waves. Anna pretended not to notice the father with his son—there was something strange about them. That frank, silent intimacy, too gentle, the man's bare feet in the water and the boy a few feet away, leaning away from his father. He was about nine years old and still his father held his hand.

A small yipping dog, a golden dog, bounded near them.

Anna turned shyly back to her reading; she did not want to have to speak to these neighbors. She saw the man's shadow falling over her legs, then over the pages of her book, and she had the idea that he wanted to see what she was reading. The dog nuzzled her; the man called him away.

She watched them walk down the beach. She was relieved that the man had not spoken to her.

She saw them in town later that day, the two of them brown-haired and patient, now wearing sandals, walking with that same look of care. The man's white shorts were soiled and a little baggy. His pullover shirt was a faded green. His face was broad, the cheekbones wide, spaced widely apart, the eyes stark in their sockets, as if they fastened onto objects for no reason, ponderous and edgy. The little boy's face was pale and sharp; his lips were perpetually parted.

Anna realized that the child was blind.

The next morning, early, she caught sight of them again. For some reason she went to the back door of her cottage. She faced the sea breeze eagerly. Her heart hammered. . . . She had been here, in her family's old house, for three days, alone, bitterly satisfied at being alone, and now it was a puzzle to her how her soul strained to fly outward, to meet with another person. She watched the man with his son, his cautious, rather stooped shoulders above the child's small shoulders.

The man was carrying something, it looked like a notebook. He sat on the sand, not far from Anna's spot of the day before, and the dog rushed up to them. The child approached the edge of the ocean, timidly. He moved in short jerky steps, his legs stiff. The dog ran around him. Anna heard the child crying out a word that sounded like "Ty"—it must have been the dog's name—and then the man joined in, his voice heavy and firm.

"Ty—"

Anna tied her hair back with a yellow scarf and went down to the beach.

The man glanced around at her. He smiled. She stared past him at the waves. To talk to him or not to talk—she had the freedom of that choice. For a moment she felt that she had made a mistake, that the child and the dog would not protect her, that behind this man's ordinary, friendly face there was a certain arrogant maleness—then she relented, she smiled shyly.

"A nice house you've got there," the man said.

She nodded her thanks.

The man pushed his sunglasses up on his forehead. Yes, she recognized the eyes of the day before—intelligent and nervous, the sockets pale, untanned.

"Is that your telephone ringing?" he said.

She did not bother to listen. "It's a wrong number," she said.

Her husband calling: she had left home for a few days, to be alone.

But the man, settling himself on the sand, seemed to misinterpret this. He smiled in surprise, one corner of his mouth higher than the other. He said nothing. Anna wondered: *What is he thinking?* The dog was leaping about her, panting against her legs, and she laughed in embarrassment. She bent to pet it, grateful for its busyness. "Don't let him jump up on you," the man said. "He's a nuisance."

The dog was a small golden retriever, a young dog. The blind child, standing now in the water, turned to call the dog to him. His voice was shrill and impatient.

"Our house is the third one down—the white one," the man said.

She turned, startled. "Oh, did you buy it from Dr. Patrick? Did he die?"

"Yes, finally. . . ."

Her eyes wandered nervously over the child and the dog. She felt the nervous beat of her heart out to the very tips of her fingers, the fleshy tips of her fingers: little hearts were there, pulsing. *What is he thinking?* The man had opened his notebook. He had a piece of charcoal and he began to sketch something.

Anna looked down at him. She saw the top of his head, his thick brown hair, the freckles on his shoulders, the quick, deft movement of his hand. Upside down, Anna herself being drawn. She smiled in surprise.

"Let me draw you. Sit down," he said.

She knelt awkwardly a few yards away. He turned the page of the sketch pad. The dog ran to her and she sat, straightening out her skirt beneath her, flinching from the dog's tongue. "Ty!" cried the child. Anna sat, and slowly the pleasure of the moment began to glow in her; her skin flushed with gratitude.

She sat there for nearly an hour. The man did not talk much. Back and forth the dog bounded, shaking itself. The child came to sit near them, in silence. Anna felt that she was drifting into a kind of trance while the man sketched her, half a dozen rapid sketches, the surface of her face given up to him. "Where are you from?" the man asked.

"Ohio. My husband lives in Ohio."

She wore no wedding band.

"Your wife—" Anna began.

"Yes?"

"Is she here?"

"Not right now."

She was silent, ashamed. She had asked an improper question. But the man did not seem to notice. He continued drawing her, bent over the sketch pad. When Anna said she had to go, he showed her the drawings—one after another of her, Anna, recognizably Anna, a woman in her early thirties, her hair smooth and flat across the top of her head, tied behind by a scarf. "Take the one you like best," he said, and she picked one of her with the dog in her lap, sitting very straight, her brows and eyes clearly defined, her lips girlishly pursed, the dog and her dress suggested by a few quick irregular lines.

"Lady with pet dog," the man said.

She spent the rest of that day reading, nearer her cottage. It was not really a cottage—it was a two-story house, large and ungainly and weathered. It was mixed up in her mind with her family, her own childhood, and she glanced up from her book, perplexed, as if waiting for one of her parents or her sister to come up to her. Then she thought of that man, the man with the blind child, the man with the dog, and she could not concentrate on her reading. Someone—probably her father—had marked a passage that must be important, but she kept reading and rereading it: *We try to discover in things, endeared to us on that account, the spiritual glamour which we ourselves have cast upon them; we are disillusioned, and learn that they are in themselves barren and devoid of the charm that they owed, in our minds, to the association of certain ideas. . . .*

She thought again of the man on the beach. She lay the book aside and thought of him: his eyes, his aloneness, his drawings of her.

They began seeing each other after that. He came to her front door in the evening, without the child; he drove her into town for dinner. She was shy and extremely pleased. The darkness of the expensive restaurant released her; she heard herself chatter; she leaned forward and seemed to be offering her face up to him, listening to him. He talked about his work on a Long Island newspaper and she seemed to be listening to him, as she stared at his face, arranging her own face into the expression she had seen in that charcoal drawing. Did he see her like that, then?—girlish and withdrawn and patrician? She felt the weight of his interest in her, a force that fell upon her like a blow. A repeated blow. Of course he was married, he had children—of course she was married, permanently married. This flight from her husband was not important. She had left him before, to be alone, it was not important. Everything in her was slender and delicate and not important.

They walked for hours after dinner, looking at the other strollers, the weekend visitors, the tourists, the couples like themselves. Surely they were mistaken for a couple, a married couple. *This is the hour in which everything is decided,* Anna thought. They had both had several drinks and they talked a great deal. Anna found herself saying too much, stopping and starting giddily. She put her hand to her forehead, feeling faint.

"It's from the sun—you've had too much sun—" he said.

At the door to her cottage, on the front porch, she heard herself asking him if he would like to come in. She allowed him to lead her inside, to close the door. *This is not important,* she thought clearly, *he doesn't mean it, he doesn't love me, nothing will come of it.* She was frightened, yet it seemed to her necessary to give in; she had to leave Nantucket with that act completed, an act of adultery, an accomplishment she would take back to Ohio and to her marriage.

Later, incredibly, she heard herself asking: "Do you . . . do you love me?"

"You're so beautiful!" he said, amazed.

She felt this beauty, shy and glowing and centered in her eyes. He stared at her. In this large, drafty house, alone together, they were like accomplices, conspirators. She could not think: how old was she? which year was this? They had done something unforgivable together, and the knowledge of it was tugging at their faces. A cloud seemed to pass over her. She felt herself smiling shrilly.

Afterward, a peculiar raspiness, a dryness of breath. He was silent. She felt a strange, idle fear, a sense of the danger outside this room and this old, comfortable bed—a danger that would not recognize her as the lady in that drawing, the lady with the pet dog. There was nothing to say to this man, this stranger. She felt the beauty draining out of her face, her eyes fading.

"I've got to be alone," she told him.

He left, and she understood that she would not see him again. She stood by the window of the room, watching the ocean. A sense of shame overpowered her: it was smeared everywhere on her body, the smell of it, the richness of it. She tried to recall him, and his face was confused in her memory: she would have to shout to him across a jumbled space, she would have to wave her arms wildly. *You love me! You must love me!* But she knew he did not love her, and she did not love him; he was a man who drew everything up into himself, like all men, walking away, free to walk away, free to have his own thoughts, free to envision her body, all the secrets of her body. . . . And she lay down again in the bed, feeling how heavy this body had become, her insides heavy with shame, the very backs of her eyelids coated with shame.

"This is the end of one part of my life," she thought.

But in the morning the telephone rang. She answered it. It was her lover: they talked brightly and happily. She could hear the eagerness in his voice, the love in his voice, that same still, sad amazement—she understood how simple life was, there were no problems.

They spent most of their time on the beach, with the child and the dog. He joked and was serious at the same time. He said, once, "You have defined my soul for me," and she laughed to hide her alarm. In a few days it was time for her to leave. He got a sitter for the boy and took the ferry with her to the mainland, then rented a car to drive her up to Albany. She kept thinking: *Now something will happen. It will come to an end.* But most of the drive was silent and hypnotic. She wanted him to joke with her, to say again that she had defined his soul for him, but he drove fast, he was serious, she distrusted the hawkish look of his profile—she did not know him at all. At a gas station she splashed her face with cold water. Alone in the grubby little rest room, shaky and very much alone. In such places are women totally alone with their bodies. The body grows heavier, more evil, in such silence. . . . On the beach everything had been noisy with sunlight and gulls and waves; here, as if run to earth, everything was cramped and silent and dead.

She went outside, squinting. There he was, talking with the station attendant. She could not think as she returned to him whether she wanted to live or not.

She stayed in Albany for a few days, then flew home to her husband. He met her at the airport, near the luggage counter, where her three pieces of pale-brown luggage were brought to him on a conveyer belt, to be claimed by him. He kissed her on the cheek. They shook hands, a little embarrassed. She had come home again.

"How will I live out the rest of my life?" she wondered.

In January her lover spied on her: she glanced up and saw him, in a public place, in the DeRoy Symphony Hall. She was paralyzed with fear. She nearly fainted. In this faint she felt her husband's body, loving her, working its love upon her, and she shut her eyes harder to keep out the certainty of his love—sometimes he failed at loving her, sometimes he succeeded, it had nothing to do with her or her pity or her ten years of love for him, it had nothing to do with a woman at all. It was a private act accomplished by a man, a husband or a lover, in communion with his own soul, his manhood.

Her husband was forty-two years old now, growing slowly into middle age, getting heavier, softer. Her lover was about the same age, narrower in the shoulders, with a full, solid chest, yet lean, nervous. She thought, in her paralysis, of men and how they love freely and eagerly so long as their bodies are capable of love, love for a woman; and then, as love fades in their bodies, it fades from their souls and they become immune and immortal and ready to die.

Her husband was a little rough with her, as if impatient with himself. "I love you," he said fiercely, angrily. And then, ashamed, he said, "Did I hurt you? . . ."

"You didn't hurt me," she said.

Her voice was too shrill for their embrace.

While he was in the bathroom she went to her closet and took out that drawing of the summer before. There she was, on the beach at Nantucket, a lady with a pet dog, her eyes large and defined, the dog in her lap hardly more than a few snarls, a few coarse soft lines of charcoal . . . her dress smeared, her arms oddly limp . . . her hands not well drawn at all. . . . She tried to think: did she love the man who had drawn this? did he love her? The fever in her husband's body had touched her and driven her temperature up, and now she stared at the drawing with a kind of lust, fearful of seeing an ugly soul in that woman's face, fearful of seeing the face suddenly through her lover's eyes. She breathed quickly and harshly, staring at the drawing.

And so, the next day, she went to him at his hotel. She wept, pressing against him, demanding of him, "What do you want? Why are you here? Why don't you let me alone?" He told her that he wanted nothing. He expected nothing. He would not cause trouble.

"I want to talk about last August," he said.

"Don't—" she said.

She was hypnotized by his gesturing hands, his nervousness, his obvious agitation. He kept saying, "I understand. I'm making no claims upon you."

They became lovers again.

He called room service for something to drink and they sat side by side on his bed, looking through a copy of *The New Yorker,* laughing at the cartoons. It was so peaceful in this room, so complete. They were on a holiday. It was a secret holiday. Four-thirty in the afternoon, on a Friday, an ordinary Friday: a secret holiday.

"I won't bother you again," he said.

He flew back to see her again in March, and in late April. He telephoned her from his hotel—a different hotel each time—and she came down to him at once. She rose to him in various elevators, she knocked on the doors of various rooms, she stepped into his embrace, breathless and guilty and already angry with him, pleading with him. One morning in May, when he telephoned, she pressed her forehead against the doorframe and could not speak. He kept saying, "What's wrong? Can't you talk? Aren't you alone?" She felt that she was going insane. Her head would burst. Why, why did he love her, why did he pursue her? Why did he want her to die?

She went to him in the hotel room. A familiar room: had they been here before? "Everything is repeating itself. Everything is stuck," she said. He framed her face in his hands and said that she looked thinner—was she sick?—what was wrong? She shook herself free. He, her lover, looked about the same. There was a small, angry pimple on his neck. He stared at her, eagerly and suspiciously. Did she bring bad news?

"So you love me? You love me?" she asked.

"Why are you so angry?"

"I want to be free of you. The two of us free of each other."

"That isn't true—you don't want that—"

He embraced her. She was wild with that old, familiar passion for him, her body clinging to his, her arms not strong enough to hold him. Ah, what despair!—what bitter hatred she felt!—she needed this man for her salvation, he was all she had to live for, and yet she could not believe in him. He embraced her thighs, her hips, kissing her, pressing his warm face against her, and yet she could not believe in him, not really. She needed him in order to live, but he was not worth her love, he was not worth her dying. . . . She promised herself this: when she got back home, when she was alone, she would draw the razor more deeply across her arm.

The telephone rang and he answered it: a wrong number.

"Jesus," he said.

They lay together, still. She imagined their posture like this, the two of them one figure, one substance; and outside this room and this bed there was a universe of disjointed, separate things, blank things, that had nothing to do with them. She would not be Anna out there, the lady in the drawing. He would not be her lover.

"I love you so much . . ." she whispered.

"Please don't cry! We have only a few hours, please. . . ."

It was absurd, their clinging together like this. She saw them as a single figure in a drawing, their arms and legs entwined, their heads pressing mutely together. Helpless substance, so heavy and warm and doomed. It was absurd that any human being should be so important to another human being. She wanted to laugh: a laugh might free them both.

She could not laugh.

Sometime later he said, as if they had been arguing, "Look. It's you. You're the one who doesn't want to get married. You lie to me—"

"Lie to you?"

"You love me but you won't marry me, because you want something left over—Something not finished—All your life you can attribute your misery to me, to our not being married—you are using me—"

"Stop it! You'll make me hate you!" she cried.

"You can say to yourself that you're miserable because of *me.* We will never be married, you will never be happy, neither one of us will ever be happy—"

"I don't want to hear this!" she said.

She pressed her hands flatly against her face.

She went to the bathroom to get dressed. She washed her face and part of her body, quickly. The fever was in her, in the pit of her belly. She would rush home and strike a razor across the inside of her arm and free that pressure, that fever.

The impatient bulging of the veins: an ordeal over.

The demand of the telephone's ringing: that ordeal over.

The nuisance of getting the car and driving home in all that five o'clock traffic: an ordeal too much for a woman.

The movement of this stranger's body in hers: over, finished.

Now, dressed, a little calmer, they held hands and talked. They had to talk swiftly, to get all their news in: he did not trust the people who worked for him, he had faith in no one, his wife had moved to a textbook publishing company and was doing well, she had inherited a Ben Shahn painting from her father and wanted to "touch it up a little"—she was crazy!—his blind son was at another school, doing fairly well, in fact his children were all doing fairly well in spite of the stupid mistake of their parents' marriage—and what about her? what about her life? She told him in a rush the one thing he wanted to hear: that she lived with her husband lovelessly, the two of them polite strangers, sharing a bed, lying side by side in the night in that bed, bodies out of which souls had fled. There was no longer even any shame between them.

"And what about me? Do you feel shame with me still?" he asked.

She did not answer. She moved away from him and prepared to leave.

Then, a minute later, she happened to catch sight of his reflection in the bureau mirror—he was glancing down at himself, checking himself mechanically, impersonally, preparing also to leave. He too would leave this room: he too was headed somewhere else.

She stared at him. It seemed to her that in this instant he was breaking from her, the image of her lover fell free of her, breaking from her . . . and she realized that he existed in a dimension quite apart from her, a mysterious being. And suddenly, joyfully, she felt a miraculous calm. This man was her husband, truly—they were truly married, here in this room—they had been married haphazardly and accidentally for a long time. In another part of the city she had another husband, a "husband," but she had not betrayed that man, not really. This man, whom she loved above any other person in the world, above even her own self-pitying sorrow and her own life, was her truest lover, her destiny. And she did not hate him, she did not hate herself any longer; she did not wish to die; she was flooded with a strange certainty, a sense of gratitude, of pure selfless energy. It was obvious to her that she had, all along, been behaving correctly; out of instinct.

What triumph, to love like this in any room, anywhere, risking even the craziest of accidents!

"Why are you so happy? What's wrong?" he asked, startled. He stared at her. She felt the abrupt concentration in him, the focusing of his vision on her, almost a bitterness in his face, as if he feared her. What, was it beginning all over again? Their love beginning again, in spite of them? "How can you look so happy?" he asked. "We don't have any right to it. Is it because . . . ?"

"Yes," she said.

QUESTIONS FOR DISCUSSION AND WRITING

1. Why does Oates begin her story at the concert? Why does she place the Nantucket episode in the middle of her story? What question is the woman answering at the end of the story?
2. How does the woman characterize the difference between her husband and her lover? How does her lover's drawing characterize her?
3. Why is the social status of these characters important to the setting of the story? How does the woman compare the atmosphere of the beach with that of the hotel rooms?
4. To what extent does the narrator encourage the reader to identify with the woman in the story? Why does the woman find it difficult to know what the male characters are thinking?
5. What is the thematic relationship between love and shame in the story? What does the woman want? Does she find it? Explain your answer.

70

FLANNERY O'CONNOR

A Good Man Is Hard to Find

FLANNERY O'CONNOR (1925–1964) was born in Savannah, Georgia, and educated at Georgia State College for Women and the University of Iowa. After completing her graduate work at the University of Iowa Writer's Workshop in 1947, she lived for two years in New York City. O'Connor returned to her mother's farm near Milledgeville, Georgia, however, when she discovered that she had contracted lupus erythematosus, the systemic disease that had

killed her father and of which she herself was to die. For the last fourteen years of her life, she lived a quiet, productive life on the farm—raising peacocks, painting, and writing the extraordinary stories and novels that won her world-wide acclaim. Her novels, *Wise Blood* (1952)—adapted to film in 1980—and *The Violent Bear It Away* (1960), both deal with fanatical preachers: one is an urban minister of the "Church of God without Christ"; the other is a rural prophet struggling to save his grandson from his atheist nephew. Both novels reveal O'Connor's preoccupation with the gothic distortions of contemporary religion as well as the profound Roman Catholic faith that is at the bottom of all her work. Her thirty-one carefully crafted stories, combining grotesque comedy and violent tragedy, appear in *A Good Man Is Hard to Find* (1955), *Everything That Rises Must Converge* (1965), and *The Complete Stories* (1971), which won the National Book Award. A selection of her letters, edited by Sally Fitzgerald, was published under the title *The Habit of Being* (1979). "A Good Man Is Hard to Find" describes the tragic fate that befalls a family on its trip to Florida. "Revelation" dramatizes the ironic discoveries a woman makes about the order of things, and "Everything That Rises Must Converge" tells of an equally fateful journey of a mother and her son on a city bus.

The grandmother didn't want to go to Florida. She wanted to visit some of her connections in east Tennessee and she was seizing at every chance to change Bailey's mind. Bailey was the son she lived with, her only boy. He was sitting on the edge of his chair at the table, bent over the orange sports section of the *Journal*. "Now look here, Bailey," she said, "see here, read this," and she stood with one hand on her thin hip and the other rattling the newspaper at his bald head. "Here this fellow that calls himself The Misfit is aloose from the Federal Pen and headed toward Florida and you read here what it says he did to these people. Just you read it. I wouldn't take my children in any direction with a criminal like that aloose in it. I couldn't answer to my conscience if I did."

Bailey didn't look up from his reading so she wheeled around then and faced the children's mother, a young woman in slacks, whose face was as broad and innocent as a cabbage and was tied around with a green head-kerchief that had two points on the top like a rabbit's ears. She was sitting on the sofa, feeding the baby his apricots out of a jar. "The children have been to Florida before," the old lady said. "You all ought to take them somewhere else for a change so they would see different parts of the world and be broad. They never have been to east Tennessee."

The children's mother didn't seem to hear her but the eight-year-old boy, John Wesley, a stocky child with glasses, said, "If you don't want to go to Florida, why dontcha stay at home?" He and the little girl, June Star, were reading the funny papers on the floor.

"She wouldn't stay at home to be queen for a day," June Star said without raising her yellow head.

"Yes and what would you do if this fellow, The Misfit, caught you?" the grandmother asked.

"I'd smack his face," John Wesley said.

"She wouldn't stay at home for a million bucks," June Star said. "Afraid she'd miss something. She has to go everywhere we go."

"All right, Miss," the grandmother said. "Just remember that the next time you want me to curl your hair."

June Star said her hair was naturally curly.

The next morning the grandmother was the first one in the car, ready to go. She had her big black valise that looked like the head of a hippopotamus in one corner, and underneath it she was hiding a basket with Pitty Sing, the cat, in it. She didn't intend for the cat to be left alone in the house for three days because he would miss her too much and she was afraid he might brush against one of the gas burners and accidentally asphyxiate himself. Her son, Bailey, didn't like to arrive at a motel with a cat.

She sat in the middle of the back seat with John Wesley and June Star on either side of her. Bailey and the children's mother and the baby sat in front and they left Atlanta at eight forty-five with the mileage on the car at 55890. The grandmother wrote this down because she thought it would be interesting to say how many miles they had been when they got back. It took them twenty minutes to reach the outskirts of the city.

The old lady settled herself comfortably, removing her white cotton gloves and putting them up with her purse on the shelf in front of the back window. The children's mother still had on slacks and still had her head tied up in a green kerchief, but the grandmother had on a navy blue straw sailor hat with a bunch of white violets on the brim and a navy blue dress with a small white dot in the print. Her collars and cuffs were white organdy trimmed with lace and at her neckline she had pinned a purple spray of cloth violets containing a sachet. In case of an accident, anyone seeing her dead on the highway would know at once that she was a lady.

She said she thought it was going to be a good day for driving, neither too hot nor too cold, and she cautioned Bailey that the speed limit was fifty-five miles an hour and that the patrolmen hid themselves behind billboards and small clumps of trees and sped out after you before you had a chance to slow down. She pointed out interesting details of the scenery: Stone Mountain; the blue granite that in some places came up to both sides of the highway; the brilliant red clay banks slightly streaked with purple; and the various crops that made rows of green lace-work on the ground. The trees were full of silver-white sunlight and the meanest of them sparkled. The children were reading comic magazines and their mother had gone back to sleep.

"Let's go through Georgia fast so we won't have to look at it much," John Wesley said.

"If I were a little boy," said the grandmother, "I wouldn't talk about my native state that way. Tennessee has the mountains and Georgia has the hills."

"Tennessee is just a hillbilly dumping ground," John Wesley said, "and Georgia is a lousy state, too."

"You said it," June Star said.

"In my time," said the grandmother, folding her thin veined fingers, "children were more respectful of their native states and their parents and everything else. People did right then. Oh look at the cute little pickaninny!" she said and pointed to a Negro child standing in the door of a shack. "Wouldn't that make a picture, now?" she asked and they all turned and looked at the little Negro out of the back window. He waved.

"He didn't have any britches on," June Star said.

"He probably didn't have any," the grandmother explained. "Little niggers in the country don't have things like we do. If I could paint, I'd paint that picture," she said.

The children exchanged comic books.

The grandmother offered to hold the baby and the children's mother passed him over the front seat to her. She set him on her knee and bounced him and told him about the things they were passing. She rolled her eyes and screwed up her mouth and stuck her leathery thin face into his smooth bland one. Occasionally he gave her a faraway smile. They passed a large cotton field with five or six graves fenced in the middle of it, like a small island. "Look at the graveyard!" the grandmother said, pointing it out. "That was the old family burying ground. That belonged to the plantation."

"Where's the plantation?" John Wesley asked.

"Gone With the Wind," said the grandmother. "Ha. Ha."

When the children finished all the comic books they had brought, they opened the lunch and ate it. The grandmother ate a peanut butter sandwich and an olive and would not let the children throw the box and the paper napkins out the window. When there was nothing else to do they played a game by choosing a cloud and making the other two guess what shape it suggested. John Wesley took one the shape of a cow and June Star guessed a cow and John Wesley said, no, an automobile, and June Star said he didn't play fair, and they began to slap each other over the grandmother.

The grandmother said she would tell them a story if they would keep quiet. When she told a story, she rolled her eyes and waved her head and was very dramatic. She said once when she was a maiden lady she had been courted by a Mr. Edgar Atkins Teagarden from Jasper, Georgia. She said he was a very good-looking man and a gentleman and that he brought her a watermelon every Saturday afternoon with his initials cut in it, E. A. T. Well, one Saturday, she said, Mr. Teagarden brought the watermelon and there was nobody at home and he left it on the front porch and returned in his buggy to Jasper, but she never got the watermelon, she said, because a nigger boy ate it when he saw the initials, E. A. T! This story tickled John Wesley's funny bone and he giggled and giggled but June Star didn't think it was any good. She said she wouldn't marry a man that just brought her a watermelon on Saturday. The grandmother said she would have done well to marry Mr. Teagarden because he was a gentleman and had bought Coca-Cola stock when it first came out and that he had died only a few years ago, a very wealthy man.

They stopped at The Tower for barbecued sandwiches. The Tower was a part stucco and part wood filling station and dance hall set in a clearing outside of Timothy. A fat man named Red Sammy Butts ran it and there were signs stuck here and there on the building and for miles up and down the highway saying, TRY RED SAMMY'S FAMOUS BARBECUE. NONE LIKE FAMOUS RED SAMMY'S! RED SAM! THE FAT BOY WITH THE HAPPY LAUGH! A VETERAN! RED SAMMY'S YOUR MAN!

Red Sammy was lying on the bare ground outside The Tower with his head under a truck while a gray monkey about a foot high, chained to a small chinaberry tree, chattered nearby. The monkey sprang back into the tree and got on the highest limb as soon as he saw the children jump out of the car and run toward him.

Inside, The Tower was a long dark room with a counter at one end and tables at the other and dancing space in the middle. They sat down at a board table next to the nickelodeon and Red Sam's wife, a tall burnt-brown woman with hair and eyes lighter than her skin, came and took their order. The children's mother put a dime in the machine and played "The Tennessee Waltz," and the grandmother said that tune always made her want to dance. She asked Bailey if he would like to dance but he only glared at her. He didn't have a naturally sunny disposition like she did and trips made him nervous. The grandmother's brown eyes were very bright. She swayed her head from side to side and pretended she was dancing in her chair. June Star said play something she could tap to so the children's mother put in another dime and played a fast number and June Star stepped out onto the dance floor and did her tap routine.

"Ain't she cute?" Red Sam's wife said, leaning over the counter. "Would you like to come be my little girl?"

"No I certainly wouldn't," June Star said. "I wouldn't live in a broken-down place like this for a million bucks!" and she ran back to the table.

"Ain't she cute?" the woman repeated, stretching her mouth politely.

"Aren't you ashamed?" hissed the grandmother.

Red Sam came in and told his wife to quit lounging on the counter and hurry up with these people's order. His khaki trousers reached just to his hip bones and his stomach hung over them like a sack of meal swaying under his shirt. He came over and sat down at a table nearby and let out a combination sigh and yodel. "You can't win," he said. "You can't win," and he wiped his sweating red face off with a gray handkerchief. "These days you don't know who to trust," he said. "Ain't that the truth?"

"People are certainly not nice like they used to be," said the grandmother.

"Two fellers come in here last week," Red Sammy said, "driving a Chrysler. It was a old beat-up car but it was a good one and these boys looked all right to me. Said they worked at the mill and you know I let them fellers charge the gas they bought? Now why did I do that?"

"Because you're a good man!" the grandmother said at once.

"Yes'm, I suppose so," Red Sam said as if he were struck with this answer.

His wife brought the orders, carrying the five plates all at once without a tray, two in each hand and one balanced on her arm. "It isn't a soul in this green world of God's that you can trust," she said. "And I don't count nobody out of that, not nobody," she repeated, looking at Red Sammy.

"Did you read about that criminal, The Misfit, that's escaped?" asked the grandmother.

"I wouldn't be a bit surprised if he didn't attack this place right here," said the woman. "If he hears about it being here, I wouldn't be none surprised to see him. If he hears it's two cent in the cash register, I wouldn't be a tall surprised if he . . ."

"That'll do," Red Sam said. "Go bring these people their Co'-Colas," and the woman went off to get the rest of the order.

"A good man is hard to find," Red Sammy said. "Everything is getting terrible. I remember the day you could go off and leave your screen door unlatched. Not no more."

He and the grandmother discussed better times. The old lady said that in her opinion Europe was entirely to blame for the way things were now. She said the way Europe acted you would think we were made of money and Red Sam said it was no use talking about it, she was exactly right. The children ran outside into the white sunlight and looked at the monkey in the lacy chinaberry tree. He was busy catching fleas on himself and biting each one carefully between his teeth as if it were a delicacy.

They drove off again into the hot afternoon. The grandmother took cat naps and woke up every few minutes with her own snoring. Outside of Toombsboro she woke up and recalled an old plantation that she had visited in this neighborhood once when she was a young lady. She said the house had six white columns across the front and that there was an avenue of oaks leading up to it and two little wooden trellis arbors on either side in front where you sat down with your suitor after a stroll in the garden. She recalled exactly which road to turn off to get to it. She knew that Bailey would not be willing to lose any time looking at an old house, but the more she talked about it, the more she wanted to see it once again and find out if the little twin arbors were still standing. "There was a secret panel in this house," she said craftily, not telling the truth but wishing that she were, "and the story went that all the family silver was hidden in it when Sherman came through but it was never found . . ."

"Hey!" John Wesley said. "Let's go see it! We'll find it! We'll poke all the woodwork and find it! Who lives there? Where do you turn off at? Hey Pop, can't we turn off there?"

"We never have seen a house with a secret panel!" June Star shrieked. "Let's go to the house with the secret panel! Hey Pop, can't we go see the house with the secret panel!"

"It's not far from here, I know," the grandmother said. "It wouldn't take over twenty minutes."

Bailey was looking straight ahead. His jaw was as rigid as a horseshoe. "No," he said.

The children began to yell and scream that they wanted to see the house with the secret panel. John Wesley kicked the back of the front seat and June Star hung over her mother's shoulder and whined desperately into her ear that they never had any fun even on their vacation, that they could never do what THEY wanted to do. The baby began to scream and John Wesley kicked the back of the seat so hard that his father could feel the blows in his kidney.

"All right!" he shouted and drew the car to a stop at the side of the road. "Will you all shut up? Will you all just shut up for one second? If you don't shut up, we won't go anywhere."

"It would be very educational for them," the grandmother murmured.

"All right," Bailey said, "but get this: this is the only time we're going to stop for anything like this. This is the one and only time."

"The dirt road that you have to turn down is about a mile back," the grandmother directed. "I marked it when we passed."

"A dirt road," Bailey groaned.

After they had turned around and were headed toward the dirt road, the grandmother recalled other points about the house, the beautiful glass over the front doorway and the candle-lamp in the hall. John Wesley said that the secret panel was probably in the fireplace.

"You can't go inside this house," Bailey said. "You don't know who lives there."

"While you all talk to the people in front, I'll run around behind and get in a window," John Wesley suggested.

"We'll all stay in the car," his mother said.

They turned onto the dirt road and the car raced roughly along in a swirl of pink dust. The grandmother recalled the times when there were no paved roads and thirty miles was a day's journey. The dirt road was hilly and there were sudden washes in it and sharp curves on dangerous embankments. All at once they would be on a hill, looking down over the blue tops of trees for miles around, then the next minute, they would be in a red depression with the dust-coated trees looking down on them.

"This place had better turn up in a minute," Bailey said, "or I'm going to turn around."

The road looked as if no one had traveled on it in months.

"It's not much farther," the grandmother said and just as she said it, a horrible thought came to her. The thought was so embarrassing that she turned red in the face and her eyes dilated and her feet jumped up, upsetting her valise in the corner. The instant the valise moved, the newspaper top she had over the basket under it rose with a snarl and Pitty Sing, the cat, sprang onto Bailey's shoulder.

The children were thrown to the floor and their mother, clutching the baby, was thrown out the door onto the ground; the old lady was thrown into the front seat. The car turned over once and landed right-side-up in a gulch off the side of the road. Bailey remained in the driver's seat with the cat—gray-striped with a broad white face and an orange nose—clinging to his neck like a caterpillar.

As soon as the children saw they could move their arms and legs, they scrambled out of the car, shouting, "We've had an ACCIDENT!" The grandmother was curled up under the dashboard, hoping she was injured so that Bailey's wrath would not come down on her all at once. The horrible thought she had had before the accident was that the house she had remembered so vividly was not in Georgia but in Tennessee.

Bailey removed the cat from his neck with both hands and flung it out the window against the side of a pine tree. Then he got out of the car and started looking for the children's mother. She was sitting against the side of the red gutted ditch, holding the screaming baby, but she only had a cut down her face and a broken shoulder. "We've had an ACCIDENT!" the children screamed in a frenzy of delight.

"But nobody's killed," June Star said with disappointment as the grandmother limped out of the car, her hat still pinned to her head but the broken front brim standing up at a jaunty angle and the violet spray hanging off the side. They all sat down in the ditch, except the children, to recover from the shock. They were all shaking.

"Maybe a car will come along," said the children's mother hoarsely.

"I believe I have injured an organ," said the grandmother, pressing her side, but no one answered her. Bailey's teeth were clattering. He had on a yellow sport shirt with bright blue parrots designed in it and his face was as yellow as the shirt. The grandmother decided that she would not mention that the house was in Tennessee.

The road was about ten feet above and they could see only the tops of the trees on the other side of it. Behind the ditch they were sitting in there were more woods, tall and dark and deep. In a few minutes they saw a car some distance away on top of a hill, coming slowly as if the occupants were watching them. The grandmother stood up and waved both arms dramatically to attract their attention. The car continued to come on slowly, disappeared around a bend and appeared again, moving even slower, on top of the hill they had gone over. It was a big black battered hearse-like automobile. There were three men in it.

It came to a stop just over them and for some minutes, the driver looked down with a steady expressionless gaze to where they were sitting, and didn't speak. Then he turned his head and muttered something to the other two and they got out. One was a fat boy in black trousers and a red sweat shirt with a silver stallion embossed on the front of it. He moved around on the right side of them and stood staring, his mouth partly open in a kind of loose grin. The other had on khaki pants and a blue striped coat and a gray hat pulled down very low, hiding most of his face. He came around slowly on the left side. Neither spoke.

The driver got out of the car and stood by the side of it, looking down at them. He was an older man than the other two. His hair was just beginning to gray and he wore silver-rimmed spectacles that gave him a scholarly look. He had a long creased face and didn't have on any shirt or undershirt. He had on blue jeans that were too tight for him and was holding a black hat and a gun. The two boys also had guns.

"We've had an ACCIDENT!" the children screamed.

The grandmother had the peculiar feeling that the bespectacled man was someone she knew. His face was as familiar to her as if she had known him all her life but she could not recall who he was. He moved away from the car and began to come down the embankment, placing his feet carefully so that he wouldn't slip. He had on tan and white shoes and no socks, and his ankles were red and thin. "Good afternoon," he said. "I see you all had you a little spill."

"We turned over twice!" said the grandmother.

"Oncet," he corrected. "We seen it happen. Try their car and see will it run, Hiram," he said quietly to the boy with the gray hat.

"What you got that gun for?" John Wesley asked. "Whatcha gonna do with that gun?"

"Lady," the man said to the children's mother, "would you mind calling them children to sit down by you? Children make me nervous. I want all you all to sit down right together there where you're at."

"What are you telling US what to do for?" June Star asked.

Behind them the line of woods gaped like a dark open mouth. "Come here," said their mother.

"Look here now," Bailey began suddenly, "we're in a predicament! We're in . . ."

The grandmother shrieked. She scrambled to her feet and stood staring. "You're The Misfit!" she said. "I recognized you at once!"

"Yes'm," the man said, smiling slightly as if he were pleased in spite of himself to be known, "but it would have been better for all of you, lady, if you hadn't of reckernized me."

Bailey turned his head sharply and said something to his mother that shocked even the children. The old lady began to cry and The Misfit reddened.

"Lady," he said, "don't you get upset. Sometimes a man says things he don't mean. I don't reckon he meant to talk to you thataway."

"You wouldn't shoot a lady, would you?" the grandmother said and removed a clean handkerchief from her cuff and began to slap at her eyes with it.

The Misfit pointed the toe of his shoe into the ground and made a little hole and then covered it up again. "I would hate to have to," he said.

"Listen," the grandmother almost screamed, "I know you're a good man. You don't look a bit like you have common blood. I know you must come from nice people!"

"Yes mam," he said, "finest people in the world." When he smiled he showed a row of strong white teeth. "God never made a finer woman than my mother and my daddy's heart was pure gold," he said. The boy with the red sweat shirt had come around behind them and was standing with his gun at his hip. The Misfit squatted down on the ground. "Watch them children, Bobby Lee," he said. "You know they make me nervous." He looked at the six of them huddled together in front of him and he seemed to be embarrassed as if he couldn't think of anything to say. "Ain't a cloud in the sky," he remarked, looking up at it. "Don't see no sun but don't see no cloud neither."

"Yes, it's a beautiful day," said the grandmother. "Listen," she said, "you shouldn't call yourself The Misfit because I know you're a good man at heart. I can just look at you and tell."

"Hush!" Bailey yelled. "Hush! Everybody shut up and let me handle this!" He was squatting in the position of a runner about to sprint forward but he didn't move.

"I pre-chate that, lady," The Misfit said and drew a little circle in the ground with the butt of his gun.

"It'll take a half a hour to fix this here car," Hiram called, looking over the raised hood of it.

"Well, first you and Bobby Lee get him and that little boy to step over yonder with you," The Misfit said, pointing to Bailey and John Wesley. "The boys want to ast you something," he said to Bailey. "Would you mind stepping back in them woods there with them?"

"Listen," Bailey began, "we're in a terrible predicament! Nobody realizes what this is," his voice cracked. His eyes were as blue and intense as the parrots in his shirt and he remained perfectly still.

The grandmother reached up to adjust her hat brim as if she were going to the woods with him but it came off in her hand. She stood staring at it and after a second she let it fall on the ground. Hiram pulled Bailey up by the arms as if he were assisting an old man. John Wesley caught hold of his father's hand and Bobby Lee followed. They went off toward the woods and just as they reached the dark edge, Bailey turned and supporting himself against a gray naked pine trunk, he shouted, "I'll be back in a minute, Mamma, wait on me!"

"Come back this instant!" his mother shrilled but they all disappeared into the woods.

"Bailey Boy!" the grandmother called in a tragic voice but she found she was looking at The Misfit squatting on the ground in front of her. "I just know you're a good man," she said desperately. "You're not a bit common!"

"Nome, I ain't a good man," The Misfit said after a second as if he had considered her statement carefully, "but I ain't the worst in the world neither. My daddy said I was a different breed of dog from my brothers and sisters. 'You know,' Daddy said, 'it's some that can live their whole life out without asking about it and it's others has to know why it is, and this boy is one of the latters. He's going to be into everything!'" He put on his black hat and looked up suddenly and then away deep into the woods as if he were embarrassed again. "I'm sorry I don't have on a shirt before you ladies," he said, hunching his shoulders slightly. "We buried our clothes that we had on when we escaped and we're just making do until we can get better. We borrowed these from some folks we met," he explained.

"That's perfectly all right," the grandmother said. "Maybe Bailey has an extra shirt in his suitcase."

"I'll look and see terrectly," The Misfit said.

"Where are they taking him?" the children's mother screamed.

"Daddy was a card himself," The Misfit said. "You couldn't put anything over on him. He never got in trouble with the Authorities though. Just had the knack of handling them."

"You could be honest too if you'd only try," said the grandmother. "Think how wonderful it would be to settle down and live a comfortable life and not have to think about somebody chasing you all the time."

The Misfit kept scratching in the ground with the butt of his gun as if he were thinking about it. "Yes'm, somebody is always after you," he murmured.

The grandmother noticed how thin his shoulder blades were just behind his hat because she was standing up looking down at him. "Do you ever pray?" she asked.

He shook his head. All she saw was the black hat wiggle between his shoulder blades. "Nome," he said.

There was a pistol shot from the woods, followed closely by another. Then silence. The old lady's head jerked around. She could hear the wind move through the tree tops like a long satisfied insuck of breath. "Bailey Boy!" she called.

"I was a gospel singer for a while," The Misfit said. "I been most everything. Been in the arm service, both land and sea, at home and abroad, been twice married, been an undertaker, been with the railroads, plowed Mother Earth, been in a tornado, seen a man burnt alive oncet," and looked up at the children's mother and the little girl who were sitting close together, their faces white and their eyes glassy; "I even seen a woman flogged," he said.

"Pray, pray," the grandmother began, "pray, pray . . ."

"I never was a bad boy that I remember of," The Misfit said in an almost dreamy voice, "but somewheres along the line I done something wrong and got sent to the penitentiary. I was buried alive," and he looked up and held her attention to him by a steady stare.

"That's when you should have started to pray," she said. "What did you do to get sent to the penitentiary that first time?"

"Turn to the right, it was a wall," The Misfit said, looking up again at the cloudless sky. "Turn to the left, it was a wall. Look up it was a ceiling, look down it was a floor. I forgot what I done, lady. I set there and set there, trying to remember what it was I done and I ain't recalled it to this day. Oncet in a while, I would think it was coming to me, but it never come."

"Maybe they put you in by mistake," the old lady said vaguely.

"Nome," he said. "It wasn't no mistake. They had the papers on me."

"You must have stolen something," she said.

The Misfit sneered slightly. "Nobody had nothing I wanted," he said. "It was a head-doctor at the penitentiary said what I had done was kill my daddy but I know that for a lie. My daddy died in nineteen ought nineteen of the epidemic flu and I never had a thing to do with it. He was buried in the Mount Hopewell Baptist churchyard and you can go there and see for yourself."

"If you would pray," the old lady said, "Jesus would help you."

"That's right," The Misfit said.

"Well then, why don't you pray?" she asked trembling with delight suddenly.

"I don't want no hep," he said. "I'm doing all right by myself."

Bobby Lee and Hiram came ambling back from the woods. Bobby Lee was dragging a yellow shirt with bright blue parrots in it.

"Throw me that shirt, Bobby Lee," The Misfit said. The shirt came flying at him and landed on his shoulder and he put it on. The grandmother couldn't name what the shirt reminded her of. "No, lady," The Misfit said while he was buttoning it up, "I found out the crime don't matter. You can do one thing or you can do another, kill a man or take a tire off his car, because sooner or later you're going to forget what it was you done and just be punished for it."

The children's mother had begun to make heaving noises as if she couldn't get her breath. "Lady," he asked, "would you and that little girl like to step off yonder with Bobby Lee and Hiram and join your husband?"

"Yes, thank you," the mother said faintly. Her left arm dangled helplessly and she was holding the baby, who had gone to sleep, in the other. "Hep that lady up, Hiram," The Misfit said as she struggled to climb out of the ditch, "and Bobby Lee, you hold onto that little girl's hand."

"I don't want to hold hands with him," June Star said. "He reminds me of a pig."

The fat boy blushed and laughed and caught her by the arm and pulled her off into the woods after Hiram and her mother.

Alone with The Misfit, the grandmother found that she had lost her voice. There was not a cloud in the sky nor any sun. There was nothing around her but woods. She wanted to tell him that he must pray. She opened and closed her mouth several times before anything came out. Finally she found herself saying, "Jesus, Jesus," meaning, Jesus will help you, but the way she was saying it, it sounded as if she might be cursing.

"Yes'm," The Misfit said as if he agreed. "Jesus thrown everything off balance. It was the same case with Him as with me except He hadn't committed any crime and they could prove I had committed one because they had the papers on me. Of course," he said, "they never shown me my papers. That's why I sign myself now. I said long ago, you get you a signature and sign everything you do and keep a copy of it. Then you'll know what you done and you can hold up the crime to the punishment and see do they match and in the end you'll have something to prove you ain't been treated right. I call myself The Misfit," he said, "because I can't make what all I done wrong fit what all I gone through in punishment."

There was a piercing scream from the woods, followed closely by a pistol report. "Does it seem right to you, lady, that one is punished a heap and another ain't punished at all?"

"Jesus!" the old lady cried. "You've got good blood! I know you wouldn't shoot a lady! I know you come from nice people! Pray! Jesus, you ought not to shoot a lady. I'll give you all the money I've got!"

"Lady," The Misfit said, looking beyond her far into the woods, "there never was a body that give the undertaker a tip."

There were two more pistol reports and the grandmother raised her head like a parched old turkey hen crying for water and called, "Bailey Boy, Bailey Boy!" as if her heart would break.

"Jesus was the only One that ever raised the dead," The Misfit continued, "and He shouldn't have done it. He thrown everything off balance. If He did what He said, then it's nothing for you to do but throw away everything and follow him, and if He didn't, then it's nothing for you to do but enjoy the few minutes you got left the best way you can—by killing somebody or burning down his house or doing some other meanness to him. No pleasure but meanness," he said and his voice had become almost a snarl.

"Maybe He didn't raise the dead," the old lady mumbled, not knowing what she was saying and feeling so dizzy that she sank down in the ditch with her legs twisted under her.

"I wasn't there so I can't say He didn't," The Misfit said. "I wisht I had of been there," he said, hitting the ground with his fist. "It ain't right I wasn't there because if I had of been there I would of known. Listen lady," he said in a high voice, "if I had of been there I would of known and I wouldn't be like I am now." His voice seemed about to crack and the grandmother's head cleared for an instant. She saw the man's face twisted close to her own as if he were going to cry and she murmured, "Why you're one of my babies. You're one of my own children!" She reached out and touched him on the shoulder. The Misfit sprang back as if a snake had bitten him and shot her three times through the chest. Then he put his gun down on the ground and took off his glasses and began to clean them.

Hiram and Bobby Lee returned from the woods and stood over the ditch, looking down at the grandmother who half sat and half lay in a puddle of blood with her legs crossed under her like a child's and her face smiling up at the cloudless sky.

Without his glasses, The Misfit's eyes were red-rimmed and pale and defenseless-looking. "Take her off and throw her where you thrown the others," he said, picking up the cat that was rubbing itself against his leg.

"She was a talker, wasn't she?" Bobby Lee said, sliding down the ditch with a yodel.

"She would have been a good woman," The Misfit said, "if it had been somebody there to shoot her every minute of her life."

"Some fun!" Bobby Lee said.

"Shut up, Bobby Lee," The Misfit said. "It's no real pleasure in life."

QUESTIONS FOR DISCUSSION AND WRITING

1. How does the grandmother's early apprehension about the trip to Florida foreshadow the major crisis in the story? Explain why the grandmother's recognition of The Misfit triggers that crisis. How do The Misfit's final comments on the grandmother bring the crisis to its denouement?

2. How does the grandmother's relationship to her family characterize her personality? What function does the character of Red Sam serve in the story? How does The Misfit's description of his life justify his name?

3. How do the grandmother's memories of other places and times lead her to the wrong place at the wrong time? In what ways do the characters' positive comments on the weather contrast with the horrible events that take place?
4. How does June Star's assertion that the grandmother is "afraid she'd miss something" help establish the grandmother's point of view in the early part of the story? Once she realizes the intentions of The Misfit, how does her point of view change?
5. How do The Misfit's final words illustrate his attitude toward the events of the afternoon? Explain how the title comments on the theme of the story. How does The Misfit define crime and punishment, goodness and evil? What does he mean when he says, "Jesus thrown everything off balance"?

71
FLANNERY O'CONNOR
Revelation

The doctor's waiting room, which was very small, was almost full when the Turpins entered and Mrs. Turpin, who was very large, made it look even smaller by her presence. She stood looming at the head of the magazine table set in the center of it, a living demonstration that the room was inadequate and ridiculous. Her little bright black eyes took in all the patients as she sized up the seating situation. There was one vacant chair and a place on the sofa occupied by a blond child in a dirty blue romper who should have been told to move over and make room for the lady. He was five or six, but Mrs. Turpin saw at once that no one was going to tell him to move over. He was slumped down in the seat, his arms idle at his sides and his eyes idle in his head; his nose ran unchecked.

Mrs. Turpin put a firm hand on Claud's shoulder and said in a voice that included anyone who wanted to listen, "Claud, you sit in that chair there," and gave him a push down into the vacant one. Claud was florid and bald and sturdy, somewhat shorter than Mrs. Turpin, but he sat down as if he were accustomed to doing what she told him to.

Mrs. Turpin remained standing. The only man in the room besides Claud was a lean stringy old fellow with a rusty hand spread out on each knee, whose eyes were closed as if he were asleep or dead or pretending to be so as not to get up and offer her his seat. Her gaze settled agreeably on a well-dressed grey-haired lady whose eyes met hers and whose expression said: if that child belonged to me, he would have some manners and move over—there's plenty of room there for you and him too.

Claud looked up with a sigh and made as if to rise.

"Sit down," Mrs. Turpin said. "You know you're not supposed to stand on that leg. He has an ulcer on his leg," she explained.

Claud lifted his foot onto the magazine table and rolled his trouser leg up to reveal a purple swelling on a plump marble-white calf.

"My!" the pleasant lady said. "How did you do that?"

"A cow kicked him," Mrs. Turpin said.

"Goodness!" said the lady.

Claud rolled his trouser leg down.

"Maybe the little boy would move over," the lady suggested, but the child did not stir.

"Somebody will be leaving in a minute," Mrs. Turpin said. She could not understand why a doctor—with as much money as they made charging five dollars a day to just stick their head in the hospital door and look at you—couldn't afford a decent-sized waiting room. This one was hardly bigger than a garage. The table was cluttered with limp-looking magazines and at one end of it there was a big green glass ash tray full of cigaret butts and cotton wads with little blood spots on them. If she had had anything to do with the running of the place, that would have been emptied every so often. There were no chairs against the wall at the head of the room. It had a rectangular-shaped panel in it that permitted a view of the office where the nurse came and went and the secretary listened to the radio. A plastic fern in a gold pot sat in the opening and trailed its fronds down almost to the floor. The radio was softly playing gospel music.

Just then the inner door opened and a nurse with the highest stack of yellow hair Mrs. Turpin had ever seen put her face in the crack and called for the next patient. The woman sitting beside Claud grasped the two arms of her chair and hoisted herself up; she pulled her dress free from her legs and lumbered through the door where the nurse disappeared.

Mrs. Turpin eased into the vacant chair, which held her tight as a corset. "I wish I could reduce," she said, and rolled her eyes and gave a comic sigh.

"Oh, *you* aren't fat," the stylish lady said.

"Ooooo I am too," Mrs. Turpin said. "Claud he eats all he wants to and never weighs over one hundred and seventy-five pounds, but me I just look at something good to eat and I gain some weight," and her stomach and shoulders shook with laughter. "You can eat all you want to, can't you, Claud?" she asked, turning to him.

Claud only grinned.

"Well, as long as you have such a good disposition," the stylish lady said, "I don't think it makes a bit of difference what size you are. You just can't beat a good disposition."

Next to her was a fat girl of eighteen or nineteen, scowling into a thick blue book which Mrs. Turpin saw was entitled *Human Development.* The girl raised her head and directed her scowl at Mrs. Turpin as if she did not like her looks. She appeared annoyed that anyone should speak while she tried to read. The poor girl's face was blue with acne and Mrs. Turpin thought how pitiful it was to have a face like that at that age. She gave the girl a friendly smile but the girl only scowled the harder. Mrs. Turpin herself was fat but she had always had good skin, and, though she was forty-seven years old, there was not a wrinkle in her face except around her eyes from laughing too much.

Next to the ugly girl was the child, still in exactly the same position, and next to him was a thin leathery old woman in a cotton print dress. She and Claud had three sacks of chicken feed in their pump house that was in the same print. She had seen from the first that the child belonged with the old woman. She could tell by the way they sat—kind of vacant and white-trashy, as if they would sit there until Doomsday if nobody called and told them to get up. And at right angles but next to the well-dressed pleasant lady was a lank-faced woman who was certainly the child's mother. She had on a yellow sweat shirt and wine-colored slacks, both gritty-looking, and the rims of her lips were stained with snuff. Her dirty yellow hair was tied behind with a little piece of red paper ribbon. Worse than niggers any day, Mrs. Turpin thought.

The gospel hymn playing was, "When I looked up and He looked down," and Mrs. Turpin, who knew it, supplied the last line mentally, "And wona these days I know I'll we-eara crown."

Without appearing to, Mrs. Turpin always noticed people's feet. The well-dressed lady had on red and grey suede shoes to match her dress. Mrs. Turpin had on her good black patent leather pumps. The ugly girl had on Girl Scout shoes and heavy socks. The old woman had on tennis shoes and the white-trashy mother had on what appeared to be bedroom slippers, black straw with gold braid threaded through them—exactly what you would have expected her to have on.

Sometimes at night when she couldn't go to sleep, Mrs. Turpin would occupy herself with the question of who she would have chosen to be if she couldn't have been herself. If Jesus had said to her before he made her, "There's only two places available for you. You can either be a nigger or white-trash," what would she have said? "Please, Jesus, please," she would have said, "just let me wait until there's another place available," and he would have said, "No, you have to go right now and I have only those two places so make up your mind." She would have wiggled and squirmed and begged and pleaded but it would have been no use and finally she would have said, "All right, make me a nigger then—but that don't mean a trashy one." And he would have made her a neat clean respectable Negro-woman, herself but black.

Next to the child's mother was a red-headed youngish woman, reading one of the magazines and working a piece of chewing gum, hell for leather, as Claud would say. Mrs. Turpin could not see the woman's feet. She was not white-trash, just common. Sometimes Mrs. Turpin occupied herself at night naming the classes of people. On the bottom of the heap were most colored people, not the kind she would have been if she had been one, but most of them; then next to them—not above, just away from—were the white-trash; then above them were the home-owners, and above them the home-and-land owners, to which she and Claud belonged. Above she and Claud were people with a lot of money and much bigger houses and much more land. But here the complexity of it would begin to bear in on her, for some of the people with a lot of money were common and ought to be below she and Claud and some of the people who had good blood had lost their money and had to rent and then there were colored people who owned their homes and land as well. There was a colored dentist in town who had two red Lincolns and a swimming pool and a farm with registered white-face cattle on it. Usually by the time she had fallen asleep all the classes of people were moiling and roiling around in her head, and she would dream they were all crammed in together in a box car, being ridden off to be put in a gas oven.

"That's a beautiful clock," she said and nodded to her right. It was a big wall clock, the face encased in a brass sunburst.

"Yes, it's very pretty," the stylish lady said agreeably. "And right on the dot too," she added, glancing at her watch.

The ugly girl beside her cast an eye upward at the clock, smirked, then looked directly at Mrs. Turpin and smirked again. Then she returned her eyes to her book. She was obviously the lady's daughter because, although they didn't look anything alike as to disposition, they both had the same shape of face and the same blue eyes. On the lady they sparkled pleasantly but in the girl's seared face they appeared alternately to smolder and to blaze.

What if Jesus had said, "All right, you can be white-trash or a nigger or ugly"!

Mrs. Turpin felt an awful pity for the girl, though she thought it was one thing to be ugly and another to act ugly.

The woman with the snuff-stained lips turned around in her chair and looked up at the clock. Then she turned back and appeared to look a little to the side of Mrs. Turpin. There was a cast in one of her eyes. "You want to know wher you can get you one of themther clocks?" she asked in a loud voice.

"No, I already have a nice clock," Mrs. Turpin said. Once somebody like her got a leg in the conversation, she would be all over it.

"You can get you one with green stamps," the woman said. "That's most likely wher he got hisn. Save you up enough, you can get you most anythang. I got me some joo'ry."

Ought to have got you a wash rag and some soap, Mrs. Turpin thought.

"I get contour sheets with mine," the pleasant lady said.

The daughter slammed her book shut. She looked straight in front of her, directly through Mrs. Turpin and on through the yellow curtain and the plate glass window which made the wall behind her. The girl's eyes seemed lit all of a sudden with a peculiar light, an unnatural light like night road signs give. Mrs. Turpin turned her head to see if there was anything going on outside that she should see, but she could not see anything. Figures passing cast only a pale shadow through the curtain. There was no reason the girl should single her out for her ugly looks.

"Miss Finley," the nurse said, cracking the door. The gum-chewing woman got up and passed in front of her and Claud and went into the office. She had on red high-heeled shoes.

Directly across the table, the ugly girl's eyes were fixed on Mrs. Turpin as if she had some very special reason for disliking her.

"This is wonderful weather, isn't it?" the girl's mother said.

"It's good weather for cotton if you can get the niggers to pick it," Mrs. Turpin said, "but niggers don't want to pick cotton any more. You can't get the white folks to pick it and now you can't get the niggers—because they got to be right up there with the white folks."

"They gonna *try* anyways," the white-trash woman said, leaning forward.

"Do you have one of those cotton-picking machines?" the pleasant lady asked.

"No," Mrs. Turpin said, "they leave half the cotton in the field. We don't have much cotton anyway. If you want to make it farming now, you have to have a little of everything. We got a couple of acres of cotton and a few hogs and chickens and just enough white-face that Claud can look after them himself."

"One thang I don't want," the white-trash woman said, wiping her mouth with the back of her hands. "Hogs. Nasty stinking things, a-gruntin and a-rootin all over the place."

Mrs. Turpin gave her the merest edge of her attention. "Our hogs are not dirty and they don't stink," she said. "They're cleaner than some children I've seen. Their feet never touch the ground. We have a pig parlor—that's where you raise them on concrete," she explained to the pleasant lady, "and Claud scoots them down with the hose every afternoon and washes off the floor." Cleaner by far than that child right there, she thought. Poor nasty little thing. He had not moved except to put the thumb of his dirty hand into his mouth.

The woman turned her face away from Mrs. Turpin. "I know I wouldn't scoot down no hog with no hose," she said to the wall.

You wouldn't have no hog to scoot down, Mrs. Turpin said to herself.

"A-gruntin and a-rootin and a-groanin," the woman muttered.

"We got a little of everything," Mrs. Turpin said to the pleasant lady. "It's no use in having more than you can handle yourself with help like it is. We found enough niggers to pick our cotton this year but Claud he has to go after them and take them home again in the evening. They can't walk that half a mile. No they can't. I tell you," she said and laughed merrily, "I sure am tired of buttering up niggers, but you got to love em if you want em to work for you. When they come in the morning, I run out and I say, 'Hi yawl this morning?' and when Claud drives them off to the field I just wave to beat the band and they just wave back." And she waved her hand rapidly to illustrate.

"Like you read out of the same book," the lady said, showing she understood perfectly.

"Child, yes," Mrs. Turpin said. "And when they come in from the field, I run out with a bucket of icewater. That's the way it's going to be from now on," she said. "You may as well face it."

"One thang I know," the white-trash woman said. "Two thangs I ain't going to do: love no niggers or scoot down no hog with no hose." And she let out a bark of contempt.

The look that Mrs. Turpin and the pleasant lady exchanged indicated they both understood that you had to *have* certain things before you could *know* certain things. But every time Mrs. Turpin exchanged a look with the lady, she was aware that the ugly girl's peculiar eyes were still on her, and she had trouble bringing her attention back to the conversation.

"When you got something," she said, "you got to look after it." And when you ain't got a thing but breath and britches, she added to herself, you can afford to come to town every morning and just sit on the Court House coping and spit.

A grotesque revolving shadow passed across the curtain behind her and was thrown palely on the opposite wall. Then a bicycle clattered down against the outside of the building. The door opened and a colored boy glided in with a tray from the drug store. It had two large red and white paper cups on it with tops on them. He was a tall, very black boy in discolored white pants and a green nylon shirt. He was chewing gum slowly, as if to music. He set the tray down in the office opening next to the fern and stuck his head through to look for the secretary. She was not in there. He rested his arms on the ledge and waited, his narrow bottom stuck out, swaying slowly to the left and right. He raised a hand over his head and scratched the base of his skull.

"You see that button there, boy?" Mrs. Turpin said. "You can punch that and she'll come. She's probably in the back somewhere."

"Is thas right?" the boy said agreeably, as if he had never seen the button before. He leaned to the right and put his finger on it. "She sometime out," he said and twisted around to face his audience, his elbows behind him on the counter. The nurse appeared and he twisted back again. She handed him a dollar and he rooted in his pocket and made the change and counted it out to her. She gave him fifteen cents for a tip and he went out with the empty tray. The heavy door swung to slowly and closed at length with the sound of suction. For a moment no one spoke.

"They ought to send all them niggers back to Africa," the white-trash woman said. "That's wher they come from in the first place."

"Oh, I couldn't do without my good colored friends," the pleasant lady said.

"There's a heap of things worse than a nigger," Mrs. Turpin agreed. "It's all kinds of them just like it's all kinds of us."

"Yes, and it takes all kinds to make the world go round," the lady said in her musical voice.

As she said it, the raw-complexioned girl snapped her teeth together. Her lower lip turned downwards and inside out, revealing the pale pink inside of her mouth. After a second it rolled back up. It was the ugliest face Mrs. Turpin had ever seen anyone make and for a moment she was certain that the girl had made it at her. She was looking at her as if she had known and disliked her all her life—all of Mrs. Turpin's life, it seemed too, not just all the girl's life. Why, girl, I don't even know you, Mrs. Turpin said silently.

She forced her attention back to the discussion. "It wouldn't be practical to send them back to Africa," she said. "They wouldn't want to go. They got it too good here."

"Wouldn't be what they wanted—if I had anythang to do with it," the woman said.

"It wouldn't be a way in the world you could get all the niggers back over there," Mrs. Turpin said. "They'd be hiding out and lying down and turning sick on you and wailing and hollering and raring and pitching. It wouldn't be a way in the world to get them over there."

"They got over here," the trashy woman said. "Get back like they got over."

"It wasn't so many of them then," Mrs. Turpin explained.

The woman looked at Mrs. Turpin as if here was an idiot indeed but Mrs. Turpin was not bothered by the look, considering where it came from.

"Nooo," she said, "they're going to stay here where they can go to New York and marry white folks and improve their color. That's what they all want to do, every one of them, improve their color."

"You know what comes of that, don't you?" Claud asked.

"No, Claud, what?" Mrs. Turpin said.

Claud's eyes twinkled. "White-faced niggers," he said with never a smile.

Everybody in the office laughed except the white-trash and the ugly girl. The girl gripped the book in her lap with white fingers. The trashy woman looked around her from face to face as if she thought they were all idiots. The old woman in the feed sack dress continued to gaze expressionless across the floor at the high-top shoes of the man opposite her, the one who had been pretending to be asleep when the Turpins came in. He was laughing heartily, his hands still spread out on his knees. The child had fallen to the side and was lying now almost face down in the old woman's lap.

While they recovered from their laughter, the nasal chorus on the radio kept the room from silence.

"You go to blank blank
And I'll go to mine
But we'll all blank along
To-geth-ther,
And all along the blank
We'll hep each other out
Smile-ling in any kind of
Weath-ther!"

Mrs. Turpin didn't catch every word but she caught enough to agree with the spirit of the song and it turned her thoughts sober. To help anybody out that needed it was her philosophy of life. She never spared herself when she found somebody in need, whether they were white or black, trash or decent. And of all she had to be thankful for, she was most thankful that this was so. If Jesus had said, "You can be high society and have all the money you want and be thin and svelte-like, but you can't be a good woman with it," she would have had to say, "Well don't make me that then. Make me a good woman and it don't matter what else, how fat or how ugly or how poor!" Her heart rose. He had not made her a nigger or white-trash or ugly! He had made her herself and given her a little of everything. Jesus, thank you! she said. Thank you thank you thank you! Whenever she counted her blessings she felt as buoyant as if she weighed one hundred and twenty-five pounds instead of one hundred and eighty.

"What's wrong with your little boy?" the pleasant lady asked the white-trashy woman.

"He has a ulcer," the woman said proudly. "He ain't give me a minute's peace since he was born. Him and her are just alike," she said, nodding at the old woman, who was running her leathery fingers through the child's pale hair. "Look like I can't get nothing down them two but Co'Cola and candy."

That's all you try to get down em, Mrs. Turpin said to herself. Too lazy to light the fire. There was nothing you could tell her about people like them that she didn't know already. And it was not just that they didn't have anything. Because if you gave them everything, in two weeks it would all be broken or filthy or they would have chopped it up for lightwood. She knew all this from her own experience. Help them you must, but help them you couldn't.

All at once the ugly girl turned her lips inside out again. Her eyes were fixed like two drills on Mrs. Turpin. This time there was no mistaking that there was something urgent behind them.

Girl, Mrs. Turpin exclaimed silently, I haven't done a thing to you! The girl might be confusing her with somebody else. There was no need to sit by and let herself be intimidated. "You must be in college," she said boldly, looking directly at the girl. "I see you reading a book there."

The girl continued to stare and pointedly did not answer.

Her mother blushed at this rudeness. "The lady asked you a question, Mary Grace," she said under her breath.

"I have ears," Mary Grace said.

The poor mother blushed again. "Mary Grace goes to Wellesley College," she explained. She twisted one of the buttons on her dress. "In Massachusetts," she added with a grimace. "And in the summer she just keeps right on studying. Just reads all the time, a real book worm. She's done real well at Wellesley; she's taking English and Math and History and Psychology and Social Studies," she rattled on, "and I think it's too much. I think she ought to get out and have fun."

The girl looked as if she would like to hurl them all through the plate glass window.

"Way up north," Mrs. Turpin murmured and thought, well, it hasn't done much for her manners.

"I'd almost rather to have him sick," the white-trash woman said, wrenching the attention back to herself. "He's so mean when he ain't. Look like some children just take natural to meanness. It's some gets bad when they get sick but he was the opposite. Took sick and turned good. He don't give me no trouble now. It's me waitin to see the doctor," she said.

If I was going to send anybody back to Africa, Mrs. Turpin thought, it would be your kind, woman. "Yes, indeed," she said aloud, but looking up at the ceiling, "it's a heap of things worse than a nigger." And dirtier than a hog, she added to herself.

"I think people with bad dispositions are more to be pitied than anyone on earth," the pleasant lady said in a voice that was decidedly thin.

"I thank the Lord he has blessed me with a good one," Mrs. Turpin said. "The day has never dawned that I couldn't find something to laugh at."

"Not since she married me anyways," Claud said with a comical straight face.

Everybody laughed except the girl and the white-trash.

Mrs. Turpin's stomach shook. "He's such a caution," she said, "that I can't help but laugh at him."

The girl made a loud ugly noise through her teeth.

Her mother's mouth grew thin and tight. "I think the worst thing in the world," she said, "is an ungrateful person. To have everything and not appreciate it. I know a girl," she said, "who has parents who would give her anything, a little brother who loves her dearly, who is getting a good education, who wears the best clothes, but who can never say a kind word to anyone, who never smiles, who just criticizes and complains all day long."

"Is she too old to paddle?" Claud asked.

The girl's face was almost purple.

"Yes," the lady said, "I'm afraid there's nothing to do but leave her to her folly. Some day she'll wake up and it'll be too late."

"It never hurt anyone to smile," Mrs. Turpin said. "It just makes you feel better all over."

"Of course," the lady said sadly, "but there are just some people you can't tell anything to. They can't take criticism."

"If it's one thing I am," Mrs. Turpin said with feeling, "it's grateful. When I think who all I could have been besides myself and what all I got, a little of everything, and a good disposition besides, I just feel like shouting, 'Thank you, Jesus, for making everything the way it is!' It could have been different!" For one thing, somebody else could have got Claud. At the thought of this, she was flooded with gratitude and a terrible pang of joy ran through her. "Oh thank you, Jesus, Jesus, thank you!" she cried aloud.

The book struck her directly over her left eye. It struck almost at the same instant that she realized the girl was about to hurl it. Before she could utter a sound, the raw face came crashing across the table toward her, howling. The girl's fingers sank like clamps into the soft flesh of her neck. She heard the mother cry out and Claud shout, "Whoa!" There was an instant when she was certain that she was about to be in an earthquake.

All at once her vision narrowed and she saw everything as if it were happening in a small room far away, or as if she were looking at it through the wrong end of a telescope. Claud's face crumpled and fell out of sight. The nurse ran in, then out, then in again. Then the gangling figure of the doctor rushed out of the inner door. Magazines flew this way and that as the table turned over. The girl fell with a thud and Mrs. Turpin's vision suddenly reversed itself and she saw everything large instead of small. The eyes of the white-trashy woman were staring hugely at the floor. There the girl, held down on one side by the nurse and on the other by her mother, was wrenching and turning in their grasp. The doctor was kneeling astride her, trying to hold her arm down. He managed after a second to sink a long needle into it.

Mrs. Turpin felt entirely hollow except for her heart which swung from side to side as if it were agitated in a great empty drum of flesh.

"Somebody that's not busy call for the ambulance," the doctor said in the off-hand voice young doctors adopt for terrible occasions.

Mrs. Turpin could not have moved a finger. The old man who had been sitting next to her skipped numbly into the office and made the call, for the secretary still seemed to be gone.

"Claud!" Mrs. Turpin called.

He was not in his chair. She knew she must jump up and find him but she felt like some one trying to catch a train in a dream, when everything moves in slow motion and the faster you try to run the slower you go.

"Here I am," a suffocated voice, very unlike Claud's, said.

He was doubled up in the corner on the floor, pale as paper, holding his leg. She wanted to get up and go to him but she could not move. Instead, her gaze was drawn slowly downward to the churning face on the floor, which she could see over the doctor's shoulder.

The girl's eyes stopped rolling and focused on her. They seemed a much lighter blue than before, as if a door that had been tightly closed behind them was now open to admit light and air.

Mrs. Turpin's head cleared and her power of motion returned. She leaned forward until she was looking directly into the fierce brilliant eyes. There was no doubt in her mind that the girl did know her, knew her in some intense and personal way, beyond time and place and condition. "What you got to say to me?" she asked hoarsely and held her breath, waiting, as for a revelation.

The girl raised her head. Her gaze locked with Mrs. Turpin's. "Go back to hell where you came from, you old wart hog," she whispered. Her voice was low but clear. Her eyes burned for a moment as if she saw with pleasure that her message had struck its target.

Mrs. Turpin sank back in her chair.

After a moment the girl's eyes closed and she turned her head wearily to the side.

The doctor rose and handed the nurse the empty syringe. He leaned over and put both hands for a moment on the mother's shoulders, which were shaking. She was sitting on the floor, her lips pressed together, holding Mary Grace's hand in her lap. The girl's fingers were gripped like a baby's around her thumb. "Go on to the hospital," he said. "I'll call and make the arrangements."

"Now let's see that neck," he said in a jovial voice to Mrs. Turpin. He began to inspect her neck with his first two fingers. Two little moon-shaped lines like pink fish bones were indented over her windpipe. There was the beginning of an angry red swelling above her eye. His fingers passed over this also.

"Lea' me be," she said thickly and shook him off. "See about Claud. She kicked him."

"I'll see about him in a minute," he said and felt her pulse. He was a thin grey-haired man, given to pleasantries. "Go home and have yourself a vacation the rest of the day," he said and patted her on the shoulder.

Quit your pattin me, Mrs. Turpin growled to herself.

"And put an ice pack over that eye," he said. Then he went and squatted down beside Claud and looked at his leg. After a moment he pulled him up and Claud limped after him into the office.

Until the ambulance came, the only sounds in the room were the tremulous moans of the girl's mother, who continued to sit on the floor. The white-trash woman did not take her eyes off the girl. Mrs. Turpin looked straight ahead at nothing. Presently the ambulance drew up, a long dark shadow, behind the curtain. The attendants came in and set the stretcher down beside the girl and lifted her expertly onto it and carried her out. The nurse helped the mother gather up her things. The shadow of the ambulance moved silently away and the nurse came back in the office

"That ther girl is going to be a lunatic, ain't she?" the white-trash woman asked the nurse, but the nurse kept on to the back and never answered her.

"Yes, she's going to be a lunatic," the white-trash woman said to the rest of them.

"Po' critter," the old woman murmured. The child's face was still in her lap. His eyes looked idly out over her knees. He had not moved during the disturbance except to draw one leg up under him.

"I thank Gawd," the white-trash woman said fervently, "I ain't a lunatic."

Claud came limping out and the Turpins went home.

As their pick-up truck turned into their own dirt road and made the crest of the hill, Mrs. Turpin gripped the window ledge and looked out suspiciously. The land sloped gracefully down through a field dotted with lavender weeds and at the start of the rise their small yellow frame house, with its little flower beds spread out around it like a fancy apron, sat primly in its accustomed place between two giant hickory trees. She would not have been startled to see a burnt wound between two blackened chimneys.

Neither of them felt like eating so they put on their house clothes and lowered the shade in the bedroom and lay down, Claud with his leg on a pillow and herself with a damp washcloth over her eye. The instant she was flat on her back, the image of a razor-backed hog with warts on its face and horns coming out behind its ears snorted into her head. She moaned, a low quiet moan.

"I am not," she said tearfully, "a wart hog. From hell." But the denial had no force. The girl's eyes and her words, even the tone of her voice, low but clear, directed only to her, brooked no repudiation. She had been singled out for the message, though there was trash in the room to whom it might justly have been applied. The full force of this fact struck her only now. There was a woman there who was neglecting her own child but she had been overlooked. The message had been given to Ruby Turpin, a respectable, hard-working, church-going woman. The tears dried. Her eyes began to burn instead with wrath.

She rose on her elbow and the washcloth fell into her hand. Claud was lying on his back, snoring. She wanted to tell him what the girl had said. At the same time, she did not wish to put the image of herself as a wart hog from hell into his mind.

"Hey, Claud," she muttered and pushed his shoulder.

Claud opened one pale baby blue eye.

She looked into it warily. He did not think about anything. He just went his way.

"Wha, whasit?" he said and closed the eye again.

"Nothing," she said. "Does your leg pain you?"

"Hurts like hell," Claud said.

"It'll quit terreckly," she said and lay back down. In a moment Claud was snoring again. For the rest of the afternoon they lay there. Claud slept. She scowled at the ceiling. Occasionally she raised her fist and made a small stabbing motion over her chest as if she was defending her innocence to invisible guests who were like the comforters of Job, reasonable-seeming but wrong.

About five-thirty Claud stirred. "Got to go after those niggers," he sighed, not moving.

She was looking straight up as if there were unintelligible handwriting on the ceiling. The protuberance over her eye had turned a greenish-blue. "Listen here," she said.

"What?"

"Kiss me."

Claud leaned over and kissed her loudly on the mouth. He pinched her side and their hands interlocked. Her expression of ferocious concentration did not change. Claud got up, groaning and growling, and limped off. She continued to study the ceiling.

She did not get up until she heard the pick-up truck coming back with the Negroes. Then she rose and thrust her feet in her brown oxfords, which she did not bother to lace, and stumped out onto the back porch and got her red plastic bucket. She emptied a tray of ice cubes into it and filled it half full of water and went out into the back yard. Every afternoon after Claud brought the hands in, one of the boys helped him put out hay and the rest waited in the back of the truck until he was ready to take them home. The truck was parked in the shade under one of the hickory trees.

"Hi yawl this evening?" Mrs. Turpin asked grimly, appearing with the bucket and the dipper. There were three women and a boy in the truck.

"Us doin nicely," the oldest woman said. "Hi you doin?" and her gaze stuck immediately on the dark lump on Mrs. Turpin's forehead. "You done fell down, ain't you?" she asked in a solicitous voice. The old woman was dark and almost toothless. She had on an old felt hat of Claud's set back on her head. The other two women were younger and lighter and they both had new bright green sun hats. One of them had hers on her head; the other had taken hers off and the boy was grinning beneath it.

Mrs. Turpin set the bucket down on the floor of the truck. "Yawl hep yourselves," she said. She looked around to make sure Claud had gone. "No. I didn't fall down," she said, folding her arms. "It was something worse than that."

"Ain't nothing bad happen to you!" the old woman said. She said it as if they all knew that Mrs. Turpin was protected in some special way by Divine Providence. "You just had you a little fall."

"We were in town at the doctor's office for where the cow kicked Mr. Turpin," Mrs. Turpin said in a flat tone that indicated they could leave off their foolishness. "And there was this girl there. A big fat girl with her face all broke out. I could look at that girl and tell she was peculiar but I couldn't tell how. And me and her mama were just talking and going along and all of a sudden WHAM! She throws this big book she was reading at me and . . ."

"Naw!" the old woman cried out.

"And then she jumps over the table and commences to choke me."

"Naw!" they all exclaimed, "naw!"

"Hi come she do that?" the old woman asked. "What ail her?"

Mrs. Turpin only glared in front of her.

"Somethin ail her," the old woman said.

"They carried her off in an ambulance," Mrs. Turpin continued, "but before she went she was rolling on the floor and they were trying to hold her down to give her a shot and she said something to me." She paused. "You know what she said to me?"

"What she say?" they asked.

"She said," Mrs. Turpin began, and stopped, her face very dark and heavy. The sun was getting whiter and whiter, blanching the sky overhead so that the leaves of the hickory tree were black in the face of it. She could not bring forth the words. "Something real ugly," she muttered.

"She sho shouldn't said nothin ugly to you," the old woman said. "You so sweet. You the sweetest lady I know."

"She pretty too," the one with the hat on said.

"And stout," the other one said. "I never knowed no sweeter white lady."

"That's the truth befo' Jesus," the old woman said. "Amen! You des as sweet and pretty as you can be."

Mrs. Turpin knew just exactly how much Negro flattery was worth and it added to her rage. "She said," she began again and finished this time with a fierce rush of breath, "that I was an old wart hog from hell."

There was an astounded silence.

"Where she at?" the youngest woman cried in a piercing voice.

"Lemme see her. I'll kill her!"

"I'll kill her with you!" the other one cried.

"She b'long in the sylum," the old woman said emphatically. "You the sweetest white lady I know."

"She pretty too," the other two said. "Stout as she can be and sweet. Jesus satisfied with her!"

"Deed he is," the old woman declared.

Idiots! Mrs. Turpin growled to herself. You could never say anything intelligent to a nigger. You could talk at them but not with them. "Yawl ain't drunk your water," she said shortly. "Leave the bucket in the truck when you're finished with it. I got more to do than just stand around and pass the time of day," and she moved off and into the house.

She stood for a moment in the middle of the kitchen. The dark protuberance over her eye looked like a miniature tornado cloud which might any moment sweep across the horizon of her brow. Her lower lip protruded dangerously. She squared her massive shoulders. Then she marched into the front of the house and out the side door and started down the road to the pig parlor. She had the look of a woman going single-handed, weaponless, into battle.

The sun was a deep yellow now like a harvest moon and was riding westward very fast over the far tree line as if it meant to reach the hogs before she did. The road was rutted and she kicked several good-sized stones out of her path as she strode along. The pig parlor was on a little knoll at the end of a lane that ran off from the side of the barn. It was a square of concrete as large as a small room, with a board fence about four feet high around it. The concrete floor sloped slightly so that the hog wash could drain off into a trench where it was carried to the field for fertilizer. Claud was standing on the outside, on the edge of the concrete, hanging onto the top board, hosing down the floor inside. The hose was connected to the faucet of a water trough nearby.

Mrs. Turpin climbed up beside him and glowered down at the hogs inside. There were seven long-snouted bristly shoats in it—tan with liver-colored spots—and an old sow a few weeks off from farrowing. She was lying on her side grunting. The shoats were running about shaking themselves like idiot children, their little slit pig eyes searching the floor for anything left. She had read that pigs were the most intelligent animal. She doubted it. They were supposed to be smarter than dogs. There had even been a pig astronaut. He had performed his assignment perfectly but died of a heart attack afterwards because they left him in his electric suit, sitting upright throughout his examination when naturally a hog should be on all fours.

A-gruntin and a-rootin and a-groanin.

"Gimme that hose," she said, yanking it away from Claud. "Go on and carry them niggers home and then get off that leg."

"You look like you might have swallowed a mad dog," Claud observed, but he got down and limped off. He paid no attention to her humors.

Until he was out of earshot, Mrs. Turpin stood on the side of the pen, holding the hose and pointing the stream of water at the hind quarters of any shoat that looked as if it might try to lie down. When he had had time to get over the hill, she turned her head slightly and her wrathful eyes scanned the path. He was nowhere in sight. She turned back again and seemed to gather herself up. Her shoulders rose and she drew in her breath.

"What do you send me a message like that for?" she said in a low fierce voice, barely above a whisper but with the force of a shout in its concentrated fury. "How am I a hog and me both? How am I saved and from hell too?" Her free fist was knotted and with the other she gripped the hose, blindly pointing the stream of water in and out of the eye of the old sow whose outraged squeal she did not hear.

The pig parlor commanded a view of the back pasture where their twenty beef cows were gathered around the hay-bales Claud and the boy had put out. The freshly cut pasture sloped down to the highway. Across it was their cotton field and beyond that a dark green dusty wood which they owned as well. The sun was behind the wood, very red, looking over the paling of trees like a farmer inspecting his own hogs.

"Why me?" she rumbled. "It's no trash around here, black or white, that I haven't given to. And break my back to the bone every day working. And do for the church."

She appeared to be the right size woman to command the arena before her. "How am I a hog?" she demanded. "Exactly how am I like them?" and she jabbed the stream of water at the shoats. "There was plenty of trash there. It didn't have to be me."

"If you like trash better, go get yourself some trash then," she railed. "You could have made me trash. Or a nigger. If trash is what you wanted why didn't you make me trash?" She shook her fist with the hose in it and a watery snake appeared momentarily in the air. "I could quit working and take it easy and be filthy," she growled. "Lounge about the sidewalks all day drinking root beer. Dip snuff and spit in every puddle and have it all over my face. I could be nasty.

"Or you could have made me a nigger. It's too late for me to be a nigger," she said with deep sarcasm, "but I could act like one. Lay down in the middle of the road and stop traffic. Roll on the ground."

In the deepening light everything was taking on a mysterious hue. The pasture was growing a peculiar glassy green and the streak of highway had turned lavender. She braced herself for a final assault and this time her voice rolled out over the pasture. "Go on," she yelled, "call me a hog! Call me a hog again. From hell. Call me a wart hog from hell. Put that bottom rail on top. There'll still be a top and bottom!"

A garbled echo returned to her.

A final surge of fury shook her and she roared, "Who do you think you are?"

The color of everything, field and crimson sky, burned for a moment with a transparent intensity. The question carried over the pasture and across the highway and the cotton field and returned to her clearly like an answer from beyond the wood.

She opened her mouth but no sound came out of it.

A tiny truck, Claud's, appeared on the highway, heading rapidly out of sight. Its gears scraped thinly. It looked like a child's toy. At any moment a bigger truck might smash into it and scatter Claud's and the niggers' brains all over the road.

Mrs. Turpin stood there, her gaze fixed on the highway, all her muscles rigid, until in five or six minutes the truck reappeared, returning. She waited until it had had time to turn into their own road. Then like a monumental statue coming to life, she bent her head slowly and gazed, as if through the very heart of mystery, down into the pig parlor at the hogs. They had settled all in one corner around the old sow who was grunting softly. A red glow suffused them. They appeared to pant with a secret life.

Until the sun slipped finally behind the tree line, Mrs. Turpin remained there with her gaze bent to them as if she were absorbing some abysmal life-giving knowledge. At last she lifted her head. There was only a purple streak in the sky, cutting through a field of crimson and leading, like an extension of the highway, into the descending dusk. She raised her hands from the side of the pen in a gesture hieratic and profound. A visionary light settled in her eyes. She saw the streak as a vast swinging bridge extending upward from the earth through a field of living fire. Upon it a vast horde of souls were rumbling toward heaven. There were whole companies of white-trash, clean for the first time in their lives, and bands of black niggers in white robes, and battalions of freaks and lunatics shouting and clapping and leaping like frogs. And bringing up the end of the procession was a tribe of people whom she recognized at once as those who, like herself and Claud, had always had a little of everything and the God-given wit to use it right. She leaned forward to observe them closer. They were marching behind the others with great dignity, accountable as they had always been for good order and common sense and respectable behavior. They alone were on key. Yet she could see by their shocked and altered faces that even their virtues were being burned away. She lowered her hands and gripped the rail of the hog pen, her eyes small but fixed unblinkingly on what lay ahead. In a moment the vision faded but she remained where she was, immobile.

At length she got down and turned off the faucet and made her slow way on the darkening path to the house. In the woods around her the invisible cricket choruses had struck up, but what she heard were the voices of the souls climbing upward into the starry field and shouting hallelujah.

QUESTIONS FOR DISCUSSION AND WRITING

1. How do the various revelations mark the development of the story? How does Mrs. Turpin's conflict with people evolve into her final conflict with God?
2. How does Mrs. Turpin characterize herself? What clues does O'Connor provide that explain why the fat girl accuses Mrs. Turpin of being a "wart hog from hell"? What does the story reveal finally about Mrs. Turpin's good disposition?
3. How does Mrs. Turpin impose her sense of social order on the group in the waiting room? In what ways is the pig parlor like the waiting room?
4. How do Mrs. Turpin's internal and external dialogues complement each other? How accurately does Mrs. Turpin report the events in the waiting room to the Negroes?
5. On what perception does Mrs. Turpin base her belief in order and goodness? How does her "revelation" alter this perception?

72

FLANNERY O'CONNOR

Everything That Rises Must Converge

Her doctor had told Julian's mother that she must lose twenty pounds on account of her blood pressure, so on Wednesday nights Julian had to take her downtown on the bus for a reducing class at the Y. The reducing class was designed for working girls over fifty, who weighed from 165 to 200 pounds. His mother was one of the slimmer ones, but she said ladies did not tell their age or weight. She would not ride the buses by herself at night since they had been integrated, and because the reducing class was one of her few pleasures, necessary for her health, and *free*, she said Julian could at least put himself out to take her, considering all she did for him. Julian did not like to consider all she did for him, but every Wednesday night he braced himself and took her.

She was almost ready to go, standing before the hall mirror, putting on her hat, while he, his hands behind him, appeared pinned to the door frame, waiting like Saint Sebastian for the arrows to begin piercing him. The hat was new and had cost her seven dollars and a half. She kept saying, "Maybe I shouldn't have paid that for it. No, I shouldn't have. I'll take it off and return it tomorrow. I shouldn't have bought it."

Julian raised his eyes to heaven. "Yes, you should have bought it," he said. "Put it on and let's go." It was a hideous hat. A purple velvet flap came down on one side of it and stood up on the other; the rest of it was green and looked like a cushion with the stuffing out. He decided it was less comical than jaunty and pathetic. Everything that gave her pleasure was small and depressed him.

She lifted the hat one more time and set it down slowly on top of her head. Two wings of gray hair protruded on either side of her florid face, but her eyes, sky-blue, were as innocent and untouched by experience as they must have been when she was ten. Were it not that she was a widow who had struggled fiercely to feed and clothe and put him through school and who was supporting him still, "until he got on his feet," she might have been a little girl that he had to take to town.

"It's all right, it's all right," he said. "Let's go." He opened the door himself and started down the walk to get her going. The sky was a dying violet and the houses stood out darkly against it, bulbous liver-colored monstrosities of a uniform ugliness though no two were alike. Since this had been a fashionable neighborhood forty years ago, his mother persisted in thinking they did well to have an apartment in it. Each house had a narrow collar of dirt around it in which sat, usually, a grubby child. Julian walked with his hands in his pockets, his head down and thrust forward and his eyes glazed with the determination to make himself completely numb during the time he would be sacrificed to her pleasure.

The door closed and he turned to find the dumpy figure, surmounted by the atrocious hat, coming toward him. "Well," she said, "you only live once and paying a little more for it, I at least won't meet myself coming and going."

"Some day I'll start making money," Julian said gloomily—he knew he never would—"and you can have one of those jokes whenever you take the fit." But first they would move. He visualized a place where the nearest neighbors would be three miles away on either side.

"I think you're doing fine," she said, drawing on her gloves. "You've only been out of school a year. Rome wasn't built in a day."

She was one of the few members of the Y reducing class who arrived in hat and gloves and who had a son who had been to college. "It takes time," she said, "and the world is in such a mess. This hat looked better on me than any of the others, though when she brought it out I said, 'Take that thing back. I wouldn't have it on my head,' and she said, 'Now wait till you see it on,' and when she put it on me, I said, 'we-ull,' and she said, 'If you ask me, that hat does something for you and you do something for that hat, and besides,' she said, 'with that hat, you won't meet yourself coming and going.'"

Julian thought he could have stood his lot better if she had been selfish, if she had been an old hag who drank and screamed at him. He walked along, saturated in depression, as if in the midst of his martyrdom he had lost his faith. Catching sight of his long, hopeless, irritated face, she stopped suddenly with a grief-stricken look, and pulled back on his arm. "Wait on me," she said. "I'm going back to the house and take this thing off and tomorrow I'm going to return it. I was out of my head. I can pay the gas bill with the seven-fifty."

He caught her arm in a vicious grip. "You are not going to take it back," he said. "I like it."

"Well," she said, "I don't think I ought . . ."

"Shut up and enjoy it," he muttered, more depressed than ever.

"With the world in the mess it's in," she said, "it's a wonder we can enjoy anything. I tell you, the bottom rail is on the top."

Julian sighed.

"Of course," she said, "if you know who you are, you can go anywhere." She said this every time he took her to the reducing class. "Most of them in it are not our kind of people," she said, "but I can be gracious to anybody. I know who I am."

"They don't give a damn for your graciousness," Julian said savagely. "Knowing who you are is good for one generation only. You haven't the foggiest idea where you stand now or who you are."

She stopped and allowed her eyes to flash at him. "I most certainly do know who I am," she said, "and if you don't know who you are, I'm ashamed of you."

"Oh hell," Julian said.

"Your great-grandfather was a former governor of this state," she said. "Your grandfather was a prosperous landowner. Your grandmother was a Godhigh."

"Will you look around you," he said tensely, "and see where you are now?" and he swept his arm jerkily out to indicate the neighborhood, which the growing darkness at least made less dingy.

"You remain what you are," she said. "Your great-grandfather had a plantation and two hundred slaves."

"There are no more slaves," he said irritably.

"They were better off when they were," she said. He groaned to see that she was off on that topic. She rolled onto it every few days like a train on an open track. He knew every stop, every junction, every swamp along the way, and knew the exact point at which her conclusion would roll majestically into the station: "It's ridiculous. It's simply not realistic. They should rise, yes, but on their own side of the fence."

"Let's skip it," Julian said.

"The ones I feel sorry for," she said, "are the ones that are half white. They're tragic."

"Will you skip it?"

"Suppose we were half white. We would certainly have mixed feelings."

"I have mixed feelings now," he groaned.

"Well let's talk about something pleasant," she said. "I remember going to Grandpa's when I was a little girl. Then the house had double stairways that went up to what was really the second floor—all the cooking was done on the first. I used to like to stay down in the kitchen on account of the way the walls smelled. I would sit with my nose pressed against the plaster and take deep breaths. Actually the place belonged to the Godhighs but your grandfather Chestny paid the mortgage and saved it for them. They were in reduced circumstances," she said, "but reduced or not, they never forgot who they were."

"Doubtless that decayed mansion reminded them," Julian muttered. He never spoke of it without contempt or thought of it without longing. He had seen it once when he was a child before it had been sold. The double stairways had rotted and been torn down. Negroes were living in it. But it remained in his mind as his mother had known it. It appeared in his dreams regularly. He would stand on the wide porch, listening to the rustle of oak leaves, then wander through the high-ceilinged hall into the parlor that opened onto it and gaze at the worn rugs and faded draperies. It occurred to him that it was he, not she, who could have appreciated it. He preferred its threadbare elegance to anything he could name and it was because of it that all the neighborhoods they had lived in had been a torment to him—whereas she had hardly known the difference. She called her insensitivity "being adjustable."

"And I remember the old darky who was my nurse, Caroline. There was no better person in the world. I've always had a great respect for my colored friends," she said. "I'd do anything in the world for them and they'd . . ."

"Will you for God's sake get off that subject?" Julian said. When he got on a bus by himself, he made it a point to sit down beside a Negro, in reparation as it were for his mother's sins.

"You're mighty touchy tonight," she said. "Do you feel all right?"

"Yes I feel all right," he said. "Now lay off."

She pursed her lips. "Well, you certainly are in a vile humor," she observed. "I just won't speak to you at all."

They had reached the bus stop. There was no bus in sight and Julian, his hands still jammed in his pockets and his head thrust forward, scowled down the empty street. The frustration of having to wait on the bus as well as ride on it began to creep up his neck like a hot hand. The presence of his mother was borne in upon him as she gave a pained sigh. He looked at her bleakly. She was holding herself very erect under the preposterous hat, wearing it like a banner of her imaginary dignity. There was in him an evil urge to break her spirit. He suddenly unloosened his tie and pulled it off and put it in his pocket.

She stiffened. "Why must you look like *that* when you take me to town?" she said. "Why must you deliberately embarrass me?"

"If you'll never learn where you are," he said, "you can at least learn where I am."

"You look like a—thug," she said.

"Then I must be one," he murmured.

"I'll just go home," she said. "I will not bother you. If you can't do a little thing like that for me . . ."

Rolling his eyes upward, he put his tie back on. "Restored to my class," he muttered. He thrust his face toward her and hissed, "True culture is in the mind, the *mind,*" he said, and tapped his head, "the mind."

"It's in the heart," she said, "and in how you do things and how you do things is because of who you *are.*"

"Nobody in the damn bus cares who you are."

"I care who I am," she said icily.

The lighted bus appeared on top of the next hill and as it approached, they moved out into the street to meet it. He put his hand under her elbow and hoisted her up on the creaking step. She entered with a little smile, as if she were going into a drawing room where everyone had been waiting for her. While he put in the tokens, she sat down on one of the broad front seats for three which faced the aisle. A thin woman with protruding teeth and long yellow hair was sitting on the end of it. His mother moved up beside her and left room for Julian beside herself. He sat down and looked at the floor across the aisle where a pair of thin feet in red and white canvas sandals were planted.

His mother immediately began a general conversation meant to attract anyone who felt like talking. "Can it get any hotter?" she said and removed from her purse a folding fan, black with a Japanese scene on it, which she began to flutter before her.

"I reckon it might could," the woman with the protruding teeth said, "but I know for a fact my apartment couldn't get no hotter."

"It must get the afternoon sun," his mother said. She sat forward and looked up and down the bus. It was half filled. Everybody was white. "I see we have the bus to ourselves," she said. Julian cringed.

"For a change," said the woman across the aisle, the owner of the red and white canvas sandals. "I come on one the other day and they were thick as fleas—up front and all through."

"The world is in a mess everywhere," his mother said. "I don't know how we've let it get in this fix."

"What gets my goat is all those boys from good families stealing automobile tires," the woman with the protruding teeth said. "I told my boy, I said you may not be rich but you been raised right and if I ever catch you in any such mess, they can send you on to the reformatory. Be exactly where you belong."

"Training tells," his mother said. "Is your boy in high school?"

"Ninth grade," the woman said.

"My son just finished college last year. He wants to write but he's selling typewriters until he gets started," his mother said.

The woman leaned forward and peered at Julian. He threw her such a malevolent look that she subsided against the seat. On the floor across the aisle there was an abandoned newspaper. He got up and got it and opened it out in front of him. His mother discreetly continued the conversation in a lower tone but the woman across the aisle said in a loud voice, "Well that's nice. Selling typewriters is close to writing. He can go right from one to the other."

"I tell him," his mother said, "that Rome wasn't built in a day."

Behind the newspaper Julian was withdrawing into the inner compartment of his mind where he spent most of his time. This was a kind of mental bubble in which he established himself when he could not bear to be a part of what was going on around him. From it he could see out and judge but in it he was safe from any kind of penetration from without. It was the only place where he felt free of the general idiocy of his fellows. His mother had never entered it but from it he could see her with absolute clarity.

The old lady was clever enough and he thought that if she had started from any of the right premises, more might have been expected of her. She lived according to the laws of her own fantasy world, outside of which he had never seen her set foot. The law of it was to sacrifice herself for him after she had first created the necessity to do so by making a mess of things. If he had permitted her sacrifices, it was only because her lack of foresight had made them necessary. All of her life had been a struggle to act like a Chestny without the Chestny goods, and to give him everything she thought a Chestny ought to have; but since, said she, it was fun to struggle, why complain? And when you had won, as she had won, what fun to look back on the hard times! He could not forgive her that she had enjoyed the struggle and that she thought *she* had won.

What she meant when she said she had won was that she had brought him up successfully and had sent him to college and that he had turned out so well—good looking (her teeth had gone unfilled so that his could be straightened), intelligent (he realized he was too intelligent to be a success), and with a future ahead of him (there was of course no future ahead of him). She excused his gloominess on the grounds that he was still growing up and his radical ideas on his lack of practical experience. She said he didn't yet know a thing about "life," that he hadn't even entered the real world—when already he was as disenchanted with it as a man of fifty.

The further irony of all this was that in spite of her, he had turned out so well. In spite of going to only a third-rate college, he had, on his own initiative, come out with a first-rate education; in spite of growing up dominated by a small mind, he had ended up with a large one; in spite of all her foolish views, he was free of prejudice and unafraid to face facts. Most miraculous of all, instead of being blinded by love for her as she was for him, he had cut himself emotionally free of her and could see her with complete objectivity. He was not dominated by his mother.

The bus stopped with a sudden jerk and shook him from his meditation. A woman from the back lurched forward with little steps and barely escaped falling in his newspaper as she righted herself. She got off and a large Negro got on. Julian kept his paper lowered to watch. It gave him a certain satisfaction to see injustice in daily operation. It confirmed his view that with a few exceptions there was no one worth knowing within a radius of three hundred miles. The Negro was well dressed and carried a briefcase. He looked around and then sat down on the other end of the seat where the woman with the red and white canvas sandals was sitting. He immediately unfolded a newspaper and obscured himself behind it. Julian's mother's elbow at once prodded insistently into his ribs. "Now you see why I won't ride on these buses by myself," she whispered.

The woman with the red and white canvas sandals had risen at the same time the Negro sat down and had gone further back in the bus and taken the seat of the woman who had got off. His mother leaned forward and cast her an approving look.

Julian rose, crossed the aisle, and sat down in the place of the woman with the canvas sandals. From this position, he looked serenely across at his mother. Her face had turned an angry red. He stared at her, making his eyes the eyes of a stranger. He felt his tension suddenly lift as if he had openly declared war on her.

He would have liked to get in conversation with the Negro and to talk with him about art or politics or any subject that would be above the comprehension of those around them, but the man remained entrenched behind his paper. He was either ignoring the change of seating or had never noticed it. There was no way for Julian to convey his sympathy.

His mother kept her eyes fixed reproachfully on his face. The woman with the protruding teeth was looking at him avidly as if he were a type of monster new to her.

"Do you have a light?" he asked the Negro.

Without looking away from his paper, the man reached in his pocket and handed him a packet of matches.

"Thanks," Julian said. For a moment he held the matches foolishly. A NO SMOKING sign looked down upon him from over the door. This alone would not have deterred him; he had no cigarettes. He had quit smoking some months before because he could not afford it. "Sorry," he muttered and handed back the matches. The Negro lowered the paper and gave him an annoyed look. He took the matches and raised the paper again.

His mother continued to gaze at him but she did not take advantage of his momentary discomfort. Her eyes retained their battered look. Her face seemed to be unnaturally red, as if her blood pressure had risen. Julian allowed no glimmer of sympathy to show on his face. Having got the advantage, he wanted desperately to keep it and carry it through. He would have liked to teach her a lesson that would last her a while, but there seemed no way to continue the point. The Negro refused to come out from behind his paper.

Julian folded his arms and looked stolidly before him, facing her but as if he did not see her, as if he had ceased to recognize her existence. He visualized a scene in which, the bus having reached their stop, he would remain in his seat and when she said, "Aren't you going to get off?" he would look at her as at a stranger who had rashly addressed him. The corner they got off on was usually deserted, but it was well lighted and it would not hurt her to walk by herself the four blocks to the Y. He decided to wait until the time came and then decide whether or not he would let her get off by herself. He would have to be at the Y at ten to bring her back, but he could leave her wondering if he was going to show up. There was no reason for her to think she could always depend on him.

He retired again into the high-ceilinged room sparsely settled with large pieces of antique furniture. His soul expanded momentarily but then he became aware of his mother across from him and the vision shriveled. He studied her coldly. Her feet in little pumps dangled like a child's and did not quite reach the floor. She was training on him an exaggerated look of reproach. He felt completely detached from her. At that moment he could with pleasure have slapped her as he would have slapped a particularly obnoxious child in his charge.

He began to imagine various unlikely ways by which he could teach her a lesson. He might make friends with some distinguished Negro professor or lawyer and bring him home to spend the evening. He would be entirely justified but her blood pressure would rise to 300. He could not push her to the extent of making her have a stroke, and moreover, he had never been successful at making any Negro friends. He had tried to strike up an acquaintance on the bus with some of the better types, with ones that looked like professors or ministers or lawyers. One morning he had sat down next to a distinguished-looking dark brown man who had answered his questions with a sonorous solemnity but who had turned out to be an undertaker. Another day he had sat down beside a cigar-smoking Negro with a diamond ring on his finger, but after a few stilted pleasantries, the Negro had rung the buzzer and risen, slipping two lottery tickets into Julian's hand as he climbed over him to leave.

He imagined his mother lying desperately ill and his being able to secure only a Negro doctor for her. He toyed with that idea for a few minutes and then dropped it for a momentary vision of himself participating as a sympathizer in a sit-in demonstration. This was possible but he did not linger with it. Instead, he approached the ultimate horror. He brought home a beautiful suspiciously Negroid woman. Prepare yourself, he said. There is nothing you can do about it. This is the woman I've chosen. She's intelligent, dignified, even good, and she's suffered and she hasn't thought it *fun*. Now persecute us, go ahead and persecute us. Drive her out of here, but remember, you're driving me too. His eyes were narrowed and through the indignation he had generated, he saw his mother across the aisle, purple-faced, shrunken to the dwarf-like proportions of her moral nature, sitting like a mummy beneath the ridiculous banner of her hat.

He was tilted out of his fantasy again as the bus stopped. The door opened with a sucking hiss and out of the dark a large, gaily dressed, sullen-looking colored woman got on with a little boy. The child, who might have been four, had on a short plaid suit and a Tyrolean hat with a blue feather in it. Julian hoped that he would sit down beside him and that the woman would push in beside his mother. He could think of no better arrangement.

As she waited for her tokens, the woman was surveying the seating possibilities—he hoped with the idea of sitting where she was least wanted. There was something familiar-looking about her but Julian could not place what it was. She was a giant of a woman. Her face was set not only to meet opposition but to seek it out. The downward tilt of her large lower lip was like a warning sign: DON'T TAMPER WITH ME. Her bulging figure was encased in a green crepe dress and her feet overflowed in red shoes. She had on a hideous hat. A purple velvet flap came down on one side of it and stood up on the other; the rest of it was green and looked like a cushion with the stuffing out. She carried a mammoth red pocketbook that bulged throughout as if it were stuffed with rocks.

To Julian's disappointment, the little boy climbed up on the empty seat beside his mother. His mother lumped all children, black and white, into the common category, "cute," and she thought little Negroes were on the whole cuter than little white children. She smiled at the little boy as he climbed on the seat.

Meanwhile the woman was bearing down upon the empty seat beside Julian. To his annoyance, she squeezed herself into it. He saw his mother's face change as the woman settled herself next to him and he realized with satisfaction that this was more objectionable to her than it was to him. Her face seemed almost gray and there was a look of dull recognition in her eyes, as if suddenly she had sickened at some awful confrontation. Julian saw that it was because she and the woman had, in a sense, swapped sons. Though his mother would not realize the symbolic significance of this, she would feel it. His amusement showed plainly on his face.

The woman next to him muttered something unintelligible to herself. He was conscious of a kind of bristling next to him, muted growling like that of an angry cat. He could not see anything but the red pocketbook upright on the bulging green thighs. He visualized the woman as she had stood waiting for her tokens—the ponderous figure, rising from the red shoes upward over the solid hips, the mammoth bosom, the haughty face, to the green and purple hat.

His eyes widened.

The vision of the two hats, identical, broke upon him with the radiance of a brilliant sunrise. His face was suddenly lit with joy. He could not believe that Fate had thrust upon his mother such a lesson. He gave a loud chuckle so that she would look at him and see that he saw. She turned her eyes on him slowly. The blue in them seemed to have turned a bruised purple. For a moment he had an uncomfortable sense of her innocence, but it lasted only a second before principle rescued him. Justice entitled him to laugh. His grin hardened until it said to her as plainly as if he were saying aloud: Your punishment exactly fits your pettiness. This should teach you a permanent lesson.

Her eyes shifted to the woman. She seemed unable to bear looking at him and to find the woman preferable. He became conscious again of the bristling presence at his side. The woman was rumbling like a volcano about to become active. His mother's mouth began to twitch slightly at one corner. With a sinking heart, he saw incipient signs of recovery on her face and realized that this was going to strike her suddenly as funny and was going to be no lesson at all. She kept her eyes on the woman and an amused smile came over her face as if the woman were a monkey that had stolen her hat. The little Negro was looking up at her with large fascinated eyes. He had been trying to attract her attention for some time.

"Carver!" the woman said suddenly. "Come heah!"

When he saw that the spotlight was on him at last, Carver drew his feet up and turned himself toward Julian's mother and giggled.

"Carver!" the woman said. "You heah me? Come heah!"

Carver slid down from the seat but remained squatting with his back against the base of it, his head turned slyly around toward Julian's mother, who was smiling at him. The woman reached a hand across the aisle and snatched him to her. He righted himself and hung backwards on her knees, grinning at Julian's mother. "Isn't he cute?" Julian's mother said to the woman with the protruding teeth.

"I reckon he is," the woman said without conviction.

The Negress yanked him upright but he eased out of her grip and shot across the aisle and scrambled, giggling wildly, onto the seat beside his love.

"I think he likes me," Julian's mother said, and smiled at the woman. It was the smile she used when she was being particularly gracious to an inferior. Julian saw everything lost. The lesson had rolled off her like rain on a roof.

The woman stood up and yanked the little boy off the seat as if she were snatching him from contagion. Julian could feel the rage in her at having no weapon like his mother's smile. She gave the child a sharp slap across his leg. He howled once and then thrust his head into her stomach and kicked his feet against her shins. "Behave," she said vehemently.

The bus stopped and the Negro who had been reading the newspaper got off. The woman moved over and set the little boy down with a thump between herself and Julian. She held him firmly by the knee. In a moment he put his hands in front of his face and peeped at Julian's mother through his fingers.

"I see yoooooooo!" she said and put her hand in front of her face and peeped at him.

The woman slapped his hand down. "Quit yo' foolishness," she said, "before I knock the living Jesus out of you!"

Julian was thankful that the next stop was theirs. He reached up and pulled the cord. The woman reached up and pulled it at the same time. Oh my God, he thought. He had the terrible intuition that when they got off the bus together, his mother would open her purse and give the little boy a nickel. The gesture would be as natural to her as breathing. The bus stopped and the woman got up and lunged to the front, dragging the child, who wished to stay on, after her. Julian and his mother got up and followed. As they neared the door, Julian tried to relieve her of her pocketbook.

"No," she murmured, "I want to give the little boy a nickel."

"No!" Julian hissed. "No!"

She smiled down at the child and opened her bag. The bus door opened and the woman picked him up by the arm and descended with him, hanging at her hip. Once in the street she set him down and shook him.

Julian's mother had to close her purse while she got down the bus step but as soon as her feet were on the ground, she opened it again and began to rummage inside. "I can't find but a penny," she whispered, "but it looks like a new one."

"Don't do it!" Julian said fiercely between his teeth. There was a streetlight on the corner and she hurried to get under it so that she could better see into her pocketbook. The woman was heading off rapidly down the street with the child still hanging backward on her hand.

"Oh little boy!" Julian's mother called and took a few quick steps and caught up with them just beyond the lamppost. "Here's a bright new penny for you," and she held out the coin, which shone bronze in the dim light.

The huge woman turned and for a moment stood, her shoulders lifted and her face frozen with frustrated rage, and stared at Julian's mother. Then all at once she seemed to explode like a piece of machinery that had been given one ounce of pressure too much. Julian saw the black fist swing out with the red pocketbook. He shut his eyes and cringed as he heard the woman shout, "He don't take nobody's pennies!" When he opened his eyes, the woman was disappearing down the street with the little boy staring wide-eyed over her shoulder. Julian's mother was sitting on the sidewalk.

"I told you not to do that," Julian said angrily. "I told you not to do that!"

He stood over her for a minute, gritting his teeth. Her legs were stretched out in front of her and her hat was on her lap. He squatted down and looked her in the face. It was totally expressionless. "You got exactly what you deserved," he said. "Now get up."

He picked up her pocketbook and put what had fallen out back in it. He picked the hat up off her lap. The penny caught his eye on the sidewalk and he picked that up and let it drop before her eyes into the purse. Then he stood up and leaned over and held his hands out to pull her up. She remained immobile. He sighed. Rising above them on either side were black apartment buildings, marked with irregular rectangles of light. At the end of the block a man came out of a door and walked off in the opposite direction. "All right," he said, "suppose somebody happens by and wants to know why you're sitting on the sidewalk?"

She took the hand and, breathing hard, pulled heavily up on it and then stood for a moment, swaying slightly as if the spots of light in the darkness were circling around her. Her eyes, shadowed and confused, finally settled on his face. He did not try to conceal his irritation. "I hope this teaches you a lesson," he said. She leaned forward and her eyes raked his face. She seemed trying to determine his identity. Then, as if she found nothing familiar about him, she started off with a headlong movement in the wrong direction.

"Aren't you going on to the Y?" he asked.

"Home," she muttered.

"Well, are we walking?"

For answer she kept going. Julian followed along, his hands behind him. He saw no reason to let the lesson she had had go without backing it up with an explanation of its meaning. She might as well be made to understand what had happened to her. "Don't think that was just an uppity Negro woman," he said. "That was the whole colored race which will no longer take your condescending pennies. That was your black double. She can wear the same hat as you, and to be sure," he added gratuitously (because he thought it was funny), "it looked better on her than it did on you. What all this means," he said, "is that the old world is gone. The old manners are obsolete and your graciousness is not worth a damn." He thought bitterly of the house that had been lost for him. "You aren't who you think you are," he said.

She continued to plow ahead, paying no attention to him. Her hair had come undone on one side. She dropped her pocketbook and took no notice. He stopped and picked it up and handed it to her but she did not take it.

"You needn't act as if the world had come to an end," he said, "because it hasn't. From now on you've got to live in a new world and face a few realities for a change. Buck up," he said, "it won't kill you."

She was breathing fast.

"Let's wait on the bus," he said.

"Home," she said thickly.

"I hate to see you behave like this," he said. "Just like a child. I should be able to expect more of you." He decided to stop where he was and make her stop and wait for a bus. "I'm not going any farther," he said, stopping. "We're going on the bus."

She continued to go on as if she had not heard him. He took a few steps and caught her arm and stopped her. He looked into her face and caught his breath. He was looking into a face he had never seen before. "Tell Grandpa to come get me," she said.

He stared, stricken.

"Tell Caroline to come get me," she said.

Stunned, he let her go and she lurched forward again, walking as if one leg were shorter than the other. A tide of darkness seemed to be sweeping her from him. "Mother!" he cried. "Darling, sweetheart, wait!" Crumpling, she fell to the pavement. He dashed forward and fell at her side, crying, "Mamma, Mamma!" He turned her over. Her face was fiercely distorted. One eye, large and staring, moved slightly to the left as if it had become unmoored. The other remained fixed on him, raked his face again, found nothing and closed.

"Wait here, wait here!" he cried and jumped up and began to run for help toward a cluster of lights he saw in the distance ahead of him. "Help, help!" he shouted, but his voice was thin, scarcely a thread of sound. The lights drifted farther away the faster he ran and his feet moved numbly as if they carried him nowhere. The tide of darkness seemed to sweep him back to her, postponing from moment to moment his entry into the world of guilt and sorrow.

QUESTIONS FOR DISCUSSION AND WRITING

1. How does Julian's mother's insistence that he accompany her to the reducing class at the Y establish the basic conflict in the story? In what way do the black woman and her child bring that conflict to its climax? How do the last paragraphs of the story resolve that conflict?

2. Is Julian's description of his mother as "innocent and undaunted by experience" an accurate assessment of her character? How well does Julian's description of his "mental bubble" define his character? In what ways are Julian's and his mother's views of the world different? In what ways are they the same?

3. How does the world of the bus serve as an appropriate setting for this story? According to Julian's mother, why is the world in such a mess? How does the mansion stand for the way the world used to be?

4. How does the author's allusion to Saint Sebastian reveal her attitude toward Julian and the world? What kind of lesson does Julian wish to teach his mother? What have Julian and his mother learned at the end of the story?

5. How does the title help explain the events in the story? In what sense have both Julian and the black woman "risen"? Why is it inevitable that Julian's mother and the black woman "converge"?

73

FRANK O'CONNOR

Guests of the Nation

FRANK O'CONNOR (1903–1966), the pen name for Michael John O'Donovan, was born in Cork, Ireland. Although he briefly attended the Christian Brothers School in Cork, his family's poverty forced him to forgo any formal education. While still in his teens, O'Connor joined the Irish Republican Army (IRA) and fought in the civil war from 1922 to 1923. Arrested and imprisoned, O'Connor continued his self-education while serving as the prison librarian until he was released in 1923. O'Connor was hired by the Irish Carnegie United Kingdom Trust to organize rural libraries, an activity that put him in contact with the leaders of the Irish Literature Revival, most notably William Butler Yeats and others associated with the Abbey Theatre Company in Dublin. In the 1930s he began publishing his short stories in American magazines such as *The New Yorker, Holiday,* and *Esquire.* His stories, which attempt to record the oral quality of the Irish people and which appear in more than twenty volumes, are most accessible in *Collected Stories* (1981). O'Connor also wrote novels, *Dutch Interior* (1940); travel literature, *Irish Miles* (1947); literary criticism, *The Lonely Voice* (1963); and two volumes of an autobiography, *An Only Child* (1961) and *My Father's Son* (1969). "Guests of the Nation," reprinted from *Collected Stories,* recounts the experiences of several Irishmen who must choose between loyalty to their guests and duty to their nation.

1

At dusk the big Englishman, Belcher, would shift his long legs out of the ashes and say "Well, chums, what about it?" and Noble or me would say "All right, chum" (for we had picked up some of their curious expressions), and the little Englishman, Hawkins, would light the lamp and bring out the cards. Sometimes Jeremiah Donovan would come up and supervise the game and get excited over Hawkins's cards, which he always played badly, and shout at him as if he was one of our own, "Ah, you divil, you, why didn't you play the tray?"

But ordinarily Jeremiah was a sober and contented poor devil like the big Englishman, Belcher, and was looked up to only because he was a fair hand at documents, though he was slow enough even with them. He wore a small cloth hat and big gaiters over his long pants, and you seldom saw him with his hands out of his pockets. He reddened when you talked to him, tilting from toe to heel and back, and looking down all the time at his big farmer's feet. Noble and me used to make fun of his broad accent, because we were from the town.

I couldn't at the time see the point of me and Noble guarding Belcher and Hawkins at all, for it was my belief that you could have planted that pair down anywhere from this to Claregalway and they'd have taken root there like a native weed. I never in my short experience seen two men to take to the country as they did.

They were handed on to us by the Second Battalion when the search for them became too hot, and Noble and myself, being young, took over with a natural feeling of responsibility, but Hawkins made us look like fools when he showed that he knew the country better than we did.

"You're the bloke they calls Bonaparte," he says to me. "Mary Brigid O'Connell told me to ask you what you done with the pair of her brother's socks you borrowed."

For it seemed, as they explained it, that the Second used to have little evenings, and some of the girls of the neighborhood turned in, and, seeing they were such decent chaps, our fellows couldn't leave the two Englishmen out of them. Hawkins learned to dance "The Walls of Limerick," "The Siege of Ennis," and "The Waves of Tory" as well as any of them, though, naturally, we couldn't return the compliment, because our lads at that time did not dance foreign dances on principle.

So whatever privileges Belcher and Hawkins had with the Second they just naturally took with us, and after the first day or two we gave up all pretense of keeping a close eye on them. Not that they could have got far, for they had accents you could cut with a knife and wore khaki tunics and overcoats with civilian pants and boots. But it's my belief that they never had any idea of escaping and were quite content to be where they were.

It was a treat to see how Belcher got off with the old woman of the house where we were staying. She was a great warrant to scold, and cranky even with us, but before ever she had a chance of giving our guests, as I may call them, a lick of her tongue, Belcher had made her his friend for life. She was breaking sticks, and Belcher, who hadn't been more than ten minutes in the house, jumped up from his seat and went over to her.

"Allow me, madam," he says, smiling his queer little smile, "please allow me"; and he takes the bloody hatchet. She was struck too paralytic to speak, and after that, Belcher would be at her heels, carrying a bucket, a basket, or a load of turf, as the case might be. As Noble said, he got into looking before she leapt, and hot water, or any little thing she wanted, Belcher would have it ready for her. For such a huge man (and though I am five foot ten myself I had to look up at him) he had an uncommon shortness—or should I say lack?—of speech. It took us some time to get used to him, walking in and out, like a ghost, without a word. Especially because Hawkins talked enough for a platoon, it was strange to hear big Belcher with his toes in the ashes come out with a solitary "Excuse me, chum," or "That's right, chum." His one and only passion was cards, and I will say for him that he was a good cardplayer. He could have fleeced myself and Noble, but whatever we lost to him Hawkins lost to us, and Hawkins played with the money Belcher gave him.

Hawkins lost to us because he had too much old gab, and we probably lost to Belcher for the same reason. Hawkins and Noble would spit at one another about religion into the early hours of the morning, and Hawkins worried the soul out of Noble, whose brother was a priest, with a string of questions that would puzzle a cardinal. To make it worse, even in treating of holy subjects, Hawkins had a deplorable tongue. I never in all my career met a man who could mix such a variety of cursing and bad language into an argument. He was a terrible man, and a fright to argue. He never did a stroke of work, and when he had no one else to talk to, he got stuck in the old woman.

He met his match in her, for one day when he tried to get her to complain profanely of the drought, she gave him a great come-down by blaming it entirely on Jupiter Pluvius (a deity neither Hawkins nor I had ever heard of, though Noble said that among the pagans it was believed that he had something to do with the rain). Another day he was swearing at the capitalists for starting the German war when the old lady laid down her iron, puckered up her little crab's mouth, and said: "Mr. Hawkins, you can say what you like about the war, and think you'll deceive me because I'm only a simple poor countrywoman, but I know what started the war. It was the Italian Count that stole the heathen divinity out of the temple in Japan. Believe me, Mr. Hawkins, nothing but sorrow and want can follow the people that disturb the hidden powers."

A queer old girl, all right.

2

We had our tea one evening, and Hawkins lit the lamp and we all sat into cards. Jeremiah Donovan came in too, and sat down and watched us for a while, and it suddenly struck me that he had no great love for the two Englishmen. It came as a great surprise to me, because I hadn't noticed anything about him before.

Late in the evening a really terrible argument blew up between Hawkins and Noble, about capitalists and priests and love of your country.

"The capitalists," says Hawkins with an angry gulp, "pays the priests to tell you about the next world so as you won't notice what the bastards are up to in this."

"Nonsense, man!" says Noble, losing his temper. "Before ever a capitalist was thought of, people believed in the next world."

Hawkins stood up as though he was preaching a sermon.

"Oh, they did, did they?" he says with a sneer. "They believed all the things you believe, isn't that what you mean? And you believe that God created Adam, and Adam created Shem, and Shem created Jehoshaphat. You believe all that silly old fairytale about Eve and Eden and the apple. Well, listen to me, chum. If you're entitled to hold a silly belief like that, I'm entitled to hold my silly belief—which is that the first thing your God created was a bleeding capitalist, with morality and Rolls-Royce complete. Am I right, chum?" he says to Belcher.

"You're right, chum," says Belcher with his amused smile, and got up from the table to stretch his long legs into the fire and stroke his moustache. So, seeing that Jeremiah Donovan was going, and that there was no knowing when the argument about religion would be over, I went out with him. We strolled down to the village together, and then he stopped and started blushing and mumbling and saying I ought to be behind, keeping guard on the prisoners. I didn't like the tone he took with me, and anyway I was bored with life in the cottage, so I replied by asking him what the hell we wanted guarding them at all for. I told him I'd talked it over with Noble, and that we'd both rather be out with a fighting column.

"What use are those fellows to us?" says I.

He looked at me in surprise and said: "I thought you knew we were keeping them as hostages."

"Hostages?" I said.

"The enemy have prisoners belonging to us," he says, "and now they're talking of shooting them. If they shoot our prisoners, we'll shoot theirs."

"Shoot them?" I said.

"What else did you think we were keeping them for?" he says.

"Wasn't it very unforeseen of you not to warn Noble and myself of that in the beginning?" I said.

"How was it?" says he. "You might have known it."

"We couldn't know it, Jeremiah Donovan," says I. "How could we when they were on our hands so long?"

"The enemy have our prisoners as long and longer," says he.

"That's not the same thing at all," says I.

"What difference is there?" says he.

I couldn't tell him, because I knew he wouldn't understand. If it was only an old dog that was going to the vet's, you'd try and not get too fond of him, but Jeremiah Donovan wasn't a man that would ever be in danger of that.

"And when is this thing going to be decided?" says I.

"We might hear tonight," he says. "Or tomorrow or the next day at latest. So if it's only hanging round here that's a trouble to you, you'll be free soon enough."

It wasn't the hanging round that was a trouble to me at all by this time. I had worse things to worry about. When I got back to the cottage the argument was still on. Hawkins was holding forth in his best style, maintaining that there was no next world, and Noble was maintaining that there was; but I could see that Hawkins had had the best of it.

"Do you know what, chum?" he was saying with a saucy smile. "I think you're just as big a bleeding unbeliever as I am. You say you believe in the next world, and you know just as much about the next world as I do, which is sweet damn-all. What's heaven? You don't know. Where's heaven? You don't know. You know sweet damn-all! I ask you again, do they wear wings?"

"Very well, then," says Noble, "they do. Is that enough for you? They do wear wings."

"Where do they get them, then? Who makes them? Have they a factory for wings? Have they a sort of store where you hands in your chit and takes your bleeding wings?"

"You're an impossible man to argue with," says Noble. "Now, listen to me—" And they were off again.

It was long after midnight when we locked up and went to bed. As I blew out the candle I told Noble what Jeremiah Donovan was after telling me. Noble took it very quietly. When we'd been in bed about an hour he asked me did I think we ought to tell the Englishmen. I didn't think we should, because it was more than likely that the English wouldn't shoot our men, and even if they did, the brigade officers, who were always up and down with the Second Battalion and knew the Englishmen well, wouldn't be likely to want them plugged. "I think so too," says Noble. "It would be great cruelty to put the wind up them now."

"It was very unforeseen of Jeremiah Donovan anyhow," says I.

It was next morning that we found it so hard to face Belcher and Hawkins. We went about the house all day scarcely saying a word. Belcher didn't seem to notice; he was stretched into the ashes as usual, with his usual look of waiting in quietness for something unforeseen to happen, but Hawkins noticed and put it down to Noble's being beaten in the argument of the night before.

"Why can't you take a discussion in the proper spirit?" he says severely. "You and your Adam and Eve! I'm a Communist, that's what I am. Communist or anarchist, it all comes to much the same thing." And for hours he went round the house, muttering when the fit took him. "Adam and Eve! Adam and Eve! Nothing better to do with their time than picking bleeding apples!"

3

I don't know how we got through that day, but I was very glad when it was over, the tea things were cleared away, and Belcher said in his peaceful way: "Well, chums, what about it?" We sat round the table and Hawkins took out the cards, and just then I heard Jeremiah Donovan's footsteps on the path and a dark presentiment crossed my mind. I rose from the table and caught him before he reached the door.

"What do you want?" I asked.

"I want those two soldier friends of yours," he says, getting red.

"Is that the way, Jeremiah Donovan?" I asked.

"That's the way. There were four of our lads shot this morning, one of them a boy of sixteen."

"That's bad," I said.

At that moment Noble followed me out, and the three of us walked down the path together, talking in whispers. Feeney, the local intelligence officer, was standing by the gate.

"What are you going to do about it?" I asked Jeremiah Donovan.

"I want you and Noble to get them out; tell them they're being shifted again; that'll be the quietest way."

"Leave me out of that," says Noble under his breath.

Jeremiah Donovan looks at him hard.

"All right," he says. "You and Feeney get a few tools from the shed and dig a hole by the far end of the bog. Bonaparte and myself will be after you. Don't let anyone see you with the tools. I wouldn't like it to go beyond ourselves."

We saw Feeney and Noble go round to the shed and went in ourselves. I left Jeremiah Donovan to do the explanations. He told them that he had orders to send them back to the Second Battalion. Hawkins let out a mouthful of curses, and you could see that though Belcher didn't say anything, he was a bit upset too. The old woman was for having them stay in spite of us, and she didn't stop advising them until Jeremiah Donovan lost his temper and turned on her. He had a nasty temper, I noticed. It was pitch-dark in the cottage by this time, but no one thought of lighting the lamp, and in the darkness the two Englishmen fetched their topcoats and said good-bye to the old woman.

"Just as a man makes a home of a bleeding place, some bastard at headquarters thinks you're too cushy and shunts you off," says Hawkins, shaking her hand.

"A thousand thanks, madam," says Belcher. "A thousand thanks for everything"—as though he'd made it up.

We went round to the back of the house and down towards the bog. It was only then that Jeremiah Donovan told them. He was shaking with excitement.

"There were four of our fellows shot in Cork this morning and now you're to be shot as a reprisal."

"What are you talking about?" snaps Hawkins. "It's bad enough being mucked about as we are without having to put up with your funny jokes."

"It isn't a joke," says Donovan. "I'm sorry, Hawkins, but it's true," and begins on the usual rigmarole about duty and how unpleasant it is.

I never noticed that people who talk a lot about duty find it much of a trouble to them.

"Oh, cut it out!" says Hawkins.

"Ask Bonaparte," says Donovan, seeing that Hawkins isn't taking him seriously. "Isn't it true, Bonaparte?"

"It is," I say, and Hawkins stops.

"Ah, for Christ's sake, chum."

"I mean it, chum," I say.

"You don't sound as if you meant it."

"If he doesn't mean it, I do," says Donovan, working himself up.

"What have you against me, Jeremiah Donovan?"

"I never said I had anything against you. But why did your people take out four of our prisoners and shoot them in cold blood?"

He took Hawkins by the arm and dragged him on, but it was impossible to make him understand that we were in earnest. I had the Smith and Wesson in my pocket and I kept fingering it and wondering what I'd do if they put up a fight for it or ran, and wishing to God they'd do one or the other. I knew if they did run for it, that I'd never fire on them. Hawkins wanted to know was Noble in it, and when we said yes, he asked why Noble wanted to plug him. Why did any of us want to plug him? What had he done to us? Weren't we all chums? Didn't we understand him and didn't he understand us? Did we imagine for an instant that he'd shoot us for all the so-and-so officers in the so-and-so British Army?

By this time we'd reached the bog, and I was so sick I couldn't even answer him. We walked along the edge of it in the darkness, and every now and then Hawkins would call a halt and begin all over again, as if he was wound up, about our being chums, and I knew that nothing but the sight of the grave would convince him that we had to do it. And all the time I was hoping that something would happen; that they'd run for it or that Noble would take over the responsibility from me. I had the feeling that it was worse on Noble than on me.

4

At last we saw the lantern in the distance and made towards it. Noble was carrying it, and Feeney was standing somewhere in the darkness behind him, and the picture of them so still and silent in the bogland brought it home to me that we were in earnest, and banished the last bit of hope I had.

Belcher, on recognizing Noble, said: "Hallo, chum," in his quiet way, but Hawkins flew at him at once, and the argument began all over again, only this time Noble had nothing to say for himself and stood with his head down, holding the lantern between his legs.

It was Jeremiah Donovan who did the answering. For the twentieth time, as though it was haunting his mind, Hawkins asked if anybody thought he'd shoot Noble.

"Yes, you would," says Jeremiah Donovan.

"No, I wouldn't, damn you!"

"You would, because you'd know you'd be shot for not doing it."

"I wouldn't, not if I was to be shot twenty times over. I wouldn't shoot a pal. And Belcher wouldn't—isn't that right, Belcher?"

"That's right, chum," Belcher said, but more by way of answering the question than of joining in the argument. Belcher sounded as though whatever unforeseen thing he'd always been waiting for had come at last.

"Anyway, who says Noble would be shot if I wasn't? What do you think I'd do if I was in his place, out in the middle of a blasted bog?"

"What would you do?" asks Donovan.

"I'd go with him wherever he was going, of course. Share my last bob with him and stick by him through thick and thin. No one can ever say of me that I let down a pal."

"We had enough of this," says Jeremiah Donovan, cocking his revolver. "Is there any message you want to send?"

"No, there isn't."

"Do you want to say your prayers?"

Hawkins came out with a cold-blooded remark that even shocked me and turned on Noble again.

"Listen to me, Noble," he says. "You and me are chums. You can't come over to my side, so I'll come over to your side. That show you I mean what I say? Give me a rifle and I'll go along with you and the other lads."

Nobody answered him. We knew that was no way out.

"Hear what I'm saying?" he says. "I'm through with it. I'm a deserter or anything else you like. I don't believe in your stuff, but it's no worse than mine. That satisfy you?"

Noble raised his head, but Donovan began to speak and he lowered it again without replying.

"For the last time, have you any messages to send?" says Donovan in a cold, excited sort of voice.

"Shut up, Donovan! You don't understand me, but these lads do. They're not the sort to make a pal and kill a pal. They're not the tools of any capitalist."

I alone of the crowd saw Donovan raise his Webley to the back of Hawkins's neck, and as he did so I shut my eyes and tried to pray. Hawkins had begun to say something else when Donovan fired, and as I opened my eyes at the bang, I saw Hawkins stagger at the knees and lie out flat at Noble's feet, slowly and as quiet as a kid falling asleep, with the lantern-light on his lean legs and bright farmer's boots. We all stood very still, watching him settle out in the last agony.

Then Belcher took out a handkerchief and began to tie it about his own eyes (in our excitement we'd forgotten to do the same for Hawkins), and, seeing it wasn't big enough, turned and asked for the loan of mine. I gave it to him and he knotted the two together and pointed with his foot at Hawkins.

"He's not quite dead," he says. "Better give him another."

Sure enough, Hawkins's left knee is beginning to rise. I bend down and put my gun to his head; then, recollecting myself, I get up again. Belcher understands what's in my mind.

"Give him his first," he says. "I don't mind. Poor bastard, we don't know what's happening to him now."

I knelt and fired. By this time I didn't seem to know what I was doing. Belcher, who was fumbling a bit awkwardly with the handkerchiefs, came out with a laugh as he heard the shot. It was the first time I heard him laugh and it sent a shudder down my back; it sounded so unnatural.

"Poor bugger!" he said quietly. "And last night he was so curious about it all. It's very queer, chums, I always think. Now he knows as much about it as they'll ever let him know, and last night he was all in the dark."

Donovan helped him to tie the handkerchiefs about his eyes. "Thanks, chum," he said. Donovan asked if there were any messages he wanted sent.

"No, chum," he says. "Not for me. If any of you would like to write to Hawkins's mother, you'll find a letter from her in his pocket. He and his mother were great chums. But my missus left me eight years ago. Went away with another fellow and took the kid with her. I like the feeling of a home, as you may have noticed, but I couldn't start again after that."

It was an extraordinary thing, but in those few minutes Belcher said more than in all the weeks before. It was just as if the sound of the shot had started a flood of talk in him and he could go on the whole night like that, quite happily, talking about himself. We stood round like fools now that he couldn't see us any longer. Donovan looked at Noble, and Noble shook his head. Then Donovan raised his Webley, and at that moment Belcher gives his queer laugh again. He may have thought we were talking about him, or perhaps he noticed the same thing I'd noticed and couldn't understand it.

"Excuse me, chums," he says. "I feel I'm talking the hell of a lot, and so silly, about my being so handy about a house and things like that. But this thing came on me suddenly. You'll forgive me, I'm sure."

"You don't want to say a prayer?" asked Donovan.

"No, chum," he says. "I don't think it would help. I'm ready, and you boys want to get it over."

"You understand that we're only doing our duty?" says Donovan.

Belcher's head was raised like a blind man's, so that you could only see his chin and the tip of his nose in the lantern-light.

"I never could make out what duty was myself," he said. "I think you're all good lads, if that's what you mean. I'm not complaining."

Noble, just as if he couldn't bear any more of it, raised his fist at Donovan, and in a flash Donovan raised his gun and fired. The big man went over like a sack of meal, and this time there was no need of a second shot.

I don't remember much about the burying, but that it was worse than all the rest because we had to carry them to the grave. It was all made lonely with nothing but a patch of lantern-light between ourselves and the dark, and birds hooting and screeching all round, disturbed by the guns. Noble went through Hawkins's belongings to find the letter from his mother, and then joined his hands together. He did the same with Belcher. Then, when we'd filled in the grave, we separated from Jeremiah Donovan and Feeney and took our tools back to the shed. All the way we didn't speak a word. The kitchen was dark and cold as we'd left it, and the old woman was sitting over the hearth, saying her beads. We walked past her into the room, and Noble struck a match to light the lamp. She rose quietly and came to the doorway with all her cantankerousness gone.

"What did ye do with them?" she asked in a whisper, and Noble started so that the match went out in his hand.

"What's that?" he asked without turning round.

"I heard ye," she said.

"What did you hear?" asked Noble.

"I heard ye. Do ye think I didn't hear ye, putting the spade back in the houseen?"

Noble struck another match and this time the lamp lit for him.

"Was that what ye did to them?" she asked.

Then, by God, in the very doorway, she fell on her knees and began praying, and after looking at her for a minute or two Noble did the same by the fireplace. I pushed my way out past her and left them at it. I stood at the door, watching the stars and listening to the shrieking of the birds dying out over the bogs. It is so strange what you feel at times like that you can't describe it. Noble says he saw everything ten times the size, as though there were nothing in the whole world but that little patch of bog with the two Englishmen stiffening into it, but with me it was as if the patch of bog where the Englishmen were was a million miles away, and even Noble and the old woman, mumbling behind me, and the birds and the bloody stars were all far away, and I was somehow very small and very lost and lonely like a child astray in the snow. And anything that happened to me afterwards, I never felt the same about again.

QUESTIONS FOR DISCUSSION AND WRITING

1. How does the card game help establish the existing relationships in the story? How does Jeremiah Donovan's revelation change those relationships and bring the story to its climax?
2. How does the narrator contrast the difference between Hawkins and Belcher? How does he characterize the difference between himself and Donovan? What function does the old woman's character have in the development of the story?
3. The setting for this story is the Anglo-Irish war in which the Irish fought for independence in 1919–1921. How do the men's arguments about religion and politics help explain the conflicts that started the war between the English and the Irish? How does the word "chum" serve as a counterpoint to these arguments?
4. What is the narrator's point of view toward his duty as guard? How does his point of view change once he realizes that he will have to kill his hostages? What do his final words reveal about what he has learned?
5. How does the title of the story establish its theme? In what sense are Hawkins and Belcher "guests"? To what extent does duty to "nation" justify their murder?

74

TILLIE OLSEN

I Stand Here Ironing

TILLIE OLSEN was born in 1913 in Omaha, Nebraska. After graduating from high school, she worked in industry and as a typist-transcriber. In the 1930s, Olsen became active in the labor movement, trying to organize a union among the meat packers in Kansas City, and wrote *Yonnondio: From the Thirties,* a novel that chronicles the struggles of a working-class family. The novel was lost before it could be published, but it was later reclaimed and acknowledged as one of the best works of fiction to emerge from the Depression. In 1936 she married Jack Olsen, a printer, and gave up writing for the next fifteen years to raise four children. In the early 1950s Olsen returned to writing, and her stories attracted a small but enthusiastic group of readers. In 1961 her novella *Tell Me a Riddle* won the O. Henry Award. On the basis of this newly established reputation, Olsen was asked to serve as writer-in-residence at Amherst College, Stanford University, the Massachusetts Institute of Technology, and the University of California at San Diego. During this period, she published the long-lost *Yonnondio* (1974), two works of nonfiction, *Rebecca Harding Davis: Life in the Iron Mills* (1972) and *Silences* (1978), and an anthology, *Mother to Daughter, Daughter to Mother* (1984). The latter is a series of meditations on the problems faced by women writers. "I Stand Here Ironing," reprinted from *Tell Me a Riddle* (1961), is a mother's attempt to explain the circumstances that shaped her daughter's character.

I stand here ironing, and what you asked me moves tormented back and forth with the iron.

"I wish you would manage the time to come in and talk with me about your daughter. I'm sure you can help me understand her. She's a youngster who needs help and whom I'm deeply interested in helping."

"Who needs help." . . . Even if I came, what good would it do? You think because I am her mother I have a key, or that in some way you could use me as a key? She has lived for nineteen years. There is all that life that has happened outside of me, beyond me.

And when is there time to remember, to sift, to weigh, to estimate, to total? I will start and there will be an interruption and I will have to gather it all together again. Or I will become engulfed with all I did or did not do, with what should have been and what cannot be helped.

She was a beautiful baby. The first and only one of our five that was beautiful at birth. You do not guess how new and uneasy her tenancy in her now-loveliness. You did not know her all those years she was thought homely, or see her poring over her baby pictures, making me tell her over and over how beautiful she had been—and would be, I would tell her—and was now, to the seeing eye. But the seeing eyes were few or non-existent. Including mine.

I nursed her. They feel that's important nowadays. I nursed all the children, but with her, with all the fierce rigidity of first motherhood, I did like the books then said. Though her cries battered me to trembling and my breasts ached with swollenness, I waited till the clock decreed.

Why do I put that first? I do not even know if it matters, or if it explains anything.

She was a beautiful baby. She blew shining bubbles of sound. She loved motion, loved light, loved color and music and textures. She would lie on the floor in her blue overalls patting the surface so hard in ecstasy her hands and feet would blur. She was a miracle to me, but when she was eight months old I had to leave her daytimes with the woman downstairs to whom she was no miracle at all, for I worked or looked for work and for Emily's father, who "could no longer endure" (he wrote in his good-bye note) "sharing want with us."

I was nineteen. It was the pre-relief, pre-WPA world of the depression. I would start running as soon as I got off the streetcar, running up the stairs, the place smelling sour, and awake or asleep to startle awake, when she saw me she would break into a clogged weeping that could not be comforted, a weeping I can hear yet.

After a while I found a job hashing at night so I could be with her days, and it was better. But it came to where I had to bring her to his family and leave her.

It took a long time to raise the money for her fare back. Then she got chicken pox and I had to wait longer. When she finally came, I hardly knew her, walking quick and nervous like her father, looking like her father, thin, and dressed in a shoddy red that yellowed her skin and glared at the pockmarks. All the baby loveliness gone.

She was two. Old enough for nursery school they said, and I did not know then what I know now—the fatigue of the long day, and the lacerations of group life in the kinds of nurseries that are only parking places for children.

Except that it would have made no difference if I had known. It was the only place there was. It was the only way we could be together, the only way I could hold a job.

And even without knowing, I knew. I knew the teacher that was evil because all these years it has curdled into my memory, the little boy hunched in the corner, her rasp, "why aren't you outside, because Alvin hits you? that's no reason, go out, scaredy." I knew Emily hated it even if she did not clutch and implore "don't go Mommy" like the other children, mornings.

She always had a reason why we should stay home. Momma, you look sick. Momma, I feel sick. Momma, the teachers aren't there today, they're sick. Momma, we can't go, there was a fire there last night. Momma, it's a holiday today, no school, they told me.

But never a direct protest, never rebellion. I think of our others in their three-, four-year-oldness—the explosions, the tempers, the denunciations, the demands—and I feel suddenly ill. I put the iron down. What in me demanded that goodness in her? And what was the cost, the cost to her of such goodness?

The old man living in the back once said in his gentle way: "You should smile at Emily more when you look at her." What *was* in my face when I looked at her? I loved her. There were all the acts of love.

It was only with the others I remembered what he said, and it was the face of joy, and not of care or tightness or worry I turned to them—too late for Emily. She does not smile easily, let alone almost always as her brothers and sisters do. Her face is closed and sombre, but when she wants, how fluid. You must have seen it in her pantomimes, you spoke of her rare gift for comedy on the stage that rouses a laughter out of the audience so dear they applaud and applaud and do not want to let her go.

Where does it come from, that comedy? There was none of it in her when she came back to me that second time, after I had had to send her away again. She had a new daddy now to learn to love, and I think perhaps it was a better time.

Except when we left her alone nights, telling ourselves she was old enough.

"Can't you go some other time, Mommy, like tomorrow?" she would ask. "Will it be just a little while you'll be gone? Do you promise?"

The time we came back, the front door open, the clock on the floor in the hall. She rigid awake. "It wasn't just a little while. I didn't cry. Three times I called you, just three times, and then I ran downstairs to open the door so you could come faster. The clock talked loud. I threw it away, it scared me what it talked."

She said the clock talked loud again that night I went to the hospital to have Susan. She was delirious with the fever that comes before red measles, but she was fully conscious all the week I was gone and the week after we were home when she could not come near the new baby or me.

She did not get well. She stayed skeleton thin, not wanting to eat, and night after night she had nightmares. She would call for me, and I would rouse from exhaustion to sleepily call back: "You're all right, darling, go to sleep, it's just a dream," and if she still called, in a sterner voice, "now go to sleep, Emily, there's nothing to hurt you." Twice, only twice, when I had to get up for Susan anyhow, I went in to sit with her.

Now when it is too late (as if she could let me hold and comfort her like I do the others) I get up and go to her at once at her moan or restless stirring. "Are you awake, Emily? Can I get you something?" And the answer is always the same: "No, I'm all right, go back to sleep, Mother."

They persuaded me at the clinic to send her away to a convalescent home in the country where "she can have the kind of food and care you can't manage for her, and you'll be free to concentrate on the new baby." They still send children to that place. I see pictures on the society page of sleek young women planning affairs to raise money for it, or dancing at the affairs, or decorating Easter eggs or filling Christmas stockings for the children.

They never have a picture of the children so I do not know if the girls still wear those gigantic red bows and the ravaged looks on the every other Sunday when parents can come to visit "unless otherwise notified"—as we were notified the first six weeks.

Oh it is a handsome place, green lawns and tall trees and fluted flower beds. High up on the balconies of each cottage the children stand, the girls in their red bows and white dresses, the boys in white suits and giant red ties. The parents stand below shrieking up to be heard and the children shriek down to be heard, and between them the invisible wall "Not To Be Contaminated by Parental Germs or Physical Affection."

There was a tiny girl who always stood hand in hand with Emily. Her parents never came. One visit she was gone. "They moved her to Rose Cottage," Emily shouted in explanation. "They don't like you to love anybody here."

She wrote once a week, the labored writing of a seven-year-old. "I am fine. How is the baby. If I write my leter nicely I will have a star. Love." There never was a star. We wrote every other day, letters she could never hold or keep but only hear read—once. "We simply do not have room for children to keep any personal possessions," they patiently explained when we pieced one Sunday's shrieking together to plead how much it would mean to Emily, who loved so to keep things, to be allowed to keep her letters and cards.

Each visit she looked frailer. "She isn't eating," they told us.

(They had runny eggs for breakfast or mush with lumps, Emily said later. I'd hold it in my mouth and not swallow. Nothing ever tasted good, just when they had chicken.)

It took us eight months to get her released home, and only the fact that she gained back so little of her seven lost pounds convinced the social worker.

I used to try to hold and love her after she came back, but her body would stay stiff, and after a while she'd push away. She ate little. Food sickened her, and I think much of life too. Oh she had physical lightness and brightness, twinkling by on skates, bouncing like a ball up and down up and down over the jump rope, skimming over the hill; but these were momentary.

She fretted about her appearance, thin and dark and foreign-looking at a time when every little girl was supposed to look or thought she should look a chubby blonde replica of Shirley Temple. The doorbell sometimes rang for her, but no one seemed to come and play in the house or be a best friend. Maybe because we moved so much.

There was a boy she loved painfully through two school semesters. Months later she told me how she had taken pennies from my purse to buy him candy. "Licorice was his favorite and I brought him some every day, but he still liked Jennifer better'n me. Why, Mommy?" The kind of question for which there is no answer.

School was a worry to her. She was not glib in a world where glibness and quickness were easily confused with ability to learn. To her overworked and exasperated teachers she was an overconscientious "slow learner" who kept trying to catch up and was absent entirely too often.

I let her be absent, though sometimes the illness was imaginary. How different from my now-strictness about attendance with the others. I wasn't working. We had a new baby, I was home anyhow. Sometimes, after Susan grew old enough, I would keep her home from school, too, to have them all together.

Mostly Emily had asthma, and her breathing, harsh and labored, would fill the house with a curiously tranquil sound. I would bring the two old dresser mirrors and her boxes of collections to her bed. She would select beads and single earrings, bottle tops and shells, dried flowers and pebbles, old postcards and scraps, all sorts of oddments; then she and Susan would play Kingdom, setting up landscapes and furniture, peopling them with action.

Those were the only times of peaceful companionship between her and Susan. I have edged away from it, that poisonous feeling between them, that terrible balancing of hurts and needs I had to do between the two, and did so badly, those earlier years.

Oh there are conflicts between the others too, each one human, needing, demanding, hurting, taking—but only between Emily and Susan, no, Emily toward Susan that corroding resentment. It seems so obvious on the surface, yet it is not obvious. Susan, the second child, Susan, golden- and curly-haired and chubby, quick and articulate and assured, everything in appearance and manner Emily was not; Susan, not able to resist Emily's precious things, losing or sometimes clumsily breaking them; Susan telling jokes and riddles to company for applause while Emily sat silent (to say to me later: that was *my* riddle, Mother, I told it to Susan); Susan, who for all the five years' difference in age was just a year behind Emily in developing physically.

I am glad for that slow physical development that widened the difference between her and her contemporaries, though she suffered over it. She was too vulnerable for that terrible world of youthful competition, of preening and parading, of constant measuring of yourself against every other, of envy, "If I had that copper hair," "If I had that skin. . . ." She tormented herself enough about not looking like the others, there was enough of the unsureness, the having to be conscious of words before you speak, the constant caring—what are they thinking of me? without having it all magnified by the merciless physical drives.

Ronnie is calling. He is wet and I change him. It is rare there is such a cry now. That time of motherhood is almost behind me when the ear is not one's own but must always be racked and listening for the child cry, the child call. We sit for a while and I hold him, looking out over the city spread in charcoal with its soft aisles of light. "*Shoogily,*" he breathes and curls closer. I carry him back to bed, asleep. *Shoogily.* A funny word, a family word, inherited from Emily, invented by her to say: *comfort.*

In this and other ways she leaves her seal, I say aloud. And startle at my saying it. What do I mean? What did I start to gather together, to try and make coherent? I was at the terrible, growing years. War years. I do not remember them well. I was working, there were four smaller ones now, there was not time for her. She had to help be a mother, and housekeeper, and shopper. She had to set her seal. Mornings of crisis and near hysteria trying to get lunches packed, hair combed, coats and shoes found, everyone to school or Child Care on time, the baby ready for transportation. And always the paper scribbled on by a smaller one, the book looked at by Susan then mislaid, the homework not done. Running out to that huge school where she was one, she was lost, she was a drop; suffering over the unpreparedness, stammering and unsure in her classes.

There was so little time left at night after the kids were bedded down. She would struggle over books, always eating (it was in those years she developed her enormous appetite that is legendary in our family) and I would be ironing, or preparing food for the next day, or writing V-mail to Bill, or tending the baby. Sometimes, to make me laugh, or out of her despair, she would imitate happenings or types at school.

I think I said once: "Why don't you do something like this in the school amateur show?" One morning she phoned me at work, hardly understandable through the weeping: "Mother, I did it. I won, I won; they gave me first prize; they clapped and clapped and wouldn't let me go."

Now suddenly she was Somebody, and as imprisoned in her difference as she had been in anonymity.

She began to be asked to perform at other high schools, even in colleges, then at city and statewide affairs. The first one we went to, I only recognized her that first moment when thin, shy, she almost drowned herself into the curtains. Then: Was this Emily? The control, the command, the convulsing and deadly clowning, the spell, then the roaring, stamping audience, unwilling to let this rare and precious laughter out of their lives.

Afterwards: You ought to do something about her with a gift like that—but without money or knowing how, what does one do? We have left it all to her, and the gift has as often eddied inside, clogged and clotted, as been used and growing.

She is coming. She runs up the stairs two at a time with her light graceful step, and I know she is happy tonight. Whatever it was that occasioned your call did not happen today.

"Aren't you ever going to finish the ironing, Mother? Whistler painted his mother in a rocker. I'd have to paint mine standing over an ironing board." This is one of her communicative nights and she tells me everything and nothing as she fixes herself a plate of food out of the icebox.

She is so lovely. Why did you want me to come in at all? Why were you concerned? She will find her way.

She starts up the stairs to bed. "Don't get me up with the rest in the morning." "But I thought you were having midterms." "Oh, those," she comes back in, kisses me, and says quite lightly, "in a couple of years when we'll all be atom-dead they won't matter a bit."

She has said it before. She *believes* it. But because I have been dredging the past, and all that compounds a human being is so heavy and meaningful in me, I cannot endure it tonight.

I will never total it all. I will never come in to say: She was a child seldom smiled at. Her father left me before she was a year old. I had to work her first six years when there was work, or I sent her home and to his relatives. There were years she had care she hated. She was dark and thin and foreign-looking in a world where the prestige went to blondeness and curly hair and dimples, she was slow where glibness was prized. She was a child of anxious, not proud, love. We were poor and could not afford for her the soil of easy growth. I was a young mother, I was a distracted mother. There were the other children pushing up, demanding. Her younger sister seemed all that she was not. There were years she did not want me to touch her. She kept too much in herself, her life was such she had to keep too much in herself. My wisdom came too late. She has much to her and probably little will come of it. She is a child of her age, of depression, of war, of fear.

Let her be. So all that is in her will not bloom—but in how many does it? There is still enough left to live by. Only help her to know—help make it so there is cause for her to know—that she is more than this dress on the ironing board, helpless before the iron.

QUESTIONS FOR DISCUSSION AND WRITING

1. How does the opening question about Emily establish the basic conflicts in the story? Why does Emily's mother think it is impossible to answer the question? In what sense do her concluding remarks provide a satisfactory resolution to the conflict?
2. How does the mother's account of Emily's childhood help characterize her daughter? How does the mother's description of her first child help define her own character? How have circumstances helped shape a different character for Susan and the other children?

3. Why is the ironing board an appropriate setting for the telling of this story? How is poverty an important condition of setting in Emily's story? How does Emily respond to the various places she must live—the nursery, the convalescent home, the school, and home?
4. How does the mother's inability to account for "all that life that has happened outside me, beyond me" explain her point of view toward the story of her daughter? To what extent does the summary paragraph retell her story? Why won't she be able to "total it all"?
5. What has Emily's mother learned as a result of her daughter's experience? Has her wisdom come "too late"? Explain your answer.

75

CYNTHIA OZICK

Puttermesser Paired

CYNTHIA OZICK was born in 1928 in New York City, and educated at New York University and Ohio State University. She worked briefly in advertising, then taught English at the City College of the City University of New York before embarking on her career as a novelist, essayist, translator, and critic. Her novels include *Trust* (1966), *The Cannibal Galaxy* (1983), and *The Messiah of Stockholm* (1987); her essays appear in *Art and Ardor: Essays* (1983) and *Metaphor and Memory* (1988); and her short stories are collected in *The Pagan Rabbi and Other Stories* (1971), *Bloodshed and Three Novellas* (1976), and *Levitation: Five Fictions* (1981). "Puttermesser Paired," reprinted from *The New Yorker,* describes how a woman and her companion "reenact" the lives of novelist George Eliot, her lover George Lewes, and her husband John Cross.

1 AN AGE OF DIVORCE

At the unsatisfying age of fifty-plus, Ruth Puttermesser, a lawyer, a rationalist, and an ex-public official, took a year off to live on her savings and think through her fate. In the second week of her freedom—no slavery of paperwork, no office to go to (she had bled out a wide tract of her life in the corridors of the Municipal Building)—it came to her that what she ought to do was marry. This was not a new idea: it had been her mother's refrain as far back as three decades ago or more, ever since Puttermesser's first year in law school.

> Ruth, Ruth [her mother wrote from Miami], there's nothing wrong with having a husband along with brains, it's not a contradiction. For God's sake pull your head out of the clouds! If you don't get married where will you be, what will happen? Alone

> is a stone as they say and believe me Ruthie Daddy agrees with me on this issue not only double but triple, we didn't come down here to live in the heat with Daddy's bursitis only in order to break his heart from you and your brains.

This innocently anti-feminist letter was now brown at the edges, brittle; in the fresh tedium of her leisure Puttermesser was sorting out the boxes stored under her bed. She was throwing things out. Her mother was dead. Her father was dead. There would be no more reports of the Florida weather, and no grandchildren to inherit these interesting out-of-date postage stamps and wrinkled complaints. Puttermesser was an elderly orphan. For the first time it struck her that her mother was right: it was possible for brains to break the heart.

She bought a copy of the *New York Review of Books* and looked through the personals. Brains, brains everywhere.

> Fit, handsome, ambitious writer/editor, militant nonsmoker, witty, imaginative, irreverent, seeks lasting relationship with nonsmoking female. Must be brilliant, unpretentious, passionate, creative. Prefer Ph.D. in Milton, Shakespeare, or Beowulf.
>
> University professor, anthropologist, 50, gentle, intellectual, youthful, author of three volumes on Aleutian Islanders, cherishes the examined life, welcomes marriage or long-term attachment to loyal, accomplished professional woman; well-analyzed (Jung only, no Freud or Reich, please). Sense of humor and love of outdoors a must.

Among dozens of these condensed portraits Puttermesser could not recognize herself. She was hostile to the outdoors; the country air—the peril of so many uneasy encounters with unidentifiable rodents, loud birds, monstrous insects, mud after fearsome Sag Harbor storms—left her moody and squeamish. She was no good at getting the points of jokes. The persecution of smokers she regarded as a civil-liberties issue. As for the examined life—enough! She was sick of examining her own and hardly needed to hear an Eskimo expert examine his. It was all fiction anyhow—those columns and columns of ads. "Vibrant, appealing, attractive, likable"—that meant divorced. Leftovers and mistakes. "Unconventional, earthy, nurturing, fascinated by Zen, Sufism, music of the spheres"—a crackpot still in sandals. "Successful achiever longing for strong woman"—watch out, probably a porn nut. Every self-indulgent type in the book turned up in these ads. Literature was no better. The great novels, rife with weirdos and misalliance—Isabel Archer entangled with the sinister Gilbert Osmond, Gwendolen Harleth's troubles with Grandcourt. Anna Karenina. Worst of all, poor Dorothea Brooke and the deadly Mr. Casaubon. All these bad characters—the men in the case absolutely, and many of the women—were brainy. Think of Shaw, a logician, refusing to allow Professor Higgins to wed Eliza, in open dread of foreordained rotten consequences. And Jane Austen: with one hand she marries Elizabeth to Darcy, clever with clever, and with the other she goes and saddles Mr. Bennet with a silly wife. People get stuck. Brains are no guarantee. Hope is slim.

The truth was this: Puttermesser had entered a new zone of being. From the Women Attorneys Association she received a questionnaire: "Aging and the Female Counsellor." Aging! Puttermesser! How could this be, when she had yet to satisfy Miss Charlotte Kuntz, her piano teacher? At Puttermesser's last lesson, forty-five years ago, Miss Kuntz had warned her sharply that such-and-such a sonatina needed work. It was just before summer vacation. Puttermesser promised to toil over the Tempo di Minuetto section all during July and August (the Andante was easier), but she put it off and put it off. Instead, she wandered in a trance in and out of the children's room of the public library; the rule was you could take out only two books at a time. Frequently Puttermesser appeared at the library twice in one day, to return two and to borrow two more. She read far into the rosy shadows of the summer twilight. The lower half of the sky was daubed with a streak of blood. "A beautiful day tomorrow," Puttermesser's mild father said. "That's what a red sunset means."

But Puttermesser's mother scolded: "In the dark! Again reading in the dark! You'll burn out your eyes! And didn't you *swear* to Miss Kuntz you'll practice every day during vacation? You're not ashamed, she'll come back and you didn't learn it yet? Nose in the book without a light!"

In late August a letter arrived. Miss Kuntz was not coming back. She was moving upstate with her elderly father. "As I have often mentioned, Ruth," she wrote, "you are intelligent, but require more diligence. Always remember: Every Great Brain Delves Furiously!"

By now, Puttermesser had put off practicing for so long that her hair was showing signs of whitening. If alive, Miss Kuntz would be a hundred and four. Puttermesser had still not perfected the Tempo di Minuetto section, so how was it possible to consider a questionnaire on aging?

> Do you encounter discrimination on the part of judges? Employers? Clients? Court personnel?
>
> Has your mental acuity or judgment noticeably slackened? If yes, how does this manifest itself?
>
> Have your earlier positions (political, moral, societal) eroded? Are you, in your opinion, capable of new ideas? Flexibility? An open mind?
>
> Have your earnings diminished? Increased? Are you treated with less respect? More? If more, how does your mature appearance contribute to this?
>
> Has the feminist movement eased your professional situation? Are you harried less? More? No difference? How many times per week do you encounter sexist or ageist remarks?
>
> Do you dye your hair? Use henna? Surrender to Mother Nature? If the latter, does this appear to augment or lessen your dignity among male colleagues? Female colleagues? The public?

Miss Kuntz was no doubt under the ground in Pleasantville, New York, together with her father. In Puttermesser's cramped apartment in the East Seventies—a neighborhood of ophthalmologists and dermatologists—there was no room for a piano; the space near her bed could barely accommodate a modest desk. At night she could hear the high-school math teacher on the other side of the wall plunge her red pencils into an electric sharpener. Sometimes the math teacher did exercises on a plastic mat—unfolding, it whacked against the baseboard. A divorcée in her middle thirties, who counted out loud with each leg stretch. She was working on her figure in the hope of attracting a lover. An announcement addressed to the math teacher had been thrust into Puttermesser's mailbox.

SINGLES EVENT!

ATTENTION! EDUCATED UNUSUAL SINGLES

TEACHERS' MIXER EVERY FRIDAY NIGHT
8:30 P.M.
MEET YOUR PEERS WITHOUT SNEERS OR TEARS
BRONX SCIENCE, HUNTER HIGH, STUYVESANT,
OTHER TOP SCHOOLS WELL REPRESENTED
$3 DONATION TO COVER PUNCH AND CHEESE
NOTE TO MALE TEACHERS: MORE MEN WANTED!
BRING YOUR (PROFESSIONAL) FRIENDS
CALL GINNY (718) 555-3000 FOR DETAILS

Puttermesser contemplated calling Ginny—she, too, was an educated unusual single. Instead, she slid the sheet under the math teacher's door. The building, with its dedication to anonymity (each mysterious soul invisible in its own cubicle), was subject to jitters and multiple confusions. Mixups, mishaps, misdeliveries, misnamings. To the doorman she was Miss Perlmutter. If you asked the super to send the plumber you would get the exterminator. Without warning, the pipes dried up for the day; you could try to run the faucet and nothing would come out. Or the lights would fail; the refrigerator fluttered its grand lung and ceased. All the refrigerators up and down the whole row of apartments on a single corridor expired together, in one extended shudder. You could feel it under your soles, right through the carpeting. The building was a nervous organism; its familiar soughings ricocheted from cranny to cranny. Puttermesser could tell which floor the elevator was stopping on by the pitch of its motor. She knew by the thump in the hall, and by the slap of sneakers heading back to the elevator, and by the rattle of all her locks, the moment when the new telephone book landed on her doormat.

Thump, slap, rattle. Something had landed there now; the sneakers were in flight. The chain lock was still swinging and tinkling. Puttermesser laboriously fiddled with it, and then with the other two locks. Each required one turn followed by a quarter turn. She worked as fast as she could. What if there were a fire? Robbery and rape or get burned alive: the New York predicament. All her neighbors had just as many locks; the math teacher had installed a steel pole that dropped into a hole in the floor.

The locks were undone. Puttermesser stuck her head out in time to see the flash of a yellow shirt at the end of the corridor. At her feet a chimney of huge, flat cardboard boxes rose up. There was a smell of noisome cheese.

"Hey!" Puttermesser yelled. "Get back here! I didn't order this stuff."

"6-C, right?" the yellow shirt yelled back. "Pizza!"

"3-C. You want the sixth floor. I didn't order any pizza," Puttermesser yelled.

"You Morgenbluth?"

"You've got the wrong apartment."

"Listen," the yellow shirt called. "Bike's in the street. Boss's bike. They take my bike, I'm finished. Half-dozen veggie pizzas for Morgenbluth, O.K.?"

"I don't know any Morgenbluth!"

Like a piece of stage machinery, the elevator hummed the yellow shirt out of sight.

Fecal smell of the stable—that cheese; some unfathomable sauce. Puttermesser kept her distance from ethnic foods. She had never tasted souvlaki; she had never tasted sushi. With the exception of chocolate fudge and Tootsie Rolls (her molars were ruined and crowned), gastronomy did not draw her. What she was concentrating on was marriage: the marriage of true minds. Reciprocal transcendence—she was not thinking of sinew, synapse, hormone-fired spasm. Those couples who saunter by with arms like serpents wrapped around each other, stopping in the middle of the sidewalk to plug mouth on mouth: biological robots, twitches powered by pitiless instinct. Puttermesser, despite everything, was not beyond idealism; she believed (admittedly the proposition wouldn't stand up under rigorous questioning) she had a soul. She dreamed—why not dream?—of a wedding of like souls.

Only the day before yesterday Puttermesser had taken out of the Society Library on East Seventy-ninth Street—an amiable walk from her apartment—a biography of George Eliot. A woman with a soul, born Mary Anne Evans, who had named herself George in sympathy with her sympathetic mate. George Eliot and George Lewes, penmen both, sat side by side every evening reading aloud to each other. They read science, philosophy, history, poetry. Once, they travelled up to Oxford to see a brain dissected. Another time, they invited Charles Dickens to lunch; he enthralled them with an eerie anecdote about Lincoln's death. They undertook feverishly cultural journeys to Spain and Italy and Germany, sightseeing with earnest thoroughness, visiting cathedrals and museums, going diligently night after night to the theatre and opera. On steamers, for relaxation, they read Walter Scott. They were strenuous naturalists, pursuing riverbanks and hillsides for shells and fungi. Their house was called the Priory; nothing not high-minded or morally or artistically serious ever happened there. The people who came on Sunday afternoons—George Eliot presided over a "salon"—were uniformly distinguished, the cream of English intellectual life: they were learned in Chaldaic, Aramaic, Amharic, Phoenician, or Sanskrit; or else they were orators, or else had invented the clinical thermometer; or were aristocrats, or Americans. The young Henry James made a pilgrimage to George Eliot's footstool, and so did Virginia Woolf's father. George Lewes was always present—small, thin, blond, quick—an impresario steering an awed room around the long-nosed sibyl in her chair. She depended on him; he protected her from slights, hurts, cruelty, shame, and from the critical doubts of John Blackwood, her publisher, who took her at first for a clergyman. It was a marriage of brain with brain, weightiness with weightiness. Dignity with dignity. And of course there was no marriage at all— not legally or officially. Lewes's wife, Agnes, was an adulteress who went on giving birth to another man's children; but it was an age of no divorce. George Lewes and George Eliot, husband and wife, a marriage of true minds admitting no impediment, were, perforce, a scandal.

All this Puttermesser knew inside out: it was her third or fourth, or perhaps fifth or sixth, George Eliot biography. She had, moreover, arrived at that season of life—its "autumn," in the language of one of these respectful old volumes—when rereading gratifies more than discovery, and there were certain familiar passages that she had assimilated word for word. "And yet brilliance conquered impropriety" gave her a shiver whenever she came on it; and also "Consider how a homely female intellectual, no longer young, falls into a happy fate." O happy fate! Somewhere on the East Side of New York, from, say, Fifty-third to Eighty-ninth, or possibly on West End Avenue between Sixty-sixth and Ninety-eighth, a latter-day George Lewes lurked: Puttermesser's own, sans scandal. It was now, after all, an age of divorce.

The shopping cart was squeezed between the refrigerator and the sink, folded up to fit into the little alley where the roaches frolicked. Wrestling it out, Puttermesser recalled her mother's phrase for a divorced man: "used goods." Yet what else was there for her in the world but used goods? Puttermesser was used goods herself, in her mother's manner of speaking: she had once had a lover. But lovers are transients: they have a way of moving on—they are subject to panicked reconsiderations, sudden depressions, cold feet. Lovers are notorious for cowardice, for returning to their wives.

Puttermesser wedged the cart against the doorjamb and bent to heave each big, flat box into it. When all the pizzas were piled up inside the wire frame, she double-locked her top lock and triple-locked her bottom lock and trundled the cart down the corridor to the elevator. It was like pushing a wheelbarrow filled with slag. The elevator smelled partly of urine and partly of pine-scented disinfectant; with the cart in it there was barely enough room to stand. She poked the button marked "6," but instead of grinding her upward, the thing headed for the lobby, now and then scraping against the shaft.

Two very tall young women were waiting down there. One of them was carrying a bottle of wine without a wrapper.

"You getting out?"

"I was on my way up," Puttermesser said. "You brought me down."

"Well, we can't all fit," said the tall young woman with the wine.

"Just *try,*" said the other tall young woman. "If you could just move your laundry—"

The tall young woman with the wine looked into the cart. "That isn't laundry. Smells like throw-up."

Puttermesser's spine pressed against the back wall of the elevator. The buttons were beyond her reach. A large black plastic triangle—an earring—swung into her face; the bottle of wine drove into her side.

"What floor?"

"Six," Puttermesser said.

"How about that. Is this stuff for Harvey's party? You going where we're going, Harvey's party?"

"No," Puttermesser said.

"Harvey Morgenbluth? On the sixth floor?"

"That's where I'm going," Puttermesser said.

The door to 6-C was propped open; all its chains were dangling free. A row of spidery plants in tiger-striped pots lined the foyer—a tropical motif. It was the sort of party, Puttermesser saw, where children run through shrieking and no one complains. Ducks in police uniforms were shooting at evil-visaged porcupines in burglars' caps on a big color television in a corner of the living room, next to a white piano, but the children were paying no attention at all. A mob of them were chasing three little boys in overalls, two of whom seemed, as they sped by, to be identical twins. They raced through the living room and out into what Puttermesser knew had to be the kitchen (6-C's layout was the same as 3-C's) and back again. "No we don't, no we don't," all three were yowling. The two very tall young women from the elevator instantly made a place for themselves on the beige tweed carpet in front of the sofa, kneeling at the coffee table and pouring wine into paper cups, instantly hilarious; it was as if they had been dawdling there for hours. The sofa itself held a tangle of five or six human forms, each with its legs in one extraordinary position or another, and each devoted to a paper cup. Behind the children's screeches, a steady sea noise burbled: the sound of a party that has been long under way, and has already secretly been defined, by the earliest arrivals, as a success or a failure.

This one was a failure; all ruined parties are alike. They pump themselves up, they are too boisterous, too frenetic, they pretend raucous pleasure. And this is true even of parties with cousins and young aunts; of families. The Morgenbluth apartment looked to be all family—husbands, wives, untamed offspring. Sisters-in-law, like the pair from the elevator. A birthday—one of the little boys', probably—but there was too much wine, and no balloons; besides, the children were being ignored. Puttermesser wheeled the cart straight toward the white piano and began lifting the boxes out onto the top of it. Cracker crumbs were scattered over the keys; a cigarette, with its snout still burning, lay directly on middle C. The boxes climbed upward in precarious steps.

"Leaning tower of pizza," someone quipped, and, from the tight little tone she caught in the voice, Puttermesser was certain that she was mistaken after all, that the noise all around was anything but domestic, that except for the children no one here belonged to anybody: no husbands, wives, cousins, aunts. It was the usual collection of the unattached. Roomful of the divorced on a Sunday afternoon in mild middle November. A "singles event": the math teacher, puffing on her mat three floors below, strained her torso in ignorance of the paradise of opportunity just overhead.

"It's about time we got some real food in here. You can't feed kids indefinitely on peanuts. Pretzels, maybe. Takes a grownup woman to remember nutrition. Any of these little sons of bitches yours?"

"I'd have to be their grandmother," Puttermesser said. It was the kind of remark she despised, and this stranger—a bearded man in his fifties, with a squashed nose and oversized, naïve eyes, gray and on guard, more suitable to a kitten—had forced her to it.

He was pecking at the peanuts in his palm. "Well, you don't look it—they say it's all in the chin line. Twins are mine, but only on alternate weekends. With me it's always a double felony. Not to mention a couple of breakups. Marital. The way you spell that is m-a-r-t-i-a-l." He put out his hand, greasy from the peanuts. "Freddy Kaplow. How long've you known Harvey?"

The New York patter. Mechanical spew of the middle-aged flirt; he was practiced enough. And too stale for such young sons. Already finished with the second wife, the mother of the twins. No doubt a grown daughter from the first marriage. The daughter and the second wife were, as usual, nearly the same age.

"Tell Mr. Morgenbluth his pizza was delivered to the wrong apartment," Puttermesser said. "Tell him 3-C corrected the error."

"3-C corrected the error. No kidding, that's how come you got here? Cute, I like that. Boy-meets-girl cute."

Puttermesser took hold of her cart and began to wheel it away.

"There goes Mother Courage," Freddy Kaplow called after her. "Hey! No guts!"

The two young women from the elevator, still curled on the carpet, were being even more hilarious than before; on the sofa the row of tangled legs had become attentive.

Three pairs of trousers (two corduroy, one blue denim), two of panty hose. One of the men on the sofa—not the one in jeans—wore his hair in a ponytail, but was mainly bald in front.

Puttermesser tugged cautiously on the cart handle. "Excuse me. If you wouldn't mind, if I could just slide through here—"

"Hello there, pizza person, when do we eat?"

The balding man with the ponytail said, "I saw a bag lady the other day with one of those. She had it filled up to the top with piles of old shoes. All mixed up, no pairs."

"What'd she think she was going to do with them?"

"God only knows. Sell 'em."

"Eat 'em."

"Boil 'em in the bowels of Grand Central Station, *then* eat 'em."

"That's not funny," said a woman on the sofa. "I *work* with the homeless."

Puttermesser stopped. Pity for the ravaged municipality—reverberations from her days in officialdom—could still beat in her.

"In our program—it's a volunteer thing—what we try to do is get them to keep diaries. We read poetry, we do E. E. Cummings. They feel it when you're spiritually *with* them."

Another version of the New York patter. The wisecrack version and the earnest version, and all of it ego and self-regard. All of it conceit. Where was virtue, where was knowledge? Puttermesser was conscious of inward heavings and longings. She thought of mutuality, of meaning. So many indolent strutters, so much babble battering at the ceiling. That white piano with the crumbs. In no more than a quarter of an hour the windows behind the piano had begun to darken to blue dusk. Harvey Morgenbluth's beige tweed carpet, his paper cups, the hysteria of those hungry half-orphaned children running loose. Oh, for a time machine! London in the grave twilight of a hundred years ago, Sunday evenings at the Priory. Cornices, massive draperies in heavy folds, ponderous tables and cupboards with carved gryphons' claws or lions' feet, old enamelled landscapes hanging on tasselled cords from high roseate ceilings. A keyboard left open for the sublime and resolute hands. And in a great stuffed armchair in a shadowed corner, away from the lamp, the noble sibyl, receiving. Lives of courtliness, distinction; clarified lives, without tumble or blur. In George Eliot's parlor, a manner, or an idea, was purely itself. Ah, to leave careless New York behind, to be restored to glad, golden Victoria, when the electric light was new and poetry unashamed!

In the foyer several of the tiger-striped pots had been overturned into puddles of wine; Puttermesser drew her cart through a patch of country mud. The spidery plants sprawled. A child's shoe lay flattened under one of the pots. A child's sock had become a glove for the doorknob.

And there, at the littered entrance of 6-C, stood a Victorian gentleman. He was not very tall; his cheeks and wrists looked thin. He was distractingly young, with a blond mustache, and he was actually wearing a hat—a formal hat, not exactly a fedora, but something more stately than a mere cap. He had on a capelike raincoat—partially unfurled at each shoulder, cola brown, and grandly punctuated by big, varnished metal buttons as shockingly bright as cymbals. Sherlock Holmes? Oscar Wilde? A dandy, in any case, self-consciously on display. One arm was held high, the other low, and in between rode a large, flat rectangle wrapped in pale-yellow paper and tied with a white string.

Puttermesser humbly backed her cart into mud to let the dandy pass. He slipped by without taking any notice of her. She saw how she was invisible to him, of less moment than the tiger-striped pots displaced in his path. *She* had given way; the pots demanded his circumspection, and obliged him to go around them. It was worse than the Women Attorneys could imagine: the humiliating equation of a counsellor of mature appearance with the walls and ceiling of 6-C's desolated vestibule. A doorknob is more engaging than a woman of fifty-plus. The man's face hurt Puttermesser; its youth hurt her. For an instant his head was perilously near hers—picking through the uprooted greenery, he tilted so close that she caught sight of the separate tender hairs of his mustache. His eyes were small and serious. Puttermesser thought with a pang how such a head, with such a dignified hat, and such snubbing colorless irises, and such an unfamiliar gravity of intent, would be out of place in Harvey Morgenbluth's living room, among the New York flirts. And that big flat package: a map? A map of the city, the world? An astronomical map. Andromeda. Ursa Major and Minor. Or a graph. A business graph. He was only a salesman, so never mind. Anyhow, it was an illicit hurt: youth is for youth. An aesthetic error, a thin-skinned moral grotesquerie, to yearn after such a head, hat, cape; that nose, that mouth, those intimate hairs.

In her own apartment Puttermesser collapsed the cart and shoved it back into the alleyway between the refrigerator and the sink. There had been, she observed, a hatching: a crowd of baby roaches milled under the ray of her flashlight, then fled with purposeful intelligence. In God's littlest, the urge toward being and enduring; a soulless mite wills its continuity with all the force and fury of our own mammoth human longing. O life, O philosophy!

All the same, Puttermesser sprayed.

In the morning she heard the brush of something in flight under her door.

> Dear 3-C:
>
> Just a note of thanx for yesterday's delivery—Freddy Kaplow (your pal and mine) gave me the dope on this. Sorry for the trouble and sorry I missed you! I'd love to return the favor, so if you ever need a passport photo in a hurry (no charge) or anything else in that line call on me. (I'm in the photography business, by the way.) I specialize in commercial reducing and enlarging but also in children's portraits. If you're interested in having a portrait done of the kids I can offer you a 25% studio discount in honor of your Good Deed!
>
> Yours hastily (scribbling this right in front of your door on my way to work)
> HARVEY MORGENBLUTH
> 6-C
>
> P.S. Hate to mention it, but your insecticide smells all the way out here in the hall! This means the little visitors get to climb the riser pipe up to yours truly! Thanx a lot, neighbor!

A page out of the *National Geographic:* a pair of civilizations adverse in temperament can live juxtaposed in identical environments. Archeologists report, for instance, that Israelites and Canaanites inhabited the same kinds of dwellings furnished with the same kinds of artifacts, and yet history testifies to intensely disparate cultures. 6-C's floor plan, Puttermesser reflected, was no different from 3-C's—she had seen that with her own eyes—but Harvey Morgenbluth had room for a piano and she did not. Harvey Morgenbluth gave parties and she did not. 6-C, the palace of exuberance. Harvey Morgenbluth had a business and Puttermesser currently had nothing.

Or, to reformulate it: despite exactly congruent apartment layouts, Harvey Morgenbluth belonged to the present decade and Puttermesser belonged to selected phantom literary flashbacks.

The day was secretly bright behind a gray fisherman's net about to dissolve into a full autumn rain. The coursing sidewalks, still dry, had the spotted look of rapid, dark rivers clogged with fish: all those young women in sneakers, clutching Channel 13 totes containing their office pumps and speeding toward desks, corridors, switchboards, computers, bosses, underlings. New York—Harvey Morgenbluth included—was going to work. And Puttermesser was idle. She was not idle: it was, instead, a meditative hiatus. She had stopped in her tracks to listen, to detect; to learn something; to study. She was holding still, waiting for life to begin to happen—why not? Venturing out for air, she was compelled to invent daily destinations. Most often it was the supermarket over on Third, if only for an extra package of potato chips; she hated to run out. Or she fell in with the aerobic walkers among the more populated paths of Central Park, close to the protective rim of Fifth Avenue. Or she went mooning through the Morgan Library, the Cooper-Hewitt, the Guggenheim, the Frick; or kept up with the special exhibits at the Jewish Museum—the pitiable history of poor, hollow Captain Dreyfus (hair-raising posters, Europe convulsed), shadowy old chronicles of the Prague Golem. New York, crazed by mental plenitude. The brain could not take in so much as a morsel of it, even at the rate of a museum a day. Paintings, jars, ornaments, armor, manuscripts, tapestries, pillars, flutes, violas, harps; the rare, the sublime, the celestial! Forms and illuminations, how was it possible to swallow it all down?

Hand in hand. The parallel gaze. No one knows lonely sorrow who has not arrived at fifty-plus without George Lewes.

From the express line in the supermarket (salty chips, cheese-flavored) Puttermesser headed for the Society Library, where she picked up the Yale "Selections from George Eliot's Letters" (pleasantly thick but portable, as against the nine-volume complete), then gravitated—why not?—to the Metropolitan Museum: the rain had started, anyhow. Among the Roman portrait busts on the main floor Puttermesser ate a clandestine potato chip. A female sculpture in a niche—hallowed serenity wearing a head shawl—who certainly ought to have been the Virgin Mary turned out to be nothing more than a regular first-century woman, non-theological; she was what the Romans had instead of Kodak. Puttermesser resisted this pleasing notion. She was unwilling, just now, to marvel at the objects and hangings and statuary glimmering all around—the rare, the sublime, the celestial—in this exalted castle of masterworks. Her mind was on the "Letters." George Eliot's own voice against Puttermesser's heart. She was tired of 3-C, of reading in bed or at the kitchen table. What she wanted was a public bench; why not?

From Rome she passed through Egypt (the little sphinx of Sesostris III; the granary official Nykairu with his tiny wife—no higher than his knee—and his tiny daughter; King Sahura in his headdress and beard; Queen Hatshepsut in *her* headdress and beard; and the great god Amun; and powerful horses, and perfect gazelles), and through polished Africa (Nigeria, Gabon, Mali), and through Southern Europe, and through Flanders and Holland, and straight through the Impressionists. Immensity opened into immensity; there were benches in all those grand halls, and streams of worshipful, pale tourists ascending and descending the high marble stair, but she did not come to the recognizable right bench until Socrates beckoned.

At least his forefinger was up in the air. The ceiling lights of that place—it was French Neoclassical Painting of the Eighteenth Century—seemed wan and overused. The room was unpopular and mostly empty—who cares about French Neoclassical? Puttermesser's bench faced Socrates on his deathbed. Even from a distance away she could see him reaching for the bowl of hemlock with a bare, muscular right arm. Socrates was stocky, healthy, in his prime. Part of a toga was slung over the other arm—and there was the forefinger sticking up. He was exhorting his disciples—a whole lamenting crowd of disciples, of all ages, in various grief-stricken poses, like draped Greek statues. A curly-haired boy, an anguished graybeard, a bowed figure in a clerical cap, a man in a red cloak gripping Socrates' leg, a man weeping against a wall. Socrates himself was naked right down to below his navel. He had little red nipples and a ruddy face and a round, blunt nose and a strawberry-blond beard. He looked a lot like Santa Claus, if you could imagine Santa Claus with armpit hair.

Puttermesser settled in. It was a good bench, exactly right. There were not too many passersby, and the guard at the other end of the long hall was as indifferent as a cardboard cutout. Now and then she foraged for a potato chip; the cellophane bag rattled and the guard did not stir.

> Assuredly [Puttermesser read in the "Letters"] if there be any one subject on which I feel no levity it is that of marriage and the relation of the sexes—if there is any one action or relation of my life which is and always has been profoundly serious, it is my relation to Mr. Lewes.
>
> I do not wish to take the ground of ignoring what is unconventional in my position. I have counted the cost of the step I have taken and am prepared to bear, without irritation or bitterness, renunciation by all my friends. I am not mistaken in the person to whom I have attached myself. He is worthy of the sacrifice I have incurred, and my only anxiety is that he should be rightly judged.
>
> We work hard in the mornings till our heads are hot, then walk out, dine at three and, if we don't go out, read diligently aloud in the evening. I think it is impossible for two human beings to be more happy in each other.

Impossible for two human beings to be more happy in each other!

A rush of movement along the far wall: a knot of starers had assembled just at "The Death of Socrates." They stared up, and then away, then up again. They were fixed on the lifted finger. Inexplicably, it was directing them to look somewhere else. The knot grew into a little, circling pack. Something was being surrounded over there, under Socrates' feet. The chips, the salt, the love adventures of the famous dead. Out of the blue, Puttermesser fell into a wild thirst—George Eliot and George Lewes were travelling on the Continent, illicitly declaring themselves husband and wife. At home in England they were scorned and condemned, but in the enlightened Europe of the eighteen-fifties the best salons welcomed them without criticism; they were introduced to poets, artists, celebrated intellectuals; Franz Liszt played for them at breakfast, smiling in rapture with his head thrown back.

That fuss around Socrates. Puttermesser got up to see—anyhow, she was in need of a water fountain. Some fellow had set up an easel. She inched her way into the starers and stared. The canvas on the easel was almost entirely covered: here were the mourning disciples; here was that prison staircase through a darkened archway; here were the visitors departing; here on the stone floor under Socrates' couch were the chain and manacle. That suffering youth hiding his eyes as he proffers the hemlock. All of it minutely identical to the painting on the wall, except that on the easel Socrates still had no face—the fellow in front of the easel was stippling out the strawberry-blond beard where it starts to curl over Socrates' clavicle. Puttermesser stared up at the painting and back down at the copy. One was the same as the other. You could not tell the difference. She stood at the rim of the crowd and through a kind of porthole watched the shadow of the lower lip gradually bloom into being; she had a better view of the easel than of the copyist. A bit of shoulder, a sleeve pushed up, a narrow hand manipulating the brush—that was all. The hand was horrifically meticulous; patient; slow; horrifically precise. It worked like some unearthly twinning machine. A machine for uncanny displacement. The brush licked and drew back, licked and drew back. The ancient strokes reappeared purely. Puttermesser took in the legend on the plaque—1787, Jacques-Louis David—and saw how, after two centuries, Socrates' nose was freshly forming, lick by lick, all over again. She licked her lip; she had never been thirstier.

The drinking fountain was on another floor. She was gone ten minutes and came back to disappointment: the show was over. The room was nearly deserted. The fellow with the easel was dropping things into a satchel—he had already loaded his canvas onto some sort of dolly. He stopped to wipe a brush with a rag; then he rolled down his shirtsleeves and buttoned them. His shoes were beautifully polished.

Puttermesser's old, neglected worldliness woke. She had not always been a loafer. Until only a little while ago she had moved among power brokers, deputies, opportunists, spoliators, the puffed up. Commissioners and chiefs. She had not always felt so meek. It is enervating to contemplate your fate too steadily, over too protracted a time: the uses of inquisitiveness begin to be forgotten. She thought of what she would ask the copyist—something about the mysteries of replication: what the point of it was. Plainly it wasn't a student exercise—not only because, though he was fairly young, he could hardly have been a student. He was well into his thirties, unless that modest, orderly mustache was designed to deceive. And, anyhow, the will to repetition—Puttermesser theorized that she had glimpsed absolute will—was too big, too indecently ambitious, for a simple exercise. It looked to be a kind of passion. The drive to reproduce what was already there, what did it hint, what could hang from it?

She asked, instead, "Did you get to finish the face?"

The young man held up an index finger in the direction of "The Death of Socrates." On the wall Socrates mimicked him. "It's finished, see for yourself."

"I mean in your version."

"What I do isn't a version. It's a different thing altogether."

An elbow poke of enchantment—aha, metaphysics! "I saw you *do* it. It comes out exactly the same. It's the same thing exactly. It's amazingly the same," Puttermesser said.

"It only looks the same."

"But you're copying!"

"I don't copy. That's not what I do."

Now he was being too metaphysical; she was confused. She was confused by delight. He stood there folding things up—first the rag, then the easel. Above the mustache his nostrils gaped in a doubling victory of their own. George Eliot's observation of Liszt—when the music was triumphant the nostrils dilated. "If you don't want to call it copying," Puttermesser almost began—it was going to be an argument—but instantly quit. The syllables stopped in her mouth. Thin cheeks. Those bright hairs under such a tidy nose. Without his hat it was hard to be sure. Nevertheless, she was sure. She had studied him, she had absorbed the veins of his right hand. She had observed him and not known him. The deceptions of dislocation, the misleadings! Uprooting dispels recognition; what is unexpected cannot be seen. The Victorian gentleman in the vestibule of 6-C. The dandy who had snubbed her because a young man is incapable of noticing a woman of fifty-plus. She knew him now. He was noticing her now. She had coerced it. She had made him look right at her.

"Aren't you a friend of Harvey Morgenbluth's? We met at his door," Puttermesser said. "In the middle of that party."

"I don't go to Harvey's parties. I go on business."

"Well, I live right under him. Three floors down." Fraudulent. It would be right to admit that she had never set eyes on Harvey Morgenbluth. "Was that a painting you had with you? In that big package?"

Clearly he did not remember her at all.

"Harvey photographs my things," he said.

"He copies your copies."

"They're not copies. I've explained that."

"But the result is just the same," Puttermesser insisted.

"I can't help the result. It's the act I care about. I don't copy, I reënact. And I do it my own way. I start from scratch and *do* it. How do I know if Socrates' face got finished first or last? You think I care about that? You think I care about what some dead painter feels? Or what anyone with a brush in his hand thought about a couple of hundred years ago? I do it my way."

Puttermesser's terrible thirst all at once rushed back; she believed it might be the wizening of her actual heart. Her organs were drinking her up and leaving her dry. She had abandoned all her acquaintance for the sake of the arrival of intellectual surprise. Mama, she called back to her mother through the dried-up marshes of so many lost decades, look, Mama, the brain is the seat of the emotions, I always told you so!

In her mother's voice, Puttermesser said, "It's used goods, isn't it? Shouldn't you begin with a new idea? With your own idea?"

"This *is* my idea. It's always my own idea. Nobody tells me what to do."

"But you don't make anything *up*—some new combination, something that never existed before," she urged.

"Whatever I do is original. Until I've done them my things don't exist."

"You can't say it's original to duplicate somebody else!"

"I don't duplicate." He was hitching his satchel onto his shoulder by its strap. "I reproduce. Can't you understand that? Babies get born all the time, don't they? And every baby's new and never existed before."

"No baby looks like any other," she protested.

"Unless they're twins." The canvas went onto the dolly. "And then they lead separate lives from the first breath."

"A painting isn't alive," she nearly shouted.

"Well, *I* am—that's the point. Whatever I do is happening for the first time. Anything I make was never made before." He gave her a suddenly speculative look; she was startled to catch a shade of jubilation in it. Did he talk like this every day of his life? She saw straight into the black zeros of his pupils, bright islands washed round by faint ink. He poked one end of the folded easel toward her—it was all contraption, with wing nuts everywhere. "What would you think," he said, "of helping me with some of this stuff?"

They walked with the contraption between them. The "Letters" were squeezed under Puttermesser's arm. Again, immensity opened into immensity, hall into hall. They passed through majesties of civilizations, maneuvering around columns like a pair of workmen, drilling aisles through clusters of mooners and gapers. Precariously they wobbled down the great staircase. It was evident he could have managed all that equipment on his own; he was used to it. She was an attachment trailing along—an impediment—but it seemed to Puttermesser that there was another purpose in this clumsy caravan. A kind of mental heat ran through the rod that linked them. He had decided to clip the two of them together for a little time. She understood that she had happened on an original. A mimic with a philosophy! A philosophy that denied mimicry! And he wasn't mistaken, he wasn't a lunatic. He was, just as he said, someone with a new idea. He had a claim on legitimacy. He was guilty with an explanation; or he wasn't guilty at all. The thing jerking and bobbing between them, with its sticks and screws, was an excitement—it made her keep her distance, but it led her. It was a sort of leash. She followed him, like an aging dog, sidelong.

Puddles on the sidewalk; she had missed the rain altogether. The street was silted with afternoon light. Puttermesser surrendered her end of the easel—she hated to give it up. Found! George Lewes, George Lewes in New York! He had a kind of thesis, a life's argument. He had nerve. "I'll come by," he said. "I'll drop in. The next time I have to be at Harvey's place. Here, take one of these. It tells all."

He set easel, satchel, dolly down on the pavement. Then he pulled out a little red case and drew from it a white card. There was a telephone number accompanied by two lines of red type:

RUPERT RABEENO
REENACTMENTS OF THE MASTERS

Puttermesser, who had not laughed in a month, laughed: she was ready to be happy. "Do people know what this means when you hand it out?"

"It's self-explanatory."

She was still laughing; it made her as bold as an old politician. "Why would you drop in?"

"To explain the card." He bent to pick up easel, satchel, dolly. "Don't you want me to? Would you rather I didn't?"

"Come right now," she said. "I'm dying of thirst. I'll make some tea."

2 THE NIGHT READERS

Puttermesser's favorite tea was Celestial Seasonings Swiss Mint—each tea bag had an instructive or uplifting quotation attached to it. Henry Ward Beecher: "Compassion will cure more sins than condemnation." Victor Hugo: "Laughter is the sun that drives winter from the human face." Ralph Waldo Emerson: "Make the most of yourself, for that is all there is of you."

The box, too, was imprinted with wisdom. Rupert Rabeeno read aloud, "'I have always thought the actions of men the best interpreters of their thoughts'—John Locke," and twisted the box around. "This next one's Nietzche. 'He who has a why to live can bear with almost any how.'"

Reading from the tea bag tags was only a joke, a diversion. What they were really reading from was "Middlemarch." This was the beginning of a project: they were going to do all of George Eliot's novels—out loud, taking turns. The early chapters galloped, but after a while talk seemed to intervene; they forgot what had happened at the start of a chapter, and had to repeat it. Sometimes they skipped the reading altogether. Rupert Rabeeno was not one of those people who allow their lives to be obscured by the vapor of the merely inferential. He was amazingly explicit: he made Puttermesser *see* things. In a month or so she had been led through all the particulars of his childhood. She knew the contents of his mother's dusty jewelry tray—her high-school class ring, four pairs of screw-on celluloid earrings, one necklace of five-and-dime pearls, one broken watch in the shape of a violin—and exactly where his father used to keep the key to the store safe (in the toe of an out-of-style Buster Brown Mary Jane). His father had run a shoe store in a town outside of Atlanta. Rupert's two married sisters, much older, grandmothers several times over, were settled in Tampa and Dallas. He claimed, besides, two mothers. The first had died when he was only nine: it became his habit to dream over the sad remnants of her few poor trinkets. He thought he could catch a reminiscent sniff of her dress fuming out of the tray in her old chifforobe. His father had put it down in the cellar of the shoe store. His father's second wife—strong and rosy—worked in the shoe store just as Rupert's mother had, and to woo his affection rushed home to give him milk and chocolate graham crackers after school, just as his mother had. But he threw over his milk glass on purpose, and his stepmother watched him drag a spiteful finger through the spill, pulling the wet lines of it into a marvel of a cat with a lifted tail. After that he was sent for "art lessons" on Thursday afternoons to a little local academy, where his classmates were mostly girls. Tap dancing was in progress just across the corridor, accompanied by a quaking piano; it was a humiliating place altogether. He didn't *sound* very Southern, Puttermesser noticed: he had left the South a long time ago, and had travelled everywhere. Some years back, he said, he had fallen into a "subject," his first, at the Louvre: it was the "Officier de Chasseurs à Cheval de la Garde Impériale Chargeant," by Théodore Géricault. And before that he had done some translating from the Catalan; and a stint, before that, in "The Changeling," on the London fringe, playing De Flores.

Puttermesser heard all this with a formidable sharpness—he was charging her with the will to take hold of him. It was as if he had given her a razor to cut him out with: the whole figuration of his history. He wanted her to know precisely what he added up to. He discharged everything he had done—he had done a lot—in a shower of color and anecdote; he was against elusiveness. Stories, worn through retelling, shot out from him: she felt the knots and burrs of reused thread. And portraits: his curly-haired sisters, their husbands (a couple of doctors, one a gastroenterologist, the other a pediatrician), their children, the strangers their children had married; but he was lost to all of them now. He had left his family behind. He spoke of the curiously perfected reflections of the bridges over the Seine, of how when you looked at them you couldn't tell which was the true world, the one in the air or the one in the river; and of the part-time job he had held at eighteen, in a grimy record-pressing plant, listening over and over again for flaws in the grooves; and of how he had once been hired to teach English in a loft on West Fifteenth Street to fearful, pathetic newcomers up from the Caribbean, under a half-mad "principal" who required every pupil to trace over the principal's model sentences in green ink; and of how the shoe store, always dark and unpopulated, like an empty movie theatre, with its double row of chairs back to back, had all at once surprisingly begun to flourish and bustle, fevered, it seemed, by his step-mother's quick run over the old brown carpeting—so that the two of them, his nearsighted father and his rubicund second mother, could dare to open a second store in the next town, called, like the first, THE PAIR FAIR.

It was almost too much. Puttermesser would not have minded a bit more mystery, the trail of something shielded, a secret stowed in a crevice. A spot, here and there, of opacity. He told her, with a compulsive comic vividness that shook her, of his clandestine night wedding, at twenty-three, to Cecilia Almendra, a little Argentine cabaret singer who turned out to be a runaway. Señor and Señora Almendra found them out and took the bride back to Buenos Aires—"before the consummation," he said. Señor Almendra (born Mandel, a refugee from the European cataclysm) raged; Señora Almendra sobbed. The girl had been registered at N.Y.U. and was supposed to be studying psychology; she never went to classes and wrote lying letters home. Her hours in the "cabaret"—a filthy bar on Avenue A—lasted until five in the morning. A bedroom farce with an unrumpled bed.

In the decade or so since, Rupert had lived without romance—not that kind, anyhow. Paris, and then London, and then Pittsburgh. He was sick of being a seedy wanderer bartering the baubles of trick and knack. In granite Pittsburgh he worked for a provincial satrap, the monarch of an intrastate railroad, and for half a dozen years threw himself into designing billboards. His grand, noisy posters, in riotous orange and purple and drumming red, jumped out at every station like oversized postage stamps connecting town with town. All the commuter lines that led to Pittsburgh were stitched together by Rupert's posters—he thought of them as brilliant beads strung on wire tracks. And he thought of himself as a polychromatic jack-in-the-box, ambushing the public. After the billboards, he switched to decorating cereal boxes. It pleased him that the selfsame jug, yellow and two-handled, overflowing with banana flakes, cropped up on tables from Tokyo to Tel Aviv; repetition wasn't far from continuity, and continuity not far from eternity. But in the end he didn't care for assignments and projects and campaigns. He disliked art directors and company bosses. Granite Pittsburgh crumbled for him; it was no better than a heap of sand draining through an hourglass. He missed being sovereign over himself.

Rupert Rabeeno was glutted with his own life—who isn't, and why not? He liked to tell it over and over, as if in the telling he could keep it from shrinking away into the smallness of the nearly forgotten. He let go of nothing he had ever known or seen or felt. Or not felt. Whatever had happened once he meant to make happen again. Reprise invigorated him. And Puttermesser was the same. It came to her in a rush of deliverance as wild as cognition, wilder than consternation—she was the same, the very same, no different! Whatever had happened once, she conspired, through a density of purposefulness, to redraw, redo, replay; to translate into the language of her own respiration. A resurrection of sorts. Wasn't her dream of having George Lewes again—a simulacrum of George Lewes—exactly the same as Rupert Rabeeno's wanting to make things happen again? Wasn't she, all on her own, a mistress of reënactment?

On a snowy afternoon in early January—Rupert Rabeeno was just back from delivering one of his great flat parcels upstairs at 6-C—Puttermesser decided to tell her idea about George Lewes. It was less an idea than an instinct; it was a burning; it made her shy. She suffered—he might mock her; she would be humiliated. And the awful discrepancy, the moat of age. The first George Lewes (would Rupert Rabeeno consent to be the second?) was born in 1817. George Eliot was born in 1819. A match altogether on the mark, generationally intelligent, so to speak; two years between them, she nearly thirty-five, he thirty-seven, as decently appropriate as could be. Puttermesser's shame stung. A hag. A crone. Estrogen dwindling in her cells. Rupert Rabeeno was too young—he was two decades too young—to be a candidate for a simulacrum of George Lewes. A gap like that is a foolishness in whatever century.

She watched him rummage in her clogged inch of pantry. He plucked up a can of tomato-and-vegetable soup and emptied it into a pot. Then he poured in some water from Puttermesser's blue teakettle and began to stir. She was used to this: he loved soup. He brought two or three cans every time he turned up.

She had calculated just how to get it said. An announcement. "October 23, 1854," she started off. And read: "'I have been long enough with Mr. Lewes to judge of his character on adequate grounds, and there is therefore no absurdity in offering my opinion as evidence that he is worthy of high respect.'" The moist smell of onions heating in the soup curled around them. "Written," she explained, "right after George Eliot and George Lewes went off to Weimar together."

The soup splashed into two of Puttermesser's china bowls. "Why Weimar?"

"Goethe's city. Lewes was working on a book about Goethe. He was always working on *some*thing."

"Sit down and eat your veggies," Rupert Rabeeno commanded. "That woman's a prig. Too damn solemn."

Puttermesser said, "It's Lewes I'm thinking of." George Lewes, lighthearted, airy, a talker!

"He's on your mind a whole lot. So is she."

A clot of embarrassment coarsened her throat. "It's only a feeling," Puttermesser said. "A sort of . . . you know, a conceit. A literary conceit." She put her head down. It was unseemly. She was too old, by twenty years. "It's about ideal friendship."

He said, "I still don't see the point of Weimar. Going off somewhere. There's no point to it. We can stay right here."

So he understood her to the marrow. He was all quicksilver; he was ready. She saw how, once she had yielded up her little burning, he could better it, he could complicate it, he could shake the ash of theory from it and fire it into life. They drove through the rest of "Middlemarch" without interruption; or almost. Often she followed him out into the wintry town—after "The Death of Socrates" he had moved over to the Frick. In his own place, on West Fifty-ninth, a studio with a Castro Convertible, he boiled up a can of mushroom-and-barley. It seemed to Puttermesser that all the singles who had ever lived in this solitary room before him were roiling like phantoms in the steam. His suitcase was tidy and waiting—fresh shirts and turtlenecks, his shoe polish and his own toothpaste. His clothes were orderly, well brushed. She asked him where he kept his valet. He laughed; he was exhilarated. "No room for Jeeves! I hide him in my sleeves!" He showed her his favorite lamp—indispensable, he said, for snugness. He carried the lamp and the suitcase, she carried the shade. Laughing, they left shoe holes in the snow; at the curb the new snow was folding itself over last week's old black humps.

Rupert Rabeeno's lampshade was as wide as a bat's wing and cast phosphorescent reflections on the walls. At night under that greenish, fishy light—3-C was now spookily undersea—they finished "The Mill on the Floss." Rupert asked what next.

Puttermesser considered. "Not 'Romola.' George Eliot said that book was what made her into an old woman."

"Let's do the life," Rupert said.

They tramped in the New York slush to the Society Library and took out all the George Eliot biographies there were, including the one Puttermesser had returned not long before. Rupert wanted to see how they matched up, whether someone writing about George Eliot in, say, the nineteen-eighties was going to turn up the same George Eliot as someone writing in the nineteen-forties, or in the eighteen-nineties. It was like reënacting a landscape a hundred years later, he said. The same grove of trees under the same sky, but different. What altered it was whoever was looking at it. Puttermesser almost followed the argument but was indifferent to it anyhow. Copyist's talk. She didn't care about any of that. She rejoiced, she was anointed. The germ of her secret seeing had breathed itself alive. Here they were, side by side, reading aloud, an indoor January pastoral; she had passed through the sacred gate, she had entered ideal friendship. Rupert's reading voice was dark, with now and then a sharp scratchy click in it, the call of some imaginary bird—it was a chirp she could not hear in ordinary conversation. It meant he was seized. Snared. Sometimes a tic convulsed his eyelid; he was agitated, he was engulfed. He surpassed her in her little burning, he urged her on.

In her cube of a kitchen she told him her convoluted work history, and admitted to sour Rappoport, a Canadian with a wife at home in Toronto, who had once been her lover. Rupert, concentrating, beat at the soup—it was lumpy—and shook the eggs in their pan. After supper he cut her hair. The wisps fell from her nape and forehead, all over her shoulders and the floor. She watched in the mirror as he snipped, evening out the sides: it struck her that she was not yet a hag. Tiny hyphens of hair-cuttings fuzzed her neck; he blew them down inside her blouse and over her back. Her mouth in the mirror was content. Her tongue slipped out like a shining lizard. He never thought of her as unnatural; he never thought of her as too old. Nothing grotesque lay between them. She believed that now. They were friends, ideal friends. She saw how he had become more zealous than she.

When he went upstairs to Harvey Morgenbluth's she stayed behind. It was all business up there. She didn't care for Rupert's business; it opened into discord and combat. His business was postcards. He copied the masters. Harvey Morgenbluth photographed Rupert's doubles, in full color and full size, and reduced the photos before they went off first to the printer and then to a jobber for distribution. This was Rupert's living. "The Death of Socrates," for instance, with Socrates' face filled in, reappeared in packets of a hundred, sealed in transparent plastic. One hundred identically lifted Socratic fingers. One hundred identical youths baring one hundred identical bowls of hemlock. There was a Rubens—"Venus and Adonis"—with a Cupid and a pair of dogs; there was van Gogh's "Irises" and Manet's "Woman with a Parrot." There was Turner's "Grand Canal, Venice," all ship and sky and water and misty distance. She thought him a genius—a genius ventriloquist; he could penetrate any style and any form, from a petal to an earlobe. He was at home in minuteness or in vista. The name of both painting and painter were printed on the back of each card—and, also, in minuscule letters: "Rupert Rabeeno, Reenactments of the Masters."

This was the subject of their small war. "If all it comes down to is postcards," Puttermesser said, "you might just as well send Harvey Morgenbluth into the Met with a camera."

"In the first place, he wouldn't be allowed. Which," Rupert said, "is beside the point anyhow."

"No, it's not. Every museum in the world sells postcards of its paintings."

"Exactly," Rupert said. "These are postcards of *my* paintings."

"It's a fraud."

This made him jolly. "Counsellor!"

"I didn't say it's illegal. I'm not talking about copyright laws. There aren't any copyright laws for French Neoclassicals. That leaves you with your conscience."

"My conscience!" He reared back as if she had smacked him, and let out a scratchy laugh. It reminded her of the snap, as of an unearthly pod bursting, of his reading voice.

"People are going to look at *your* Grand Canal and think it's Turner's."

"I made it," he said, with so much clarity that Puttermesser felt she could stare right through the unpainted circles of his eyes into whatever murmured behind them.

This murmur swept her. She brought his whole head into her arms. "Rupert, Rupert," she said. A fabricator of doubles, but he had no duplicity. She nearly believed in his case: that these weren't doubles he fabricated. It wasn't a manner or mannerisms he took from his prototypes. It was—could it be true?—their power.

She recited: " 'To see Kean act was like reading Shakespeare by flashes of lightning.' "

"What's that?"

"Coleridge said it about some famous actor."

And so their skirmish ended. She could not keep it up. If he didn't invent the work of his hands, he had, anyhow, invented himself. He wasn't a swindler, he wasn't an impostor. The postcards were his very own. She came on them in bookshops, and realized she had often seen them there before. A rack of his cards stood near the door when she went into a stationer's for a typewriter ribbon. There on the top tier was Picasso's "Gertrude Stein"—that autonomous skull, tile forehead, mouse's chin. But Rupert had made it.

3 THE UNSPEAKABLE JOY

Their night reading under the sea-green lamp: the names of the long, long dead. Brabant, Bray, Chapman, Rufa, Cara, Sara, Barbara Bodichon, Edith Simcox, Johnny Cross. Spectres. Of these, only Herbert Spencer survives recognizably on his own. George Eliot dared to beg him to marry her: she was infatuated. She had not yet met George Lewes. "I promise not to sin any more in the same way," she pleaded when Spencer turned her down; she could not imagine that he would end his days a bachelor. The philosopher of evolution could not evolve. "If you become attached to someone else, then I must die, but until then I could gather courage to work and make life valuable, if only I had you near me. I do not ask you to sacrifice anything—I would be very good and cheerful and never annoy you."

Rupert was reading this from the "Letters." Puttermesser slammed down her eyelids. She had those pitiful phrases by heart. The abjectness, the yearning. Dry Herbert Spencer, a man shut off; no feeling could invade him. But one day he brought George Lewes with him to the *Westminster Review,* where George Eliot—she was still plain Miss Evans—was working as editor. Lewes was playful, impudent, jokey; his face was pitted, he had a little, neat nose with big nostrils. He was an apt mimic and told clever stories without a speck of meanness. George Eliot at first thought him ugly; she was ugly enough herself. People said he resembled a monkey; they said she resembled a horse. He had free tickets to the theatre and invited her along. He reviewed plays, books, art, music. His mind was all worldly versatility. He wrote on French and German literature, he wrote plays, he made a study of insanity, he wrote on history and science and philosophy, on anemones and Comte and Charlotte Brontë. She translated Strauss, Feuerbach, Spinoza; she wrote on Matthew Arnold, Tennyson, Browning, Thoreau, Ruskin. She read Homer, Plato, Aristophanes, Theocritus; she read Drayton and a history of Sanskrit.

"What a pair, what a pair," Puttermesser said.

She had discovered something disconcerting: Rupert confessed that until now George Eliot had been no more than a rumor for him. In high school in the town near Atlanta they had read "Silas Marner" in sophomore year. That was all of George Eliot he was acquainted with. The rest was new. He had never before looked into a biography of George Eliot. He had never heard of George Lewes or Johnny Cross or all those others.

"Why didn't you say so when we began? When we started the reading?"

"I thought you could tell." He put his hand on her hand. How dependable he was; how eager to satisfy. "Anyhow, I'm catching up. In fact I'm *caught* up. What do you know that I don't?"

She could not contradict him. It was as if he had swum into her brain and swallowed up its spiny fish, great and small, as they flickered by. Puttermesser was ravished: it was true, there was no difference between them. Under the sea-green lamp he was caught, he knew what she knew.

It was Lewes she wanted him to know.

They read until they were dried up. They read until their eyes skittered and swelled. The strangeness in it did not elude them: where George Eliot and George Lewes in their nighttime coziness had taken up Scott, Trollope, Balzac, Turgenev, Daudet, Sainte-Beuve, Madame D'Agoult (Lewes recorded all this in his diary), she and Rupert read only the two Georges. Puttermesser discussed what this might mean. It wasn't for "inspiration," she pointed out—she certainly wasn't mixing herself up with a famous dead Victorian. She was conscious of her Lilliputian measure: a worn-out city lawyer, stunted as to real experience, a woman lately secluded, eaten up with loneliness, melancholia ground into the striations of her face. The object was not inspiration but something sterner. The object was just what it had been for the two Georges—study. What Puttermesser and Rupert were studying was a pair of heroic boon companions. Boon companions! It was fellowship they were studying, it was nearness.

"George and George," Rupert said. "Practically a couple of twins."

"They were *lovers,*" Puttermesser corrected.

In the mornings he snatched up his satchel and dolly and clattering easel and headed for the Frick. Puttermesser marvelled at the soaked threads of the canvas, glistening with bright, heavy oil. In the evenings, after supper, they pushed on with the two Georges. A history of money and family. The money went to Agnes, Lewes's easygoing, adulterous wife, and her brood of children by another man. Agnes in old age, unrepentant and very fat, with small, fat fingers twiddling in her lap, supported until her death by George Eliot's earnings: they mooned over her photo in one of those bricklike volumes that littered the kitchen chairs. But to Lewes's sons George Eliot was "Mutter." One died young she nursed and mourned him as if he were her own. Another was attached to her all her life. Lewes, meanwhile, was coaxing her to try her hand at writing stories, though privately he doubted whether she could master drama. Overnight she bloomed into greatness. And was a pariah all the same. Her brother Isaac, still in the Midlands of their childhood, would have nothing to do with her. She wrote him and he refused to answer. His sister was living with a man who had a wife. His sister could not be received in respectable drawing rooms. In the end the world came to her. A daughter of Queen Victoria contrived to be presented to George Eliot.

Rupert read: "'Our unspeakable joy in each other has no other alloy than the sense that it must one day end in parting.'" For twenty-five years George Eliot and George Lewes had their unspeakable joy—each other, and fame, and homage, and Europe, and a carriage of their own, and comforts, and the admiration of the best minds, and the hoverings and adorations of the young, among them Johnny Cross. Johnny Cross helped Lewes find a house in the country—he was good at all sorts of practical things. George Eliot called him nephew. "My dear Nephew," her letters to him began; and ended, "Your affectionate Aunt." He was a tall, comely young man of twenty-nine, introduced to her by his mother on a holiday in Rome. After Rugby, he went to New York to work in a branch of the family bank, and returned to London to do the same. George Eliot met Nephew Johnny Cross on George Lewes's fifty-second birthday.

4 THE AWFUL DISCREPANCY

The death scenes and their aftermath fell to Puttermesser. They were familiar to her, and unimportant. It was the living Lewes she cared for, the salvational Lewes, the merry Lewes of transformation. George Lewes died at sixty-one, in a dank November. He had always been sickly. During his final hours the doctors bustled in and out. In front of the Priory their coachmen cracked noisy jokes. George Eliot did not go to the funeral. Day after day she shut herself up in her bedroom with Lewes's books and microscope; she howled and howled. Only the servants heard.

Here Puttermesser stopped. It was over.

Rupert said, "We ought to do it."

"Do what?"

"Get married."

"*They* didn't marry," Puttermesser said, and closed the book.

"Hey, don't quit—there's more."

"No more Lewes."

"There's all the rest."

"You don't like her on her own. You called her a prig."

"That was before I knew her. Do the rest," he persisted.

So she went on with it. Two months after Lewes's death, George Eliot wrote to Johnny Cross, "Dearest Nephew, I do need your affection. Every sign of care for me from the beings I respect and love is a help to me. . . . In a week or two I think I shall want to see you. Sometimes even now I have a longing. . . . Your affectionate Aunt." And on a brilliant May day, at St. George's Church in Hanover Square, eighteen months after she had howled over the parting from Lewes, George Eliot married Johnny Cross. The new wife was sixty. Johnny's mother had died within days of Lewes. He was an orphan of forty.

Rupert danced around Puttermesser's tiny bedroom, where they had set up the sea-green lamp on Puttermesser's teak desk. "Look at that, look at that!"

"She needed someone to lean on," Puttermesser said. "It was her temperament."

"The body was hardly cold!"

"You can't lean on a dead man."

"*Aha.*" Now he took her by the wrists. "Didn't I tell you that from the start? That first day in the Met? I told you—*I'm* the one who's alive!"

Puttermesser wondered at this. "Well, there's the honeymoon."

"I'll do the honeymoon!" Rupert said.

She watched him reconstruct Johnny Cross. Johnny Cross was, anyhow, a puzzlement. No one knew him, really. He was expected to be "deep," and he wasn't. He was handsome and genial and athletic and rich. He was no intellectual, though he worked at it gamely, in the same plucky way he chopped down a clump of trees or devoutly smacked at a tennis ball. He was a tremendous swimmer. He wasn't even remotely a writer, but he did turn out one astonishing book—astonishing chiefly because Johnny Cross had written it: "George Eliot's Life." The title was as obvious and direct as he was. He plugged away at it after she died: it was a genuflection.

Rupert saw quickly that the heap of biographies they had been reciting from—including Johnny Cross's—were useless. Johnny Cross appeared in all of them to be sure—which didn't signify he was *there.* You might find him but you couldn't get hold of him. Rupert did what he could to conjure up the true Johnny. In a way, he remade him—Puttermesser thought it was a kind of plunder. Rupert was being preposterous and unfair, but she had to acknowledge that he was ingenious. He went after unheard-of combinations and juxtapositions: a letter, then a paragraph from one of the biographies, then again a letter. He threaded in and out of whatever was at hand. And what emerged from all that prestidigitation was Johnny Cross in love—but not with George Eliot.

"Good God," Puttermesser said. "The one thing everybody knows for sure about Johnny Cross is that he loved George Eliot. He adored her! There never *was* anybody else for him. When she died he never married again. You can't just contradict what everybody absolutely *knows.*"

But Rupert pressed on with his evidence. It was, he said, right there in Johnny's unnatural behavior in the first weeks after Lewes's funeral. George Eliot had pleaded with him to come and help her with the business matters George Lewes had always taken care of: Johnny was good at money. He arrived carrying Dante's Inferno. George Eliot was in her sitting room rereading the Iliad—in Greek, of course—to take her mind off her sorrow. Johnny said he was hoping to get started on Dante to take his mind off *his* sorrow; he was mourning his mother. The trouble was, he had to read Dante in Carlyle's translation. The Italian he had picked up in Rome, with his mother, wasn't up to snuff. "Oh," George Eliot cried out to Nephew Johnny, "I must read that with you!"—she liked Dante better than accounting. They went at it word by word. She was massively patient. He was painfully attentive—this was his design.

Rupert held up "George Eliot's Life" under the sea-green lamp and chanted: "'The divine poet took us into a new world. It was a renovation of life.' There, that's Johnny confessing."

"Right! You see?" Puttermesser said. "A renovation of life! He's telling us how he adored her—"

"You're not getting it," Rupert said. "The fellow was infatuated. With Lewes."

"Rupert, that's ridiculous."

"I don't mean what you think. I mean incarnation. He was trying to jump right into Lewes's shoes—whatever Lewes was good at, Johnny was going to do. He was out for that. He was going to be Lewes for her. A reasonable facsimile. The idea was to impress on her that Lewes was still around. Accessible, in a manner of speaking. In another packet of flesh. The face was the face of Johnny, but the soul was the soul of Lewes. *That's* the point."

"Oh, I don't know," Puttermesser said, weakening. It was ridiculous, and it was not.

"And the night readings. He kept a record, just like Lewes. First Dante. Then she took him through Chaucer, Shakespeare, Wordsworth. The basics. He had to sweat it out. All of it right there in her sitting room in the Priory, right smack under a big blown-up photo of Lewes. For all I know he had his bottom in the same chair Lewes used to put *his* bottom in. And doesn't he ask her to play the piano for him? The same music she played for Lewes? Then she turns sixty, and Johnny kisses her hand."

"And then he marries her. George Lewes never did that! You keep ignoring that," Puttermesser said. "Marrying her isn't jumping into George Lewes's shoes!"

"You think she wouldn't have had a big church wedding with Lewes if she'd had a chance to? If the law had allowed it? Look, the minute such a thing gets to be possible—Johnny's definitely single—what does she do? She runs out to buy a trousseau."

Rupert plucked up a book from the stack on Puttermesser's teak desk and wet his thumb. "They're sending letters right and left behind her back. Churning up the gossip. 'George Eliot had been seen at all the fashionable milliners and dressmakers in London. . . . Whatever money and taste could do to make her look not too unsuitable a bride for a man of forty had been done.' And after a quarter of a century of snubbing her for living in sin with Lewes, brother Isaac writes to congratulate her on her marriage to Johnny! And she's *grateful.* These are conventional folks, Ruthie, believe me. It's Johnny you've got to keep your eye on."

Puttermesser stared. "Why?"

"I'm telling you why. Watch him make himself into a second Lewes."

"*You're* doing that. You're making him into Johnny Cross, Reënactments." Puttermesser drew back. Her lungs felt fat from too much air. "You're making him into a copyist!"

Rupert gave out a paradisal smile. "Isn't that what he had in mind?"

"He was in love! And she was lonely, she was missing connubial love. She'd been happy with Lewes, she wanted to be happy again—" Puttermesser seized the "Letters" and shook out the pages with a ferocity. "Damn it, Rupert, *listen!*

> A great momentous change is taking place in my life—a sort of miracle in which I could never have believed, and under which I still sit amazed. If it alters your conception of me so thoroughly that you must henceforth regard me as a new person, a stranger to you, I shall not take it hardly, for I myself a little while ago should have said this thing could not be.
>
> I am going to be married to Mr. Cross. . . . He has been a devoted friend for years, much loved and trusted by Mr. Lewes, and now that I am alone, he sees his only longed-for happiness in dedicating his life to me. . . . Explanations of these crises, which seem sudden though they are slowly dimly prepared, are impossible. . . . We are going away tomorrow and shall be abroad two or three months.

"And then they went off together. That's how it is," Puttermesser finished. "A pair of married lovers. You can't just go and twist it into something else. You want to hear how she'd been feeling? *Here's* how she'd been feeling!" She was as pitiless as a conqueror. It was Rupert she wanted to conquer—Rupert's plan for Johnny Cross. She thumped a fist on the "Letters" and read out furiously, "'Blessed are the dead who rest from their labors, and have not to dread a barren, useless survival.' That's why she married Johnny Cross!"

Rupert looked meditative; he looked serious. Puttermesser took him in all over again—he was narrow, and blond, and burnished, and small. He was brushed and orderly.

The clear, blank circles of his eyes were needled through by the fierce points of the pupils. They punctuated; they punctured.

"*We* ought to do that," Rupert said. "Not the going away part. The great momentous change—that part."

He *was* serious. It wasn't a snicker, it wasn't a crack tossed off. Puttermesser hated banter and flippancy; she had fled Harvey Morgenbluth's party because of banter and flippancy. Rupert was a Southerner—he wasn't infected by the New York patter. "Like a few other people in the world, he is much better than he seems—a man of heart and conscience wearing a mask of flippancy." This was how George Eliot had once described George Lewes—though not right away. Her first impression was of a miniature fop, gyrating his arms, too talkative, shallow. But Rupert was serious through and through.

"O.K.," Puttermesser said. "Let's do it."

She wasn't sure whether she had at just that moment agreed to marry Rupert Rabeeno.

"Let's not forget the honeymoon," he said.

"O.K.," she said. "The honeymoon. You do it."

She watched him do the honeymoon. He did it fastidiously, with a sort of military instinct for the organization of it—slips of paper to mark the pages, volumes set in consecutive order ready to hand, quotations culled on cards. It was curious how well he had prepared himself. Out of the jumble they drew from every night—maps, letters, journals, biographies, memoirs, pamphlets, books and more books!—he was fashioning something clever, something out of the ordinary. A destiny. Rupert went about doing the honeymoon with the same heat of immanence he had blown into "The Death of Socrates." He read, yelled, sang, beamed. It was all for Johnny Cross—for Rupert's theory of Johnny Cross, and Johnny Cross was only footnote and anticlimax. He wouldn't let her ride over his theory; she hadn't been able to deflect him. Puttermesser was jealous. Rupert had lavished nothing like this on George Lewes. Yet it really *was* happening again, a second round. Puttermesser was obliged to admit to herself the possibility that Rupert might be on the right track. The honeymoon of Johnny Cross and George Eliot was turning out to be purest mimicry of the honeymoon of George Lewes and George Eliot—the honeymoon that couldn't be called a honeymoon because there had never been a wedding.

Rupert did the wedding first. It was plausible to begin there, at the church at quarter past ten in the morning. Lewes's son, two years younger than Johnny, gave George Eliot away. All of Johnny's relatives came—his sisters, and their husbands, and his cousins, and his cousins' children. After the ceremony the bride and groom went back to the Priory with a pair of solicitors to sign their wills. Then they set out for Dover, to catch the next day's Channel steamer for Calais. In Dover they spent the night at the same hotel where George Eliot and George Lewes had once sojourned. ("When Johnny was still a schoolboy!" Rupert crowed. "The same hotel!") When they reached Calais Johnny noticed how much younger and healthier George Eliot was looking—it was as if she were being renewed by every familiar mile along the old route. ("It *was* the old route," Rupert pointed out.) They were heading for Venice. Johnny took them down to Milan through Grenoble and Mount Cenis, exactly the itinerary Lewes had designed for what George Eliot had called their "deep wedded happiness." A week in Milan, as before; and then Venice.

Venice! "What stillness! What beauty!" George Eliot whispered. (Rupert, reading from George Eliot's journal, was whispering, too.) "Looking out from the high window of our hotel on the Grand Canal, I felt that it was a pity to go to bed. Venice was more beautiful than romances had feigned. And that was the impression that remained and even deepened during our stay of eight days." But that was long ago, with Lewes. Their room was dizzily distant above the glistering water. In the afternoons, the two Georges meandered through the basilica of San Marco, thinking it resplendent but barbaric. In the Scuola di San Rocco they were transfixed by the homely Mary of Tintoretto's "Annunciation." They bought lace and glass and jewelry, and floated around the lagoon in a gondola decked out with colored lanterns. Under the Rialto bridge the gondoliers rested their poles and warbled their lungs out, to bring an echo out of the waves. ("'*O sole mio,*" Rupert sang. "Now watch-a John-nee," he sang.) Johnny Cross and George Eliot reached Venice a month after their wedding. It was fragrant early June. Sunlight and speckled cream palaces with ancient cracks running down their walls, and darkling shadows under the bridges—they intended to linger for an indefinite stretch of summer.

Instead, they quit Venice in the second week.

"Panic," said Rupert. "The honeymoon's secret shock. Its mystery, its enigma."

"All right," Puttermesser said. "Get it over with. You don't have to milk it."

5 THE HONEYMOON

They took a hotel directly on the Grand Canal, and had all their meals brought to their room. Much of George Eliot's new wardrobe had come with them in trunks. She was cunningly and handsomely dressed, the elderly erupting collarbone covered by the lightest of wraps, the youthful waist disclosed. Lewes's death had left her ailing and frail; now she was marvelously restored. She was robust, she was tireless. She marched Johnny out to churches and galleries, and lectured him on architecture, painting, sculpture, history. He followed her ardently. He was proud of her, he was proud of himself. It was achieved. It was all exactly as it had been with Lewes. They stood before the same ugly Tintoretto Madonna and circled the gaudy bowels of San Marco. The June heat thickened; it began to feel tropical, though inside the old stone churches it was cool enough.

But there was something amiss with the air; the air was strange, and bad; there was something amiss with the drains. The view (though not so high up) from the windows of the Hôtel de l'Europe was just what it had been for that earlier pair, the two Georges—the Grand Canal knife-bright in the morning, blood-streaked at sundown, glowering at dusk. The canal below was itself no better than a drain. The air that rose from it was a sick cloud, a pustule of spew, a fume. The open windows gulped it in, especially at night when there was a flicker of wind. At night, the stillness, the beauty: a pity to go to bed. Day after day the pair searched out gonging campaniles, out-of-the-way chapels, glazed portraits of holy babes and saints and bishops and doges, and when the heat ebbed slightly they rode round and round in gondolas, dazed by the blinding white cheeks of the palazzi. The beauty, the beauty!

In the evenings they settled in for supper at the snug oval table in their room. The napery was always blue, though the cloth, sweetened by some herbal soap, was changed daily, and a bowl of flowers, cut every afternoon, was set down on it to obscure the drifting smells of the canal. When the porter came to remove the trays—they ate simply, bread and fish and tea—Johnny and George Eliot were already sunk back into the Inferno. They had returned to Dante because it was clear that Johnny needed to brush up on his Italian now more than ever. Again, she was lavishly attentive, especially to the difficulties of the syntax. She saw a kind of phrenological sturdiness in the coronal arch as his head lowered to the discipline of the page, a dolichocephalic head belonging to a long-boned six-footer. She was glad that he was as different in appearance from Lewes as could be—nothing about him was a reminder. Lewes had been little and vivacious—occasionally too quick—and brilliant and versatile. Johnny wasn't quick, but he was worldly enough; he was a banker who could tell when a man was bluffing. "Thou dost not know," she teased him once, "anything of verbs in Hiphil and Hophal or the history of metaphysics or the position of Kepler in science, but thou knowest best things of another sort, such as belong to the manly heart—secrets of lovingness and rectitude."

His character was solid, well tried, he was steady and affectionate. It hurt her that she was so old, though *he* never thought of it. In Venice, despite all their happiness, she was consumed by it. Nothing could make her young again for Johnny; she knew it whenever she combed through the gray in her hair, or held the mirror to her eyes, with their bruised fleshiness run wild in the caverns beneath. Johnny was already well into balding, but the hair around his ears was dark and bunched with curls. His beard was frizzy. Behind it (his lovely mouth lost in the frizz) there perspired a striving boy with a nervous look. She noticed the look and understood. It was five weeks—almost six—since the wedding. They went to their beds every night as friends—he was her noble companion, her squire, her loyal pupil. How hard he tried! But he faltered over the Dante; she pointed with her finger, and he corrected himself. He was beginning to languish a little. The more she bloomed, the sounder she grew, the more he drooped. They had not yet lain as husband and wife.

It was exercise he was missing. He was, after all, a man of the outdoors, he played tennis and football, and rowed and swam. Venice, all that water, and no rowing—it was only the sunburned gondoliers and their indolent poles, it was only the dreamy floating, it was churches and galleries and pictures and history. Endless, endless history. Endless art. Endless beauty. He wanted some clean air, he wanted something strenuous.

("Pretty strenuous," Rupert intervened, "to keep on walking every minute in Lewes's shoes!")

Johnny said he needed a swim. The Grand Canal was a cesspool; it was right at their doorstep, just under their windows, but you couldn't swim in the canal. The Lido wasn't far. They ought to get over to the Lido, the other side of it, where there was a good sandy beach. On the other side of the Lido they sat sedately on a bench, among ladies and their parasols, and watched the line of tidal waves. Johnny said he longed for a sea bath. The bathhouses were nearby, and he had brought along his swimming costume. He would dash into the sea, have a decent splash, loosen up his limbs, and dash out again; it wouldn't occupy more than a quarter of an hour. She thought the weather wasn't suitable for such a venture: see, she said, raising the pedagogic finger that had so often guided him through the Inferno, you can feel the wind. I'm dying for a bathe, he said, it's the middle of June and hot as Hades. "Though the temperature is agreeable," she argued pleasantly, in that even, courteous contralto cherished by Lewes, and now cherished again by Johnny, "it has not the sort of heat that makes a plunge in cold water"—here she struggled to uncover a just simile—"as good as a drink to the thirsty."

They went back to their hotel. Johnny ordered an elaborate supper of lamb and tomatoes and pudding. The sommelier followed behind the porter with two small ruby bottles. She drank a glassful. Johnny drank several. He seemed roused, alert. She caught the thirst in his eye, and knew it was a shy celebration. The time had come. Over the last days she had observed his inwardness, his delicacy, his brooding. He had stood despondently before the very shapes and pictures that Lewes had looked on years before with so much brio and worshipful wit. Johnny was distracted. She was not surprised when, after the porter returned to clear the table, Johnny wiped his fingers with his blue napkin and declined to take up the Dante. She thought to tempt him with Comte—a diversion—but he turned away. She was discreet. The diffidence between them was natural. Until a month ago he had been a bachelor, doubtless no more celibate than any other handsome young fellow. But unlike herself—she had gone to bed with George Lewes for twenty-five years—he was new to the dignified rituals of conjugal intimacy. She made out some fresh tentativeness in him, a drawing away. It was restraint, it was mindfulness: he was whipping down animal nature until she was ready to give him a signal. She was a little frightened that he put the responsibility on her; but also excited. She, who was accustomed to leaning on a husband!

She retired into her dressing closet, a mirrored nook set apart, and chose a nightgown she had never worn before. She shut the door so that he would not see her too soon, and let down her hair. The nightgown feathered her bony shoulders with masses of concealing lace. It all at once struck her that, with her pleasant figure and loosened hair, she had, in the looking glass, the sweetness of a bride of twenty-two: she did not feel old at all.

When she came back to him she was disappointed that he was in his own bed. Nothing was different, it was like other nights. She had imagined he would be loitering at the window, say, listening for her, watching the black spirals the gondoliers' poles lanced into the water. She had imagined that he would wait until she hid herself—her little bride-self—under her own coverlet, and then, hesitantly, tenderly, silently, he would set his limbs against her limbs at last. Instead, he was a stiff hunch in the other bed. His trousers were folded on a chair. The small wind sent the window curtains grazing over his head.

On second thought she was charmed by this backwardness. She reminded herself that the initiative was hers, and how could it be otherwise? He was reticent, he was a boy. Perhaps she had been mistaken—possibly he had no experience at all. Below, sliding along the Grand Canal, a convoy of gondolas was flinging up laughter and voices and loud singing in an Italian remote from Dante's. Some locals on a lark, or a party of gondoliers and their wild girls. The air, bad as it was, swelled every sound into a roar. Then the line of gondolas passed and she was alone with him in the quiet. "*Bester Mann,*" she murmured, and added some syllables from Goethe—Goethe, whom Lewes had so much loved.

She sat on the bed beside him and caressed the circle of his ear. "Dearest, dearest John," she said. He kept his back to her, and did not stir. She lifted the coverlet, and lay down close against him. He had not put on his nightdress; he was still in that morning's shirt. He had discarded his cravat—it was a thick serpent on the floor. She touched her naked toes to the naked bulge of his calf; with one bold arm she embraced his wide chest. His upper body was hot. The leg was cold. She was right to have discouraged a swim—was he ill? "Johnny, dear," she said. He did not answer. She was alarmed and faintly shamed; she removed her foot from his calf, and put her hand to the thigh of the other leg. It was cold, cold. Despite the trail of wind, the night was warm. It was growing warmer and warmer. The grooves flowing from her nose to the corners of her mouth, an old woman's creases, ran with sudden sweat; her armpits were sweated. She was not doing what he wished. She was too immodest, there was some direction he mutely intended which she could not interpret. "Johnny," she pleaded, "dear boy, are you unwell? Look at me, Johnny, dear, let me see your eyes."

He turned to her then, and showed her his eyes. They were unrecognizable—the rims of the lids as raw and bloody as meat, stretched apart like an animal's freshly slaughtered throat. Only the whites were there—the eyeballs had rolled off under the skin. An old secret shot through her like an intuition: a thing she had forgotten she knew. Johnny had a mad brother who was put away somewhere; Lewes had told her this long ago. Abruptly, the eyeballs fell back into place. He was not normal. He was unwell. The bitter, putrid wind, the drains, the polluted canal, the open window. He was breathing with an urgency; every inhalation seemed hard won. She could not get enough air for herself. They were entombed in a furnace. Down below, the fleet of gondolas was returning, the raucous party from before, or another just as noisy—she heard blasts of laughter, and common street voices, and singing, and this time a tremulous guitar. She was standing now; her brain was shuttling so rapidly that it shook her—there was a doctor in Venice, Dr. Ricchetti, whom English people consulted. She ran to the bellpull on the far wall, a little distance from the windows, to ring for the hall porter.

A tremendous swipe—the scream of a huge bullwhip or instant cyclone—cut through naked space. A projectile of some kind—she had seen the smudge of it fly past her own back. A stone—a ball, a bone—tossed up by some loutish member of the crew below. Straight through the window. But the bed was empty. Johnny was not in it. The curtain was ripped away. The projectile had flown not into but out of the window. The projectile was Johnny. She bent over the windowsill and shrieked. His elbows in their shirtsleeves dipped and rose, dipped and rose, like white fins. He was having his swim in the Grand Canal. The gondoliers mocked her cry: "Gianni, Gianni!" They leaped into the night water after him, but he would not be caught. For ten minutes they chased the white fins, and fished poor Johnny out by hooking his collar on one of their poles.

6 THE MARRIAGE

Puttermesser had always hated that part. It was too ugly. She didn't like to think about it. Everything bright had ended with George Lewes's funeral. The rest was nothing. The rest didn't count. Johnny Cross, diagnosed as having been subject to "acute mental depression" on a single night of his life, came back to normal, never again had even a moment's worth of derangement, and died in 1924 at the age of eighty-four. But George Eliot weakened and failed. Six months after Johnny threw himself out of the window, she was dead.

Rupert remained cheerful. He didn't miss George Eliot; he had never admired her. Puttermesser, too, under Rupert's influence, had begun to withdraw a little. Possibly George Eliot *was* a prig. She shouldn't have kept Johnny from bathing at the Lido; it was preposterous. She knew he was no good at foreign languages—he couldn't master Hebrew, and mixed up *hiphil* and *hophal.* Then why did she terrorize him with Dante? But Rupert was still harping on his idea—Johnny impersonating Lewes. After Venice, Rupert persisted, in the little time left to their marriage, George Eliot and Johnny Cross went back to the *very same house* Johnny had once helped Lewes buy. "The identical four walls!" he said. "Proof! What more do you want?"

Puttermesser was impatient. She was getting sick of Rupert's idea.

"George Lewes didn't jump into the Grand Canal, did he?" She pushed away the last volume of Johnny Cross's biography. "Johnny just couldn't face sex," she accused.

She looked around her bedroom. A flood of disorder. Heaps of those biographies and maps and memoirs and diaries. An engulfing crust on desk and dresser and floor. Miniature skyscrapers on the windowsills. It was enough. She wanted all those books out. Out, out! Back to the Society Library! The only tidy corner was over near her bed, where Rupert had stored several stacks of his postcards, straight as dominoes.

Puttermesser felt routed. It was as if they had come through a riot. Something tumultuous had happened; she was exhausted, as after intoxication or trance. Rupert had made it happen: this shivering precariousness, this tumult. He had cast out George Lewes, bright-souled George Lewes, and hauled Johnny Cross in. Rupert's impersonation of Johnny Cross impersonating Lewes! It was too alive. It jarred, it aroused. All through his telling the honeymoon she fidgeted, she kindled, she smarted. Rupert was a wizard. He made the honeymoon happen under her fingernails, at the root of her spine. She suffered. It was Lewes she wanted, only Lewes. Didn't the two of them—herself and Rupert—put their heads together under the lamp? Didn't they ignite every passage between them? Yet Rupert took Lewes from her and gave her Cross. Done! The honeymoon was done. Ugly, ugly. She hated it. She had always hated the honeymoon. Rupert pressed it under her fingernails; it was a pole piercing her spine.

Rupert said, "I finished up that Frick thing. Vegetarian tomato, all right?"

Puttermesser said she wasn't hungry for soup.

"Finished up yesterday. A nice Dutch landscape. I have to see Harvey about it when it dries—I'll ask him then. What's wrong with vegetarian tomato?"

"Ask Harvey what?"

"Well, it takes two witnesses. I'll get Harvey next time I'm up there. You figure out who else."

Puttermesser concentrated. "Two witnesses?"

"That's how many you need to get married."

So he meant it. She saw that he meant it. He had been serious about it before. He was serious about it now. Lewes! Lewes, after all! Lewes had inspired him to it. Lewes had seduced him to it. Johnny Cross had got in the way, but the victory belonged to Lewes. Ideal friendship!

"I don't know anybody to ask," Puttermesser said.

"You know a lot of people."

"Not lately. Not this year."

"What about all those politicos in the Municipal Building?"

"I don't work there anymore and I'll never work there again. It was stupid to think I'd ever go back." She reflected on the webwork of her life. Her aunts and uncles were dead. The cousins, once a numerous and jolly gang, were scattered and aging. Half of them had been swallowed up by California—San Diego, Berkeley, Santa Monica, Lake Tahoe. By now most were senior citizens. And the receding gallery of all her old society: there they were, page after page in her little Woolworth address book, those ghosts of classrooms past and half-remembered offices, the detritus of her ascent to fifty-plus. Superannuated fellowship of gossip. Movie companions of yesteryear. They were all distant: either they were wrangling toward divorce, or they lived for their jobs, or they were tanning in the Caribbean, or they were absorbed in their children and their children's babies. Their children: the great genetic tide—the torrent—that separates those with offspring from those without. Three or four of Puttermesser's friends had already died in the lottery of early disease. In the roster of the living, there was not a soul she might want as witness to her wedding. Everyone was obsolete. She was clearing the way. A new life. Clean, pristine.

"But no, Rupert, you're the only one. It's only you. I don't have anybody else."

"I'm in lieu of the world," Rupert said.

She looked to see the mask of flippancy. But there was none.

"Oh, no," she protested, and let his tidy head come into her arms. "You're not in lieu of anything."

Late on a Monday afternoon they took the subway all the way downtown to the Brooklyn Bridge station and went up to the second floor of the Municipal Building. The familiar corridors were wide, battered, gritty; it was as if the walls repelled light. To Puttermesser's surprise, the Marriage License Bureau was no longer there. It had crossed the road to Chambers Street and settled in a former bank the color of an elderly cat's scarred hide. On their way out, Puttermesser surveyed her old territory; inside what had been her own office only months ago, motes hung languidly on smuggled beads of illicit sun. Somewhere a toilet was running. It was relieving that no one recognized her. She was now among the generations of the politically vanished. Estrangement narrowed her throat; her eyes stung in the dimness. She marvelled that she had once disgorged her lawyerly brain into this moribund organism, with its system of secretaries, clerks, assistants, its iron arteries shuffling with underlings.

On the trip back on the No. 6 line in the rush-hour crush, enveloped by the tunnel's grinding thunder, Puttermesser found herself smashed up against Rupert. The car swung like a cradle inside a concussion. Sunk into Rupert's warm shoulder, she felt herself without a past.

"A tomb," she told Rupert. "That place is a tomb."

"What?" he yelled out of the thunder.

"I'm thinking," Puttermesser shouted back, "that my savings are going down. I'll have to start again somewhere pretty soon. You, too, Rupert."

"I don't *have* any savings."

The car screeched around a turn. "You can't do postcards forever," Puttermesser yelled. "Your talent's too big."

"It's just the right size to fit on a postcard. You should see the nice job Harvey's doing on the Frick thing," he yelled back. "Harvey says O.K., did I tell you? About being a witness. And he knows two rabbis—one on the West Side who married him the first time, and one on the East Side who married him the second time. On Second Avenue, in fact," Rupert hollered.

"You should give up the postcards. You should give up Harvey."

The train, arriving at a station, came to a violent stop. Puttermesser was catapulted away. A river of bodies rushed for the door. A forest of bodies sprang up between herself and Rupert.

"All right," Rupert mouthed from across the car. "I'll give up Harvey."

The wedding day was Wednesday—the rabbi on Second Avenue was free that night—and by then they had found the second witness.

Puttermesser said, "There used to be a thumping sound, remember? No, it was before you got here."

"Thumping sound?"

"Well, it's gone. It's been gone for weeks. She's quit doing it. I bet she wouldn't refuse us. She's the one," Puttermesser said. "She's right next *door.*"

The math teacher explained that she had folded up her exercise mat for good. It was hard work, and didn't do the job. Anyhow, it was too lonely. She was enrolled nowadays in one of those new health clubs for singles over on Madison. Her name was Raya Lieberman; she wouldn't at all mind, she said, helping out at a wedding, as long as it was after school. It was true she had Math Club on Wednesdays, but she was perfectly happy to skip it for once. "I've got as good an extracurric supervisory attendance record as anybody, believe me," she assured Puttermesser. "The best, considering what comes down the pike these days."

The rabbi's study was on East Ninetieth, in his apartment. On the telephone he had inquired whether a modest ceremony at 9:30 P.M. in his study at home would be satisfactory, given that it was such a small wedding party and given also—he had a homiletic inflection—that the congregational sanctuary couldn't in any case be secured in the evening on such short notice; and Rupert had agreed. It was beginning to snow again, so the four of them went by taxi—the bride and groom, and the two witnesses. Puttermesser sat in the back seat between the math teacher and Harvey Morgenbluth. Rupert, straight-spined in his stately hat and capelike raincoat, was up front with the driver. Puttermesser had on her best black patent-leather high heels. Rupert and the two witnesses were all wearing their galoshes.

"You ever done a thing like this before?" Harvey Morgenbluth asked Raya Lieberman, leaning across Puttermesser.

"I've been a bride, but not a witness. You?"

"Never done anything like this. How many times?"

"How many times what?"

"How many times you been married?" Harvey Morgenbluth urged across Puttermesser's lap.

"Once."

"With me, it's twice. This is my second rabbi we're on the way to."

It surprised Puttermesser that Harvey Morgenbluth was a familiar apparition. She was habituated to his camel's walk and translucent, flushed ears and phlegmatic, oxlike forehead, well scored by parallel clef lines. It was not unusual for her to run into the math teacher on the way to the incinerator closet or the elevator, but now it dawned on Puttermesser that the flustered-seeming man whom she had often noticed weaving among the shabby old sofas in the lobby, hauling big, square cartons, was Harvey Morgenbluth. Occasionally he pushed them on a dolly. No doubt some of those cartons contained Rupert's postcards. A sourness rose in her. Four inches by six; that was their size. That Frick landscape, a spacious van Ruysdael—a bridge, the gnarled roots of a tree, dark clouds, strange light (dawn or dusk or afternoon before rain), a hunter, a fisherman, a long road, deep vista, two riders, one mounted, the other standing by, red cloak thrown over a shoulder (Rupert loved cloaks, capes, togas), black horse crosswise in the road, blocking it, blacking it, dotting it, swallowing up sky and earth—all that mastery shrunk to four inches by six. Rupert on the side of diminishment, how could it be? At the Met, that first time, hadn't she seen in him voluminous will, the will to be proxy for the punctilious windings and reverberations of huge precursors? Was Rupert with all his amplitude always to be reduced via the technologies of Harvey Morgenbluth? He had promised on the subway to give up Harvey Morgenbluth. Rupert had never explained why a reënactment had to be a dwindling. If it was a dwindling, how could you call it a reënactment?

Puttermesser reminded herself that it was normal to be jittery on the way to one's wedding. Who knew what unhappy divinations Rupert was hurling at her in the front seat, from under his cloak?

Harvey Morgenbluth, still heavy across Puttermesser's knees, was trying to find out from the math teacher if she was available for dinner and a movie next Sunday. "We could go over to the Baronet on Third, or the Beekman on Second. Or look, I've got 'Gone with the Wind' on tape, how about it?"

Puttermesser said briskly, "Don't you do those Sunday parties anymore?"

"Winding down, haven't had one in a bunch of weeks. The kids drove everybody crazy. And you couldn't get a type like Rupert—Rupert's a pretty open guy, but he wasn't interested. Nobody would open up."

Raya Lieberman said, "Nobody opens up nowadays. It's hard for people to be in touch. Everyone's a lonesome atom."

Harvey Morgenbluth whistled. "A lonesome atom, my God. You *said* it." He turned to Puttermesser. His flushed ears were all attention. "By the way, how's the roach problem? You really want to beat 'em, try sodium fluoride around the pipes."

The rabbi's name was Stewart Sonnenfeld. He introduced his wife, Jill, and his teenage son, Seth, who was at that moment writing a report on Chaucer's "Prologue" for his English class. The four poles of the wedding canopy were held up by Harvey Morgenbluth, Raya Lieberman, Jill Sonnenfeld, and Seth Sonnenfeld. Puttermesser had retrieved her mother's wedding ring from an old felt wallet she kept inside an empty plastic margarine container at the back of the vegetable bin in the refrigerator to foil a burglar. The rabbi had cautioned Rupert to bring along his own wineglass for the ceremony, so that morning Puttermesser had hurried into Woolworth to buy one. Jill Sonnenfeld wrapped it in a paper napkin inside a paper bag, and Rupert stamped on it with his galosh. It exploded with a gratifying convulsion. In Puttermesser's apartment afterward Harvey Morgenbluth and Raya Lieberman each drank a Styrofoam cup of champagne (Harvey's present) and ate a piece of wedding cake—Puttermesser made do with an Entenmann's chocolate layer from the supermarket on Third—and then the two witnesses went off together.

"Into the night," Puttermesser said. "They've gone off into the night, imagine that. Maybe it'll take."

Rupert was poking in the corner closet where he kept his equipment; he was dragging out his satchel. "Maybe into the night," Rupert said. "More likely upstairs to 6-C."

"*We* took," Puttermesser said.

Her heart—her fleshly heart—was curled around itself, like a spiralled loaf of hot, new bread. Inside the cavity that rocked it, this good bread was swelling. Puttermesser waited for Rupert's head to come into her arms, against her heart's loaf. She waited for his voice, his dark reading voice, with its sharp click that could cut her with happiness, like a beak. The living, plain, painful flesh. Sometimes, for all the tumult of his history (he had handed over every winding of his life to her, he kept nothing back), he seemed new-made—as if she had ejected him from a secret spectral egg lodged in her frontal lobe, or under her tongue where the sour saliva gave birth to desire. He was her own shadow and fingerprint. She had painted him on her retina in her sleep. She felt him to be the smothered croak in her throat, a phlegm of chaos burst out of her lung. He had lived too long in her nerves, and her nerves were all wired to the transcendent. Desire, desire! She and Rupert—both of them—were too tentative.

He had pulled out his easel, and left it on the floor with the satchel. He crossed the living room to stand at the window. A hard wind hit the glass. There he was, mooning down at the snowy street below; she wondered if he was looking to see whether Harvey Morgenbluth and Raya Lieberman had really gone off into the night. The loaf in the middle of her chest ballooned; it grew and grew. Jealousy. Rupert's head struck her as still another loaf, all brightly honeyed against the snow-streaked panes. He had been born into the world two decades after her own birth. A long, long meadow, all grassy-green, stretched before him. Under his mustache the two points of his mouth were as elastic as a child's.

She saw that he was dusted over with gloom. He unbuckled one of his galoshes. He seemed indecisive about the other, but he shook it free. The race was behind them, the dream was dreamed. They had arrived at arrival. All wedding nights taste of letdown.

Puttermesser took off her black patent-leather high heels. They had walked in the snow only a little—out of the taxi, into the lobby—but her feet were still damp. She shivered from the feet up. She went into the bedroom to fetch her furry winter slippers. The dresser mirror arrested, fleetingly, the figure of a woman. How quickly that woman fled!

When she came back into the living room, Rupert was wearing his galoshes again. He was wearing his capelike raincoat and his stately hat. He had his folded-up easel under one arm and his satchel in his hand.

There was something in his face she recognized. An indifference had seeped into the gloom. It was as if she had turned invisible. It was as if he did not recognize her: *that* was what she recognized. A snub—almost a snub. His face hurt her. His youth hurt her.

"Rupert," she said. "What are you doing, Rupert?"

"I can't stay."

"You have to."

"I can't. I can't, Ruth. I can't stay."

"Rupert, take off your coat. Please. Rupert, please."

"No," he said. It was not indifference. It was a burning. He was inside a furnace; he was speaking out of a furnace.

Puttermesser called after him, "Rupert! What are you *doing?*"

"I can't stay."

In the little vestibule he set down his satchel and aimed the easel directly in front of him, clutching it like a burning beam; like a spear. He raised it high and plummeted after it back into the living room. He was running for the window. Puttermesser feared he would fling his lance straight through the glass. But he stopped. He put down the easel and with both hands lifted the window wide. A shock of wind knocked over the stack of Styrofoam cups on the sill. The snow flew in, wet as a waterfall.

"Rupert, Rupert," Puttermesser pleaded. "Take off your coat. Shut the window. For God's sake, shut the window!"

He gave her his whole look then. She was falling into the tiny black holes at the center of his clean, powerful eyes. She was falling and falling, but instead of vertigo or delirium or disorder, there was only the candor of her own intelligence. She understood that he was altogether sane, altogether calculating, and as jubilant as a mathematician in the act of confirming an equation.

He picked up his things and walked out the door.

At the open window, hanging over the sill to catch sight of him dwindling in the street, Puttermesser squinted into the snow. It was pointless to call down to him as George Eliot had called down into the Grand Canal, but anyhow she called and called; the snow blew into her mouth. It was starting to stick to her hair. She leaned into the wetness until her hair was all white with snow.

A copyist, a copyist!

QUESTIONS FOR DISCUSSION AND WRITING

1. How do the titles of the six divisions of the story provide an ironic structure for the plot? How does the last line of the story serve as a climax?
2. What is the difference between George Eliot's relationship to George Lewes and Eliot's relationship to Johnny Cross? Why does Ruth prefer the first while Rupert identifies with the second?
3. How does Ruth use the setting of her apartment (3-C) to recreate the setting of the Priory? Why was Venice an important setting in George Eliot's life?
4. How do the quotations and paraphrases provide a second point of view in the story? What is the difference between the way the two "night readers" use the Eliot material?
5. What does Rupert's art suggest about his views of life and relationships? How do Ruth's "brains" create problems in her life and relationships?

76

DOROTHY PARKER

The Waltz

DOROTHY PARKER (1893–1967) was born in West End, New Jersey, grew up on Manhattan's West Side, and was educated at a private school in Morristown, New Jersey. In the 1920s, she began her literary career at *Vogue,* where she published her samples of witty verse. Next, she worked as the drama critic for *Vanity Fair* before joining the staff of *The New Yorker,* where her caustic wit earned her a place at the famous "round table" that met at the Algonquin Hotel. In the 1930s, she moved to Hollywood where she wrote a series of film scripts, until she was blacklisted in the early 1950s for her alleged Communist sympathies. Her poems appear in *Enough Rope* (1926), *Sunset Over* (1928), and *Death and Taxes* (1931). Her stories, which originally appeared in magazines such as *The New Yorker* and *Esquire,* are collected in *Laments for the Living* (1930), *After Such Pleasures* (1933), and *Here Lies* (1939). "The Waltz," reprinted from *Here Lies,* recounts a woman's private observations on the social ritual she performs.

Why, thank you so much. I'd adore to.

I don't want to dance with him. I don't want to dance with anybody. And even if I did, it wouldn't be him. He'd be well down among the last ten. I've seen the way he dances; it looks like something you do on Saint Walpurgis Night. Just think, not a quarter of an hour ago, here I was sitting, feeling so sorry for the poor girl he was dancing with. And now *I'm* going to be the poor girl. Well, well. Isn't it a small world?

And a peach of a world, too. A true little corker. Its events are so fascinatingly unpredictable, are not they? Here I was, minding my own business, not doing a stitch of harm to any living soul. And then he comes into my life, all smiles and city manners, to sue me for the favor of one memorable mazurka. Why, he scarcely knows my name, let alone what it stands for. It stands for Despair, Bewilderment, Futility, Degradation, and Premeditated Murder, but little does he wot. I don't wot his name, either; I haven't any idea what it is. Jukes, would be my guess from the look in his eyes. How do you do, Mr. Jukes? And how is that dear little brother of yours, with the two heads?

Ah, now why did he have to come around me, with his low requests? Why can't he let me lead my own life? I ask so little—just to be left alone in my quiet corner of the table, to do my evening brooding over all my sorrows. And he must come, with his bows and his scrapes and his may-I-have-this-ones. And I had to go and tell him that I'd adore to dance with him. I cannot understand why I wasn't struck right down dead. Yes, and being struck dead would look like a day in the country, compared to struggling out a dance with this boy. But what could I do? Everyone else at the table had got up to dance, except him and me. There was I, trapped. Trapped like a trap in a trap.

What can you say, when a man asks you to dance with him? I most certainly will *not* dance with you, I'll see you in hell first. Why, thank you, I'd like to awfully, but I'm having labor pains. Oh, yes, *do* let's dance together—it's so nice to meet a man who isn't a scaredy-cat about catching my beri-beri. No. There was nothing for me to do, but say I'd adore to. Well, we might as well get it over with. All right, Cannonball, let's run out on the field. You won the toss; you can lead.

Why, I think it's more of a waltz, really. Isn't it? We might just listen to the music a second. Shall we? Oh, yes, it's a waltz. Mind? Why, I'm simply thrilled. I'd love to waltz with you.

I'd love to waltz with you. I'd love to waltz with you. I'd love to have my tonsils out, I'd love to be in a midnight fire at sea. Well, it's too late now. We're getting under way. *Oh.* Oh, dear. Oh, dear, dear, dear. Oh, this is even worse than I thought it would be. I suppose that's the one dependable law of life—everything is always worse than you thought it was going to be. Oh, if I had any real grasp of what this dance would be like, I'd have held out for sitting it out. Well, it will probably amount to the same thing in the end. We'll be sitting it out on the floor in a minute, if he keeps this up.

I'm so glad I brought it to his attention that this is a waltz they're playing. Heaven knows what might have happened, if he had thought it was something fast; we'd have blown the sides right out of the building. Why does he always want to be somewhere that he isn't? Why can't we stay in one place just long enough to get acclimated? It's this constant rush, rush, rush, that's the curse of American life. That's the reason that we're all of us so—*Ow!* For God's sake, don't *kick,* you idiot; this is only second down. Oh, my shin. My poor, poor shin, that I've had ever since I was a little girl!

Oh, no, no, no. Goodness, no. It didn't hurt the least little bit. And anyway it was my fault. Really it was. Truly. Well, you're just being sweet, to say that. It really was all my fault.

I wonder what I'd better do—kill him this instant, with my naked hands, or wait and let him drop in his traces. Maybe it's best not to make a scene. I guess I'll just lie low, and watch the pace get him. He can't keep this up indefinitely—he's only flesh and blood. Die he must, and die he shall, for what he did to me. I don't want to be of the over-sensitive type, but you can't tell me that kick was unpremeditated. Freud says there are no accidents. I've led no cloistered life, I've known dancing partners who have spoiled my slippers and torn my dress; but when it comes to kicking, I am Outraged Womanhood. When you kick me in the shin, *smile.*

Maybe he didn't do it maliciously. Maybe it's just his way of showing his high spirits. I suppose I ought to be glad that one of us is having such a good time. I suppose I ought to think myself lucky if he brings me back alive. Maybe it's captious to demand of a practically strange man that he leave your shins as he found them. After all, the poor boy's doing the best he can. Probably he grew up in the hill country, and never had no larnin'. I bet they had to throw him on his back to get shoes on him.

Yes, it's lovely, isn't it? It's simply lovely. It's the loveliest waltz. Isn't it? Oh, I think it's lovely, too.

Why, I'm getting positively drawn to the Triple Threat here. He's my hero. He has the heart of a lion, and the sinews of a buffalo. Look at him—never a thought of the consequences, never afraid of his face, hurling himself into every scrimmage, eyes shining, cheeks ablaze. And shall it be said that I hung back? No, a thousand times no. What's it to me if I have to spend the next couple of years in a plaster cast? Come on, Butch, right through them! Who wants to live forever?

Oh. Oh, dear. Oh, he's all right, thank goodness. For a while I thought they'd have to carry him off the field. Ah, I couldn't bear to have anything happen to him. I love him. I love him better than anybody in the world. Look at the spirit he gets into a dreary, commonplace waltz; how effete the other dancers seem, beside him. He is youth and vigor and courage, he is strength and gaiety and—*Ow!* Get off my instep, you hulking peasant! What do you think I am, anyway—a gangplank? *Ow!*

No, of course it didn't hurt. Why, it didn't a bit. Honestly. And it was all my fault. You see, that little step of yours—well, it's perfectly lovely, but it's just a tiny bit tricky to follow at first. Oh, did you work it up yourself? You really did? Well, aren't you amazing! Oh, now I think I've got it. Oh, I think it's lovely. I was watching you do it when you were dancing before. It's awfully effective when you look at it.

It's awfully effective when you look at it. I bet I'm awfully effective when you look at me. My hair is hanging along my cheeks, my skirt is swaddled about me, I can feel the cold damp of my brow. I must look like something out of the "Fall of the House of Usher." This sort of thing takes a fearful toll of a woman my age. And he worked up his little step himself, he with his degenerate cunning. And it was just a tiny bit tricky at first, but now I think I've got it. Two stumbles, slip, and a twenty-yard dash; yes. I've got it. I've got several other things, too, including a split shin and a bitter heart. I hate this creature I'm chained to. I hated him the moment I saw his leering, bestial face. And here I've been locked in his noxious embrace for the thirty-five years this waltz has lasted. Is that orchestra never going to stop playing? Or must this obscene travesty of a dance go on until hell burns out?

Oh, they're going to play another encore. Oh, goody. Oh, that's lovely. Tired? I should say I'm not tired. I'd like to go on like this forever.

I should say I'm not tired. I'm dead, that's all I am. Dead, and in what a cause! And the music is never going to stop playing, and we're going on like this, Double-Time Charlie and I, throughout eternity. I suppose I won't care any more, after the first hundred thousand years. I suppose nothing will matter then, not heat nor pain nor broken heart nor cruel, aching weariness. Well. It can't come too soon for me.

I wonder why I didn't tell him I was tired. I wonder why I didn't suggest going back to the table. I could have said let's just listen to the music. Yes, and if he would, that would be the first bit of attention he had given it all evening. George Jean Nathan said that the lovely rhythms of the waltz should be listened to in stillness and not be accompanied by strange gyrations of the human body. I think that's what he said. I think it was George Jean Nathan. Anyhow, whatever he said and whoever he was and whatever he's doing now, he's better off than I am. That's safe. Anybody who isn't waltzing with this Mrs. O'Leary's cow I've got here is having a good time.

Still if we were back at the table, I'd probably have to talk to him. Look at him—what could you say to a thing like that! Did you go to the circus this year, what's your favorite kind of ice cream, how do you spell cat? I guess I'm as well off here. As well off as if I were in a cement mixer in full action.

I'm past all feeling now. The only way I can tell when he steps on me is that I can hear the splintering of bones. And all the events of my life are passing before my eyes.

There was the time I was in a hurricane in the West Indies, there was the day I got my head cut open in the taxi smash, there was the night the drunken lady threw a bronze ash-tray at her own true love and got me instead, there was that summer that the sailboat kept capsizing. Ah, what an easy, peaceful time was mine, until I fell in with Swifty, here. I didn't know what trouble was, before I got drawn into this *danse macabre.* I think my mind is beginning to wander. It almost seems to me as if the orchestra were stopping. It couldn't be, of course; it could never, never be. And yet in my ears there is a silence like the sound of angel voices. . . .

Oh, they've stopped, the mean things. They're not going to play any more. Oh, darn. Oh, do you think they would? Do you really think so, if you gave them twenty dollars? Oh, that would be lovely. And look, do tell them to play this same thing. I'd simply adore to go on waltzing.

QUESTIONS FOR DISCUSSION AND WRITING

1. How does the behavior of the two dancers mark the development of the plot? Why does the narrator decide to go on?
2. How do the narrator's exaggerations develop her character? Does Parker expect her readers to see the woman narrator as a sympathetic character? What do we know about her male partner?
3. How does the narrator's use of slang—e.g., "it's a peach"; "I fell in with Swifty here"—create and/or date the setting of the story?
4. How does Parker contrast the external dialogue and the internal monologue in the story?
5. How accurate is the story in its depiction of the difference between what we think and what we say? How much of this depiction depends on stereotypical attitudes toward gender?

77

EDGAR ALLAN POE

The Fall of the House of Usher

EDGAR ALLAN POE (1809–1849) was born in Boston, Massachusetts, the son of traveling actors. Before he was three, his father deserted the family, his mother died, and he was adopted by John Allan of Richmond, Virginia, who saw to Poe's education in England, at the University of Virginia, and finally at West Point. Poe's drinking and gambling constantly strained his relationship with his foster father and eventually resulted in his dismissal from the Academy. He then moved to Baltimore to live with his aunt and to devote himself to a literary career. In 1832 he published five of his stories in the *Saturday Courier,* and in 1833 he won first prize

in a short-story contest sponsored by a Baltimore newspaper. Encouraged by this success, he returned to Richmond in 1835 to edit *The Southern Literary Messenger,* in which he published highly influential literary criticism. In 1836 he married Virginia Clemm, his cousin, then not quite fourteen. Although Poe's work for the *Messenger* helped make it a leading critical magazine, his salary was so low that he resigned and moved to New York to look for work. His addiction to drink and drugs was a constant source of difficulty for him, contributing to his poverty, poor health, and early death. Nevertheless, in the next ten years he was able to publish his classic novel *The Narrative of Arthur Gordon Pym* (1838), famous poems, *The Raven and Other Poems* (1845), and stories in two notable forms: tales of gothic terror and tales of deduction or ratiocination (the precursor of the modern detective story). "The Fall of the House of Usher," reprinted from *Tales of the Grotesque and Arabesque* (1839), describes the terrifying collapse of an ancient family and its mansion. "The Cask of Amontillado," first published in *Godey's Lady's Book* (November, 1846), is the dramatic retelling of the murder of a man unaware of his own fate.

Son cœur est un luth suspendu;
Sitôt qu'on le touche il résonne.
—de Béranger

During the whole of a dull, dark, and soundless day in the autumn of the year, when the clouds hung oppressively low in the heavens, I had been passing alone, on horseback, through a singularly dreary tract of country, and at length found myself, as the shades of the evening drew on, within view of the melancholy House of Usher. I know not how it was—but, with the first glimpse of the building, a sense of insufferable gloom pervaded my spirit. I say insufferable; for the feeling was unrelieved by any of that half-pleasurable, because poetic, sentiment with which the mind usually receives even the sternest natural images of the desolate or terrible. I looked upon the scene before me—upon the mere house, and the simple landscape features of the domain—upon the bleak walls—upon the vacant eye-like windows—upon a few rank sedges—and upon a few white trunks of decayed trees—with an utter depression of soul which I can compare to no earthly sensation more properly than to the afterdream of the reveller upon opium—the bitter lapse into everyday life—the hideous dropping off of the veil. There was an iciness, a sinking, a sickening of the heart—an unredeemed dreariness of thought which no goading of the imagination could torture into aught of the sublime. What was it—I paused to think—what was it that so unnerved me in the contemplation of the House of Usher? It was a mystery all insoluble; nor could I grapple with the shadowy fancies that crowded upon me as I pondered. I was forced to fall back upon the unsatisfactory conclusion, that while, beyond doubt, there *are* combinations of very simple natural objects which have the power of thus affecting us, still the analysis of this power lies among considerations beyond our depth. It was possible, I reflected, that a mere different arrangement of the particulars of the scene, of the details of the picture, would be sufficient to modify, or perhaps to annihilate its capacity for sorrowful impression; and, acting upon this idea, I reined my horse to the precipitous brink of a black and lurid tarn that lay in unruffled lustre by the dwelling, and gazed down—but with a shudder even more thrilling than before—upon the remodelled and inverted images of the gray sedge, and the ghastly tree-stems, and the vacant and eye-like windows.

Nevertheless, in this mansion of gloom I now proposed to myself a sojourn of some weeks. Its proprietor, Roderick Usher, had been one of my boon companions in boyhood; but many years had elapsed since our last meeting. A letter, however, had lately reached me in a distant part of the country—a letter from him—which, in its wildly importunate nature, had admitted of no other than a personal reply. The MS. gave evidence of nervous agitation. The writer spoke of acute bodily illness—of a mental disorder which oppressed him—and of an earnest desire to see me, as his best and, indeed, his only personal friend, with a view of attempting, by the cheerfulness of my society, some alleviation of his malady. It was the manner in which all this, and much more, was said—it was the apparent heart that went with his request—which allowed me no room for hesitation; and I accordingly obeyed forthwith what I still considered a very singular summons.

Although as boys, we had been even intimate associates, yet I really knew little of my friend. His reserve had been always excessive and habitual. I was aware, however, that his very ancient family had been noted, time out of mind, for a peculiar sensibility of temperament, displaying itself, through long ages, in many works of exalted art, and manifested, of late, in repeated deeds of munificent yet unobtrusive charity, as well as in a passionate devotion to the intricacies, perhaps even more than to the orthodox and easily recognizable beauties, of musical science. I had heard, too, the very remarkable fact, that the stem of the Usher race, all time-honored as it was, had put forth, at no period, any enduring branch; in other words, that the entire family lay in the direct line of descent, and had always, with very trifling and very temporary variations, so lain. It was this deficiency, I considered, while running over in thought the perfect keeping of the character of the premises with the accredited character of the people, and while speculating upon the possible influence which the one, in the long lapse of centuries, might have exercised upon the other—it was this deficiency, perhaps, of collateral issue, and the consequent undeviating transmission, from sire to son, of the patrimony with the name, which had, at length, so identified the two as to merge the original title of the estate in the quaint and equivocal appellation of the "House of Usher"—an appellation which seemed to include, in the minds of the peasantry who used it, both the family and the family mansion.

I have said that the sole effect of my somewhat childish experiment—that of looking down within the tarn—had been to deepen the first singular impression. There can be no doubt that the consciousness of the rapid increase of my superstition—for why should I not so term it?—served mainly to accelerate the increase itself. Such, I have long known, is the paradoxical law of all sentiments having terror as a basis. And it might have been for this reason only, that, when I again uplifted my eyes to the house itself, from its image in the pool, there grew in my mind a strange fancy—a fancy so ridiculous, indeed, that I but mention it to show the vivid force of the sensations which oppressed me. I had so worked upon my imagination as really to believe that about the whole mansion and domain there hung an atmosphere peculiar to themselves and their immediate vicinity—an atmosphere which had no affinity with the air of heaven, but which had reeked up from the decayed trees, and the gray wall, and the silent tarn—a pestilent and mystic vapor, dull, sluggish, faintly discernible and leaden-hued.

Shaking off from my spirit what *must* have been a dream, I scanned more narrowly the real aspect of the building. Its principal feature seemed to be that of an excessive antiquity. The discoloration of ages had been great. Minute fungi overspread the whole exterior, hanging in a fine tangled web-work from the eaves. Yet all this was apart from any extraordinary dilapidation. No portion of the masonry had fallen; and there appeared to be a wild inconsistency between its still perfect adaptation of parts, and the crumbling condition of the individual stones. In this there was much that reminded me of the specious totality of old woodwork which has rotted for long years in some neglected vault, with no disturbance from the breath of the external air. Beyond this indication of extensive decay, however, the fabric gave little token of instability. Perhaps the eye of a scrutinizing observer might have discovered a barely perceptible fissure, which extending from the roof of the building in front, made its way down the wall in a zigzag direction, until it became lost in the sullen waters of the tarn.

Noticing these things, I rode over a short causeway to the house. A servant in waiting took my horse, and I entered the Gothic archway of the hall. A valet, of stealthy step, thence conducted me, in silence, through many dark and intricate passages in my progress to the *studio* of his master. Much that I encountered on the way contributed, I know not how, to heighten the vague sentiments of which I have already spoken. While the objects around me—while the carvings of the ceilings, the sombre tapestries of the walls, the ebon blackness of the floors, and the phantasmagoric armorial trophies which rattled as I strode, were but matters to which, or to such as which, I had been accustomed from my infancy—while I hesitated not to acknowledge how familiar was all this—I still wondered to find how unfamiliar were the fancies which ordinary images were stirring up. On one of the staircases, I met the physician of the family. His countenance, I thought, wore a mingled expression of low cunning and perplexity. He accosted me with trepidation and passed on. The valet now threw open a door and ushered me into the presence of his master.

The room in which I found myself was very large and lofty. The windows were long, narrow, and pointed, and at so vast a distance from the black oaken floor as to be altogether inaccessible from within. Feeble gleams of encrimsoned light made their way through the trellised panes, and served to render sufficiently distinct the more prominent objects around; the eye, however, struggled in vain to reach the remoter angles of the chamber, or the recesses of the vaulted and fretted ceiling. Dark draperies hung upon the walls. The general furniture was profuse, comfortless, antique, and tattered. Many books and musical instruments lay scattered about, but failed to give any vitality to the scene. I felt that I breathed an atmosphere of sorrow. An air of stern, deep, and irredeemable gloom hung over and pervaded all.

Upon my entrance, Usher arose from a sofa on which he had been lying at full length, and greeted me with a vivacious warmth which had much in it, I at first thought, of an overdone cordiality—of the constrained effort of the *ennuyé* man of the world. A glance, however, at his countenance convinced me of his perfect sincerity. We sat down;

and for some moments, while he spoke not, I gazed upon him with a feeling half of pity, half of awe. Surely, man had never before so terribly altered, in so brief a period, as had Roderick Usher! It was with difficulty that I could bring myself to admit the identity of the wan being before me with the companion of my early boyhood. Yet the character of his face had been at all times remarkable. A cadaverousness of complexion; an eye large, liquid, and luminous beyond comparison; lips somewhat thin and very pallid, but of a surpassingly beautiful curve; a nose of a delicate Hebrew model, but with a breadth of nostril unusual in similar formations; a finely molded chin, speaking, in its want of prominence, of a want of moral energy; hair of a more than web-like softness and tenuity;—these features, with an inordinate expansion above the regions of the temple, made up altogether a countenance not easily to be forgotten. And now in the mere exaggeration of the prevailing character of these features, and of the expression they were wont to convey, lay so much of change that I doubted to whom I spoke. The now ghastly pallor of the skin, and the now miraculous lustre of the eye, above all things startled and even awed me. The silken hair, too, had been suffered to grow all unheeded, and as, in its wild gossamer texture, it floated rather than fell about the face, I could not, even with effort, connect its Arabesque expression with any idea of simple humanity.

In the manner of my friend I was at once struck with an incoherence—an inconsistency; and I soon found this to arise from a series of feeble and futile struggles to overcome an habitual trepidancy—an excessive nervous agitation. For something of this nature I had indeed been prepared, no less by his letter, than by reminiscences of certain boyish traits, and by conclusions deduced from his peculiar physical conformation and temperament. His action was alternately vivacious and sullen. His voice varied rapidly from a tremulous indecision (when the animal spirits seemed utterly in abeyance) to that species of energetic concision—that abrupt, weighty, unhurried, and hollow-sounding enunciation—that leaden, self-balanced, and perfectly modulated guttural utterance, which may be observed in the lost drunkard, or the irreclaimable eater of opium, during the periods of his most intense excitement.

It was thus that he spoke of the object of my visit, of his earnest desire to see me, and of the solace he expected me to afford him. He entered, at some length, into what he conceived to be the nature of his malady. It was, he said, a constitutional and a family evil and one for which he despaired to find a remedy—a mere nervous affection, he immediately added, which would undoubtedly soon pass off. It displayed itself in a host of unnatural sensations. Some of these, as he detailed them, interested and bewildered me; although, perhaps, the terms and the general manner of their narration had their weight. He suffered much from a morbid acuteness of the senses; the most insipid food was alone endurable; he could wear only garments of certain texture; the odors of all flowers were oppressive; his eyes were tortured by even a faint light; and there were but peculiar sounds, and these from stringed instruments, which did not inspire him with horror.

To an anomalous species of terror, I found him a bounden slave. "I shall perish," said he, "I *must* perish in this deplorable folly. Thus, thus, and not otherwise, shall I be lost. I dread the events of the future, not in themselves, but in their results. I shudder at the thought of any, even the most trivial, incident, which may operate upon this intolerable agitation of soul. I have, indeed, no abhorrence of danger, except in its absolute effect—

in terror. In this unnerved, in this pitiable condition I feel that the period will sooner or later arrive when I must abandon life and reason together, in some struggle with the grim phantasm, Fear."

I learned, moreover, at intervals, and through broken and equivocal hints, another singular feature of his mental condition. He was enchained by certain superstitious impressions in regard to the dwelling which he tenanted, and whence, for many years, he had never ventured forth—in regard to an influence whose suppositious force was conveyed in terms too shadowy here to be re-stated—an influence which some peculiarities in the mere form and substance of his family mansion had, by dint of long sufferance, he said, obtained over his spirit—an effect which the *physique* of the gray walls and turrets, and of the dim tarn into which they all looked down, had, at length, brought about upon the *morale* of his existence.

He admitted, however, although with hesitation, that much of the peculiar gloom which thus afflicted him could be traced to a more natural and far more palpable origin—to the severe and long-continued illness—indeed to the evidently approaching dissolution—of a tenderly beloved sister, his sole companion for long years, his last and only relative on earth. "Her decease," he said, with a bitterness which I can never forget, "would leave him (him, the hopeless and the frail) the last of the ancient race of the Ushers." While he spoke, the lady Madeline (for so was she called) passed through a remote portion of the apartment, and, without having noticed my presence, disappeared. I regarded her with an utter astonishment not unmingled with dread and yet I found it impossible to account for such feelings. A sensation of stupor oppressed me as my eyes followed her retreating steps. When a door, at length, closed upon her, my glance sought instinctively and eagerly the countenance of the brother; but he had buried his face in his hands, and I could only perceive that a far more than ordinary wanness had overspread the emaciated fingers through which trickled many passionate tears.

The disease of the lady Madeline had long baffled the skill of her physicians. A settled apathy, a gradual wasting away of the person, and frequent although transient affections of a partially cataleptical character were the usual diagnosis. Hitherto she had steadily borne up against the pressure of her malady, and had not betaken herself finally to bed; but on the closing in of the evening of my arrival at the house, she succumbed (as her brother told me at night with inexpressible agitation) to the prostrating power of the destroyer; and I learned that the glimpse I had obtained of her person would thus probably be the last I should obtain—that the lady, at least while living, would be seen by me no more.

For several days ensuing, her name was unmentioned by either Usher or myself; and during this period I was busied in earnest endeavors to alleviate the melancholy of my friend. We painted and read together, or I listened, as if in a dream, to the wild improvisations of his speaking guitar. And thus, as a closer and still closer intimacy admitted me more unreservedly into the recesses of his spirit, the more bitterly did I perceive the futility of all attempts at cheering a mind from which darkness, as if an inherent positive quality, poured forth upon all objects of the moral and physical universe in one unceasing radiation of gloom.

I shall ever bear about me a memory of the many solemn hours I thus spent alone with the master of the House of Usher. Yet I should fail in any attempt to convey an idea of the exact character of the studies, or of the occupations, in which he involved me, or led me the way. An excited and highly distempered ideality threw a sulphureous lustre over all. His long improvised dirges will ring forever in my ears. Among other things, I hold painfully in mind a certain singular perversion and amplification of the wild air of the last waltz of Von Weber. From the painting over which his elaborate fancy brooded, and which grew, touch by touch, into vagueness at which I shuddered the more thrillingly, because I shuddered knowing not why—from these paintings (vivid as their images now are before me) I would in vain endeavor to educe more than a small portion which should lie within the compass of merely written words. By the utter simplicity, by the nakedness of his designs, he arrested and overawed attention. If ever mortal painted an idea, that mortal was Roderick Usher. For me at least, in the circumstances then surrounding me, there arose out of the pure abstractions which the hypochondriac contrived to throw upon his canvas, an intensity of intolerable awe, no shadow of which felt I ever yet in the contemplation of the certainly glowing yet too concrete reveries of Fuseli.

One of the phantasmagoric conceptions of my friend, partaking not so rigidly of the spirit of abstraction, may be shadowed forth, although feebly, in words. A small picture presented the interior of an immensely long and rectangular vault or tunnel, with low walls, smooth, white and without interruption or device. Certain accessory points of the design served well to convey the idea that this excavation lay at an exceeding depth below the surface of the earth. No outlet was observed in any portion of its vast extent, and no torch or other artificial source of light was discernible; yet a flood of intense rays rolled throughout, and bathed the whole in a ghastly and inappropriate splendor.

I have just spoken of that morbid condition of the auditory nerve which rendered all music intolerable to the sufferer, with the exception of certain effects of stringed instruments. It was, perhaps, the narrow limits to which he thus confined himself upon the guitar which gave birth, in great measure, to the fantastic character of his performances. But the fervid *facility* of his *impromptus* could not be so accounted for. They must have been, and were, in the notes, as well as in the words of his wild fantasies (for he not unfrequently accompanied himself with rhymed verbal improvisations), the result of that intense mental collectedness and concentration to which I have previously alluded as observable only in particular moments of the highest artificial excitement. The words of one of these rhapsodies I have easily remembered. I was, perhaps, the more forcibly impressed with it as he gave it, because, in the under or mystic current of its meaning, I fancied that I perceived, and for the first time, a full consciousness on the part of Usher of the tottering of his lofty reason upon her throne. The verses, which were entitled "The Haunted Palace," ran very nearly, if not accurately, thus:

I

In the greenest of our valleys,
 By good angels tenanted,
Once a fair and stately palace—
 Radiant palace—reared its head.
In the monarch Thought's dominion—
 It stood there!
Never seraph spread a pinion
 Over fabric half so fair.

II

Banners yellow, glorious, golden,
On its roof did float and flow
(This—all this—was in the olden
Time long ago);
And every gentle air that dallied,
In that sweet day,
Along the ramparts plumed and pallid,
A wingèd odor went away.

III

Wanderers in that happy valley
Through two luminous windows saw
Spirits moving musically
To a lute's well-tuned law;
Round about a throne, where sitting
(Porphyrogene!)
In state his glory well befitting,
The ruler of the realm was seen.

IV

And all with pearl and ruby glowing
Was the fair palace door,
Through which came flowing, flowing, flowing
And sparkling evermore,
A troop of Echoes whose sweet duty
Was but to sing,
In voices of surpassing beauty,
The wit and wisdom of their king.

V

But evil things, in robes of sorrow,
Assailed the monarch's high estate;
(Ah, let us mourn, for never morrow
Shall dawn upon him, desolate!)
And, round about his home, the glory
That blushed and bloomed
Is but a dim-remembered story
Of the old time entombed.

VI

And travellers now within that valley,
Through the red-litten windows see
Vast forms that move fantastically
To a discordant melody;
While, like a rapid ghastly river,
Through the pale door,

A hideous throng rush out forever,
And laugh—but smile no more.

I well remember that suggestions arising from this ballad led us into a train of thought wherein there became manifest an opinion of Usher's, which I mention not so much on account of its novelty (for other men have thought thus), as on account of the pertinacity with which he maintained it. This opinion, in its general form, was that of the sentience of all vegetable things. But, in his disordered fancy, the idea had assumed a more daring character, and trespassed, under certain conditions, upon the kingdom of inorganization. I lack words to express the full extent, or the earnest *abandon* of his persuasion. The belief, however, was connected (as I have previously hinted) with the gray stones of the home of his forefathers. The conditions of the sentience had been here, he imagined, fulfilled in the method of collocation of these stones—in the order of their arrangement, as well as in that of the many *fungi* which overspread them, and of the decayed trees which stood around—above all, in the long undisturbed endurance of this arrangement, and in its reduplication in the still waters of the tarn. Its evidence—the evidence of the sentience—was to be seen, he said (and I here started as he spoke), in the gradual yet certain condensation of an atmosphere of their own about the waters and the walls. The result was discoverable, he added, in that silent yet importunate and terrible influence which for centuries had molded the destinies of his family, and which made *him* what I now saw him—what he was. Such opinions need no comment, and I will make none.

Our books—the books which, for years, had formed no small portion of the mental existence of the invalid—were, as might be supposed, in strict keeping with this character of phantasm. We pored together over such works as the "Ververt et Chartreuse" of Gresset; the "Belphegor" of Machiavelli; the "Heaven and Hell" of Swedenborg; the "Subterranean Voyage of Nicholas Klimm" by Holberg; the "Chiromancy" of Robert Flud, of Jean D'Indaginé and Dela Chambre; the "Journey into the Blue Distance" of Tieck; and the "City of the Sun" of Campanella. One favorite volume was a small octavo edition of the "Directorium Inquisitorium," by the Dominican Eymeric de Gironne; and there were passages in Pomponius Mela, about the old African Satyrs and Oegipans, over which Usher would sit dreaming for hours. His chief delight, however, was found in the perusal of an exceedingly rare and curious book in quarto Gothic— the manual of a forgotten church—the *Vigiliae Mortuorum secundum Chorum Ecclesiae Maguntinae.*

I could not help thinking of the wild ritual of this work, and of its probable influence upon the hypochondriac, when, one evening, having informed me abruptly that the lady Madeline was no more, he stated his intention of preserving her corpse for a fortnight (previously to its final interment), in one of the numerous vaults within the main walls of the building. The worldly reason, however, assigned for this singular proceeding, was one which I did not feel at liberty to dispute. The brother had been led to his resolution (so he told me) by consideration of the unusual character of the malady of the deceased, of certain obtrusive and eager inquiries on the part of her medical men, and of the remote and exposed situation of the burial-ground of the family. I will not deny that when I called to mind the sinister countenance of the person whom I met upon the staircase, on the day of my arrival at the house, I had no desire to oppose what I regarded as at best but a harmless, and by no means an unnatural, precaution.

At the request of Usher, I personally aided him in the arrangements for the temporary entombment. The body having been encoffined, we two alone bore it to its rest. The vault in which we placed it (and which had been so long unopened that our torches, half smothered in its oppressive atmosphere, gave us little opportunity for investigation) was small, damp, and entirely without means of admission for light; lying, at great depth, immediately beneath that portion of the building in which was my own sleeping apartment. It had been used, apparently, in remote feudal times, for the worst purposes of a donjon-keep, and, in later days, as a place of deposit for powder, or some other highly combustible substance, as a portion of its floor, and the whole interior of a long archway through which we reached it, were carefully sheathed with copper. The door, of massive iron, had been, also, similarly protected. Its immense weight caused an unusually sharp, grating sound, as it moved upon its hinges.

Having deposited our mournful burden upon tressels within this region of horror, we partially turned aside the yet unscrewed lid of the coffin, and looked upon the face of the tenant. A striking similitude between the brother and sister now first arrested my attention; and Usher, divining, perhaps, my thoughts, murmured out some few words from which I learned that the deceased and himself had been twins, and that sympathies of a scarcely intelligible nature had always existed between them. Our glances, however, rested not long upon the dead—for we could not regard her unawed. The disease which had thus entombed the lady in the maturity of youth, had left, as usual in all maladies of a strictly cataleptical character, the mockery of a faint blush upon the bosom and the face, and that suspiciously lingering smile upon the lip which is so terrible in death. We replaced and screwed down the lid, and, having secured the door of iron, made our way, with toil, into the scarcely less gloomy apartments of the upper portion of the house.

And now, some days of bitter grief having elapsed, an observable change came over the features of the mental disorder of my friend. His ordinary manner had vanished. His ordinary occupations were neglected or forgotten. He roamed from chamber to chamber with hurried, unequal, and objectless step. The pallor of his countenance had assumed, if possible, a more ghastly hue—but the luminousness of his eye had utterly gone out. The once occasional huskiness of his tone was heard no more; and a tremulous quaver, as if of extreme terror, habitually characterized his utterance. There were times, indeed, when I thought his unceasingly agitated mind was laboring with some oppressive secret, to divulge which he struggled for the necessary courage. At times, again, I was obliged to resolve all into the mere inexplicable vagaries of madness, for I beheld him gazing upon vacancy for long hours, in an attitude of the profoundest attention, as if listening to some imaginary sound. It was no wonder that his condition terrified—that it infected me. I felt creeping upon me, by slow yet certain degrees, the wild influences of his own fantastic yet impressive superstitions.

It was, especially, upon retiring to bed late in the night of the seventh or eighth day after the placing of the lady Madeline within the donjon, that I experienced the full power of such feelings. Sleep came not near my couch—while the hours waned and waned away. I struggled to reason off the nervousness which had dominion over me. I endeavored to believe that much, if not all of what I felt, was due to the bewildering influence of the gloomy furniture of the room—of the dark and tattered draperies, which, tortured into motion by the breath of a rising tempest, swayed fitfully to and fro upon the walls, and rustled uneasily about the decorations of the bed. But my efforts were fruitless. An irrepressible tremor gradually pervaded my frame; and, at length, there sat upon my very heart an incubus of utterly causeless alarm. Shaking this off with a gasp and a struggle, I uplifted myself upon the pillows, and, peering earnestly within the intense darkness of the chamber, harkened—I know not why, except that an instinctive spirit prompted me—to certain low and indefinite sounds which came, through the pauses of the storm, at long intervals, I knew not whence. Overpowered by an intense sentiment of horror, unaccountable yet unendurable, I threw on my clothes with haste (for I felt that I should sleep no more during the night), and endeavored to arouse myself from the pitiable condition into which I had fallen by pacing rapidly to and fro through the apartment.

I had taken but few turns in this manner, when a light step on an adjoining staircase arrested my attention. I presently recognized it as that of Usher. In an instant afterward he rapped, with a gentle touch, at my door, and entered, bearing a lamp. His countenance was, as usual, cadaverously wan—but, moreover, there was a species of mad hilarity in his eyes—an evidently restrained *hysteria* in his whole demeanor. His air appalled me—but anything was preferable to the solitude which I had so long endured, and I even welcomed his presence as a relief.

"And you have not seen it?" he said abruptly, after having stared about him for some moments in silence—"you have not then seen it?—but, stay! you shall." Thus speaking, and having carefully shaded his lamp, he hurried to one of the casements, and threw it freely open to the storm.

The impetuous fury of the entering gust nearly lifted us from our feet. It was, indeed, a tempestuous yet sternly beautiful night, and one wildly singular in its terror and its beauty. A whirlwind had apparently collected its force in our vicinity; for there were frequent and violent alterations in the direction of the wind; and the exceeding density of the clouds (which hung so low as to press upon the turrets of the house) did not prevent our perceiving the lifelike velocity with which they flew careering from all points against each other, without passing away into the distance. I say that even their exceeding density did not prevent our perceiving this—yet we had no glimpse of the moon or stars, nor was there any flashing forth of the lightning. But the under surfaces of the huge masses of agitated vapor, as well as all terrestrial objects immediately around us, were glowing in the unnatural light of a faintly luminous and distinctly visible gaseous exhalation which hung about and enshrouded the mansion.

"You must not—you shall not behold this!" said I, shuddering, to Usher, as I led him, with a gentle violence, from the window to a seat. "These appearances, which bewilder you, are merely electrical phenomena not uncommon—or it may be that they have their ghastly origin in the rank miasma of the tarn. Let us close this casement; —the air is chilling and dangerous to your frame. Here is one of your favorite romances. I will read, and you shall listen:—and so we will pass away this terrible night together."

The antique volume which I had taken up was the "Mad Trist" of Sir Launcelot Canning but I had called it a favorite of Usher's more in sad jest than in earnest; for, in truth, there is little in its uncouth and unimaginative prolixity which could have had interest for the lofty and spiritual ideality of my friend. It was, however, the only book immediately at hand; and I indulged a vague hope that the excitement which now agitated the hypochondriac, might find relief (for the history of mental disorder is full of similar anomalies) even in the extremeness of the folly which I should read. Could I have judged, indeed, by the wild overstrained air of vivacity with which he hearkened, or apparently hearkened, to the words of the tale, I might well have congratulated myself upon the success of my design.

I had arrived at the well-known portion of the story where Ethelred, the hero of the Trist, having sought in vain for peaceable admission to the dwelling of the hermit, proceeds to make good an entrance by force. Here, it will be remembered, the words of the narrative run thus:

"And Ethelred, who was by nature of a doughty heart, and who was now mighty withal, on account of the powerfulness of the wine which he had drunken, waited no longer to hold parley with the hermit, who, in sooth, as of an obstinate and maliceful turn, but feeling the rain upon his shoulders, and fearing the rising of the tempest, uplifted his mace outright, and, with blows, made quickly room in the plankings of the door for his gauntleted hand; and now pulling therewith sturdily, he so cracked, and ripped, and tore all asunder, that the noise of the dry and hollow-sounding wood alarmed and reverberated throughout the forest."

At the termination of this sentence I started and, for a moment, paused; for it appeared to me (although I at once concluded that my excited fancy had deceived me)—it appeared to me that, from some very remote portion of the mansion, there came, indistinctly to my ears, what might have been, in its exact similarity of character, the echo (but a stifled and dull one certainly) of the very cracking and ripping sound which Sir Launcelot had so particularly described. It was, beyond doubt, the coincidence alone which had arrested my attention; for, amid the rattling of the sashes of the casements, and the ordinary commingled noises of the still increasing storm, the sound, in itself, had nothing, surely, which should have interested or disturbed me. I continued the story:

"But the good champion Ethelred, now entered within the door, was sore enraged and amazed to perceive no signal of the maliceful hermit; but, in the stead thereof, a dragon of a scaly and prodigious demeanor, and of a fiery tongue, which sate in guard before a palace of gold, with a floor of silver; and upon the wall there hung a shield of shining brass with this legend enwritten—

> Who entereth herein, a conqueror hath bin;
> Who slayeth the dragon, the shield he shall win.

And Ethelred uplifted his mace, and struck upon the head of the dragon, which fell before him, and gave up his pesty breath, with a shriek so horrid and harsh, and withal so piercing, that Ethelred had fain to close his ears with his hands against the dreadful noise of it, the like whereof was never before heard."

Here again I paused abruptly, and now with a feeling of wild amazement—for there could be no doubt whatever that, in this instance, I did actually hear (although from what direction it proceeded I found it impossible to say) a low and apparently distant, but harsh, protracted, and most unusual screaming or grating sound—the exact counterpart of what my fancy had already conjured up for the dragon's unnatural shriek as described by the romancer.

Oppressed, as I certainly was, upon the extraordinary coincidence, by a thousand conflicting sensations, in which wonder and extreme terror were predominant, I still retained sufficient presence of mind to avoid exciting, by an observation, the sensitive nervousness of my companion. I was by no means certain that he had noticed the sounds in question; although, assuredly, a strange alteration had, during the last few minutes, taken place in his demeanor. From a position fronting my own, he had gradually brought round his chair, so as to sit with his face to the door of the chamber; and thus I could but partially perceive his features, although I saw that his lips trembled as if he were murmuring inaudibly. His head had dropped upon his breast—yet I knew that he was not asleep, from the wide and rigid opening of the eye as I caught a glance of it in profile. The motion of his body, too, was at variance with this idea—for he rocked from side to side with a gentle yet constant and uniform sway. Having rapidly taken notice of all this, I resumed the narrative of Sir Launcelot, which thus proceeded:

"And now, the champion, having escaped from the terrible fury of the dragon, bethinking himself of the brazen shield, and of the breaking up of the enchantment which was upon it, removed the carcass from out of the way before him, and approached valorously over the silver pavement of the castle to where the shield was upon the wall; which in sooth tarried not for his full coming, but fell down at his feet upon the silver floor, with a mighty great and terrible ringing sound."

No sooner had these syllables passed my lips, than—as if a shield of brass had indeed, at the moment, fallen heavily upon a floor of silver—I became aware of a distinct, hollow, metallic, and clangorous, yet apparently muffled, reverberation. Completely unnerved, I leaped to my feet; but the measured rocking movement of Usher was undisturbed. I rushed to the chair in which he sat. His eyes were bent fixedly before him, and throughout this whole countenance there reigned a stony rigidity. But, as I placed my hand upon his shoulder, there came a strong shudder over his whole person; a sickly smile quivered about his lips; and I saw that he spoke in a low, hurried, and glibbering murmur, as if unconscious of my presence. Bending closely over him I at length drank in the hideous import of his words.

"Not hear it?—yes, I hear it, and *have* heard it. Long—long—long—many minutes, many hours, many days, have I heard it—yet I dared not—oh, pity me, miserable wretch that I am!—I dared not—I *dared* not speak! *We have put her living in the tomb!* Said I not that my senses were acute? I *now* tell you that I heard her first feeble movements in the hollow coffin. I heard them—many, many days ago—yet I dared not—*I dared not speak!* And now—to-night—Ethelred—ha! ha!—the breaking of the hermit's door, and the death-cry of the dragon, and the clangor of the shield—say, rather, the rending of her coffin, and the grating of the iron hinges of her prison, and her struggles within the coppered archway of the vault! Oh! whither shall I fly? Will she not be here anon? Is she not hurrying to upbraid me for my haste? Have I not heard her footstep on the stair? Do I not distinguish that heavy and horrible beating of her heart? Madman!"—here he sprang furiously to his feet, and shrieked out his syllables, as if in the effort he were giving up his soul—"*Madman! I tell you that she now stands without the door!*"

As if in the superhuman energy of his utterance there had been found the potency of a spell, the huge antique panels to which the speaker pointed threw slowly back, upon the instant, their ponderous and ebony jaws. It was the work of the rushing gust—but then without those doors there *did* stand the lofty and enshrouded figure of the lady Madeline of Usher. There was blood upon her white robes, and the evidence of some bitter struggle upon every portion of her emaciated frame. For a moment she remained trembling and reeling to and fro upon the threshold—then, with a low moaning cry, fell heavily inward upon the person of her brother, and in her violent and now final death-agonies, bore him to the floor a corpse, and a victim of the terrors he had anticipated.

From that chamber, and from that mansion, I fled aghast. The storm was still abroad in all its wrath as I found myself crossing the old causeway. Suddenly there shot along the path a wild light, and I turned to see whence a gleam so unusual could have issued, for the vast house and its shadows were alone behind me. The radiance was that of the full, setting, and blood-red moon, which now shone vividly through that once barely discernible fissure, of which I have before spoken as extending from the roof of the building, in a zigzag direction, to the base. While I gazed, this fissure rapidly widened—there came a fierce breath of the whirlwind—the entire orb of the satellite burst at once upon my sight—my brain reeled as I saw the mighty walls rushing asunder—there was a long tumultuous shouting sound like the voice of a thousand waters—and the deep and dank tarn at my feet closed sullenly and silently over the fragments of the "*House of Usher.*"

QUESTIONS FOR DISCUSSION AND WRITING

1. How does the narrator's description of his approach to the mansion foreshadow the conflicts in the story? How does the narrator's reading of the story of Ethelred bring the story to its climax? In what ways does the final catastrophe resolve the story's central conflict?

2. How does the quotation at the beginning of the story—"His heart is a suspended lute/The moment one touches it, it responds"—help characterize Roderick Usher? In what ways do Roderick and Madeline resemble one another? How do the narrator's actions during his stay at the House of Usher help characterize him?

3. How do certain details of physical setting—such as the fissure, the grey stones, and the luminous gas—suggest a resemblance between Roderick and his house? How does the setting of the story make Madeline's reappearance seem credible?

4. What is the role of the narrator in this story? He arrives at the house to help a boyhood friend, views the events he witnesses during his stay with some skepticism, and then by the end of the tale undergoes a soul-shaking transformation. What specific events account for his change in attitude?

5. What does this story tell us about the causes and effects of terror? What, specifically, terrifies Roderick Usher? How does his twin sister contribute to his terror? How does the narrator's telling of the story intensify this terror for the reader?

78

EDGAR ALLAN POE

The Cask of Amontillado

The thousand injuries of Fortunato I had borne as I best could, but when he ventured upon insult I vowed revenge. You, who so well know the nature of my soul, will not suppose, however, that I gave utterance to a threat. *At length* I would be avenged; this was a point definitely settled—but the very definitiveness with which it was resolved precluded the idea of risk. I must not only punish but punish with impunity. A wrong is unredressed when retribution overtakes its redresser. It is equally unredressed when the avenger fails to make himself felt as such to him who has done the wrong.

It must be understood that neither by word nor deed had I given Fortunato cause to doubt my good will. I continued, as was my wont, to smile in his face, and he did not perceive that my smile *now* was at the thought of his immolation.

He had a weak point—this Fortunato—although in other regards he was a man to be respected and even feared. He prided himself on his connoisseurship in wine. Few Italians have the true virtuoso spirit. For the most part their enthusiasm is adopted to suit the time and opportunity, to practice imposture upon the British and Austrian millionaires. In painting and gemmary, Fortunato, like his countrymen, was quack, but in the matter of old wines he was sincere. In this respect I did not differ from him materially;—I was skillful in the Italian vintages myself, and bought largely whenever I could.

It was about dusk, one evening during the supreme madness of the carnival season, that I encountered my friend. He accosted me with excessive warmth, for he had been drinking much. The man wore motley. He had on a tight-fitting parti-striped dress, and his head was surmounted by the conical cap and bells. I was so pleased to see him that I thought I should never have done wringing his hand.

I said to him—"My dear Fortunato, you are luckily met. How remarkably well you are looking to-day. But I have received a pipe of what passes for Amontillado, and I have my doubts."

"How?" said he. "Amontillado? A pipe? Impossible! And in the middle of the carnival!"

"I have my doubts," I replied; "and I was silly enough to pay the full Amontillado price without consulting you in the matter. You were not to be found, and I was fearful of losing a bargain."

"Amontillado!"

"I have my doubts."

"Amontillado!"

"And I must satisfy them."

"Amontillado!"

"As you are engaged, I am on my way to Luchresi. If any one has a critical turn, it is he. He will tell me———"

"Luchresi cannot tell Amontillado from Sherry."

"And yet some fools will have it that his taste is a match for your own."

"Come, let us go."

"Whither?"

"To your vaults."

"My friend, no; I will not impose upon your good nature. I perceive you have an engagement. Luchresi———"

"I have no engagement;—come."

"My friend, no. It is not the engagement, but the severe cold with which I perceive you are afflicted. The vaults are insufferably damp. They are encrusted with nitre."

"Let us go, nevertheless. The cold is merely nothing. Amontillado! You have been imposed upon. And as for Luchresi, he cannot distinguish Sherry from Amontillado."

Thus speaking, Fortunato possessed himself of my arm; and putting on a mask of black silk and drawing a *roquelaire* closely about my person, I suffered him to hurry me to my palazzo.

There were no attendants at home; they had absconded to make merry in honor of the time. I had told them that I should not return until the morning, and had given them explicit orders not to stir from the house. These orders were sufficient, I well knew, to insure their immediate disappearance, one and all, as soon as my back was turned.

I took from their sconces two flambeaux, and giving one to Fortunato, bowed him through several suites of rooms to the archway that led into the vaults. I passed down a long and winding staircase, requesting him to be cautious as he followed. We came at length to the foot of the descent, and stood together on the damp ground of the catacombs of the Montresors.

The gait of my friend was unsteady, and the bells upon his cap jingled as he strode.

"The pipe?" said he.

"It is farther on," said I; "but observe the white web-work which gleams from these cavern walls."

He turned towards me, and looked into my eyes with two filmy orbs that distilled the rheum of intoxication.

"Nitre?" he asked at length.

"Nitre," I replied. "How long have you had that cough?"

"Ugh! ugh! ugh!—ugh! ugh! ugh!—ugh! ugh! ugh! ugh! ugh! ugh!—ugh! ugh! ugh!"

My poor friend found it impossible to reply for many minutes.

"It is nothing," he said, at last.

"Come," I said, with decision, "we will go back; your health is precious. You are rich, respected, admired, beloved; you are happy, as once I was. You are a man to be missed. For me it is no matter. We will go back; you will be ill, and I cannot be responsible. Besides, there is Luchresi———"

"Enough," he said; "the cough is a mere nothing; it will not kill me. I shall not die of a cough."

"True—true," I replied; "and, indeed, I had no intention of alarming you unnecessarily—but you should use all proper caution. A draft of this Medoc will defend us from the damps."

Here I knocked off the neck of a bottle which I drew from a long row of its fellows that lay upon the mold.

"Drink," I said, presenting him the wine.

He raised it to his lips with a leer. He paused and nodded to me familiarly, while his bells jingled.

"I drink," he said, "to the buried that repose around us."

"And I to your long life."

He again took my arm, and we proceeded.

"These vaults," he said, "are extensive."

"The Montresors," I replied, "were a great and numerous family."

"I forget your arms."

"A huge human foot d'or, in a field azure; the foot crushes a serpent rampant whose fangs are imbedded in the heel."

"And the motto?"

"*Nemo me impune lacessit.*"

"Good!" he said.

The wine sparkled in his eyes and the bells jingled. My own fancy grew warm with the Medoc. We had passed through long walls of piled skeletons, with casks and puncheons intermingling, into the inmost recesses of the catacombs. I paused again, and this time I made bold to seize Fortunato by an arm above the elbow.

"The nitre!" I said; "see, it increases. It hangs like moss upon the vaults. We are below the river's bed. The drops of moisture trickle among the bones. Come, we will go back ere it is too late. Your cough———"

"It is nothing," he said; "let us go on. But first, another draft of the Medoc."

I broke and reached him a flagon of De Grâve. He emptied it at a breath. His eyes flashed with a fierce light. He laughed and threw the bottle upward with a gesticulation I did not understand.

I looked at him in surprise. He repeated the movement—a grotesque one.

"You do not comprehend?" he said.

"Not I," I replied.

"Then you are not of the brotherhood."

"How?"

"You are not of the masons."

"Yes, yes," I said; "yes, yes."

"You? Impossible! A mason?"

"A mason," I replied.

"A sign," he said, "a sign."

"It is this," I answered, producing from beneath the folds of my *roquelaire* a trowel.

"You jest," he exclaimed, recoiling a few paces. "But let us proceed to the Amontillado."

"Be it so," I said, replacing the tool beneath the cloak and again offering him my arm. He leaned upon it heavily. We continued our route in search of the Amontillado. We passed through a range of low arches, descended, passed on, and descending again, arrived at a deep crypt, in which the foulness of the air caused our flambeaux rather to glow than flame.

At the most remote end of the crypt there appeared another less spacious. Its walls had been lined with human remains, piled to the vault overhead, in the fashion of the great catacombs of Paris. Three sides of this interior crypt were still ornamented in this manner. From the fourth the bones had been thrown down, and lay promiscuously upon the earth, forming at one point a mound of some size. Within the wall thus exposed by the displacing of the bones, we perceived a still interior crypt or recess, in depth about four feet, in width three, in height six or seven. It seemed to have been constructed for no especial use within itself, but formed merely the interval between two of the colossal supports of the roof of the catacombs, and was backed by one of their circumscribing walls of solid granite.

It was in vain that Fortunato, uplifting his dull torch, endeavored to pry into the depth of the recess. Its termination the feeble light did not enable us to see.

"Proceed," I said; "herein is the Amontillado. As for Luchresi———"

"He is an ignoramus," interrupted my friend, as he stepped unsteadily forward, while I followed immediately at his heels. In an instant he had reached the extremity of the niche, and finding his progress arrested by the rock, stood stupidly bewildered. A moment more and I had fettered him to the granite. In its surface were two iron staples, distant from each other about two feet, horizontally. From one of these depended a short chain, from the other a padlock. Throwing the links about his waist, it was but the work of a few seconds to secure it. He was too much astounded to resist. Withdrawing the key I stepped back from the recess.

"Pass your hand," I said, "over the wall; you cannot help feeling the nitre. Indeed it is *very* damp. Once more let me *implore* you to return. No? Then I must positively leave you. But I must first render you all the little attentions in my power."

"The Amontillado!" ejaculated my friend, not yet recovered from his astonishment.

"True," I replied; "the Amontillado."

As I said these words I busied myself among the pile of bones of which I have before spoken. Throwing them aside, I soon uncovered a quantity of building stone and mortar. With these materials and with the aid of my trowel, I began vigorously to wall up the entrance of the niche.

I had scarcely laid the first tier of the masonry when I discovered that the intoxication of Fortunato had in a great measure worn off. The earliest indication I had of this was a low moaning cry from the depth of the recess. It was *not* the cry of a drunken man. There was then a long and obstinate silence. I laid the second tier, and the third, and the fourth; and then I heard the furious vibrations of the chain. The noise lasted for several minutes, during which, that I might hearken to it with the more satisfaction, I ceased my labors and sat down upon the bones. When at last the clanking subsided, I resumed the trowel, and finished without interruption the fifth, the sixth, and the seventh tier. The wall was now nearly upon a level with my breast. I again paused, and holding the flambeaux over the masonwork, threw a few feeble rays upon the figure within.

A succession of loud and shrill screams, bursting suddenly from the throat of the chained form, seemed to thrust me violently back. For a brief moment I hesitated, I trembled. Unsheathing my rapier, I began to grope with it about the recess; but the thought of an instant reassured me. I placed my hand upon the solid fabric of the catacombs, and felt satisfied. I reapproached the wall. I replied to the yells of him who clamored. I reechoed, I aided, I surpassed them in volume and in strength. I did this, and the clamorer grew still.

It was now midnight, and my task was drawing to a close. I had completed the eighth, the ninth and the tenth tier. I had finished a portion of the last and the eleventh; there remained but a single stone to be fitted and plastered in. I struggled with its weight; I placed it partially in its destined position. But now there came from out the niche a low laugh that erected the hairs upon my head. It was succeeded by a sad voice, which I had difficulty in recognizing as that of the noble Fortunato. The voice said—

"Ha! ha! ha!—he! he! he!—a very good joke, indeed—an excellent jest. We will have many a rich laugh about it at the palazzo—he! he! he!—over our wine—he! he! he!"

"The Amontillado!" I said.

"He! he! he!—he! he! he!—yes, the Amontillado. But is it not getting late? Will not they be awaiting us at the palazzo, the Lady Fortunato and the rest? Let us be gone."

"Yes," I said, "let us be gone."

"*For the love of God, Montresor!*"

"Yes," I said, "for the love of God!"

But to these words I hearkened in vain for a reply. I grew impatient. I called aloud—

"Fortunato!"

No answer. I called again—

"Fortunato!"

No answer still. I thrust a torch through the remaining aperture and let it fall within. There came forth in return only a jingling of the bells. My heart grew sick; it was the dampness of the catacombs that made it so. I hastened to make an end of my labor. I forced the last stone into its position; I plastered it up. Against the new masonry I re-erected the old rampart of bones. For the half of a century no mortal has disturbed them. *In pace requiescat!*

QUESTIONS FOR DISCUSSION AND WRITING

1. How does Montresor's opening paragraph explain the conflict in the story and foreshadow its resolution? How does Montresor's apparent concern for Fortunato's health enhance the suspense of the inevitable climax?
2. How do Montresor's name, attire, coat of arms, and family motto—"No one provokes me with impunity"—help to establish his character? Explain how Fortunato's name, costume, and love of wine help define his character. How does Montresor use his knowledge of Fortunato's character to manipulate him?
3. How does "the supreme madness of the carnival season" provide an appropriate environment for Montresor to initiate his plot? How do the catacombs provide the appropriate setting for Montresor's revenge?
4. What does Montresor assume his "reader" knows about "the nature of [his] soul"? What do Montresor's own screams reveal about his point of view toward his revenge? Why has he waited a half-century to tell this story?

5. How does the opening paragraph define the conditions for satisfactory revenge? In what ways does Montresor's scheme fulfill those conditions? How might the final "*In pace requiescat*" ("May he rest in peace") apply to the narrator as well as his victim?

79

KATHERINE ANNE PORTER

The Jilting of Granny Weatherall

KATHERINE ANNE PORTER (1890–1980) was born in Indian Creek, Texas, and was educated at a Catholic convent and a series of private schools in Texas and Louisiana. She married at the age of sixteen, but left her husband five years later to pursue a career in journalism, working on newspapers in Chicago, San Antonio, and Denver. Surviving a near-fatal attack of influenza in 1919, she worked as a ghost writer in Greenwich Village, where she became acquainted with Mexican artists. In 1920, she went to Mexico to study art and became involved in revolutionary political movements. It was during this period that she began publishing short stories in various national magazines. In 1930 she collected those stories in *Flowering Judas*. The success of this volume enabled her to take a boat from Vera Cruz, Mexico, to Bremerhaven, Germany, a cruise that became the basis of her best-selling novel, *Ship of Fools* (1962). After several years abroad and a second marriage, Porter returned to the United States in 1937 and soon thereafter published three novellas in *Pale Horse, Pale Rider* (1939). During her third marriage, to a professor at Louisiana State University, she wrote the stories that were collected in *The Leaning Tower* (1944). In the 1950s Porter was a lecturer at Stanford, the University of Michigan, and other universities while she worked on *Ship of Fools*. In the 1960s Porter published her *Collected Stories* (1965), which won both the Pulitzer Prize and the National Book Award. Her later books are *Collected Essays* (1970) and an account of her participation in the protest over the Sacco-Vanzetti Trial in the 1920s, *The Never Ending Wrong* (1977). "The Jilting of Granny Weatherall," reprinted from *Flowering Judas,* describes an old woman's deathbed memories. "The Grave," reprinted from *The Leaning Tower,* evokes a significant experience from a woman's childhood. "Holiday," reprinted from *Collected Stories,* describes a woman's attempt to understand another family.

She flicked her wrist neatly out of Doctor Harry's pudgy careful fingers and pulled the sheet up to her chin. The brat ought to be in knee breeches. Doctoring around the country with spectacles on his nose! "Get along now, take your schoolbooks and go. There's nothing wrong with me."

Doctor Harry spread a warm paw like a cushion on her forehead where the forked green vein danced and made her eyelids twitch. "Now, now, be a good girl, and we'll have you up in no time."

"That's no way to speak to a woman nearly eighty years old just because she's down. I'd have you respect your elders, young man."

"Well, Missy, excuse me." Doctor Harry patted her cheek. "But I've got to warn you, haven't I? You're a marvel, but you must be careful or you're going to be good and sorry."

"Don't tell me what I'm going to be. I'm on my feet now, morally speaking. It's Cornelia. I had to go to bed to get rid of her."

Her bones felt loose, and floated around in her skin, and Doctor Harry floated like a balloon around the foot of the bed. He floated and pulled down his waistcoat and swung his glasses on a cord. "Well, stay where you are, it certainly can't hurt you."

"Get along and doctor your sick," said Granny Weatherall. "Leave a well woman alone. I'll call for you when I want you. . . . Where were you forty years ago when I pulled through milk-leg and double pneumonia? You weren't even born. Don't let Cornelia lead you on," she shouted, because Doctor Harry appeared to float up to the ceiling and out. "I pay my own bills, and I don't throw my money away on nonsense!"

She meant to wave good-by, but it was too much trouble. Her eyes closed of themselves, it was like a dark curtain drawn around the bed. The pillow rose and floated under her, pleasant as a hammock in a light wind. She listened to the leaves rustling outside the window. No, somebody was swishing newspapers: no, Cornelia and Doctor Harry were whispering together. She leaped broad awake, thinking they whispered in her ear.

"She was never like this, *never* like this!" "Well, what can we expect?" "Yes, eighty years old. . . ."

Well, and what if she was? She still had ears. It was like Cornelia to whisper around doors. She always kept things secret in such a public way. She was always being tactful and kind. Cornelia was dutiful; that was the trouble with her. Dutiful and good: "So good and dutiful," said Granny, "that I'd like to spank her." She saw herself spanking Cornelia and making a fine job of it.

"What'd you say, Mother?"

Granny felt her face tying up in hard knots.

"Can't a body think, I'd like to know?"

"I thought you might want something."

"I do. I want a lot of things. First off, go away and don't whisper."

She lay and drowsed, hoping in her sleep that the children would keep out and let her rest a minute. It had been a long day. Not that she was tired. It was always pleasant to snatch a minute now and then. There is always so much to be done, let me see: tomorrow.

Tomorrow was far away and there was nothing to trouble about. Things were finished somehow when the time came; thank God there was always a little margin over for peace: then a person could spread out the plan of life and tuck in the edges orderly. It was good to have everything clean and folded away, with the hair brushes and tonic bottles sitting straight on the white embroidered linen: the day started without fuss and the pantry shelves laid out with rows of jelly glasses and brown jugs and white stone-china jars with blue whirligigs and words painted on them: coffee, tea, sugar, ginger, cinnamon, allspice: and the bronze clock with the lion on top nicely dusted off. The dust that lion could collect in twenty-four hours! The box in the attic with all those letters tied up, well she'd have to go through that tomorrow. All those letters—George's letters and John's letters and her letters to them both—lying around for the children to find afterwards made her uneasy. Yes, that would be tomorrow's business. No use to let them know how silly she had been once.

While she was rummaging around she found death in her mind and it felt clammy and unfamiliar. She had spent so much time preparing for death there was no need for bringing it up again. Let it take care of itself now. When she was sixty she had felt very old, finished, and went around making farewell trips to see her children and grandchildren, with a secret in her mind: This is the very last of your mother, children! Then she made her will and came down with a long fever. That was all just a notion like a lot of other things, but it was lucky too, for she had once and for all got over the idea of dying for a long time. Now she couldn't be worried. She hoped she had better sense now. Her father had lived to be one hundred and two years old and had drunk a noggin of strong hot toddy on his last birthday. He told the reporters it was his daily habit, and he owed his long life to that. He had made quite a scandal and was very pleased about it. She believed she'd just plague Cornelia a little.

"Cornelia! Cornelia!" No footsteps, but a sudden hand on her cheek. "Bless you, where have you been?"

"Here, mother."

"Well, Cornelia, I want a noggin of hot toddy."

"Are you cold, darling?"

"I'm chilly, Cornelia. Lying in bed stops the circulation. I must have told you that a thousand times."

Well, she could just hear Cornelia telling her husband that Mother was getting childish and they'd have to humor her. The thing that most annoyed her was that Cornelia thought she was deaf, dumb, and blind. Little hasty glances and tiny gestures tossed around her and over her head saying, "Don't cross her, let her have her way, she's eighty years old," and she sitting there as if she lived in a thin glass cage. Sometimes Granny almost made up her mind to pack up and move back to her own house where nobody could remind her every minute that she was old. Wait, wait, Cornelia, till your own children whisper behind your back!

In her day she had kept a better house and had got more work done. She wasn't too old yet for Lydia to be driving eighty miles for advice when one of the children jumped the track, and Jimmy still dropped in and talked things over: "Now, Mammy, you've a good business head, I want to know what you think of this? . . ." Old Cornelia couldn't change the furniture around without asking. Little things, little things! They had been so sweet when they were little. Granny wished the old days were back again with the children young and everything to be done over. It had been a hard pull, but not too much for her.

When she thought of all the food she had cooked, and all the clothes she had cut and sewed, and all the gardens she had made—well, the children showed it. There they were, made out of her, and they couldn't get away from that. Sometimes she wanted to see John again and point to them and say, Well, I didn't do so badly, did I? But that would have to wait. That was for tomorrow. She used to think of him as a man, but now all the children were older than their father, and he would be a child beside her if she saw him now. It seemed strange and there was something wrong in the idea. Why, he couldn't possibly recognize her. She had fenced in a hundred acres once, digging the post holes herself and clamping the wires with just a negro boy to help. That changed a woman. John would be looking for a young woman with the peaked Spanish comb in her hair and the painted fan. Digging post holes changed a woman. Riding country roads in the winter when women had their babies was another thing: sitting up nights with sick horses and sick negroes and sick children and hardly ever losing one. John, I hardly ever lost one of them! John would see that in a minute, that would be something he could understand, she wouldn't have to explain anything!

It made her feel like rolling up her sleeves and putting the whole place to rights again. No matter if Cornelia was determined to be everywhere at once, there were a great many things left undone on this place. She would start tomorrow and do them. It was good to be strong enough for everything, even if all you made melted and changed and slipped under your hands, so that by the time you finished you almost forgot what you were working for. What was it I set out to do? she asked herself intently, but she could not remember. A fog rose over the valley, she saw it marching across the creek swallowing the trees and moving up the hill like an army of ghosts. Soon it would be at the near edge of the orchard, and then it was time to go in and light the lamps. Come in, children, don't stay out in the night air.

Lighting the lamps had been beautiful. The children huddled up to her and breathed like little calves waiting at the bars in the twilight. Their eyes followed the match and watched the flame rise and settle in a blue curve, then they moved away from her. The lamp was lit, they didn't have to be scared and hang on to mother any more. Never, never, never more. God, for all my life I thank Thee. Without Thee, my God, I could never have done it. Hail, Mary, full of grace.

I want you to pick all the fruit this year and see that nothing is wasted. There's always someone who can use it. Don't let good things rot for want of using. You waste life when you waste good food. Don't let things get lost. It's bitter to lose things. Now, don't let me get to thinking, not when I am tired and taking a little nap before supper. . . .

The pillow rose about her shoulders and pressed against her heart and the memory was being squeezed out of it: oh, push down the pillow, somebody: it would smother her if she tried to hold it. Such a fresh breeze blowing and such a green day with no threats in it. But he had not come, just the same. What does a woman do when she has put on the white veil and set out the white cake for a man and he doesn't come? She tried to remember. No, I swear he never harmed me but in that. He never harmed me but in that . . . and what if he did? There was the day, the day, but a whirl of dark smoke rose and covered it, crept up and over into the bright field where everything was planted so carefully in orderly rows. That was hell, she knew hell when she saw it. For sixty years she had prayed against remembering him and against losing her soul in the deep pit of hell, and now the two things were mingled in one and the thought of him was a smoky cloud from hell that moved and crept in her head when she had just got rid of Doctor Harry and was trying to rest a minute. Wounded vanity, Ellen, said a sharp voice in the top of her mind. Don't let your wounded vanity get the upper hand of you. Plenty of girls get jilted. You were jilted, weren't you? Then stand up to it. Her eyelids wavered and let in streamers of blue-gray light like tissue paper over her eyes. She must get up and pull the shades down or she'd never sleep. She was in bed again and the shades were not down. How could that happen? Better turn over, hide from the light, sleeping in the light gave you nightmares. "Mother, how do you feel now?" and a stinging wetness on her forehead. But I don't like having my face washed in cold water!

Hapsy? George? Lydia? Jimmy? No, Cornelia, and her features were swollen and full of little puddles. "They're coming, darling, they'll all be here soon." Go wash your face, child, you look funny.

Instead of obeying, Cornelia knelt down and put her head on the pillow. She seemed to be talking but there was no sound. "Well, are you tongue-tied? Whose birthday is it? Are you going to give a party?"

Cornelia's mouth moved urgently in strange shapes. "Don't do that, you bother me, daughter."

"Oh, no, Mother. Oh, no. . . ."

Nonsense. It was strange about children. They disputed your every word. "No what, Cornelia?"

"Here's Doctor Harry."

"I won't see that boy again. He just left five minutes ago."

"That was this morning, Mother. It's night now. Here's the nurse."

"This is Doctor Harry, Mrs. Weatherall. I never saw you look so young and happy!"

"Ah, I'll never be young again—but I'd be happy if they'd let me lie in peace and get rested."

She thought she spoke up loudly, but no one answered. A warm weight on her forehead, a warm bracelet on her wrist, and a breeze went on whispering, trying to tell her something. A shuffle of leaves in the everlasting hand of God. He blew on them and they danced and rattled. "Mother, don't mind, we're going to give you a little hypodermic." "Look here, daughter, how do ants get in this bed? I saw sugar ants yesterday." Did you send for Hapsy too?

It was Hapsy she really wanted. She had to go a long way back through a great many rooms to find Hapsy standing with a baby on her arm. She seemed to herself to be Hapsy also, and the baby on Hapsy's arm was Hapsy and himself and herself, all at once, and there was no surprise in the meeting. Then Hapsy melted from within and turned flimsy as gray gauze and the baby was a gauzy shadow, and Hapsy came up close and said, "I thought you'd never come," and looked at her very searchingly and said, "You haven't changed a bit!" They leaned forward to kiss, when Cornelia began whispering from a long way off, "Oh, is there anything you want to tell me? Is there anything I can do for you?"

Yes, she had changed her mind after sixty years and she would like to see George. I want you to find George. Find him and be sure to tell him I forgot him. I want him to know I had my husband just the same and my children and my house like any other woman. A good house too and a good husband that I loved and fine children out of him. Better than I hoped for even. Tell him I was given back everything he took away and more. Oh, no, oh, God, no, there was something else besides the house and the man and the children. Oh, surely they were not all? What was it? Something not given back. . . . Her breath crowded down under her ribs and grew into a monstrous frightening shape with cutting edges; it bored up into her head, and the agony was unbelievable: Yes, John, get the doctor now, no more talk, my time has come.

When this one was born it should be the last. The last. It should have been born first, for it was the one she had truly wanted. Everything came in good time. Nothing left out, left over. She was strong, in three days she would be as well as ever. Better. A woman needed milk in her to have her full health.

"Mother, do you hear me?"

"I've been telling you—"

"Mother, Father Connolly's here."

"I went to Holy Communion only last week. Tell him I'm not so sinful as all that."

"Father just wants to speak to you."

He could speak as much as he pleased. It was like him to drop in and inquire about her soul as if it were a teething baby, and then stay on for a cup of tea and a round of cards and gossip. He always had a funny story of some sort, usually about an Irishman who made his little mistakes and confessed them, and the point lay in some absurd thing he would blurt out in the confessional showing his struggles between native piety and original sin. Granny felt easy about her soul. Cornelia, where are your manners? Give Father Connolly a chair. She had her secret comfortable understanding with a few favorite saints who cleared a straight road to God for her. All as surely signed and sealed as the papers for the new Forty Acres. Forever . . . heirs and assigns forever. Since the day the wedding cake was not cut, but thrown out and wasted. The whole bottom dropped out of the world, and there she was blind and sweating with nothing under her feet and the walls falling away. His hand had caught her under the breast, she had not fallen, there was the freshly polished floor with the green rug on it, just as before. He had cursed like a sailor's parrot and said, "I'll kill him for you." Don't lay a hand on him, for my sake leave something to God. "Now, Ellen, you must believe what I tell you. . . ."

So there was nothing, nothing to worry about any more, except sometimes in the night one of the children screamed in a nightmare, and they both hustled out shaking and hunting for the matches and calling, "There, wait a minute, here we are!" John, get the doctor now, Hapsy's time has come. But there was Hapsy standing by the bed in a white cap. "Cornelia, tell Hapsy to take off her cap. I can't see her plain."

Her eyes opened very wide and the room stood out like a picture she had seen somewhere. Dark colors with the shadows rising towards the ceiling in long angles. The tall black dresser gleamed with nothing on it but John's picture, enlarged from a little one, with John's eyes very black when they should have been blue. You never saw him, so how do you know how he looked? But the man insisted the copy was perfect, it was very rich and handsome. For a picture, yes, but it's not my husband. The table by the bed had a linen cover and a candle and a crucifix. The light was blue from Cornelia's silk lampshades.

No sort of light at all, just frippery. You had to live forty years with kerosene lamps to appreciate honest electricity. She felt very strong and she saw Doctor Harry with a rosy nimbus around him.

"You look like a saint, Doctor Harry, and I vow that's as near as you'll ever come to it."

"She's saying something."

"I heard you, Cornelia. What's all this carrying-on?"

"Father Connolly's saying—"

Cornelia's voice staggered and bumped like a cart in a bad road. It rounded corners and turned back again and arrived nowhere. Granny stepped up in the cart very lightly and reached for the reins, but a man sat beside her and she knew him by his hands, driving the cart. She did not look in his face, for she knew without seeing, but looked instead down the road where the trees leaned over and bowed to each other and a thousand birds were singing a Mass. She felt like singing too, but she put her hand in the bosom of her dress and pulled out a rosary, and Father Connolly murmured Latin in a very solemn voice and tickled her feet. My God, will you stop that nonsense? I'm a married woman. What if he did run away and leave me to face the priest by myself? I found another a whole world better. I wouldn't have exchanged my husband for anybody except St. Michael himself, and you may tell him that for me with a thank you in the bargain.

Light flashed on her closed eyelids, and a deep roaring shook her. Cornelia, is that lightning? I hear thunder. There's going to be a storm. Close all the windows. Call the children in. . . . "Mother, here we are, all of us." "Is that you, Hapsy?" "Oh no, I'm Lydia. We drove as fast as we could." Their faces drifted above her, drifted away. The rosary fell out of her hands and Lydia put it back. Jimmy tried to help, their hands fumbled together, and Granny closed two fingers around Jimmy's thumb. Beads wouldn't do, it must be something alive. She was so amazed her thoughts ran round and round. So, my dear Lord, this is my death and I wasn't even thinking about it. My children have come to see me die. But I can't, it's not time. Oh, I always hated surprises. I wanted to give Cornelia the amethyst set—Cornelia, you're to have the amethyst set, but Hapsy's to wear it when she wants, and, Doctor Harry, do shut up. Nobody sent for you. Oh, my dear Lord, do wait a minute. I meant to do something about the Forty Acres, Jimmy doesn't need it and Lydia will later on, with that worthless husband of hers. I meant to finish the altar cloth and send six bottles of wine to Sister Borgia for her dyspepsia. I want to send six bottles of wine to Sister Borgia, Father Connolly, now don't let me forget.

Cornelia's voice made short turns and tilted over and crashed. "Oh, Mother, oh, Mother, oh, Mother. . . ."

"I'm not going, Cornelia. I'm taken by surprise. I can't go."

You'll see Hapsy again. What about her? "I thought you'd never come." Granny made a long journey outward, looking for Hapsy. What if I don't find her? What then? Her heart sank down and down, there was no bottom to death, she couldn't come to the end of it. The blue light from Cornelia's lampshade drew into a tiny point in the center of her brain, it flickered and winked like an eye, quietly it fluttered and dwindled. Granny lay curled down within herself, amazed and watchful, staring at the point of light that was herself; her body was now only a deeper mass of shadow in an endless darkness and this darkness would curl around the light and swallow it up. God, give a sign!

For the second time there was no sign. Again no bridegroom and the priest in the house. She could not remember any other sorrow because this grief wiped them all away. Oh, no, there's nothing more cruel than this—I'll never forgive it. She stretched herself with a deep breath and blew out the light.

QUESTIONS FOR DISCUSSION AND WRITING

1. How does Granny's opening conversation with Doctor Harry establish the situation to be dramatized in the story? How do Granny's memories prepare her for her death?
2. How does Granny's last name, "Weatherall," describe her character? How does Granny characterize her husband and children? What does she want to tell George?
3. How does Granny's concern for order help portray the environment she wanted to create for her life? In particular, how does Granny describe the bedroom where she is dying?
4. How do the comments of the doctor, the priest, and Cornelia help establish the restricted focus of Granny's point of view? In what manner does Granny's preoccupation with the "point of light" toward the end of the story heighten the difference between her point of view and the points of view of those who are attending her?
5. How does Granny compare the experience of being jilted with the experience of death? What will she "never forgive"?

80

KATHERINE ANNE PORTER

The Grave

The grandfather, dead for more than thirty years, had been twice disturbed in his long repose by the constancy and possessiveness of his widow. She removed his bones first to Louisiana and then to Texas as if she had set out to find her own burial place, knowing well she would never return to the places she had left. In Texas she set up a small cemetery in a corner of her first farm, and as the family connection grew, and oddments of relations came over from Kentucky to settle, it contained at last about twenty graves. After the grandmother's death, part of her land was to be sold for the benefit of certain of her children, and the cemetery happened to lie in the part set aside for sale. It was necessary to take up the bodies and bury them again in the family plot in the big new public cemetery, where the grandmother had been buried. At last her husband was to lie beside her for eternity, as she had planned.

The family cemetery had been a pleasant small neglected garden of tangled rose bushes and ragged cedar trees and cypress, the simple flat stones rising out of uncropped sweet-smelling wild grass. The graves were lying open and empty one burning day when Miranda and her brother Paul, who often went together to hunt rabbits and doves, propped their twenty-two Winchester rifles carefully against the rail fence, climbed over and explored among the graves. She was nine years old and he was twelve.

They peered into the pits all shaped alike with such purposeful accuracy, and looking at each other with pleased adventurous eyes, they said in solemn tones: "These were graves!" trying by words to shape a special, suitable emotion in their minds, but they felt nothing except an agreeable thrill of wonder: they were seeing a new sight, doing something they had not done before. In them both there was also a small disappointment at the entire commonplaceness of the actual spectacle. Even if it had once contained a coffin for years upon years, when the coffin was gone a grave was just a hole in the ground. Miranda leaped into the pit that had held her grandfather's bones. Scratching around aimlessly and pleasurably as any young animal, she scooped up a lump of earth and weighed it in her palm. It had a pleasantly sweet, corrupt smell, being mixed with cedar needles and small leaves, and as the crumbs fell apart, she saw a silver dove no larger than a hazel nut, with spread wings and a neat fan-shaped tail. The breast had a deep round hollow in it. Turning it up to the fierce sunlight, she saw that the inside of the hollow was cut in little whorls. She scrambled out, over the pile of loose earth that had fallen back into one end of the grave, calling to Paul that she had found something, he must guess what . . . His head appeared smiling over the rim of another grave. He waved a closed hand at her. "I've got something too!" They ran to compare treasures, making a game of it, so many guesses each, all wrong, and a final show-down with opened palms. Paul had found a thin wide gold ring carved with intricate flowers and leaves. Miranda was smitten at sight of the ring and wished to have it. Paul seemed more impressed by the dove. They made a trade, with some little bickering. After he had got the dove in his hand, Paul said, "Don't you know what this is? This is a screw head for a *coffin!* . . . I'll bet nobody else in the world has one like this!"

Miranda glanced at it without covetousness. She had the gold ring on her thumb; it fitted perfectly. "Maybe we ought to go now," she said, "maybe one of the niggers 'll see us and tell somebody." They knew the land had been sold, the cemetery was no longer theirs, and they felt like trespassers. They climbed back over the fence, slung their rifles loosely under their arms—they had been shooting at targets with various kinds of firearms since they were seven years old—and set out to look for the rabbits and doves or whatever small game might happen along. On these expeditions Miranda always followed at Paul's heels along the path, obeying instructions about handling her gun when going through fences; learning how to stand it up properly so it would not slip and fire unexpectedly; how to wait her time for a shot and not just bang away in the air without looking, spoiling shots for Paul, who really could hit things if given a chance. Now and then, in her excitement at seeing birds whizz up suddenly before her face, or a rabbit leap across her very toes, she lost her head, and almost without sighting she flung her rifle up and pulled the trigger. She hardly ever hit any sort of mark. She had no proper sense of hunting at all. Her brother would be often completely disgusted with her. "You don't care whether you get your bird or not," he said. "That's no way to hunt." Miranda could not understand his indignation. She had seen him smash his hat and yell with fury when he had missed his aim. "What I like about shooting," said Miranda, with exasperating inconsequence, "is pulling the trigger and hearing the noise."

"Then, by golly," said Paul, "whyn't you go back to the range and shoot at bulls-eyes?"

"I'd just as soon," said Miranda, "only like this, we walk around more."

"Well, you just stay behind and stop spoiling my shots," said Paul, who, when he made a kill, wanted to be certain he had made it. Miranda, who alone brought down a bird once in twenty rounds, always claimed as her own any game they got when they fired at the same moment. It was tiresome and unfair and her brother was sick of it.

"Now, the first dove we see, or the first rabbit, is mine," he told her. "And the next will be yours. Remember that and don't get smarty."

"What about snakes?" asked Miranda idly. "Can I have the first snake?"

Waving her thumb gently and watching her gold ring glitter, Miranda lost interest in shooting. She was wearing her summer roughing outfit: dark blue overalls, a light blue shirt, a hired-man's straw hat, and thick brown sandals. Her brother had the same outfit except his was a sober hickory-nut color. Ordinarily Miranda preferred her overalls to any other dress, though it was making rather a scandal in the countryside, for the year was 1903, and in the back country the law of female decorum had teeth in it. Her father had been criticized for letting his girls dress like boys and go careering around astride bare-backed horses. Big sister Maria, the really independent and fearless one, in spite of her rather affected ways, rode at a dead run with only a rope knotted around her horse's nose. It was said the motherless family was running down, with the grandmother no longer there to hold it together. It was known that she had discriminated against her son Harry in her will, and that he was in straits about money. Some of his old neighbors reflected with vicious satisfaction that now he would probably not be so stiff-necked, nor have any more high-stepping horses either. Miranda knew this, though she could not say how. She had met along the road old women of the kind who smoked corn-cob pipes, who had treated her grandmother with most sincere respect. They slanted their gummy old eyes side-ways at the granddaughter and said, "Ain't you ashamed of yoself, Missy? It's aginst the Scriptures to dress like that. Whut yo Pappy thinkin about?" Miranda, with her powerful social sense, which was like a fine set of antennae radiating from every pore of her skin, would feel ashamed because she knew well it was rude and ill-bred to shock anybody, even bad-tempered old crones, though she had faith in her father's judgment and was perfectly comfortable in the clothes. Her father had said, "They're just what you need, and they'll save your dresses for school . . ." This sounded quite simple and natural to her. She had been brought up in rigorous economy. Wastefulness was vulgar. It was also a sin. These were truths; she had heard them repeated many times and never once disputed.

Now the ring, shining with the serene purity of fine gold on her rather grubby thumb, turned her feelings against her overalls and sockless feet, toes sticking through the thick brown leather straps. She wanted to go back to the farmhouse, take a good cold bath, dust herself with plenty of Maria's violet talcum powder—provided Maria was not present to object, of course—put on the thinnest, most becoming dress she owned, with a big sash, and sit in a wicker chair under the trees . . . These things were not all she wanted, of course; she had vague stirrings of desire for luxury and a grand way of living which could not take precise form in her imagination but were founded on family legend of past wealth and leisure. These immediate comforts were what she could have, and she wanted them at once. She lagged rather far behind Paul, and once she thought of just turning back without a word and going home. She stopped, thinking that Paul would never do that to her, and so she would have to tell him. When a rabbit leaped, she let Paul have it without dispute. He killed it with one shot.

When she came up with him, he was already kneeling, examining the wound, the rabbit trailing from his hands. "Right through the head," he said complacently, as if he had aimed for it. He took out his sharp, competent bowie knife and started to skin the body. He did it very cleanly and quickly. Uncle Jimbilly knew how to prepare the skins so that Miranda always had fur coats for her dolls, for though she never cared much for her dolls she liked seeing them in fur coats. The children knelt facing each other over the dead animal. Miranda watched admiringly while her brother stripped the skin away as if he were taking off a glove. The flayed flesh emerged dark scarlet, sleek, firm; Miranda with thumb and finger felt the long fine muscles with the silvery flat strips binding them to the joints. Brother lifted the oddly bloated belly. "Look," he said, in a low amazed voice. "It was going to have young ones."

Very carefully he slit the thin flesh from the center ribs to the flanks, and a scarlet bag appeared. He slit again and pulled the bag open, and there lay a bundle of tiny rabbits, each wrapped in a thin scarlet veil. The brother pulled these off and there they were, dark gray, their sleek wet down lying in minute even ripples, like a baby's head just washed, their unbelievably small delicate ears folded close, their little blind faces almost featureless.

Miranda said, "Oh, I want to *see*," under her breath. She looked and looked—excited but not frightened, for she was accustomed to the sight of animals killed in hunting—filled with pity and astonishment and a kind of shocked delight in the wonderful little creatures for their own sakes, they were so pretty. She touched one of them ever so carefully, "Ah, there's blood running over them," she said and began to tremble without knowing why. Yet she wanted most deeply to see and to know. Having seen, she felt at once as if she had known all along. The very memory of her former ignorance faded, she had always known just this. No one had ever told her anything outright, she had been rather unobservant of the animal life around her because she was so accustomed to animals. They seemed simply disorderly and unaccountably rude in their habits, but altogether natural and not very interesting. Her brother had spoken as if he had known about everything all along. He may have seen all this before. He had never said a word to her, but she knew now a part at least of what he knew. She understood a little of the secret, formless intuitions in her own mind and body, which had been clearing up, taking form, so gradually and so steadily she had not realized that she was learning what she had to know. Paul said cautiously, as if he were talking about something forbidden: "They were just about ready to be born." His voice dropped on the last word. "I know," said Miranda, "like kittens. I know, like babies." She was quietly and terribly agitated, standing again with her rifle under her arm, looking down at the bloody heap. "I don't want the skin," she said, "I won't have it." Paul buried the young rabbits again in their mother's body, wrapped the skin around her, carried her to a clump of sage bushes, and hid her away. He came out again at once and said to Miranda, with an eager friendliness, a confidential tone quite unusual in him, as if he were taking her into an important secret on equal terms: "Listen now. Now you listen to me, and don't ever forget. Don't you ever tell a living soul that you saw this. Don't tell a soul. Don't tell Dad because I'll get into trouble. He'll say I'm leading you into things you ought not to do. He's always saying that. So now don't you go and forget and blab out sometime the way you're always doing . . . Now, that's a secret. Don't you tell."

Miranda never told, she did not even wish to tell anybody. She thought about the whole worrisome affair with confused unhappiness for a few days. Then it sank quietly into her mind and was heaped over by accumulated thousands of impressions, for nearly twenty years. One day she was picking her path among the puddles and crushed refuse of a market street in a strange city of a strange country, when without warning, plain and clear in its true colors as if she looked through a frame upon a scene that had not stirred nor changed since the moment it happened, the episode of that far-off day leaped from its burial place before her mind's eye. She was so reasonlessly horrified she halted suddenly staring, the scene before her eyes dimmed by the vision back of them. An Indian vendor had held up before her a tray of dyed sugar sweets, in the shapes of all kinds of small creatures: birds, baby chicks, baby rabbits, lambs, baby pigs. They were in gay colors and smelled of vanilla, maybe. . . . It was a very hot day and the smell in the market, with its piles of raw flesh and wilting flowers, was like the mingled sweetness and corruption she had smelled that other day in the empty cemetery at home: the day she had remembered always until now vaguely as the time she and her brother had found treasure in the opened graves. Instantly upon this thought the dreadful vision faded, and she saw clearly her brother, whose childhood face she had forgotten, standing again in the blazing sunshine, again twelve years old, a pleased sober smile in his eyes, turning the silver dove over and over in his hands.

QUESTIONS FOR DISCUSSION AND WRITING

1. What does Miranda discover buried in the grave? How does she react to what is hidden in the rabbit's body and describe what she discovers. What does she discover concealed in her own memory? Explain the connection among the three discoveries.
2. What evidence does Porter provide to show why Miranda is strong and unconventional even as a child? Why does Paul insist that Miranda not tell?
3. What physical sense provides the link between the setting of the grave at the beginning and the Indian market at the conclusion?
4. What does Porter accomplish by beginning her story with a historical point of view? What does she accomplish by shifting the point forward twenty years in the last paragraph of the story?
5. By the end of the story, what is the symbolic significance of the golden ring and the silver dove? What images throughout the story convey the sense of "mingled sweetness and corruption of life"?

81

KATHERINE ANNE PORTER

Holiday

At that time I was too young for some of the troubles I was having, and I had not yet learned what to do with them. It no longer can matter what kind of troubles they were, or what finally became of them. It seemed to me then there was nothing to do but run away from them, though all my tradition, background, and training had taught me unanswerably that no one except a coward ever runs away from anything. What nonsense! They should have taught me the difference between courage and foolhardiness, instead of leaving me to find it out for myself. I learned finally that if I still had the sense I was born with, I would take off like a deer at the first warning of certain dangers. But this story I am about to tell you happened before this great truth impressed itself upon me—that we do not run from the troubles and dangers that are truly ours, and it is better to learn what they are earlier than later, and if we don't run from the others, we are fools.

I confided to my friend Louise, a former schoolmate about my own age, not my troubles but my little problem: I wanted to go somewhere for a spring holiday, by myself, to the country, and it should be very simple and nice and, of course, not expensive, and she was not to tell anyone where I had gone; but if she liked, I would send her word now and then, if anything interesting was happening. She said she loved getting letters but hated answering them; and she knew the very place for me, and she would not tell anybody anything. Louise had then—she has it still—something near to genius for making improbable persons, places, and situations sound attractive. She told amusing stories that did not turn grim on you until a little while later, when by chance you saw and heard for yourself. So with this story. Everything was just as Louise had said, if you like, and everything was, at the same time, quite different.

"I know the very place," said Louise, "a family of real old-fashioned German peasants, in the deep blackland Texas farm country, a household in real patriarchal style—the kind of thing you'd hate to live with but is very nice to visit. Old father, God Almighty himself, with whiskers and all; Old mother, matriarch in men's shoes; endless daughters and sons and sons-in-law and fat babies falling about the place; and fat puppies—my favourite was a darling little black thing named Kuno—cows, calves, and sheep and lambs and goats and turkeys and guineas roaming up and down the shallow green hills, ducks and geese on the ponds. I was there in the summer when the peaches and watermelons were in——"

"This is the end of March," I said, doubtfully.

"Spring comes early there," said Louise. "I'll write to the Müllers about you, you just get ready to go."

"Just where is this paradise?"

"Not far from the Louisiana line," said Louise. "I'll ask them to give you my attic—oh, that was a sweet place! It's a big room, with the roof sloping to the floor on each side, and the roof leaks a little when it rains, so the shingles are all stained in beautiful streaks, all black and grey and mossy green, and in one corner there used to be a stack of dime novels, *The Duchess,* Ouida, Mrs. E.D.E.N. Southworth, Ella Wheeler Wilcox's poems—one summer they had a lady boarder who was a great reader, and she went off and left her library. I loved it! And everybody was so healthy and good-hearted, and the weather was perfect. . . . How long do you want to stay?"

I hadn't thought of this, so I said at random, "About a month."

A few days later I found myself tossed off like an express package from a dirty little crawling train onto the sodden platform of a country station, where the stationmaster emerged and locked up the waiting room before the train had got round the bend. As he clumped by me he shifted his wad of tobacco to his cheek and asked, "Where you goin'?"

"To the Müller farm," I said, standing beside my small trunk and suitcase with the bitter wind cutting through my thin coat.

"Anybody meet you?" he asked, not pausing.

"They *said* so."

"All right," he said, and got into his little ragged buckboard with a sway-backed horse and drove away.

I turned my trunk on its side and sat on it facing the wind and the desolate mud-colored shapeless scene and began making up my first letter to Louise. First I was going to tell her that unless she was to be a novelist, there was no excuse for her having so much imagination. In daily life, I was going to tell her, there are also such useful things as the plain facts that should be stuck to, through thick and thin. Anything else led to confusion like this. I was beginning to enjoy my letter to Louise when a sturdy boy about twelve years old crossed the platform. As he neared me, he took off his rough cap and bunched it in his thick hand, dirt-stained at the knuckles. His round cheeks, his round nose, his round chin were a cool, healthy red. In the globe of his face, as neatly circular as if drawn in bright crayon, his narrow, long, tip-tilted eyes, clear as pale-blue water, seemed out of place, as if two incompatible strains had collided in making him. They were beautiful eyes, and the rest of the face was not to be taken seriously. A blue woollen blouse buttoned up to his chin ended abruptly at his waist as if he would outgrow it in another half hour, and his blue drill breeches flapped about his ankles. His old clodhopper shoes were several sizes too big for him. Altogether, it was plain he was not the first one to wear his clothes. He was a cheerful, detached, self-possessed apparition against the tumbled brown earth and ragged dark sky, and I smiled at him as well as I could with a face that felt like wet clay.

He smiled back slightly without meeting my eye, motioning for me to take up my suitcase. He swung my trunk to his head and tottered across the uneven platform, down the steps slippery with mud where I expected to see him crushed beneath his burden like an ant under a stone. He heaved the trunk into the back of his wagon with a fine smash, took my suitcase and tossed it after, then climbed up over one front wheel while I scrambled my way up over the other.

The pony, shaggy as a wintering bear, eased himself into a grudging trot, while the boy, bowed over with his cap pulled down over his ears and eyebrows, held the reins slack and fell into a brown study. I studied the harness, a real mystery. It met and clung in all sorts of unexpected places; it parted company in what appeared to be strategic seats of jointure. It was mended sketchily in risky places with bits of hairy rope. Other seemingly unimportant parts were bound together irrevocably with wire. The bridle was too long for the pony's stocky head, so he had shaken the bit out of his mouth at the start, apparently, and went his own way at his own pace.

Our vehicle was an exhausted specimen of something called a spring wagon, who knows why? There were no springs, and the shallow enclosed platform at the back, suitable for carrying various plunder, was worn away until it barely reached midway of the back wheels, one side of it steadily scraping the iron tire. The wheels themselves spun not dully around and around in the way of common wheels, but elliptically, being loosened at the hubs, so that we proceeded with a drunken, hilarious swagger, like the rolling motion of a small boat on a choppy sea.

The soaked brown fields fell away on either side of the lane, all rough with winter-worn stubble ready to sink and become earth again. The scanty leafless woods ran along an edge of the field nearby. There was nothing beautiful in those woods now except the promise of spring, for I detested bleakness, but it gave me pleasure to think that beyond this there might be something else beautiful in its own being, a river shaped and contained by its banks, or a field stripped down to its true meaning, ploughed and ready for the seed. The road turned abruptly and was almost hidden for a moment, and we were going through the woods. Closer sight of the crooked branches assured me that spring was beginning, if sparely, reluctantly: the leaves were budding in tiny cones of watery green besprinkling all the new shoots; a thin sedate rain began again to fall, not so opaque as a fog, but a mist that merely deepened overhead, and lowered, until the clouds became rain in one swathing, delicate grey.

As we emerged from the woods, the boy roused himself and pointed forward, in silence. We were approaching the farm along the skirts of a fine peach orchard, now faintly colored with young bud, but there was nothing to disguise the gaunt and aching ugliness of the farmhouse itself. In this Texas valley, so gently modulated with small crests and shallows, "rolling country" as the farmers say, the house was set on the peak of the barest rise of ground, as if the most infertile spot had been thriftily chosen for building a shelter. It stood there staring and naked, an intruding stranger, strange even beside the barns ranged generously along the back, low-eaved and weathered to the color of stone.

The narrow windows and the steeply sloping roof oppressed me; I wished to turn away and go back. I had come a long way to be so disappointed, I thought, and yet I must go on, for there could be nothing here for me more painful than what I had left. But as we drew near the house, now hardly visible except for the yellow lamplight in the back, perhaps in the kitchen, my feelings changed again toward warmth and tenderness, or perhaps just an apprehension that I could feel so, maybe, again.

The wagon drew up before the porch, and I started climbing down. No sooner had my foot touched ground than an enormous black dog of the detestable German shepherd breed leaped silently at me, and as silently I covered my face with my arms and leaped back. "Kuno, down!" shouted the boy, lunging at him. The front door flew open and a young girl with yellow hair ran down the steps and seized the ugly beast by the scruff. "He does not mean anything," she said seriously in English. "He is only a dog."

Just Louise's darling little puppy Kuno, I thought, a year or so older. Kuno whined, apologized by bowing and scraping one front paw on the ground, and the girl holding his scruff said, shyly and proudly, "I teach him that. He has always such bad manners, but I teach him!"

I had arrived, it seemed, at the moment when the evening chores were about to begin. The entire Müller household streamed out of the door, each man and woman going about the affairs of the moment. The young girl walked with me up the porch and said, "This is my brother Hans," and a young man paused to shake hands and passed by. "This is my brother Fritz," she said, and Fritz took my hand and dropped it as he went. "My sister Annetje," said the young girl, and a quiet young woman with a baby draped loosely like a scarf over her shoulder smiled and held out her hand. Hand after hand went by, their palms variously younger or older, broad or small, male or female, but all thick hard decent peasant hands, warm and strong. And in every face I saw again the pale, tilted eyes, on every head that taffy-colored hair, as though they might all be brothers and sisters, though Annetje's husband and still another daughter's husband had gone by after greeting me. In the wide hall with a door at front and back, full of cloudy light and the smell of soap, the old mother, also on her way out, stopped to offer her hand. She was a tall strong-looking woman wearing a three-cornered black wool shawl on her head, her skirts looped up over a brown flannel petticoat. Not from her did the young ones get those water-clear eyes. Hers were black and shrewd and searching, a band of hair showed black streaked with grey, her seamed dry face was brown as seasoned bark, and she walked in her rubber boots with the stride of a man. She shook my hand briefly and said in German English that I was welcome, smiling and showing her blackened teeth.

"This is my girl Hatsy," she told me, "and she will show you to your room." Hatsy took my hand as if I were a child needing a guide. I followed her up a flight of steps steep as a ladder, and there we were, in Louise's attic room, with the sloping roof. Yes, the shingles were stained all the colors she had said. There were the dime novels heaped in the corner. For once, Louise had got it straight, and it was homely and familiar, as if I had seen it before. "My mother says we could give you a better place on the downstairs," said Hatsy, in her soft blurred English, "but *she* said in her letter you would like it so." I told her indeed I did like it so. She went down the steep stairs then, and her brother came up as if he were climbing a tree, with the trunk on his head and the suitcase in his right hand, and I could not see what kept the trunk from crashing back to the bottom, as he used the left hand to climb with. I wished to offer help but feared to insult him, having noted well the tremendous ease and style with which he had hurled the luggage around before, a strong man doing his turn before a weakling audience. He put his burden down and straightened up, wriggling his shoulders and panting only a little. I thanked him and he pushed his cap back and pulled it forward again, which I took for some sort of polite response, and clattered out hugely. Looking out of my window a few minutes later, I saw him setting off across the fields carrying a lighted lantern and a large steel trap.

I began changing my first letter to Louise. "I'm going to like it here. I don't quite know why, but it's going to be all right. Maybe I can tell you later——"

The sound of the German speech in the household below was part of the pleasantness, for they were not talking to me and did not expect me to answer. All the German I understood then was contained in five small deadly sentimental songs of Heine's, learned by heart; and this was a very different tongue, Low German corrupted by three generations in a foreign country. A dozen miles away, where Texas and Louisiana melted together in a rotting swamp whose sluggish under-tow of decay nourished the roots of pine and cedar, a colony of French emigrants had lived out two hundred years of exile, not wholly incorruptible, but mystically faithful to the marrow of their bones, obstinately speaking their old French by then as strange to the French as it was to the English. I had known many of these families during a certain long summer happily remembered, and here again, listening to another language nobody could understand except those of this small farming community, I knew that I was again in a house of perpetual exile. These were solid, practical, hard-bitten, land-holding German peasants, who struck their mattocks into the earth deep and held fast wherever they were, because to them life and the land were one indivisible thing; but never in any wise did they confuse nationality with habitation.

I liked the thick warm voices, and it was good not to have to understand what they were saying. I loved that silence which means freedom from the constant pressure of other minds and other opinions and other feelings, that freedom to fold up in quiet and go back to my own center, to find out again, for it is always a rediscovery, what kind of creature it is that rules me finally, makes all the decisions no matter who thinks they make them, even I; who little by little takes everything away except the one thing I cannot live without, and who will one day say, "Now I am all you have left—take me." I paused there a good while listening to this muted unknown language which was silence with music in it; I could be moved and touched but not troubled by it, as by the crying of frogs or the wind in the trees.

The catalpa tree at my window would, I noticed, when it came into leaf, shut off my view of the barns and the fields beyond. When in bloom the branches would almost reach through the window. But now they were a thin screen through which the calves, splotchy red and white, moved prettily against the weathered darkness of the sheds. The brown fields would soon be green again; the sheep washed by the rains and become clean grey. All the beauty of the landscape now was in the harmony of the valley rolling fluently away to the wood's edge. It was an inland country, with the forlorn look of all unloved things; winter in this part of the south is a moribund coma, not the northern death sleep with the sure promise of resurrection. But in my south, my loved and never-forgotten country, after her long sickness, with only a slight stirring, an opening of the eyes between one breath and the next, between night and day, the earth revives and bursts into the plenty of spring with fruit and flowers together, spring and summer at once under the hot shimmering blue sky.

The freshening wind promised another light sedate rain to come at evening. The voices below stairs dispersed, rose again, separately calling from the yards and barns. The old woman strode down the path toward the cow sheds, Hatsy running behind her. The woman wore her wooden yoke, with the milking pails covered and closed with iron hasps, slung easily across her shoulders, but her daughter carried two tin milking pails on her arm. When they pushed back the bars of cedar which opened onto the fields, the cows came through lowing and crowding, and the calves scampered each to his own dam with reaching, opened mouths. Then there was the battle of separating the hungry children from their mothers when they had taken their scanty share. The old woman slapped their little haunches with her open palm, Hatsy dragged at their halters, her feet slipping wide in the mud, the cows bellowed and brandished their horns, the calves bawled like rebellious babies. Hatsy's long yellow braids whisked around her shoulders, her laughter was a shrill streak of gaiety above the angry cow voices and the raucous shouting of the old woman.

From the kitchen porch below came the sound of splashing water, the creaking of the pump handle, and the stamping boots of men. I sat in the window watching the darkness come on slowly, while all the lamps were being lighted. My own small lamp had a handle on the oil bowl, like a cup's. There was also a lantern with a frosted chimney hanging by a nail on the wall. A voice called to me from the foot of my stairs and I looked down into the face of a dark-skinned, flaxen-haired young woman, far advanced in pregnancy, and carrying a prosperous year-old boy on her hip, one arm clutching him to her, the other raised above her head so that her lantern shone upon their heads. "The supper is now ready," she said, and waited for me to come down before turning away.

In the large square room the whole family was gathering at a long table covered with a red checkered cotton cloth, with heaped-up platters of steaming food at either end. A crippled and badly deformed servant girl was setting down pitchers of milk. Her face was so bowed over it was almost hidden, and her whole body was maimed in some painful, mysterious way, probably congenital, I supposed, though she seemed wiry and tough. Her knotted hands shook continually, her wagging head kept pace with her restless elbows. She ran unsteadily around the table scattering plates, dodging whoever stood in her way; no one moved aside for her, or spoke to her, or even glanced after her when she vanished into the kitchen.

The men then moved forward to their chairs. Father Müller took his patriarch's place at the head of the table, Mother Müller looming behind him like a dark boulder. The younger men ranged themselves about on one side, the married ones with their wives standing back of their chairs to serve them, for three generations in this country had not made them self-conscious or disturbed their ancient customs. The two sons-in-law and three sons rolled down their shirt sleeves before beginning to eat. Their faces were polished with recent scrubbing and their open collars were damp.

Mother Müller pointed to me, then waved her hand at her household, telling off their names rapidly. I was a stranger and a guest, so was seated on the men's side of the table, and Hatsy, whose real name turned out to be Huldah, the maiden of the family, was seated on the children's side of the board, attending to them and keeping them in order. These infants ranged from two years to ten, five in number—not counting the one still straddling his mother's hip behind his father's chair—divided between the two married daughters. The children ravened and gorged and reached their hands into the sugar bowl to sprinkle sugar on everything they ate, solemnly elated over their food and paying no attention to Hatsy, who struggled with them only a little less energetically than she did with the calves, and ate almost nothing. She was about seventeen years old, pale-lipped and too thin, and her sleek fine butter-yellow hair, streaked light and dark, real German peasant hair, gave her an air of fragility. But she shared the big-boned structure and the enormous energy and animal force that was like a bodily presence itself in the room; and seeing Father Müller's pale-grey deep-set choleric eyes and high cheekbones, it was easy to trace the family resemblance around the table: it was plain that poor Mother Müller had never had a child of her own—black-eyed, black-haired South Germany people. True, she had borne them, but that was all; they belonged to their father. Even the tawny

Gretchen, expecting another baby, obviously the pet of the family, with the sly smiling manner of a spoiled child, who wore the contented air of a lazy, healthy young animal, seeming always about to yawn, had hair like pulled taffy and those slanted clear eyes. She stood now easing the weight of her little boy on her husband's chair back, reaching with her left arm over his shoulder to refill his plate from time to time.

Annetje, the eldest daughter, carried her newly born baby over her shoulder, where he drooled comfortably down her back, while she spooned things from platters and bowls for her husband. Whenever their eyes met, they smiled with a gentle, reserved warmth in their eyes, the smile of long and sure friendship.

Father Müller did not in the least believe in his children's marrying and leaving home. Marry, yes, of course; but must that take a son or daughter from him? He always could provide work and a place in the household for his daughters' husbands, and in time he would do the same for his sons' wives. A new room had lately been built on, to the northeast, Annetje explained to me, leaning above her husband's head and talking across the table, for Hatsy to live in when she should be married. Hatsy turned very beautifully pink and ducked her head almost into her plate, then looked up boldly and said, "Jah, jah, I am marrit now soon!" Everybody laughed except Mother Müller, who said in German that girls at home never knew when they were well off—no, they must go bringing in husbands. This remark did not seem to hurt anybody's feelings, and Gretchen said it was nice that I was going to be here for the wedding. This reminded Annetje of something, and she spoke in English to the table at large, saying that the Lutheran pastor had advised her to attend church oftener and put her young ones in Sunday school, so that God would give her a blessing with her fifth child. I counted around again, and sure enough, with Gretchen's unborn, there were eight children at that table under the age of ten; somebody was going to need a blessing in all that crowd, no doubt. Father Müller delivered a short speech to his daughter in German, then turned to me and said, "What I say iss, it iss all craziness to go to church and pay a preacher goot money to talk his nonsense. Say rather that he pay me to come and lissen, then I vill go!" His eyes glared with sudden fierceness above his square speckled grey and yellow beard that sprouted directly out from the high cheekbones. "He thinks, so, that my time maybe costs nothing? That iss goot! Let him pay me!"

Mother Müller snorted and shuffled her feet. "Ach, you talk, you talk. Now you vill make the pastor goot and mad if he hears. Vot ve do, if he vill not chrissen the babies?"

"You give him goot money, he vill chrissen," shouted Father Müller. "You vait and see!"

"Ah sure, dot iss so," agreed Mother Müller. "Only do not let him hear!"

There was a gust of excited talk in German, with much rapping of knife handles on the table. I gave up trying to understand, but watched their faces. It sounded like a pitched battle, but they were agreeing about something. They were united in their tribal scepticisms, as in everything else. I got a powerful impression that they were all, even the sons-in-law, one human being divided into several separate appearances. The crippled servant girl brought in more food and gathered up plates and went away in her limping run, and she seemed to me the only individual in the house. Even I felt divided into many fragments, having left or lost a part of myself in every place I had travelled, in every life mine had touched, above all, in every death of someone near to me that had carried into the grave some part of my living cells. But the servant, she was whole, and belonged nowhere.

I settled easily enough into the marginal life of the household ways and habits. Day began early at the Müllers', and we ate breakfast by yellow lamplight, with the grey damp winds blowing with spring softness through the open windows. The men swallowed their last cups of steaming coffee standing, with their hats on, and went out to harness the horses to the ploughs at sunrise. Annetje, with her fat baby slung over her shoulder, could sweep a room or make a bed with one hand, all finished before the day was well begun; and she spent the rest of the day outdoors, caring for the chickens and the pigs. Now and then she came in with a shallow boxful of newly hatched chickens, abject dabs of wet fluff, and put them on a table in her bedroom where she might tend them carefully on their first day. Mother Müller strode about hugely, giving orders right and left, while Father Müller, smoothing his whiskers and lighting his pipe, drove away to town with Mother Müller calling out after him final directions and instructions about household needs. He never spoke a word to her and appeared not to be listening, but he always returned in a few hours with every commission and errand performed exactly. After I had made my own bed and set my attic in order, there was nothing at all for me to do, and I walked out of this enthusiastic bustle into the lane, feeling extremely useless. But the repose, the almost mystical inertia of their minds in the midst of this muscular life, communicated itself to me little by little, and I absorbed it gratefully in silence and felt all the hidden knotted painful places in my own mind beginning to loosen. It was easier to breathe, and I might even weep, if I pleased. In a very few days I no longer felt like weeping.

One morning I saw Hatsy spading up the kitchen garden plot, and my offer to help, to spread the seeds and cover them, was accepted. We worked at this for several hours each morning, until the warmth of the sun and the stooping posture induced in me a comfortable vertigo. I forgot to count the days, they were one like the other except as the colors of the air changed, deepening and warming to keep step with the advancing season, and the earth grew firmer underfoot with the swelling tangle of crowding roots.

The children, so hungry and noisy at the table, were peaceable little folk who played silent engrossed games in the front yard. They were always kneading mud into loaves and pies and carrying their battered dolls and cotton rag animals through the operations of domestic life. They fed them, put them to bed; they got them up and fed them again, set them to their chores making more mud loaves; or they would harness themselves to their carts and gallop away to a great shady chestnut tree on the opposite side of the house. Here the tree became the *Turnverein,* and they themselves were again human beings, solemnly ambling about in a dance and going through the motions of drinking beer. Miraculously changed once more into horses, they harnessed themselves and galloped home. They came at call to be fed and put to sleep with the docility of their own toys or animal playmates. Their mothers handled them with instinctive, constant gentleness; they never seemed to be troubled by them. They were as devoted and caretaking as a cat with her kittens.

Sometimes I took Annetje's next to youngest child, a baby of two years, in her little wagon, and we would go down through the orchard, where the branches were beginning to sprout in cones of watery green, and into the lane for a short distance. I would turn again into a smaller lane, smoother because less travelled, and we would go slowly between the aisle of mulberry trees where the fruit was beginning to hang and curl like green furry worms. The baby would sit in a compact mound of flannel and calico, her pale-blue eyes tilted and shining under her cap, her two lower teeth showing in a rapt smile. Sometimes several of the other children would follow along quietly. When I turned, they all turned without question, and we would proceed back to the house as sedately as we had set out.

The narrow lane, I discovered, led to the river, and it became my favorite walk. Almost every day I went along the edge of the naked wood, passionately occupied with looking for signs of spring. The changes there were so subtle and gradual I found one day that branches of willows and sprays of blackberry vine alike were covered with fine points of green; the color had changed overnight, or so it seemed, and I knew that tomorrow the whole valley and wood and edge of the river would be quick and feathery with golden green blowing in the winds.

And it was so. On that day I did not leave the river until after dark and came home through the marsh with the owls and night jars crying over my head, calling in a strange and broken chorus in the woods until the farthest answering cry was a ghostly echo. When I went through the orchard the trees were all abloom with fireflies. I stopped and looked at it for a long time, then walked slowly, amazed, for I had never seen anything that was more beautiful to me. The trees were freshly budded out with pale bloom, the branches were immobile in the thin darkness, but the flower clusters shivered in a soundless dance of delicately woven light, whirling as airily as leaves in a breeze, as rhythmically as water in a fountain. Every tree was budded out with this living, pulsing fire as fragile and cool as bubbles. When I opened the gate their light shone on my hands like fox fire. When I looked back, the shimmer of golden light was there, it was no dream.

Hatsy was on her knees in the dining room, washing the floor with heavy dark rags. She always did this work at night, so the men with their heavy boots would not be tracking it up again and it would be immaculate in the morning. She turned her young face to me in a stupor of fatigue. "Ottilie! Ottilie!" she called, loudly, and before I could speak, she said, "Ottilie will give you supper. It is waiting, all ready." I tried to tell her that I was not hungry, but she wished to reassure me. "Look, we all must eat. Now or then, it's no trouble." She sat back on her heels, and raising her head, looked over the window sill at the orchard. She smiled and paused for a moment and said happily, "Now it is come spring. Every spring we have that." She bent again over the great pail of water with her mops.

The crippled servant came in, stumbling perilously on the slippery floor, and set a dish before me, lentils with sausage and red chopped cabbage. It was hot and savory and I was truly grateful, for I found I was hungry, after all. I looked at her—so her name was Ottilie?—and said, "Thank you." "She can't talk," said Hatsy, simply stating a fact that need not be emphasized. The blurred, dark face was neither young nor old, but crumpled into criss cross wrinkles, irrelevant either to age or suffering; simply wrinkles, patternless blackened seams as if the perishable flesh had been wrung in a hard cruel fist. Yet in that mutilated face I saw high cheekbones, slanted water-blue eyes, the pupils very large and strained with the anxiety of one peering into a darkness full of danger. She jarred heavily against the table as she turned, her bowed back trembling with the perpetual working of her withered arms, and ran away in aimless, driven haste.

Hatsy sat on her heels again for a moment, tossed her braids back over her shoulder and said, "That is Ottilie. She is not sick now. She is only like that since she was sick when she was a baby. But she can work so well as I can. She cooks. But she cannot talk so you can understand." She went up on her knees, bowed over, and began to scrub again, with new energy. She was really a network of thin taut ligaments and long muscles elastic as woven steel. She would always work too hard, and be tired all her life, and never know that this was anything but perfectly natural; everybody worked all the time, because there was always more work waiting when they had finished what they were doing then. I ate my supper and took my plate to the kitchen and set it on the table. Ottilie was sitting in a kitchen chair with her feet in the open oven, her arms folded and her head waggling a little. She did not see or hear me.

At home, Hatsy wore an old brown corduroy dress and galoshes without stockings. Her skirts were short enough to show her thin legs, slightly crooked below the knees, as if she had walked too early. "Hatsy, she's a good, quick girl," said Mother Müller, to whom praising anybody or anything did not come easily. On Saturdays, Hatsy took a voluminous bath in a big tub in the closet back of the kitchen, where also were stored the extra chamber pots, slop jars, and water jugs. She then unplaited her yellow hair and bound up the crinkled floss with a wreath of pink cotton rosebuds, put on her pale-blue China silk dress, and went to the *Turnverein* to dance and drink a seidel of dark-brown beer with her suitor, who resembled her brothers enough to be her brother, though I think nobody ever noticed this except myself, and I said nothing because it would have been the remark of a stranger and hopeless outsider. On Sundays, the entire family went to the *Turnverein* after copious washings, getting into starched dresses and shirts, and getting the baskets of food stored in the wagons. The servant, Ottilie, would rush out to see them off, standing with both shaking arms folded over her forehead, shading her troubled eyes to watch them to the turn of the lane. Her muteness seemed nearly absolute; she had no coherent language of signs. Yet three times a day she spread that enormous table with solid food, freshly baked bread, huge platters of vegetables, immoderate roasts of meat, extravagant tarts, strudels, pies—enough for twenty people. If neighbors came in for an afternoon on some holiday, Ottilie would stumble into the big north room, the parlor, with its golden oak melodeon, a harsh-green Brussels carpet, Nottingham lace curtains, crocheted lace antimacassars on the chair backs, to serve them coffee with cream and sugar and thick slices of yellow cake.

Mother Müller sat but seldom in her parlor, and always with an air of formal unease, her knotted big fingers cramped in a cluster. But Father Müller often sat there in the evenings, where no one ventured to follow him unless commanded; he sometimes played chess with his elder son-in-law, who had learned a good while ago that Father Müller was a good player who abhorred an easy victory, and he dared not do less than put up the best fight he was able, but even so, if Father Müller felt himself winning too often, he would roar, "No, you are not trying! You are not doing your best. Now we stop this nonsense!" and son-in-law would find himself dismissed in temporary disgrace.

Most evenings, however, Father Müller sat by himself and read *Das Kapital.* He would settle deeply into the red plush base rocker and spread the volume upon a low table before him. It was an early edition in blotty black German type, stained and ragged in its leather cover, the pages falling apart, a very bible. He knew whole chapters almost by heart, and added nothing to, took nothing from, the canonical, once-delivered text. I cannot say at that time of my life I had never heard of *Das Kapital,* but I had certainly never known anyone who had read it, though if anyone mentioned it, it was always with profound disapproval. It was not a book one had to read in order to reject it. And here was this respectable old farmer who accepted its dogma as a religion—that is to say, its legendary inapplicable precepts were just, right, proper, one must believe in them, of course, but life, everyday living, was another and unrelated thing. Father Müller was the richest man in his community; almost every neighboring farmer rented land from him, and some of them worked it on the share system. He explained this to me one evening after he had given up trying to teach me chess. He was not surprised that I could not learn, at least not in one lesson, and he was not surprised either that I knew nothing about *Das Kapital.* He explained his own arrangements to me thus: "These men, they cannot buy their land. The land must be bought, for Kapital owns it, and Kapital will not give back to the worker the land that is his. Well, somehow, I can always buy land. Why? I do not know. I only know that with my first land here I made good crops to buy more land, and so I rent it cheap, more than anybody else I rent it cheap, I lend money so my neighbors do not fall into the hands of the bank, and so I am not Kapital. Someday these workers, they can buy land from me, for less than they can get it anywhere else. Well, that is what I can do, that is all." He turned over a page, and his angry grey eyes looked out at me under his shaggy brows. "I buy my land with my hard work, all my life, and I rent it cheap to my neighbors, and then they say they will not elect my son-in-law, my Annetje's husband, to be sheriff because I am atheist. So then I say, all right, but next year you pay more for your land or more shares of your crops. If I am atheist I will act like one. So, my Annetje's husband is sheriff, that is all."

He had put a stubby forefinger on a line to mark his place, and now he sank himself into his book and I left quietly without saying good night.

The *Turnverein* was an octagonal pavilion set in a cleared space in a patch of woods belonging to Father Müller. The German colony came here to sit about in the cool shade, while a small brass band played cloppity country dances. The girls danced with energy and direction, their starched petticoats rustling like dry leaves. The boys were more awkward, but willing; they clutched their partners' waists and left crumpled sweaty spots where they clutched. Here Mother Müller took her ease after a hard week. Her gaunt limbs would relax, her knees spread squarely apart, and she would gossip over her beer with the women of her own generation. They would cast an occasional caretaking glance at the children playing nearby, allowing the younger mothers freedom to dance or sit in peace with their own friends.

On the other side of the pavilion, Father Müller would sit with the sober grandfathers, their long curved pipes wagging on their chests as they discussed local politics with profound gravity, their hard peasant fatalism tempered only a little by a shrewd worldly distrust of all officeholders not personally known to them, all political plans except their own immediate ones. When Father Müller talked, they listened respectfully, with faith in him as a strong man, head of his own house and his community. They nodded slowly whenever he took his pipe from his mouth and gestured, holding it by the bowl as if it were a stone he was getting ready to throw. On our way back from the *Turnverein* one evening, Mother Müller said to me, "Well, now, by the grace of Gott it is all settled between Hatsy and her man. It is next Sunday by this time they will be marrit."

All the folk who usually went to the *Turnverein* on Sundays came instead to the Müller house for the wedding. They brought useful presents, mostly bed linen, pillow covers, a white counterpane, with a few ornaments for the bridal chamber—a home-braided round rug in many colors, a brass-bottomed lamp with a round pink chimney decorated with red roses, a stone china washbowl and pitcher also covered with red roses; and the bridegroom's gift to the bride was a necklace, a double string of red coral twigs. Just before the short ceremony began, he slipped the necklace over her head with trembling hands. She smiled up at him shakily and helped him disentangle her short veil from the coral, then they joined hands and turned their faces to the pastor, not letting go until time for the exchange of rings—the widest, thickest, reddest gold bands to be found, no doubt—and at that moment they both stopped smiling and turned a little pale. The groom recovered first, and bent over—he was considerably taller than she—and kissed her on the forehead. His eyes were a deep blue, and his hair not really Müller taffy color, but a light chestnut; a good-looking, gentle-tempered boy, I decided, and he looked at Hatsy as if he liked what he saw. They knelt and clasped hands again for the final prayer, then stood together and exchanged the bridal kiss, a very chaste reserved one, still not on the lips. Then everybody came to shake hands and the men all kissed the bride and the women all kissed the groom. Some of the women whispered in Hatsy's ear, and all burst out laughing except Hatsy, who turned red from her forehead to her throat. She whispered in turn to her husband, who nodded in agreement. She then tried to slip away quietly, but the watchful young girls were after her, and shortly we saw her running through the blossoming orchard, holding up her white ruffled skirts, with all the girls in pursuit, shrieking and calling like excited hunters, for the first to overtake and touch her would be the next bride. They returned, breathless, dragging the lucky one with them, and held her against her ecstatic resistance, while all the young boys kissed her.

The guests stayed on for a huge supper, and Ottilie came in, wearing a fresh blue apron, sweat beaded in the wrinkles of her forehead and around her formless mouth, and passed the food around the table. The men ate first and then Hatsy came in with the women for the first time, still wearing her square little veil of white cotton net bound on her hair with peach blossoms shattered in the bride's race. After supper, one of the girls played waltzes and polkas on the melodeon, and everyone danced. The bridegroom drew gallons of beer from a keg set up in the hall, and at midnight everybody went away, warmly emotional and happy. I went down to the kitchen for a pitcher of hot water. The servant was still setting things to rights, hobbling between table and cupboard. Her face was a brown smudge of anxiety, her eyes were wide and dazed. Her uncertain hands rattled among the pans, but nothing could make her seem real, or in any way connected with the life around her. Yet when I set my pitcher on the stove, she lifted the heavy kettle and poured the scalding water into it without spilling a drop.

The clear honey green of the early morning sky was a mirror of the bright earth. At the edge of the woods there had sprung a reticent blooming of small white and pale-colored flowers. The peach trees were now each a separate nosegay of shell rose and white. I left the house, meaning to take the short path across to the lane of mulberries. The women were deep in the house, the men were away to the fields, the animals were turned into the pastures, and only Ottilie was visible, sitting on the steps of the back porch peeling potatoes. She gazed in my direction with eyes that fell short of me, and seemed to focus on a point midway between us, and gave no sign. Then she dropped her knife and rose, her mouth opened and closed several times, she strained toward me, motioning with her right hand. I went to her, her hands came out and clutched my sleeve, and for a moment I feared to hear her voice. There was no sound from her, but she drew me along after her, full of some mysterious purpose of her own. She opened the door of a dingy bitter-smelling room, windowless, which opened off the kitchen, beside the closet where Hatsy took her baths. A lumpy narrow cot and chest of drawers supporting a blistered looking-glass almost filled the space. Ottilie's lips moved, struggling for speech, as she pulled and tumbled over a heap of rubbish in the top drawer. She took out a photograph and put it in my hands. It was in the old style, faded to a dirty yellow, mounted on cardboard elaborately clipped and gilded at the edges.

I saw a girl child about five years old, a pretty smiling German baby, looking curiously like a slightly elder sister of Annetje's two-year-old, wearing a frilled frock and a prodigious curl of blonde hair, called a roach, on the crown of her head. The strong legs, round as sausages, were encased in long white ribbed stockings, and the square firm feet were laced into old-fashioned soft-soled black boots. Ottilie peered over the picture, twisted her neck, and looked up into my face. I saw the slanted water-blue eyes and the high cheekbones of the Müllers again, mutilated, almost destroyed, but unmistakable. This child was what she had been, and she was without doubt the elder sister of Annetje and Gretchen and Hatsy; in urgent pantomime she insisted that this was so—she patted the picture and her own face, and strove terribly to speak. She pointed to the name written carefully on the back, Ottilie, and touched her mouth with her bent knuckles. Her head wagged in her perpetual nod; her shaking hand seemed to flap the photograph at me in a roguish humor. The bit of cardboard connected her at once somehow to the world of human beings I knew; for an instant some filament lighter than cobweb spun itself out between that living center in her and in me, a filament from some center that held us all bound to our unescapable common source, so that her life and mine were kin, even a part of each other, and the painfulness and strangeness of her vanished. She knew well that she had been Ottilie, with those steady legs and watching eyes, and she was Ottilie still within herself. For a moment, being alive, she knew she suffered, for she stood and shook with silent crying, smearing away her tears with the open palm of her hand. Even while her cheeks were wet, her face changed. Her eyes cleared and fixed themselves upon that point in space which seemed for her to contain her unaccountable and terrible troubles. She turned her head as if she had heard a voice and disappeared in her staggering run into the kitchen, leaving the drawer open and the photograph face downward on the chest.

At midday meal she came hurrying and splashing coffee on the white floor, restored to her own secret existence of perpetual amazement, and again I had been a stranger to her like all the rest but she was no stranger to me, and could not be again.

The youngest brother came in, holding up an opossum he had caught in his trap. He swung the furry body from side to side, his eyes fairly narrowed with pride as he showed us the mangled creature. "No, it is cruel, even for the wild animals," said gentle Annetje to me, "but boys love to kill, they love to hurt things. I am always afraid he will trap poor Kuno." I thought privately that Kuno, a wolfish, ungracious beast, might well prove a match for any trap. Annetje was full of silent, tender solicitudes. The kittens, the puppies, the chicks, the lambs and calves were her special care. She was the only one of the women who caressed the weanling calves when she set the pans of milk before them. Her child seemed as much a part of her as if it were not yet born. Still, she seemed to have forgotten that Ottilie was her sister. So had all the others. I remembered how Hatsy had spoken her name but had not said she was her sister. Their silence about her was, I realized, exactly that—simple forgetfulness. She moved among them as invisible to their imaginations as a ghost. Ottilie their sister was something painful that had happened long ago and now was past and done for; they could not live with that memory or its visible reminder—they forgot her in pure self-defense. But I could not forget her. She drifted into my mind like a bit of weed carried in a current and caught there, floating but fixed, refusing to be carried away. I reasoned it out. The Müllers, what else could they have done with Ottilie? By a physical accident in her childhood she had been stripped of everything but her mere existence. It was not a society or a class that pampered its invalids and the unfit. So long as one lived, one did one's share. This was her place, in this family she had been born and must die; did she suffer? No one asked, no one looked to see. Suffering went with life, suffering and labor. While one lived one worked, that was all, and without complaints, for no one had time to listen, and everybody had his own troubles. So, what else could they have done with Ottilie? As for me, I could do nothing but promise myself that I would forget her, too; and to remember her for the rest of my life.

Sitting at the long table, I would watch Ottilie clattering about in her tormented haste, bringing in that endless food that represented all her life's labors. My mind would follow her into the kitchen where I could see her peering into the great simmering kettles, the crowded oven, her whole body a mere machine of torture. Straight up to the surface of my mind the thought would come urgently, clearly, as if driving time toward the desired event: Let it be now, let it be *now.* Not even tomorrow, no, today. Let her sit down quietly in her rickety chair by the stove and fold those arms, and let us find her there like that, with her head fallen forward on her knees. She will rest then. I would wait, hoping she might not come again, ever again, through that door I gazed at with wincing eyes, as if I might see something unendurable enter through it. Then she would come, and it was only Ottilie, after all, in the bosom of her family, and one of its most useful and competent members; and they with a deep right instinct had learned to live with her disaster on its own terms, and hers; they had accepted and then made use of what was for them only one more painful event in a world full of troubles, many of them much worse than this. So, a step at a time, I followed the Müllers as nearly as I could in their acceptance of Ottilie, and the use they made of her life, for in some way that I could not quite explain to myself, I found great virtue and courage in their steadiness and refusal to feel sorry for anybody, least of all for themselves.

Gretchen bore her child, a son, conveniently between the hours of supper and bedtime, one evening of friendly and domestic-sounding rain. The next day brought neighboring women from miles around, and the child was bandied about among them as if he were a new kind of medicine ball. Sedate and shy at dances, emotional at weddings, they were ribald and jocose at births. Over coffee and beer the talk grew broad, the hearty gutturals were swallowed in the belly of laughter; those honest hard-working wives and mothers saw life for a few hours as a hearty low joke, and it did them good. The baby bawled and suckled like a young calf, and the men of the family came in for a look and added their joyful improprieties.

Cloudy weather drove them home earlier than they had meant to go. The whole sky was lined with smoky black and grey vapor hanging in ragged wisps like soot in a chimney. The edges of the woods turned dull purple as the horizon reddened slowly, then faded, and all across the sky ran a deep shuddering mumble of thunder. All the Müllers hurried about getting into rubber boots and oilcloth overalls, shouting to each other, making their plan of action. The youngest boy came over the ridge of the hill with Kuno helping him to drive the sheep down into the fold. Kuno was barking, the sheep were baaing and bleating, the horses freed from the ploughs were excited; they whinnied and trotted at the lengths of their halters, their ears laid back. The cows were bawling in distress and the calves cried back to them. All the men went out among the animals to round them up and quiet them and get them enclosed safely. Even as Mother Müller, her half-dozen petticoats looped about her thighs and tucked into her hip boots, was striding to join them in the barns, the cloud rack was split end to end by a shattering blow of lightning, and the cloudburst struck the house with the impact of a wave against a ship. The wind broke the windowpanes and the floods poured through. The roof beams strained and the walls bent inward, but the house stood to its foundations. The children were huddled into the inner bedroom with Gretchen. "Come and sit on the bed with me now," she told them calmly, "and be still." She sat up with a shawl around her, suckling the baby. Annetje came then and left her baby with Gretchen, too; and standing at the doorsteps with one arm caught over the porch rail, reached down into the furious waters which were rising to the very threshold and dragged in a half-drowned lamb. I followed her. We could not make ourselves heard above the cannonade of thunder, but together we carried the creature into the hall under the stairs, where we rubbed the drowned fleece with rags and pressed his stomach to free him from the water and finally got him sitting up with his feet tucked under him. Annetje was merry with triumph and kept saying in delight, "Alive, alive! look!"

We left him there when we heard the men shouting and beating at the kitchen door and ran to open it for them. They came in, Mother Müller among them, wearing her yoke and milk pails. She stood there with the water pouring from her skirts, the three-cornered piece of black oilcloth on her head dripping, her rubber boots wrinkled down with the weight of her petticoats stuffed into them. She and Father Müller stood near each other, looking like two gnarled lightning-struck old trees, his beard and oilcloth garments streaming, both their faces suddenly dark and old and tired, tired once for all; they would never be rested again in their lives. Father Müller suddenly roared at her, "Go get yourself dry clothes. Do you want to make yourself sick?"

"Ho," she said, taking off her milk yoke and setting the pails on the floor. "Go change yourself. I bring you dry socks." One of the boys told me she had carried a day-old calf on her back up a ladder against the inside wall of the barn and had put it safely in the hayloft behind a barricade of bales. Then she had lined up the cows in the stable, and, sitting on her milking stool in the rising water, she had milked them all. She seemed to think nothing of it.

"Hatsy!" she called, "come help with this milk!" Little pale Hatsy came flying barefoot because she had been called in the midst of taking off her wet shoes, her thick yellow and silver braids thumping on her shoulders as she ran. Her new husband followed her, rather shy of his mother-in-law.

"Let me," he said, wishing to spare his dear bride such heavy work, and started to lift the great pails. "No!" shouted Mother Müller, so the poor young man nearly jumped out of his shirt, "Not you. The milk is not business for a man." He fell back and stood there with dark rivulets of mud seeping from his boots, watching Hatsy pour the milk into pans. Mother Müller started to follow her husband to attend him, but said at the door, turning back, "Where is Ottilie?", and no one knew, no one had seen her. "Find her," said Mother Müller, going. "Tell her we want supper now."

Hatsy motioned to her husband, and together they tiptoed to the door of Ottilie's room and opened it silently. The light from the kitchen showed them Ottilie, sitting by herself, folded up on the edge of the bed. Hatsy threw the door wide open for more light and called in a high penetrating voice as if to a deaf person or one at a great distance, "Ottilie! Suppertime. We are hungry!", and the young pair left the kitchen to look under the stairway to see how Annetje's lamb was getting on. Then Annetje, Hatsy, and I got brooms and began sweeping the dirty water and broken glass from the floors of the hall and dining room.

The storm lightened gradually, but the flooding rain continued. At supper there was talk about the loss of animals and their replacement. All the crops must be replanted, the season's labor was for nothing. They were all tired and wet, but they ate heartily and calmly, to strengthen themselves against all the labor of repairing and restoring which must begin early tomorrow morning.

By morning the drumming on the roof had almost ceased; from my window I looked upon a sepia-colored plain of water moving slowly to the valley. The roofs of the barns sagged like the ridge poles of a tent, and a number of drowned animals floated or were caught against the fences. At breakfast Mother Müller sat groaning over her coffee cup. "Ach," she said, "what it is to have such a pain in the head. Here too," she thumped her chest. "All over. Ach, Gott, I'm sick." She got up sighing hoarsely, her cheeks flushed, calling Hatsy and Annetje to help her in the barn.

They all came back very soon, their skirts draggled to the knees, and the two sisters were supporting their mother, who was speechless and could hardly stand. They put her to bed, where she lay without moving, her face scarlet. Everybody was confused, no one knew what to do. They tucked the quilts about her, and she threw them off. They offered her coffee, cold water, beer, but she turned her head away. The sons came in and stood beside her, and joined the cry: "*Mutterchen, Mutti, Mutti,* what can we do? Tell us, what do you need?" But she could not tell them. It was impossible to ride the twelve miles to town for a doctor; fences and bridges were down, the roads were washed out. The family crowded into the room, unnerved in panic, lost unless the sick woman should come to herself and tell them what to do for her. Father Müller came in and, kneeling beside her, he took hold of her hands and spoke to her most lovingly, and when she did not answer him he broke out crying openly in a loud voice, the great tears rolling, "Ach, Gott, Gott. A hundert tousand tollars in the bank"—he glared around at his family and spoke broken English to them, as if he were a stranger to himself and had forgotten his own language—"and tell me, tell, what goot does it do?"

This frightened them, and all at once, together, they screamed and called and implored her in a tumult utterly beyond control. The noise of their grief and terror filled the place. In the midst of this, Mother Müller died.

In the midafternoon the rain passed, and the sun was a disc of brass in a cruelly bright sky. The waters flowed thickly down to the river, leaving the hill bald and brown, with the fences lying in a flattened tangle, the young peach trees stripped of bloom and sagging at the roots. In the woods had occurred a violent eruption of ripe foliage of a jungle thickness, glossy and burning, a massing of hot peacock green with cobalt shadows.

The household was in such silence, I had to listen carefully to know that anyone lived there. Everyone, even the younger children, moved on tiptoe and spoke in whispers. All afternoon the thud of hammers and the whine of a saw went on monotonously in the barn loft. At dark the men brought in a shiny coffin of new yellow pine with rope handles and set it in the hall. It lay there on the floor for an hour or so, where anyone passing had to step over it. Then Annetje and Hatsy, who had been washing and dressing the body, appeared in the doorway and motioned: "You may bring it in now."

Mother Müller lay in state in the parlor throughout the night, in her black silk dress with a scrap of white lace at the collar and a small lace cap on her hair. Her husband sat in the plush chair near her, looking at her face, which was very contemplative, gentle, and remote. He wept at intervals, silently, wiping his face and head with a big handkerchief. His daughters brought him coffee from time to time. He fell asleep there toward morning.

The light burned in the kitchen nearly all night, too, and the sound of Ottilie's heavy boots thumping about unsteadily was accompanied by the locust whirring of the coffee mill and the smell of baking bread. Hatsy came to my room. "There's coffee and cake," she said, "you'd better have some," and turned away crying, crumbling her slice in her hand. We stood about and ate in silence. Ottilie brought in a fresh pot of coffee, her eyes bleared and fixed, her gait as aimless-looking and hurried as ever, and when she spilled some on her own hand, she did not seem to feel it.

For a day longer they waited; then the youngest boy went to fetch the Lutheran pastor, and a few neighbors came back with them. By noon many more had arrived, spattered with mud, the horses heaving and sweating. At every greeting the family gave way and wept afresh, as naturally and openly as children. Their faces were drenched and soft with their tears; there was a comfortable relaxed look in the muscles of their faces. It was good to let go, to have something to weep for that nobody need excuse or explain. Their tears were at once a luxury and a cure of souls. They wept away the hard core of secret trouble that is in the heart of each separate man, secure in a communal grief; in sharing it, they consoled each other. For a while they would visit the grave and remember, and then life would arrange itself again in another order, yet it would be the same. Already the thoughts of the living were turning to tomorrow, when they would be at the work of rebuilding and replanting and repairing—even now, today, they would hurry back from the burial to milk the cows and feed the chickens, and they might weep again and again for several days, until their tears could heal them at last.

On that day I realized, for the first time, not death, but the terror of dying. When they took the coffin out to the little country hearse and I saw that the procession was about to form, I went to my room and lay down. Staring at the ceiling, I heard and felt the ominous order and purpose in the movements and sounds below—the creaking harness and hoofbeats and grating wheels, the muted grave voices—and it was as if my blood fainted and receded with fright, while my mind stayed wide awake to receive the awful impress. Yet when I knew they were leaving the yard, the terror began to leave me. As the sounds receded, I lay there not thinking, not feeling, in a mere drowse of relief and weariness.

Through my half-sleep I heard the howling of a dog. It seemed to be a dream, and I was troubled to awaken. I dreamed that Kuno was caught in the trap; then I thought he was really caught, it was no dream and I must wake, because there was no one but me to let him out. I came broad awake, the cry rushed upon me like a wind, and it was not the howl of a dog. I ran downstairs and looked into Gretchen's room. She was curled up around her baby, and they were both asleep. I ran to the kitchen.

Ottilie was sitting in her broken chair with her feet on the edge of the open oven, where the heat had died away. Her hands hung at her sides, the fingers crooked into the palm; her head lay back on her shoulders, and she howled with a great wrench of her body, an upward reach of the neck, without tears. At sight of me she got up and came over to me and laid her head on my breast, and her hands dangled forward a moment. Shuddering, she babbled and howled and waved her arms in a frenzy through the open window over the stripped branches of the orchard toward the lane where the procession had straightened out into formal order. I took hold of her arms where the unnaturally corded muscles clenched and strained under her coarse sleeves; I led her out to the steps and left her sitting there, her head wagging.

In the barnyard there remained only the broken-down spring wagon and the shaggy pony that had brought me to the farm on the first day. The harness was still a mystery, but somehow I managed to join pony, harness, and wagon not too insecurely, or so I could only hope; and I pushed and hauled and tugged at Ottilie and lifted her until she was in the seat and I had the reins in hand. We careened down the road at a grudging trot, the pony jolting like a churn, the wheels spinning elliptically in a truly broad comedy swagger. I watched the jovial antics of those wheels with attention, hoping for the best. We slithered into round pits of green mud, and jogged perilously into culverts where small bridges had been. Once, in what was left of the main road, I stood up to see if I might overtake the funeral train; yes, there it was, going inchmeal up the road over the little hill, a bumbling train of black beetles crawling helter-skelter over clods.

Ottilie, now silent, was doubled upon herself, slipping loosely on the edge of the seat. I caught hold of her stout belt with my free hand, and my fingers slipped between her clothes and bare flesh, ribbed and gaunt and dry against my knuckles. My sense of her realness, her humanity, this shattered being that was a woman, was so shocking to me that a howl as doglike and despairing as her own rose in me unuttered and died again, to be a perpetual ghost. Ottilie slanted her eyes and peered at me, and I gazed back. The knotted wrinkles of her face were grotesquely changed, she gave a choked little whimper, and suddenly she laughed out, a kind of yelp but unmistakably laughter, and clapped her hands for joy, the grinning mouth and suffering eyes turned to the sky. Her head nodded and wagged with the clownish humor of our trundling lurching progress. The feel of the hot sun on her back, the bright air, the jolly senseless staggering of the wheels, the peacock green of the heavens: something of these had reached her. She was happy and gay, and she gurgled and rocked in her seat, leaning upon me and waving loosely around her as if to show me what wonders she saw.

Drawing the pony to a standstill, I studied her face for a while and pondered my ironical mistake. There was nothing I could do for Ottilie, selfishly as I wished to ease my heart of her; she was beyond my reach as well as any other human reach, and yet, had I not come nearer to her than I had to anyone else in my attempt to deny and bridge the distance between us, or rather, her distance from me? Well, we were both equally the fools of life, equally fellow fugitives from death. We had escaped for one day more at least. We would celebrate our good luck, we would have a little stolen holiday, a breath of spring air and freedom on this lovely, festive afternoon.

Ottilie fidgeted, uneasy at our stopping. I flapped the reins, the pony moved on, we turned across the shallow ditch where the small road divided from the main travelled one. I measured the sun westering gently; there would be time enough to drive to the river down the lane of mulberries and to get back to the house before the mourners returned. There would be plenty of time for Ottilie to have a fine supper ready for them. They need not even know she had been gone.

QUESTIONS FOR DISCUSSION AND WRITING

1. How does the development of the season up to and including the storm provide a sense of organic structure for the plot?
2. How does the narrator make the reader see the Müllers as one character in spite of her presentation of them as distinct individuals?
3. Why does the narrator create so many detailed settings in the story—her room, the parlor, the kitchen, the *Turnverein*? What characters does she associate with each setting?
4. How does the opening paragraph establish the narrator's point of view? In what ways does the final episode clarify or change that point of view?
5. In what sense has the narrator had a "holiday"? What does the narrator mean at the end of the story when she says that both she and Ottilie are "fools of life"?

82

PHILIP ROTH

Defender of the Faith

PHILIP ROTH was born in 1933 in Newark, New Jersey, and educated at Rutgers, Bucknell, and the University of Chicago. As a graduate student, he worked as an instructor in the University of Chicago's humanities program and began publishing stories in magazines such as *Paris Review, The New Yorker,* and *Harper's.* In 1959, he collected five of his stories and a novella in *Goodbye, Columbus,* a volume which won the National Book Award. The success of his first book encouraged Roth to give up graduate study and teaching to pursue a full-time career as a writer. In 1962 he published his first full-length novel, *Letting Go,* followed by *When She Was Good* (1967) and his controversial best-seller *Portnoy's Complaint* (1969). Roth often indulges his strong satiric impulse, as in *Our Gang (Starring Tricky and His Friends)* (1971), *The Breast* (1972), and *The Great American Novel* (1973). But he is also interested in the personal and cultural dilemmas of the Jewish American writer, as is evident in his critical self-appraisal *Reading Myself and Others* (1975) and in his semi-autobiographical novels *The Professor of Desire* (1977), *The Ghost Writer* (1979), *Zuckerman Unbound* (1981), and *The Anatomy Lesson* (1983). His most recent novels include *The Counterlife* (1986) and *Deception* (1990). Roth continues to be a prolific writer of short fiction, but many of his stories remain uncollected. "Defender of the Faith," reprinted from *Goodbye, Columbus,* tells of an Army sergeant's dilemma defending the values of his religion and his profession.

In May of 1945, only a few weeks after the fighting had ended in Europe, I was rotated back to the States, where I spent the remainder of the war with a training company at Camp Crowder, Missouri. Along with the rest of the Ninth Army, I had been racing across Germany so swiftly during the late winter and spring that when I boarded the plane, I couldn't believe its destination lay to the west. My mind might inform me otherwise, but there was an inertia of the spirit that told me we were flying to a new front, where we would disembark and continue our push eastward—eastward until we'd circled the globe, marching through villages along whose twisting, cobbled streets crowds of the enemy would watch us take possession of what, up till then, they'd considered their own. I had changed enough in two years not to mind the trembling of old people, the crying of the very young, the uncertainty and fear in the eyes of the once arrogant. I had been fortunate enough to develop an infantryman's heart, which, like his feet, at first aches and swells but finally grows horny enough for him to travel the weirdest paths without feeling a thing.

Captain Paul Barrett was my C.O. in Camp Crowder. The day I reported for duty, he came out of his office to shake my hand. He was short, gruff, and fiery, and—indoors or out—he wore his polished helmet liner pulled down to his little eyes. In Europe, he had received a battlefield commission and a serious chest wound, and he'd been returned to the States only a few months before. He spoke easily to me, and at the evening formation he introduced me to the troops. "Gentlemen," he said. "Sergeant Thurston, as you know, is no longer with this company. Your new first sergeant is Sergeant Nathan Marx, here. He is a veteran of the European theater, and consequently will expect to find a company of soldiers here, and not a company of *boys*."

I sat up late in the orderly room that evening, trying half-heartedly to solve the riddle of duty rosters, personnel forms, and morning reports. The Charge of Quarters slept with his mouth open on a mattress on the floor. A trainee stood reading the next day's duty roster, which was posted on the bulletin board just inside the screen door. It was a warm evening, and I could hear radios playing dance music over in the barracks. The trainee, who had been staring at me whenever he thought I wouldn't notice, finally took a step in my direction.

"Hey, Sarge—we having a G.I. party tomorrow night?" he asked. A G.I. party is a barracks cleaning.

"You usually have them on Friday nights?" I asked him.

"Yes," he said, and then he added, mysteriously, "that's the whole thing."

"Then you'll have a G.I. party."

He turned away, and I heard him mumbling. His shoulders were moving and I wondered if he was crying.

"What's your name, soldier?" I asked.

He turned, not crying at all. Instead, his green-speckled eyes, long and narrow, flashed like fish in the sun. He walked over to me and sat on the edge of my desk. He reached out a hand. "Sheldon," he said.

"Stand on your feet, Sheldon."

Getting off the desk, he said, "Sheldon Grossbart." He smiled at the familiarity into which he'd led me.

"You against cleaning the barracks Friday night, Grossbart?" I said. "Maybe we shouldn't have G.I. parties. Maybe we should get a maid." My tone startled me. I felt I sounded like every top sergeant I had ever known.

"No, Sergeant." He grew serious, but with a seriousness that seemed to be only the stifling of a smile. "It's just—G.I. parties on Friday night, of all nights."

He slipped up onto the corner of the desk again—not quite sitting, but not quite standing, either. He looked at me with those speckled eyes flashing, and then made a gesture with his hand. It was very slight—no more than a movement back and forth of the wrist—and yet it managed to exclude from our affairs everything else in the orderly room, to make the two of us the center of the world. It seemed, in fact, to exclude everything even about the two of us except our hearts.

"Sergeant Thurston was one thing," he whispered, glancing at the sleeping C.Q., "but we thought that with you here things might be a little different."

"We?"

"The Jewish personnel."

"Why?" I asked, harshly. "What's on your mind?" Whether I was still angry at the "Sheldon" business, or now at something else, I hadn't time to tell, but clearly I was angry.

"We thought you—Marx, you know, like Karl Marx. The Marx Brothers. Those guys are all—M-a-r-x. Isn't that how *you* spell it, Sergeant?"

"M-a-r-x."

"Fishbein said—" He stopped. "What I mean to say, Sergeant—" His face and neck were red, and his mouth moved but no words came out. In a moment, he raised himself to attention, gazing down at me. It was as though he had suddenly decided he could expect no more sympathy from me than from Thurston, the reason being that I was of Thurston's faith, and not his. The young man had managed to confuse himself as to what my faith really was, but I felt no desire to straighten him out. Very simply, I didn't like him.

When I did nothing but return his gaze, he spoke, in an altered tone. "You see, Sergeant," he explained to me, "Friday nights, Jews are supposed to go to services."

"Did Sergeant Thurston tell you you couldn't go to them when there was a G.I. party?"

"No."

"Did he say you had to stay and scrub the floors?"

"No, Sergeant."

"Did the Captain say you had to stay and scrub the floors?"

"That isn't it, Sergeant. It's the other guys in the barracks." He leaned toward me. "They think we're goofing off. But we're not. That's when Jews go to services, Friday night. We have to."

"Then go."

"But the other guys make accusations. They have no right."

"That's not the Army's problem, Grossbart. It's a personal problem you'll have to work out yourself."

"But it's *unfair*."

I got up to leave. "There's nothing I can do about it," I said.

Grossbart stiffened and stood in front of me. "But this is a matter of *religion,* sir."

"Sergeant," I said.

"I mean, 'Sergeant,'" he said, almost snarling.

"Look, go see the chaplain. You want to see Captain Barrett, I'll arrange an appointment."

"No, no. I don't want to make trouble, Sergeant. That's the first thing they throw up to you. I just want my rights!"

"Damn it, Grossbart, stop whining. You have your rights. You can stay and scrub floors or you can go to shul—"

The smile swam in again. Spittle gleamed at the corners of his mouth. "You mean church, Sergeant."

"I mean shul, Grossbart!"

I walked past him and went outside. Near me, I heard the scrunching of the guard's boots on gravel. Beyond the lighted windows of the barracks, young men in T shirts and fatigue pants were sitting on their bunks, polishing their rifles. Suddenly there was a light rustling behind me. I turned and saw Grossbart's dark frame fleeing back to the barracks, racing to tell his Jewish friends that they were right—that, like Karl and Harpo, I was one of them.

The next morning, while chatting with Captain Barrett, I recounted the incident of the previous evening. Somehow, in the telling, it must have seemed to the Captain that I was not so much explaining Grossbart's position as defending it. "Marx, I'd fight side by side with a nigger if the fella proved to me he was a man. I pride myself," he said, looking out the window, "that I've got an open mind. Consequently, Sergeant, nobody gets special treatment here, for the good *or* the bad. All a man's got to do is prove himself. A man fires well on the range, I give him a weekend pass. He scores high in P.T., he gets a weekend pass. He *earns* it." He turned from the window and pointed a finger at me. "You're a Jewish fella, am I right, Marx?"

"Yes, sir."

"And I admire you. I admire you because of the ribbons on your chest. I judge a man by what he shows me on the field of battle, Sergeant. It's what he's got *here,*" he said, and then, though I expected he would point to his chest, he jerked a thumb toward the buttons straining to hold his blouse across his belly. "Guts," he said.

"O.K., sir. I only wanted to pass on to you how the men felt."

"Mr. Marx, you're going to be old before your time if you worry about how the men feel. Leave that stuff to the chaplain—that's his business, not yours. Let's us train these fellas to shoot straight. If the Jewish personnel feels the other men are accusing them of goldbricking—well, I just don't know. Seems awful funny that suddenly the Lord is calling so loud in Private Grossman's ear he's just got to run to church."

"Synagogue," I said.

"Synagogue is right, Sergeant. I'll write that down for handy reference. Thank you for stopping by."

That evening, a few minutes before the company gathered outside the orderly room for the chow formation, I called the C.Q., Corporal Robert LaHill, in to see me. LaHill was a dark, burly fellow whose hair curled out of his clothes wherever it could. He had a glaze in his eyes that made one think of caves and dinosaurs. "LaHill," I said, "when you take the formation, remind the men that they're free to attend church services *whenever* they are held, provided they report to the orderly room before they leave the area."

LaHill scratched his wrist, but gave no indication that he'd heard or understood.

"LaHill," I said, "*church.* You remember? Church, priest, Mass, confession."

He curled one lip into a kind of smile; I took it for a signal that for a second he had flickered back up into the human race.

"Jewish personnel who want to attend services this evening are to fall out in front of the orderly room at 1900," I said. Then, as an afterthought, I added, "By order of Captain Barrett."

A little while later, as the day's last light—softer than any I had seen that year—began to drop over Camp Crowder, I heard LaHill's thick, inflectionless voice outside my window: "Give me your ears, troopers. Toppie says for me to tell you that at 1900 hours all Jewish personnel is to fall out in front, here, if they want to attend the Jewish Mass."

At seven o'clock, I looked out the orderly-room window and saw three soldiers in starched khakis standing on the dusty quadrangle. They looked at their watches and fidgeted while they whispered back and forth. It was getting dimmer, and, alone on the otherwise deserted field, they looked tiny. When I opened the door, I heard the noise of the G.I. party coming from the surrounding barracks—bunks being pushed to the walls, faucets pounding water into buckets, brooms whisking at the wooden floors, cleaning the dirt away for Saturday's inspection. Big puffs of cloth moved round and round on the windowpanes. I walked outside, and the moment my foot hit the ground I thought I heard Grossbart call to the others, "'Ten-*hut!*" Or maybe, when they all three jumped to attention, I imagined I heard the command.

Grossbart stepped forward, "Thank you, sir," he said.

"'Sergeant,' Grossbart," I reminded him. "You call officers 'sir.' I'm not an officer. You've been in the Army three weeks—you know that."

He turned his palms out at his sides to indicate that, in truth, he and I lived beyond convention. "Thank you anyway," he said.

"Yes," a tall boy behind him said. "Thanks a lot."

And the third boy whispered, "Thank you," but his mouth barely fluttered, so that he did not alter by more than a lip's movement his posture of attention.

"For what?" I asked.

Grossbart snorted happily. "For the announcement. The Corporal's announcement. It helped. It made it—"

"Fancier." The tall boy finished Grossbart's sentence.

Grossbart smiled. "He means formal, sir. Public," he said to me. "Now it won't seem as though we're just taking off—goldbricking because the work has begun."

"It was by order of Captain Barrett," I said.

"Aaah, but you pull a little weight," Grossbart said. "So we thank you." Then he turned to his companions. "Sergeant Marx, I want you to meet Larry Fishbein."

The tall boy stepped forward and extended his hand. I shook it. "You from New York?" he asked.

"Yes."

"Me, too." He had a cadaverous face that collapsed inward from his cheekbone to his jaw, and when he smiled—as he did at the news of our communal attachment—revealed a mouthful of bad teeth. He was blinking his eyes a good deal, as though he were fighting back tears. "What borough?" he asked.

I turned to Grossbart. "It's five after seven. What time are services?"

"Shul," he said, smiling, "is in ten minutes. I want you to meet Mickey Halpern. This is Nathan Marx, our sergeant."

The third boy hopped forward. "Private Michael Halpern." He saluted.

"Salute officers, Halpern," I said. The boy dropped his hand, and, on its way down, in his nervousness, checked to see if his shirt pockets were buttoned.

"Shall I march them over, sir?" Grossbart asked. "Or are you coming along?"

From behind Grossbart, Fishbein piped up. "Afterward, they're having refreshments. A ladies auxiliary from St. Louis, the rabbi told us last week."

"The chaplain," Halpern whispered.

"You're welcome to come along," Grossbart said.

To avoid his plea, I looked away, and saw, in the windows of the barracks, a cloud of faces staring out at the four of us. "Hurry along, Grossbart," I said.

"O.K., then," he said. He turned to the others. "Double time, *march!*"

They started off, but ten feet away Grossbart spun around and, running backward, called to me, "Good *shabbus,* sir!" And then the three of them were swallowed into the alien Missouri dusk.

Even after they had disappeared over the parade ground, whose green was now a deep blue, I could hear Grossbart singing the double-time cadence, and as it grew dimmer and dimmer, it suddenly touched a deep memory—as did the slant of the light—and I was remembering the shrill sounds of a Bronx playground where, years ago, beside the Grand Concourse, I had played on long spring evenings such as this. It was a pleasant memory for a young man so far from peace and home, and it brought so many recollections with it that I began to grow exceedingly tender about myself. In fact, I indulged myself in a reverie so strong that I felt as though a hand were reaching down inside me. It had to reach so very far to touch me! It had to reach past those days in the forests of Belgium, and past the dying I'd refused to weep over; past the nights in German farmhouses whose books we'd burned to warm us; past endless stretches when I had shut off all softness I might feel for my fellows, and had managed even to deny myself the posture of a conqueror—the swagger that I, as a Jew, might well have worn as my boots whacked against the rubble of Wesel, Münster, and Braunschweig.

But now one night noise, one rumor of home and time past, and memory plunged down through all I had anesthetized, and came to what I suddenly remembered was myself. So it was not altogether curious that, in search of more of me, I found myself following Grossbart's tracks to Chapel No. 3, where the Jewish services were being held.

I took a seat in the last row, which was empty. Two rows in front of me sat Grossbart, Fishbein, and Halpern, holding little white Dixie cups. Each row of seats was raised higher than the one in front of it, and I could see clearly what was going on. Fishbein was pouring the contents of his cup into Grossbart's, and Grossbart looked mirthful as the liquid made a purple arc between Fishbein's hand and his. In the glaring yellow light, I saw the chaplain standing on the platform at the front; he was chanting the first line of the responsive reading. Grossbart's prayer book remained closed on his lap; he was swishing the cup around. Only Halpern responded to the chant by praying. The fingers of his right hand were spread wide across the cover of his open book. His cap was pulled down low onto his brow, which made it round, like a yarmulke. From time to time, Grossbart wet his lips at the cup's edge; Fishbein, his long yellow face a dying light bulb, looked from here to there, craning forward to catch sight of the faces down the row, then of those in front of him, then behind. He saw me, and his eyelids beat a tattoo. His elbow slid into Grossbart's side, his neck inclined toward his friend, he whispered something, and then, when the congregation next responded to the chant, Grossbart's voice was among the others. Fishbein looked into his book now, too; his lips, however, didn't move.

Finally, it was time to drink the wine. The chaplain smiled down at them as Grossbart swigged his in one long gulp, Halpern sipped, meditating, and Fishbein faked devotion with an empty cup. "As I look down amongst the congregation"—the chaplain grinned at the word—"this night, I see many new faces, and I want to welcome you to Friday-night services here at Camp Crowder. I am Major Leo Ben Ezra, your chaplain." Though an American, the chaplain spoke deliberately—syllable by syllable, almost—as though to communicate, above all, with the lip readers in his audience. "I have only a few words to say before we adjourn to the refreshment room, where the kind ladies of the Temple Sinai, St. Louis, Missouri, have a nice setting for you."

Applause and whistling broke out. After another momentary grin, the chaplain raised his hands, palms out, his eyes flicking upward a moment, as if to remind the troops where they were and Who Else might be in attendance. In the sudden silence that followed, I thought I heard Grossbart cackle, "Let the goyim clean the floors!" Were those the words? I wasn't sure, but Fishbein, grinning, nudged Halpern. Halpern looked dumbly at him, then went back to his prayer book, which had been occupying him all through the rabbi's talk. One hand tugged at the black kinky hair that stuck out under his cap. His lips moved.

The rabbi continued. "It is about the food that I want to speak to you for a moment. I know, I know, I know," he intoned, wearily, "how in the mouths of most of you the *trafe* food tastes like ashes. I know how you gag, some of you, and how your parents suffer to think of their children eating foods unclean and offensive to the palate. What can I tell you? I can only say, close your eyes and swallow as best you can. Eat what you must to live, and throw away the rest. I wish I could help more. For those of you who find this impossible, may I ask that you try and try, but then come to see me in private. If your revulsion is so great, we will have to seek aid from those higher up."

A round of chatter rose and subsided. Then everyone sang "Ain Kelohainu"; after all those years, I discovered I still knew the words. Then, suddenly, the service over, Grossbart was upon me. "Higher up? He means the General?"

"Hey, Shelly," Fishbein said, "he means God." He smacked his face and looked at Halpern. "How high can you go!"

"Sh-h-h!" Grossbart said. "What do you think Sergeant?"

"I don't know," I said. "You better ask the chaplain."

"I'm going to. I'm making an appointment to see him in private. So is Mickey."

Halpern shook his head. "No, no, Sheldon—"

"You have rights, Mickey," Grossbart said. "They can't push us around."

"It's O.K.," said Halpern. "It bothers my mother, not me."

Grossbart looked at me. "Yesterday he threw up. From the hash. It was all ham and God knows what else."

"I have a cold—that was why," Halpern said. He pushed his yarmulke back into a cap.

"What about you, Fishbein?" I asked. "You kosher, too?"

He flushed. "A little. But I'll let it ride. I have a very strong stomach, and I don't eat a lot anyway." I continued to look at him, and he held up his wrist to reinforce what he'd just said; his watch strap was tightened to the last hole, and he pointed that out to me.

"But services are important to you?" I asked him.

He looked at Grossbart. "Sure, sir."

"'Sergeant.'"

"Not so much at home," said Grossbart, stepping between us, "but away from home it gives one a sense of his Jewishness."

"We have to stick together," Fishbein said.

I started to walk toward the door; Halpern stepped back to make way for me.

"That's what happened to Germany," Grossbart was saying, loud enough for me to hear. "They didn't stick together. They let themselves get pushed around."

I turned. "Look, Grossbart. This is the Army, not summer camp."

He smiled. "So?"

Halpern tried to sneak off, but Grossbart held his arm.

"Grossbart, how old are you?" I asked.

"Nineteen."

"And you?" I said to Fishbein.

"The same. The same month, even."

"And what about him?" I pointed to Halpern, who had by now made it safely to the door.

"Eighteen," Grossbart whispered. "But like he can't tie his shoes or brush his teeth himself. I feel sorry for him."

"I feel sorry for all of us, Grossbart," I said, "but just act like a man. Just don't overdo it."

"Overdo what, sir?"

"The 'sir' business, for one thing. Don't overdo that," I said.

I left him standing there. I passed by Halpern, but he did not look at me. Then I was outside, but, behind, I heard Grossbart call, "Hey, Mickey, my *leben,* come on back. Refreshments!"

"*Leben!*" My grandmother's word for me!

One morning a week later, while I was working at my desk, Captain Barrett shouted for me to come into his office. When I entered, he had his helmet liner squashed down so far on his head that I couldn't even see his eyes. He was on the phone, and when he spoke to me, he cupped one hand over the mouthpiece. "Who the hell is Grossbart?"

"Third platoon, Captain," I said. "A trainee."

"What's all this stink about food? His mother called a goddam congressman about the food." He uncovered the mouthpiece and slid his helmet up until I could see his bottom eyelashes. "Yes, sir," he said into the phone. "Yes, sir. I'm still here, sir. I'm asking Marx, here, right now—"

He covered the mouthpiece again and turned his head back toward me. "Lightfoot Harry's on the phone," he said, between his teeth. "This congressman calls General Lyman, who calls Colonel Sousa, who calls the Major, who calls me. They're just dying to stick this thing on me. Whatsa matter?" He shook the phone at me. "I don't feed the troops? What is this?"

"Sir, Grossbart is strange—" Barrett greeted that with a mockingly indulgent smile. I altered my approach. "Captain, he's a very orthodox Jew, and so he's only allowed to eat certain foods."

"He throws up, the congressman said. Every time he eats something, his mother says, he throws up!"

"He's accustomed to observing the dietary laws, Captain."

"So why's his old lady have to call the White House?"

"Jewish parents, sir—they're apt to be more protective than you expect. I mean, Jews have a very close family life. A boy goes away from home, sometimes the mother is liable to get very upset. Probably the boy mentioned something in a letter, and his mother misinterpreted."

"I'd like to punch him one right in the mouth," the Captain said. "There's a war on, and he wants a silver platter!"

"I don't think the boy's to blame, sir. I'm sure we can straighten it out by just asking him. Jewish parents worry—"

"*All* parents worry, for Christ's sake. But they don't get on their high horse and start pulling strings—"

I interrupted, my voice higher, tighter than before. "The home life, Captain, is very important—but you're right, it may sometimes get out of hand. It's a very wonderful thing, Captain, but because it's so close, this kind of thing . . ."

He didn't listen any longer to my attempt to present both myself and Lightfoot Harry with an explanation for the letter. He turned back to the phone. "Sir?" he said. "Sir—Marx, here, tells me Jews have a tendency to be pushy. He says he thinks we can settle it right here in the company . . . Yes, sir . . . I *will* call back, sir, soon as I can." He hung up. "Where are the men, Sergeant?"

"On the range."

With a whack on the top of his helmet, he crushed it down over his eyes again, and charged out of his chair. "We're going for a ride," he said.

The Captain drove, and I sat beside him. It was a hot spring day, and under my newly starched fatigues I felt as though my armpits were melting down into my sides and chest. The roads were dry, and by the time we reached the firing range, my teeth felt gritty with dust, though my mouth had been shut the whole trip. The Captain slammed the brakes on and told me to get the hell out and find Grossbart.

I found him on his belly, firing wildly at the five-hundred-feet target. Waiting their turns behind him were Halpern and Fishbein. Fishbein, wearing a pair of steel-rimmed G.I. glasses I hadn't seen on him before, had the appearance of an old peddler who would gladly have sold you his rifle and the cartridges that were slung all over him. I stood back by the ammo boxes, waiting for Grossbart to finish spraying the distant target. Fishbein straggled back to stand near me.

"Hello, Sergeant Marx," he said.

"How are you?" I mumbled.

"Fine, thank you. Sheldon's really a good shot."

"I didn't notice."

"I'm not so good, but I think I'm getting the hang of it now. Sergeant, I don't mean to, you know, ask what I shouldn't—" The boy stopped. He was trying to speak intimately, but the noise of the shooting forced him to shout at me.

"What is it?" I asked. Down the range, I saw Captain Barrett standing up in the jeep, scanning the line for me and Grossbart.

"My parents keep asking and asking where we're going," Fishbein said. "Everybody says the Pacific. I don't care, but my parents—If I could relieve their minds, I think I could concentrate more on my shooting."

"I don't know where, Fishbein. Try to concentrate anyway."

"Sheldon says you might be able to find out."

"I don't know a thing, Fishbein. You just take it easy, and don't let Sheldon—"

"*I'm* taking it easy, Sergeant. It's at home—"

Grossbart had finished on the line, and was dusting his fatigues with one hand. I called to him. "Grossbart, the Captain wants to see you."

He came toward us. His eyes blazed and twinkled. "Hi!"

"Don't point that rifle!" I said.

"I wouldn't shoot you, Sarge." He gave me a smile as wide as a pumpkin, and turned the barrel aside.

"Damn you, Grossbart, this is no joke! Follow me."

I walked ahead of him, and had the awful suspicion that, behind me, Grossbart was *marching,* his rifle on his shoulder as though he were a one-man detachment. At the jeep, he gave the Captain a rifle salute. "Private Sheldon Grossbart, sir."

"At ease, Grossman." The Captain sat down, slid over the empty seat, and, crooking a finger, invited Grossbart closer.

"Bart, sir. Sheldon Gross*bart.* It's a common error." Grossbart nodded at me: *I* understood, he indicated. I looked away just as the mess truck pulled up to the range, disgorging a half-dozen K.P.s with rolled-up sleeves. The mess sergeant screamed at them while they set up the chow line equipment.

"Grossbart, your mama wrote some congressman that we don't feed you right. Do you know that?" the Captain said.

"It was my father, sir. He wrote to Representative Franconi that my religion forbids me to eat certain foods."

"What religion is that, Grossbart?"

"Jewish."

" 'Jewish, *sir,*' " I said to Grossbart.

"Excuse me, sir, Jewish, sir."

"What have you been living on?" the Captain asked. "You've been in the Army a month already. You don't look to me like you're falling to pieces."

"I eat because I have to, sir. But Sergeant Marx will testify to the fact that I don't eat one mouthful more than I need to in order to survive."

"Is that so, Marx?" Barrett asked.

"I've never seen Grossbart eat, sir," I said.

"But you heard the rabbi," Grossbart said. "He told us what to do, and I listened."

The Captain looked at me. "Well, Marx?"

"I still don't know what he eats and doesn't eat, sir."

Grossbart raised his arms to plead with me, and it looked for a moment as though he were going to hand me his weapon to hold. "But, Sergeant—"

"Look, Grossbart, just answer the Captain's questions," I said sharply.

Barrett smiled at me, and I resented it. "All right, Grossbart," he said. "What is it you want? The little piece of paper? You want out?"

"No, sir. Only to be allowed to live as a Jew. And for the others, too."

"What others?"

"Fishbein, sir, and Halpern."

"They don't like the way we serve, either?"

"Halpern throws up, sir. I've seen it."

"I thought *you* throw up."

"Just once, sir. I didn't know the sausage was sausage."

"We'll give menus, Grossbart. We'll show training films about the food, so you can identify when we're trying to poison you."

Grossbart did not answer. The men had been organized into two long chow lines. At the tail end of one, I spotted Fishbein—or, rather, his glasses spotted me. They winked sunlight back at me. Halpern stood next to him, patting the inside of his collar with a khaki handkerchief. They moved with the line as it began to edge up toward the food. The mess sergeant was still screaming at the K.P.s. For a moment, I was actually terrified by the thought that somehow the mess sergeant was going to become involved in Grossbart's problem.

"Marx," the Captain said, "you're a Jewish fella—am I right?"

I played straight man. "Yes, sir."

"How long you been in the Army? Tell this boy."

"Three years and two months."

"A year in combat, Grossbart. Twelve goddam months in combat all through Europe. I admire this man." The Captain snapped a wrist against my chest. "Do you hear him peeping about the food? Do you? I want an answer, Grossbart. Yes or no."

"No, sir."

"And why not? He's a Jewish fella."

"Some things are more important to some Jews than other things to other Jews."

Barrett blew up. "Look, Grossbart. Marx, here, is a good man—a goddam hero. When you were in high school, Sergeant Marx was killing Germans. Who does more for the Jews—you, by throwing up over a lousy piece of sausage, a piece of first-cut meat, or Marx, by killing those Nazi bastards? If I was a Jew, Grossbart, I'd kiss this man's feet. He's a goddam hero, and *he* eats what we give him. Why do you have to cause trouble is what I want to know! What is it you're buckin' for—a discharge?"

"No, sir."

"I'm talking to a wall! Sergeant, get him out of my way." Barrett swung himself back into the driver's seat. "I'm going to see the chaplain." The engine roared, the jeep spun around in a whirl of dust, and the Captain was headed back to camp.

For a moment, Grossbart and I stood side by side, watching the jeep. Then he looked at me and said, "I don't want to start trouble. That's the first thing they toss up to us."

When he spoke, I saw that his teeth were white and straight, and the sight of them suddenly made me understand that Grossbart actually did have parents—that once upon a time someone had taken little Sheldon to the dentist. He was their son. Despite all the talk about his parents, it was hard to believe in Grossbart as a child, an heir—as related by blood to anyone, mother, father, or, above all, to me. This realization led me to another.

"What does your father do, Grossbart?" I asked as we started to walk back toward the chow line.

"He's a tailor."

"An American?"

"Now, yes. A son in the Army," he said, jokingly.

"And your mother?" I asked.

He winked. "A *ballabusta*. She practically sleeps with a dustcloth in her hand."

"She's also an immigrant?"

"All she talks is Yiddish, still."

"And your father, too?"

"A little English, 'Clean,' 'Press,' 'Take the pants in.' That's the extent of it. But they're good to me."

"Then, Grossbart—" I reached out and stopped him. He turned toward me, and when our eyes met, his seemed to jump back, to shiver in their sockets. "Grossbart—you were the one who wrote that letter, weren't you?"

It took only a second or two for his eyes to flash happy again. "Yes." He walked on, and I kept pace. "It's what my father *would* have written if he had known how. It was his name, though. *He* signed it. He even mailed it. I sent it home. For the New York postmark."

I was astonished, and he saw it. With complete seriousness, he thrust his right arm in front of me. "Blood is blood, Sergeant," he said, pinching the blue vein in his wrist.

"What the hell *are* you trying to do, Grossbart?" I asked. "I've seen you eat. Do you know that? I told the Captain I don't know what you eat, but I've seen you eat like a hound at chow."

"We work hard, Sergeant. We're in training. For a furnace to work, you've got to feed it coal."

"Why did you say in the letter that you threw up all the time?"

"I was really talking about Mickey there. I was talking *for* him. He would never write, Sergeant, though I pleaded with him. He'll waste away to nothing if I don't help. Sergeant, I used my name—my father's name—but it's Mickey, and Fishbein, too, I'm watching out for."

"You're a regular Messiah, aren't you?"

We were at the chow line now.

"That's a good one, Sergeant," he said, smiling. "But who knows? Who can tell? Maybe you're the Messiah—a little bit. What Mickey says is the Messiah is a collective idea. He went to Yeshiva, Mickey, for a while. He says *together* we're the Messiah. Me a little bit, you a little bit. You should hear that kid talk, Sergeant, when he gets going."

"Me a little bit, you a little bit," I said. "You'd like to believe that, wouldn't you, Grossbart? That would make everything so clean for you."

"It doesn't seem too bad a thing to believe, Sergeant. It only means we should all *give* a little, is all."

I walked off to eat my rations with the other noncoms.

Two days later, a letter addressed to Captain Barrett passed over my desk. It had come through the chain of command—from the office of Congressman Franconi, where it had been received, to General Lyman, to Colonel Sousa, to Major Lamont, now to Captain Barrett. I read it over twice. It was dated May 14, the day Barrett had spoken with Grossbart on the rifle range.

Dear Congressman:

First let me thank you for your interest in behalf of my son, Private Sheldon Grossbart. Fortunately, I was able to speak with Sheldon on the phone the other night, and I think I've been able to solve our problem. He is, as I mentioned in my last letter, a very religious boy, and it was only with the greatest difficulty that I could persuade him that the religious thing to do—what God Himself would want Sheldon to do—would be to suffer the pangs of religious remorse for the good of his country and all mankind. It took some doing, Congressman, but finally he saw the light. In fact, what he said (and I wrote down the words on a scratch pad so as never to forget), what he said was "I guess you're right, Dad. So many millions of my fellow-Jews gave up their lives to the enemy, the least I can do is live for a while minus a bit of my heritage so as to help end this struggle and regain for all the children of God dignity and humanity." That, Congressman, would make any father proud.

By the way, Sheldon wanted me to know—and to pass on to you—the name of a soldier who helped him reach this decision: SERGEANT NATHAN MARX. Sergeant Marx is a combat veteran who is Sheldon's first sergeant. This man has helped Sheldon over some of the first hurdles he's had to face in the Army, and is in part responsible for Sheldon's changing his mind about the dietary laws. I know Sheldon would appreciate any recognition Marx could receive.

Thank you and good luck. I look forward to seeing your name on the next election ballot.

Respectfully,
Samuel E. Grossbart

Attached to the Grossbart communiqué was another, addressed to General Marshall Lyman, the post commander, and signed by Representative Charles E. Franconi, of the House of Representatives. The communiqué informed General Lyman that Sergeant Nathan Marx was a credit to the U.S. Army and the Jewish people.

What was Grossbart's motive in recanting? Did he feel he'd gone too far? Was the letter a strategic retreat—a crafty attempt to strengthen what he considered our alliance? Or had he actually changed his mind, via an imaginary dialogue between Grossbart *père* and Grossbart *fils?* I was puzzled, but only for a few days—that is, only until I realized that, whatever his reasons, he had actually decided to disappear from my life; he was going to allow himself to become just another trainee. I saw him at inspection, but he never winked; at chow formations, but he never flashed me a sign. On Sunday, with the other trainees, he would sit around watching the noncoms' softball team, for which I pitched, but not once did he speak an unnecessary word to me. Fishbein and Halpern retreated, too—at Grossbart's command, I was sure. Apparently he had seen that wisdom lay in turning back before he plunged over into the ugliness of privilege undeserved. Our separation allowed me to forgive him our past encounters, and finally, to admire him for his good sense.

Meanwhile, free of Grossbart, I grew used to my job and my administrative tasks. I stepped on a scale one day, and discovered I had truly become a noncombatant; I had gained seven pounds. I found patience to get past the first three pages of a book. I thought about the future more and more, and wrote letters to girls I'd known before the war. I even got a few answers. I sent away to Columbia for a Law School catalogue. I continued to follow the war in the Pacific, but it was not my war. I thought I could see the end, and sometimes, at night, I dreamed that I was walking on the streets of Manhattan—Broadway, Third Avenue, 116th Street, where I had lived the three years I attended Columbia. I curled myself around these dreams and I began to be happy.

And then, one Sunday, when everybody was away and I was alone in the orderly room reading a month-old copy of the *Sporting News,* Grossbart reappeared.

"You a baseball fan, Sergeant?"

I looked up. "How are you?"

"Fine," Grossbart said. "They're making a soldier out of me."

"How are Fishbein and Halpern?"

"Coming along," he said. "We've got no training this afternoon. They're at the movies."

"How come you're not with them?"

"I wanted to come over and say hello."

He smiled—a shy, regular-guy smile, as though he and I well knew that our friendship drew its sustenance from unexpected visits, remembered birthdays, and borrowed lawnmowers. At first it offended me, and then the feeling was swallowed by the general uneasiness I felt at the thought that everyone on the post was locked away in a dark movie theater and I was here alone with Grossbart. I folded up my paper.

"Sergeant," he said, "I'd like to ask a favor. It is a favor, and I'm making no bones about it."

He stopped, allowing me to refuse him a hearing—which, of course, forced me into a courtesy I did not intend. "Go ahead."

"Well, actually, it's two favors."

I said nothing.

"The first one's about these rumors. Everybody says we're going to the Pacific."

"As I told your friend Fishbein, I don't know," I said. "You'll just have to wait to find out. Like everybody else."

"You think there's a chance of any of us going East?"

"Germany?" I said. "Maybe."

"I meant New York."

"I don't think so, Grossbart. Offhand."

"Thanks for the information, Sergeant," he said.

"It's not information, Grossbart. Just what I surmise."

"It certainly would be good to be near home. My parents—you know." He took a step toward the door and then turned back. "Oh, the other thing. May I ask the other?"

"What is it?"

"The other thing is—I've got relatives in St. Louis, and they say they'll give me a whole Passover dinner if I can get down there. God, Sergeant, that'd mean an awful lot to me."

I stood up. "No passes during basic, Grossbart."

"But we're off from now till Monday morning, Sergeant. I could leave the post and no one would even know."

"I'd know. You'd know."

"But that's all. Just the two of us. Last night, I called my aunt, and you should have heard her. 'Come—come,' she said. 'I got gefilte fish, *chrain*—the works!' Just a day, Sergeant. I'd take the blame if anything happened."

"The Captain isn't here to sign a pass."

"You could sign."

"Look, Grossbart—"

"Sergeant, for two months, practically, I've been eating *trafe* till I want to die."

"I thought you'd made up your mind to live with it. To be minus a little bit of heritage."

He pointed a finger at me. "You!" he said. "That wasn't for you to read."

"I read it. So what?"

"The letter was addressed to a congressman."

"Grossbart, don't feed me any baloney. You *wanted* me to read it."

"Why are you persecuting me, Sergeant?"

"Are you kidding!"

"I've run into this before," he said, "but never from my own!"

"Get out of here, Grossbart! Get the hell out of my sight!"

He did not move. "Ashamed, that's what you are," he said. "So you take it out on the rest of us. They say Hitler himself was half a Jew. Hearing you, I wouldn't doubt it."

"What are you trying to do with me, Grossbart?" I asked him. "What are you after? You want me to give you special privileges, to change the food, to find out about your orders, to give you weekend passes."

"You even talk like a goy!" Grossbart shook his fist. "Is this just a weekend pass I'm asking for? Is a Seder sacred, or not?"

Seder! It suddenly occurred to me that Passover had been celebrated weeks before. I said so.

"That's right," he replied. "Who says no? A month ago—and I was in the field eating hash! And now all I ask is a simple favor. A Jewish boy I thought would understand. My aunt's willing to go out of her way—to make a Seder a month later . . ." He turned to go, mumbling.

"Come back here!" I called. He stopped and looked at me. "Grossbart, why can't you be like the rest? Why do you have to stick out like a sore thumb?"

"Because I'm a Jew, Sergeant. I *am* different. Better, maybe not. But different."

"This is a war, Grossbart. For the time being *be* the same."

"I refuse."

"What?"

"I refuse. I can't stop being me, that's all there is to it." Tears came to his eyes. "It's a hard thing to be a Jew. But now I understand what Mickey says—it's a harder thing to stay one." He raised a hand sadly toward me. "Look at *you*."

"Stop crying!"

"Stop this, stop that, stop the other thing! *You* stop, Sergeant. Stop closing your heart to your own!" And, wiping his face with his sleeve, he ran out the door. "The least we can do for one another—the least . . ."

An hour later, looking out of the window, I saw Grossbart headed across the field. He wore a pair of starched khakis and carried a little leather ditty bag. I went out into the heat of the day. It was quiet; not a soul was in sight except, over by the mess hall, four K.P.'s sitting around a pan, sloped forward from their waists, gabbing and peeling potatoes in the sun.

"Grossbart!" I called.

He looked toward me and continued walking.

"Grossbart, get over here!"

He turned and came across the field. Finally, he stood before me.

"Where are you going?" I asked.

"St. Louis. I don't care."

"You'll get caught without a pass."

"So I'll get caught without a pass."

"You'll go to the stockade."

"I'm *in* the stockade." He made an about-face and headed off.

I let him go only a step or two. "Come back here," I said, and he followed me into the office, where I typed out a pass and signed the Captain's name, and my own initials after it.

He took the pass and then, a moment later, reached out and grabbed my hand. "Sergeant, you don't know how much this means to me."

"O.K.," I said. "Don't get in any trouble."

"I wish I could show you how much this means to me."

"Don't do me any favors. Don't write any more congressmen for citations."

He smiled. "You're right. I won't. But let me do something."

"Bring me a piece of that gefilte fish. Just get out of here."

"I will!" he said. "With a slice of carrot and a little horseradish. I won't forget."

"All right. Just show your pass at the gate. And don't tell *anybody*."

"I won't. It's a month late, but a good Yom Tov to you."

"Good Yom Tov, Grossbart," I said.

"You're a good Jew, Sergeant. You like to think you have a hard heart, but underneath you're a fine, decent man. I mean that."

Those last three words touched me more than any words from Grossbart's mouth had the right to. "All right, Grossbart," I said. "Now call me 'sir,' and get the hell out of here."

He ran out the door and was gone. I felt very pleased with myself; it was a great relief to stop fighting Grossbart, and it had cost me nothing. Barrett would never find out, and if he did, I could manage to invent some excuse. For a while, I sat at my desk, comfortable in my decision. Then the screen door flew back and Grossbart burst in again. "Sergeant!" he said. Behind him I saw Fishbein and Halpern, both in starched khakis, both carrying ditty bags like Grossbart's.

"Sergeant, I caught Mickey and Larry coming out of the movies. I almost missed them."

"Grossbart—did I say to tell no one?" I said.

"But my aunt said I could bring friends. That I should, in fact."

"*I'm* the Sergeant, Grossbart—not your aunt!"

Grossbart looked at me in disbelief. He pulled Halpern up by his sleeve. "Mickey, tell the Sergeant what this would mean to you."

Halpern looked at me and, shrugging, said, "A lot."

Fishbein stepped forward without prompting. "This would mean a great deal to me and my parents, Sergeant Marx."

"No!" I shouted.

Grossbart was shaking his head. "Sergeant, I could see you denying me, but how can you deny Mickey, a Yeshiva boy—that's beyond me."

"I'm not denying Mickey anything," I said. "You just pushed a little too hard, Grossbart. *You* denied him."

"I'll give him my pass, then," Grossbart said. "I'll give him my aunt's address and a little note. At least let him go."

In a second, he had crammed the pass into Halpern's pants pocket. Halpern looked at me, and so did Fishbein. Grossbart was at the door, pushing it open. "Mickey, bring me a piece of gefilte fish, at least," he said, and then he was outside again.

The three of us looked at one another, and then I said, "Halpern, hand that pass over."

He took it from his pocket and gave it to me. Fishbein had now moved to the doorway, where he lingered. He stood there for a moment with his mouth slightly open, and then he pointed to himself. "And me?" he asked.

His utter ridiculousness exhausted me. I slumped down in my seat and felt pulses knocking at the back of my eyes. "Fishbein," I said, "you understand I'm not trying to deny you anything, don't you? If it was my Army, I'd serve gefilte fish in the mess hall. I'd sell *kugel* in the PX, honest to God."

Halpern smiled.

"You understand, don't you, Halpern?"

"Yes, Sergeant."

"And you, Fishbein? I don't want enemies. I'm just like you—I want to serve my time and go home. I miss the same things you miss."

"Then, Sergeant," Fishbein said, "why don't you come, too?"

"Where?"

"To St. Louis. To Shelly's aunt. We'll have a regular Seder. Play hide-the-matzoh." He gave me a broad, black-toothed smile.

I saw Grossbart again, on the other side of the screen.

"Psst!" He waved a piece of paper. "Mickey, here's the address. Tell her I couldn't get away."

Halpern did not move. He looked at me, and I saw the shrug moving up his arms into his shoulders again. I took the cover off my typewriter and made out passes for him and Fishbein. "Go," I said. "The three of you."

I thought Halpern was going to kiss my hand.

That afternoon, in a bar in Joplin, I drank beer and listened with half an ear to the Cardinal game. I tried to look squarely at what I'd become involved in, and began to wonder if perhaps the struggle with Grossbart wasn't as much my fault as his. What was I that I had to *muster* generous feelings? Who was I to have been feeling so grudging, so tight-hearted? After all, I wasn't being asked to move the world. Had I a right, then, or a reason, to clamp down on Grossbart, when that meant clamping down on Halpern, too? And Fishbein—that ugly, agreeable soul? Out of the many recollections of my childhood that had tumbled over me these past days I heard my grandmother's voice: "What are you making a *tsimmes?*" It was what she would ask my mother when, say, I cut myself while doing something I shouldn't have done, and her daughter was busy bawling me out. I needed a hug and a kiss, and my mother would moralize. But my grandmother knew—mercy overrides justice. I should have known it, too. Who was Nathan Marx to be such a penny pincher with kindness? Surely, I thought, the Messiah himself—if He should ever come—won't niggle over nickels and dimes. God willing, he'll hug and kiss.

The next day, while I was playing softball over on the parade ground, I decided to ask Bob Wright, who was noncom in charge of Classification and Assignment, where he thought our trainees would be sent when their cycle ended, in two weeks. I asked casually, between innings, and he said, "They're pushing them all into the Pacific. Shulman cut the orders on your boys the other day."

The news shocked me, as though I were the father of Halpern, Fishbein, and Grossbart.

That night, I was just sliding into sleep when someone tapped on my door. "Who is it?" I asked.

"Sheldon."

He opened the door and came in. For a moment, I felt his presence without being able to see him. "How was it?" I asked.

He popped into sight in the near-darkness before me. "Great, Sergeant." Then he was sitting on the edge of the bed. I sat up.

"How about you?" he asked. "Have a nice weekend?"

"Yes."

"The others went to sleep." He took a deep, paternal breath. We sat silent for a while, and a homey feeling invaded my ugly little cubicle; the door was locked, the cat was out, the children were safely in bed.

"Sergeant, can I tell you something? Personal?"

I did not answer, and he seemed to know why. "Not about me. About Mickey. Sergeant, I never felt for anybody like I feel for him. Last night I heard Mickey in the bed next to me. He was crying so, it could have broken your heart. Real sobs."

"I'm sorry to hear that."

"I had to talk to him to stop him. He held my hand, Sergeant—he wouldn't let it go. He was almost hysterical. He kept saying if he only knew where we were going. Even if he knew it *was* the Pacific, that would be better than nothing. Just to know."

Long ago, someone had taught Grossbart the sad rule that only lies can get the truth. Not that I couldn't believe in the fact of Halpern's crying; his eyes *always* seemed red-rimmed. But, fact or not, it became a lie when Grossbart uttered it. He was entirely strategic. But then—it came with the force of indictment—so was I! There are strategies of aggression, but there are strategies of retreat as well. And so, recognizing that I myself had not been without craft and guile, I told him what I knew. "It is the Pacific."

He let out a small gasp, which was not a lie. "I'll tell him. I wish it was otherwise."

"So do I."

He jumped on my words. "You mean you think you could do something? A change, maybe?"

"No, I couldn't do a thing."

"Don't you know anybody over at C. and A.?"

"Grossbart, there's nothing I can do," I said. "If your orders are for the Pacific, then it's the Pacific."

"But Mickey—"

"Mickey, you, me—everybody, Grossbart. There's nothing to be done. Maybe the war'll end before you go. Pray for a miracle."

"But—"

"Good night, Grossbart." I settled back, and was relieved to feel the springs unbend as Grossbart rose to leave. I could see him clearly now; his jaw had dropped, and he looked like a dazed prizefighter. I noticed for the first time a little paper bag in his hand.

"Grossbart." I smiled. "My gift?"

"Oh, yes, Sergeant. Here—from all of us." He handed me the bag. "It's egg roll."

"Egg roll?" I accepted the bag and felt a damp grease spot on the bottom. I opened it, sure that Grossbart was joking.

"We thought you'd probably like it. You know—Chinese egg roll. We thought you'd probably have a taste for—"

"Your aunt served egg roll?"

"She wasn't home."

"Grossbart, she invited you. You told me she invited you and your friends."

"I know," he said. "I just reread the letter. *Next* week."

I got out of bed and walked to the window. "Grossbart," I said. But I was not calling to him.

"What?"

"What are you, Grossbart? Honest to God, what are you?"

I think it was the first time I'd asked him a question for which he didn't have an immediate answer.

"How can you do this to people?" I went on.

"Sergeant, the day away did us all a world of good. Fishbein, you should see him, he *loves* Chinese food."

"But the Seder," I said.

"We took second best, Sergeant."

Rage came charging at me. I didn't sidestep. "Grossbart, you're a liar!" I said. "You're a schemer and a crook. You've got no respect for anything. Nothing at all. Not for me, the truth—not even for poor Halpern. You use us all—"

"Sergeant, Sergeant, I feel for Mickey. Honest to God, I do. I *love* Mickey. I try—"

"You try! You feel!" I lurched toward him and grabbed his shirt front. I shook him furiously. "Grossbart, get out! Get out and stay the hell away from me. Because if I see you, I'll make your life miserable. *You understand that?*"

"Yes."

I let him free, and when he walked from the room, I wanted to spit on the floor where he had stood. I couldn't stop the fury. It engulfed me, owned me, till it seemed I could only rid myself of it with tears or an act of violence. I snatched from the bed the bag Grossbart had given me and, with all my strength, threw it out the window. And the next morning, as the men policed the area around the barracks, I heard a great cry go up from one of the trainees, who had been anticipating only his morning handful of cigarette butts and candy wrappers. "Egg roll!" he shouted. "Holy Christ, Chinese goddam egg roll!"

A week later, when I read the orders that had come down from C. and A., I couldn't believe my eyes. Every single trainee was to be shipped to Camp Stoneman, California, and from there to the Pacific—every trainee but one. Private Sheldon Grossbart. He was to be sent to Fort Monmouth, New Jersey. I read the mimeographed sheet several times. Dee, Farrell, Fishbein, Fuselli, Fylypowycz, Glinicki, Gromke, Gucwa, Halpern, Hardy, Helebrandt, right down to Anton Zygadlo—all were to be headed West before the month was out. All except Grossbart. He had pulled a string, and I wasn't it.

I lifted the phone and called C. and A.

The voice on the other end said smartly, "Corporal Shulman, sir."

"Let me speak to Sergeant Wright."

"Who is this calling, sir?"

"Sergeant Marx."

And, to my surprise, the voice said, "*Oh!*" Then, "Just a minute, Sergeant."

Shulman's "*Oh!*" stayed with me while I waited for Wright to come to the phone. Why "*Oh!*"? Who was Shulman? And then, so simply, I knew I'd discovered the string that Grossbart had pulled. In fact, I could hear Grossbart the day he'd discovered Shulman in the PX, or in the bowling alley, or maybe even at services. "Glad to meet you. Where you from? Bronx? Me, too. Do you know So-and-So? And So-and-So? Me, too! You work at C. and A.? Really? Hey, how's chances of getting East? Could you do something? Change something? Swindle, cheat, lie? We gotta help each other, you know. If the Jews in Germany . . ."

Bob Wright answered the phone. "How are you, Nate? How's the pitching arm?"

"Good. Bob, I wonder if you could do me a favor." I heard clearly my own words, and they so reminded me of Grossbart that I dropped more easily than I could have imagined into what I had planned. "This may sound crazy, Bob, but I got a kid here on orders to Monmouth who wants them changed. He had a brother killed in Europe, and he's hot to go to the Pacific. Says he'd feel like a coward if he wound up Stateside. I don't know, Bob—can anything be done? Put somebody else in the Monmouth slot?"

"Who?" he asked cagily.

"Anybody. First guy in the alphabet. I don't care. The kid just asked if something could be done."

"What's his name?"

"Grossbart, Sheldon."

Wright didn't answer.

"Yeah," I said. "He's a Jewish kid, so he thought I could help him out. You know."

"I guess I can do something," he finally said. "The Major hasn't been around for weeks. Temporary duty to the golf course. I'll try, Nate, that's all I can say."

"I'd appreciate it, Bob. See you Sunday." And I hung up, perspiring.

The following day, the corrected orders appeared: Fishbein, Fuselli, Fylypowycz, Glinicki, Gromke, Grossbart, Gucwa, Halpern, Hardy . . . Lucky Private Harley Alton was to go to Fort Monmouth, New Jersey, where, for some reason or other, they wanted an enlisted man with infantry training.

After chow that night, I stopped back at the orderly room to straighten out the guard-duty roster. Grossbart was waiting for me. He spoke first.

"You son of a bitch!"

I sat down at my desk, and while he glared at me, I began to make the necessary alterations in the duty roster.

"What do you have against me?" he cried. "Against my family? Would it kill you for me to be near my father, God knows how many months he has left to him?"

"Why so?"

"His heart," Grossbart said. "He hasn't had enough troubles in a lifetime, you've got to add to them. I curse the day I ever met you, Marx! Shulman told me what happened over there. There's no limit to your anti-Semitism, is there? The damage you've done here isn't enough. You have to make a special phone call! You really want me dead!"

I made the last notations in the duty roster and got up to leave. "Good night, Grossbart."

"You owe me an explanation!" He stood in my path.

"Sheldon, you're the one who owes explanations."

He scowled. "To *you?*"

"To me, I think so—yes. Mostly to Fishbein and Halpern."

"That's right, twist things around. I owe nobody nothing. I've done all I could for them. Now I think I've got the right to watch out for myself."

"For each other we have to learn to watch out, Sheldon. You told me yourself."

"You call this watching out for me—what you did?"

"No. For all of us."

I pushed him aside and started for the door. I heard his furious breathing behind me, and it sounded like steam rushing from an engine of terrible strength.

"*You'll* be all right," I said from the door. And, I thought, so would Fishbein and Halpern be all right, even in the Pacific, if only Grossbart continued to see—in the obsequiousness of the one, the soft spirituality of the other—some profit for himself.

I stood outside the orderly room, and I heard Grossbart weeping behind me. Over in the barracks, in the lighted windows, I could see the boys in their T shirts sitting on their bunks talking about their orders, as they'd been doing for the past two days. With a kind of quiet nervousness, they polished shoes, shined belt buckles, squared away underwear, trying as best they could to accept their fate. Behind me, Grossbart swallowed hard, accepting his. And then, resisting with all my will an impulse to turn and seek pardon for my vindictiveness, I accepted my own.

QUESTIONS FOR DISCUSSION AND WRITING

1. How many different conflicts does Sheldon Grossbart create in attempting to claim his rights? Explain how Grossbart's trip to St. Louis brings these conflicts to a crisis. How does Marx resolve the trouble Grossbart causes?

2. How does Marx characterize the three Jewish recruits to Captain Barrett? How does Captain Barrett describe Marx to the three recruits? What specific features of Grossbart's character does Marx find most exasperating?
3. What details in the story best reveal the value of army life as Marx sees it? What past life has he "anesthetized" in order to pursue his life in the army? How does Grossbart's attempt to evoke that other life give him a momentary advantage in his attempt to manipulate Marx?
4. How does Marx's first-person narration help characterize the dilemmas Grossbart forces him to face? How do Marx's actions and judgments alter his initial description of his "infantryman's heart"? To what extent does his final decision reestablish that point of view?
5. Why does Grossbart's defense of his faith seem "entirely strategic"? How many different "faiths" is Marx asked to defend in this story? Is he able to defend them all? Explain your answer.

83

ISAAC BASHEVIS SINGER

Gimpel the Fool

ISAAC BASHEVIS SINGER (1904–1991) was born in Radzymin, Poland, and educated at Tachkemoni Rabbinical Seminary in Warsaw. After working for over a decade as translator and editor for the Polish press, he emigrated to the United States in 1935 and worked for the *Jewish Daily Forward* in New York City, where he began publishing his stories and sketches in Yiddish. Before he felt sufficiently fluent in English, Singer had to rely on other people to translate his writing. In 1950 he published his first novel in America, *The Family Moskat,* but his discovery by American readers was probably initiated in 1953 by Saul Bellow's magnificent translation of "Gimpel the Fool" for *Partisan Review*. Most of Singer's works draw upon his experiences in the Yiddish-speaking Jewish ghettos of Poland and are preoccupied with the problems of sin and the character of the religious life. His novels include *The Magician of Lublin* (1960), *The Slave* (1962), *The Manor* (1968), *Enemies: A Love Story* (1972), and *Shosha* (1978). He is also the author of an award-winning children's book, *A Day of Pleasure* (1970), and an autobiography, *In My Father's Court* (1966). Singer's many stories are collected in volumes such as *The Spinoza of Market Street and Other Stories* (1961), *A Friend of Kafka's* (1970), and *A Crown of Feathers* (1973), which won the National Book Award. His *Collected Stories* (1981) won the Pulitzer Prize. In 1978, Singer was

awarded the Nobel Prize for Literature. "Gimpel the Fool," reprinted from *A Treasury of Yiddish Stories* (1953), tells of a man who was thought a fool because of his belief that "everything is possible."

1

I am Gimpel the fool. I don't think myself a fool. On the contrary. But that's what folks call me. They gave me the name while I was still in school. I had seven names in all: imbecile, donkey, flax-head, dope, glump, ninny, and fool. The last name stuck. What did my foolishness consist of? I was easy to take in. They said, "Gimpel, you know the rabbi's wife has been brought to childbed?" So I skipped school. Well, it turned out to be a lie. How was I supposed to know? She hadn't had a big belly. But I never looked at her belly. Was that really so foolish? The gang laughed and hee-hawed, stomped and danced and chanted a good-night prayer. And instead of the raisins they give when a woman's lying in, they stuffed my hand full of goat turds. I was no weakling. If I slapped someone he'd see all the way to Cracow. But I'm really not a slugger by nature. I think to myself: Let it pass. So they take advantage of me.

I was coming home from school and heard a dog barking. I'm not afraid of dogs, but of course I never want to start up with them. One of them may be mad, and if he bites there's not a Tartar in the world who can help you. So I made tracks. Then I looked around and saw the whole market place wild with laughter. It was no dog at all but Wolf-Leib the Thief. How was I supposed to know it was he? It sounded like a howling bitch.

When the pranksters and leg-pullers found that I was easy to fool, every one of them tried his luck with me. "Gimpel, the Czar is coming to Frampol; Gimpel, the moon fell down in Turbeen; Gimpel, little Hodel Furpiece found a treasure behind the bathhouse." And I like a golem believed everyone. In the first place, everything is possible, as it is written in the Wisdom of the Fathers, I've forgotten just how. Second, I had to believe when the whole town came down on me! If I ever dared to say, "Ah, you're kidding!" there was trouble. People got angry. "What do you mean! You want to call everyone a liar?" What was I to do? I believed them, and I hope at least that did them some good.

I was an orphan. My grandfather who brought me up was already bent toward the grave. So they turned me over to a baker, and what a time they gave me there! Every woman or girl who came to bake a batch of noodles had to fool me at least once. "Gimpel, there's a fair in heaven; Gimpel, the rabbi gave birth to a calf in the seventh month; Gimpel, a cow flew over the roof and laid brass eggs." A student from the yeshiva came once to buy a roll, and he said, "You, Gimpel, while you stand here scraping with your baker's shovel the Messiah has come. The dead have arisen." "What do you mean?" I said. "I heard no one blowing the ram's horn!" He said, "Are you deaf?" And all began to cry, "We heard it, we heard!" Then in came Rietze the Candle-dipper and called out in her hoarse voice, "Gimpel, your father and mother have stood up from the grave. They're looking for you."

To tell the truth, I knew very well that nothing of the sort had happened, but all the same, as folks were talking, I threw on my wool vest and went out. Maybe something had happened. What did I stand to lose by looking? Well, what a cat music went up! And then I took a vow to believe nothing more. But that was no go either. They confused me so that I didn't know the big end from the small.

I went to the rabbi to get some advice. He said, "It is written, better to be a fool all your days than for one hour to be evil. You are not a fool. They are the fools. For he who causes his neighbor to feel shame loses Paradise himself." Nevertheless the rabbi's daughter took me in. As I left the rabbinical court she said, "Have you kissed the wall yet?" I said, "No; what for?" She answered, "It's the law; you've got to do it after every visit." Well, there didn't seem to be any harm in it. And she burst out laughing. It was a fine trick. She put one over on me, all right.

I wanted to go off to another town, but then everyone got busy matchmaking, and they were after me so they nearly tore my coat tails off. They talked at me and talked until I got water on the ear. She was no chaste maiden, but they told me she was virgin pure. She had a limp, and they said it was deliberate, from coyness. She had a bastard, and they told me the child was her little brother. I cried, "You're wasting your time. I'll never marry that whore." But they said indignantly, "What a way to talk! Aren't you ashamed of yourself? We can take you to the rabbi and have you fined for giving her a bad name." I saw then that I wouldn't escape them so easily and I thought: They're set on making me their butt. But when you're married the husband's the master, and if that's all right with her it's agreeable to me too. Besides, you can't pass through life unscathed, nor expect to.

I went to her clay house, which was built on the sand, and the whole gang hollering and chorusing, came after me. They acted like bear-baiters. When we came to the well they stopped all the same. They were afraid to start anything with Elka. Her mouth would open as if it were on a hinge, and she had a fierce tongue. I entered the house. Lines were strung from wall to wall and clothes were drying. Barefoot she stood by the tub, doing the wash. She was dressed in a worn hand-me-down gown of plush. She had her hair put up in braids and pinned across her head. It took my breath away, almost, the reek of it all.

Evidently she knew who I was. She took a look at me and said, "Look who's here! He's come, the drip. Grab a seat."

I told her all; I denied nothing. "Tell me the truth," I said, "are you really a virgin; and is that mischievous Yechiel actually your little brother? Don't be deceitful with me, for I'm an orphan."

"I'm an orphan myself," she answered, "and whoever tries to twist you up, may the end of his nose take a twist. But don't let them think they can take advantage of me. I want a dowry of fifty guilders, and let them take up a collection besides. Otherwise they can kiss my you-know-what." She was very plainspoken. I said, "It's the bride and not the groom who gives a dowry." Then she said, "Don't bargain with me. Either a flat 'yes' or a flat 'no'—Go back where you came from."

I thought: No bread will ever be baked from *this* dough. But ours is not a poor town. They consented to everything and proceeded with the wedding. It so happened that there was a dysentery epidemic at the time. The ceremony was held at the cemetery gates, near the little corpse-washing hut. The fellows got drunk. While the marriage contract was being drawn up I heard the most pious high rabbi ask, "Is the bride a widow or a divorced woman?" And the sexton's wife answered for her, "Both a widow and divorced." It was a black moment for me. But what was I to do, run away from under the marriage canopy?

There was singing and dancing. An old granny danced opposite me, hugging a braided white *chalah*. The master of revels made a "God 'a mercy" in memory of the bride's parents. The schoolboys threw burrs, as on Tishe b'Av fast day. There were a lot of gifts after the sermon: a noodle board, a kneading trough, a bucket, brooms, ladles, household articles galore. Then I took a look and saw two strapping young men carrying a crib. "What do we need this for?" I asked. So they said, "Don't rack your brains about it. It's all right, it'll come in handy." I realized I was going to be rooked. Take it another way though, what did I stand to lose? I reflected: I'll see what comes of it. A whole town can't go altogether crazy.

2

At night I came where my wife lay, but she wouldn't let me in. "Say, look here, is this what they married us for?" I said. And she said, "My monthly has come." "But yesterday they took you to the ritual bath, and that's afterward, isn't it supposed to be?" "Today isn't yesterday," said she, "and yesterday's not today. You can beat it if you don't like it." In short, I waited.

Not four months later she was in childbed. The townsfolk hid their laughter with their knuckles. But what could I do? She suffered intolerable pains and clawed at the walls. "Gimpel," she cried, "I'm going. Forgive me!" The house filled with women. They were boiling pans of water. The screams rose to the welkin.

The thing to do was to go to the House of Prayer to repeat Psalms, and that was what I did.

The townsfolk liked that, all right. I stood in a corner saying Psalms and prayers, and they shook their heads at me. "Pray, pray!" they told me. "Prayer never made any woman pregnant." One of the congregation put a straw to my mouth and said, "Hay for the cows." There was something to that too, by God!

She gave birth to a boy. Friday at the synagogue the sexton stood up before the Ark, pounded on the reading table, and announced, "The wealthy Reb Gimpel invites the congregation to a feast in honor of the birth of a son." The whole House of Prayer rang with laughter. My face was flaming. But there was nothing I could do. After all, I *was* the one responsible for the circumcision honors and rituals.

Half the town came running. You couldn't wedge another soul in. Women brought peppered chick-peas, and there was a keg of beer from the tavern. I ate and drank as much as anyone, and they all congratulated me. Then there was a circumcision, and I named the boy after my father, may he rest in peace. When all were gone and I was left with my wife alone, she thrust her head through the bed-curtain and called me to her.

"Gimpel," said she, "why are you silent? Has your ship gone and sunk?"

"What shall I say?" I answered. "A fine thing you've done to me! If my mother had known of it she'd have died a second time."

She said, "Are you crazy, or what?"

"How can you make such a fool," I said, "of one who should be the lord and master?"

"What's the matter with you?" she said. "What have you taken it into your head to imagine?"

I saw that I must speak bluntly and openly. "Do you think this is the way to use an orphan?" I said. "You have borne a bastard."

She answered, "Drive this foolishness out of your head. The child is yours."

"How can he be mine?" I argued. "He was born seventeen weeks after the wedding."

She told me then that he was premature. I said, "Isn't he a little too premature?" She said, she had had a grandmother who carried just as short a time and she resembled this grandmother of hers as one drop of water does another. She swore to it with such oaths that you would have believed a peasant at the fair if he had used them. To tell the plain truth, I didn't believe her; but when I talked it over next day with the schoolmaster he told me that the very same thing had happened to Adam and Eve. Two they went up to bed, and four they descended.

"There isn't a woman in the world who is not the granddaughter of Eve," he said.

That was how it was; they argued me dumb. But then, who really knows how such things are?

I began to forget my sorrow. I loved the child madly, and he loved me too. As soon as he saw me he'd wave his little hands and want me to pick him up, and when he was colicky I was the only one who could pacify him. I bought him a little bone teething ring and a little gilded cap. He was forever catching the evil eye from someone, and then I had to run to get one of those abracadabras for him that would get him out of it. I worked like an ox. You know how expenses go up when there's an infant in the house. I don't want to lie about it; I didn't dislike Elka either, for that matter. She swore at me and cursed, and I couldn't get enough of her. What strength she had! One of her looks could rob you of the power of speech. And her orations! Pitch and sulphur, that's what they were full of, and yet somehow also full of charm. I adored her every word. She gave me bloody wounds though.

In the evening I brought her a white loaf as well as a dark one, and also poppyseed rolls I baked myself. I thieved because of her and swiped everything I could lay hands on: macaroons, raisins, almonds, cakes. I hope I may be forgiven for stealing from the Saturday pots the women left to warm in the baker's oven. I would take out scraps of meat, a chunk of pudding, a chicken leg or head, a piece of tripe, whatever I could nip quickly. She ate and became fat and handsome.

I had to sleep away from home all during the week, at the bakery. On Friday nights when I got home she always made an excuse of some sort. Either she had heartburn, or a stitch in the side, or hiccups, or headaches. You know what women's excuses are. I had a bitter time of it. It was rough. To add to it, this little brother of hers, the bastard, was growing bigger. He'd put lumps on me, and when I wanted to hit back she'd open her mouth and curse so powerfully I saw a green haze floating before my eyes. Ten times a day she threatened to divorce me. Another man in my place would have taken French leave and disappeared. But I'm the type that bears it and says nothing. What's one to do? Shoulders are from God, and burdens too.

One night there was a calamity in the bakery; the oven burst, and we almost had a fire. There was nothing to do but go home, so I went home. Let me, I thought, also taste the joy of sleeping in bed in mid-week. I didn't want to wake the sleeping mite and tiptoed into the house. Coming in, it seemed to me that I heard not the snoring of one but, as it were, a double snore, one a thin enough snore and the other like the snoring of a slaughtered ox. Oh, I didn't like that! I didn't like it at all. I went up to the bed, and things suddenly turned black. Next to Elka lay a man's form. Another in my place would have made an uproar, and enough noise to rouse the whole town, but the thought occurred to me that I might wake the child. A little thing like that—why frighten a little swallow, I thought. All right then, I went back to the bakery and stretched out on a sack of flour and till morning I never shut an eye. I shivered as if I had had malaria. "Enough of being a donkey," I said to myself. "Gimpel isn't going to be a sucker all his life. There's a limit even to the foolishness of a fool like Gimpel."

In the morning I went to the rabbi to get advice, and it made a great commotion in the town. They sent the beadle for Elka right away. She came, carrying the child. And what do you think she did? She denied it, denied everything, bone and stone! "He's out of his head," she said. "I know nothing of dreams or divinations." They yelled at her, warned her, hammered on the table, but she stuck to her guns: it was a false accusation, she said.

The butchers and the horse-traders took her part. One of the lads from the slaughterhouse came by and said to me, "We've got our eye on you, you're a marked man." Meanwhile the child started to bear down and soiled itself. In the rabbinical court there was an Ark of the Covenant, and they couldn't allow that, so they sent Elka away.

I said to the rabbi, "What shall I do?"

"You must divorce her at once," said he.

"And what if she refuses?" I asked.

He said, "You must serve the divorce. That's all you'll have to do."

I said, "Well, all right, Rabbi. Let me think about it."

"There's nothing to think about," said he. "You mustn't remain under the same roof with her."

"And if I want to see the child?" I asked

"Let her go, the harlot," said he, "and her brood of bastards with her."

The verdict he gave was that I mustn't even cross her threshold—never again, as long as I should live.

During the day it didn't bother me so much. I thought: It was bound to happen, the abscess had to burst. But at night when I stretched out upon the sacks I felt it all very bitterly. A longing took me, for her and for the child. I wanted to be angry, but that's my misfortune exactly, I don't have it in me to be really angry. In the first place—this was how my thoughts went—there's bound to be a slip sometimes. You can't live without errors. Probably that lad who was with her led her on and gave her presents and what not, and women are often long on hair and short on sense, and so he got around her. And then since she denies it so, maybe I was only seeing things? Hallucinations do happen. You see a figure or a mannikin or something, but when you come up closer it's nothing, there's not a thing there. And if that's so, I'm doing her an injustice. And when I got so far in my thoughts I started to weep. I sobbed so that I wet the flour where I lay. In the morning I went to the rabbi and told him that I had made a mistake. The rabbi wrote on with his quill, and he said that if that were so he would have to reconsider the whole case. Until he had finished I wasn't to go near my wife, but I might send her bread and money by messenger.

3

Nine months passed before all the rabbis could come to an agreement. Letters went back and forth. I hadn't realized that there could be so much erudition about a matter like this.

Meanwhile Elka gave birth to still another child, a girl this time. On the Sabbath I went to the synagogue and invoked a blessing on her. They called me up to the Torah, and I named the child for my mother-in-law—may she rest in peace. The louts and loudmouths of the town who came into the bakery gave me a going over. All Frampol refreshed its spirits because of my trouble and grief. However, I resolved that I would always believe what I was told. What's the good of *not* believing? Today it's your wife you don't believe; tomorrow it's God Himself you won't take stock in.

By an apprentice who was her neighbor I sent her daily a corn or a wheat loaf, or a piece of pastry, rolls or bagels, or, when I got the chance, a slab of pudding, a slice of honeycake, or wedding strudel—whatever came my way. The apprentice was a good-hearted lad, and more than once he added something on his own. He had formerly annoyed me a lot, plucking my nose and digging me in the ribs, but when he started to be a visitor to my house he became kind and friendly. "Hey, you, Gimpel," he said to me, "you have a very decent little wife and two fine kids. You don't deserve them."

"But the things people say about her," I said.

"Well, they have long tongues," he said, "and nothing to do with them but babble. Ignore it as you ignore the cold of last winter."

One day the rabbi sent for me and said, "Are you certain, Gimpel, that you were wrong about your wife?"

I said, "I'm certain."

"Why, but look here! You yourself saw it."

"It must have been a shadow," I said.

"The shadow of what?"

"Just one of the beams, I think."

"You can go home then. You owe thanks to the Yanover rabbi. He found an obscure reference in Maimonides that favored you."

I seized the rabbi's hand and kissed it.

I wanted to run home immediately. It's no small thing to be separated for so long a time from wife and child. Then I reflected: I'd better go back to work now, and go home in the evening. I said nothing to anyone, although as far as my heart was concerned it was like one of the Holy Days. The women teased and twitted me as they did every day, but my thought was: Go on, with your loose talk. The truth is out, like the oil upon the water. Maimonides says it's right, and therefore it is right!

At night, when I had covered the dough to let it rise, I took my share of bread and a little sack of flour and started homeward. The moon was full and the stars were glistening, something to terrify the soul. I hurried onward, and before me darted a long shadow. It was winter, and a fresh snow had fallen. I had a mind to sing, but it was growing late and I didn't want to wake the householders. Then I felt like whistling, but I remembered that you don't whistle at night because it brings the demons out. So I was silent and walked as fast as I could.

Dogs in the Christian yards barked at me when I passed, but I thought: Bark your teeth out! What are you but mere dogs? Whereas I am a man, the husband of a fine wife, the father of promising children.

As I approached the house my heart started to pound as though it were the heart of a criminal. I felt no fear, but my heart went thump! thump! Well, no drawing back. I quietly lifted the latch and went in. Elka was asleep. I looked at the infant's cradle. The shutter was closed, but the moon forced its way through the cracks. I saw the newborn child's face and loved it as soon as I saw it—immediately—each tiny bone.

Then I came nearer to the bed. And what did I see but the apprentice lying there beside Elka. The moon went out all at once. It was utterly black, and I trembled. My teeth chattered. The bread fell from my hands, and my wife waked and said, "Who is that, ah?"

I muttered, "It's me."

"Gimpel?" she asked. "How come you're here? I thought it was forbidden."

"The rabbi said," I answered and shook as with a fever.

"Listen to me, Gimpel," she said, "go out to the shed and see if the goat's all right. It seems she's been sick." I have forgotten to say that we had a goat. When I heard she was unwell I went into the yard. The nanny goat was a good little creature. I had a nearly human feeling for her.

With hesitant steps I went up to the shed and opened the door. The goat stood there on her four feet. I felt her everywhere, drew her by the horns, examined her udders, and found nothing wrong. She had probably eaten too much bark. "Good night, little goat," I said. "Keep well." And the little beast answered with a "Maa" as though to thank me for the good will.

I went back. The apprentice had vanished.

"Where," I asked, "is the lad?"

"What lad?" my wife answered.

"What do you mean?" I said. "The apprentice. You were sleeping with him."

"The things I have dreamed this night and the night before," she said, "may they come true and lay you low, body and soul! An evil spirit has taken root in you and dazzles your sight." She screamed out, "You hateful creature! You moon calf! You spook! You uncouth man! Get out, or I'll scream all Frampol out of bed!"

Before I could move, her brother sprang out from behind the oven and struck me a blow on the back of the head. I thought he had broken my neck. I felt that something about me was deeply wrong, and I said, "Don't make a scandal. All that's needed now is that people should accuse me of raising spooks and *dybbuks*." For that was what she had meant. "No one will touch bread of my baking."

In short, I somehow calmed her.

"Well," she said, "that's enough. Lie down, and be shattered by wheels."

Next morning I called the apprentice aside. "Listen here, brother!" I said. And so on and so forth. "What do you say?" He stared at me as though I had dropped from the roof or something.

"I swear," he said, "you'd better go to an herb doctor or some healer. I'm afraid you have a screw loose, but I'll hush it up for you." And that's how the thing stood.

To make a long story short, I lived twenty years with my wife. She bore me six children, four daughters and two sons. All kinds of things happened, but I neither saw nor heard. I believed, and that's all. The rabbi recently said to me, "Belief in itself is beneficial. It is written that a good man lives by his faith."

Suddenly my wife took sick. It began with a trifle, a little growth upon the breast. But she evidently was not destined to live long; she had no years. I spent a fortune on her. I have forgotten to say that by this time I had a bakery of my own and in Frampol was considered to be something of a rich man. Daily the healer came, and every witch doctor in the neighborhood was brought. They decided to use leeches, and after that to try cupping. They even called a doctor from Lublin, but it was too late. Before she died she called me to her bed and said, "Forgive me, Gimpel."

I said, "What is there to forgive? You have been a good and faithful wife."

"Woe, Gimpel!" she said. "It was ugly how I deceived you all these years. I want to go clean to my Maker, and so I have to tell you that the children are not yours."

If I had been clouted on the head with a piece of wood it couldn't have bewildered me more.

"Whose are they?" I asked.

"I don't know," she said. "There were a lot . . . but they're not yours." And as she spoke she tossed her head to the side, her eyes turned glassy, and it was all up with Elka. On her whitened lips there remained a smile.

I imagined that, dead as she was, she was saying, "I deceived Gimpel. That was the meaning of my brief life."

4

One night, when the period of mourning was done, as I lay dreaming on the flour sacks, there came the Spirit of Evil himself and said to me, "Gimpel, why do you sleep?"

I said, "What should I be doing? Eating *kreplach?*"

"The whole world deceives you," he said, "and you ought to deceive the world in your turn."

"How can I deceive the world?" I asked him.

He answered, "You might accumulate a bucket of urine every day and at night pour it into the dough. Let the sages of Frampol eat filth."

"What about the judgment in the world to come?" I said.

"There is no world to come," he said. "They've sold you a bill of goods and talked you into believing you carried a cat in your belly. What nonsense!"

"Well then," I said, "and is there a God?"

He answered, "There is no God either."

"What," I said, "*is* there, then?"

"A thick mire."

He stood before my eyes with a goatish beard and horn, long-toothed, and with a tail. Hearing such words, I wanted to snatch him by the tail, but I tumbled from the flour sacks and nearly broke a rib. Then it happened that I had to answer the call of nature, and, passing, I saw the risen dough, which seemed to say to me, "Do it!" In brief, I let myself be persuaded.

At dawn the apprentice came. We kneaded the bread, scattered caraway seeds on it, and set it to bake. Then the apprentice went away, and I was left sitting in the little trench by the oven, on a pile of rags. Well, Gimpel, I thought, you've revenged yourself on them for all the shame they've put on you. Outside the frost glittered, but it was warm beside the oven. The flames heated my face. I bent my head and fell into a doze.

I saw in a dream, at once, Elka in her shroud. She called to me, "What have you done, Gimpel?"

I said to her, "It's all your fault," and started to cry.

"You fool!" she said. "You fool! Because I was false is everything false too? I never deceived anyone but myself. I'm paying for it all, Gimpel. They spare you nothing here."

I looked at her face. It was black; I was startled and waked, and remained sitting dumb. I sensed that everything hung in the balance. A false step now and I'd lose Eternal Life. But God gave me His help. I seized the long shovel and took out the loaves, carried them into the yard, and started to dig a hole in the frozen earth.

My apprentice came back as I was doing it. "What are you doing, boss?" he said, and grew pale as a corpse.

"I know what I'm doing," I said, and I buried it all before his very eyes.

Then I went home, took my hoard from its hiding place, and divided it among the children. "I saw your mother tonight," I said. "She's turning black, poor thing."

They were so astounded they couldn't speak a word.

"Be well," I said, "and forget that such a one as Gimpel ever existed." I put on my short coat, a pair of boots, took the bag that held my prayer shawl in one hand, my stock in the other, and kissed the *mezzuzah*. When people saw me in the street they were greatly surprised.

"Where are you going?" they said.

I answered, "Into the world." And so I departed from Frampol.

I wandered over the land, and good people did not neglect me. After many years I became old and white; I heard a great deal, many lies and falsehoods, but the longer I lived the more I understood that there were really no lies. Whatever doesn't really happen is dreamed at night. It happens to one if it doesn't happen to another, tomorrow if not today, or a century hence if not next year. What difference can it make? Often I heard tales of which I said, "Now this is a thing that cannot happen." But before a year had elapsed I heard that it actually had come to pass somewhere.

Going from place to place, eating at strange tables, it often happens that I spin yarns—improbable things that could never have happened—about devils, magicians, windmills, and the like. The children run after me, calling, "Grandfather, tell us a story." Sometimes they ask for particular stories, and I try to please them. A fat young boy once said to me, "Grandfather, it's the same story you told us before." The little rogue, he was right.

So it is with dreams too. It is many years since I left Frampol, but as soon as I shut my eyes I am there again. And whom do you think I see? Elka. She is standing by the washtub, as at our first encounter, but her face is shining and her eyes are as radiant as the eyes of a saint, and she speaks outlandish words to me, strange things. When I wake I have forgotten it all. But while the dream lasts I am comforted. She answers all my queries, and what comes out is that all is right. I weep and implore, "Let me be with you." And she consoles me and tells me to be patient. The time is nearer than it is far. Sometimes she strokes and kisses me and weeps upon my face. When I awaken I feel her lips and taste the salt of her tears.

No doubt the world is entirely an imaginary world, but it is only once removed from the true world. At the door of the hovel where I lie, there stands the plank on which the dead are taken away. The gravedigger Jew has his spade ready. The grave waits and the worms are hungry; the shrouds are prepared—I carry them in my beggar's sack. Another *shnorrer* is waiting to inherit my bed of straw. When the time comes I will go joyfully. Whatever may be there, it will be real, without complication, without ridicule, without deception. God be praised: there even Gimpel cannot be deceived.

QUESTIONS FOR DISCUSSION AND WRITING

1. How do Gimpel's first two sentences establish the conflict in his story? Why does Gimpel finally decide to resist the devil's temptation? How does Gimpel's final dream of Elka bring the story to an appropriate conclusion?
2. How does Gimpel's belief that "everything is possible" help perpetuate his friends' perception of him as a fool? In what way does Gimpel's marriage to Elka portray the ancient stereotype of the husband as cuckold? How does Gimpel's treatment of Elka and her children suggest that he may be wise rather than foolish?
3. How does the small village of Frampol contribute to the social and psychological forces that form Gimpel? Why does he decide to leave Frampol? How is he treated outside his native setting?
4. Why does Gimpel's explanation of his own point of view help us see him as something more than a fool? How do his trips to the Rabbi help confirm his belief in his own point of view?
5. What does Gimpel's experience suggest about the relationship of wisdom and ignorance, faith and doubt? How does Gimpel's discovery "that there were really no lies" help him come to terms with his life in this world and prepare him for the world hereafter?

84

JOHN STEINBECK

The Chrysanthemums

JOHN STEINBECK (1902–1968) was born in Salinas, California, and intermittently attended Stanford University, leaving in 1925 to work his way to New York on a cattle boat to pursue a writing career. He was unable to find sufficient employment, so he returned to California and worked throughout the depression at

various jobs: fruit picker, surveyor, chemical-laboratory assistant, and caretaker for a large estate on Lake Tahoe. Steinbeck's first novels, such as *Cup of Gold* (1929) and *To a God Unknown* (1933), attracted little attention. But with the publication of *Tortilla Flat* (1935), *In Dubious Battle* (1936), and *The Grapes of Wrath* (1939), his classic account of the Joad family's journey from Oklahoma to California, Steinbeck established himself as one of America's major literary talents. During World War II, he served as a journalist in Italy and Russia, continuing to publish noteworthy fiction such as *Cannery Row* (1945) and *The Wayward Bus* (1947), as well as several works of nonfiction such as *Bombs Away* (1942) and *Russian Journal* (1948). After the war Steinbeck published two major novels, *East of Eden* (1952), a national best-seller, and *Winter of Our Discontent* (1961). In 1962, Steinbeck was awarded the Nobel Prize for Literature. The same year marked the publication of *Travels with Charley: In Search of America,* a journal of his tour across America in a camper with his pet poodle. Steinbeck's best-known short stories appear in *The Long Valley* (1938). "The Chrysanthemums," reprinted from that collection, describes a woman's momentary attraction to a freer, more fulfilling life.

The high grey-flannel fog of winter closed off the Salinas Valley from the sky and from all the rest of the world. On every side it sat like a lid on the mountains and made of the great valley a closed pot. On the broad, level land floor the gang plows bit deep and left the black earth shining like metal where the shares had cut. On the foothill ranches across the Salinas River, the yellow stubble fields seemed to be bathed in pale cold sunshine, but there was no sunshine in the valley now in December. The thick willow scrub along the river flamed with sharp and positive yellow leaves.

It was a time of quiet and of waiting. The air was cold and tender. A light wind blew up from the southwest so that the farmers were mildly hopeful of a good rain before long; but fog and rain do not go together.

Across the river, on Henry Allen's foothill ranch there was little work to be done, for the hay was cut and stored and the orchards were plowed up to receive the rain deeply when it should come. The cattle on the higher slopes were becoming shaggy and rough-coated.

Elisa Allen, working in her flower garden, looked down across the yard and saw Henry, her husband, talking to two men in business suits. The three of them stood by the tractor shed, each man with one foot on the side of the little Fordson. They smoked cigarettes and studied the machine as they talked.

Elisa watched them for a moment and then went back to her work. She was thirty-five. Her face was lean and strong and her eyes were as clear as water. Her figure looked blocked and heavy in her gardening costume, a man's black hat pulled low down over her eyes, clod-hopper shoes, a figured print dress almost completely covered by a big corduroy apron with four big pockets to hold the snips, the trowel and scratcher, the seeds and the knife she worked with. She wore heavy leather gloves to protect her hands while she worked.

She was cutting down the old year's chrysanthemum stalks with a pair of short and powerful scissors. She looked down toward the men by the tractor shed now and then. Her face was eager and mature and handsome; even her work with the scissors was over-eager, over-powerful. The chrysanthemum stems seemed too small and easy for her energy.

She brushed a cloud of hair out of her eyes with the back of her glove, and left a smudge of earth on her cheek in doing it. Behind her stood the neat white farm house with red geraniums close-banked around it as high as the windows. It was a hard-swept looking little house with hard-polished windows, and a clean mud-mat on the front steps.

Elisa cast another glance toward the tractor shed. The strangers were getting into their Ford coupe. She took off a glove and put her strong fingers down into the forest of new green chrysanthemum sprouts that were growing around the old roots. She spread the leaves and looked down among the close-growing stems. No aphids were there, no sowbugs or snails or cutworms. Her terrier fingers destroyed such pests before they could get started.

Elisa started at the sound of her husband's voice. He had come near quietly, and he leaned over the wire fence that protected her flower garden from cattle and dogs and chickens.

"At it again," he said. "You've got a strong new crop coming."

Elisa straightened her back and pulled on the gardening glove again. "Yes. They'll be strong this coming year." In her tone and on her face there was a little smugness.

"You've got a gift with things," Henry observed. "Some of those yellow chrysanthemums you had this year were ten inches across. I wish you'd work out in the orchard and raise some apples that big."

Her eyes sharpened. "Maybe I could do it, too. I've a gift with things, all right. My mother had it. She could stick anything in the ground and make it grow. She said it was having planters' hands that knew how to do it."

"Well, it sure works with flowers," he said.

"Henry, who were those men you were talking to?"

"Why, sure, that's what I came to tell you. They were from the Western Meat Company. I sold those thirty head of three-year-old steers. Got nearly my own price, too."

"Good," she said. "Good for you."

"And I thought," he continued, "I thought how it's Saturday afternoon, and we might go into Salinas for dinner at a restaurant, and then to a picture show—to celebrate, you see."

"Good," she repeated. "Oh, yes. That will be good."

Henry put on his joking tone. "There's fights tonight. How'd you like to go to the fights?"

"Oh, no," she said breathlessly. "No, I wouldn't like fights."

"Just fooling, Elisa. We'll go to a movie. Let's see. It's two now. I'm going to take Scotty and bring down those steers from the hill. It'll take us maybe two hours. We'll go in town about five and have dinner at the Cominos Hotel. Like that?"

"Of course I'll like it. It's good to eat away from home."

"All right, then. I'll go get up a couple of horses."

She said, "I'll have plenty of time to transplant some of these sets, I guess."

She heard her husband calling Scotty down by the barn. And a little later she saw the two men ride up the pale yellow hillside in search of the steers.

There was a little square sandy bed kept for rooting the chrysanthemums. With her trowel she turned the soil over and over, and smoothed it and patted it firm. Then she dug ten parallel trenches to receive the sets. Back at the chrysanthemum bed she pulled out the little crisp shoots, trimmed off the leaves of each one with her scissors and laid it on a small orderly pile.

A squeak of wheels and plod of hoofs came from the road. Elisa looked up. The country road ran along the dense bank of willows and cottonwoods that bordered the river, and up this road came a curious vehicle, curiously drawn. It was an old spring-wagon, with a round canvas top on it like the corner of a prairie schooner. It was drawn by an old bay horse and a little grey-and-white burro. A big stubble-bearded man sat between the cover flaps and drove the crawling team. Underneath the wagon, between the hind wheels, a lean and rangy mongrel dog walked sedately. Words were painted on the canvas, in clumsy, crooked letters. "Pots, pans, knives, sisors, lawn mores, Fixed." Two rows of articles, and the triumphantly definitive "Fixed" below. The black paint had run down in little sharp points beneath each letter.

Elisa, squatting on the ground, watched to see the crazy, loose-jointed wagon pass by. But it didn't pass. It turned into the farm road in front of her house, crooked old wheels skirling and squeaking. The rangy dog darted from between the wheels and ran ahead. Instantly the two ranch shepherds flew out at him. Then all three stopped, and with stiff and quivering tails, with taut straight legs, with ambassadorial dignity, they slowly circled, sniffing daintily. The caravan pulled up to Elisa's wire fence and stopped. Now the newcomer dog, feeling out-numbered, lowered his tail and retired under the wagon with raised hackles and bared teeth.

The man on the wagon seat called out, "That's a bad dog in a fight when he gets started."

Elisa laughed. "I see he is. How soon does he generally get started?"

The man caught up her laughter and echoed it heartily. "Sometimes not for weeks and weeks," he said. He climbed stiffly down, over the wheel. The horse and the donkey drooped like unwatered flowers.

Elisa saw that he was a very big man. Although his hair and beard were greying, he did not look old. His worn black suit was wrinkled and spotted with grease. The laughter had disappeared from his face and eyes the moment his laughing voice ceased. His eyes were dark, and they were full of the brooding that gets in the eyes of teamsters and of sailors. The calloused hands he rested on the wire fence were cracked, and every crack was a black line. He took off his battered hat.

"I'm off my general road, ma'am," he said. "Does this dirt road cut over across the river to the Los Angeles highway?"

Elisa stood up and shoved the thick scissors in her apron pocket. "Well, yes, it does, but it winds around and then fords the river. I don't think your team could pull through the sand."

He replied with some asperity, "It might surprise you what them beasts can pull through."

"When they get started?" she asked.

He smiled for a second. "Yes. When they get started."

"Well," said Elisa, "I think you'll save time if you go back to the Salinas road and pick up the highway there."

He drew a big finger down the chicken wire and made it sing. "I ain't in any hurry, ma'am. I go from Seattle to San Diego and back every year. Takes all my time. About six months each way. I aim to follow nice weather."

Elisa took off her gloves and stuffed them in the apron pocket with the scissors. She touched the under edge of her man's hat, searching for fugitive hairs. "That sounds like a nice kind of a way to live," she said.

He leaned confidentially over the fence. "Maybe you noticed the writing on my wagon. I mend pots and sharpen knives and scissors. You got any of them things to do?"

"Oh, no," she said, quickly. "Nothing like that." Her eyes hardened with resistance.

"Scissors is the worst thing," he explained. "Most people just ruin scissors trying to sharpen 'em, but I know how. I got a special tool. It's a little bobbit kind of thing, and patented. But it sure does the trick."

"No. My scissors are all sharp."

"All right, then. Take a pot," he continued earnestly, "a bent pot, or a pot with a hole. I can make it like new so you don't have to buy no new ones. That's a saving for you."

"No," she said shortly. "I tell you I have nothing like that for you to do."

His face fell to an exaggerated sadness. His voice took on a whining undertone. "I ain't had a thing to do today. Maybe I won't have no supper tonight. You see I'm off my regular road. I know folks on the highway clear from Seattle to San Diego. They save their things for me to sharpen up because they know I do it so good and save them money."

"I'm sorry," Elisa said irritably. "I haven't anything for you to do."

His eyes left her face and fell to searching the ground. They roamed about until they came to the chrysanthemum bed where she had been working. "What's them plants, ma'am?"

The irritation and resistance melted from Elisa's face. "Oh, those are chrysanthemums, giant whites and yellows. I raise them every year, bigger than anybody around here."

"Kind of a long-stemmed flower? Looks like a quick puff of colored smoke?" he asked.

"That's it. What a nice way to describe them."

"They smell kind of nasty till you get used to them," he said.

"It's a good bitter smell," she retorted, "not nasty at all."

He changed his tone quickly. "I like the smell myself."

"I had ten-inch blooms this year," she said.

The man leaned farther over the fence. "Look. I know a lady down the road a piece, has got the nicest garden you ever seen. Got nearly every kind of flower but no chrysanthemums. Last time I was mending a copper-bottom washtub for her (that's a hard job but I do it good), she said to me, 'If you ever run acrost some nice chrysanthemums I wish you'd try to get me a few seeds.' That's what she told me."

Elisa's eyes grew alert and eager. "She couldn't have known much about chrysanthemums. You *can* raise them from seed, but it's much easier to root the little sprouts you see there."

"Oh," he said. "I s'pose I can't take none to her, then."

"Why yes you can," Elisa cried. "I can put some in damp sand, and you can carry them right along with you. They'll take root in the pot if you keep them damp. And then she can transplant them."

"She'd sure like to have some, ma'am. You say they're nice ones?"

"Beautiful," she said. "Oh, beautiful." Her eyes shone. She tore off the battered hat and shook out her dark pretty hair. "I'll put them in a flower pot, and you can take them right with you. Come into the yard."

While the man came through the picket gate Elisa ran excitedly along the geranium-bordered path to the back of the house. And she returned carrying a big red flower pot. The gloves were forgotten now. She kneeled on the ground by the starting bed and dug up the sandy soil with her fingers and scooped it into the bright new flower pot. Then she picked up the little pile of shoots she had prepared. With her strong fingers she pressed them into the sand and tamped around them with her knuckles. The man stood over her. "I'll tell you what to do," she said. "You remember so you can tell the lady."

"Yes, I'll try to remember."

"Well, look. These will take root in about a month. Then she must set them out, about a foot apart in good rich earth like this, see?" She lifted a handful of dark soil for him to look at. "They'll grow fast and tall. Now remember this: In July tell her to cut them down, about eight inches from the ground."

"Before they bloom?" he asked.

"Yes, before they bloom." Her face was tight with eagerness. "They'll grow right up again. About the last of September the buds will start."

She stopped and seemed perplexed. "It's the budding that takes the most care," she said hesitantly. "I don't know how to tell you." She looked deep into his eyes, searchingly. Her mouth opened a little, and she seemed to be listening. "I'll try to tell you," she said. "Did you ever hear of planting hands?"

"Can't say I have, ma'am."

"Well, I can only tell you what it feels like. It's when you're picking off the buds you don't want. Everything goes right down into your fingertips. You watch your fingers work. They do it themselves. You can feel how it is. They pick and pick the buds. They never make a mistake. They're with the plant. Do you see? Your fingers and the plant. You can feel that, right up your arm. They know. They never make a mistake. You can feel it. When you're like that you can't do anything wrong. Do you see that? Can you understand that?"

She was kneeling on the ground looking up at him. Her breast swelled passionately.

The man's eyes narrowed. He looked away self-consciously. "Maybe I know," he said. "Sometimes in the night in the wagon there—"

Elisa's voice grew husky. She broke in on him, "I've never lived as you do, but I know what you mean. When the night is dark—why, the stars are sharp-pointed, and there's quiet. Why, you rise up and up! Every pointed star gets driven into your body. It's like that. Hot and sharp and—lovely."

Kneeling there, her hand went out toward his leg in the greasy black trousers. Her hesitant fingers almost touched the cloth. Then her hand dropped to the ground. She crouched low like a fawning dog.

He said, "It's nice, just like you say. Only when you don't have no dinner, it ain't."

She stood up then, very straight, and her face was ashamed. She held the flower pot out to him and placed it gently in his arms. "Here. Put it in your wagon, on the seat, where you can watch it. Maybe I can find something for you to do."

At the back of the house she dug in the can pile and found two old and battered aluminum saucepans. She carried them back and gave them to him. "Here, maybe you can fix these."

His manner changed. He became professional. "Good as new I can fix them." At the back of his wagon he set a little anvil, and out of an oily tool box dug a small machine hammer. Elisa came through the gate to watch him while he pounded out the dents in the kettles. His mouth grew sure and knowing. At a difficult part of the work he sucked his upper-lip.

"You sleep right in the wagon?" Elisa asked.

"Right in the wagon, ma'am. Rain or shine I'm dry as a cow in there."

"It must be nice," she said. "It must be very nice. I wish women could do such things."

"It ain't the right kind of a life for a woman."

Her upper lip raised a little, showing her teeth. "How do you know? How can you tell?" she said.

"I don't know, ma'am," he protested. "Of course I don't know. Now here's your kettles, done. You don't have to buy no new ones."

"How much?"

"Oh, fifty cents'll do. I keep my prices down and my work good. That's why I have all them satisfied customers up and down the highway."

Elisa brought him a fifty-cent piece from the house and dropped it in his hand. "You might be surprised to have a rival some time. I can sharpen scissors, too. And I can beat the dents out of little pots. I could show you what a woman might do."

He put his hammer back in the oily box and shoved the little anvil out of sight. "It would be a lonely life for a woman, ma'am, and a scarey life, too, with animals creeping under the wagon all night." He climbed over the singletree, steadying himself with a hand on the burro's white rump. He settled himself in the seat, picked up the lines. "Thank you kindly, ma'am," he said. "I'll do like you told me; I'll go back and catch the Salinas road."

"Mind," she called, "if you're long in getting there, keep the sand damp."

"Sand, ma'am? . . . Sand? Oh, sure. You mean around the chrysanthemums. Sure I will." He clucked his tongue. The beasts leaned luxuriously into their collars. The mongrel dog took his place between the back wheels. The wagon turned and crawled out the entrance road and back the way it had come, along the river.

Elisa stood in front of her wire fence watching the slow progress of the caravan. Her shoulders were straight, her head thrown back, her eyes half-closed, so that the scene came vaguely into them. Her lips moved silently, forming the words "Good-bye—good-bye." Then she whispered, "That's a bright direction. There's a glowing there." The sound of her whisper startled her. She shook herself free and looked about to see whether anyone had been listening. Only the dogs had heard. They lifted their heads toward her from their sleeping in the dust, and then stretched out their chins and settled asleep again. Elisa turned and ran hurriedly into the house.

In the kitchen she reached behind the stove and felt the water tank. It was full of hot water from the noonday cooking. In the bathroom she tore off her soiled clothes and flung them into the corner. And then she scrubbed herself with a little block of pumice, legs and thighs, loins and chest and arms, until her skin was scratched and red. When she had dried herself she stood in front of a mirror in her bedroom and looked at her body. She tightened her stomach and threw out her chest. She turned and looked over her shoulder at her back.

After a while she began to dress, slowly. She put on her newest underclothing and her nicest stockings and the dress which was the symbol of her prettiness. She worked carefully on her hair, penciled her eyebrows and rouged her lips.

Before she was finished she heard the little thunder of hoofs and the shouts of Henry and his helper as they drove the red steers into the corral. She heard the gate bang shut and set herself for Henry's arrival.

His step sounded on the porch. He entered the house calling, "Elisa, where are you?"

"In my room, dressing. I'm not ready. There's hot water for your bath. Hurry up. It's getting late."

When she heard him splashing in the tub, Elisa laid his dark suit on the bed, and shirt and socks and tie beside it. She stood his polished shoes on the floor beside the bed. Then she went to the porch and sat primly and stiffly down. She looked toward the river road where the willow-line was still yellow with frosted leaves so that under the high grey fog they seemed a thin band of sunshine. This was the only color in the grey afternoon. She sat unmoving for a long time. Her eyes blinked rarely.

Henry came banging out of the door, shoving his tie inside his vest as he came. Elisa stiffened and her face grew tight. Henry stopped short and looked at her. "Why—why, Elisa. You look so nice!"

"Nice? You think I look nice? What do you mean by 'nice'?"

Henry blundered on. "I don't know. I mean you look different, strong and happy."

"I am strong? Yes, strong. What do you mean 'strong'?"

He looked bewildered. "You're playing some kind of a game," he said helplessly. "It's a kind of play. You look strong enough to break a calf over your knee, happy enough to eat it like a watermelon."

For a second she lost her rigidity. "Henry! Don't talk like that. You didn't know what you said." She grew complete again. "I'm strong," she boasted. "I never knew before how strong."

Henry looked down toward the tractor shed, and when he brought his eyes back to her, they were his own again. "I'll get out the car. You can put on your coat while I'm starting."

Elisa went into the house. She heard him drive to the gate and idle down his motor, and then she took a long time to put on her hat. She pulled it here and pressed it there. When Henry turned the motor off she slipped into her coat and went out.

The little roadster bounced along on the dirt road by the river, raising the birds and driving the rabbits into the brush. Two cranes flapped heavily over the willow-line and dropped into the river-bed.

Far ahead on the road Elisa saw a dark speck. She knew.

She tried not to look as they passed it, but her eyes would not obey. She whispered to herself sadly, "He might have thrown them off the road. That wouldn't have been much trouble, not very much. But he kept the pot," she explained. "He had to keep the pot. That's why he couldn't get them off the road."

The roadster turned a bend and she saw the caravan ahead. She swung full around toward her husband so she could not see the little covered wagon and the mismatched team as the car passed them.

In a moment it was over. The thing was done. She did not look back.

She said loudly, to be heard above the motor, "It will be good, tonight, a good dinner."

"Now you're changed again," Henry complained. He took one hand from the wheel and patted her knee. "I ought to take you in to dinner oftener. It would be good for both of us. We get so heavy out on the ranch."

"Henry," she asked, "could we have wine at dinner?"

"Sure we could. Say! That will be fine."

She was silent for a while; then she said, "Henry, at those prize fights, do the men hurt each other very much?"

"Sometimes a little, not often. Why?"

"Well, I've read how they break noses, and blood runs down their chests. I've read how the fighting gloves get heavy and soggy with blood."

He looked around at her. "What's the matter, Elisa? I didn't know you read things like that." He brought the car to a stop, then turned to the right over the Salinas River bridge.

"Do any women ever go to the fights?" she asked.

"Oh, sure, some. What's the matter, Elisa? Do you want to go? I don't think you'd like it, but I'll take you if you really want to go."

She relaxed limply in the seat. "Oh, no. No. I don't want to go. I'm sure I don't." Her face was turned away from him. "It will be enough if we can have wine. It will be plenty." She turned up her coat collar so he could not see that she was crying weakly—like an old woman.

QUESTIONS FOR DISCUSSION AND WRITING

1. How does Elisa's meeting with the tinker produce the conflict in the story? How does that conflict reach its climax when Elisa and Henry pass the tinker on the way to town? To what extent does Elisa's statement, "It will be enough if we can have wine. It will be plenty," resolve that conflict?

2. How does Steinbeck's description of Elisa's attire and "gift" help establish her character? What hidden qualities in her character are revealed in her conversation with the tinker? What two character transformations does Henry notice in his wife toward the end of the story?

3. How does Steinbeck's initial description of the Salinas Valley as a "closed pot" help establish the mood of the story? How does Elisa's speculation about the tinker's travels reveal her dissatisfaction with her life?
4. In what ways does Elisa's observation of her husband and the two men from behind the wire fence of her flower garden establish her point of view in this story? How does her observation of herself in the mirror after her bath suggest a change in her point of view?
5. What do the chrysanthemums symbolize at the beginning of the story, at the time when Elisa gives them to the tinker, and at the end when she suspects he has discarded them? How do the tinker's description of the flower as a "quick puff of colored smoke" and Elisa's description of it as having a "good bitter smell" suggest ways to interpret its symbolic significance?

85

JAMES THURBER

The Catbird Seat

JAMES THURBER (1894–1961) was born in Columbus, Ohio, and attended Ohio State University. Accidentally blinded in one eye as a child, Thurber was rejected for military service in World War I, but he worked briefly for the State Department in Paris as a code clerk. After the war, he returned home to write for the Columbus *Dispatch* and to compose and direct musical comedies for a theatrical group at Ohio State University. In 1924 he traveled to Paris as a correspondent for the Chicago *Tribune* and the next year to New York to work for the New York *Evening Post.* In 1927 Thurber joined the staff of *The New Yorker* and remained there as a writer and editor until 1935, when he resigned to work on his own writing. But he continued to contribute stories, prose sketches, and drawings to the magazine until his death. His recollections of *The New Yorker* are contained in his book *The Years with Ross* (1959). In 1929 Thurber published his first book, *Is Sex Necessary?,* in collaboration with E. B. White. In the 1930s he published his *New Yorker* writings and drawings in volumes such as *The Owl in the Attic and Other Perplexities* (1931), *The Seal in the Bedroom and Other Predicaments* (1932), *The Middle-Aged Man on the Flying Trapeze* (1935), and *Let Your Mind Alone!* (1937). In 1940 Thurber collaborated with Elliott Nugent on the successful Broadway play *The Male Animal.* Despite his failing eyesight, Thurber continued writing humor and satire until his death. Other books of his include *Fables for Our Time and Famous Poems Illustrated* (1940), *The Beast in Me and Other Animals* (1948), *Thurber Country* (1953), and *Lanterns and Lances* (1961). "The Catbird Seat," reprinted from *The Thurber Carnival* (1945), recounts the attempt of an exemplary employee to "rub out" his office enemy.

Mr. Martin bought the pack of Camels on Monday night in the most crowded cigar store on Broadway. It was theater time and seven or eight men were buying cigarettes. The clerk didn't even glance at Mr. Martin, who put the pack in his overcoat pocket and went out. If any of the staff at F & S had seen him buy the cigarettes, they would have been astonished, for it was generally known that Mr. Martin did not smoke, and never had. No one saw him.

It was just a week to the day since Mr. Martin had decided to rub out Mrs. Ulgine Barrows. The term "rub out" pleased him because it suggested nothing more than the correction of an error—in this case an error of Mr. Fitweiler. Mr. Martin had spent each night of the past week working out his plan and examining it. As he walked home now he went over it again. For the hundredth time he resented the element of imprecision, the margin of guesswork that entered into the business. The project as he had worked it out was casual and bold, the risks were considerable. Something might go wrong anywhere along the line. And therein lay the cunning of his scheme. No one would ever see in it the cautious, painstaking hand of Erwin Martin, head of the filing department at F & S of whom Mr. Fitweiler had once said, "Man is fallible but Martin isn't." No one would see his hand, that is, unless it were caught in the act.

Sitting in his apartment, drinking a glass of milk, Mr. Martin reviewed his case against Mrs. Ulgine Barrows, as he had every night for seven nights. He began at the beginning. Her quacking voice and braying laugh had first profaned the halls of F & S on March 7, 1941 (Mr. Martin had a head for dates). Old Roberts, the personnel chief, had introduced her as the newly appointed special adviser to the president of the firm, Mr. Fitweiler. The woman had appalled Mr. Martin instantly, but he hadn't shown it. He had given her his dry hand, a look of studious concentration, and a faint smile. "Well," she had said, looking at the papers on his desk, "are you lifting the oxcart out of the ditch?" As Mr. Martin recalled the moment, over his milk, he squirmed slightly. He must keep his mind on her crimes as a special adviser, not on her peccadillos as a personality. This he found difficult to do, in spite of entering an objection and sustaining it. The faults of the woman as a woman kept chattering on in his mind like an unruly witness. She had, for almost two years now, baited him. In the halls, in the elevator, even in his own office, into which she romped now and then like a circus horse, she was constantly shouting these silly questions at him. "Are you lifting the oxcart out of the ditch? Are you tearing up the pea patch? Are you hollering down the rain barrel? Are you scraping around the bottom of the pickle barrel? Are you sitting in the catbird seat?"

It was Joey Hart, one of Mr. Martin's two assistants, who had explained what the gibberish meant. "She must be a Dodger fan," he had said. "Red Barber announces the Dodger games over the radio and he uses those expressions—picked 'em up down South." Joey had gone on to explain one or two. "Tearing up the pea patch" meant going on a rampage; "sitting in the catbird seat" meant sitting pretty, like a batter with three balls and no strikes on him. Mr. Martin dismissed all this with an effort. It had been annoying, it had driven him near to distraction, but he was too solid a man to be moved to murder by anything so childish. It was fortunate, he reflected as he passed on to the important charges against Mrs. Barrows, that he had stood up under it so well. He had maintained always an outward appearance of polite tolerance. "Why, I even believe you like the woman," Miss Paird, his other assistant, had once said to him. He had simply smiled.

A gavel rapped in Mr. Martin's mind and the case was resumed. Mrs. Ulgine Barrows stood charged with willful, blatant, and persistent attempts to destroy the efficiency and system of F & S. It was competent, material, and relevant to review her advent and rise to power. Mr. Martin had got the story from Miss Paird, who seemed always able to find things out. According to her, Mrs. Barrows had met Mr. Fitweiler at a party, where she had rescued him from the embraces of a powerfully built drunken man who had mistaken the president of F & S for a famous retired Middle Western football coach. She had led him to a sofa and somehow worked upon him a monstrous magic. The aging gentleman had jumped to the conclusion there and then that this was a woman of singular attainments, equipped to bring out the best in him and the firm. A week later he had introduced her into F & S as his special adviser. On that day confusion got its foot in the door. After Miss Tyson, Mr. Brundage and Mr. Bartlett had been fired and Mr. Munson had taken his hat and stalked out, mailing in his resignation later, old Roberts had been emboldened to speak to Mr. Fitweiler. He mentioned that Mr. Munson's department had been "a little disrupted" and hadn't they perhaps better resume the old system there? Mr. Fitweiler had said certainly not. He had the greatest faith in Mrs. Barrows' idea. "They require a little seasoning, a little seasoning, is all," he had added. Mr. Roberts had given it up. Mr. Martin reviewed in detail all the changes wrought by Mrs. Barrows. She had begun chipping at the cornices of the firm's edifice and now she was swinging at the foundation with a pickaxe.

Mr. Martin came now, in his summing up, to the afternoon of Monday, November 2, 1942—just one week ago. On that day, at 3 P.M., Mrs. Barrows had bounced into his office. "Boo!" she had yelled. "Are you scraping around the bottom of the pickle barrel?" Mr. Martin had looked at her from under his green eyeshade, saying nothing. She had begun to wander about the office, taking it in with her great, popping eyes. "Do you really need *all* these filing cabinets?" she had demanded suddenly. Mr. Martin's heart had jumped. "Each of these files," he had said, keeping his voice even, "plays an indispensable part in the system of F & S." She had brayed at him, "Well, don't tear up the pea patch!" and gone to the door. From there she had bawled, "But you sure have got a lot of fine scrap in here!" Mr. Martin could no longer doubt that the finger was on his beloved department. Her pickaxe was on the upswing, poised for the first blow. It had not come yet; he had received no blue memo from the enchanted Mr. Fitweiler bearing nonsensical instructions deriving from the obscene woman. But there was no doubt in Mr. Martin's mind that one would be forthcoming. He must act quickly. Already a precious week had gone by. Mr. Martin stood up in his living room, still holding his milk glass. "Gentlemen of the jury," he said to himself, "I demand the death penalty for this horrible person."

The next day Mr. Martin followed his routine, as usual. He polished his glasses more often and once sharpened an already sharp pencil, but not even Miss Paird noticed. Only once did he catch sight of his victim; she swept past him in the hall with a patronizing "Hi!" At five-thirty he walked home, as usual, and had a glass of milk, as usual. He had never drunk anything stronger in his life—unless you could count ginger ale. The late Sam Schlosser, the S of F & S, had praised Mr. Martin at a staff meeting several years before for his temperate habits. "Our most efficient worker neither drinks nor smokes," he had said. "The results speak for themselves." Mr. Fitweiler had sat by, nodding approval.

Mr. Martin was still thinking about that red-letter day as he walked over to Schrafft's on Fifth Avenue near Forty-sixth Street. He got there, as he always did, at eight o'clock. He finished his dinner and the financial page of the *Sun* at a quarter to nine, as he always did. It was his custom after dinner to take a walk. This time he walked down Fifth Avenue at a casual pace. His gloved hands felt moist and warm, his forehead cold. He transferred the Camels from his overcoat to a jacket pocket. He wondered, as he did so, if they did not represent an unnecessary note of strain. Mrs. Barrows smoked only Luckies. It was his idea to puff a few puffs on a Camel (after the rubbing-out), stub it out in the ashtray holding her lipstick-stained Luckies, and thus drag a small red herring across the trail. Perhaps it was not a good idea. It would take time. He might even choke, too loudly.

Mr. Martin had never seen the house on West Twelfth Street where Mrs. Barrows lived, but he had a clear enough picture of it. Fortunately, she had bragged to everybody about her ducky first-floor apartment in the perfectly darling three-story red-brick. There would be no doorman or other attendants; just the tenants of the second and third floors. As he walked along, Mr. Martin realized that he would get there before nine-thirty. He had considered walking north on Fifth Avenue from Schrafft's to a point from which it would take him until ten o'clock to reach the house. At that hour people were less likely to be coming in or going out. But the procedure would have made an awkward loop in the straight thread of his casualness, and he had abandoned it. It was impossible to figure when people would be entering or leaving the house, anyway. There was a great risk at any hour. If he ran into anybody, he would simply have to place the rubbing-out of Ulgine Barrows in the inactive file forever. The same thing would hold true if there were someone in her apartment. In that case he would just say that he had been passing by, recognized her charming house, and thought to drop in.

It was eighteen minutes after nine when Mr. Martin turned into Twelfth Street. A man passed him, and a man and a woman, talking. There was no one within fifty paces when he came to the house, halfway down the block. He was up the steps and in the small vestibule in no time, pressing the bell under the card that said "Mrs. Ulgine Barrows." When the clicking in the lock started he jumped forward against the door. He got inside fast, closing the door behind him. A bulb in a lantern hung from the hall ceiling on a chain seemed to give a monstrously bright light. There was nobody on the stair, which went up ahead of him along the left wall. A door opened down the hall in the wall on the right. He went toward it swiftly, on tiptoe.

"Well, for God's sake, look who's here!" bawled Mrs. Barrows, and her braying laugh rang out like the report of a shotgun. He rushed past her like a football tackle, bumping her. "Hey, quit shoving!" she said, closing the door behind them. They were in her living room, which seemed to Mr. Martin to be lighted by a hundred lamps. "What's after you?" she said. "You're as jumpy as a goat." He found he was unable to speak. His heart was wheezing in his throat. "I—yes," he finally brought out. She was jabbering and laughing as she started to help him off with his coat. "No, no," he said. "I'll put it here." He took it off and put it on a chair near the door. "Your hat and gloves, too," she said. "You're in a lady's house." He put his hat on top of the coat. Mrs. Barrows seemed larger than he had thought. He kept his gloves on. "I was passing by," he said. "I recognized—is there anyone here?" She laughed louder than ever. "No," she said, "we're all alone. You're as white as a sheet, you funny man. Whatever *has* come over you? I'll mix you a toddy." She started toward a door across the room. "Scotch-and-soda be all right? But say, you don't drink, do you?" She turned and gave him her amused look. Mr. Martin pulled himself together. "Scotch-and-soda will be all right," he heard himself say. He could hear her laughing in the kitchen.

Mr. Martin looked quickly around the living room for the weapon. He had counted on finding one there. There were andirons and a poker and something in a corner that looked like an Indian club. None of them would do. It couldn't be that way. He began to pace around. He came to a desk. On it lay a metal paper knife with an ornate handle. Would it be sharp enough? He reached for it and knocked over a small brass jar. Stamps spilled out of it and it fell to the floor with a clatter. "Hey," Mrs. Barrows yelled from the kitchen, "are you tearing up the pea patch?" Mr. Martin gave a strange laugh. Picking up the knife, he tried its point against his left wrist. It was blunt. It wouldn't do.

When Mrs. Barrows reappeared, carrying two highballs, Mr. Martin, standing there with his gloves on, became acutely conscious of the fantasy he had wrought. Cigarettes in his pocket, a drink prepared for him—it was all too grossly improbable. It was more than that; it was impossible. Somewhere in the back of his mind a vague idea stirred, sprouted. "For heaven's sake, take off those gloves," said Mrs. Barrows. "I always wear them in the house," said Mr. Martin. The idea began to bloom, strange and wonderful. She put the glasses on a coffee table in front of a sofa and sat on the sofa. "Come over here, you odd little man," she said. Mr. Martin went over and sat beside her. It was difficult getting a cigarette out of the pack of Camels, but he managed it. She held a match for him, laughing. "Well," she said, handing him his drink, "this is perfectly marvelous. You with a drink and a cigarette."

Mr. Martin puffed, not too awkwardly, and took a gulp of the highball. "I drink and smoke all the time," he said. He clinked his glass against hers. "Here's nuts to that old windbag, Fitweiler," he said, and gulped again. The stuff tasted awful, but he made no grimace. "Really, Mr. Martin," she said, her voice and posture changing, "you are insulting our employer." Mrs. Barrows was now all special adviser to the president. "I am preparing a bomb," said Mr. Martin, "which will blow the old goat higher than hell." He had only had a little of the drink, which was not strong. It couldn't be that. "Do you take dope or something?" Mrs. Barrows asked coldly. "Heroin," said Mr. Martin. "I'll be coked to the gills when I bump the old buzzard off." "Mr. Martin!" she shouted, getting to her feet. "That will be all of that. You must go at once." Mr. Martin took another swallow of his drink. He tapped his cigarette out in the ashtray and put the pack of Camels on the coffee table. Then he got up. She stood glaring at him. He walked over and put on his hat and coat. "Not a word about this," he said, and laid an index finger against his lips. All Mrs. Barrows could bring out was "Really!" Mr. Martin put his hand on the doorknob. "I'm sitting in the catbird seat," he said. He stuck his tongue out at her and left. Nobody saw him go.

Mr. Martin got to his apartment, walking, well before eleven. No one saw him go in. He had two glasses of milk after brushing his teeth, and he felt elated. It wasn't tipsiness, because he hadn't been tipsy. Anyway, the walk had worn off all effects of the whiskey. He got in bed and read a magazine for a while. He was asleep before midnight.

Mr. Martin got to the office at eight-thirty the next morning, as usual. At a quarter to nine, Ulgine Barrows, who had never before arrived at work before ten, swept into his office. "I'm reporting to Mr. Fitweiler now!" she shouted. "If he turns you over to the police, it's no more than you deserve!" Mr. Martin gave her a look of shocked surprise. "I beg your pardon?" he said. Mrs. Barrows snorted and bounced out of the room, leaving Miss Paird and Joey Hart staring after her. "What's the matter with that old devil now?" asked Miss Paird. "I have no idea," said Mr. Martin, resuming his work. The other two looked at him and then at each other. Miss Paird got up and went out. She walked slowly past the closed door of Mr. Fitweiler's office. Mrs. Barrows was yelling inside, but she was not braying. Miss Paird could not hear what the woman was saying. She went back to her desk.

Forty-five minutes later, Mrs. Barrows left the president's office and went into her own, shutting the door. It wasn't until half an hour later that Mr. Fitweiler sent for Mr. Martin. The head of the filing department, neat, quiet, attentive, stood in front of the old man's desk. Mr. Fitweiler was pale and nervous. He took his glasses off and twiddled them. He made a small, bruffing sound in his throat. "Martin," he said, "you have been with us more than twenty years." "Twenty-two, sir," said Mr. Martin. "In that time," pursued the president, "your work and your—uh—manner have been exemplary." "I trust so, sir," said Mr. Martin. "I have understood, Martin," said Mr. Fitweiler, "that you have never taken a drink or smoked." "That is correct, sir," said Mr. Martin. "Ah, yes." Mr. Fitweiler polished his glasses. "You may describe what you did after leaving the office yesterday, Martin," he said. Mr. Martin allowed less than a second for his bewildered pause. "Certainly, sir," he said. "I walked home. Then I went to Schrafft's for dinner. Afterward I walked home again. I went to bed early, sir, and read a magazine for a while. I was asleep before eleven." "Ah, yes," said Mr. Fitweiler again. He was silent for a moment, searching for the proper words to say to the head of the filing department. "Mrs. Barrows," he said finally, "Mrs. Barrows has worked hard, Martin, very hard. It grieves me to report that she has suffered a severe breakdown. It has taken the form of a persecution complex accompanied by distressing hallucinations." "I am very sorry, sir," said Mr. Martin. "Mrs. Barrows is under the delusion," continued Mr. Fitweiler, "that you visited her last evening and behaved yourself in an—uh—unseemly manner." He raised his hand to silence Mr. Martin's little pained outcry. "It is the nature of these psychological diseases," Mr. Fitweiler said, "to fix upon the least likely and most innocent party as the—uh—source of persecution. These matters are not for the lay mind to grasp, Martin. I've just had my psychiatrist, Dr. Fitch, on the phone. He would not, of course, commit himself, but he made enough generalizations to substantiate my suspicions. I suggested to Mrs. Barrows, when she had completed her—uh—story to me this morning, that she visit Dr. Fitch, for I suspected a condition at once. She flew, I regret to say, into a rage, and demanded—uh—requested that I call you on the carpet. You may not know, Martin, but Mrs. Barrows had planned a reorganization of your department—subject to my approval, of course, subject to my approval. This brought you, rather than anyone else, to her mind—but again that is a phenomenon for Dr. Fitch and not for us. So, Martin, I am afraid Mrs. Barrows' usefulness here is at an end." "I am dreadfully sorry, sir," said Mr. Martin.

It was at this point that the door to the office blew open with the suddenness of a gas-main explosion and Mrs. Barrows catapulted through it. "Is the little rat denying it?" she screamed. "He can't get away with that!" Mr. Martin got up and moved discreetly to a point beside Mr. Fitweiler's chair. "You drank and smoked at my apartment," she bawled at Mr. Martin, "and you know it! You called Mr. Fitweiler an old windbag and said you were going to blow him up when you got coked to the gills on your heroin!" She stopped yelling to catch her breath and a new glint came into her popping eyes. "If you weren't such a drab, ordinary little man," she said, "I'd think you'd planned it all. Sticking your tongue out, saying you were sitting in the catbird seat, because you thought no one would believe me when I told it! My God, it's really too perfect!" she brayed loudly and hysterically, and the fury was on her again. She glared at Mr. Fitweiler. "Can't you see how he has tricked us, you old fool? Can't you see his little game?" But Mr. Fitweiler had been surreptitiously pressing all the buttons under the top of his desk and employees of F & S began pouring into the room. "Stockton," said Mr. Fitweiler, "you and Fishbein will take Mrs. Barrows to her home. Mrs. Powell, you will go with them." Stockton, who had played a little football in high school, blocked Mrs. Barrows as she made for Mr. Martin. It took him and Fishbein together to force her out of the door into the hall, crowded with stenographers and office boys. She was still screaming imprecations at Mr. Martin, tangled and contradictory imprecations. The hubbub finally died out down the corridor.

"I regret that this has happened," said Mr. Fitweiler. "I shall ask you to dismiss it from your mind, Martin," "Yes, sir," said Mr. Martin, anticipating his chief's "That will be all" by moving to the door. "I will dismiss it." He went out and shut the door, and his step was light and quick in the hall. When he entered his department he had slowed down to his customary gait, and he walked quietly across the room to the W20 file, wearing a look of studious concentration.

QUESTIONS FOR DISCUSSION AND WRITING

1. What events have caused Mr. Martin to arrive at his decision to "rub out" Mrs. Ulgine Barrows? How does Mr. Martin's unsuccessful search for a weapon at Mrs. Barrows' apartment delay the climax of the story? How does Mr. Fitweiler's decision to send Mrs. Barrows to see Dr. Fitch provide the story with an appropriate denouement?
2. How does Mr. Fitweiler's statement that "Man is fallible but Martin isn't" establish Martin's character? How does Martin's description of Mrs. Barrows' language and behavior make the infallible Martin a sympathetic character? What is ironic about Mrs. Barrows' description of Martin as an "odd little man"?
3. How do Martin's office and filing cabinets represent the precision of the F and S system? How do Martin's personal habits establish the stable boundaries of his existence? Is Martin right to see Mrs. Barrows as a threat to this orderly world? Explain your answer.
4. How does Martin's presentation of his case to an imaginary jury establish the humorous point of view in this story? Why would the story cease to be humorous if it were told from Mrs. Barrows' point of view?
5. In what ways does this story comment on the battles between tradition and change, dullness and imagination, men and women? According to the story, what is the most effective way to win these battles, to be "sitting in the catbird seat"?

86

LEO TOLSTOY

The Death of Ivan Ilych

LEO TOLSTOY (1828–1910) was born into the Russian nobility at Yasnaya Polyana, his family's estate south of Moscow, and was privately tutored through his restless and reckless youth. After a brief stay at Kazan University, he joined the Russian Army and began writing sketches of military life during the Crimean War (1835–1856), as well as three autobiographical novels, *Childhood* (1852), *Boyhood* (1854), and *Youth* (1857). Tolstoy left the army in 1856 and traveled in Europe before returning to his family estate to start a progressive school for children. In 1862 he married, published a novel, *The Cossacks,* and began work on his epic of the Napoleonic wars, *War and Peace,* which was finally published in 1869. Tolstoy spent the next eight years completing his second masterpiece, *Anna Karenina* (1876), the story of a woman who is destroyed by her passions and society's hypocrisy. About 1889, Tolstoy underwent a religious conversion and dedicated his life to propagating his own version of radical Christianity. He published his new views in volumes of nonfiction such as *What Men Live By* (1881), *My Confession* (1882), *What I Believe* (1884), and *The Kingdom of God Is Within You* (1893). Tolstoy's fiction during this period, *The Death of Ivan Ilych* (1886), *The Kreutzer Sonata* (1890), and *Resurrection* (1899), is powerful as literature, if on a much smaller scale than his two great works. Troubled by his spiritual turmoil, Tolstoy left his home and family to seek exile in a monastery. But he never reached his destination, dying in the waiting room of a railway station. *The Death of Ivan Ilych* records the tragic life of a man who discovers too late that he did not live as he ought to have lived.

1

During an interval in the Melvinski trial in the large building of the Law Courts the members and public prosecutor met in Ivan Egorovich Shebek's private room, where the conversation turned on the celebrated Krasovski case. Fedor Vasilievich warmly maintained that it was not subject to their jurisdiction, Ivan Egorovich maintained the contrary, while Peter Ivanovich, not having entered into the discussion at the start, took no part in it but looked through the *Gazette* which had just been handed in.

"Gentlemen," he said, "Ivan Ilych has died!"

"You don't say so!"

"Here, read it yourself," replied Peter Ivanovich, handing Fedor Vasilievich the paper still damp from the press. Surrounded by a black border were the words "Praskovya Fedorovna Golovina, with profound sorrow, informs relatives and friends of the demise of her beloved husband Ivan Ilych Golovin, Member of the Court of Justice, which occurred on February the 4th of this year 1882. The funeral will take place on Friday at one o'clock in the afternoon."

Ivan Ilych had been a colleague of the gentlemen present and was liked by them all. He had been ill for some weeks with an illness said to be incurable. His post had been kept open for him, but there had been conjectures that in case of his death Alexeev might receive his appointment, and that either Vinnikov or Shtabel would succeed Alexeev. So on receiving the news of Ivan Ilych's death the first thought of each of the gentlemen in that private room was of the changes and promotions it might occasion among themselves or their acquaintances.

"I shall be sure to get Shtabel's place or Vinnikov's," thought Fedor Vasilievich. "I was promised that long ago, and the promotion means an extra eight hundred rubles a year for me besides the allowance."

"Now I must apply for my brother-in-law's transfer from Kaluga," thought Peter Ivanovich. "My wife will be very glad, and then she won't be able to say that I never do anything for her relations."

"I thought he would never leave his bed again," said Peter Ivanovich aloud. "It's very sad."

"But what really was the matter with him?"

"The doctors couldn't say—at least they could, but each of them said something different. When last I saw him I thought he was getting better."

"And I haven't been to see him since the holidays. I always meant to go."

"Had he any property?"

"I think his wife had a little—but something quite trifling."

"We shall have to go see her, but they live so terribly far away."

"Far away from you, you mean. Everything's far away from your place."

"You see, he never can forgive my living on the other side of the river," said Peter Ivanovich, smiling at Shebek. Then, still talking of the distances between different parts of the city, they returned to the Court.

Besides considerations as to the possible transfers and promotions likely to result from Ivan Ilych's death, the mere fact of the death of a near acquaintance aroused, as usual, in all who heard of it the complacent feeling that "it is he who is dead and not I."

Each one thought or felt, "Well, he's dead but I'm alive!" But the more intimate of Ivan Ilych's acquaintances, his so-called friends, could not help thinking also that they would now have to fulfill the very tiresome demands of propriety by attending the funeral service and paying a visit of condolence to the widow.

Fedor Vasilievich and Peter Ivanovich had been his nearest acquaintances. Peter Ivanovich had studied law with Ivan Ilych and had considered himself to be under obligations to him.

Having told his wife at dinner-time of Ivan Ilych's death, and of his conjecture that it might be possible to get her brother transferred to their circuit, Peter Ivanovich sacrificed his usual nap, put on his evening clothes, and drove to Ivan Ilych's house.

At the entrance stood a carriage and two cabs. Leaning against the wall in the hall downstairs near the cloak-stand was a coffin-lid covered with cloth of gold, ornamented with gold cord and tassels, that had been polished up with metal powder. Two ladies in black were taking off their fur cloaks. Peter Ivanovich recognized one of them as Ivan Ilych's sister, but the other was a stranger to him. His colleague Schwartz was just coming downstairs, but on seeing Peter Ivanovich enter he stopped and winked at him, as if to say: "Ivan Ilych has made a mess of things—not like you and me."

Schwartz's face with his Piccadilly whiskers, and his slim figure in evening dress, had as usual an air of elegant solemnity which contrasted with the playfulness of his character and had a special piquancy here, or so it seemed to Peter Ivanovich.

Peter Ivanovich allowed the ladies to precede him and slowly followed them upstairs. Schwartz did not come down but remained where he was, and Peter Ivanovich understood that he wanted to arrange where they should play bridge that evening. The ladies went upstairs to the widow's room, and Schwartz with seriously compressed lips but a playful look in his eyes, indicated by a twist of his eye-brows the room to the right where the body lay.

Peter Ivanovich, like everyone else on such occasions, entered feeling uncertain what he would have to do. All he knew was that at such times it is always safe to cross oneself. But he was not quite sure whether one should make obeisances while doing so. He therefore adopted a middle course. On entering the room he began crossing himself and made a slight movement resembling a bow. At the same time, as far as the motion of his head and arm allowed, he surveyed the room. Two young men—apparently nephews, one of whom was a high school pupil—were leaving the room, crossing themselves as they did so. An old woman was standing motionless, and a lady with strangely arched eyebrows was saying something to her in a whisper. A vigorous, resolute Church Reader, in a frock-coat, was reading something in a loud voice with an expression that precluded any contradiction. The butler's assistant, Gerasim, stepping lightly in front of Peter Ivanovich, was strewing something on the floor. Noticing this, Peter Ivanovich was immediately aware of a faint odour of a decomposing body.

The last time he had called on Ivan Ilych, Peter Ivanovich had seen Gerasim in the study. Ivan Ilych had been particularly fond of him and he was performing the duty of a sick nurse.

Peter Ivanovich continued to make the sign of the cross slightly inclining his head in an intermediate direction between the coffin, the Reader, and the icons on the table in a corner of the room. Afterwards, when it seemed to him that this movement of his arm in crossing himself had gone on too long, he stopped and began to look at the corpse.

The dead man lay, as dead men always lie, in a specially heavy way, his rigid limbs sunk in the soft cushions of the coffin, with the head forever bowed on the pillow. His yellow waxen brow with bald patches over his sunken temples was thrust up in the way peculiar to the dead, the protruding nose seeming to press on the upper lip. He was much changed and had grown even thinner since Peter Ivanovich had last seen him, but, as is always the case with the dead, his face was handsomer and above all more dignified than when he was alive. The expression on the face said that what was necessary had been accomplished, and accomplished rightly. Besides this there was in that expression a reproach and a warning to the living. This warning seemed to Peter Ivanovich out of place, or at least not applicable to him. He felt a certain discomfort and so he hurriedly crossed himself once more and turned and went out of the door—too hurriedly and too regardless of propriety, as he himself was aware.

Schwartz was waiting for him in the adjoining room with legs spread wide apart and both hands toying with his top-hat behind his back. The mere sight of that playful, well-groomed, and elegant figure refreshed Peter Ivanovich. He felt that Schwartz was above all these happenings and would not surrender to any depressing influences. His very look said that this incident of a church service for Ivan Ilych could not be a sufficient reason for infringing the order of the session—in other words, that it would certainly not prevent his unwrapping a new pack of cards and shuffling them that evening while a footman placed four fresh candles on the table: in fact, there was no reason for supposing that this incident would hinder their spending the evening agreeably. Indeed he said this in a whisper as Peter Ivanovich passed him, proposing that they should meet for a game at Fedor Vasilievich's. But apparently Peter Ivanovich was not destined to play bridge that evening. Praskovya Fedorovna (a short, fat woman who despite all efforts to the contrary had continued to broaden steadily from her shoulders downwards and who had the same extraordinarily arched eyebrows as the lady who had been standing by the coffin), dressed all in black, her head covered with lace, came out of her own room with some other ladies, conducted them to the room where the dead body lay, and said: "The service will begin immediately. Please go in."

Schwartz, making an indefinite bow, stood still, evidently neither accepting nor declining this invitation. Praskovya Fedorovna, recognizing Peter Ivanovich, sighed, went close up to him, took his hand, and said: "I know you were a true friend to Ivan Ilych . . ." and looked at him awaiting some suitable response. And Peter Ivanovich knew that, just as it had been the right thing to cross himself in that room, so what he had to do here was to press her hand, sigh, and say, "Believe me . . ." So he did all this and as he did it felt that the desired result had been achieved: that both he and she were touched.

"Come with me. I want to speak to you before it begins," said the widow. "Give me your arm."

Peter Ivanovich gave her his arm and they went to the inner room, passing Schwartz who winked at Peter Ivanovich compassionately.

"That does for our bridge! Don't object if we find another player. Perhaps you can cut in when you do escape," said his playful look.

Peter Ivanovich sighed still more deeply and despondently, and Praskovya Fedorovna pressed his arm gratefully. When they reached the drawing-room, upholstered in pink cretonne and lighted by a dim lamp, they sat down at the table—she on a sofa and Peter Ivanovich on a low pouffe, the springs of which yielded spasmodically under his weight. Praskovya Fedorovna had been on the point of warning him to take another seat, but felt that such a warning was out of keeping with her present condition and so changed her mind. As he sat down on the pouffe Peter Ivanovich recalled how Ivan Ilych had arranged this room and had consulted him regarding this pink cretonne with green leaves. The whole room was full of furniture and knick-knacks, and on her way to the sofa the lace of the widow's black shawl caught on the carved edge of the table. Peter Ivanovich rose to detach it, and the springs on the pouffe, relieved of his weight, rose also and gave him a push. The widow began detaching her shawl herself, and Peter Ivanovich again sat down, suppressing the rebellious springs of the pouffe under him. But the widow had not quite freed herself and Peter Ivanovich got up again, and again the pouffe rebelled and even creaked. When this was all over she took out a clean cambric handkerchief and began to weep. The episode with the shawl and the struggle with the pouffe had cooled Peter Ivanovich's emotions and he sat there with a sullen look on his face. This awkward situation was interrupted by Sokolov, Ivan Ilych's butler, who came to report that the plot in the cemetery that Praskovya Fedorovna had chosen would cost two hundred rubles. She stopped weeping and, looking at Peter Ivanovich with the air of a victim, remarked in French that it was very hard for her. Peter Ivanovich made a silent gesture signifying his full conviction that it must indeed be so.

"Please smoke," she said in a magnanimous yet crushed voice, and turned to discuss with Sokolov the price of the plot for the grave.

Peter Ivanovich while lighting his cigarette heard her inquiring very circumstantially into the price of different plots in the cemetery and finally decide which she would take. When that was done she gave instructions about engaging the choir. Sokolov then left the room.

"I look after everything myself," she told Peter Ivanovich, shifting the albums that lay on the table; and noticing that the table was endangered by his cigarette-ash, she immediately passed him an ashtray, saying as she did so: "I consider it an affectation to say that my grief prevents my attending to practical affairs. On the contrary, if anything can—I won't say console me, but—distract me, it is seeing to everything concerning him." She again took out her handkerchief as if preparing to cry, but suddenly, as if mastering her feeling, she shook herself and began to speak calmly. "But there is something I want to talk to you about."

Peter Ivanovich bowed, keeping control of the springs of the pouffe, which immediately began quivering under him.

"He suffered terribly the last few days."

"Did he?" said Peter Ivanovich.

"Oh, terribly! He screamed unceasingly, not for minutes but for hours. For the last three days he screamed incessantly. It was unendurable. I cannot understand how I bore it; you could hear him three rooms off. Oh, what I have suffered!"

"Is it possible that he was conscious all that time?" asked Peter Ivanovich.

"Yes," she whispered. "To the last moment. He took leave of us a quarter of an hour before he died, and asked us to take Volodya away."

The thought of the sufferings of this man he had known so intimately, first as a merry little boy, then as a school-mate, and later as a grown-up colleague, suddenly struck Peter Ivanovich with horror, despite an unpleasant consciousness of his own and this woman's dissimulation. He again saw that brow, and that nose pressing down on the lip, and felt afraid for himself.

"Three days of frightful suffering and then death! Why, that might suddenly, at any time, happen to me," he thought, and for a moment felt terrified. But—he did not himself know how—the customary reflection at once occurred to him that this had happened to Ivan Ilych and not to him, and that it should not and could not happen to him, and that to think that it could would be yielding to depression which he ought not to do, as Schwartz's expression plainly showed. After which reflection Peter Ivanovich felt reassured, and began to ask with interest about the details of Ivan Ilych's death, as though death was an accident natural to Ivan Ilych but certainly not to himself.

After many details of the really dreadful physical sufferings Ivan Ilych had endured (which details he learnt only from the effect those sufferings had produced on Praskovya Fedorovna's nerves) the widow apparently found it necessary to get to business.

"Oh, Peter Ivanovich, how hard it is! How terribly, terribly hard!" and she again began to weep.

Peter Ivanovich sighed and waited for her to finish blowing her nose. When she had done so he said, "Believe me . . ." and she again began talking and brought out what was evidently her chief concern with him—namely, to question him as to how she could obtain a grant of money from the government on the occasion of her husband's death. She made it appear that she was asking Peter Ivanovich's advice about her pension, but he soon saw that she already knew about that to the minutest detail, more even than he did himself. She knew how much could be got out of the government in consequence of her husband's death, but wanted to find out whether she could not possibly extract something more. Peter Ivanovich tried to think of some means of doing so, but after reflecting for a while and, out of propriety, condemning the government for its niggardliness, he said he thought that nothing more could be got. Then she sighed and evidently began to devise means of getting rid of her visitor. Noticing this, he put out his cigarette, rose, pressed her hand, and went out into the anteroom.

In the dining-room where the clock stood that Ivan Ilych had liked so much and had bought at an antique shop, Peter Ivanovich met a priest and a few acquaintances who had come to attend the service, and he recognized Ivan Ilych's daughter, a handsome young woman. She was in black and her slim figure appeared slimmer than ever. She had a gloomy, determined, almost angry expression, and bowed to Peter Ivanovich as though he were in some way to blame. Behind her, with the same offended look, stood a wealthy young man, an examining magistrate, whom Peter Ivanovich also knew and who was her fiancé, as he had heard. He bowed mournfully to them and was about to pass into the death-chamber, when from under the stairs appeared the figure of Ivan Ilych's schoolboy son, who was extremely like his father. He seemed a little Ivan Ilych, such as Peter Ivanovich remembered when they studied law together. His tear-stained eyes had in them the look that is seen in the eyes of boys of thirteen or fourteen who are not pure-minded. When he saw Peter Ivanovich he scowled morosely and shame-facedly. Peter Ivanovich nodded to him and entered the death-chamber. The service began: candles, groans, incense, tears, and sobs. Peter Ivanovich stood looking gloomily down at his feet. He did not look once at the dead man, did not yield to any depressing influence, and was one of the first to leave the room. There was no one in the anteroom, but Gerasim darted out of the dead man's room, rummaged with his strong hands among the fur coats to find Peter Ivanovich's and helped him on with it.

"Well, friend Gerasim," said Peter Ivanovich, so as to say something. "It's a sad affair, isn't it?"

"It's God's will. We shall all come to it some day," said Gerasim, displaying his teeth—the even, white teeth of a healthy peasant—and, like a man in the thick of urgent work, he briskly opened the front door, called the coachman, helped Peter Ivanovich into the sledge, and sprang back to the porch as if in readiness for what he had to do next.

Peter Ivanovich found the fresh air particularly pleasant after the smell of incense, the dead body, and carbolic acid.

"Where to, sir?" asked the coachman.

"It's not too late even now. . . . I'll call around on Fedor Vasilievich."

He accordingly drove there and found them just finishing the first rubber, so that it was quite convenient for him to cut in.

2

Ivan Ilych's life had been most simple and most ordinary and therefore most terrible.

He had been a member of the Court of Justice, and died at the age of forty-five. His father had been an official who after serving in various ministries and departments of Petersburg had made the sort of career which brings men to positions from which by reason of their long service they cannot be dismissed, though they are obviously unfit to hold any responsible position, and for whom therefore posts are specially created, which though fictitious carry salaries of from six to ten thousand rubles that are not fictitious, and in receipt of which they live on to a great age.

Such was the Privy Councillor and superfluous member of various superfluous institutions, Ilya Epimovich Golovin.

He had three sons, of whom Ivan Ilych was the second. The eldest son was following in his father's footsteps only in another department, and was already approaching that stage in the service at which a similar sinecure would be reached. The third son was a failure. He had ruined his prospects in a number of positions and was now serving in the railway department. His father and brothers, and still more their wives, not merely disliked meeting him, but avoided remembering his existence unless compelled to do so. His sister had married Baron Greff, a Petersburg official of her father's type. Ivan Ilych was *le phénix de la famille* as people said. He was neither as cold and formal as his elder brother nor as wild as the younger, but was a happy mean between them—an intelligent, polished, lively and agreeable man. He had studied with his younger brother at the School of Law, but the latter had failed to complete the course and was expelled when he was in the fifth class. Ivan Ilych finished the course well. Even when he was at the School of Law he was just what he remained for the rest of his life: a capable, cheerful, good-natured, and social man, though strict in the fulfilment of what he considered to be his duty: and he considered his duty to be what was so considered by those in authority. Neither as a boy nor as a man was he a toady, but from early youth was by nature attracted to people of high station as a fly is drawn to the light, assimilating their ways and views of life and establishing friendly relations with them. All the enthusiasms of childhood and youth passed without leaving much trace on him; he succumbed to sensuality, to vanity, and latterly among the highest classes to liberalism, but always within limits which his instinct unfailingly indicated to him as correct.

At school he had done things which had formerly seemed to him very horrid and made him feel disgusted with himself when he did them; but when later on he saw that such actions were done by people of good position and that they did not regard them as wrong, he was able not exactly to regard them as right, but to forget about them entirely or not be at all troubled at remembering them.

Having graduated from the School of Law and qualified for the tenth rank of civil service, and having received money from his father for his equipment, Ivan Ilych ordered himself clothes at Scharmer's, the fashionable tailor, hung a medallion inscribed *respice finem* on his watch-chain, took leave of his professor and the prince who was patron of the school, had a farewell dinner with his comrades at Donon's first-class restaurant, and with his new and fashionable portmanteau, linen, clothes, shaving and other toilet appliances, and a travelling rug, all purchased at the best shops, he set off for one of the provinces where, through his father's influence, he had been attached to the Governor as an official for special service.

In the province Ivan Ilych soon arranged as easy and agreeable a position for himself as he had had at the School of Law. He performed his official tasks, made his career, and at the same time amused himself pleasantly and decorously. Occasionally he paid official visits to country districts, where he behaved with dignity both to his superiors and inferiors, and performed the duties entrusted to him, which related chiefly to the sectarians, with an exactness and incorruptible honesty of which he could not but feel proud.

In official matters, despite his youth and taste for frivolous gaiety, he was exceedingly reserved, punctilious, and even severe; but in society he was often amusing and witty, and always good-natured, correct in his manner, and *bon enfant,* as the governor and his wife—with whom he was like one of the family—used to say of him.

In the provinces he had an affair with a lady who made advances to the elegant young lawyer, and there was also a milliner; and there were carousals with aides-de-camp who visited the district, and after-supper visits to a certain outlying street of doubtful reputation; and there was too some obsequiousness to his chief and even to his chief's wife, but all this was done with such a tone of good breeding that no hard names could be applied to it. It all came under the heading of the French saying: "Il faut que jeunesse se passe." It was all done with clean hands, in clean linen, with French phrases, and above all among people of the best society and consequently with the approval of people of rank.

So Ivan Ilych served for five years and then came a change in his official life. The new and reformed judicial institutions were introduced, and new men were needed. Ivan Ilych became such a new man. He was offered the post of Examining Magistrate, and he accepted it though the post was in another province and obliged him to give up the connexions he had formed and to make new ones. His friends met to give him a send-off; they had a group-photograph taken and presented him with a silver cigarette-case, and he set off to his new post.

As examining magistrate Ivan Ilych was just as *comme il faut* and decorous a man, inspiring general respect and capable of separating his official duties from his private life, as he had been when acting as an official on special service. His duties now as examining magistrate were far more interesting and attractive than before. In his former position it had been pleasant to wear an undress uniform made by Scharmer, and to pass through the crowd of petitioners and officials who were timorously awaiting an audience with the governor, and who envied him as with free and easy gait he went straight into his chief's private room to have a cup of tea and a cigarette with him. But not many people had then been directly dependent on him—only police officials and the sectarians when he went on special missions—and he liked to treat them politely, almost as comrades, as if he were letting them feel that he who had the power to crush them was treating them in this simple, friendly way. There were then but few such people. But now, as an examining magistrate, Ivan Ilych felt that everyone without exception, even the most important and self-satisfied, was in his power, and that he need only write a few words on a sheet of paper with a certain heading, and this or that important, self-satisfied person would be brought before him in the role of an accused person or a witness, and if he did not choose to allow him to sit down, would have to stand before him and answer his questions. Ivan Ilych never abused his power; he tried on the contrary to soften its expression, but the consciousness of it and of the possibility of softening its effect, supplied the chief interest and attraction of his office. In his work itself, especially in his examinations, he very soon acquired a method of eliminating all considerations irrelevant to the legal aspect of the case, and reducing even the most complicated case to a form in which it would be presented on paper only in its externals, completely excluding his personal opinion of the matter, while above all observing every prescribed formality. The work was new and Ivan Ilych was one of the first men to apply the new Code of 1864.

On taking up the post of examining magistrate in a new town, he made new acquaintances and connexions, placed himself on a new footing, and assumed a somewhat different tone. He took up an attitude of rather dignified aloofness towards the provincial authorities, but picked out the best circle of legal gentlemen and wealthy gentry living in the town and assumed a tone of slight dissatisfaction with the government, of moderate liberalism, and of enlightened citizenship. At the same time, without at all altering the elegance of his toilet, he ceased shaving his chin and allowed his beard to grow as it pleased.

Ivan Ilych settled down very pleasantly in this new town. The society there, which inclined towards opposition to the Governor, was friendly, his salary was larger, and he began to play *vint,* which he found added not a little to the pleasure of life, for he had a capacity for cards, played good-humouredly, and calculated rapidly and astutely, so that he usually won.

After living there for two years he met his future wife, Praskovya Fedorovna Mikhel, who was the most attractive, clever, and brilliant girl of the set in which he moved, and among other amusements and relaxations from his labours as examining magistrate, Ivan Ilych established light and playful relations with her.

While he had been an official on special service he had been accustomed to dance, but now as an examining magistrate it was exceptional for him to do so. If he danced now, he did it as if to show that though he served under the reformed order of things, and had reached the fifth official rank, yet when it came to dancing he could do it better than most people. So at the end of an evening he sometimes danced with Praskovya Fedorovna, and it was chiefly during these dances that he captivated her. She fell in love with him. Ivan Ilych had at first no definite intention of marrying, but when the girl fell in love with him he said to himself: "Really, why shouldn't I marry?"

Praskovya Fedorovna came of a good family, was not bad looking and had some little property. Ivan Ilych might have aspired to a more brilliant match, but even this was good.

He had his salary, and she, he hoped, would have an equal income. She was well connected, and was a sweet, pretty, and thoroughly correct young woman. To say that Ivan Ilych married because he fell in love with Praskovya Fedorovna and found that she sympathized with his views of life would be as incorrect as to say that he married because his social circle approved of the match. He was swayed by both these considerations: the marriage gave him personal satisfaction, and at the same time it was considered the right thing by the most highly placed of his associates.

So Ivan Ilych got married.

The preparations for marriage and the beginning of married life, with its conjugal caresses, the new furniture, new crockery, and new linen, were very pleasant until his wife became pregnant—so that Ivan Ilych had begun to think that marriage would not impair the easy, agreeable, gay and always decorous character of his life, approved of by society and regarded by himself as natural, but would even improve it. But from the first months of his wife's pregnancy, something new, unpleasant, depressing, and unseemly, and from which there was no way of escape, unexpectedly showed itself.

His wife, without any reason—*de gaieté de coeur* as Ivan Ilych expressed it to himself—began to disturb the pleasure and propriety of their life. She began to be jealous without any cause, expected him to devote his whole attention to her, found fault with everything, and made coarse and ill-mannered scenes.

At first Ivan Ilych hoped to escape from the unpleasantness of this state of affairs by the same easy and decorous relation to life that had served him heretofore: he tried to ignore his wife's disagreeable moods, continued to live in his usual easy and pleasant way, invited friends to his house for a game of cards, and also tried going out to his club or spending his evenings with friends. But one day his wife began upbraiding him so vigorously, using such coarse words, and continued to abuse him every time he did not fulfil her demands, so resolutely and with such evident determination not to give way till he submitted—that is, till he stayed at home and was bored just as she was—that he became alarmed. He now realized that matrimony—at any rate with Praskovya Fedorovna—was not always conducive to the pleasures and amenities of life but on the contrary often infringed both comfort and propriety, and that he must therefore entrench himself against such infringement. And Ivan Ilych began to seek for means of doing so. His official duties were the one thing that imposed upon Praskovya Fedorovna, and by means of his official work and the duties attached to it he began struggling with his wife to secure his own independence.

With the birth of their child, the attempts to feed it and the various failures in doing so, and with the real and imaginary illnesses of mother and child, in which Ivan Ilych's sympathy was demanded but about which he understood nothing, the need of securing for himself an existence outside his family life became still more imperative.

As his wife grew more irritable and exacting and Ivan Ilych transferred the centre of gravity of his life more and more to his official work, so did he grow to like his work better and became more ambitious than before.

Very soon, within a year of his wedding, Ivan Ilych had realized that marriage, though it may add some comforts to life, is in fact a very intricate and difficult affair towards which in order to perform one's duty, that is, to lead a decorous life approved of by society, one must adopt a definite attitude just as towards one's official duties.

And Ivan Ilych evolved such an attitude towards married life. He only required of it those conveniences—dinner at home, housewife, and bed—which it could give him, and above all that propriety of external forms required by public opinion. For the rest he looked for light-hearted pleasure and propriety, and was very thankful when he found them, but if he met with antagonism and querulousness he at once retired into his separate fenced-off world of official duties, where he found satisfaction.

Ivan Ilych was esteemed a good official, and after three years was made Assistant Public Prosecutor. His new duties, their importance, the possibility of indicting and imprisoning anyone he chose, the publicity his speeches received, and the success he had in all these things, made his work still more attractive.

More children came. His wife became more and more querulous and ill-tempered, but the attitude Ivan Ilych had adopted towards his home life rendered him almost impervious to her grumbling.

After seven years' service in that town he was transferred to another province as Public Prosecutor. They moved, but were short of money and his wife did not like the place they moved to. Though the salary was higher the cost of living was greater, besides which two of their children died and family life became still more unpleasant for him.

Praskovya Fedorovna blamed her husband for every inconvenience they encountered in their new home. Most of the conversations between husband and wife, especially as to the children's education, led to topics which recalled former disputes, and those disputes were apt to flare up again at any moment. There remained only those rare periods of amorousness which still came to them at times but did not last long. These were islets at which they anchored for a while and then again set out upon that ocean of veiled hostility which showed itself in their aloofness from one another. This aloofness might have grieved Ivan Ilych had he considered that it ought not to exist, but he now regarded the position as normal, and even made it the goal at which he aimed in family life. His aim was to free himself more and more from those unpleasantnesses and to give them a semblance of harmlessness and propriety. He attained this by spending less and less time with his family, and when obliged to be at home he tried to safeguard his position by the presence of outsiders. The chief thing, however, was that he had his official duties. The whole interest of his life now centered in the official world and that interest absorbed him. The consciousness of his power, being able to ruin anybody he wished to ruin, the importance, even the external dignity of his entry into court, or meetings with his subordinates, his success with superiors and inferiors, and above all his masterly handling of cases, of which he was conscious—all this gave him pleasure and filled his life, together with chats with his colleagues, dinners, and bridge. So that on the whole Ivan Ilych's life continued to flow as he considered it should do—pleasantly and properly.

So things continued for another seven years. His eldest daughter was already sixteen, another child had died, and only one son was left, a schoolboy and a subject of dissension. Ivan Ilych wanted to put him in the School of Law, but to spite him Praskovya Fedorovna entered him at the High School. The daughter had been educated at home and had turned out well: the boy did not learn badly either.

3

So Ivan Ilych lived for seventeen years after his marriage. He was already a Public Prosecutor of long standing, and had declined several proposed transfers while awaiting a more desirable post, when an unanticipated and unpleasant occurrence quite upset the peaceful course of his life. He was expecting to be offered the post of presiding judge in a University town, but Happe somehow came to the front and obtained the appointment instead. Ivan Ilych became irritable, reproached Happe, and quarrelled both with him and with his immediate superiors—who became colder to him and again passed him over when other appointments were made.

This was in 1880, the hardest year of Ivan Ilych's life. It was then that it became evident on the one hand that his salary was insufficient for them to live on, and on the other that he had been forgotten, and not only this, but that what was for him the greatest and most cruel injustice appeared to others a quite ordinary occurrence. Even his father did not consider it his duty to help him. Ivan Ilych felt himself abandoned by everyone, and that they regarded his position with a salary of 3,500 rubles as quite normal and even fortunate. He alone knew that with the consciousness of the injustices done him, with his wife's incessant nagging, and with the debts he had contracted by living beyond his means, his position was far from normal.

In order to save money that summer he obtained leave of absence and went with his wife to live in the country at her brother's place.

In the country, without his work, he experienced *ennui* for the first time in his life, and not only *ennui* but intolerable depression, and he decided that it was impossible to go on living like that, and that it was necessary to take energetic measures.

Having passed a sleepless night pacing up and down the veranda, he decided to go to Petersburg and bestir himself, in order to punish those who had failed to appreciate him and to get transferred to another ministry.

Next day, despite many protests from his wife and her brother, he started for Petersburg with the sole object of obtaining a post with a salary of five thousand rubles a year. He was no longer bent on any particular department, or tendency, or kind of activity. All he now wanted was an appointment to another post with a salary of five thousand rubles, either in the administration, in the banks, with the railways, in one of the Empress Marya's Institutions, or even in the customs—but it had to carry with it a salary of five thousand rubles and be in a ministry other than that in which they had failed to appreciate him.

And this quest of Ivan Ilych's was crowned with remarkable and unexpected success. At Kursk an acquaintance of his, F. I. Ilyin, got into the first-class carriage, sat down beside Ivan Ilych, and told him of a telegram just received by the Governor of Kursk announcing that a change was about to take place in the ministry: Peter Ivanovich was to be superseded by Ivan Semenovich.

The proposed change, apart from its significance for Russia, had a special significance for Ivan Ilych, because by bringing forward a new man, Peter Petrovich, and consequently his friend Zachar Ivanovich, it was highly favourable for Ivan Ilych, since Zachar Ivanovich was a friend and colleague of his.

In Moscow this news was confirmed, and on reaching Petersburg Ivan Ilych found Zachar Ivanovich and received a definite promise of an appointment in his former Department of Justice.

A week later he telegraphed to his wife: "Zachar in Miller's place. I shall receive appointment on presentation of report."

Thanks to this change of personnel, Ivan Ilych had unexpectedly obtained an appointment in his former ministry which placed him two stages above his former colleagues besides giving him five thousand rubles salary and three thousand five hundred rubles for expenses connected with his removal. All his ill humour towards his former enemies and the whole department vanished, and Ivan Ilych was completely happy.

He returned to the country more cheerful and contented than he had been for a long time. Praskovya Fedorovna also cheered up and a truce was arranged between them. Ivan Ilych told of how he had been feted by everybody in Petersburg, how all those who had been his enemies were put to shame and now fawned on him, how envious they were of his appointment, and how much everybody in Petersburg had liked him.

Praskovya Fedorovna listened to all this and appeared to believe it. She did not contradict anything, but only made plans for her life in the town to which they were going. Ivan Ilych saw with delight that these plans were his plans, that he and his wife agreed, and that, after a stumble, his life was regaining its due and natural character of pleasant lightheartedness and decorum.

Ivan Ilych had come back for a short time only, for he had to take up his new duties on the 10th of September. Moreover, he needed time to settle into the new place, to move all his belongings from the province, and to buy and order many additional things: in a word, to make such arrangements as he had resolved on, which were almost exactly what Praskovya Fedorovna too had decided on.

Now that everything had happened so fortunately, and that he and his wife were at one in their aims and moreover saw so little of one another, they got on together better than they had done since the first years of marriage. Ivan Ilych had thought of taking his family away with him at once, but the insistence of his wife's brother and her sister-in-law, who had suddenly become particularly amiable and friendly to him and his family, induced him to depart alone.

So he departed, and the cheerful state of mind induced by his success and by the harmony between his wife and himself, the one intensifying the other, did not leave him. He found a delightful house, just the thing both he and his wife had dreamt of. Spacious, lofty reception rooms in the old style, a convenient and dignified study, rooms for his wife and daughter, a study for his son—it might have been specially built for them. Ivan Ilych himself superintended the arrangement, chose the wall-papers, supplemented the furniture (preferably with antiques which he considered particularly *comme il faut*), and supervised the upholstering. Everything progressed and progressed and approached the ideal he had set himself: even when things were only half completed they exceeded his expectations. He saw what a refined and elegant character, free from vulgarity, it would all have when it was ready. On falling asleep he pictured to himself how the reception-room would look. Looking at the yet unfinished drawing-room he could see the fireplace, the screen, the what-not, the little chairs dotted here and there, the dishes and plates on the walls, and the bronzes, as they would be when everything was in place. He was pleased by the thought of how his wife and daughter, who shared his taste in this matter, would be impressed by it. They were certainly not expecting as much. He had been particularly successful in finding, and buying cheaply, antiques which gave a particularly aristocratic character to the whole place. But in his letters he intentionally understated everything in order to be able to surprise them. All this so absorbed him that his new duties—though he liked his official work—interested him less than he had expected. Sometimes he even had moments of absentmindedness during the Court Sessions, and would consider whether he should have straight or curved cornices for his curtains. He was so interested in it all that he often did things himself, rearranging the furniture, or rehanging the curtains. Once when mounting a step-ladder to show the upholsterer, who did not understand, how he wanted the hangings draped, he made a false step and slipped, but being a strong and agile man he clung on and only knocked his side against the knob of the window frame. The bruised place was painful but the pain soon passed, and he felt particularly bright and well just then. He wrote: "I feel fifteen years younger." He thought he would have everything ready by September, but it dragged on till mid-October. But the result was charming not only in his eyes but to everyone who saw it.

In reality it was just what is usually seen in the houses of people of moderate means who want to appear rich, and therefore succeed only in resembling others like themselves: there were damasks, dark wood, plants, rugs, and dull and polished bronzes—all the things people of a certain class have in order to resemble other people of that class. His house was so like the others that it would never have been noticed, but to him it all seemed to be quite exceptional. He was very happy when he met his family at the station and brought them to the newly furnished house all lit up, where a footman in a white tie opened the door into the hall decorated with plants, and when they went on into the drawing-room and the study uttering exclamations of delight. He conducted them everywhere, drank in their praises eagerly, and beamed with pleasure. At tea that evening, when Praskovya Fedorovna among other things asked him about his fall, he laughed, and showed them how he had gone flying and had frightened the upholsterer.

"It's a good thing I'm a bit of an athlete. Another man might have been killed, but I merely knocked myself, just here; it hurts when it's touched, but it's passing off already—it's only a bruise."

So they began living in their new home—in which, as always happens, when they got thoroughly settled in they found they were just one room short—and with the increased income, which as always was just a little (some five hundred rubles) too little, but it was all very nice.

Things went particularly well at first, before everything was finally arranged and while something had still to be done: this thing bought, that thing ordered, another thing moved, and something else adjusted. Though there were some disputes between husband and wife, they were both so well satisfied and had so much to do that it all passed off without any serious quarrels. When nothing was left to arrange it became rather dull and something seemed to be lacking, but they were then making acquaintances, forming habits, and life was growing fuller.

Ivan Ilych spent his mornings at the law court and came home to dinner, and at first he was generally in a good humour, though he occasionally became irritable just on account of his house. (Every spot on the tablecloth or the upholstery, and every broken window-blind string, irritated him. He had devoted so much trouble to arranging it all that every disturbance of it distressed him.) But on the whole his life ran its course as he believed life should do: easily, pleasantly, and decorously.

He got up at nine, drank his coffee, read the paper, and then put on his undress uniform and went to the law courts. There the harness in which he worked had already been stretched to fit him and he donned it without a hitch: petitioners, inquiries at the chancery, the chancery itself, and the sittings public and administrative. In all this the thing was to exclude everything fresh and vital, which always disturbs the regular course of official business, and to admit only official relations with people, and then only on official grounds. A man would come, for instance, wanting some information. Ivan Ilych, as one in whose sphere the matter did not lie, would have nothing to do with him: but if the man had some business with him in his official capacity, something that could be expressed on officially stamped paper, he would do everything, positively everything he could within the limits of such relations, and in doing so would maintain the semblance of friendly human relations, that is, would observe the courtesies of life. As soon as the official relations ended, so did everything else. Ivan Ilych possessed this capacity to separate his real life from the official side of affairs and not mix the two, in the highest degree, and by long practice and natural aptitude had brought it to such a pitch that sometimes, in the manner of a virtuoso, he would even allow himself to let the human and official relations mingle. He let himself do this just because he felt that he could at any time he chose resume the strictly official attitude again and drop the human relation. And he did it all easily, pleasantly, correctly, and even artistically. In the intervals between the sessions he smoked, drank tea, chatted a little about politics, a little about general topics, a little about cards, but most of all about official appointments. Tired, but with the feelings of a virtuoso—one of the first violins who has played his part in an orchestra with precision—he would return home to find that his wife and daughter had been out paying calls, or had a visitor, and that his son had been to school, had done his homework with his tutor, and was duly learning what is taught at High Schools. Everything was as it should be. After dinner, if they had no visitors, Ivan Ilych sometimes read a book that was being much discussed at the time, and in the evening settled down to work, that is, read official papers, compared the depositions of witnesses, and noted paragraphs of the Code applying to them. This was neither dull nor amusing. It was dull when he might have been playing bridge, but if no bridge was available it was at any rate better than doing nothing or sitting with his wife. Ivan Ilych's chief pleasure was giving little dinners to which he invited men and women of good social position, and just as his drawing-room resembled all other drawing-rooms so did his enjoyable little parties resemble all other such parties.

Once they even gave a dance. Ivan Ilych enjoyed it and everything went off well, except that it led to a violent quarrel with his wife about the cakes and sweets. Praskovya Fedorovna had made her own plans, but Ivan Ilych insisted on getting everything from an expensive confectioner and ordered too many cakes, and the quarrel occurred because some of those cakes were left over and the confectioner's bill came to forty-five rubles. It was a great and disagreeable quarrel. Praskovya Fedorovna called him "a fool and an imbecile," and he clutched at his head and made angry allusions to divorce.

But the dance itself had been enjoyable. The best people were there, and Ivan Ilych had danced with Princess Trufonova, a sister of the distinguished founder of the Society "Bear my Burden."

The pleasures connected with his work were pleasures of ambition; his social pleasures were those of vanity; but Ivan Ilych's greatest pleasure was playing bridge. He acknowledged that whatever disagreeable incident happened in his life, the pleasure that beamed like a ray of light above everything else was to sit down to bridge with good players, not noisy partners, and of course to four-handed bridge (with five players it was annoying to have to stand out, though one pretended not to mind), to play a clever and serious game (when the cards allowed it) and then to have supper and drink a glass of wine. After a game of bridge, especially if he had won a little (to win a large sum was unpleasant), Ivan Ilych went to bed in specially good humour.

So they lived. They formed a circle of acquaintances among the best people and were visited by people of importance and by young folk. In their views as to their acquaintances, husband, wife and daughter were entirely agreed, and tacitly and unanimously kept at arm's length and shook off the various shabby friends and relations who, with much show of affection, gushed into the drawing-room with its Japanese plates on the walls. Soon these shabby friends ceased to obtrude themselves and only the best people remained in the Golovins' set.

Young men made up to Lisa, and Petrishchev, an examining magistrate and Dmitri Ivanovich Petrishchev's son and sole heir, began to be so attentive to her that Ivan Ilych had already spoken to Praskovya Fedorovna about it, and considered whether they should not arrange a party for them or get up some private theatricals.

So they lived, and all went well, without change, and life flowed pleasantly.

4

They were all in good health. It could not be called ill health if Ivan Ilych sometimes said that he had a queer taste in his mouth and felt some discomfort in his left side.

But this discomfort increased and, though not exactly painful, grew into a sense of pressure in his side accompanied by ill humour. And his irritability became worse and worse and began to mar the agreeable, easy, and correct life that had established itself in the Golovin family. Quarrels between husband and wife became more and more frequent, and soon the ease and amenity disappeared and even the decorum was barely maintained. Scenes again became frequent, and very few of those islets remained on which husband and wife could meet without an explosion. Praskovya Fedorovna now had good reason to say that her husband's temper was trying. With characteristic exaggeration she said he had always had a dreadful temper, and that it had needed all her good nature to put up with it for twenty years. It was true that now the quarrels were started by him. His bursts of temper always came just before dinner, often just as he began to eat his soup. Sometimes he noticed that a plate or dish was chipped, or the food was not right, or his son put his elbow on the table, or his daughter's hair was not done as he liked it, and for all this he blamed Praskovya Fedorovna. At first she retorted and said disagreeable things to him, but once or twice he fell into such a rage at the beginning of dinner that she realized it was due to some physical derangement brought on by taking food, and so she restrained herself and did not answer, but only hurried to get the dinner over. She regarded this self-restraint as highly praiseworthy. Having come to the conclusion that her husband had a dreadful temper and made her life miserable, she began to feel sorry for herself, and the more she pitied herself the more she hated her husband. She began to wish he would die; yet she did not want him to die because then his salary would cease. And this irritated her against him still more. She considered herself dreadfully unhappy just because not even his death could save her, and though she concealed her exasperation, that hidden exasperation of hers increased his irritation also.

After one scene in which Ivan Ilych had been particularly unfair and after which he had said in explanation that he certainly was irritable but that it was due to his not being well, she said that if he was ill it should be attended to, and insisted on his going to see a celebrated doctor.

He went. Everything took place as he had expected and as it always does. There was the usual waiting and the important air assumed by the doctor, with which he was so familiar (resembling that which he himself assumed in court), and the sounding and listening, and the questions which called for answers that were foregone conclusions and were evidently unnecessary, and the look of importance which implied that "if only you put yourself in our hands we will arrange everything—we know indubitably how it has to be done, always in the same way for everybody alike." It was all just as it was in the law courts. The doctor put on just the same air towards him as he himself put on towards an accused person.

The doctor said that so-and-so indicated that there was so-and-so inside the patient, but if the investigation of so-and-so did not confirm this, then he must assume that and that. If he assumed that and that, then . . . and so on. To Ivan Ilych only one question was important: was his case serious or not? But the doctor ignored that inappropriate question. From his point of view it was not the one under consideration, the real question was to decide between a floating kidney, chronic catarrh, or appendicitis. It was not a question of Ivan Ilych's life or death, but one between a floating kidney and appendicitis. And that question the doctor solved brilliantly, as it seemed to Ivan Ilych, in favour of the appendix, with the reservation that should an examination of the urine give fresh indications the matter would be reconsidered. All this was just what Ivan Ilych had himself brilliantly accomplished a thousand times in dealing with men on trial. The doctor summed up just as brilliantly, looking over his spectacles triumphantly and even gaily at the accused. From the doctor's summing up Ivan Ilych concluded that things were bad, but that for the doctor, and perhaps for everybody else, it was a matter of indifference, though for him it was bad. And this conclusion struck him painfully, arousing in him a great feeling of pity for himself and of bitterness towards the doctor's indifference to a matter of such importance.

He said nothing of this, but rose, placed the doctor's fee on the table, and remarked with a sigh: "We sick people probably often put inappropriate questions. But tell me, in general, is this complaint dangerous, or not? . . ."

The doctor looked at him sternly over his spectacles with one eye, as if to say: "Prisoner, if you will not keep to the questions put to you, I shall be obliged to have you removed from the court."

"I have already told you what I consider necessary and proper. The analysis may show something more." And the doctor bowed.

Ivan Ilych went out slowly, seated himself disconsolately in his sledge, and drove home. All the way home he was going over what the doctor had said, trying to translate those complicated, obscure, scientific phrases into plain language and find in them an answer to the question: "Is my condition bad? Is it very bad? Or is there as yet nothing much wrong?" And it seemed to him that the meaning of what the doctor had said was that it was very bad. Everything in the streets seemed depressing. The cabmen, the houses, the passers-by, and the shops, were dismal. His ache, this dull gnawing ache that never ceased for a moment, seemed to have acquired a new and more serious significance from the doctor's dubious remarks. Ivan Ilych now watched it with a new and oppressive feeling.

He reached home and began to tell his wife about it. She listened, but in the middle of his account his daughter came in with her hat on, ready to go out with her mother. She sat down reluctantly to listen to this tedious story, but could not stand it long, and her mother too did not hear him to the end.

"Well, I am very glad," she said. "Mind now to take your medicine regularly. Give me the prescription and I'll send Gerasim to the chemist's." And she went to get ready to go out.

While she was in the room Ivan Ilych had hardly taken time to breathe, but he sighed deeply when she left it.

"Well," he thought, "perhaps it isn't so bad after all."

He began taking his medicine and following the doctor's directions, which had been altered after the examination of the urine. But then it happened that there was a contradiction between the indications drawn from the examination of the urine and the symptoms that showed themselves. It turned out that what was happening differed from what the doctor had told him, and that he had either forgotten, or blundered, or hidden something from him. He could not, however, be blamed for that, and Ivan Ilych still obeyed his orders implicitly and at first derived some comfort from doing so.

From the time of his visit to the doctor, Ivan Ilych's chief occupation was the exact fulfilment of the doctor's instructions regarding hygiene and the taking of medicine, and the observation of his pain and his excretions. His chief interests came to be people's ailments and people's health. When sickness, deaths, or recoveries were mentioned in his presence, especially when the illness resembled his own, he listened with agitation which he tried to hide, asked questions, and applied what he heard to his own case.

The pain did not grow less, but Ivan Ilych made efforts to force himself to think that he was better. And he could do this so long as nothing agitated him. But as soon as he had any unpleasantness with his wife, any lack of success in his official work, or held bad cards at bridge, he was at once acutely sensible of his disease. He had formerly borne such mischances, hoping soon to adjust what was wrong, to master it and attain success, or make a grand slam. But now every mischance upset him and plunged him into despair. He would say to himself: "There now, just as I was beginning to get better and the medicine had begun to take effect, comes this accursed misfortune, or unpleasantness . . ." And he was furious with the mishap, or with the people who were causing the unpleasantness and killing him, for he felt that this fury was killing him but could not restrain it. One would have thought that it should have been clear to him that this exasperation with circumstances and people aggravated his illness, and that he ought therefore to ignore unpleasant occurrences. But he drew the very opposite conclusion: he said that he needed peace, and he watched for everything that might disturb it and became irritable at the slightest infringement of it. His condition was rendered worse by the fact that he read medical books and consulted doctors. The progress of his disease was so gradual that he could deceive himself when comparing one day with another—the difference was so slight. But when he consulted the doctors it seemed to him that he was getting worse, and even very rapidly. Yet despite this he was continually consulting them.

That month he went to see another celebrity, who told him almost the same as the first had done but put his questions rather differently, and the interview with this celebrity only increased Ivan Ilych's doubts and fears. A friend of a friend of his, a very good doctor, diagnosed his illness again quite differently from the others, and though he predicted recovery, his questions and suppositions bewildered Ivan Ilych still more and increased his doubts. A homeopathist diagnosed the disease in yet another way, and prescribed medicine which Ivan Ilych took secretly for a week. But after a week, not feeling any improvement and having lost confidence both in the former doctor's treatment and in this one's, he became still more despondent. One day a lady acquaintance mentioned a cure effected by a wonder-working icon. Ivan Ilych caught himself listening attentively and beginning to believe that it had occurred. This incident alarmed him. "Has my mind really weakened to such an extent?" he asked himself. "Nonsense! It's all rubbish. I mustn't give way to nervous fears but having chosen a doctor must keep strictly to his treatment. That is what I will do. Now it's all settled. I won't think about it, but will follow the treatment seriously till summer, and then we shall see. From now there must be no more of this wavering!" This was easy to say but impossible to carry out. The pain in his side oppressed him and seemed to grow worse and more incessant, while the taste in his mouth grew stranger and stranger. It seemed to him that his breath had a disgusting smell, and he was conscious of a loss of appetite and strength. There was no deceiving himself: something terrible, new, and more important than anything before in his life, was taking place within him of which he alone was aware. Those about him did not understand or would not understand it, but thought everything in the world was going on as usual. That tormented Ivan Ilych more than anything. He saw that his household, especially his wife and daughter who were in a perfect whirl of visiting, did not understand anything of it and were annoyed that he was so depressed and so exacting, as if he were to blame for it. Though they tried to disguise it he saw that he was an obstacle in their path, and that his wife had adopted a definite line in regard to his illness and kept to it regardless of anything he said or did. Her attitude was this: "You know," she would say to her friends, "Ivan Ilych can't do as other people do, and keep to the treatment prescribed for him. One day he'll take his drops and keep strictly to his diet and go to bed in good time, but the next day unless I watch him he'll suddenly forget his medicine, eat sturgeon—which is forbidden—and sit up playing cards till one o'clock in the morning."

"Oh, come, when was that?" Ivan Ilych would ask in vexation. "Only once at Peter Ivanovich's."

"And yesterday with Shebek."

"Well, even if I hadn't stayed up, this pain would have kept me awake."

"Be that as it may you'll never get well like that, but will always make us wretched."

Praskovya Fedorovna's attitude to Ivan Ilych's illness, as she expressed it both to others and to him, was that it was his own fault and was another of the annoyances he caused her. Ivan Ilych felt that this opinion escaped her involuntarily—but that did not make it easier for him.

At the law courts too, Ivan Ilych noticed, or thought he noticed, a strange attitude towards himself. It sometimes seemed to him that people were watching him inquisitively as a man whose place might soon be vacant. Then again, his friends would suddenly begin to chaff him in a friendly way about his low spirits, as if the awful, horrible, and unheard-of thing that was going on within him, incessantly gnawing at him and irresistibly drawing him away, was a very agreeable subject for jests. Schwartz in particular irritated him by his jocularity, vivacity, and *savoir-faire,* which reminded him of what he himself had been ten years ago.

Friends came to make up a set and they sat down to cards. They dealt, bending the new cards to soften them, and he sorted the diamonds in his hand and found he had seven. His partner said "No trumps" and supported him with two diamonds. What more could be wished for? It ought to be jolly and lively. They would make a grand slam. But suddenly Ivan Ilych was conscious of that gnawing pain, that taste in his mouth, and it seemed ridiculous that in such circumstances he should be pleased to make a grand slam.

He looked at his partner Mikhail Mikhaylovich, who rapped the table with his strong hand and instead of snatching up the tricks pushed the cards courteously and indulgently towards Ivan Ilych that he might have the pleasure of gathering them up without the trouble of stretching out his hand for them. "Does he think I am too weak to stretch out my arm?" thought Ivan Ilych, and forgetting what he was doing he over-trumped his partner, missing the grand slam by three tricks. And what was most awful of all was that he saw how upset Mikhail Mikhaylovich was about it but did not himself care. And it was dreadful to realize why he did not care.

They all saw that he was suffering, and said: "We can stop if you are tired. Take a rest." Lie down? No, he was not at all tired, and he finished the rubber. All were gloomy and silent. Ivan Ilych felt that he diffused this gloom over them and could not dispel it. They had supper and went away, and Ivan Ilych was left alone with the consciousness that his life was poisoned and was poisoning the lives of others, and that this poison did not weaken but penetrated more and more deeply into his whole being.

With this consciousness, and with physical pain besides the terror, he must go to bed, often to lie awake the greater part of the night. Next morning he had to get up again, dress, go to the law courts, speak, and write; or if he did not go out, spend at home those twenty-four hours a day each of which was a torture. And he had to live thus all alone on the brink of an abyss, with no one who understood or pitied him.

5

So one month passed and then another. Just before the New Year his brother-in-law came to town and stayed at their house. Ivan Ilych was at the law courts and Praskovya Fedorovna had gone shopping. When Ivan Ilych came home and entered his study he found his brother-in-law there—a healthy, florid man—unpacking his portmanteau himself. He raised his head on hearing Ivan Ilych's footsteps and looked up at him for a moment without a word. That stare told Ivan Ilych everything. His brother-in-law opened his mouth to utter an exclamation of surprise but checked himself, and that action confirmed it all.

"I have changed, eh?"

"Yes, there is a change."

And after that, try as he would to get his brother-in-law to return to the subject of his looks, the latter would say nothing about it. Praskovya Fedorovna came home and her brother went out to her. Ivan Ilych locked the door and began to examine himself in the glass, first full face, then in profile. He took up a portrait of himself taken with his wife, and compared it with what he saw in the glass. The change in him was immense. Then he bared his arms to the elbow, looked at them, drew the sleeves down again, sat down on an ottoman, and grew blacker than night.

"No, no, this won't do!" he said to himself, and jumped up, went to the table, took up some law papers and began to read them, but could not continue. He unlocked the door and went into the reception-room. The door leading to the drawing-room was shut. He approached it on tiptoe and listened.

"No, you are exaggerating!" Praskovya Fedorovna was saying.

"Exaggerating! Don't you see it? Why, he's a dead man! Look at his eyes—there's no light in them. But what is it that is wrong with him?"

"No one knows. Nikolaevich (that was another doctor) said something, but I don't know what. And Leshchetitsky (this was the celebrated specialist) said quite the contrary . . ."

Ivan Ilych walked away, went to his own room, lay down, and began musing: "The kidney, a floating kidney." He recalled all the doctors had told him of how it detached itself and swayed about. And by an effort of imagination he tried to catch that kidney and arrest it and support it. So little was needed for this, it seemed to him. "No, I'll go to see Peter Ivanovich again."(That was the friend whose friend was a doctor.) He rang, ordered the carriage, and got ready to go.

"Where are you going, Jean?" asked his wife, with a specially sad and exceptionally kind look.

This exceptionally kind look irritated him. He looked morosely at her.

"I must go to see Peter Ivanovich."

He went to see Peter Ivanovich, and together they went to see his friend, the doctor. He was in, and Ivan Ilych had a long talk with him.

Reviewing the anatomical and physiological details of what in the doctor's opinion was going on inside him, he understood it all.

There was something, a small thing, in the vermiform appendix. It might all come right. Only stimulate the energy of one organ and check the activity of another, then absorption would take place and everything would come right. He got home rather late for dinner, ate his dinner, and conversed cheerfully, but could not for a long time bring himself to go back to work in his room. At last, however, he went to his study and did what was necessary, but the consciousness that he had put something aside—an important, intimate matter which he would revert to when his work was done—never left him. When he had finished his work he remembered that this intimate matter was the thought of his vermiform appendix. But he did not give himself up to it, and went to the drawing-room for tea. There were callers there, including the examining magistrate who was a desirable match for his daughter, and they were conversing, playing the piano and singing. Ivan Ilych, as Praskovya Fedorovna remarked, spent that evening more cheerfully than usual, but he never for a moment forgot that he had postponed the important matter of the appendix. At eleven o'clock he said good-night and went to his bedroom. Since his illness he had slept alone in a small room next to his study. He undressed and took up a novel by Zola, but instead of reading it he fell into thought, and in his imagination that desired improvement in the vermiform appendix occurred. There was the absorption and evacuation and the reestablishment of normal activity. "Yes, that's it!" he said to himself. "One need only assist nature, that's all." He remembered his medicine, rose, took it, and lay down on his back watching for the beneficient action of the medicine and for it to lessen the pain. "I need only take it regularly and avoid all injurious influences. I am already feeling better, much better." He began touching his side: it was not painful to the touch. "There, I really don't feel it. It's much better already." He put out the light and turned on his side . . . "The appendix is getting better, absorption is occurring." Suddenly he felt the old, familiar, dull, gnawing pain, stubborn and serious. There was the same familiar loathsome taste in his mouth. His heart sank and he felt dazed. "My God! My God!" he muttered. "Again, again! And it will never cease." And suddenly the matter presented itself in a quite different aspect. "Vermiform appendix! Kidney!" he said to himself. "It's not a question of appendix or kidney, but of life and . . . death. Yes, life was there and now it is going, going and I cannot stop it. Yes. Why deceive myself? Isn't it obvious to everyone but me that I'm dying, and that it's only a question of weeks, days . . . it may happen this moment. There was light and now there is darkness. I was here and now I'm going there! Where?" A chill came over him, his breathing ceased, and he felt only the throbbing of his heart.

"When I am not, what will there be? There will be nothing. Then where shall I be when I am no more? Can this be dying? No, I don't want to!" He jumped up and tried to light the candle, felt for it with trembling hands, dropped candle and candlestick on the floor, and fell back on his pillow.

"What's the use? It makes no difference," he said to himself, staring with wide-open eyes into the darkness. "Death. Yes, death. And none of them know or wish to know it, and they have no pity for me. Now they are playing." (He heard through the door the distant sound of a song and its accompaniment.) "It's all the same to them, but they will die too! Fools! I first, and they later, but it will be the same for them. And now they are merry . . . the beasts!"

Anger choked him and he was agonizingly, unbearably miserable. "It is impossible that all men have been doomed to suffer this awful horror!" He raised himself.

"Something must be wrong. I must calm myself—must think it all over from the beginning." And he again began thinking. "Yes, the beginning of my illness: I knocked my side, but I was still quite well that day and the next. It hurt a little, then rather more. I saw the doctors, then followed despondency and anguish, more doctors, and I drew nearer to the abyss. My strength grew less and I kept coming nearer and nearer, and now I have wasted away and there is no light in my eyes. I think of the appendix—but this is death! I think of mending the appendix, and all the while here is death! Can it really be death?" Again terror seized him and he gasped for breath. He leant down and began feeling for the matches, pressing with his elbow on the stand beside the bed. It was in his way and hurt him, he grew furious with it, pressed on it still harder, and upset it. Breathless and in despair he fell on his back, expecting death to come immediately.

Meanwhile the visitors were leaving. Praskovya Fedorovna was seeing them off. She heard something fall and came in.

"What has happened?"

"Nothing. I knocked it over accidentally."

She went out and returned with a candle. He lay there panting heavily, like a man who has run a thousand yards, and stared upwards at her with a fixed look.

"What is it, Jean?"

"No . . . o . . . thing. I upset it." ("Why speak of it? She won't understand," he thought.)

And in truth she did not understand. She picked up the stand, lit his candle, and hurried away to see another visitor off. When she came back he still lay on his back looking upwards.

"What is it? Do you feel worse?"

"Yes."

She shook her head and sat down.

"Do you know, Jean, I think we must ask Leshchetitsky to come and see you here."

This meant calling in the famous specialist, regardless of expense. He smiled malignantly and said "No." She remained a little longer and then went up to him and kissed his forehead.

While she was kissing him he hated her from the bottom of his soul and with difficulty refrained from pushing her away.

"Good-night. Please God you'll sleep."

"Yes."

6

Ivan Ilych saw that he was dying, and he was in continual despair.

In the depth of his heart he knew he was dying, but not only was he not accustomed to the thought, he simply did not and could not grasp it.

The syllogism he had learnt from Kiezewetter's Logic: "Caius is a man, men are mortal, therefore Caius is mortal," had always seemed to him correct as applied to Caius, but certainly not as applied to himself. That Caius—man in the abstract—was mortal, was perfectly correct, but he was not Caius, not an abstract man, but a creature quite, quite separate from all others. He had been little Vanya, with a mamma and a papa; with Mitya and Volodya, and the toys, a coachman and a nurse, afterwards with Katenka and with all the joys, griefs, and delights of childhood, boyhood, and youth. What did Caius know of the smell of that striped leather ball Vanya had been so fond of? Had Caius kissed his mother's hand like that, and did the silk of her dress rustle so for Caius? Had he rioted like that at school when the pastry was bad? Had Caius been in love like that? Could Caius preside at a session as he did? "Caius really was mortal, and it was right for him to die; but for me, little Vanya, Ivan Ilych, with all my thoughts and emotions, it's altogether a different matter. It cannot be that I ought to die. That would be too terrible"

Such was his feeling.

"If I had to die like Caius I should have known it was so. An inner voice would have told me so, but there was nothing of the sort in me and I and all my friends felt that our case was quite different from that of Caius. And now here it is!" he said to himself. "It can't be. It's impossible! But here it is. How is this? How is one to understand it?"

He could not understand it, and tried to drive this false, incorrect, morbid thought away and to replace it by other proper and healthy thoughts. But that thought and not the thought only but the reality itself, seemed to come and confront him.

And to replace that thought he called up a succession of others, hoping to find in them some support. He tried to get back into the former current of thoughts that had once screened the thought of death from him. But strange to say, all that had formerly shut off, hidden, and destroyed, his consciousness of death, no longer had that effect. Ivan Ilych now spent most of his time in attempting to re-establish that old current. He would say to himself: "I will take up my duties again—after all I used to live by them." And banishing all doubts he would go to the law courts, enter into conversation with his colleagues, and sit carelessly as was his wont, scanning the crowd with a thoughtful look and leaning both his emaciated arms on the arms of his oak chair; bending over as usual to a colleague and drawing his papers nearer he would interchange whispers with him, and then suddenly raising his eyes and sitting erect would pronounce certain words and open the proceedings. But suddenly in the midst of those proceedings the pain in his side, regardless of the stage the proceedings had reached, would begin its own gnawing work. Ivan Ilych would turn his attention to it and try to drive the thought of it away, but without success. *It* would come and stand before him and look at him, and he would be petrified and the light would die out of his eyes, and he would again begin asking himself whether *It* alone was true. And his colleagues and subordinates would see with surprise and distress that he, the brilliant and subtle judge, was becoming confused and making mistakes. He would shake himself, try to pull himself together, manage somehow to bring the sitting to a close, and return home with the sorrowful consciousness that his judicial labours could not as formerly hide from him what he wanted them to hide, and could not deliver him from *It*. And what was worst of all was that *It* drew his attention to itself not in order to make him take some action but only that he should look at *It,* look it straight in the face: look at it and without doing anything, suffer inexpressibly.

And to save himself from this condition Ivan Ilych looked for consolations—new screens—and new screens were found and for a while seemed to save him, but then they immediately fell to pieces or rather became transparent, as if *It* penetrated them and nothing could veil *It*.

In these latter days he would go into the drawing-room he had arranged—that drawing-room where he had fallen and for the sake of which (how bitterly ridiculous it seemed) he had sacrificed his life—for he knew that his illness originated with that knock. He would enter and see that something had scratched the polished table. He would look for the cause of this and find that it was the bronze ornamentation of an album, that had got bent. He would take up the expensive album which he had lovingly arranged, and feel vexed with his daughter and her friends for their untidiness—for the album was torn here and there and some of the photographs turned upside down. He would put it carefully in order and bend the ornamentation back into position. Then it would occur to him to place all those things in another corner of the room, near the plants. He could call the footman, but his daughter or wife would come to help him. They would not agree, and his wife would contradict him, and he would dispute and grow angry. But that was all right, for then he did not think about *It*. *It* was invisible.

But then, when he was moving something himself, his wife would say: "Let the servants do it. You will hurt yourself again." And suddenly *It* would flash through the screen and he would see it. It was just a flash, and he hoped it would disappear, but he would involuntarily pay attention to his side. "It sits there as before, gnawing just the same!" And he could no longer forget *It*, but could distinctly see it looking at him from behind the flowers. "What is it all for?"

"It really is so! I lost my life over that curtain as I might have done when storming a fort. Is that possible? How terrible and how stupid. It can't be true! It can't, but it is!"

He would go to his study, lie down, and again be alone with *It*: face to face with *It*. And nothing could be done with *It* except to look at it and shudder.

7

How it happened it is impossible to say because it came about step by step, unnoticed, but in the third month of Ivan Ilych's illness, his wife, his daughter, his son, his acquaintances, the doctors, the servants, and above all he himself, were aware that the whole interest he had for other people was whether he would soon vacate his place, and at last release the living from the discomfort caused by his presence and be himself released from his sufferings.

He slept less and less. He was given opium and hypodermic injections of morphine, but this did not relieve him. The dull depression he experienced in a somnolent condition at first gave him a little relief, but only as something new, afterwards it became as distressing as the pain itself or even more so.

Special foods were prepared for him by the doctors' orders, but all those foods became increasingly distasteful and disgusting to him.

For his excretions also special arrangements had to be made, and this was a torment to him every time—a torment from the uncleanliness, the unseemliness, and the smell, and from knowing that another person had to take part in it.

But just through this most unpleasant matter Ivan Ilych obtained comfort. Gerasim, the butler's young assistant, always came in to carry the things out. Gerasim was a clean, fresh peasant lad, grown stout on town food and always cheerful and bright. At first the sight of him, in his clean Russian peasant costume, engaged on that disgusting task embarrassed Ivan Ilych.

Once when he got up from the commode too weak to draw up his trousers, he dropped into a soft armchair and looked with horror at his bare, enfeebled thighs with the muscles so sharply marked on them.

Gerasim with a firm light tread, his heavy boots emitting a pleasant smell of tar and fresh winter air, came in wearing a clean Hessian apron, the sleeves of his print shirt tucked up over his strong bare young arms; and refraining f om looking at his sick master out of consideration for his feelings, and restraining the joy of life that beamed from his face, went up to the commode.

"Gerasim!" said Ivan Ilych in a weak voice.

Gerasim started, evidently afraid he might have committed some blunder, and with a rapid movement turned his fresh, kind, simple young face which just showed the first downy signs of a beard.

"Yes, sir?"

"That must be very unpleasant for you. You must forgive me. I am helpless."

"Oh, why, sir," and Gerasim's eyes beamed and he showed his glistening white teeth, "what's a little trouble? It's a case of illness with you, sir."

And his deft strong hands did their accustomed task, and he went out of the room stepping lightly. Five minutes later he was lightly returned.

Ivan Ilych was still sitting in the same position in the armchair.

"Gerasim," he said when the latter had replaced the freshly-washed utensil. "Please come here and help me." Gerasim went up to him. "Lift me up. It is hard for me to get up, and I have sent Dmitri away."

Gerasim went up to him, grasped his master with his strong arms deftly but gently, in the same way that he stepped—lifted him, supported him with one hand, and with the other drew up his trousers and would have set him down again, but Ivan Ilych asked to be led to the sofa. Gerasim, without an effort and without apparent pressure, led him, almost lifting him, to the sofa and placed him on it.

"Thank you. How easily and well you do it all!"

Gerasim smiled again and turned to leave the room. But Ivan Ilych felt his presence such a comfort that he did not want to let him go.

"One thing more, please move up that chair. No, the other one—under my feet. It is easier for me when my feet are raised."

Gerasim brought the chair, set it down gently in place, and raised Ivan Ilych's legs on to it. It seemed to Ivan Ilych that he felt better while Gerasim was holding up his legs.

"It's better when my legs are higher," he said. "Place that cushion under them."

Gerasim did so. He again lifted the legs and placed them, and again Ivan Ilych felt better while Gerasim held his legs. When he set them down Ivan Ilych fancied he felt worse.

"Gerasim," he said. "Are you busy now?"

"Not at all, sir," said Gerasim, who had learnt from the townsfolk how to speak to gentlefolk.

"What have you still to do?"

"What have I to do? I've done everything except chopping the logs for tomorrow."

"Then hold my legs up a bit higher, can you?"

"Of course I can. Why not?" And Gerasim raised his master's legs higher and Ivan Ilych thought that in that position he did not feel any pain at all.

"And how about the logs?"

"Don't trouble about that, sir. There's plenty of time."

Ivan Ilych told Gerasim to sit down and hold his legs, and began to talk to him. And strange to say it seemed to him that he felt better while Gerasim held his legs up.

After that Ivan Ilych would sometimes call Gerasim and get him to hold his legs on his shoulders, and he liked talking to him. Gerasim did it all easily, willingly, simply, and with a good nature that touched Ivan Ilych. Health, strength, and vitality in other people were offensive to him, but Gerasim's strength and vitality did not mortify but soothed him.

What tormented Ivan Ilych most was the deception, the lie, which for some reason they all accepted, that he was not dying but was simply ill, and that he only need keep quiet and undergo a treatment and then something very good would result. He however knew that do what they would nothing would come of it, only still more agonizing suffering and death. This deception tortured him—their not wishing to admit what they all knew and what he knew, but wanting to lie to him concerning his terrible condition, and wishing and forcing him to participate in that lie. Those lies—lies enacted over him on the eve of his death and destined to degrade this awful, solemn act to the level of their visitings, their curtains, their sturgeon for dinner—were a terrible agony for Ivan Ilych. And strangely enough, many times when they were going through their antics over him he had been within a hairbreadth of calling out to them: "Stop lying! You know and I know that I am dying. Then at least stop lying about it!" But he had never had the spirit to do it. The awful, terrible act of his dying was, he could see, reduced by those about him to the level of a casual, unpleasant, and almost indecorous incident (as if someone entered a drawing-room diffusing an unpleasant odour) and this was done by that very decorum which he had served all his life long. He saw that no one felt for him, because no one even wished to grasp his position. Only Gerasim recognized it and pitied him. And so Ivan Ilych felt at ease only with him. He felt comforted when Gerasim supported his legs (sometimes all night long) and refused to go to bed, saying: "Don't you worry, Ivan Ilych. I'll get sleep enough later on," or when he suddenly became familiar and exclaimed: "If you weren't sick it would be another matter, but as it is, why should I grudge a little trouble?" Gerasim alone did not lie; everything showed that he alone understood the facts of the case and did not consider it necessary to disguise them, but simply felt sorry for his emaciated and enfeebled master. Once when Ivan Ilych was sending him away he even said straight out: "We shall all of us die, so why should I grudge a little trouble?"—expressing the fact that he did not think his work burdensome, because he was doing it for a dying man and hoped someone would do the same for him when his time came.

Apart from this lying, or because of it, what most tormented Ivan Ilych was that no one pitied him as he wished to be pitied. At certain moments after prolonged suffering he wished most of all (though he would have been ashamed to confess it) for someone to pity him as a sick child is pitied. He longed to be petted and comforted. He knew he was an important functionary, that he had a beard turning grey, and that therefore what he longed for was impossible, but still he longed for it. And in Gerasim's attitude towards him there was something akin to what he wished for, and so that attitude comforted him. Ivan Ilych wanted to weep, wanted to be petted and cried over, and then his colleague Shebek would come, and instead of weeping and being petted, Ivan Ilych would assume a serious, and profound air, and by force of habit would express his opinion on a decision of the Court of Cassation and would stubbornly insist on that view. This falsity around him and within him did more than anything else to poison his last days.

8

It was morning. He knew it was morning because Gerasim had gone, and Peter the footman had come and put out the candles, drawn back one of the curtains, and begun quietly to tidy up. Whether it was morning or evening, Friday or Sunday, made no difference, it was all just the same: the gnawing, unmitigated, agonizing pain, never ceasing for an instant, the consciousness of life inexorably waning but not yet extinguished, the approach of that ever dreaded and hateful Death which was the only reality, and always the same falsity. What were days, weeks, hours, in such a case?

"Will you have some tea, sir?"

"He wants things to be regular, and wishes the gentlefolk to drink tea in the morning," thought Ivan Ilych, and only said "No."

"Wouldn't you like to move onto the sofa, sir?"

"He wants to tidy up the room, and I'm in the way. I am uncleanliness and disorder," he thought, and said only:

"No, leave me alone."

The man went on bustling about. Ivan Ilych stretched out his hand. Peter came up, ready to help.

"What is it, sir?"

"My watch."

Peter took the watch which was close at hand and gave it to his master.

"Half-past eight. Are they up?"

"No sir, except Vladimir Ivanich" (the son) "who has gone to school. Praskovya Fedorovna ordered me to wake her if you asked for her. Shall I do so?"

"No, there's no need to." "Perhaps I'd better have some tea," he thought, and added aloud: "Yes, bring me some tea."

Peter went to the door but Ivan Ilych dreaded being left alone. "How can I keep him here? Oh yes, my medicine." "Peter, give me my medicine." "Why not? Perhaps it may still do me some good." He took a spoonful and swallowed it. "No, it won't help. It's all tomfoolery, all deception," he decided as soon as he became aware of the familiar, sickly, hopeless taste. "No, I can't believe in it any longer. But the pain, why this pain? If it would only cease just for a moment!" And he moaned. Peter turned towards him. "It's all right. Go and fetch me some tea."

Peter went out. Left alone Ivan Ilych groaned not so much with pain, terrible though that was, as from mental anguish. Always and for ever the same, always these endless days and nights. If only it would come quicker! If only *what* would come quicker? Death, darkness? . . . No, no! Anything rather than death!

When Peter returned with the tea on a tray, Ivan Ilych stared at him for a time in perplexity, not realizing who and what he was. Peter was disconcerted by that look and his embarrassment brought Ivan Ilych to himself.

"Oh, tea! All right, put it down. Only help me to wash and put on a clean shirt."

And Ivan Ilych began to wash. With pauses for rest, he washed his hands and then his face, cleaned his teeth, brushed his hair, and looked in the glass. He was terrified by what he saw, especially by the limp way in which his hair clung to his pallid forehead.

While his shirt was being changed he knew he would be still more frightened at the sight of his body, so he avoided looking at it. Finally he was ready. He drew on a dressing-gown, wrapped himself in a plaid, and sat down in the armchair to take his tea. For a moment he felt refreshed, but as soon as he began to drink the tea he was again aware of the same taste, and the pain also returned. He finished it with an effort, and then lay down stretching out his legs, and dismissed Peter.

Always the same. Now a spark of hope flashes up, then a sea of despair rages, and always pain; always pain, always despair, and always the same. When alone he had a dreadful and distressing desire to call someone, but he knew beforehand that with others present it would be still worse. "Another dose of morphine—to lose consciousness. I will tell him, the doctor, that he must think of something else. It's impossible, impossible, to go on like this."

An hour and another pass like that. But now there is a ring at the door bell. Perhaps it's the doctor? It is. He comes in fresh, hearty, plump, and cheerful, with that look on his face that seems to say: "There now, you're in a panic about something, but we'll arrange it all for you directly?" The doctor knows this expression is out of place here, but he has put it on once for all and can't take it off—like a man who has put on a frock-coat in the morning to pay a round of calls.

The doctor rubs his hands vigorously and reassuringly.

"Brr! How cold it is! There's such a sharp frost; just let me warm myself!" he says, as if it were only a matter of waiting till he was warm, and then he would put everything right.

"Well now, how are you?"

Ivan Ilych feels that the doctor would like to say: "Well, how are your affairs?" but that even he feels that this would not do, and says instead: "What sort of a night have you had?"

Ivan Ilych looks at him as much as to say: "Are you really never ashamed of lying?" But the doctor does not wish to understand this question, and Ivan Ilych says: "Just as terrible as ever. The pain never leaves me and never subsides. If only something . . ."

"Yes, you sick people are always like that. . . . There, now I think I am warm enough. Even Praskovya Fedorovna, who is so particular, could find no fault with my temperature. Well, now I can say good-morning," and the doctor presses his patient's hand.

Then, dropping his former playfulness, he begins with a most serious face to examine the patient, feeling his pulse and taking his temperature, and then begins the sounding and auscultation.

Ivan Ilych knows quite well and definitely that all this is nonsense and pure deception, but when the doctor, getting down on his knee, leans over him, putting his ear first higher then lower, and performs various gymnastic movements over him with a significant expression on his face, Ivan Ilych submits to it all as he used to submit to the speeches of the lawyers, though he knew very well that they were all lying and why they were lying.

The doctor, kneeling on the sofa, is still sounding him when Praskovya Fedorovna's silk dress rustles at the door and she is heard scolding Peter for not having let her know of the doctor's arrival.

She comes in, kisses her husband, and at once proceeds to prove that she has been up a long time already, and only owing to a misunderstanding failed to be there when the doctor arrived.

Ivan Ilych looks at her, scans her all over, sets against her the whiteness and plumpness and cleanness of her hands and neck, the gloss of her hair, and the sparkle of her vivacious eyes. He hates her with his whole soul. And the thrill of hatred he feels for her makes him suffer from her touch.

Her attitude towards him and his disease is still the same. Just as the doctor had adopted a certain relation to his patient which he could not abandon, so had she formed one towards him—that he was not doing something he ought to do and was himself to blame, and that she reproached him lovingly for this—and she could not now change that attitude.

"You see he doesn't listen to me and doesn't take his medicine at the proper time. And above all he lies in a position that is no doubt bad for him—with his legs up."

She described how he made Gerasim hold his legs up.

The doctor smiled with a contemptuous affability that said: "What's to be done? These sick people do have foolish fancies of that kind, but we must forgive them."

When the examination was over the doctor looked at his watch, and then Praskovya Fedorovna announced to Ivan Ilych that it was of course as he pleased, but she had sent to-day for a celebrated specialist who would examine him and have a consultation with Michael Danilovich (their regular doctor).

"Please don't raise any objections. I am doing this for my own sake," she said ironically, letting it be felt that she was doing it all for his sake and only said that to leave him no right to refuse. He remained silent, knitting his brows. He felt that he was so surrounded and involved in a mesh of falsity that it was hard to unravel anything.

Everything she did for him was entirely for her own sake, and she told him she was doing for herself what she actually was doing for herself, as if that was so incredible that he must understand the opposite.

At half-past eleven the celebrated specialist arrived. Again the sounding began and the significant conversations in his presence and in another room, about the kidneys and the appendix, and the questions and answers, with such an air of importance that again, instead of the real question of life and death which now alone confronted him, the question arose of the kidney and appendix which were not behaving as they ought to and would now be attacked by Michael Danilovich and the specialist and forced to amend their ways.

The celebrated specialist took leave of him with a serious though not hopeless look, and in reply to the timid question Ivan Ilych, with eyes glistening with fear and hope, put to him as to whether there was a chance of recovery, said that he could not vouch for it but there was a possibility. The look of hope with which Ivan Ilych watched the doctor out was so pathetic that Praskovya Fedorovna, seeing it, even wept as she left the room to hand the doctor his fee.

The gleam of hope kindled by the doctor's encouragement did not last long. The same room, the same pictures, curtains, wall-paper, medicine bottles, were all there, and the same aching suffering body, and Ivan Ilych began to moan. They gave him a subcutaneous injection and he sank into oblivion.

It was twilight when he came to. They brought him his dinner and he swallowed some beef tea with difficulty, and then everything was the same again and night was coming on.

After dinner, at seven o'clock, Praskovya Fedorovna came into the room in evening dress, her full bosom pushed up by her corset, and with traces of powder on her face. She had reminded him in the morning that they were going to the theatre. Sarah Bernhardt was visiting the town and they had a box, which he had insisted on their taking. Now he had forgotten about it and her toilet offended him, but he concealed his vexation when he remembered that he had himself insisted on their securing a box and going because it would be an instructive and aesthetic pleasure for the children.

Praskovya Fedorovna came in, self-satisfied but yet with a rather guilty air. She sat down and asked how he was but, as he saw, only for the sake of asking and not in order to learn about it, knowing that there was nothing to learn—and then went on to what she really wanted to say: that she would not on any account have gone but that the box had been taken and Helen and their daughter were going, as well as Petrishchev (the examining magistrate, their daughter's fiancé) and that it was out of the question to let them go alone; but that she would have much preferred to sit with him for a while; and he must be sure to follow the doctor's orders while she was away.

"Oh, and Fedor Petrovich" (the fiancé) "would like to come in. May he? And Lisa?"

"All right."

Their daughter came in in full evening dress, her fresh young flesh exposed (making a show of that very flesh which in his own case caused so much suffering), strong, healthy, evidently in love, and impatient with illness, suffering, and death, because they interfered with her happiness.

Fedor Petrovich came in too, in evening dress, his hair curled *á la Capoul,* a tight stiff collar round his long sinewy neck, an enormous white shirt-front and narrow black trousers tightly stretched over his strong thighs. He had one white glove tightly drawn on, and was holding his opera hat in his hand.

Following him the schoolboy crept in unnoticed, in a new uniform, poor little fellow, and wearing gloves. Terribly dark shadows showed under his eyes, the meaning of which Ivan Ilych knew well.

His son had always seemed pathetic to him, and now it was dreadful to see the boy's frightened look of pity. It seemed to Ivan Ilych that Vasya was the only one besides Gerasim who understood and pitied him.

They all sat down and again asked how he was. A silence followed. Lisa asked her mother about the opera-glasses, and there was an altercation between mother and daughter as to who had taken them and where they had been put. This occasioned some unpleasantness.

Fedor Petrovich inquired of Ivan Ilych whether he had ever seen Sarah Bernhardt. Ivan Ilych did not at first catch the question, but then replied: "No, have you seen her before?"

"Yes, in *Adrienne Lecouvreur.*"

Praskovya Fedorovna mentioned some roles in which Sarah Bernhardt was particularly good. Her daughter disagreed. Conversation sprang up as to the elegance and realism of her acting—the sort of conversation that is always repeated and is always the same.

In the midst of the conversation Fedor Petrovich glanced at Ivan Ilych and became silent. The others also looked at him and grew silent. Ivan Ilych was staring with glittering eyes straight before him, evidently indignant with them. This had to be rectified, but it was impossible to do so. The silence had to be broken, but for a time no one dared to break it and they all became afraid that the conventional deception would suddenly become obvious and the truth become plain to all. Lisa was the first to pluck up courage and break that silence, but by trying to hide what everybody was feeling, she betrayed it.

"Well, if we are going it's time to start," she said, looking at her watch, a present from her father, and with a faint and significant smile at Fedor Petrovich relating to something known only to them. She got up with a rustle of her dress.

They all rose, said good-night, and went away.

When they had gone it seemed to Ivan Ilych that he felt better; the falsity had gone with them. But the pain remained—that same pain and that same fear that made everything monotonously alike, nothing harder and nothing easier. Everything was worse.

Again minute followed minute and hour followed hour. Everything remained the same and there was no cessation. And the inevitable end of it all became more and more terrible.

"Yes, send Gerasim here," he replied to a question Peter asked.

9

His wife returned late at night. She came in on tiptoe, but he heard her, opened his eyes, and made haste to close them again. She wished to send Gerasim away and to sit with him herself, but he opened his eyes and said: "No, go away."

"Are you in great pain?"

"Always the same."

"Take some opium."

He agreed and took some. She went away.

Till about three in the morning he was in a state of stupefied misery. It seemed to him that he and pain were being thrust into a narrow, deep black sack, but though they were pushed further and further in they could not be pushed to the bottom. And this, terrible enough in itself, was accompanied by suffering. He was frightened yet wanted to fall through the sack, he struggled but yet co-operated. And suddenly he broke through, fell, and regained consciousness. Gerasim was sitting at the foot of the bed dozing quietly and patiently, while he himself lay with his emaciated stockinged legs resting on Gerasim's shoulders; the same shaded candle was there and the same unceasing pain.

"Go away, Gerasim," he whispered.

"It's all right, sir. I'll stay a while."

"No. Go away."

He removed his legs from Gerasim's shoulders, turned sideways onto his arm, and felt sorry for himself. He only waited till Gerasim had gone into the next room and then restrained himself no longer but wept like a child. He wept on account of his helplessness, his terrible loneliness, the cruelty of man, the cruelty of God, and the absence of God.

"Why hast Thou done all this? Why hast Thou brought me here? Why, why dost Thou torment me so terribly?"

He did not expect an answer and yet wept because there was no answer and could be none. The pain again grew more acute, but he did not stir and did not call. He said to himself: "Go on! Strike me! But what is it for? What have I done to Thee? What is it for?"

Then he grew quiet and not only ceased weeping but even held his breath and became all attention. It was as though he were listening not to an audible voice but to the voice of his soul, to the current of thoughts arising within him.

"What is it you want?" was the clear conception capable of expression in words, that he heard.

"What do you want? What do you want?" he repeated to himself.

"What do I want? To live and not to suffer," he answered.

And again he listened with such concentrated attention that even his pain did not distract him.

"To live? How?" asked his inner voice.

"Why, to live as I used to—well and pleasantly."

"As you lived before, well and pleasantly?" the voice repeated.

And in imagination he began to recall the best moments of his pleasant life. But strange to say none of these best moments of his pleasant life now seemed at all what they had then seemed—none of them except the first recollections of childhood. There, in childhood, there had been something really pleasant with which it would be possible to live if it could return. But the child who had experienced that happiness existed no longer, it was like a reminiscence of somebody else.

As soon as the period began which had produced the present Ivan Ilych, all that had then seemed joys now melted before his sight and turned into something trivial and often nasty.

And the further he departed from childhood and the nearer he came to the present the more worthless and doubtful were the joys. This began with the School of Law. A little that was really good was still found there—there was light-heartedness, friendship, and hope. But in the upper classes there had already been fewer of such good moments. Then during the first years of his official career, when he was in the service of the Governor, some pleasant moments again occurred: They were the memories of love for a woman. Then all became confused and there was still less of what was good; later on again there was still less that was good, and the further he went the less there was. His marriage, a mere accident, then the disenchantment that followed it, his wife's bad breath and the sensuality and hypocrisy: then that deadly official life and those preoccupations about money, a year of it, and two, and ten, and twenty, and always the same thing. And the longer it lasted the more deadly it became. "It is as if I had been going downhill while I imagined I was going up. And that is really what it was. I was going up in public opinion, but to the same extent life was ebbing away from me. And now it is all done and there is only death."

"Then what does it mean? Why? It can't be that life is so senseless and horrible. But if it really has been so horrible and senseless, why must I die and die in agony? There is something wrong!"

"Maybe I did not live as I ought to have done," it suddenly occurred to him. "But how could that be, when I did everything properly?" he replied, and immediately dismissed from his mind this, the sole solution of all the riddles of life and death, as something quite impossible.

"Then what do you want now? To live? Live how? Live as you lived in the law courts when the usher proclaimed 'The judge is coming!' " "The judge is coming, the judge!" he repeated to himself. "Here he is, the judge. But I am not guilty!" he exclaimed angrily. "What is it for?" And he ceased crying, but turning his face to the wall continued to ponder on the same question: Why, and for what purpose, is there all this horror? But however much he pondered he found no answer. And whenever the thought occurred to him, as it often did, that it all resulted from his not having lived as he ought to have done, he at once recalled the correctness of his whole life and dismissed so strange an idea.

10

Another fortnight passed. Ivan Ilych now no longer left his sofa. He would not lie in bed but lay on the sofa, facing the wall nearly all the time. He suffered ever the same unceasing agonies and in his loneliness pondered always on the same insoluble question: "What is this? Can it be that it is Death?" And the inner voice answered: "Yes, it is Death."

"Why these sufferings?" And the voice answered, "For no reason—they just are so." Beyond and besides this there was nothing.

From the very beginning of his illness, ever since he had first been to see the doctor, Ivan Ilych's life had been divided between two contrary and alternating moods: now it was despair and the expectation of this uncomprehended and terrible death, and now hope and an intently interested observation of the functioning of his organs. Now before his eyes there was only a kidney or an intestine that temporarily evaded its duty, and now only that incomprehensible and dreadful death from which it was impossible to escape.

These two states of mind had alternated from the very beginning of his illness, but the further it progressed the more doubtful and fantastic became the conception of the kidney, and the more real the sense of impending death.

He had but to call to mind what he had been three months before and what he was now, to call to mind with what regularity he had been going downhill, for every possibility of hope to be shattered.

Latterly during that loneliness in which he found himself as he lay facing the back of the sofa, a loneliness in the midst of a populous town and surrounded by numerous acquaintances and relations but that yet could not have been more complete anywhere—either at the bottom of the sea or under the earth—during that terrible loneliness Ivan Ilych had lived only in memories of the past. Pictures of his past rose before him one after another. They always began with what was nearest in time and then went back to what was more remote—to his childhood—and rested there. If he thought of the stewed prunes that had been offered him that day, his mind went back to the raw shrivelled French plums of his childhood, their peculiar flavour and the flow of saliva when he sucked their stones, and along with the memory of that taste came a whole series of memories of those days: his nurse, his brother, and their toys. "No, I mustn't think of that. . . . It is too painful," Ivan Ilych said to himself, and brought himself back to the present—to the bottom of the back of the sofa and the creases in its morocco. "Morocco is expensive, but it does not wear well: There had been a quarrel about it. It was a different kind of quarrel and a different kind of morocco that time when we tore father's portfolio and were punished, and mamma brought us some tarts. . . ." And again his thoughts dwelt on his childhood, and again it was painful and he tried to banish them and fix his mind on something else.

Then again together with that chain of memories another series passed through his mind—of how his illness had progressed and grown worse. There also the further back he looked the more life there had been. There had been more of what was good in life and more of life itself. The two merged together. "Just as the pain went on getting worse and worse so my life grew worse and worse," he thought. "There is one bright spot there at the back, at the beginning of life, and afterwards all becomes blacker and blacker and proceeds more and more rapidly—in inverse ratio to the square of the distance from death," thought Ivan Ilych. And the example of a stone falling downwards with increasing velocity entered his mind. Life, a series of increasing sufferings, flies, further and further towards its end—the most terrible suffering. "I am flying. . . ." He shuddered, shifted himself, and tried to resist, but was already aware that resistance was impossible, and again with eyes weary of gazing but unable to cease seeing what was before them, he stared at the back of the sofa and waited—awaiting the dreadful fall and shock and destruction.

"Resistance is impossible!" he said to himself. "If I could only understand what it is all for! But that too is impossible. An explanation would be possible if it could be said that I have not lived as I ought to. But it is impossible to say that," and he remembered all the legality, correctitude, and propriety of his life. "That at any rate can certainly not be admitted," he thought, and his lips smiled ironically as if someone could see that smile and be taken in by it. "There is no explanation! Agony, death. . . . What for?"

11

Another two weeks went by in this way and during that fortnight an event occurred that Ivan Ilych and his wife had desired. Petrishchev formally proposed. It happened in the evening. The next day Praskovya Fedorovna came into her husband's room considering how best to inform him of it, but that very night there had been a fresh change for the worse in his condition. She found him still lying on the sofa but in a different position. He lay on his back, groaning and staring fixedly straight in front of him.

She began to remind him of his medicines, but he turned his eyes towards her with such a look that she did not finish what she was saying; so great an animosity, to her in particular, did that look express.

"For Christ's sake, let me die in peace!" he said.

She would have gone away, but just then their daughter came in and went up to say good morning. He looked at her as he had done at his wife, and in reply to her inquiry about his health said dryly that he would soon free them all of himself. They were both silent and after sitting with him for a while went away.

"Is it our fault?" Lisa said to her mother. "It's as if we were to blame! I am sorry for papa, but why should we be tortured?"

The doctor came at his usual time. Ivan Ilych answered "Yes" and "No," never taking his angry eyes from him, and at last said: "You know you can do nothing for me, so leave me alone."

"We can ease your sufferings."

"You can't even do that. Let me be."

The doctor went into the drawing-room and told Praskovya Fedorovna that the case was very serious and that the only resource left was opium to allay her husband's sufferings, which must be terrible.

It was true, as the doctor said, that Ivan Ilych's physical sufferings were terrible, but worse than the physical sufferings were his mental sufferings which were his chief torture.

His mental sufferings were due to the fact that that night, as he looked at Gerasim's sleepy, good-natured face with its prominent cheek-bones, the question suddenly occurred to him: "What if my whole life has really been wrong?"

It occurred to him that what had appeared perfectly impossible before, namely that he had not spent his life as he could have done, might after all be true. It occurred to him that his scarcely perceptible attempts to struggle against what was considered good by the most highly placed people, those scarcely noticeable impulses which he had immediately suppressed, might have been the real thing, and all the rest false. And his professional duties and the whole arrangement of his life and of his family, and all his social and official interests, might all have been false. He tried to defend all those things to himself and suddenly felt the weakness of what he was defending. There was nothing to defend.

"But if that is so," he said to himself, "and I am leaving this life with the consciousness that I have lost all that was given me and it is impossible to rectify it—what then?"

He lay on his back and began to pass his life in review in quite a new way. In the morning when he saw first his footman, then his wife, then his daughter, and then the doctor, their every word and movement confirmed to him the awful truth that had been revealed to him during the night. In them he saw himself—all that for which he had lived—and saw clearly that it was not real at all, but a terrible and huge deception which had hidden both life and death. This consciousness intensified his physical suffering tenfold. He groaned and tossed about, and pulled at his clothing which choked and stifled him. And he hated them on that account.

He was given a large dose of opium and became unconscious, but at noon his sufferings began again. He drove everybody away and tossed from side to side.

His wife came to him and said:

"Jean, my dear, do this for me. It can't do any harm and often helps. Healthy people often do it."

He opened his eyes wide.

"What? Take communion? Why? It's unnecessary! However. . . ."

She began to cry.

"Yes, do, my dear. I'll send for our priest. He is such a nice man."

"All right. Very well," he muttered.

When the priest came and heard his confession, Ivan Ilych was softened and seemed to feel a relief from his doubts and consequently from his sufferings, and for a moment there came a ray of hope. He again began to think of the vermiform appendix and the possibility of correcting it. He received the sacrament with tears in his eyes.

When they laid him down again afterwards he felt a moment's ease, and the hope that he might live awoke in him again. He began to think of the operation that had been suggested to him. "To live! I want to live!" he said to himself.

His wife came in to congratulate him after his communion, and when uttering the usual conventional words she added:

"You feel better, don't you?"

Without looking at her he said "Yes."

Her dress, her figure, the expression of her face, the tone of her voice, all revealed the same thing. "This is wrong, it is not as it should be. All you have lived for and still live for is falsehood and deception, hiding life and death from you." And as soon as he admitted that thought, his hatred and his agonizing physical suffering again sprang up, and with that suffering a consciousness of the unavoidable, approaching end. And to this was added a new sensation of grinding shooting pain and a feeling of suffocation.

The expression of his face when he uttered that "yes" was dreadful. Having uttered it, he looked her straight in the eyes, turned on his face with a rapidity extraordinary in his weak state and shouted:

"Go away! Go away and leave me alone!"

12

From that moment the screaming began that continued for three days, and was so terrible that one could not hear it through two closed doors without horror. At the moment he answered his wife he realized that he was lost, that there was no return, that the end had come, the very end, and his doubts were still unsolved and remained doubts.

"Oh! Oh! Oh!" he cried in various intonations. He had begun by screaming "I won't!" and continued screaming on the letter "o."

For three whole days, during which time did not exist for him, he struggled in that black sack into which he was being thrust by an invisible, resistless force. He struggled as a man condemned to death struggles in the hands of the executioner, knowing that he cannot save himself. And every moment he felt that despite all his efforts he was drawing nearer and nearer to what terrified him. He felt that his agony was due to his being thrust into that black hole and still more to his not being able to get right into it. He was hindered from getting into it by his conviction that his life had been a good one. That very justification of his life held him fast and prevented his moving forward, and it caused him most torment of all.

Suddenly some force struck him in the chest and side, making it still harder to breathe, and he fell through the hole and there at the bottom was a light. What had happened to him was like the sensation one sometimes experiences in a railway carriage when one thinks one is going backwards while one is really going forwards and suddenly becomes aware of the real direction.

"Yes, it was all not the right thing," he said to himself, "but that's no matter. It can be done. But what *is* the right thing?" he asked himself, and suddenly grew quiet.

This occurred at the end of the third day, two hours before his death. Just then his schoolboy son had crept softly in and gone up to the bedside. The dying man was still screaming desperately and waving his arms. His hand fell on the boy's head, and the boy caught it, pressed it to his lips, and began to cry.

At that very moment Ivan Ilych fell through and caught sight of the light, and it was revealed to him that though his life had not been what it should have been, this could still be rectified. He asked himself, "What *is* the right thing?" and grew still, listening. Then he felt that someone was kissing his hand. He opened his eyes, looked at his son, and felt sorry for him. His wife came up to him and he glanced at her. She was gazing at him open-mouthed, with undried tears on her nose and cheek and a despairing look on her face. He felt sorry for her too.

"Yes, I am making them wretched," he thought. "They are sorry, but it will be better for them when I die." He wished to say this but had not the strength to utter it. "Besides, why speak? I must act," he thought. With a look at his wife he indicated his son and said: "Take him away . . . sorry for him . . . sorry for you too. . . ." He tried to add, "forgive me," but said "forego" and waved his hand, knowing that He whose understanding mattered would understand.

And suddenly it grew clear to him that what had been oppressing him and would not leave him was all dropping away at once from two sides, from ten sides, and from all sides. He was sorry for them, he must act so as not to hurt them: release them and free himself from these sufferings. "How good and how simple!" he thought. "And the pain?" he asked himself. "What has become of it? Where are you, pain?"

He turned his attention to it.

"Yes, here it is. Well, what of it? Let the pain be."

"And death . . . where is it?"

He sought his former accustomed fear of death and did not find it. "Where is it? What death?" There was no fear because there was no death.

In place of death there was light.

"So that's what it is!" he suddenly exclaimed aloud. "What joy!"

To him all this happened in a single instant, and the meaning of that instant did not change. For those present his agony continued for another two hours. Something rattled in his throat, his emaciated body twitched, then the gasping and rattle became less and less frequent.

"It is finished!" said someone near him.

He heard these words and repeated them in his soul.

"Death is finished," he said to himself. "It is no more!"

He drew in a breath, stopped in the midst of a sigh, stretched out, and died.

QUESTIONS FOR DISCUSSION AND WRITING

1. How does the response of Ivan's associates to the news of his death introduce the conflicts that will be revealed in the story? How does Ivan's fall from the stepladder mark a turning point in his life? What conclusions does Ivan come to during his three days of screaming?

2. How does Ivan characterize himself through his decisions about his career, wife, children, and amusements? In what ways does his character change once he becomes ill? How does Gerasim reveal the limitations in Ivan and his family?

3. How does Ivan's preoccupation with his social and physical setting help explain the difficulty he has in coming to terms with his death? How does the bridge game symbolize the kind of life Ivan and his friends value?

4. In what ways do Peter Ivanovich and Ivan Ilych share a similar point of view toward life? How does Ivan's ability to eliminate "all considerations irrelevant to the legal aspect of the case" reveal his attitude toward his clients? How does he react when his doctors exhibit a similar attitude toward him?

5. The first sentence of part 2 seems at first to be a paradox: "Ivan Ilych's life had been most simple and most ordinary and therefore most terrible." In what ways does the rest of the story explain how a simple and ordinary life can be terrible? Does Ivan's perception of this truth come too late to redeem him? Explain your answer.

87

WILLIAM TREVOR

The Ballroom of Romance

WILLIAM TREVOR was born in 1928 in Mitchelstown, County Cork, Ireland, and educated at St. Columba's College and Trinity College, Dublin. In the 1950s he taught school in Northern Ireland and England where he also pursued a career as an artist. In the 1960s, he worked as an advertising copywriter in London, before deciding to become a writer. Since that time he has quietly created an impressive body of Anglo-Irish literature. His novels include *The Old Boys* (1964), *Miss Eckdorf in O'Neill's Hotel* (1969), *Elizabeth Alone* (1973), *Other People's Worlds* (1980), and *Fools of Fortune* (1983). He has also written several plays—*A Perfect Relationship* (1973), *Scenes from an Album* (1981); a work on nonfiction—*A Writer's Ireland: Landscape in Literature* (1986); and numerous television plays for the BBC. "The Ballroom of Romance," which is reprinted from *The Stories of William Trevor* (1983) and which was adapted for the BBC in 1982, describes a woman's evening at a dance "where people who did not often see other people met."

On Sundays, or on Mondays if he couldn't make it and often he couldn't, Sunday being his busy day, Canon O'Connell arrived at the farm in order to hold a private service with Bridie's father, who couldn't get about any more, having had a leg amputated after gangrene had set in. They'd had a pony and cart then and Bridie's mother had been alive: it hadn't been difficult for the two of them to help her father on to the cart in order to make the journey to Mass. But two years later the pony had gone lame and eventually had to be destroyed; not long after that her mother had died. 'Don't worry about it at all,' Canon O'Connell had said, referring to the difficulty of transporting her father to Mass. 'I'll slip up by the week, Bridie.'

The milk lorry called daily for the single churn of milk, Mr Driscoll delivered groceries and meal in his van, and took away the eggs that Bridie had collected during the week. Since Canon O'Connell had made his offer, in 1953, Bridie's father hadn't left the farm.

As well as Mass on Sundays and her weekly visits to a wayside dance-hall Bridie went shopping once every month, cycling to the town early on a Friday afternoon. She bought things for herself, material for a dress, knitting wool, stockings, a newspaper, and paper-backed Wild West novels for her father. She talked in the shops to some of the girls she'd been at school with, girls who had married shop-assistants or shopkeepers, or had become assistants themselves. Most of them had families of their own by now. 'You're lucky to be peaceful in the hills,' they said to Bridie, 'instead of stuck in a hole like this.' They had a tired look, most of them, from pregnancies and their efforts to organize and control their large families.

As she cycled back to the hills on a Friday Bridie often felt that they truly envied her her life, and she found it surprising that they should do so. If it hadn't been for her father she'd have wanted to work in the town also, in the tinned-meat factory maybe, or in a shop. The town had a cinema called the Electric, and a fish-and-chip shop where people met at night, eating chips out of newspaper on the pavement outside. In the evenings, sitting in the farmhouse with her father, she often thought about the town, imagining the shop-windows lit up to display their goods and the sweet-shops still open so that people could purchase chocolates or fruit to take with them to the Electric cinema. But the town was eleven miles away, which was too far to cycle, there and back, for an evening's entertainment.

'It's a terrible thing for you, girl,' her father used to say, genuinely troubled, 'tied up to a one-legged man.' He would sigh heavily, hobbling back from the fields, where he managed as best he could. 'If your mother hadn't died,' he'd say, not finishing the sentence.

If her mother hadn't died her mother could have looked after him and the scant acres he owned, her mother could somehow have lifted the milk-churn on to the collection platform and attended to the few hens and the cows. 'I'd be dead without the girl to assist me,' she'd heard her father saying to Canon O'Connell, and Canon O'Connell replied that he was certainly lucky to have her.

'Amn't I as happy here as anywhere?' she'd say herself, but her father knew she was pretending and was saddened because the weight of circumstances had so harshly interfered with her life.

Although her father still called her a girl, Bridie was thirty-six. She was tall and strong: the skin of her fingers and her palms were stained, and harsh to touch. The labour they'd experienced had found its way into them, as though juices had come out of vegetation and pigment out of soil: since childhood she'd torn away the rough scotch grass that grew each spring among her father's mangolds and sugar beet; since childhood she'd harvested potatoes in August, her hands daily rooting in the ground she loosened and turned. Wind had toughened the flesh of her face, sun had browned it; her neck and nose were lean, her lips touched with early wrinkles.

But on Saturday nights Bridie forgot the scotch grass and the soil. In different dresses she cycled to the dance-hall, encouraged to make the journey by her father. 'Doesn't it do you good, girl?' he'd say, as though he imagined she begrudged herself the pleasure. 'Why wouldn't you enjoy yourself?' She'd cook him his tea and then he'd settle down with the wireless, or maybe a Wild West novel. In time, while still she danced, he'd stoke the fire up and hobble his way upstairs to bed.

The dance-hall, owned by Mr Justin Dwyer, was miles from anywhere, a lone building by the roadside with treeless boglands all around and a gravel expanse in front of it. On pink pebbled cement its title was painted in an azure blue that matched the depth of the background shade yet stood out well, unfussily proclaiming *The Ballroom of Romance.* Above these letters four coloured bulbs—in red, green, orange and mauve—were lit at appropriate times, an indication that the evening rendezvous was open for business. Only the façade of the building was pink, the other walls being a more ordinary grey. And inside, except for pink swing-doors, everything was blue.

On Saturday nights Mr Justin Dwyer, a small, thin man, unlocked the metal grid that protected his property and drew it back, creating an open mouth from which music would later pour. He helped his wife to carry crates of lemonade and packets of biscuits from their car, and then took up a position in the tiny vestibule between the drawn-back grid and the pink swing-doors. He sat at a card-table, with money and tickets spread out before him. He'd made a fortune, people said: he owned other ballrooms also.

People came on bicycles or in old motor-cars, country people like Bridie from remote hill farms and villages. People who did not often see other people met there, girls and boys, men and women. They paid Mr Dwyer and passed into his dance-hall, where shadows were cast on pale-blue walls and light from a crystal bowl was dim. The band, known as the Romantic Jazz Band, was composed of clarinet, drums and piano. The drummer sometimes sang.

Bridie had been going to the dance-hall since first she left the Presentation Nuns, before her mother's death. She didn't mind the journey, which was seven miles there and seven back: she'd travelled as far every day to the Presentation Nuns on the same bicycle, which had once been the property of her mother, an old Rudge purchased originally in 1936. On Sundays she cycled six miles to Mass, but she never minded either: she'd grown quite used to all that.

'How're you, Bridie?' inquired Mr Justin Dwyer when she arrived in a new scarlet dress one autumn evening. She said she was all right and in reply to Mr Dwyer's second query she said that her father was all right also. 'I'll go up one of these days,' promised Mr Dwyer, which was a promise he'd been making for twenty years.

She paid the entrance fee and passed through the pink swing-doors. The Romantic Jazz Band was playing a familiar melody of the past, 'The Destiny Waltz'. In spite of the band's title, jazz was not ever played in the ballroom: Mr Dwyer did not personally care for that kind of music, nor had he cared for various dance movements that had come and gone over the years. Jiving, rock and roll, twisting and other such variations had all been resisted by Mr Dwyer, who believed that a ballroom should be, as much as possible, a dignified place. The Romantic Jazz Band consisted of Mr Maloney, Mr Swanton, and Dano Ryan on drums. They were three middle-aged men who drove out from the town in Mr Maloney's car, amateur performers who were employed otherwise by the tinned-meat factory, the Electricity Supply Board and the County Council.

'How're you, Bridie?' inquired Dano Ryan as she passed him on her way to the cloakroom. He was idle for a moment with his drums, 'The Destiny Waltz' not calling for much attention from him.

'I'm all right, Dano,' she said. 'Are you fit yourself? Are the eyes better?' The week before he'd told her that he'd developed a watering of the eyes that must have been some kind of cold or other. He'd woken up with it in the morning and it had persisted until the afternoon: it was a new experience, he'd told her, adding that he'd never had a day's illness or discomfort in his life.

'I think I need glasses,' he said now, and as she passed into the cloakroom she imagined him in glasses, repairing the roads, as he was employed to do by the County Council. You hardly ever saw a road-mender with glasses, she reflected, and she wondered if all the dust that was inherent in his work had perhaps affected his eyes.

'How're you, Bridie?' a girl called Eenie Mackie said in the cloakroom, a girl who'd left the Presentation Nuns only a year ago.

'That's a lovely dress, Eenie,' Bridie said. 'Is it nylon, that?'

'Tricel actually. Drip-dry.'

Bridie took off her coat and hung it on a hook. There was a small washbasin in the cloakroom above which hung a discoloured oval mirror. Used tissue and pieces of cotton-wool, cigarette-butts and matches covered the concrete floor. Lengths of green-painted timber partitioned off a lavatory in a corner.

'Jeez, you're looking great, Bridie,' Madge Dowding remarked, waiting for her turn at the mirror. She moved towards it as she spoke, taking off a pair of spectacles before endeavouring to apply make-up to the lashes of her eye. She stared myopically into the oval mirror, humming while the other girls became restive.

'Will you hurry up, for God's sake!' shouted Eenie Mackie. 'We're standing here all night, Madge.'

Madge Dowding was the only one who was older than Bridie. She was thirty-nine, although often she said she was younger. The girls sniggered about that, saying that Madge Dowding should accept her condition—her age and her squint and her poor complexion—and not make herself ridiculous going out after men. What man would be bothered with the like of her anyway? Madge Dowding would do better to give herself over to do Saturday-night work for the Legion of Mary: wasn't Canon O'Connell always looking for aid?

'Is that fellow there?' she asked now, moving away from the mirror. 'The guy with the long arms. Did anyone see him outside?'

'He's dancing with Cat Bolger,' one of the girls replied. 'She has herself glued to him.'

'Lover boy,' remarked Patty Byrne, and everyone laughed because the person referred to was hardly a boy any more, being over fifty it was said, a bachelor who came only occasionally to the dance-hall.

Madge Dowding left the cloakroom rapidly, not bothering to pretend she wasn't anxious about the conjunction of Cat Bolger and the man with the long arms. Two sharp spots of red had come into her cheeks, and when she stumbled in her haste the girls in the cloakroom laughed. A younger girl would have pretended to be casual.

Bridie chatted, waiting for the mirror. Some girls, not wishing to be delayed, used the mirrors of their compacts. Then in twos and threes, occasionally singly, they left the cloakroom and took their places on upright wooden chairs at one end of the dance-hall, waiting to be asked to dance. Mr Maloney, Mr Swanton and Dano Ryan played 'Harvest Moon' and 'I Wonder Who's Kissing Her Now' and 'I'll Be Around'.

Bridie danced. Her father would be falling asleep by the fire; the wireless, tuned in to Radio Eireann, would be murmuring in the background. Already he'd have listened to *Faith and Order* and *Spot the Talent.* His Wild West novel, *Three Rode Fast* by Jake Matall, would have dropped from his single knee on to the flagged floor. He would wake with a jerk as he did every night and, forgetting what night it was, might be surprised not to see her, for usually she was sitting there at the table, mending clothes or washing eggs. 'Is it time for the news?' he'd automatically say.

Dust and cigarette smoke formed a haze beneath the crystal bowl, feet thudded, girls shrieked and laughed, some of them dancing together for want of a male partner. The music was loud, the musicians had taken off their jackets. Vigorously they played a number of tunes from *State Fair* and then, more romantically, 'Just One of Those Things'. The tempo increased for a Paul Jones, after which Bridie found herself with a youth who told her he was saving up to emigrate, the nation in his opinion being finished. 'I'm up in the hills with the uncle,' he said, 'labouring fourteen hours a day. Is it any life for a young fellow?' She knew his uncle, a hill farmer whose stony acres were separated from her father's by one other farm only. 'He has me gutted with work,' the youth told her. 'Is there sense in it at all, Bridie?'

At ten o'clock there was a stir, occasioned by the arrival of three middle-aged bachelors who'd cycled over from Carey's public house. They shouted and whistled, greeting other people across the dancing area. They smelt of stout and sweat and whiskey.

Every Saturday at just this time they arrived, and, having sold them their tickets, Mr Dwyer folded up his card-table and locked the tin box that held the evening's takings: his ballroom was complete.

'How're you, Bridie?' one of the bachelors, known as Bowser Egan, inquired. Another one, Tim Daly, asked Patty Byrne how she was. 'Will we take the floor?' Eyes Horgan suggested to Madge Dowding, already pressing the front of his navy-blue suit against the net of her dress. Bridie danced with Bowser Egan, who said she was looking great.

The bachelors would never marry, the girls of the dance-hall considered: they were wedded already, to stout and whiskey and laziness, to three old mothers somewhere up in the hills. The man with the long arms didn't drink but he was the same in all other ways: he had the same look of a bachelor, a quality in his face.

'Great,' Bowser Egan said, feather-stepping in an inaccurate and inebriated manner. 'You're a great little dancer, Bridie.'

'Will you lay off that!' cried Madge Dowding, her voice shrill above the sound of the music. Eyes Horgan had slipped two fingers into the back of her dress and was now pretending they'd got there by accident. He smiled blearily, his huge red face streaming with perspiration, the eyes which gave him his nickname protuberant and bloodshot.

'Watch your step with that one,' Bowser Egan called out, laughing so that spittle sprayed on to Bridie's face. Eenie Mackie, who was also dancing near the incident, laughed also and winked at Bridie. Dano Ryan left his drums and sang. 'Oh, how I miss your gentle kiss,' he crooned, 'and long to hold you tight.'

Nobody knew the name of the man with the long arms. The only words he'd ever been known to speak in the Ballroom of Romance were the words that formed his invitation to dance. He was a shy man who stood alone when he wasn't performing on the dance-floor. He rode away on his bicycle afterwards, not saying good-night to anyone.

'Cat has your man leppin' tonight,' Tim Daly remarked to Patty Byrne, for the liveliness that Cat Bolger had introduced into foxtrot and waltz was noticeable.

'I think of you only,' sang Dano Ryan. 'Only wishing, wishing you were by my side.'

Dano Ryan would have done, Bridie often thought, because he was a different kind of bachelor: he had a lonely look about him, as if he'd become tired of being on his own. Every week she thought he would have done, and during the week her mind regularly returned to that thought. Dano Ryan would have done because she felt he wouldn't mind coming to live in the farmhouse while her one-legged father was still about the place. Three could live as cheaply as two where Dano Ryan was concerned because giving up the wages he earned as a road-worker would be balanced by the saving made on what he paid for lodgings. Once, at the end of an evening, she'd pretended that there was a puncture in the back wheel of her bicycle and he'd concerned himself with it while Mr Maloney and Mr Swanton waited for him in Mr Maloney's car. He'd blown the tyre up with the car pump and had said he thought it would hold.

It was well known in the dance-hall that she fancied her chances with Dano Ryan. But it was well known also that Dano Ryan had got into a set way of life and had remained in it for quite some years. He lodged with a widow called Mrs Griffin and Mrs Griffin's mentally affected son, in a cottage on the outskirts of the town. He was said to be good to the affected child, buying him sweets and taking him out for rides on the crossbar of his bicycle. He gave an hour or two of his time every week to the Church of Our Lady Queen of Heaven, and he was loyal to Mr Dwyer. He performed in the two other rural dance-halls that Mr Dwyer owned, rejecting advances from the town's more sophisticated dance-hall, even though it was more conveniently situated for him and the fee was more substantial than that paid by Mr Dwyer. But Mr Dwyer had discovered Dano Ryan and Dano had not forgotten it, just as Mr Maloney and Mr Swanton had not forgotten their discovery by Mr Dwyer either.

'Would we take a lemonade?' Bowser Egan suggested. 'And a packet of biscuits, Bridie?'

No alcoholic liquor was ever served in the Ballroom of Romance, the premises not being licensed for this added stimulant. Mr Dwyer in fact had never sought a licence for any of his premises, knowing that romance and alcohol were difficult commodities to mix, especially in a dignified ballroom. Behind where the girls sat on the wooden chairs Mr Dwyer's wife, a small stout woman, served the bottles of lemonade, with straws, and the biscuits, and crisps. She talked busily while doing so, mainly about the turkeys she kept. She'd once told Bridie that she thought of them as children.

'Thanks,' Bridie said, and Bowser Egan led her to the trestle table. Soon it would be the intermission: soon the three members of the band would cross the floor also for refreshment. She thought up questions to ask Dano Ryan.

When first she'd danced in the Ballroom of Romance, when she was just sixteen, Dano Ryan had been there also, four years older than she was, playing the drums for Mr Maloney as he played them now. She'd hardly noticed him then because of his not being one of the dancers: he was part of the ballroom's scenery, like the trestle table and the lemonade bottles, and Mrs Dwyer and Mr Dwyer. The youths who'd danced with her then in their Saturday-night blue suits had later disappeared into the town, or to Dublin or Britain, leaving behind them those who became the middle-aged bachelors of the hills. There'd been a boy called Patrick Grady whom she had loved in those days. Week after week she'd ridden away from the Ballroom of Romance with the image of his face in her mind, a thin face, pale beneath black hair. It had been different, dancing with Patrick Grady, and she'd felt that he found it different dancing with her, although he'd never said so. At night she'd dreamed of him and in the daytime too, while she helped her mother in the kitchen or her father with the cows. Week by week she'd returned to the ballroom, delighting in its pink façade and dancing in the arms of Patrick Grady. Often they'd stood together drinking lemonade, not saying anything, not knowing what to say. She knew he loved her, and she believed then that he would lead her one day from the dim, romantic ballroom, from its blueness and its pinkness and its crystal bowl of light and its music. She believed he would lead her into sunshine, to the town and the Church of Our Lady Queen of Heaven, to marriage and smiling faces. But someone else had got Patrick Grady, a girl from the town who'd never danced in the wayside ballroom. She'd scooped up Patrick Grady when he didn't have a chance.

Bridie had wept, hearing that. By night she'd lain in her bed in the farmhouse, quietly crying, the tears rolling into her hair and making the pillow damp. When she woke in the early morning the thought was still naggingly with her and it remained with her by day, replacing her daytime dreams of happiness. Someone told her later on that he'd crossed to Britain, to Wolverhampton, with the girl he'd married, and she imagined him there, in a place she wasn't able properly to visualize, labouring in a factory, his children being born and acquiring the accent of the area. The Ballroom of Romance wasn't the same without him, and when no one else stood out for her particularly over the years and when no one offered her marriage, she found herself wondering about Dano Ryan. If you couldn't have love, the next best thing was surely a decent man.

Bowser Egan hardly fell into that category, nor did Tim Daly. And it was plain to everyone that Cat Bolger and Madge Dowding were wasting their time over the man with the long arms. Madge Dowding was already a figure of fun in the ballroom, the way she ran after the bachelors; Cat Bolger would end up the same if she wasn't careful. One way or another it wasn't difficult to be a figure of fun in the ballroom, and you didn't have to be as old as Madge Dowding: a girl who'd just left the Presentation Nuns had once asked Eyes Horgan what he had in his trouser pocket and he told her it was a penknife. She'd repeated this afterwards in the cloakroom, how she'd requested Eyes Horgan not to dance so close to her because his penknife was sticking into her. 'Jeez, aren't you the right baby!' Patty Byrne had shouted delightedly; everyone had laughed, knowing that Eyes Horgan only came to the ballroom for stuff like that. He was no use to any girl.

'Two lemonades, Mrs Dwyer,' Bowser Egan said, 'and two packets of Kerry Creams. Is Kerry Creams all right, Bridie?'

She nodded, smiling. Kerry Creams would be fine, she said.

'Well, Bridie, isn't that the great outfit you have!' Mrs Dwyer remarked. 'Doesn't the red suit her, Bowser?'

By the swing-doors stood Mr Dwyer, smoking a cigarette that he held cupped in his left hand. His small eyes noted all developments. He had been aware of Madge Dowding's anxiety when Eyes Horgan had inserted two fingers into the back opening of her dress. He had looked away, not caring for the incident, but had it developed further he would have spoken to Eyes Horgan, as he had on other occasions. Some of the younger lads didn't know any better and would dance very close to their partners, who generally were too embarrassed to do anything about it, being young themselves. But that, in Mr Dwyer's opinion, was a different kettle of fish altogether because they were decent young lads who'd in no time at all be doing a steady line with a girl and would end up as he had himself with Mrs Dwyer, in the same house with her, sleeping in a bed with her, firmly married. It was the middle-aged bachelors who required the watching: they came down from the hills like mountain goats, released from their mammies and from the smell of animals and soil. Mr Dwyer continued to watch Eyes Horgan, wondering how drunk he was.

Dano Ryan's song came to an end, Mr Swanton laid down his clarinet, Mr Maloney rose from the piano. Dano Ryan wiped sweat from his face and the three men slowly moved towards Mrs Dwyer's trestle table.

'Jeez, you have powerful legs,' Eyes Horgan whispered to Madge Dowding, but Madge Dowding's attention was on the man with the long arms, who had left Cat Bolger's side and was proceeding in the direction of the men's lavatory. He never took refreshments. She moved, herself, towards the men's lavatory, to take up a position outside it, but Eyes Horgan followed her. 'Would you take a lemonade, Madge?' he asked. He had a small bottle of whiskey on him: if they went into a corner they could add a drop of it to the lemonade. She didn't drink spirits, she reminded him, and he went away.

'Excuse me a minute,' Bowser Egan said, putting down his bottle of lemonade. He crossed the floor to the lavatory. He too, Bridie knew, would have a small bottle of whiskey on him. She watched while Dano Ryan, listening to a story Mr Maloney was telling, paused in the centre of the ballroom, his head bent to hear what was being said. He was a big man, heavily made, with black hair that was slightly touched with grey, and big hands. He laughed when Mr Maloney came to the end of his story and then bent his head again, in order to listen to a story told by Mr Swanton.

'Are you on your own, Bridie?' Cat Bolger asked, and Bridie said she was waiting for Bowser Egan. 'I think I'll have a lemonade,' Cat Bolger said.

Younger boys and girls stood with their arms still around one another, queuing up for refreshments. Boys who hadn't danced at all, being nervous because they didn't know any steps, stood in groups, smoking and making jokes. Girls who hadn't been danced with yet talked to one another, their eyes wandering. Some of them sucked at straws in lemonade bottles.

Bridie, still watching Dano Ryan, imagined him wearing the glasses he'd referred to, sitting in the farmhouse kitchen, reading one of her father's Wild West novels. She imagined the three of them eating a meal she'd prepared, fried eggs and rashers and fried potato-cakes, and tea and bread and butter and jam, brown bread and soda and shop bread. She imagined Dano Ryan leaving the kitchen in the morning to go out to the fields in order to weed the mangolds, and her father hobbling off behind him, and the two men working together. She saw hay being cut, Dano Ryan with the scythe that she'd learned to use herself, her father using a rake as best he could. She saw herself, because of the extra help, being able to attend to things in the farmhouse, things she'd never had time for because of the cows and the hens and the fields. There were bedroom curtains that needed repairing where the net had ripped, and wallpaper that had become loose and needed to be stuck up with flour paste. The scullery required white-washing.

The night he'd blown up the tyre of her bicycle she'd thought he was going to kiss her. He'd crouched on the ground in the darkness with his ear to the tyre, listening for escaping air. When he could hear none he'd straightened up and said he thought she'd be all right on the bicycle. His face had been quite close to hers and she'd smiled at him. At that moment, unfortunately, Mr Maloney had blown an impatient blast on the horn of his motor-car.

Often she'd been kissed by Bowser Egan, on the nights when he insisted on riding part of the way home with her. They had to dismount in order to push their bicycles up a hill and the first time he'd accompanied her he'd contrived to fall against her, steadying himself by putting a hand on her shoulder. The next thing she was aware of was the moist quality of his lips and the sound of his bicycle as it clattered noisily on the road. He'd suggested then, regaining his breath, that they should go into a field.

That was nine years ago. In the intervening passage of time she'd been kissed as well, in similar circumstances, by Eyes Horgan and Tim Daly. She'd gone into fields with them and permitted them to put their arms about her while heavily they breathed. At one time or another she had imagined marriage with one or other of them, seeing them in the farmhouse with her father, even though the fantasies were unlikely.

Bridie stood with Cat Bolger, knowing that it would be some time before Bowser Egan came out of the lavatory. Mr Maloney, Mr Swanton and Dano Ryan approached, Mr Maloney insisting that he would fetch three bottles of lemonade from the trestle table.

'You sang the last one beautifully,' Bridie said to Dano Ryan. 'Isn't it a beautiful song?'

Mr Swanton said it was the finest song ever written, and Cat Bolger said she preferred 'Danny Boy', which in her opinion was the finest song ever written.

'Take a suck of that,' said Mr Maloney, handing Dano Ryan and Mr Swanton bottles of lemonade. 'How's Bridie tonight? Is your father well, Bridie?'

Her father was all right, she said.

'I hear they're starting a cement factory,' said Mr Maloney. 'Did anyone hear talk of that? They're after striking some commodity in the earth that makes good cement. Ten feet down, over at Kilmalough.'

'It'll bring employment,' said Mr Swanton. 'It's employment that's necessary in this area.'

'Canon O'Connell was on about it,' Mr Maloney said. 'There's Yankee money involved.'

'Will the Yanks come over?' inquired Cat Bolger. 'Will they run it themselves, Mr Maloney?'

Mr Maloney, intent on his lemonade, didn't hear the questions and Cat Bolger didn't repeat them.

'There's stuff called Optrex,' Bridie said quietly to Dano Ryan, 'that my father took the time he had a cold in his eyes. Maybe Optrex would settle the watering, Dano.'

'Ah sure, it doesn't worry me that much—'

'It's terrible, anything wrong with the eyes. You wouldn't want to take a chance. You'd get Optrex in a chemist, Dano, and a little bowl with it so that you can bathe the eyes.'

Her father's eyes had become red-rimmed and unsightly to look at. She'd gone into Riordan's Medical Hall in the town and had explained what the trouble was, and Mr Riordan had recommended Optrex. She told this to Dano Ryan, adding that her father had had no trouble with his eyes since. Dano Ryan nodded.

'Did you hear that, Mrs Dwyer?' Mr Maloney called out. 'A cement factory for Kilmalough.'

Mrs Dwyer wagged her head, placing empty bottles in a crate. She'd heard references to the cement factory, she said: it was the best news for a long time.

'Kilmalough won't know itself,' her husband commented, joining her in her task with the empty lemonade bottles.

''Twill bring prosperity certainly,' said Mr Swanton. 'I was saying just there, Justin, that employment's what's necessary.'

'Sure, won't the Yanks—' began Cat Bolger, but Mr Maloney interrupted her.

'The Yanks'll be in at the top, Cat, or maybe not here at all—maybe only inserting money into it. It'll be local labour entirely.'

'You'll not marry a Yank, Cat,' said Mr Swanton, loudly laughing. 'You can't catch those fellows.'

'Haven't you plenty of homemade bachelors?' suggested Mr Maloney. He laughed also, throwing away the straw he was sucking through and tipping the bottle into his mouth. Cat Bolger told him to get on with himself. She moved towards the men's lavatory and took up a position outside it, not speaking to Madge Dowding, who was still standing there.

'Keep a watch on Eyes Horgan,' Mrs Dwyer warned her husband, which was advice she gave him at this time every Saturday night, knowing that Eyes Horgan was drinking in the lavatory. When he was drunk Eyes Horgan was the most difficult of the bachelors.

'I have a drop of it left, Dano,' Bridie said quietly. 'I could bring it over on Saturday. The eye stuff.'

'Ah, don't worry yourself, Bridie—'

'No trouble at all. Honestly now—'

'Mrs Griffin has me fixed up for a test with Dr Cready. The old eyes are no worry, only when I'm reading the paper or at the pictures. Mrs Griffin says I'm only straining them due to lack of glasses.'

He looked away while he said that, and she knew at once that Mrs Griffin was arranging to marry him. She felt it instinctively: Mrs Griffin was going to marry him because she was afraid that if he moved away from her cottage, to get married to someone else, she'd find it hard to replace him with another lodger who'd be good to her affected son. He'd become a father to Mrs Griffin's affected son, to whom already he was kind. It was a natural outcome, for Mrs Griffin had all the chances, seeing him every night and morning and not having to make do with weekly encounters in a ballroom.

She thought of Patrick Grady, seeing in her mind his pale, thin face. She might be the mother of four of his children now, or seven or eight maybe. She might be living in Wolverhampton, going out to the pictures in the evenings, instead of looking after a one-legged man. If the weight of circumstances hadn't intervened she wouldn't be standing in a wayside ballroom, mourning the marriage of a road-mender she didn't love. For a moment she thought she might cry, standing there thinking of Patrick Grady in Wolverhampton. In her life, on the farm and in the house, there was no place for tears. Tears were a luxury, like flowers would be in the fields where the mangolds grew, or fresh whitewash in the scullery. It wouldn't have been fair ever to have wept in the kitchen while her father sat listening to *Spot the Talent*: her father had more right to weep, having lost a leg. He suffered in a greater way, yet he remained kind and concerned for her.

In the Ballroom of Romance she felt behind her eyes the tears that it would have been improper to release in the presence of her father. She wanted to let them go, to feel them streaming on her cheeks, to receive the sympathy of Dano Ryan and of everyone else. She wanted them all to listen to her while she told them about Patrick Grady who was now in Wolverhampton and about the death of her mother and her own life since. She wanted Dano Ryan to put his arm around her so that she could lean her head against it. She wanted him to look at her in his decent way and to stroke with his road-mender's fingers the backs of her hands. She might wake in a bed with him and imagine for a moment that he was Patrick Grady. She might bathe his eyes and pretend.

'Back to business,' said Mr Maloney, leading his band across the floor to their instruments.

'Tell your father I was asking for him,' Dano Ryan said. She smiled and she promised, as though nothing had happened, that she would tell her father that.

She danced with Tim Daly and then again with the youth who'd said he intended to emigrate. She saw Madge Dowding moving swiftly towards the man with the long arms as he came out of the lavatory, moving faster than Cat Bolger. Eyes Horgan approached Cat Bolger. Dancing with her, he spoke earnestly, attempting to persuade her to permit him to ride part of the way home with her. He was unaware of the jealousy that was coming from her as she watched Madge Dowding holding close to her the man with the long arms while they performed a quickstep. Cat Bolger was in her thirties also.

'Get away out of that,' said Bowser Egan, cutting in on the youth who was dancing with Bridie. 'Go home to your mammy, boy.' He took her into his arms, saying again that she was looking great tonight. 'Did you hear about the cement factory?' he said. 'Isn't it great for Kilmalough?'

She agreed. She said what Mr Swanton and Mr Maloney had said: that the cement factory would bring employment to the neighbourhood.

'Will I ride home with you a bit, Bridie?' Bowser Egan suggested, and she pretended not to hear him. 'Aren't you my girl, Bridie, and always have been?' he said, a statement that made no sense at all.

His voice went on whispering at her, saying he would marry her tomorrow only his mother wouldn't permit another woman in the house. She knew what it was like herself, he reminded her, having a parent to look after: you couldn't leave them to rot, you had to honour your father and your mother.

She danced to 'The Bells Are Ringing', moving her legs in time with Bowser Egan's while over his shoulder she watched Dano Ryan softly striking one of his smaller drums. Mrs Griffin had got him even though she was nearly fifty, with no looks at all, a lumpish woman with lumpish legs and arms. Mrs Griffin had got him just as the girl had got Patrick Grady.

The music ceased, Bowser Egan held her hard against him, trying to touch her face with his. Around them, people whistled and clapped: the evening had come to an end. She walked away from Bowser Egan, knowing that not ever again would she dance in the Ballroom of Romance. She'd been a figure of fun, trying to promote a relationship with a middle-aged County Council labourer, as ridiculous as Madge Dowding dancing on beyond her time.

"I'm waiting outside for you, Cat,' Eyes Horgan called out, lighting a cigarette as he made for the swing-doors.

Already the man with the long arms—made long, so they said, from carrying rocks off his land—had left the ballroom. Others were moving briskly. Mr Dwyer was tidying the chairs.

In the cloakroom the girls put on their coats and said they'd see one another at Mass the next day. Madge Dowding hurried. 'Are you OK, Bridie?' Patty Byrne asked and Bridie said she was. She smiled at little Patty Byrne, wondering if a day would come for the younger girl also, if one day she'd decide that she was a figure of fun in a wayside ballroom.

'Good-night so,' Bridie said, leaving the cloakroom, and the girls who were still chatting there wished her good-night. Outside the cloakroom she paused for a moment. Mr Dwyer was still tidying the chairs, picking up empty lemonade bottles from the floor, setting the chairs in a neat row. His wife was sweeping the floor. 'Good-night, Bridie,' Mr Dwyer said. 'Good-night, Bridie,' his wife said.

Extra lights had been switched on so that the Dwyers could see what they were doing. In the glare the blue walls of the ballroom seemed tatty, marked with hair-oil where men had leaned against them, inscribed with names and initials and hearts with arrows through them. The crystal bowl gave out a light that was ineffective in the glare; the bowl was broken here and there, which wasn't noticeable when the other lights weren't on.

'Good-night so,' Bridie said to the Dwyers. She passed through the swing-doors and descended the three concrete steps on the gravel expanse in front of the ballroom. People were gathered on the gravel, talking in groups, standing with their bicycles. She saw Madge Dowding going off with Tim Daly. A youth rode away with a girl on the crossbar of his bicycle. The engines of motor-cars started.

'Good-night, Bridie,' Dano Ryan said.

'Good-night, Dano,' she said.

She walked across the gravel towards her bicycle, hearing Mr Maloney, somewhere behind her, repeating that no matter how you looked at it the cement factory would be a great thing for Kilmalough. She heard the bang of a car door and knew it was Mr Swanton banging the door of Mr Maloney's car because he always gave it the same loud bang. Two other doors banged as she reached her bicycle and then the engine started up and the headlights went on. She touched the two tyres of the bicycle to make certain she hadn't a puncture. The wheels of Mr Maloney's car traversed the gravel and were silent when they reached the road.

'Good-night, Bridie,' someone called, and she replied, pushing her bicycle towards the road.

'Will I ride a little way with you?' Bowser Egan asked.

They rode together and when they arrived at the hill for which it was necessary to dismount she looked back and saw in the distance the four coloured bulbs that decorated the façade of the Ballroom of Romance. As she watched, the lights went out, and she imagined Mr Dwyer pulling the metal grid across the front of his property and locking the two padlocks that secured it. His wife would be waiting with the evening's takings, sitting in the front of their car.

'D'you know what it is, Bridie,' said Bowser Egan, 'you were never looking better than tonight.' He took from a pocket of his suit the small bottle of whiskey he had. He uncorked it and drank some and then handed it to her. She took it and drank. 'Sure, why wouldn't you?' he said, surprised to see her drinking because she never had in his company before. It was an unpleasant taste, she considered, a taste she'd experienced only twice before, when she'd taken whiskey as a remedy for toothache. 'What harm would it do you?' Bowser Egan said as she raised the bottle again to her lips. He reached out a hand for it, though, suddenly concerned lest she should consume a greater share than he wished her to.

She watched him drinking more expertly than she had. He would always be drinking, she thought. He'd be lazy and useless, sitting in the kitchen with the *Irish Press.* He'd waste money buying a secondhand motor-car in order to drive into the town to go to the public houses on fair-days.

'She's shook these days,' he said, referring to his mother. 'She'll hardly last two years, I'm thinking.' He threw the empty whiskey bottle into the ditch and lit a cigarette. They pushed their bicycles. He said:

'When she goes, Bridie, I'll sell the bloody place up. I'll sell the pigs and the whole damn one and twopence worth.' He paused in order to raise the cigarette to his lips. He drew in smoke and exhaled it. 'With the cash that I'll get I could improve some place else, Bridie.'

They reached a gate on the left-hand side of the road and automatically they pushed their bicycles towards it and leaned them against it. He climbed over the gate into the field and she climbed after him. 'Will we sit down here, Bridie?' he said, offering the suggestion as one that had just occurred to him, as though they'd entered the field for some other purpose.

'We could improve a place like your own one,' he said, putting his right arm around her shoulders. 'Have you a kiss in you, Bridie?' He kissed her, exerting pressure with his teeth. When his mother died he would sell his farm and spend the money in the town. After that he would think of getting married because he'd have nowhere to go, because he'd want a fire to sit at and a woman to cook food for him. He kissed her again, his lips hot, the sweat on his cheeks sticking to her. 'God, you're great at kissing,' he said.

She rose, saying it was time to go, and they climbed over the gate again. 'There's nothing like a Saturday,' he said. 'Good-night to you so, Bridie.'

He mounted his bicycle and rode down the hill, and she pushed hers to the top and then mounted it also. She rode through the night as on Saturday nights for years she had ridden and never would ride again because she'd reached a certain age. She would wait now and in time Bowser Egan would seek her out because his mother would have died. Her father would probably have died also by then. She would marry Bowser Egan because it would be lonesome being by herself in the farmhouse.

QUESTIONS FOR DISCUSSION AND WRITING

1. What are Bridie's expectations for *this* evening at *The Ballroom of Romance?* How does her decision to drink from Bowser Egan's flask mark the climax of the plot?
2. How does Trevor characterize the three bachelors, the Romantic Jazz Band, and the man with long arms? What do Canon O'Connell and Dano Ryan represent to Bridie? How does Bridie characterize "the figure of fun" she is afraid she will become?
3. How does Bridie compare life in the town with life on the farm? How does Mr. Dwyer control the environment of *The Ballroom of Romance?*
4. Where does Trevor shift briefly the point of view from Bridie to Mr. Dwyer's perspective? What does this shift accomplish for the reader?
5. What values are necessary for survival in Bridie's world? What is the ironic significance of Bridie's observation that "you had to honour your father and your mother"?

88

JOHN UPDIKE

A & P

JOHN UPDIKE was born in 1932 in Shillington, Pennsylvania, and educated at Harvard University. Upon graduation, he spent a year at Oxford studying at the Ruskin School of Drawing and Fine Arts. In 1955 he returned from England and joined the staff of *The New Yorker,* where he published his first stories, but two years later he left the magazine to pursue a full-time writing career. Updike's first book, *The Poorhouse Fair* (1959), was a moderate success, but his next novel, *Rabbit, Run* (1960), was acclaimed one of the best novels of the decade. His fascination with the leading character in this novel, Harry ("Rabbit") Angstrom, prompted Updike to write three sequels, *Rabbit Redux* (1971) and *Rabbit Is Rich* (1981), and *Rabbit at Rest* (1990). The first of these was awarded both the National Book Award and the Pulitzer Prize. His other novels

include *The Centaur* (1963), which won Updike's first National Book Award, *Couples* (1968), *A Month of Sundays* (1975), *The Coup* (1978), *The Witches of Eastwick* (1984), *Roger's Version* (1986), and *S.* (1988). Updike's poetry appeared in *The Carpentered Hen and Other Tame Creatures* (1958), *Telephone Poles and Other Poems* (1963), *Midpoint and Other Poems* (1969), and *Tossing and Turning* (1977). Updike's finely crafted short stories have been collected in *The Same Door* (1959), *Pigeon Feathers* (1962), *The Music School* (1966), *Museums and Women* (1972), *Too Far to Go* (1979), and *Trust Me* (1987). "A & P," reprinted from *Pigeon Feathers,* recounts a young boy's attempt to make a heroic stand. "A Sandstone Farmhouse," reprinted from *The Best American Short Stories 1991,* describes an older man's attempt to understand his mother and her "private paradise."

In walks these three girls in nothing but bathing suits. I'm in the third checkout slot, with my back to the door, so I don't see them until they're over by the bread. The one that caught my eye first was the one in the plaid green two-piece. She was a chunky kid, with a good tan and a sweet broad soft-looking can with those two crescents of white just under it, where the sun never seems to hit, at the top of the backs of her legs. I stood there with my hand on a box of HiHo crackers trying to remember if I rang it up or not. I ring it up again and the customer starts giving me hell. She's one of these cash-register-watchers, a witch about fifty with rouge on her cheekbones and no eyebrows, and I know it made her day to trip me up. She'd been watching cash registers for fifty years and probably never seen a mistake before.

By the time I got her feathers smoothed and her goodies into a bag—she gives me a little snort in passing, if she'd been born at the right time they would have burned her over in Salem—by the time I get her on her way the girls had circled around the bread and were coming back, without a pushcart, back my way along the counters, in the aisle between the checkouts and the Special bins. They didn't even have shoes on. There was this chunky one, with the two-piece—it was bright green and the seams on the bra were still sharp and her belly was still pretty pale so I guessed she just got it (the suit)—there was this one, with one of those chubby berry-faces, the lips all bunched together under her nose, this one, and a tall one, with black hair that hadn't quite frizzed right, and one of these sunburns right across under the eyes, and a chin that was too long—you know, the kind of girl other girls think is very "striking" and "attractive" but never quite makes it, as they very well know, which is why they like her so much—and then the third one, that wasn't quite so tall. She was the queen. She kind of led them, the other two peeking around and making their shoulders round. She didn't look around, not this queen, she just walked straight on slowly, on these long white prima-donna legs. She came down a little hard on her heels, as if she didn't walk in her bare feet that much, putting down her heels and then letting the weight move along to her toes as if she was testing the floor with every step, putting a little deliberate extra action into it. You never know for sure how girls' minds work (do you really think it's a mind in there or just a little buzz like a bee in a glass jar?) but you got the idea she had talked the other two into coming in here with her, and now she was showing them how to do it, walk slow and hold yourself straight.

She had on a kind of dirty-pink—beige maybe, I don't know—bathing suit with a little nubble all over it and, what got me, the straps were down. They were off her shoulders looped loose around the cool tops of her arms, and I guess as a result the suit had slipped a little on her, so all around the top of the cloth there was this shining rim. If it hadn't been there you wouldn't have known there could have been anything whiter than those shoulders. With the straps pushed off, there was nothing between the top of the suit and the top of her head except just *her,* this clean bare plane of the top of her chest down from the shoulder bones like a dented sheet of metal tilted in the light. I mean, it was more than pretty.

She had sort of oaky hair that the sun and salt had bleached, done up in a bun that was unravelling, and a kind of prim face. Walking into the A & P with your straps down, I suppose it's the only kind of face you *can* have. She held her head so high her neck, coming up out of those white shoulders, looked kind of stretched, but I didn't mind. The longer her neck was, the more of her there was.

She must have felt in the corner of her eye me and over my shoulder Stokesie in the second slot watching, but she didn't tip. Not this queen. She kept her eyes moving across the racks, and stopped, and turned so slow it made my stomach rub the inside of my apron, and buzzed to the other two, who kind of huddled against her for relief, and then they all three of them went up the cat-and-dog-food-breakfast-cereal-macaroni-rice-raisins-seasonings-spreads-spaghetti-soft-drinks-crackers-and-cookies aisle. From the third slot I look straight up this aisle to the meat counter, and I watched them all the way. The fat one with the tan sort of fumbled with the cookies, but on second thought she put the package back. The sheep pushing their carts down the aisle—the girls were walking against the usual traffic (not that we have one-way signs or anything)—were pretty hilarious. You could see them, when Queenie's white shoulders dawned on them, kind of jerk, or hop, or hiccup, but their eyes snapped back to their own baskets and on they pushed. I bet you could set off dynamite in an A & P and the people would by and large keep reaching and checking oatmeal off their lists and muttering "Let me see, there was a third thing, began with A, asparagus, no, ah, yes, applesauce!" or whatever it is they do mutter. But there was no doubt, this jiggled them. A few houseslaves in pin curlers even looked around after pushing their carts past to make sure what they had seen was correct.

You know, it's one thing to have a girl in a bathing suit down on the beach, where what with the glare nobody can look at each other much anyway, and another thing in the cool of the A & P, under the fluorescent lights, against all those stacked packages, with her feet paddling along naked over our checkerboard green-and-cream rubber-tile floor.

"Oh Daddy," Stokesie said beside me. "I feel so faint."

"Darling," I said. "Hold me tight." Stokesie's married, with two babies chalked up on his fuselage already, but as far as I can tell that's the only difference. He's twenty-two, and I was nineteen this April.

"Is it done?" he asks, the responsible married man finding his voice. I forgot to say he thinks he's going to be manager some sunny day, maybe in 1990 when it's called the Great Alexandrov and Petrooshki Tea Company or something.

What he meant was, our town is five miles from a beach, with a big summer colony out on the Point, but we're right in the middle of town, and the women generally put on a shirt or shorts or something before they get out of the car into the street. And anyway these are usually women with six children and varicose veins mapping their legs and nobody, including them, could care less. As I say, we're right in the middle of town, and if you stand at our front doors you can see two banks and the Congregational church and the newspaper store and the three real-estate offices and about twenty-seven old freeloaders tearing up Central Street because the sewer broke again. It's not as if we're on the Cape, we're north of Boston and there's people in this town haven't seen the ocean for twenty years.

The girls had reached the meat counter and were asking McMahon something. He pointed, they pointed, and they shuffled out of sight behind a pyramid of Diet Delight peaches. All that was left for us to see was old McMahon patting his mouth and looking after them sizing up their joints. Poor kids, I began to feel sorry for them, they couldn't help it.

Now here comes the sad part of the story, at least my family says it's sad, but I don't think it's so sad myself. The store's pretty empty, it being Thursday afternoon, so there was nothing much to do except lean on the register and wait for the girls to show up again. The whole store was like a pinball machine and I didn't know which tunnel they'd come out of. After a while they came around out of the far aisle, around the light bulbs, records at discount of the Caribbean Six or Tony Martin Sings or some such gunk you wonder they waste the wax on, sixpacks of candy bars, and plastic toys done up in cellophane that fall apart when a kid looks at them anyway. Around they come, Queenie still leading the way, and holding a little gray jar in her hand. Slots Three through Seven are unmanned and I could see her wondering between Stokes and me, but Stokesie with his usual luck draws an old party in baggy gray pants who stumbles up with four giant cans of pineapple juice (what do these bums *do* with all that pineapple juice? I've often asked myself) so the girls come to me. Queenie puts down the jar and I take it into my fingers icy cold. Kingfish Fancy Herring Snacks in Pure Sour Cream: 49¢. Now her hands are empty, not a ring or a bracelet, bare as God made them, and I wonder where the money's coming from. Still with that prim look she lifts a folded dollar bill out of the hollow at the center of her nubbled pink top. The jar went heavy in my hand. Really, I thought that was so cute.

Then everybody's luck begins to run out. Lengel comes in from haggling with a truck full of cabbages on the lot and is about to scuttle into that door marked MANAGER behind which he hides all day when the girls touch his eye. Lengel's pretty dreary, teaches Sunday school and the rest, but he doesn't miss that much. He comes over and says, "Girls, this isn't the beach."

Queenie blushes, though maybe it's just a brush of sunburn I was noticing for the first time, now that she was so close. "My mother asked me to pick up a jar of herring snacks." Her voice kind of startled me, the way voices do when you see the people first, coming out so flat and dumb yet kind of tony, too, the way it ticked over "pick up" and "snacks." All of a sudden I slid right down her voice into her living room. Her father and the other men were standing around in ice-cream coats and bow ties and the women were in sandals picking up herring snacks on toothpicks off a big glass plate and they were all holding drinks the color of water with olives and sprigs of mint in them. When my parents have somebody over they get lemonade and if it's a real racy affair Schlitz in tall glasses with "They'll Do It Every Time" cartoons stencilled on.

"That's all right," Lengel said. "But this isn't the beach." His repeating this struck me as funny, as if it had just occurred to him, and he had been thinking all these years the A & P was a great big dune and he was the head lifeguard. He didn't like my smiling—as I say he doesn't miss much—but he concentrates on giving the girls that sad Sunday-school-superintendent stare.

Queenie's blush is no sunburn now, and the plump one in plaid, that I liked better from the back—a really sweet can—pipes up, "We weren't doing any shopping. We just came in for one thing."

"That makes no difference," Lengel tells her, and I could see from the way his eyes went that he hadn't noticed she was wearing a two-piece before. "We want you decently dressed when you come in here."

"We *are* decent," Queenie says suddenly, her lower lip pushing, getting sore now that she remembers her place, a place from which the crowd that runs the A & P must look pretty crummy. Fancy Herring Snacks flashed in her very blue eyes.

"Girls, I don't want to argue with you. After this come in here with your shoulders covered. It's our policy." He turns his back. That's policy for you. Policy is what the kingpins want. What the others want is juvenile delinquency.

All this while, the customers had been showing up with their carts but, you know, sheep, seeing a scene, they had all bunched up on Stokesie, who shook open a paper bag as gently as peeling a peach, not wanting to miss a word. I could feel in the silence everybody getting nervous, most of all Lengel, who asks me, "Sammy, have you rung up their purchase?"

I thought and said "No" but it wasn't about that I was thinking. I go through the punches, 4, 9, GROC, TOT—it's more complicated than you think, and after you do it often enough, it begins to make a little song, that you hear words to, in my case "Hello (*bing*) there, you (*gung*) hap-py *pee*-pul (*splat*)!"—the *splat* being the drawer flying out. I uncrease the bill, tenderly as you may imagine, it just having come from between the two smoothest scoops of vanilla I had ever known were there, and pass a half and a penny into her narrow pink palm, and nestle the herrings in a bag and twist its neck and hand it over, all the time thinking.

The girls, and who'd blame them, are in a hurry to get out, so I say "I quit" to Lengel quick enough for them to hear, hoping they'll stop and watch me, their unsuspected hero. They keep right on going, into the electric eye; the door flies open and they flicker across the lot to their car, Queenie and Plaid and Big Tall Goony-Goony (not that as raw material she was so bad), leaving me with Lengel and a kink in his eyebrow.

"Did you say something, Sammy?"

"I said I quit."

"I thought you did."

"You didn't have to embarrass them."

"It was they who were embarrassing us."

I started to say something that came out "Fiddle-de-doo." It's a saying of my grandmother's, and I know she would have been pleased.

"I don't think you know what you're saying," Lengel said.

"I know you don't," I said. "But I do." I pull the bow at the back of my apron and start shrugging it off my shoulders. A couple customers that had been heading for my slot begin to knock against each other, like scared pigs in a chute.

Lengel sighs and begins to look very patient and old and gray. He's been a friend of my parents for years. "Sammy, you don't want to do this to your Mom and Dad," he tells me. It's true, I don't. But it seems to me that once you begin a gesture it's fatal not to go through with it. I fold the apron, "Sammy" stitched in red on the pocket, and put it on the counter, and drop the bow tie on top of it. The bow tie is theirs, if you've ever wondered. "You'll feel this for the rest of your life," Lengel says, and I know it's true, too, but remembering how he made the pretty girl blush makes me so scrunchy inside I punch the No Sale tab and the machine whirs "pee-pul" and the drawer splats out. One advantage to this scene taking place in summer, I can follow this up with a clean exit, there's no fumbling around getting your coat and galoshes, I just saunter into the electric eye in my white shirt that my mother ironed the night before, and the door heaves itself open, and outside the sunshine is skating around on the asphalt.

I look around for my girls, but they're gone, of course. There wasn't anybody but some young married screaming with her children about some candy they didn't get by the door of a powder-blue Falcon station wagon. Looking back in the big windows, over the bags of peat moss and aluminum lawn furniture stacked on the pavement, I could see Lengel in my place in the slot, checking the sheep through. His face was dark gray and his back stiff, as if he'd just had an injection of iron, and my stomach kind of fell as I felt how hard the world was going to be to me hereafter.

QUESTIONS FOR DISCUSSION AND WRITING

1. How does the appearance of three girls in bathing suits in the A & P create the initial conflict in this story? What other conflicts does Sammy's confrontation with Lengel produce? To what extent does Sammy's decision to quit provide a satisfactory resolution to those conflicts?
2. How does Sammy's characterization of the three girls help describe him? How does his name for the third girl, Queenie, justify his lengthy description of her? How does Queenie's purchase reveal the difference between her world and Sammy's world?
3. How does the title of the story call attention to its setting? What assumptions does Sammy make about his readers' familiarity with this setting? How does he compare his store to those nearer the beach?
4. What is the ironic difference between the narrator's view of himself and the reader's view of him? How do the comments of Stokesie and Lengel help qualify Sammy's first-person presentation of the events in the story?
5. What does the story reveal about the causes and effects of "heroic" action? Why has his experience led Sammy to conclude that the world was going to be hard to him "hereafter"?

89

JOHN UPDIKE

A Sandstone Farmhouse

Joey's first glimpse of the house was cloudy in his memory, like an old photo mottled by mildew. During the Second World War, his family owned no car, and renting one, for their infrequent excursions out of the compact brick city where his father worked, embarrassed the twelve-year-old boy to the point that he didn't see clearly through the windows, or was not conscious of much beyond his internal struggle not to be carsick. He fought the swaying, jiggling motion, which was mixed with the warm confluent smells of rubber floor mat and petroleum combustion, and the patient pale veiny look of his father's hand on the gear-shift knob. Farm country, miles of it, poured past. Depressing, monotonous fields moved up and down beneath their hazy burden of crops. A winding asphalt highway climbed a hill, passed a lumpy stone church, then settled into a flat stretch where they slowed to turn left down a dirt washboard road that shook the car sickeningly. Not a building in sight. No sign of civilization but telephone poles carrying a single wire. Another turn, right this time, down an even smaller dirt road, and they stopped, and in the sudden flood of fresh air as Joey opened the car door, the green of the grass rose waxy and bright to greet his giddiness, his nausea. In his cloudy memory, they went up to the house and there were people in it, farm people, wearing cotton and thick muddy shoes, shyly trying to get out of their way, like animals. There was a front porch, he remembered that much. With a banister upheld by boards jigsawed into an ornamental shape, and a secret space underneath, of weeds and pebbly dirt. A space where chickens could scratch and dogs could lie and pant during hot weather, the kind of space that is friendly and inviting to a boy of the age he was just outgrowing.

By the time they had bought the house with its surrounding eighty acres and moved in, he was thirteen, and the front porch had vanished, leaving a space between the front of the house and the cement walk where they eventually planted crocuses and tulips and erected a grape arbor. Joey as an adult could not remember how or when it had happened, their tearing down the rotten old porch. Pieces of it remained in the barn—segments of banister with the ornamental balusters cut of inch-thick pine. Once he even took a baluster home with him, back to New York City, as some kind of memento, or sample of folk art. The pattern held a circle in the center, a circle with a hole, between two shapes jigsawed into the wood, one like an arrow and one like a fish. Different-colored flakes fell dryly from it, brittle layers of old-time lead paint. The object, not quite of art, rested sideways on the black marble mantel of his apartment for a while, then found its way to the back of a closet, with broken squash rackets and college textbooks and table lamps that might someday be made to glow again. Like his mother, he had trouble throwing anything away.

If he and his father and grandfather had torn the porch down themselves, he would have remembered so heroic a labor, as he did the smashing of the lath-and-plaster partition that separated the two small parlors downstairs, making one big living room, or the tearing out of the big stone kitchen fireplace and its chimney, right up into the attic. Joey remembered swinging the great stones out the attic window, he and his grandfather pushing, trying not to pinch their fingers, while his father, his face white with the effort, held the rope of a makeshift pulley rigged over a rafter. Once clear of the sill, the heavy stones fell with a ghostly slowness, seen from above, and accumulated into a kind of mountain it became Joey's summer job to clear away. He learned a valuable lesson, that first summer on the farm, while he turned fourteen: even if you manage to wrestle only one stone into the wheelbarrow and sweatily, staggeringly trundle it down to the swampy area this side of the springhouse, eventually the entire mountain will be taken away. On the same principle, an invisible giant, removing only one day at a time, will eventually dispose of an entire life.

When, over forty years later, his mother died, and the at last uninhabited house yielded up its long-buried treasures, he came upon a photograph of her at the age of ten, posing in front of the porch. Someone in pencil, in a flowing handwriting not his mother's—hers was tiny, and cramped, and back-slanted—had marked on the back "Taken August 1914. Enlarged August 1917." Someone had loved this snapshot enough to have it enlarged and mounted on thick gray cardboard: who?

His mother, wearing a low-waisted dress, dark stockings, and black shoes with big, thick heels, her hair done up in a long braid that hangs over one shoulder, is holding the collar of a young medium-sized dog, part collie. Both the child and the dog are looking straight into the camera with similar half-smiles and wide-spaced, trusting eyes. They are standing on a cement walk that is still there, uncracked; behind them the porch balusters repeat their simple artful pattern and a small rosebush blooms. The long-dead dog, the recently dead human female look identically happy. Joey would hardly have recognized his mother but for the thick abundance of her hair—a chestless cheerful little girl in old woman's shoes. Beyond the edge of the barn to her right, ghostly in the enlargement, are fences and trees of which no trace remains and, just barely visible, an entire building that has vanished—a tobacco shed, perhaps. The lawn is edged around the walk, and the fences look trim. This was the private paradise, then, to which she attempted to return, buying back the old sandstone farmhouse that her parents, feeling full enough of tobacco profits to retire, had sold while she was innocently off at normal school. Precocious, she had been skipped, and was sent off at the age of twelve, and hated it, hated it all, including the hour-long trolley ride to Kutztown. The swaying, the ozone, the drunk men who sat down beside her made her sick.

She loved the old house; she loved the *idea* of it. For most of her life, except for the twenty years of exile in her young womanhood, when she went to normal school, then to college, and married a man she met there, and traveled with him until the Depression cost him his traveling job, and bore him a son, in the heart of the Depression, while they were all living with her parents in the brick city house—except for these twenty years, she happily inhabited an idea. The sandstone house was built, her fond research discovered, in 1812. In that era, teams of masons and stonelayers roamed the countryside, erecting these Pennsylvania farmhouses on principles of an elegant simplicity. Their ground plan was square, set square to the compass. The south face basked in the maximum of sunshine; the east windows framed the sunrise, and the west the sunset. The cornerstones were cut at a slightly acute angle, to emphasize the edge. The stout scaffolding was rooted in holes in the thirty-inch walls as they rose, and these holes were plugged with stones four inches square as the masonry was pointed, and the scaffolding dismantled, from the top down. In the mortar, lime from the lime kiln was mixed with sand from creek beds, to match the stones. Though the size of the stones raised and fitted into place was prodigious, the real feats of leverage occurred in the quarrying. Sandstone exposed in an outcropping was rendered useless by weather, but underneath the earth the sound stone slept, to be painstakingly split by star drills and wedges and "feathers" of steel, and then hauled out by teams of horses, on wagons or sleds. Sometimes the wagons shattered under the load of a single great stone. But this vast hauling and lifting continued, a tidal movement like that of the glaciers which here and there had deposited huge moraines, acres frightening in their sheer stoniness, in the middle of the forests—heaped-up depths of boulders in which no tree could take root, barren geological deposits fascinating and bewildering to nineteenth-century minds, so eager to see God's hand everywhere.

For sensitive, asthmatic Joey, removed from a brick semidetached city house where he had felt snug, where he could hear through his bedroom walls the neighbors stirring as he awoke, and the milk being delivered on the porch, and the trolley cars clanging at the corner a block away, the silent thickness of stones just behind the old plaster and wallpaper, and the rough hearths and fireplaces visible within the country house, seemed to harbor nature's damp and cold. A sullen held breath dwelled in the walls. The summer's heat brought swarms of wasps, millipedes, carpenter ants, and silverfish out from the crannies. That first winter in the house, before an oil furnace was installed in the basement, a kerosene-burning stove in the living room provided the only heat. Joey remembered the stove clearly; it was painted chocolate brown, and stood on little bent legs on an asbestos sheet papered with imitation wood grain. He spent days huddled in blankets next to this stove, on a grease-spotted sofa that had been brought close. With his constant cold, he missed days of school, and hated to, for it was warm at school, and there was running water, and flush toilets. And girls in long pleated skirts and fuzzy sweaters and bobby socks, who belonged to the modern era, to civilization. He clung to civilization by reading; huddled in the brown stove's aura of coal oil, he read anything—P. G. Wodehouse, Ellery Queen, John Dickson Carr, Thorne Smith—that savored of cities and took him out of this damp, cold little stone house.

His mother remembered that first winter with rueful pleasure, as a set of tribulations blithely overcome. "It was really very hard, I suppose, on everybody—you were *so* sick, and your father had to struggle so to get to work in that old Chevrolet that was all we could afford, and for my parents it was a terrible defeat, to come back to the farm when they had gotten away; they would hide together in the corner just like children—but I was so happy to be here I hardly noticed. The movers had broken the large pane of glass in the front door, and for some reason that whole first winter we never managed to replace it; we lived with a sheet of cardboard wedged over the hole. It's incredible that we survived." And she would laugh gaily, remembering. "We tried to light fires in the living-room fireplace, but all the wood the Schellenbargers had left us in the basement was moldy elm, and that fireplace never did draw well, even when the swifts' nests weren't plugging it up. Smoke leaks out into the room, I've never understood why. If you look up the flue with a flashlight, the stonework has a twist."

Joey seemed to remember, though, waking upstairs and putting his feet onto the bare wood floor and grabbing his school clothes and hurrying in his pajamas down the narrow stairs—the treads worn in two troughs by generations of footsteps, the nailheads protruding and shiny and dangerous—to dress in front of the fireplace, where logs were crackling. The freezing upstairs air would lick at his skin like flame, like the endless conversations between his mother and her parents, incessant flowing exchanges that would ripple into quarrel and chuckle back again into calm while he focused, when he was home, into the pages of his book. His grandfather had a beautiful, patient, elocutionary voice; his grandmother spoke little, in guttural responses. His mother, unlike most adults, hadn't parted from her parents, and clung to them with old tales and grievances, like someone adding up the same set of figures day after day and always expecting a different answer. As Joey huddled by the stove, heated conversations were in his ears as the smell of coal oil was in his nostrils, but always, those five years (only five!) that he lived in the sandstone house with four adults, his attention was aimed elsewhere—on schoolwork, on the future. He tried to ignore what was around him. The house, even when plumbing and central heating and a telephone were installed, and new wallpaper made the repainted rooms pretty, embarrassed him.

He was never more embarrassed than in that summer before they moved in, before they owned even the erratic old Chevrolet. Several times, his mother made him travel with her by bus out to the farm they already owned. She had a vision of a windbreak of pines rimming the big field, along the road, and she and Joey carried seedlings in boxes, and shovels, and pruners, and a watering can—all this humiliating apparatus dragged onto a city bus by a redfaced middle-aged woman and a skinny boy with ears that stuck out and dungarees that were too short. His mother wore a checked shirt like a man's and a straw sun hat and a pair of light-blue overalls with a bib; she looked like a farmer in a Hollywood musical comedy. There was no space inside the bus for the shovels; the driver had to store them in the luggage compartment and then stop and get out in the middle of nowhere to hand the tools over. It was a relief when the bus, headed south toward Washington, D.C., disappeared around a bend in the highway.

Joey and his mother walked down the dirt washboard road in the heat, carrying their equipment. He had never been so humiliated, so ridiculous, and vowed never to be again. He couldn't blame his mother, he still needed her too much, so he blamed the place—its hazy, buggy fields, its clouds of blowing pollen that made him sneeze and his eyes water, its little sandstone house like a cube of brown sugar melting in the heat, in a little dip of hillside beneath an overgrown, half-dead apple orchard. All through noon and into the afternoon they cleared little spaces at the edge of the field, where the Schellenbargers' last crop of field corn was pushing up in limp green rows, and cut away burdock and poison ivy and honeysuckle, and dug holes, and set in each hole a little six-inch puff of pine tree, and sprinkled water over the socket of sandy red earth. Moving a few paces farther on to plant the next tree, Joey could no longer see the last one amid the weeds and wild grass. The work seemed hopeless. Yet when the afternoon breeze came up, he felt a purity of silence—perhaps one car an hour passed, the people staring at this woman and boy in clothes neither country nor city—that didn't exist in his beloved street of semidetached houses. And there was a kind of heroism to his periodic trudge, with the empty sprinkling can, the half-mile along the edge of the cornfields to the empty house, with its rusty iron pump on the back porch, and then the long haul back, the sloshing can as heavy as a stone.

He felt heroic to himself. Space for heroism existed out here. He was determined to impress his mother—to win her back, since here on this farm he for the first time encountered something she apparently loved as much as she loved him.

At last, the weeds threw feathery long shadows upon one another and the tiny pines were all planted in the hopeless roadside jungle and it was time to walk back up the dusty washboard road to wait for the bus from Washington to round the corner. Having gone and come so far, the bus could be as much as an hour late, and their eyes would sting, staring down the gray highway for it, and his stomach would sink at the thought that they had missed it and were stranded. But not even this possibility daunted him, for he had forged a mood of defiant collusion in which he was numbed to humiliation and played a role both stoic and comic, costarring with his heavy mother in her straw sun hat and his lanky, sharp-faced sidekicks, the clippers and the shovel. Years later, he could even laugh with her about it, those awkward hot trips to plant a line of trees most of which never thrived, choked by thistles and bindweed or severed by a too zealous mower. Yet a few of the pines, perhaps six or seven, did live to tower along the road bank—shaggy-headed apparitions taller than a ship's mast, swaying in the wind. By this time, the dirt road was macadamized and hummed with traffic, and the bus route to Washington had long ago been abandoned as unprofitable.

Five years after the September when they had moved, Joey went to college and, essentially, never returned. He married in his senior year, and after graduation moved to New York City. Another of his mother's visions, along with that of the farm as paradise, was of him as a poet; he fulfilled this heroic task as best he could, by going to work for an ad agency and devoting himself to the search for the arresting phrase and image, on the edge of the indecent, that incites people to buy—that gives them permission, from the mythic world above, to buy. The business was like poetry in that you needed only a few lucky hits, and he had his share, and couldn't complain. He never again had to get on a bus with a shovel.

The numbers attached to the years and decades slowly changed and with them the numbers in his bank account and on his apartment building. His first marriage took place in three different apartments, his turbulent second in four, his short-lived third in only one, and now he wondered if women had not quite been his thing all along. He had always felt most at ease, come to think of it, in the company of men, especially those who reminded him of his father. But it was the AIDS-conscious eighties by then, and his hair had passed through gray into virtual white, and he found the personalities of young men an effective barrier to thinking about their bodies, and he was content to share his life with his books, his CDs (compact disks, certificates of deposit), his modest little art collection mixed of watery commercialism and icy minimalism. On the other side of the white walls of his apartment he could hear the mumble and thump of his neighbors, and he liked that. He was home.

Three hours away, his widowed mother lived alone in the sandstone house. Joey had been the first to depart, and then a few years later his grandfather died, suddenly, with a stroke like a thunderclap, and then, after a bedridden year, his grandmother. This created an extra room upstairs, so Joey and his first wife and young children, when they came to visit in the sixties, no longer had to camp out downstairs, on cots and the sofa spotted by the peanut-butter crackers he used to eat when sick and consigned to reading the days away. The upstairs had two real bedrooms, to which the doors could be closed, and a kind of hallway beside the head of the stairs where he had slept for five years, listening to the four adults rustle and snore and creak while girls and prayers and the beginnings of poems all ran together in his brain. His grandfather, on his way downstairs in the early morning, would ruffle the hair on the sleeping boy's head, and the gathering sounds of family breakfast, as Joey's grandmother and parents followed, would rise under him with the smell of toast, a doughy warmth of life rising beneath the cold bare floorboards.

There was a fourth room, a small room in the northwest corner, where his mother had once been born, in a long agony of labor—a rural calvary, as Joey imagined it, with flickering lamps and steaming kettles and ministering cousins arriving by horse and buggy—that shaped her relations with her own mother into, it seemed, a ferocious apology, a futile undying adhesion in an attempt to make amends. She nursed her mother in the old woman's long paralyzed agony of dying, but not always patiently, or tenderly, and when the ordeal at last was over she was left with additional cause for self-blame, more sorry images. "I spent my whole life," she concluded, "trying to please my mother, and never did."

Joey would ask, irritated by these pat surges of self-dramatization, "Did she ever say so?"

"No, but you knew her. She never said anything."

"Unlike *my* mother," he said, with an ironic pretense of gallantry.

She heard the irony. "Yes, I inherited Pop's gift of gab," she said. "It's been a curse, really. If you talk enough, you don't feel you have to *do* anything."

This fourth room had become the bathroom, with a tub but no shower, a basin but no cabinet. Toothpaste, sun lotion, hand creams, razors, dental floss, slivers of soap thriftily stuck together all accumulated on the deep sill overlooking the blackening shingles of the back-porch roof. After his father died, in the early seventies, the house gradually lost the power to purge itself of accumulation. Their occupancy, which had begun with removal of the porch and the chimney stones, now silted the attic and cellar and windowsills full with souvenirs of his mother's lengthening residence. On the theory that it would save the wild birds from being eaten, she had fed a stray cat that came to the back porch; this cat then became several, and the several became as many as forty. The kitchen became choked with stacked cases of cat food, and a site in the woods, at the end of a path overgrown with raspberry canes, became a mountain of empty cat-food cans. Tin Mountain, Joey's children called it. Magazines and junk mail and church pamphlets sat around on tables and chairs waiting to be bundled and taken to the barn, to wait there for the Boy Scouts' next paper drive. Photographs of Joey and his children, Christmas cards and valentines from relations and neighbors, piled up on available spaces like a kind of moss. Even the table where his mother ate had room eventually for only one plate and cup and saucer, her own. The house was clogging up, Joey felt, much as her heart—

coronary angiography had revealed—was plugging with arteriosclerosis, and her weakly pumped lungs were filling with water.

His arrivals, as the years went on, seemed to accumulate. He would park his car by the barn and pick his way across the line of steppingstones that in the decades since they were laid (even Granny, stiff and bent over, helping with the crowbar) had been silted over by the sandy soil and its crabgrass. On the back porch there would be a puddle of cats and kittens mewing to be fed. Entering the back door with his suitcase was like stepping into a quicksand smelling of cat food and damp cardboard. His mother saved, in separate sections of the floor, the plastic bags the supermarket bagged her groceries in, and slippery stacks of mail-order catalogues, and a bucketful of maddeningly snarled baling twine, to make bundles for the barn with. He recognized in this accumulation a superstition he had to fight within himself—the belief that everything has value. The birds in the trees, the sunflower at the edge of the orchard, the clumsily pasted-up valentine received years ago from a distant grandchild—all have a worth that might at any moment be called into account. It was a way of saying that one's own life was infinitely precious.

There would be a peck of a kiss at the door, and he would carry the suitcase upstairs, past the whirling, nipping mongrel bitch, who was thrilled to have a man in the house. The guest room had been his parents' old room. When she became a widow, his mother had moved into her parents' old room, closer to the room in which she had been born. The move was part, Joey felt, of an obscure religious system that had nothing to do with Christianity. He remembered how, in a surprising rite of that system, his parents, the day after his grandmother died, took her stained, urine-soaked mattress outdoors and burned it, down near the stones he had dumped, darkening the sky all morning with the smoke.

Here, in this guest room, at night, without a wife to distract and comfort him, he would begin to fight for his breath. The bed sagged so that his back hurt. The pillow felt heavy and dense. The sandstone hearth of the never-used fireplace in the room would emit an outdoor dampness. Birds and bats and mice would stir in the porous walls, and his mother's motions would make her bed beyond the thin wall creak. Was she awake, or asleep? He could relax deeply only in the early morning, when the dog would wake her, scrabbling on the bare boards with her claws, and the two of them would slowly, noisily head downstairs, and the can opener would rhythmically begin to chew through the first installment of cat-food cans.

The guest room for some reason had no curtains; in the dead of the night the moon burned on the wide sills as if calling to him, calling him back to a phase his whole adult life had been an effort to obliterate. The asthma, the effect of inner tightening and complication, wasn't so bad, usually, the first two nights; he might manage five or six hours of sleep each if he could then get away, back to cozy, salubrious New York. But on long holiday weekends he would struggle through the whole third night with the accumulated house dust and pollen in his lungs, and the damp hard pillow, and the obdurate moonlight, so accusatory in its white silence.

He was aware of his mother and himself, lying each in bed, as survivors of the larger party that had once occupied this house. It was as if, on a snowy pass, they had killed and eaten the others, and now one of the two remaining must perish next. She, too, in her eighties, had breathing problems, and slept with her head up on two pillows. One night she woke him with the soft words, "Joey. I'm not doing so well. Put on your daddy's old overcoat and come downstairs with me."

He was awake, his head clear as moonlight, in an instant. "Shall we call the hospital?"

"No, I just need to sit up. You know which overcoat, it hangs at the foot of the stairs."

It had hung there for years, one of those curious comforting rags his father would acquire in thrift shops or outlet stores. Joey had often seen it on him, in the last year of the old man's life, when his legs turned white and phlebitic and his nose turned blue with poor circulation and his eyes sank deeper and deeper into his head and his deafness worsened. But to the end his father had held his head high, and took a lively interest in the world. Once a social-science teacher, he continued to read fat history books, and wrote Joey, in one of his rare letters, in his patient, legible schoolteacher's hand, that being deaf made it easier for him to concentrate.

Joey wondered why his mother was being so insistent about the coat, but obediently put it on. It had a fuzziness unusual in dark overcoats, and was big for him, since his father had been bigger than he. She was right; once it was on, over his pajamas, he became a child again, and calm, and trusting. They went downstairs and turned up the thermostat and sat in the dark living room together, he on the sofa and she in her television-watching chair, and he watched her struggle for breath, in little sudden shuddering gasps like the desperate heaves of a bird caught in the chimney.

"Do you hurt?" he asked.

She had little breath for speaking, and shook her head no, and her head underwent again the convulsion, as if trying to keep above water. "It's like," she gasped, "a squeezing."

"Sure you wouldn't like to drive to the hospital?"

A vigorous headshake again. "What can they do, but torture you?"

So he sat there, in his father's overcoat, fighting sleepiness, wondering if his mother would die before his eyes. The dog, agitated at first by this predawn rising, wheezed and resettled on the floor. The moonlight weakened on the sills across the room, with their potted geraniums and violets and a night-blooming cereus that had been allowed to grow grotesquely long, so that its stem filled the window. His mother's shudders lessened, and eventually she told him to go upstairs, she would sit here a while longer. In her old age she had become almost grafted onto this chair of hers. On a previous visit, she had shocked him by refusing, when the evening run of television comedies that she faithfully watched was over, to come upstairs at all; morning found her still sitting there, in her clothes. This irritated him, along with her television watching. "Why do you watch all these idiots?" he once asked her. "They seem realer to you than I am."

She did not deny it. "Well," she had answered, "they're always here."

Now, her crisis past, he accepted her dismissal gratefully and yet reluctantly. He went upstairs feeling that this hour had been the most purely companionable he had ever spent with her in this house. To Joey in his father's fuzzy, overlarge coat, as he silently watched his mother struggle and the dog stir and doze and the night-blooming cereus cast its gawky shadow in the deep window recess beyond the tasseled bridge lamp and the upright piano, it had been like one of those scenes we witness in childhood, from under the table or over the edge of the crib, understanding nothing except that large forces are moving around us—that there is a heavy dynamism from which we are, as children, sheltered.

When she had her next attack of breathlessness, he was not there, and she called the neighbors, and they called the township ambulance, which came at five in the morning. For all her talk of "torture," she seemed to settle gratefully into the hospital's ministrations. "They said I was quite blue, the oxygen in my blood was down to nothing." Rather gaily, she described the emergency-room doctors thrusting some violent sucking instrument down her throat and into her lungs.

Her bathrobe was turquoise with a maroon hem; she ordered her clothes from catalogues now and was attracted to decisive colors. With her white hair all about her on the pillow, and the baby-blue tubes of oxygen making a mustache, and the identification bracelet looped on her wrist, she looked festive and hectic and feminized. All day, young men in antiseptic garb came and tended to her, cutting her toenails, interrogating her bowels. Her bowels, to Joey's embarrassment, had become a topic of supreme fascination to her. Her insides in general were brought uncomfortably close to the surface by the wearing away of her body. His father's method of coping with what seemed to Joey her unaccountable whims, including moving them all to the farm, had been to say, "She's a femme. Your mother's a real femme. What can you do?" He would shrug, and sometimes add, "I should have put her on the burleycue stage."

This had seemed one of the man's lofty, pained jokes; but now her femininity, which Joey's father and succession of wives had shielded him from, was upon him. In her slightly disheveled, revealing gowns, in her gracefully accepted helplessness and fragility, in this atmosphere of frank bodily event, his mother had her sex on her mind. She told him, remembering the first years of her marriage in Pittsburgh, "There was this young doctor, Dr. Langhorne over on Sixth Street, who when I went to him with these pains on my chest I couldn't understand told me to take off my clothes. Well, I trusted him, and did, and he looked me over for the longest time, and then told me, 'You're not obese.' That was all he said."

His own birth, her conviction that she couldn't do such a normal thing as conceive and bear a child, recurred in her self-accounting; old Dr. Berthoff, who kept brusquely calming her fears, who treated her as a normal woman and not as the monstrous product of her own mother's agony, emerged as a kind of erotic hero, and Joey suddenly saw that his own self, which he had imagined she cherished for qualities all his own, was lovable to her above all as a piece of her body, as a living proof of her womanhood.

And she recalled, of those straitened Depression days when he was an infant, how she left him in the care of his grandparents and went off on the trolley car to work in the drapes department of the department store downtown. She had lost a tooth, a bicuspid, and the upper partial plate containing its replacement was uncomfortable, and one day she didn't wear it to work and was chastised by the department manager, Mr. Wirtheimer, for not wearing it. The image of her missing tooth, this tidy black hole leaping up within her young woman's smile, seemed erotic, too, along with the thought of his then-slender mother's charm as a saleswoman. "On my good days," she said, "I could sell anything. But then the people would bring it all back for exchange on Monday. As if I had bewitched them. Mr. Wirtheimer said there was such a thing as being *too* good."

But not all her days were good days, she told Joey. She took her periods too hard, they knocked her flat for thirty-six, forty-eight hours; and this brought the conversation back to her body, her body arching over his life like a firmament, and he would leave the hospital building and find relief in the reality of the city, Alton, with its close-packed suburbs, which he loved as his mother loved her farm, because it had formed his first impressions, when the wax was soft. He ate at aluminum diners, shopped at hardware stores for parts and tools the sandstone farmhouse in its long decrepitude needed, and bought a new vacuum cleaner, since his mother's old Hoover had hardly been used for years. He even got himself a haircut in a front-parlor barbershop—the kind of shop, with a radio playing and a baby crying in rooms out of sight, and a spiral pole out front, that he thought had disappeared, because such shops had disappeared in New York. A small child of his, years ago, had knocked the porcelain lid off the toilet water tank and it had shattered. Now, between visits to his mother, he went about the city with the cardboard box of fragments, dusty and cobweb-ridden after years in the attic, to plumbing-supply houses, where overweight, hard-smoking, not quite sardonic men would return from digging in their cavernous storerooms and give him, free, old spare lids that did not, it would turn out, quite fit. He kept trying. Alton had lost factories and population since he was a boy, and appeared in smaller letters on the maps of Pennsylvania, but it was still a place where things were made and handled, where brute matter got its honest due, and he recognized as still alive in himself the city's blue-collar faith in hardware and industry and repair, a humble faith that had survived all his heady traffic in imagery.

Life was a series of plumbing problems. After a week, the hospital had cleared out his mother's lungs, and now the cardiologists wanted to operate on the malfunctioning heart that had let the pulmonary edema occur. The angiography had revealed coronary arteries stenosed almost shut. "Oh, Joey—I could go any day," she blurted to him after the test results had been described to her. She showed him with a forefinger and thumb how small the lumen had become. "Worse than they thought." She was sitting on the bed with her hair wild and one shoulder bared by a loose tie in the hospital johnny, and her facial expression was girlish, womanhood's acquired composure all dissolved. Their intermittently shared life was being lifted into new octaves, and they seemed in these moments of hospital conference simply a man and a woman, both with more white hairs than dark, taking counsel because no one else who mattered was left. They were it.

To his relief, she did not want the open-heart operation, sparing him the trouble, the expense, the tests, the trips to Philadelphia. He tried to suppress his relief and to argue for the coronary bypass that was recommended. She said, making a wryly twisted mouth just as her father used to when discussing the county's politicians, "Of course *they* recommend it. It's what they have to sell. They're in business, just like their fathers, only peddling different things. They pass me around, one to another; I've yet to see a Christian."

In the frankness that her closeness to death allowed, as her composed womanhood melted, an anti-Semitism was one of the things that emerged, shockingly. She could not see the doctors as saviors and allies but only as opportunists and exploiters. She even developed with one solemn young cardiologist a banter that cast her as a Palestinian: "You've taken me away from my village," she said. Joey was dismayed; his third wife, the briefest one, had been Jewish, and she and his mother had seemed especially friendly, and as he imagined now his mother's suppressed feelings in those years it was like seeing silverfish tumble out of old books. On her less lucid days, she seemed to think that the doctors and their allies ("One big fella, looked just like Danny Thomas, came and cut my toenails; now how much do you think *that's* going to add to the bill?") were scheming to do her out of her house and its priceless eighty acres—that she was territory they wanted to seize and develop. Each day she spent in the hospital, the little sandstone house pulled at her harder. "Get me home," she begged Joey.

"And then what?"

"Then we'll take what comes." Her eyes widened, watching his, and her mouth as it clamped shut over "what comes" was very like a child's, stubborn in its fright. For, however close their consultation and their agreements, both were aware that she was the star and he merely the prompter: though his turn would come, the spotlight burned upon her.

When, six months later, she died—instantly, it seemed to the coroner—in the kitchen, just under the room where she had been born, the neighbors, who were patient Mennonites and Lutherans, took a day to find her and another twelve hours to find him in at his apartment telephone number. It was midnight when he let himself into the house. The door keys had been lost long ago, in that distant, fabulous era after they had moved. When his mother would be away for more than a day, she would lock the doors from the inside and go out through the cellar bulkhead. Her neighbors knew this and had left the house that way after her body was removed. Joey had brought no flashlight; after parking the car by the barn, he walked to the slanted cellar doors by moonlight, and within the dark cellar was guided by memory. A Lally column here, a pyramid of paint cans there. His father and he had laid this cement floor one frantic long day when three cubic yards of ready-mix concrete were delivered in a giant gob by a truck. He would have been fifteen or so, his father in his late forties. The cellar floor of these old farmhouses was typically dirt, the red clay of the region packed more or less hard, except when the foundation walls wept in the spring and it turned to mud. His father had talked with construction men, and set out boards to frame the platform for the furnace, and dug a clay pipe into the dirt for drainage, and stretched strings here and there to determine the level and pitch, but none of these preparations encompassed the alarming dimensions of the slowly hardening concrete when it arrived early that Saturday morning. With rakes and shovels and boards and trowels they pushed and tugged the sluggish stuff level, into the far corners, around the furnace and the mouth of the drainage pipe. His father's face went white with effort, as it had when struggling with the chimney stones several years before, and the ordeal went on and on, by the light of a few bare bulbs, this panicky race with time and matter, as the concrete grew stiffer and stiffer, and in drying pushed its water toward the surface, and exuded its sonorous underground smell, its inexorable stony scent. The floor had come out surprisingly well, out of that day's sweaty panic—smooth and gray and delicately sloped so that hardly a puddle lingered after a flooding. It sometimes seemed, in the mottled perspectives of hindsight, that there had been a third man in the cellar with them, something of a professional, for it seemed unlikely that he and his father, a history teacher and a would-be poet, could have made such a satisfactory cellar floor. But if there had been such a man, Joey had mentally erased him, jealous of this arduous day at his father's side fending off disaster, doing a man's job. He was just becoming a man, and his father was wearying of being one; this was the last project so ambitious that he tackled around the house.

In the blackness, Joey's city shoes slithered on the smooth cement, and then thumped on the echoing wooden cellar stairs; he pushed the door open into the moon-striped kitchen, and a warm whimpering hairy body hurtled up against him, and he thought that his mother had not died after all. But it was the dog, who took his hand in her mouth and unstoppably whimpered and whined as if telling him a long story, the story of her hours alone in the house with her mistress, with the body, with her hunger and bafflement.

Things work out. One of his former wives, who had remarried into the Connecticut suburbs, agreed to take the dog. The cats a man from the county Humane Society came and trapped and carried away to be gassed, a few each day. Joey stacked the magazines and catalogues and Christmas cards and tied them with baling twine from the bucket and carried them to the barn to be trucked to a landfill. The Boy Scouts no longer collected paper and bottles; nothing was precious anymore. As his family assembled, Joey impressed them with his efficiency, portioning out the furniture and heirlooms among his children, his ex-wives, the local auctioneer, the junkman.

For himself he kept little but odd small items that reached back into his boyhood in the brick house they moved to the farm from—a brass tiger that sat on the piano there, when he still took piano lessons, and a curved leather-backed brush he remembered his grandfather using on his black hightop shoes before setting off to the Lutheran church. He kept some of his father's college notebooks, preserved in the attic, penned in a more rounded version of his legible schoolteacherish hand. A set of Shakespeare, with limp red covers, of which the silverfish had nibbled some pages into lace. His mother's sun hats—these were hard to throw away, though none of the assembled females wanted them. His daughters sorted through the clothes for him. He couldn't bear to touch and sort the dresses hanging in the closet, dozens of garments pressed together in an anthology of past fashions, all the way back to a fox-trimmed spring coat whose collar he remembered close to his face, its tingling black-tipped red-brown hairs. In the toolhouse, where his father had left a pathetic legacy of rusty screws and nails neatly arranged in jars, and oily tools, half of them broken, mounted on pegboard, there were also antique implements worn like prehistoric artifacts: an ancient oblong pink whetstone pointed at either end and soapily warped by all its use, and an old-fashioned square hoe worn into a lopsided metal oval, its edges had struck so many stones. Such wear couldn't have occurred in the merely forty years they were here, but must have been the work of generations; these tools had traveled back and forth across the county, surviving many moves, to end in his impatient hands. They seemed sacred—runes no one else could decipher. He was the last of his line to have ever hoed a row of carrots or sharpened a scythe.

Relatives and neighbors spoke to him with a curious soft gravity, as if he were fragile in grief. He knew he and his mother were regarded as having been unusually, perhaps unnaturally close; when in fact between themselves the fear was that they were not close enough. Why grieve? She was old, in pain, worn-out. She was too frail in her last half-year to walk to the mailbox or lift a case of cat food or pull a clump of burdock: it was time; dying is the last favor we do the world, the last tax we pay. He cried only once, during the funeral, quite unexpectedly, having taken his seat at the head of his raggedly extended family, suddenly free, for the moment, of arrangements and decisions, and seeing an arm's reach away the gleaming cherry-wood casket he had picked out in the undertaker's satiny showroom three days before. The lustrous well-joined wood, soon to be buried; the sumptuous waste of it; and the image of his mother as he first remembered her, a young slim woman dressed in a navy-blue suit, with white at her throat, to go off to her job at the downtown department store, hurrying to catch the trolley car. She had once reminisced, "Oh, how you'd run, and if you just missed it, there wouldn't be another for twenty minutes, and you wanted to cry." She had laughed, remembering.

His tears came and kept coming, in a kind of triumph, a breakthrough, a torrent of empathy and pity for that lost young woman running past the row houses, under the horse-chestnut trees, running to catch the trolley, the world of the thirties shabby and solid around her, the porches, the blue midsummer hydrangeas, this tiny well-dressed figure in her diminishing pocket of time, her future unknown, her death, her farm, far from her mind. This was the mother, apparently, he had loved, the young woman living with him and others in a brick semidetached house, a part of the world, youthfully finding her way. During the war she worked in a parachute factory, wearing a bandanna on her head like the other women, plump like them by this time, merging with them and their chatter one lunch break when he, somehow, had bicycled to the side entrance to see her. She was not like them, the tough other women, he knew, but for the moment had blended with them, did a job alongside them, and this too renewed his tears, his naive pride in her then, when he was ten or eleven. She had tried to be a person, she had lived. There was something amazing, something immortal to him in the image of her running. He remembered, from their first years on the farm, a crisis with the roof; it was being reshingled by a team of Amishmen and they had left it partially open to the weather on the night of a thunderstorm. Crashes, flashes. Joey's parents and grandparents were all awake, and he, boy though he still was, was expected now to wake and help too; they rushed up and down the attic stairs with buckets, to save the plaster of the walls and ceilings below. There was a tarpaulin in the barn that might help; he found himself outdoors, in the downpour, and he had retained an image of his mother running across the lawn in a flash of lightning that caught the white of her legs. She would not have been much over forty, and was still athletic; perhaps his father was included in this unsteady glimpse; there was a hilarity to it all, a violent health. Working his way, after her death, through all the accumulated souvenirs of her life, Joey was fascinated by the college yearbooks that preserved her girlish image above a line or two of verse:

> She's blest with temper, whose unclouded ray
> Can make tomorrow cheerful as today.

Group photographs showed his mother as part of the hockey team, the hiking club. With a magnifying glass he studied her unsmiling, competitive face, with her hair in two balls at her ears and a headband over her bangs. Her face seemed slightly larger than the other girls', a childlike oval broadest at the brow, its defenses relatively unevolved. As he sat there beside the cherry casket crying, his former wives and adult children stealing nervous peeks at him, the young woman ran for the trolley car, her breath catching, her panting mixed with a sighing laughter at herself, and the image was as potent, as fertile, as a classic advertisement, which endlessly taps something deep and needy within us. The image of her running down the street, away from him, trailed like a comet's tail the maternal enactments of those misty years when he was a child—crayoning with him on the living-room floor, sewing him Halloween costumes in the shape of Disney creatures, having him lift what she called the "skirts" of the bushes in the lawn while she pushed the old reel mower under them—but from her point of view; he seemed to feel from within his mother's head the situation, herself and this small son, this defenseless gurgling hatched creature, and the tentative motions of her mind and instincts as she, as new to mothering as he was to being a child, explored the terrain between them. In the attic he had found a padded baby-blue scrapbook, conscientiously maintained, containing his first words, the date of his first crawl, and his hospital birth certificate imprinted with his inky day-old feet. The baths. The cod-liver oil. Trying to do the right thing, the normal thing, running toward her farm, her death. In his vision of her running she was bright and quick and small, like an animal in a trap. This was the mother he had loved, the mother before they moved, before she betrayed him with the farm and its sandstone house.

Ruthlessly, vengefully, weekend by weekend, he cleaned the place out—disconnecting the phone, giving the auctioneer the run of the attic, seeing the refrigerator and stove hauled off for a few dollars each, by a truck that got stuck in the muddy winter lawn. With his new vacuum cleaner Joey attacked the emptying rooms, sucking up the allergen-laden dust from the cracks between the floorboards, sweeping the walls and ceilings clean of their veils of cobwebs upon cobwebs. How satisfying this was, one room after another that he would not have to do again. Joey discovered that his mother had been far from alone in the house; while the cats mewed and milled outside on the porch, a tribe of mice, year after year, ancestors and descendants, had been fed sunflower seeds, whose accumulated stored husks burst forth by the bucketful from behind where the stained-pine corner cupboard had stood, and the back of the dishtowel drawer of the kitchen sink. He set traps for the mice. He set out d-Con, and the next weekend tossed their small stiff bodies, held gingerly by the tail, down into the swamp, where the rocks were, and the ashes of his grandmother's mattress.

The old house had curious small cabinets built into the stone thickness, and they disgorged packets of his father's index cards, riddled with anxious, harried reminder notes to himself, and pads of old high-school permission slips, and small boxes of dull pencils and hardened erasers, and playing cards from the remote days when he and his parents played three-handed pinochle at the dining table. At first, he could scarcely hold the cards, sixteen fanned in one little hand, and would stifle tears when his meld was poor and he lost. Once at the farm they never played cards again. There were animals of petrified Play-Doh made by Joey's children, and useless pretty vases and bowls sent distractedly as seasonal gifts, and plush-bound old-fashioned albums, with little mildewed mirrors on the covers, of stiffly posed ancestors he could not identify. His mother had offered, over the years, to teach him their names and relation to him, but he had not been interested, and now she was not there to ask, and his ancestors floated free and nameless like angels.

There were things she had offered to tell him he had not wanted to hear. "What didn't you like about him?" he had once asked her—a bit impatiently, wearying of her voice—about his father.

Sitting in her television-watching chair, her weight and strength so wasted that only her mouth and mind could move, she had been telling him about her youthful romantic life. She had gone to a one room country school—when she was dead, he came upon a photograph of the student body and its corpulent mustachioed instructor, his mother's broad little face squinting toward the camera under a ponderous crown of wound braids. Among the other children there had been a dark-haired, dark-eyed boy she had fancied, and who had fancied her. But her parents had disapproved of the boy's "people," and of several other dark-eyed substitutes that over the years she had offered them. But no, not until Joey's blondish, pale-eyed father did she bring home a suitor they could endorse. "They liked him, and he liked them. I'll say this for your father, not every man could have lived with his inlaws that cheerfully all those years. He really admired my mother, that style of little woman. He loved energetic little women. He thought they could make money for him. It's true, Mother was a money-maker. She was the one who got up in the dark to drive the cart into Alton to market. The tobacco they retired on had been her project. But admiring Mother was no reason to marry me. I was *big.* It was a mistake, and we both knew it. We knew it the first day of our honeymoon." Joey had often heard his mother's views on little women, how they have the best of it, and take the men from the big women like herself, big women who have tortured their little mothers in the birthing. Behind these formulations there was something—about sex, he believed—that he didn't want, as a boy or a man, to hear. *A real femme.* Even as a very small child he had been aware of a weight of anger his mother carried; he had quickly evolved—first word, first crawl—an adroitness at staying out of her way when she was heavy with it, and a wish to amuse her, to keep her light. But now as they were nearing the end, and her flesh was dissolving, and her inner self rising to the surface, he had become more daring, less catering, even challenging. Her own blue eyes, that had never needed a cataract operation, widened at his question as if she were seeing ghosts over his shoulder. "Oh, Joey," she said, "don't ask. It was un*speak*able."

He had to smile at the old-fashioned concept. "Unspeakable? Daddy?"

A bit of flush had crept into her colorless creased cheeks. She was getting angry, once again. She kept staring, not so much at him as at the space in his vicinity. She knew from watching television what the talk shows permitted people to say these days. "Well, maybe you're old enough. Maybe I *should* speak it."

"Oh, no, no thanks, that's all right," he said, jumping up from his chair and heading into the kitchen, much as his father used to in the middle of a marital exchange. *Poor Daddy,* was his thought. Let the dead alone. Now she too was dead, and there were many things Joey would never know. Though he grew used to the sandstone house without her in it, he still found it strange, back in his Manhattan apartment, that she never called on Saturday mornings the way she used to, with her playful, self-mocking account of her week. The dead can't even telephone. The phone's silence more than any other conveyed the peace of the dead, their absolute and, as it were, hostile withdrawal.

The real-estate appraiser, an old high-school classmate, stood in his gray suit in the cobwebbed cellar, next to the rickety furnace, among the paint cans and rusty hot-air ducts, and said to Joey, "Seventeen years here alone. It took a lot of guts." Yes, she had been brave, he could now afford to see, all those years alone, alone but for the animals she fed, and the ghosts on television. Over the telephone, even when reporting an insomniac night of breathlessness and terror, she had tried to keep it light for his sake, and mocked herself, mocking her very will, at the age of eighty-five, to live. "It's strange, but I really don't intend to die. Though a lot of people would like me to."

"Really? Who?"

"The real-estate developers. The neighbors. They think it's time for this old lady to move over and make some room."

"Do they really?" He was grateful she had not included him among the many who wished her dead.

"*Really,*" she mocked. "But I have a responsibility here. The place still needs me."

"We all need you," Joey said, sighing, giving up. The fate of the place was another unspeakable matter. She wanted the place to go on and on, as it was in her idea of it.

He had scanned her in vain for some sign of sunset resignation. She had choked down her pills and vitamins to the end, and her fear of life's sensations ceasing had seemed as pure as a child's. The last time he had visited, on a cool fall day, she came outdoors to supervise his planting, in two arcs by a curve of the cement walk, two dozen tulip bulbs she had ordered from a catalogue. At first he had arranged the bulbs point down, and then realized that the point was what would grow upward, toward the sun. His mother had stood there on her unsteady feet, in her gaudy bathrobe, looking down; the sight of the fat cream-white bulbs nested in the turned red earth startled a kind of grunt out of her. "Oh, how dear they look," she said. To Joey she added, "How nicely you do things."

In all of her leavings that came to light he was most touched by her accounts—her tax forms and used checkbooks, meticulously kept, even though her tiny backward-slanting hand had become spasmodic and shaky. (Could that big penciled handwriting on the back of the enlarged photograph have been hers after all, at the age of thirteen?) She had kept, on a large pad of green paper, spreadsheets of her monthly expenses, ruled off by hand at the beginning of each month. The last entries had been made the day before the morning of her death. This financial and mathematical niceness of hers was something quite unpredictable, like a musical passion in a banker. Among the stored sheets of figures were several drawn up before they moved, with lists of expenses side by side, taxes, heating, utilities, upkeep—absurdly small amounts they now seemed, from that frozen wartime world. By her calculations, their reduced costs in the little sandstone house, and the projected rentals of their eighty acres to the neighboring farmers, would save them five hundred dollars—a third of her husband's salary. It had never really occurred to Joey that their move here had had a practical side. When he came to sheets showing how the money for his college education could be squeezed out among their other expenses, he couldn't bear to keep reading.

Gradually, through the stark months of a winter that was, according to the forecasters, unseasonably cold, and then unseasonably warm, he reduced the house to its essence, removing every trace, even a rusty pencil sharpener screwed to a windowsill, of his life and the four lives that had ended. Here on this patch of now uncarpeted wood his grandfather had fallen, having convulsively leaped from the bed where, a year later, his widow would breathe her last. Here, in the bedroom adjacent, his father had sat up with such pains in his chest that he told his wife to call the ambulance. He had died in the ambulance. Here in this same space Joey had lain sleepless, wondering how to tell his mother of his next divorce. Here on the other side of the wall he would lie after a date, his head still whirling with cigarette smoke and the perfume-counter smell of the girl. Here on the worn linoleum his mother had died, at the base of a wall she had had the Amish carpenters make of old chestnut boards, boards left in the barn from the era before the blight, to cover the rough stones exposed when the big kitchen chimney had been removed. The rooms had a soft beauty, empty. The uncovered floorboards drank the sunlight. Joey looked through the curtainless windows, seeing what his mother had seen—the sloping old orchard to the north, the barn and road and fields to the east, the lilac bushes and bird feeder and meadow to the south, the woods and the tall blue spruce to the west.

On his final cleanup visit, Joey found something devil-like—a small dark stiff shape, in size between a mouse and a rat, its legs attached by webs—floating in the bathroom toilet. A flying squirrel. It had come down from the attic and drowned, sick and thirsty from the d-Con. Joey remembered watching at twilight, that summer he moved the stones, a pair of flying squirrels sail, as if sliding swiftly on a wire, from the attic window over to the blue spruce. The house had stood empty before his family had moved in the previous fall, and this pair had moved in ahead of them.

He had bought a padlock for the cellar bulkhead, and closed the house with a key, having installed new locks. The house was ready for sale in the spring. But in the meantime, as he lay awake in his apartment three hours away, its emptiness called to him. It needed him. Suppose a fire, or local vandals, jealous of the price the place would fetch . . . Housing developments were all around, and even Philadelphians were moving into the area. His mother had made a shrewd investment, buying back paradise.

Those weekends alone in the house, sorting, cleaning, staying away from the motel until moonlight had replaced sunlight on the floors, he had discovered himself talking aloud, as if in response to a friendly presence just behind the dry old wallpaper, in the thick sandstone walls. His own uncluttered rooms, suspended above Manhattan's steady roar, with an ornamental piece of porch banister hidden at the back of a closet, felt as if they were flying somewhere. He felt guilty, anxious, displaced. He had always wanted to be where the action was, and what action there was, it turned out, had been back there.

QUESTIONS FOR DISCUSSION AND WRITING

1. How do the various transactions with regard to the farmhouse establish the structure of the plot? How does Joey's new vision of the farmhouse at the end serve as a climax for the story?
2. Why is Joey's mother so preoccupied with her physical size? What does his father mean when he says Joey's mother is *a real femme?*
3. What does Joey's New York apartment reveal about the man he has become? How does the farmhouse become a "[s]pace for heroism"?
4. What effect does the third person point of view have on the reader's relationship to Joey? Why would Joey make an ineffective narrator of his own story?
5. Why does Joey have to strip the house to its essence to understand its meaning for his mother? How does this understanding compare to his earlier image of his mother as a "running woman"?

90

ABRAHAM VERGHESE

Lilacs

ABRAHAM VERGHESE was born in 1955 in Addis Ababa, Ethiopia, and was educated at the Medical School in Madras, India, and East Tennessee State University and Boston University Schools of Medicine. He also attended the University of Iowa Writer's Workshop. Although Verghese is presently Professor of Medicine and Chief of Infectious Diseases at Texas Tech University and has published scientific research in journals such as *Annals of Internal Medicine, Journal of the American Medical Association,* and *Archives of Internal Medicine,* he remains active as a creative writer. He has published essays and fiction in magazines such as *Sports Illustrated, Black Warrior Review, North American Review,* and *The New Yorker.* "Lilacs," reprinted from *The New Yorker,* dramatizes the attempts of an AIDS "survivor" to explain and control his life.

Bobby sits up on the side of the bed. He feels weak, spinny-headed and hollow. In a little while he tugs at the bedspread and wraps it around himself. Using the chest of drawers and the television for handholds, he stumbles to the air-conditioning unit below the window. He leans over the gray box, turning his head away from the cold blast, fumbling till he finds the concealed door to the control panel, and then blindly punches buttons till it turns off.

He draws the curtain back cautiously. He stares out at the motel parking lot for several minutes, focussing on any movement that might suggest he is being watched. Over the high wall behind the parking lot he sees the blue-green span of Tobin Bridge and, beyond that, the Boston skyline. The parking lot has filled up overnight. He sees Massachusetts plates, New Hampshire plates—an Indiana plate on a jeep reads "HOOSIER HOSPITALITY."

"FIRST IN THE WAITING ROOM." That would be on his license plate. If he had a car. When he walked into the motel lobby the previous night, it had smelled of coriander. The manager, an Indian, had stared at him with alarm. "No vehicle?" he said. Behind the counter, a door stood open, revealing a woman's fat leg on a recliner; a silver toe ring looked welded onto her second toe. There were the murmurs of a TV and the shrill voices of children speaking in another language. Bobby peeled three hundred-dollar bills from his roll, and the man's manner softened considerably. "What it is happened to your face?" the man asked, coming close to Bobby. The woman in the recliner stuck her head around to look.

"Oh, I was born this way," Bobby had answered. He had smiled at the fat woman, who quickly retracted her head.

The bathroom is cold. He brushes his teeth with the bedspread still wrapped around him. He tries not to look into the mirror. Why look? Better to remember himself as he used to be. As he is in the photograph in the briefcase—a photograph Primo took. It is from Myrtle Beach, the summer of 1973, when he was twenty-one years old. In the photograph his hair comes down to his shoulders. He is bare-chested, sitting sideways on Primo's '64 Harley, one hand on the tank and the other resting lightly on his thigh—his own thigh. He is smiling—a strong smile, a smile of certainty. Primo had said something to make him smile, something flattering, and his Fu Manchu mustache looks innocent, young. In the background is Primo's airplane, and beyond that, faintly, the sea, though in the photograph it blurs with the blue of the sky. Carolina blue.

In those days, Bobby worked as a manager in the Myrtle Mystery Mall, selling tokens for the peephole dioramas, supervising the soda and trinket concessions, keeping the lines flowing through the Dinosaur Cyclorama, shooing out the couples who lingered in the dark recesses of the Polynesian Fire-Walk of Love. He was ten years old the first summer his parents brought him to Myrtle Beach. They drove down from Spartanburg and rented a "cottage" (in reality, a double-wide trailer) for two weeks in late July, in what became an annual family ritual. Bobby, an only child, distracted, suffering again that summer with bad eczema, spent most of his time and all of his allowance in the Myrtle Mystery Mall. He thrilled to its dark, panelled interiors, the dim, red glow of the Chinese lanterns, the labyrinth of doors and corridors leading to exhibits, but most of all he thrilled to being part of the clique of boys who hung around in their flowery sports shirts and shades and seemed unofficially to preside over the whole phantasmagoria. They encouraged him to disobey the "HANDS OFF" sign on the Iron Maiden in the Gallery of Torture; they laughed when he tested the blade edge of the guillotine with his tongue; and later, sitting in a prop room, they let him sip from the silver hip flask that they were passing around—a mark of his acceptance. He much preferred their company to baking on the beach with his parents or sitting mute in the back seat while his father, talking nonstop, inched the Buick into the family cavalcade that went up and down the Strip in search of a different fast-food joint for the evening.

The year his father died, Bobby dropped out of the English Honors program at Appalachian State and moved to Myrtle Beach, landing a job in his old hangout. Every day, Bobby caught triptychs of himself in the Distortion Gallery; Bobbys were catapulted out of one mirror and reeled back into another: thin Bobbys, fat Bobbys. In the evenings, Bobby went to the Connection, and there he saw himself reflected in the eyes of guys from Johnson City, Fayetteville, Raleigh, wherever. They would cluster around him, buy him drinks, while he looked over the tops of their heads. One night he saw Primo come in, look around, and leave before Bobby could get near him—it was the only time Bobby had seen a better-looking man than himself in the place. Primo had returned in an hour, dressed in leather. This time Bobby walked over, scattering the people around them.

"If I had known," Bobby said, fingering the straps on Primo's shoulders, "I would have worn my skins."

"It's not too late," Primo said. They didn't make it out of the parking lot.

He rinses off the toothbrush. He has no razor, and, in any case, his beard barely grows anymore. He runs a washcloth over his face and works the corners of his eyes. His eyelashes have grown long and translucent and have curled up at the ends—a side effect of AZT, according to Dr. Chatupadia. Of the six doctors in the clinic at Boston Metropolitan, four are from India, one is from Pakistan, and one is a Palestinian. Chatupadia, who has been Bobby's physician ever since Bobby moved to Boston nine years ago, took a photograph of Bobby's closed eyelids with the eyelashes dangling and sent it to *The New England Journal of Medicine.* Chatupadia was disappointed when they sent the photograph back, saying that what it showed was now a well-described side effect of AZT. He showed the letter to Bobby. "'Well-described,' they are calling it, Bobby!" he said, pronouncing it *Boobee.* "These people," Chatupadia said, and he wagged his head from side to side, letting the silence stand for all the injustice in his life and Bobby's life. Bobby agreed. *These people . . .*

These people had no place for Bobby. These people were waiting for him to die. Even Chatupadia seemed to regard his longevity, his hanging on despite plummeting weight and daily fevers, as an aberration. He was a bird without wings, suspended in midair, defying the ground below. His Social Security supplement, even with Medicaid, could not support him. It didn't cover the medications for the infections—the opportunists—that threatened to kill him before the AIDS virus did. Five days earlier, after waiting for three months, Bobby was turned down from the only multicenter interferon trial in Boston. Because his white-blood-cell count was too low, Chatupadia said.

"But my count is low *because* of the AIDS!"

"So sorry, Boobee. They won't allow it."

The other interferon trial in the United States was in Durham. He didn't have the money to go to Durham, but he called anyway, not telling them his white count. "Sorry, we are fully enrolled," a tired male voice had said. "And the study protocol only allows our own patients—our own AZT failures—to be enrolled."

"What if I came down there and waited on your doorstep?" Bobby asked.

They had a waiting list of three hundred. The doorstep was full.

"Just give me *some* of the drug! You don't understand—I have no more rope to hang on to."

But they couldn't. Protocol.

These people . . . But Bobby cannot give up. He cannot. He will not give them that satisfaction. He will go to the clinic today, as he has done every Wednesday these nine years. He will be first in the waiting room, as always. He will sit there and show everyone that he lacks neither determination nor, as of last night, money. And he will remind them of their impotence.

"We are an army of Boobees, an army with overgrown eyelashes," Bobby says to the shrouded figure in the mirror. His voice echoes in the bathroom, and he speaks even louder: "Across this great country, our army is converging on city hospitals. We will assemble in the waiting rooms. We will wait for the clinics to open. We will be treated—we Americans—by our Indian, our Pakistani, our Filipino, our Palestinian doctors: the drones. Upstairs, the queen bees will be working on the cure, appearing on television, writing for the journals."

Someone bangs on the wall next door. "Fuck you!" Bobby shouts, but he has lost enthusiasm for his speech.

He pulls his T-shirt on, trying not to snag it on his Hickman catheter. The catheter enters above his right nipple and then tunnels under the skin to pierce the large vein beneath his collarbone and extend through it till it reaches the vein just above his heart. For two years the Hickman has been his lifeline. It has spared him countless needles; blood for testing has been drawn out of it, and all his intravenous medicine, at home and in the hospital, administered through it. He has not used the catheter in two days; the solution he injects to keep it open is in the refrigerator in the South End apartment he abandoned in such haste the previous day. The catheter has probably clotted off, he thinks.

He turns on the TV as he dresses. He flips past the local news stations, half expecting to see his mug flash on the screen, and stops at CNN. He presses the "Mute" button as Miss Cheekbones talks. He speaks for her: "An overgrowth of eyelashes is being described among persons infected with the AIDS virus who are on the anti-AIDS drug AZT." Here she flashes her dimples, and Bobby continues. "Concern is being expressed by advocates that this will result in people being identified in their workplace as infected with the AIDS virus. . . ." He remembers his father watching boxing on television with the volume turned off, providing ringside commentary in his loud voice: "Muñoz, once again pounding the body, coming straight ahead, hooking to the ribs—Styles make fights, wouldn't you say, Marv? You couldn't find two more different fighters. Concinni hasn't stopped moving, dodging, backpedalling, weaving—Oh! Concinni is tagged with a left! He's in trouble! He's down! Good night, sweet prince!"

He picks up the briefcase. It is burgundy and made of soft leather; it belonged to Michael. Michael moved into the apartment soon after Primo moved out. Michael did research on mice at the Genecor Research Center—mice with heart disease. He got sick and moved back to Iowa, leaving everything: his medicine, his furniture, his briefcase.

The bag has handles that slide out. In the outer, zippered pocket is Bobby's birth certificate, his living will, his prescriptions, a yellow pad, and a pen. Inside the bag is the gun. And thick wads of hundred-dollar bills. He takes the gun out—Primo's gun. In his hand it looks animate and repulsive. He regrets having it; he regrets having needed it. He walks around the room, looking for a place to hide it. He has a vision of a child discovering the gun, examining it, playing with it. Reluctantly, he puts it back in the briefcase.

He leaves the motel after a last look around. He takes a bus and gets off near M.I.T., near the hospital. A mist is rising off the river. He walks onto the bridge on Massachusetts Avenue. Halfway across, the muscles of his calves begin to hurt. These are not my muscles, he thinks as he reaches down to touch them. This is not my pain. He leans over the railing and looks down at the water. A purple reflection of his face flashes at him, and he pulls away from the railing.

He starts walking again, watching his feet: one boot with silver chain, the other plain; left, right, left, right. This is the only way to do it, he thinks—something Primo never understood. He is angry when he thinks of Primo, and Michael. Primo gave up almost at once. Primo had made the move to Boston with Bobby, in search of better AIDS care, but had bolted from the clinic after the first visit, terrified by the sight of a cachectic young man in the waiting room. Primo's only fight—before he was hospitalized—was to take wild risks in his plane. He tried Dead Man's Stalls and Cuban 8s in the Cessna until they took away his license. Later, Bobby heard from others—because they had separated by then; the path Bobby had chosen to deal with the disease made Primo and his fatalism impossible to be around—that Primo began to cruise, spreading it, poisoning as many others as he could, as if it would ease his own pain. This had enraged Bobby so much that he did not attend Primo's funeral. Primo's mother called him afterward, screamed at him, accused him of killing her son. Michael gave up in a different way: he left one morning, saying that the magic of being in Waterloo, Iowa, eating his mama's cooking, going to the high-school ballgames, doing whatever one did in Waterloo, Iowa, would somehow save him. It didn't.

Meanwhile, Bobby had tried it all: AZT, then DDI, now DDC. And ganciclovir. And the underground Compound Q. And intravenous protein feeds. And aerosol pentamidine. He had meditated—he still did. He had gone macrobiotic until he could no longer swallow. "Oh, I may die," he shouts at a car that passes by, "but not without a goddam fight!"

Near the Christian Science Building, Bobby jams one toe between the stones of the retaining wall and climbs up to reach some lilacs that hang from a bush. It is more effort than he thought it would be. He gets the flowers, but his shoulder hurts. He hears the woman's voice before he sees her. "Those are pretty flowers. But you should leave them on the tree."

She wears a track suit and tennis shoes; her gray hair peeks out from under a scarf. A handkerchief is tightly wadded in her hand, and she is breathless. Bobby holds the flowers out to her; it freezes whatever else she was going to say, and she breaks into a shy smile. He drops slowly to one knee. He imagines he catches the scent of her perspiration, sees the steam rising off her body. "The official flower of our state, Ma'am."

"You shouldn't have done that," she says, her hands reaching for one cluster, "but they are beautiful."

"Aren't you going to ask me what state?"

"Are you all right?"

He gets up and rubs his shoulder. It is on his tongue to say "the State of Immunodeficiency." Instead, he says, "No, I'm not all right."

Her smile melts into an expression of concern. She moves her feet, conscious that she has tarried too long already, but feels obliged to ask: "Can I do anything?"

"Are you a magician?" Bobby asks. "Never mind. No, you can't do anything. Thank you for stopping, though. Thank you."

She waves and walks away briskly, her elbows pumping high, her lockstep gait quickening; she turns when she nears the bridge, and smiles.

Bobby watches her till she is out of sight; he feels the anger return again. It comes in waves and crashes over him. Yesterday, rage at the mindless bills, the dunning letters, and—finally—the cutting off of his telephone and electricity had carried him downtown. He had seen his reflection as he tore into the Bank of Boylston—a whirling dervish in a black coat, with gun drawn. He almost shot at the reflection. Could a face really be that purple? He braced himself, expecting to be challenged at any moment. Instead, they pushed money bundles at him, even gave him a bag to stuff them in. When the bag was full, he shouted, "What now? What now?" but none of the prone figures would move. "What now?" he cried to the camera on the ceiling.

Too late he remembers that he could have given the woman some of the money.

He rests outside the hospital by the dry fountain that is full of butts and matchsticks. Then he starts walking again, against the flow of traffic as the eleven-to-seven nurses head for the parking lot. He bypasses the main entrance and goes into the tunnel and walks down it to the Kass Memorial Building and then takes the elevator to the fifth floor. He walks past patients' rooms smelling of Lysol and bacon. In the nurses' lounge the coffee is fresh, and he pours himself a cup, then snaps open drawer after drawer until he finds some sugar. He empties six packets into his cup.

Two people in white come in. One male, one female. One black, one white.

"Who are you?" one asks.

"Who are you?" he replies.

"We work here."

"*We work here,*" Bobby says. Such complacency, such arrogance, he thinks. "And I am a walking skeleton. I'm a voodoo doll. I own this hospital." They look confused. He explains: "I'm your three square meals a day."

His hands are full now, what with the lilacs and the coffee and the briefcase. He moves toward the nurses and they step quickly aside.

Bobby goes down the stairs to the second floor and then through a long hallway, past dark labs and locked offices, until he reaches the clinic waiting room. Before the first sip of coffee is past his throat, before he can even sit down, he feels his intestines start to writhe, and he hurries for the men's room.

Back in the waiting room he takes one lilac stalk and leans over the counter, over the patient-register book, and wedges the stalk between the printer stand and the printer. Laurelei will keep it there all day. She says that whenever she thinks of lilacs or smells them she thinks of him.

He tries breathing and meditation. He wants to feel the prana ebb and flow. *Ommmmm.* His mind strays and he brings it back. *Ommmmm.* But there is only anger. *Ommmmm.* He thinks of his job as a short-order cook in Hoboken, ten years ago, while Primo was enrolled in a six-month course for his commercial license. It was fluid motion for Bobby—a moving line walked past him and they called the tune while he danced. He was the ballerina of Niko's in Hoboken, cracking eggs, flipping hotcakes, buttering toast, sliding the dishes down the counter. Oronfrio, the manager, said he didn't know why Bobby bothered with the men when he could have had any of the women. "Because I can have any of the men," Bobby would say, flipping a morsel of scrambled egg into the air and catching it on his tongue, all the while looking into Oronfrio's eyes. *Ommmmm.* He thinks of his mother in Spartanburg and how she must shudder when she thinks of him with Primo. *That's right, Mama. I was his blushing bride. He did to me more or less what Dad did to you.* She will be surprised when she gets the money he sent her. She will draw the shades and walk around the living room talking to herself, tormented by the knowledge of where the money came from and what she ought to do, and by her greed for the money and her wish to burrow in her house and deny his existence. He laughs aloud, and gives up the idea of meditation.

Three guys come in; two of them are a couple he knows from the waiting room. They run a bar in the South End. Bobby remembers buying some dope from one of them a year ago. The third one—the new one—is not quite with them. He signs in and sits two seats away from Bobby while the couple sign in. Bobby smells aftershave on the new guy, but beneath it is a sour, unwashed smell. It is the smell of fear, Bobby thinks; it irritates him. Laurelei arrives behind the desk and turns pale when she sees Bobby.

"Thanks," she stammers when the dope dealer comments on the flowers. "Bobby brings them in," she adds, and looks at Bobby fearfully. Bobby waves back and points at the rest of the flowers, which he has arranged in a soda can on the windowsill, but Laurelei runs into the inner office.

"The official AIDS flower," Bobby says to the new guy, pointing to the lilacs. The new guy looks at the lilacs and then at the purple growths on Bobby's face. "Get it?" Bobby asks, touching the biggest growth, over his right eyelid. "Lilacs out of the dead land. Get it?"

The new guy just blinks. The disease is not choosy, Bobby thinks; this kid is dumb as a coal bucket.

The new guy tries to ignore Bobby. He shakes out a cigarette with trembling fingers. There is a ring with a turquoise stone on his pinky, and his nails are long. They would be elegant in a different setting from the Metropolitan Hospital clinic. His brown hair is slicked back in a "wet look"—a style that Primo favored years before it became commonplace. Bobby moves over to sit next to him.

"You didn't really have a bath, did you?" Bobby asks. "Your hair looks like you had a bath, but you didn't. And you hurried with your breakfast—Doughnuts on the way? How did I know? The powdered sugar on your mustache. I'm Bobby, by the way." The new guy has the cigarette in one hand and a lighter in the other. "You can't smoke here. You can shake my hand, though. You can't get it by shaking my hand. Besides, you already got it."

The new guy puts the lighter away and Bobby shakes his hand. The hand feels crumbly, fragile, but it is its sweatiness that primes Bobby, forces him to take more interest in this boy.

"You must be Clovis," Bobby says. "I saw the register. 'Clovis: Forty-five.' Forty-five minutes is for new patients. Must be you. Let me guess. You tested positive—what, two years ago? And you were positive before that but didn't want the test. And now you wake up in the night and you feel cold and you put on socks and wrap your head up, and then in an hour you drench the sheets. And then you feel cold again. That's why you didn't shower, right? You were cold when it was time to have the shower. Am I right? You're shit scared, am I right?"

Clovis tries to get up. "Sit down," Bobby says to him. "You can't afford not to listen to me. You need to listen to me. I'm a survivor—nine years. If you don't want to live, just keep walking. That's better. Let's begin." Bobby puts both his hands round Clovis's forearm and twists the skin in opposite directions; Clovis yelps. "That's called a barber's twist, Clovis. Keep your eyes on the skin." A shower of fine red dots makes a bracelet on Clovis's forearm. "Oh, oh! You know what that means, don't you? Your platelets are low. You're farther along than you thought, Clovis. Good thing you came today." Clovis's face shrivels.

Clovis's acquaintances are getting out. Clovis tries to rise again. His eyes plead with the couple, who are standing at the door, but Bobby takes the gun out of the briefcase and sets it on the chair. "Clovis is with me," Bobby tells them. "And don't roll your eyes at me, honey. You guys don't look so hot yourselves. You got a way to make him live? I can make him live. What have you got?" The couple hurry out.

Bobby looks at Clovis; he wonders why he is bothering with this kid. Has Clovis become his hostage? In return for what? Bobby gets up and bolts the door. He paces around and then sits down. He has no doubt the police will be here soon. He takes one of Clovis's cigarettes and lights it and hands it to Clovis. "You can smoke now, Clovis. Everything has changed." He sits down and thinks awhile and then picks his words carefully.

"You don't know how special I am, Clovis. I am a nine-year survivor. I've beaten the odds; I am way over the median survival. Look it up, if you want. I'm the only nine-year guy in this clinic. And it wasn't luck either, Clovis. I fought for every fucking bit of it; I *scrapped* for it; I *took* all the responsibility."

Clovis is listening; the fear and gloom that were on his face are momentarily erased.

"Level with me, Clovis. What is the scariest thing about this whole business? That you can die from it? Death? Bang, bang? You probably will die from it, right?" Clovis's eyes get big. "And that fear is what kept you from being tested? And that fear is still there—right?" Clovis's eyes get even wider. Bobby takes out his yellow pad and pencil. He pats Clovis's hand. "The only way to beat this is to lose your fear, Clovis," he says kindly. "The fear doesn't do you any good. In fact the fear can kill you before the disease does. It's like most anything else in life: lose your fear and it can't touch you."

Bobby massages Clovis's hand, trying to imagine what it is like to be a Clovis. What does a Clovis really feel? He sees a "LOSER, LOSER, LOSER" sign flash across Clovis's face. Clovis is giving up, retreating again. Clovis is ugly, Bobby thinks. The dimples are really pimples, he has dandruff on his eyelashes, his face is oily. Clovis tries to withdraw his hand. Bobby considers stopping but feels obliged to continue; let the kid have the message, for what it's worth.

"It's not illegal to hold hands—is it, Clovis? O.K., I'm going to let go of your hand. I want you to answer a series of questions for me. I'll write down your answers on paper, and then you put that paper in your pocket and carry it with you. Then—trust me—you will have conquered death. It worked for me. O.K.? First of all, where do you want to die?"

Clovis's chin is quivering. Bobby makes lines and draws columns on the paper. He is aware of the absolute silence in the building. "I'm asking you where you want to die? In the hospital? At home? On the street? You live with those guys, right? You all came in the same car, right? You work in the bar for them, right? A little dope, a little head—Hey, *I* know. So, you ready to die with them, in their apartment? In the South End? Or you want to die at your own house, in your mama's arms? Or do you want to die with me?" Clovis begins to open his mouth, but no answer seems forthcoming. "With Mama," Bobby whispers for him. He uses a Southern accent. Childlike and *very* Southern. "With Mama? Let me guess—Alabama? Tennessee? O.K., you want to die with Mama? You need to write that down, Clovis. Get that down on paper. Otherwise they'll dump you in Roxbury Cemetery. O.K., so you want to die at home. Now, what do you want them to do with your body?"

Clovis is weeping now, his face in his hands, and Bobby strokes the ducktail, his fingers coming away greasy. "It boils down to do you want to be cremated or buried?" Bobby busies himself writing on the yellow sheet. He is aware of the sirens approaching the parking lot outside, but he concentrates on the paper:

BODY	Home	x	Away	
DISPOSAL	Bury		Cremate	x
SERVICE	Yes	x	No	
MUSIC				
TOMBSTONE				

"I personally can't stand the thought of waking up one day to find I'm locked in a pine box with rats nibbling at my eye sockets. If I was you I would go for cremation. It's cheaper, easier for your family."

Clovis is sniffling and carrying on. Bobby lets the "X" remain where it is. Cremation for Clovis.

"Music? I assume you want a service—so, music. See, that's something you can control. Music: what do you want them to play? Come on, Clovis—music?

" 'Rocky Top,' Clovis? 'Rocky Top you'll always be, Home sweet home to me, Good old Rocky Top, Rocky Top, Tennessee.' " Singing the song makes Bobby laugh. He gets up and tries to clog but can't move his feet quickly enough. "Good choice, Clovis! 'Rocky Top' it shall be." He writes in "Rocky Top." He lets go of the pad to hold Clovis's hand again, because Clovis is trying to get away. Clovis sits downs on the floor, his hand in Bobby's grasp.

"The eulogy, Clovis! Don't forget the eulogy. What do you want them to say? O.K., O.K., you can think about that. But the tombstone, the grave marker. That *has* to be your choice. 'Clovis. Our beloved son—' "

Clovis breaks loose. He unbolts the door, pulls it open, and runs around the corner.

"Wait, Clovis! Put this paper in your pocket."

Bobby picks up the gun but then tosses it out the window. He sits on the floor and carefully folds the paper into an airplane. His body is rocking back and forth with concentration. When he is done, he stands up and looks out the window. He is astonished by the crowd below. He sees Chatupadia and waves. He slowly pushes the window wide open and stands on a chair. With a flick of the wrist he sails the plane out. It is a wonderful plane—the best he has ever made. It catches an updraft and rises in a tight spiral. Bobby is drawn to the window: the yellow plane is still climbing. Bobby steps out on the sill and cranes his neck to follow it. Finally, when it can climb no more, it banks into a lazy left turn. He is aware of voices yelling at him, but they are drowned out by the roar of the plane's engine. He imagines himself as the pilot. The plane finds another updraft. Bobby increases the power to full throttle and points the nose straight up. Gravity works against him, and he watches the airspeed indicator drop rapidly. Just before the plane shudders to a stop, he applies full rudder. He has timed it exactly, and his plane makes a perfect Hammerhead turn, rotating on the tip of one wing. Now he points the nose at the crowd below. He sees his airspeed rise again. The wings shudder and the wind whips at his face. He puts his finger on the "Fire" button. "Coming at you!" he shouts.

QUESTIONS FOR DISCUSSION AND WRITING

1. Who are "these people"? How do they represent the forces against which Bobby must struggle? In what sense does he control his struggle?

2. What qualities of character have enabled Bobby to beat the odds for nine years? How do Primo and Michael characterize themselves by their responses to their disease?
3. How do the three settings—Myrtle Beach, the Boston motel room, and the hospital waiting room—create the shifting atmosphere in the story?
4. How does Verghese keep the reader at an emotional distance from Bobby? Why does he want the reader to maintain that objectivity?
5. What themes are developed by the following images in the story—reflections and photographs, lilacs, and the list?

91

KURT VONNEGUT, JR.

Harrison Bergeron

KURT VONNEGUT, JR., was born in 1922 in Indianapolis, Indiana, and attended Cornell University, where he studied biochemistry before being drafted into the infantry in World War II. Vonnegut was captured by the Germans at the Battle of the Bulge and sent to Dresden where he worked in the underground meat locker of a slaughterhouse. He miraculously survived the Allied firebombing of Dresden and, following the war, returned to the United States to study anthropology at the University of Chicago and to work for a local news bureau. In 1947 Vonnegut accepted a position writing publicity for the General Electric Research Laboratory in Schenectady, New York, but left the company in 1950 to work on his own writing. His first three novels, *Player Piano* (1952), a satire on the tyrannies of corporate automation, *The Sirens of Titan* (1959), a science-fiction comedy on the themes of free will and determination, and *Cat's Cradle* (1963), a science fantasy on the amorality of atomic scientists, established Vonnegut's reputation as a writer who could blend humor with serious insights into the human experience. His most successful novel, *Slaughterhouse-Five, or the Children's Crusade* (1969), is based on his wartime experiences in Dresden. His other works include *God Bless You, Mr. Rosewater* (1966), *Breakfast of Champions* (1973), *Jailbird* (1979), *Palm Sunday* (1981), *Galapagos* (1985), and *Hocus Pocus* (1990). His best-known short stories are collected in *Canary in the Cat House* (1961) and *Welcome to the Monkey House* (1968). "Harrison Bergeron," reprinted from the latter collection, is the story of the apparatus a future society must create to make everyone equal.

The year was 2081, and everybody was finally equal. They weren't only equal before God and the law. They were equal every which way. Nobody was smarter than anybody else. Nobody was better looking than anybody else. Nobody was stronger or quicker than anybody else. All this equality was due to the 211th, 212th, and 213th Amendments to the Constitution, and to the unceasing vigilance of agents of the United States Handicapper General.

Some things about living still weren't quite right, though. April, for instance, still drove people crazy by not being springtime. And it was in that clammy month that the H-G men took George and Hazel Bergeron's fourteen-year-old son, Harrison, away.

It was tragic, all right, but George and Hazel couldn't think about it very hard. Hazel had a perfectly average intelligence, which meant she couldn't think about anything except in short bursts. And George, while his intelligence was way above normal, had a little mental handicap radio in his ear. He was required by law to wear it at all times. It was tuned to a government transmitter. Every twenty seconds or so, the transmitter would send out some sharp noise to keep people like George from taking unfair advantage of their brains.

George and Hazel were watching television. There were tears on Hazel's cheeks, but she'd forgotten for the moment what they were about.

On the television screen were ballerinas.

A buzzer sounded in George's head. His thoughts fled in panic, like bandits from a burglar alarm.

"That was a real pretty dance, that dance they just did," said Hazel.

"Huh?" said George.

"That dance—it was nice," said Hazel.

"Yup," said George. He tried to think a little about the ballerinas. They weren't really very good—no better than anybody else would have been, anyway. They were burdened with sashweights and bags of birdshot, and their faces were masked, so that no one, seeing a free and graceful gesture or a pretty face, would feel like something the cat drug in. George was toying with the vague notion that maybe dancers shouldn't be handicapped. But he didn't get very far with it before another noise in his ear radio scattered his thoughts.

George winced. So did two of the eight ballerinas.

Hazel saw him wince. Having no mental handicap herself, she had to ask George what the latest sound had been.

"Sounded like somebody hitting a milk bottle with a ball peen hammer," said George.

"I'd think it would be real interesting, hearing all the different sounds," said Hazel, a little envious. "All the things they think up."

"Um," said George.

"Only, if I was Handicapper General, you know what I would do?" said Hazel. Hazel, as a matter of fact, bore a strong resemblance to the Handicapper General, a woman named Diana Moon Glampers. "If I was Diana Moon Glampers," said Hazel, "I'd have chimes on Sunday—just chimes. Kind of in honor of religion."

"I could think, if it was just chimes," said George.

"Well—maybe make 'em real loud," said Hazel. "I think I'd make a good Handicapper General."

"Good as anybody else," said George.

"Who knows better'n I do what normal is?" said Hazel.

"Right," said George. He began to think glimmeringly about his abnormal son who was now in jail, about Harrison, but a twenty-one-gun salute in his head stopped that.

"Boy!" said Hazel, "that was a doozy, wasn't it?"

It was such a doozy that George was white and trembling, and tears stood on the rims of his red eyes. Two of the eight ballerinas had collapsed to the studio floor, were holding their temples.

"All of a sudden you look so tired," said Hazel. "Why don't you stretch out on the sofa, so's you can rest your handicap bag on the pillows, honeybunch." She was referring to the forty-seven pounds of birdshot in a canvas bag, which was padlocked around George's neck. "Go on and rest the bag for a little while," she said. "I don't care if you're not equal to me for a while."

George weighed the bag with his hands. "I don't mind it," he said. "I don't notice it any more. It's just a part of me."

"You been so tired lately—kind of wore out," said Hazel. "If there was just some way we could make a little hole in the bottom of the bag, and just take out a few of them lead balls. Just a few."

"Two years in prison and two thousand dollars fine for every ball I took out," said George. "I don't call that a bargain."

"If you could just take a few out when you came home from work," said Hazel. "I mean—you don't compete with anybody around here. You just set around."

"If I tried to get away with it," said George, "then other people'd get away with it—and pretty soon we'd be right back to the dark ages again, with everybody competing against everybody else. You wouldn't like that, would you?"

"I'd hate it," said Hazel.

"There you are," said George. "The minute people start cheating on laws, what do you think happens to society?"

If Hazel hadn't been able to come up with an answer to this question, George couldn't have supplied one. A siren was going off in his head.

"Reckon it'd fall all apart," said Hazel.

"What would?" said George blankly.

"Society," said Hazel uncertainly. "Wasn't that what you just said?"

"Who knows?" said George.

The television program was suddenly interrupted for a news bulletin. It wasn't clear at first as to what the bulletin was about, since the announcer, like all announcers, had a serious speech impediment. For about half a minute, and in a state of high excitement, the announcer tried to say, "Ladies and gentlemen—"

He finally gave up, handed the bulletin to a ballerina to read.

"That's all right—" Hazel said of the announcer, "he tried. That's the big thing. He tried to do the best he could with what God gave him. He should get a nice raise for trying so hard."

"Ladies and gentlemen—" said the ballerina, reading the bulletin. She must have been extraordinarily beautiful, because the mask she wore was hideous. And it was easy to see that she was the strongest and most graceful of all the dancers, for her handicap bags were as big as those worn by two-hundred-pound men.

And she had to apologize at once for her voice, which was a very unfair voice for a woman to use. Her voice was a warm, luminous, timeless melody. "Excuse me—" she said, and she began again, making her voice absolutely uncompetitive.

"Harrison Bergeron, age fourteen," she said in a grackle squawk, "has just escaped from jail, where he was held on suspicion of plotting to overthrow the government. He is a genius and an athlete, is under-handicapped, and should be regarded as extremely dangerous."

A police photograph of Harrison Bergeron was flashed on the screen upside down, then sideways, upside down again, then right side up. The picture showed the full length of Harrison against a background calibrated in feet and inches. He was exactly seven feet tall.

The rest of Harrison's appearance was Halloween and hardware. Nobody had ever borne heavier handicaps. He had outgrown hindrances faster than the H-G men could think them up. Instead of a little ear radio for a mental handicap, he wore a tremendous pair of earphones, and spectacles with thick wavy lenses. The spectacles were intended to make him not only half blind, but to give him whanging headaches besides.

Scrap metal was hung all over him. Ordinarily, there was a certain symmetry, a military neatness to the handicaps issued to strong people, but Harrison looked like a walking junkyard. In the race of life, Harrison carried three hundred pounds.

And to offset his good looks, the H-G men required that he wear at all times a red rubber ball for a nose, keep his eyebrows shaved off, and cover his even white teeth with black caps at snaggle-tooth random.

"If you see this boy," said the ballerina, "do not—I repeat, do not—try to reason with him."

There was the shriek of a door being torn from its hinges.

Screams and barking cries of consternation came from the television set. The photograph of Harrison Bergeron on the screen jumped again and again, as though dancing to the tune of an earthquake.

George Bergeron correctly identified the earthquake, and well he might have—for many was the time his own home had danced to the same crashing tune. "My God—" said George, "that must be Harrison!"

The realization was blasted from his mind instantly by the sound of an automobile collision in his head.

When George could open his eyes again, the photograph of Harrison was gone. A living, breathing Harrison filled the screen.

Clanking, clownish, and huge, Harrison stood in the center of the studio. The knob of the uprooted studio door was still in his hand. Ballerinas, technicians, musicians, and announcers cowered on their knees before him, expecting to die.

"I am the Emperor!" cried Harrison. "Do you hear? I am the Emperor! Everybody must do what I say at once!" He stamped his foot and the studio shook.

"Even as I stand here—" he bellowed, "crippled, hobbled, sickened—I am a greater ruler than any man who ever lived! Now watch me become what I *can* become!"

Harrison tore the straps of his handicap harness like wet tissue paper, tore straps guaranteed to support five thousand pounds.

Harrison's scrap-iron handicaps crashed to the floor.

Harrison thrust his thumbs under the bars of the padlock that secured his head harness. The bar snapped like celery. Harrison smashed his headphones and spectacles against the wall.

He flung away his rubber-ball nose, revealed a man that would have awed Thor, the god of thunder.

"I shall now select my Empress!" he said, looking down on the cowering people. "Let the first woman who dares rise to her feet claim her mate and her throne!"

A moment passed, and then a ballerina arose, swaying like a willow.

Harrison plucked the mental handicap from her ear, snapped off her physical handicaps with marvelous delicacy. Last of all, he removed her mask.

She was blindingly beautiful.

"Now—" said Harrison, taking her hand, "shall we show the people the meaning of the word dance? Music!" he commanded.

The musicians scrambled back into their chairs, and Harrison stripped them of their handicaps, too. "Play your best," he told them, "and I'll make you barons and dukes and earls."

The music began. It was normal at first—cheap, silly, false. But Harrison snatched two musicians from their chairs, waved them like batons as he sang the music as he wanted it played. He slammed them back into their chairs.

The music began again and was much improved.

Harrison and his Empress merely listened to the music for a while—listened gravely, as though synchronizing their heartbeats with it.

They shifted their weights to their toes.

Harrison placed his big hands on the girl's tiny waist, letting her sense the weightlessness that would soon be hers.

And then, in an explosion of joy and grace, into the air they sprang!

Not only were the laws of the land abandoned, but the law of gravity and the laws of motion as well.

They reeled, whirled, swiveled, flounced, capered, gamboled, and spun.

They leaped like deer on the moon.

The studio ceiling was thirty feet high, but each leap brought the dancers nearer to it.

It became their obvious intention to kiss the ceiling.

They kissed it.

And then, neutralizing gravity with love and pure will, they remained suspended in air inches below the ceiling, and they kissed each other for a long, long time.

It was then that Diana Moon Glampers, the Handicapper General, came into the studio with a double-barreled ten-gauge shotgun. She fired twice, and the Emperor and the Empress were dead before they hit the floor.

Diana Moon Glampers loaded the gun again. She aimed it at the musicians and told them they had ten seconds to get their handicaps back on.

It was then that the Bergerons' television tube burned out.

Hazel turned to comment about the blackout to George. But George had gone out into the kitchen for a can of beer.

George came back in with the beer, paused while a handicap signal shook him up. And then he sat down again. "You been crying?" he said to Hazel.

"Yup," she said.

"What about?" he said.

"I forgot," she said. "Something real sad on television."

"What was it?" he said.

"It's all kind of mixed up in my mind," said Hazel.

"Forget sad things," said George.

"I always do," said Hazel.

"That's my girl," said George. He winced. There was the sound of a rivetting gun in his head.

"Gee—I could tell that one was a doozy," said Hazel.

"You can say that again," said George.

"Gee—" said Hazel, "I could tell that one was a doozy."

QUESTIONS FOR DISCUSSION AND WRITING

1. How does George and Hazel's conversation while watching television reflect the larger social conflicts portrayed in the story? How does Harrison's attempt to become Emperor bring those conflicts to a climax? To what extent does George and Hazel's response to their son's death resolve those conflicts?

2. How does the handicapping system work to regulate characters such as George, the ballerina, and the television announcer? Why does Vonnegut devote so much attention to describing the transformation of Harrison Bergeron's character? Why does he devote so little attention to describing the character of Diana Moon Glampers?

3. How does the first paragraph of the story establish the social setting of the story? How do the scenes with George and Hazel personalize this future society? How do George and Hazel describe the setting of former societies?

4. Although the point of view in this story is objective, some of it is told from George's perspective. What situation would make it impossible for the story to be told completely from George's point of view? Why is it appropriate that Harrison's story is portrayed on television?

5. What does this story reveal about equality as a valuable social objective? To what extent does Harrison's attempt to become Emperor fulfill George's suggestion that competition would take us back to the dark ages?

92

ALICE WALKER

Everyday Use

ALICE WALKER was born in 1944 in Eatonton, Georgia, attended Spelman College, and graduated from Sarah Lawrence College. She then became active in the Civil Rights movement, helping to register voters in Georgia, teaching in the Head Start program in Mississippi, and working on the staff of the New York City welfare department. In 1968 Walker joined the faculty at Jackson State College to teach writing and black literature. In subsequent years she began her own writing career while working as a writer-in-residence at Wellesley College, the University of California, Berkeley, and Brandeis University. She has also been a scholar at the Bread Loaf Writers' Conference and a fellow at the Radcliffe Institute. Walker has contributed her stories, poems, and essays to magazines such as *Negro Digest, Harper's,* and *Black World* and serves as a contributing editor to *Freedomways* and *Ms.* She has written a children's biography, *Langston Hughes, American Poet* (1973), edited an important literary anthology, *I Love Myself When I'm Laughing . . . And Then Again When I'm Looking Mean and Impressive: A Zora Neale Hurston Reader* (1979), and compiled two collections of her essays, *In Search of Our Mothers' Gardens* (1983) and *Living By the Word* (1988). These works reveal her interest in the themes of sexism and racism, themes she embodies in her three widely acclaimed novels: *The Third Life of Grange Copeland* (1970), *Meridian* (1976), and especially *The Color Purple* (1982), which received both the American Book Award and the Pulitzer Prize. Her most recent novel, published in 1992, is *Possessing the Secret of Joy.* Her stories, collected in *In Love and Trouble: Stories of Black Women* (1973) and *You Can't Keep a Good Woman Down* (1981), also examine the complex experiences of black women. "Everyday Use" focuses on a family reunion that produces a conflict between two definitions of the family's heritage. "To Hell with Dying" documents a family's attempt to conquer death through love. "Really, *Doesn't* Crime Pay?" provides an ironic commentary on "The Black Woman's Resistance to Creativity in the Arts."

I will wait for her in the yard that Maggie and I made so clean and wavy yesterday afternoon. A yard like this is more comfortable than most people know. It is not just a yard. It is like an extended living room. When the hard clay is swept clean as a floor and the fine sand around the edges lined with tiny, irregular grooves anyone can come and sit and look up into the elm tree and wait for the breezes that never come inside the house.

Maggie will be nervous until after her sister goes: she will stand hopelessly in corners homely and ashamed of the burn scars down her arms and legs, eyeing her sister with a mixture of envy and awe. She thinks her sister has held life always in the palm of one hand, that "no" is a word the world never learned to say to her.

You've no doubt seen those TV shows where the child who has "made it" is confronted, as a surprise, by her own mother and father, tottering in weakly from backstage. (A pleasant surprise, of course: What would they do if parent and child came on the show only to curse out and insult each other?) On TV mother and child embrace and smile into each other's faces. Sometimes the mother and father weep, the child wraps them in her arms and leans across the table to tell how she would not have made it without their help. I have seen these programs.

Sometimes I dream a dream in which Dee and I are suddenly brought together on a TV program of this sort. Out of a dark and soft-seated limousine I am ushered into a bright room filled with many people. There I meet a smiling, gray, sporty man like Johnny Carson who shakes my hand and tells me what a fine girl I have. Then we are on the stage and Dee is embracing me with tears in her eyes. She pins on my dress a large orchid, even though she has told me once that she thinks orchids are tacky flowers.

In real life I am a large, big-boned woman with rough, man-working hands. In the winter I wear flannel nightgowns to bed and overalls during the day. I can kill and clean a hog as mercilessly as a man. My fat keeps me hot in zero weather. I can work all day, breaking ice to get water for washing. I can eat pork liver cooked over the open fire minutes after it comes steaming from the hog. One winter I knocked a bull calf straight in the brain between the eyes with a sledge hammer and had the meat hung up to chill before nightfall. But of course all this does not show on television. I am the way my daughter would want me to be: a hundred pounds lighter, my skin like an uncooked barley pancake. My hair glistens in the hot bright lights. Johnny Carson has much to do to keep up with my quick and witty tongue.

But that is a mistake. I know even before I wake up. Who ever knew a Johnson with a quick tongue? Who can even imagine me looking a strange white man in the eye? It seems to me I have talked to them always with one foot raised in flight, with my head turned in whichever way is farthest from them. Dee, though. She would always look anyone in the eye. Hesitation was no part of her nature.

"How do I look, Mama?" Maggie says, showing just enough of her thin body enveloped in pink skirt and red blouse for me to know she's there, almost hidden by the door.

"Come out into the yard," I say.

Have you ever seen a lame animal, perhaps a dog run over by some careless person rich enough to own a car, sidle up to someone who is ignorant enough to be kind to him? That is the way my Maggie walks. She has been like this, chin on chest, eyes on ground, feet in shuffle, ever since the fire that burned the other house to the ground.

Dee is lighter than Maggie, with nicer hair and a fuller figure. She's a woman now, though sometimes I forget. How long ago was it that the other house burned? Ten, twelve years? Sometimes I can still hear the flames and feel Maggie's arm sticking to me, her hair smoking and her dress falling off her in little black papery flakes. Her eyes seemed stretched open, blazed open by the flames reflected in them. And Dee. I see her standing off under the sweet gum tree she used to dig gum out of; a look of concentration on her face as she watched the last dingy gray board of the house fall in toward the red-hot brick chimney. Why don't you do a dance around the ashes? I'd wanted to ask her. She had hated the house that much.

I used to think she hated Maggie, too. But that was before we raised the money, the church and me, to send her to Augusta to school. She used to read to us without pity; forcing words, lies, other folks' habits, whole lives upon us two, sitting trapped and ignorant underneath her voice. She washed us in a river of make-believe, burned us with a lot of knowledge we didn't necessarily need to know. Pressed us to her with the serious way she read, to shove us away at just the moment, like dimwits, we seemed about to understand.

Dee wanted nice things. A yellow organdy dress to wear to her graduation from high school; black pumps to match a green suit she'd made from an old suit somebody gave me. She was determined to stare down any disaster in her efforts. Her eyelids would not flicker for minutes at a time. Often I fought off the temptation to shake her. At sixteen she had a style of her own: and knew what style was.

I never had an education myself. After second grade the school was closed down. Don't ask me why: in 1927 colored asked fewer questions than they do now. Sometimes Maggie reads to me. She stumbles along good-naturedly but can't see well. She knows she is not bright. Like good looks and money, quickness passed her by. She will marry John Thomas (who has mossy teeth in an earnest face) and then I'll be free to sit here and I guess just sing church songs to myself. Although I never was a good singer. Never could carry a tune. I was always better at a man's job. I used to love to milk till I was hoofed in the side in '49. Cows are soothing and slow and don't bother you, unless you try to milk them the wrong way.

I have deliberately turned my back on the house. It is three rooms, just like the one that burned, except the roof is tin; they don't make shingle roofs any more. There are no real windows, just some holes cut in the sides, like the portholes in a ship, but not round and not square, with rawhide holding the shutters up on the outside. This house is in a pasture, too, like the other one. No doubt when Dee sees it she will want to tear it down. She wrote me once that no matter where we "choose" to live, she will manage to come see us. But she will never bring her friends. Maggie and I thought about this and Maggie asked me, "Mama, when did Dee ever *have* any friends?"

She had a few. Furtive boys in pink shirts hanging about on washday after school. Nervous girls who never laughed. Impressed with her they worshiped the well-turned phrase, the cute shape, the scalding humor that erupted like bubbles in lye. She read to them.

When she was courting Jimmy T she didn't have much time to pay to us, but turned all her faultfinding power on him. He *flew* to marry a cheap gal from a family of ignorant flashy people. She hardly had time to recompose herself.

When she comes I will meet—but there they are!

Maggie attempts to make a dash for the house, in her shuffling way, but I stay her with my hand. "Come back here," I say. And she stops and tries to dig a well in the sand with her toe.

It is hard to see them clearly through the strong sun. But even the first glimpse of leg out of the car tells me it is Dee. Her feet were always neat-looking, as if God himself had shaped them with a certain style. From the other side of the car comes a short, stocky man. Hair is all over his head a foot long and hanging from his chin like a kinky mule tail. I hear Maggie suck in her breath. "Uhnnnh," is what it sounds like. Like when you see the wriggling end of a snake just in front of your foot on the road. "Uhnnnh."

Dee next. A dress down to the ground, in this hot weather. A dress so loud it hurts my eyes. There are yellows and oranges enough to throw back the light of the sun. I feel my whole face warming from the heat waves it throws out. Earrings, too, gold and hanging down to her shoulders. Bracelets dangling and making noises when she moves her arm up to shake the folds of the dress out of her armpits. The dress is loose and flows, and as she walks closer, I like it. I hear Maggie go "Uhnnnh" again. It is her sister's hair. It stands straight up like the wool on a sheep. It is black as night and around the edges are two long pigtails that rope about like small lizards disappearing behind her ears.

"Wa-su-zo–Tean-o!" she says, coming on in that gliding way the dress makes her move. The short stocky fellow with the hair to his navel is all grinning and he follows up with "Asalamalakim, my mother and sister!" He moves to hug Maggie but she falls back, right up against the back of my chair. I feel her trembling there and when I look up I see the perspiration falling off her chin.

"Don't get up," says Dee. Since I am stout it takes something of a push. You can see me trying to move a second or two before I make it. She turns, showing white heels through her sandals, and goes back to the car. Out she peeks next with a Polaroid. She stoops down quickly and lines up picture after picture of me sitting there in front of the house with Maggie cowering behind me. She never takes a shot without making sure the house is included. When a cow comes nibbling around the edge of the yard she snaps it and me and Maggie *and* the house. Then she puts the Polaroid in the back seat of the car, and comes up and kisses me on the forehead.

Meanwhile Asalamalakim is going through the motions with Maggie's hand. Maggie's hand is as limp as a fish, and probably as cold, despite the sweat, and she keeps trying to pull it back. It looks like Asalamalakim wants to shake hands but wants to do it fancy. Or maybe he don't know how people shake hands. Anyhow, he soon gives up on Maggie.

"Well," I say. "Dee."

"No, Mama," she says. "Not 'Dee,' Wangero Leewanika Kemanjo!"

"What happened to 'Dee'?" I wanted to know.

"She's dead," Wangero said. "I couldn't bear it any longer being named after the people who oppress me."

"You know as well as me you was named after your aunt Dicie," I said. Dicie is my sister. She named Dee. We called her "Big Dee" after Dee was born.

"But who was *she* named after?" asked Wangero.

"I guess after Grandma Dee," I said.

"And who was she named after?" asked Wangero.

"Her mother," I said, and saw Wangero was getting tired. "That's about as far back as I can trace it," I said. Though, in fact, I probably could have carried it back beyond the Civil War through the branches.

"Well," said Asalamalakim, "there you are."

"Uhnnnh," I heard Maggie say.

"There I was not," I said, "before 'Dicie' cropped up in our family, so why should I try to trace it that far back?"

He just stood there grinning, looking down on me like somebody inspecting a Model A car. Every once in a while he and Wangero sent eye signals over my head.

"How do you pronounce this name?" I asked.

"You don't have to call me by it if you don't want to," said Wangero.

"Why shouldn't I?" I asked. "If that's what you want us to call you, we'll call you."

"I know it might sound awkward at first," said Wangero.

"I'll get used to it," I said. "Ream it out again."

Well, soon we got the name out of the way. Asalamalakim had a name twice as long and three times as hard. After I tripped over it two or three times he told me just call him Hakim-a-barber. I wanted to ask him was he a barber, but I didn't really think he was, so I didn't ask.

"You must belong to those beef-cattle peoples down the road," I said. They said "Asalamalakim" when they met you, too, but they didn't shake hands. Always too busy: feeding the cattle, fixing the fences, putting up salt-lick shelters, throwing down hay. When the white folks poisoned some of the herd the men stayed up all night with rifles in their hands. I walked a mile and a half just to see the sight.

Hakim-a-barber said, "I accept some of their doctrines, but farming and raising cattle is not my style." (They didn't tell me, and I didn't ask, whether Wangero [Dee] had really gone and married him.)

We sat down to eat and right away he said he didn't eat collards and pork was unclean. Wangero, though, went on through the chitlins and corn bread, the greens and everything else. She talked a blue streak over the sweet potatoes. Everything delighted her. Even the fact that we still used the benches her daddy made for the table when we couldn't afford to buy chairs.

"Oh, Mama!" she cried. Then turned to Hakim-a-barber. "I never knew how lovely these benches are. You can feel the rump prints," she said, running her hands underneath her and along the bench. Then she gave a sigh and her hand closed over Grandma Dee's butter dish. "That's it!" she said. "I knew there was something I wanted to ask you if I could have." She jumped up from the table and went over in the corner where the churn stood, the milk in its clabber by now. She looked at the churn and looked at it.

"This churn top is what I need," she said. "Didn't Uncle Buddy whittle it out of a tree you all used to have?"

"Yes," I said.

"Uh huh," she said happily. "And I want the dasher, too."

"Uncle Buddy whittle that, too?" asked the barber.

Dee (Wangero) looked up at me.

"Aunt Dee's first husband whittled the dash," said Maggie so low you almost couldn't hear her. "His name was Henry, but they called him Stash."

"Maggie's brain is like an elephant's," Wangero said, laughing. "I can use the churn top as a centerpiece for the alcove table," she said, sliding a plate over the churn, "and I'll think of something artistic to do with the dasher."

When she finished wrapping the dasher the handle stuck out. I took it for a moment in my hands. You didn't even have to look close to see where hands pushing the dasher up and down to make butter had left a kind of sink in the wood. In fact, there were a lot of small sinks; you could see where thumbs and fingers had sunk into the wood. It was beautiful light yellow wood, from a tree that grew in the yard where Big Dee and Stash had lived.

After dinner Dee (Wangero) went to the trunk at the foot of my bed and started rifling through it. Maggie hung back in the kitchen over the dishpan. Out came Wangero with two quilts. They had been pieced by Grandma Dee and then Big Dee and me had hung them on the quilt frames on the front porch and quilted them. One was in the Lone Star pattern. The other was Walk Around the Mountain. In both of them were scraps of dresses Grandma Dee had worn fifty and more years ago. Bits and pieces of Grandpa Jarrell's Paisley shirts. And one teeny faded blue piece, about the size of a penny matchbox, that was from Great Grandpa Ezra's uniform that he wore in the Civil War.

"Mama," Wangero said sweet as a bird. "Can I have these old quilts?"

I heard something fall in the kitchen, and a minute later the kitchen door slammed.

"Why don't you take one or two of the others?" I asked. "These old things was just done by me and Big Dee from some tops your grandma pieced before she died."

"No," said Wangero. "I don't want those. They are stitched around the borders by machine."

"That's made them last better," I said.

"That's not the point," said Wangero. "These are all pieces of dresses Grandma used to wear. She did all this stitching by hand. Imagine!" She held the quilts securely in her arms, stroking them.

"Some of the pieces, like those lavender ones, come from old clothes her mother handed down to her," I said, moving up to touch the quilts. Dee (Wangero) moved back just enough so that I couldn't reach the quilts. They already belonged to her.

"Imagine!" she breathed again, clutching them closely to her bosom.

"The truth is," I said, "I promised to give them quilts to Maggie, for when she marries John Thomas."

She gasped like a bee had stung her.

"Maggie can't appreciate these quilts!" she said. "She'd probably be backward enough to put them to everyday use."

"I reckon she would," I said. "God knows I been saving 'em for long enough with nobody using 'em. I hope she will!" I didn't want to bring up how I had offered Dee (Wangero) a quilt when she went away to college. Then she had told me they were old-fashioned, out of style.

"But they're *priceless!*" she was saying now, furiously; for she has a temper. "Maggie would put them on the bed and in five years they'd be in rags. Less than that!"

"She can always make some more," I said. "Maggie knows how to quilt."

Dee (Wangero) looked at me with hatred. "You just will not understand. The point is these quilts, *these* quilts!"

"Well," I said, stumped. "What would *you* do with them?"

"Hang them," she said. As if that was the only thing you *could* do with quilts.

Maggie by now was standing in the door. I could almost hear the sound her feet made as they scraped over each other.

"She can have them, Mama," she said, like somebody used to never winning anything, or having anything reserved for her. "I can 'member Grandma Dee without the quilts."

I looked at her hard. She had filled her bottom lip with checkerberry snuff and it gave her face a kind of dopey, hangdog look. It was Grandma Dee and Big Dee who taught her how to quilt herself. She stood there with her scarred hands hidden in the folds of her skirt. She looked at her sister with something like fear but she wasn't mad at her. This was Maggie's portion. This was the way she knew God to work.

When I looked at her like that something hit me in the top of my head and ran down to the soles of my feet. Just like when I'm in church and the spirit of God touches me and I get happy and shout. I did something I never had done before: hugged Maggie to me, then dragged her on into the room, snatched the quilts out of Miss Wangero's hands and dumped them into Maggie's lap. Maggie just sat there on my bed with her mouth open.

"Take one or two of the others," I said to Dee.

But she turned without a word and went out to Hakim-a-barber.

"You just don't understand," she said, as Maggie and I came out to the car.

"What don't I understand?" I wanted to know.

"Your heritage," she said. And then she turned to Maggie, kissed her, and said, "You ought to try to make something of yourself, too, Maggie. It's really a new day for us. But from the way you and Mama still live you'd never know it."

She put on some sunglasses that hid everything above the tip of her nose and her chin.

Maggie smiled; maybe at the sunglasses. But a real smile, not scared. After we watched the car dust settle I asked Maggie to bring me a dip of snuff. And then the two of us sat there just enjoying, until it was time to go in the house and go to bed.

QUESTIONS FOR DISCUSSION AND WRITING

1. How do the mother's observations about the family reunions presented on television introduce the conflicts in the story? Why does the mother's decision to give the quilts to Maggie mark the climax of the story? How do Wangero's comments about heritage and advancement bring the story to its ironic conclusion?

2. How does the mother's description of her working ability help to establish her character? How do Maggie's scars explain her apprehension about her sister's visit? In what way do Dee's attire, boyfriend, and new name comment on her mother's observation that Dee "knew what style was"?

3. How do the mother's opening and closing references to the yard evoke the setting of the story? Why does the mother suspect that Wangero will want to "tear down" the house?

Why does Wangero photograph the house and pay so much attention to the benches, the churn, and the quilts?

4. What is the mother's point of view toward Maggie's accident and Wangero's education? How does she explain the cause of her dramatic decision at the end of the story?

5. How do the quilts symbolize the conflict of tradition and progress? For example, why did Wangero refuse the quilt when she went to college? Why does she now suggest that putting them to "everyday use" is backward? How would you compare the mother's comment that "Maggie knows how to quilt" with Wangero's comment that her sister should "make something" of herself?

93

ALICE WALKER

To Hell with Dying

"To hell with dying," my father would say. "These children want Mr. Sweet!"

Mr. Sweet was a diabetic and an alcoholic and a guitar player and lived down the road from us on a neglected cotton farm. My older brothers and sisters got the most benefit from Mr. Sweet, for when they were growing up he had quite a few years ahead of him and so was capable of being called back from the brink of death any number of times—whenever the voice of my father reached him as he lay expiring. "To hell with dying, man," my father would say, pushing the wife away from the bedside (in tears although she knew the death was not necessarily the last one unless Mr. Sweet really wanted it to be). "These children want Mr. Sweet!" And they did want him, for at a signal from Father they would come crowding around the bed and throw themselves on the covers, and whoever was the smallest at the time would kiss him all over his wrinkled brown face and tickle him so that he would laugh all down in his stomach, and his mustache, which was long and sort of straggly, would shake like Spanish moss and was also that color.

Mr. Sweet had been ambitious as a boy, wanted to be a doctor or lawyer or sailor, only to find that black men fare better if they are not. Since he could become none of these things he turned to fishing as his only earnest career and playing the guitar as his only claim to doing anything extraordinarily well. His son, the only one that he and his wife, Miss Mary, had, was shiftless as the day is long and spent money as if he were trying to see the bottom of the mint, which Mr. Sweet would tell him was the clean brown palm of his hand. Miss Mary loved her "baby," however, and worked hard to get him the "li'l necessaries" of life, which turned out mostly to be women.

Mr. Sweet was a tall, thinnish man with thick kinky hair going dead white. He was dark brown, his eyes were squinty and sort of bluish, and he chewed Brown Mule tobacco. He was constantly on the verge of being blind drunk, for he brewed his own liquor and was not in the least a stingy sort of man, and was always very melancholy and sad, though frequently when he was "feelin' good" he'd dance around the yard with us, usually keeling over just as my mother came to see what the commotion was.

Toward all of us children he was very kind, and had the grace to be shy with us, which is unusual in grown-ups. He had great respect for my mother for she never held his drunkenness against him and would let us play with him even when he was about to fall in the fireplace from drink. Although Mr. Sweet would sometimes lose complete or nearly complete control of his head and neck so that he would loll in his chair, his mind remained strangely acute and his speech not too affected. His ability to be drunk and sober at the same time made him an ideal playmate, for he was as weak as we were and we could usually best him in wrestling, all the while keeping a fairly coherent conversation going.

We never felt anything of Mr. Sweet's age when we played with him. We loved his wrinkles and would draw some on our brows to be like him, and his white hair was my special treasure and he knew it and would never come to visit us just after he had had his hair cut off at the barbershop. Once he came to our house for something, probably to see my father about fertilizer for his crops because, although he never paid the slightest attention to his crops, he liked to know what things would be best to use on them if he ever did. Anyhow, he had not come with his hair since he had just had it shaved off at the barbershop. He wore a huge straw hat to keep off the sun and also to keep his head away from me. But as soon as I saw him I ran up and demanded that he take me up and kiss me with his funny beard which smelled so strongly of tobacco. Looking forward to burying my small fingers into his woolly hair I threw away his hat only to find he had done something to his hair, that it was no longer there! I let out a squall which made my mother think that Mr. Sweet had finally dropped me in the well or something and from that day I've been wary of men in hats. However, not long after, Mr. Sweet showed up with his hair grown out and just as white and kinky and impenetrable as it ever was.

Mr. Sweet used to call me his princess, and I believed it. He made me feel pretty at five and six, and simply outrageously devastating at the blazing age of eight and a half. When he came to our house with his guitar the whole family would stop whatever they were doing to sit around him and listen to him play. He liked to play "Sweet Georgia Brown," that was what he called me sometimes, and also he liked to play "Caldonia" and all sorts of sweet, sad, wonderful songs which he sometimes made up. It was from one of these songs that I heard that he had had to marry Miss Mary when he had in fact loved somebody else (now living in Chi-ca-go, or De-stroy, Michigan). He was not sure that Joe Lee, her "baby," was also his baby. Sometimes he would cry and that was an indication that he was about to die again. And so we would all get prepared, for we were sure to be called upon.

I was seven the first time I remember actually participating in one of Mr. Sweet's "revivals"—my parents told me I had participated before, I had been the one chosen to kiss him and tickle him long before I knew the rite of Mr. Sweet's rehabilitation. He had come to our house, it was a few years after his wife's death, and was very sad, and also, typically, very drunk. He sat on the floor next to me and my older brother, the rest of the children were grown up and lived elsewhere, and began to play his guitar and cry. I held his woolly head in my arms and wished I could have been old enough to have been the woman he loved so much and that I had not been lost years and years ago.

When he was leaving, my mother said to us that we'd better sleep light that night for we'd probably have to go over to Mr. Sweet's before daylight. And we did. For soon after we had gone to bed one of the neighbors knocked on our door and called my father and said that Mr. Sweet was sinking fast and if he wanted to get in a word before the crossover he'd better shake a leg and get over to Mr. Sweet's house. All the neighbors knew to come to our house if something was wrong with Mr. Sweet, but they did not know how we always managed to make him well, or at least stop him from dying, when he was so often near death. As soon as we heard the cry we got up, my brother and I and my mother and father, and put on our clothes. We hurried out of the house and down the road for we were always afraid that we might someday be too late and Mr. Sweet would get tired of dallying.

When we got to the house, a very poor shack really, we found the front room full of neighbors and relatives and someone met us at the door and said it was all very sad that old Mr. Sweet Little (for Little was his family name, although we mostly ignored it) was about to kick the bucket. My parents were advised not to take my brother and me into the "death room," seeing we were so young and all, but we were so much more accustomed to the death room than he that we ignored him and dashed in without giving his warnings a second thought. I was almost in tears, for these deaths upset me fearfully, and the thought of how much depended on me and my brother (who was such a ham most of the time) made me very nervous.

The doctor was bending over the bed and turned back to tell us for at least the tenth time in the history of my family that, alas, old Mr. Sweet Little was dying and that the children had best not see the face of implacable death (I didn't know what "implacable" was, but whatever it was, Mr. Sweet was not!). My father pushed him rather abruptly out of the way saying, as he always did and very loudly for he was saying it to Mr. Sweet, "To hell with dying, man, these children want Mr. Sweet"—which was my cue to throw myself upon the bed and kiss Mr. Sweet all around the whiskers and under the eyes and around the collar of his nightshirt where he smelled so strongly of all sorts of things, mostly liniment.

I was very good at bringing him around, for as soon as I saw that he was struggling to open his eyes I knew he was going to be all right, and so could finish my revival sure of success. As soon as his eyes were open he would begin to smile and that way I knew that I had surely won. Once, though, I got a tremendous scare, for he could not open his eyes and later I learned that he had had a stroke and that one side of his face was stiff and hard to get into motion. When he began to smile I could tickle him in earnest because I was sure that nothing would get in the way of his laughter, although once he began to cough so hard that he almost threw me off his stomach, but that was when I was very small, little more than a baby, and my bushy hair had gotten in his nose.

When we were sure he would listen to us we would ask him why he was in bed and when he was coming to see us again and could we play his guitar, which more than likely would be leaning against the bed. His eyes would get all misty and he would sometimes cry out loud, but we never let it embarrass us, for he knew that we loved him and that we sometimes cried too for no reason. My parents would leave the room to just the three of us; Mr. Sweet, by that time, would be propped up in bed with a number of pillows behind his head and with me sitting and lying on his shoulder and along his chest. Even when he had trouble breathing he would not ask me to get down. Looking into my eyes he would shake his white head and run a scratchy old finger all around my hairline, which was rather low down, nearly to my eyebrows, and made some people say I looked like a baby monkey.

My brother was very generous in all this, he let me do all the revivaling—he had done it for years before I was born and so was glad to be able to pass it on to someone new. What he would do while I talked to Mr. Sweet was pretend to play the guitar, in fact pretend that he was a young version of Mr. Sweet, and it always made Mr. Sweet glad to think that someone wanted to be like him—of course, we did not know this then, we played the thing by ear, and whatever he seemed to like, we did. We were desperately afraid that he was just going to take off one day and leave us.

It did not occur to us that we were doing anything special; we had not learned that death was final when it did come. We thought nothing of triumphing over it so many times, and in fact became a trifle contemptuous of people who let themselves be carried away. It did not occur to us that if our father had been dying we could not have stopped it, that Mr. Sweet was the only person over whom we had power.

When Mr. Sweet was in his eighties I was studying in the university many miles from home. I saw him whenever I went home, but he was never on the verge of dying that I could tell and I began to feel that my anxiety for his health and psychological well-being was unnecessary. By this time he not only had a mustache but a long flowing snow-white beard, which I loved and combed and braided for hours. He was very peaceful, fragile, gentle, and the only jarring note about him was his old steel guitar, which he still played in the old sad, sweet, down-home blues way.

On Mr. Sweet's ninetieth birthday I was finishing my doctorate in Massachusetts and had been making arrangements to go home for several weeks' rest. That morning I got a telegram telling me that Mr. Sweet was dying again and could I please drop everything and come home. Of course I could. My dissertation could wait and my teachers would understand when I explained to them when I got back. I ran to the phone, called the airport, and within four hours I was speeding along the dusty road to Mr. Sweet's.

The house was more dilapidated than when I was last there, barely a shack, but it was overgrown with yellow roses which my family had planted many years ago. The air was heavy and sweet and very peaceful. I felt strange walking through the gate and up the old rickety steps. But the strangeness left me as I caught sight of the long white beard I loved so well flowing down the thin body over the familiar quilt coverlet. Mr. Sweet!

His eyes were closed tight and his hands, crossed over his stomach, were thin and delicate, no longer scratchy. I remembered how always before I had run and jumped up on him just anywhere; now I knew he would not be able to support my weight. I looked around at my parents, and was surprised to see that my father and mother also looked old and frail. My father, his own hair very gray, leaned over the quietly sleeping old man, who, incidentally, smelled still of wine and tobacco, and said, as he'd done so many times, "To hell with dying, man! My daughter is home to see Mr. Sweet!" My brother had not been able to come as he was in the war in Asia. I bent down and gently stroked the closed eyes and gradually they began to open. The closed, wine-stained lips twitched a little, then parted in a warm, slightly embarrassed smile. Mr. Sweet could see me and he recognized me and his eyes looked very spry and twinkly for a moment. I put my head down on the pillow next to his and we just looked at each other for a long time. Then he began to trace my peculiar hairline with a thin, smooth finger. I closed my eyes when his finger halted above my ear (he used to rejoice at the dirt in my ears when I was little), his hand stayed cupped around my cheek. When I opened my eyes, sure that I had reached him in time, his were closed.

Even at twenty-four how could I believe that I had failed? that Mr. Sweet was really gone? He had never gone before. But when I looked at my parents I saw that they were holding back tears. They had loved him dearly. He was like a piece of rare and delicate china which was always being saved from breaking and which finally fell. I looked long at the old face, the wrinkled forehead, the red lips, the hands that still reached out to me. Soon I felt my father pushing something cool into my hands. It was Mr. Sweet's guitar. He had asked them months before to give it to me; he had known that even if I came next time he would not be able to respond in the old way. He did not want me to feel that my trip had been for nothing.

The old guitar! I plucked the strings, hummed "Sweet Georgia Brown." The magic of Mr. Sweet lingered still in the cool steel box. Through the window I could catch the fragrant delicate scent of tender yellow roses. The man on the high old-fashioned bed with the quilt coverlet and the flowing white beard had been my first love.

QUESTIONS FOR DISCUSSION AND WRITING

1. How do the three presentations of the ritualistic revivals form the dramatic structure of the story? In what way does playing the guitar mark the success of the revival? How does playing the guitar provide an appropriate ending for the last attempt to revive Mr. Sweet?

2. How does Mr. Sweet's name suggest his character? What qualities does he possess that make everyone love him in spite of his weaknesses? How does the narrator respond to Mr. Sweet's description of her as a "princess"?

3. How do Mr. Sweet's dreams and disappointments help establish the setting of the story? How does his relationship with the narrator's family evoke a world of abundant life in spite of his failures?

4. At the beginning of the story, the narrator seems to be speaking collectively for all the children in her family. At what point in the story does the point of view shift from "we" to "I"? How do the narrator's growth and education affect her point of view in the last scene?

5. What does the ritual of revival suggest about the restorative powers of love? What other assumptions about death does the narrator form as a result of her experience with Mr. Sweet? Why is it significant that she does not understand the meaning of the word "implacable"?

94
ALICE WALKER
"Really, Doesn't *Crime Pay?"*
(Myrna)

SEPTEMBER, 1961

page 118

I sit here by the window in a house with a thirty-year mortgage, writing in this notebook, looking down at my Helena Rubenstein hands . . . and why not? Since I am not a serious writer my nails need not be bitten off, my cuticles need not have jagged edges. I can indulge myself—my hands—in Herbessence nail-soak, polish, lotions, and creams. The result is a truly beautiful pair of hands: sweet-smelling, small, and soft. . . .

I lift them from the page where I have written the line "Really, *Doesn't* Crime Pay?" and send them seeking up my shirt front (it is a white and frilly shirt) and smoothly up the column of my throat, where gardenia scent floats beneath my hairline. If I should spread my arms and legs or whirl, just for an instant, the sweet smell of my body would be more than I could bear. But I fit into my new surroundings perfectly; like a jar of cold cream melting on a mirrored vanity shelf.

page 119

"I have a surprise for you," Ruel said, the first time he brought me here. And you know how sick he makes me now when he grins.

"What is it?" I asked, not caring in the least.

And that is how we drove up to the house. Four bedrooms and two toilets and a half.

"Isn't it a beauty?" he said, not touching me, but urging me out of the car with the phony enthusiasm of his voice.

"Yes," I said. It is "a beauty." Like new Southern houses everywhere. The bricks resemble cubes of raw meat; the roof pressed down, a field hat made of iron. The windows are narrow, beady eyes; the aluminum glints. The yard is a long undressed wound, the few trees as bereft of foliage as hairpins stuck in a mud cake.

"Yes," I say, "it sure is a beauty." He beams, in his chill and reassured way. I am startled that he doesn't still wear some kind of military uniform. But no. He came home from Korea a hero, and a glutton for sweet smells.

"Here we can forget the past," he says.

page 120

We have moved in and bought new furniture. The place reeks of newness, the green walls turn me bilious. He stands behind me, his hands touching the edges of my hair. I pick up my hairbrush and brush his hands away. I have sweetened my body to such an extent that even he (especially he) may no longer touch it.

I do not want to forget the past; but I say "Yes," like a parrot. "We can forget the past here."

The past of course is Mordecai Rich, the man who, Ruel claims, caused my breakdown. The past is the night I tried to murder Ruel with one of his chain saws.

MAY, 1958

page 2

Mordecai Rich

Mordecai does not believe Ruel Johnson is my husband. "*That* old man," he says, in a mocking, cruel way.

"Ruel is not old," I say. "Looking old is just his way." Just as, I thought, looking young is your way, although you're probably not much younger than Ruel.

Maybe it is just that Mordecai is a vagabond, scribbling down impressions of the South, from no solid place, going to none . . . and Ruel has never left Hancock County, except once, when he gallantly went off to war. He claims travel broadened him, especially his two months of European leave. He married me because although my skin is brown he thinks I look like a Frenchwoman. Sometimes he tells me I look Oriental: Korean or Japanese. I console myself with this thought: My family tends to darken and darken as we get older. One day he may wake up in bed with a complete stranger.

"He works in the store," I say. "He also raises a hundred acres of peanuts." Which is surely success.

"That many," muses Mordecai.

It is not pride that makes me tell him what my husband does, is. It is a way I can tell him about myself.

page 4

Today Mordecai is back. He tells a funny/sad story about a man in town who could not move his wife. "He huffed and puffed," laughed Mordecai, "to no avail." Then one night as he was sneaking up to her bedroom he heard joyous cries. Rushing in he found his wife in the arms of another woman! The wife calmly dressed and began to pack her bags. The husband begged and pleaded. "Anything you want," he promised. "What *do* you want?" he pleaded. The wife began to chuckle and, laughing, left the house with her friend.

Now the husband gets drunk every day and wants an ordinance passed. He cannot say what the ordinance will be against, but that is what he buttonholes people to say: "I want a goddam ordinance passed!" People who know the story make jokes about him. They pity him and give him enough money to keep him drunk.

page 5

I think Mordecai Rich has about as much heart as a dirt-eating toad. Even when he makes me laugh I know that nobody ought to look on other people's confusion with that cold an eye.

"But that's what I am," he says, flipping through the pages of his scribble pad. "A cold eye. An eye looking for Beauty. An eye looking for Truth."

"Why don't you look for other things?" I want to know. "Like neither Truth nor Beauty, but places in people's lives where things have just slipped a good bit off the track."

"That's too vague," said Mordecai, frowning.

"So is Truth," I said. "Not to mention Beauty."

page 10

Ruel wants to know why "the skinny black tramp"—as he calls Mordecai—keeps hanging around. I made the mistake of telling him Mordecai is thinking of using our house as the setting for one of his Southern country stories.

"Mordecai is from the North," I said. "He never saw a wooden house with a toilet in the yard."

"Well maybe he better go back where he's from," said Ruel, "and shit the way he's used to."

It's Ruel's pride that is hurt. He's ashamed of this house that seems perfectly adequate to me. One day we'll have a new house, he says, of brick, with a Japanese bath. How should I know why?

page 11

When I told Mordecai what Ruel said he smiled in that snake-eyed way he has and said, "Do *you* mind me hanging around?"

I didn't know what to say. I stammered something. Not because of his question but because he put his hand point-blank on my left nipple. He settled his other hand deep in my hair.

"I am married more thoroughly than a young boy like you could guess," I told him. But I don't expect that to stop him. Especially since the day he found out I wanted to be a writer myself.

It happened this way: I was writing in the grape arbor, on the ledge by the creek that is hidden from the house by trees. He was right in front of me before I could put my notebook away. He snatched it from me and began to read. What is worse, he read aloud. I was embarrassed to death.

"No wife of mine is going to embarrass me with a lot of foolish, vulgar stuff," Mordecai read. (This is Ruel's opinion of my writing.) *Every time he tells me how peculiar I am for wanting to write stories he brings up having a baby or going shopping, as if these things are the same. Just something to occupy my time.*

"If you have time on your hands," he said today, "why don't you go shopping in that new store in town."

I went. I bought six kinds of face cream, two eyebrow pencils, five nightgowns and a longhaired wig. Two contour sticks and a pot of gloss for my lips.

And all the while I was grieving over my last story. Outlined—which is as far as I take stories now—but dead in embryo. My hand stilled by cowardice, my heart the heart of a slave.

page 14

Of course Mordecai wanted to see the story. What did I have to lose?

"Flip over a few pages," I said. "It is the very skeleton of a story, but one that maybe someday I will write."

"The One-Legged Woman," Mordecai began to read aloud, then continued silently.

> The characters are poor dairy farmers. One morning the husband is too hung over to do the milking. His wife does it and when she has finished the cows are frightened by thunder and stampede, trampling her. She is also hooked severely in one leg. Her husband is asleep and does not hear her cry out. Finally she drags herself home and wakes him up. He washes her wounds and begs her to forgive him. He does not go for a doctor because he is afraid the doctor will accuse him of being lazy and a drunk, undeserving of his good wife. He wants the doctor to respect him. The wife, understanding, goes along with this.
>
> However, gangrene sets in and the doctor comes. He lectures the husband and amputates the leg of the wife. The wife lives and tries to forgive her husband for his weakness.
>
> While she is ill the husband tries to show he loves her, but cannot look at the missing leg. When she is well he finds he can no longer make love to her. The wife, sensing his revulsion, understands her sacrifice was for nothing. She drags herself to the barn and hangs herself.
>
> The husband, ashamed that anyone should know he was married to a one-legged woman, buries her himself and later tells everyone that she is visiting her mother.

While Mordecai was reading the story I looked out over the fields. If he says one good thing about what I've written, I promised myself, I will go to bed with him. (How else could I repay him? All I owned in any supply were my jars of cold cream!) As if he read my mind he sank down on the seat beside me and looked at me strangely.

"*You* think about things like this?" he asked.

He took me in his arms, right there in the grape arbor. "You sure do have a lot of heavy, sexy hair," he said, placing me gently on the ground. After that, a miracle happened. Under Mordecai's fingers my body opened like a flower and carefully bloomed. And it was strange as well as wonderful. For I don't think love had anything to do with this at all.

page 17

After that, Mordecai praised me for my intelligence, my sensitivity, the depth of the work he had seen—and naturally I showed him everything I had: old journals from high school, notebooks I kept hidden under tarpaulin in the barn, stories written on paper bags, on table napkins, even on shelf paper from over the sink. I am amazed—even more amazed than Mordecai—by the amount of stuff I have written. It is over twenty years' worth, and would fill, easily, a small shed.

"You must give these to me," Mordecai said finally, holding three notebooks he selected from the rather messy pile. "I will see if something can't be done with them. You could be another Zora Hurston—" he smiled—"another Simone de Beauvoir!"

Of course I am flattered. "Take it! Take it!" I cry. Already I see myself as he sees me. A famous authoress, miles away from Ruel, miles away from anybody. I am dressed in dungarees, my hands are a mess. I smell of sweat. I glow with happiness.

"How could such pretty brown fingers write such ugly, deep stuff?" Mordecai asks, kissing them.

page 20

For a week we deny each other nothing. If Ruel knows (how could he not know? His sheets are never fresh), he says nothing. I realize now that he never considered Mordecai a threat. Because Mordecai seems to have nothing to offer but his skinny self and his funny talk. I gloat over this knowledge. Now Ruel will find that I am not a womb without a brain that can be bought with Japanese bathtubs and shopping sprees. The moment of my deliverance is at hand!

page 24

Mordecai did not come today. I sit in the arbor writing down those words and my throat begins to close up. I am nearly strangled by my fear.

page 56

I have not noticed anything for weeks. Not Ruel, not the house. Everything whispers to me that Mordecai has forgotten me. Yesterday Ruel told me not to go into town and I said I wouldn't, for I have been hunting Mordecai up and down the streets. People look at me strangely, their glances slide off me in a peculiar way. It is as if they see something on my face that embarrasses them. Does everyone know about Mordecai and me? Does good loving show so soon? . . . But it is not soon. He has been gone already longer than I have known him.

page 61

Ruel tells me I act like my mind's asleep. It is asleep, of course. Nothing will wake it but a letter from Mordecai telling me to pack my bags and fly to New York.

page 65

If I could have read Mordecai's scribble pad I would know exactly what he thought of me. But now I realize he never once offered to show it to me, though he had a chance to read every serious thought I ever had. I'm afraid to know what he thought. I feel crippled, deformed. But if he ever wrote it down, that would make it true.

page 66

Today Ruel brought me in from the grape arbor, out of the rain. I didn't know it was raining. "Old folks like us might catch rheumatism if we don't be careful," he joked. I don't know what he means. I am thirty-two. He is forty. I never felt old before this month.

page 79

Ruel came up to bed last night and actually cried in my arms! He would give anything for a child, he says.

"Do you think we could have one?" he said.

"Sure," I said. "Why not?"

He began to kiss me and carry on about my goodness. I began to laugh. He became very angry, but finished what he started. He really does intend to have a child.

page 80

I must really think of something better to do than kill myself.

page 81

Ruel wants me to see a doctor about speeding up conception of the child.

"Will you go, honey?" he asks, like a beggar.

"Sure," I say. "Why not?"

page 82

Today at the doctor's office the magazine I was reading fell open at a story about a one-legged woman. They had a picture of her, drawn by someone who painted the cows orange and green, and painted the woman white, like a white cracker, with little slit-blue eyes. Not black and heavy like she was in the story I had in mind. But it is still my story, filled out and switched about as things are. The author is said to be Mordecai Rich. They show a little picture of him on a back page. He looks severe and has grown a beard. And underneath his picture there is that same statement he made to me about going around looking for Truth.

They say his next book will be called "The Black Woman's Resistance to Creativity in the Arts."

page 86

Last night while Ruel snored on his side of the bed I washed the prints of his hands off my body. Then I plugged in one of his chain saws and tried to slice off his head. This failed because of the noise. Ruel woke up right in the nick of time.

page 95

The days pass in a haze that is not unpleasant. The doctors and nurses do not take me seriously. They fill me full of drugs and never even bother to lock the door. When I think of Ruel I think of the song the British sing: "Ruel Britannia"! I can even whistle it, or drum it with my fingers.

SEPTEMBER, 1961

page 218

People tell my husband all the time that I do not look crazy. I have been out for almost a year and he is beginning to believe them. Nights, he climbs on me with his slobber and his hope, cursing Mordecai Rich for messing up his life. I wonder if he feels our wills clashing in the dark. Sometimes I see the sparks fly inside my head. It is amazing how normal everything is.

page 223

The house still does not awaken to the pitter-patter of sweet little feet, because I religiously use the Pill. It is the only spot of humor in my entire day, when I am gulping that little yellow tablet and washing it down with soda pop or tea. Ruel spends long hours at the store and in the peanut field. He comes in sweaty, dirty, tired, and I wait for him smelling of Arpège, My Sin, Wind Song, and Jungle Gardenia. The women of the community feel sorry for him, to be married to such a fluff of nothing.

I wait, beautiful and perfect in every limb, cooking supper as if my life depended on it. Lying unresisting on his bed like a drowned body washed to shore. But he is not happy. For he knows now that I intend to do nothing but say yes until he is completely exhausted.

I go to the new shopping mall twice a day now; once in the morning and once in the afternoon, or at night. I buy hats I would not dream of wearing, or even owning. Dresses that are already on their way to Goodwill. Shoes that will go to mold and mildew in the cellar. And I keep the bottles of perfume, the skin softeners, the pots of gloss and eye shadow. I amuse myself painting my own face.

When he is quite, quite tired of me I will tell him how long I've relied on the security of the Pill. When I am quite, quite tired of the sweet, sweet smell of my body and the softness of these Helena Rubenstein hands I will leave him and this house. Leave them forever without once looking back.

QUESTIONS FOR DISCUSSION AND WRITING

1. How does the first section of the story (September, 1961) introduce the conflicts reported in the middle section of the story (May, 1958)? How does the narrator's discovery of Mordecai Rich's "story" in the magazine mark the crisis? In the last section (September, 1961), how does the narrator decide to resolve that crisis?

2. Given the events in the story, what is ironic about the narrator's initial statement that she is "not a serious writer"? What is Ruel's opinion of his wife's desire to be a writer? How does Mordecai's statement that he is "a cold eye" help explain his motives? To what extent is Ruel correct in his assessment of Mordecai as a "skinny black tramp"?

3. How do the two houses—the old one where the narrator meets Mordecai, and the new one where she is supposed to forget the past—embody the major conflicts in the story? How does the narrator's preoccupation with beauty products suggest the degree to which she is at odds with her setting?

4. How does the narrator's journal trace the growing awareness of her loss? For example, what kind of emotions and observations has she probably documented in the missing pages of her journal? How does her story of the one-legged lady comment on her own "sacrifice"?

5. How does the title of the story establish its theme? How does the discussion of the artist's search for Truth and Beauty comment on Mordecai's crime? How many other crimes are committed in the story? Which ones seem to "pay"?

95

EUDORA WELTY

A Worn Path

EUDORA WELTY was born in 1909 in Jackson, Mississippi, and educated at Mississippi State College for Women, the University of Wisconsin, and, for a brief period, the School of Business at Columbia University. During the Depression, Welty returned to Mississippi to write for newspapers and radio stations and to photograph and interview local residents for the Works Progress Administration. Welty's photographs were exhibited in New York City in 1936. During the 1930s Welty also began to publish her short stories in magazines such as *The Southern Review, The New Yorker,* and *The Atlantic Monthly,* winning the 1941 O. Henry Award for "A Worn Path." Welty has continued to live in Jackson, where she has written an impressive body of fiction that evokes a strong sense of her "place." Her stories have been collected in *A Curtain of Green and Other Stories* (1941), *The Wide Net and Other Stories* (1943), *The Golden Apples* (1949), *The Bride of the Innisfallen and Other Stories* (1955), and *The Collected Stories of Eudora Welty* (1980). Welty is also the author of three longer works of fiction, *The Ponder Heart* (1954), *Losing Battles* (1970), and *The Optimist's Daughter* (1972), which was awarded the Pulitzer Prize. Welty's collection of essays and reviews, *The Eye of the Story,* appeared in 1977. In her most recent book, *One Writer's Beginnings* (1984), she discusses the origins of her craft. "A Worn Path," "Petrified Man," and "Why I Live at the P.O." are reprinted from *A Curtain of Green.* The first documents an old woman's arduous journey to accomplish an important mission; the second reveals the lives of several women through their dialogue in a beauty parlor; and the third dramatizes the comic conflicts in an extended Southern family.

It was December—a bright frozen day in the early morning. Far out in the country there was an old Negro woman with her head tied in a red rag, coming along a path through the pinewoods. Her name was Phoenix Jackson. She was very old and small and she walked slowly in the dark pine shadows, moving a little from side to side in her steps, with the balanced heaviness and lightness of a pendulum in a grandfather clock. She carried a thin, small cane made from an umbrella, and with this she kept tapping the frozen earth in front of her. This made a grave and persistent noise in the still air, that seemed meditative like the chirping of a solitary little bird.

She wore a dark striped dress reaching down to her shoe tops, and an equally long apron of bleached sugar sacks, with a full pocket: all neat and tidy, but every time she took a step she might have fallen over her shoelaces, which dragged from her unlaced shoes. She looked straight ahead. Her eyes were blue with age. Her skin had a pattern all its own of numberless branching wrinkles and as though a whole little tree stood in the middle of her forehead, but a golden color ran underneath, and the two knobs of her cheeks were illuminated by a yellow burning under the dark. Under the red rag her hair came down on her neck in the frailest of ringlets, still black, and with an odor like copper.

Now and then there was a quivering in the thicket. Old Phoenix said, "Out of my way, all you foxes, owls, beetles, jack rabbits, coons and wild animals! . . . Keep out from under these feet, little bob-whites. . . . Keep the big wild hogs out of my path. Don't let none of those come running my direction. I got a long way." Under her small black-freckled hand her cane, limber as a buggy whip, would switch at the brush as if to rouse up any hiding things.

On she went. The woods were deep and still. The sun made the pine needles almost too bright to look at, up where the wind rocked. The cones dropped as light as feathers. Down in the hollow was the mourning dove—it was not too late for him.

The path ran up a hill. "Seem like there is chains about my feet, time I get this far," she said, in the voice of argument old people keep to use with themselves. "Something always take a hold of me on this hill—pleads I should stay."

After she got to the top she turned and gave a full, severe look behind her where she had come. "Up through pines," she said at length. "Now down through oaks."

Her eyes opened their widest, and she started down gently. But before she got to the bottom of the hill a bush caught her dress.

Her fingers were busy and intent, but her skirts were full and long, so that before she could pull them free in one place they were caught in another. It was not possible to allow the dress to tear. "I in the thorny bush," she said. "Thorns, you doing your appointed work. Never want to let folks pass, no sir. Old eyes thought you was a pretty little *green* bush."

Finally, trembling all over, she stood free, and after a moment dared to stoop for her cane.

"Sun so high!" she cried, leaning back and looking, while the thick tears went over her eyes. "The time getting all gone here."

At the foot of this hill was a place where a log was laid across the creek.

"Now comes the trial," said Phoenix.

Putting her right foot out, she mounted the log and shut her eyes. Lifting her skirt, leveling her cane fiercely before her, like a festival figure in some parade, she began to march across. Then she opened her eyes and she was safe on the other side.

"I wasn't as old as I thought," she said.

But she sat down to rest. She spread her skirts on the bank around her and folded her hands over her knees. Up above her was a tree in a pearly cloud of mistletoe. She did not dare to close her eyes, and when a little boy brought her a plate with a slice of marble-cake on it she spoke to him. "That would be acceptable," she said. But when she went to take it there was just her own hand in the air.

So she left that tree, and had to go through a barbed-wire fence. There she had to creep and crawl, spreading her knees and stretching her fingers like a baby trying to climb the steps. But she talked loudly to herself: she could not let her dress be torn now, so late in the day, and she could not pay for having her arm or her leg sawed off if she got caught fast where she was.

At last she was safe through the fence and risen up out in the clearing. Big dead trees, like black men with one arm, were standing in the purple stalks of the withered cotton field. There sat a buzzard.

"Who you watching?"

In the furrow she made her way along.

"Glad this not the season for bulls," she said, looking sideways, "and the good Lord made his snakes to curl up and sleep in the winter. A pleasure I don't see no two-headed snake coming around that tree, where it come once. It took a while to get by him, back in the summer."

She passed through the old cotton and went into a field of dead corn. It whispered and shook and was taller than her head. "Through the maze now," she said, for there was no path.

Then there was something tall, black, and skinny there, moving before her.

At first she took it for a man. It could have been a man dancing in the field. But she stood still and listened, and it did not make a sound. It was as silent as a ghost.

"Ghost," she said sharply, "who be you the ghost of? For I have heard of nary death close by."

But there was no answer—only the ragged dancing in the wind.

She shut her eyes, reached out her hand, and touched a sleeve. She found a coat and inside that an emptiness, cold as ice.

"You scarecrow," she said. Her face lighted. "I ought to be shut up for good," she said with laughter. "My senses is gone. I too old. I the oldest people I ever know. Dance, old scarecrow," she said, "while I dancing with you."

She kicked her foot over the furrow, and with mouth drawn down, shook her head once or twice in a little strutting way. Some husks blew down and whirled in streamers about her skirts.

Then she went on, parting her way from side to side with the cane, through the whispering field. At last she came to the end, to a wagon track where the silver grass blew between the red ruts. The quail were walking around like pullets, seeming all dainty and unseen.

"Walk pretty," she said. "This the easy place. This the easy going."

She followed the track, swaying through the quiet bare fields, through the little strings of trees silver in their dead leaves, past cabins silver from weather, with the doors and windows boarded shut, all like old women under a spell sitting there. "I walking in their sleep," she said, nodding her head vigorously.

In a ravine she went where a spring was silent flowing through a hollow log. Old Phoenix bent and drank. "Sweet-gum makes the water sweet," she said, and drank more. "Nobody know who made this well, for it was here when I was born."

The track crossed a swampy part where the moss hung as white as lace from every limb. "Sleep on, alligators, and blow your bubbles." Then the track went into the road.

Deep, deep the road went down between the high green-colored banks. Overhead the live-oaks met, and it was as dark as a cave.

A black dog with a lolling tongue came up out of the weeds by the ditch. She was meditating, and not ready, and when he came at her she only hit him a little with her cane. Over she went in the ditch, like a little puff of milkweed.

Down there, her senses drifted away. A dream visited her, and she reached her hand up, but nothing reached down and gave her a pull. So she lay there and presently went to talking. "Old woman," she said to herself, "that black dog come up out of the weeds to stall you off, and now there he sitting on his fine tail, smiling at you."

A white man finally came along and found her—a hunter, a young man, with his dog on a chain.

"Well, Granny!" he laughed. "What are you doing there?"

"Lying on my back like a June-bug waiting to be turned over, mister," she said, reaching up her hand.

He lifted her up, gave her a swing in the air, and set her down. "Anything broken, Granny?"

"No, sir, them old dead weeds is springy enough," said Phoenix, when she had got her breath. "I thank you for your trouble."

"Where do you live, Granny?" he asked, while the two dogs were growling at each other.

"Away back yonder, sir, behind the ridge. You can't even see it from here."

"On your way home?"

"No sir, I going to town."

"Why, that's too far! That's as far as I walk when I come out myself, and I get something for my trouble." He patted the stuffed bag he carried, and there hung down a little closed claw. It was one of the bob-whites, and its beak hooked bitterly to show it was dead. "Now you go home, Granny!"

"I bound to go to town, mister," said Phoenix. "The time come around."

He gave another laugh, filling the whole landscape. "I know you old colored people! Wouldn't miss going to town to see Santa Claus!"

But something held old Phoenix very still. The deep lines in her face went into a fierce and different radiation. Without warning, she had seen with her own eyes a flashing nickel fall out of the man's pocket onto the ground.

"How old are you, Granny?" he was saying.

"There is no telling, mister," she said, "no telling."

Then she gave a little cry and clapped her hands and said, "Git on away from here, dog! Look! Look at that dog!" She laughed as if in admiration. "He ain't scared of nobody. He a big black dog." She whispered, "Sic him!"

"Watch me get rid of that cur," said the man. "Sic him, Pete! Sic him!"

Phoenix heard the dogs fighting, and heard the man running and throwing sticks. She even heard a gunshot. But she was slowly bending forward by that time, further and further forward, the lids stretched down over her eyes, as if she were doing this in her sleep. Her chin was lowered almost to her knees. The yellow palm of her hand came out from the fold of her apron. Her fingers slid down and along the ground under the piece of money with the grace and care they would have in lifting an egg from under a setting hen. Then she slowly straightened up, she stood erect, and the nickel was in her apron pocket. A bird flew by. Her lips moved. "God watching me the whole time. I come to stealing."

The man came back, and his own dog panted about them. "Well, I scared him off that time," he said, and then he laughed and lifted his gun and pointed it at Phoenix.

She stood straight and faced him.

"Doesn't the gun scare you?" he said, still pointing it.

"No, sir, I seen plenty go off closer by, in my day, and for less than what I done," she said, holding utterly still.

He smiled, and shouldered the gun. "Well, Granny," he said, "you must be a hundred years old, and scared of nothing. I'd give you a dime if I had any money with me. But you take my advice and stay home, and nothing will happen to you."

"I bound to go on my way, mister," said Phoenix. She inclined her head in the red rag. Then they went in different directions, but she could hear the gun shooting again and again over the hill.

She walked on. The shadows hung from the oak trees to the road like curtains. Then she smelled wood-smoke, and smelled the river, and she saw a steeple and the cabins on their steep steps. Dozens of little black children whirled around her. There ahead was Natchez shining. Bells were ringing. She walked on.

In the paved city it was Christmas time. There were red and green electric lights strung and criss-crossed everywhere, and all turned on in the daytime. Old Phoenix would have been lost if she had not distrusted her eyesight and depended on her feet to know where to take her.

She paused quietly on the sidewalk where people were passing by. A lady came along in the crowd, carrying an armful of red-, green- and silver-wrapped presents; she gave off perfume like the red roses in hot summer, and Phoenix stopped her.

"Please, missy, will you lace up my shoe?" She held up her foot.

"What do you want, Grandma?"

"See my shoe," said Phoenix. "Do all right for out in the country, but wouldn't look right to go in a big building."

"Stand still then, Grandma," said the lady. She put her packages down on the sidewalk beside her and laced and tied both shoes tightly.

"Can't lace 'em with a cane," said Phoenix. "Thank you, missy. I doesn't mind asking a nice lady to tie up my shoe, when I gets out on the street."

Moving slowly and from side to side, she went into the big building, and into a tower of steps, where she walked up and around and around until her feet knew to stop.

She entered a door, and there she saw nailed up on the wall the document that had been stamped with the gold seal and framed in the gold frame, which matched the dream that was hung up in her head.

"Here I be," she said. There was a fixed and ceremonial stiffness over her body.

"A charity case, I suppose," said an attendant who sat at the desk before her.

But Phoenix only looked above her head. There was sweat on her face, the wrinkles in her skin shone like a bright net.

"Speak up, Grandma," the woman said. "What's your name? We must have your history, you know. Have you been here before? What seems to be the trouble with you?"

Old Phoenix only gave a twitch to her face as if a fly were bothering her.

"Are you deaf?" cried the attendant.

But then the nurse came in.

"Oh, that's just old Aunt Phoenix," she said. "She doesn't come for herself—she has a little grandson. She makes these trips just as regular as clockwork. She lives away back off the Old Natchez Trace." She bent down. "Well, Aunt Phoenix, why don't you just take a seat? We won't keep you standing after your long trip." She pointed.

The old woman sat down, bolt upright in the chair.

"Now, how is the boy?" asked the nurse.

Old Phoenix did not speak.

"I said, how is the boy?"

But Phoenix only waited and stared straight ahead, her face very solemn and withdrawn into rigidity.

"Is his throat any better?" asked the nurse. "Aunt Phoenix, don't you hear me? Is your grandson's throat any better since the last time you came for the medicine?"

With her hands on her knees, the old woman waited, silent, erect and motionless, just as if she were in armor.

"You mustn't take up our time this way, Aunt Phoenix," the nurse said. "Tell us quickly about your grandson, and get it over. He isn't dead, is he?"

At last there came a flicker and then a flame of comprehension across her face, and she spoke.

"My grandson. It was my memory had left me. There I sat and forgot why I made my long trip."

"Forgot?" The nurse frowned. "After you came so far?"

Then Phoenix was like an old woman begging a dignified forgiveness for waking up frightened in the night. "I never did go to school, I was too old at the Surrender," she said in a soft voice. "I'm an old woman without an education. It was my memory fail me. My little grandson, he is just the same, and I forgot it in the coming."

"Throat never heals, does it?" said the nurse, speaking in a loud, sure voice to old Phoenix. By now she had a card with something written on it, a little list. "Yes. Swallowed lye. When was it?—January—two-three years ago—"

Phoenix spoke unasked now. "No, missy, he not dead, he just the same. Every little while his throat begin to close up again, and he not able to swallow. He not get his breath. He not able to help himself. So the time come around, and I go on another trip for the soothing medicine."

"All right. The doctor said as long as you came to get it, you could have it," said the nurse. "But it's an obstinate case."

"My little grandson, he sit up there in the house all wrapped up, waiting by himself," Phoenix went on. "We is the only two left in the world. He suffer and it don't seem to put him back at all. He got a sweet look. He going to last. He wear a little patch quilt and peep out holding his mouth open like a little bird. I remembers so plain now. I not going to forget him again, no, the whole enduring time. I could tell him from all the others in creation."

"All right." The nurse was trying to hush her now. She brought her a bottle of medicine. "Charity," she said, making a check mark in a book.

Old Phoenix held the bottle close to her eyes, and then carefully put it into her pocket.

"I thank you," she said.

"It's Christmas time, Grandma," said the attendant. "Could I give you a few pennies out of my purse?"

"Five pennies is a nickel," said Phoenix stiffly.

"Here's a nickel," said the attendant.

Phoenix rose carefully and held out her hand. She received the nickel and then fished the other nickel out of her pocket and laid it beside the new one. She stared at her palm closely, with her head on one side.

Then she gave a tap with her cane on the floor.

"This is what come to me to do," she said. "I going to the store and buy my child a little windmill they sells, made out of paper. He going to find it hard to believe there such a thing in the world. I'll march myself back where he waiting, holding it straight up in his hand."

She lifted her free hand, gave a little nod, turned around, and walked out of the doctor's office. Then her slow step began on the stairs, going down.

QUESTIONS FOR DISCUSSION AND WRITING

1. What does Welty accomplish by withholding the purpose of Phoenix's journey until the end of the story? To what extent does the hunter's comment about "getting something for his trouble" foreshadow the climax of the story? Why does Phoenix's decision to buy a paper windmill bring the story to a satisfactory conclusion?
2. What specific details of Phoenix's external appearance and behavior help establish her character? In what ways does Phoenix's name provide a clue to her character? How do the attendant and nurse characterize themselves and Phoenix during their conversation about the grandson?
3. How does the title define the setting of the story? What landmarks on the path are familiar to Phoenix? What objects and events surprise her? How does her concern about tying her shoes signal her arrival in a new setting?
4. What effect does Welty create by using an objective rather than first-person point of view in this story? What does Phoenix's conversation with herself reveal about her attitude toward herself and her journey?
5. What does this story reveal about the trials, wisdom, and dignity of old age? To what extent does the hunter's allusion to Santa Claus or the nurse's notation of "charity" demean the achievement of Phoenix's journey?

96

EUDORA WELTY

Petrified Man

"Reach in my purse and git me a cigarette without no powder in it if you kin, Mrs. Fletcher, honey," said Leota to her ten o'clock shampoo-and-set customer. "I don't like no perfumed cigarettes."

Mrs. Fletcher gladly reached over to the lavender shelf under the lavender-framed mirror, shook a hair net loose from the clasp of the patent-leather bag, and slapped her hand down quickly on a powder puff which burst out when the purse was opened.

"Why, look at the peanuts, Leota!" said Mrs. Fletcher in her marvelling voice.

"Honey, them goobers has been in my purse a week if they's been in it a day. Mrs. Pike bought them peanuts."

"Who's Mrs. Pike?" asked Mrs. Fletcher, settling back. Hidden in this den of curling fluid and henna packs, separated by a lavender swing-door from the other customers, who were being gratified in other booths, she could give her curiosity its freedom. She looked expectantly at the black part in Leota's yellow curls as she bent to light the cigarette.

"Mrs. Pike is this lady from New Orleans," said Leota, puffing, and pressing into Mrs. Fletcher's scalp with strong red-nailed fingers. "A friend, not a customer. You see, like maybe I told you last time, me and Fred and Sal and Joe all had us a fuss, so Sal and Joe up and moved out, so we didn't do a thing but rent out their room. So we rented it to Mrs. Pike. And Mr. Pike." She flicked an ash into the basket of dirty towels. "Mrs. Pike is a very decided blonde. *She* bought me the peanuts."

"She must be cute," said Mrs. Fletcher.

"Honey, 'cute' ain't the word for what she is. I'm tellin' you, Mrs. Pike is attractive. She has her a good time. She's got a sharp eye out, Mrs. Pike has."

She dashed the comb through the air, and paused dramatically as a cloud of Mrs. Fletcher's hennaed hair floated out of the lavender teeth like a small storm-cloud.

"Hair fallin'."

"Aw, Leota."

"Uh-huh, commencin' to fall out," said Leota, combing again, and letting fall another cloud.

"Is it any dandruff in it?" Mrs. Fletcher was frowning, her hair-line eyebrows diving down toward her nose, and her wrinkled, beady-lashed eyelids batting with concentration.

"Nope." She combed again. "Just fallin' out."

"Bet it was that last perm'nent you gave me that did it," Mrs. Fletcher said cruelly. "Remember you cooked me fourteen minutes."

"You had fourteen minutes comin' to you," said Leota with finality.

"Bound to be somethin'," persisted Mrs. Fletcher. "Dandruff, dandruff. I couldn't of caught a thing like that from Mr. Fletcher, could I?"

"Well," Leota answered at last, "you know what I heard in here yestiddy, one of Thelma's ladies was settin' over yonder in Thelma's booth gittin' a machineless, and I don't mean to insist or insinuate or anything, Mrs. Fletcher, but Thelma's lady just happ'ned to throw out—I forgotten what she was talkin' about at the time—that you was p-r-e-g., and lots of times that'll make your hair do awful funny, fall out and God knows what all. It just ain't our fault, is the way I look at it."

There was a pause. The women stared at each other in the mirror.

"Who was it?" demanded Mrs. Fletcher.

"Honey, I really couldn't say," said Leota. "Not that you look it."

"Where's Thelma? I'll get it out of her," said Mrs. Fletcher.

"Now, honey, I wouldn't go and git mad over a little thing like that," Leota said, combing hastily, as though to hold Mrs. Fletcher down by the hair. "I'm sure it was somebody didn't mean no harm in the world. How far gone are you?"

"Just wait," said Mrs. Fletcher, and shrieked for Thelma, who came in and took a drag from Leota's cigarette.

"Thelma, honey, throw your mind back to yestiddy if you kin," said Leota, drenching Mrs. Fletcher's hair with a thick fluid and catching the overflow in a cold wet towel at her neck.

"Well, I got my lady half wound for a spiral," said Thelma doubtfully.

"This won't take but a minute," said Leota. "Who is it you got in there, old Horse Face? Just cast your mind back and try to remember who your lady was yestiddy who happ'm to mention that my customer was pregnant, that's all. She's dead to know."

Thelma drooped her blood-red lips and looked over Mrs. Fletcher's head into the mirror. "Why, honey, I ain't got the faintest," she breathed. "I really don't recollect the faintest. But I'm sure she meant no harm. I declare, I forgot my hair finally got combed and thought it was a stranger behind me."

"Was it that Mrs. Hutchinson?" Mrs. Fletcher was tensely polite.

"Mrs. Hutchinson? Oh, Mrs. Hutchinson." Thelma batted her eyes. "Naw, precious, she come in Thursday and didn't ev'm mention your name. I doubt if she ev'm knows you're on the way."

"Thelma!" cried Leota staunchly.

"All I know is, whoever it is 'll be sorry some day. Why, I just barely knew it myself!" cried Mrs. Fletcher. "Just let her wait!"

"Why? What're you gonna do to her?"

It was a child's voice, and the women looked down. A little boy was making tents with aluminum wave pinchers on the floor under the sink.

"Billy Boy, hon, mustn't bother nice ladies," Leota smiled. She slapped him brightly and behind her back waved Thelma out of the booth. "Ain't Billy Boy a sight? Only three years old and already just nuts about the beauty-parlor business."

"I never saw him here before," said Mrs. Fletcher, still unmollified.

"He ain't been here before, that's how come," said Leota. "He belongs to Mrs. Pike. She got her a job but it was Fay's Millinery. He oughtn't to try on those ladies' hats, they come down over his eyes like I don't know what. They just git to look ridiculous, that's what, an' of course he's gonna put 'em on: hats. They tole Mrs. Pike they didn't appreciate him hangin' around there. Here, he couldn't hurt a thing."

"Well! I don't like children that much," said Mrs. Fletcher.

"Well!" said Leota moodily.

"Well! I'm almost tempted not to have this one," said Mrs. Fletcher. "That Mrs. Hutchinson! Just looks straight through you when she sees you on the street and then spits at you behind your back."

"Mr. Fletcher would beat you on the head if you didn't have it now," said Leota reasonably. "After going this far."

Mrs. Fletcher sat up straight. "Mr. Fletcher can't do a thing with me."

"He can't!" Leota winked at herself in the mirror.

"No, siree, he can't. If he so much as raises his voice against me, he knows good and well I'll have one of my sick headaches, and then I'm just not fit to live with. And if I really look that pregnant already—"

"Well, now, honey, I just want you to know—I habm't told any of my ladies and I ain't goin' to tell 'em—even that you're losin' your hair. You just get you one of those Stork-a-Lure dresses and stop worryin'. What people don't know don't hurt nobody, as Mrs. Pike says."

"Did you tell Mrs. Pike?" asked Mrs. Fletcher sulkily.

"Well, Mrs. Fletcher, look, you ain't ever goin' to lay eyes on Mrs. Pike or her lay eyes on you, so what diffunce does it make in the long run?"

"I knew it!" Mrs. Fletcher deliberately nodded her head so as to destroy a ringlet Leota was working on behind her ear. "Mrs. Pike!"

Leota sighed. "I reckon I might as well tell you. It wasn't any more Thelma's lady tole me you was pregnant than a bat."

"Not Mrs. Hutchinson?"

"Naw, Lord! It was Mrs. Pike."

"Mrs. Pike!" Mrs. Fletcher could only sputter and let curling fluid roll into her ear. "How could Mrs. Pike possibly know I was pregnant or otherwise, when she doesn't even know me? The nerve of some people!"

"Well, here's how it was. Remember Sunday?"

"Yes," said Mrs. Fletcher.

"Sunday, Mrs. Pike an' me was all by ourself. Mr. Pike and Fred had gone over to Eagle Lake, sayin' they was goin' to catch 'em some fish, but they didn't a course. So we was settin' in Mrs. Pike's car, it's a 1939 Dodge—"

"1939, eh," said Mrs. Fletcher.

"—An' we was gettin' us a Jax beer apiece—that's the beer that Mrs. Pike says is made right in N.O., so she won't drink no other kind. So I seen you drive up to the drugstore an' run in for just a secont, leavin' I reckon Mr. Fletcher in the car, an' come runnin' out with looked like a perscription. So I says to Mrs. Pike, just to be makin' talk, 'Right yonder's Mrs. Fletcher, and I reckon that's Mr. Fletcher—she's one of my regular customers,' I says."

"I had on a figured print," said Mrs. Fletcher tentatively.

"You sure did," agreed Leota. "So Mrs. Pike, she give you a good look—she's very observant, a good judge of character, cute as a minute, you know—and she says, 'I bet you another Jax that lady's three months on the way.'"

"What gall!" said Mrs. Fletcher. "Mrs. Pike!"

"Mrs. Pike ain't goin' to bite you," said Leota. "Mrs. Pike is a lovely girl, you'd be crazy about her, Mrs. Fletcher. But she can't sit still a minute. We went to the travellin' freak show yestiddy after work. I got through early—nine o'clock. In the vacant store next door. What, you ain't been?"

"No, I despise freaks," declared Mrs. Fletcher.

"Aw. Well, honey, talkin' about bein' pregnant an' all, you ought to see those twins in a bottle, you really owe it to yourself."

"What twins?" asked Mrs. Fletcher out of the side of her mouth.

"Well, honey, they got these two twins in a bottle, see? Born joined plumb together—dead a course." Leota dropped her voice into a soft lyrical hum. "They was about this long—pardon—must of been full time, all right, wouldn't you say?—an' they had these two heads an' two faces an' four arms an' four legs, all kind of joined *here*. See, this face looked this-a-way, and the other face looked that-a-way, over their shoulder, see. Kinda pathetic."

"Glah!" said Mrs. Fletcher disapprovingly.

"Well, ugly? Honey, I mean to tell you—their parents was first cousins and all like that. Billy Boy, git me a fresh towel from off Teeny's stack—this 'n's wringin' wet—an' quit ticklin' my ankles with that curler. I declare! He don't miss nothin'."

"Me and Mr. Fletcher aren't one speck of kin, or he could never of had me," said Mrs. Fletcher placidly.

"Of course not!" protested Leota. "Neither is me an' Fred, not that we know of. Well, honey, what Mrs. Pike liked was the pygmies. They've got these pygmies down there, too, an' Mrs. Pike was just wild about 'em. You know, the teeniest men in the universe? Well, honey, they can just rest back on their little bohunkus an' roll around an' you can't hardly tell if they're sittin' or standin'. That'll give you some idea. They're about forty-two years old. Just suppose it was your husband!"

"Well, Mr. Fletcher is five foot nine and one half," said Mrs. Fletcher quickly.

"Fred's five foot ten," said Leota, "but I tell him he's still a shrimp, account of I'm so tall." She made a deep wave over Mrs. Fletcher's other temple with the comb. "Well, these pygmies are a kind of a dark brown, Mrs. Fletcher. Not bad lookin' for what they are, you know."

"I wouldn't care for them," said Mrs. Fletcher. "What does that Mrs. Pike see in them?"

"Aw, I don't know," said Leota. "She's just cute, that's all. But they got this man, this petrified man, that ever'thing ever since he was nine years old, when it goes through his digestion, see, somehow Mrs. Pike says it goes to his joints and has been turning to stone."

"How awful!" said Mrs. Fletcher.

"He's forty-two too. That looks like a bad age."

"Who said so, that Mrs. Pike? I bet she's forty-two," said Mrs. Fletcher.

"Naw," said Leota, "Mrs. Pike's thirty-three, born in January, an Aquarian. He could move his head—like this. A course his head and mind ain't a joint, so to speak, and I guess his stomach ain't, either—not yet, anyways. But see—his food, he eats it, and it goes down, see, and then he digests it"—Leota rose on her toes for an instant—"and it goes out to his joints and before you can say 'Jack Robinson,' it's stone—pure stone. He's turning to stone. How'd you like to be married to a guy like that? All he can do, he can move his head just a quarter of an inch. A course he *looks* just *terrible*."

"I should think he would," said Mrs. Fletcher frostily. "Mr. Fletcher takes bending exercises every night of the world. I make him."

"All Fred does is lay around the house like a rug. I wouldn't be surprised if he woke up some day and couldn't move. The petrified man just sat there moving his quarter of an inch though," said Leota reminiscently.

"Did Mrs. Pike like the petrified man?" asked Mrs. Fletcher.

"Not as much as she did the others," said Leota deprecatingly. "And then she likes a man to be a good dresser, and all that."

"Is Mr. Pike a good dresser?" asked Mrs. Fletcher sceptically.

"Oh, well, yeah," said Leota, "but he's twelve or fourteen years older'n her. She ast Lady Evangeline about him."

"Who's Lady Evangeline?" asked Mrs. Fletcher.

"Well, it's this mind reader they got in the freak show," said Leota. "Was real good. Lady Evangeline is her name, and if I had another dollar I wouldn't do a thing but have my other palm read. She had what Mrs. Pike said was the 'sixth mind' but she had the worst manicure I ever saw on a living person."

"What did she tell Mrs. Pike?" asked Mrs. Fletcher.

"She told her Mr. Pike was as true to her as he could be and besides, would come into some money."

"Humph!" said Mrs. Fletcher. "What does he do?"

"I can't tell," said Leota, "because he don't work. Lady Evangeline didn't tell me enough about my nature or anything. And I would like to go back and find out some more about this boy. Used to go with this boy until he got married to this girl. Oh, shoot, that was about three and a half years ago, when you was still goin' to the Robert E. Lee Beauty Shop in Jackson. He married her for her money. Another fortune-teller tole me that at the time. So I'm not in love with him any more, anyway, besides being married to Fred, but Mrs. Pike thought, just for the hell of it, see, to ask Lady Evangeline was he happy."

"Does Mrs. Pike know everything about you already?" asked Mrs. Fletcher unbelievingly. "Mercy!"

"Oh, yeah, I tole her ever'thing about ever'thing, from now on back to I don't know when—to when I first started goin' out," said Leota. "So I ast Lady Evangeline for one of my questions, was he happily married, and she says, just like she was glad I ask her, 'Honey,' she says, 'naw, he idn't. You write down this day, March 8, 1941,' she says, 'and mock it down: three years from today him and her won't be occupyin' the same bed.' There it is, up on the wall with them other dates—see, Mrs. Fletcher? And she says, 'Child, you ought to be glad you didn't git him, because he's so mercenary.' So I'm glad I married Fred. He sure ain't mercenary, money don't mean a thing to him. But I sure would like to go back and have my other palm read."

"Did Mrs. Pike believe in what the fortune-teller said?" asked Mrs. Fletcher in a superior tone of voice.

"Lord, yes, she's from New Orleans. Ever'body in New Orleans believes ever'thing spooky. One of 'em in New Orleans before it was raided says to Mrs. Pike one summer she was goin' to go from State to State and meet some grey-headed men, and, sure enough, she says she went on a beautician convention up to Chicago. . . ."

"Oh!" said Mrs. Fletcher. "Oh, is Mrs. Pike a beautician too?"

"Sure she is," protested Leota. "She's a beautician. I'm going to git her in here if I can. Before she married. But it don't leave you. She says sure enough, there was three men who was a very large part of making her trip what it was, and they all three had grey in their hair and they went in six States. Got Christmas cards from 'em. Billy Boy, go see if Thelma's got any dry cotton. Look how Mrs. Fletcher's a-drippin'."

"Where did Mrs. Pike meet Mr. Pike?" asked Mrs. Fletcher primly.

"On another train," said Leota.

"I met Mr. Fletcher, or rather he met me, in a rental library," said Mrs. Fletcher with dignity, as she watched the net come down over her head.

"Honey, me an' Fred, we met in a rumble seat eight months ago and we was practically on what you might call the way to the altar inside of half an hour," said Leota in a guttural voice, and bit a bobby pin open. "Course it don't last. Mrs. Pike says nothin' like that ever lasts."

"Mr. Fletcher and myself are as much in love as the day we married," said Mrs. Fletcher belligerently as Leota stuffed cotton into her ears.

"Mrs. Pike says it don't last," repeated Leota in a louder voice. "Now go git under the dryer. You can turn yourself on, can't you? I'll be back to comb you out. Durin' lunch I promised to give Mrs. Pike a facial. You know—free. Her bein' in the business, so to speak."

"I bet she needs one," said Mrs. Fletcher, letting the swing-door fly back against Leota. "Oh, pardon me."

A week later, on time for her appointment, Mrs. Fletcher sank heavily into Leota's chair after first removing a drug-store rental book, called *Life Is Like That,* from the seat. She stared in a discouraged way into the mirror.

"You can tell it when I'm sitting down, all right," she said.

Leota seemed preoccupied and stood shaking out a lavender cloth. She began to pin it around Mrs. Fletcher's neck in silence.

"I said you sure can tell it when I'm sitting straight on and coming at you this way," Mrs. Fletcher said.

"Why, honey, naw you can't," said Leota gloomily. "Why, I'd never know. If somebody was to come up to me on the street and say, 'Mrs. Fletcher is pregnant!' I'd say, 'Heck, she don't look it to me.'"

"If a certain party hadn't found it out and spread it around, it wouldn't be too late even now," said Mrs. Fletcher frostily, but Leota was almost choking her with the cloth, pinning it so tight, and she couldn't speak clearly. She paddled her hands in the air until Leota wearily loosened her.

"Listen, honey, you're just a virgin compared to Mrs. Montjoy," Leota was going on, still absent-minded. She bent Mrs. Fletcher back in the chair and, sighing, tossed liquid from a teacup on to her head and dug both hands into her scalp. "You know Mrs. Montjoy—her husband's that premature-grey-headed fella?"

"She's in the Trojan Garden Club, is all I know," said Mrs. Fletcher.

"Well, honey," said Leota, but in a weary voice, "she come in here not the week before and not the day before she had her baby—she come in here the very selfsame day, I mean to tell you. Child, we was all plumb scared to death. There she was! Come for her shampoo an' set. Why, Mrs. Fletcher, in an hour an' twenty minutes she was layin' up there in the Babtist Hospital with a seb'm-pound son. It was that close a shave. I declare, if I hadn't been so tired I would of drank up a bottle of gin that night."

"What gall," said Mrs. Fletcher. "I never knew her at all well."

"See, her husband was waitin' outside in the car, and her bags was all packed an' in the back seat, an' she was all ready, 'cept she wanted her shampoo an' set. An' havin' one pain right after another. Her husband kep' comin' in here, scared-like, but couldn't do nothin' with her a course. She yelled bloody murder, too, but she always yelled her head off when I give her a perm'nent."

"She must of been crazy," said Mrs. Fletcher. "How did she look?"

"Shoot!" said Leota.

"Well, I can guess," said Mrs. Fletcher. "Awful."

"Just wanted to look pretty while she was havin' her baby, is all," said Leota airily. "Course, we was glad to give the lady what she was after—that's our motto—but I bet a hour later she wasn't payin' no mind to them little end curls. I bet she wasn't thinkin' about she ought to have on a net. It wouldn't of done her no good if she had."

"No, I don't suppose it would," said Mrs. Fletcher.

"Yeah man! She was a-yellin'. Just like when I give her perm'nent."

"Her husband ought to make her behave. Don't it seem that way to you?" asked Mrs. Fletcher. "He ought to put his foot down."

"Ha," said Leota. "A lot he could do. Maybe some women is soft."

"Oh, you mistake me, I don't mean for her to get soft—far from it! Women have to stand up for themselves, or there's just no telling. But now you take me—I ask Mr. Fletcher's advice now and then, and he appreciates it, especially on something important, like is it time for a permanent—not that I've told him about the baby. He says, 'Why, dear, go ahead!' Just ask their *advice*."

"Huh! If I ever ast Fred's advice we'd be floatin' down the Yazoo River on a houseboat or somethin' by this time," said Leota. "I'm sick of Fred. I told him to go over to Vicksburg."

"Is he going?" demanded Mrs. Fletcher.

"Sure. See, the fortune-teller—I went back and had my other palm read, since we've got to rent the room agin—said my lover was goin' to work in Vicksburg, so I don't know who she could mean, unless she meant Fred. And Fred ain't workin' here—that much is so."

"Is he going to work in Vicksburg?" asked Mrs. Fletcher. "And—"

"Sure. Lady Evangeline said so. Said the future is going to be brighter than the present. He don't want to go, but I ain't gonna put up with nothin' like that. Lays around the house an' bulls—did bull—with that good-for-nothin' Mr. Pike. He says if he goes who'll cook, but I says I never get to eat anyway—not meals. Billy Boy, take Mrs. Grover that *Screen Secrets* and leg it."

Mrs. Fletcher heard stamping feet go out the door.

"Is that that Mrs. Pike's little boy here again?" she asked, sitting up gingerly.

"Yeah, that's still him." Leota stuck out her tongue.

Mrs. Fletcher could hardly believe her eyes. "Well! How's Mrs. Pike, your attractive new friend with the sharp eyes who spreads it around town that perfect strangers are pregnant?" she asked in a sweetened tone.

"Oh, Mizziz Pike." Leota combed Mrs. Fletcher's hair with heavy strokes.

"You act like you're tired," said Mrs. Fletcher.

"Tired? Feel like it's four o'clock in the afternoon, already," said Leota. "I ain't told you the awful luck we had, me and Fred? It's the worst thing you ever heard of. Maybe *you* think Mrs. Pike's got sharp eyes. Shoot, there's a limit! Well, you know, we rented out our room to this Mr. and Mrs. Pike from New Orleans when Sal an' Joe Fentress got mad at us 'cause they drank up some home-brew we had in the closet—Sal an' Joe did. So, a week ago Sat'day Mr. and Mrs. Pike moved in. Well, I kinda fixed up the room, you know—put a sofa pillow on the couch and picked some ragged robbins and put in a vase, but they never did say they appreciated it. Anyway, then I put some old magazines on the table."

"I think that was lovely," said Mrs. Fletcher.

"Wait. So, come night 'fore last, Fred and this Mr. Pike, who Fred just took up with, was back from they said they was fishin', bein' as neither one of 'em has got a job to his name, and we was all settin' around in their room. So Mrs. Pike was settin' there readin' a old *Startling G-Man Tales* that was mine, mind you, I'd bought it myself, and all of a sudden she jumps!—into the air—you'd 'a' thought she'd set on a spider—an' says, 'Canfield'—ain't that silly, that's Mr. Pike—'Canfield, my God A'mighty,' she says, 'honey,' she says, 'we're rich, and you won't have to work.' Not that he turned one hand anyway. Well, me and Fred rushes over to her, and Mr. Pike, too, and there she sets, pointin' her finger at a photo in my copy of *Startling G-Man*. 'See that man?' yells Mrs. Pike. 'Remember him, Canfield?' 'Never forget a face,' says Mr. Pike. 'It's Mr. Petrie, that we stayed with him in the apartment next to ours in Toulouse Street in N.O. for six weeks. Mr. Petrie.' 'Well,' says Mrs. Pike, like she can't hold out one secont longer, 'Mr. Petrie is wanted for five hundred dollars cash, for rapin' four women in California, and I know where he is.' "

"Mercy!" said Mrs. Fletcher. "Where was he?"

At some time Leota had washed her hair and now she yanked her up by the back locks and sat her up.

"Know where he was?"

"I certainly don't," Mrs. Fletcher said. Her scalp hurt all over.

Leota flung a towel around the top of her customer's head. "Nowhere else but in that freak show! I saw him just as plain as Mrs. Pike. *He* was the petrified man!"

"Who would ever have thought that?" cried Mrs. Fletcher sympathetically.

"So Mr. Pike says, 'Well whatta you know about that,' an' he looks real hard at the photo and whistles. And she starts dancin' and singin' about their good luck. She meant our bad luck! I made a point of tellin' that fortune-teller the next time I saw her. I said, 'Listen, that magazine was layin' around the house for a month, and there was the freak show runnin' night an' day, not two steps away from my own beauty parlor, with Mr. Petrie just settin' there waitin'. An' it had to be Mr. and Mrs. Pike, almost perfect strangers.' "

"What gall," said Mrs. Fletcher. She was only sitting there, wrapped in a turban, but she did not mind.

"Fortune-tellers don't care. And Mrs. Pike, she goes around actin' like she thinks she was Mrs. God," said Leota. "So they're goin' to leave tomorrow, Mr. and Mrs. Pike. And in the meantime I got to keep that mean, bad little ole kid here, gettin' under my feet ever' minute of the day an' talkin' back too."

"Have they gotten the five hundred dollars' reward already?" asked Mrs. Fletcher.

"Well," said Leota, "at first Mr. Pike didn't want to do anything about it. Can you feature that? Said he kinda liked that ole bird and said he was real nice to 'em, lent 'em money or somethin'. But Mrs. Pike simply tole him he could just go to hell, and I can see her point. She says, 'You ain't worked a lick in six months, and here I make five hundred dollars in two seconts, and what thanks do I get for it? You go to hell, Canfield,' she says. "So," Leota went on in a despondent voice, "they called up the cops and they caught the ole bird, all right, right there in the freak show where I saw him with my own eyes, thinkin' he was petrified. He's the one. Did it under his real name—Mr. Petrie. Four women in California, all in the month of August. So Mrs. Pike gits five hundred dollars. And my magazine, and right next door to my beauty parlor. I cried all night, but Fred said it wasn't a bit of use and to go to sleep, because the whole thing was just a sort of coincidence—you know: can't do nothin' about it. He says it put him clean out of the notion of goin' to Vicksburg for a few days till we rent out the room again—no tellin' who we'll git this time."

"But can you imagine anybody knowing this old man, that's raped four women?" persisted Mrs. Fletcher, and she shuddered audibly. "Did Mrs. Pike *speak* to him when she met him in the freak show?"

Leota had begun to comb Mrs. Fletcher's hair. "I says to her, I says, 'I didn't notice you fallin' on his neck when he was the petrified man—don't tell me you didn't recognize your fine friend?' And she says, 'I didn't recognize him with that white powder all over his face. He just looked familiar.' Mrs. Pike says, 'and lots of people look familiar.' But she says that ole petrified man did put her in mind of somebody. She wondered who it was! Kep' her awake, which man she'd ever knew it reminded her of. So when she seen the photo, it all come to her. Like a flash. Mr. Petrie. The way he'd turn his head and look at her when she took him in his breakfast."

"Took him in his breakfast!" shrieked Mrs. Fletcher. "Listen—don't tell me. I'd a' felt something."

"Four women. I guess those women didn't have the faintest notion at the time they'd be worth a hundred an' twenty-five bucks a piece some day to Mrs. Pike. We ast her how old the fella was then, an' she says he musta had one foot in the grave, at least. Can you beat it?"

"Not really petrified at all, of course," said Mrs. Fletcher meditatively. She drew herself up. "I'd a' felt something," she said proudly.

"Shoot! I did feel somethin'," said Leota. "I tole Fred when I got home I felt so funny. I said, 'Fred, that ole petrified man sure did leave me with a funny feelin'.' He says, 'Funny-haha or funny-peculiar?' and I says, 'Funny-peculiar.'" She pointed her comb into the air emphatically.

"I'll bet you did," said Mrs. Fletcher.

They both heard a crackling noise.

Leota screamed. "Billy Boy! What you doin' in my purse?"

"Aw, I'm just eatin' these ole stale peanuts up," said Billy Boy.

"You come here to me!" screamed Leota, recklessly flinging down the comb, which scattered a whole ashtray full of bobby pins and knocked down a row of Coca-Cola bottles. "This is the last straw!"

"I caught him! I caught him!" giggled Mrs. Fletcher. "I'll hold him on my lap. You bad, bad boy, you! I guess I better learn how to spank little old bad boys," she said.

Leota's eleven o'clock customer pushed open the swing-door upon Leota paddling him heartily with the brush, while he gave angry but belittling screams which penetrated beyond the booth and filled the whole curious beauty parlor. From everywhere ladies began to gather round to watch the paddling. Billy Boy kicked both Leota and Mrs. Fletcher as hard as he could, Mrs. Fletcher with her new fixed smile.

Billy Boy stomped through the group of wildhaired ladies and went out the door, but flung back the words, "If you're so smart, why ain't you rich?"

QUESTIONS FOR DISCUSSION AND WRITING

1. What conflicts are revealed in Leota and Mrs. Fletcher's first conversation? What has happened between the first and second visit to bring these conflicts to a crisis? Why does the spanking of Billy Boy provide an appropriate conclusion to the story?
2. What specific features of Leota's conversation with Mrs. Fletcher help establish her character? How does Mrs. Fletcher characterize herself by her response to the public acknowledgment of her pregnancy? What causes Leota to change the assessment of Mrs. Pike's character?
3. What physical details does Welty use to evoke the environment of the beauty parlor? How do Leota's attitudes about men, appearance, and amusement establish her social class? In what ways is Mrs. Fletcher similar to and different from Leota?
4. How does Welty's choice of an objective point of view help reinforce the themes of the story? For example, why does Welty focus her attention on what Leota and Mrs. Fletcher say and do rather than what they think?
5. How does this story comment on the traditional attitudes toward love, marriage, and children? To what extent have all the men (and women) in the story become "petrified"? How does Billy Boy's final statement comment on the people and activity in the story?

97

EUDORA WELTY

Why I Live at the P.O.

I was getting along fine with Mama, Papa-Daddy and Uncle Rondo until my sister Stella-Rondo just separated from her husband and came back home again. Mr. Whitaker! Of course I went with Mr. Whitaker first, when he first appeared here in China Grove, taking "Pose Yourself!" photos, and Stella-Rondo broke us up. Told him I was one-sided. Bigger on one side than the other, which is a deliberate, calculated falsehood: I'm the same. Stella-Rondo is exactly twelve months to the day younger than I am and for that reason she's spoiled.

She's always had anything in the world she wanted and then she'd throw it away. Papa-Daddy gave her this gorgeous Add-a-Pearl necklace when she was eight years old and she threw it away playing baseball when she was nine, with only two pearls.

So as soon as she got married and moved away from home the first thing she did was separate! From Mr. Whitaker! This photographer with the popeyes she said she trusted. Came home from one of those towns up in Illinois and to our complete surprise brought this child of two.

Mama said she like to made her drop dead for a second. "Here you had this marvelous blonde child and never so much as wrote your mother a word about it," says Mama. "I'm thoroughly ashamed of you." But of course she wasn't.

Stella-Rondo just calmly takes off this *hat,* I wish you could see it. She says, "Why, Mama, Shirley-T.'s adopted, I can prove it."

"How?" says Mama, but all I says was, "H'm!" There I was over the hot stove, trying to stretch two chickens over five people and a completely unexpected child into the bargain, without one moment's notice.

"What do you mean—'H'm!'?" says Stella-Rondo, and Mama says, "I heard that, Sister."

I said that oh, I didn't mean a thing, only that whoever Shirley-T. was, she was the spit-image of Papa-Daddy if he'd cut off his beard, which of course he'd never do in the world. Papa-Daddy's Mama's papa and sulks.

Stella-Rondo got furious! She said, "Sister, I don't need to tell you you got a lot of nerve and always did have and I'll thank you to make no future reference to my adopted child whatsoever."

"Very well," I said. "Very well, very well. Of course I noticed at once she looks like Mr. Whitaker's side too. That frown. She looks like a cross between Mr. Whitaker and Papa-Daddy."

"Well, all I can say is she isn't."

"She looks exactly like Shirley Temple to me," says Mama, but Shirley-T. just ran away from her.

So the first thing Stella-Rondo did at the table was turn Papa-Daddy against me.

"Papa-Daddy," she says. He was trying to cut up his meat. "Papa-Daddy!" I was taken completely by surprise. Papa-Daddy is about a million years old and's got this long-long beard. "Papa-Daddy, Sister says she fails to understand why you don't cut off your beard."

So Papa-Daddy l-a-y-s down his knife and fork! He's real rich. Mama says he is, he says he isn't. So he says, "Have I heard correctly? You don't understand why I don't cut off my beard?"

"Why," I says, "Papa-Daddy, of course I understand, I did not say any such of a thing, the idea!"

He says, "Hussy!"

I says, "Papa-Daddy, you know I wouldn't any more want you to cut off your beard than the man in the moon. It was the farthest thing from my mind! Stella-Rondo sat there and made that up while she was eating breast of chicken."

But he says, "So the postmistress fails to understand why I don't cut off my beard. Which job I got you through my influence with the government. 'Bird's nest'—is that what you call it?"

Not that it isn't the next to smallest P.O. in the entire state of Mississippi.

I says, "Oh, Papa-Daddy," I says, "I didn't say any such of a thing, I never dreamed it was a bird's nest, I have always been grateful though this is the next to smallest P.O. in the state of Mississippi, and I do not enjoy being referred to as a hussy by my own grandfather."

But Stella-Rondo says, "Yes, you did say it too. Anybody in the world could of heard you, that had ears."

"Stop right there," says Mama, looking at *me*.

So I pulled my napkin straight back through the napkin ring and left the table.

As soon as I was out of the room Mama says, "Call her back, or she'll starve to death," but Papa-Daddy says, "This is the beard I started growing on the Coast when I was fifteen years old." He would of gone on till nightfall if Shirley-T. hadn't lost the Milky Way she ate in Cairo.

So Papa-Daddy says, "I am going out and lie in the hammock, and you can all sit here and remember my words. I'll never cut off my beard as long as I live, even one inch, and I don't appreciate it in you at all." Passed right by me in the hall and went straight out and got in the hammock.

It would be a holiday. It wasn't five minutes before Uncle Rondo suddenly appeared in the hall in one of Stella-Rondo's flesh-colored kimonos, all cut on the bias, like something Mr. Whitaker probably thought was gorgeous.

"Uncle Rondo!" I says. "I didn't know who that was! Where are you going?"

"Sister," he says, "get out of my way, I'm poisoned."

"If you're poisoned stay away from Papa-Daddy," I says. "Keep out of the hammock. Papa-Daddy will certainly beat you on the head if you come within forty miles of him. He thinks I deliberately said he ought to cut off his beard after he got me the P.O., and I've told him and told him and told him, and he acts like he just don't hear me. Papa-Daddy must of gone stone deaf."

"He picked a fine day to do it then," says Uncle Rondo, and before you could say "Jack Robinson" flew out in the yard.

What he'd really done, he'd drunk another bottle of that prescription. He does it every single Fourth of July as sure as shooting, and it's horribly expensive. Then he falls over in the hammock and snores. So he insisted on zigzagging right on out to the hammock, looking like a half-wit.

Papa-Daddy woke up with this horrible yell and right there without moving an inch he tried to turn Uncle Rondo against me. I heard every word he said. Oh, he told Uncle Rondo I didn't learn to read till I was eight years old and he didn't see how in the world I ever got the mail put up at the P.O., much less read it all, and he said if Uncle Rondo could only fathom the lengths he had gone to get me that job! And he said on the other hand he thought Stella-Rondo had a brilliant mind and deserved credit for getting out of town. All the time he was just lying there swinging as pretty as you please and looping out his beard, and poor Uncle Rondo was *pleading* with him to slow down the hammock, it was making him dizzy as a witch to watch it. But that's what Papa-Daddy likes about a hammock. So Uncle Rondo was too dizzy to get turned against me for the time being. He's Mama's only brother and is a good case of a one-track mind. Ask anybody. A certified pharmacist.

Just then I heard Stella-Rondo raising the upstairs window. While she was married she got this peculiar idea that it's cooler with the windows shut and locked. So she has to raise the window before she can make a soul hear her outdoors.

So she raises the window and says, "*Oh!*" You would have thought she was mortally wounded.

Uncle Rondo and Papa-Daddy didn't even look up, but kept right on with what they were doing. I had to laugh.

I flew up the stairs and threw the door open! I says, "What in the wide world's the matter, Stella-Rondo? You mortally wounded?"

"No," she says, "I am not mortally wounded but I wish you would do me the favor of looking out that window there and telling me what you see."

So I shade my eyes and look out the window.

"I see the front yard," I says.

"Don't you see any human beings?" she says.

"I see Uncle Rondo trying to run Papa-Daddy out of the hammock," I says. "Nothing more. Naturally, it's so suffocating-hot in the house, with all the windows shut and locked, everybody who cares to stay in their right mind will have to go out and get in the hammock before the Fourth of July is over."

"Don't you notice anything different about Uncle Rondo?" asks Stella-Rondo.

"Why, no, except he's got on some terrible-looking flesh-colored contraption I wouldn't be found dead in, is all I can see," I says.

"Never mind, you won't be found dead in it, because it happens to be part of my trousseau, and Mr. Whitaker took several dozen photographs of me in it," says Stella-Rondo. "What on earth could Uncle Rondo *mean* by wearing part of my trousseau out in the broad open daylight without saying so much as 'Kiss my foot,' *knowing* I only got home this morning after my separation and hung my negligee up on the bathroom door, just as nervous as I could be?"

"I'm sure I don't know, and what do you expect me to do about it?" I says. "Jump out the window?"

"No, I expect nothing of the kind. I simply declare that Uncle Rondo looks like a fool in it, that's all," she says. "It makes me sick to my stomach."

"Well, he looks as good as he can," I says. "As good as anybody in reason could." I stood up for Uncle Rondo, please remember. And I said to Stella-Rondo, "I think I would do well not to criticize so freely if I were you and came home with a two-year-old child I had never said a word about, and no explanation whatever about my separation."

"I asked you the instant I entered this house not to refer one more time to my adopted child, and you gave me your word of honor you would not," was all Stella-Rondo would say, and started pulling out every one of her eyebrows with some cheap Kress tweezers.

So I merely slammed the door behind me and went down and made some green-tomato pickle. Somebody had to do it. Of course Mama had turned both the niggers loose; she always said no earthly power could hold one anyway on the Fourth of July, so she wouldn't even try. It turned out that Jaypan fell in the lake and came within a very narrow limit of drowning.

So Mama trots in. Lifts up the lid and says, "H'm! Not very good for your Uncle Rondo in his precarious condition, I must say. Or poor little adopted Shirley-T. Shame on you!"

That made me tired. I says, "Well, Stella-Rondo had better thank her lucky stars it was her instead of me came trotting in with that very peculiar-looking child. Now if it had been me that trotted in from Illinois and brought a peculiar-looking child of two, I shudder to think of the reception I'd of got, much less controlled the diet of an entire family."

"But you must remember, Sister, that you were never married to Mr. Whitaker in the first place and didn't go up to Illinois to live," says Mama, shaking a spoon in my face. "If you had I would of been just as overjoyed to see you and your little adopted girl as I was to see Stella-Rondo, when you wound up with your separation and came on back home."

"You would not," I says.

"Don't contradict me, I would," says Mama.

But I said she couldn't convince me though she talked till she was blue in the face. Then I said, "Besides, you know as well as I do that that child is not adopted."

"She most certainly is adopted," says Mama, stiff as a poker.

I says, "Why, Mama, Stella-Rondo had her just as sure as anything in this world, and just too stuck up to admit it."

"Why, Sister," said Mama. "Here I thought we were going to have a pleasant Fourth of July, and you start right out not believing a word your own baby sister tells you!"

"Just like Cousin Annie Flo. Went to her grave denying the facts of life," I remind Mama.

"I told you if you ever mentioned Annie Flo's name I'd slap your face," says Mama, and slaps my face.

"All right, you wait and see," I says.

"I," says Mama, "*I* prefer to take my children's word for anything when it's humanly possible." You ought to see Mama, she weighs two hundred pounds and has real tiny feet.

Just then something perfectly horrible occurred to me.

"Mama," I says, "can that child talk?" I simply had to whisper! "Mama, I wonder if that child can be—you know—in any way? Do you realize," I says, "that she hasn't spoken one single, solitary word to a human being up to this minute? This is the way she looks," I says, and I looked like this.

Well, Mama and I just stood there and stared at each other. It was horrible!

"I remember well that Joe Whitaker frequently drank like a fish," says Mama. "I believed to my soul he drank *chemicals*." And without another word she marches to the foot of the stairs and calls Stella-Rondo.

"Stella-Rondo? O-o-o-o-o! Stella-Rondo!"

"What?" says Stella-Rondo from upstairs. Not even the grace to get up off the bed.

"Can that child of yours talk?" asks Mama.

Stella-Rondo says, "Can she what?"

"Talk! Talk!" says Mama. "Burdyburdyburdyburdy!"

So Stella-Rondo yells back, "Who says she can't talk?"

"Sister says so," says Mama.

"You didn't have to tell me, I know whose word of honor don't mean a thing in this house," says Stella-Rondo.

And in a minute the loudest Yankee voice I ever heard in my life yells out, "OE'm Pop-OE the Sailor-r-r-r Ma-a-an!" and then somebody jumps up and down in the upstairs hall. In another second the house would of fallen down.

"Not only talks, she can tap-dance!" calls Stella-Rondo. "Which is more than some people I won't name can do."

"Why, the little precious darling thing!" Mama says, so surprised. "Just as smart as she can be!" Starts talking baby talk right there. Then she turns on me. "Sister, you ought to be thoroughly ashamed! Run upstairs this instant and apologize to Stella-Rondo and Shirley-T."

"Apologize for what?" I says. "I merely wondered if the child was normal, that's all. Now that she's proved she is, why, I have nothing further to say."

But Mama just turned on her heel and flew out, furious. She ran right upstairs and hugged the baby. She believed it was adopted. Stella-Rondo hadn't done a thing but turn her against me from upstairs while I stood there helpless over the hot stove. So that made Mama, Papa-Daddy and the baby all on Stella-Rondo's side.

Next, Uncle Rondo.

I must say that Uncle Rondo has been marvelous to me at various times in the past and I was completely unprepared to be made to jump out of my skin, the way it turned out. Once Stella-Rondo did something perfectly horrible to him—broke a chain letter from Flanders Field—and he took the radio back he had given her and gave it to me. Stella-Rondo was furious! For six months we all had to call her Stella instead of Stella-Rondo, or she wouldn't answer. I always thought Uncle Rondo had all the brains of the entire family. Another time he sent me to Mammoth Cave, with all expenses paid.

But this would be the day he was drinking that prescription, the Fourth of July.

So at supper Stella-Rondo speaks up and says she thinks Uncle Rondo ought to try to eat a little something. So finally Uncle Rondo said he would try a little cold biscuits and ketchup, but that was all. So *she* brought it to him.

"Do you think it wise to disport with ketchup in Stella-Rondo's flesh-colored kimono?" I says. Trying to be considerate! If Stella-Rondo couldn't watch out for her trousseau, somebody had to.

"Any objections?" asks Uncle Rondo, just about to pour out all the ketchup.

"Don't mind what she says, Uncle Rondo," says Stella-Rondo. "Sister has been devoting this solid afternoon to sneering out my bedroom window at the way you look."

"What's that?" says Uncle Rondo. Uncle Rondo has got the most terrible temper in the world. Anything is liable to make him tear the house down if it comes at the wrong time.

So Stella-Rondo says, "Sister says, 'Uncle Rondo certainly does look like a fool in that pink kimono!'"

Do you remember who it was really said that?

Uncle Rondo spills out all the ketchup and jumps out of his chair and tears off the kimono and throws it down on the dirty floor and puts his foot on it. It had to be sent all the way to Jackson to the cleaners and re-pleated.

"So that's your opinion of your Uncle Rondo, is it?" he says. "I look like a fool, do I? Well, that's the last straw. A whole day in this house with nothing to do, and then to hear you come out with a remark like that behind my back!"

"I didn't say any such of a thing, Uncle Rondo," I says, "and I'm not saying who did, either. Why, I think you look all right. Just try to take care of yourself and not talk and eat at the same time," I says. "I think you better go lie down."

"Lie down my foot," says Uncle Rondo. I ought to of known by that he was fixing to do something perfectly horrible.

So he didn't do anything that night in the precarious state he was in—just played Casino with Mama and Stella-Rondo and Shirley-T. and gave Shirley-T. a nickel with a head on both sides. It tickled her nearly to death, and she called him "Papa." But at 6:30 A.M. the next morning, he threw a whole five cent package of some unsold one-inch firecrackers from the store as hard as he could into my bedroom and they every one went off. Not one bad one in the string. Anybody else, there'd be one that wouldn't go off.

Well, I'm just terribly susceptible to noise of any kind, the doctor has always told me I was the most sensitive person he had ever seen in his whole life, and I was simply prostrated. I couldn't eat! People tell me they heard it as far as the cemetery, and old Aunt Jep Patterson, that had been holding her own so good, thought it was Judgment Day and she was going to meet her whole family. It's usually so quiet here.

And I'll tell you it didn't take me any longer than a minute to make up my mind what to do. There I was with the whole entire house on Stella-Rondo's side and turned against me. If I have anything at all I have pride.

So I just decided I'd go straight down to the P.O. There's plenty of room there in the back, I says to myself.

Well! I made no bones about letting the family catch on to what I was up to. I didn't try to conceal it.

The first thing they knew, I marched in where they were all playing Old Maid and pulled the electric oscillating fan out by the plug, and everything got real hot. Next I snatched the pillow I'd done the needlepoint on right off the davenport from behind

Papa-Daddy. He went "Ugh!" I beat Stella-Rondo up the stairs and finally found my charm bracelet in her bureau drawer under a picture of Nelson Eddy.

"So that's the way the land lies," says Uncle Rondo. There he was, piecing on the ham. "Well, Sister, I'll be glad to donate my army cot if you got any place to set it up, providing you'll leave right this minute and let me get some peace." Uncle Rondo was in France.

"Thank you kindly for the cot and 'peace' is hardly the word I would select if I had to resort to firecrackers at 6:30 A.M. in a young girl's bedroom," I says back to him. "And as to where I intend to go, you seem to forget my position as postmistress of China Grove, Mississippi," I says. "I've always got the P.O."

Well, that made them all sit up and take notice.

I went out front and started digging up some four-o'clocks to plant around the P.O.

"Ah-ah-ah!" says Mama, raising the window. "Those happen to be my four-o'clocks. Everything planted in that star is mine. I've never known you to make anything grow in your life."

"Very well," I says. "But I take the fern. Even you, Mama, can't stand there and deny that I'm the one watered that fern. And I happen to know where I can send in a box top and get a packet of one thousand mixed seeds, no two the same kind, free."

"Oh, where?" Mama wants to know.

But I says, "Too late. You 'tend to your house, and I'll 'tend to mine. You hear things like that all the time if you know how to listen to the radio. Perfectly marvelous offers. Get anything you want free."

So I hope to tell you I marched in and got that radio, and they could of all bit a nail in two, especially Stella-Rondo, that it used to belong to, and she well knew she couldn't get it back, I'd sue for it like a shot. And I very politely took the sewing-machine motor I helped pay the most on to give Mama for Christmas back in 1929, and a good big calendar, with the first-aid remedies on it. The thermometer and the Hawaiian ukulele certainly were rightfully mine, and I stood on the step-ladder and got all my watermelon-rind preserves and every fruit and vegetable I'd put up, every jar. Then I began to pull the tacks out of the bluebird wall vases on the archway to the dining room.

"Who told you you could have those, Miss Priss?" says Mama, fanning as hard as she could.

"I bought 'em and I'll keep track of 'em," I says. "I'll tack 'em up one on each side the post-office window, and you can see 'em when you come to ask me for your mail, if you're so dead to see 'em."

"Not I! I'll never darken the door to that post office again if I live to be a hundred," Mama says. "Ungrateful child! After all the money we spent on you at the Normal."

"Me either," says Stella-Rondo. "You can just let my mail lie there and *rot*, for all I care. I'll never come and relieve you of a single, solitary piece."

"I should worry," I says. "And who you think's going to sit down and write you all those big fat letters and postcards, by the way? Mr. Whitaker? Just because he was the only man ever dropped down in China Grove and you got him—unfairly—is he going to sit down and write you a lengthy correspondence after you come home giving no rhyme nor reason whatsoever for your separation and no explanation for the presence of that child? I may not have your brilliant mind, but I fail to see it."

So Mama says, "Sister, I've told you a thousand times that Stella-Rondo simply got homesick, and this child is far too big to be hers," and she says, "Now, why don't you all just sit down and play Casino?"

Then Shirley-T. sticks out her tongue at me in this perfectly horrible way. She has no more manners than the man in the moon. I told her she was going to cross her eyes like that some day and they'd stick.

"It's too late to stop me now," I says. "You should have tried that yesterday. I'm going to the P.O. and the only way you can possibly see me is to visit me there."

So Papa-Daddy says, "You'll never catch me setting foot in that post office, even if I should take a notion into my head to write a letter some place." He says, "I won't have you reachin' out of that little old window with a pair of shears and cuttin' off any beard of mine. I'm too smart for you!"

"We all are," says Stella-Rondo.

But I said, "If you're so smart, where's Mr. Whitaker?"

So then Uncle Rondo says, "I'll thank you from now on to stop reading all the orders I get on postcards and telling everybody in China Grove what you think is the matter with them," but I says, "I draw my own conclusions and will continue in the future to draw them." I says, "if people want to write their inmost secrets on penny postcards, there's nothing in the wide world you can do about it, Uncle Rondo."

"And if you think we'll ever *write* another postcard you're sadly mistaken," says Mama.

"Cutting off your nose to spite your face then," I says. "But if you're all determined to have no more to do with the U.S. mail, think of this: What will Stella-Rondo do now, if she wants to tell Mr. Whitaker to come after her?"

"Wah!" says Stella-Rondo. I knew she'd cry. She had a conniption fit right there in the kitchen.

"It will be interesting to see how long she holds out," I says. "And now—I am leaving."

"Good-bye," says Uncle Rondo.

"Oh, I declare," says Mama, "to think that a family of mine should quarrel on the Fourth of July, or the day after, over Stella-Rondo leaving old Mr. Whitaker and having the sweetest little adopted child! It looks like we'd all be glad!"

"Wah!" says Stella-Rondo, and has a fresh conniption fit.

"*He* left *her*—you mark my words," I says. "That's Mr. Whitaker. I know Mr. Whitaker. After all, I knew him first. I said from the beginning he'd up and leave her. I foretold every single thing that's happened."

"Where did he go?" asks Mama.

"Probably to the North Pole, if he knows what's good for him," I says.

But Stella-Rondo just bawled and wouldn't say another word. She flew to her room and slammed the door.

"Now look what you've gone and done, Sister," says Mama. "You go apologize."

"I haven't got time, I'm leaving," I says.

"Well, what are you waiting around for?" asks Uncle Rondo.

So I just picked up the kitchen clock and marched off, without saying "Kiss my foot" or anything, and never did tell Stella-Rondo good-bye.

There was a nigger girl going along on a little wagon right in front.

"Nigger girl," I says, "come help me haul these things down the hill, I'm going to live in the post office."

Took her nine trips in her express wagon. Uncle Rondo came out on the porch and threw her a nickel.

And that's the last I've laid eyes on any of my family or my family laid eyes on me for five solid days and nights. Stella-Rondo may be telling the most horrible tales in the world about Mr. Whitaker, but I haven't heard them. As I tell everybody, I draw my own conclusions.

But oh, I like it here. It's ideal, as I've been saying. You see, I've got everything cater-cornered, the way I like it. Hear the radio? All the war news. Radio, sewing machine, book ends, ironing board and that great big piano lamp—peace, that's what I like. Butter-bean vines planted all along the front where the strings are.

Of course, there's not much mail. My family are naturally the main people in China Grove, and if they prefer to vanish from the face of the earth, for all the mail they get or the mail they write, why, I'm not going to open my mouth. Some of the folks here in town are taking up for me and some turned against me. I know which is which. There are always people who will quit buying stamps just to get on the right side of Papa-Daddy.

But here I am, and here I'll stay. I want the world to know I'm happy.

And if Stella-Rondo should come to me this minute, on bended knees, and *attempt* to explain the incidents of her life with Mr. Whitaker, I'd simply put my fingers in both my ears and refuse to listen.

QUESTIONS FOR DISCUSSION AND WRITING

1. How does the return of Stella-Rondo reestablish the conflicts in the family? How does the discussion of Uncle Rondo's attire bring these conflicts to a crisis?
2. What do we learn about the character of the narrator by the ways in which she describes: Mr. Whitaker, Papa-Daddy, and Shirley-T.? How do her judgments justify Stella-Rondo's accusation that she is "one-sided"?
3. What aspects of the setting would have to be explained to someone not familiar with the American South in the 1940s? In what sense is the P.O. an "ideal" setting for the narrator at the end of the story?
4. Who seems to be the audience for the story? How do we know the narrator is unreliable?
5. What does this story reveal about the nature of family life? Why do the weaknesses and failures in this family seem funny rather than tragic or pathetic?

98

EDITH WHARTON

Roman Fever

EDITH WHARTON (1862–1937) was born in New York City and educated by private tutors in her family's homes in Paris, New York City, and Newport, Rhode Island. She published her first poems anonymously in *The Atlantic Monthly* in 1880 and collected them into a small volume of verse which she arranged to have published privately. Her marriage in 1885 to Boston banker Edward Wharton gave her the leisure to pursue her writing. She began writing stories for the popular magazines, and published her first collection, *The Greater Inclination,* in 1899. In a sense, her prolific writing was therapy for her troubled marriage, which finally ended in divorce in 1913. The publication of *The House of Mirth* (1905) established her reputation as a major talent and led to other masterpieces such as *Ethan Frome* (1911), *The Custom of the Country* (1913), *Summer* (1917), and *The Age of Innocence* (1920), for which she was awarded the Pulitzer Prize. After her divorce, Wharton lived most of her life in France. During World War I, she worked on behalf of Belgian orphans and wrote propaganda for the Allied cause, as in *Fighting France, From Dunkerque to Belfort* (1915), and *The Marne* (1918), a war novel. She was awarded the French Cross of the Legion of Honor for her efforts. In 1924 Wharton published four novelettes, *Old New York,* the second of which (*Old Maid*) won a Pulitzer Prize when it was adapted for the stage under the title *The Fifties* (1935). Her numerous short stories appear in volumes such as *Crucial Instances* (1901), *The Hermit and the Wild Woman* (1908), and *Tales of Men and Ghosts* (1910). "Roman Fever," reprinted from *The World Over* (1936), dramatizes the story of two women, each of whom has spent most of her life seeing the other "through the wrong end of her little telescope."

1

From the table at which they had been lunching two American ladies of ripe but well-cared-for middle age moved across the lofty terrace of the Roman restaurant and, leaning on its parapet, looked first at each other, and then down on the outspread glories of the Palatine and the Forum, with the same expression of vague but benevolent approval.

As they leaned there a girlish voice echoed up gaily from the stairs leading to the court below. "Well, come along, then," it cried, not to them but to an invisible companion, "and let's leave the young things to their knitting"; and a voice as fresh laughed back: "Oh, look here, Babs, not actually *knitting*—" "Well, I mean figuratively," rejoined the first. "After all, we haven't left our poor parents much else to do. . . ." and at that point the turn of the stairs engulfed the dialogue.

The two ladies looked at each other again, this time with a tingle of smiling embarrassment, and the smaller and paler one shook her head and colored slightly.

"Barbara!" she murmured, sending an unheard rebuke after the mocking voice in the stairway.

The other lady, who was fuller, and higher in color, with a small determined nose supported by vigorous black eyebrows, gave a good-humored laugh. "That's what our daughters think of us!"

Her companion replied by a deprecating gesture. "Not of us individually. We must remember that. It's just the collective modern idea of Mothers. And you see—" Half-guiltily she drew from her handsomely mounted black handbag a twist of crimson silk run through by two fine knitting needles. "One never knows," she murmured. "The new system has certainly given us a good deal of time to kill; and sometimes I get tired just looking—even at this." Her gesture was now addressed to the stupendous scene at their feet.

The dark lady laughed again, and they both relapsed upon the view, contemplating it in silence, with a sort of diffused serenity which might have been borrowed from the spring effulgence of the Roman skies. The luncheon hour was long past, and the two had their end of the vast terrace to themselves. At its opposite extremity a few groups, detained by a lingering look at the outspread city, were gathering up guidebooks and fumbling for tips. The last of them scattered, and the two ladies were alone on the air-washed height.

"Well, I don't see why we shouldn't just stay here," said Mrs. Slade, the lady of the high color and energetic brows. Two derelict basket chairs stood near, and she pushed them into the angle of the parapet, and settled herself in one, her gaze upon the Palatine. "After all, it's still the most beautiful view in the world."

"It always will be, to me," assented her friend Mrs. Ansley, with so slight a stress on the "me" that Mrs. Slade, though she noticed it, wondered if it were not merely accidental, like the random underlinings of old-fashioned letter writers.

"Grace Ansley was always old-fashioned," she thought; and added aloud, with a retrospective smile: "It's a view we've both been familiar with for a good many years. When we first met here we were younger than our girls are now. You remember?"

"Oh, yes, I remember," murmured Mrs. Ansley, with the same undefinable stress. "There's that headwaiter wondering," she interpolated. She was evidently far less sure than her companion of herself and of her rights in the world.

"I'll cure him of wondering," said Mrs. Slade, stretching her hand toward a bag as discreetly opulent-looking as Mrs. Ansley's. Signing to the headwaiter, she explained that she and her friend were old lovers of Rome, and would like to spend the end of the afternoon looking down on the view—that is, if it did not disturb the service? The headwaiter, bowing over her gratuity, assured her that the ladies were most welcome, and would be still more so if they would condescend to remain for dinner. A full-moon night, they would remember. . . .

Mrs. Slade's black brows drew together, as though references to the moon were out of place and even unwelcome. But she smiled away her frown as the headwaiter retreated. "Well, why not? We might do worse. There's no knowing, I suppose, when the girls will be back. Do you even know back from *where*? I don't!"

Mrs. Ansley again colored slightly. "I think those young Italian aviators we met at the Embassy invited them to fly to Tarquinia for tea. I suppose they'll want to wait and fly back by moonlight."

"Moonlight—moonlight! What a part it still plays. Do you suppose they're as sentimental as we were?"

"I've come to the conclusion that I don't in the least know what they are," said Mrs. Ansley. "And perhaps we didn't know much more about each other."

"No; perhaps we didn't."

Her friend gave her a shy glance. "I never should have supposed you were sentimental, Alida."

"Well, perhaps I wasn't." Mrs. Slade drew her lids together in retrospect; and for a few moments the two ladies, who had been intimate since childhood, reflected how little they knew each other. Each one, of course, had a label ready to attach to the other's name; Mrs. Delphin Slade, for instance, would have told herself, or anyone who asked her, that Mrs. Horace Ansley, twenty-five years ago, had been exquisitely lovely—no, you wouldn't believe it, would you? . . . though, of course, still charming, distinguished. . . . Well, as a girl she had been exquisite; far more beautiful than her daughter Barbara, though certainly Babs, according to the new standards at any rate, was more effective—had more *edge*, as they say. Funny where she got it, with those two nullities as parents. Yes; Horace Ansley was—well, just the duplicate of his wife. Museum specimens of old New York. Good-looking, irreproachable, exemplary. Mrs. Slade and Mrs. Ansley had lived opposite each other—actually as well as figuratively—for years. When the drawing-room curtains in No. 20 East 73rd Street were renewed, No. 23, across the way, was always aware of it. And of all the movings, buyings, travels, anniversaries, illnesses—the tame chronicle of an estimable pair. Little of it escaped Mrs. Slade. But she had grown bored with it by the time her husband made his big *coup* in Wall Street, and when they bought in upper Park Avenue had already begun to think: "I'd rather live opposite a speakeasy for a change; at least one might see it raided." The idea of seeing Grace raided was so amusing that (before the move) she launched it at a woman's lunch. It made a hit, and went the rounds—she sometimes wondered if it had crossed the street, and reached Mrs. Ansley. She hoped not, but didn't much mind. Those were the days when respectability was at a discount, and it did the irreproachable no harm to laugh at them a little.

A few years later, and not many months apart, both ladies lost their husbands. There was an appropriate exchange of wreaths and condolences, and a brief renewal of intimacy in the half-shadow of their mourning; and now, after another interval, they had run across each other in Rome, at the same hotel, each of them the modest appendage of a salient daughter. The similarity of their lot had again drawn them together, lending itself to mild jokes, and the mutual confession that, if in old days it must have been tiring to "keep up" with daughters, it was now, at times, a little dull not to.

No doubt, Mrs. Slade reflected, she felt her unemployment more than poor Grace ever would. It was a big drop from being the wife of Delphin Slade to being his widow.

She had always regarded herself (with a certain conjugal pride) as his equal in social gifts, as contributing her full share to the making of the exceptional couple they were: but the difference after his death was irremediable. As the wife of the famous corporation lawyer, always with an international case or two on hand, every day brought its exciting and unexpected obligation: the impromptu entertaining of eminent colleagues from abroad, the hurried dashes on legal business to London, Paris or Rome, where the entertaining was so handsomely reciprocated; the amusement of hearing in her wake: "What, that handsome woman with the good clothes and the eyes is Mrs. Slade—*the* Slade's wife? Really? Generally the wives of celebrities are such frumps."

Yes; being *the* Slade's widow was a dullish business after that. In living up to such a husband all her faculties had been engaged; now she had only her daughter to live up to, for the son who seemed to have inherited his father's gifts had died suddenly in boyhood. She had fought through that agony because her husband was there, to be helped and to help; now, after the father's death, the thought of the boy had become unbearable. There was nothing left but to mother her daughter; and dear Jenny was such a perfect daughter that she needed no excessive mothering. "Now with Babs Ansley I don't know that I *should* be so quiet," Mrs. Slade sometimes half-enviously reflected; but Jenny, who was younger than her brilliant friend, was that rare accident, an extremely pretty girl who somehow made youth and prettiness seem as safe as their absence. It was all perplexing—and to Mrs. Slade a little boring. She wished that Jenny would fall in love—with the wrong man, even; that she might have to be watched, out-maneuvered, rescued. And instead, it was Jenny who watched her mother, kept her out of drafts, made sure that she had taken her tonic. . . .

Mrs. Ansley was much less articulate than her friend, and her mental portrait of Mrs. Slade was slighter, and drawn with fainter touches. "Alida Slade's awfully brilliant; but not as brilliant as she thinks," would have summed it up; though she would have added, for the enlightenment of strangers, that Mrs. Slade had been an extremely dashing girl; much more so than her daughter, who was pretty, of course, and clever in a way, but had none of her mother's—well, "vividness," someone had once called it. Mrs. Ansley would take up current words like this, and cite them in quotation marks, as unheard-of audacities. No; Jenny was not like her mother. Sometimes Mrs. Ansley thought Alida Slade was disappointed; on the whole she had had a sad life. Full of failures and mistakes; Mrs. Ansley had always been rather sorry for her. . . .

So these two ladies visualized each other, each through the wrong end of her little telescope.

2

For a long time they continued to sit side by side without speaking. It seemed as though, to both, there was a relief in laying down their somewhat futile activities in the presence of the vast Memento Mori which faced them. Mrs. Slade sat quite still, her eyes fixed on the golden slope of the Palace of the Caesars, and after a while Mrs. Ansley ceased to fidget with her bag, and she too sank into meditation. Like many intimate friends, the two ladies had never before had occasion to be silent together, and Mrs.

Ansley was slightly embarrassed by what seemed, after so many years, a new stage in their intimacy, and one with which she did not yet know how to deal.

Suddenly the air was full of that deep clangor of bells which periodically covers Rome with a roof of silver. Mrs. Slade glanced at her wristwatch. "Five o'clock already," she said, as though surprised.

Mrs. Ansley suggested interrogatively: "There's bridge at the Embassy at five." For a long time Mrs. Slade did not answer. She appeared to be lost in contemplation, and Mrs. Ansley thought the remark had escaped her. But after a while she said, as if speaking out of a dream: "Bridge, did you say? Not unless you want to. . . . But I don't think I will, you know."

"Oh, no," Mrs. Ansley hastened to assure her. "I don't care to at all. It's so lovely here; and so full of old memories, as you say." She settled herself in her chair, and almost furtively drew forth her knitting. Mrs. Slade took sideway note of this activity, but her own beautifully cared-for hands remained motionless on her knee.

"I was just thinking," she said slowly, "what different things Rome stands for to each generation of travelers. To our grandmothers, Roman fever; to our mothers, sentimental dangers—how we used to be guarded!—to our daughters, no more dangers than the middle of Main Street. They don't know it—but how much they're missing!"

The long golden light was beginning to pale, and Mrs. Ansley lifted her knitting a little closer to her eyes. "Yes; how we were guarded!"

"I always used to think," Mrs. Slade continued, "that our mothers had a much more difficult job than our grandmothers. When Roman fever stalked the streets it must have been comparatively easy to gather in the girls at the danger hour; but when you and I were young, with such beauty calling us, and the spice of disobedience thrown in, and no worse risk than catching cold during the cool hour after sunset, the mothers used to be put to it to keep us in—didn't they?"

She turned again toward Mrs. Ansley, but the latter had reached a delicate point in her knitting. "One, two, three—slip two; yes, they must have been," she assented, without looking up.

Mrs. Slade's eyes rested on her with a deepened attention. "She can knit—in the face of *this*! How like her. . . ."

Mrs. Slade leaned back, brooding, her eyes ranging from the ruins which faced her to the long green hollow of the Forum, the fading glow of the church fronts beyond it, and the outlying immensity of the Colosseum. Suddenly she thought: "It's all very well to say that our girls have done away with sentiment and moonlight. But if Babs Ansley isn't out to catch that young aviator—the one who's a Marchese—then I don't know anything. And Jenny has no chance beside her. I know that too. I wonder if that's why Grace Ansley likes the two girls to go everywhere together? My poor Jenny as a foil—!" Mrs. Slade gave a hardly audible laugh, and at the sound Mrs. Ansley dropped her knitting.

"Yes—?"

"I—oh, nothing. I was only thinking how your Babs carries everything before her. That Campolieri boy is one of the best matches in Rome. Don't look so innocent, my dear—you know he is. And I was wondering, ever so respectfully, you understand . . . wondering how two such exemplary characters as you and Horace had managed to produce anything quite so dynamic." Mrs. Slade laughed again, with a touch of asperity.

Mrs. Ansley's hands lay inert across her needles. She looked straight out at the great accumulated wreckage of passion and splendor at her feet. But her small profile was almost expressionless. At length she said: "I think you overrate Babs, my dear."

Mrs. Slade's tone grew easier. "No; I don't. I appreciate her. And perhaps envy you. Oh, my girl's perfect; if I were a chronic invalid I'd—well, I think I'd rather be in Jenny's hands. There must be times . . . but there! I always wanted a brilliant daughter . . . and never quite understood why I got an angel instead."

Mrs. Ansley echoed her laugh in a faint murmur. "Babs is an angel too."

"Of course—of course! But she's got rainbow wings. Well, they're wandering by the sea with their young men; and here we sit . . . and it all brings back the past a little too acutely."

Mrs. Ansley had resumed her knitting. One might almost have imagined (if one had known her less well, Mrs. Slade reflected) that, for her also, too many memories rose from the lengthening shadows of those august ruins. But no; she was simply absorbed in her work. What was there for her to worry about? She knew that Babs would almost certainly come back engaged to the extremely eligible Campolieri. "And she'll sell the New York house, and settle down near them in Rome, and never be in their way . . . she's much too tactful. But she'll have an excellent cook, and just the right people in for bridge and cocktails . . . and a perfectly peaceful old age among her grandchildren."

Mrs. Slade broke off this prophetic flight with a recoil of self-disgust. There was no one of whom she had less right to think unkindly than of Grace Ansley. Would she never cure herself of envying her? Perhaps she had begun too long ago.

She stood up and leaned against the parapet, filling her troubled eyes with the tranquilizing magic of the hour. But instead of tranquilizing her the sight seemed to increase her exasperation. Her gaze turned toward the Colosseum. Already its golden flank was drowned in purple shadow, and above it the sky curved crystal clear, without light or color. It was the moment when afternoon and evening hang balanced in mid-heaven.

Mrs. Slade turned back and laid her hand on her friend's arm. The gesture was so abrupt that Mrs. Ansley looked up, startled.

"The sun's set. You're not afraid, my dear?"

"Afraid—?"

"Of Roman fever or pneumonia? I remember how ill you were that winter. As a girl you had a very delicate throat, hadn't you?"

"Oh, we're all right up here. Down below, in the Forum, it does get deathly cold, all of a sudden . . . but not here."

"Ah, of course you know because you had to be so careful." Mrs. Slade turned back to the parapet. She thought: "I must make one more effort not to hate her." Aloud she said: "Whenever I look at the Forum from up here, I remember that story about a great-aunt of yours, wasn't she? A dreadfully wicked great-aunt?"

"Oh, yes; great-aunt Harriet. The one who was supposed to have sent her young sister out to the Forum after sunset to gather a night-blooming flower for her album. All our great-aunts and grandmothers used to have albums of dried flowers."

Mrs. Slade nodded. "But she really sent her because they were in love with the same man—"

"Well, that was the family tradition. They said Aunt Harriet confessed it years afterward. At any rate, the poor little sister caught the fever and died. Mother used to frighten us with the story when we were children."

"And you frightened *me* with it, that winter when you and I were here as girls. The winter I was engaged to Delphin."

Mrs. Ansley gave a faint laugh. "Oh, did I? Really frighten you? I don't believe you're easily frightened."

"Not often; but I was then. I was easily frightened because I was too happy. I wonder if you know what that means?"

"I—yes . . ." Mrs. Ansley faltered.

"Well, I suppose that was why the story of your wicked aunt made such an impression on me. And I thought: 'There's no more Roman fever, but the Forum is deathly cold after sunset—especially after a hot day. And the Colosseum's even colder and damper'."

"The Colosseum—?"

"Yes. It wasn't easy to get in, after the gates were locked for the night. Far from easy. Still, in those days it could be managed; it *was* managed, often. Lovers met there who couldn't meet elsewhere. You knew that?"

"I—I dare say. I don't remember."

"You don't remember? You don't remember going to visit some ruins or other one evening, just after dark, and catching a bad chill? You were supposed to have gone to see the moon rise. People always said that expedition was what caused your illness."

There was a moment's silence; then Mrs. Ansley rejoined: "Did they? It was all so long ago."

"Yes. And you got well again—so it didn't matter. But I suppose it struck your friends—the reason given for your illness, I mean—because everybody knew you were so prudent on account of your throat, and your mother took such care of you. . . . You *had* been out late sight-seeing, hadn't you, that night?"

"Perhaps I had. The most prudent girls aren't always prudent. What made you think of it now?"

Mrs. Slade seemed to have no answer ready. But after a moment she broke out: "Because I simply can't bear it any longer—!"

Mrs. Ansley lifted her head quickly. Her eyes were wide and very pale. "Can't bear what?"

"Why—your not knowing that I've always known why you went."

"Why I went—?"

"Yes. You think I'm bluffing, don't you? Well, you went to meet the man I was engaged to—and I can repeat every word of the letter that took you there."

While Mrs. Slade spoke Mrs. Ansley had risen unsteadily to her feet. Her bag, her knitting and gloves, slid in a panic-stricken heap to the ground. She looked at Mrs. Slade as though she were looking at a ghost.

"No, no—don't," she faltered out.

"Why not? Listen, if you don't believe me. 'My one darling, things can't go on like this. I must see you alone. Come to the Colosseum immediately after dark tomorrow. There will be somebody to let you in. No one whom you need fear will suspect'—but perhaps you've forgotten what the letter said?"

Mrs. Ansley met the challenge with an unexpected composure. Steadying herself against the chair she looked at her friend, and replied: "No; I know it by heart too."

"And the signature? 'Only *your* D.S.' Was that it? I'm right, am I? That was the letter that took you out that evening after dark?"

Mrs. Ansley was still looking at her. It seemed to Mrs. Slade that a slow struggle was going on behind the voluntarily controlled mask of her small quiet face. "I shouldn't have thought she had herself so well in hand," Mrs. Slade reflected, almost resentfully. But at this moment Mrs. Ansley spoke. "I don't know how you knew. I burnt that letter at once."

"Yes; you would, naturally—you're so prudent!" The sneer was open now. "And if you burnt the letter you're wondering how on earth I know what was in it. That's it, isn't it?"

Mrs. Slade waited, but Mrs. Ansley did not speak.

"Well, my dear, I know what was in that letter because I wrote it!"

"You wrote it?"

"Yes."

The two women stood for a minute staring at each other in the last golden light. Then Mrs. Ansley dropped back into her chair. "Oh," she murmured, and covered her face with her hands.

Mrs. Slade waited nervously for another word or movement. None came, and at length she broke out: "I horrify you."

Mrs. Ansley's hands dropped to her knee. The face they uncovered was streaked with tears. "I wasn't thinking of you. I was thinking—it was the only letter I ever had from him!"

"And I wrote it. Yes; I wrote it! But I was the girl he was engaged to. Did you happen to remember that?"

Mrs. Ansley's head drooped again. "I'm not trying to excuse myself . . . I remembered. . . ."

"And still you went?"

"Still I went."

Mrs. Slade stood looking down on the small bowed figure at her side. The flame of her wrath had already sunk, and she wondered why she had ever thought there would be any satisfaction in inflicting so purposeless a wound on her friend. But she had to justify herself.

"You do understand? I'd found out—and I hated you, hated you. I knew you were in love with Delphin—and I was afraid; afraid of you, of your quiet ways, your sweetness . . . your . . . well, I wanted you out of the way, that's all. Just for a few weeks; just till I was sure of him. So in a blind fury I wrote that letter . . . I don't know why I'm telling you now."

"I suppose," said Mrs. Ansley slowly, "it's because you've gone on hating me."

"Perhaps. Or because I wanted to get the whole thing off my mind." She paused. "I'm glad you destroyed the letter. Of course I never thought you'd die."

Mrs. Ansley relapsed into silence, and Mrs. Slade, leaning over her, was conscious of a strange sense of isolation, of being cut off from the warm current of human communion. "You think me a monster!"

"I don't know. . . . It was the only letter I had, and you say he didn't write it?"

"Ah, how you care for him still!"

"I cared for that memory," said Mrs. Ansley.

Mrs. Slade continued to look down at her. She seemed physically reduced by the blow—as if, when she got up, the wind might scatter her like a puff of dust. Mrs. Slade's jealousy suddenly leapt up again at the sight. All these years the woman had been living on that letter. How she must have loved him, to treasure the mere memory of its ashes! The letter of the man her friend was engaged to. Wasn't it she who was the monster?

"You tried your best to get him away from me, didn't you? But you failed; and I kept him. That's all."

"Yes. That's all."

"I wish now I hadn't told you. I'd no idea you'd feel about it as you do; I thought you'd be amused. It all happened so long ago, as you say; and you must do me the justice to remember that I had no reason to think you'd ever taken it seriously. How could I, when you were married to Horace Ansley two months afterward? As soon as you could get out of bed your mother rushed you off to Florence and married you. People were rather surprised—they wondered at its being done so quickly; but I thought I knew. I had an idea you did it out of *pique*—to be able to say you'd got ahead of Delphin and me. Girls have such silly reasons for doing the most serious things. And your marrying so soon convinced me that you'd never really cared."

"Yes. I suppose it would," Mrs. Ansley assented.

The clear heaven overhead was emptied of all its gold. Dusk spread over it, abruptly darkening the Seven Hills. Here and there lights began to twinkle through the foliage at their feet. Steps were coming and going on the deserted terrace—waiters looking out of the doorway at the head of the stairs, then reappearing with trays and napkins and flasks of wine. Tables were moved, chairs straightened. A feeble string of electric lights flickered out. Some vases of faded flowers were carried away, and brought back replenished. A stout lady in a dust coat suddenly appeared, asking in broken Italian if anyone had seen the elastic band which held together her tattered Baedeker. She poked with her stick under the table at which she had lunched, the waiters assisting.

The corner where Mrs. Slade and Mrs. Ansley sat was still shadowy and deserted. For a long time neither of them spoke. At length Mrs. Slade began again: "I suppose I did it as a sort of joke—"

"A joke?"

"Well, girls are ferocious sometimes, you know. Girls in love especially. And I remember laughing to myself all that evening at the idea that you were waiting around there in the dark, dodging out of sight, listening for every sound, trying to get in—Of course I was upset when I heard you were so ill afterward."

Mrs. Ansley had not moved for a long time. But now she turned slowly toward her companion. "But I didn't wait. He'd arranged everything. He was there. We were let in at once," she said.

Mrs. Slade sprang up from her leaning position. "Delphin there? They let you in?—Ah, now you're lying!" she burst out with violence.

Mrs. Ansley's voice grew clearer, and full of surprise. "But of course he was there. Naturally he came—"

"Came? How did he know he'd find you there? You must be raving!"

Mrs. Ansley hesitated, as though reflecting. "But I answered the letter. I told him I'd be there. So he came."

Mrs. Slade flung her hands up to her face. "Oh, God—you answered! I never thought of your answering. . . ."

"It's odd you never thought of it, if you wrote the letter."

"Yes. I was blind with rage."

Mrs. Ansley rose, and drew her fur scarf about her. "It is cold here. We'd better go. . . . I'm sorry for you," she said, as she clasped the fur about her throat.

The unexpected words sent a pang through Mrs. Slade. "Yes; we'd better go." She gathered up her bag and cloak. "I don't know why you should be sorry for me," she muttered.

Mrs. Ansley stood looking away from her toward the dusky secret mass of the Colosseum. "Well—because I didn't have to wait that night."

Mrs. Slade gave an unquiet laugh. "Yes; I was beaten there. But I oughtn't to begrudge it to you, I suppose. At the end of all these years. After all, I had everything; I had him for twenty-five years. And you had nothing but that one letter that he didn't write."

Mrs. Ansley was again silent. At length she turned toward the door of the terrace. She took a step, and turned back, facing her companion.

"I had Barbara," she said, and began to move ahead of Mrs. Slade toward the stairway.

QUESTIONS FOR DISCUSSION AND WRITING

1. How does the departure of Jenny and Babs evoke their mothers' feelings of discontent? How does Mrs. Slade's confession about the letter bring the story to its climax? How does Mrs. Ansley's final confession provide the story with its denouement?

2. How does Mrs. Slade characterize herself, Jenny, Babs, and Mrs. Ansley in the first part of the story? Although "less articulate," how does Mrs. Ansley's initial characterization of Mrs. Slade provide early clues to her hidden wisdom? How do the revelations in the second part of the story alter our perception of these two middle-aged women?

3. What has Rome represented to the grandmothers, mothers, and daughters in this story? What did Mrs. Ansley's wicked great-aunt contribute to the folklore of "Roman fever"? Why do the time (late afternoon) and the place (a terrace overlooking the Colosseum) provide an appropriate setting for this story?

4. Although Wharton's point of view in the story is objective, she devotes more of her attention to the "vivid" Mrs. Slade. How does this emphasis enhance the power of the paler Mrs. Ansley's revelation?

5. Why does the apparently stronger Mrs. Slade envy Mrs. Ansley? Why does the apparently slighter Mrs. Ansley pity Mrs. Slade? What does this story suggest about the ability of intimate friends to know and understand one another?

99

RICHARD WRIGHT

The Man Who Was Almost a Man

RICHARD WRIGHT (1908–1960) was born in Natchez, Mississippi, and spent most of his childhood traveling through the South as his mother looked for work as a cook or maid. The family soon dissolved, and Richard was forced into a series of orphanages and foster homes. After the ninth grade, he struck out on his own, living briefly in Memphis before traveling to Chicago where he worked as a postal clerk. During the Depression, Wright became associated with writers and politicians of the radical left and began to publish poems in *Left Front*. He also wrote a series of short stories, *Uncle Tom's Children* (1938), which won first prize in a WPA competition. In 1937 Wright moved to New York, where he wrote for *New Masses* and *The Daily Worker*. But as he pointed out in a famous *Harper's* article, "I Tried to Be a Communist" (1944), Wright preferred to tell stories of individuals rather than preach propaganda to the masses. In 1940 he published his brutally realistic novel *Native Son*, establishing himself as America's foremost black writer. In 1945 he published his autobiography, *Black Boy*. After World War II, at the invitation of Gertrude Stein, Wright moved to Paris, where he found the racial atmosphere more conducive to his literary and political interests. His later novels, *The Outsider* (1953) and *The Long Dream* (1958), were mainly influenced by the philosophy of French existentialism. And his nonfiction, such as *Black Power* (1954), reveals his growing interest in the politics of Africa. "The Man Who Was Almost a Man," reprinted from *Eight Men* (1940), is an account of a young boy's attempt to prove his maturity.

Dave struck out across the fields, looking homeward through paling light. Whut's the use talkin wid em niggers in the field? Anyhow, his mother was putting supper on the table. Them niggers can't understan nothing. One of these days he was going to get a gun and practice shooting, then they couldn't talk to him as though he were a little boy. He slowed, looking at the ground. Shucks, Ah ain scareda them even ef they are biggern me! Aw, Ah know whut Ahma do. Ahm going by ol Joe's sto n git that Sears Roebuck catlog n look at them guns. Mebbe Ma will lemme buy one when she gits mah pay from ol man Hawkins. Ahma beg her t gimme some money. Ahm ol ernough to hava gun.

Ahm seventeen. Almost a man. He strode, feeling his long loose-jointed limbs. Shucks, a man oughta hava little gun aftah he done worked hard all day.

He came in sight of Joe's store. A yellow lantern glowed on the front porch. He mounted steps and went through the screen door, hearing it bang behind him. There was a strong smell of coal oil and mackerel fish. He felt very confident until he saw fat Joe walk in through the rear door, then his courage began to ooze.

"Howdy, Dave! Whutcha want?"

"How yuh, Mistah Joe? Aw, Ah don wanna buy nothing. Ah jus wanted t see ef yuhd lemme look at tha catlog erwhile."

"Sure! You wanna see it here?"

"Nawsuh. Ah wants t take it home wid me. Ah'll bring it back termorrow when Ah come in from the fiels."

"You plannin on buying something?"

"Yessuh."

"Your ma lettin you have your own money now?"

"Shucks. Mistah Joe, Ahm gittin t be a man like anybody else!"

Joe laughed and wiped his greasy white face with a red bandanna.

"What you plannin on buyin?"

Dave looked at the floor, scratched his head, scratched his thigh, and smiled. Then he looked up shyly.

"Ah'll tell yuh, Mistah Joe, ef yuh promise yuh won't tell."

"I promise."

"Waal, Ahma buy a gun."

"A gun? What you want with a gun?"

"Ah wanna keep it."

"You ain't nothing but a boy. You don't need a gun."

"Aw, lemme have the catlog, Mistah Joe. Ah'll bring it back."

Joe walked through the rear door. Dave was elated. He looked around at barrels of sugar and flour. He heard Joe coming back. He craned his neck to see if he were bringing the book. Yeah, he's got it. Gawddog, he's got it!

"Here, but be sure you bring it back. It's the only one I got."

"Sho, Mistah Joe."

"Say, if you wanna buy a gun, why don't you buy one from me? I gotta gun to sell."

"Will it shoot?"

"Sure it'll shoot."

"Whut kind is it?"

"Oh, it's kinda old . . . a left-hand Wheeler. A pistol. A big one."

"Is it got bullets in it?"

"It's loaded."

"Kin Ah see it?"

"Where's your money?"

"What yuh wan fer it?"

"I'll let you have it for two dollars."

"Just two dollahs? Shucks, Ah could buy tha when Ah git mah pay."

"I'll have it here when you want it."

"Awright, suh. Ah be in fer it."

He went through the door, hearing it slam again behind him. Ahma git some money from Ma n buy me a gun! Only two dollahs! He tucked the thick catalogue under his arm and hurried.

"Where yuh been, boy?" His mother held a steaming dish of black-eyed peas.

"Aw, Ma, Ah just stopped down the road t talk wid the boys."

"Yuh know bettah t keep suppah waiting."

He sat down, resting the catalogue on the edge of the table.

"Yuh git up from there and git to the well n wash yosef! Ah ain feedin no hogs in mah house!"

She grabbed his shoulder and pushed him. He stumbled out of the room, then came back to get the catalogue.

"Whut this?"

"Aw, Ma, it's jusa catlog."

"Who yuh git it from?"

"From Joe, down at the sto."

"Waal, thas good. We kin use it in the outhouse."

"Naw, Ma." He grabbed for it. "Gimme ma catlog, Ma."

She held onto it and glared at him.

"Quit hollerin at me! Whut's wrong wid yuh? Yuh crazy?"

"But Ma, please. It ain mine! It's Joe's! He tol me t bring it back t im termorrow."

She gave up the book. He stumbled down the back steps, hugging the thick book under his arm. When he had splashed water on his face and hands, he groped back to the kitchen and fumbled in a corner for the towel. He bumped into a chair; it clattered to the floor. The catalogue sprawled at his feet. When he had dried his eyes he snatched up the book and held it again under his arms. His mother stood watching him.

"Now, ef yuh gonna act a fool over that ol book, Ah'll take it n burn it up."

"Naw, Ma, please."

"Waal, set down n be still!"

He sat down and drew the oil lamp close. He thumbed page after page, unaware of the food his mother set on the table. His father came in. Then his small brother.

"Whutcha got there, Dave?" his father asked.

"Jusa catlog," he answered, not looking up.

"Yeah, here they is!" His eyes glowed at blue-and-black revolvers. He glanced up, feeling sudden guilt. His father was watching him. He eased the book under the table and rested it on his knees. After the blessing was asked, he ate. He scooped up peas and swallowed fat meat without chewing. Buttermilk helped to wash it down. He did not want to mention money before his father. He would do much better by cornering his mother when she was alone. He looked at his father uneasily out of the edge of his eye.

"Boy, how come yuh don quit foolin wid tha book n eat yo suppah?"

"Yessuh."

"How you n ol man Hawkins gitten erlong?"

"Suh?"

"Can't yuh hear? Why don yuh listen? Ah ast yu how wuz yuh n ol man Hawkins gittin erlong?"

"Oh, swell, Pa. Ah plows mo lan than anybody over there."

"Waal, yuh oughta keep you mind on whut yuh doin."

"Yessuh."

He poured his plate full of molasses and sopped it up slowly with a chunk of cornbread. When his father and brother had left the kitchen, he still sat and looked again at the guns in the catalogue, longing to muster courage enough to present his case to his mother. Lawd, ef Ah only had tha pretty one! He could almost feel the slickness of the weapon with his fingers. If he had a gun like that he would polish it and keep it shining so it would never rust. N Ah'd keep it loaded, by Gawd!

"Ma?" His voice was hesitant.

"Hunh?"

"Ol man Hawkins give yuh mah money yit?"

"Yeah, but ain no usa yuh thinking about throwin nona it erway. Ahm keepin tha money sos yuh kin have cloes t go to school this winter."

He rose and went to her side with the open catalogue in his palms. She was washing dishes, her head bent low over a pan. Shyly he raised the book. When he spoke, his voice was husky, faint.

"Ma, Gawd knows Ah wans one of these."

"One of whut?" she asked, not raising her eyes.

"One of these," he said again, not daring even to point. She glanced up at the page, then at him with wide eyes.

"Nigger, is yuh gone plumb crazy?"

"Aw, Ma—"

"Git outta here! Don yuh talk t me bout no gun! Yuh a fool!"

"Ma, Ah kin buy one fer two dollahs."

"Not ef Ah knows it, yuh ain!"

"But yuh promised me one—"

"Ah don care what Ah promised! Yuh ain nothing but a boy yit!"

"Ma ef yuh lemme buy one Ah'll *never* ast yuh fer nothing no mo."

"Ah tol yuh t git outta here! Yuh ain gonna toucha penny of tha money fer no gun! Thas how come Ah has Mistah Hawkins t pay yu wages t me, cause Ah knows yuh ain got no sense."

"But, Ma, we needa gun. Pa ain got no gun. We needa gun in the house. Yuh kin never tell whut might happen."

"Now don yuh try to maka fool outta me, boy! Ef we did hava gun, yuh wouldn't have it!"

He laid the catalogue down and slipped his arm around her waist.

"Aw, Ma, Ah done worked hard alla summer n ain ast yuh fer nothing, is Ah, now?"

"Thas whut yuh spose t do!"

"But Ma, Ah wans a gun. Yuh kin lemme have two dollahs outta mah money. Please, Ma. I kin give it to Pa . . . Please, Ma! Ah loves yuh, Ma."

When she spoke her voice came soft and low.

"What yu wan wida gun, Dave? Yuh don need no gun. Yuh'll git in trouble. N ef yo pa jus thought Ah let yuh have money t buy a gun he'd hava fit."

"Ah'll hide it, Ma. It ain but two dollahs."

"Lawd, chil, whut's wrong wid yuh?"

"Ain nothin wrong, Ma. Ahm almos a man now. Ah wans a gun."

"Who gonna sell yuh a gun?"

"Ol Joe at the sto."

"N it don cos but two dollahs?"

"Thas all, Ma. Jus two dollahs. Please, Ma."

She was stacking the plates away; her hands moved slowly, reflectively. Dave kept an anxious silence. Finally, she turned to him.

"Ah'll let yuh git tha gun ef yuh promise me one thing."

"Whut's tha, Ma?"

"Yuh bring it straight back t me, yuh hear? It be fer Pa."

"Yessum! Lemme go now, Ma."

She stooped, turned slightly to one side, raised the hem of her dress, rolled down the top of her stocking, and came up with a slender wad of bills.

"Here," she said. "Lawd knows yuh don need no gun. But yer pa does. Yuh bring it right back t me, yuh hear? Ahma put it up. Now ef yuh don, Ahma have yuh pa lick yuh so hard yuh won fergit it."

"Yessum."

He took the money, ran down the steps, and across the yard.

"Dave! Yuuuuu Daaaaave!"

He heard, but he was not going to stop now. "Naw, Lawd!"

The first movement he made the following morning was to reach under his pillow for the gun. In the gray light of dawn he held it loosely, feeling a sense of power. Could kill a man with a gun like this. Kill anybody, black or white. And if he were holding his gun in his hand, nobody could run over him; they would have to respect him. It was a big gun, with a long barrel and a heavy handle. He raised and lowered it in his hand, marveling at its weight.

He had not come straight home with it as his mother had asked; instead he had stayed out in the fields, holding the weapon in his hand, aiming it now and then at some imaginary foe. But he had not fired it; he had been afraid that his father might hear. Also he was not sure he knew how to fire it.

To avoid surrendering the pistol he had not come into the house until he knew that they were all asleep. When his mother had tiptoed to his bedside late that night and demanded the gun, he had first played possum; then he had told her that the gun was hidden outdoors, that he would bring it to her in the morning. Now he lay turning it slowly in his hands. He broke it, took out the cartridges, felt them, and then put them back.

He slid out of bed, got a long strip of old flannel from a trunk, wrapped the gun in it, and tied it to his naked thigh while it was still loaded. He did not go in to breakfast. Even though it was not yet daylight, he started for Jim Hawkins' plantation. Just as the sun was rising he reached the barns where the mules and plows were kept.

"Hey! That you, Dave?"

He turned. Jim Hawkins stood eying him suspiciously.

"What're yuh doing here so early?"

"Ah didn't know Ah wuz gittin up so early, Mistah Hawkins. Ah was fixin t hitch up ol Jenny n take her t the fiels."

"Good. Since you're so early, how about plowing that stretch down by the woods?"

"Suits me, Mistah Hawkins."

"O.K. Go to it!"

He hitched Jenny to a plow and started across the fields. Hot dog! This was just what he wanted. If he could get down by the woods, he could shoot his gun and nobody would hear. He walked behind the plow, hearing the traces creaking, feeling the gun tied tight to his thigh.

When he reached the woods, he plowed two whole rows before he decided to take out the gun. Finally, he stopped, looked in all directions, then untied the gun and held it in his hand. He turned to the mule and smiled.

"Know whut this is, Jenny? Naw, yuh wouldn know! Yuhs jusa ol mule! Anyhow, this is a gun, n it kin shoot, by Gawd!"

He held the gun at arm's length. Whut t hell, Ahma shoot this thing! He looked at Jenny again.

"Lissen here, Jenny! When Ah pull this ol trigger, Ah don wan yuh to run n acka fool now?"

Jenny stood with head down, her short ears pricked straight. Dave walked off about twenty feet, held the gun far out from him at arm's length, and turned his head. Hell, he told himself, Ah ain afraid. The gun felt loose in his fingers; he waved it wildly for a moment. Then he shut his eyes and tightened his forefinger. Bloom! A report half deafened him and he thought his right hand was torn from his arm. He heard Jenny whinnying and galloping over the field, and he found himself on his knees, squeezing his fingers hard between his legs. His hand was numb; he jammed it into his mouth, trying to warm it, trying to stop the pain. The gun lay at his feet. He did not quite know what had happened. He stood up and stared at the gun as though it were a living thing. He gritted his teeth and kicked the gun. Yuh almos broke mah arm! He turned to look for Jenny; she was far over the fields, tossing her head and kicking wildly.

"Hol on there, ol mule!"

When he caught up with her she stood trembling, walling her big white eyes at him. The plow was far away; the traces had broken. Then Dave stopped short, looking, not believing. Jenny was bleeding. Her left side was red and wet with blood. He went closer. Lawd, have mercy! Wondah did Ah shoot this mule? He grabbed for Jenny's mane. She flinched, snorted, whirled, tossing her head.

"Hol on now! Hol on."

Then he saw the hole in Jenny's side, right between the ribs. It was round, wet, red. A crimson stream streaked down the front leg, flowing fast. Good Gawd! Ah wuzn't shootin at tha mule. He felt panic. He knew he had to stop that blood, or Jenny would bleed to death. He had never seen so much blood in all his life. He chased the mule for half a mile, trying to catch her. Finally she stopped, breathing hard, stumpy tail half arched. He caught her mane and led her back to where the plow and gun lay. Then he stooped and grabbed handfuls of damp black earth and tried to plug the bullet hole. Jenny shuddered, whinnied, and broke from him.

"Hol on! Hol on now!"

He tried to plug it again, but blood came anyhow. His fingers were hot and sticky. He rubbed dirt into his palms, trying to dry them. Then again he attempted to plug the bullet hole, but Jenny shied away, kicking her heels high. He stood helpless. He had to do something. He ran at Jenny; she dodged him. He watched a red stream of blood flow down Jenny's leg and form a bright pool at her feet.

"Jenny . . . Jenny," he called weakly.

His lips trembled. She's bleeding t death! He looked in the direction of home, wanting to go back, wanting to get help. But he saw the pistol lying in the damp black clay. He had a queer feeling that if he only did something, this would not be; Jenny would not be there bleeding to death.

When he went to her this time, she did not move. She stood with sleepy, dreamy eyes; and when he touched her she gave a low-pitched whinny and knelt to the ground, her front knees slopping in blood.

"Jenny . . . Jenny . . ." he whispered.

For a long time she held her neck erect; then her head sank, slowly. Her ribs swelled with a mighty heave and she went over.

Dave's stomach felt empty, very empty. He picked up the gun and held it gingerly between his thumb and forefinger. He buried it at the foot of a tree. He took a stick and tried to cover the pool of blood with dirt—but what was the use? There was Jenny lying with her mouth open and her eyes walled and glassy. He could not tell Jim Hawkins he had shot his mule. But he had to tell something. Yeah, Ah'll tell em Jenny started gittin wil n fell on the joint of the plow. . . . But that would hardly happen to a mule. He walked across the field slowly, head down.

It was sunset. Two of Jim Hawkins' men were over near the edge of the woods digging a hole in which to bury Jenny. Dave was surrounded by a knot of people, all of whom were looking down at the dead mule.

"I don't see how in the world it happened," said Jim Hawkins for the tenth time.

The crowd parted and Dave's mother, father, and small brother pushed into the center.

"Where Dave?" his mother called.

"There he is," said Jim Hawkins.

His mother grabbed him.

"Whut happened, Dave? Whut yuh done?"

"Nothin."

"C'mon, boy, talk," his father said.

Dave took a deep breath and told the story he knew nobody believed.

"Waal," he drawled. "Ah brung ol Jenny down here sos Ah could do mah plowin. Ah plowed bout two rows, just like yuh see." He stopped and pointed at the long rows of upturned earth. "Then somethin musta been wrong wid ol Jenny. She wouldn ack right a-tall. She started snortin n kickin her heels. Ah tried t hol her, but she pulled erway, rearin n goin in. Then when the point of the plow was stickin up in the air, she swung erroun n twisted herself back on it . . . She stuck herself n started t bleed. N fo Ah could do anything, she wuz dead."

"Did you ever hear of anything like that in all your life?" asked Jim Hawkins.

There were white and black standing in the crowd. They murmured. Dave's mother came close to him and looked hard into his face. "Tell the truth, Dave," she said.

"Looks like a bullet hole to me," said one man.

"Dave, whut yuh do wid tha gun?" his mother asked.

The crowd surged in, looking at him. He jammed his hands into his pockets, shook his head slowly from left to right, and backed away. His eyes were wide and painful.

"Did he hava gun?" asked Jim Hawkins.

"By Gawd, Ah tol yuh tha wuz a gun wound," said a man, slapping his thigh.

His father caught his shoulders and shook him till his teeth rattled.

"Tell whut happened, yuh rascal! Tell whut . . ."

Dave looked at Jenny's stiff legs and began to cry.

"Whu yuh do wid tha gun?" his mother asked.

"Whut wuz he doin wida gun?" his father asked.

"Come on and tell the truth," said Hawkins. "Ain't nobody going to hurt you . . ."

His mother crowded close to him.

"Did yuh shoot tha mule, Dave?"

Dave cried, seeing blurred white and black faces.

"Ahh ddinn gggo tt sshooot hher . . . Ah sswear tt Gawd Ahh ddin. . . . Ah wuz a-tryin t ssee ef the gggun would sshoot—"

"Where yuh git the gun from?" his father asked.

"Ah got it from Joe, at the sto."

"Where yuh git the money?"

"Ma give it t me."

"He kept worryin me, Bob. Ah had t. Ah tol im t bring the gun right back t me . . . It was fer yuh, the gun."

"But how yuh happen to shoot that mule?" asked Jim Hawkins.

"Ah wuzn shootin at the mule, Mistah Hawkins! The gun jumped when Ah pulled the trigger . . . N fo Ah knowed anythin Jenny was there a-bleedin."

Somebody in the crowd laughed. Jim Hawkins walked close to Dave and looked into his face.

"Well, looks like you have bought you a mule, Dave."

"Ah swear fo Gawd. Ah didn go t kill the mule, Mistah Hawkins!"

"But you killed her!"

All the crowd was laughing now. They stood up tiptoe and poked heads over one another's shoulders.

"Well, boy, looks like yuh done bought a dead mule! Hahaha!"

"Ain tha ershame."

"Hohohohoho."

Dave stood, head down, twisting his feet in the dirt.

"Well, you needn't worry about it, Bob," said Jim Hawkins to Dave's father. "Just let the boy keep on working and pay me two dollars a month."

"Whut yuh wan fer yo mule, Mistah Hawkins?"

Jim Hawkins screwed up his eyes.

"Fifty dollars."

"Whut yuh do wid tha gun?" Dave's father demanded.

Dave said nothing.

"Yuh wan me t take a tree n beat yuh till yuh talk!"

"Nawsuh!"

"Whut yuh do wid it?"

"Ah throwed it erway."

"Where?"

"Ah . . . Ah throwed it in the creek."

"Waal, c mon home. N firs thing in the mawnin git to tha creek n fin tha gun."

"Yessuh."

"Whut yuh pay fer it?"

"Two dollahs."

"Take tha gun n git yo money back n carry it t Mistah Hawkins, yuh hear? N don fergit Ahma lam you black bottom good fer this! Now march yoself on home, suh!"

Dave turned and walked slowly. He heard people laughing. Dave glared, his eyes welling with tears. Hot anger bubbled in him. Then he swallowed and stumbled on.

That night Dave did not sleep. He was glad that he had gotten out of killing the mule so easily, but he was hurt. Something hot seemed to turn over inside him each time he remembered how they had laughed. He tossed on his bed, feeling his hard pillow. N Pa says he's gonna beat me . . . He remembered other beatings, and his back quivered. Naw, naw, Ah sho don wan im t beat me tha way no mo. Dam em all! Nobody ever gave him anything. All he did was work. They treat me like a mule, n then they beat me. He gritted his teeth. N Ma had t tell on me.

Well, if he had to, he would take old man Hawkins that two dollars. But that meant selling the gun. And he wanted to keep that gun. Fifty dollars for a dead mule.

He turned over, thinking how he had fired the gun. He had an itch to fire it again. Ef other men kin shoota gun, by Gawd, Ah kin! He was still, listening. Mebbe they all sleepin now. The house was still. He heard the soft breathing of his brother. Yes, now! He would go down and get that gun and see if he could fire it! He eased out of bed and slipped into overalls.

The moon was bright. He ran almost all the way to the edge of the woods. He stumbled over the ground, looking for the spot where he had buried the gun. Yeah, here it is. Like a hungry dog scratching for a bone, he pawed it up. He puffed his black cheeks and blew dirt from the trigger and barrel. He broke it and found four cartridges unshot. He looked around; the fields were filled with silence and moonlight. He clutched the gun stiff and hard in his fingers. But, as soon as he wanted to pull the trigger, he shut his eyes and turned his head. Naw, Ah can't shoot wid mah eyes closed n mah head turned. With effort he held his eyes open; then he squeezed. *Blooooom!* He was stiff, not breathing. The gun was still in his hands. Dammit, he'd done it! He fired again. *Blooooom!* He smiled. *Bloooom! Blooooom! Click, click.* There! It was empty. If anybody could shoot a gun, he could. He put the gun into his hip pocket and started across the field.

When he reached the top of a ridge he stood straight and proud in the moonlight, looking at Jim Hawkins' big white house, feeling the gun sagging in his pocket. Lawd, ef Ah had just one mo bullet Ah'd taka shot at tha house. Ah'd like t scare ol man Hawkins jusa little . . . Jusa enough t let im know Dave Saunders is a man.

To his left the road curved, running to the tracks of the Illinois Central. He jerked his head, listening. From far off came a faint *hoooof-hoooof; hoooof-hoooof* . . . He stood rigid. Two dollahs a mont. Les see now . . . Tha means it'll take bout two years. Shucks! Ah'll be dam!

He started down the road, toward the tracks. Yeah, here she comes! He stood beside the track and held himself stiffly. Here she comes, erroun the ben . . . C mon, yuh slow poke! C mon! He had his hand on his gun; something quivered in his stomach. Then the train thundered past, the gray and brown box cars rumbling and clinking. He gripped the gun tightly; then he jerked his hand out of his pocket. Ah betcha Bill wouldn't do it! Ah betcha . . . The cars slid past, steel grinding upon steel. Ahm ridin yuh ternight, so hep me Gawd! He was hot all over. He hesitated just a moment; then he grabbed, pulled atop of a car, and lay flat. He felt his pocket; the gun was still there. Ahead the long rails were glinting in the moonlight, stretching away, away to somewhere, somewhere where he could be a man . . .

QUESTIONS FOR DISCUSSION AND WRITING

1. How does Dave's desire to own a gun reveal the essential conflict in the story? How does his accidental shooting of Jenny the mule bring that conflict to a crisis? To what extent does Dave's decision to jump a freight provide a satisfactory solution to that conflict?
2. How do the other characters in the story—Mr. Joe, Jim Hawkins, and Dave's mother and father—see Dave? How does he see himself? What does the crowd's laughter reveal about the limits of Dave's self-perception?
3. What does Wright's description of the field, the store, and the house suggest about the nature of Dave's environment? How does the financial arrangement about the dead mule intensify Dave's hostility toward his environment? What kind of environment does Dave hope to find at the end of his train ride?
4. How does the shift from standard English to dialect enhance the reader's understanding of Dave's point of view? In particular, how does Wright use dialect to document Dave's anguished attempt to save Jenny and his angry response to his public humiliation?
5. What does the title suggest about the theme of the story? What are the conditions and responsibilities for manhood? Is Dave correct in assuming that he can achieve his manhood only in some other place? Explain your answer.

Glossary of Critical Terms

ALLEGORY A story in which the characters and their actions are equated with general truths about human conduct. The characters in an allegory often represent abstract concepts, such as faith, innocence, or evil. See *SYMBOL*.

ALLUSION A reference to a famous historical, fictional, or mythological person, place, or event outside the story. Allusions enrich a story by suggesting similarities to comparable circumstances in another time or place.

ANTAGONIST The character (or force) that is in direct conflict with the protagonist. An antagonist may be another person, the physical or social environment, or some aspect of the protagonist's own personality. See *PROTAGONIST*.

ANTICLIMAX A ludicrous or trivial incident that occurs instead of an expected event of significance. Sometimes the anticlimax appears in the middle of the story as an intentional digression. More often it takes place after the story has reached its climax. See *CLIMAX*.

ARCHETYPE An image, plot pattern, or character type that recurs frequently in myth, religion, folklore, or literature. According to the psychologist Carl Jung, archetypal experiences such as birth and death form part of the "collective unconscious" that the mind inherits from its racial or cultural past.

AUTHORIAL STATEMENT An interpretation of the events in a story stated directly by the author or indirectly by one of the characters. See *THEME*.

CHARACTER A person in the story. Most stories contain one or more major characters and several minor characters.

DYNAMIC CHARACTER A person who undergoes significant development or change during the story.

FLAT CHARACTER A person with little depth or complexity, who may be described in one or two phrases.

ROUND CHARACTER A person with a fully developed, complex (even contradictory) personality, who defies simple analysis or description.

STATIC CHARACTER A person who remains essentially unchanged throughout the story.

CHARACTERIZATION The methods by which writers create, reveal, or develop their characters. Writers can focus on the *external reality* of their characters by describing their appearance, actions, or manner of speech. They can also portray the *inner reality* of their characters by revealing their thoughts and feelings.

CLIMAX The moment in the story when the major action reaches its turning point. The climax (also called the *crisis*) marks the end of the story's development and propels it toward its conclusion. See *ANTICLIMAX*.

COMPLICATION That part of the plot where the various conflicts that have been introduced in the exposition are developed in greater detail before they reach the climax.

CONFLICT The struggle that grows out of the collision of various forces within a story. Although such conflicts may be many, often clashing with one another on several levels, they usually occur in three patterns: (1) the conflict between one person and another, (2) the conflict between a person and that person's physical or social environment, (3) the conflict between a person and some aspect of his or her personality. See *ANTAGONIST; PROTAGONIST.*

CONNOTATION The suggested or implied meaning of a word, as contrasted with its literal meaning or *denotation.* These additional associations may be personal (the result of individual experience) or universal (the product of the collective human experience). See *DENOTATION.*

CRISIS See *CLIMAX.*

CRITICAL ANALYSIS The systematic division of a work of literature (in this case a short story) into its various parts (or elements) in order to achieve a better understanding of the whole.

DENOTATION The literal dictionary definition of a word, apart from any emotional or intellectual association or *connotation* it may evoke. See *CONNOTATION.*

DENOUEMENT A French word meaning the untangling of a knot. As applied to fiction, the term refers to the conclusion of a story where the various conflicts (knots) are resolved (untangled). The denouement may add a surprising twist to the story, but it does not usually add new information. See *RESOLUTION.*

DIALOGUE The direct speech of characters in a story, punctuated by quotation marks. Dialogue can be used to introduce or explain the conflict in a plot, to represent the qualities of various characters, or to reveal the point of view of the central character or narrator.

DRAMATIC IRONY See *IRONY.*

DYNAMIC CHARACTER See *CHARACTER.*

EPISODE A brief period of action, often complete in itself, that forms part of a larger narrative. A story may contain several related episodes that advance the plot toward the single scene or episode that marks the climax.

EXPOSITION The part of the story, near the beginning, that introduces ("exposes") the elements of setting, character, and conflict that exist prior to the major action of the story.

FABLE A brief narrative devised to illustrate a moral lesson. The chief characters in a fable are often animals who talk and act like human beings. The plots of many fables come from folklore or superstition and focus on unusual or supernatural events.

FLASHBACK An interruption in the flow of a story to introduce an earlier scene or episode. Various devices ranging from simple recollection to dream sequences can be used to present information from the past that helps explain or comment on the present situation in the narrative.

FLAT CHARACTER See *CHARACTER.*

FOIL A character who enhances and clarifies the features of the protagonist by providing a direct and distinctive contrast to the major character.

FORESHADOWING The introduction of clues early in the story to suggest or anticipate significant events that will develop later.

IMAGERY The use of words or figures of speech to create a mental picture. Imagery exploits all five senses to produce a single powerful impression or to create a cluster of impressions that convey a dominant mood.

IRONY A term that suggests some sort of discrepancy between appearance and reality. Although irony is a broad term that can be applied to events both trivial and tragic, it depends on the ability of the reader to recognize contradictions and incongruities. Irony usually takes three forms:

1. *VERBAL IRONY* is speech in which what is said is directly opposite to what is meant. Verbal irony differs from sarcasm in that the tone of the speaker is lighter, even though the effect produced may be just as devastating.
2. *DRAMATIC IRONY* is a circumstance in which characters reveal their inability to understand their own situation. Dramatic irony is most effective when characters make fateful choices based on information the reader realizes is incorrect.
3. *SITUATIONAL IRONY* is a situation that demonstrates an incongruity between what the reader expects or presumes to be appropriate and what actually occurs.

METAPHOR A figure of speech in which an imaginative comparison is made between two dissimilar things without the use of the words *like* or *as*.

MOTIVATION The character traits, environmental forces, desires, and goals that alone or in combination explain a character's pattern of behavior

NARRATOR The person who tells the story. The narrator may be a character who is directly or indirectly involved in the action, or a detached observer who wants to explain what happened. See also *POINT OF VIEW*.

OBJECTIVE POINT OF VIEW See *POINT OF VIEW*.

OMNISCIENT POINT OF VIEW See *POINT OF VIEW*.

PACE The speed with which events are narrated. Some stories can be told quickly, with details omitted, time compressed, and events summarized. Others must be told slowly, with all details included, time extended, and events dramatized as scenes. The pace of a story will vary according to the nature of the events being recounted and their importance to the plot.

PARABLE A short narrative offered as an answer to a difficult moral question or to illustrate a moral truth. See *FABLE*.

PARADOX A rhetorical device making an assertion which on one level appears to be a contradiction but which on another level may be actually true.

PARODY A composition that imitates the distinctive features of a serious piece of writing for comic or satiric purposes. See *SATIRE*.

PLOT The essential structure of a story arranged according to a coherent sequence of events. The plot is usually divided into three major parts: (1) the *EXPOSITION*, where the existing conflicts are established; (2) the *COMPLICATION*, where new conflicts are introduced or old conflicts are increased in intensity until they reach a *CLIMAX* or *CRISIS*; and (3) the *DENOUEMENT*, where the conflicts are resolved.

POINT OF VIEW The vantage point or perspective from which the story is told. Point of view refers to both position (the narrator's proximity to the action in time and space) and person (the narrator's character and attitude). See also *NARRATOR*. There are four basic points of view:

1. *THIRD-PERSON OMNISCIENT* The narrator, usually assumed to be the author, tells the story. He or she can move at will through time, across space, and into the mind of each character to tell us anything we need to know to understand the story.
2. *THIRD-PERSON LIMITED OMNISCIENT* Although the author is still the narrator, he or she gives up total omniscience and limits the point of view to the experience and perception of one character in the story. Instead of knowing everything, the reader knows only what this one character knows or is able to learn.

3. *FIRST-PERSON* The author selects one of the characters in the narrative to tell the story. This character may be involved in the action or may view it from the position of an observer. This character may tell about events as they are happening or many years after they have taken place.

4. *OBJECTIVE* The author presents the external action of the story as if it were being filmed by a movie camera. The story is presented without any attempt to comment on or interpret the characters' private thoughts or feelings. All that the reader knows about the event must be inferred from the characters' public words and deeds.

PROTAGONIST The character who is engaged in the central conflict of the story, sometimes called the hero or heroine. See *ANTAGONIST; CHARACTER; CONFLICT; FOIL.*

REFLEXIVE FICTION Fiction in which the reader is reminded directly or indirectly that the story is artifice, the creation of a writer who is consciously shaping all the narrative elements, not reporting facts. The effect is to draw the reader into a consideration of the creative process as well as that which is created; it is an increasingly common approach in modern writing, especially in experimental fiction. See *VERISIMILITUDE.*

RESOLUTION The events that occur after the climax and bring the conflicts in the story to an appropriate conclusion. See *DENOUEMENT; PLOT.*

REVERSAL A sudden change or turnabout in the fortunes of the protagonist.

ROUND CHARACTER See *CHARACTER.*

SATIRE A work of literature that ridicules vice or folly in ideas, institutions, or individuals. Although a satiric work treats its subject with varying degrees of amusement and scorn, its ultimate purpose is to bring about improvement by calling attention—either directly or indirectly—to higher standards of human behavior. See *PARODY.*

SETTING The time, place, and social reality within which a story takes place. In a limited sense, setting refers to the physical landscape; in a broader sense, setting refers to the cultural landscape—the assumptions, rituals, and shared beliefs that shape the characters and their world.

STATIC CHARACTER See *CHARACTER.*

STEREOTYPE An oversimplified character who recurs so frequently in literary works that his or her behavior has become predictable.

STYLE A writer's distinctive manner of expression. Among the many features that characterize a writer's style are diction, sentence structure, and strategies for selecting, analyzing, and interpreting experience. See *TONE; VOICE.*

SYMBOL A person, act, or thing that has both literal significance and additional abstract meanings. Unlike an allegory, where such things are equated with one or two abstract ideas, a symbol usually refers to several complex ideas that may radiate contradictory or ambiguous meanings. See *ALLEGORY.*

THEME The central or unifying idea about human experience that grows out of all the other elements in the story. Occasionally the theme may be stated directly by the author or indirectly by one of the characters. More often the theme must be derived from an attempt to understand the complex interaction of forces within the narrative.

TONE The author's attitude toward the situations and characters in the story. By combining a variety of verbal strategies—diction, sentence structure, imagery, symbolism—authors create a tone that establishes the mood, atmosphere, or emotional coloring of a story. See *STYLE; VOICE.*

VERISIMILITUDE The attempt to make fictional elements seem lifelike and real rather than creations of the writer. Until very recently, most fiction aimed at a sense of verisimilitude. See *REFLEXIVE FICTION.*

VOICE The personality of the author or narrator that is revealed through a distinctive and habitual mode of expression. See *STYLE; TONE.*

Copyrights and Acknowledgments

CHINUA ACHEBE "Vengeful Creditor" from GIRLS AT WAR AND OTHER STORIES. Copyright © 1972, 1973 by Chinua Achebe. Used by permission of Doubleday, a division of Bantam Doubleday Dell Publishing Group, Inc.

ISABEL ALLENDE, translated from the Spanish by Margaret Sayers Peden, "Walimai" and "Two Words" from THE STORIES OF EVA LUNA by Isabel Allende. Copyright © 1989 by Isabel Allende. English translation copyright © 1991 by Macmillan Publishing Company. Reprinted with the permission of Atheneum Publishers, an imprint of Macmillan Publishing Company.

SHERWOOD ANDERSON "The Egg" from THE TRIUMPH OF THE EGG. Copyright © 1921 by B.W. Huebsch, Inc. Copyright renewed 1949 by Eleanor C. Anderson. Reprinted by permission of Harold Ober Associates Incorporated.

MARGARET ATWOOD "The Age of Lead" from WILDERNESS TIPS. Copyright © 1991 by O. W. Toad Limited. Used by permission of Doubleday, a division of Bantam Doubleday Dell Publishing Group, Inc.

JAMES BALDWIN "Sonny's Blues" from GOING TO MEET THE MAN. Copyright © 1957 by James Baldwin. Used by permission of Doubleday, a division of Bantam Doubleday Dell Publishing Group, Inc.

TONI CADE BAMBARA "The Lesson" from GORILLA, MY LOVE. Copyright © 1972 by Toni Cade Bambara. Reprinted by permission of Random House, Inc.

HEINRICH BÖLL "Christmas Not Just Once a Year" from THE STORIES OF HEINRICH BÖLL, translated by L. Vennewitz. Translation Copyright © 1986 by Leila Vennewitz and the Estate of Heinrich Böll. Reprinted by permission of Alfred A. Knopf, Inc.

ARNA BONTEMPS "A Summer Tragedy" from THE OLD SOUTH. Copyright © 1933 by Arna Bontemps, renewed. Reprinted by permission of Harold Ober Associates Incorporated.

JORGE LUIS BORGES "The Garden of Forking Paths" from LABYRINTHS. Copyright © 1963, 1964 by New Directions Publishing Corp. Reprinted by permission of New Directions Publishing Corp.

ELIZABETH BOWEN "The Demon Lover" from THE COLLECTED STORIES OF ELIZABETH BOWEN. Copyright 1946 and renewed 1974 by Elizabeth Bowen. Reprinted by permission of Alfred A. Knopf, Inc.

KAY BOYLE "Astronomer's Wife" from THE WHITE HORSES OF VIENNA AND OTHER STORIES. Copyright ©1936, 1964 by Kay Boyle. Reprinted by permission of A. Watkins, Inc., agents for Kay Boyle.

LARRY BROWN "Kubuku Rides (This Is It)" from FACING THE MUSIC. Copyright © 1984, 1985, 1986, 1988 by Larry Brown, published by Algonquin Books of Chapel Hill, a division of Workman Publishing Company, New York. Reprinted by permission of the publisher.

ALBERT CAMUS "The Guest" from EXILE AND THE KINGDOM, translated by Justin O'Brien. Copyright © 1957 by Alfred A. Knopf, Inc. Reprinted by permission of the publisher.

ETHAN CANIN "We Are Nighttime Travelers" and "The Year of Getting to Know Us" from EMPEROR OF THE AIR. Copyright © 1988 by Ethan Canin. Reprinted by permission of Houghton Mifflin Company. All rights reserved.

RAYMOND CARVER "A Small, Good Thing" from CATHEDRAL. Copyright © 1981, 1982, 1983 by Raymond Carver. Reprinted by permission of Alfred A. Knopf, Inc.

JOHN CHEEVER "The Swimmer" from STORIES OF JOHN CHEEVER. Copyright © 1964 by John Cheever. Reprinted by permission of Alfred A. Knopf, Inc.

SANDRA CISNEROS "Never Marry a Mexican" from WOMAN HOLLERING CREEK. Copyright © by Sandra Cisneros 1991. Published by Vintage Books, a division of Random House, Inc., New York and simultaneously in Canada by Random House of Canada Limited, Toronto. Originally published in hardcover by Random House, Inc., New York in 1991. Reprinted by permission of Susan Bergholz Literary Services, New York.

RALPH ELLISON "Battle Royal" from INVISIBLE MAN. Copyright © 1948 by Ralph Ellison. Reprinted by permission of Random House, Inc.

RALPH ELLISON "King of the Bingo Game." Copyright © 1944 by Ralph Ellison. Reprinted by permission of the William Morris Agency, Inc. on behalf of the author.

WILLIAM FAULKNER "A Rose for Emily" from COLLECTED STORIES OF WILLIAM FAULKNER. Copyright © 1930 and renewed 1958 by William Faulkner. Reprinted by permission of Random House, Inc.

WILLIAM FAULKNER "Barn Burning" from COLLECTED STORIES OF WILLIAM FAULKNER. Copyright © 1950 by Random House, Inc. Copyright renewed 1977 by Jill Faulkner Summers. Reprinted by permission of Random House, Inc.

F. SCOTT FITZGERALD "Babylon Revisited" from TAPS AT REVEILLE. Copyright © 1931 by The Curtis Publishing Company; renewal copyright © 1959 by Frances Scott Fitzgerald Lanahan. Reprinted by permission of Charles Scribner's Sons, an imprint of Macmillan Publishing Company.

ERNEST J. GAINES "The Sky Is Gray" from BLOODLINE. Copyright © 1963 by Ernest J. Gaines. Used by permission of Doubleday, a division of Bantam Doubleday Dell Publishing Group, Inc.

GABRIEL GARCIA MARQUEZ "A Very Old Man with Enormous Wings" from LEAF STORM. English translation copyright © 1972 by Gabriel García Márquez. Originally appeared in NEW AMERICAN REVIEW. Reprinted by permission of HarperCollins Publishers Inc.

ELLEN GILCHRIST "Revenge" from IN THE LAND OF DREAMY DREAMS. Copyright © 1981 by Ellen Gilchrist. Reprinted by permission of Little, Brown and Company.

URSULA K. LE GUIN "The Ones Who Walk Away from Omelas." Copyright © 1973 by Ursula K. Le Guin; first appeared in NEW DIMENSIONS 3. Reprinted by permission of the author and the author's agent, Virginia Kidd.

DORIS LESSING "A Woman on a Roof." Copyright © 1963 by Doris Lessing. Reprinted by permission of Jonathan Clowes Ltd., London, on behalf of Doris Lessing.

CARSON McCULLERS "A Tree, a Rock, a Cloud" from THE BALLAD OF THE SAD CAFE. Copyright 1936, 1941, 1942, 1950, © 1955 by Carson McCullers. Copyright © renewed 1979 by Floria V. Lasky. Reprinted by permission of Houghton Mifflin Company. All rights reserved.

DENNIS McFARLAND "Nothing To Ask For." Copyright © 1989 by Dennis McFarland. First appeared in THE NEW YORKER. Reprinted by permission of Brandt & Brandt Literary Agents, Inc.

JAMES ALAN McPHERSON "The Silver Bullet" from ELBOW ROOM. Copyright © 1972 by James Alan McPherson. First appeared in PLAYBOY MAGAZINE. Reprinted by permission of Little, Brown and Company.

BERNARD MALAMUD "The Magic Barrel" from THE MAGIC BARREL by Bernard Malamud. Copyright © 1954, 1958 and copyright renewed © 1982, 1986 by Bernard Malamud. Reprinted by permission of Farrar, Straus & Giroux, Inc.

KATHERINE MANSFIELD "Her First Ball" from THE SHORT STORIES OF KATHERINE MANSFIELD. Copyright 1922 by Alfred A. Knopf, Inc. and renewed 1950 by John Middleton Murry. Reprinted by permission of the publisher.

BOBBIE ANN MASON "Shiloh" from SHILOH AND OTHER STORIES. Copyright © 1982 by Bobbie Ann Mason. Originally appeared in THE NEW YORKER. Reprinted by permission of HarperCollins Publishers Inc.

YUKIO MISHIMA "Patriotism" from DEATH IN MIDSUMMER. Copyright © 1966 by New Directions Publishing Corp. Reprinted by permission of New Directions Publishing Corp.

ALICE MUNRO "How I Met My Husband" from SOMETHING I'VE BEEN MEANING TO TELL YOU AND OTHER STORIES. Copyright © 1974 by Alice Munro. Reprinted by arrangement with Virginia Barber Literary Agency Inc.

JOYCE CAROL OATES "Where Are You Going, Where Have You Been?" from THE WHEEL OF LOVE AND OTHER STORIES. Copyright © 1970 by Joyce Carol Oates. Reprinted by permission of John Hawkins & Associates, Inc.

JOYCE CAROL OATES "The Lady with the Pet Dog" from MARRIAGES AND INFIDELITIES. Copyright © 1972 by Joyce Carol Oates. Reprinted by permission of John Hawkins & Associates, Inc.

FLANNERY O'CONNOR "A Good Man is Hard to Find" from A GOOD MAN IS HARD TO FIND AND OTHER STORIES. Copyright © 1953 by Flannery O'Connor, renewed 1981 by Mrs. Regina O'Connor. Reprinted by permission of Harcourt Brace & Company.

FLANNERY O'CONNOR "Everything That Rises Must Converge" and "Revelation" from THE COMPLETE STORIES by Flannery O'Connor. Copyright © 1961, 1964, 1965 by The Estate of Mary Flannery O'Connor. Reprinted by permission of Farrar, Straus & Giroux, Inc.

FRANK O'CONNOR "Guests of the Nation" from COLLECTED STORIES by Frank O'Connor. Copyright © 1981 by Harriet O'Donovan Sheehy, Executrix of the Estate of Frank O'Connor. Reprinted by permission of Alfred A. Knopf, Inc.

TILLIE OLSEN "I Stand Here Ironing" from TELL ME A RIDDLE. Copyright © 1956, 1957, 1960, 1961 by Tillie Olsen. Used by permission of Delacorte Press/Seymour Lawrence, a division of Bantam Doubleday Dell Publishing Group, Inc.

CYNTHIA OZICK "Puttermesser Paired" from THE NEW YORKER MAGAZINE, October 8, 1990. Copyright © 1990 Cynthia Ozick. Reprinted by permission of Cynthia Ozick and her Agents, Raines & Raines, 71 Park Ave., New York, N.Y. 10016.

DOROTHY PARKER "The Waltz" from THE PORTABLE DOROTHY PARKER, Introduction by Brendan Gill. Copyright 1933, renewed © 1961 by Dorothy Parker. Used by permission of Viking Penguin, a division of Penguin Books USA Inc.

KATHERINE ANNE PORTER "The Jilting of Granny Weatherall" from FLOWERING JUDAS AND OTHER STORIES. Copyright © 1930, renewed 1958 by Katherine Anne Porter. Reprinted by permission of Harcourt Brace & Company.

KATHERINE ANNE PORTER "The Grave" from THE LEANING TOWER AND OTHER STORIES. Copyright 1944, renewed 1972 by Katherine Anne Porter. Reprinted by permission of Harcourt Brace & Company.

KATHERINE ANNE PORTER "Holiday" from COLLECTED STORIES OF KATHERINE ANNE PORTER. Copyright © 1958, 1960, 1963, 1965 by Katherine Anne Porter. Reprinted by permission of W. H. Bayley, Literary Estate of Katherine Anne Porter.

PHILIP ROTH "Defender of the Faith" from GOODBYE, COLUMBUS. Copyright © 1959, renewed 1987 by Philip Roth. Reprinted by permission of Houghton Mifflin Co. All rights reserved.

ISAAC BASHEVIS SINGER "Gimpel the Fool," Saul Bellow, translator, copyright 1953 by The Partisan Review, renewed © 1981 by Isaac Bashevis Singer, from A TREASURY OF YIDDISH STORIES edited by Irving Howe and Eliezer Greenberg. Used by permission of Viking Penguin, a division of Penguin Books USA Inc.

JOHN STEINBECK "The Chrysanthemums" from THE LONG VALLEY. Copyright © 1937, renewed © 1965 by John Steinbeck. Used by permission of Viking Penguin, a division of Penguin Books USA Inc.

JAMES THURBER "The Catbird Seat" from THE THURBER CARNIVAL. Copyright © 1945 by James Thurber, renewed 1973 by Helen W. Thurber and Rosemary T. Sauers. Reprinted by permission of Mrs. James Thurber.

WILLIAM TREVOR "The Ballroom of Romance" from THE BALLROOM OF ROMANCE. Copyright © 1965, 1966, 1969, 1971, 1972 by William Trevor. Used by permission of Viking Penguin, a division of Penguin Books USA Inc.

JOHN UPDIKE "A & P" from PIGEON FEATHERS AND OTHER STORIES. Copyright © 1962 by John Updike. Originally appeared in THE NEW YORKER. Reprinted by permission of Alfred A. Knopf, Inc.

JOHN UPDIKE "A Sandstone Farmhouse," originally in THE NEW YORKER, June 11, 1990. Copyright © 1990 John Updike. Reprinted by permission of The New Yorker and the author.